ADVENTURES

COLLECTOR'S EDITION

CONTENTS

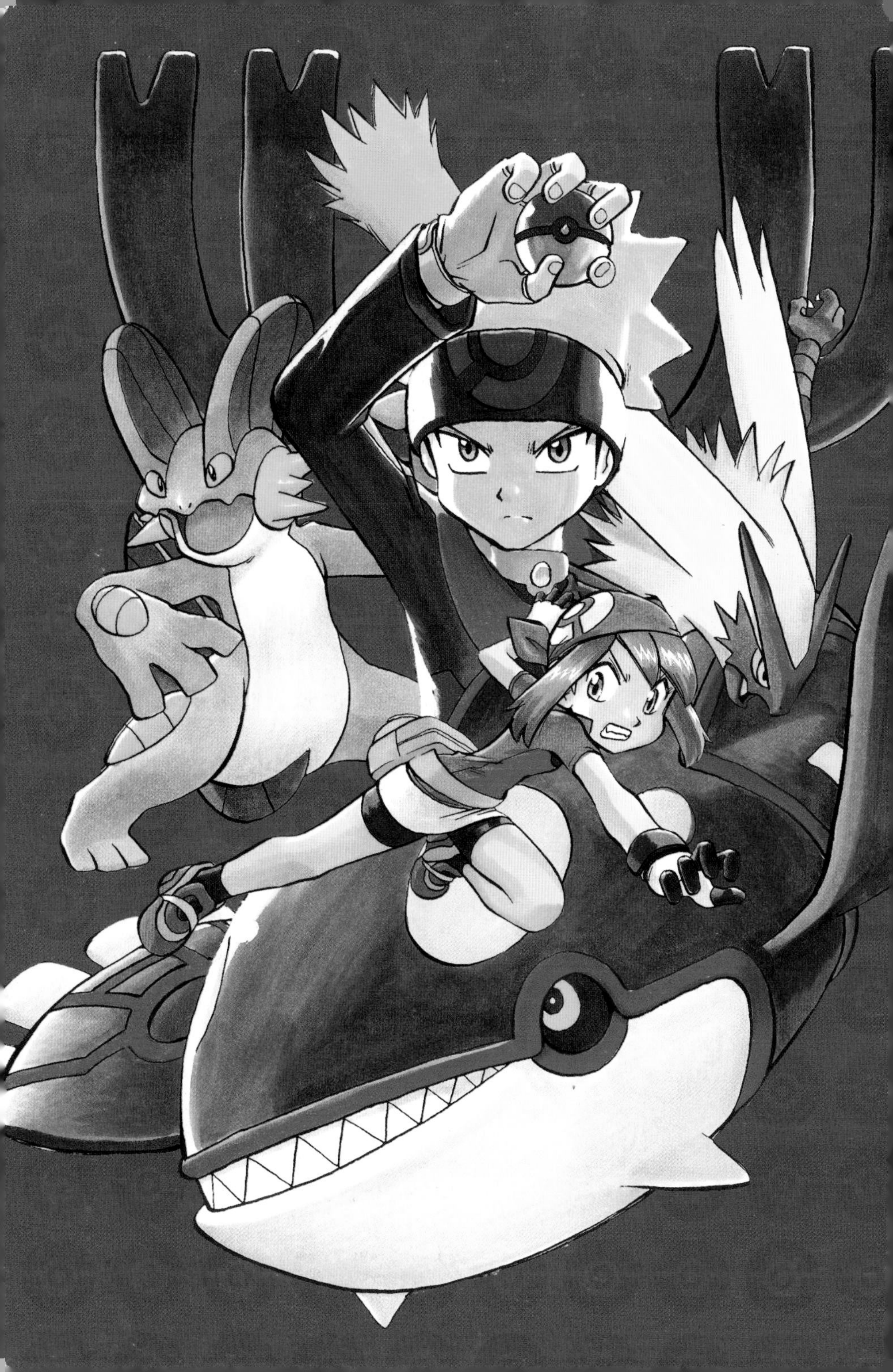

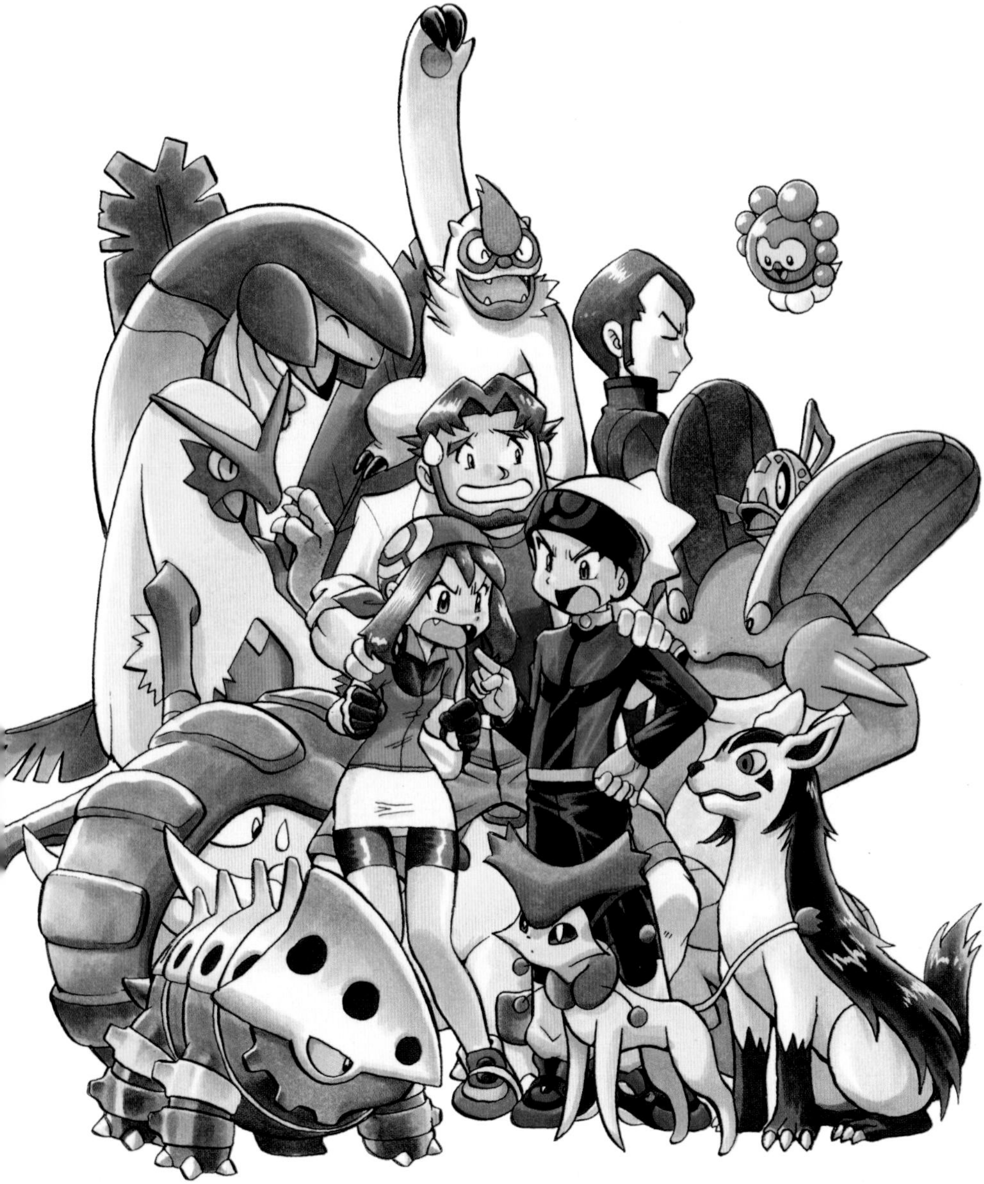

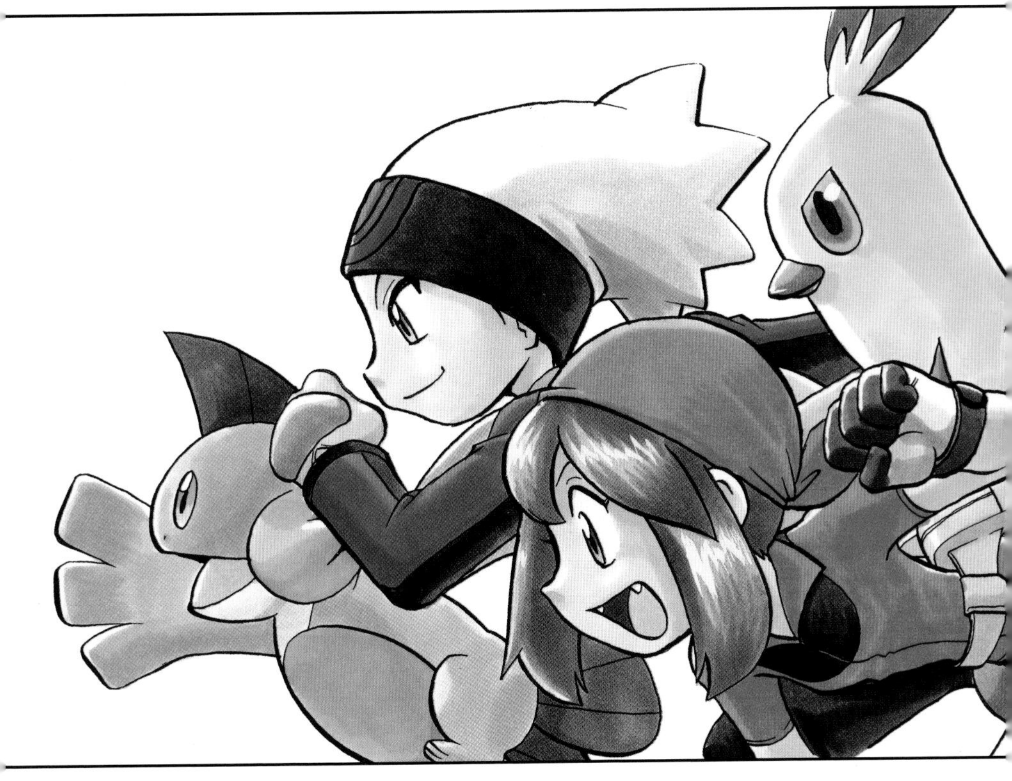

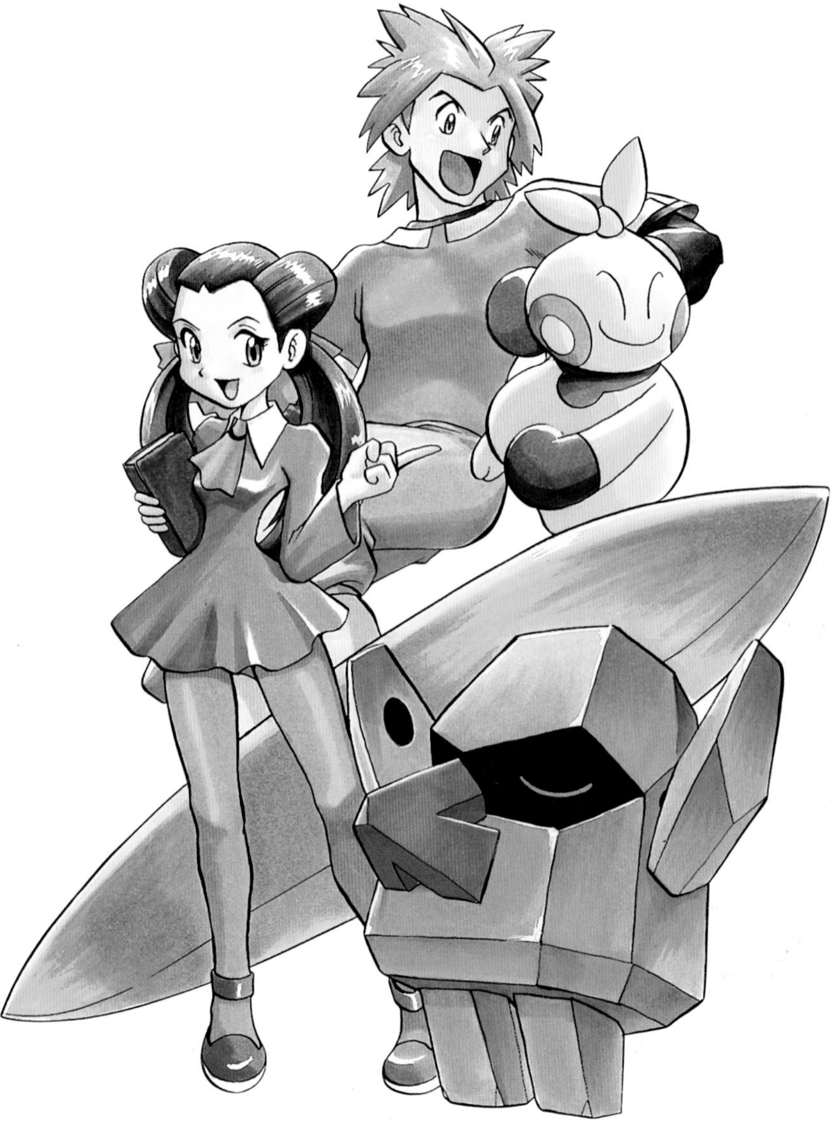

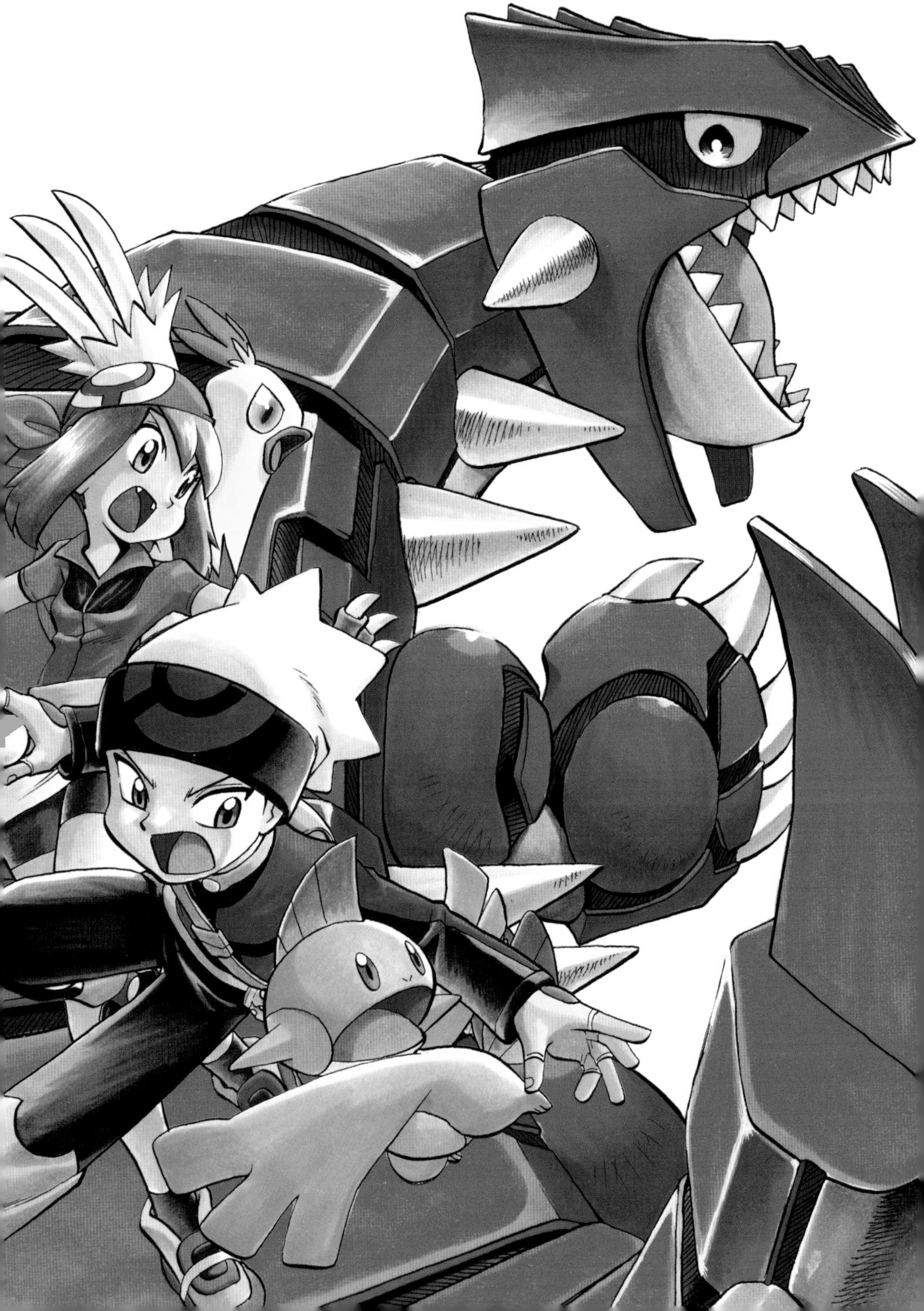

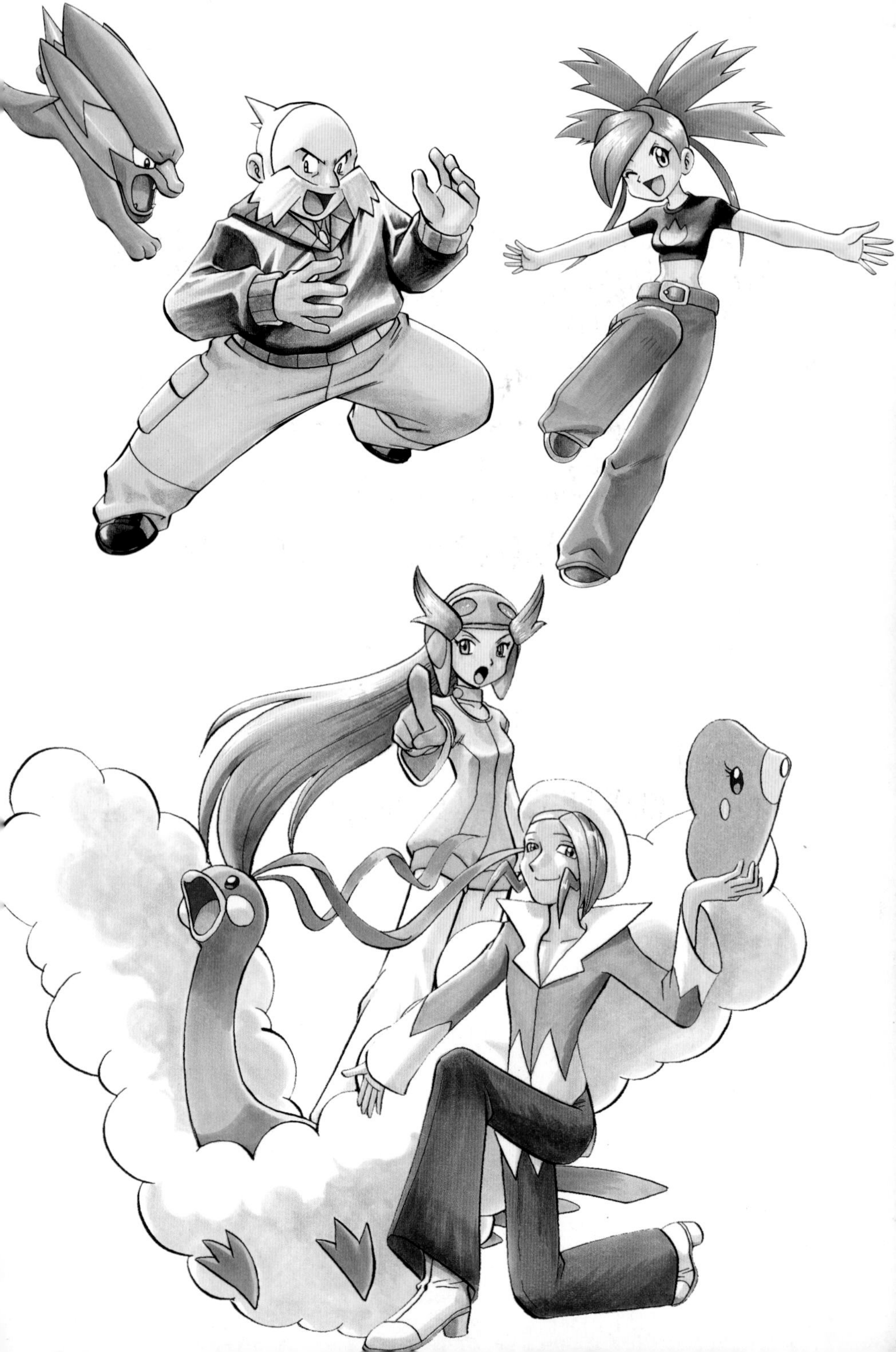

COLLECTOR'S EDITION

06

Story by **HIDENORI KUSAKA**   Art by **SATOSHI YAMAMOTO**

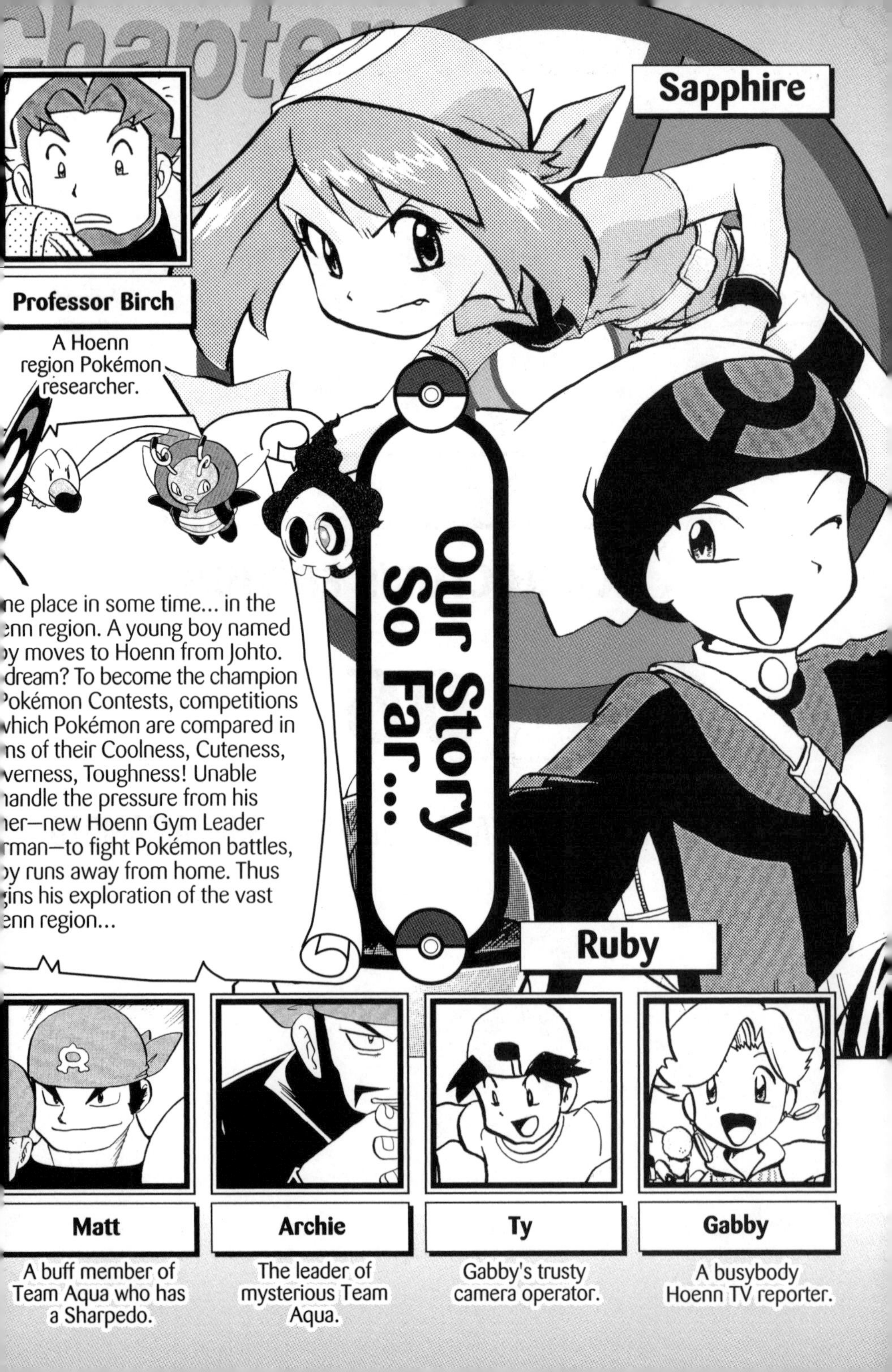
Chapter
Sapphire
Professor Birch
A Hoenn region Pokémon researcher.
Our Story So Far...
ne place in some time... in the
enn region. A young boy named
y moves to Hoenn from Johto.
dream? To become the champion
Pokémon Contests, competitions
which Pokémon are compared in
ns of their Coolness, Cuteness,
verness, Toughness! Unable
handle the pressure from his
her—new Hoenn Gym Leader
rman—to fight Pokémon battles,
y runs away from home. Thus
gins his exploration of the vast
enn region...
Ruby
Gabby
A busybody Hoenn TV reporter.
Ty
Gabby's trusty camera operator.
Archie
The leader of mysterious Team Aqua.
Matt
A buff member of Team Aqua who has a Sharpedo.

Story of The Four

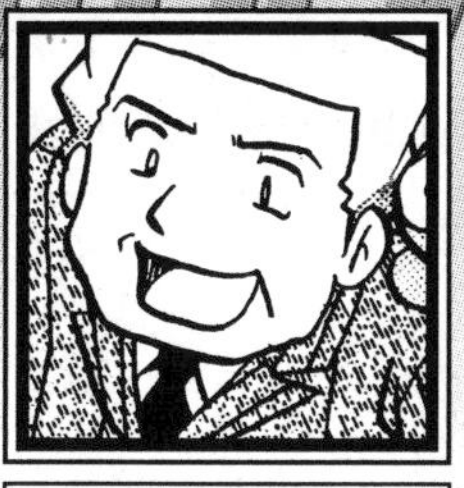

President Stone

C.E.O. of the giant Devon Corporation. Currently unconscious.

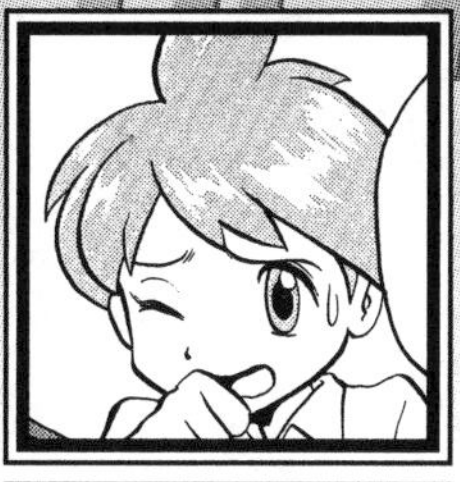

Wally

A frail boy who longs for a Pokémon of his own.

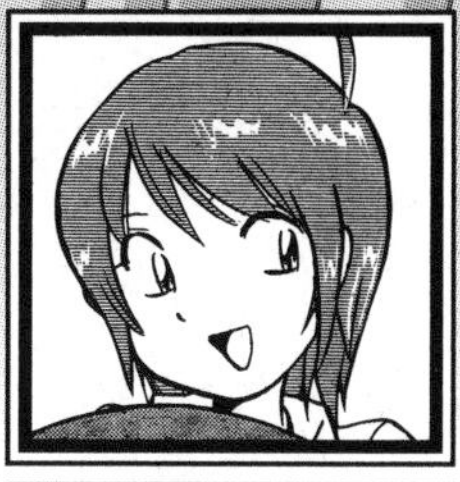

Mother

Ruby's mother, a sweet and gentle homemaker.

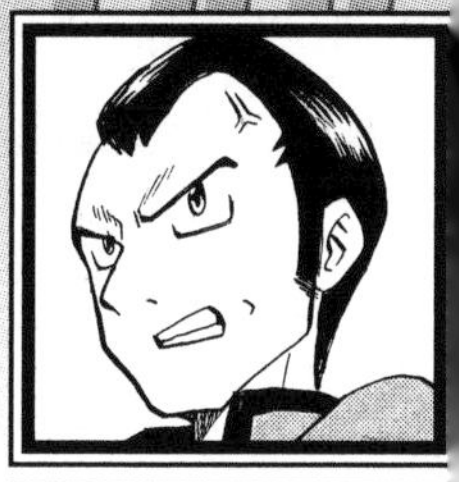

Norman

Ruby's father, the Gym Leader of Petalburg City.

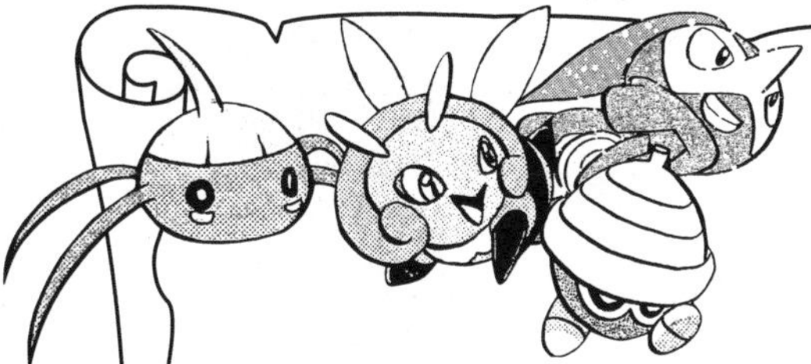

Ruby meets a girl named Sapphire who lives in a cave. Like Ruby, she has a dream. Hers is to defeat all the Gym Leaders in the Hoenn region. The two agree to pursue their dreams for 80 days, then reunite at the spot where they first met. And thus, Ruby and Sapphire's 80-day journey through Hoenn begins.

First, Ruby helps a frail boy named Wally capture his first Pokémon near Petalburg City. But then Ruby is washed away by a tsunami caused by a mysterious earthquake! Meanwhile, Sapphire faces her first Gym Leader near Rustboro City...

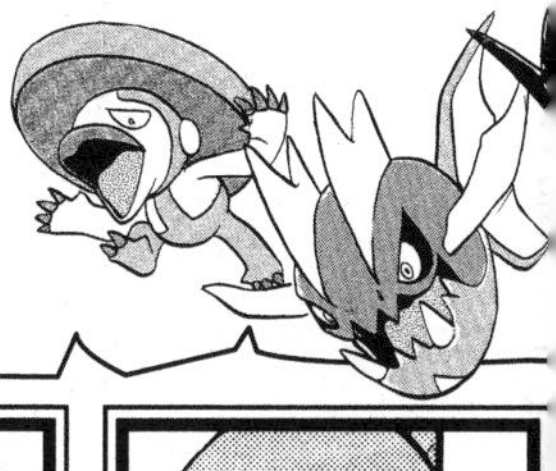

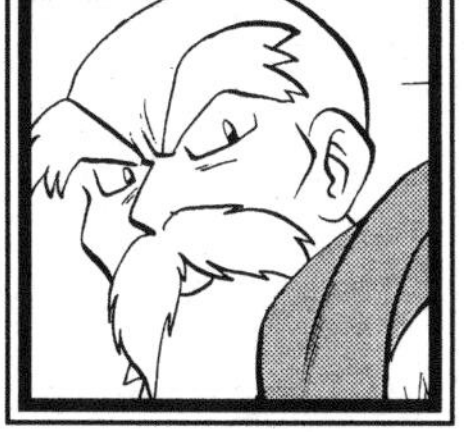

Mr. Briney

A former sailor, skilled in the ways of the maritime.

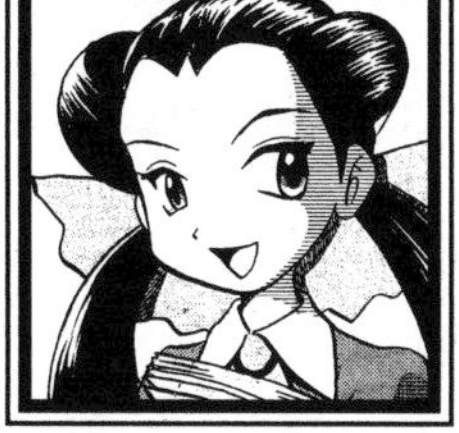

Roxanne

The Gym Leader of Rustboro City. She loves to study and learn.

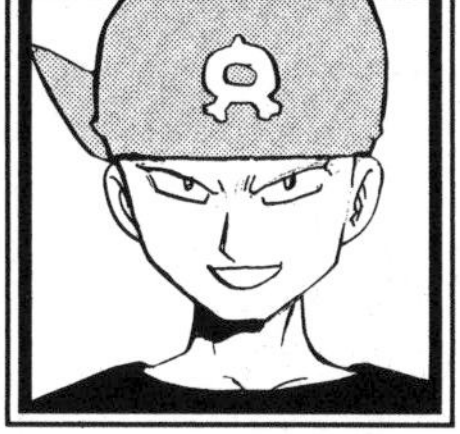

Amber

Archie's most trusted follower. He has a Carvanha.

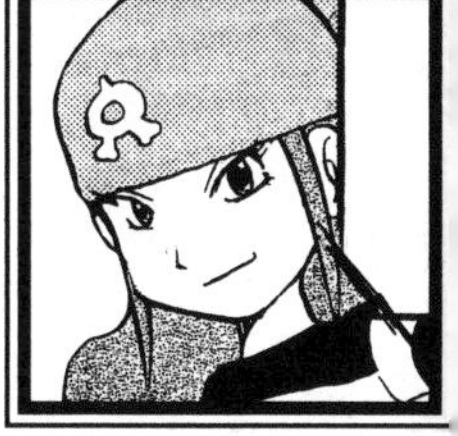

Shelly

A member of Team Aqua who has a Ludicolo.

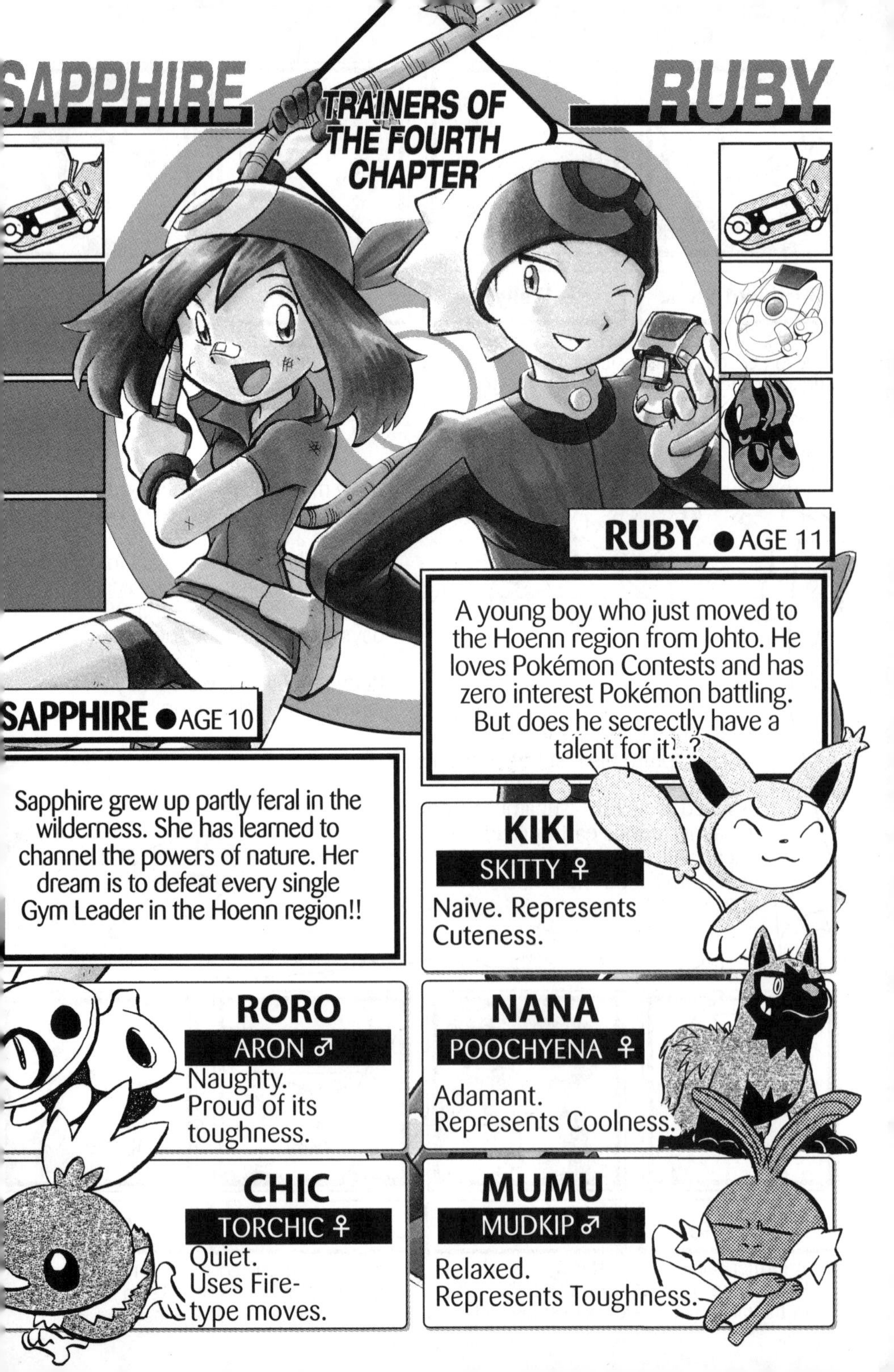
TRAINERS OF THE FOURTH CHAPTER
RUBY
SAPPHIRE
RUBY ●AGE 11
A young boy who just moved to the Hoenn region from Johto. He loves Pokémon Contests and has zero interest Pokémon battling. But does he secrectly have a talent for it!..?
SAPPHIRE ●AGE 10
Sapphire grew up partly feral in the wilderness. She has learned to channel the powers of nature. Her dream is to defeat every single Gym Leader in the Hoenn region!!
KIKI
SKITTY ♀
Naive. Represents Cuteness.
NANA
POOCHYENA ♀
Adamant. Represents Coolness.
MUMU
MUDKIP ♂
Relaxed. Represents Toughness.
RORO
ARON ♂
Naughty. Proud of its toughness.
CHIC
TORCHIC ♀
Quiet. Uses Fire-type moves.

Message from
Hidenori Kusaka

The Ruby and Sapphire story arc is unfolding rapidly as our two heroes press on toward the deadline of their competition! The Gym battle against Roxanne at Rustboro and Brawly at Dewford... The battles at the Abandoned Ship and Slateport City... This volume is chock-full of my favorite episodes! I hope you enjoy Ruby and Sapphire's high-speed journey too!

—2003

Message from
Satoshi Yamamoto

Ruby, a city boy, loves beautiful things and prefers to avoid conflict and trouble. Sapphire, a wild girl from the woods, loves battles and action. These two main characters have very different personalities—but I love complex personalities. As I write, I enjoy starting each chapter wondering what the two of them will get up to next. To tell the truth, though, I think both of them would be really hard to get along with in real life.

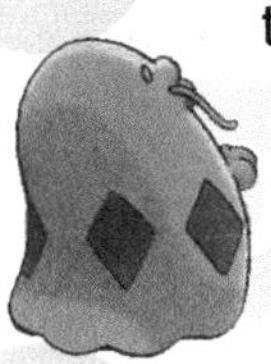

—2003

● Adventure 191 ●
Blowing Past Nosepass, Part 2

Pokémon™ Adventures Ruby & Sapphire
The Fourth Chapter

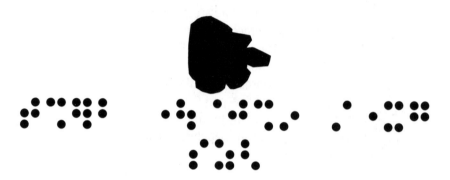

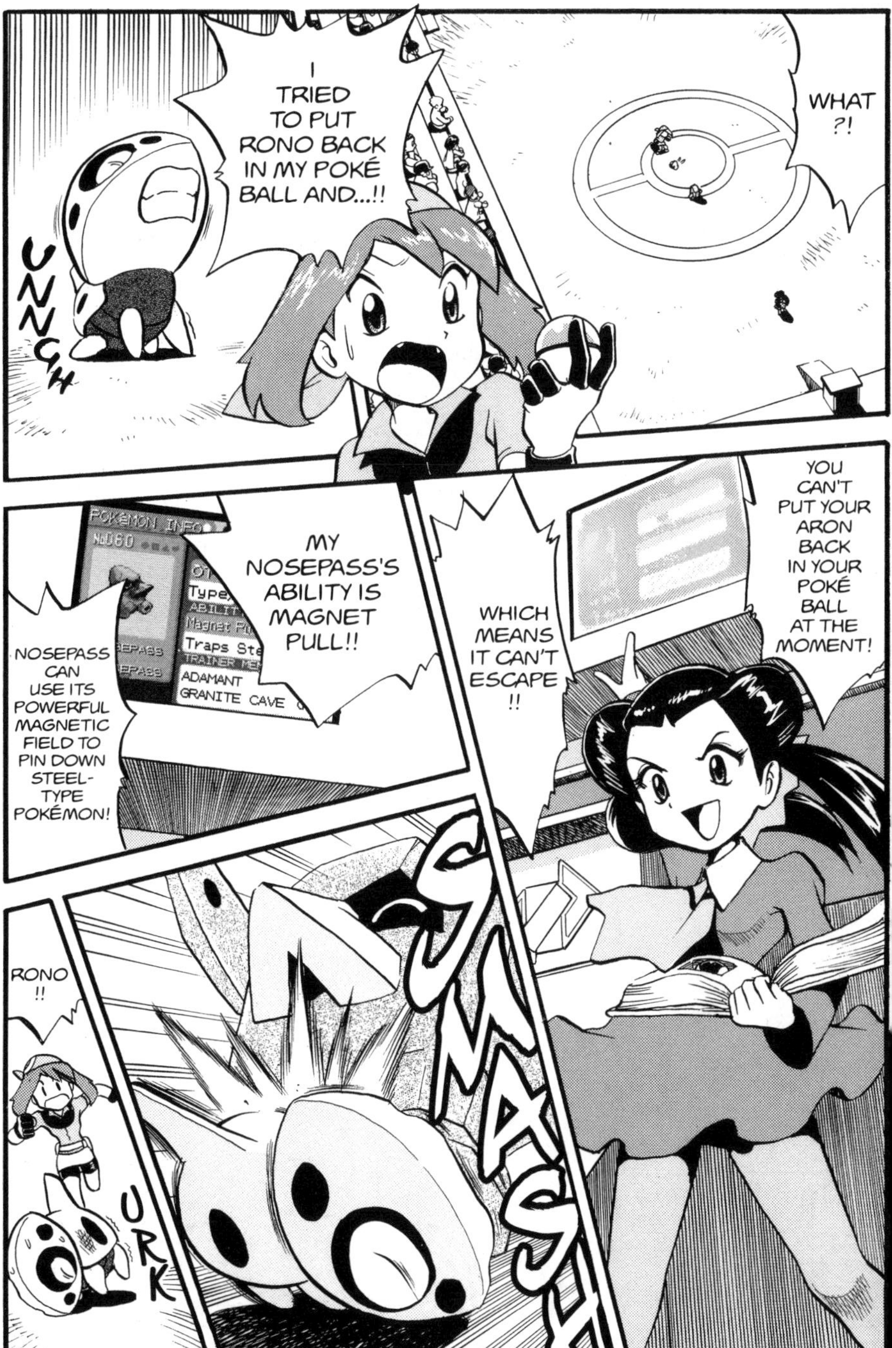
WHAT ?!
I TRIED TO PUT RONO BACK IN MY POKÉ BALL AND...!!
UNNNGH
YOU CAN'T PUT YOUR ARON BACK IN YOUR POKÉ BALL AT THE MOMENT!
WHICH MEANS IT CAN'T ESCAPE !!
MY NOSEPASS'S ABILITY IS MAGNET PULL!!
POKÉMON INFO
ADAMANT
GRANITE CAVE
NOSEPASS CAN USE ITS POWERFUL MAGNETIC FIELD TO PIN DOWN STEEL-TYPE POKÉMON!
SMASH
RONO !!
URK

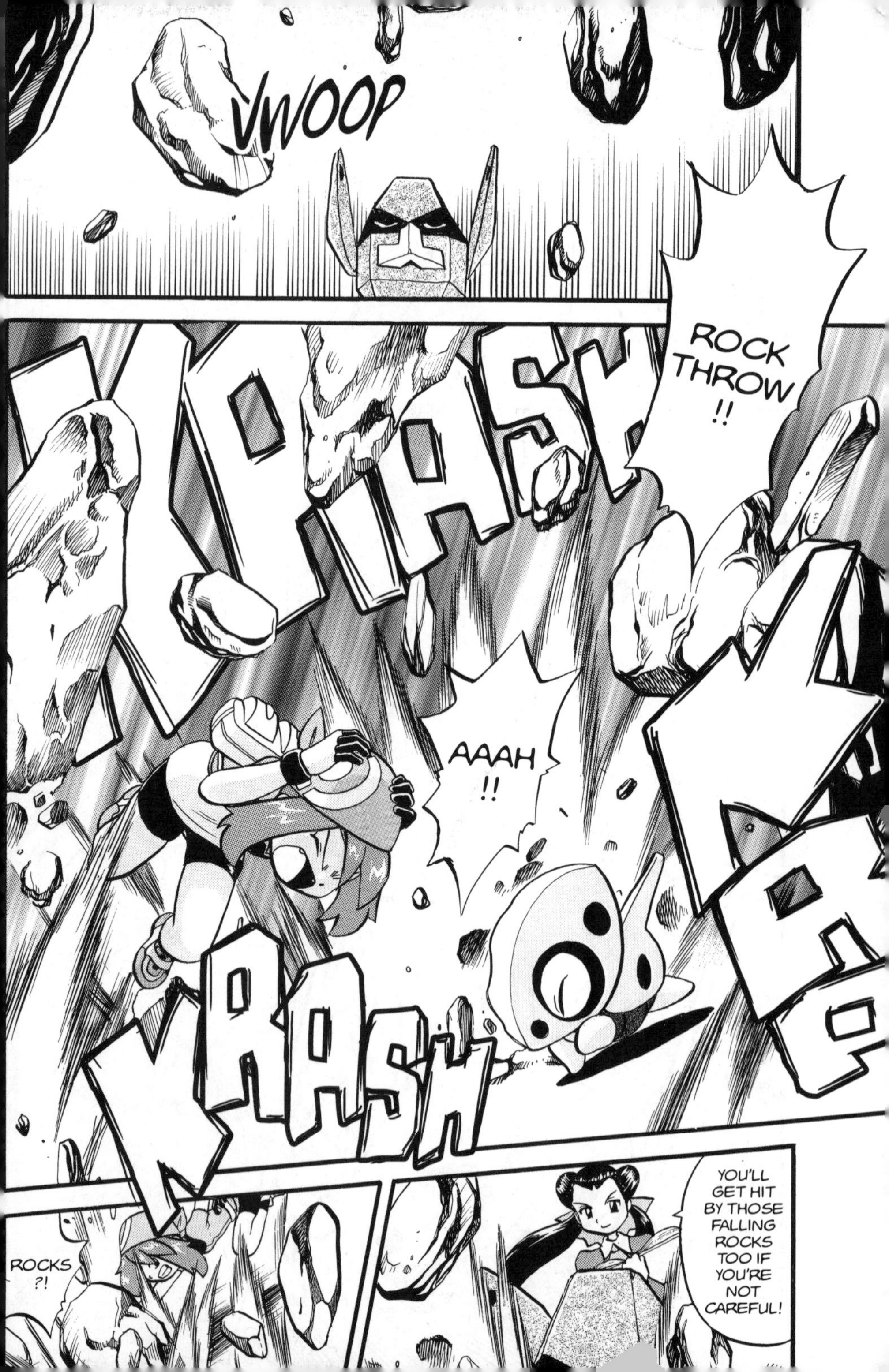
VWOOP
ROCK THROW!!
KRASH
AAAH!!
KRASH
YOU'LL GET HIT BY THOSE FALLING ROCKS TOO IF YOU'RE NOT CAREFUL!
ROCKS?!

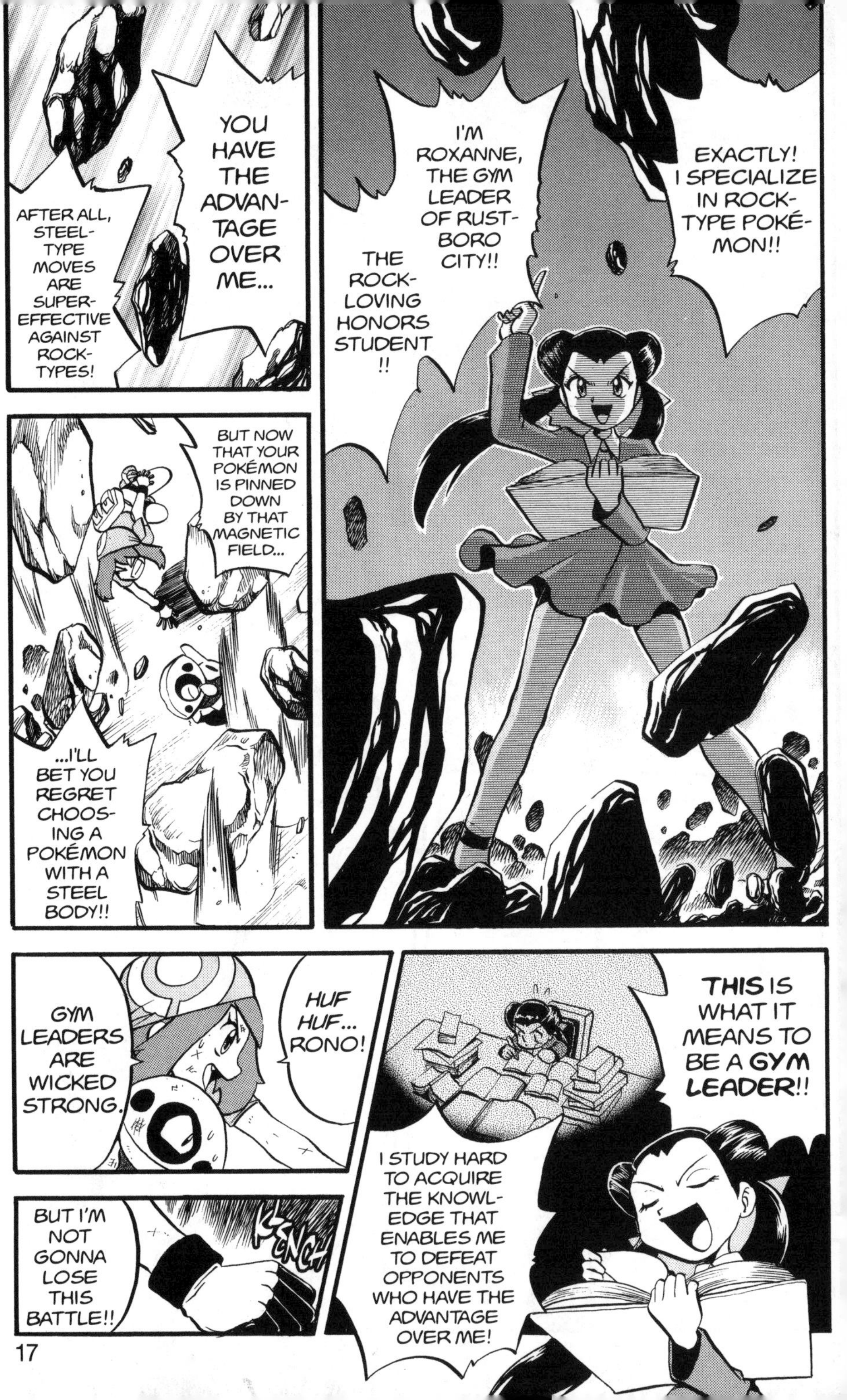
EXACTLY! I SPECIALIZE IN ROCK-TYPE POKÉMON!!
I'M ROXANNE, THE GYM LEADER OF RUSTBORO CITY!!
THE ROCK-LOVING HONORS STUDENT!!
YOU HAVE THE ADVANTAGE OVER ME...
AFTER ALL, STEEL-TYPE MOVES ARE SUPER-EFFECTIVE AGAINST ROCK-TYPES!
BUT NOW THAT YOUR POKÉMON IS PINNED DOWN BY THAT MAGNETIC FIELD...
...I'LL BET YOU REGRET CHOOSING A POKÉMON WITH A STEEL BODY!!
THIS IS WHAT IT MEANS TO BE A **GYM LEADER**!!
I STUDY HARD TO ACQUIRE THE KNOWLEDGE THAT ENABLES ME TO DEFEAT OPPONENTS WHO HAVE THE ADVANTAGE OVER ME!
HUF HUF... RONO!
GYM LEADERS ARE WICKED STRONG.
KLENCH
BUT I'M NOT GONNA LOSE THIS BATTLE!!

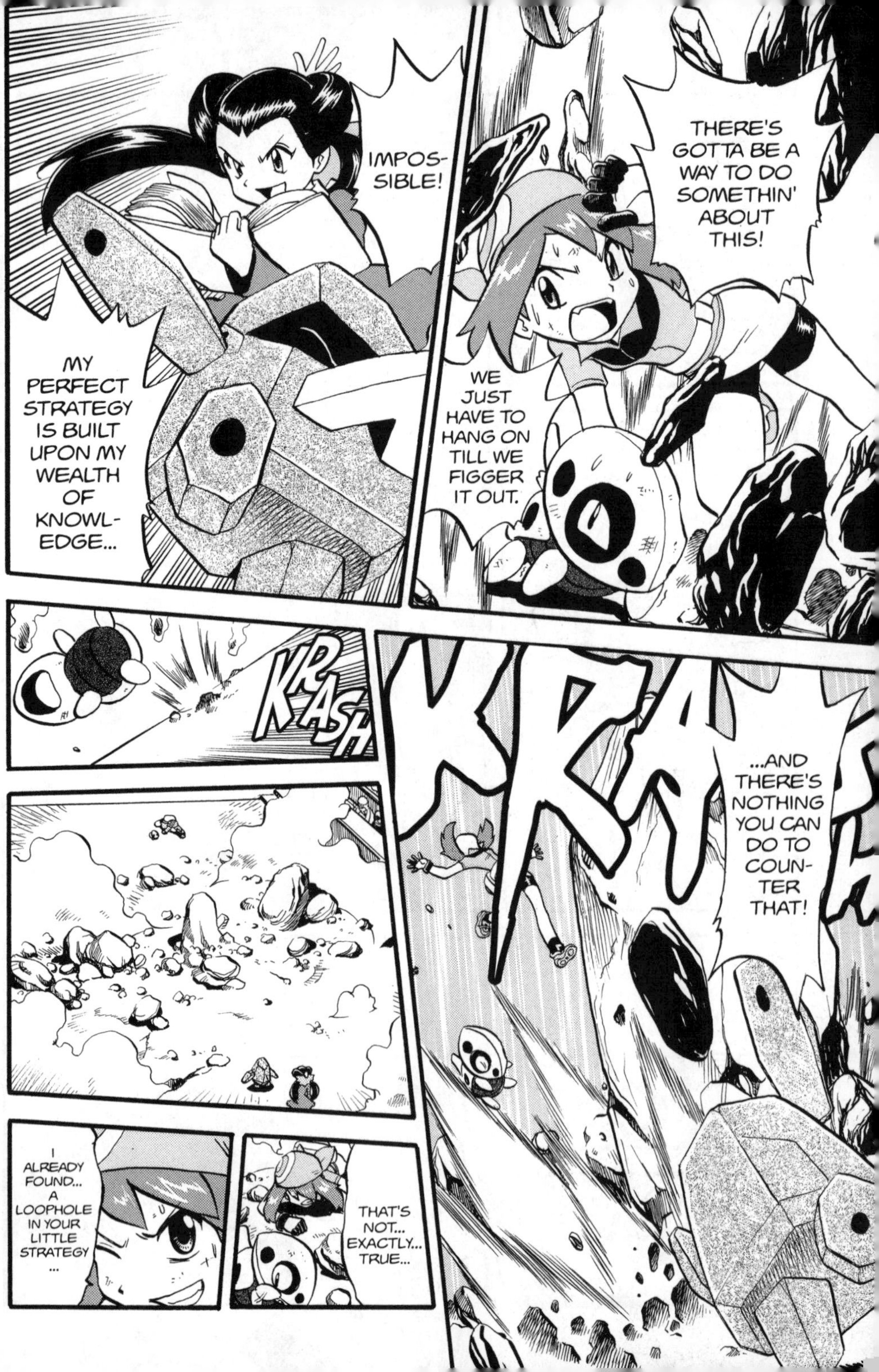
THERE'S GOTTA BE A WAY TO DO SOMETHIN' ABOUT THIS!
WE JUST HAVE TO HANG ON TILL WE FIGGER IT OUT.
IMPOSSIBLE!
MY PERFECT STRATEGY IS BUILT UPON MY WEALTH OF KNOWLEDGE...
...AND THERE'S NOTHING YOU CAN DO TO COUNTER THAT!
KRASH
THAT'S NOT... EXACTLY... TRUE...
I ALREADY FOUND... A LOOPHOLE IN YOUR LITTLE STRATEGY ...

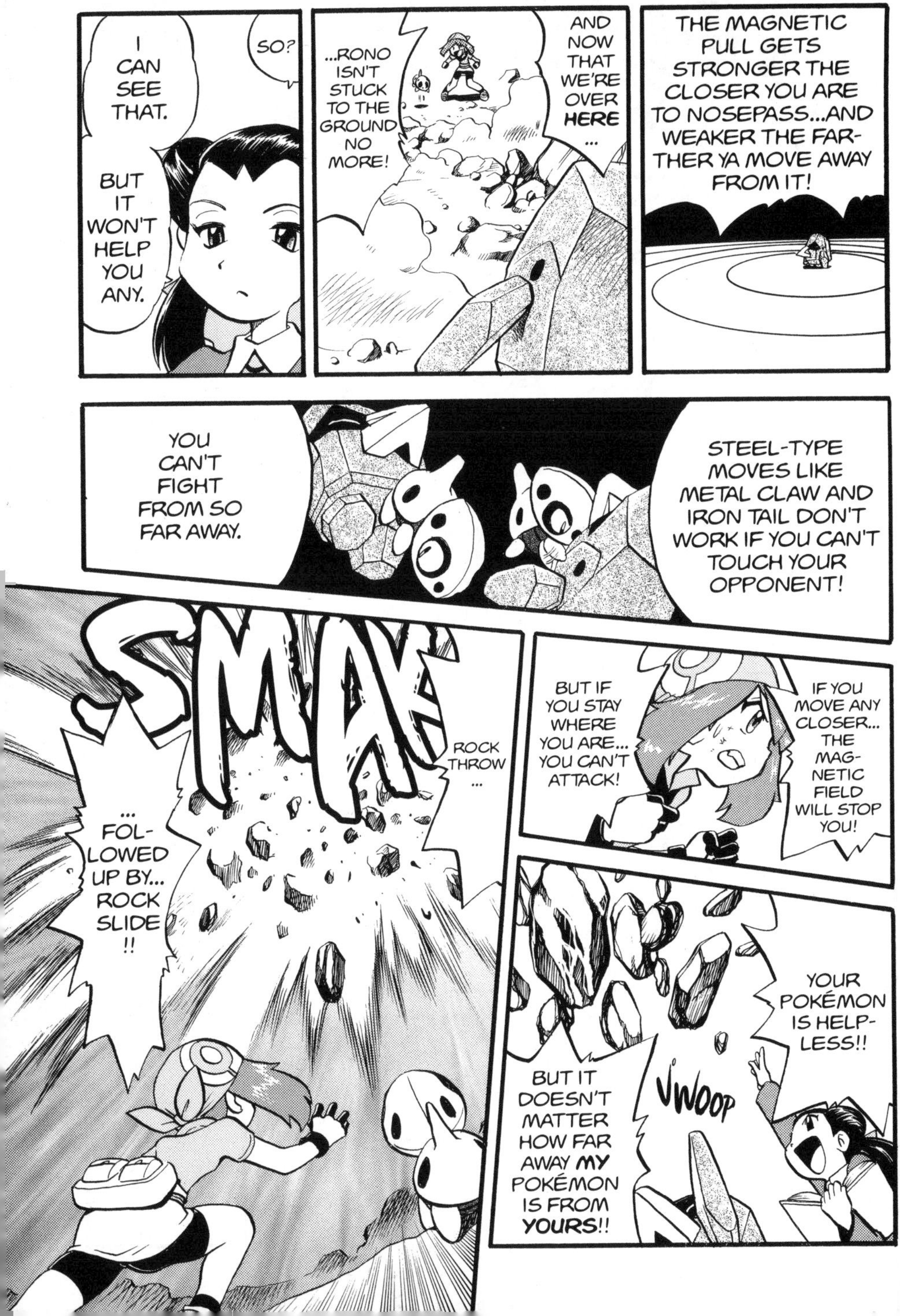
THE MAGNETIC PULL GETS STRONGER THE CLOSER YOU ARE TO NOSEPASS...AND WEAKER THE FARTHER YA MOVE AWAY FROM IT!
AND NOW THAT WE'RE OVER **HERE**...
...RONO ISN'T STUCK TO THE GROUND NO MORE!
SO?
I CAN SEE THAT.
BUT IT WON'T HELP YOU ANY.
STEEL-TYPE MOVES LIKE METAL CLAW AND IRON TAIL DON'T WORK IF YOU CAN'T TOUCH YOUR OPPONENT!
YOU CAN'T FIGHT FROM SO FAR AWAY.
IF YOU MOVE ANY CLOSER... THE MAGNETIC FIELD WILL STOP YOU!
BUT IF YOU STAY WHERE YOU ARE... YOU CAN'T ATTACK!
YOUR POKÉMON IS HELPLESS!!
VWOOP
BUT IT DOESN'T MATTER HOW FAR AWAY **MY** POKÉMON IS FROM **YOURS**!!
SMAK
ROCK THROW...
...FOLLOWED UP BY... ROCK SLIDE!!

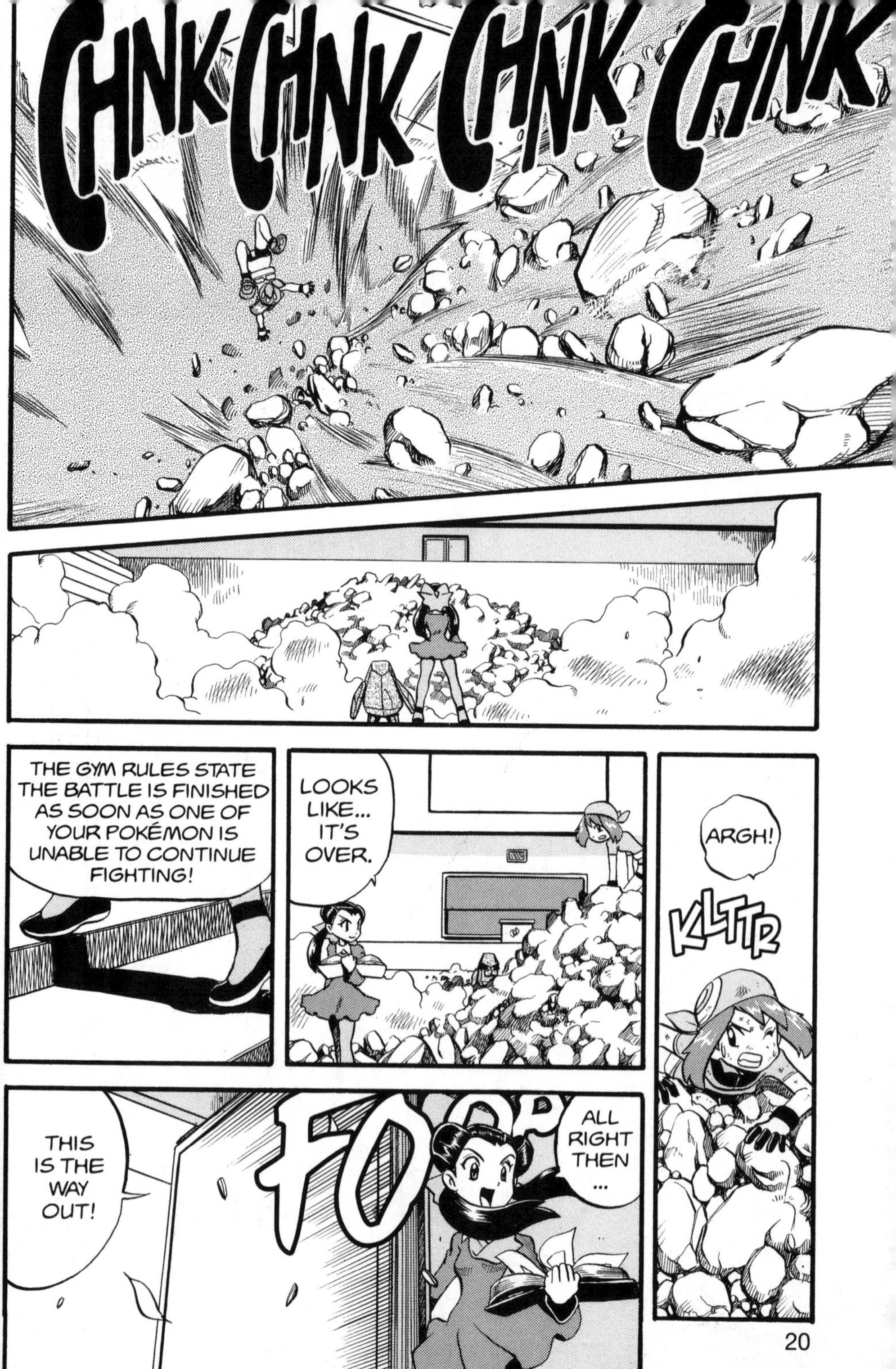
CHNK CHNK CHNK CHNK
ARGH!
KLTTR
LOOKS LIKE... IT'S OVER.
THE GYM RULES STATE THE BATTLE IS FINISHED AS SOON AS ONE OF YOUR POKÉMON IS UNABLE TO CONTINUE FIGHTING!
ALL RIGHT THEN ...
FO
THIS IS THE WAY OUT!

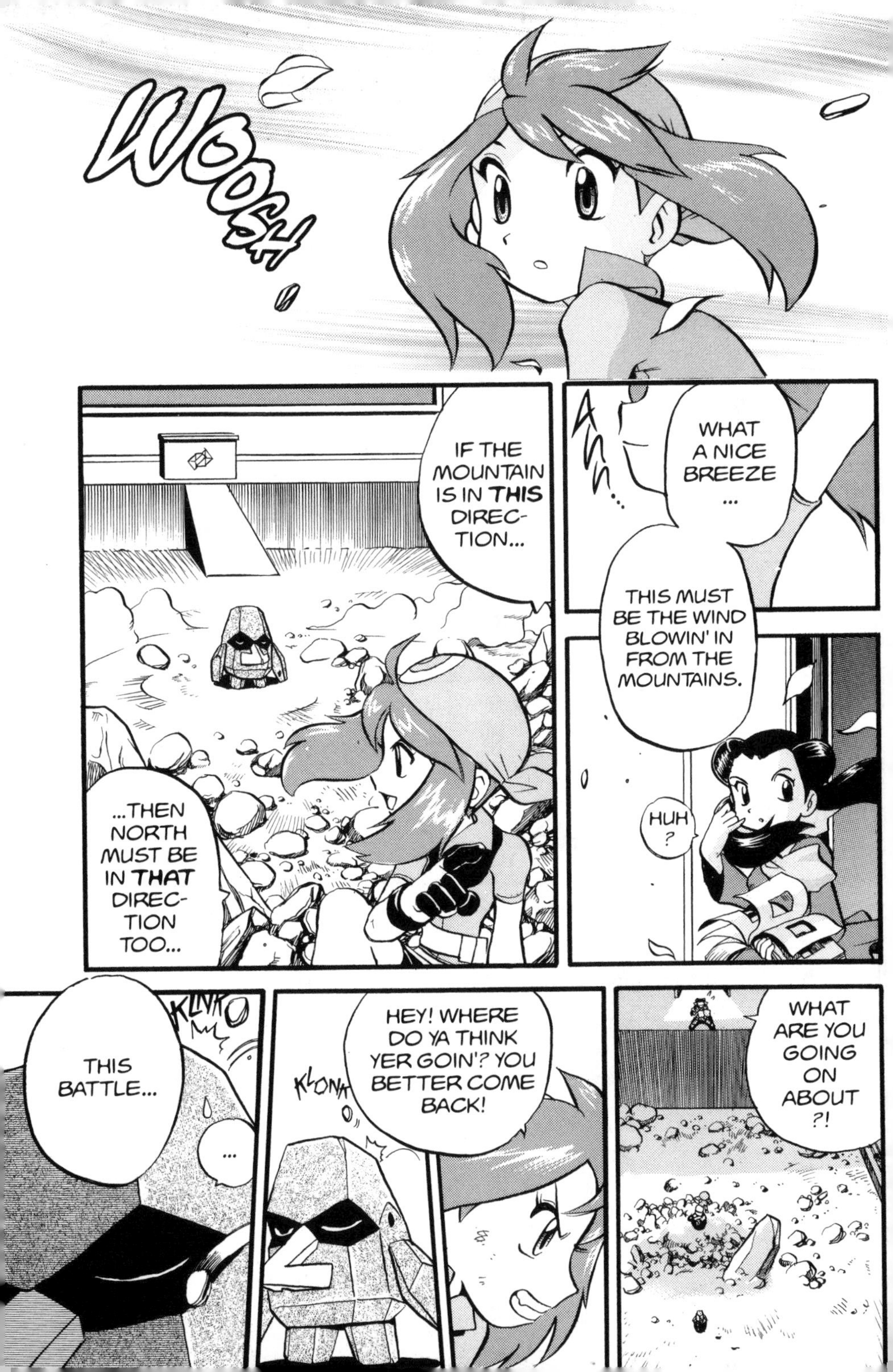
WOOSH
WHAT A NICE BREEZE...
THIS MUST BE THE WIND BLOWIN' IN FROM THE MOUNTAINS.
HUH?
IF THE MOUNTAIN IS IN **THIS** DIRECTION...
...THEN NORTH MUST BE IN **THAT** DIRECTION TOO...
WHAT ARE YOU GOING ON ABOUT?!
KLONK
HEY! WHERE DO YA THINK YER GOIN'? YOU BETTER COME BACK!
KLINK
THIS BATTLE...
...

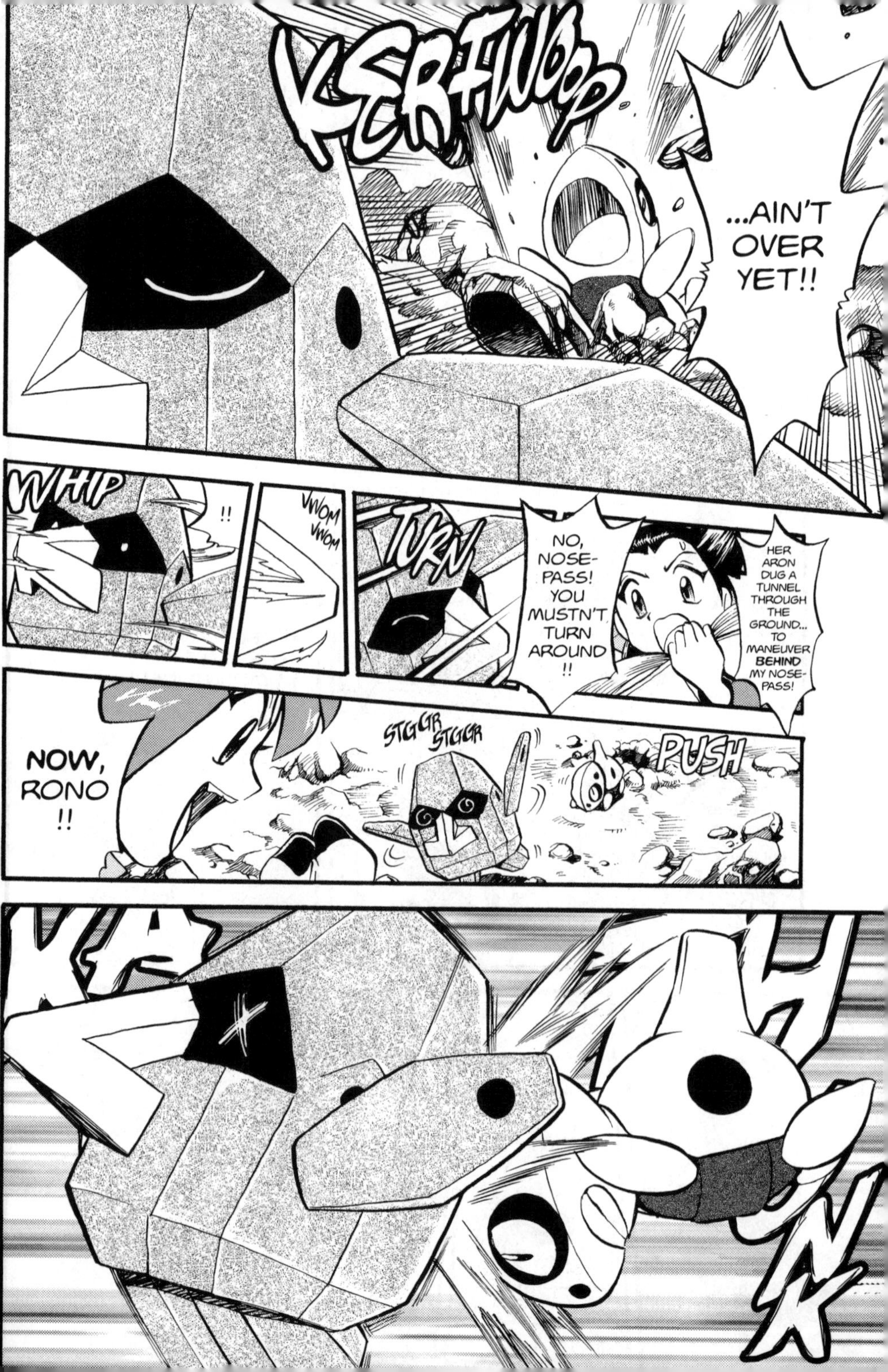
KERFWOOP
...AIN'T OVER YET!!
HER ARON DUG A TUNNEL THROUGH THE GROUND... TO MANEUVER **BEHIND** MY NOSE-PASS!
NO, NOSE-PASS! YOU MUSTN'T TURN AROUND!!
TURN
VWOM VWOM
!!
WHIP
PUSH
STGGR STGGR
NOW, RONO!!

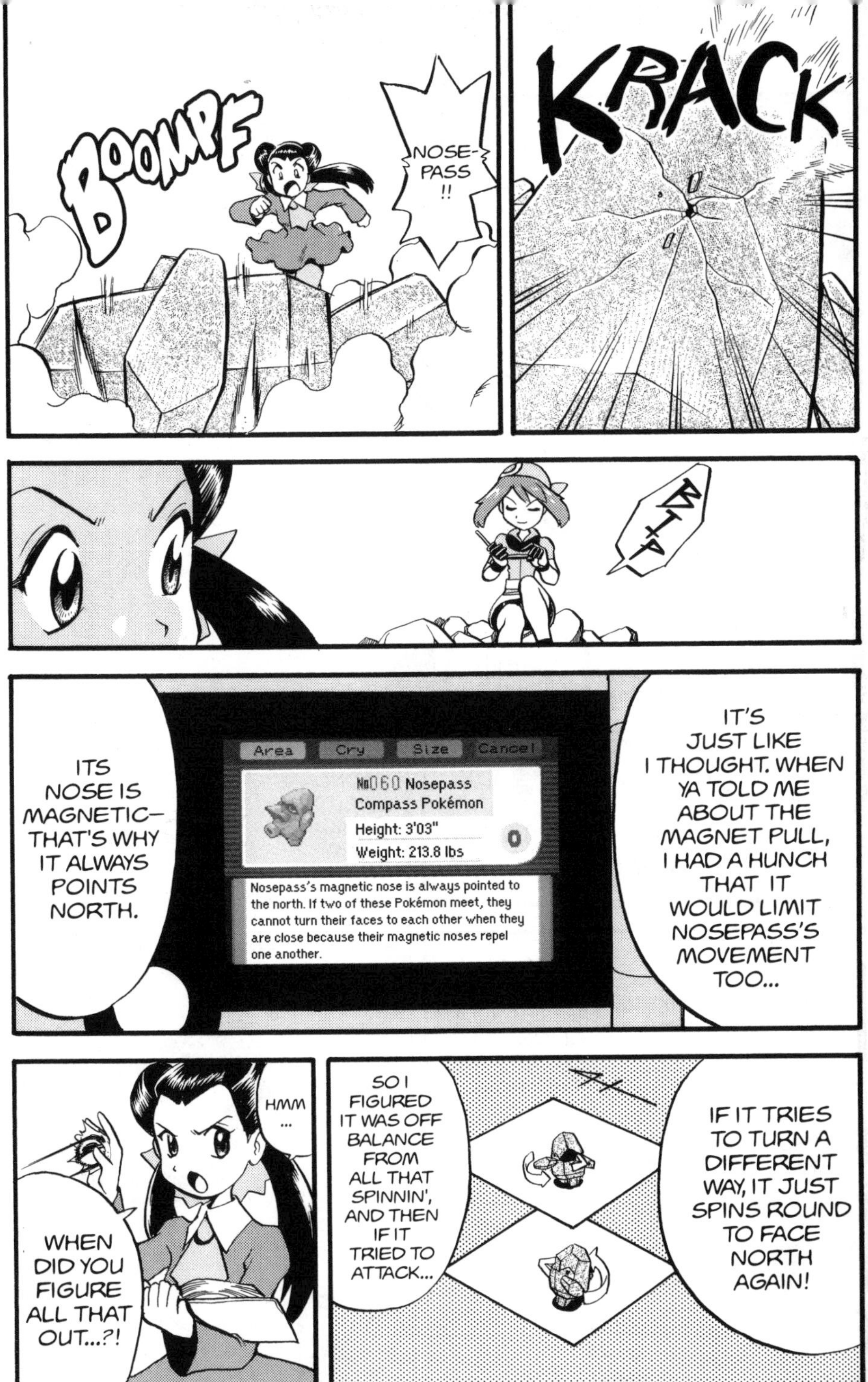
KRACK
NOSE-PASS !!
BOOMPF
BLIP
IT'S JUST LIKE I THOUGHT. WHEN YA TOLD ME ABOUT THE MAGNET PULL, I HAD A HUNCH THAT IT WOULD LIMIT NOSEPASS'S MOVEMENT TOO...
Area Cry Size Cancel
No060 Nosepass
Compass Pokémon
Height: 3'03"
Weight: 213.8 lbs
Nosepass's magnetic nose is always pointed to the north. If two of these Pokémon meet, they cannot turn their faces to each other when they are close because their magnetic noses repel one another.
ITS NOSE IS MAGNETIC— THAT'S WHY IT ALWAYS POINTS NORTH.
IF IT TRIES TO TURN A DIFFERENT WAY, IT JUST SPINS ROUND TO FACE NORTH AGAIN!
SO I FIGURED IT WAS OFF BALANCE FROM ALL THAT SPINNIN', AND THEN IF IT TRIED TO ATTACK...
HMM ...
WHEN DID YOU FIGURE ALL THAT OUT...?!

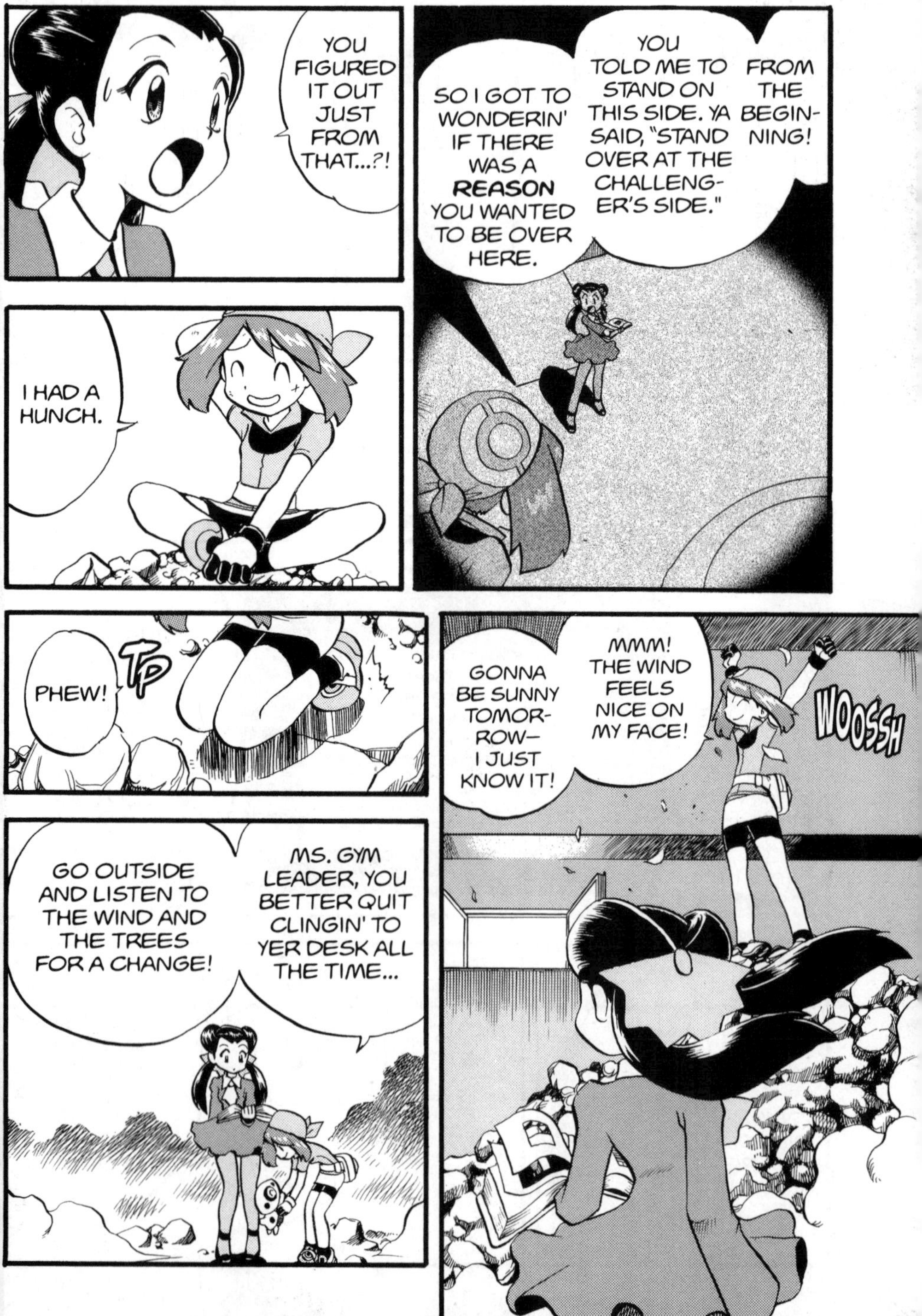
YOU TOLD ME TO STAND ON THIS SIDE. YA SAID, "STAND OVER AT THE CHALLENGER'S SIDE." FROM THE BEGINNING!
SO I GOT TO WONDERIN' IF THERE WAS A **REASON** YOU WANTED TO BE OVER HERE.
YOU FIGURED IT OUT JUST FROM THAT...?!
I HAD A HUNCH.
MMM! THE WIND FEELS NICE ON MY FACE!
GONNA BE SUNNY TOMORROW— I JUST KNOW IT!
WOOSSH
TP
PHEW!
MS. GYM LEADER, YOU BETTER QUIT CLINGIN' TO YER DESK ALL THE TIME...
GO OUTSIDE AND LISTEN TO THE WIND AND THE TREES FOR A CHANGE!

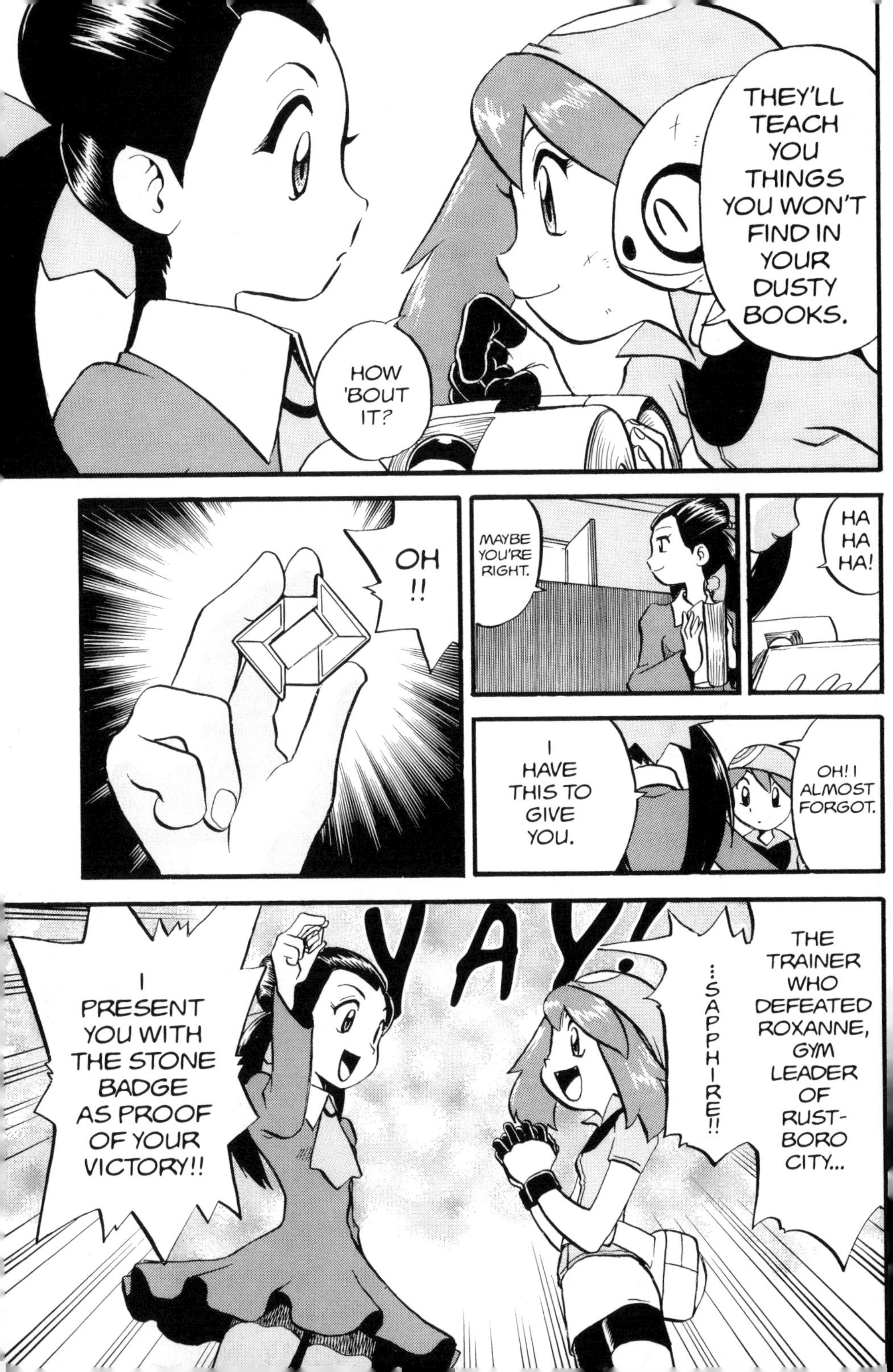
THEY'LL TEACH YOU THINGS YOU WON'T FIND IN YOUR DUSTY BOOKS.
HOW 'BOUT IT?
HA HA HA!
MAYBE YOU'RE RIGHT.
OH! I ALMOST FORGOT.
I HAVE THIS TO GIVE YOU.
OH !!
THE TRAINER WHO DEFEATED ROXANNE, GYM LEADER OF RUST-BORO CITY...
...SAPPHIRE!!
YAY!
I PRESENT YOU WITH THE STONE BADGE AS PROOF OF YOUR VICTORY!!

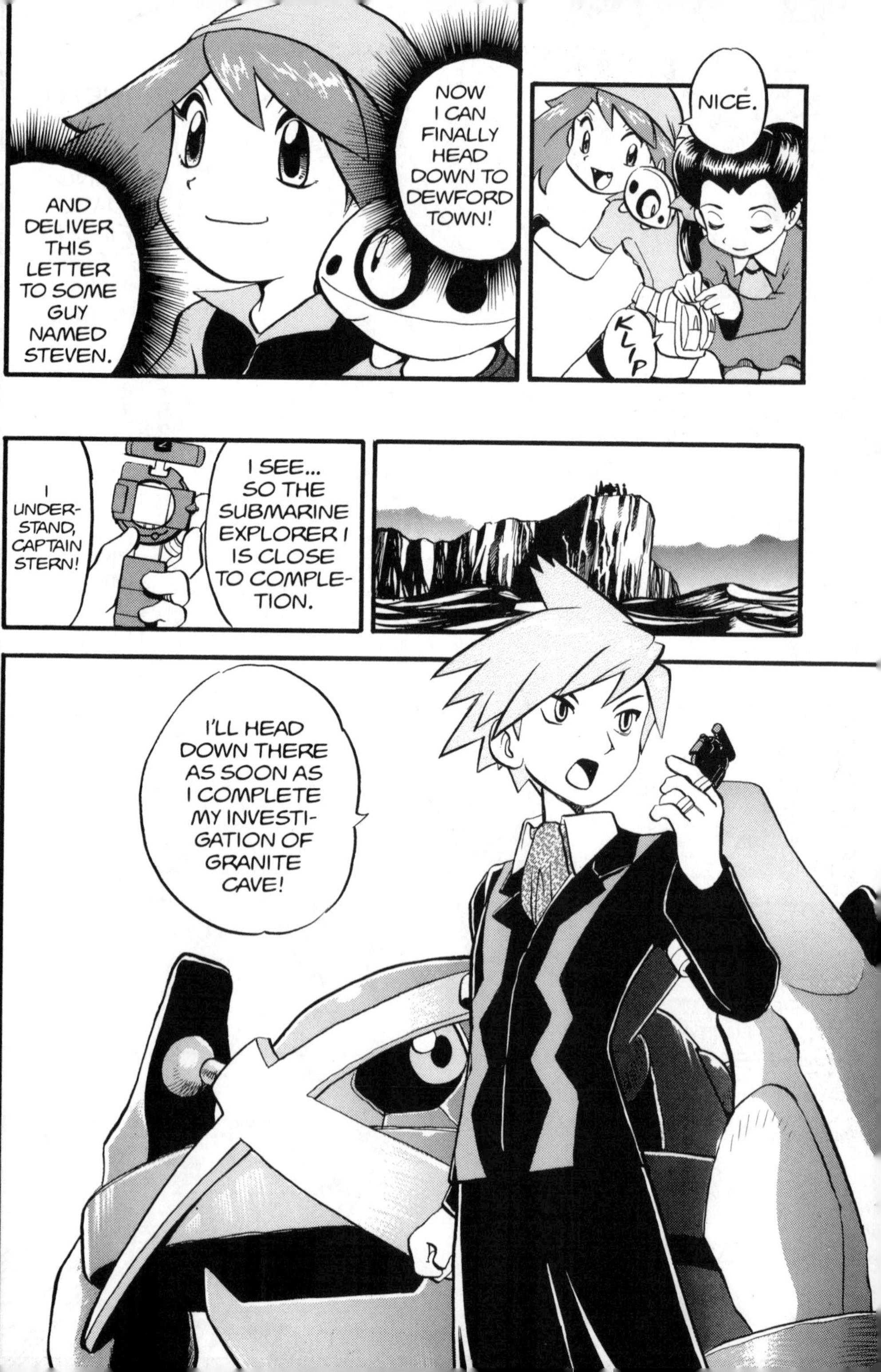
NICE.
KLIP
NOW I CAN FINALLY HEAD DOWN TO DEWFORD TOWN!
AND DELIVER THIS LETTER TO SOME GUY NAMED STEVEN.
I SEE... SO THE SUBMARINE EXPLORER I IS CLOSE TO COMPLE-TION.
I UNDER-STAND, CAPTAIN STERN!
I'LL HEAD DOWN THERE AS SOON AS I COMPLETE MY INVESTI-GATION OF GRANITE CAVE!

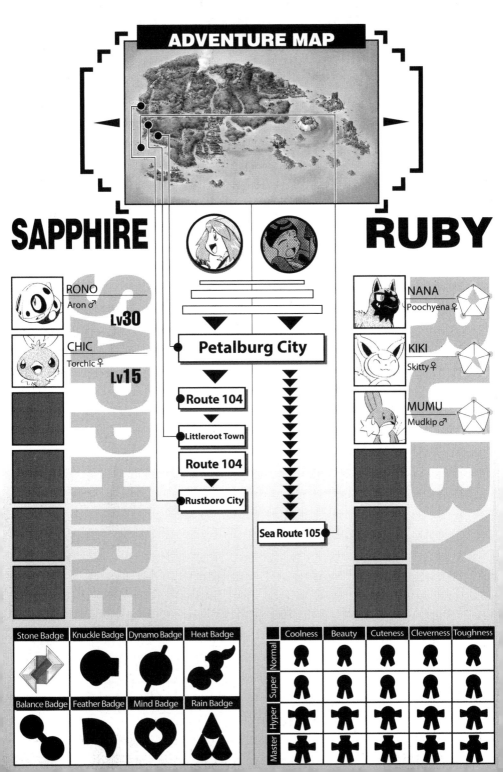

ADVENTURE MAP

SAPPHIRE

RONO
Aron ♂
Lv30

CHIC
Torchic ♀
Lv15

RUBY

NANA
Poochyena ♀

KIKI
Skitty ♀

MUMU
Mudkip ♂

Petalburg City

Route 104

Littleroot Town

Route 104

Rustboro City

Sea Route 105

Stone Badge	Knuckle Badge	Dynamo Badge	Heat Badge
Balance Badge	Feather Badge	Mind Badge	Rain Badge

	Coolness	Beauty	Cuteness	Cleverness	Toughness
Normal					
Super					
Hyper					
Master					

● Adventure 192 ●
Stick This in Your Craw, Crawdaunt! Part 1

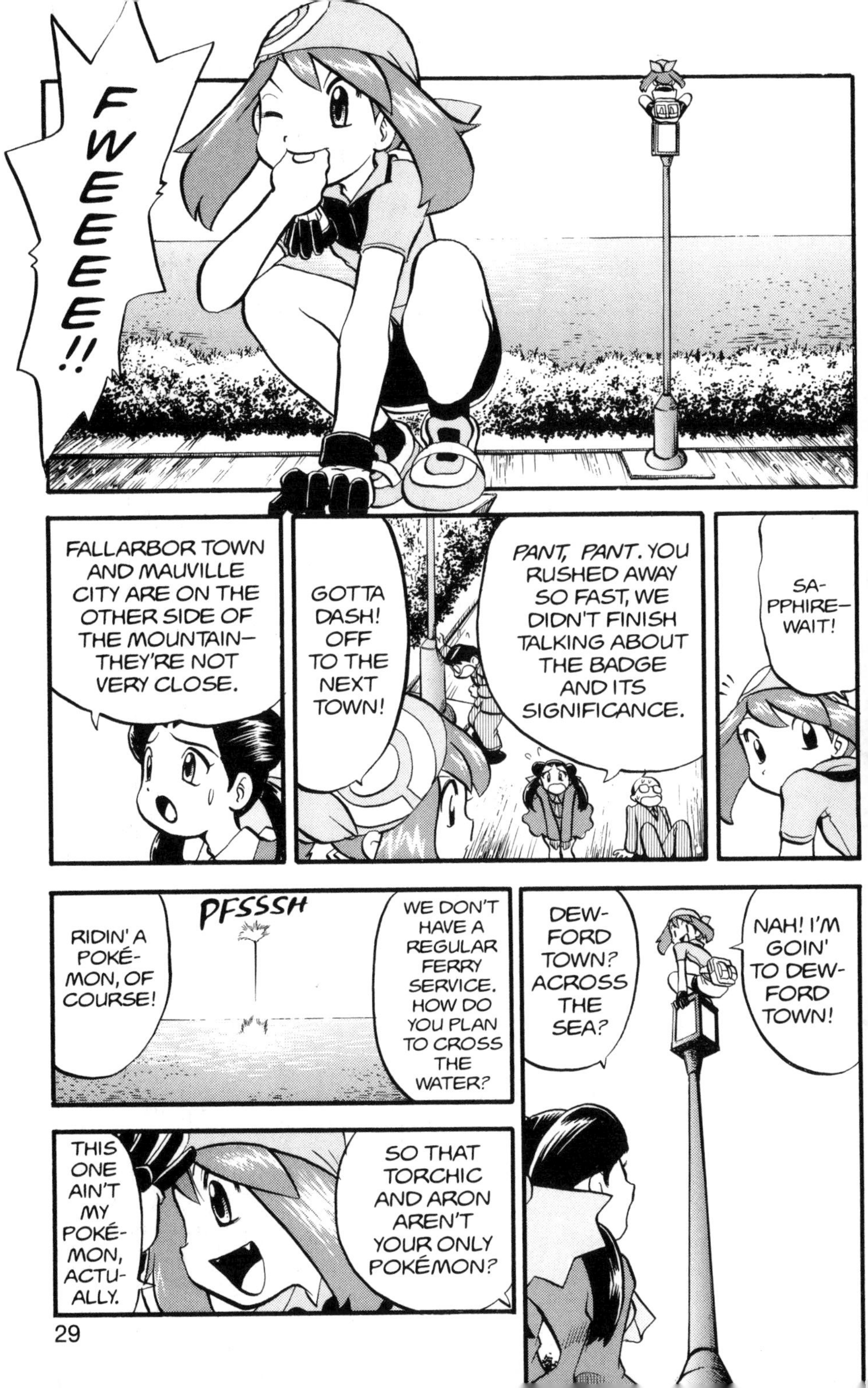
FWEEEEE!!
SAPPHIRE—WAIT!
PANT, PANT. YOU RUSHED AWAY SO FAST, WE DIDN'T FINISH TALKING ABOUT THE BADGE AND ITS SIGNIFICANCE.
GOTTA DASH! OFF TO THE NEXT TOWN!
FALLARBOR TOWN AND MAUVILLE CITY ARE ON THE OTHER SIDE OF THE MOUNTAIN—THEY'RE NOT VERY CLOSE.
NAH! I'M GOIN' TO DEWFORD TOWN!
DEWFORD TOWN? ACROSS THE SEA?
WE DON'T HAVE A REGULAR FERRY SERVICE. HOW DO YOU PLAN TO CROSS THE WATER?
PFSSSH
RIDIN' A POKÉMON, OF COURSE!
SO THAT TORCHIC AND ARON AREN'T YOUR ONLY POKÉMON?
THIS ONE AIN'T MY POKÉMON, ACTUALLY.

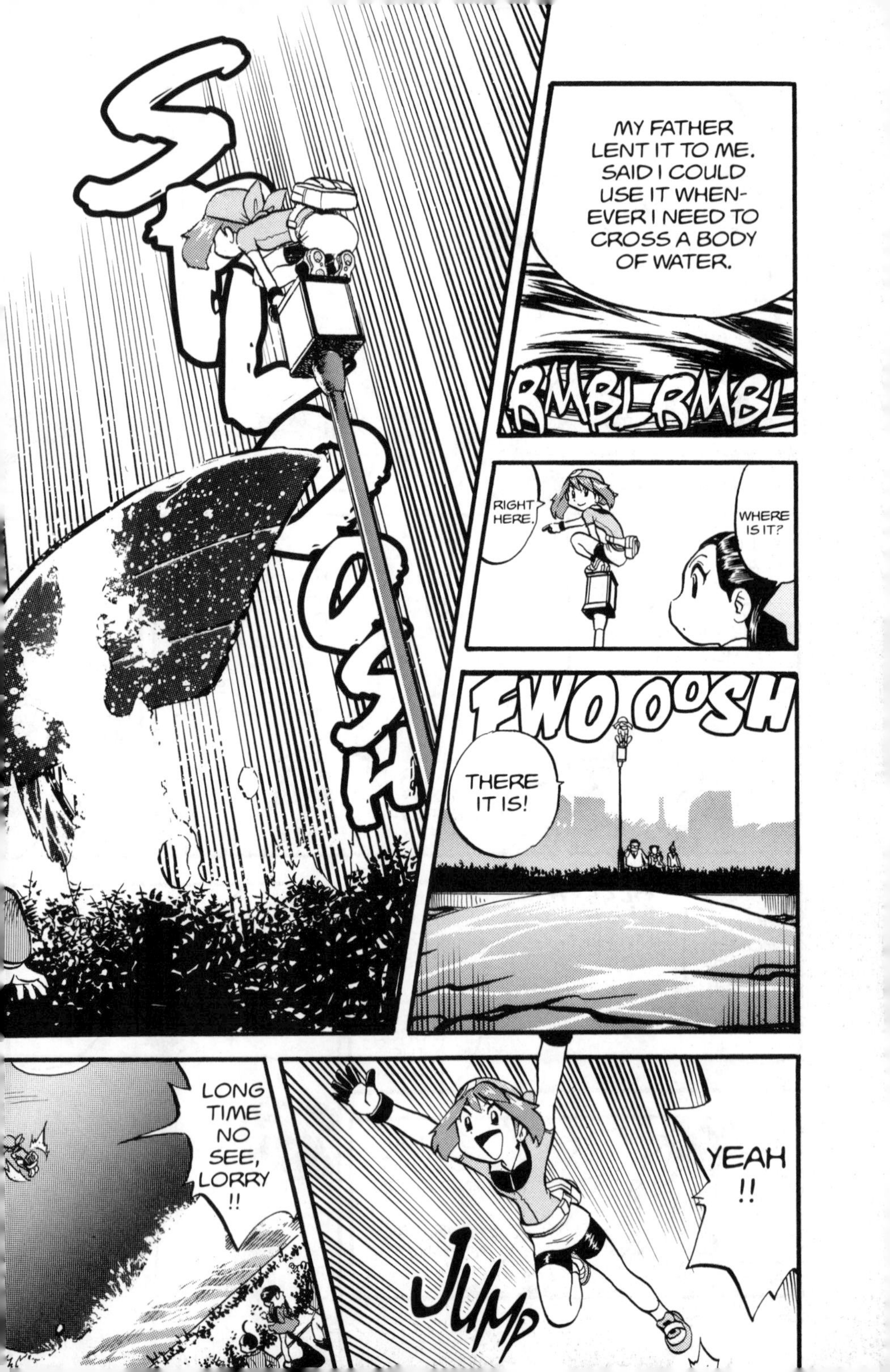
MY FATHER LENT IT TO ME. SAID I COULD USE IT WHEN-EVER I NEED TO CROSS A BODY OF WATER.
RMBLRMBL
WHERE IS IT?
RIGHT HERE.
WO OOSH
THERE IT IS!
S
OOSH
YEAH!!
JUMP
LONG TIME NO SEE, LORRY!!

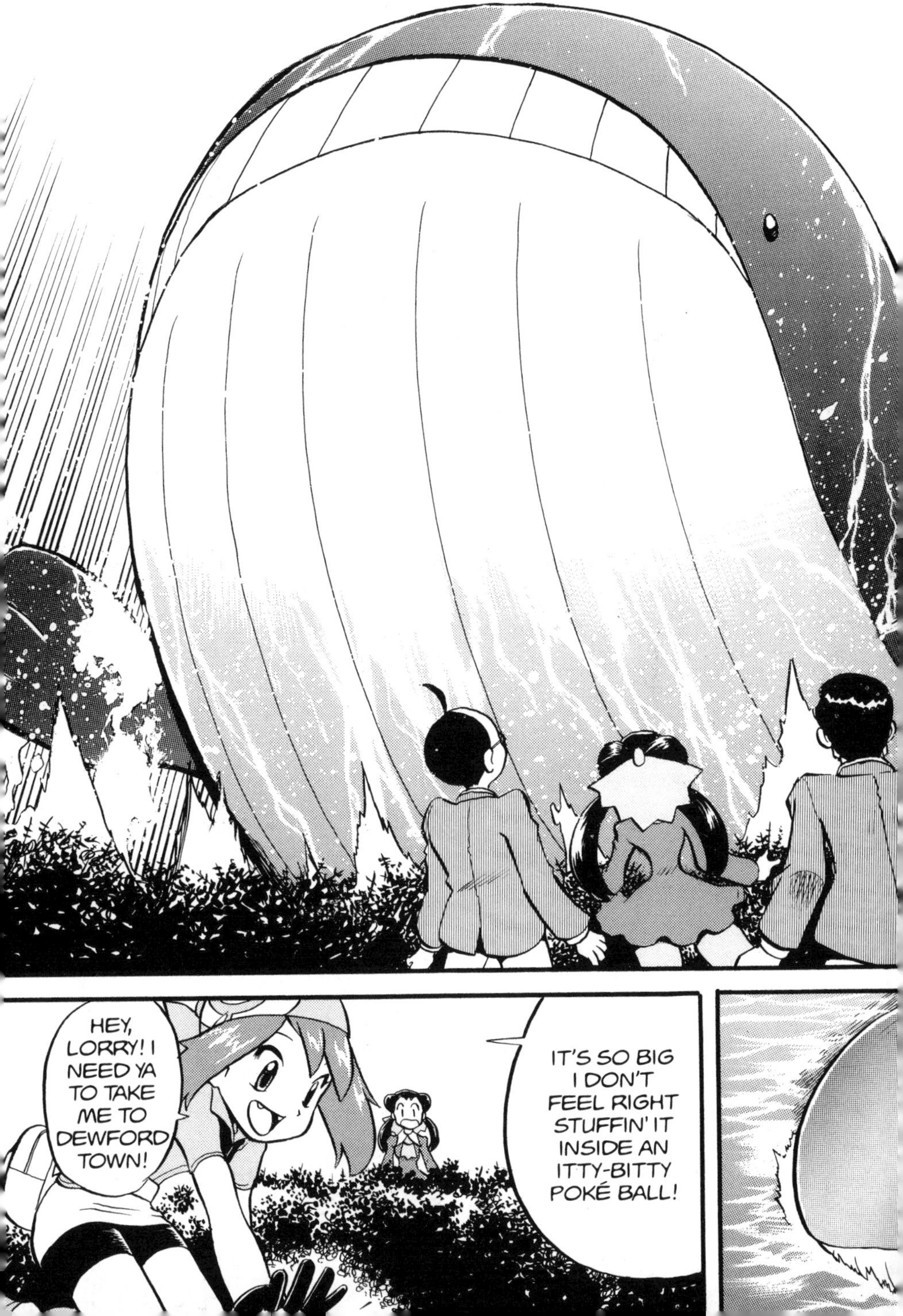
IT'S SO BIG I DON'T FEEL RIGHT STUFFIN' IT INSIDE AN ITTY-BITTY POKÉ BALL!
HEY, LORRY! I NEED YA TO TAKE ME TO DEWFORD TOWN!

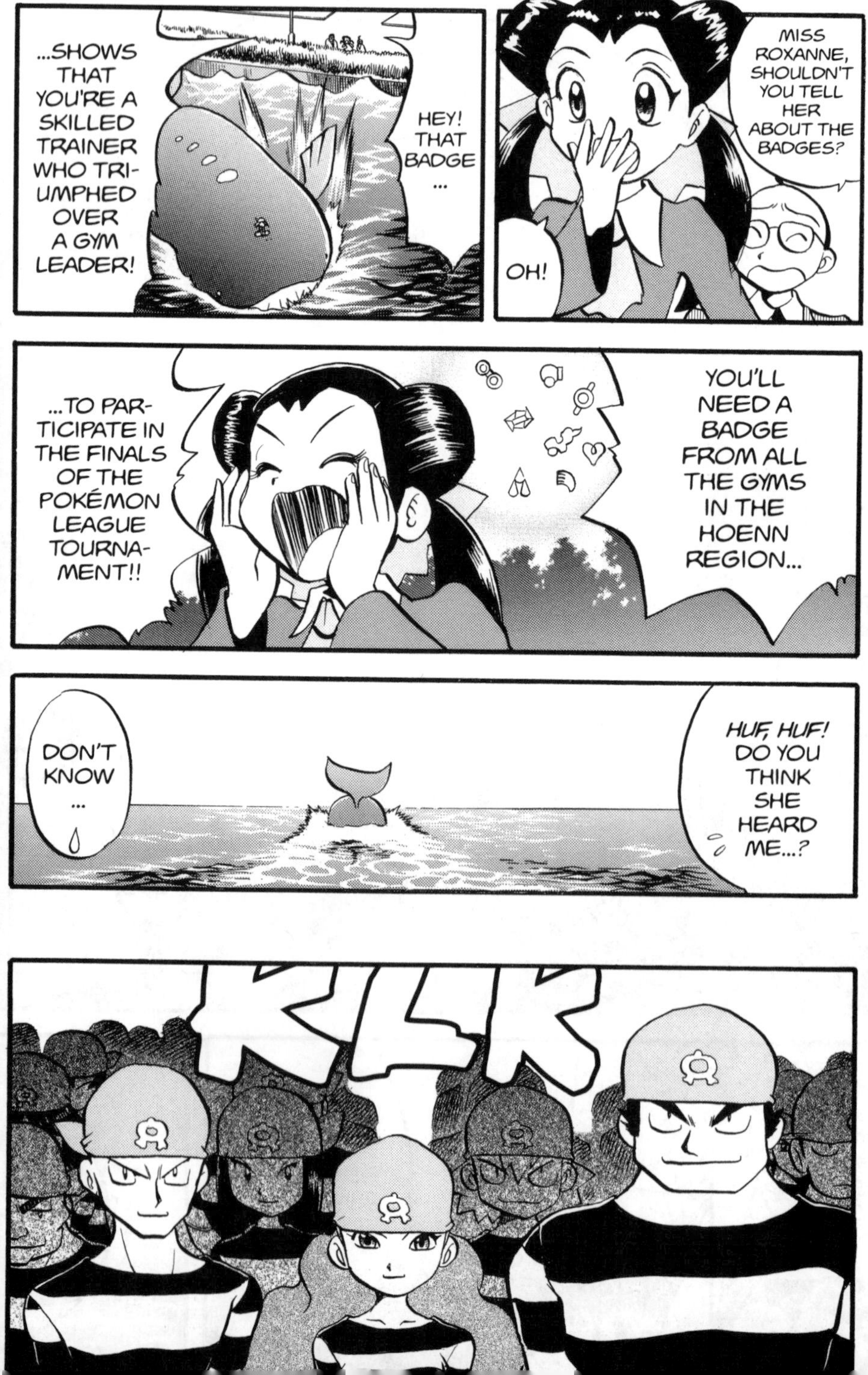
HEY! THAT BADGE ...
...SHOWS THAT YOU'RE A SKILLED TRAINER WHO TRIUMPHED OVER A GYM LEADER!
MISS ROXANNE, SHOULDN'T YOU TELL HER ABOUT THE BADGES?
OH!
YOU'LL NEED A BADGE FROM ALL THE GYMS IN THE HOENN REGION...
...TO PARTICIPATE IN THE FINALS OF THE POKÉMON LEAGUE TOURNAMENT!!
HUF, HUF! DO YOU THINK SHE HEARD ME...?
DON'T KNOW ...
KLK

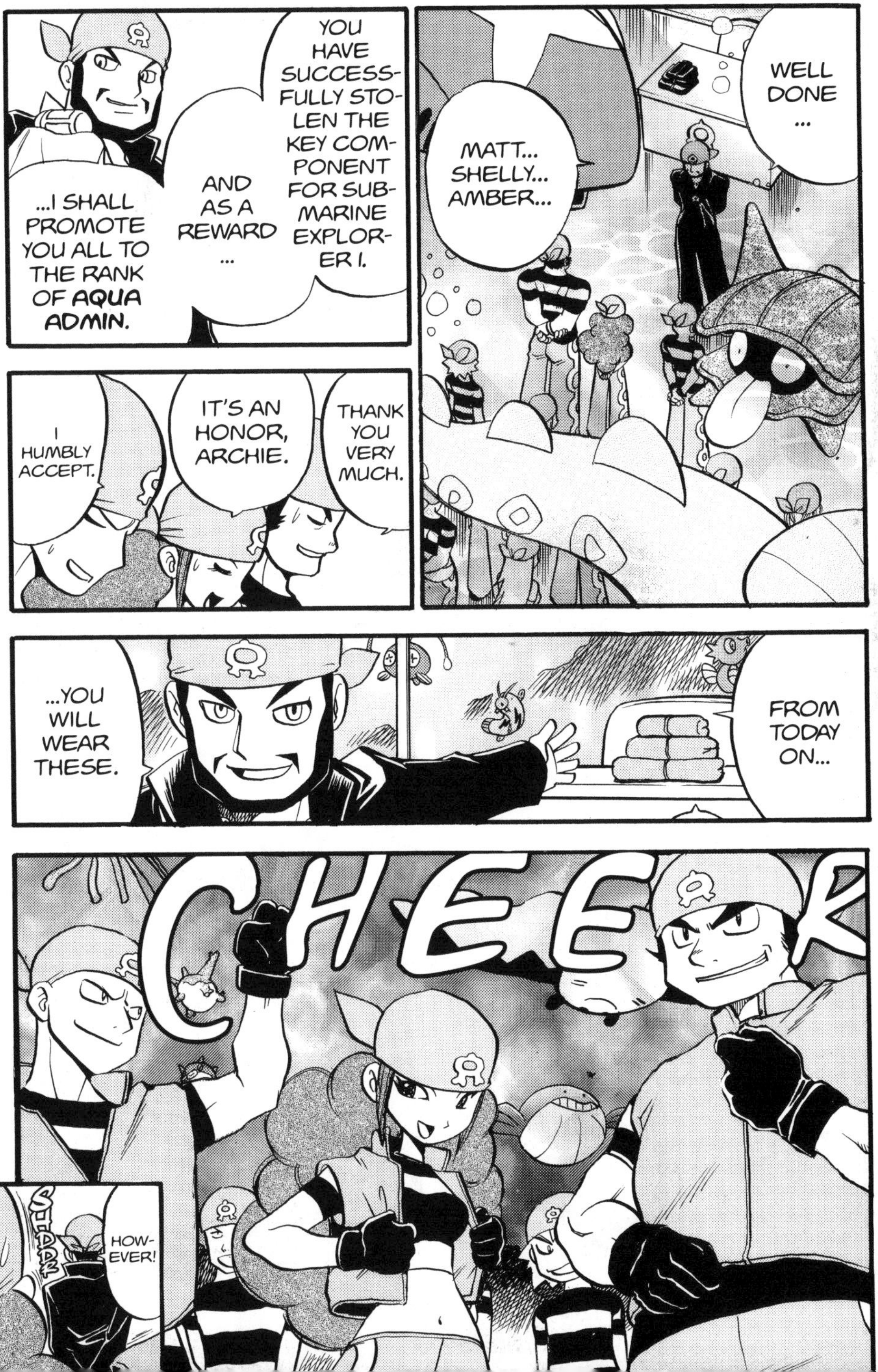
WELL DONE ...
MATT... SHELLY... AMBER...
YOU HAVE SUCCESS-FULLY STO-LEN THE KEY COM-PONENT FOR SUB-MARINE EXPLOR-ER I.
AND AS A REWARD ...
...I SHALL PROMOTE YOU ALL TO THE RANK OF **AQUA ADMIN**.
THANK YOU VERY MUCH.
IT'S AN HONOR, ARCHIE.
I HUMBLY ACCEPT.
FROM TODAY ON...
...YOU WILL WEAR THESE.
CHEER
HOW-EVER!

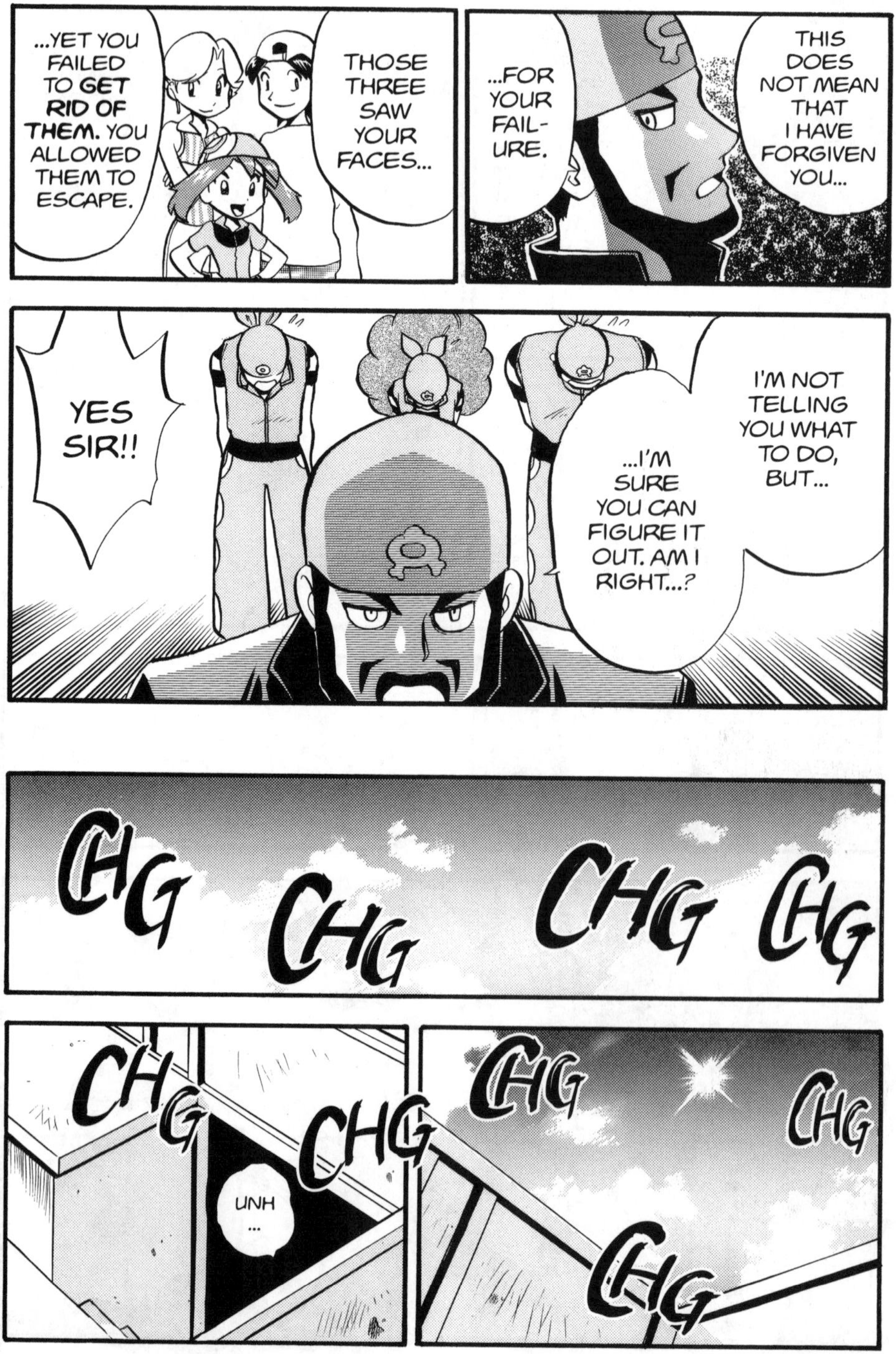
THIS DOES NOT MEAN THAT I HAVE FORGIVEN YOU...
...FOR YOUR FAIL-URE.
THOSE THREE SAW YOUR FACES...
...YET YOU FAILED TO GET RID OF THEM. YOU ALLOWED THEM TO ESCAPE.
I'M NOT TELLING YOU WHAT TO DO, BUT...
...I'M SURE YOU CAN FIGURE IT OUT. AM I RIGHT...?
YES SIR!!
CHG
CHG
CHG
CHG
CHG
CHG
CHG
CHG
UNH ...
CHG

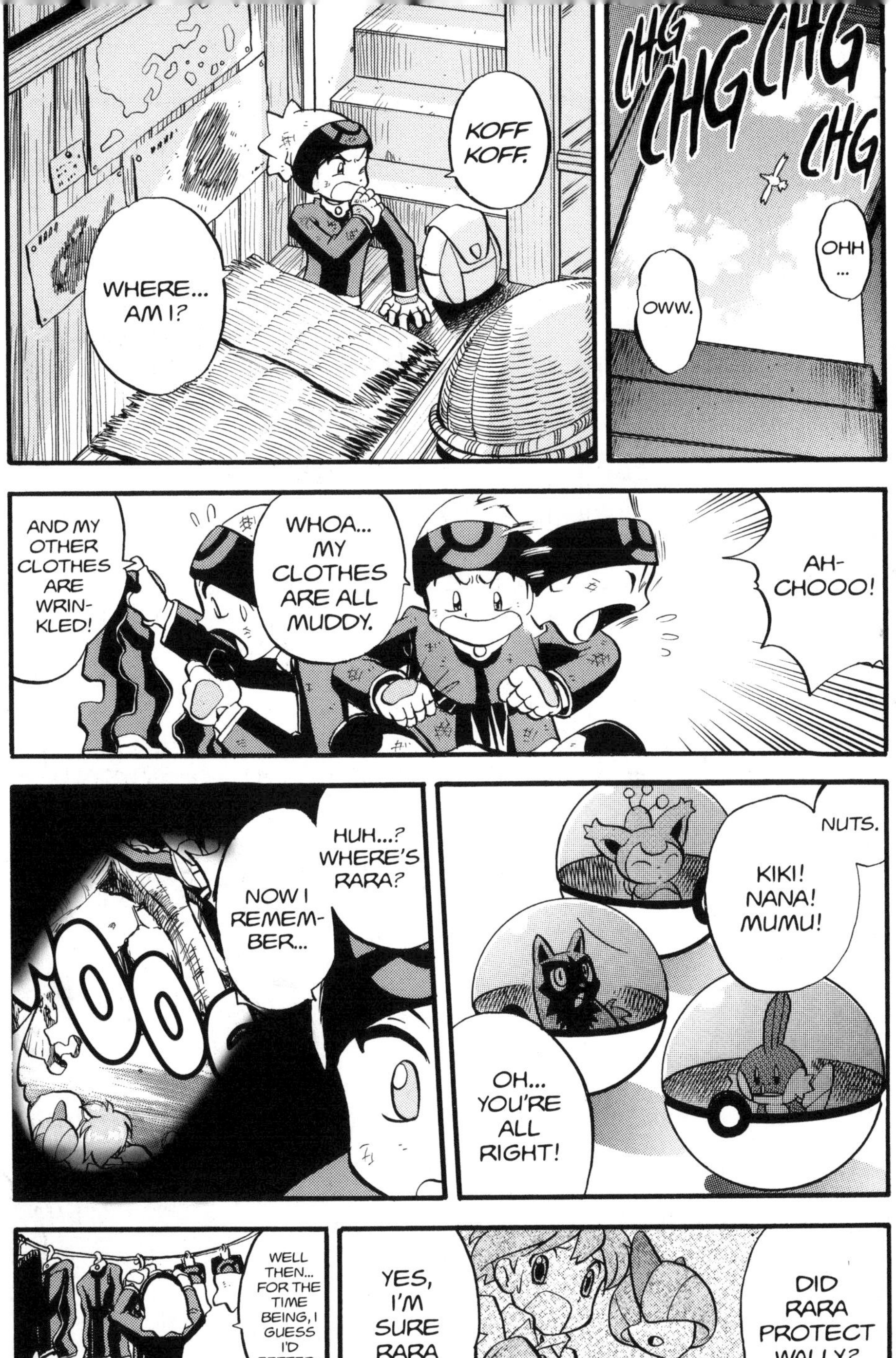
CHG CHG CHG CHG
OHH ...
OWW.
KOFF KOFF.
WHERE... AM I?
AH-CHOOO!
WHOA... MY CLOTHES ARE ALL MUDDY.
AND MY OTHER CLOTHES ARE WRIN-KLED!
NUTS.
KIKI! NANA! MUMU!
OH... YOU'RE ALL RIGHT!
HUH...? WHERE'S RARA?
NOW I REMEM-BER...
DID RARA PROTECT WALLY?
YES, I'M SURE RARA DID.
WELL THEN... FOR THE TIME BEING, I GUESS I'D BETTER-

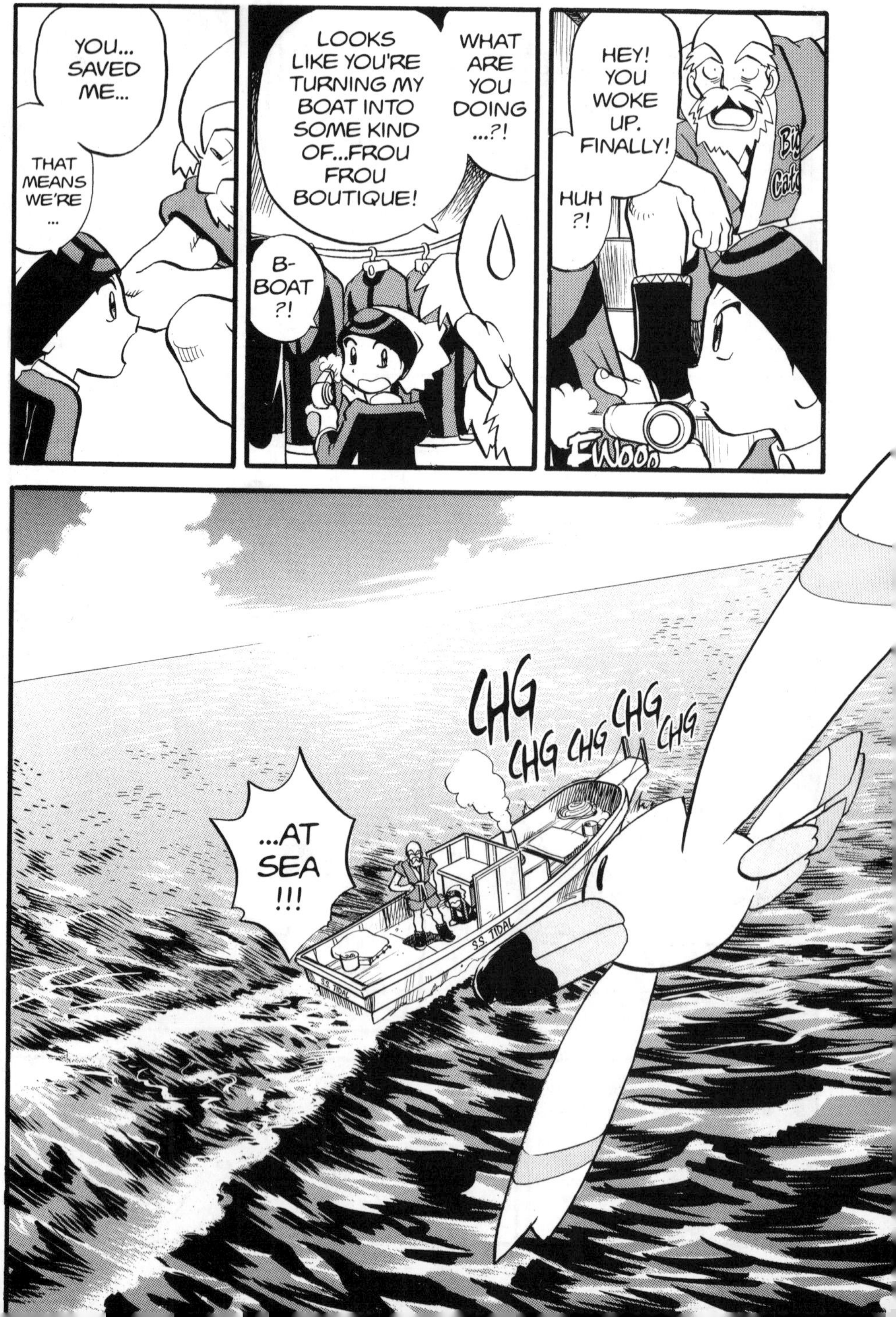
HEY! YOU WOKE UP. FINALLY!
HUH ?!
WHAT ARE YOU DOING ...?!
LOOKS LIKE YOU'RE TURNING MY BOAT INTO SOME KIND OF...FROU FROU BOUTIQUE!
B-BOAT ?!
YOU... SAVED ME...
THAT MEANS WE'RE ...
CHG CHG CHG CHG CHG
S.S. TIDAL
S.S. TIDAL
...AT SEA !!!

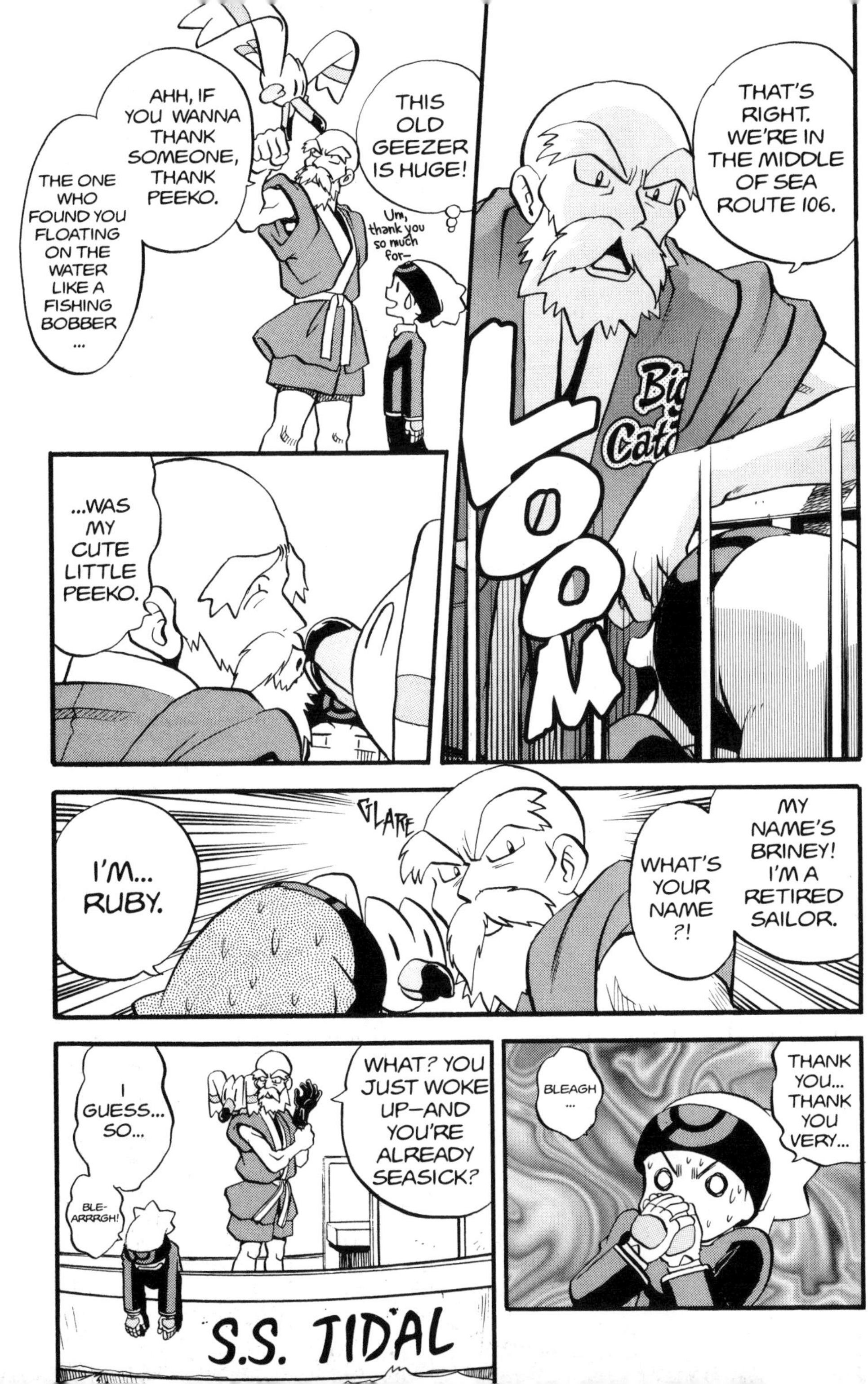
THAT'S RIGHT. WE'RE IN THE MIDDLE OF SEA ROUTE 106.
LOOM
THIS OLD GEEZER IS HUGE!
Um, thank you so much for—
AHH, IF YOU WANNA THANK SOMEONE, THANK PEEKO.
THE ONE WHO FOUND YOU FLOATING ON THE WATER LIKE A FISHING BOBBER ...
...WAS MY CUTE LITTLE PEEKO.
MY NAME'S BRINEY! I'M A RETIRED SAILOR.
WHAT'S YOUR NAME ?!
GLARE
I'M... RUBY.
THANK YOU... THANK YOU VERY...
BLEAGH ...
WHAT? YOU JUST WOKE UP—AND YOU'RE ALREADY SEASICK?
I GUESS... SO...
BLE-ARRRGH!
S.S. TIDAL

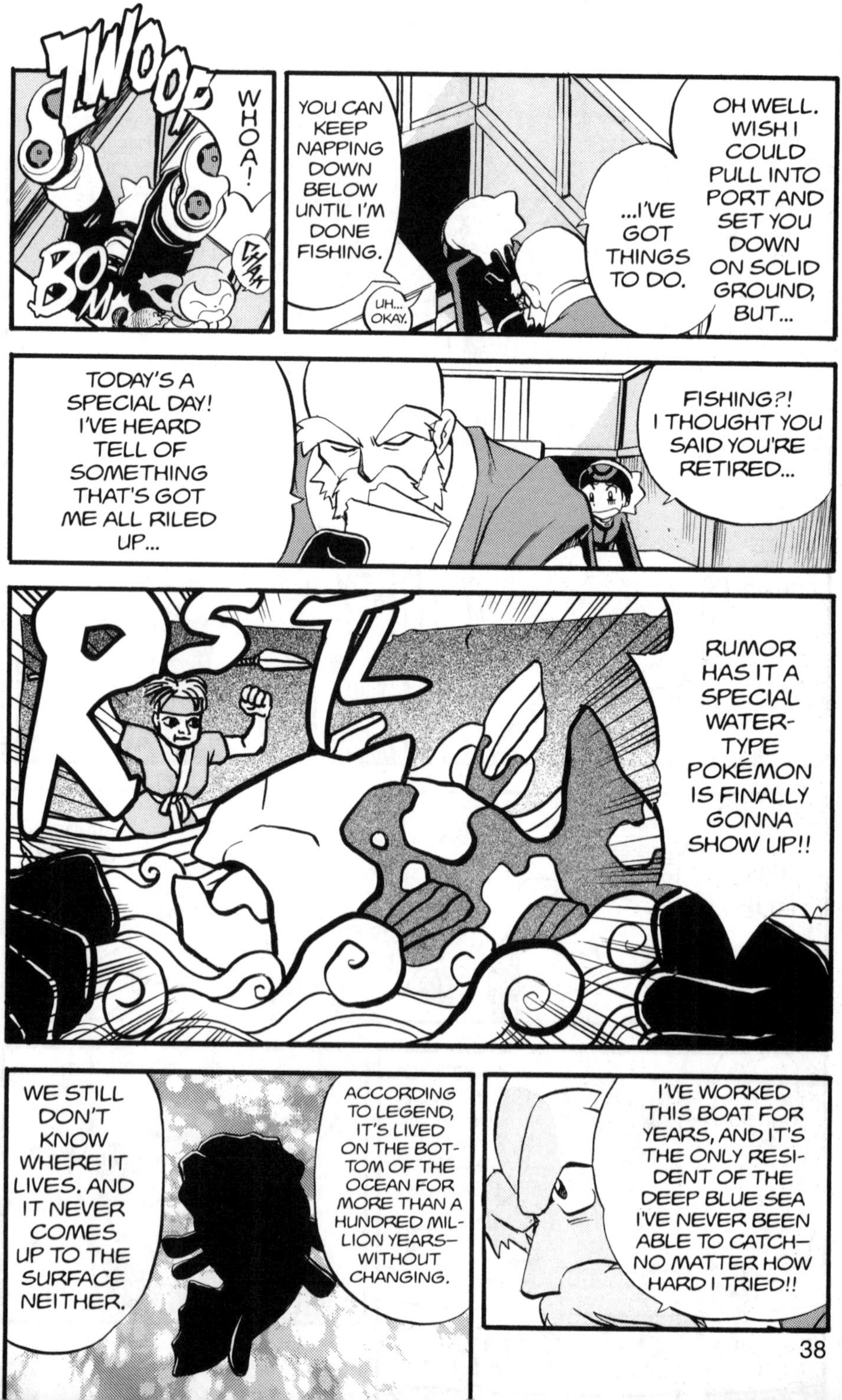
OH WELL. WISH I COULD PULL INTO PORT AND SET YOU DOWN ON SOLID GROUND, BUT...
...I'VE GOT THINGS TO DO.
YOU CAN KEEP NAPPING DOWN BELOW UNTIL I'M DONE FISHING.
UH... OKAY.
WHOA!
ZWOOP
CHAK
BOOM
FISHING?! I THOUGHT YOU SAID YOU'RE RETIRED...
TODAY'S A SPECIAL DAY! I'VE HEARD TELL OF SOMETHING THAT'S GOT ME ALL RILED UP...
RUMOR HAS IT A SPECIAL WATER-TYPE POKÉMON IS FINALLY GONNA SHOW UP!!
RSTL
I'VE WORKED THIS BOAT FOR YEARS, AND IT'S THE ONLY RESIDENT OF THE DEEP BLUE SEA I'VE NEVER BEEN ABLE TO CATCH—NO MATTER HOW HARD I TRIED!!
ACCORDING TO LEGEND, IT'S LIVED ON THE BOTTOM OF THE OCEAN FOR MORE THAN A HUNDRED MILLION YEARS—WITHOUT CHANGING.
WE STILL DON'T KNOW WHERE IT LIVES. AND IT NEVER COMES UP TO THE SURFACE NEITHER.

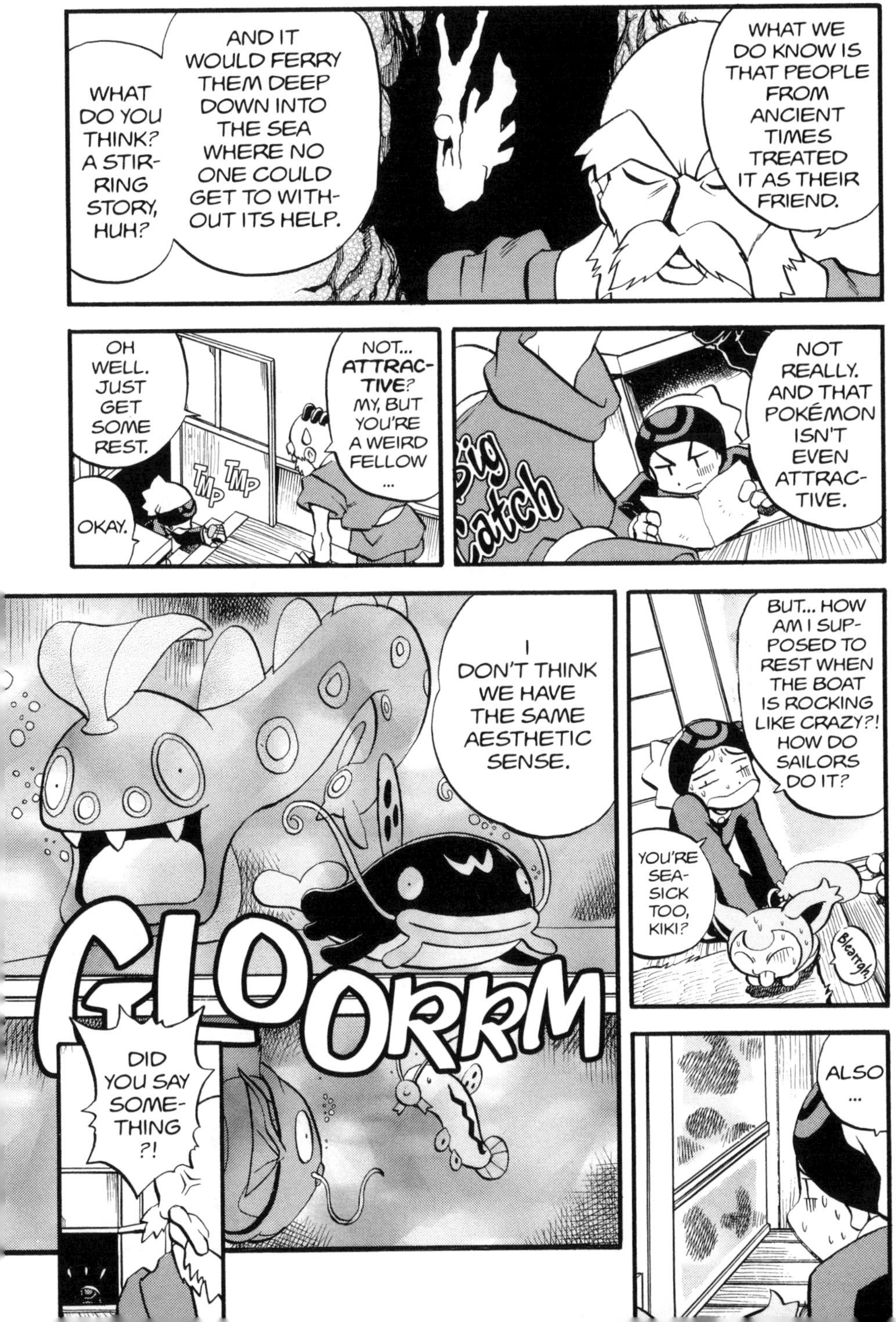
WHAT WE DO KNOW IS THAT PEOPLE FROM ANCIENT TIMES TREATED IT AS THEIR FRIEND.
AND IT WOULD FERRY THEM DEEP DOWN INTO THE SEA WHERE NO ONE COULD GET TO WITHOUT ITS HELP.
WHAT DO YOU THINK? A STIRRING STORY, HUH?
NOT REALLY. AND THAT POKÉMON ISN'T EVEN ATTRACTIVE.
Big Catch
NOT... ATTRACTIVE? MY, BUT YOU'RE A WEIRD FELLOW...
OH WELL. JUST GET SOME REST.
TMP TMP
OKAY.
BUT... HOW AM I SUPPOSED TO REST WHEN THE BOAT IS ROCKING LIKE CRAZY?! HOW DO SAILORS DO IT?
YOU'RE SEASICK TOO, KIKI?
Blearrgh
ALSO...
I DON'T THINK WE HAVE THE SAME AESTHETIC SENSE.
GLOORRKM
DID YOU SAY SOMETHING?!

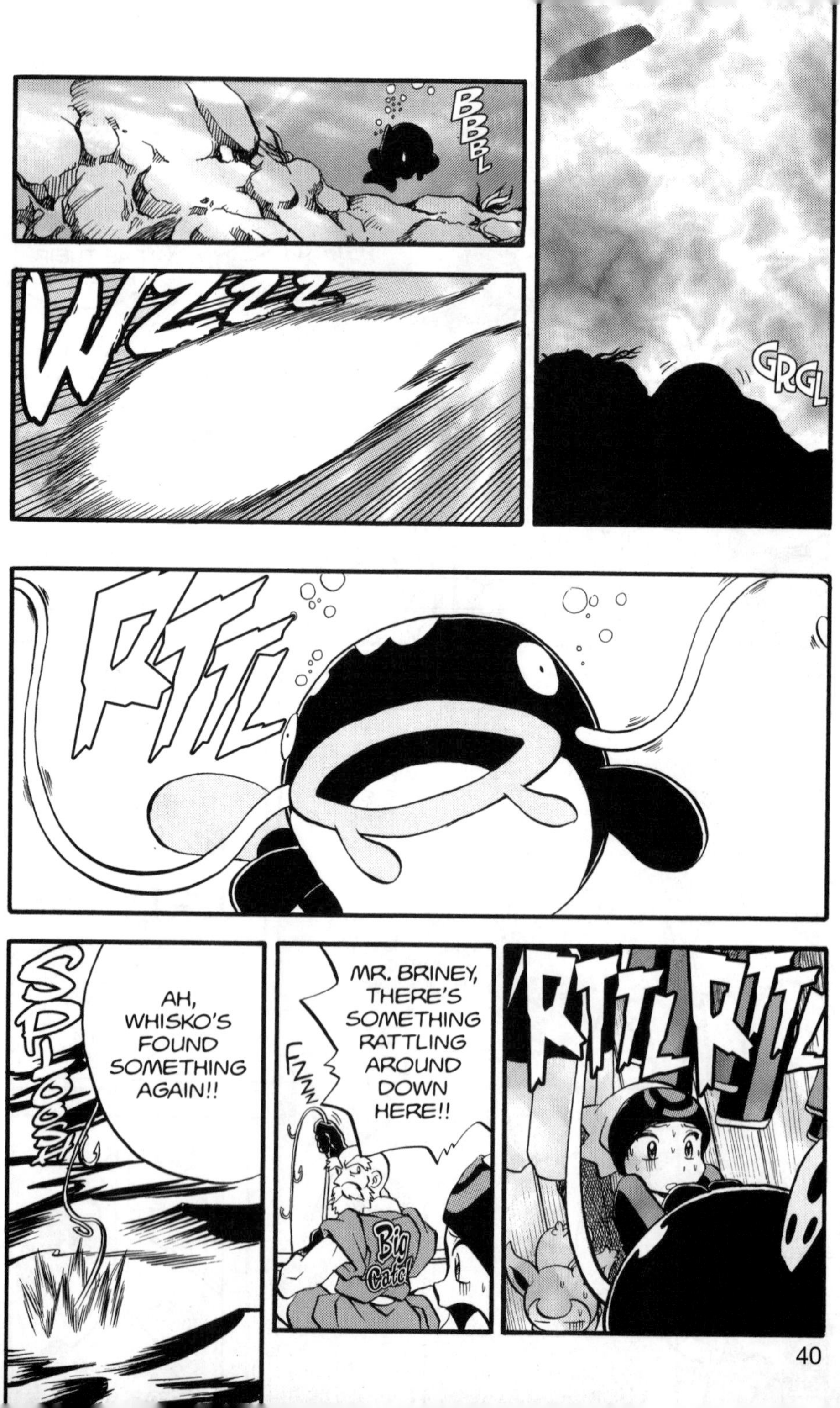
GRGL
BBBL
WZZZ
RTTL
RTTL RTTL
MR. BRINEY, THERE'S SOMETHING RATTLING AROUND DOWN HERE!!
FZZZ
Big Catch
AH, WHISKO'S FOUND SOMETHING AGAIN!!
SPLOOSH

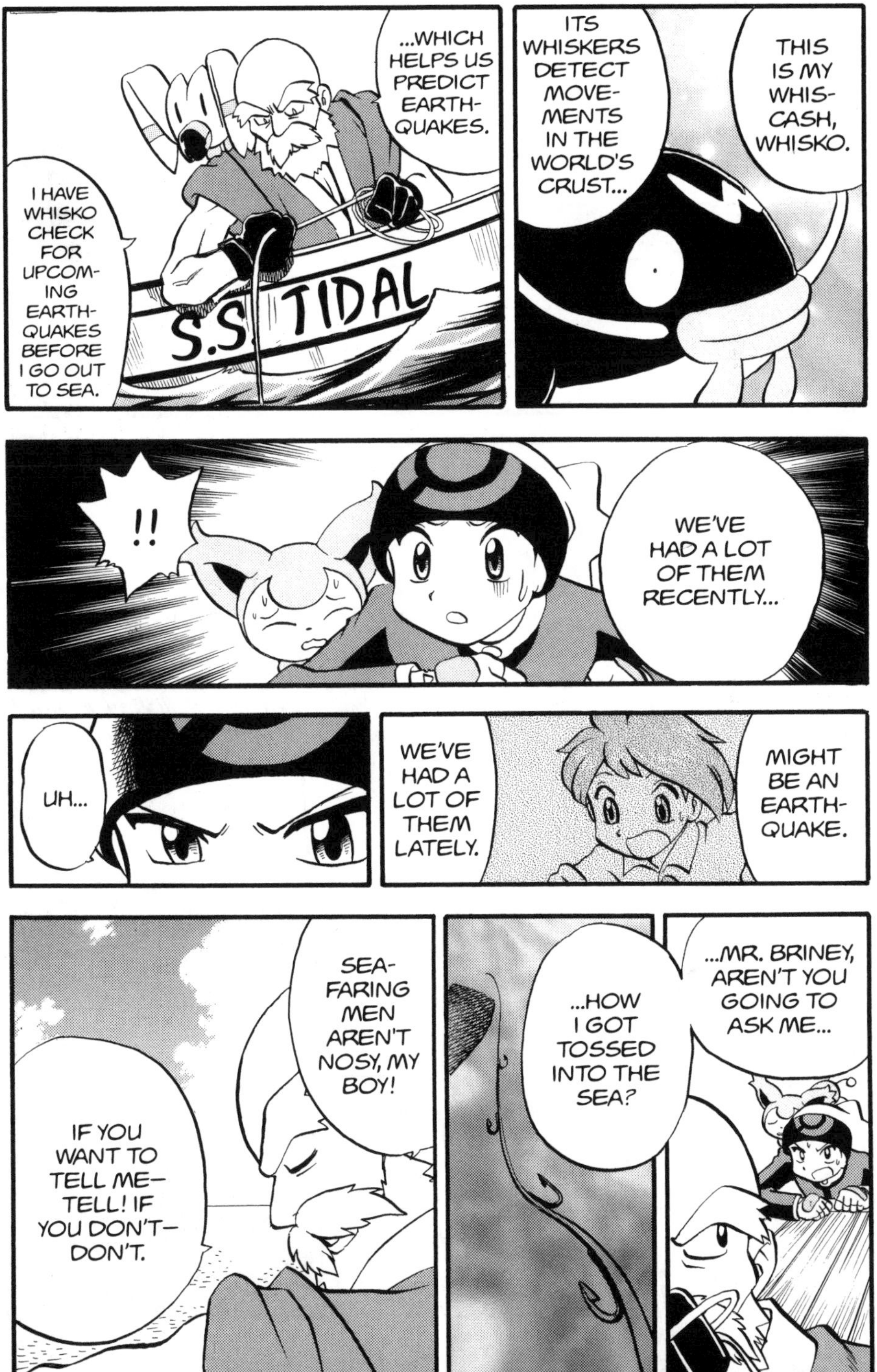
THIS IS MY WHISCASH, WHISKO.
ITS WHISKERS DETECT MOVEMENTS IN THE WORLD'S CRUST...
...WHICH HELPS US PREDICT EARTHQUAKES.
I HAVE WHISKO CHECK FOR UPCOMING EARTHQUAKES BEFORE I GO OUT TO SEA.
S.S TIDAL
WE'VE HAD A LOT OF THEM RECENTLY...
!!
MIGHT BE AN EARTHQUAKE.
WE'VE HAD A LOT OF THEM LATELY.
UH...
...MR. BRINEY, AREN'T YOU GOING TO ASK ME...
...HOW I GOT TOSSED INTO THE SEA?
SEAFARING MEN AREN'T NOSY, MY BOY!
IF YOU WANT TO TELL ME—TELL! IF YOU DON'T—DON'T.

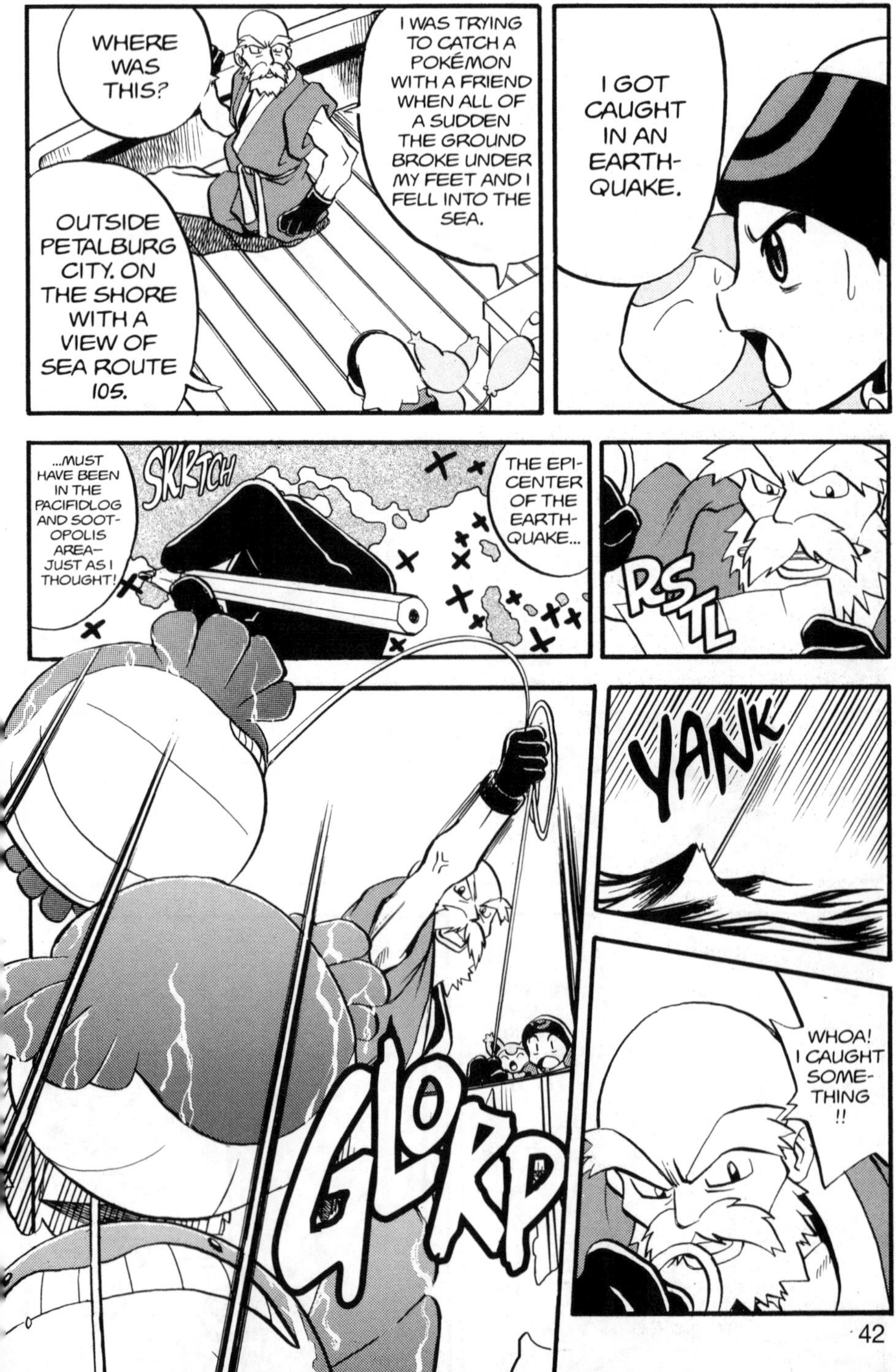
I GOT CAUGHT IN AN EARTH-QUAKE.
I WAS TRYING TO CATCH A POKÉMON WITH A FRIEND WHEN ALL OF A SUDDEN THE GROUND BROKE UNDER MY FEET AND I FELL INTO THE SEA.
WHERE WAS THIS?
OUTSIDE PETALBURG CITY. ON THE SHORE WITH A VIEW OF SEA ROUTE 105.
RSTL
THE EPI-CENTER OF THE EARTH-QUAKE...
SKRTCH
...MUST HAVE BEEN IN THE PACIFIDLOG AND SOOT-OPOLIS AREA— JUST AS I THOUGHT!
YANK
WHOA! I CAUGHT SOME-THING !!
GLORP

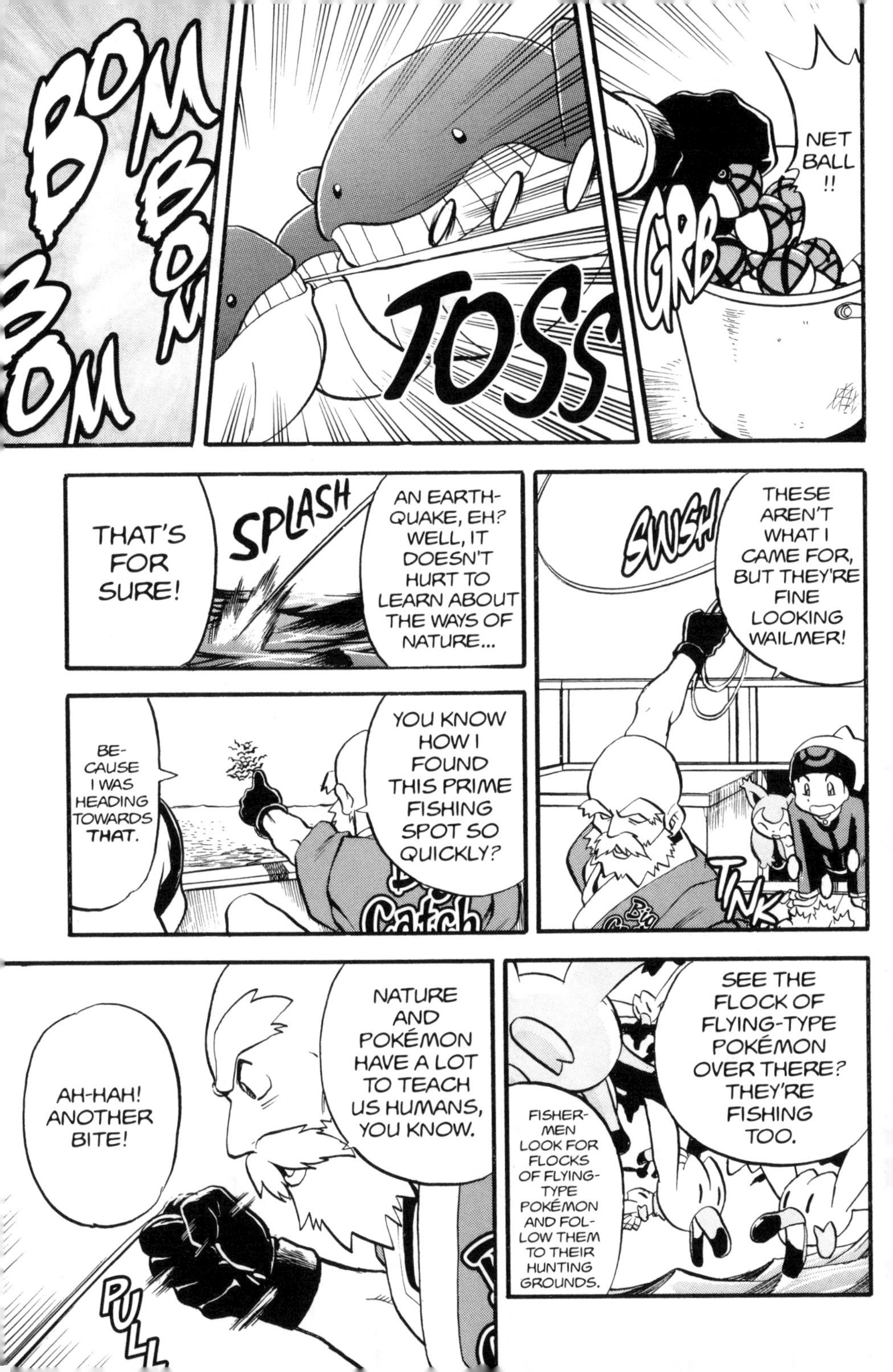
NET BALL !!
GRB
TOSS
BOM BOM BOM
SWISH
THESE AREN'T WHAT I CAME FOR, BUT THEY'RE FINE LOOKING WAILMER!
TNK
AN EARTH-QUAKE, EH? WELL, IT DOESN'T HURT TO LEARN ABOUT THE WAYS OF NATURE...
SPLASH
THAT'S FOR SURE!
YOU KNOW HOW I FOUND THIS PRIME FISHING SPOT SO QUICKLY?
BE-CAUSE I WAS HEADING TOWARDS THAT.
SEE THE FLOCK OF FLYING-TYPE POKÉMON OVER THERE? THEY'RE FISHING TOO.
FISHER-MEN LOOK FOR FLOCKS OF FLYING-TYPE POKÉMON AND FOL-LOW THEM TO THEIR HUNTING GROUNDS.
NATURE AND POKÉMON HAVE A LOT TO TEACH US HUMANS, YOU KNOW.
AH-HAH! ANOTHER BITE!
PULL

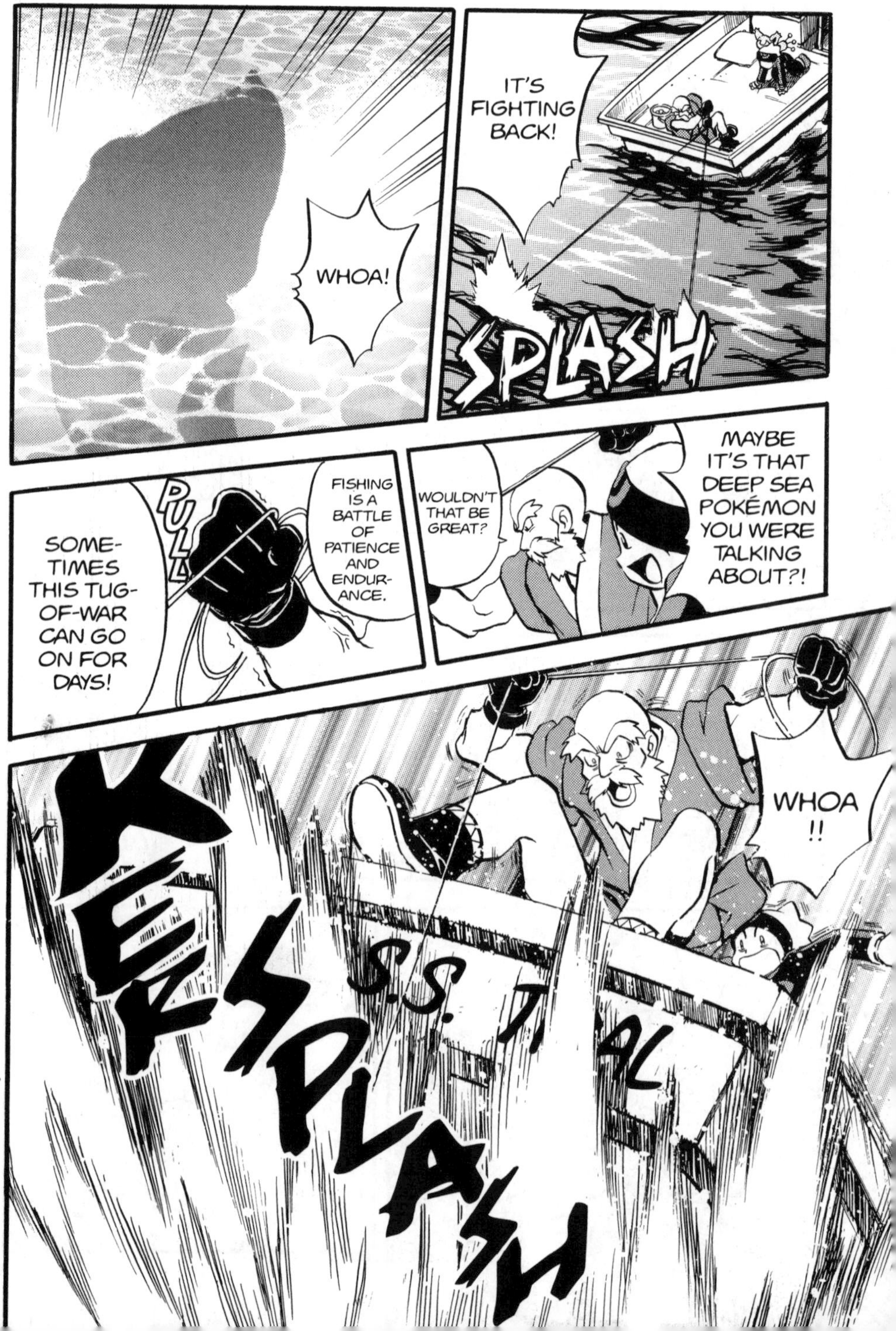
IT'S FIGHTING BACK!
SPLASH
WHOA!
MAYBE IT'S THAT DEEP SEA POKÉMON YOU WERE TALKING ABOUT?!
WOULDN'T THAT BE GREAT?
FISHING IS A BATTLE OF PATIENCE AND ENDUR-ANCE.
PULL
SOME-TIMES THIS TUG-OF-WAR CAN GO ON FOR DAYS!
WHOA !!
KERSPLASH

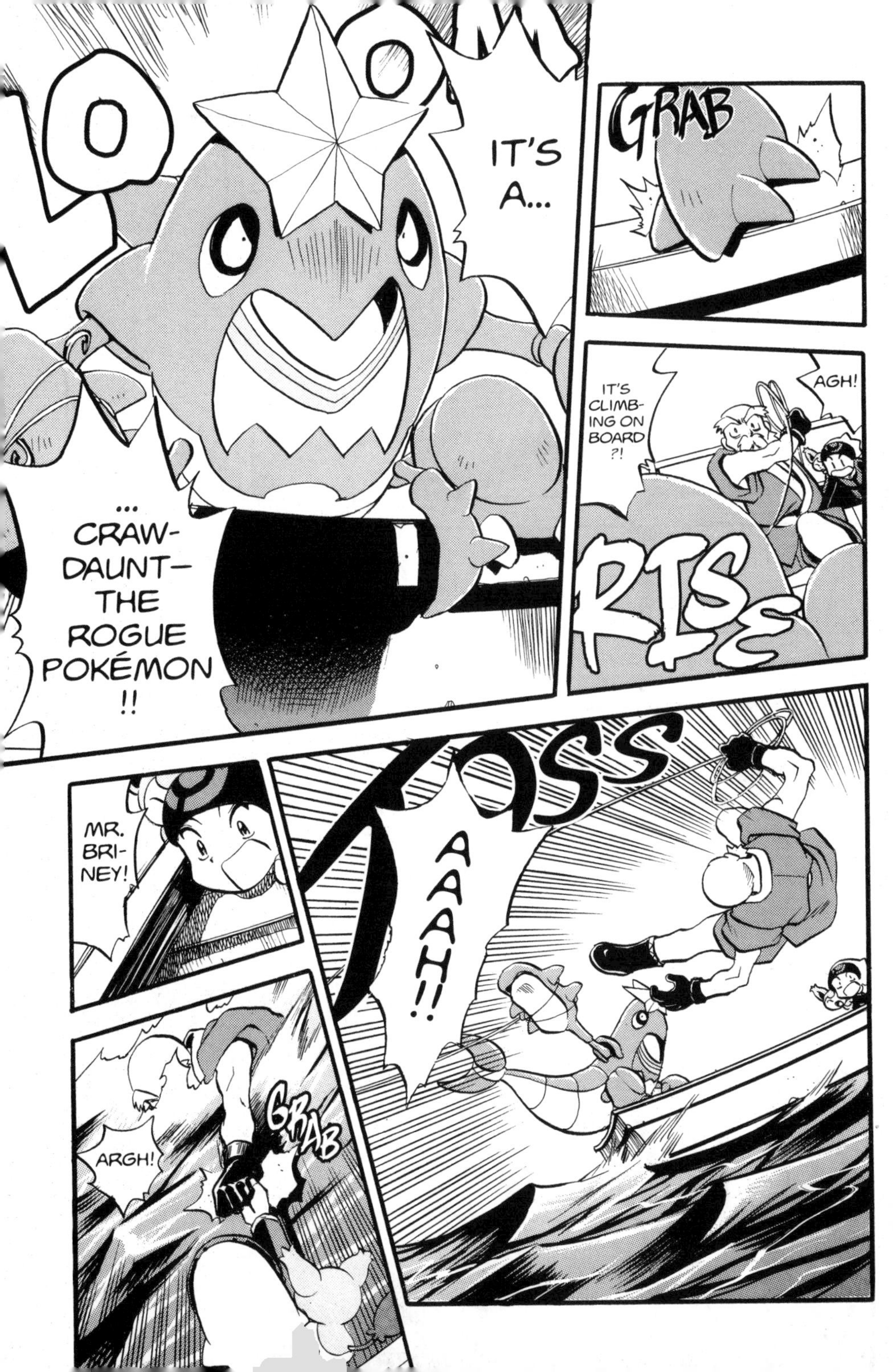
GRAB
AGH!
IT'S CLIMBING ON BOARD ?!
RISE
IT'S A...
...CRAWDAUNT—THE ROGUE POKÉMON !!
AAAAH!!
MR. BRINEY!
ARGH!
GRAB

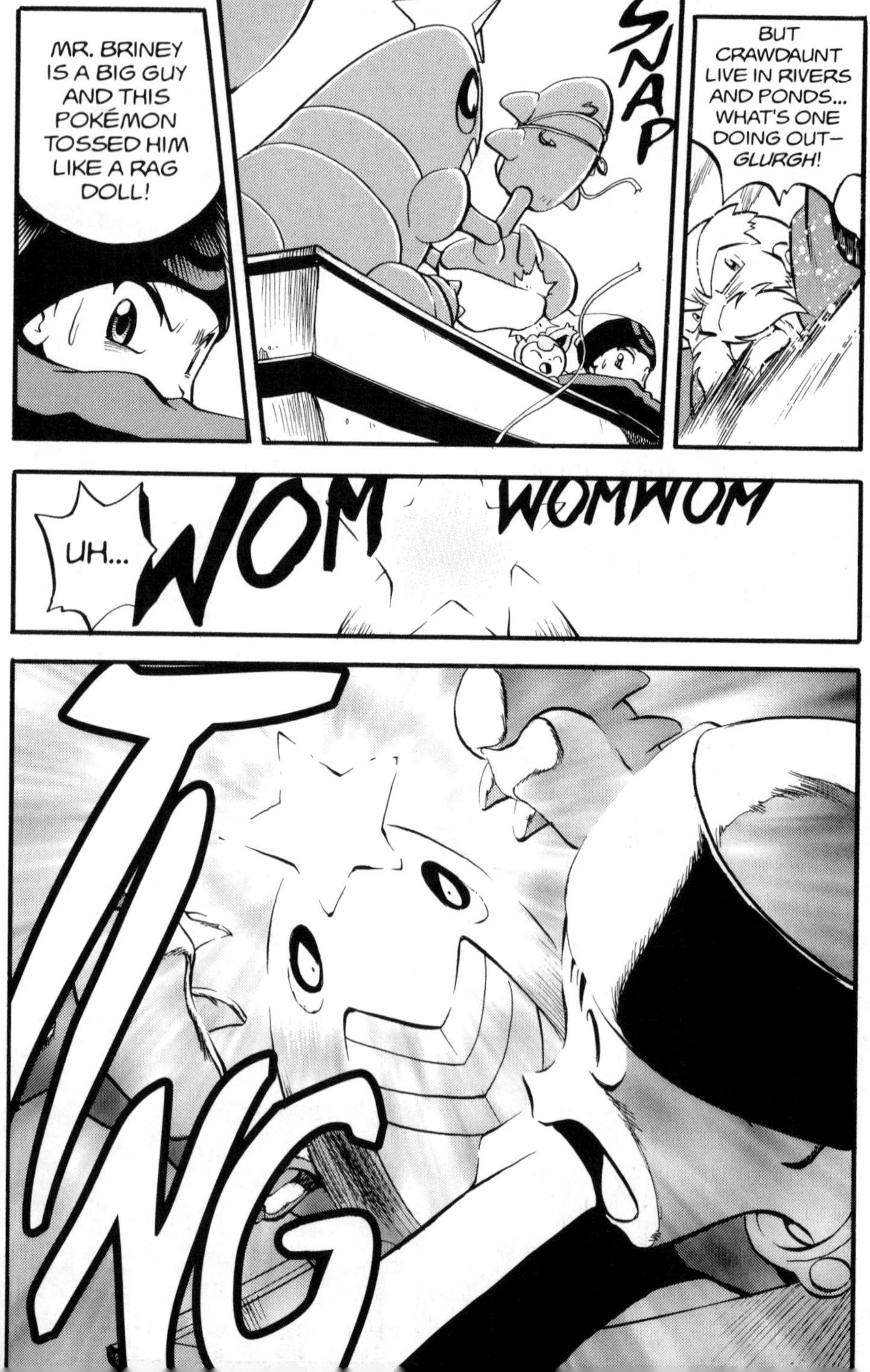
BUT CRAWDAUNT LIVE IN RIVERS AND PONDS... WHAT'S ONE DOING OUT— GLURGH!
SNAP
MR. BRINEY IS A BIG GUY AND THIS POKÉMON TOSSED HIM LIKE A RAG DOLL!
WOMWOM
WOM
UH...
TWNG

ADVENTURE MAP

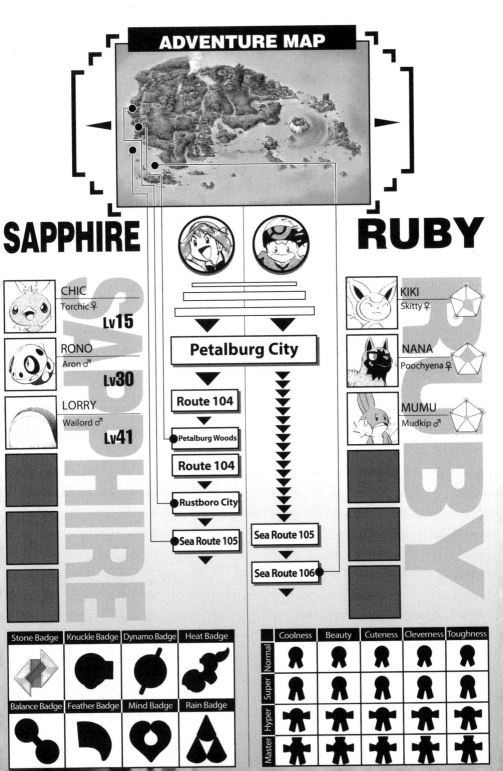

SAPPHIRE

Name	Pokémon	Level
CHIC	Torchic ♀	Lv15
RONO	Aron ♂	Lv30
LORRY	Wailord ♂	Lv41

RUBY

Name	Pokémon
KIKI	Skitty ♀
NANA	Poochyena ♀
MUMU	Mudkip ♂

Petalburg City

Sapphire: Route 104 → Petalburg Woods → Route 104 → Rustboro City → Sea Route 105

Ruby: Sea Route 105 → Sea Route 106

Stone Badge	Knuckle Badge	Dynamo Badge	Heat Badge
Balance Badge	Feather Badge	Mind Badge	Rain Badge

	Coolness	Beauty	Cuteness	Cleverness	Toughness
Normal					
Super					
Hyper					
Master					

● Adventure 193 ●
Stick This in Your Craw, Crawdaunt! Part 2

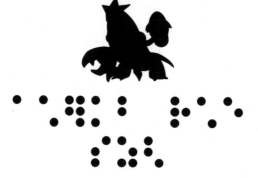

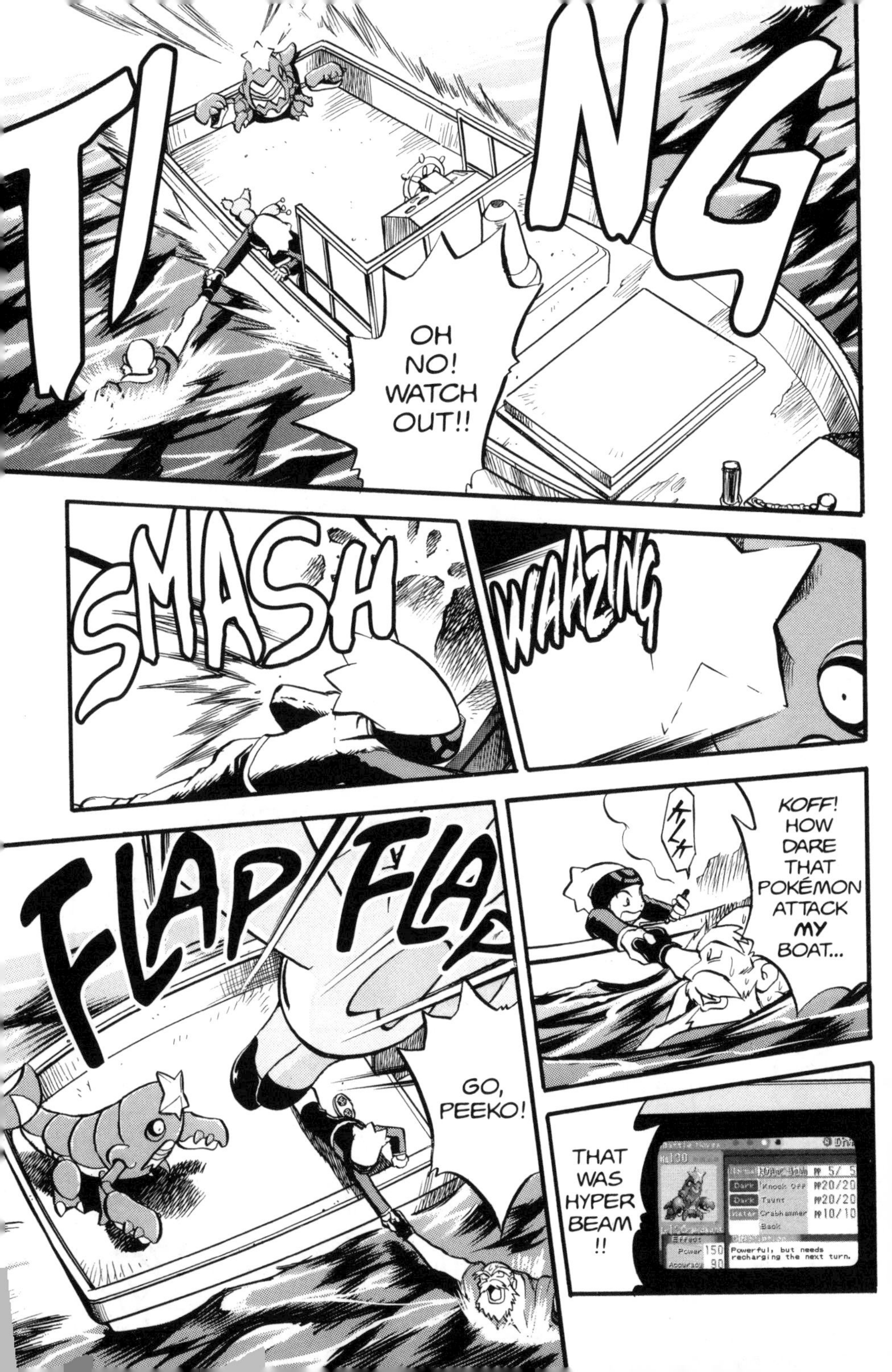
TING
OH NO! WATCH OUT!!
WAAZING
SMASH
K-LK
KOFF! HOW DARE THAT POKÉMON ATTACK MY BOAT...
THAT WAS HYPER BEAM!!
Dark Knock Off PP20/20
Dark Taunt PP20/20
Crabhammer PP10/10
Back
Power 150
Accuracy 90
Powerful, but needs recharging the next turn.
FLAP FLAP
GO, PEEKO!

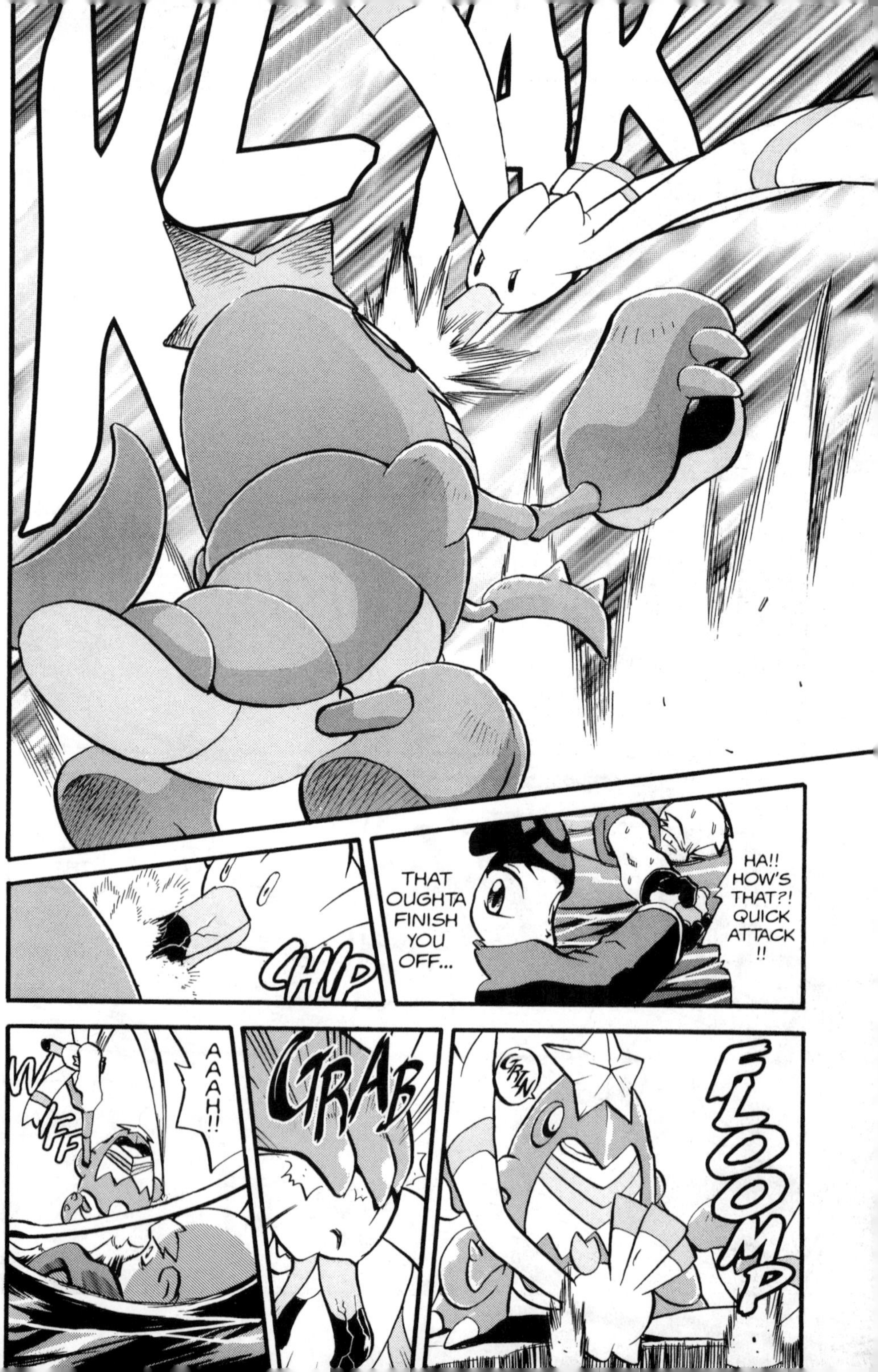
KLAK
HA!! HOW'S THAT?! QUICK ATTACK!!
THAT OUGHTA FINISH YOU OFF...
CHIP
FLOOMP
GRIN
GRAB
AAAH!!
WIFF

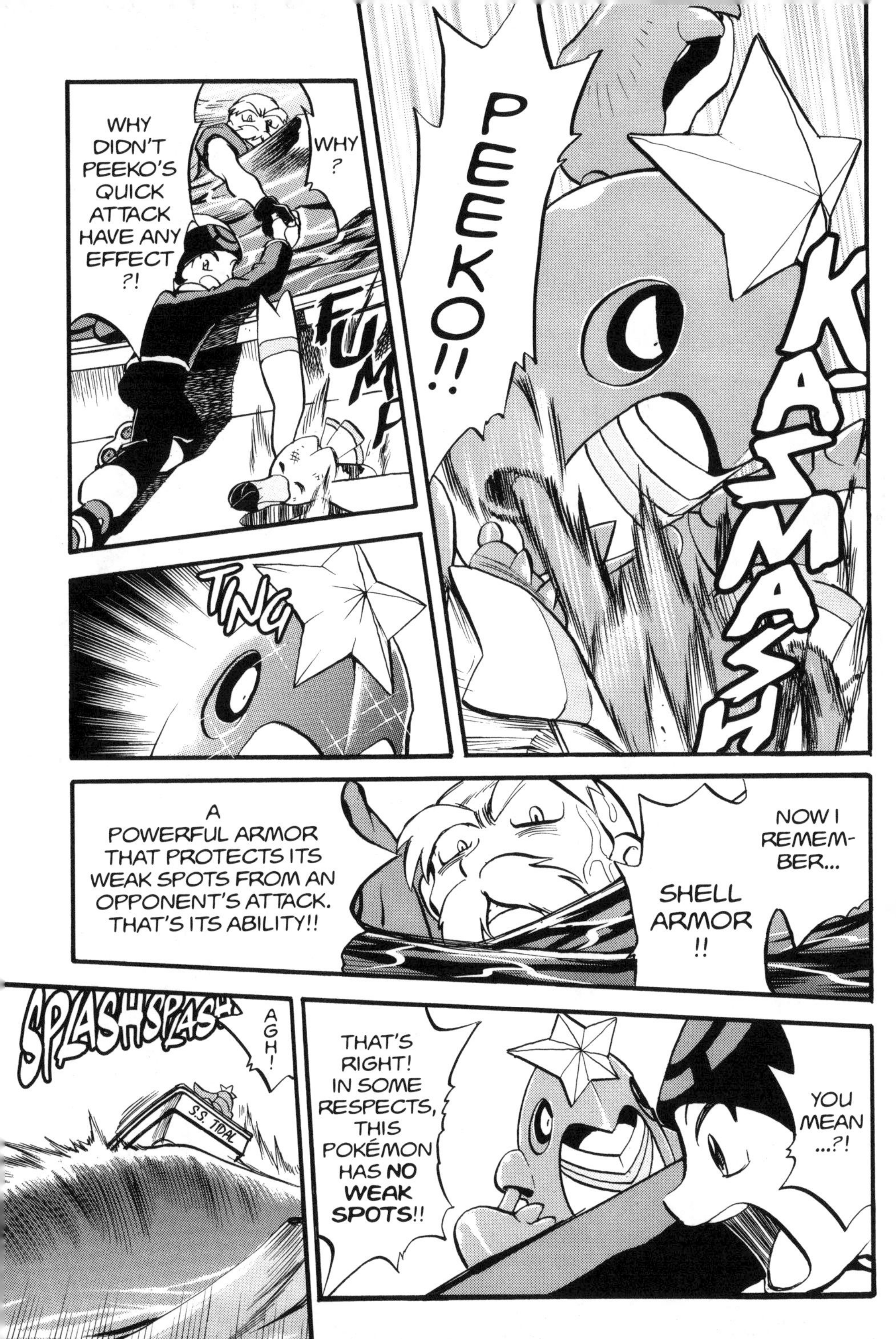
PEEKO!!
KA-SMASH
WHY?
WHY DIDN'T PEEKO'S QUICK ATTACK HAVE ANY EFFECT?!
FUMP
TING
NOW I REMEMBER...
SHELL ARMOR!!
A POWERFUL ARMOR THAT PROTECTS ITS WEAK SPOTS FROM AN OPPONENT'S ATTACK. THAT'S ITS ABILITY!!
YOU MEAN...?!
THAT'S RIGHT! IN SOME RESPECTS, THIS POKÉMON HAS **NO WEAK SPOTS**!!
AGH!
S.S. TIDAL
SPLASH SPLASH

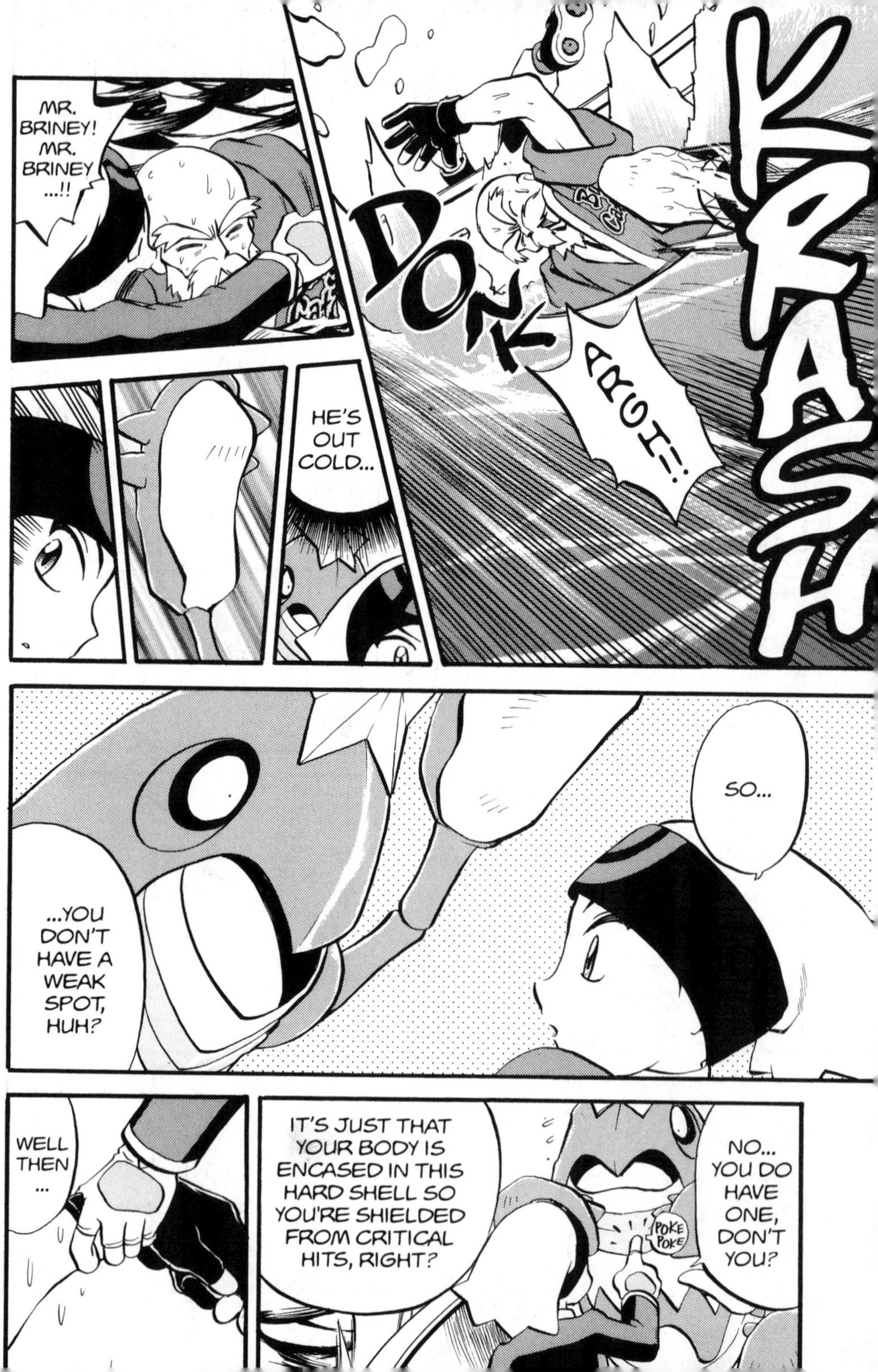
KRASH
DONK
ARGH!!
MR. BRINEY! MR. BRINEY ...!!
HE'S OUT COLD...
SO...
...YOU DON'T HAVE A WEAK SPOT, HUH?
NO... YOU DO HAVE ONE, DON'T YOU?
POKE POKE
IT'S JUST THAT YOUR BODY IS ENCASED IN THIS HARD SHELL SO YOU'RE SHIELDED FROM CRITICAL HITS, RIGHT?
WELL THEN ...

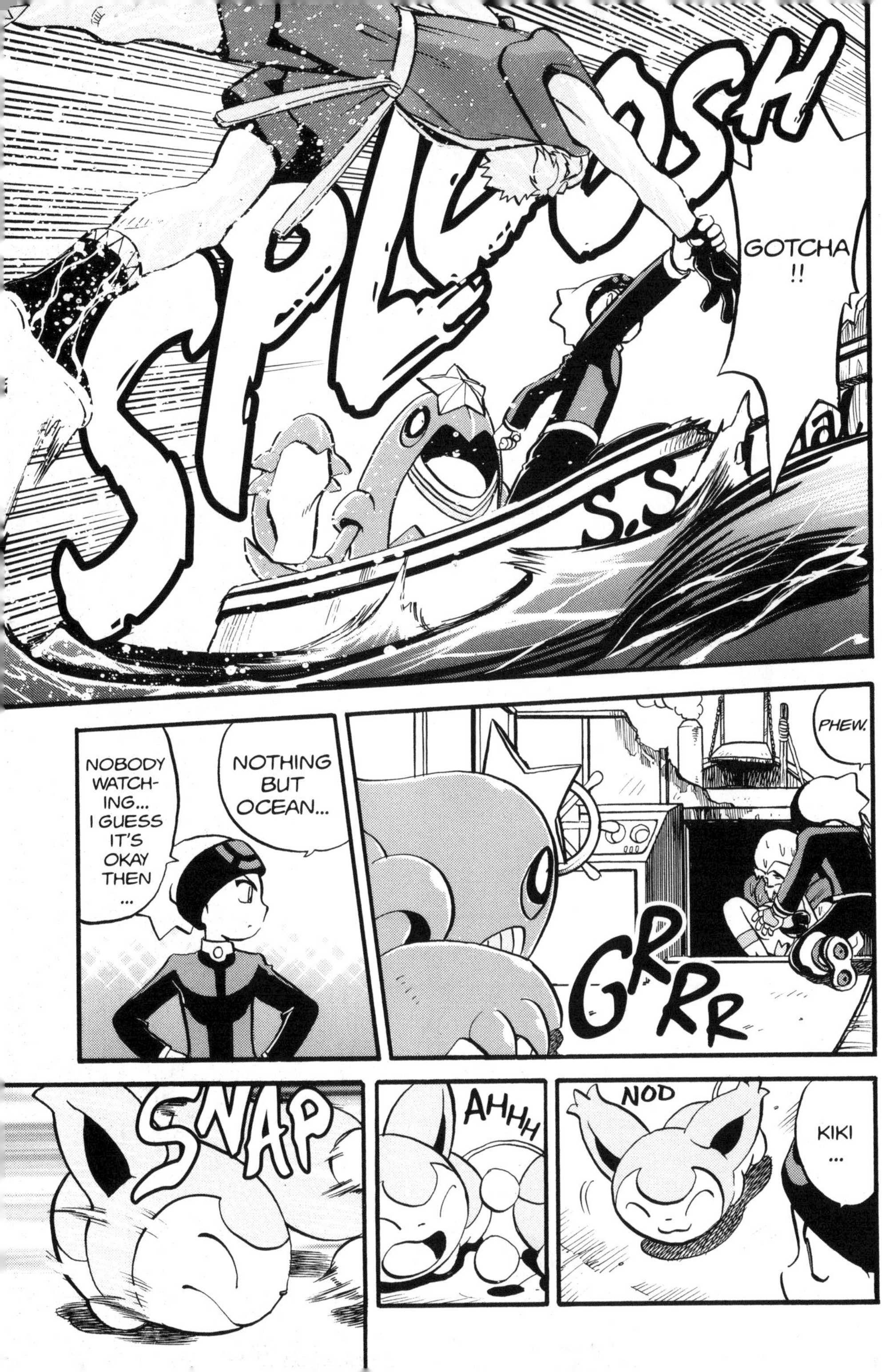
SPL OSH
GOTCHA!!
S.S.
PHEW.
GRRR
NOTHING BUT OCEAN...
NOBODY WATCHING... I GUESS IT'S OKAY THEN...
KIKI...
NOD
AHHH
SNAP

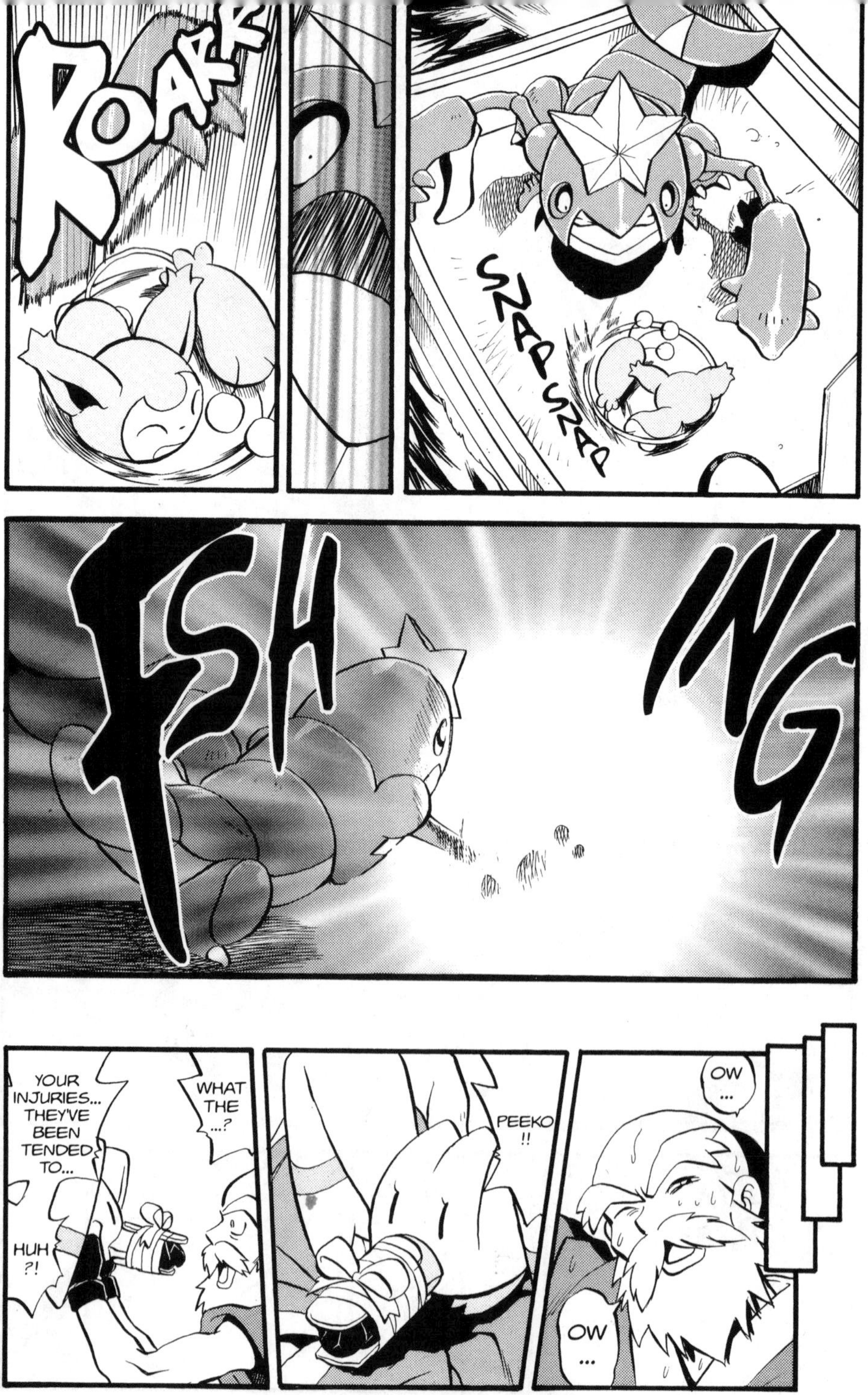
SNAP SNAP
ROARK
FSH ING
OW ...
OW ...
PEEKO !!
WHAT THE ...?
YOUR INJURIES... THEY'VE BEEN TENDED TO...
HUH ?!

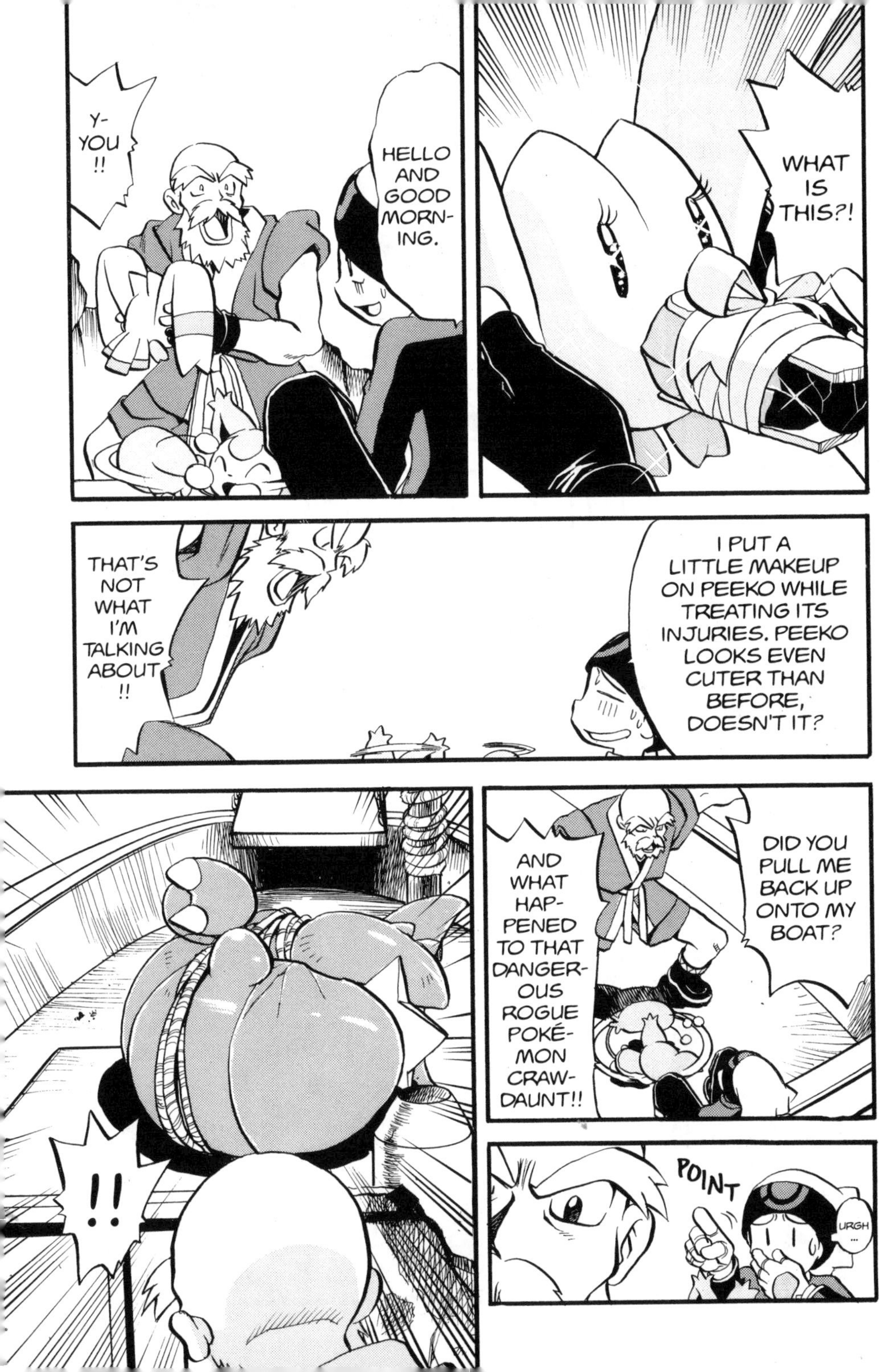
WHAT IS THIS?!
HELLO AND GOOD MORN-ING.
Y-YOU!!
I PUT A LITTLE MAKEUP ON PEEKO WHILE TREATING ITS INJURIES. PEEKO LOOKS EVEN CUTER THAN BEFORE, DOESN'T IT?
THAT'S NOT WHAT I'M TALKING ABOUT!!
DID YOU PULL ME BACK UP ONTO MY BOAT?
AND WHAT HAP-PENED TO THAT DANGER-OUS ROGUE POKÉ-MON CRAW-DAUNT!!
POINT
URGH...
!!

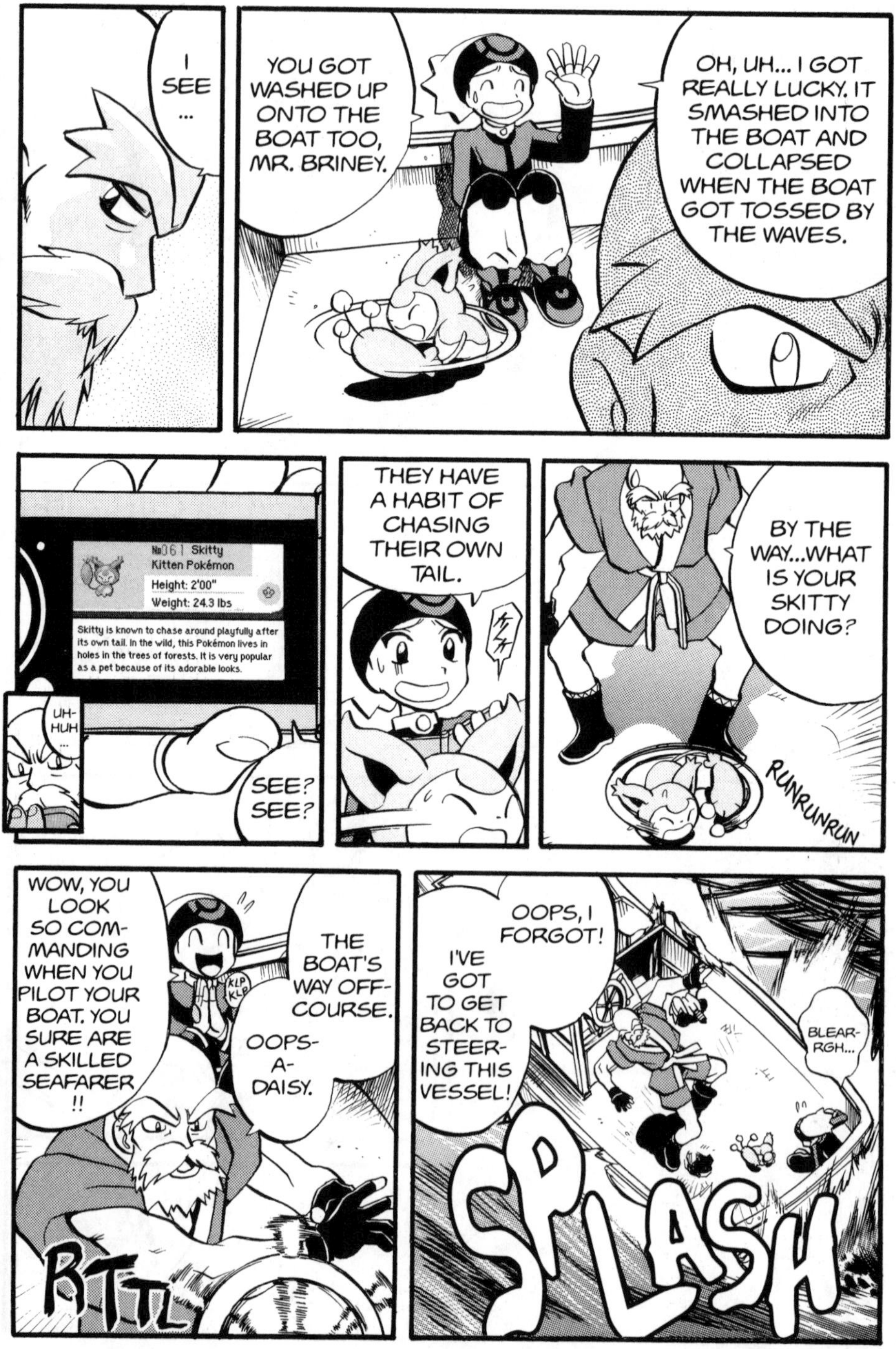
OH, UH... I GOT REALLY LUCKY. IT SMASHED INTO THE BOAT AND COLLAPSED WHEN THE BOAT GOT TOSSED BY THE WAVES.
YOU GOT WASHED UP ONTO THE BOAT TOO, MR. BRINEY.
I SEE ...
BY THE WAY...WHAT IS YOUR SKITTY DOING?
RUNRUNRUN
THEY HAVE A HABIT OF CHASING THEIR OWN TAIL.
№061 Skitty
Kitten Pokémon
Height: 2'00"
Weight: 24.3 lbs
Skitty is known to chase around playfully after its own tail. In the wild, this Pokémon lives in holes in the trees of forests. It is very popular as a pet because of its adorable looks.
UH-HUH ...
SEE? SEE?
OOPS, I FORGOT!
I'VE GOT TO GET BACK TO STEERING THIS VESSEL!
BLEAR-RGH...
SPLASH
THE BOAT'S WAY OFF-COURSE.
WOW, YOU LOOK SO COMMANDING WHEN YOU PILOT YOUR BOAT. YOU SURE ARE A SKILLED SEAFARER !!
KLP KLP
OOPS-A-DAISY.
RTTL

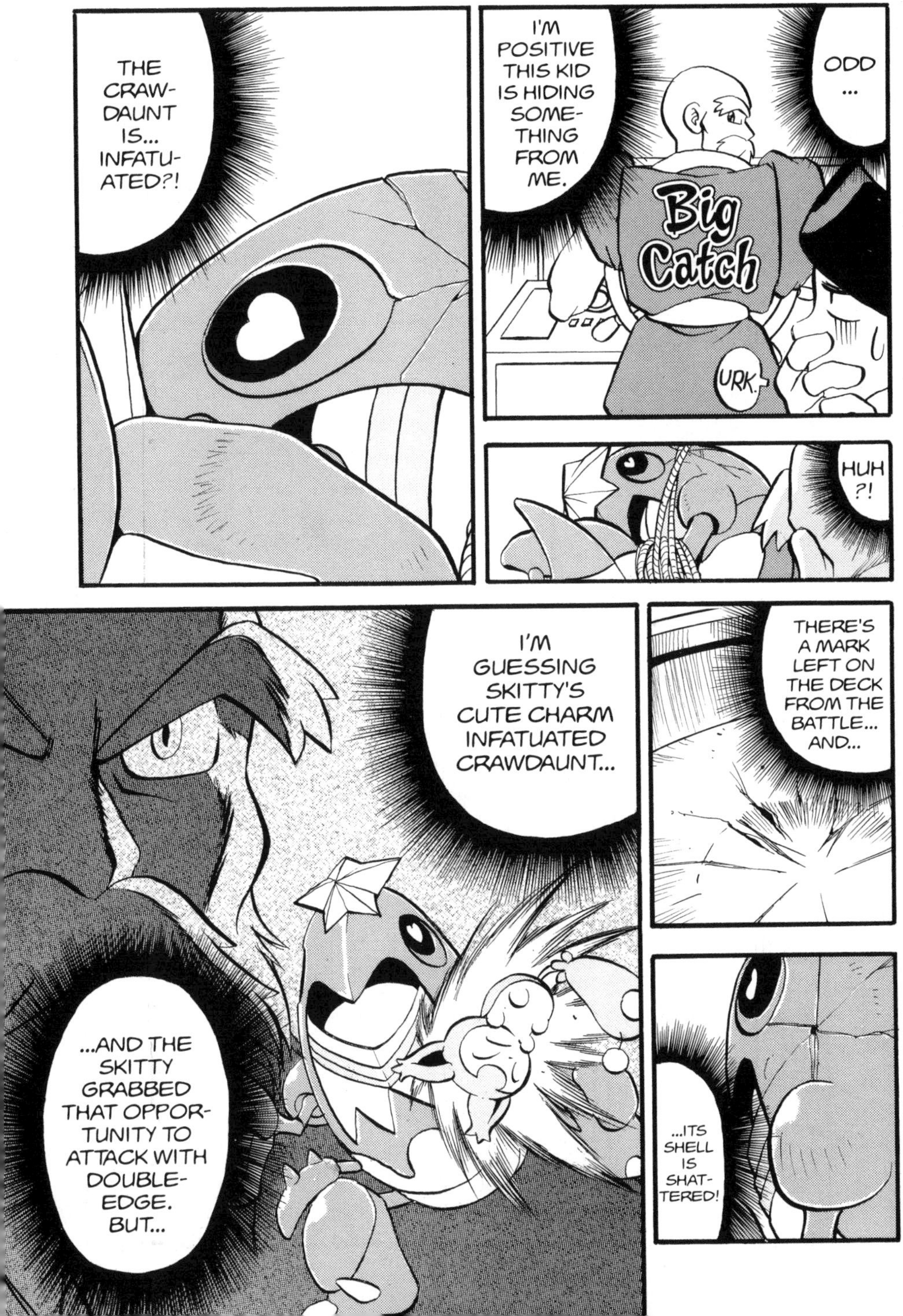
ODD...
I'M POSITIVE THIS KID IS HIDING SOMETHING FROM ME.
Big Catch
URK.
HUH?!
THE CRAWDAUNT IS... INFATUATED?!
THERE'S A MARK LEFT ON THE DECK FROM THE BATTLE... AND...
...ITS SHELL IS SHATTERED!
I'M GUESSING SKITTY'S CUTE CHARM INFATUATED CRAWDAUNT...
...AND THE SKITTY GRABBED THAT OPPORTUNITY TO ATTACK WITH DOUBLE-EDGE. BUT...

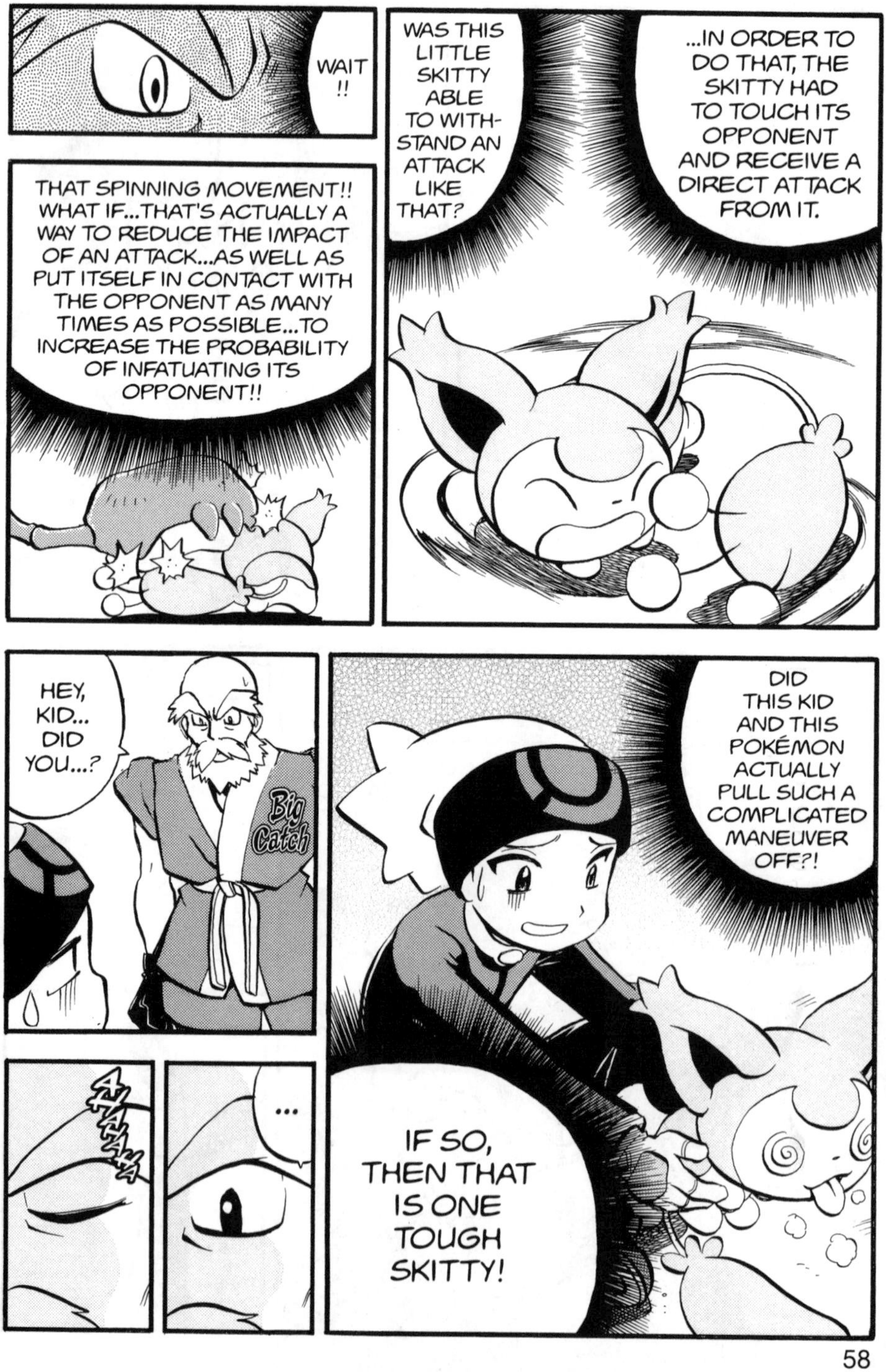

...IN ORDER TO DO THAT, THE SKITTY HAD TO TOUCH ITS OPPONENT AND RECEIVE A DIRECT ATTACK FROM IT.
WAS THIS LITTLE SKITTY ABLE TO WITH-STAND AN ATTACK LIKE THAT?
WAIT !!
THAT SPINNING MOVEMENT!! WHAT IF...THAT'S ACTUALLY A WAY TO REDUCE THE IMPACT OF AN ATTACK...AS WELL AS PUT ITSELF IN CONTACT WITH THE OPPONENT AS MANY TIMES AS POSSIBLE...TO INCREASE THE PROBABILITY OF INFATUATING ITS OPPONENT!!
DID THIS KID AND THIS POKÉMON ACTUALLY PULL SUCH A COMPLICATED MANEUVER OFF?!
IF SO, THEN THAT IS ONE TOUGH SKITTY!
HEY, KID... DID YOU...?
Big Catch
...
AHAHAHA

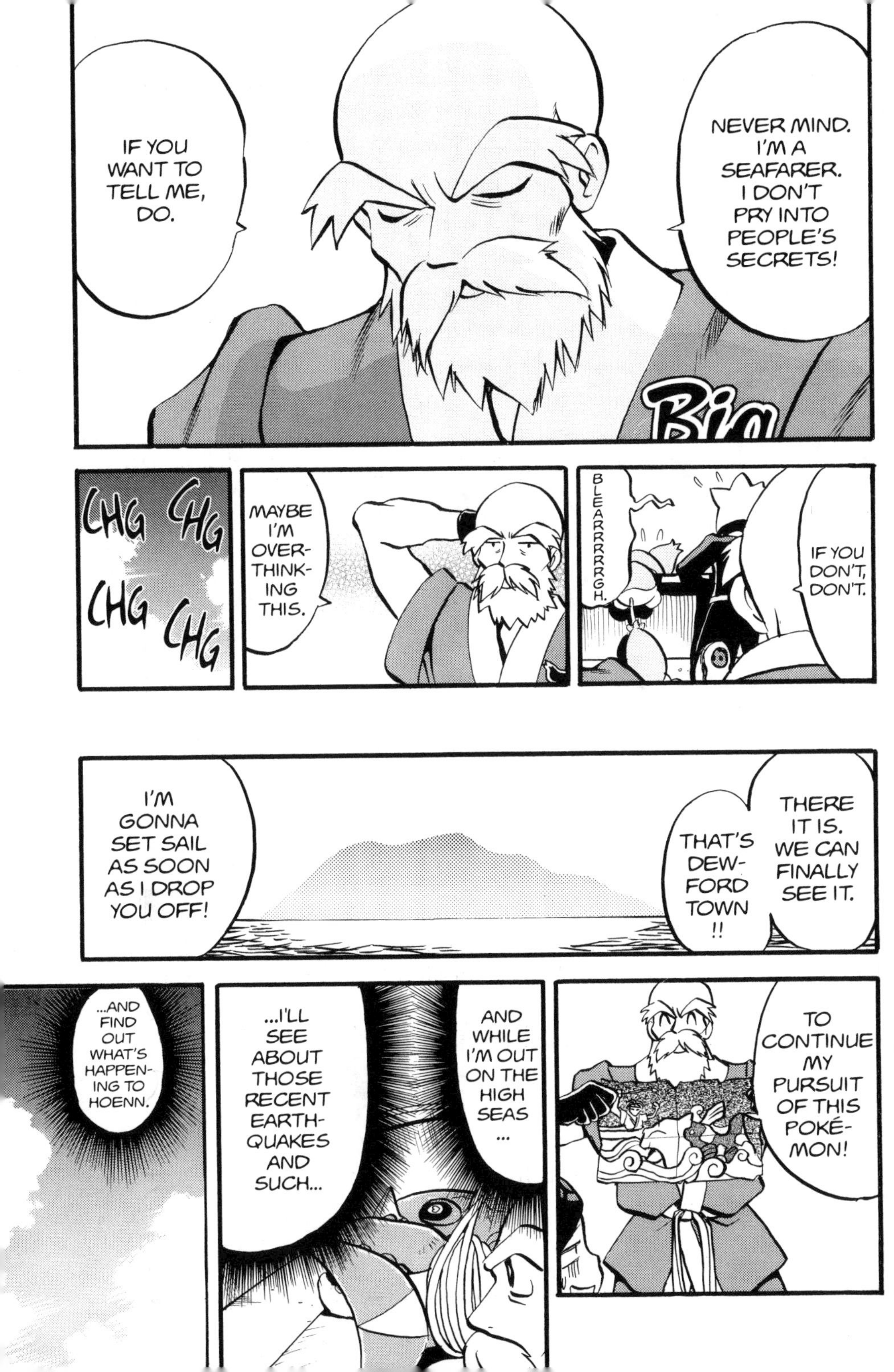
NEVER MIND. I'M A SEAFARER. I DON'T PRY INTO PEOPLE'S SECRETS!
IF YOU WANT TO TELL ME, DO.
IF YOU DON'T, DON'T.
BLEARRRRRGH.
MAYBE I'M OVER-THINKING THIS.
CHG CHG CHG CHG
THERE IT IS. WE CAN FINALLY SEE IT.
THAT'S DEW-FORD TOWN !!
I'M GONNA SET SAIL AS SOON AS I DROP YOU OFF!
TO CONTINUE MY PURSUIT OF THIS POKÉ-MON!
AND WHILE I'M OUT ON THE HIGH SEAS ...
...I'LL SEE ABOUT THOSE RECENT EARTH-QUAKES AND SUCH...
...AND FIND OUT WHAT'S HAPPEN-ING TO HOENN.

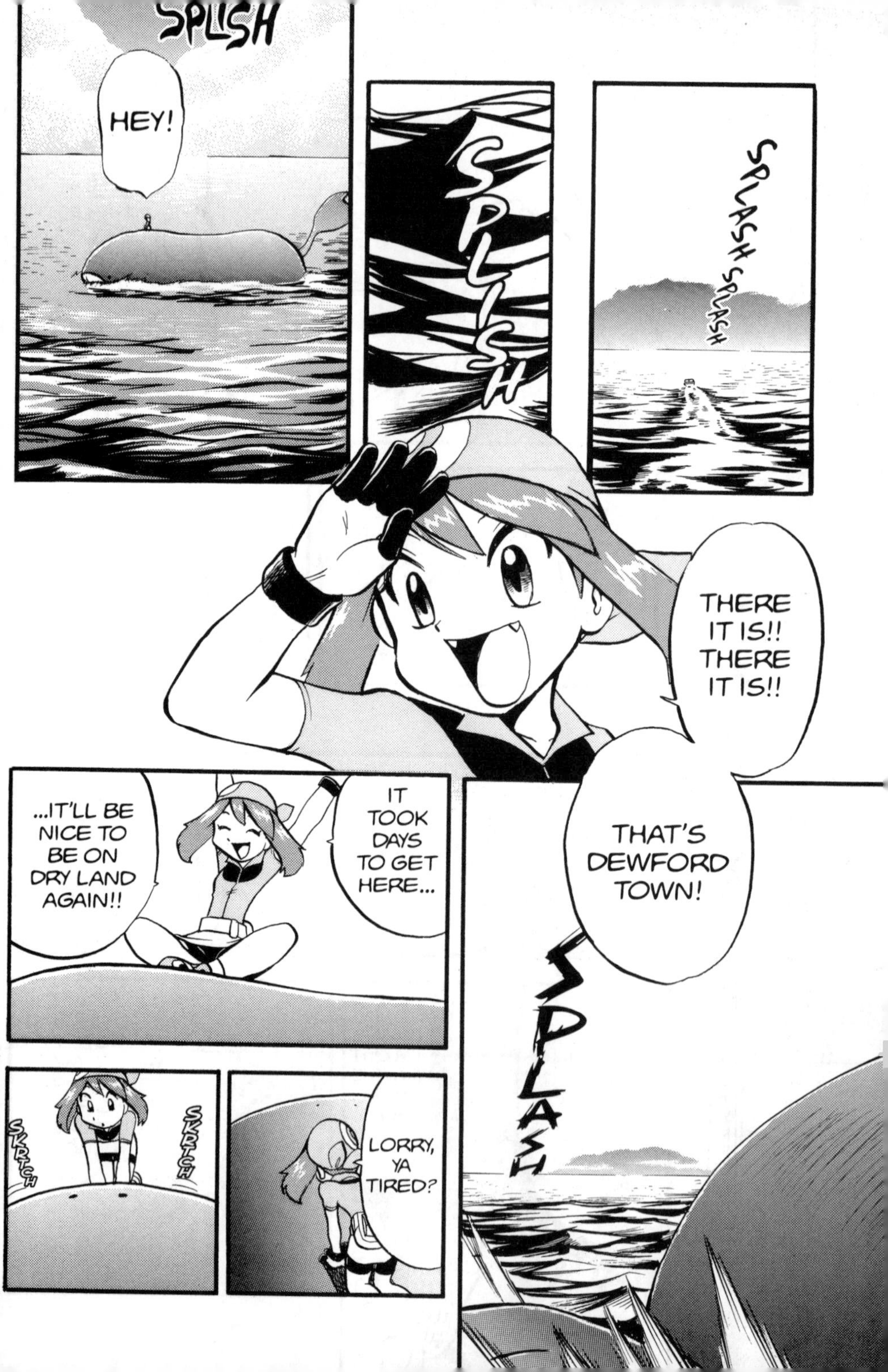
SPLASH SPLASH
SPLISH
SPLISH
HEY!
THERE IT IS!! THERE IT IS!!
THAT'S DEWFORD TOWN!
SPLASH
IT TOOK DAYS TO GET HERE...
...IT'LL BE NICE TO BE ON DRY LAND AGAIN!!
LORRY, YA TIRED?
SKRTCH
SKRTCH

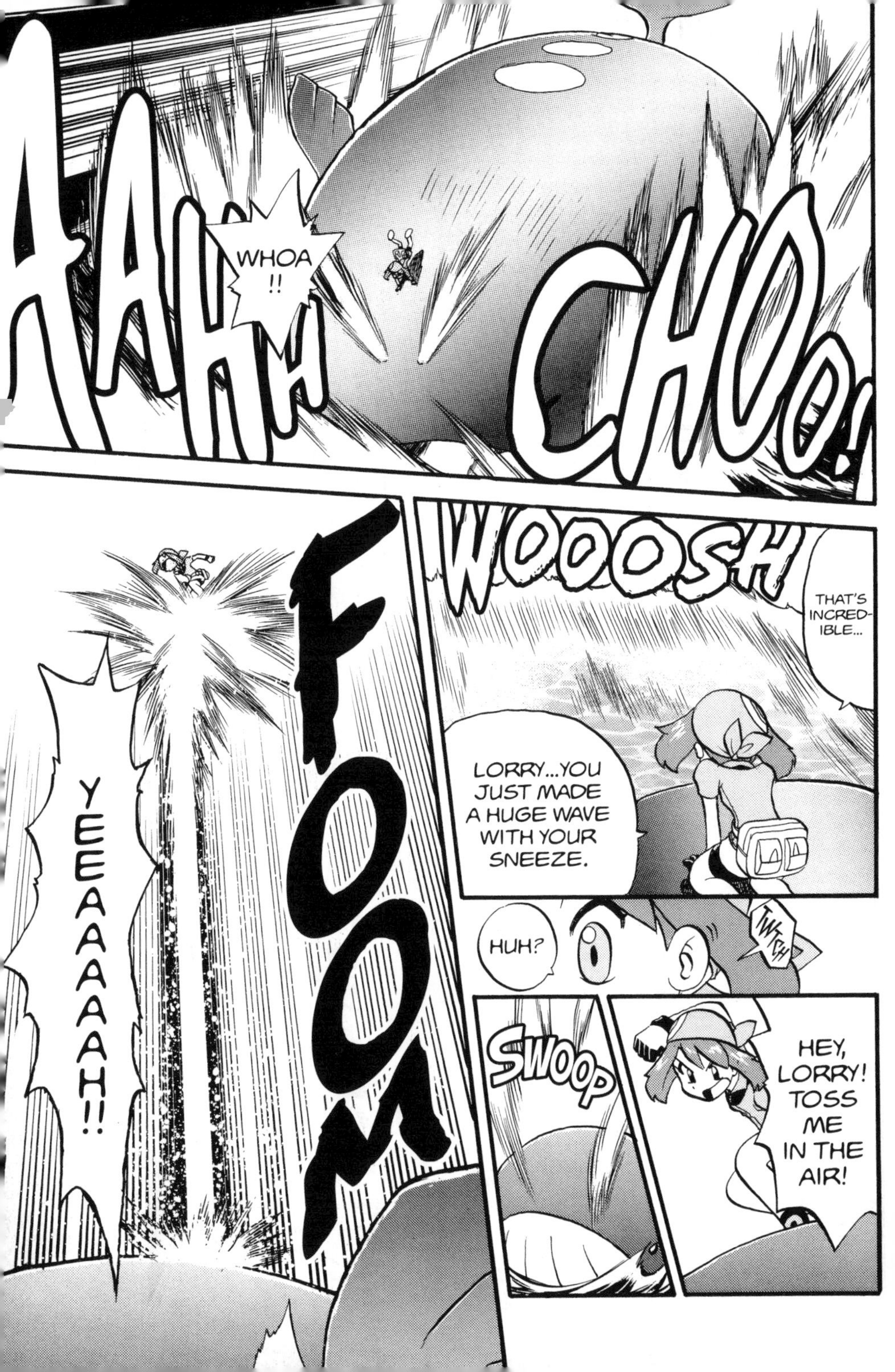
AAHH
CHOO
WHOA!!
WOOOSH
THAT'S INCREDIBLE...
LORRY...YOU JUST MADE A HUGE WAVE WITH YOUR SNEEZE.
TWITCH
HUH?
HEY, LORRY! TOSS ME IN THE AIR!
SWOOP
FOOM
YEEAAAAAAAH!!

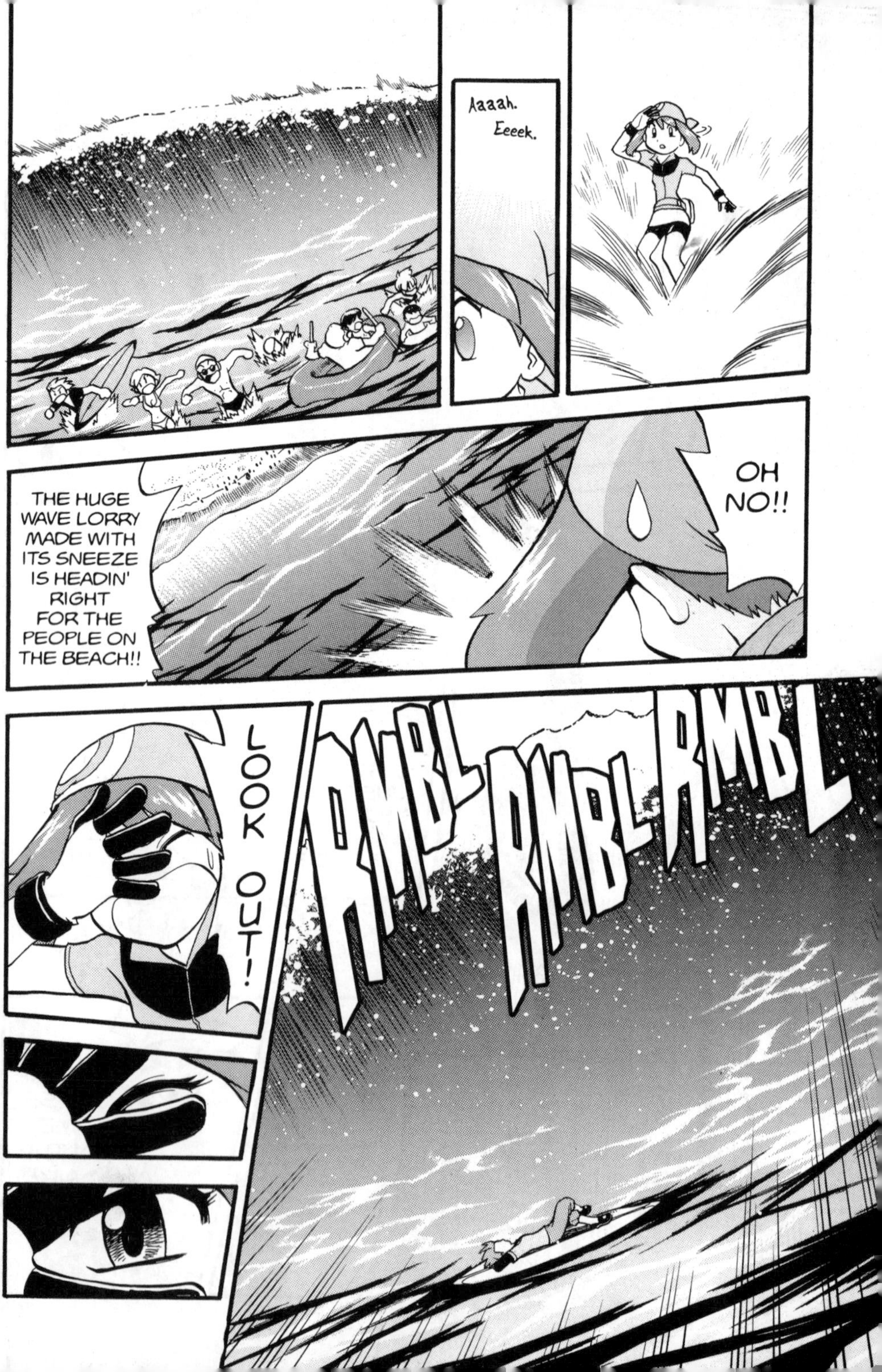
Aaaah.
Eeeek.
OH NO!!
THE HUGE WAVE LORRY MADE WITH ITS SNEEZE IS HEADIN' RIGHT FOR THE PEOPLE ON THE BEACH!!
RMBL RMBL RMBL
LOOK OUT!

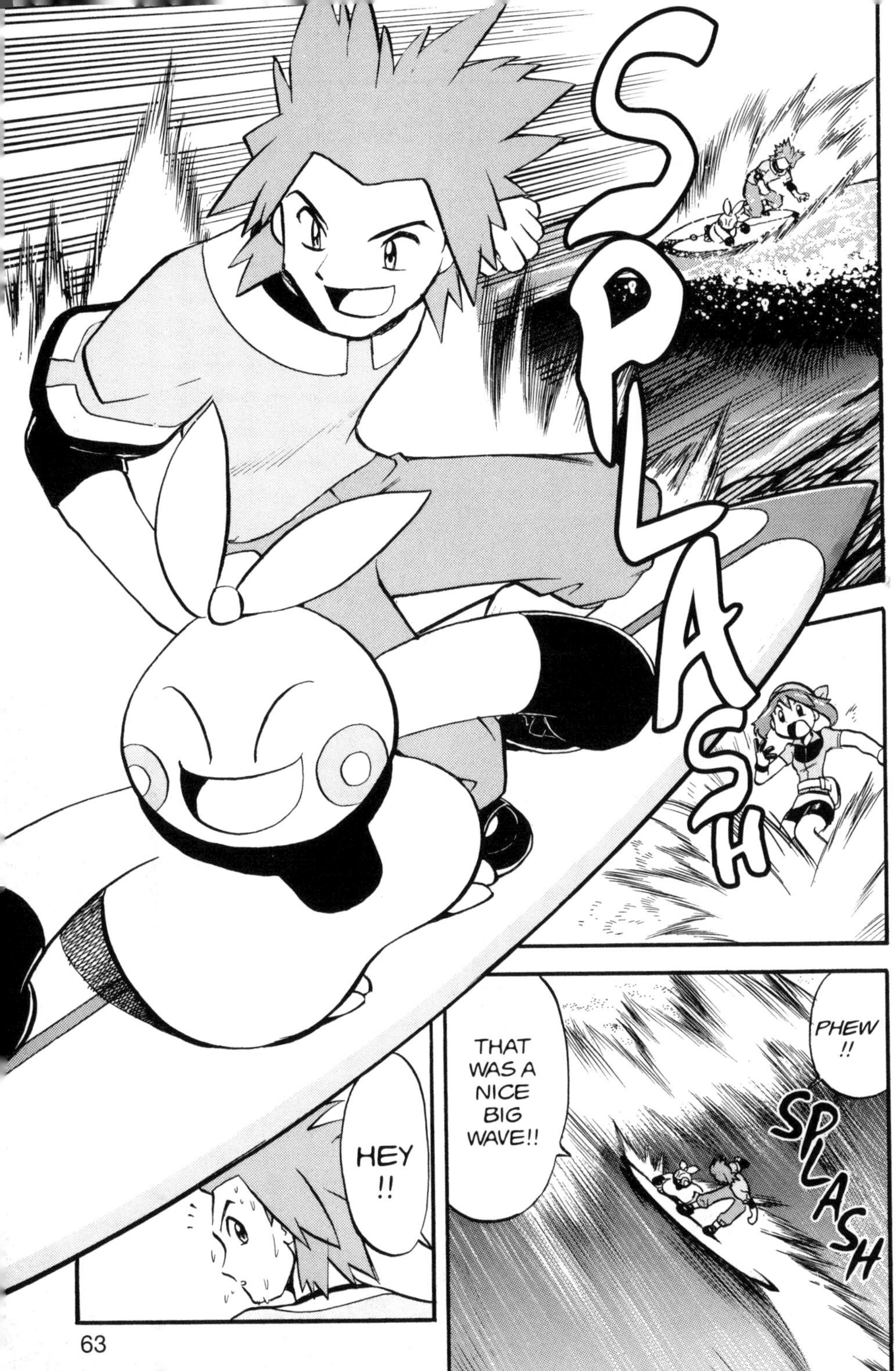
SPLASH
PHEW!!
THAT WAS A NICE BIG WAVE!!
SPLASH
HEY!!

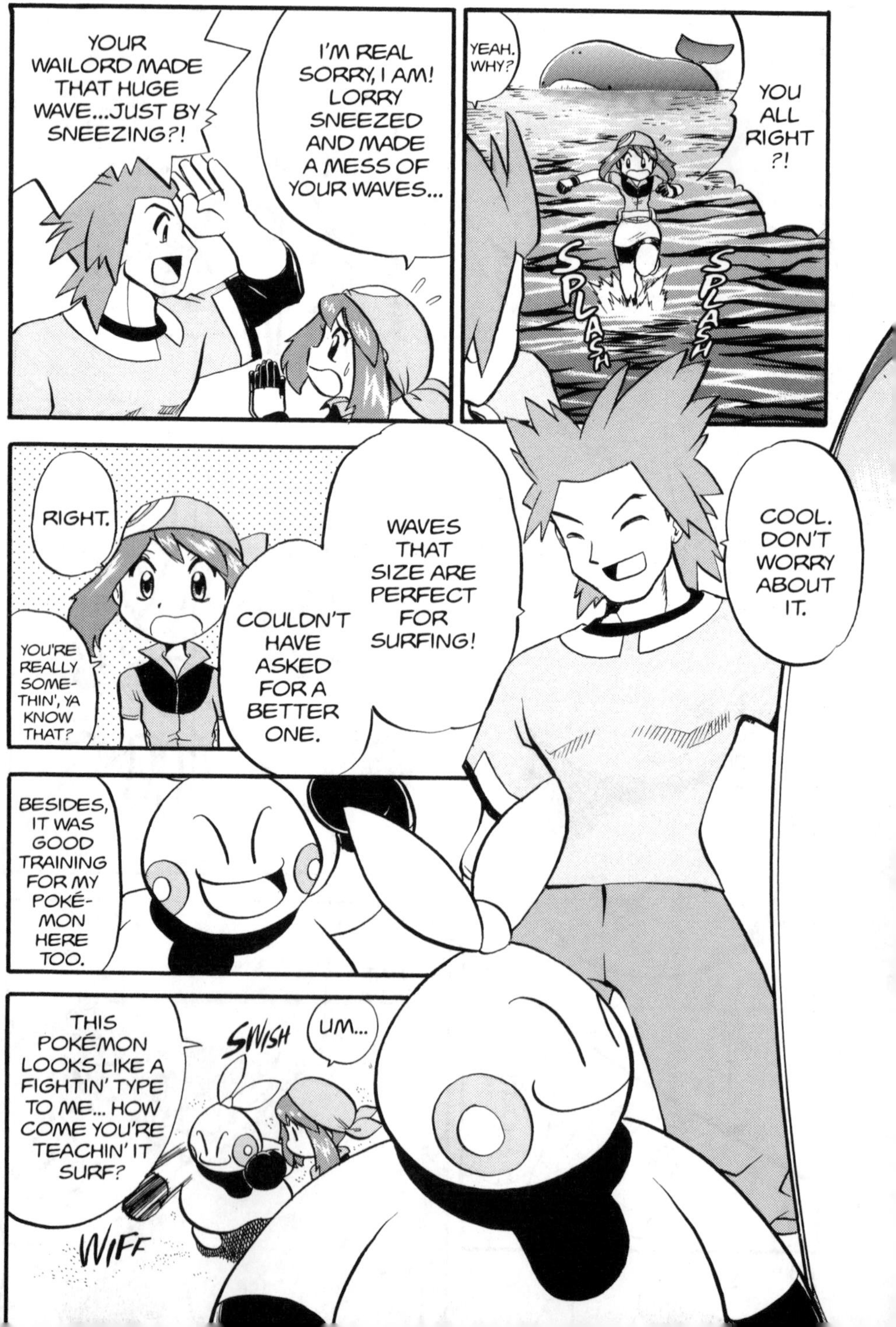
YOU ALL RIGHT?!
YEAH. WHY?
SPLASH
SPLASH
I'M REAL SORRY, I AM! LORRY SNEEZED AND MADE A MESS OF YOUR WAVES...
YOUR WAILORD MADE THAT HUGE WAVE...JUST BY SNEEZING?!
COOL. DON'T WORRY ABOUT IT.
WAVES THAT SIZE ARE PERFECT FOR SURFING!
COULDN'T HAVE ASKED FOR A BETTER ONE.
RIGHT.
YOU'RE REALLY SOME-THIN', YA KNOW THAT?
BESIDES, IT WAS GOOD TRAINING FOR MY POKÉ-MON HERE TOO.
UM...
SWISH
THIS POKÉMON LOOKS LIKE A FIGHTIN' TYPE TO ME... HOW COME YOU'RE TEACHIN' IT SURF?
WIFF

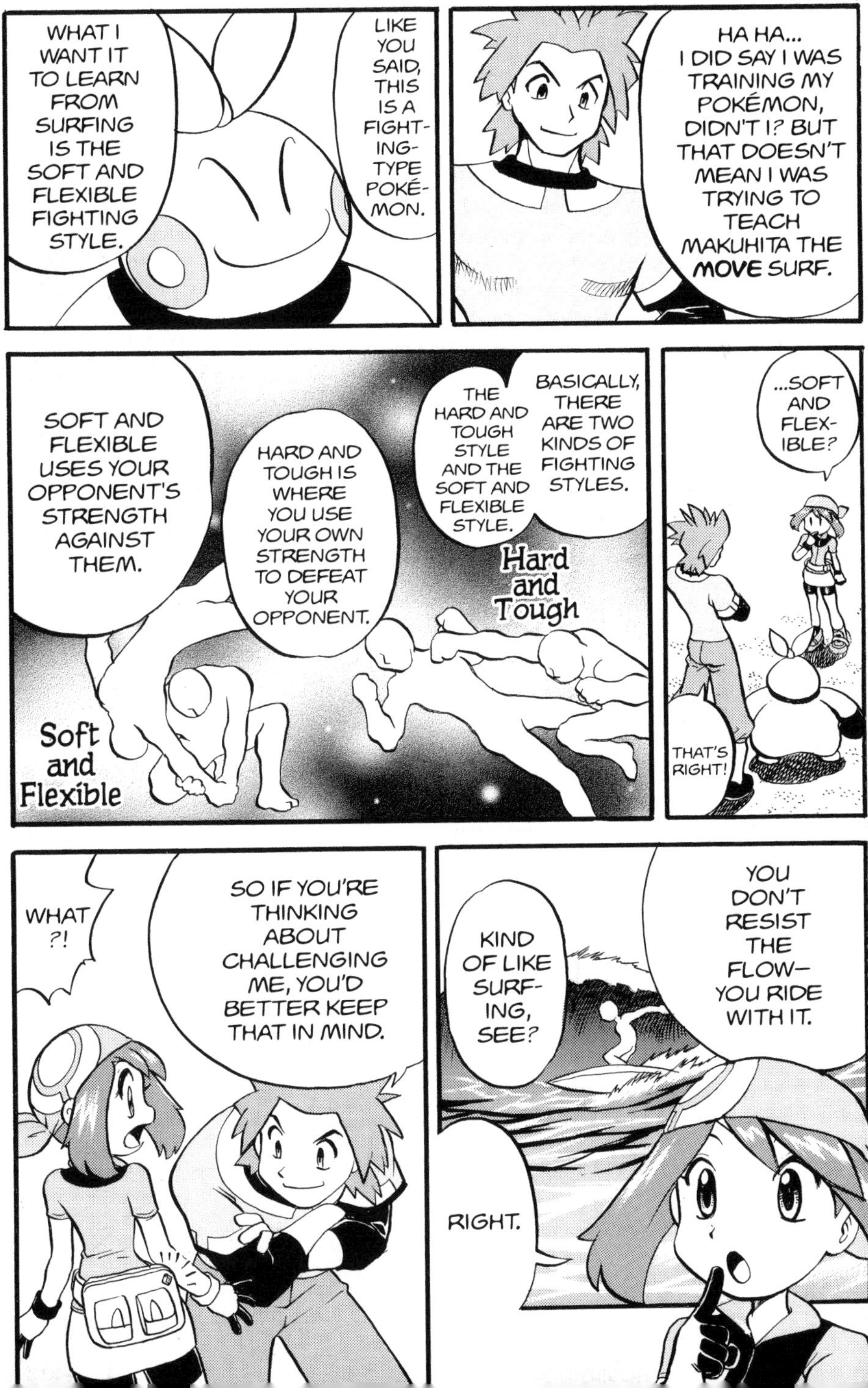
HA HA... I DID SAY I WAS TRAINING MY POKÉMON, DIDN'T I? BUT THAT DOESN'T MEAN I WAS TRYING TO TEACH MAKUHITA THE **MOVE** SURF.
LIKE YOU SAID, THIS IS A FIGHTING-TYPE POKÉMON.
WHAT I WANT IT TO LEARN FROM SURFING IS THE SOFT AND FLEXIBLE FIGHTING STYLE.
...SOFT AND FLEXIBLE?
THAT'S RIGHT!
BASICALLY, THERE ARE TWO KINDS OF FIGHTING STYLES.
THE HARD AND TOUGH STYLE AND THE SOFT AND FLEXIBLE STYLE.
HARD AND TOUGH IS WHERE YOU USE YOUR OWN STRENGTH TO DEFEAT YOUR OPPONENT.
SOFT AND FLEXIBLE USES YOUR OPPONENT'S STRENGTH AGAINST THEM.
Hard and Tough
Soft and Flexible
YOU DON'T RESIST THE FLOW—YOU RIDE WITH IT.
KIND OF LIKE SURFING, SEE?
RIGHT.
SO IF YOU'RE THINKING ABOUT CHALLENGING ME, YOU'D BETTER KEEP THAT IN MIND.
WHAT?!

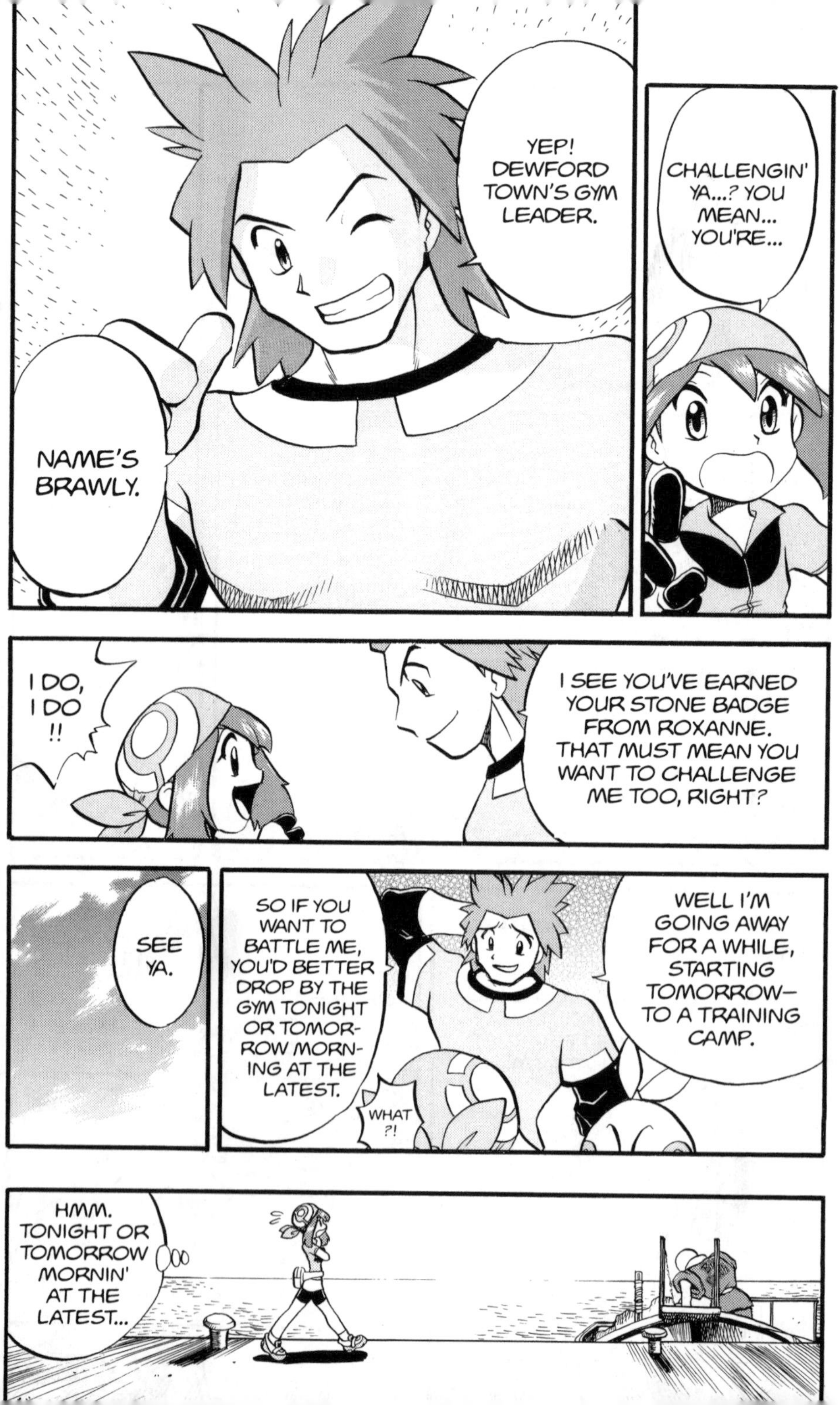
CHALLENGIN' YA...? YOU MEAN... YOU'RE...
YEP! DEWFORD TOWN'S GYM LEADER.
NAME'S BRAWLY.
I SEE YOU'VE EARNED YOUR STONE BADGE FROM ROXANNE. THAT MUST MEAN YOU WANT TO CHALLENGE ME TOO, RIGHT?
I DO, I DO !!
WELL I'M GOING AWAY FOR A WHILE, STARTING TOMORROW— TO A TRAINING CAMP.
SO IF YOU WANT TO BATTLE ME, YOU'D BETTER DROP BY THE GYM TONIGHT OR TOMOR-ROW MORN-ING AT THE LATEST.
WHAT ?!
SEE YA.
HMM. TONIGHT OR TOMORROW MORNIN' AT THE LATEST...

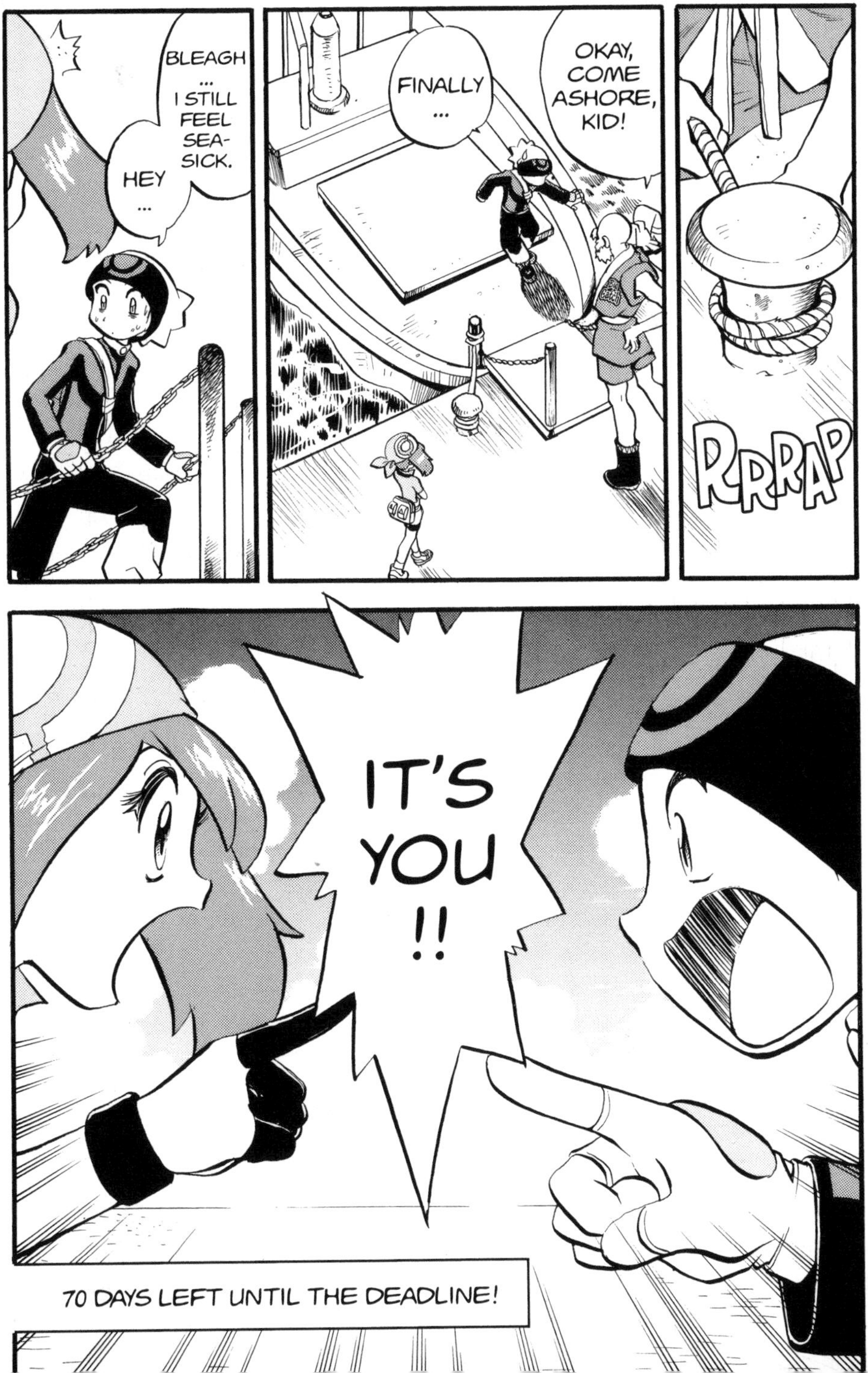
RRRAP
OKAY, COME ASHORE, KID!
FINALLY ...
BLEAGH ... I STILL FEEL SEA-SICK.
HEY ...
IT'S YOU !!
70 DAYS LEFT UNTIL THE DEADLINE!

● Adventure 194 ●
Guile from Mawile

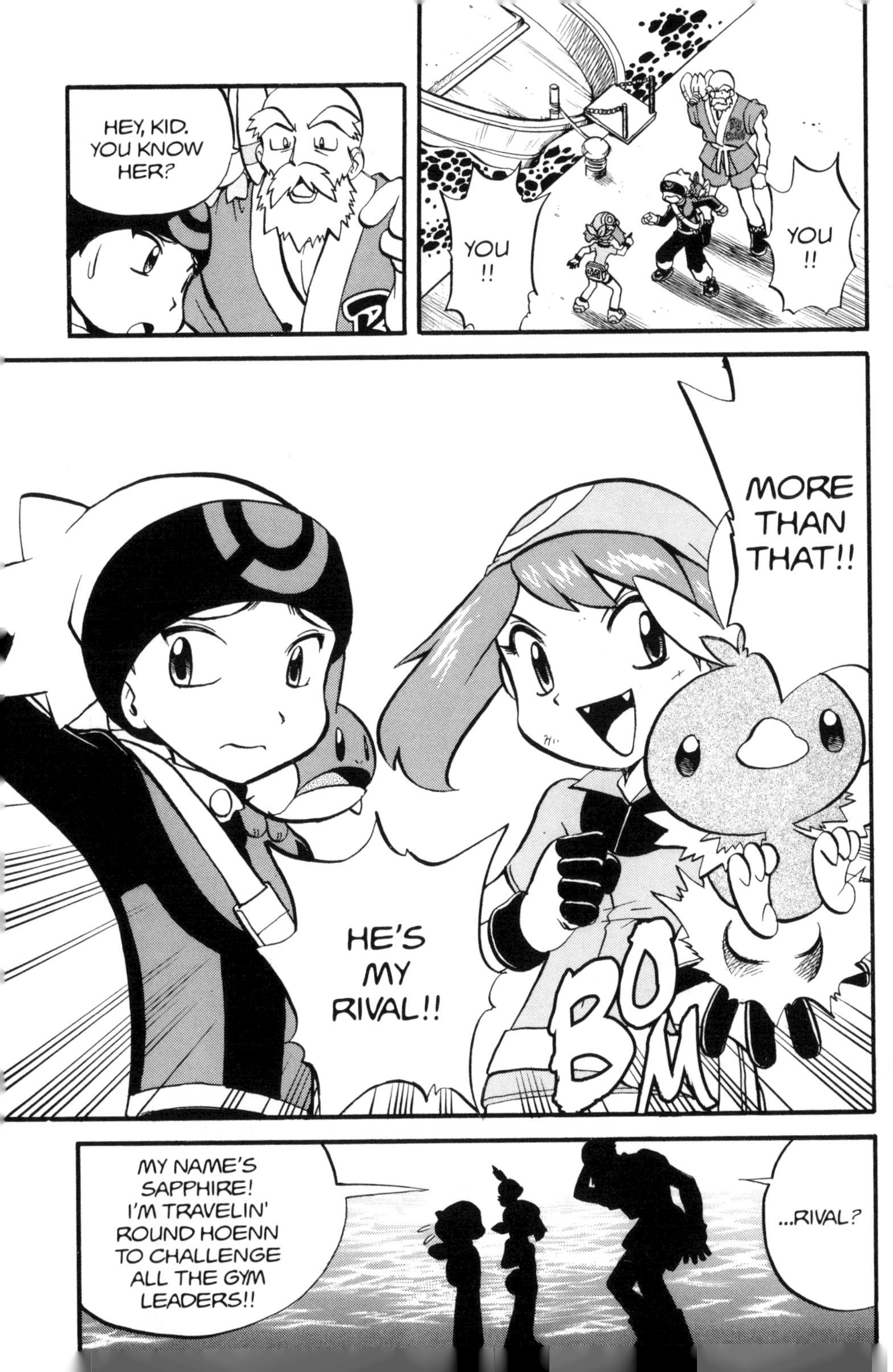
YOU !!
YOU !!
HEY, KID. YOU KNOW HER?
MORE THAN THAT!!
BOM
HE'S MY RIVAL!!
...RIVAL?
MY NAME'S SAPPHIRE! I'M TRAVELIN' ROUND HOENN TO CHALLENGE ALL THE GYM LEADERS!!

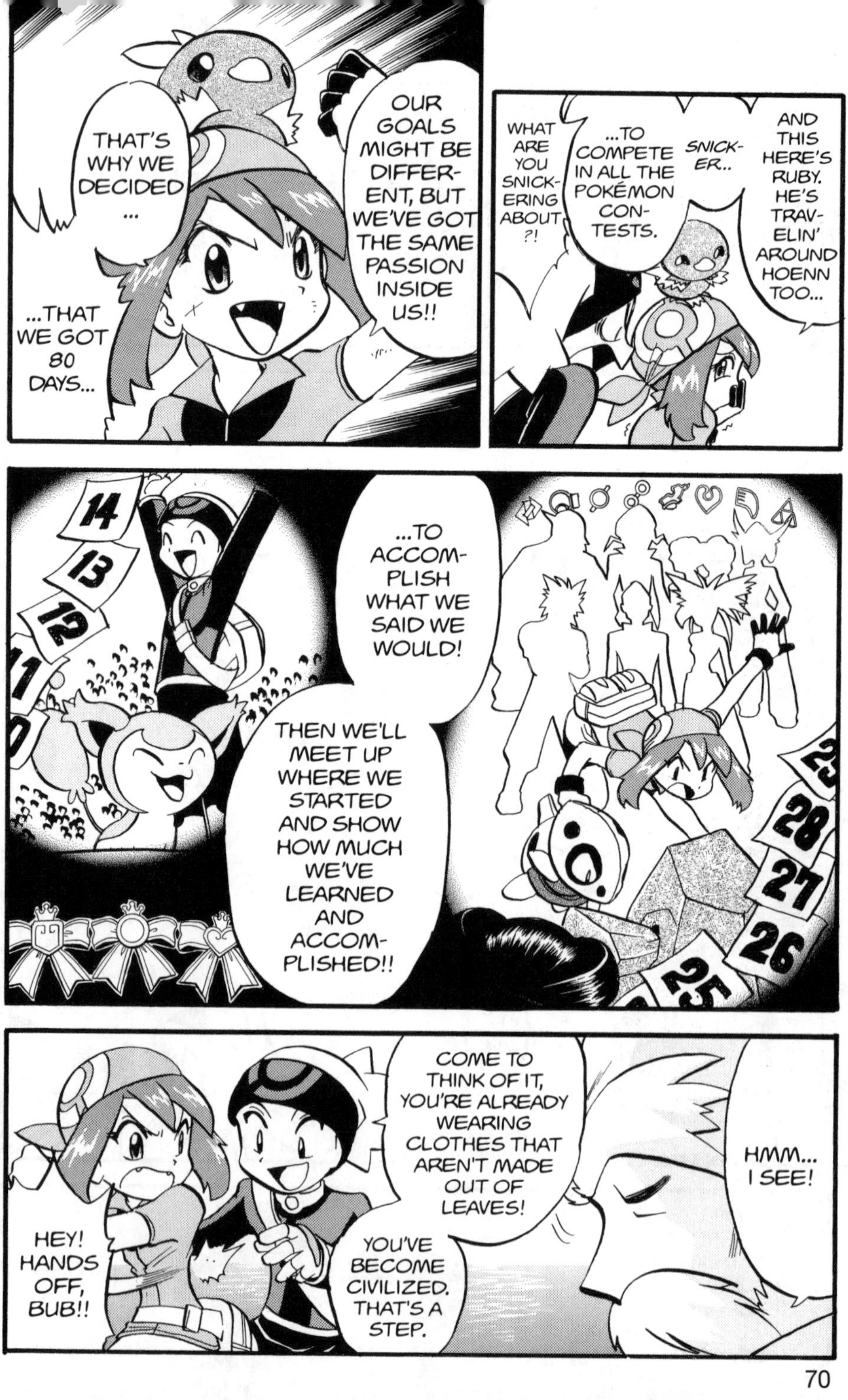
AND THIS HERE'S RUBY. HE'S TRAVELIN' AROUND HOENN TOO...
SNICKER...
...TO COMPETE IN ALL THE POKÉMON CONTESTS.
WHAT ARE YOU SNICKERING ABOUT?!
OUR GOALS MIGHT BE DIFFERENT, BUT WE'VE GOT THE SAME PASSION INSIDE US!!
THAT'S WHY WE DECIDED...
...THAT WE GOT 80 DAYS...
14
13
12
11
...TO ACCOMPLISH WHAT WE SAID WE WOULD!
THEN WE'LL MEET UP WHERE WE STARTED AND SHOW HOW MUCH WE'VE LEARNED AND ACCOMPLISHED!!
28
27
26
25
HMM... I SEE!
COME TO THINK OF IT, YOU'RE ALREADY WEARING CLOTHES THAT AREN'T MADE OUT OF LEAVES!
YOU'VE BECOME CIVILIZED. THAT'S A STEP.
HEY! HANDS OFF, BUB!!

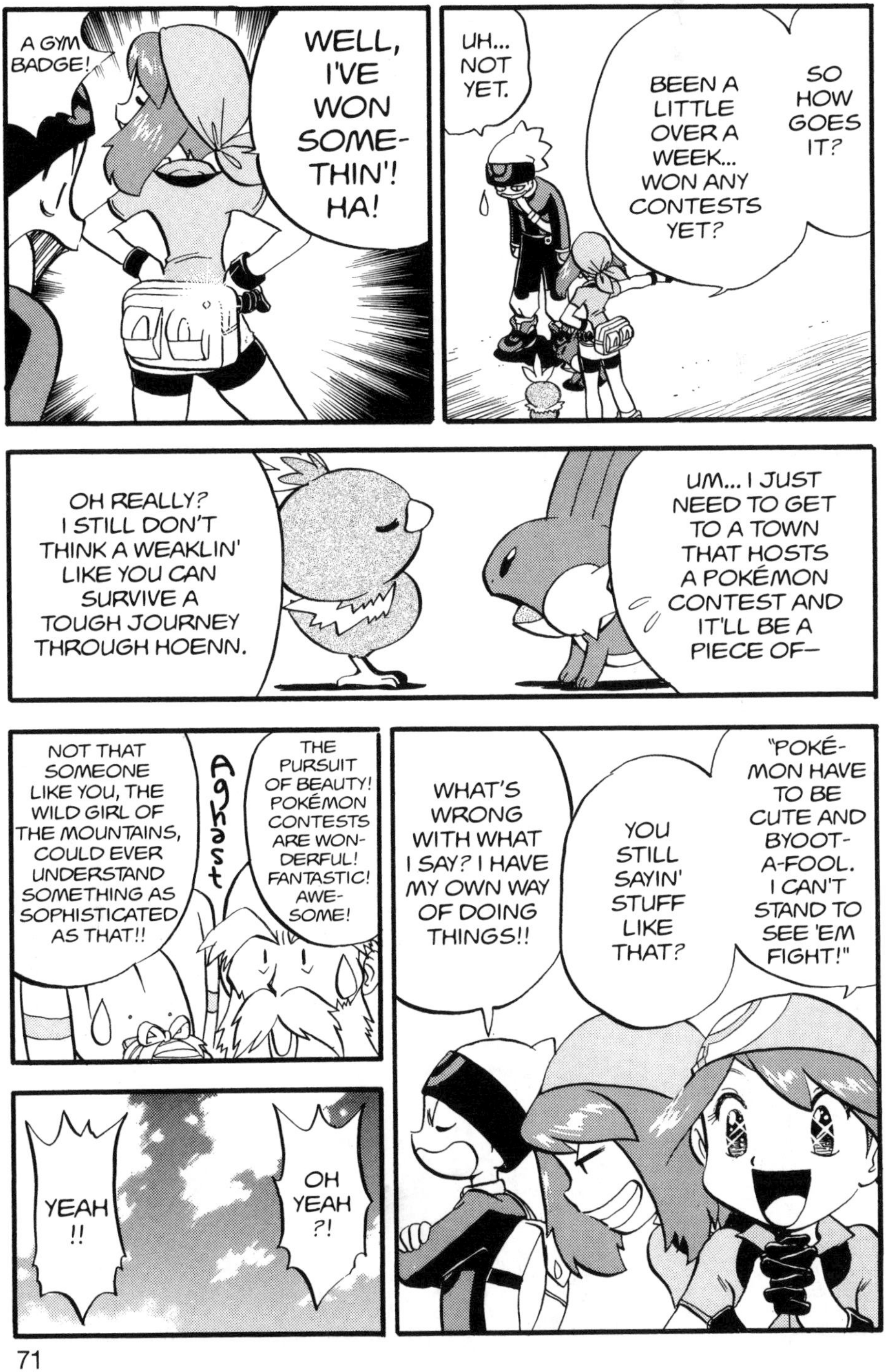
SO HOW GOES IT?
BEEN A LITTLE OVER A WEEK... WON ANY CONTESTS YET?
UH... NOT YET.
WELL, I'VE WON SOME-THIN'! HA!
A GYM BADGE!
UM... I JUST NEED TO GET TO A TOWN THAT HOSTS A POKÉMON CONTEST AND IT'LL BE A PIECE OF–
OH REALLY? I STILL DON'T THINK A WEAKLIN' LIKE YOU CAN SURVIVE A TOUGH JOURNEY THROUGH HOENN.
"POKÉ-MON HAVE TO BE CUTE AND BYOOT-A-FOOL. I CAN'T STAND TO SEE 'EM FIGHT!"
YOU STILL SAYIN' STUFF LIKE THAT?
WHAT'S WRONG WITH WHAT I SAY? I HAVE MY OWN WAY OF DOING THINGS!!
THE PURSUIT OF BEAUTY! POKÉMON CONTESTS ARE WON-DERFUL! FANTASTIC! AWE-SOME!
Aghast
NOT THAT SOMEONE LIKE YOU, THE WILD GIRL OF THE MOUNTAINS, COULD EVER UNDERSTAND SOMETHING AS SOPHISTICATED AS THAT!!
OH YEAH ?!
YEAH !!

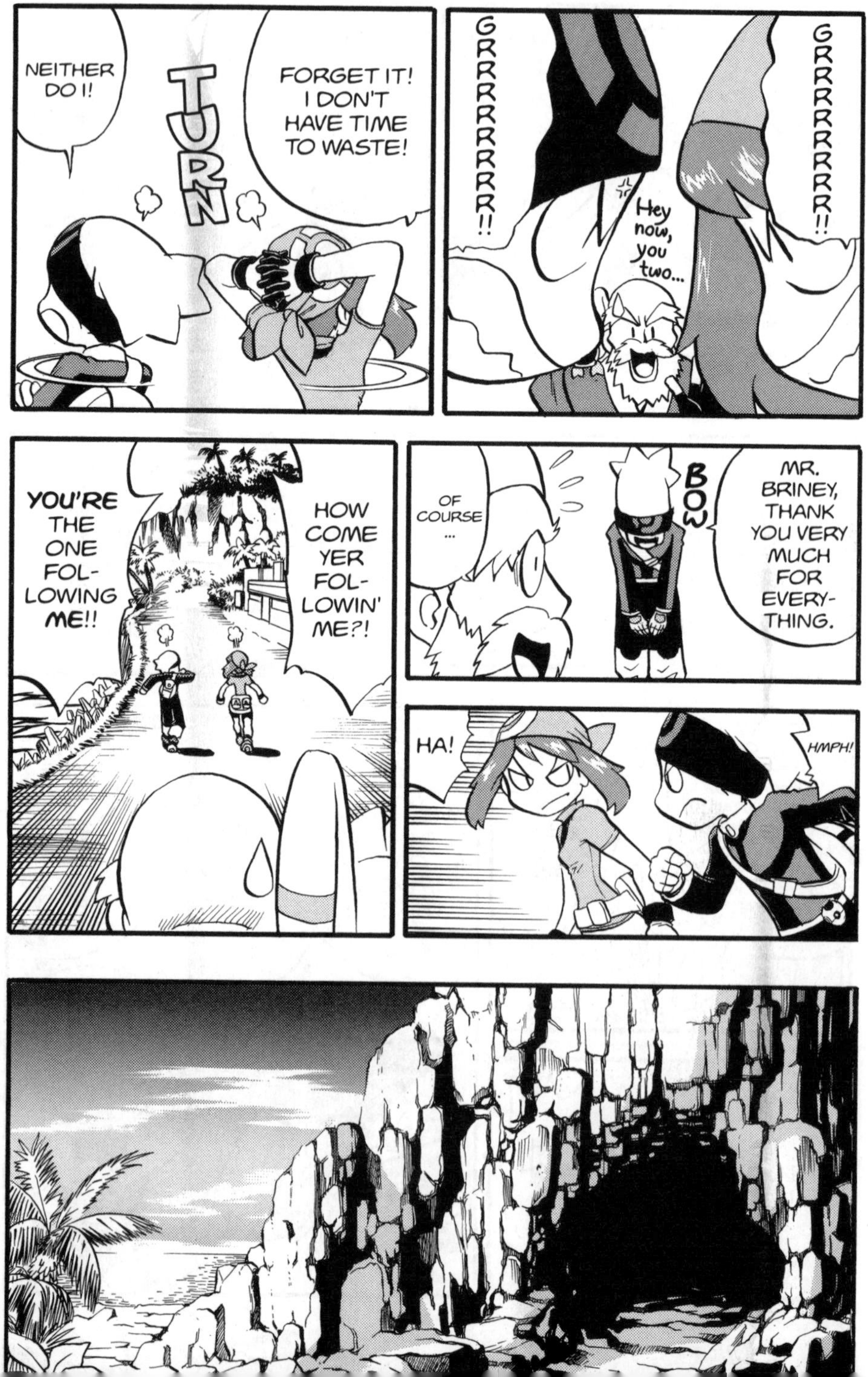
GRRRRRRRR!!
GRRRRRRRR!!
Hey now, you two...
FORGET IT! I DON'T HAVE TIME TO WASTE!
TURN
NEITHER DO I!
MR. BRINEY, THANK YOU VERY MUCH FOR EVERY-THING.
BOW
OF COURSE...
HMPH!
HA!
HOW COME YER FOL-LOWIN' ME?!
YOU'RE THE ONE FOL-LOWING ME!!

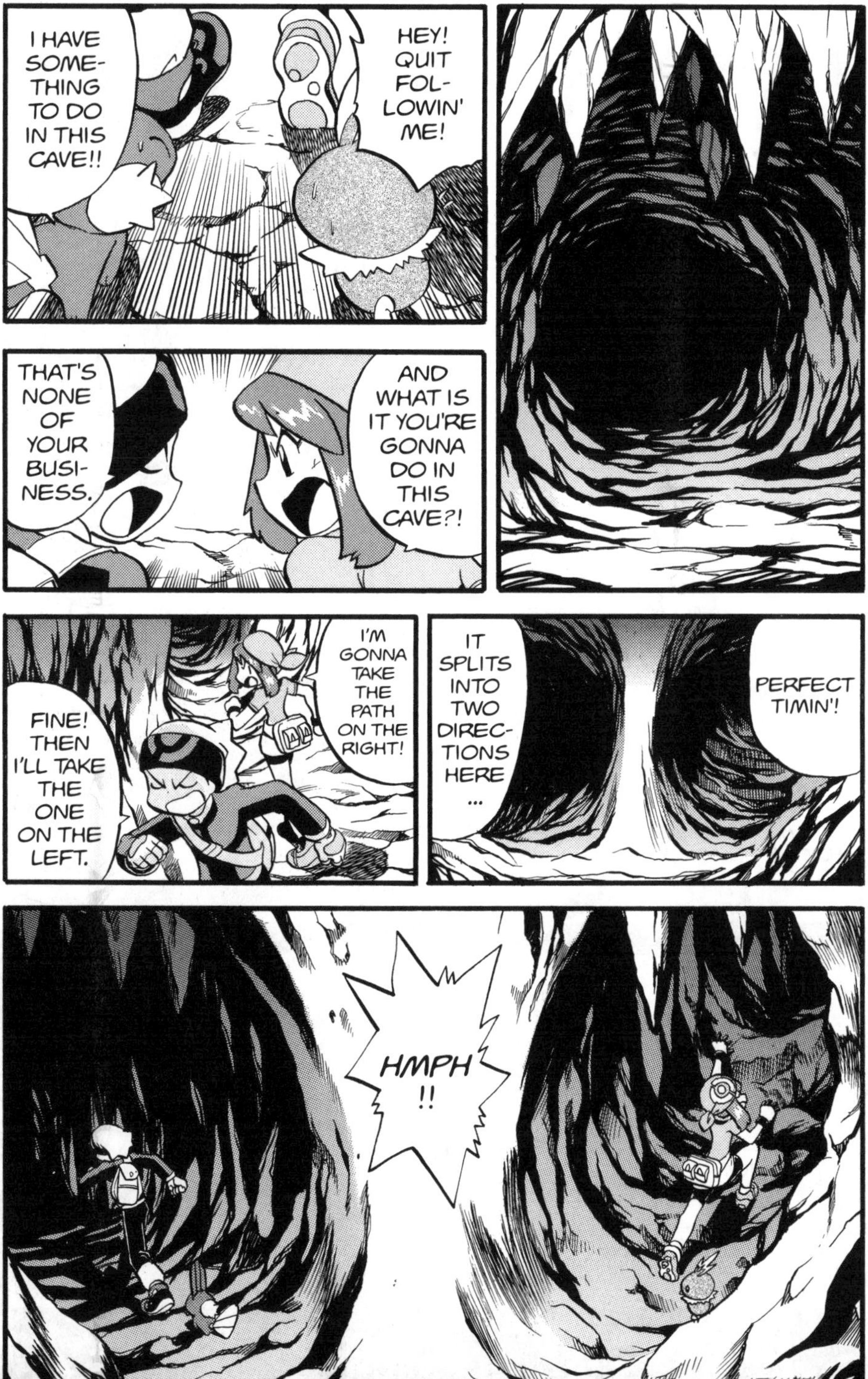
HEY! QUIT FOL-LOWIN' ME!
I HAVE SOME-THING TO DO IN THIS CAVE!!
AND WHAT IS IT YOU'RE GONNA DO IN THIS CAVE?!
THAT'S NONE OF YOUR BUSI-NESS.
PERFECT TIMIN'!
IT SPLITS INTO TWO DIREC-TIONS HERE ...
I'M GONNA TAKE THE PATH ON THE RIGHT!
FINE! THEN I'LL TAKE THE ONE ON THE LEFT.
HMPH!!

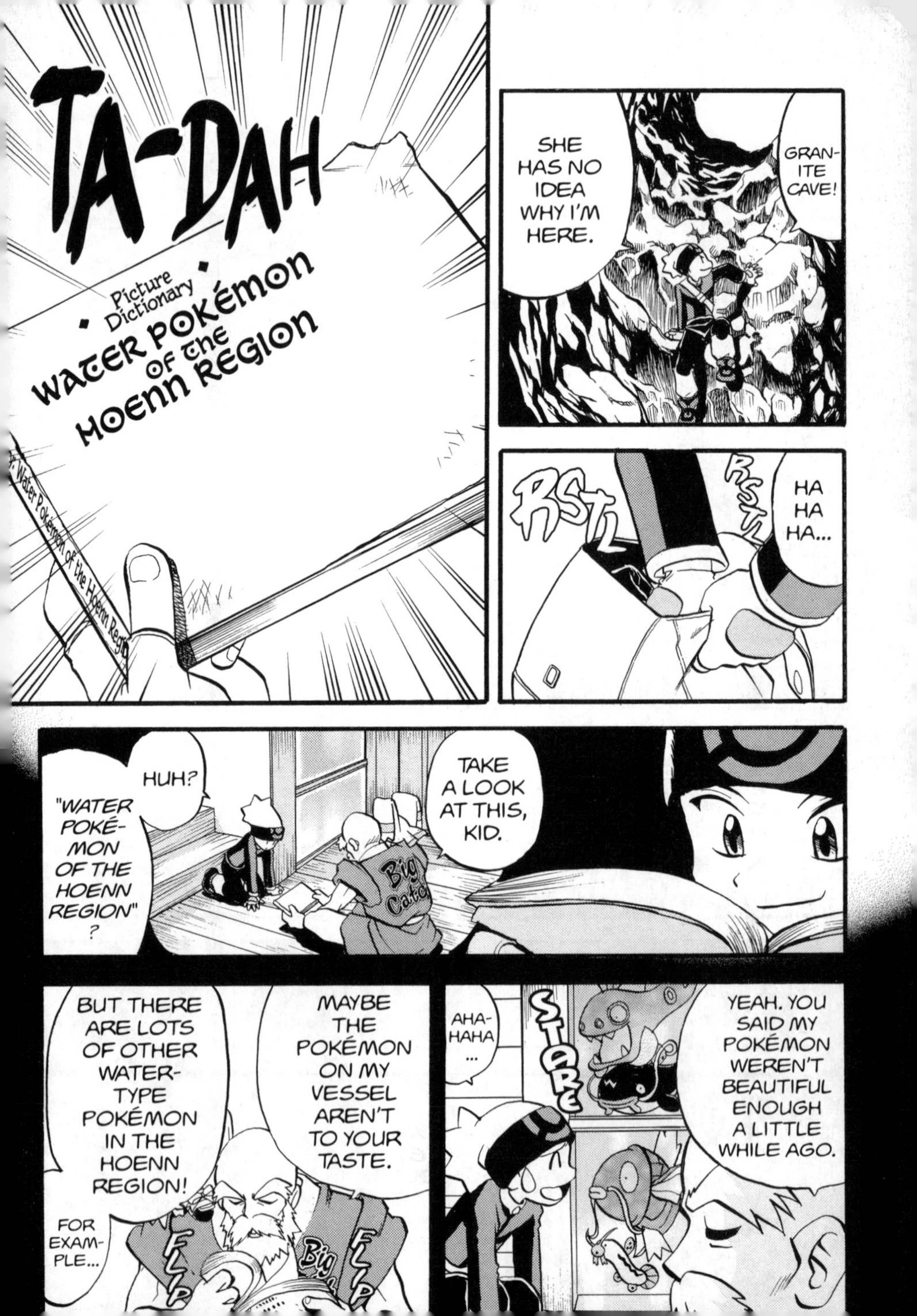
GRANITE CAVE!
SHE HAS NO IDEA WHY I'M HERE.
RSTL
HA HA HA...
RSTL
TA-DAH
Picture Dictionary
WATER POKÉMON OF THE HOENN REGION
Water Pokémon of the Hoenn Region
TAKE A LOOK AT THIS, KID.
HUH?
"WATER POKÉMON OF THE HOENN REGION"?
YEAH. YOU SAID MY POKÉMON WEREN'T BEAUTIFUL ENOUGH A LITTLE WHILE AGO.
STARE
AHAHAHA...
MAYBE THE POKÉMON ON MY VESSEL AREN'T TO YOUR TASTE.
BUT THERE ARE LOTS OF OTHER WATER-TYPE POKÉMON IN THE HOENN REGION!
FOR EXAMPLE...
FLIP
FLIP

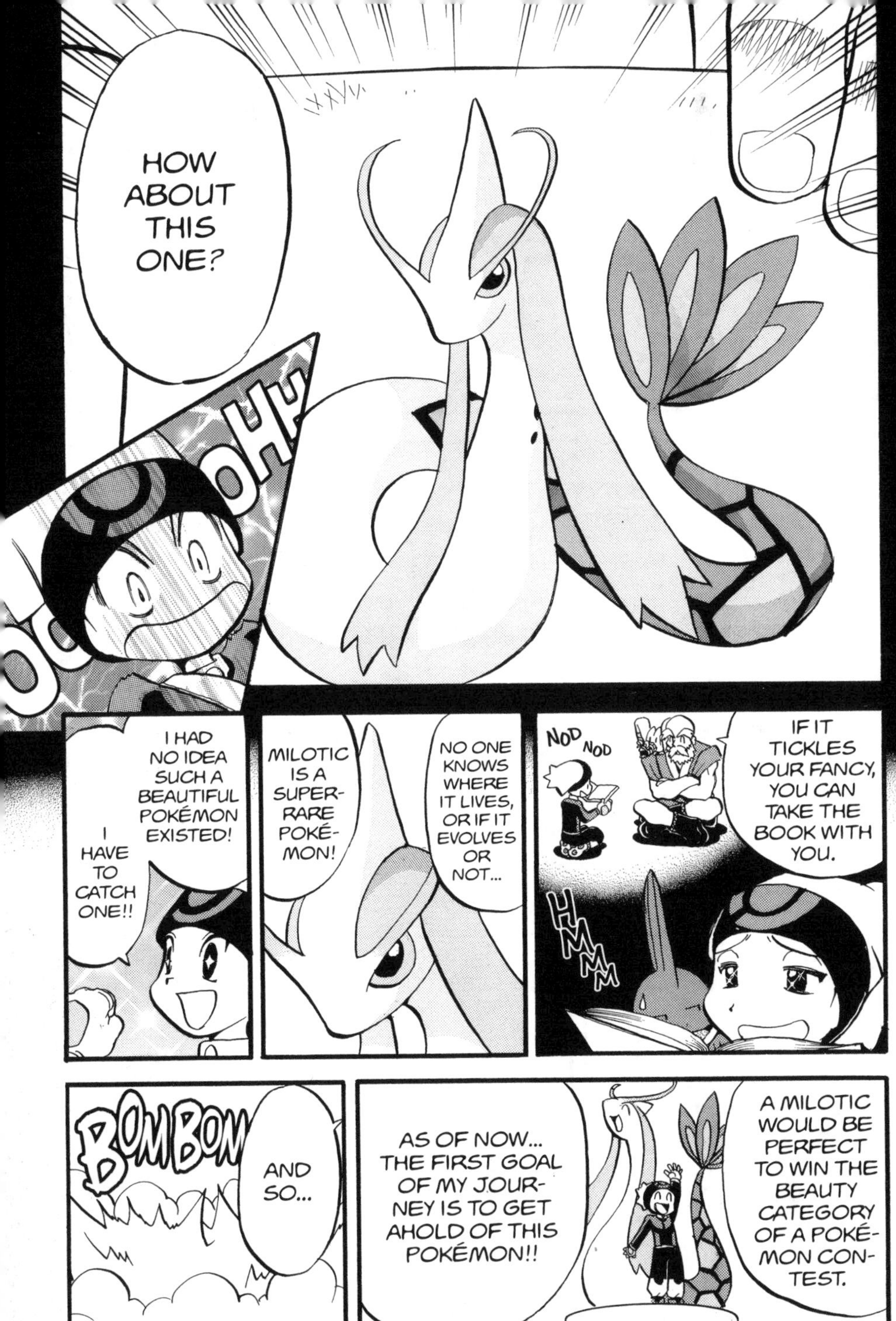
HOW ABOUT THIS ONE?
OOOHH
IF IT TICKLES YOUR FANCY, YOU CAN TAKE THE BOOK WITH YOU.
NOD NOD
HMMMM
NO ONE KNOWS WHERE IT LIVES, OR IF IT EVOLVES OR NOT...
MILOTIC IS A SUPER-RARE POKÉMON!
I HAD NO IDEA SUCH A BEAUTIFUL POKÉMON EXISTED!
I HAVE TO CATCH ONE!!
A MILOTIC WOULD BE PERFECT TO WIN THE BEAUTY CATEGORY OF A POKÉMON CONTEST.
AS OF NOW... THE FIRST GOAL OF MY JOURNEY IS TO GET AHOLD OF THIS POKÉMON!!
AND SO...
BOM BOM

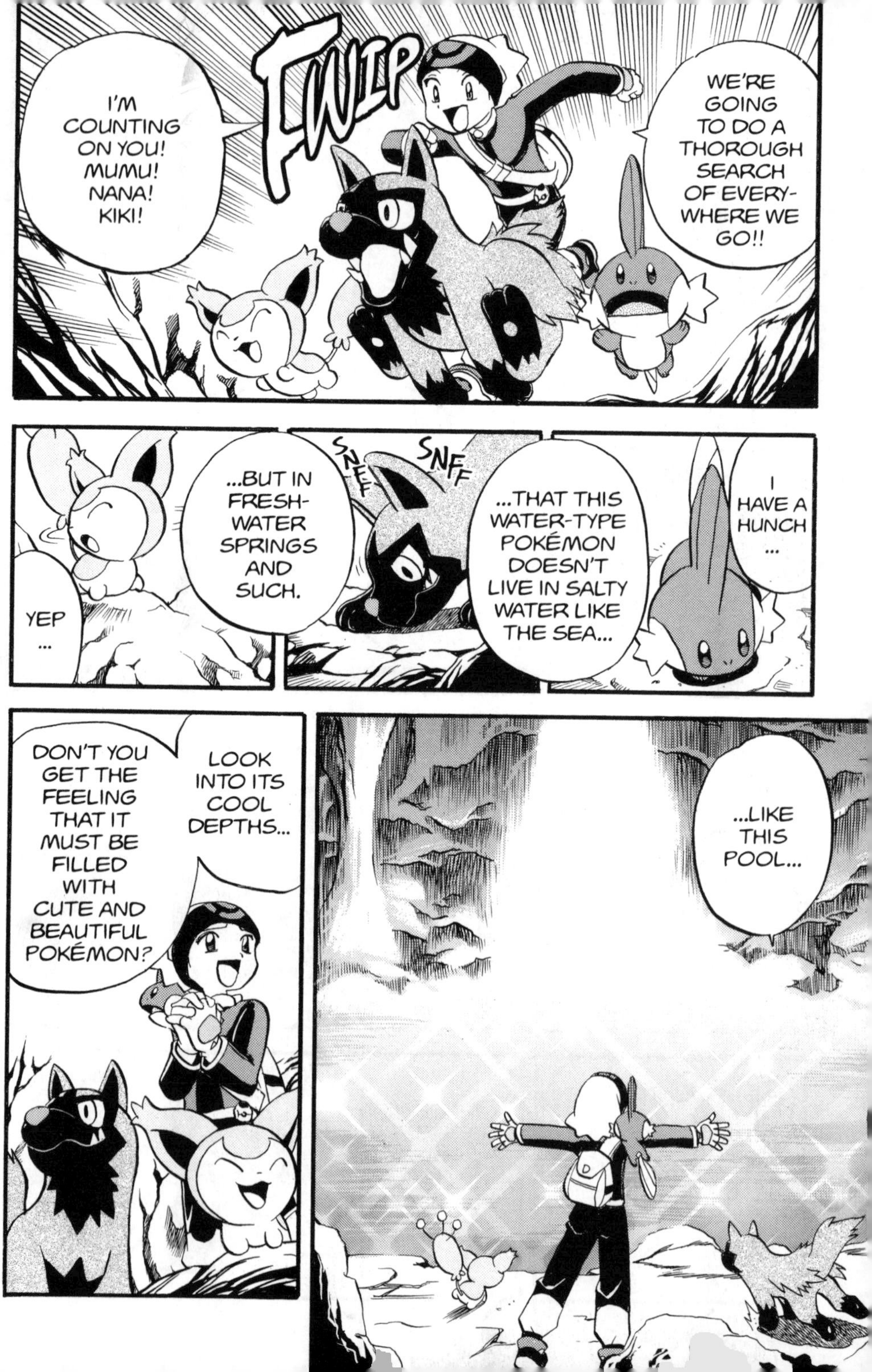
WE'RE GOING TO DO A THOROUGH SEARCH OF EVERY-WHERE WE GO!!
FWIP
I'M COUNTING ON YOU! MUMU! NANA! KIKI!
I HAVE A HUNCH ...
...THAT THIS WATER-TYPE POKÉMON DOESN'T LIVE IN SALTY WATER LIKE THE SEA...
SNFF
SNFF
...BUT IN FRESH-WATER SPRINGS AND SUCH.
YEP ...
...LIKE THIS POOL...
LOOK INTO ITS COOL DEPTHS...
DON'T YOU GET THE FEELING THAT IT MUST BE FILLED WITH CUTE AND BEAUTIFUL POKÉMON?

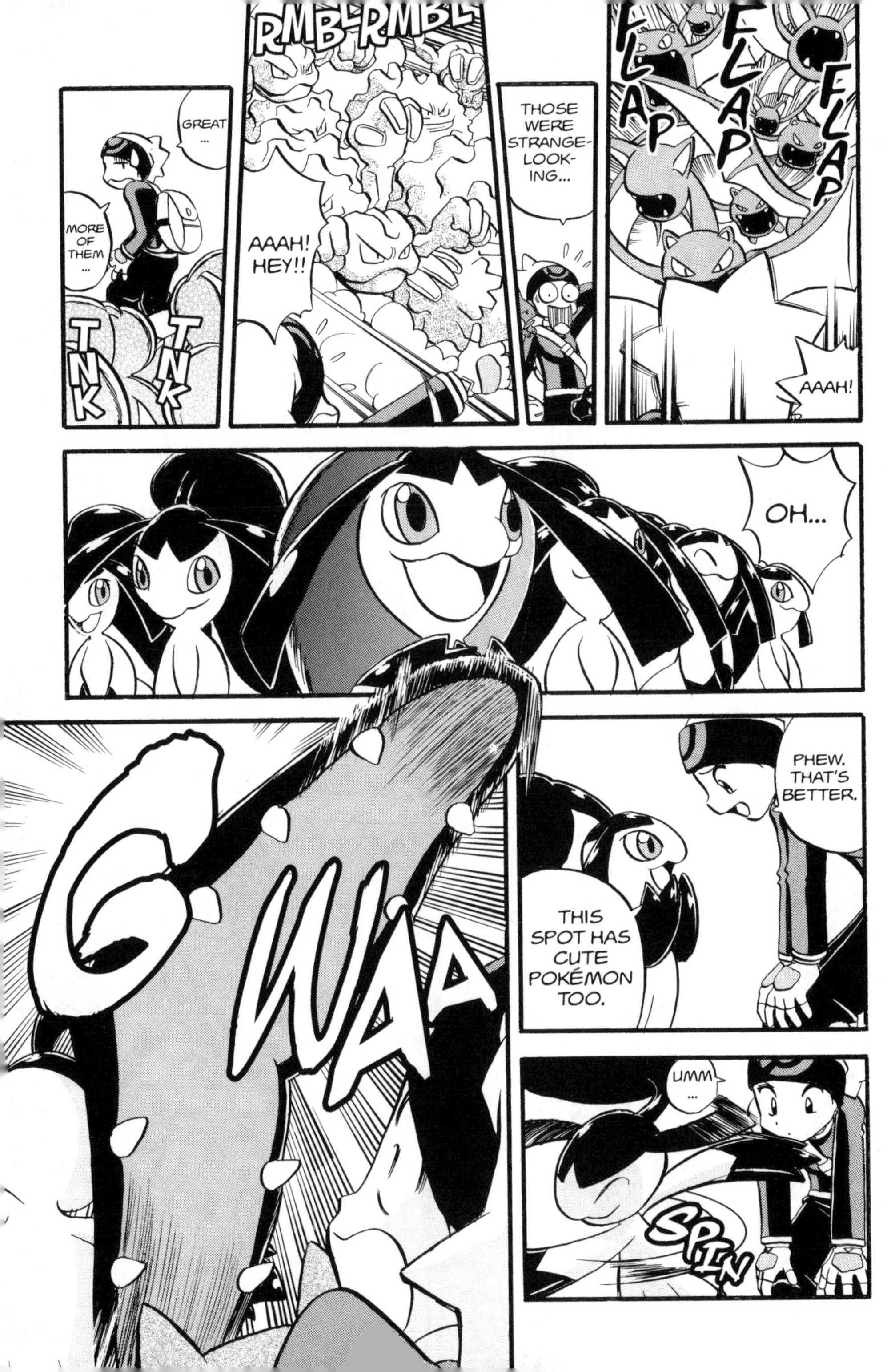
FLAP
FLAP
FLAP
AAAH!
THOSE WERE STRANGE-LOOKING...
RMBL RMBL
AAAH! HEY!!
GREAT...
MORE OF THEM...
TNK
TNK
OH...
PHEW. THAT'S BETTER.
THIS SPOT HAS CUTE POKÉMON TOO.
UMM...
SPIN
GWAA

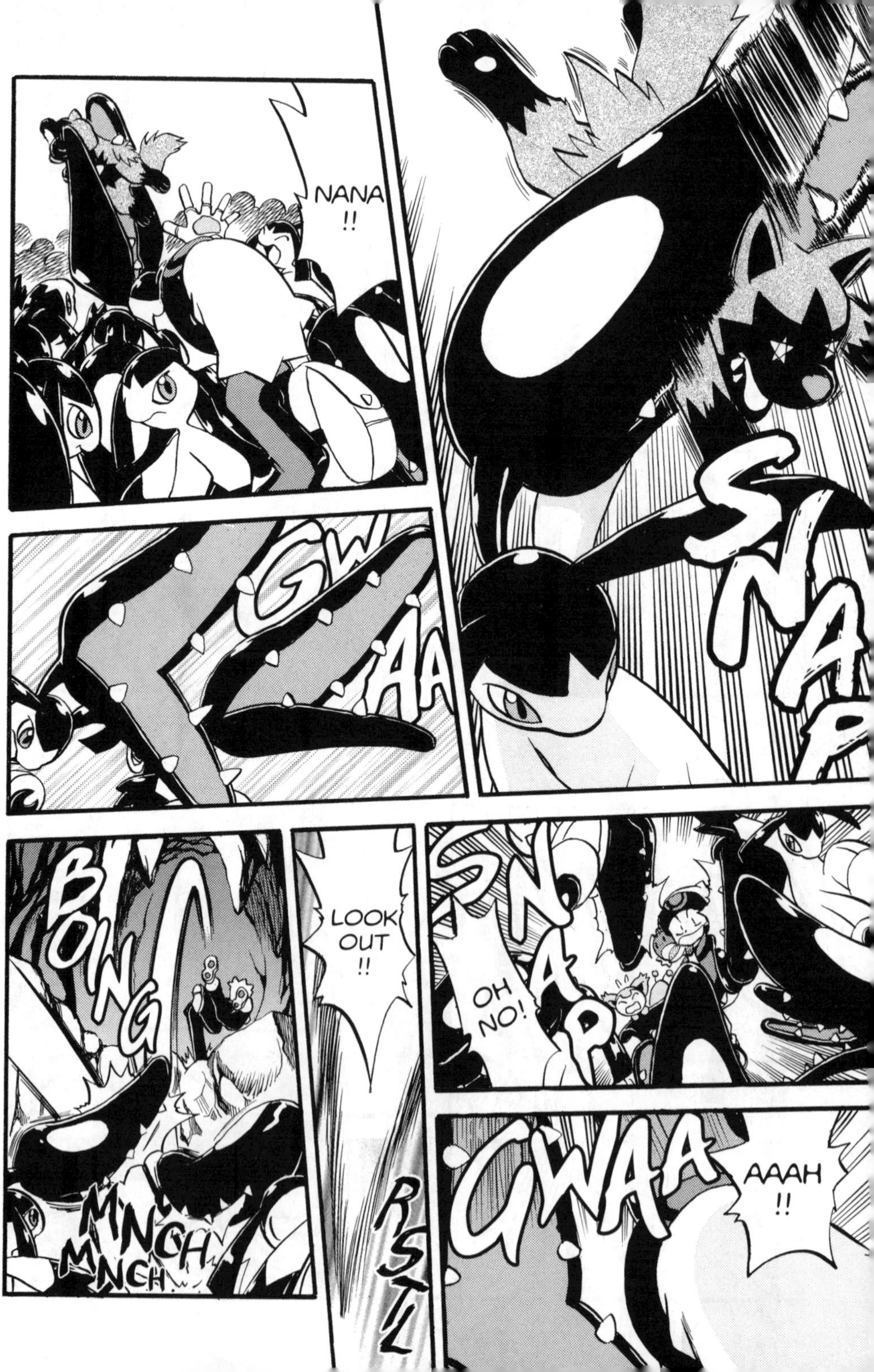
SNAP
NANA !!
GWAA
SNAP
OH NO!
GWAA
AAAH !!
LOOK OUT !!
RSTL
BOING
MNCH MNCH

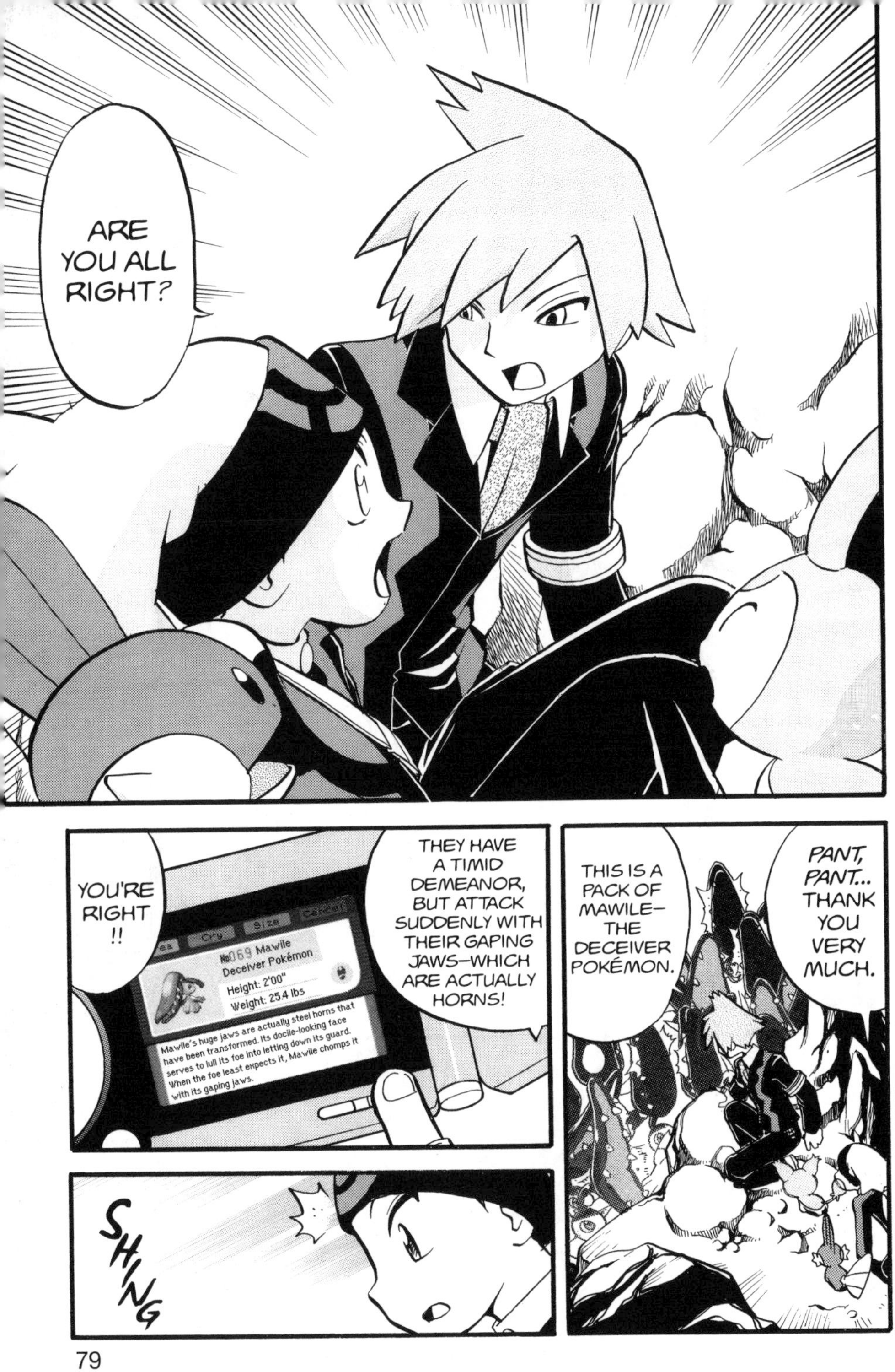
ARE YOU ALL RIGHT?
PANT, PANT... THANK YOU VERY MUCH.
THIS IS A PACK OF MAWILE—THE DECEIVER POKÉMON.
THEY HAVE A TIMID DEMEANOR, BUT ATTACK SUDDENLY WITH THEIR GAPING JAWS—WHICH ARE ACTUALLY HORNS!
YOU'RE RIGHT !!
Cry
Size
Cancel
No069 Mawile
Deceiver Pokémon
Height: 2'00"
Weight: 25.4 lbs
Mawile's huge jaws are actually steel horns that have been transformed. Its docile-looking face serves to lull its foe into letting down its guard. When the foe least expects it, Mawile chomps it with its gaping jaws.
SHING

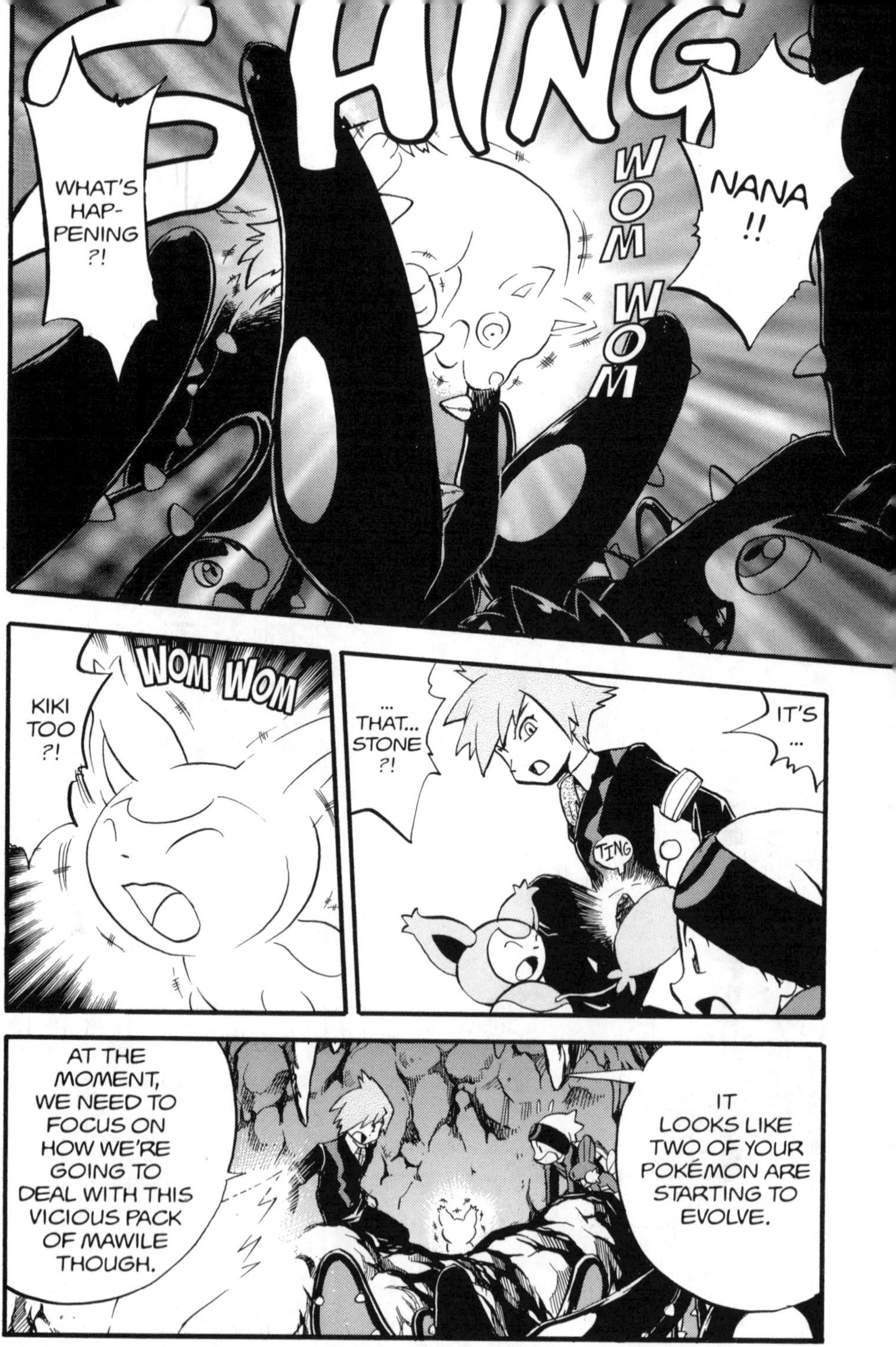
CHING
NANA !!
WOM WOM WOM WOM
WHAT'S HAP-PENING ?!
IT'S ...
TING
... THAT... STONE ?!
WOM WOM
KIKI TOO ?!
IT LOOKS LIKE TWO OF YOUR POKÉMON ARE STARTING TO EVOLVE.
AT THE MOMENT, WE NEED TO FOCUS ON HOW WE'RE GOING TO DEAL WITH THIS VICIOUS PACK OF MAWILE THOUGH.

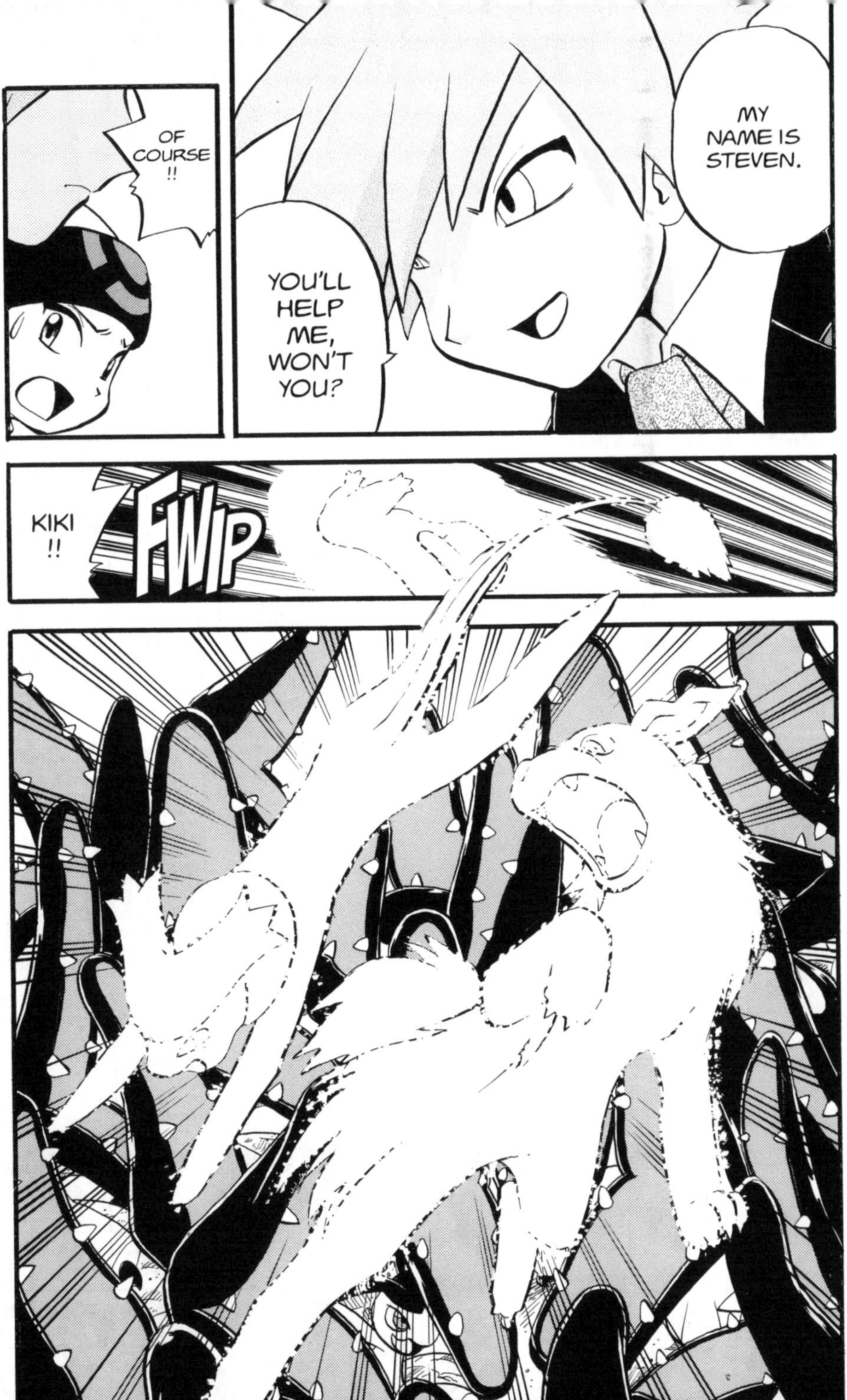
MY NAME IS STEVEN.
YOU'LL HELP ME, WON'T YOU?
OF COURSE !!
FWIP
KIKI !!

ADVENTURE MAP

SAPPHIRE

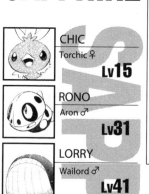

CHIC
Torchic ♀
Lv15

RONO
Aron ♂
Lv31

LORRY
Wailord ♂
Lv41

Sea Route 105	Sea Route 105
▼	▼
Sea Route 106	Sea Route 106
▼	▼
Dewford Town	
▼	▼
●Granite Cave	●Granite Cave

RUBY

NANA
? ♀

KIKI
? ♀

MUMU
Mudkip ♂

Stone Badge	Knuckle Badge	Dynamo Badge	Heat Badge
Balance Badge	Feather Badge	Mind Badge	Rain Badge

		Coolness	Beauty	Cuteness	Cleverness	Toughness
Normal	Super	🎗	🎗	🎗	🎗	🎗
		🎗	🎗	🎗	🎗	🎗
Hyper	Master	🎗	🎗	🎗	🎗	🎗
		🎗	🎗	🎗	🎗	🎗

● Adventure 195 ●
Mashing Makuhita

Pokémon™ Adventures Ruby & Sapphire
The Fourth Chapter

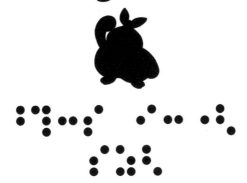

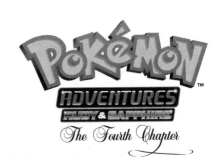

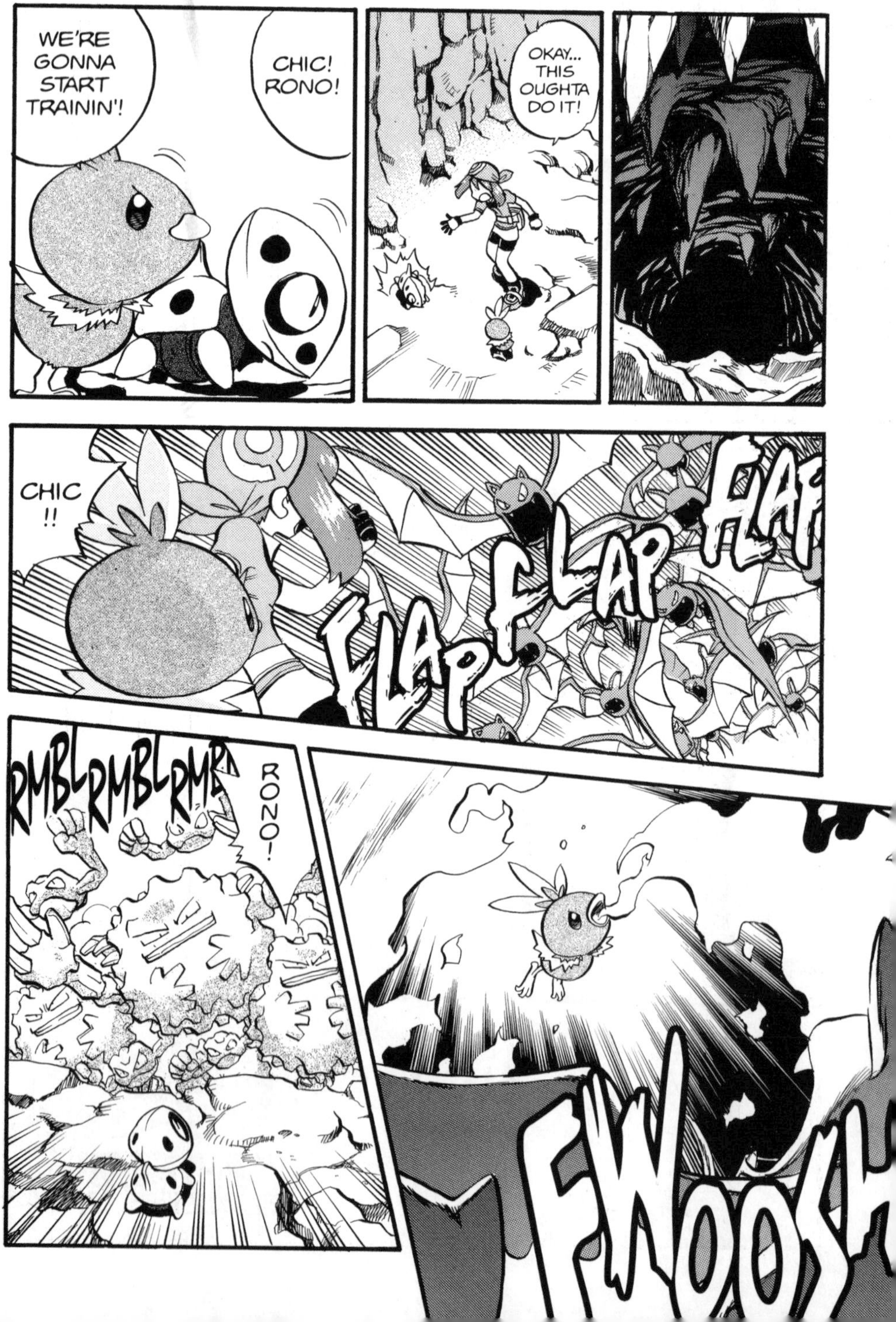

OKAY... THIS OUGHTA DO IT!
CHIC! RONO!
WE'RE GONNA START TRAININ'!
FLAP FLAP FLAP
CHIC !!
FWOOSH
RONO!
RMBL RMBL RMBL

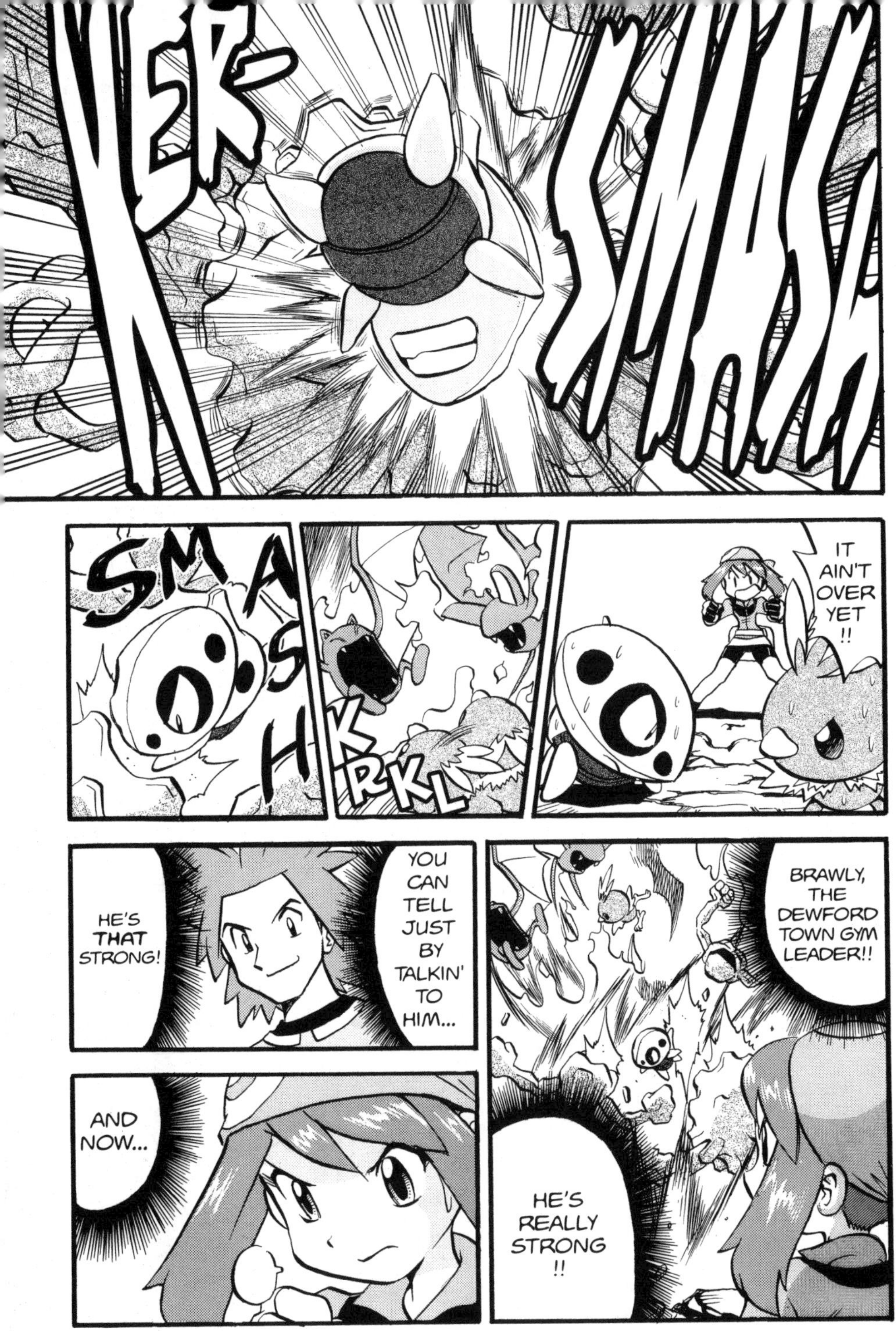
KER-
SMASH
IT AIN'T OVER YET!!
KRKL
SMASH
BRAWLY, THE DEWFORD TOWN GYM LEADER!!
HE'S REALLY STRONG!!
YOU CAN TELL JUST BY TALKIN' TO HIM...
HE'S THAT STRONG!
AND NOW...

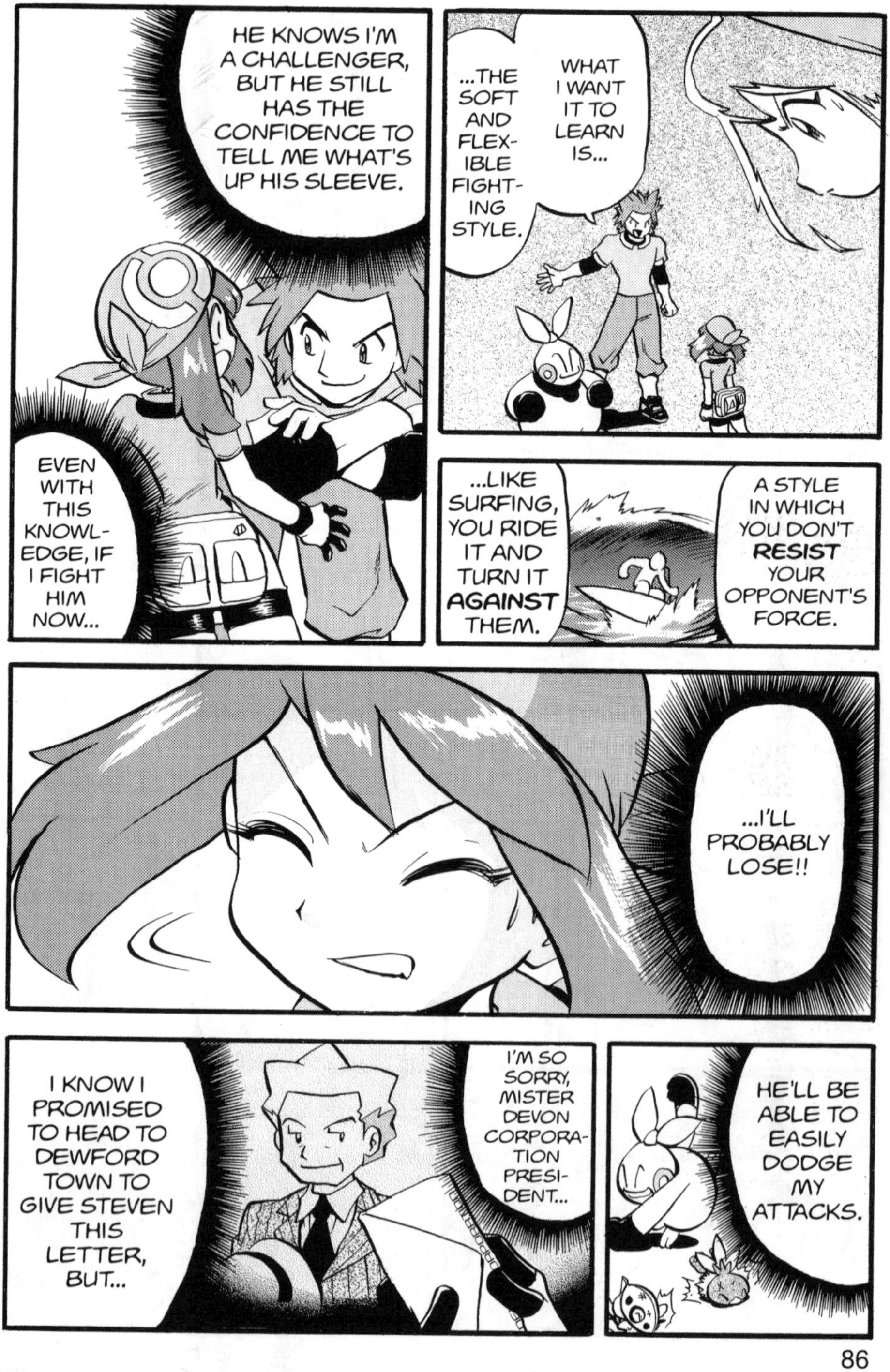

WHAT I WANT IT TO LEARN IS...
...THE SOFT AND FLEX-IBLE FIGHT-ING STYLE.
A STYLE IN WHICH YOU DON'T **RESIST** YOUR OPPONENT'S FORCE.
...LIKE SURFING, YOU RIDE IT AND TURN IT **AGAINST** THEM.
HE KNOWS I'M A CHALLENGER, BUT HE STILL HAS THE CONFIDENCE TO TELL ME WHAT'S UP HIS SLEEVE.
EVEN WITH THIS KNOWL-EDGE, IF I FIGHT HIM NOW...
...I'LL PROBABLY LOSE!!
HE'LL BE ABLE TO EASILY DODGE MY ATTACKS.
I'M SO SORRY, MISTER DEVON CORPORA-TION PRESI-DENT...
I KNOW I PROMISED TO HEAD TO DEWFORD TOWN TO GIVE STEVEN THIS LETTER, BUT...

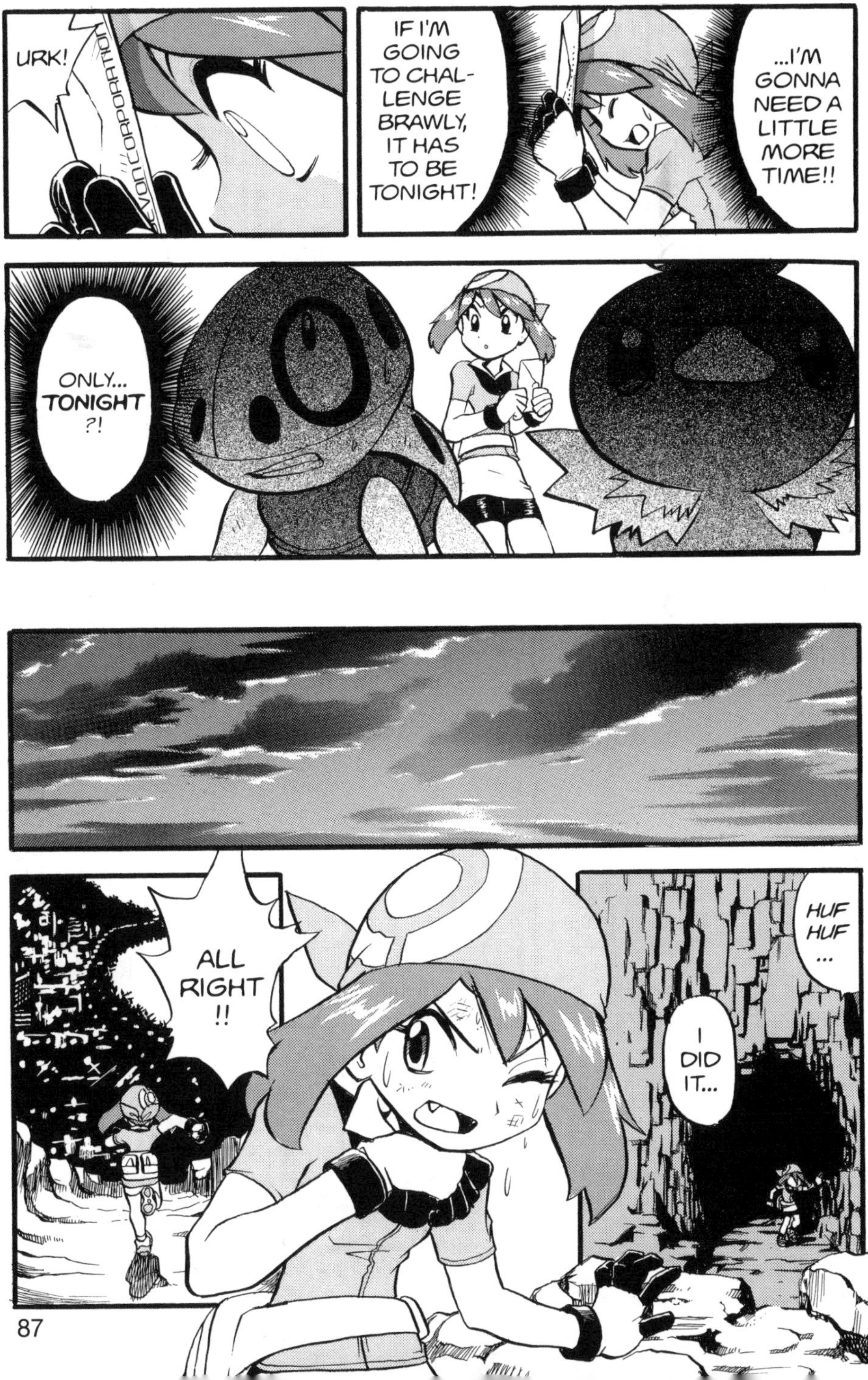

...I'M GONNA NEED A LITTLE MORE TIME!!
IF I'M GOING TO CHALLENGE BRAWLY, IT HAS TO BE TONIGHT!
URK!
DEVON CORPORATION
ONLY... **TONIGHT** ?!
HUF HUF ...
I DID IT...
ALL RIGHT !!

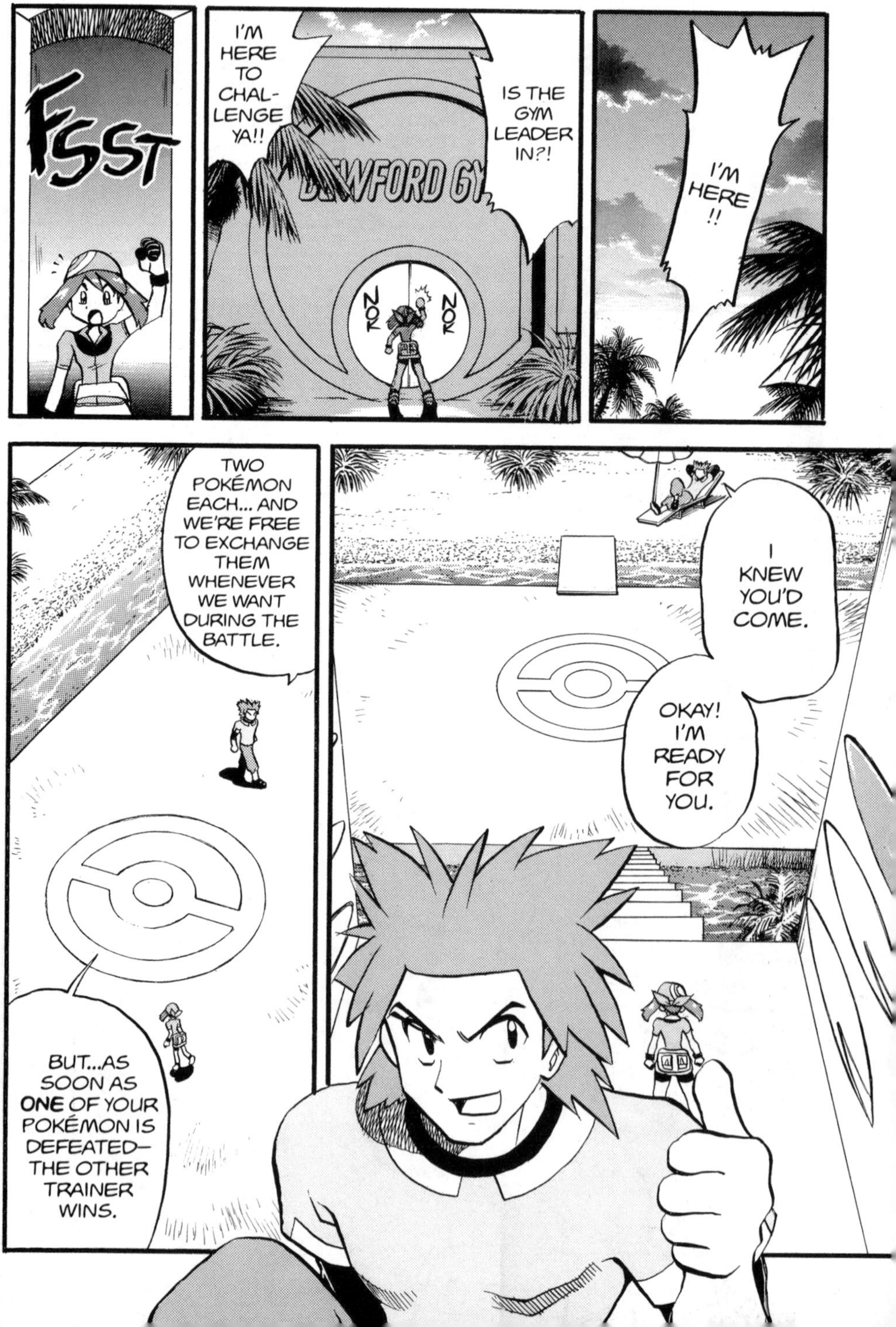
I'M HERE !!
IS THE GYM LEADER IN?!
I'M HERE TO CHAL-LENGE YA!!
DEWFORD GY
NOK
NOK
FSST
I KNEW YOU'D COME.
OKAY! I'M READY FOR YOU.
TWO POKÉMON EACH... AND WE'RE FREE TO EXCHANGE THEM WHENEVER WE WANT DURING THE BATTLE.
BUT...AS SOON AS **ONE** OF YOUR POKÉMON IS DEFEATED—THE OTHER TRAINER WINS.

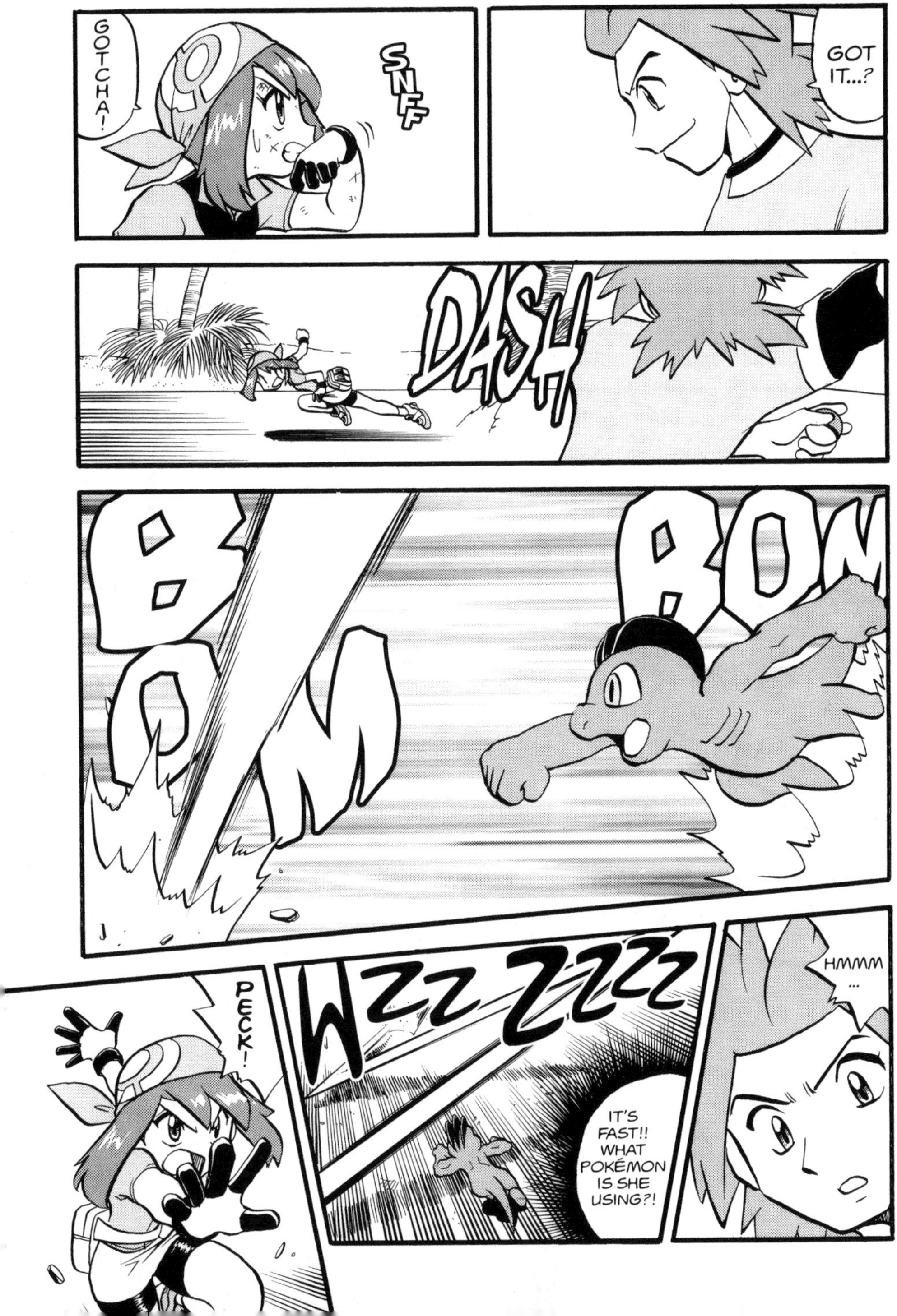
GOT IT...?
SNFF
GOTCHA!
DASH
BOM
BOM
HMMM ...
WZZ ZZZZ
IT'S FAST!! WHAT POKÉMON IS SHE USING?!
PECK!

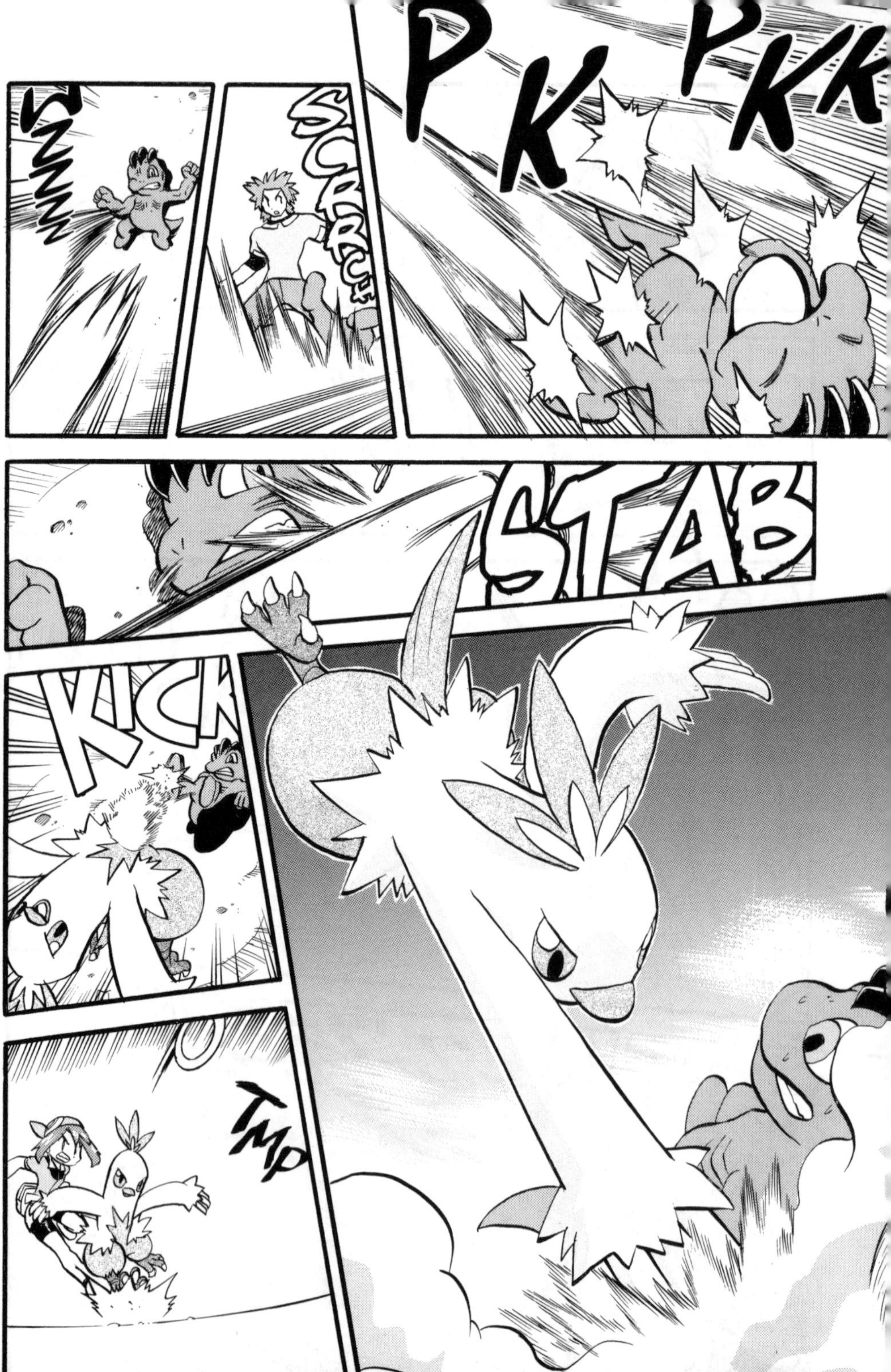
PK
PKK
SCRRCH
STAB
KICK
TMP

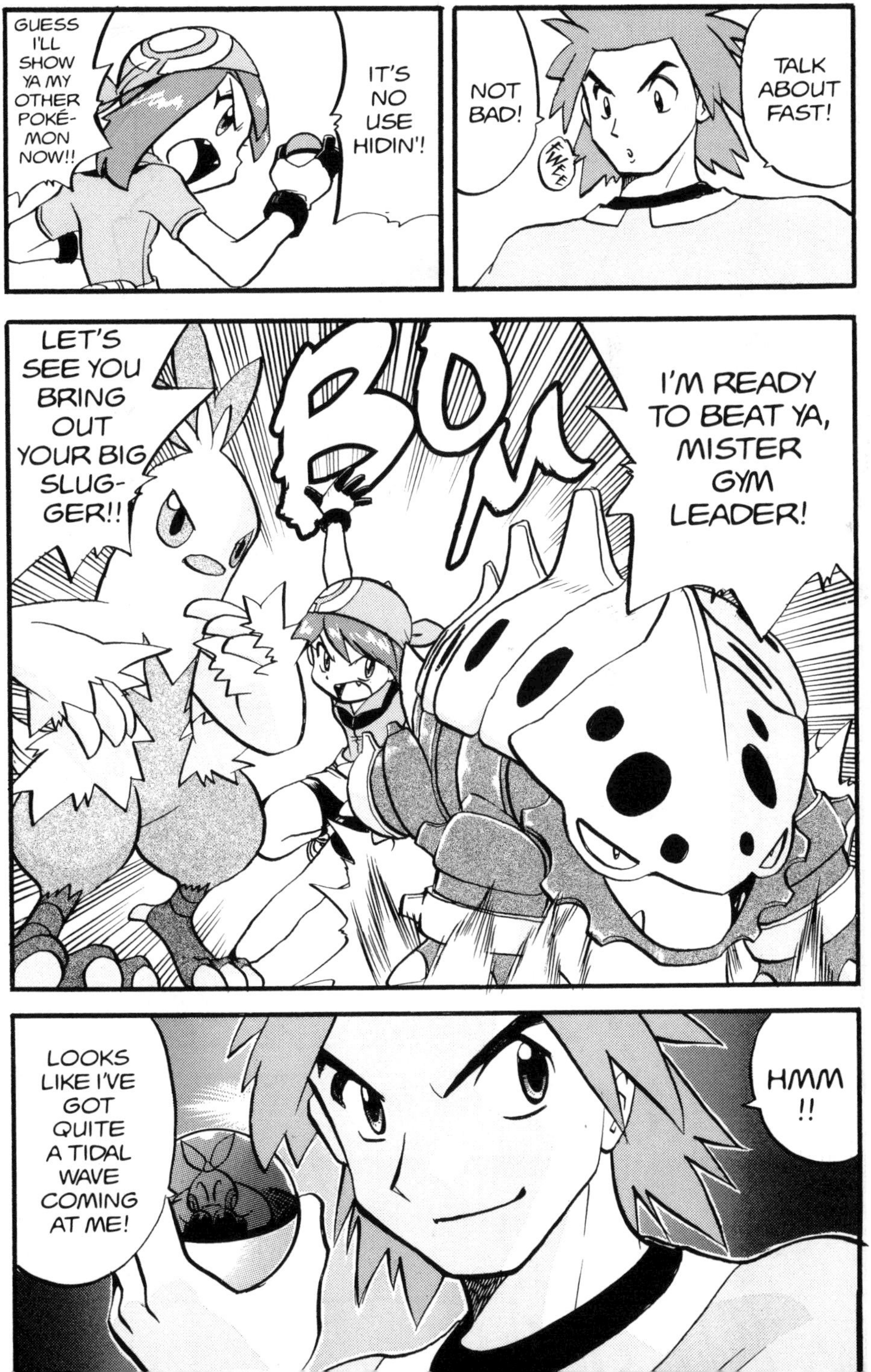
TALK ABOUT FAST!
NOT BAD!
FWEE
IT'S NO USE HIDIN'!
GUESS I'LL SHOW YA MY OTHER POKÉ-MON NOW!!
I'M READY TO BEAT YA, MISTER GYM LEADER!
BOM
LET'S SEE YOU BRING OUT YOUR BIG SLUG-GER!!
HMM!!
LOOKS LIKE I'VE GOT QUITE A TIDAL WAVE COMING AT ME!

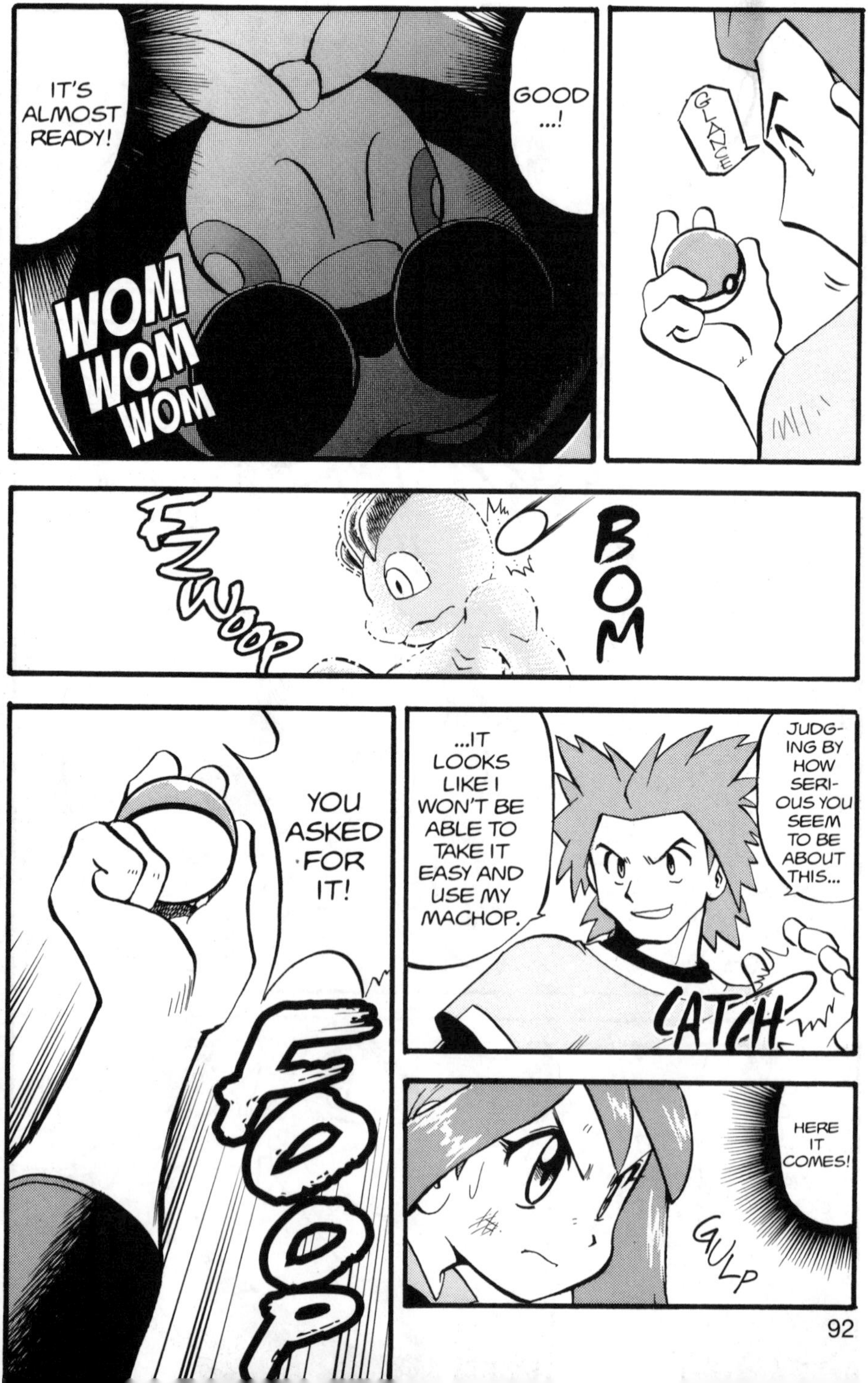
GLANCE
GOOD ...!
IT'S ALMOST READY!
WOM WOM WOM
BOM
FZWOOP
JUDGING BY HOW SERIOUS YOU SEEM TO BE ABOUT THIS...
...IT LOOKS LIKE I WON'T BE ABLE TO TAKE IT EASY AND USE MY MACHOP.
CATCH
HERE IT COMES!
GULP
YOU ASKED FOR IT!
FOOOP

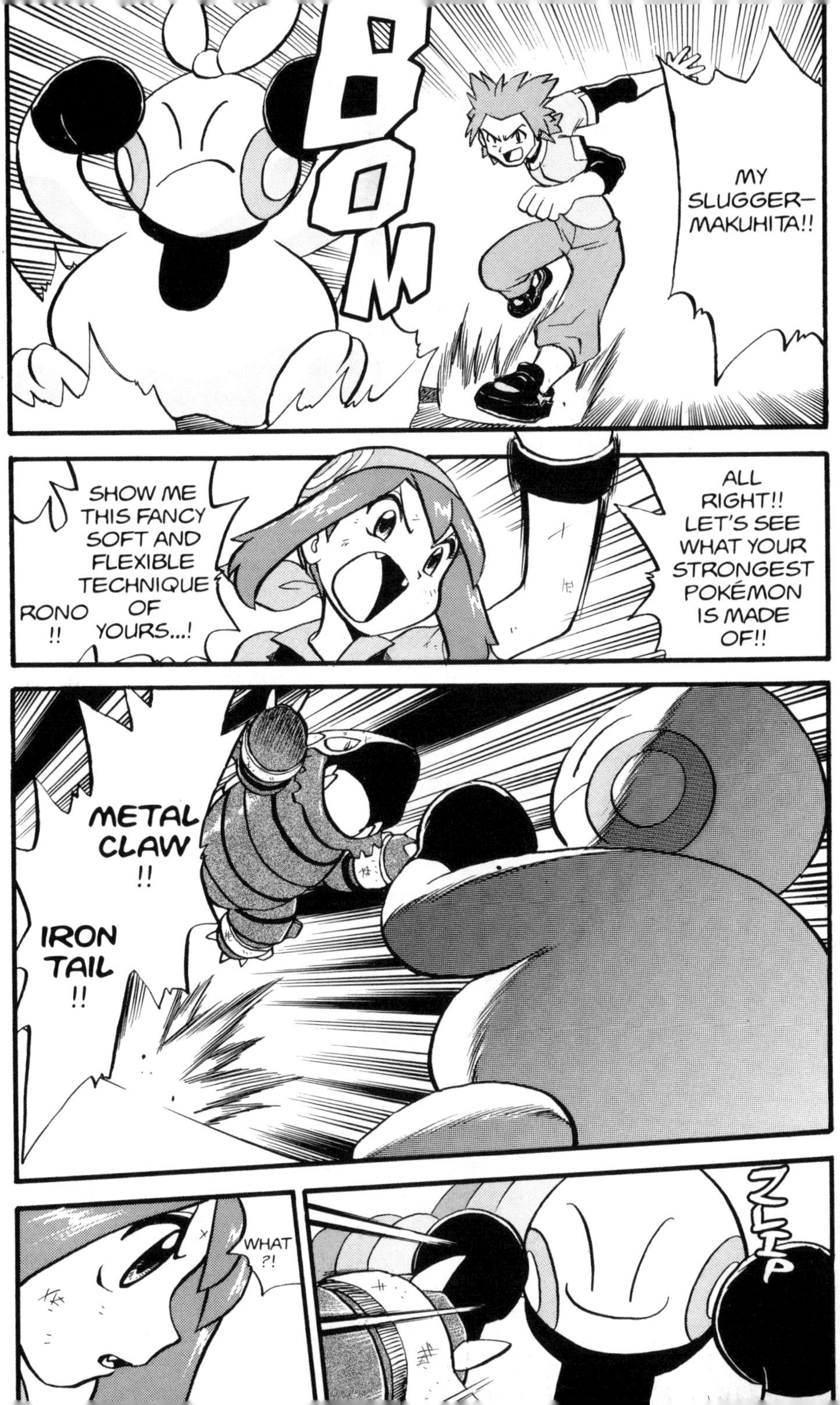
BOOM
MY SLUGGER—MAKUHITA!!
ALL RIGHT!! LET'S SEE WHAT YOUR STRONGEST POKÉMON IS MADE OF!!
SHOW ME THIS FANCY SOFT AND FLEXIBLE TECHNIQUE OF YOURS...!
RONO!!
METAL CLAW!!
IRON TAIL!!
ZLIP
WHAT?!

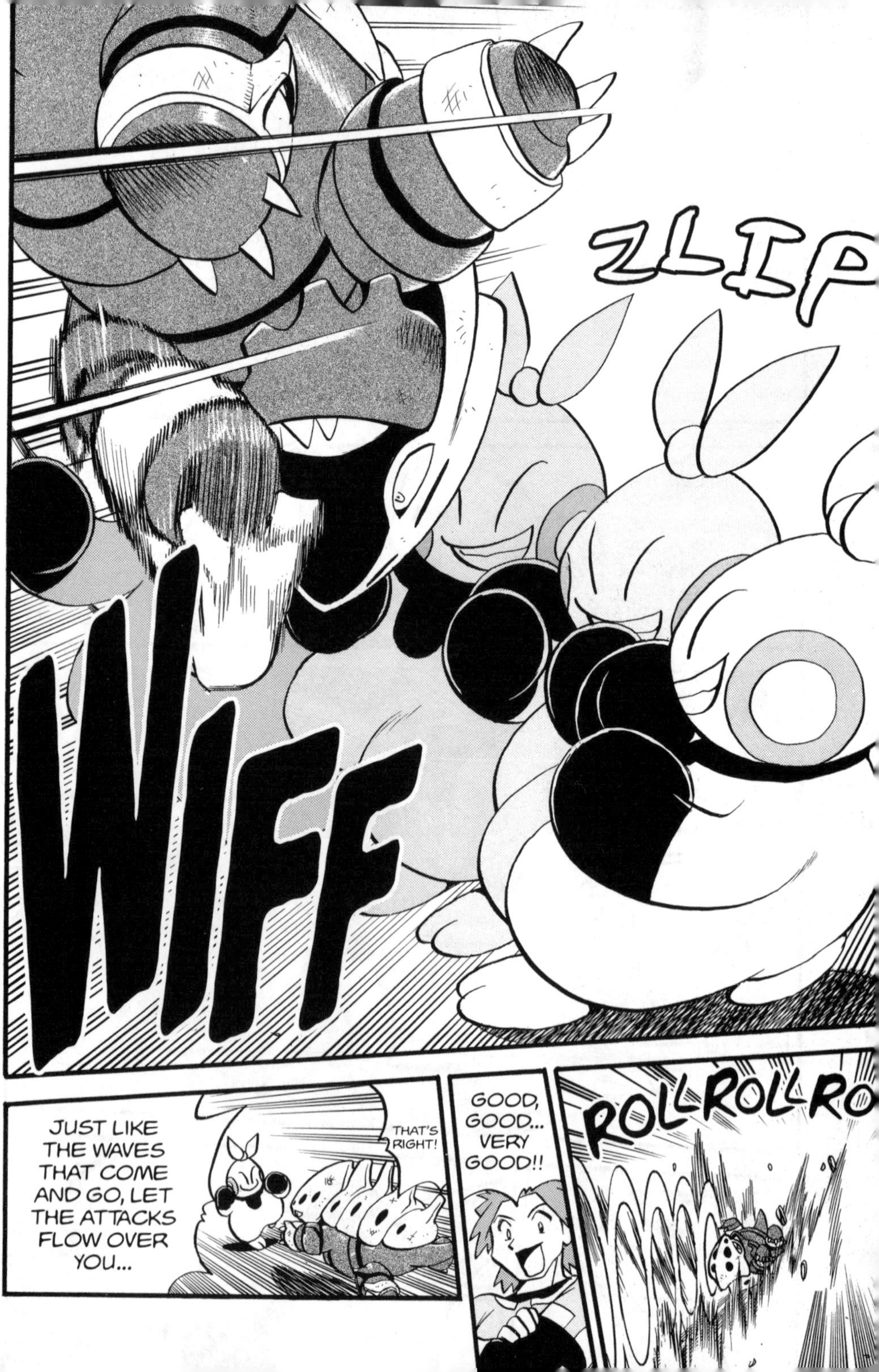
ZLIP
WIFF
ROLLROLLRO
GOOD, GOOD... VERY GOOD!!
THAT'S RIGHT!
JUST LIKE THE WAVES THAT COME AND GO, LET THE ATTACKS FLOW OVER YOU...

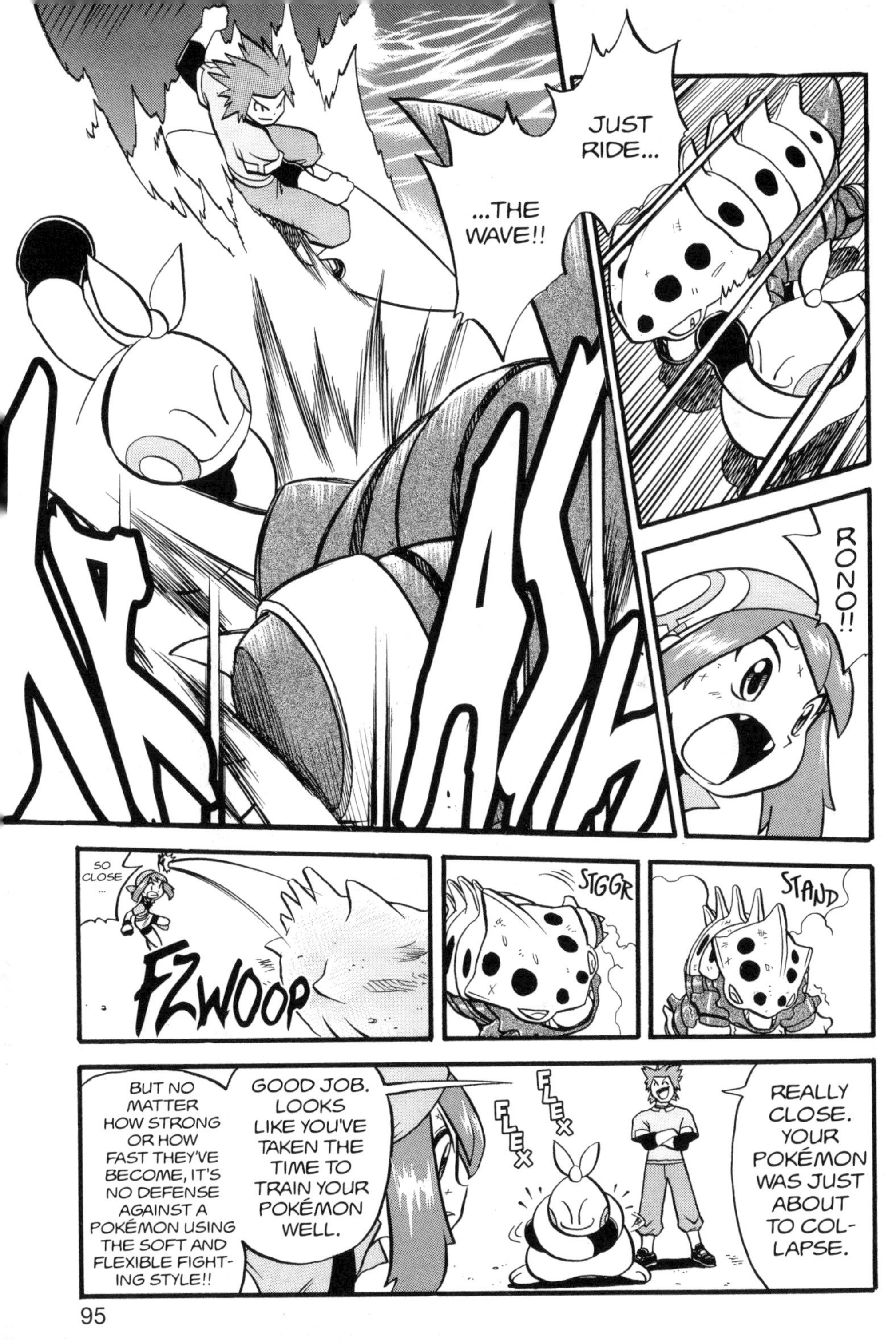
JUST RIDE...
...THE WAVE!!
RONO!!
STAND
STGGR
SO CLOSE ...
FZWOOP
REALLY CLOSE. YOUR POKÉMON WAS JUST ABOUT TO COL-LAPSE.
FLEX FLEX
GOOD JOB. LOOKS LIKE YOU'VE TAKEN THE TIME TO TRAIN YOUR POKÉMON WELL.
BUT NO MATTER HOW STRONG OR HOW FAST THEY'VE BECOME, IT'S NO DEFENSE AGAINST A POKÉMON USING THE SOFT AND FLEXIBLE FIGHT-ING STYLE!!

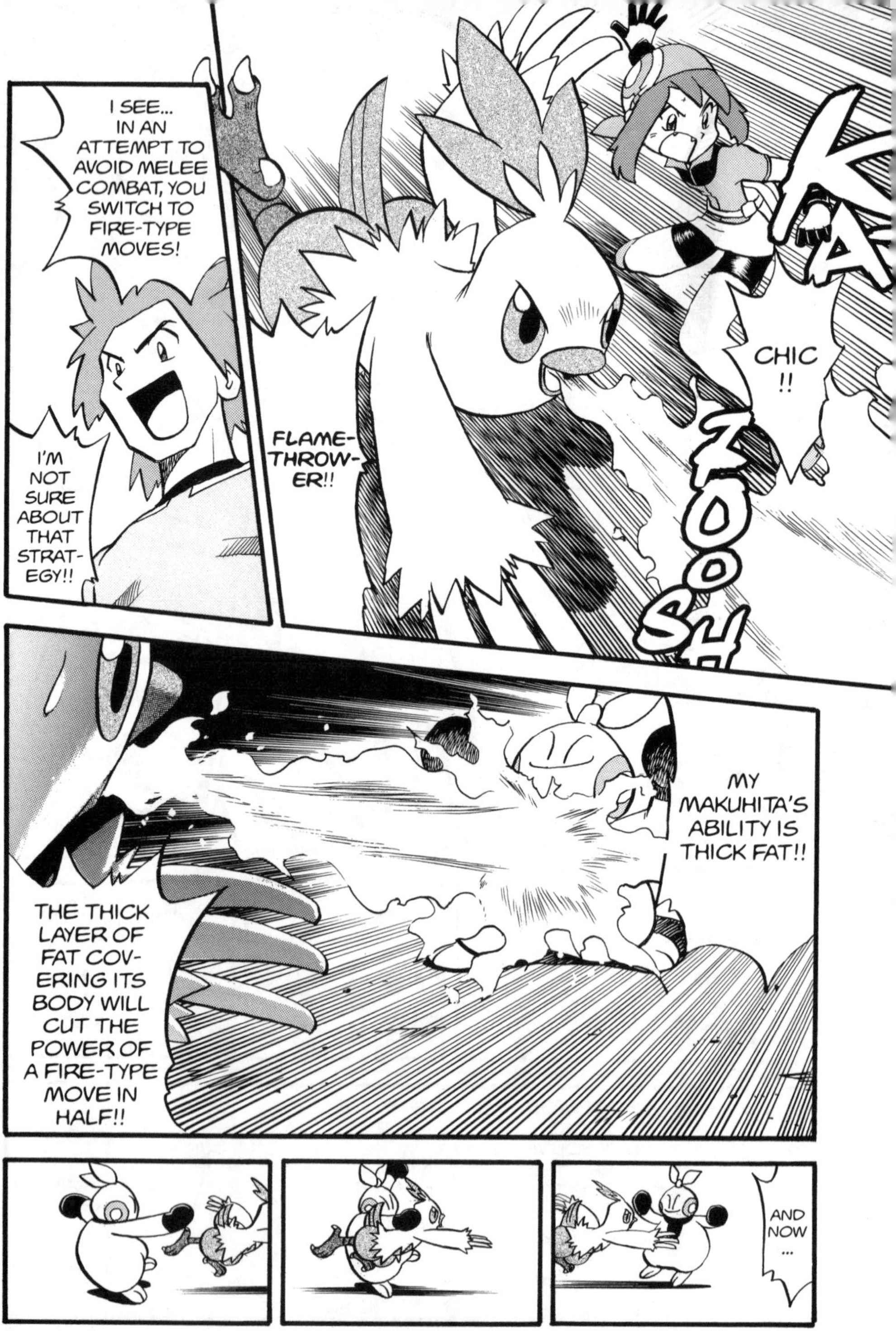
CHIC !!
FLAME-THROWER!!
I SEE... IN AN ATTEMPT TO AVOID MELEE COMBAT, YOU SWITCH TO FIRE-TYPE MOVES!
I'M NOT SURE ABOUT THAT STRATEGY!!
MY MAKUHITA'S ABILITY IS THICK FAT!!
THE THICK LAYER OF FAT COVERING ITS BODY WILL CUT THE POWER OF A FIRE-TYPE MOVE IN HALF!!
AND NOW ...

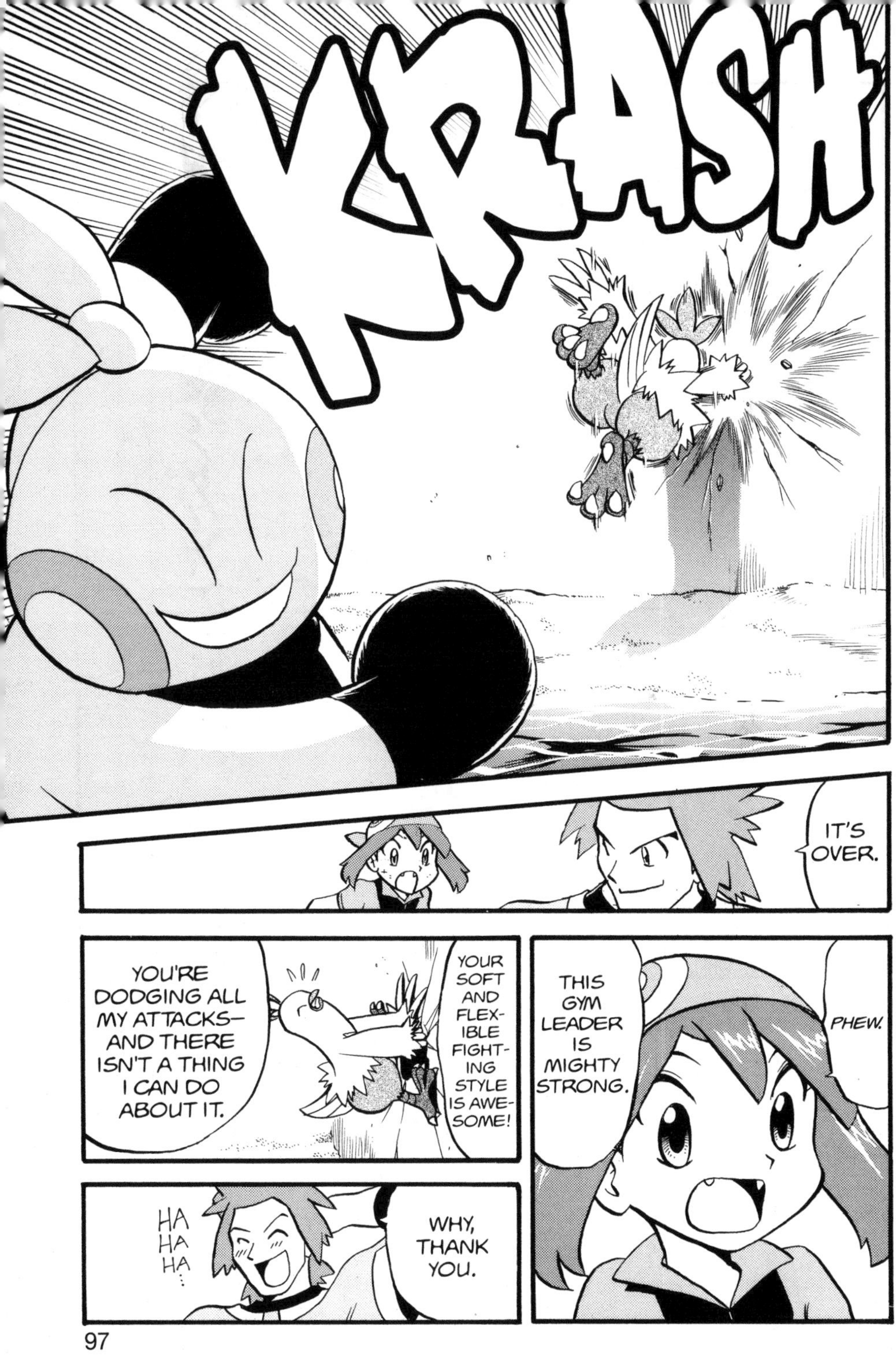
KRASH
IT'S OVER.
PHEW.
THIS GYM LEADER IS MIGHTY STRONG.
YOUR SOFT AND FLEXIBLE FIGHTING STYLE IS AWESOME!
YOU'RE DODGING ALL MY ATTACKS— AND THERE ISN'T A THING I CAN DO ABOUT IT.
WHY, THANK YOU.
HA HA HA...

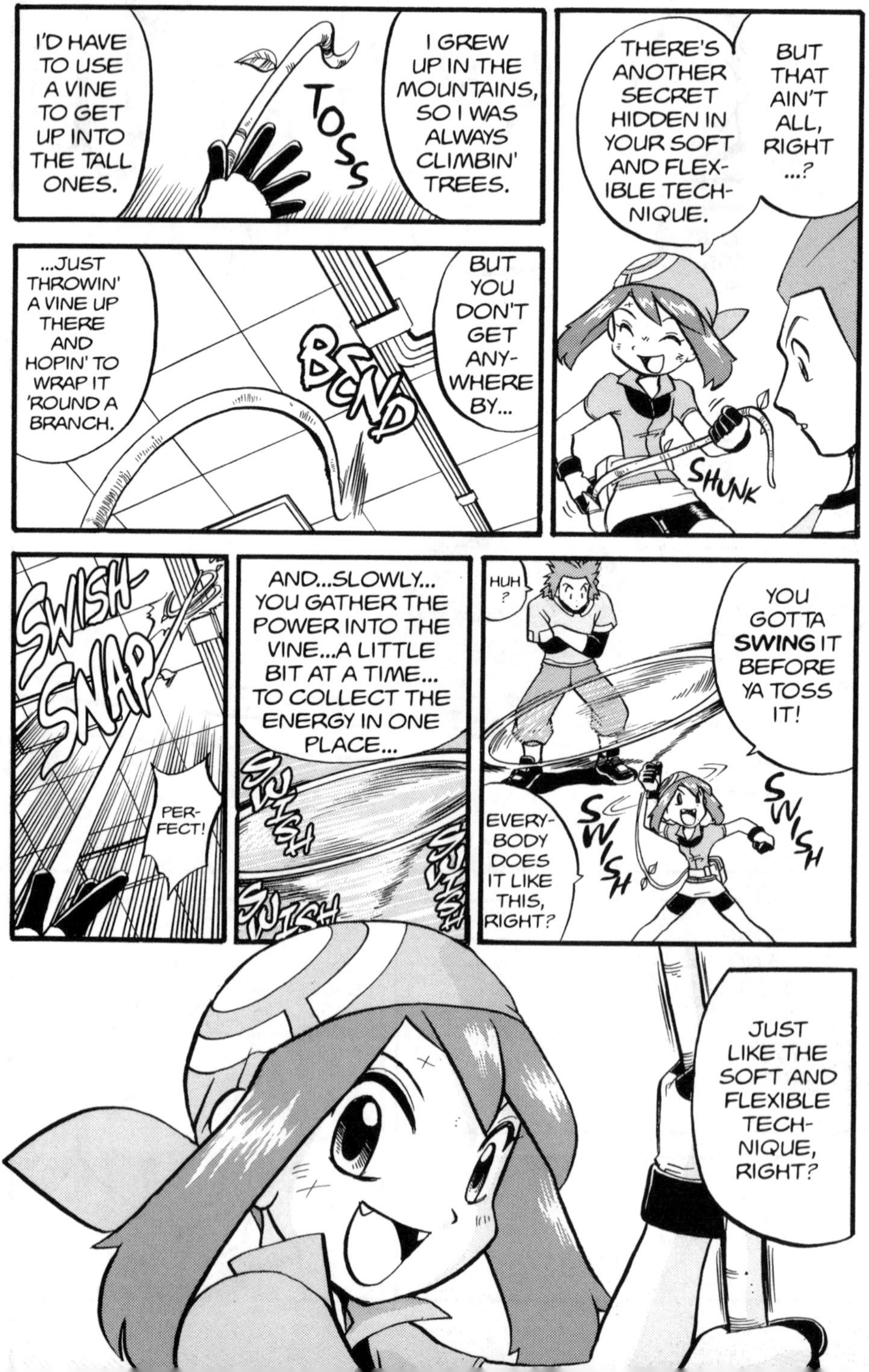
BUT THAT AIN'T ALL, RIGHT ...?
THERE'S ANOTHER SECRET HIDDEN IN YOUR SOFT AND FLEX-IBLE TECH-NIQUE.
SHUNK
I GREW UP IN THE MOUNTAINS, SO I WAS ALWAYS CLIMBIN' TREES.
TOSS
I'D HAVE TO USE A VINE TO GET UP INTO THE TALL ONES.
BUT YOU DON'T GET ANY-WHERE BY...
BEND
...JUST THROWIN' A VINE UP THERE AND HOPIN' TO WRAP IT 'ROUND A BRANCH.
YOU GOTTA **SWING** IT BEFORE YA TOSS IT!
HUH?
SWISH
SWISH
EVERY-BODY DOES IT LIKE THIS, RIGHT?
AND...SLOWLY... YOU GATHER THE POWER INTO THE VINE...A LITTLE BIT AT A TIME... TO COLLECT THE ENERGY IN ONE PLACE...
SWISH
SWISH
SWISH
SWISH-SNAP
PER-FECT!
JUST LIKE THE SOFT AND FLEXIBLE TECH-NIQUE, RIGHT?

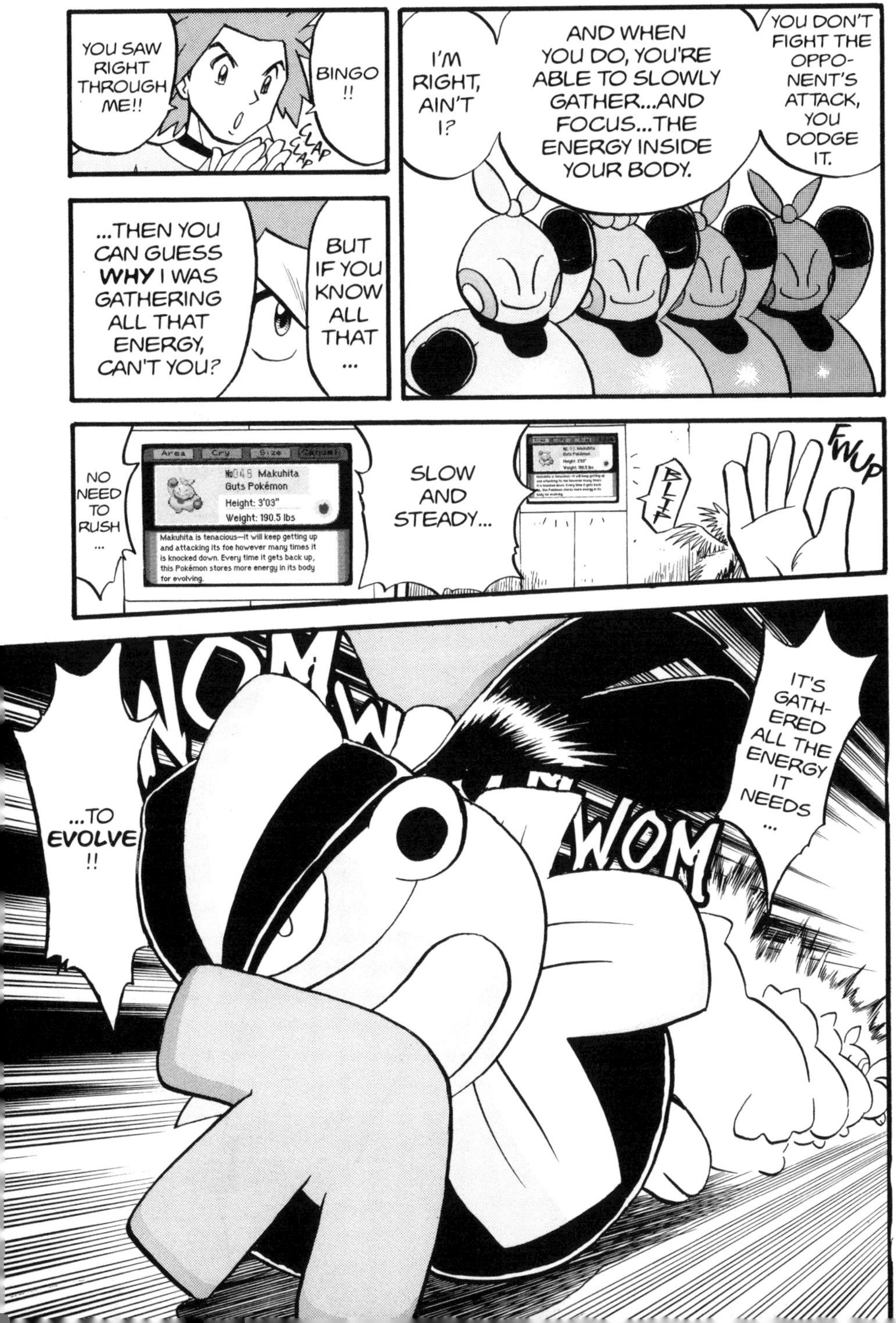
YOU DON'T FIGHT THE OPPONENT'S ATTACK, YOU DODGE IT.
AND WHEN YOU DO, YOU'RE ABLE TO SLOWLY GATHER...AND FOCUS...THE ENERGY INSIDE YOUR BODY.
I'M RIGHT, AIN'T I?
BINGO!!
CLAP CLAP
YOU SAW RIGHT THROUGH ME!!
BUT IF YOU KNOW ALL THAT...
...THEN YOU CAN GUESS **WHY** I WAS GATHERING ALL THAT ENERGY, CAN'T YOU?
FWUP
BLIP
SLOW AND STEADY...
Area Cry Size
No048 Makuhita
Guts Pokémon
Height: 3'03"
Weight: 190.5 lbs
Makuhita is tenacious—it will keep getting up and attacking its foe however many times it is knocked down. Every time it gets back up, this Pokémon stores more energy in its body for evolving.
NO NEED TO RUSH...
WOM
IT'S GATHERED ALL THE ENERGY IT NEEDS...
WOM
...TO **EVOLVE**!!

● Adventure 196 ●
Ring Ring Goes Beldum

Pokémon Adventures Ruby & Sapphire
The Fourth Chapter

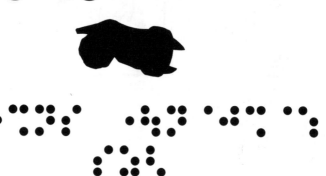

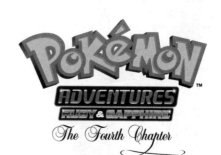

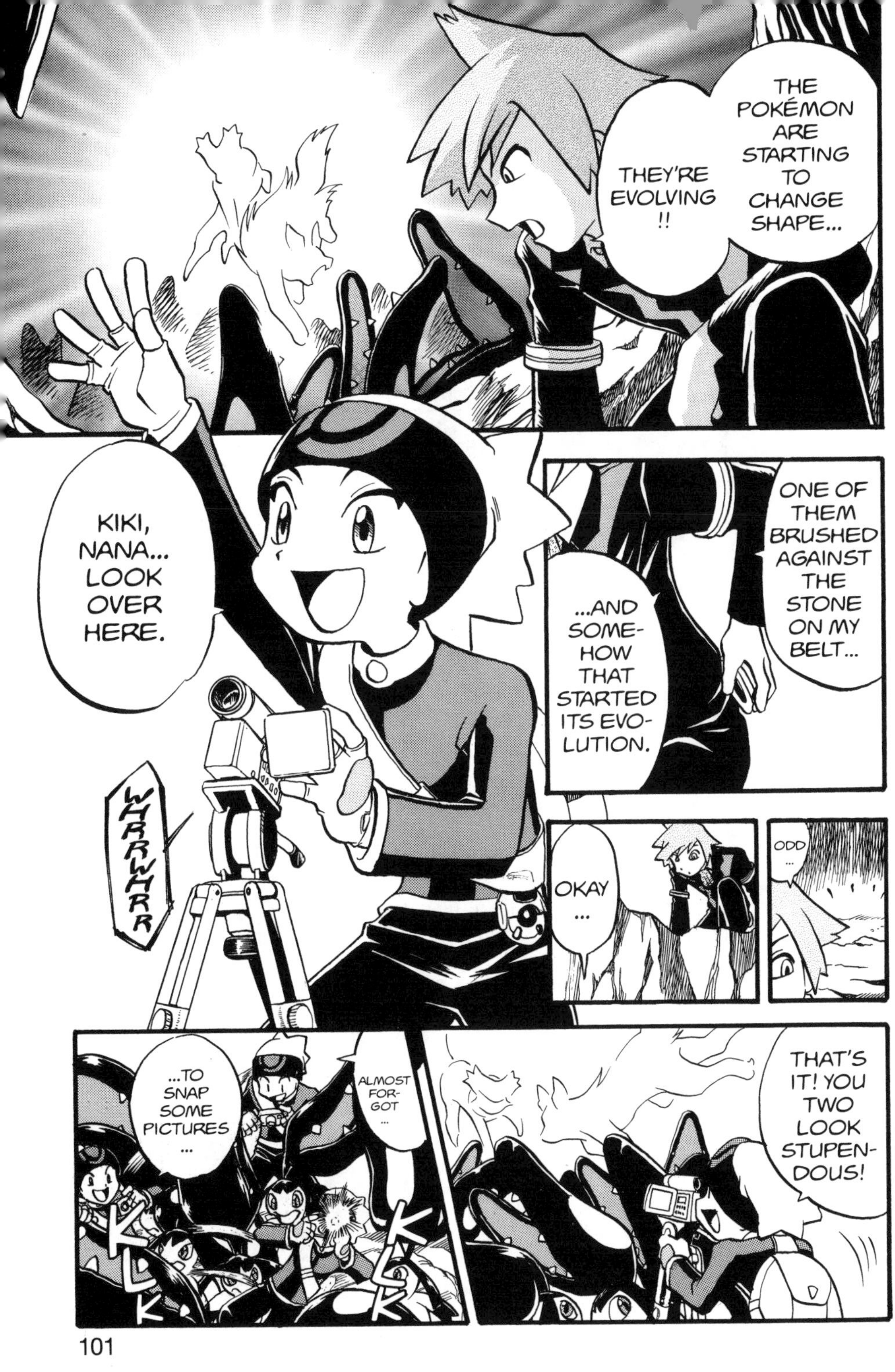
THE POKÉMON ARE STARTING TO CHANGE SHAPE...
THEY'RE EVOLVING !!
ONE OF THEM BRUSHED AGAINST THE STONE ON MY BELT...
...AND SOMEHOW THAT STARTED ITS EVOLUTION.
ODD ...
OKAY ...
KIKI, NANA... LOOK OVER HERE.
WHRRWHRR
THAT'S IT! YOU TWO LOOK STUPENDOUS!
ALMOST FORGOT ...
...TO SNAP SOME PICTURES ...
KLIK
KLIK

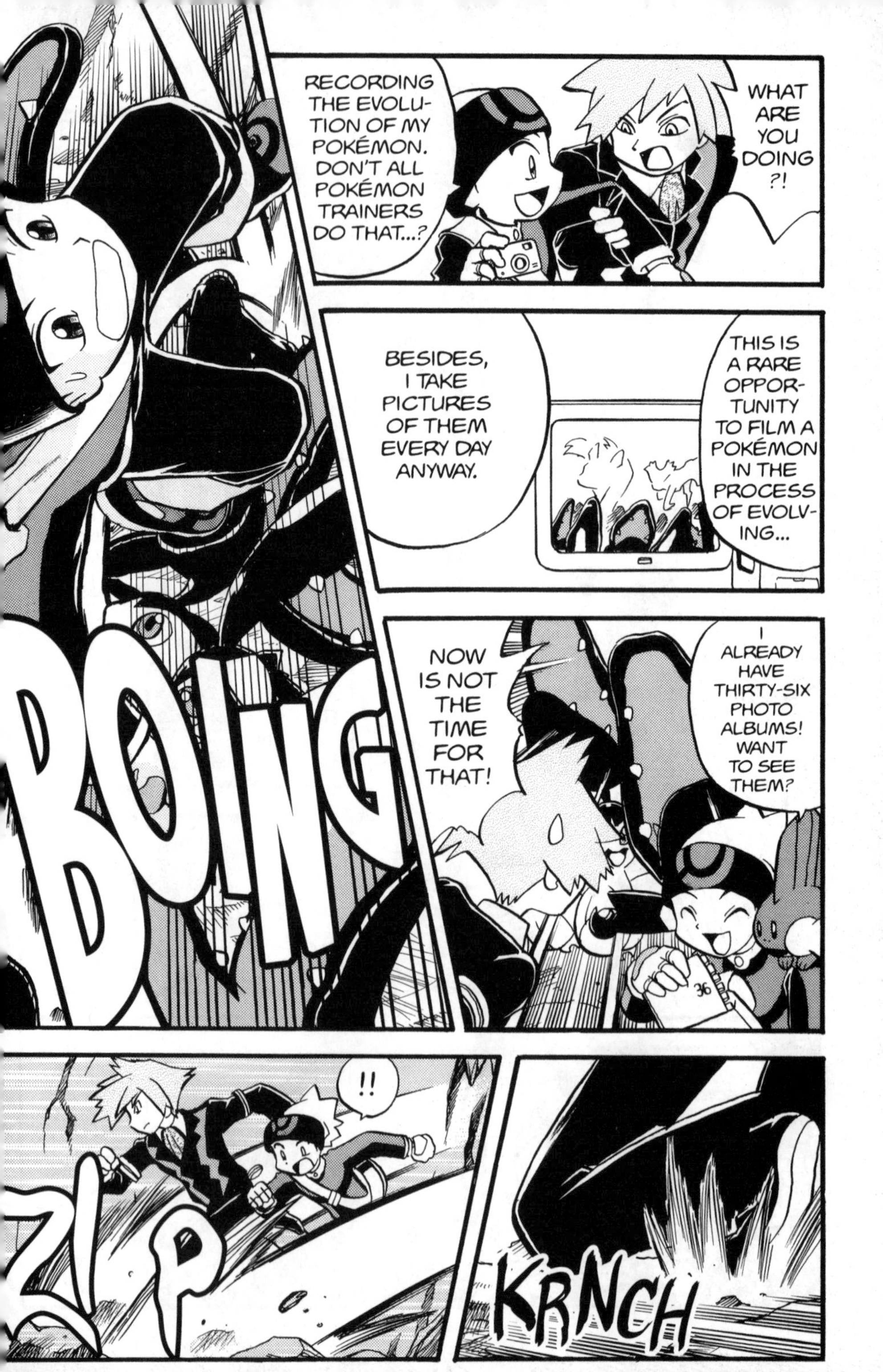
WHAT ARE YOU DOING?!
RECORDING THE EVOLUTION OF MY POKÉMON. DON'T ALL POKÉMON TRAINERS DO THAT...?
THIS IS A RARE OPPORTUNITY TO FILM A POKÉMON IN THE PROCESS OF EVOLVING...
BESIDES, I TAKE PICTURES OF THEM EVERY DAY ANYWAY.
I ALREADY HAVE THIRTY-SIX PHOTO ALBUMS! WANT TO SEE THEM?
NOW IS NOT THE TIME FOR THAT!
BOING
KRNCH
!!
ZIP

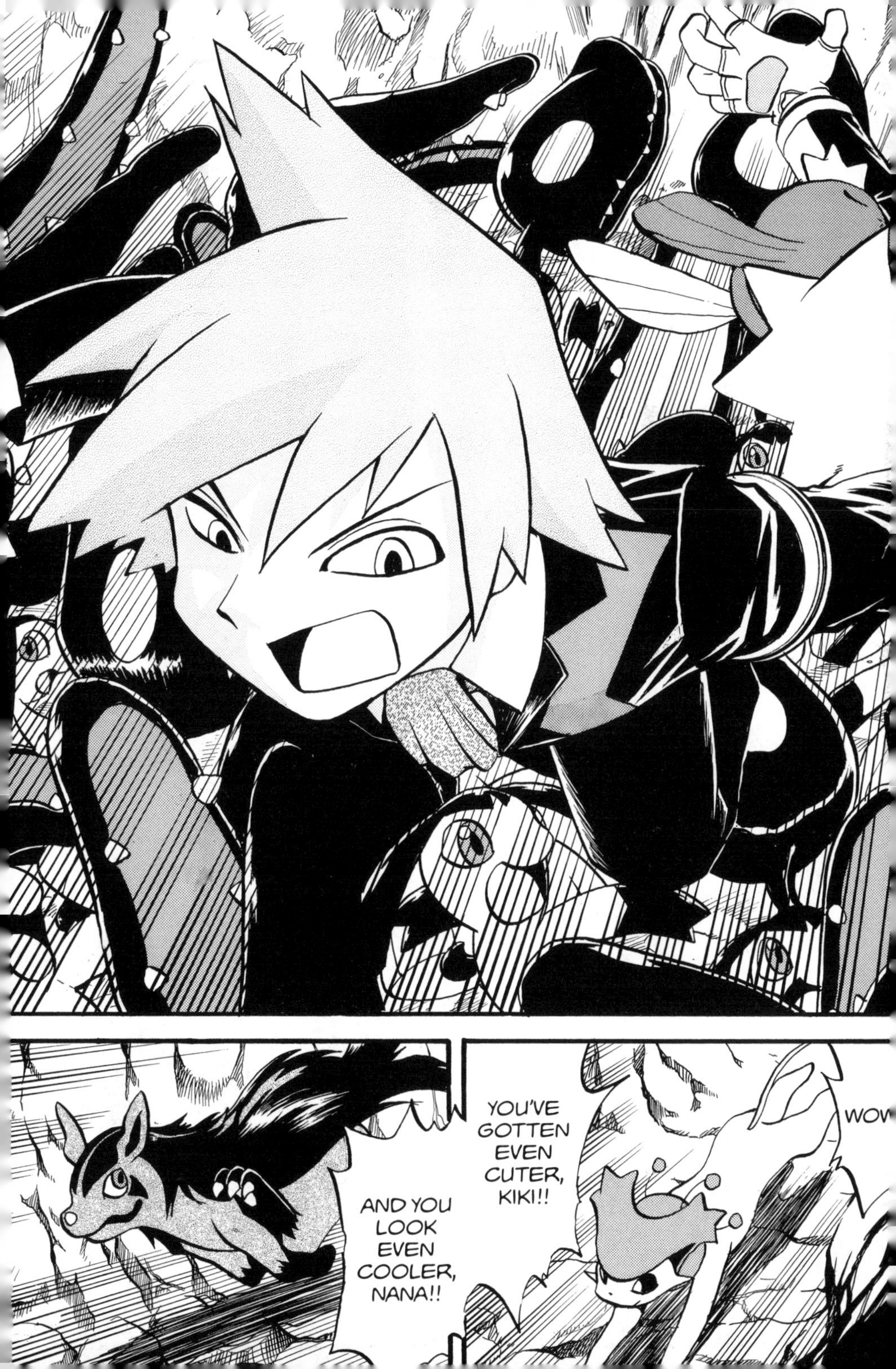

WOW
YOU'VE GOTTEN EVEN CUTER, KIKI!!
AND YOU LOOK EVEN COOLER, NANA!!

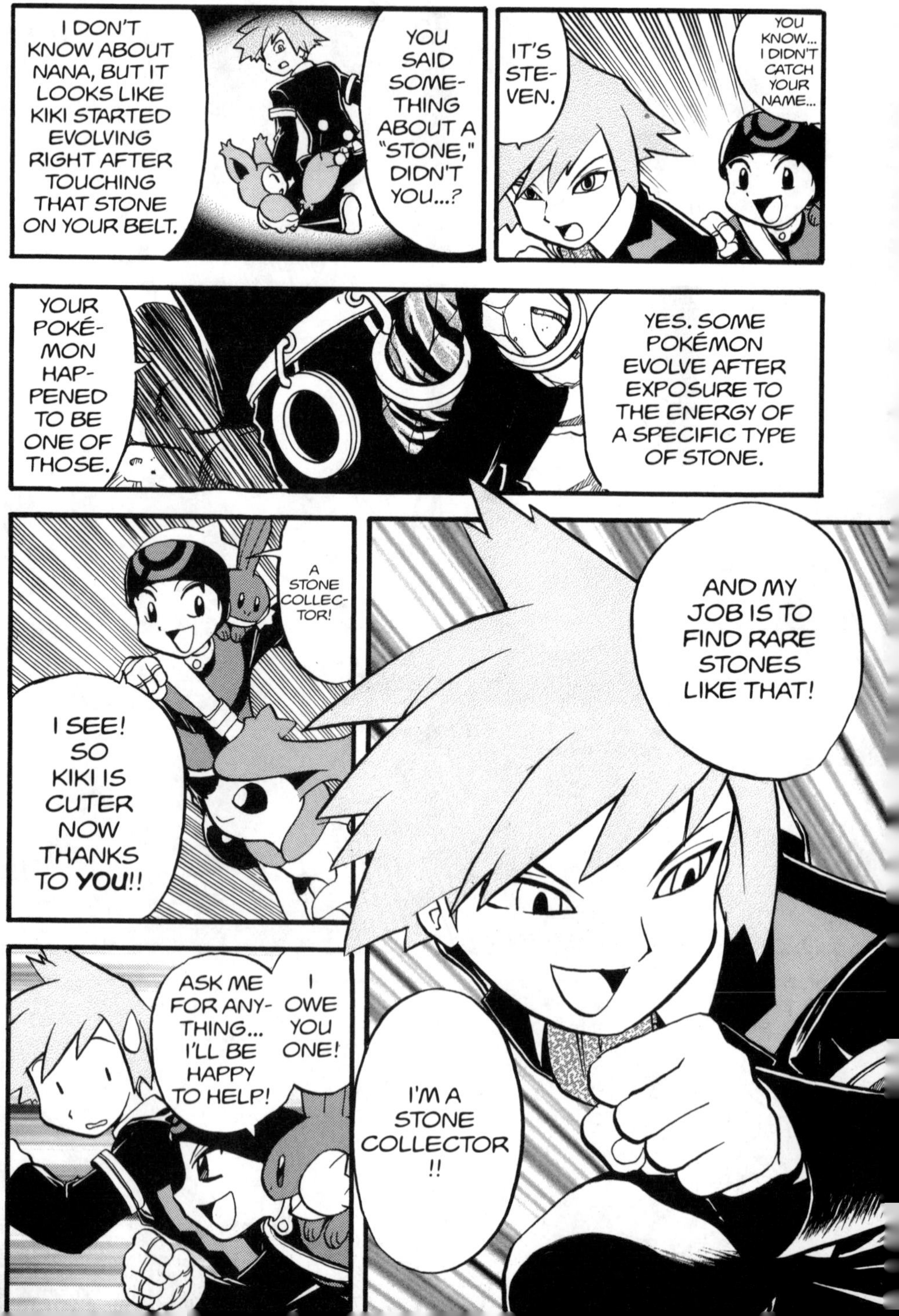
YOU KNOW... I DIDN'T CATCH YOUR NAME...
IT'S STE-VEN.
YOU SAID SOME-THING ABOUT A "STONE," DIDN'T YOU...?
I DON'T KNOW ABOUT NANA, BUT IT LOOKS LIKE KIKI STARTED EVOLVING RIGHT AFTER TOUCHING THAT STONE ON YOUR BELT.
YES. SOME POKÉMON EVOLVE AFTER EXPOSURE TO THE ENERGY OF A SPECIFIC TYPE OF STONE.
YOUR POKÉ-MON HAP-PENED TO BE ONE OF THOSE.
AND MY JOB IS TO FIND RARE STONES LIKE THAT!
I'M A STONE COLLECTOR!!
A STONE COLLEC-TOR!
I SEE! SO KIKI IS CUTER NOW THANKS TO **YOU**!!
I OWE YOU ONE!
ASK ME FOR ANY-THING... I'LL BE HAPPY TO HELP!

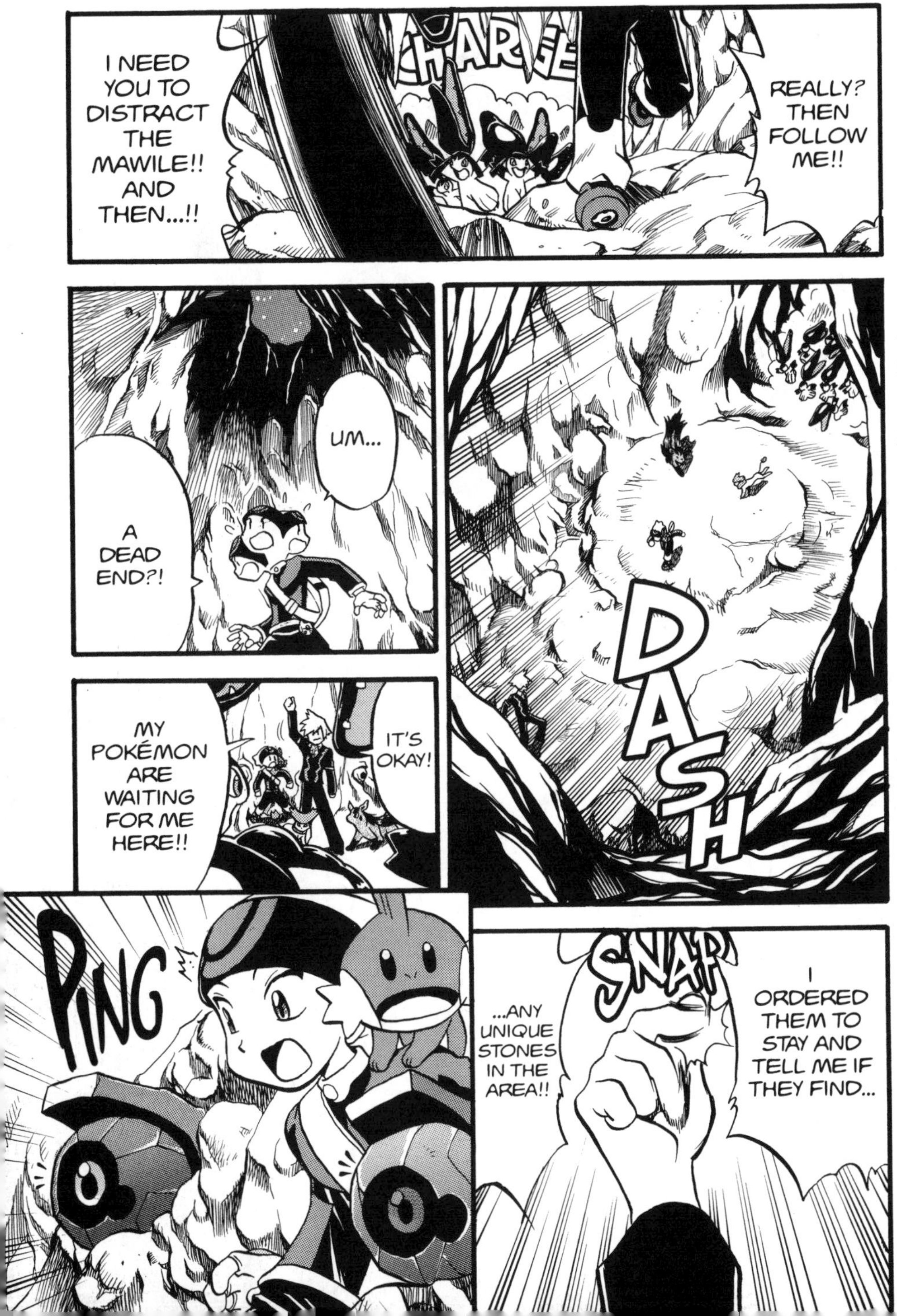
REALLY? THEN FOLLOW ME!!
CHARGE
I NEED YOU TO DISTRACT THE MAWILE!! AND THEN...!!
DASH
UM...
A DEAD END?!
IT'S OKAY!
MY POKéMON ARE WAITING FOR ME HERE!!
SNAP
I ORDERED THEM TO STAY AND TELL ME IF THEY FIND...
...ANY UNIQUE STONES IN THE AREA!!
PING

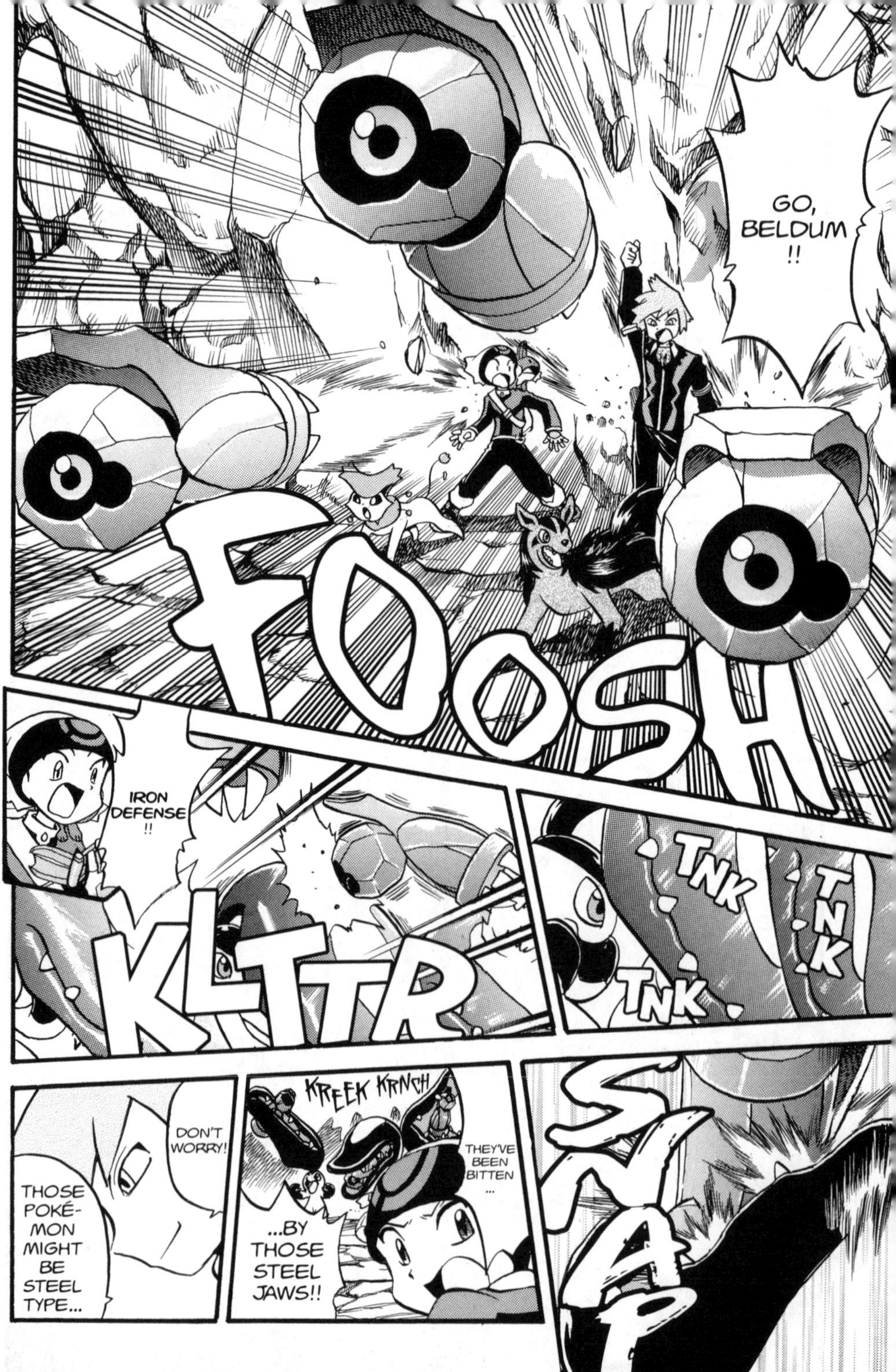
GO, BELDUM !!
FOOSH
TNK TNK TNK
IRON DEFENSE !!
KLTTR
SNAP
KREEK KRNCH
THEY'VE BEEN BITTEN ...
...BY THOSE STEEL JAWS!!
DON'T WORRY!
THOSE POKÉMON MIGHT BE STEEL TYPE...

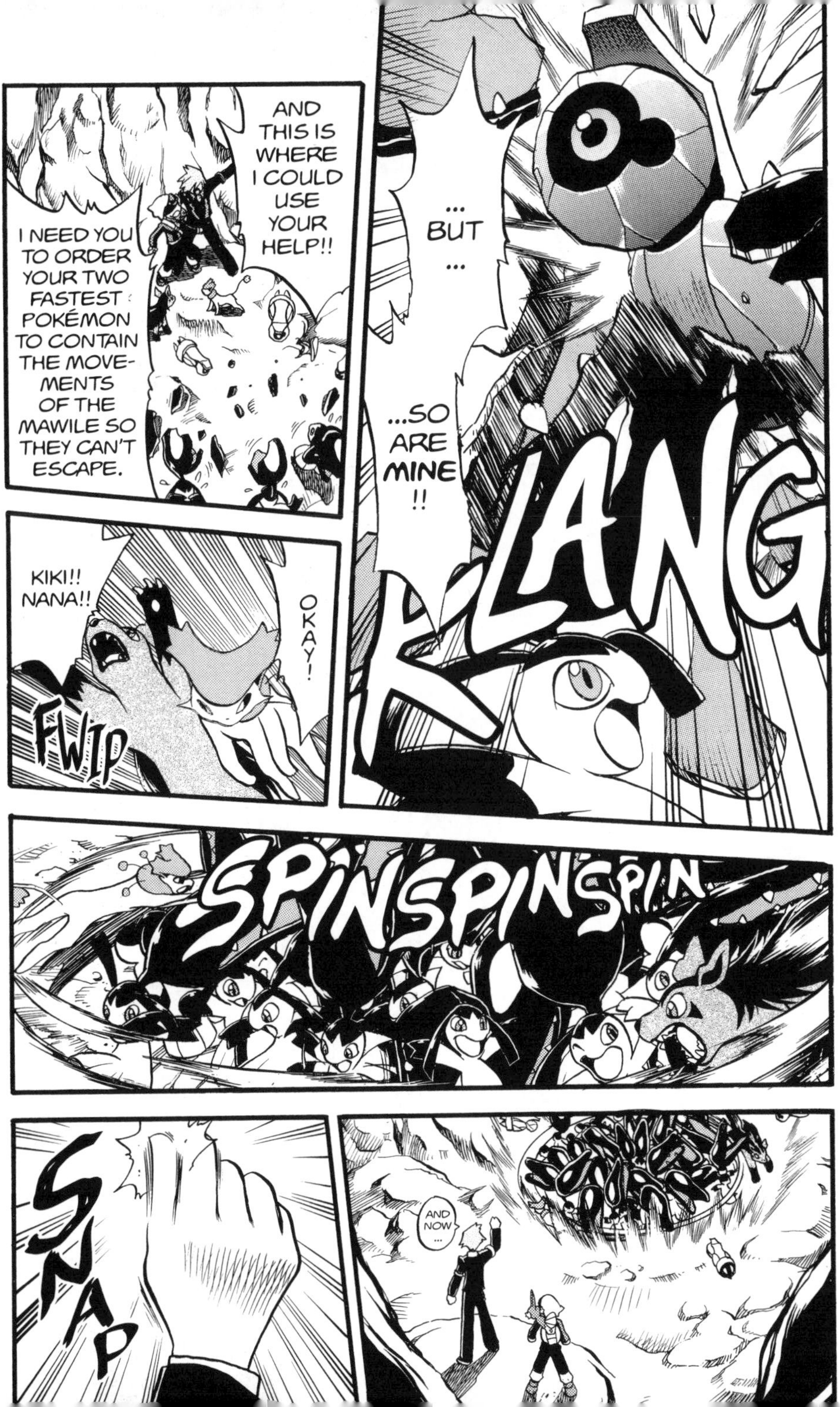
... BUT ...
...SO ARE MINE !!
KLANG
AND THIS IS WHERE I COULD USE YOUR HELP!!
I NEED YOU TO ORDER YOUR TWO FASTEST POKÉMON TO CONTAIN THE MOVEMENTS OF THE MAWILE SO THEY CAN'T ESCAPE.
KIKI!! NANA!!
OKAY!
FWIP
SPINSPINSPIN
AND NOW ...
SNAP

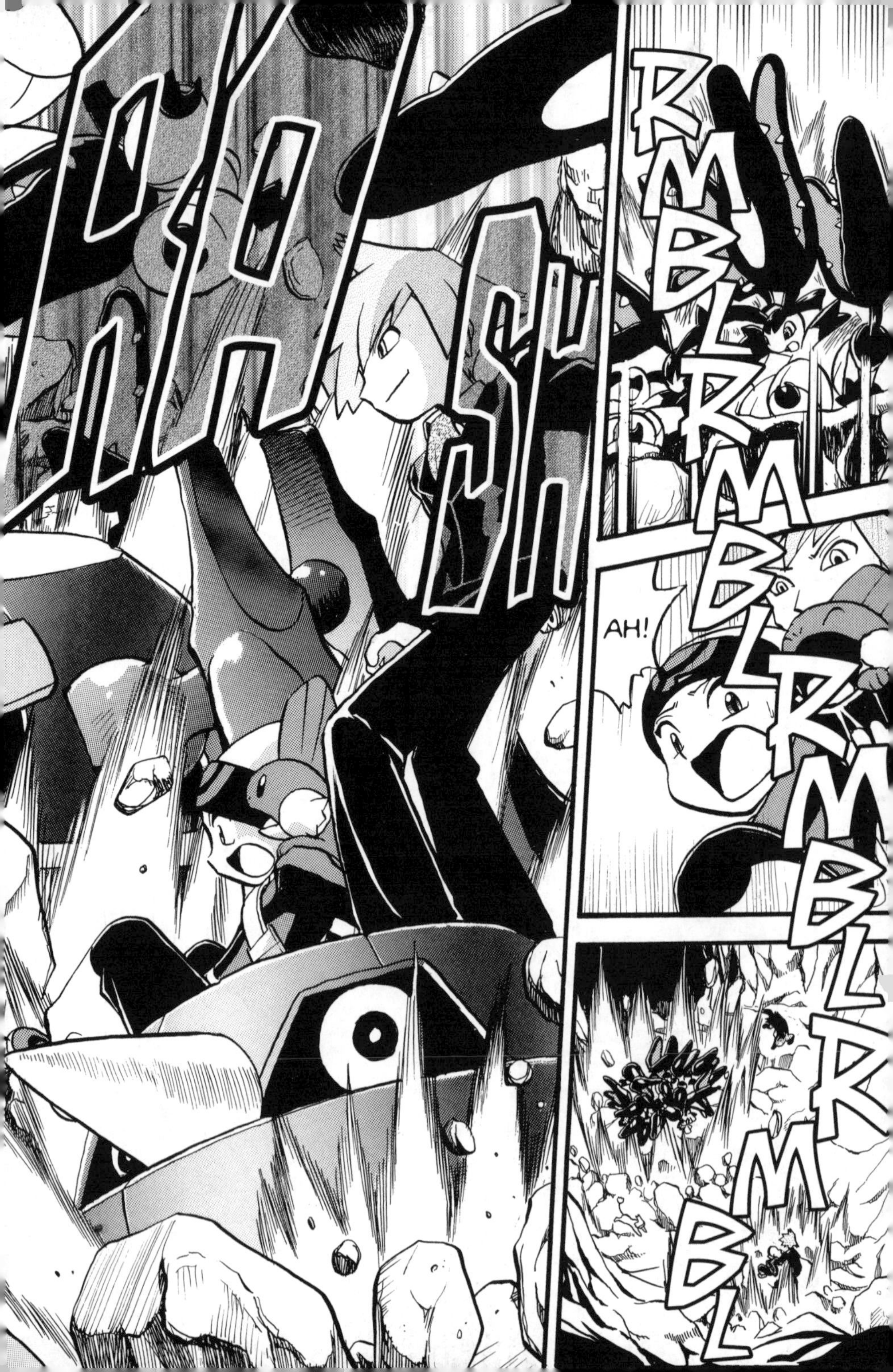
RMBLRMBLRMBLRMBL
AH!

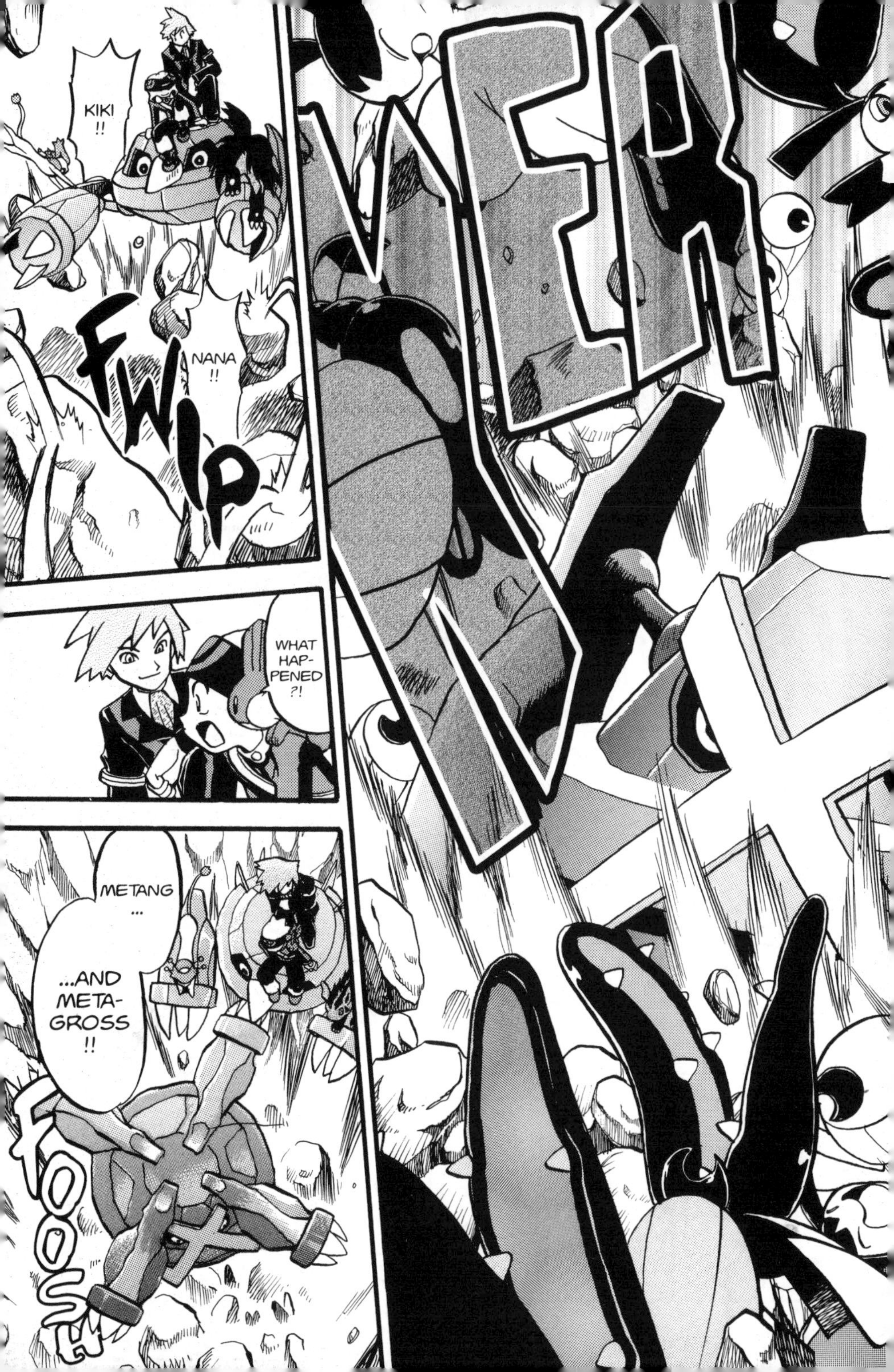
KIKI!!
NANA!!
FWIP
WHAT HAPPENED?!
METANG...
...AND METAGROSS!!
FOOOSH

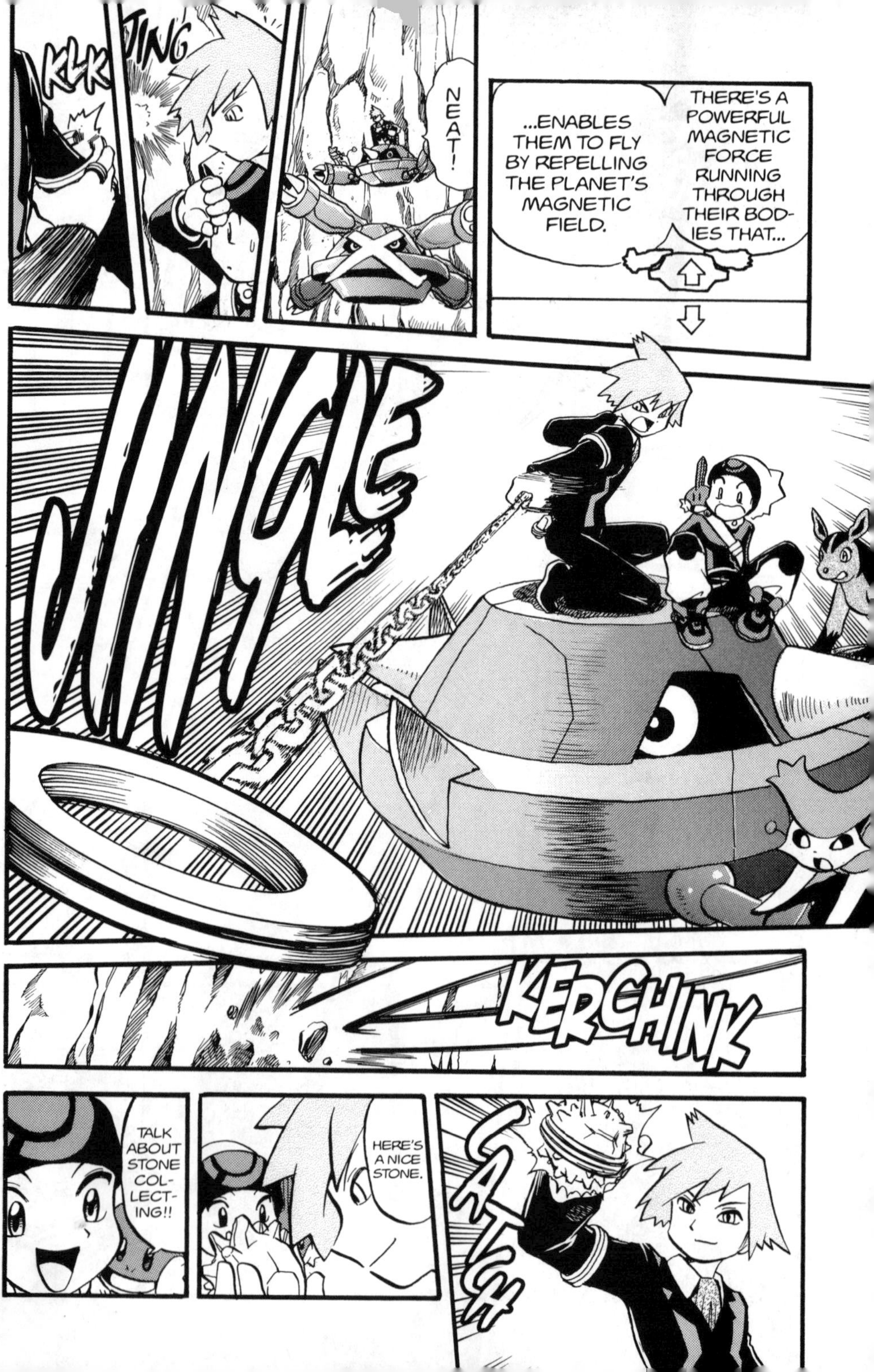
THERE'S A POWERFUL MAGNETIC FORCE RUNNING THROUGH THEIR BODIES THAT...
...ENABLES THEM TO FLY BY REPELLING THE PLANET'S MAGNETIC FIELD.
NEAT!
JING
KLK
JINGLE
KERCHINK
CATCH
HERE'S A NICE STONE.
TALK ABOUT STONE COLLECTING!!

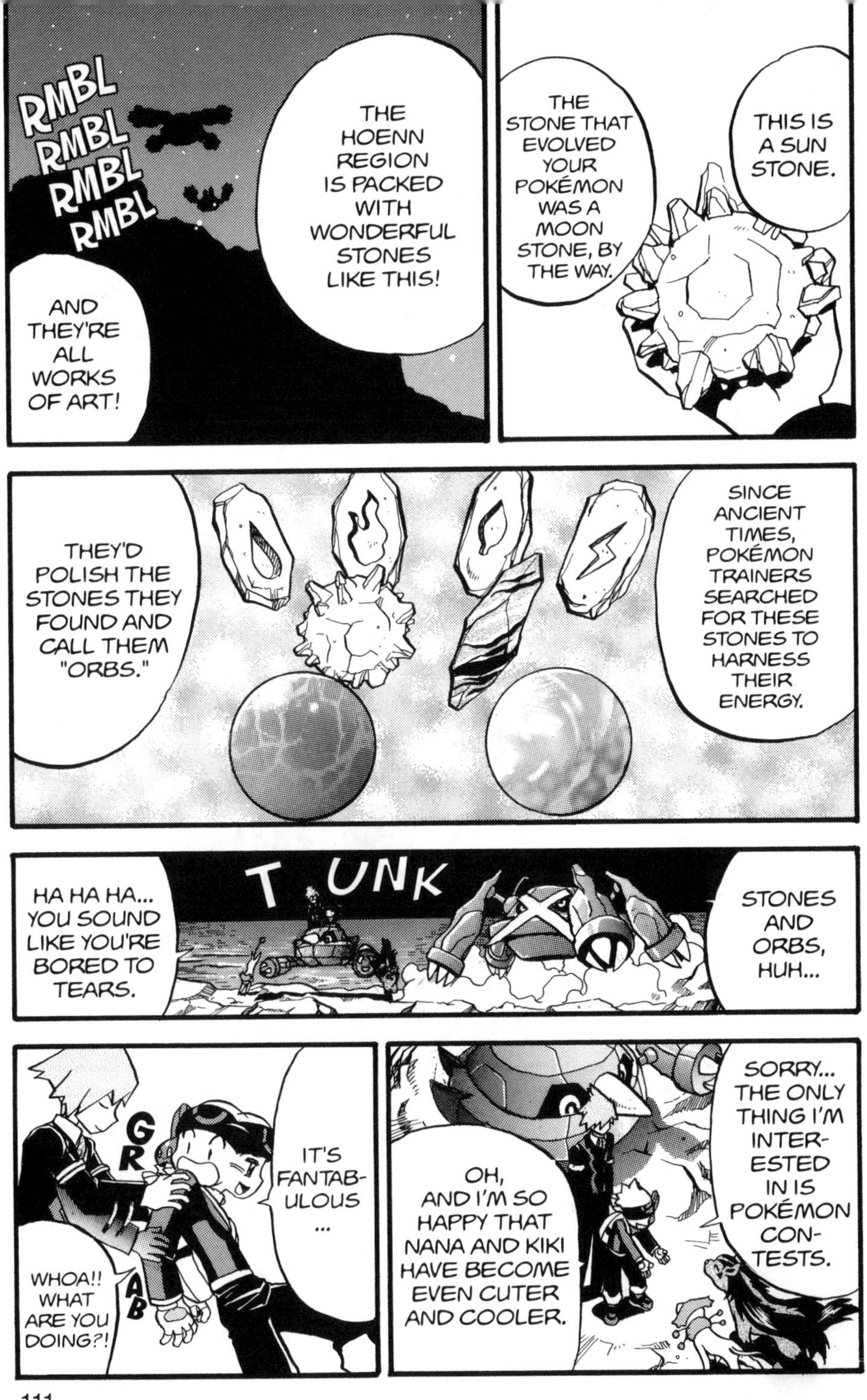
THIS IS A SUN STONE.
THE STONE THAT EVOLVED YOUR POKÉMON WAS A MOON STONE, BY THE WAY.
THE HOENN REGION IS PACKED WITH WONDERFUL STONES LIKE THIS!
RMBL RMBL RMBL RMBL
AND THEY'RE ALL WORKS OF ART!
SINCE ANCIENT TIMES, POKÉMON TRAINERS SEARCHED FOR THESE STONES TO HARNESS THEIR ENERGY.
THEY'D POLISH THE STONES THEY FOUND AND CALL THEM "ORBS."
STONES AND ORBS, HUH...
T UNK
HA HA HA... YOU SOUND LIKE YOU'RE BORED TO TEARS.
SORRY... THE ONLY THING I'M INTER-ESTED IN IS POKÉMON CON-TESTS.
OH, AND I'M SO HAPPY THAT NANA AND KIKI HAVE BECOME EVEN CUTER AND COOLER.
IT'S FANTAB-ULOUS ...
GRAB
WHOA!! WHAT ARE YOU DOING?!

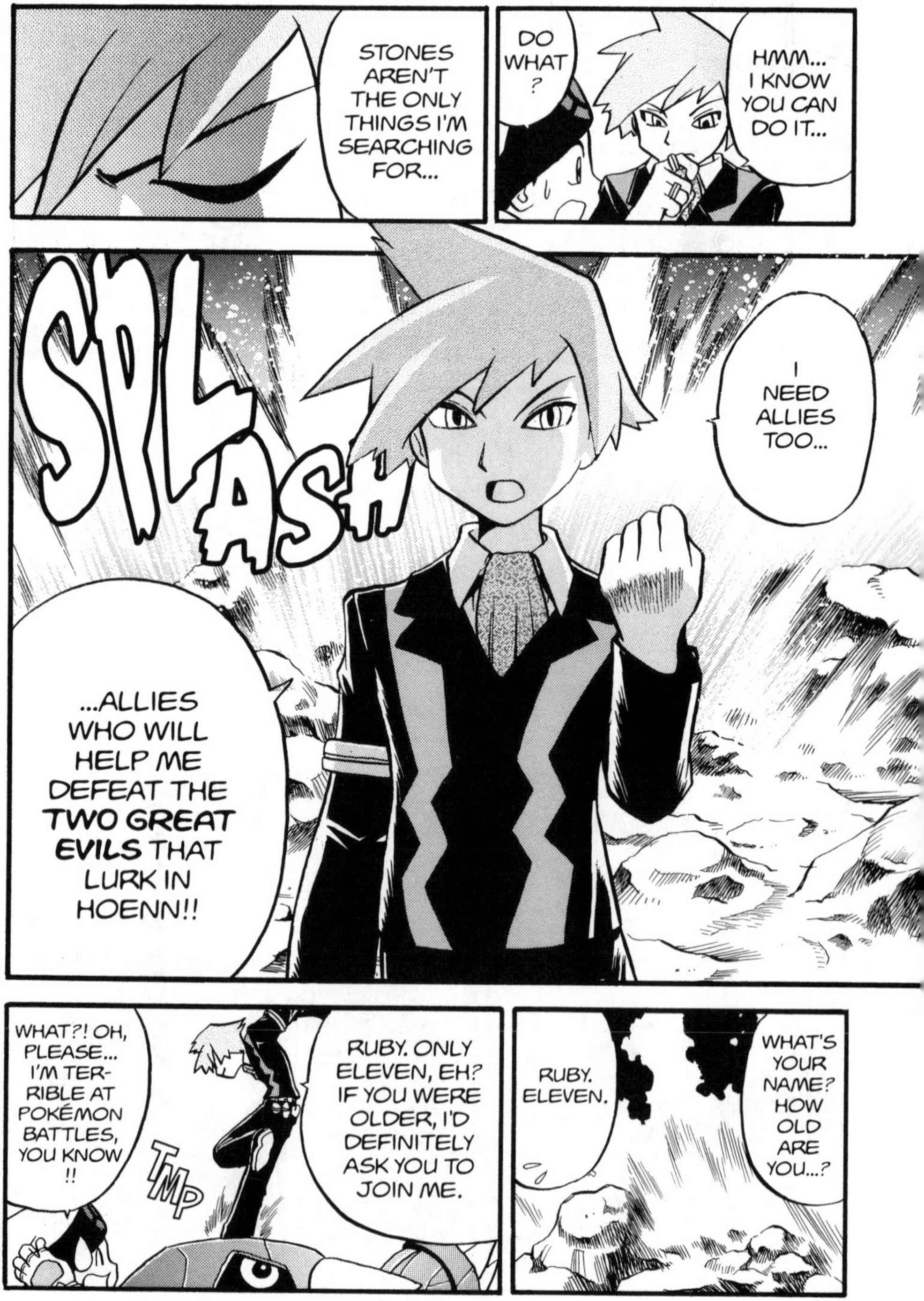
HMM... I KNOW YOU CAN DO IT...
DO WHAT?
STONES AREN'T THE ONLY THINGS I'M SEARCHING FOR...
I NEED ALLIES TOO...
SPLASH
...ALLIES WHO WILL HELP ME DEFEAT THE **TWO GREAT EVILS** THAT LURK IN HOENN!!
WHAT'S YOUR NAME? HOW OLD ARE YOU...?
RUBY. ELEVEN.
RUBY. ONLY ELEVEN, EH? IF YOU WERE OLDER, I'D DEFINITELY ASK YOU TO JOIN ME.
WHAT?! OH, PLEASE... I'M TERRIBLE AT POKÉMON BATTLES, YOU KNOW!!
TMP

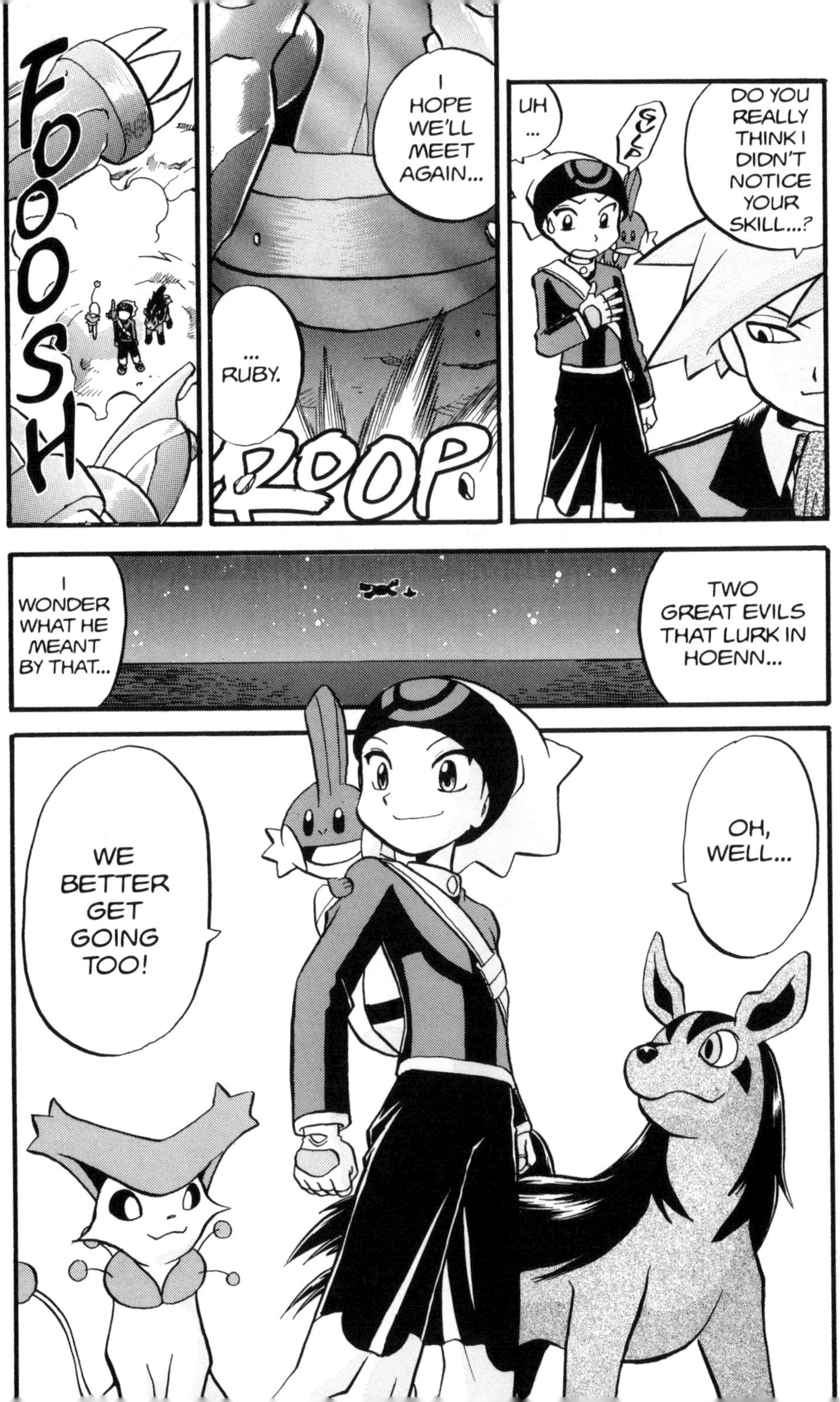
DO YOU REALLY THINK I DIDN'T NOTICE YOUR SKILL...?
UH ...
GULP
I HOPE WE'LL MEET AGAIN...
... RUBY.
ROOP
FOOOSH
TWO GREAT EVILS THAT LURK IN HOENN...
I WONDER WHAT HE MEANT BY THAT...
OH, WELL...
WE BETTER GET GOING TOO!

● Adventure 197 ●
Heavy-Hitting Hariyama

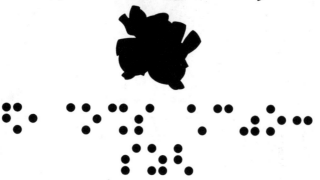

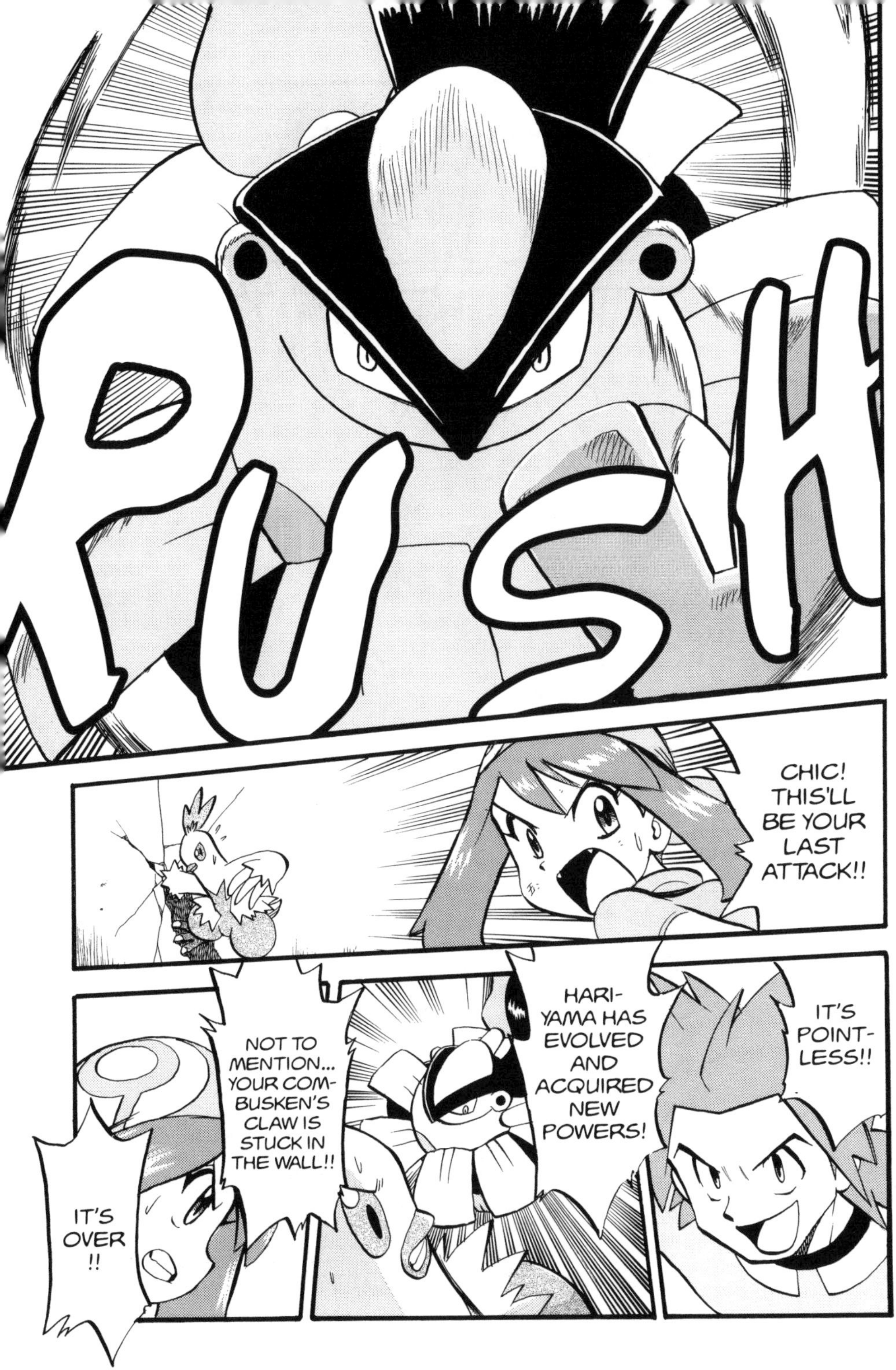
RUSH
CHIC! THIS'LL BE YOUR LAST ATTACK!!
IT'S POINT-LESS!!
HARI-YAMA HAS EVOLVED AND ACQUIRED NEW POWERS!
NOT TO MENTION... YOUR COM-BUSKEN'S CLAW IS STUCK IN THE WALL!!
IT'S OVER !!

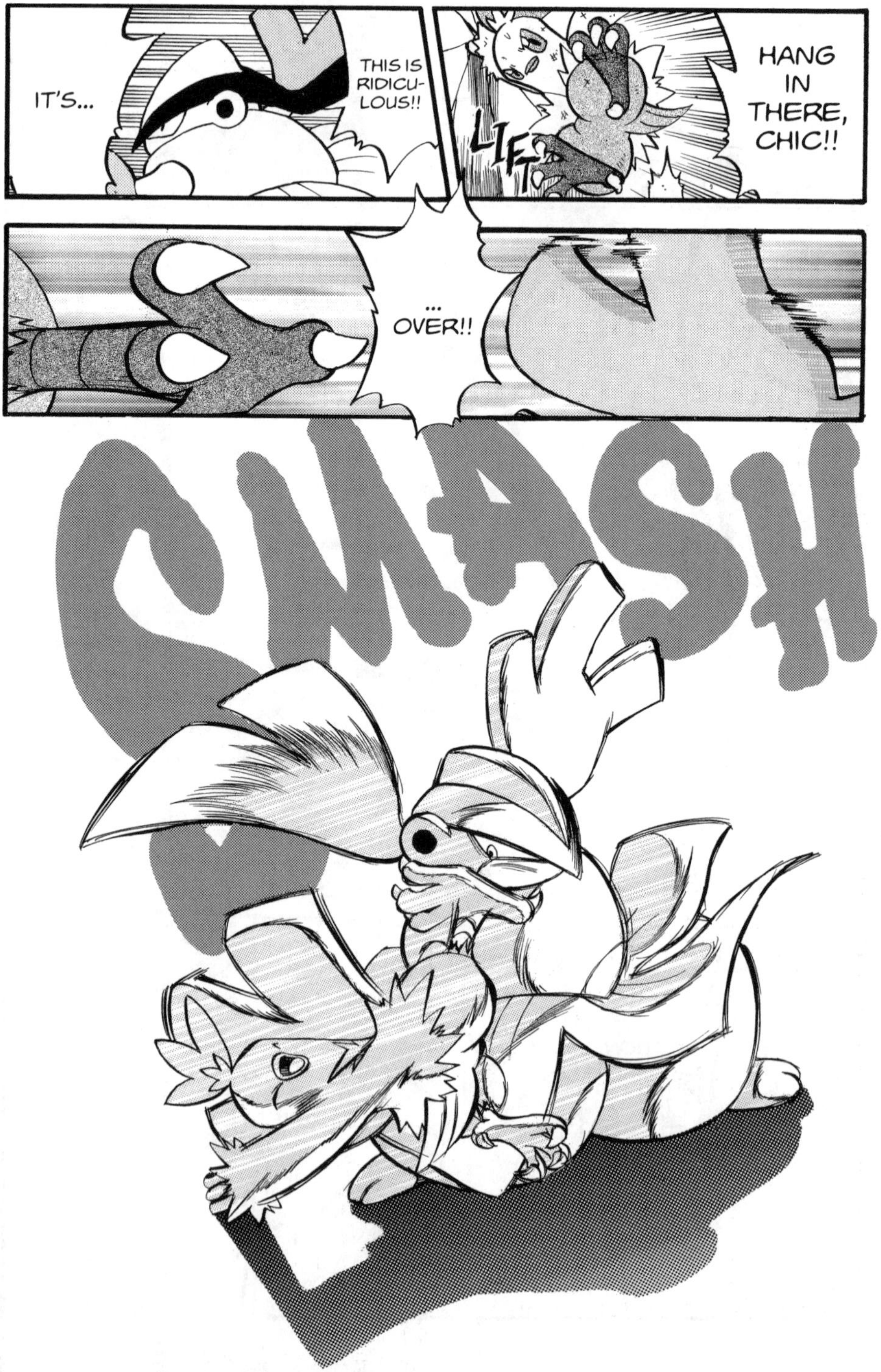
HANG IN THERE, CHIC!!
LIFT
THIS IS RIDICULOUS!!
IT'S...
... OVER!!
SMASH

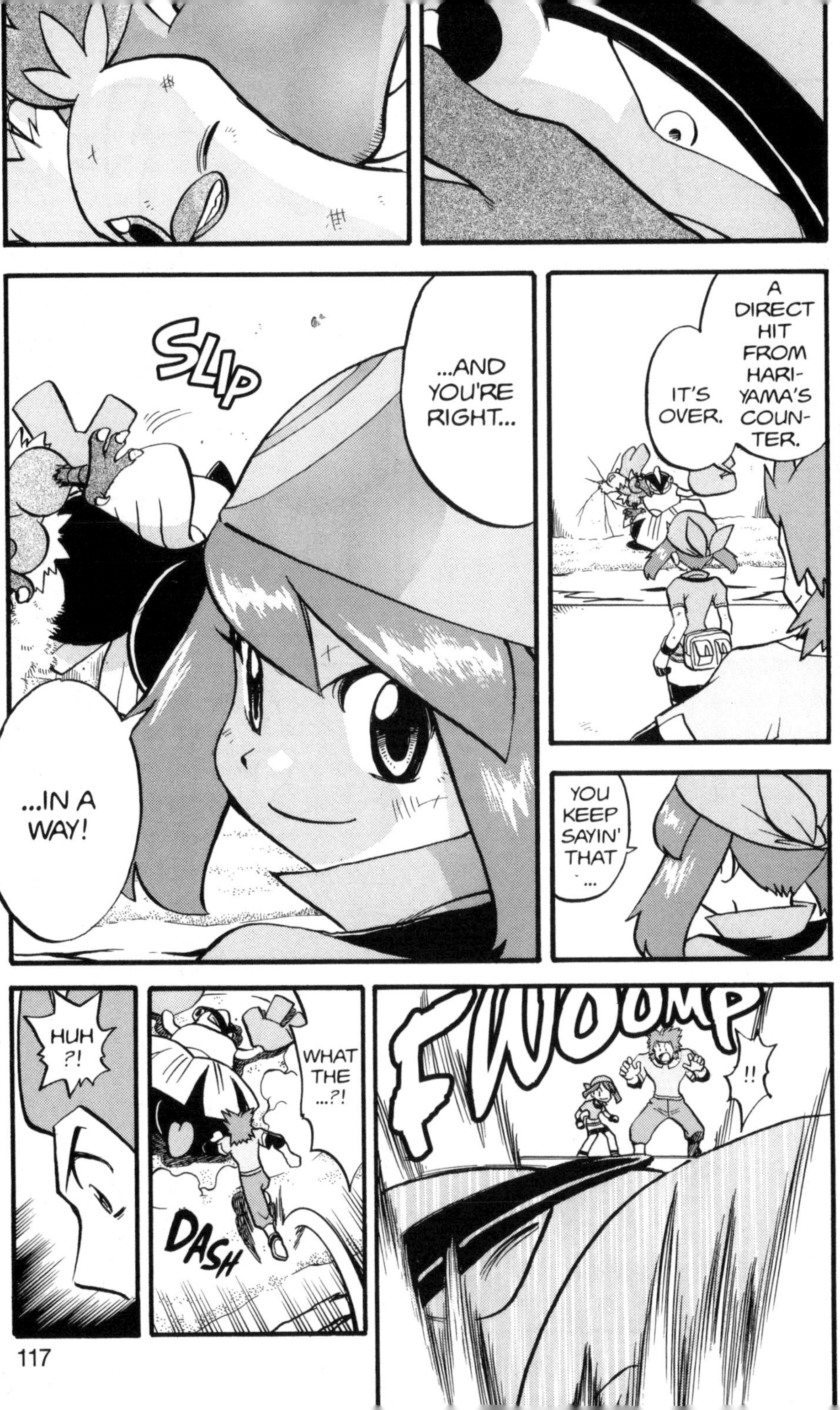
A DIRECT HIT FROM HARIYAMA'S COUNTER.
IT'S OVER.
YOU KEEP SAYIN' THAT...
...AND YOU'RE RIGHT...
SLIP
...IN A WAY!
FWOOMP
!!
WHAT THE...?!
DASH
HUH?!

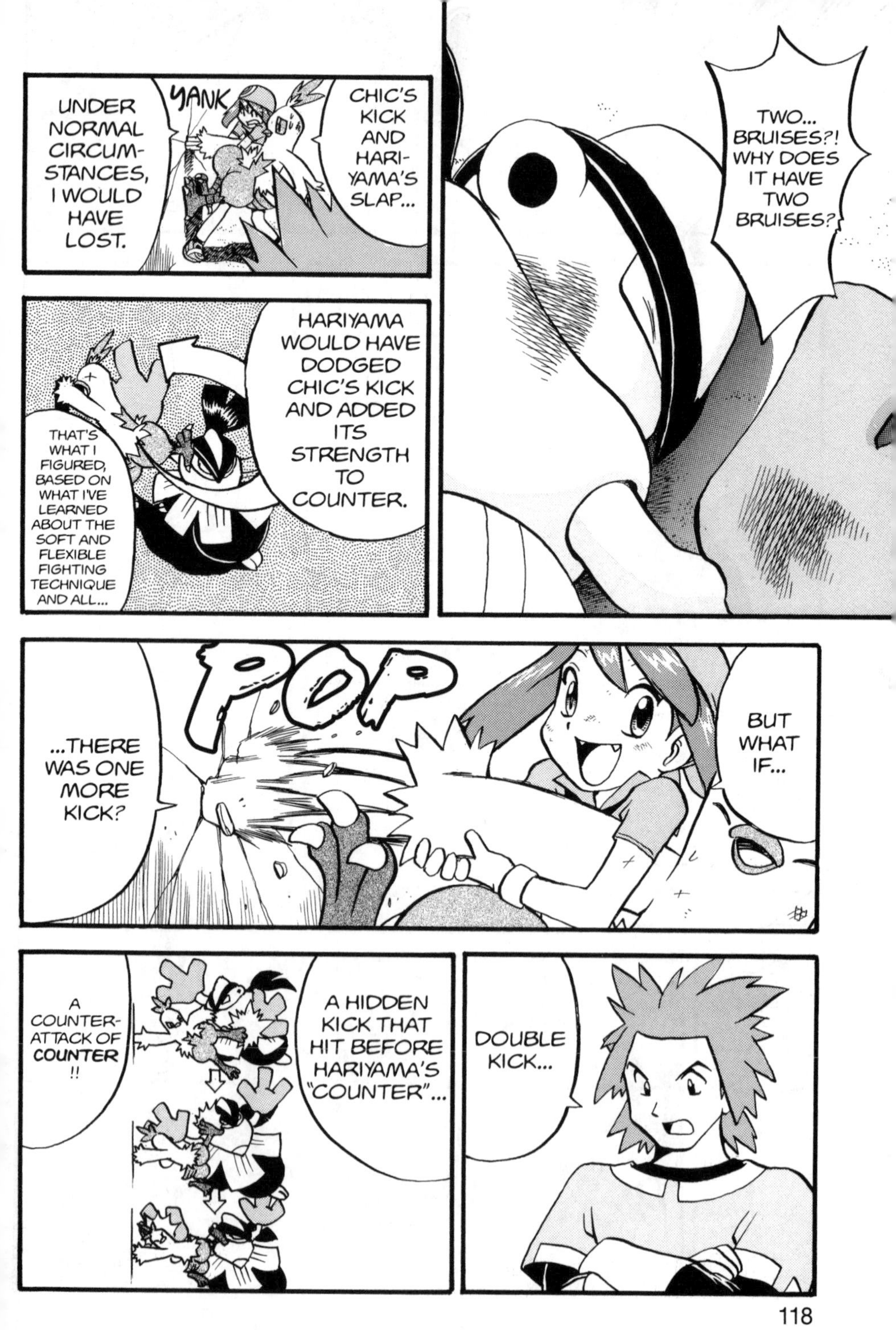
TWO... BRUISES?! WHY DOES IT HAVE TWO BRUISES?
CHIC'S KICK AND HARI-YAMA'S SLAP...
YANK
UNDER NORMAL CIRCUM-STANCES, I WOULD HAVE LOST.
HARIYAMA WOULD HAVE DODGED CHIC'S KICK AND ADDED ITS STRENGTH TO COUNTER.
THAT'S WHAT I FIGURED, BASED ON WHAT I'VE LEARNED ABOUT THE SOFT AND FLEXIBLE FIGHTING TECHNIQUE AND ALL...
BUT WHAT IF...
POP
...THERE WAS ONE MORE KICK?
DOUBLE KICK...
A HIDDEN KICK THAT HIT BEFORE HARIYAMA'S "COUNTER"...
A COUNTER-ATTACK OF COUNTER !!

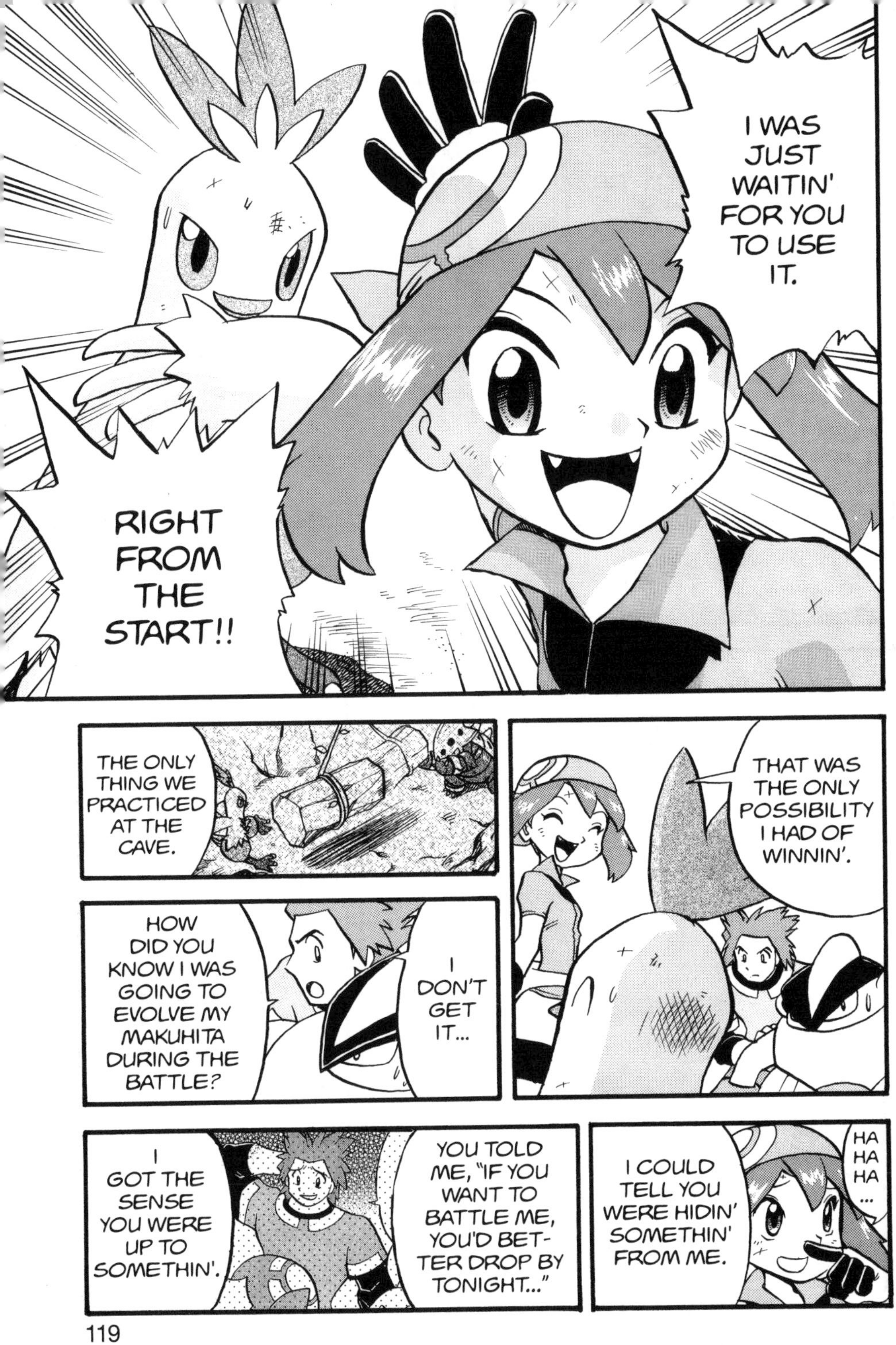
I WAS JUST WAITIN' FOR YOU TO USE IT.
RIGHT FROM THE START!!
THAT WAS THE ONLY POSSIBILITY I HAD OF WINNIN'.
THE ONLY THING WE PRACTICED AT THE CAVE.
I DON'T GET IT...
HOW DID YOU KNOW I WAS GOING TO EVOLVE MY MAKUHITA DURING THE BATTLE?
HA HA HA...
I COULD TELL YOU WERE HIDIN' SOMETHIN' FROM ME.
YOU TOLD ME, "IF YOU WANT TO BATTLE ME, YOU'D BETTER DROP BY TONIGHT..."
I GOT THE SENSE YOU WERE UP TO SOMETHIN'.

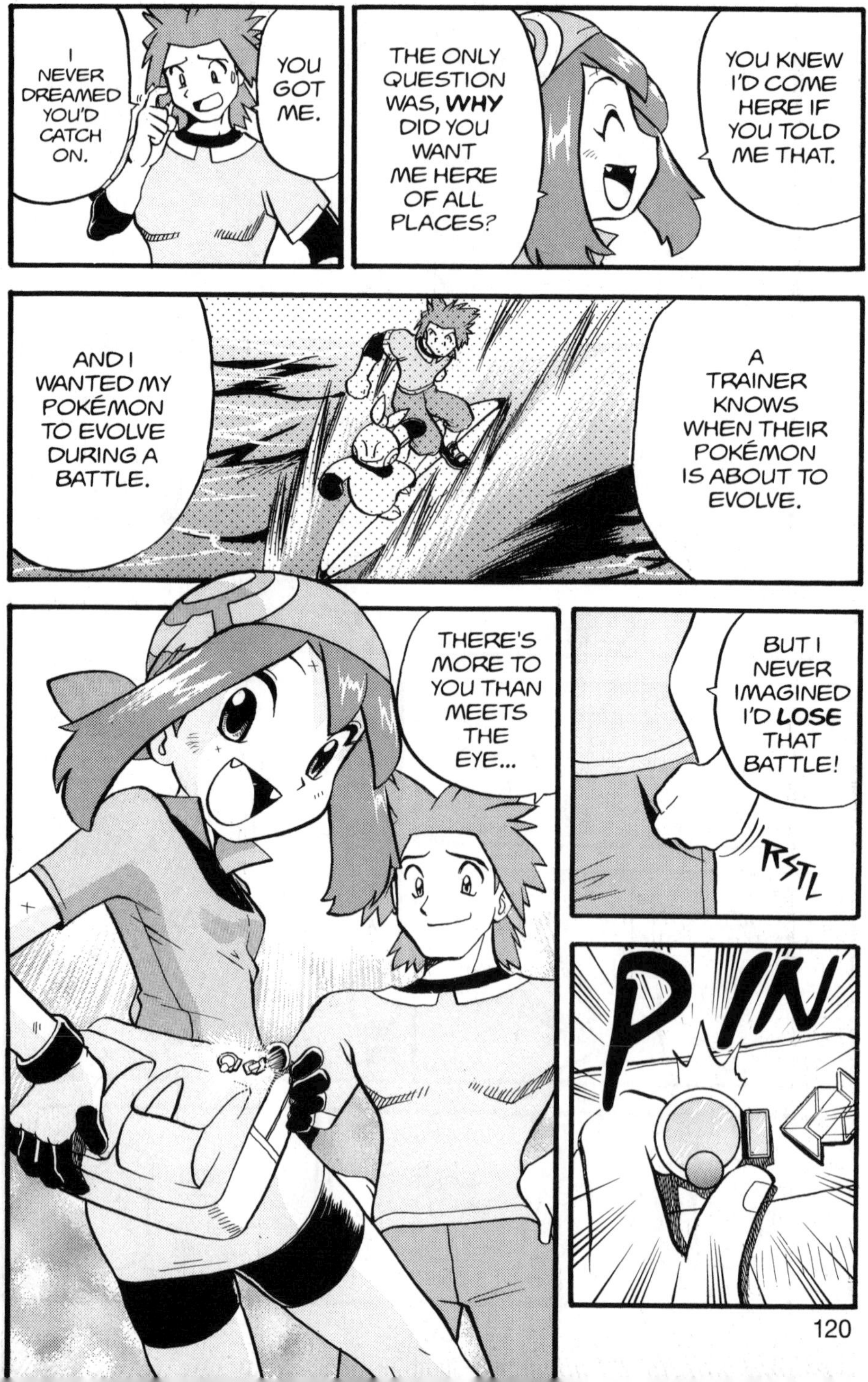
YOU KNEW I'D COME HERE IF YOU TOLD ME THAT.
THE ONLY QUESTION WAS, **WHY** DID YOU WANT ME HERE OF ALL PLACES?
YOU GOT ME.
I NEVER DREAMED YOU'D CATCH ON.
A TRAINER KNOWS WHEN THEIR POKÉMON IS ABOUT TO EVOLVE.
AND I WANTED MY POKÉMON TO EVOLVE DURING A BATTLE.
BUT I NEVER IMAGINED I'D **LOSE** THAT BATTLE!
RSTL
PIN
THERE'S MORE TO YOU THAN MEETS THE EYE...

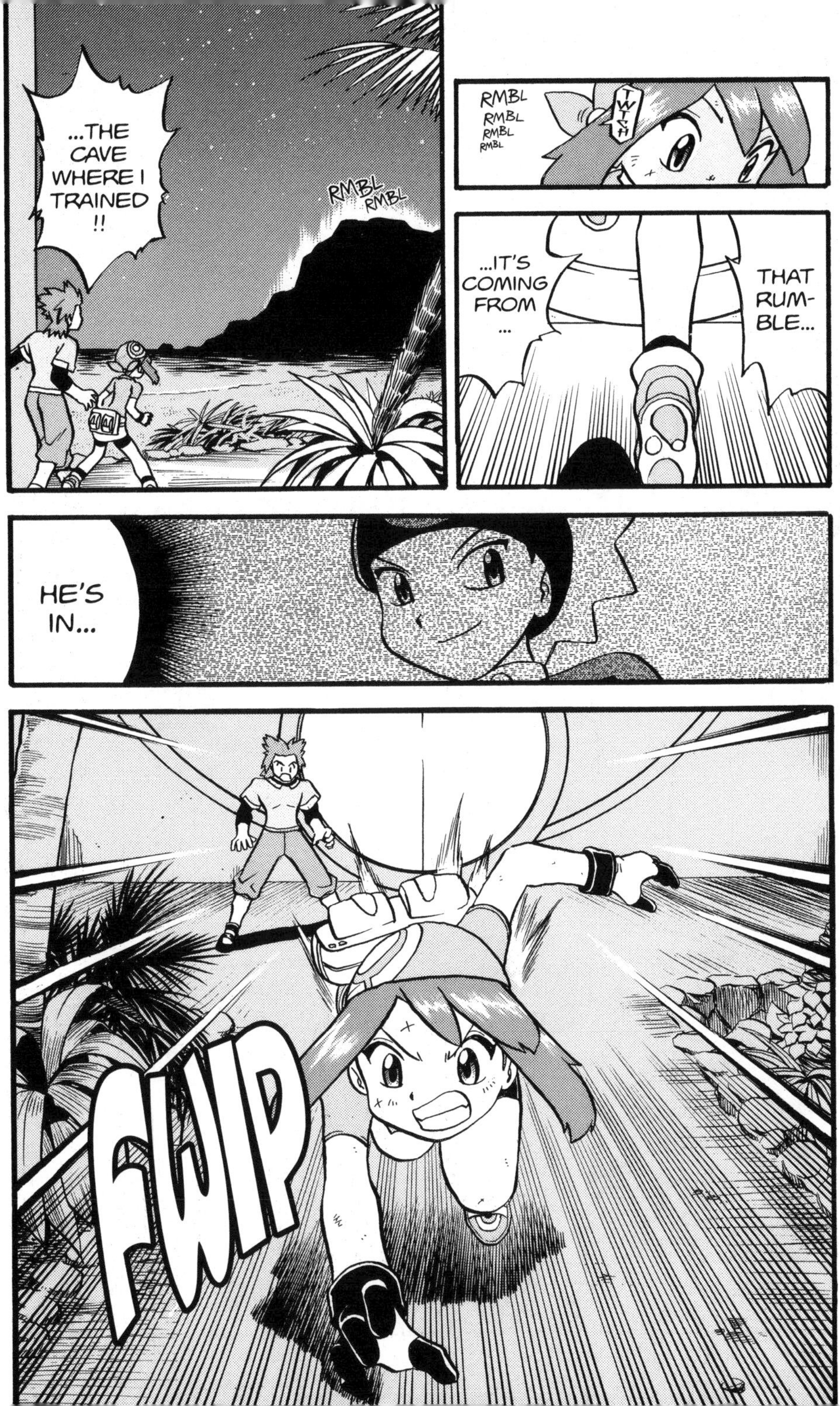
TWITCH
RMBL RMBL RMBL RMBL
THAT RUMBLE...
...IT'S COMING FROM ...
RMBL RMBL
...THE CAVE WHERE I TRAINED !!
HE'S IN...
FWIP

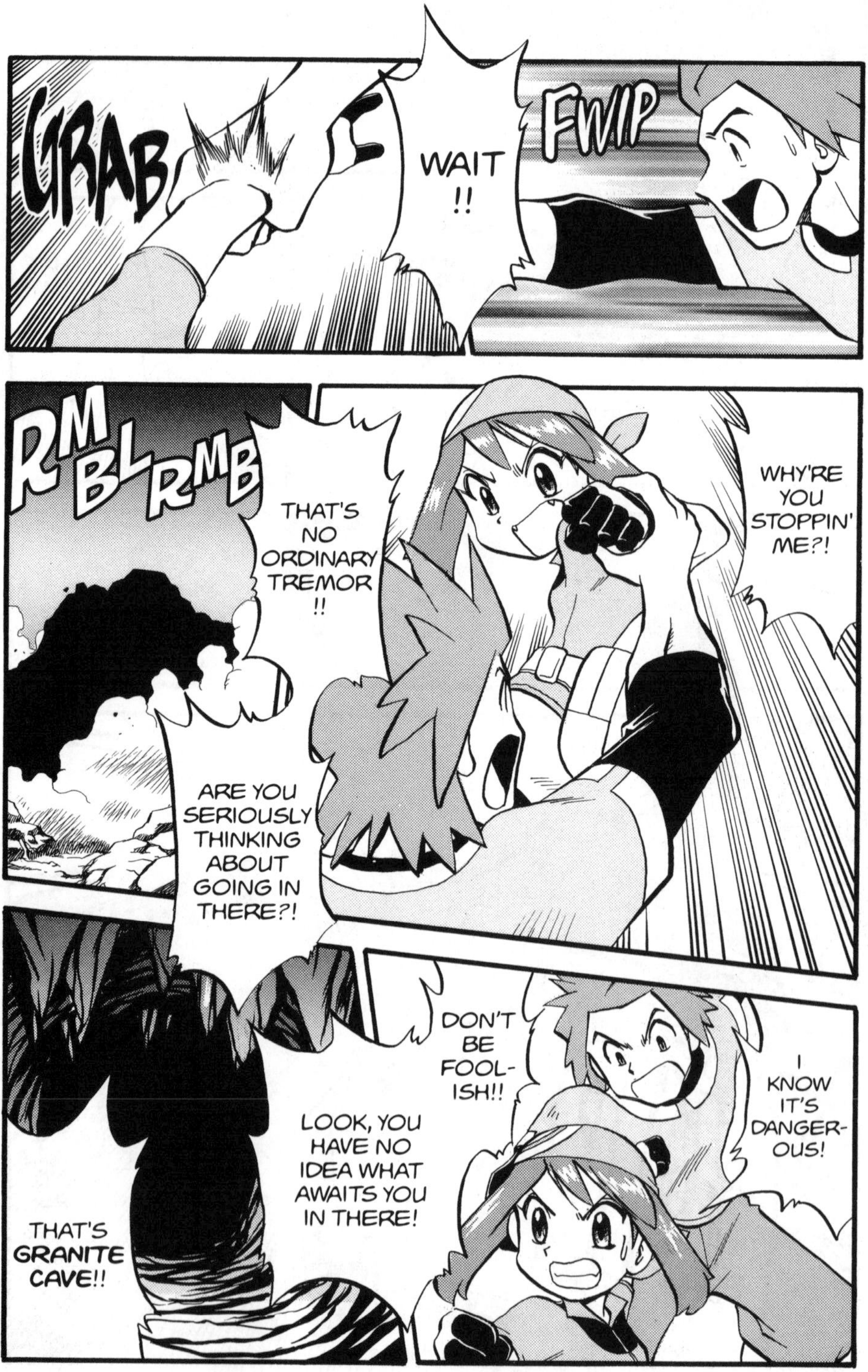
FWIP
WAIT!!
GRAB
WHY'RE YOU STOPPIN' ME?!
ARE YOU SERIOUSLY THINKING ABOUT GOING IN THERE?!
RMBLRMB
THAT'S NO ORDINARY TREMOR!!
I KNOW IT'S DANGEROUS!
DON'T BE FOOLISH!!
LOOK, YOU HAVE NO IDEA WHAT AWAITS YOU IN THERE!
THAT'S GRANITE CAVE!!

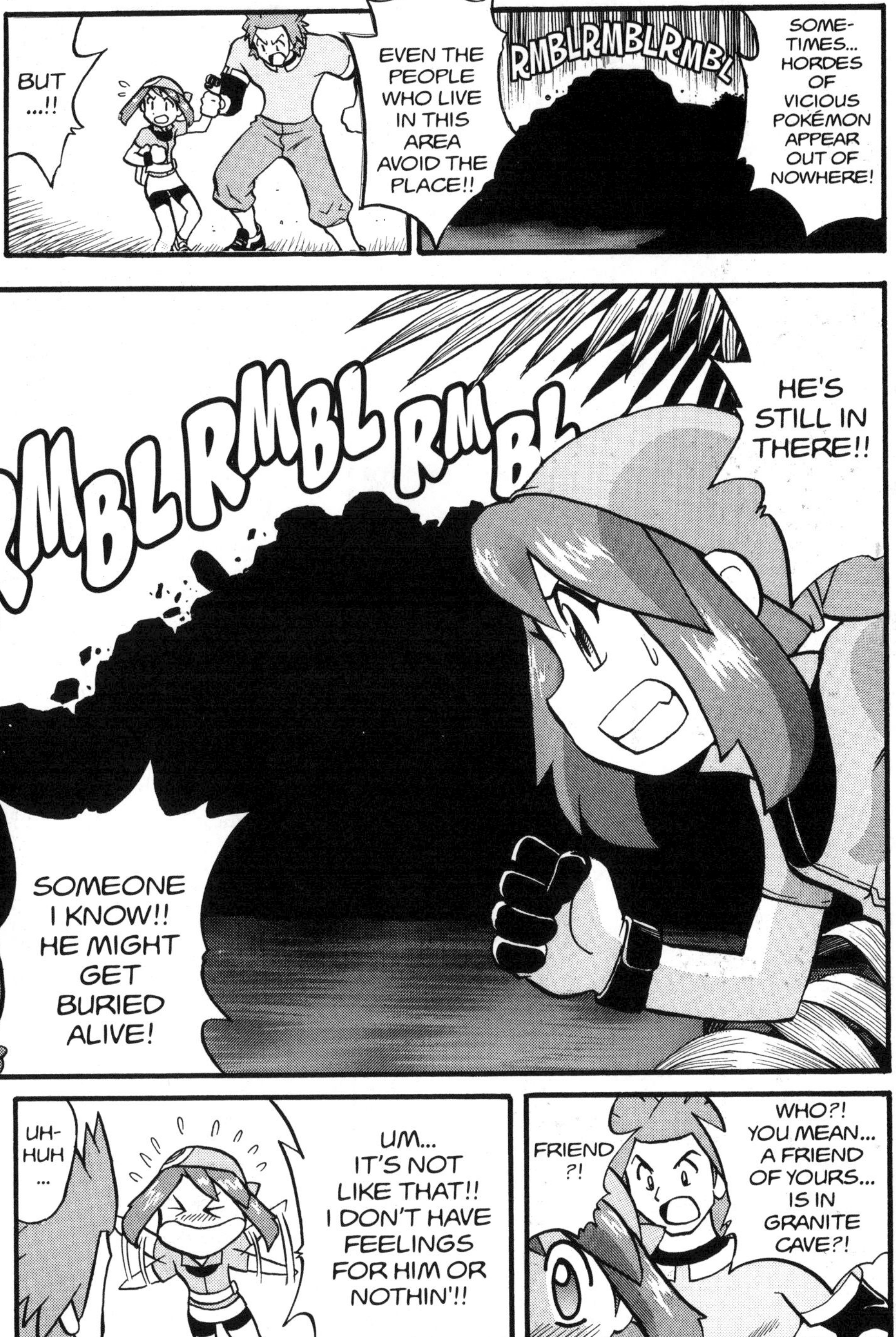
SOMETIMES... HORDES OF VICIOUS POKÉMON APPEAR OUT OF NOWHERE!
RMBLRMBLRMBL
EVEN THE PEOPLE WHO LIVE IN THIS AREA AVOID THE PLACE!!
BUT ...!!
HE'S STILL IN THERE!!
RMBLRMBLRMBL
SOMEONE I KNOW!! HE MIGHT GET BURIED ALIVE!
WHO?! YOU MEAN... A FRIEND OF YOURS... IS IN GRANITE CAVE?!
FRIEND ?!
UM... IT'S NOT LIKE THAT!! I DON'T HAVE FEELINGS FOR HIM OR NOTHIN'!!
UH-HUH ...

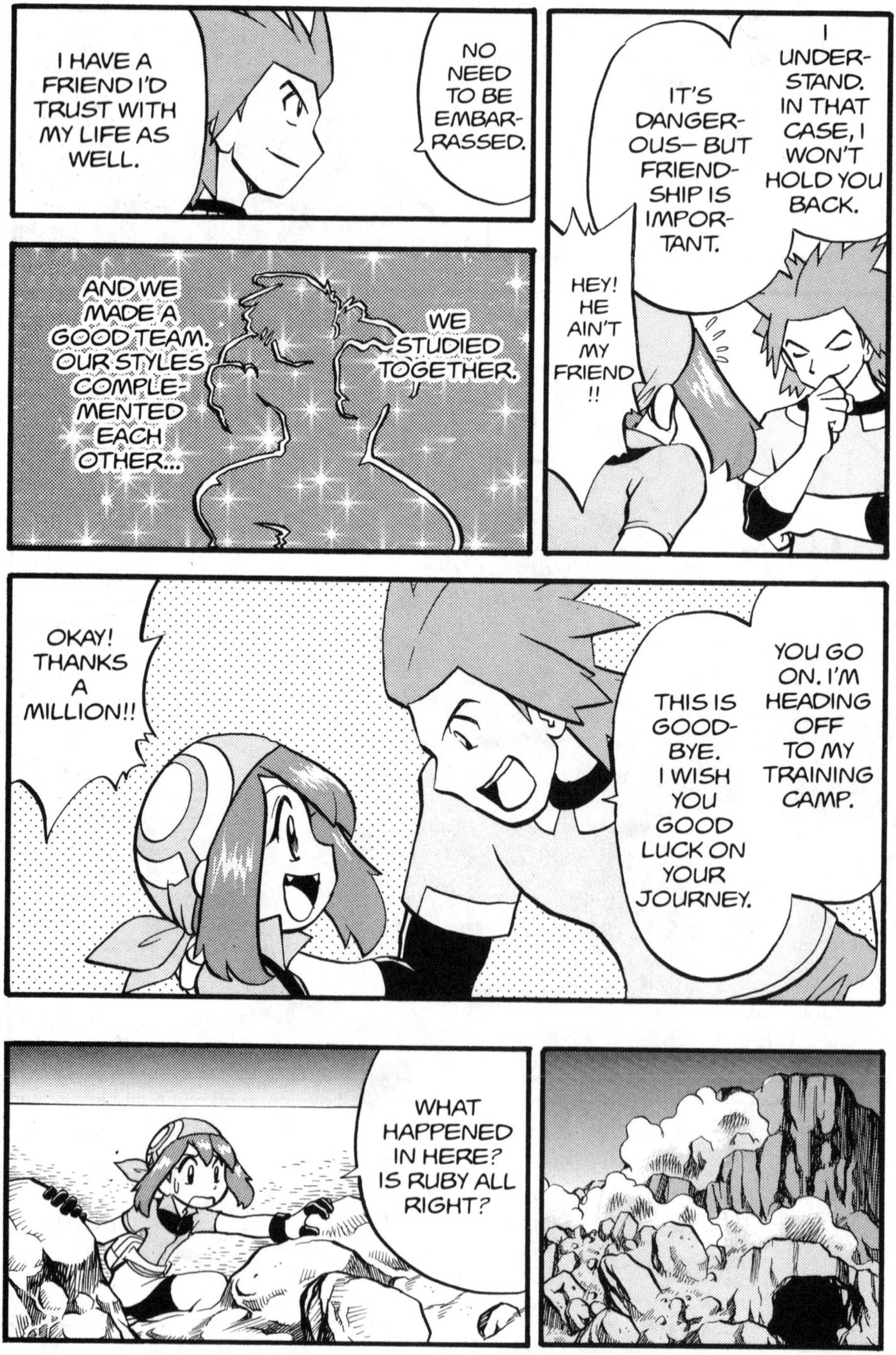
I UNDERSTAND. IN THAT CASE, I WON'T HOLD YOU BACK.
IT'S DANGEROUS— BUT FRIENDSHIP IS IMPORTANT.
HEY! HE AIN'T MY FRIEND!!
NO NEED TO BE EMBARRASSED.
I HAVE A FRIEND I'D TRUST WITH MY LIFE AS WELL.
WE STUDIED TOGETHER.
AND WE MADE A GOOD TEAM. OUR STYLES COMPLEMENTED EACH OTHER...
YOU GO ON. I'M HEADING OFF TO MY TRAINING CAMP.
THIS IS GOODBYE. I WISH YOU GOOD LUCK ON YOUR JOURNEY.
OKAY! THANKS A MILLION!!
WHAT HAPPENED IN HERE? IS RUBY ALL RIGHT?

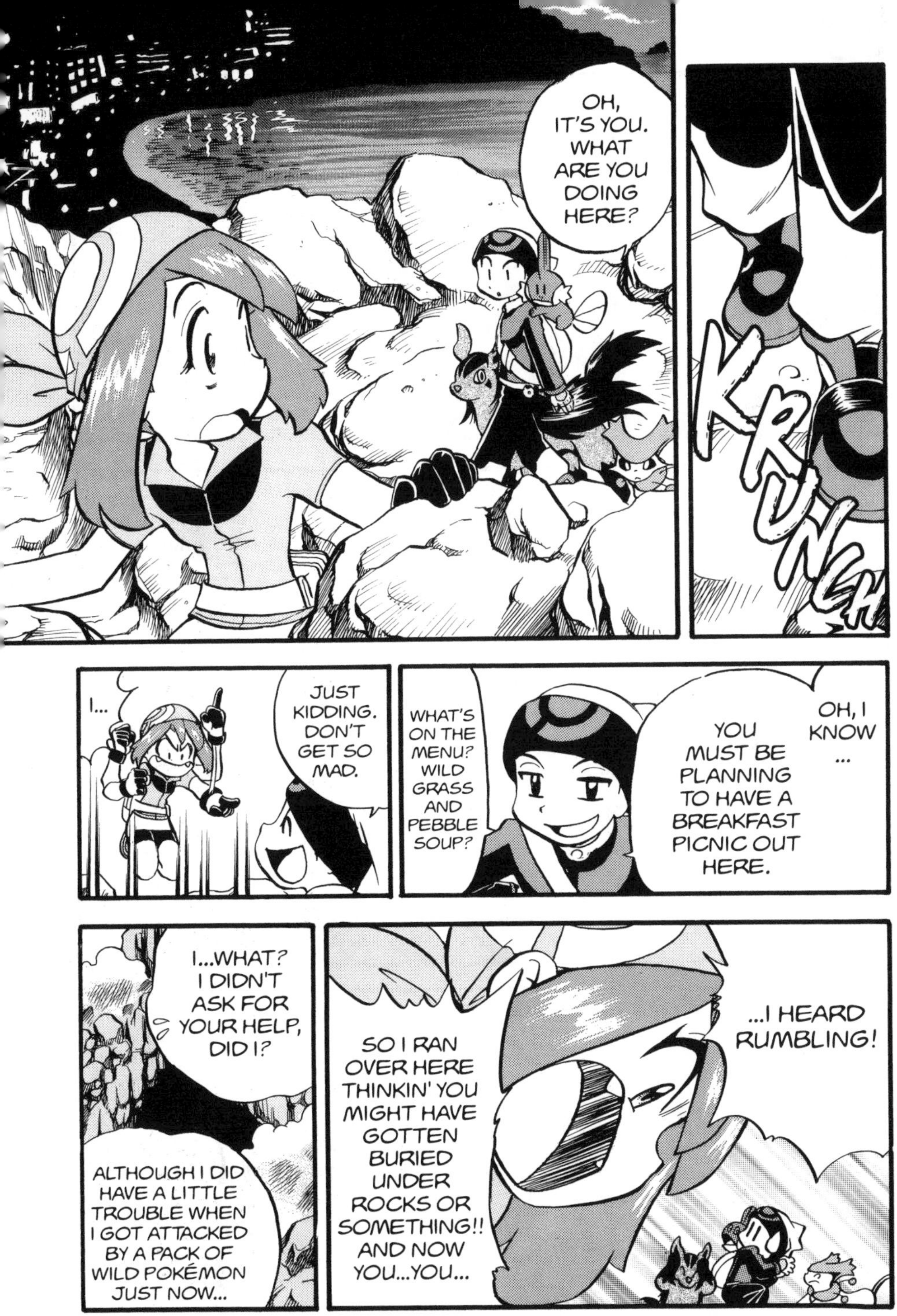
KRUNCH
OH, IT'S YOU. WHAT ARE YOU DOING HERE?
OH, I KNOW ...
YOU MUST BE PLANNING TO HAVE A BREAKFAST PICNIC OUT HERE.
WHAT'S ON THE MENU? WILD GRASS AND PEBBLE SOUP?
JUST KIDDING. DON'T GET SO MAD.
I...
...I HEARD RUMBLING!
SO I RAN OVER HERE THINKIN' YOU MIGHT HAVE GOTTEN BURIED UNDER ROCKS OR SOMETHING!! AND NOW YOU...YOU...
I...WHAT? I DIDN'T ASK FOR YOUR HELP, DID I?
ALTHOUGH I DID HAVE A LITTLE TROUBLE WHEN I GOT ATTACKED BY A PACK OF WILD POKÉMON JUST NOW...

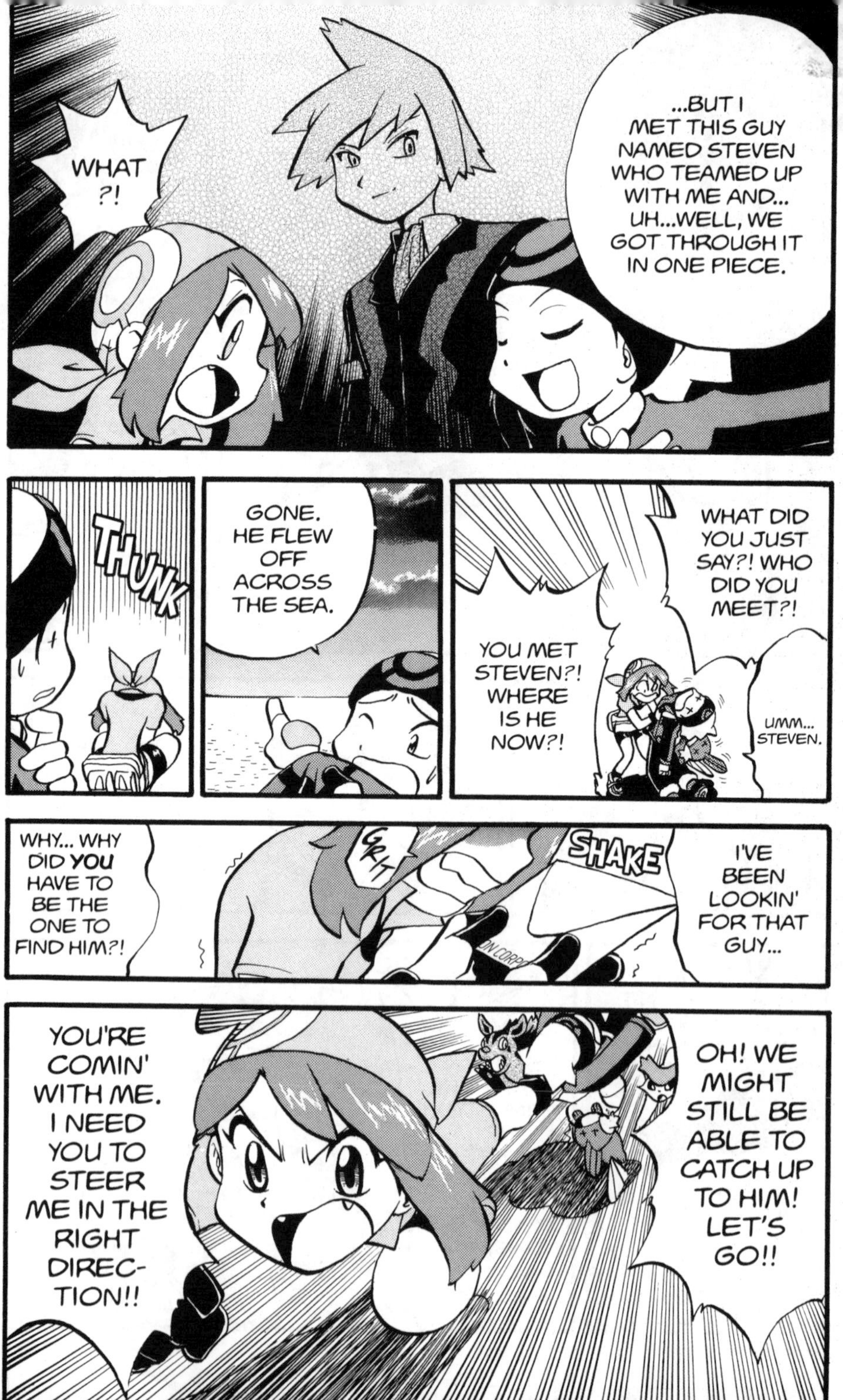
...BUT I MET THIS GUY NAMED STEVEN WHO TEAMED UP WITH ME AND... UH...WELL, WE GOT THROUGH IT IN ONE PIECE.
WHAT?!
WHAT DID YOU JUST SAY?! WHO DID YOU MEET?!
UMM... STEVEN.
YOU MET STEVEN?! WHERE IS HE NOW?!
GONE. HE FLEW OFF ACROSS THE SEA.
THUNK
I'VE BEEN LOOKIN' FOR THAT GUY...
SHAKE
GRIT
WHY... WHY DID **YOU** HAVE TO BE THE ONE TO FIND HIM?!
OH! WE MIGHT STILL BE ABLE TO CATCH UP TO HIM! LET'S GO!!
YOU'RE COMIN' WITH ME. I NEED YOU TO STEER ME IN THE RIGHT DIREC-TION!!

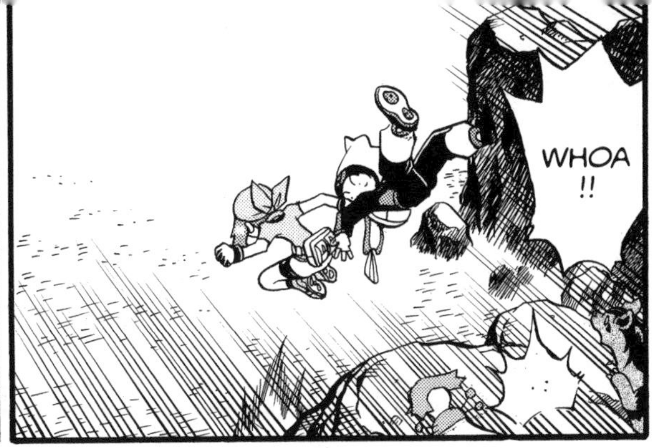
WHOA !!

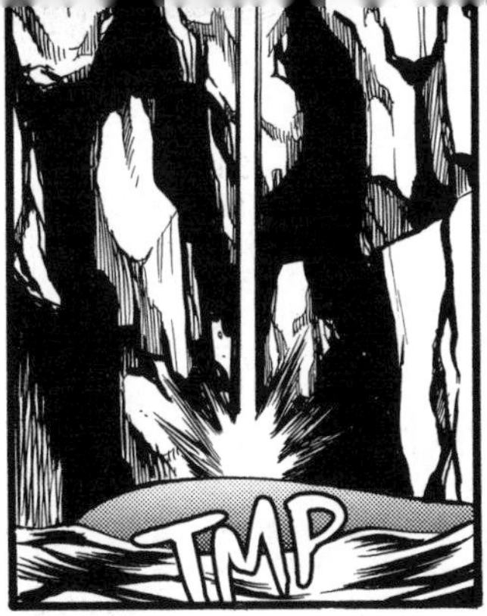
TMP

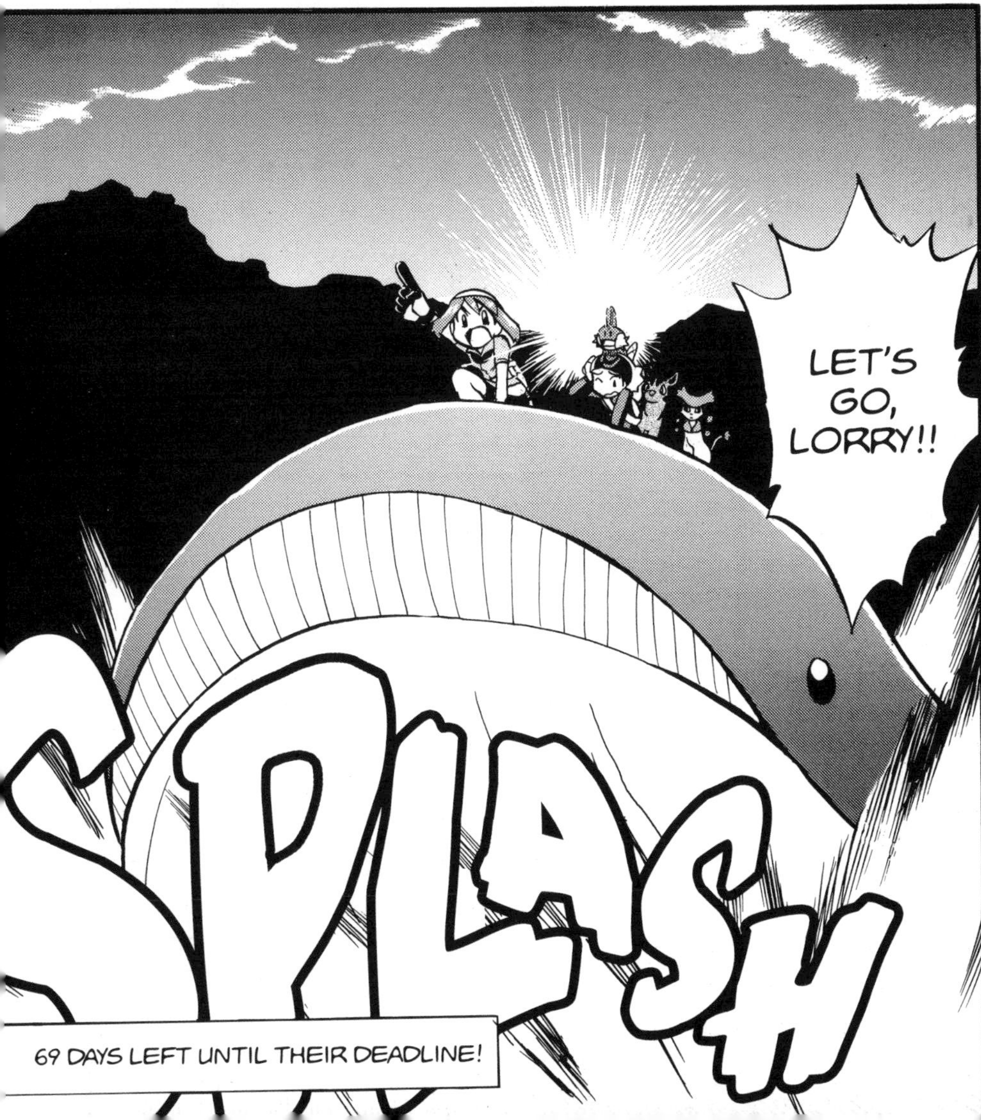
LET'S GO, LORRY!!
SPLASH
69 DAYS LEFT UNTIL THEIR DEADLINE!

● Adventure 198 ●

Adding It Up with Plusle and Minun, Part 1

Pokémon™ Adventures Ruby & Sapphire The Fourth Chapter

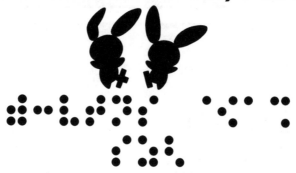

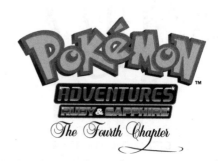

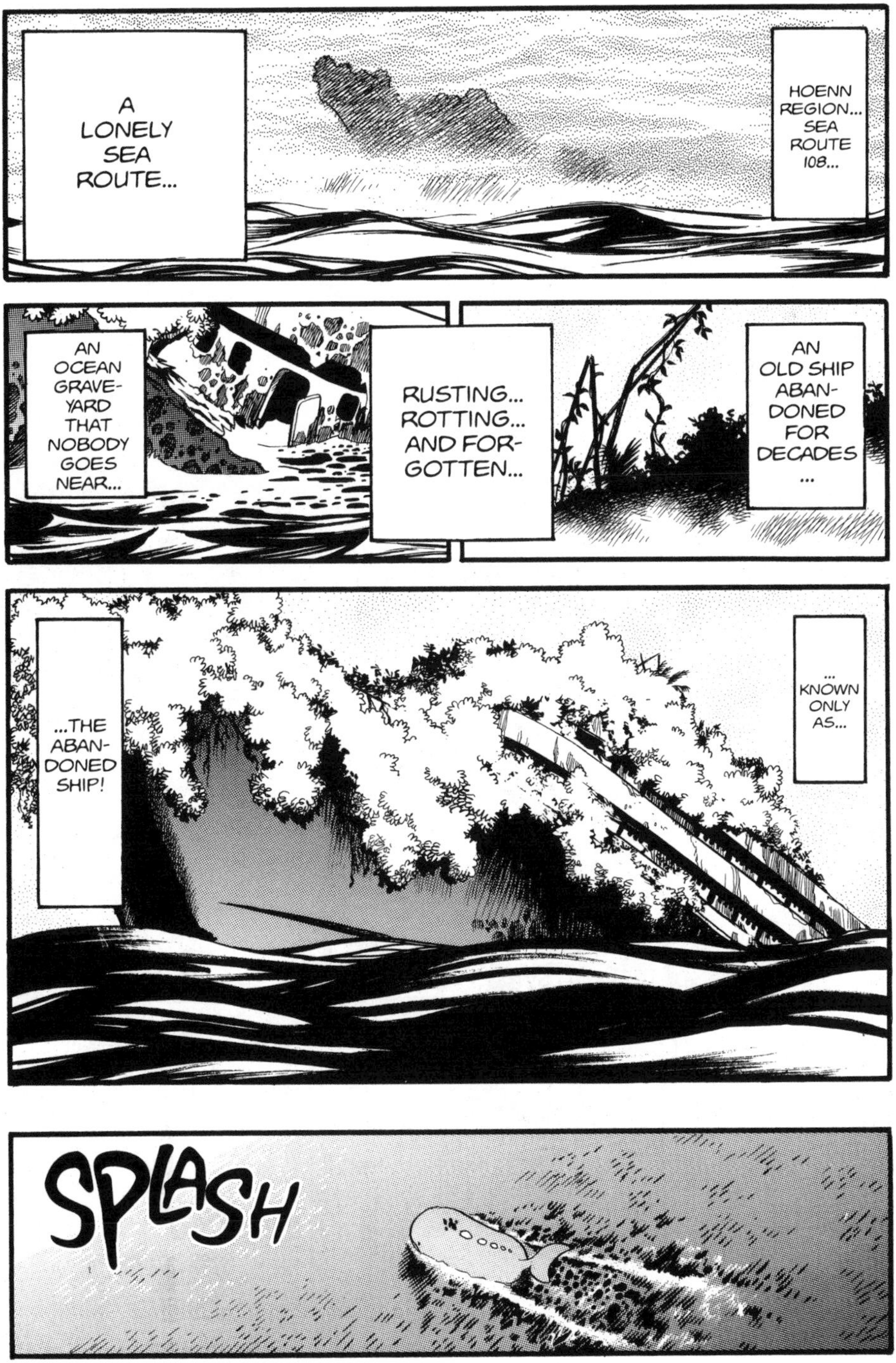

HOENN REGION... SEA ROUTE 108...
A LONELY SEA ROUTE...
AN OLD SHIP ABANDONED FOR DECADES...
RUSTING... ROTTING... AND FORGOTTEN...
AN OCEAN GRAVEYARD THAT NOBODY GOES NEAR...
...KNOWN ONLY AS...
...THE ABANDONED SHIP!
SPLASH

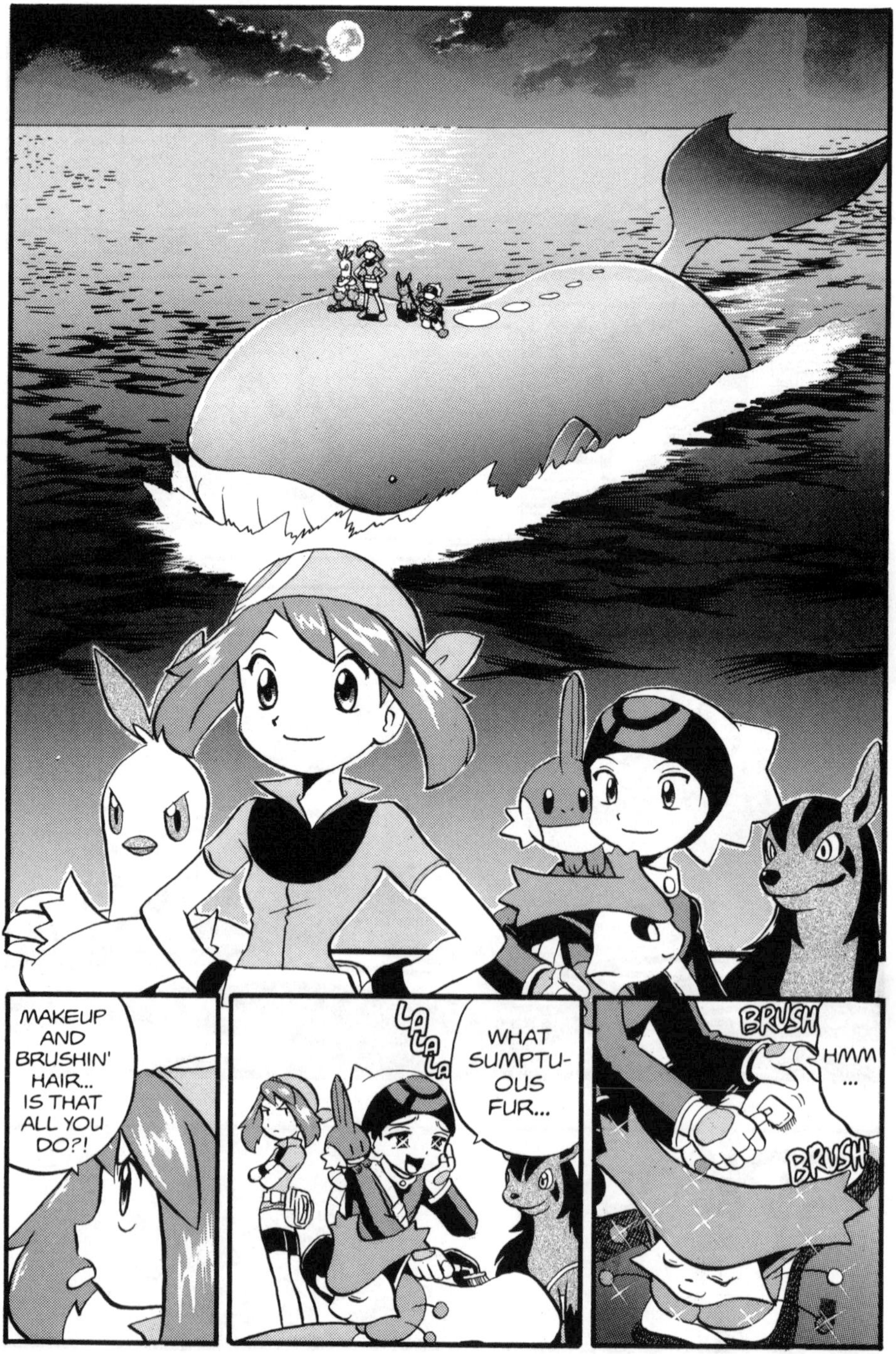
BRUSH
HMM...
BRUSH
LA LA LA
WHAT SUMPTUOUS FUR...
MAKEUP AND BRUSHIN' HAIR... IS THAT ALL YOU DO?!

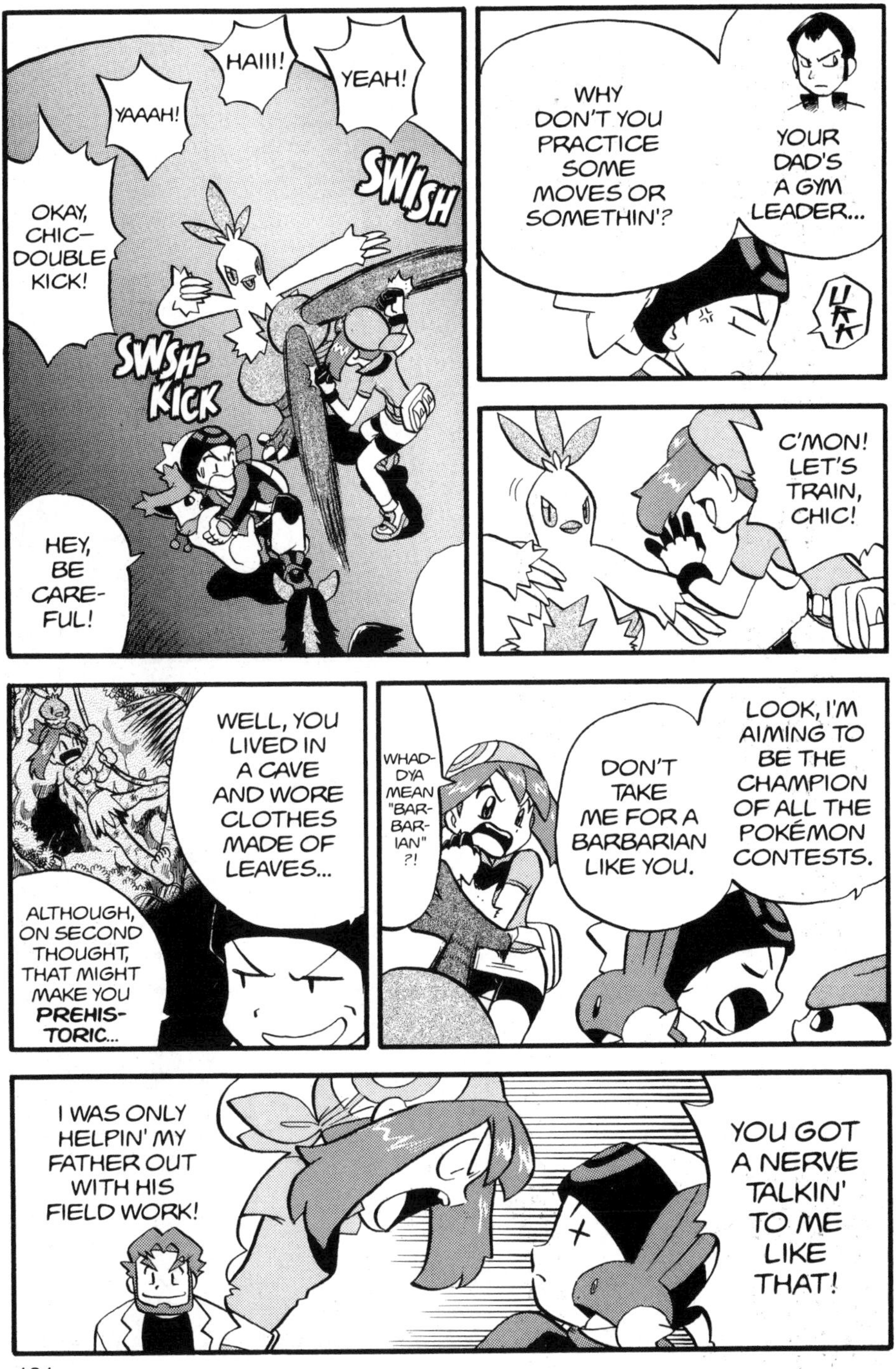
YOUR DAD'S A GYM LEADER...
WHY DON'T YOU PRACTICE SOME MOVES OR SOMETHIN'?
URK
C'MON! LET'S TRAIN, CHIC!
YEAH!
HAIII!
YAAAH!
SWISH
OKAY, CHIC— DOUBLE KICK!
SWSH-KICK
HEY, BE CARE-FUL!
LOOK, I'M AIMING TO BE THE CHAMPION OF ALL THE POKÉMON CONTESTS.
DON'T TAKE ME FOR A BARBARIAN LIKE YOU.
WHAD-DYA MEAN "BAR-BAR-IAN" ?!
WELL, YOU LIVED IN A CAVE AND WORE CLOTHES MADE OF LEAVES...
ALTHOUGH, ON SECOND THOUGHT, THAT MIGHT MAKE YOU **PREHIS-TORIC**...
YOU GOT A NERVE TALKIN' TO ME LIKE THAT!
I WAS ONLY HELPIN' MY FATHER OUT WITH HIS FIELD WORK!

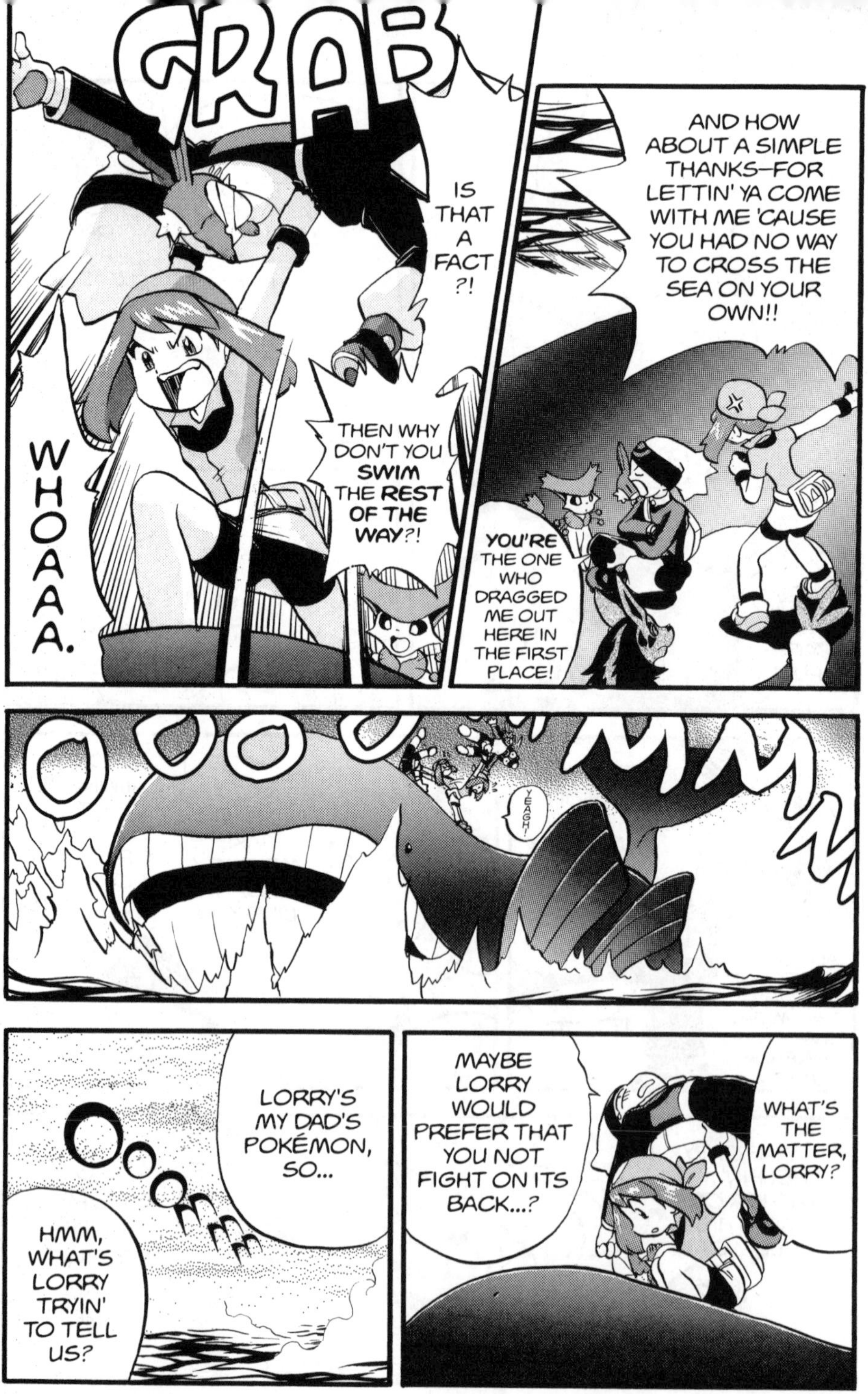

AND HOW ABOUT A SIMPLE THANKS—FOR LETTIN' YA COME WITH ME 'CAUSE YOU HAD NO WAY TO CROSS THE SEA ON YOUR OWN!!
YOU'RE THE ONE WHO DRAGGED ME OUT HERE IN THE FIRST PLACE!
GRAB
IS THAT A FACT?!
THEN WHY DON'T YOU SWIM THE REST OF THE WAY?!
WHOAAAA.
OOOOMMMM
YEAGH!
WHAT'S THE MATTER, LORRY?
MAYBE LORRY WOULD PREFER THAT YOU NOT FIGHT ON ITS BACK...?
LORRY'S MY DAD'S POKÉMON, SO...
OOOMM
HMM, WHAT'S LORRY TRYIN' TO TELL US?

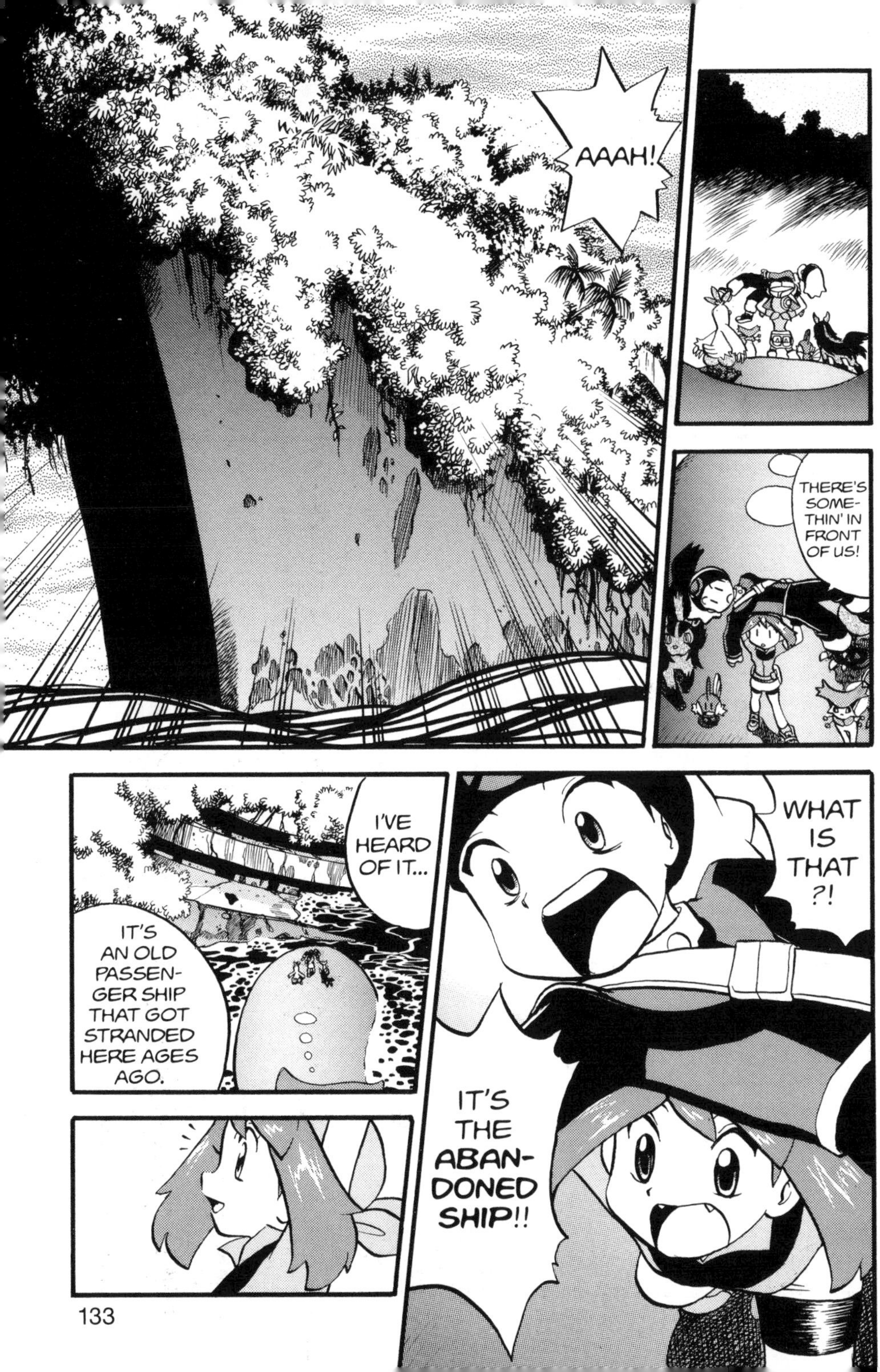
THERE'S SOMETHIN' IN FRONT OF US!
AAAH!
WHAT IS THAT?!
IT'S THE ABANDONED SHIP!!
I'VE HEARD OF IT...
IT'S AN OLD PASSENGER SHIP THAT GOT STRANDED HERE AGES AGO.

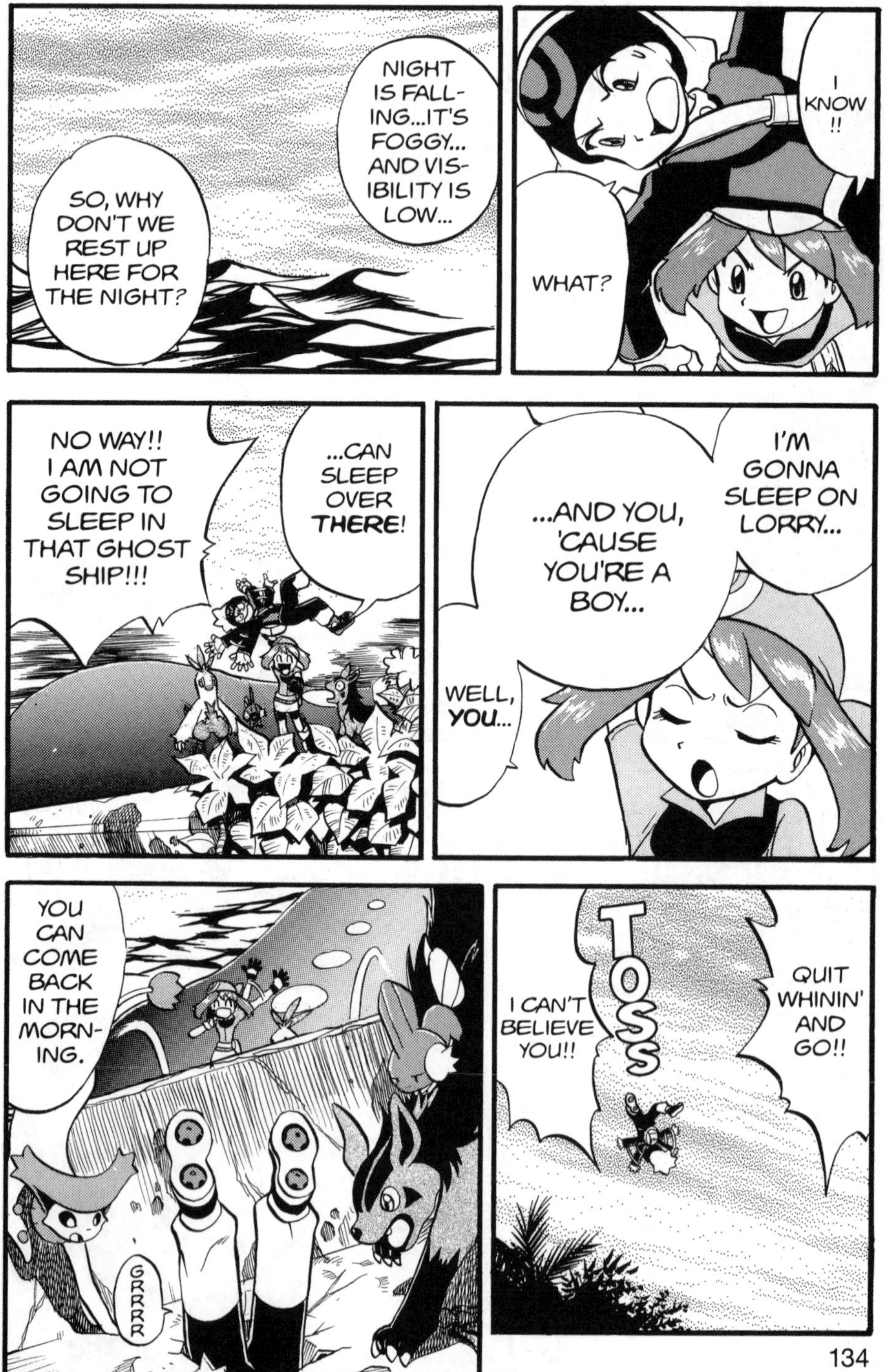

I KNOW!!
WHAT?
NIGHT IS FALLING...IT'S FOGGY... AND VISIBILITY IS LOW...
SO, WHY DON'T WE REST UP HERE FOR THE NIGHT?
I'M GONNA SLEEP ON LORRY...
...AND YOU, 'CAUSE YOU'RE A BOY...
WELL, YOU...
...CAN SLEEP OVER THERE!
NO WAY!! I AM NOT GOING TO SLEEP IN THAT GHOST SHIP!!!
QUIT WHININ' AND GO!!
TOSS
I CAN'T BELIEVE YOU!!
YOU CAN COME BACK IN THE MORNING.
GRRRR

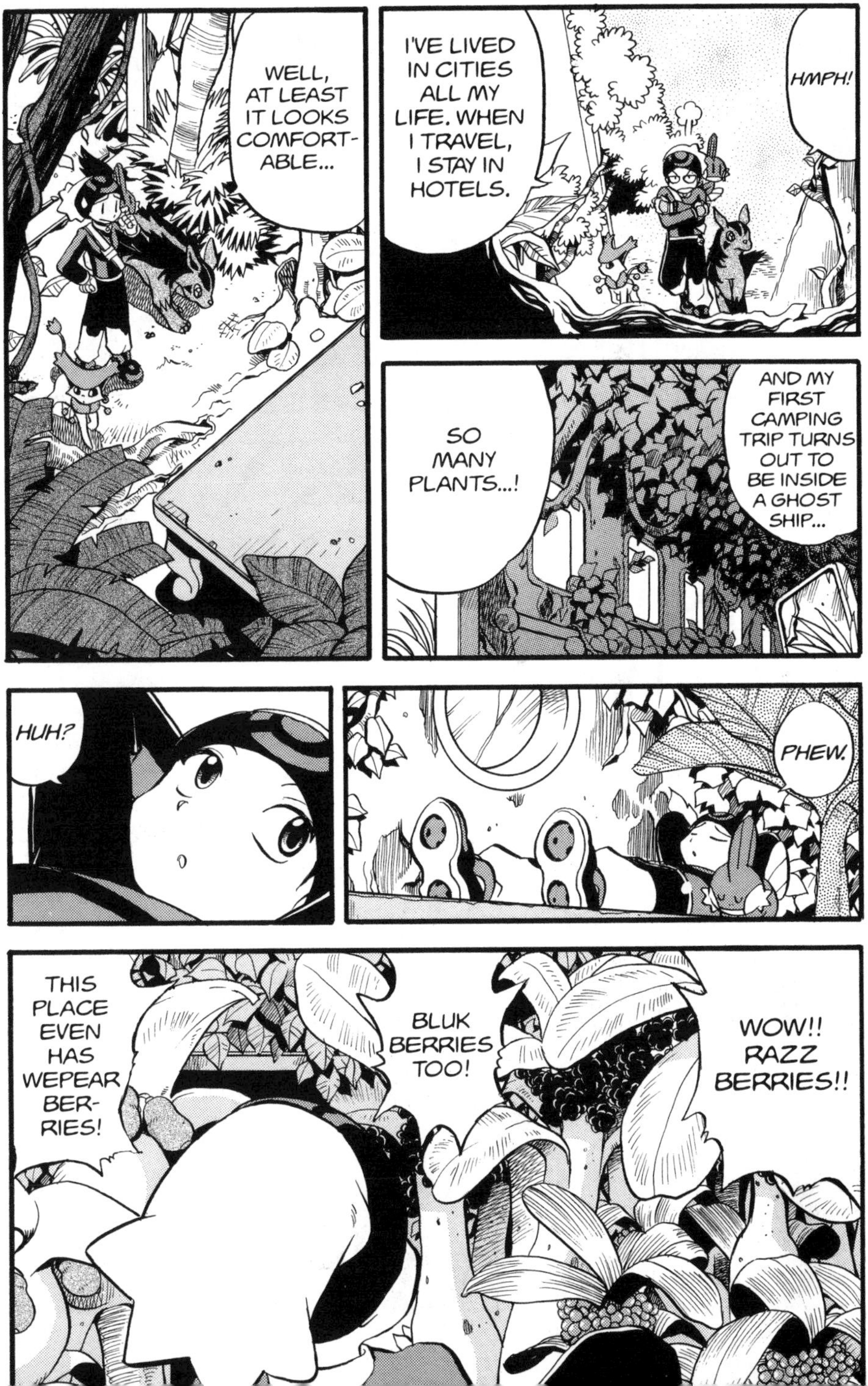
HMPH!
I'VE LIVED IN CITIES ALL MY LIFE. WHEN I TRAVEL, I STAY IN HOTELS.
AND MY FIRST CAMPING TRIP TURNS OUT TO BE INSIDE A GHOST SHIP...
SO MANY PLANTS...!
WELL, AT LEAST IT LOOKS COMFORT-ABLE...
PHEW.
HUH?
WOW!! RAZZ BERRIES!!
BLUK BERRIES TOO!
THIS PLACE EVEN HAS WEPEAR BER-RIES!

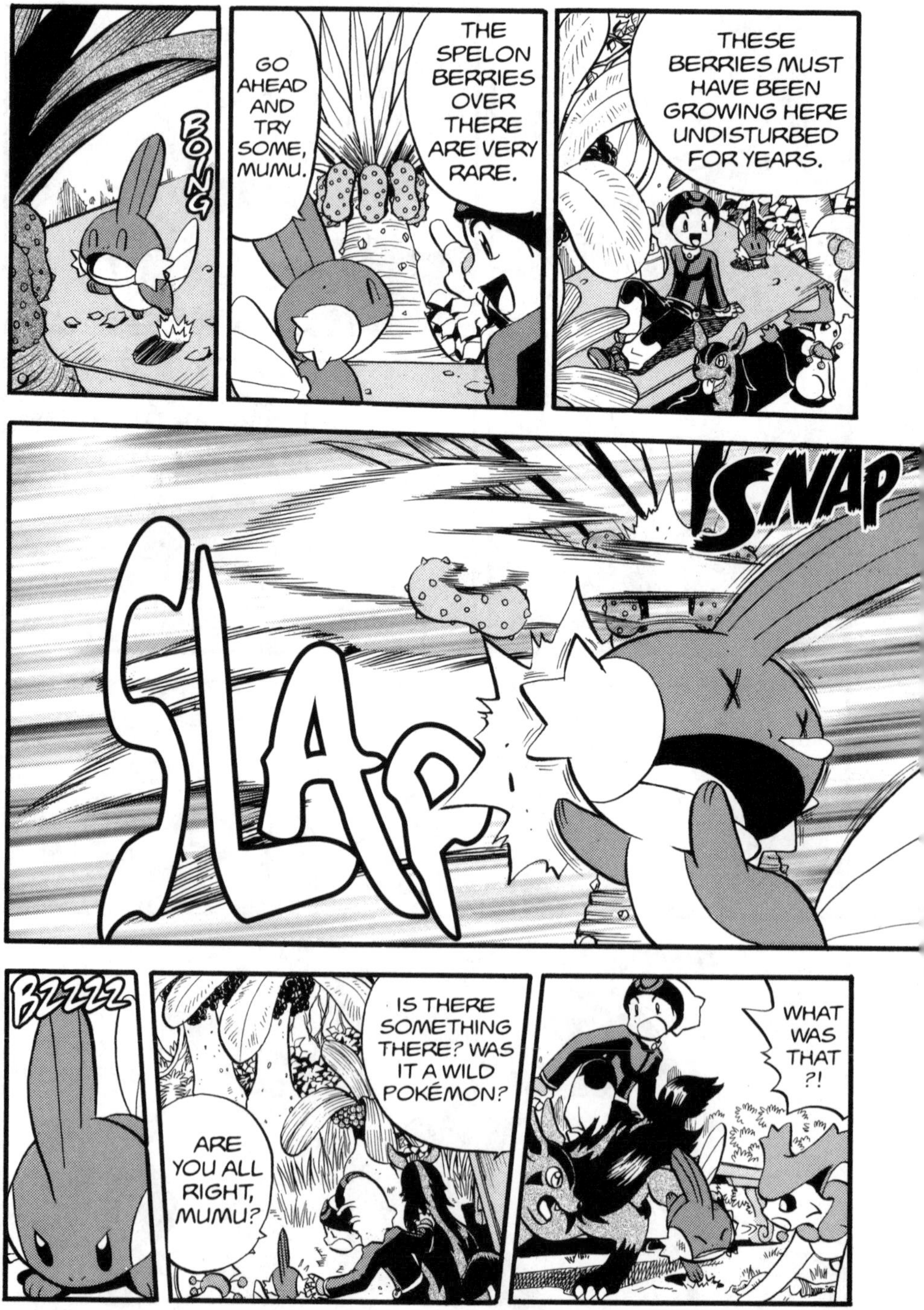
THESE BERRIES MUST HAVE BEEN GROWING HERE UNDISTURBED FOR YEARS.
THE SPELON BERRIES OVER THERE ARE VERY RARE.
GO AHEAD AND TRY SOME, MUMU.
BOING
SNAP
SLAP
WHAT WAS THAT?!
IS THERE SOMETHING THERE? WAS IT A WILD POKÉMON?
ARE YOU ALL RIGHT, MUMU?
BZZZZ

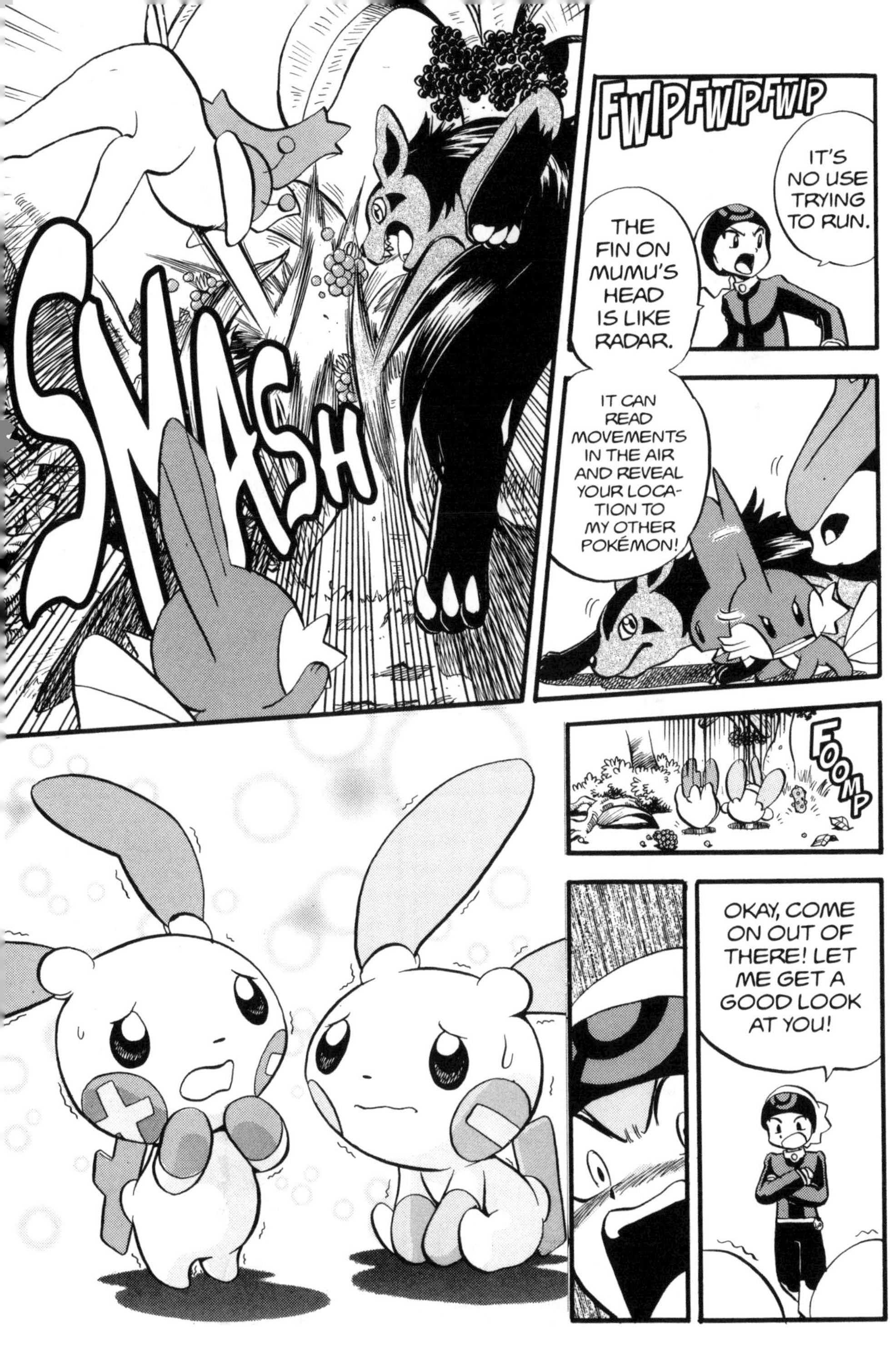
FWIP FWIP FWIP
IT'S NO USE TRYING TO RUN.
THE FIN ON MUMU'S HEAD IS LIKE RADAR.
IT CAN READ MOVEMENTS IN THE AIR AND REVEAL YOUR LOCA-TION TO MY OTHER POKÉMON!
SMASH
FOOMP
OKAY, COME ON OUT OF THERE! LET ME GET A GOOD LOOK AT YOU!

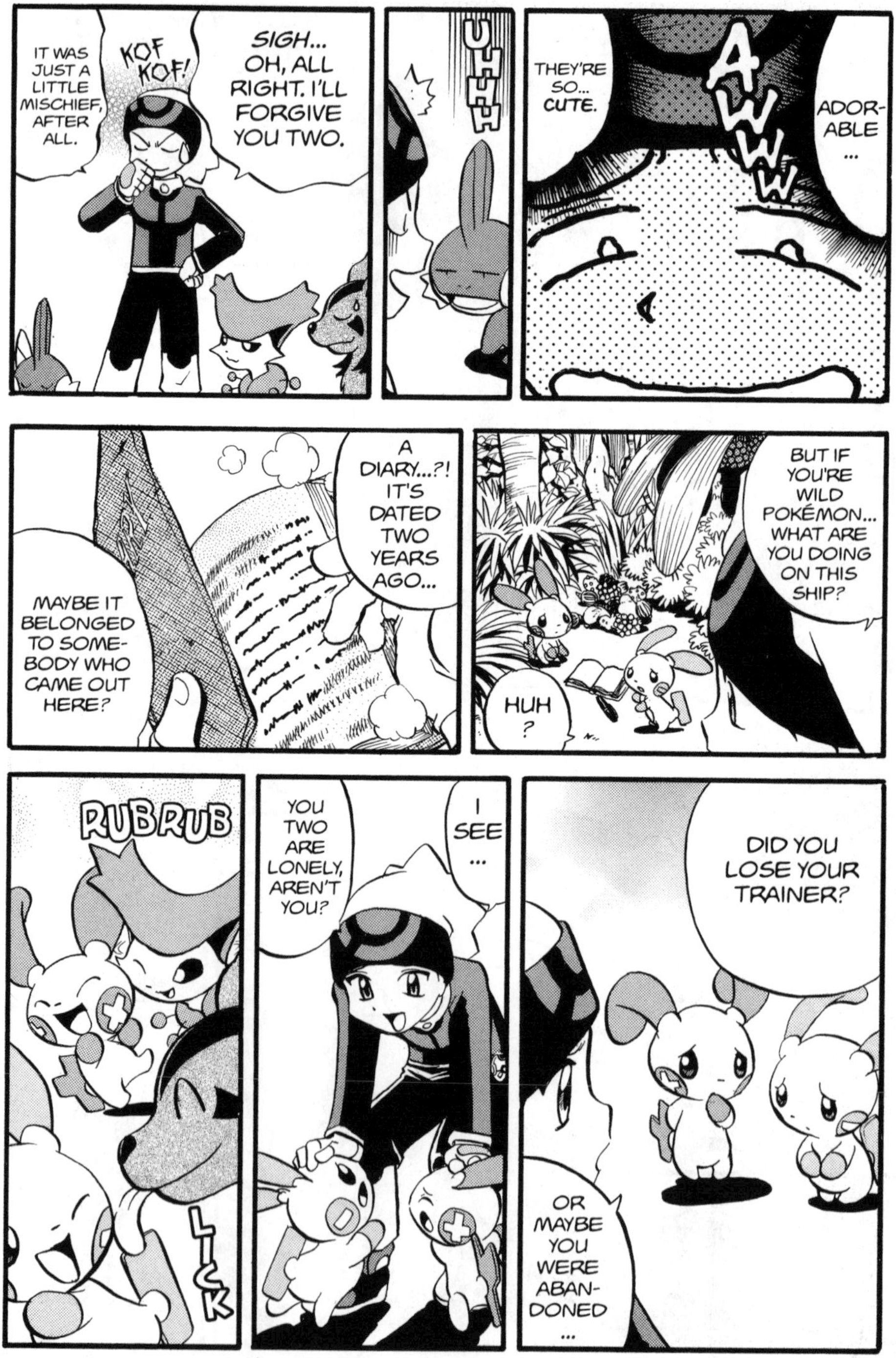
ADORABLE...
AWWW
THEY'RE SO... CUTE.
UHHHH
SIGH... OH, ALL RIGHT. I'LL FORGIVE YOU TWO.
KOF KOF!
IT WAS JUST A LITTLE MISCHIEF, AFTER ALL.
BUT IF YOU'RE WILD POKÉMON... WHAT ARE YOU DOING ON THIS SHIP?
HUH?
A DIARY...?! IT'S DATED TWO YEARS AGO...
MAYBE IT BELONGED TO SOMEBODY WHO CAME OUT HERE?
DID YOU LOSE YOUR TRAINER?
OR MAYBE YOU WERE ABANDONED...
I SEE...
YOU TWO ARE LONELY, AREN'T YOU?
RUB RUB
LICK

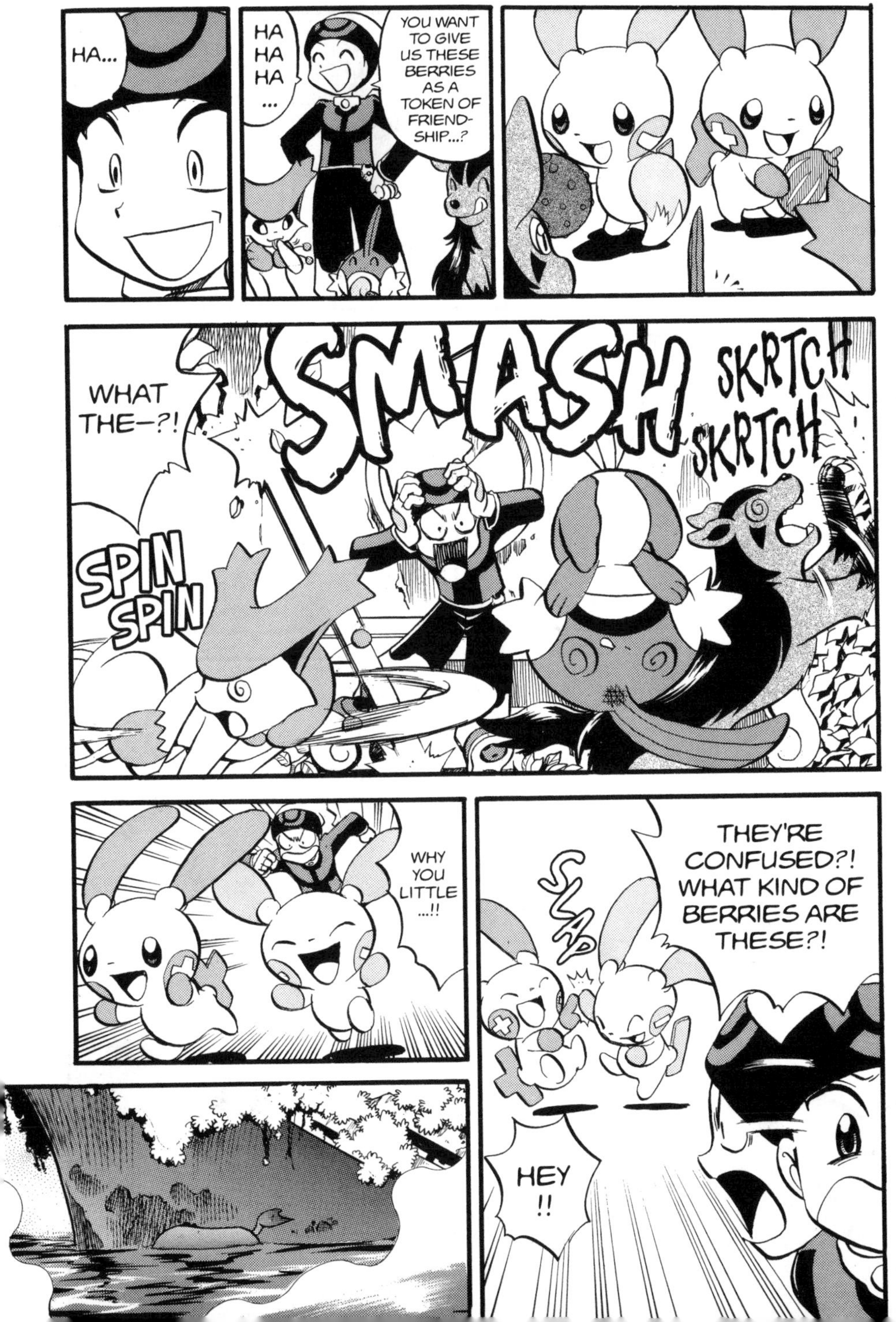
YOU WANT TO GIVE US THESE BERRIES AS A TOKEN OF FRIENDSHIP...?
HA HA HA ...
HA...
SKRTCH SKRTCH
SMASH
WHAT THE—?!
SPIN SPIN
THEY'RE CONFUSED?! WHAT KIND OF BERRIES ARE THESE?!
SLAP
HEY !!
WHY YOU LITTLE ...!!

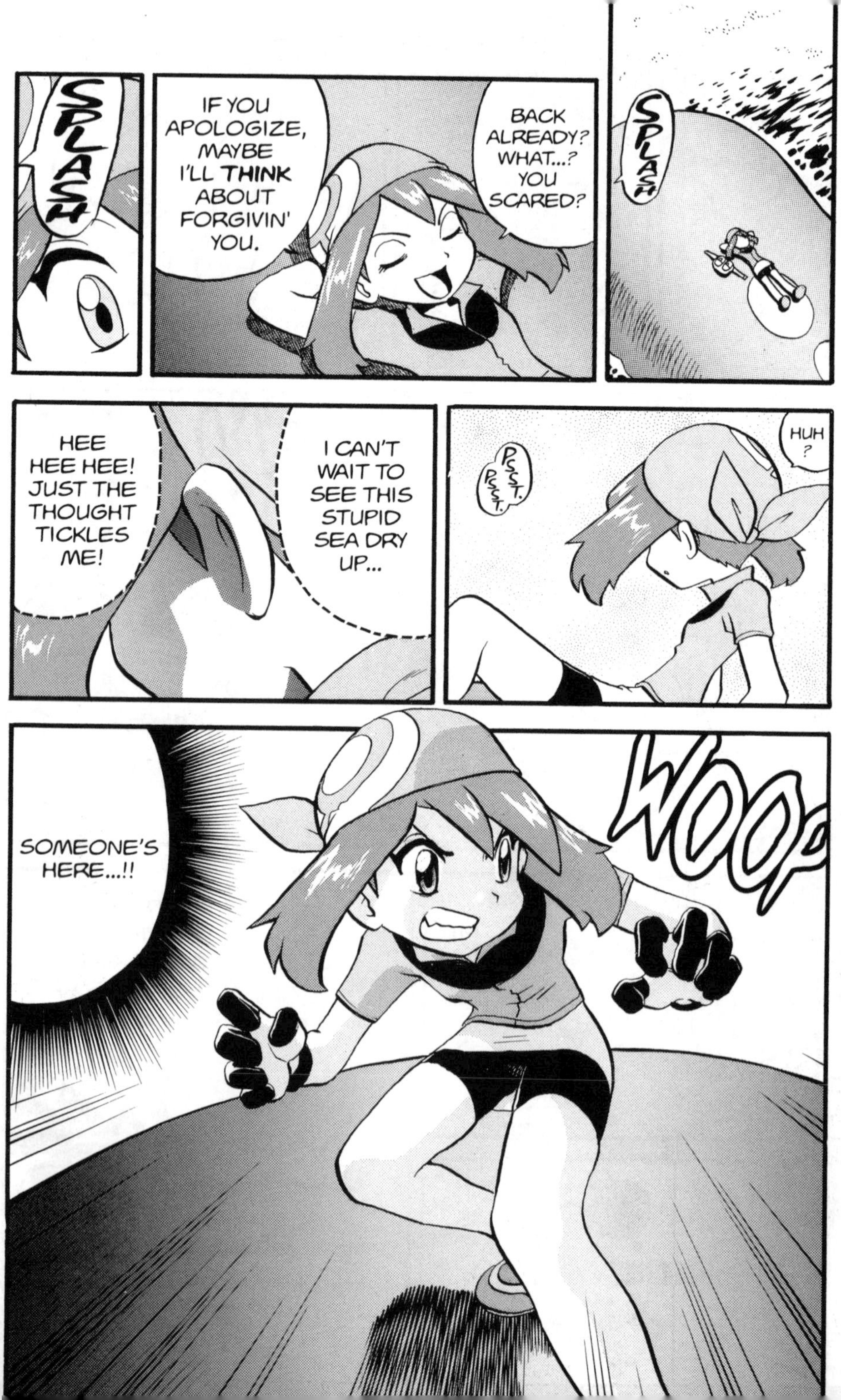
SPLASH
BACK ALREADY? WHAT...? YOU SCARED?
IF YOU APOLOGIZE, MAYBE I'LL **THINK** ABOUT FORGIVIN' YOU.
SPLASH
HUH?
PSST. PSST.
I CAN'T WAIT TO SEE THIS STUPID SEA DRY UP...
HEE HEE HEE! JUST THE THOUGHT TICKLES ME!
WOOP
SOMEONE'S HERE...!!

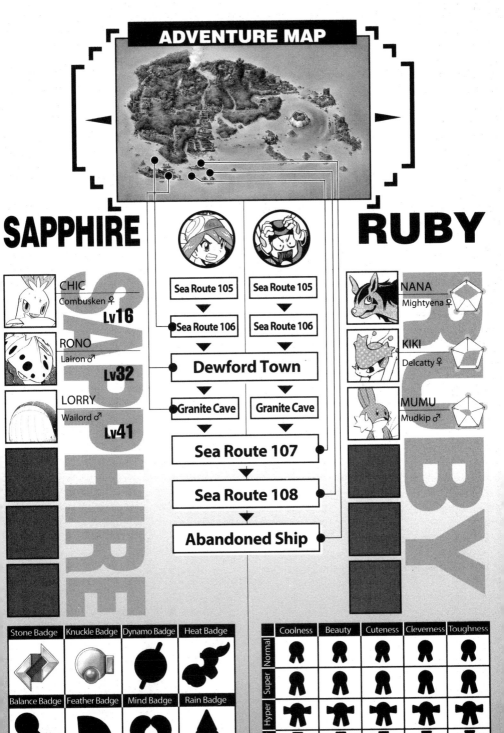

ADVENTURE MAP

SAPPHIRE

- Sea Route 105
- Sea Route 106
- Dewford Town
- Granite Cave
- Sea Route 107
- Sea Route 108
- Abandoned Ship

CHIC
Combusken ♀
Lv16

RONO
Lairon ♂
Lv32

LORRY
Wailord ♂
Lv41

RUBY

- Sea Route 105
- Sea Route 106
- Dewford Town
- Granite Cave
- Sea Route 107
- Sea Route 108
- Abandoned Ship

NANA
Mightyena ♀

KIKI
Delcatty ♀

MUMU
Mudkip ♂

Stone Badge	Knuckle Badge	Dynamo Badge	Heat Badge
Balance Badge	Feather Badge	Mind Badge	Rain Badge

	Coolness	Beauty	Cuteness	Cleverness	Toughness
Normal					
Super					
Hyper					
Master					

● Adventure 199 ●
Adding It Up with
Plusle and Minun, Part 2

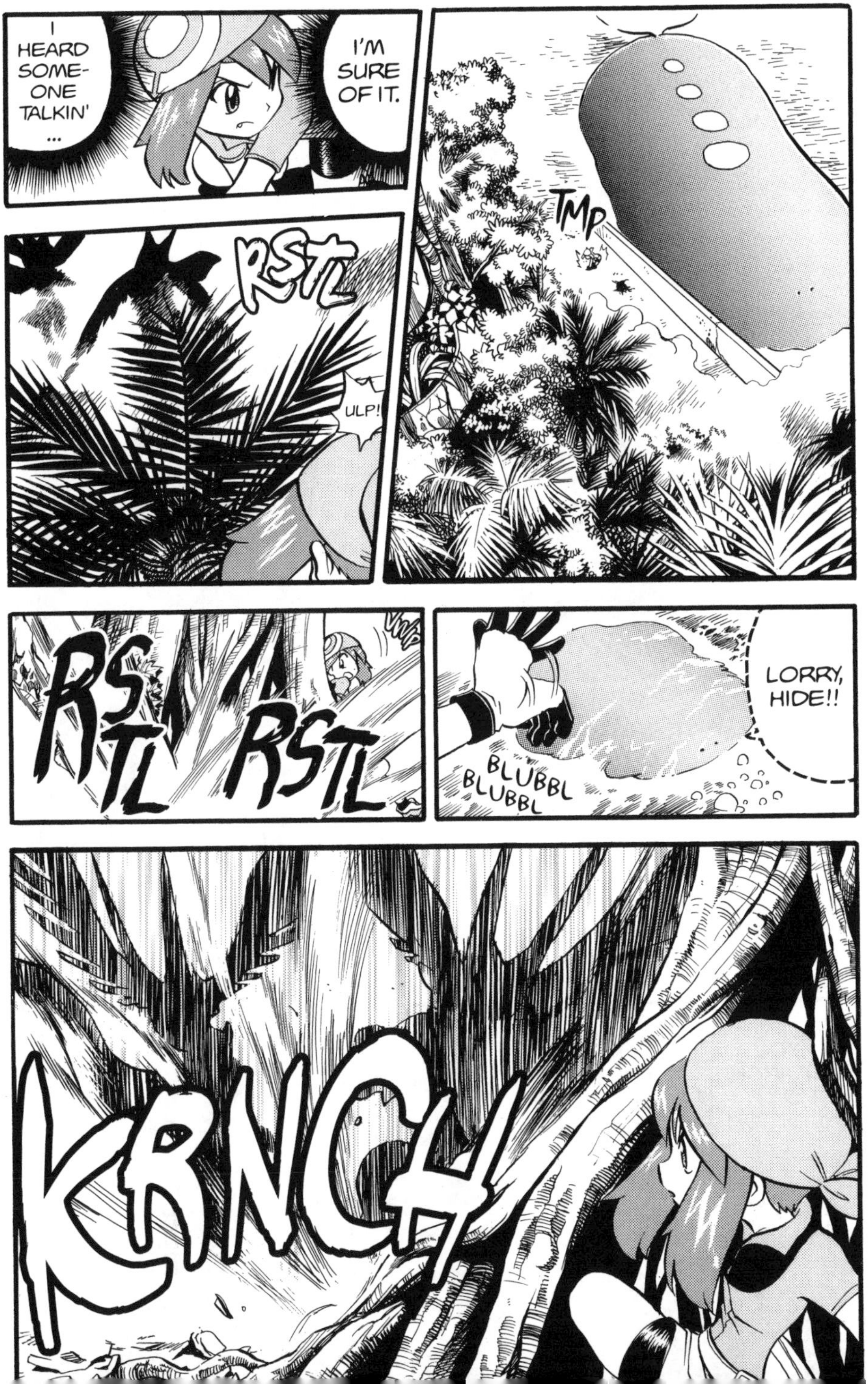

TMP
I'M SURE OF IT.
I HEARD SOME-ONE TALKIN' ...
RSTL
ULP!
LORRY, HIDE!!
BLUBBL BLUBBL
RSTL
RSTL
KRNCH

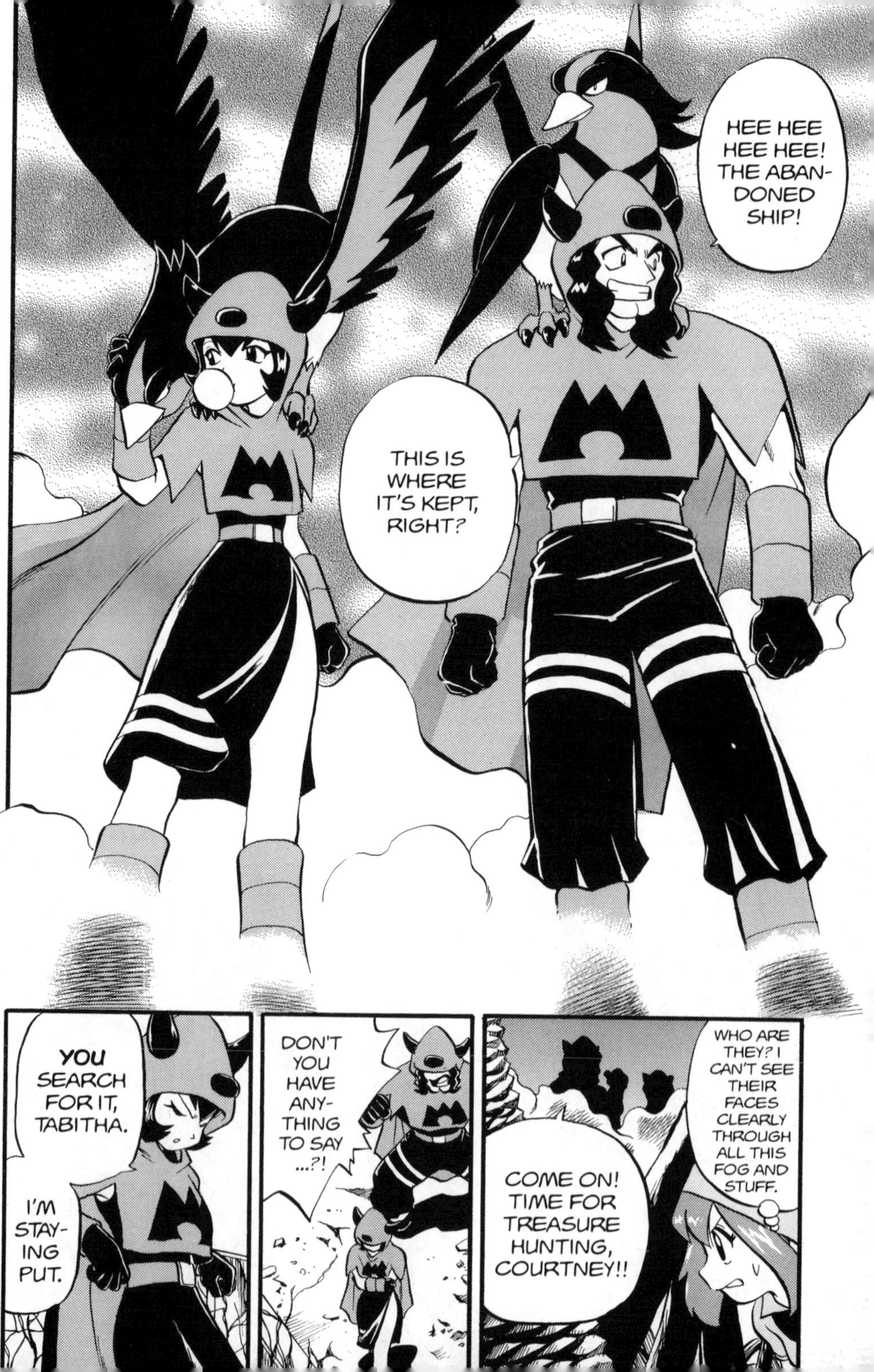
HEE HEE HEE HEE! THE ABAN-DONED SHIP!
THIS IS WHERE IT'S KEPT, RIGHT?
WHO ARE THEY? I CAN'T SEE THEIR FACES CLEARLY THROUGH ALL THIS FOG AND STUFF.
COME ON! TIME FOR TREASURE HUNTING, COURTNEY!!
DON'T YOU HAVE ANY-THING TO SAY ...?!
...
YOU SEARCH FOR IT, TABITHA.
I'M STAY-ING PUT.

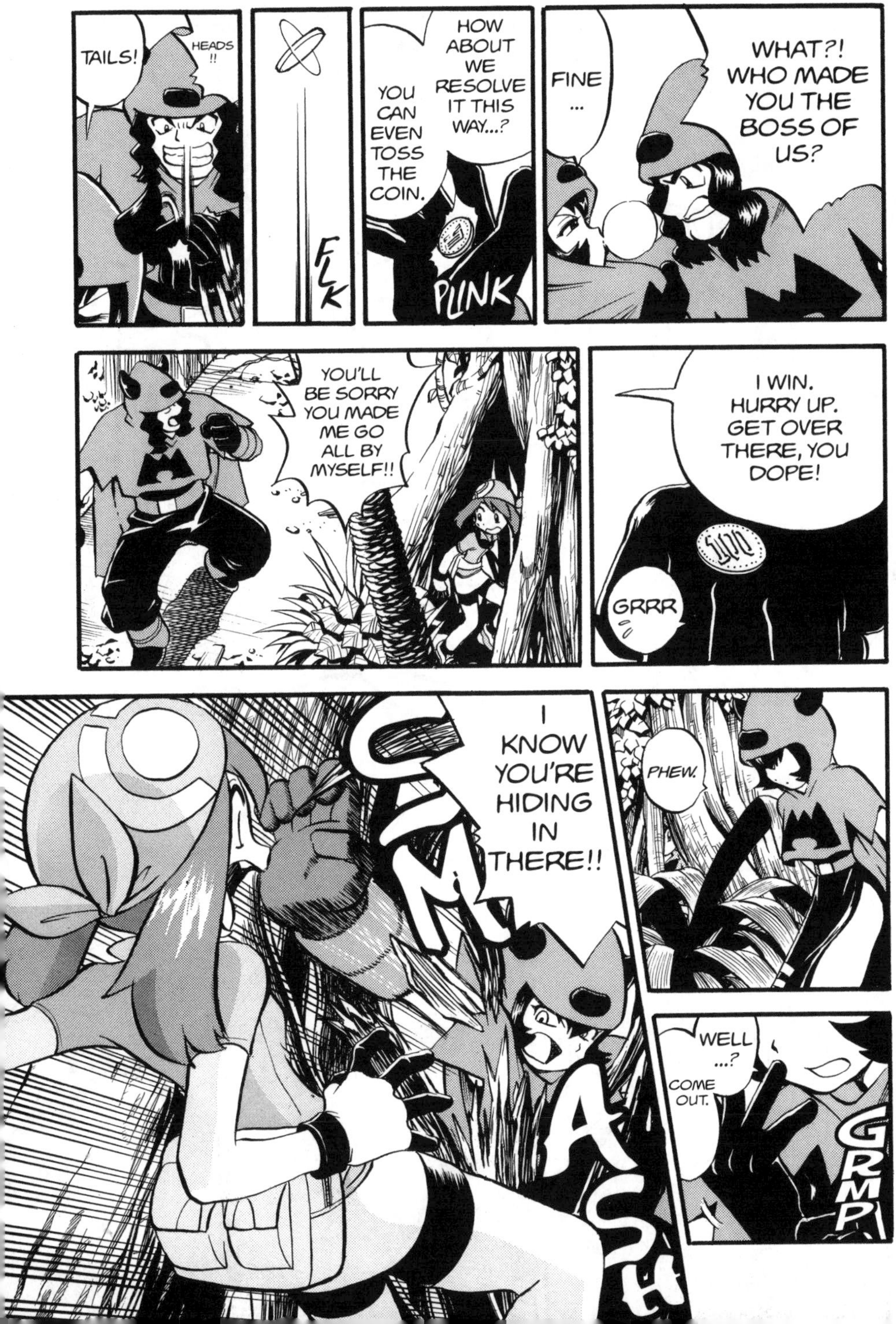
WHAT?! WHO MADE YOU THE BOSS OF US?
FINE ...
HOW ABOUT WE RESOLVE IT THIS WAY...?
YOU CAN EVEN TOSS THE COIN.
PLINK
FLK
HEADS!!
TAILS!
I WIN. HURRY UP. GET OVER THERE, YOU DOPE!
GRRR
YOU'LL BE SORRY YOU MADE ME GO ALL BY MYSELF!!
PHEW.
WELL ...?
COME OUT.
GRMP
I KNOW YOU'RE HIDING IN THERE!!
SMASH

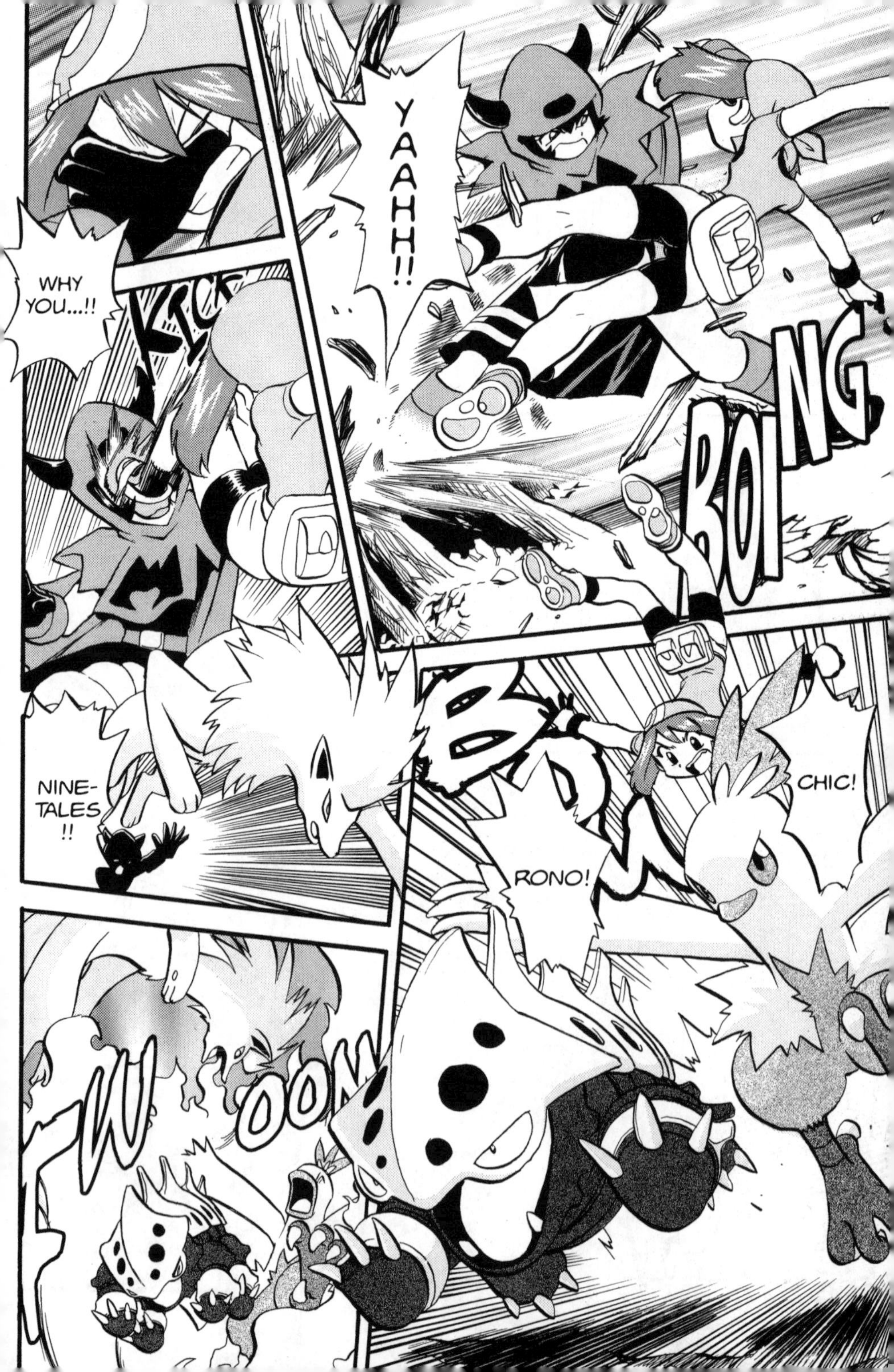

YAAAHH!!
BOING
WHY YOU...!!
CHIC!
RONO!
NINE-TALES!!

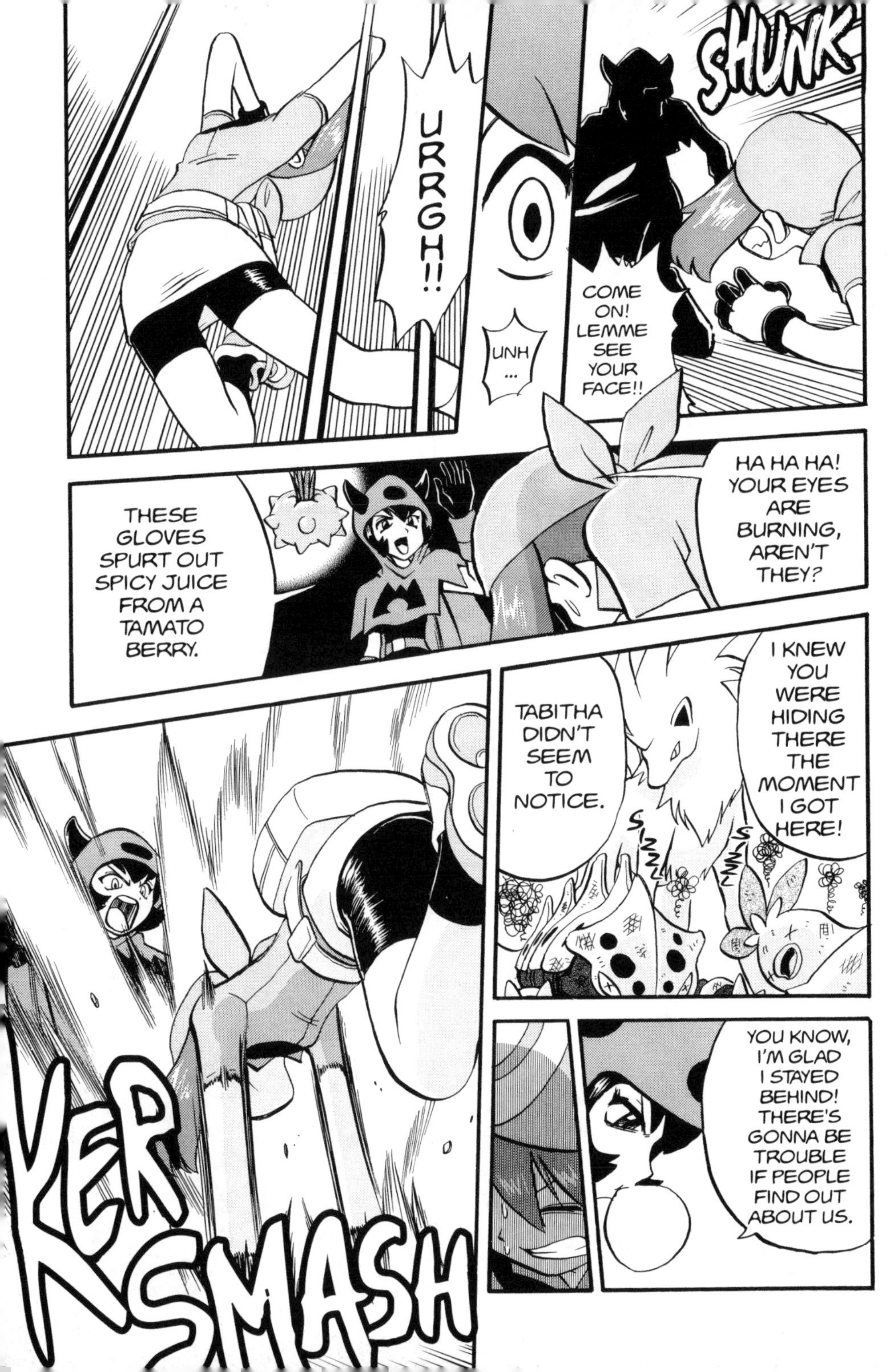
SHUNK
COME ON! LEMME SEE YOUR FACE!!
UNH ...
URRGH!!
HA HA HA! YOUR EYES ARE BURNING, AREN'T THEY?
THESE GLOVES SPURT OUT SPICY JUICE FROM A TAMATO BERRY.
I KNEW YOU WERE HIDING THERE THE MOMENT I GOT HERE!
TABITHA DIDN'T SEEM TO NOTICE.
YOU KNOW, I'M GLAD I STAYED BEHIND! THERE'S GONNA BE TROUBLE IF PEOPLE FIND OUT ABOUT US.
KER SMASH

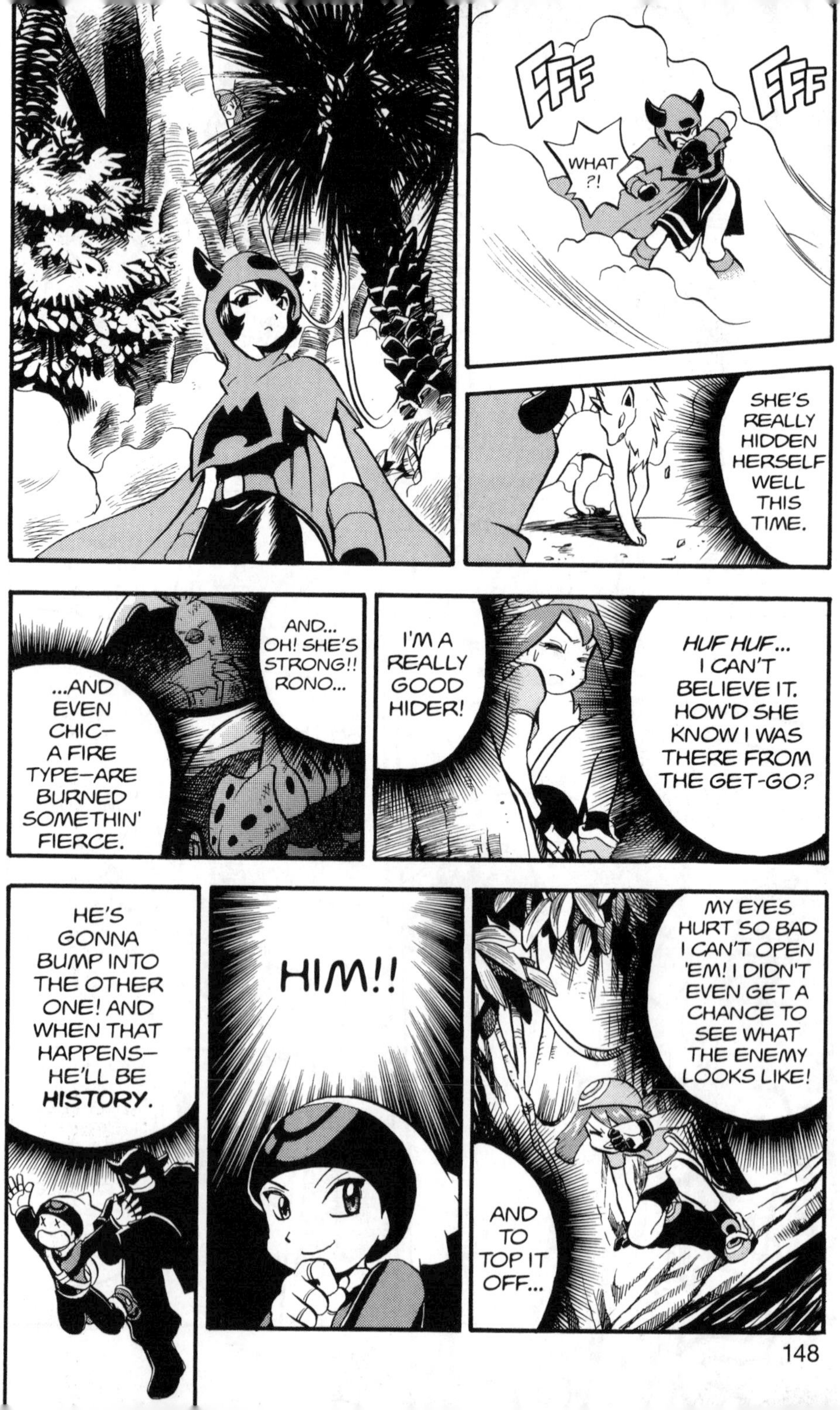
FFF
FFF
WHAT ?!
SHE'S REALLY HIDDEN HERSELF WELL THIS TIME.
HUF HUF... I CAN'T BELIEVE IT. HOW'D SHE KNOW I WAS THERE FROM THE GET-GO?
I'M A REALLY GOOD HIDER!
AND... OH! SHE'S STRONG!! RONO...
...AND EVEN CHIC—A FIRE TYPE—ARE BURNED SOMETHIN' FIERCE.
MY EYES HURT SO BAD I CAN'T OPEN 'EM! I DIDN'T EVEN GET A CHANCE TO SEE WHAT THE ENEMY LOOKS LIKE!
AND TO TOP IT OFF...
HIM!!
HE'S GONNA BUMP INTO THE OTHER ONE! AND WHEN THAT HAPPENS—HE'LL BE **HISTORY**.

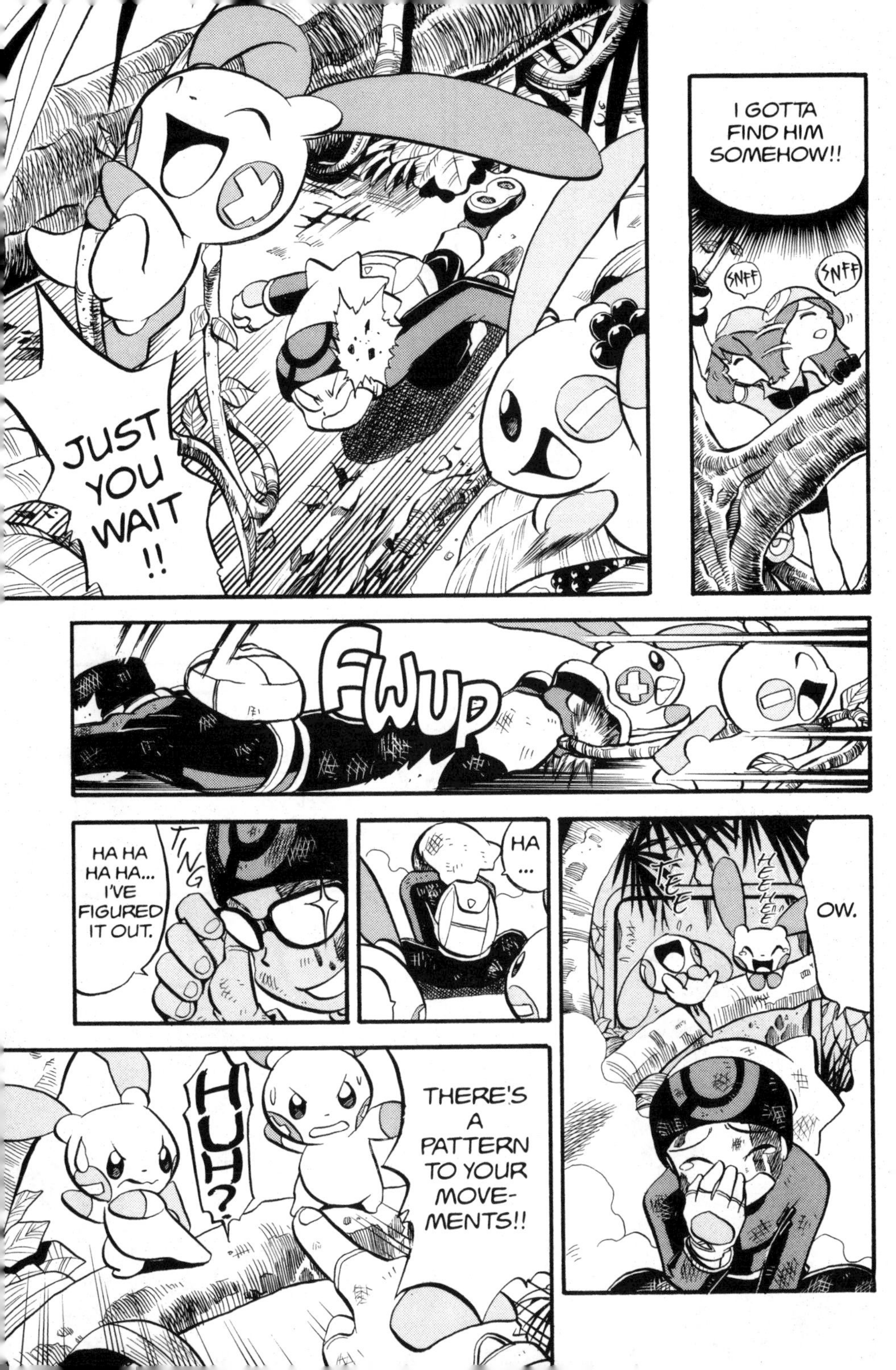
I GOTTA FIND HIM SOMEHOW!!
SNFF
SNFF
JUST YOU WAIT!!
FWUP
OW.
HEEHEEHEE
TEE
HA ...
HA HA HA HA... I'VE FIGURED IT OUT.
TING
THERE'S A PATTERN TO YOUR MOVE-MENTS!!
HUH?

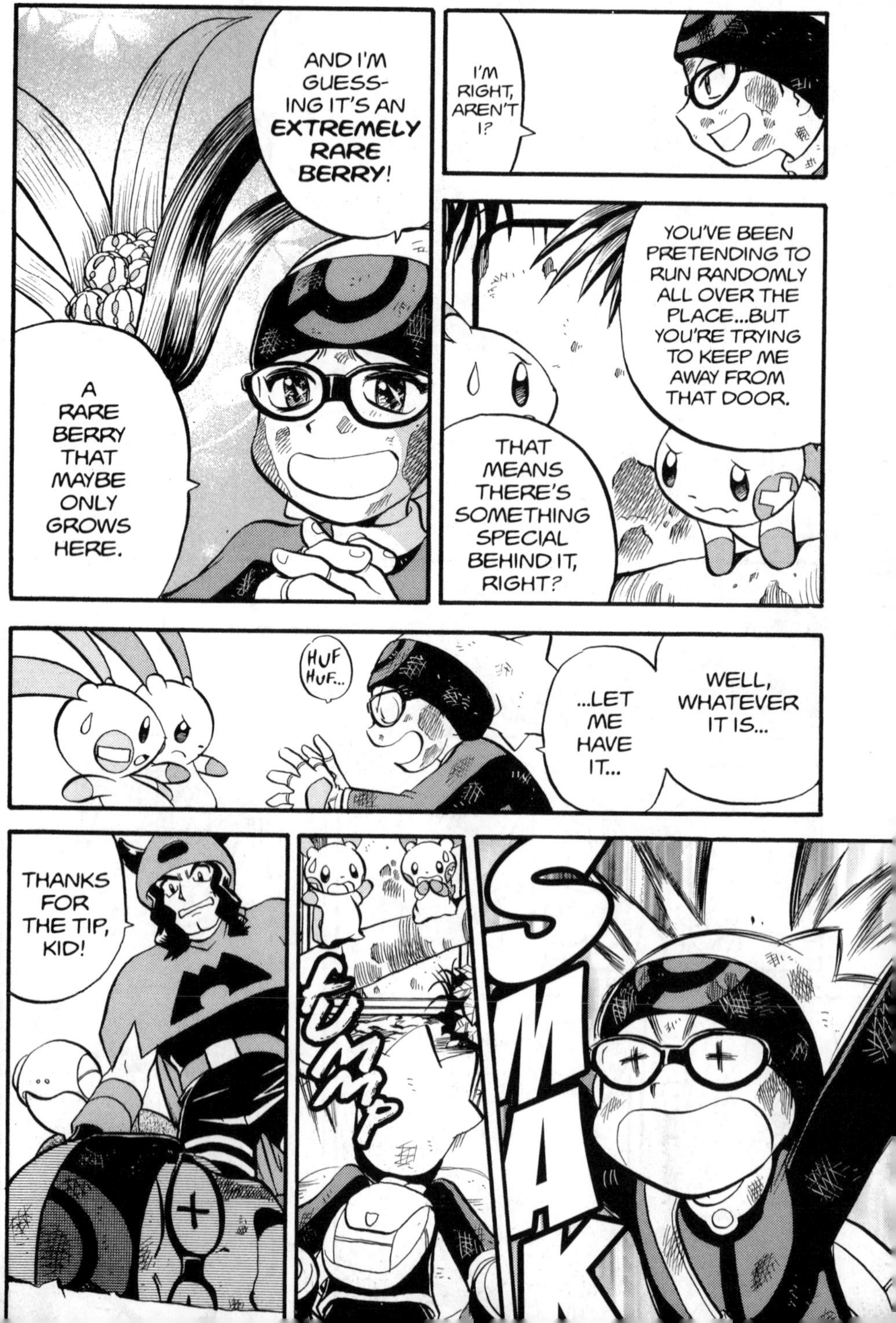
I'M RIGHT, AREN'T I?
YOU'VE BEEN PRETENDING TO RUN RANDOMLY ALL OVER THE PLACE...BUT YOU'RE TRYING TO KEEP ME AWAY FROM THAT DOOR.
THAT MEANS THERE'S SOMETHING SPECIAL BEHIND IT, RIGHT?
AND I'M GUESS-ING IT'S AN **EXTREMELY RARE BERRY**!
A RARE BERRY THAT MAYBE ONLY GROWS HERE.
WELL, WHATEVER IT IS...
...LET ME HAVE IT...
HUF HUF...
SMAK
FUMP
THANKS FOR THE TIP, KID!

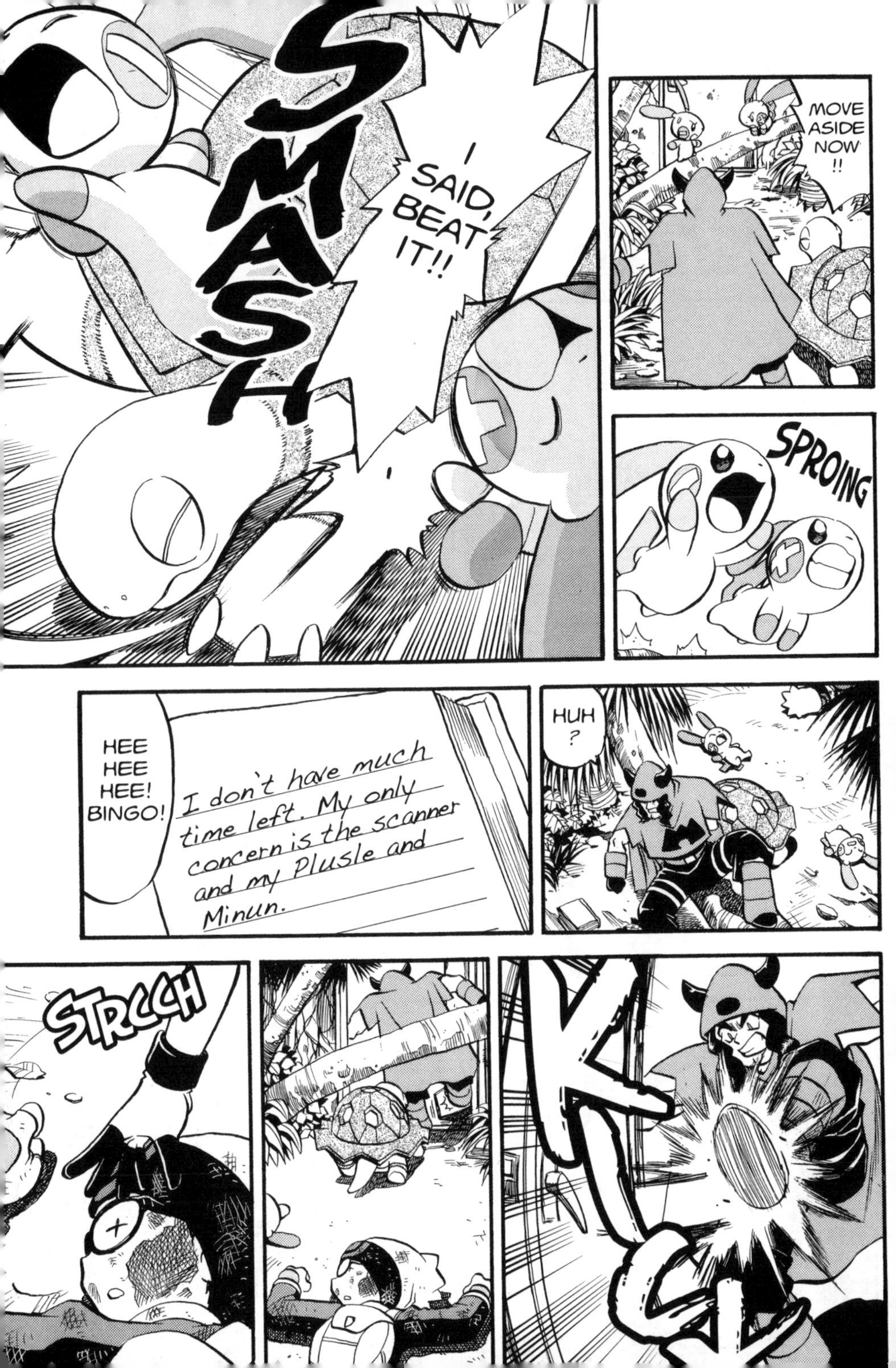
MOVE ASIDE NOW!!
SPROING
SMASH
I SAID, BEAT IT!!
HUH?
HEE HEE HEE! BINGO!
I don't have much time left. My only concern is the scanner and my Plusle and Minun.
STRCCH

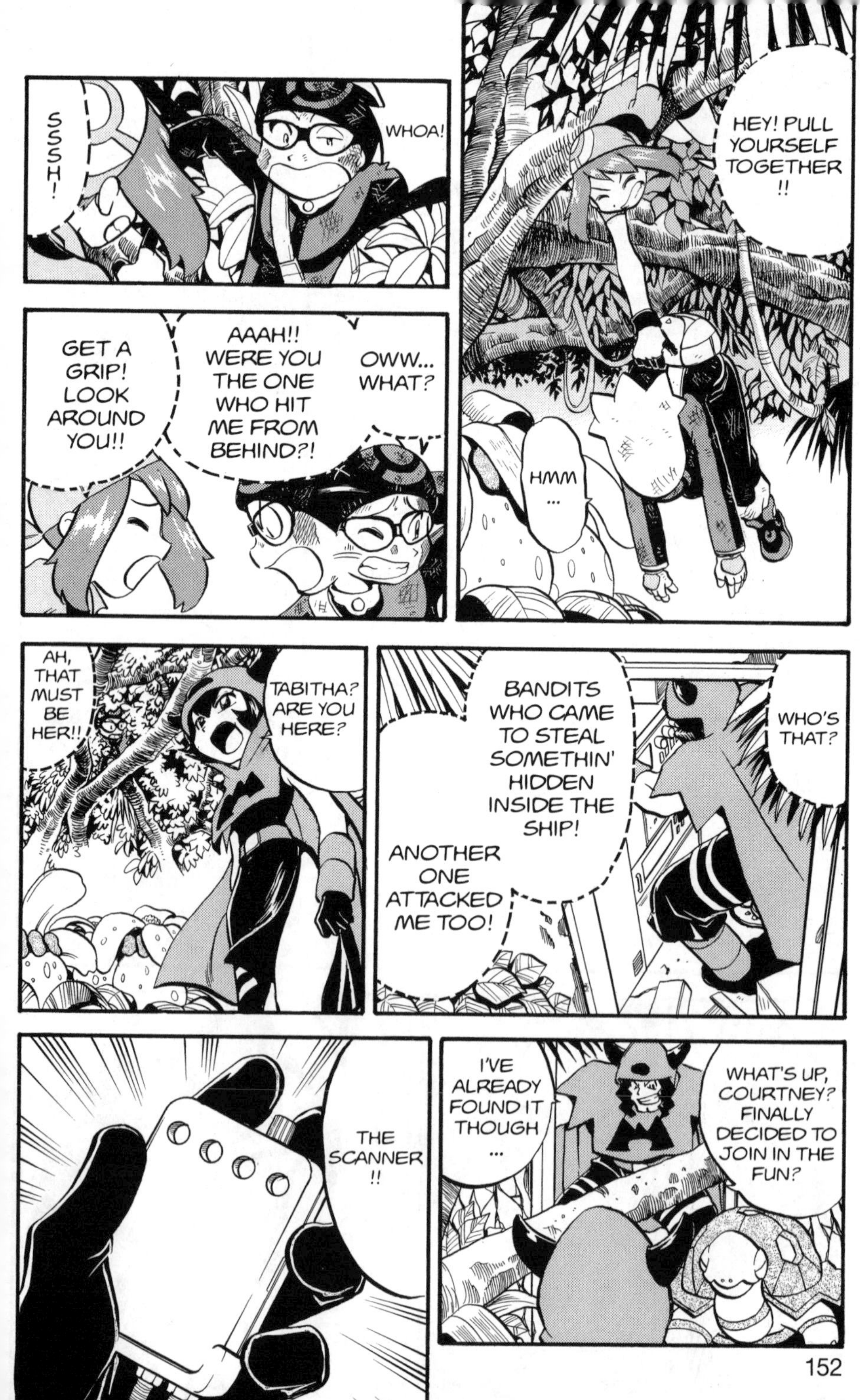
HEY! PULL YOURSELF TOGETHER!!
HMM...
WHOA!
SSSH!
OWW... WHAT?
AAAH!! WERE YOU THE ONE WHO HIT ME FROM BEHIND?!
GET A GRIP! LOOK AROUND YOU!!
WHO'S THAT?
BANDITS WHO CAME TO STEAL SOMETHIN' HIDDEN INSIDE THE SHIP!
ANOTHER ONE ATTACKED ME TOO!
TABITHA? ARE YOU HERE?
AH, THAT MUST BE HER!!
WHAT'S UP, COURTNEY? FINALLY DECIDED TO JOIN IN THE FUN?
I'VE ALREADY FOUND IT THOUGH...
THE SCANNER!!

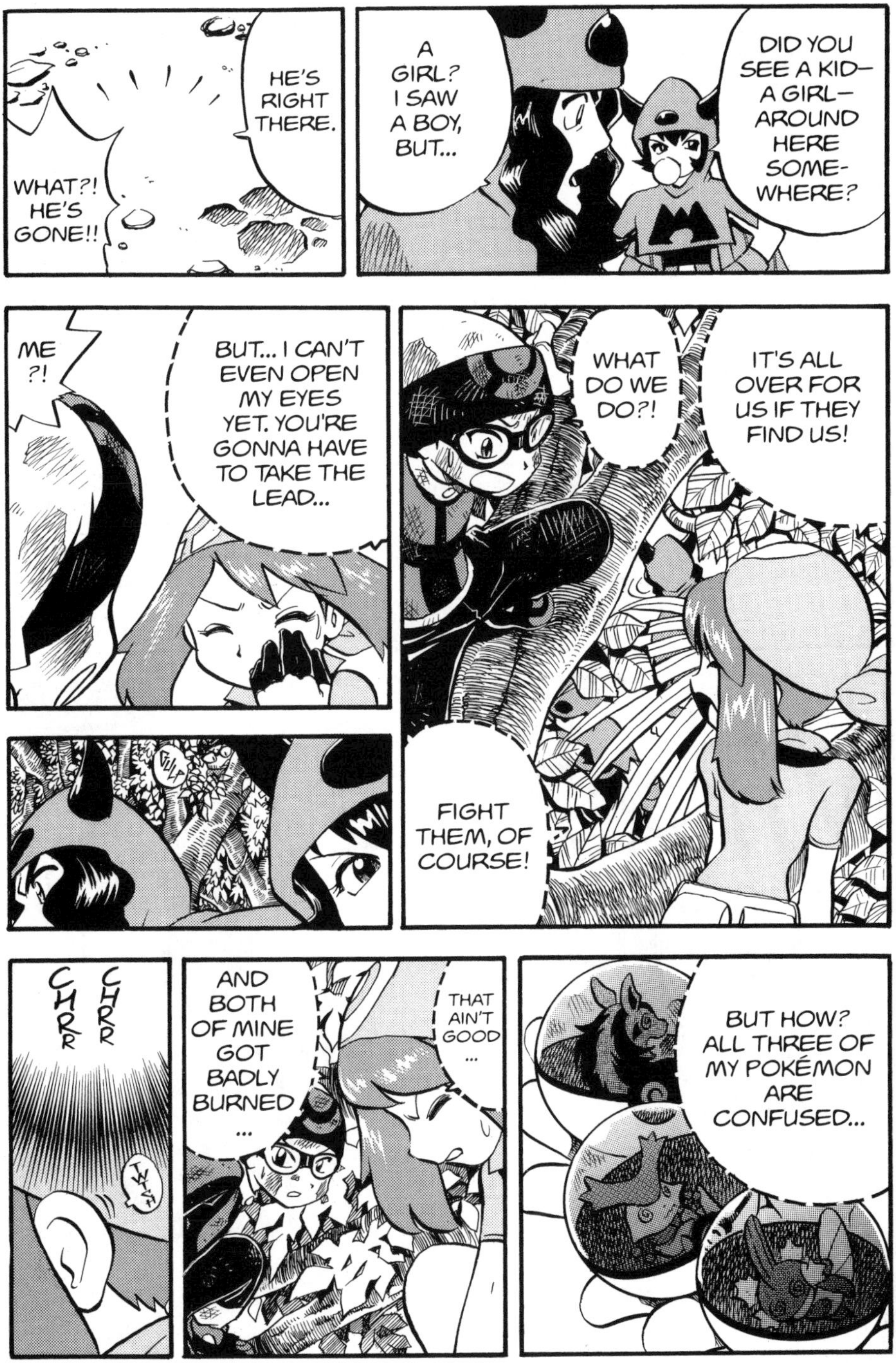
DID YOU SEE A KID— A GIRL— AROUND HERE SOME- WHERE?
A GIRL? I SAW A BOY, BUT...
HE'S RIGHT THERE.
WHAT?! HE'S GONE!!
IT'S ALL OVER FOR US IF THEY FIND US!
WHAT DO WE DO?!
FIGHT THEM, OF COURSE!
BUT... I CAN'T EVEN OPEN MY EYES YET. YOU'RE GONNA HAVE TO TAKE THE LEAD...
ME ?!
BUT HOW? ALL THREE OF MY POKÉMON ARE CONFUSED...
THAT AIN'T GOOD ...
AND BOTH OF MINE GOT BADLY BURNED ...
CHRR CHRR

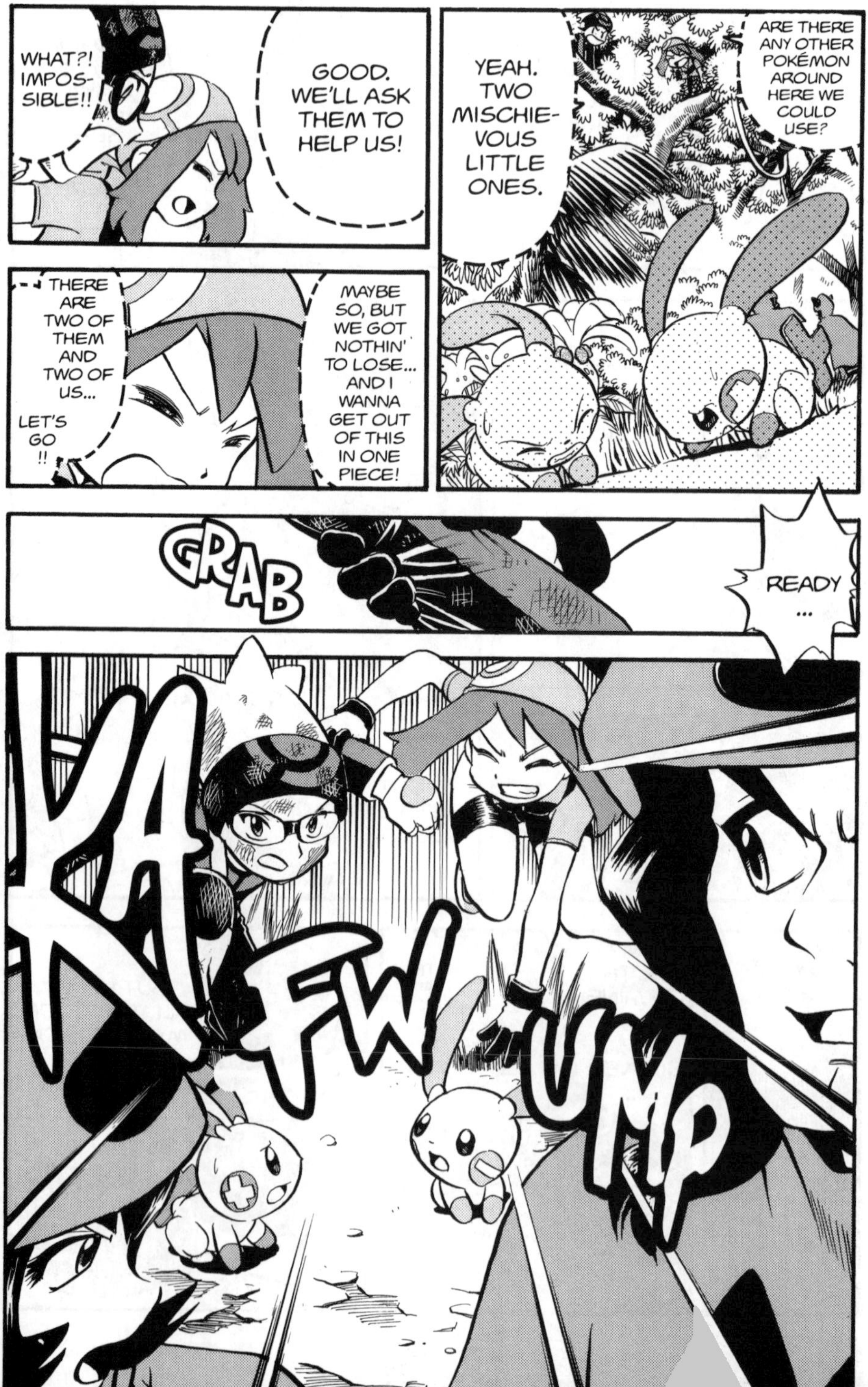
ARE THERE ANY OTHER POKÉMON AROUND HERE WE COULD USE?
YEAH. TWO MISCHIE-VOUS LITTLE ONES.
GOOD. WE'LL ASK THEM TO HELP US!
WHAT?! IMPOS-SIBLE!!
MAYBE SO, BUT WE GOT NOTHIN' TO LOSE... AND I WANNA GET OUT OF THIS IN ONE PIECE!
THERE ARE TWO OF THEM AND TWO OF US...
LET'S GO!!
READY...
GRAB
KA FWUMP

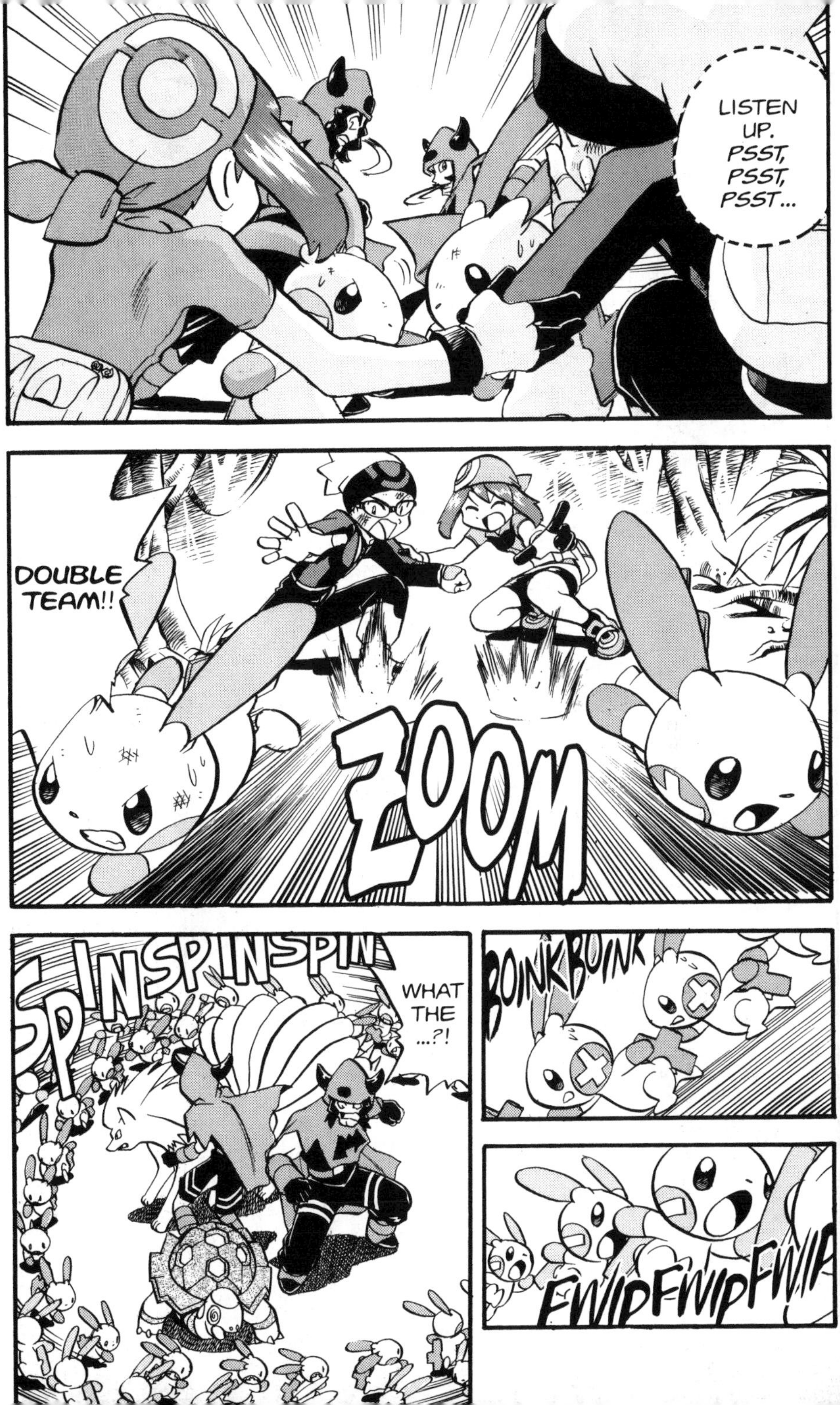
LISTEN UP. PSST, PSST, PSST...
DOUBLE TEAM!!
ZOOM
BOINKBOINK
FWIPFWIPFWIP
SPINSPINSPIN
WHAT THE ...?!

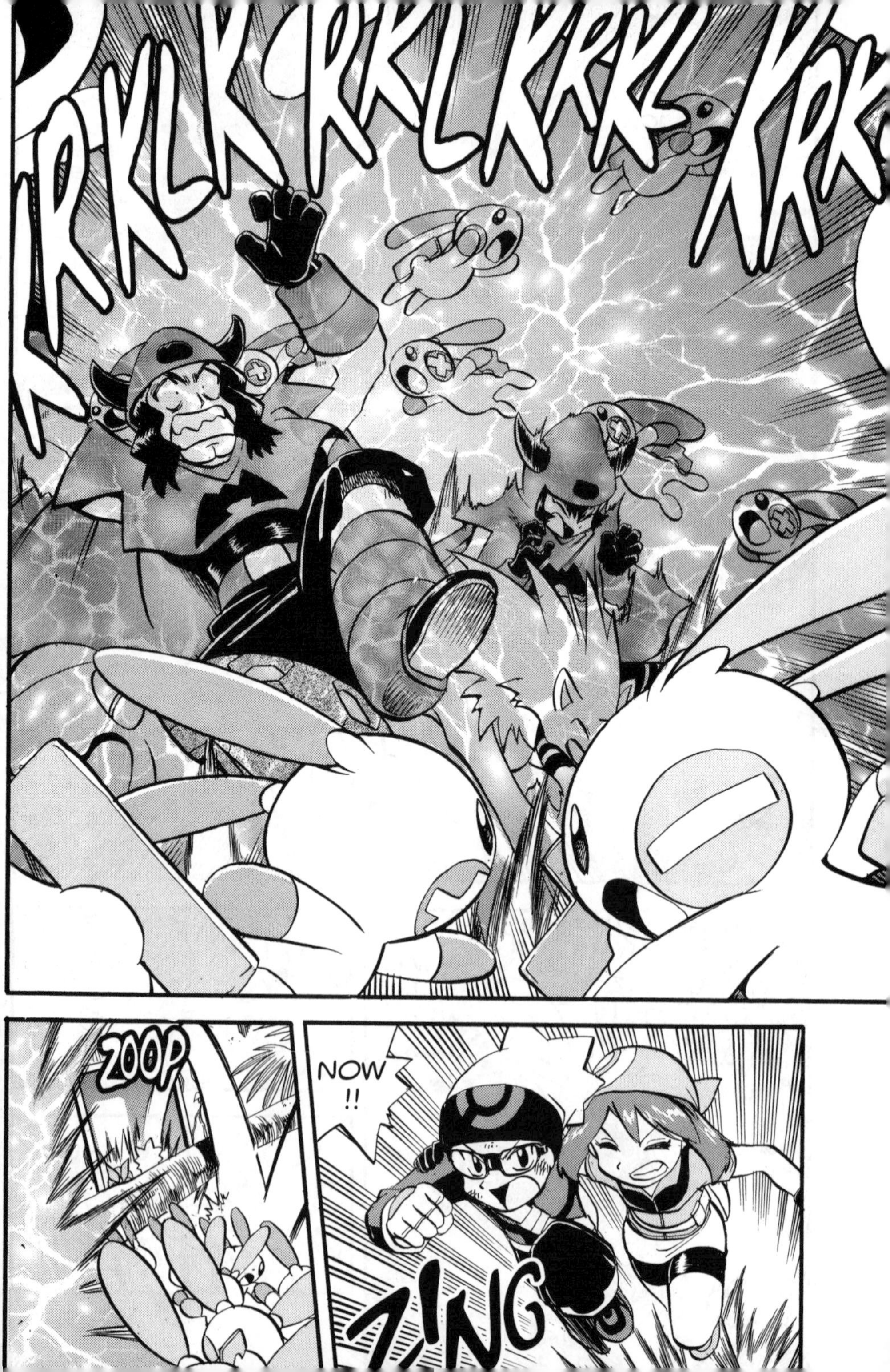
RKLK CRKKL KRKKL KRK
NOW!!
ZING
ZOOP

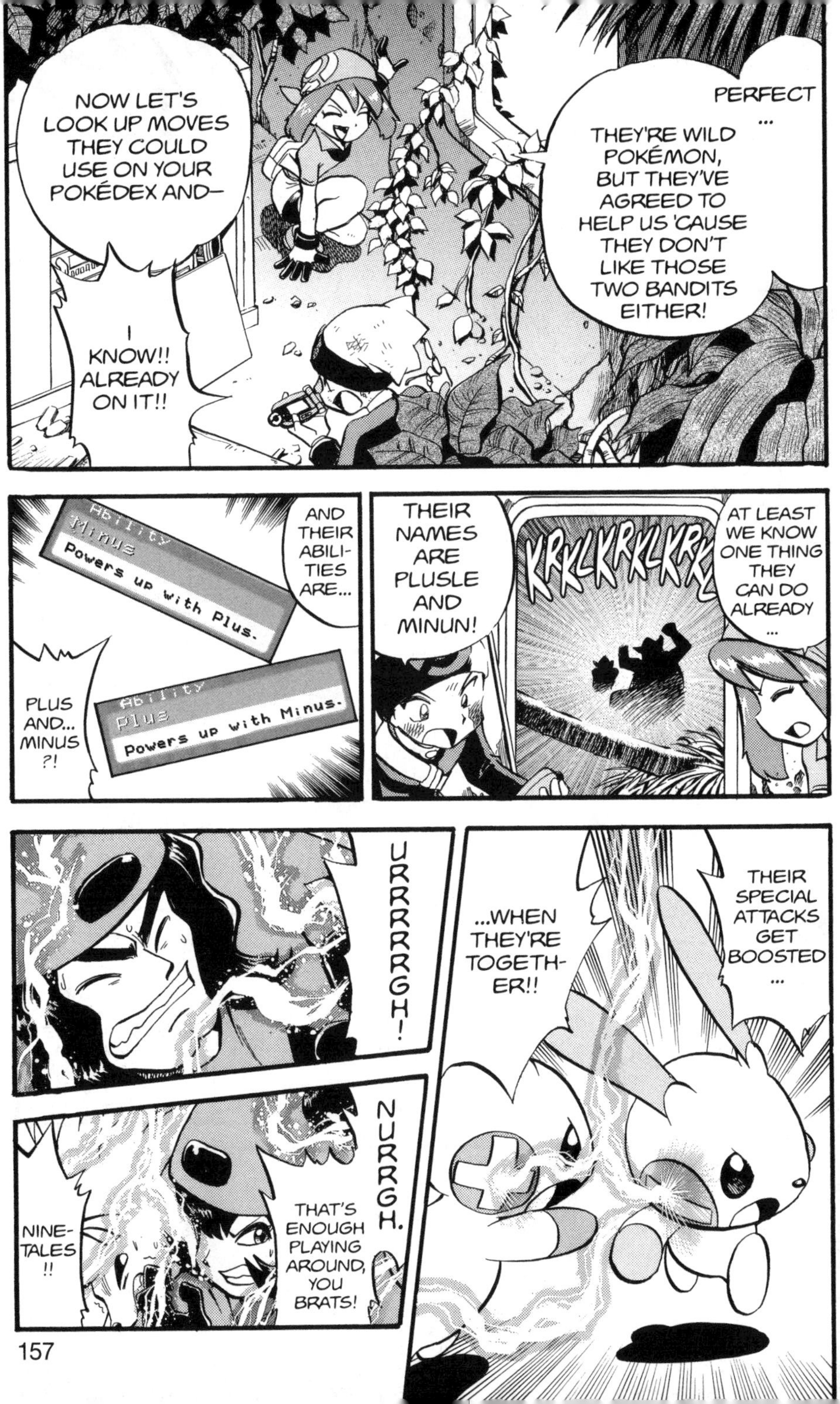
PERFECT...
THEY'RE WILD POKÉMON, BUT THEY'VE AGREED TO HELP US 'CAUSE THEY DON'T LIKE THOSE TWO BANDITS EITHER!
NOW LET'S LOOK UP MOVES THEY COULD USE ON YOUR POKÉDEX AND—
I KNOW!! ALREADY ON IT!!
AT LEAST WE KNOW ONE THING THEY CAN DO ALREADY...
KRKLKRKLKRK
THEIR NAMES ARE PLUSLE AND MINUN!
AND THEIR ABILI-TIES ARE...
Ability
Minus
Powers up with Plus.
Ability
Plus
Powers up with Minus.
PLUS AND... MINUS?!
THEIR SPECIAL ATTACKS GET BOOSTED...
...WHEN THEY'RE TOGETH-ER!!
URRRRRGH!
NURRGH.
THAT'S ENOUGH PLAYING AROUND, YOU BRATS!
NINE-TALES!!

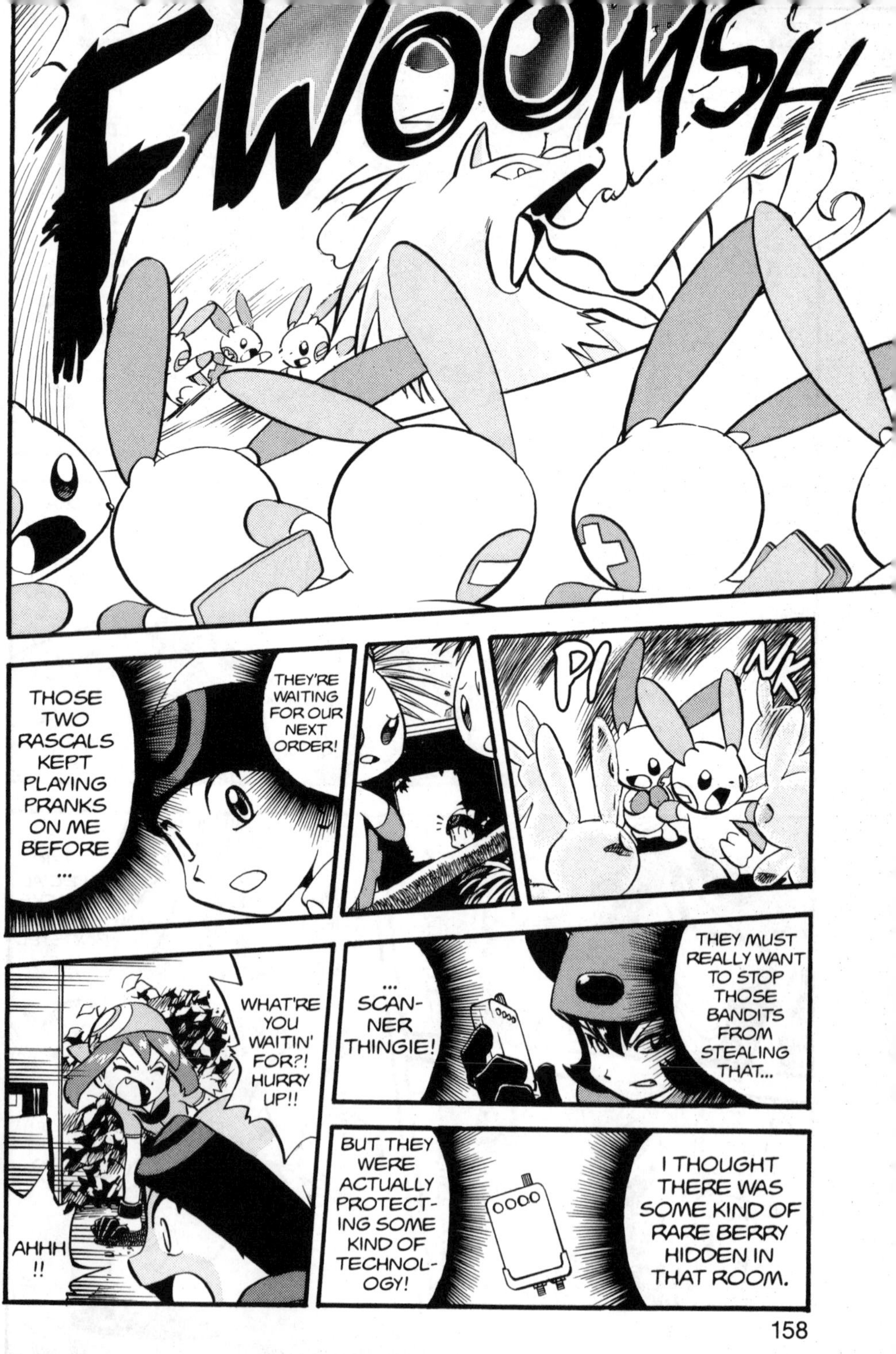
FWOOMSH
PINK
THEY'RE WAITING FOR OUR NEXT ORDER!
THOSE TWO RASCALS KEPT PLAYING PRANKS ON ME BEFORE ...
THEY MUST REALLY WANT TO STOP THOSE BANDITS FROM STEALING THAT...
... SCANNER THINGIE!
I THOUGHT THERE WAS SOME KIND OF RARE BERRY HIDDEN IN THAT ROOM.
BUT THEY WERE ACTUALLY PROTECTING SOME KIND OF TECHNOLOGY!
WHAT'RE YOU WAITIN' FOR?! HURRY UP!!
AHHH!!

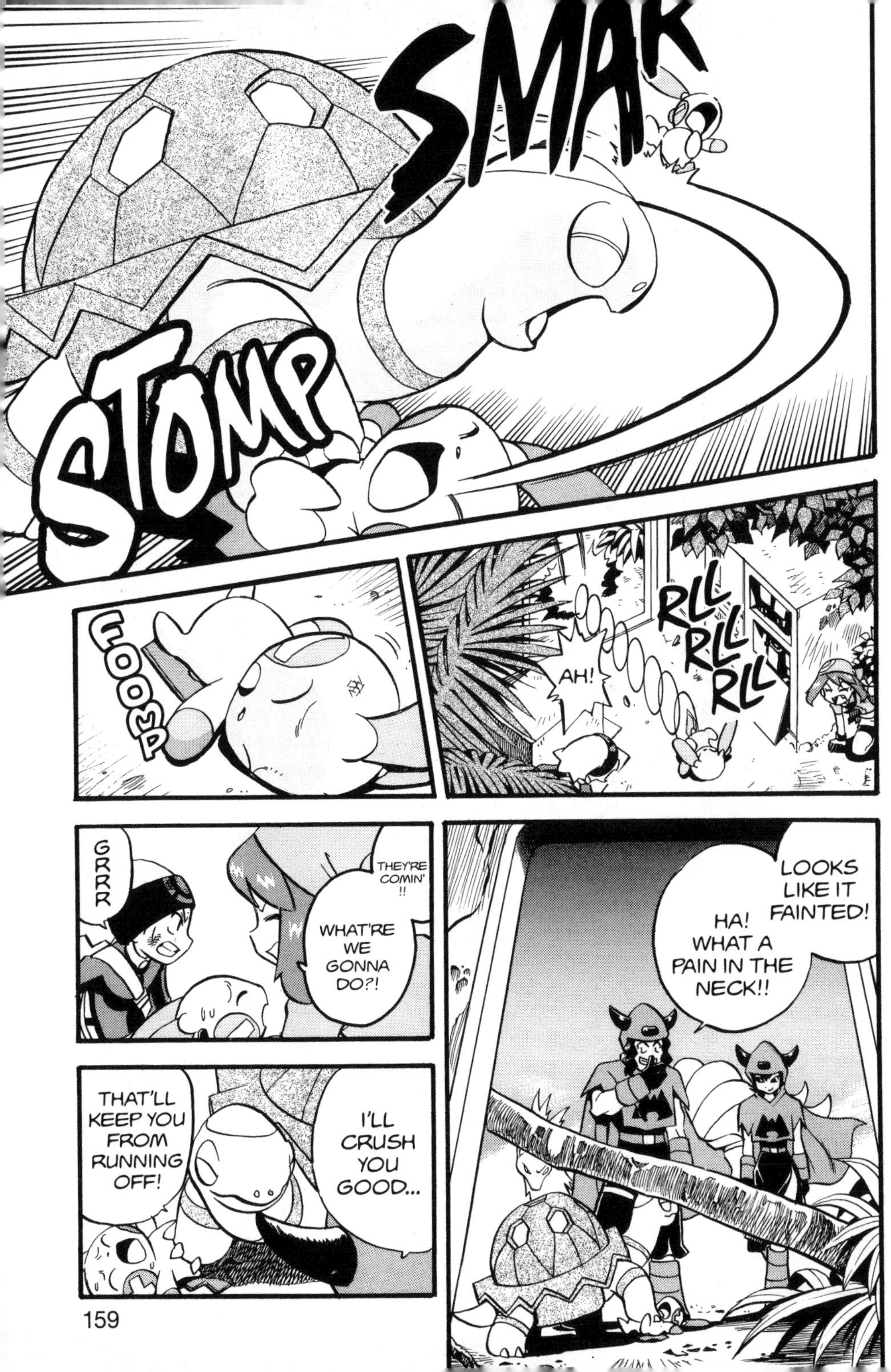
SMAK
STOMP
RLL RLL RLL
AH!
FOOMP
LOOKS LIKE IT FAINTED!
HA! WHAT A PAIN IN THE NECK!!
THEY'RE COMIN'!!
WHAT'RE WE GONNA DO?!
GRRR
I'LL CRUSH YOU GOOD...
THAT'LL KEEP YOU FROM RUNNING OFF!

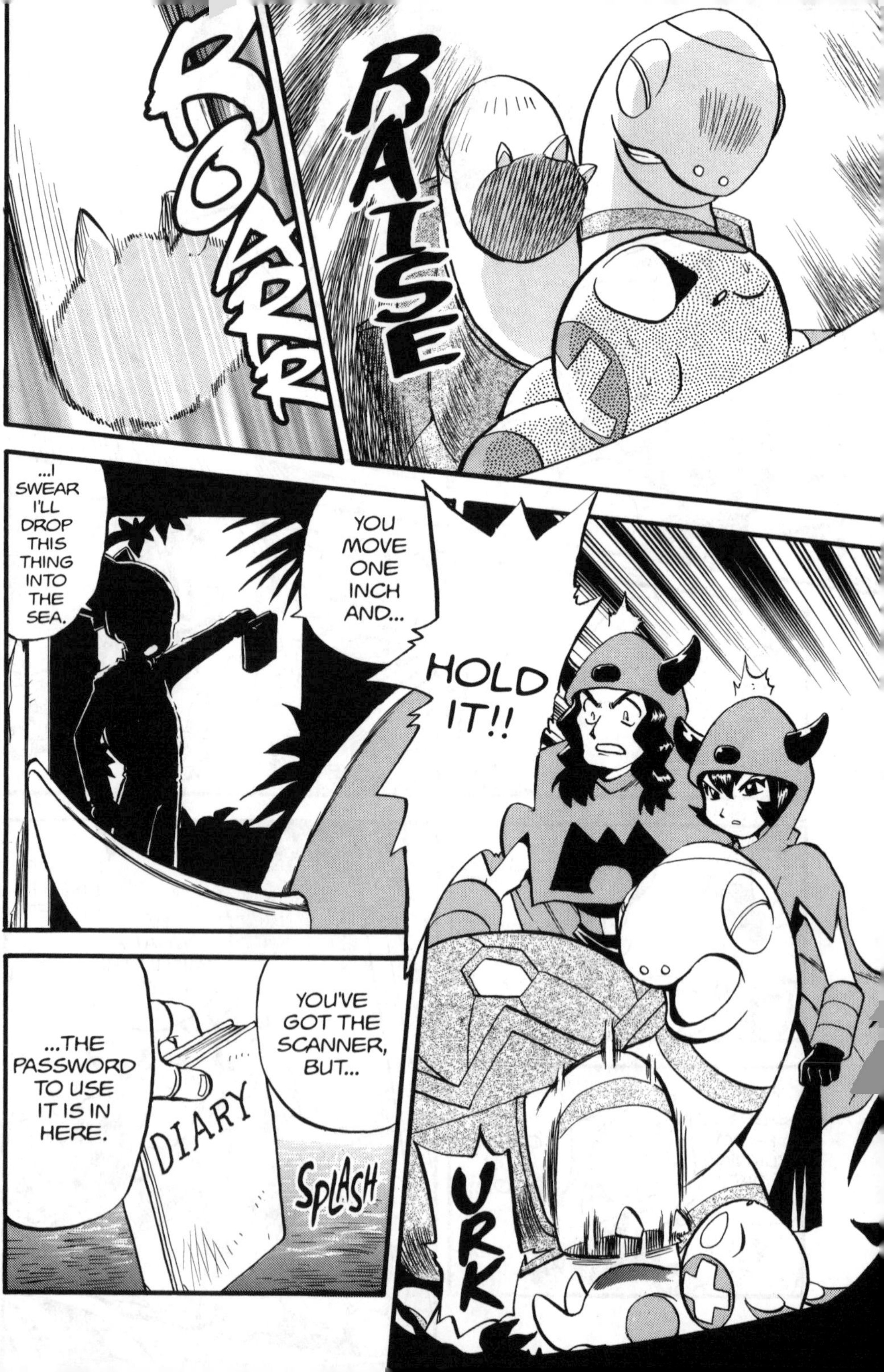
RAISE
ROARR
HOLD IT!!
URK
YOU MOVE ONE INCH AND...
...I SWEAR I'LL DROP THIS THING INTO THE SEA.
YOU'VE GOT THE SCANNER, BUT...
...THE PASSWORD TO USE IT IS IN HERE.
DIARY
SPLASH

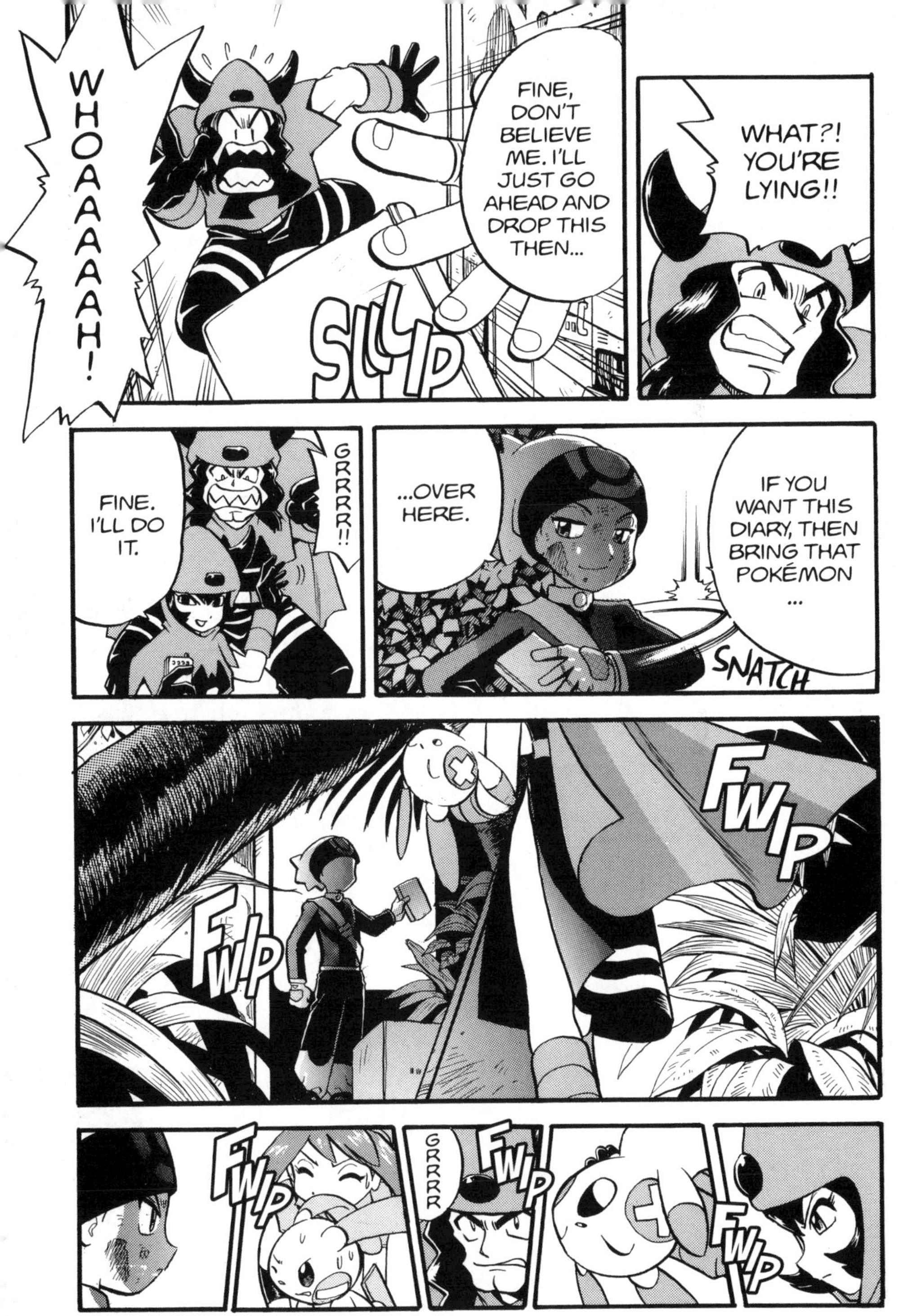
WHAT?! YOU'RE LYING!!
FINE, DON'T BELIEVE ME. I'LL JUST GO AHEAD AND DROP THIS THEN...
SLLLIP
WHOAAAAAAAH!
IF YOU WANT THIS DIARY, THEN BRING THAT POKÉMON ...
SNATCH
...OVER HERE.
GRRRRR!!
FINE. I'LL DO IT.
FWIP
FWIP
FWIP
FWIP
GRRRR
FWIP

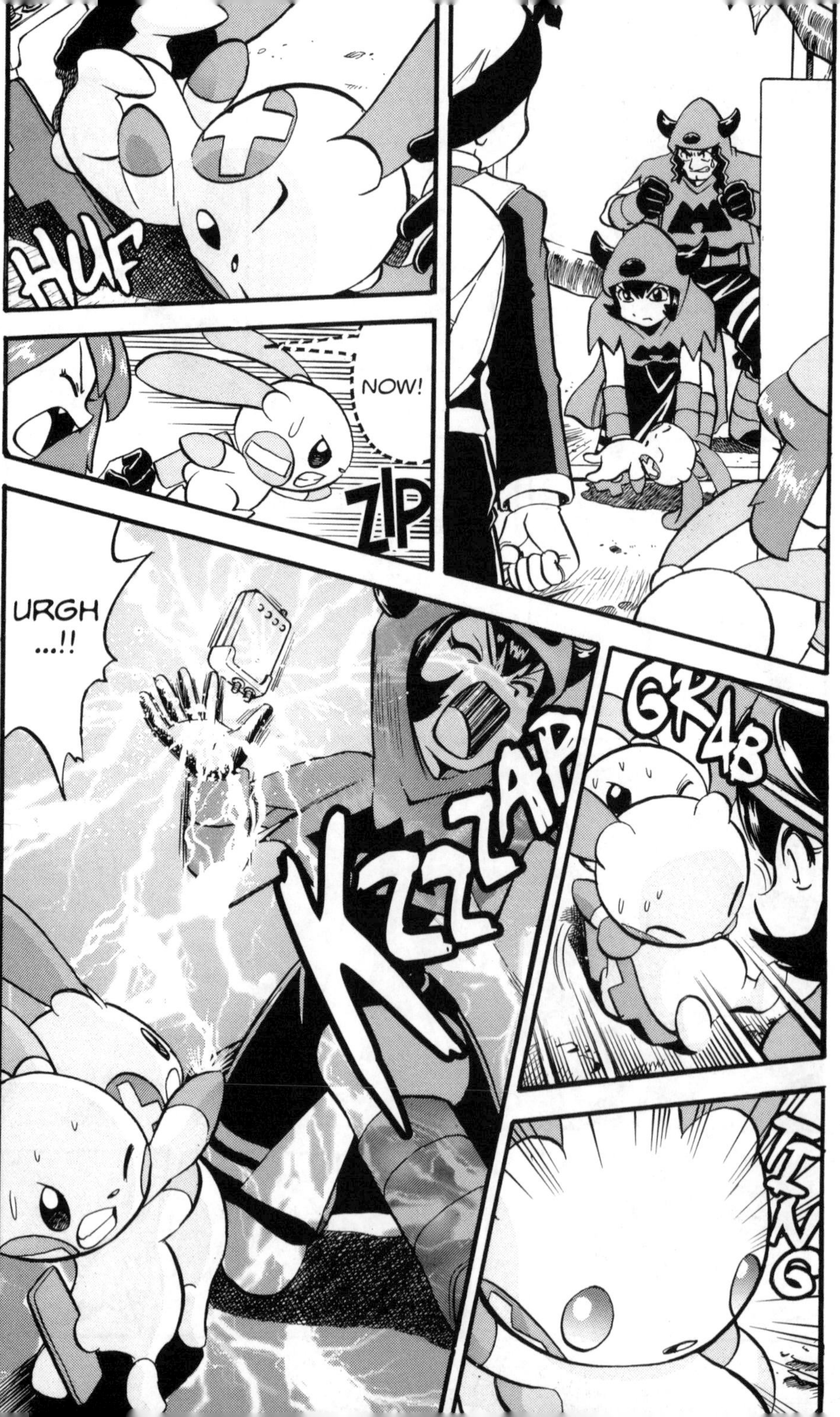

HUF
NOW!
ZIP
GRAB
TING
URGH ...!!
ZZZZAP

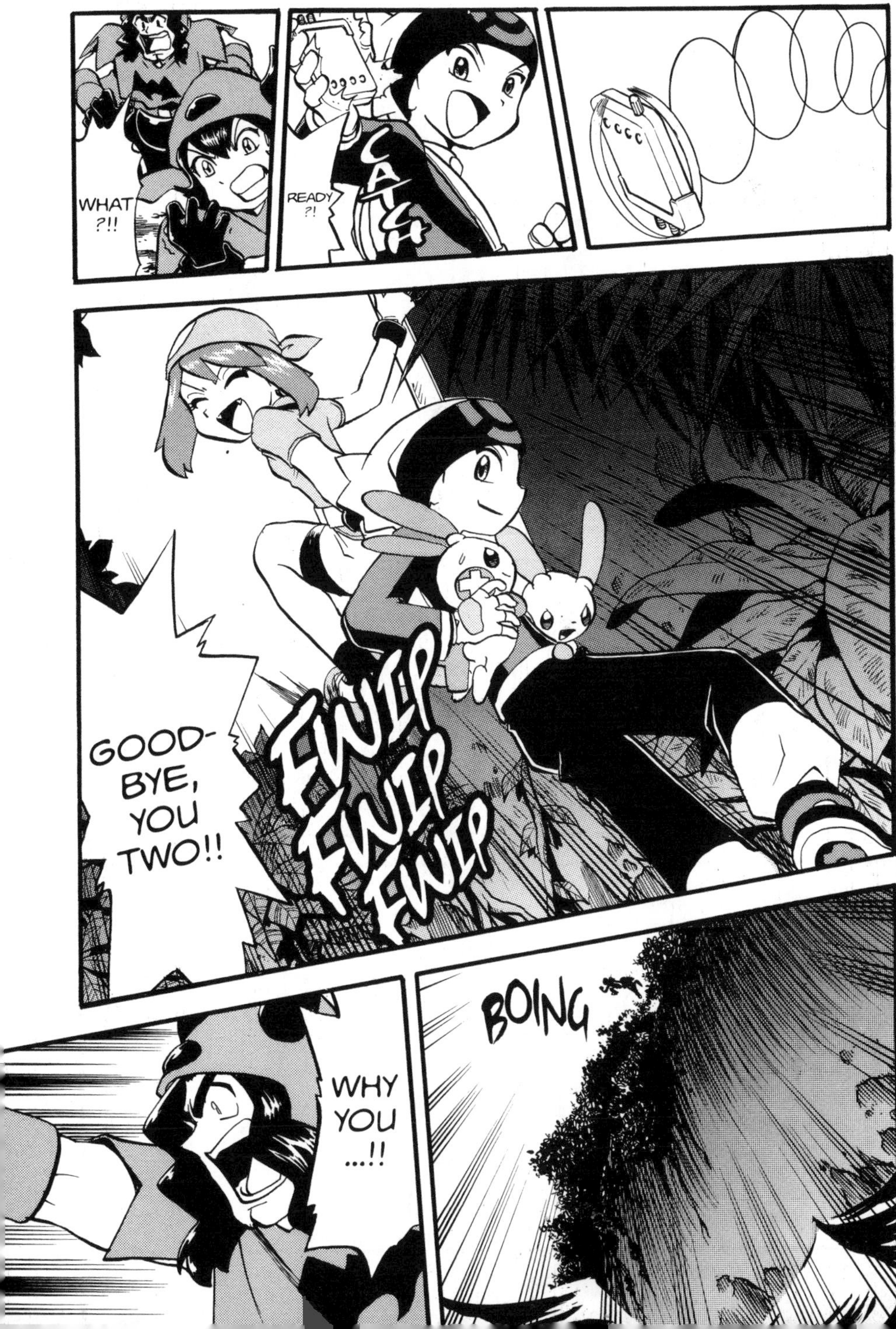
READY ?!
CATCH
WHAT ?!!
FWIP FWIP FWIP
GOOD-BYE, YOU TWO!!
BOING
WHY YOU ...!!

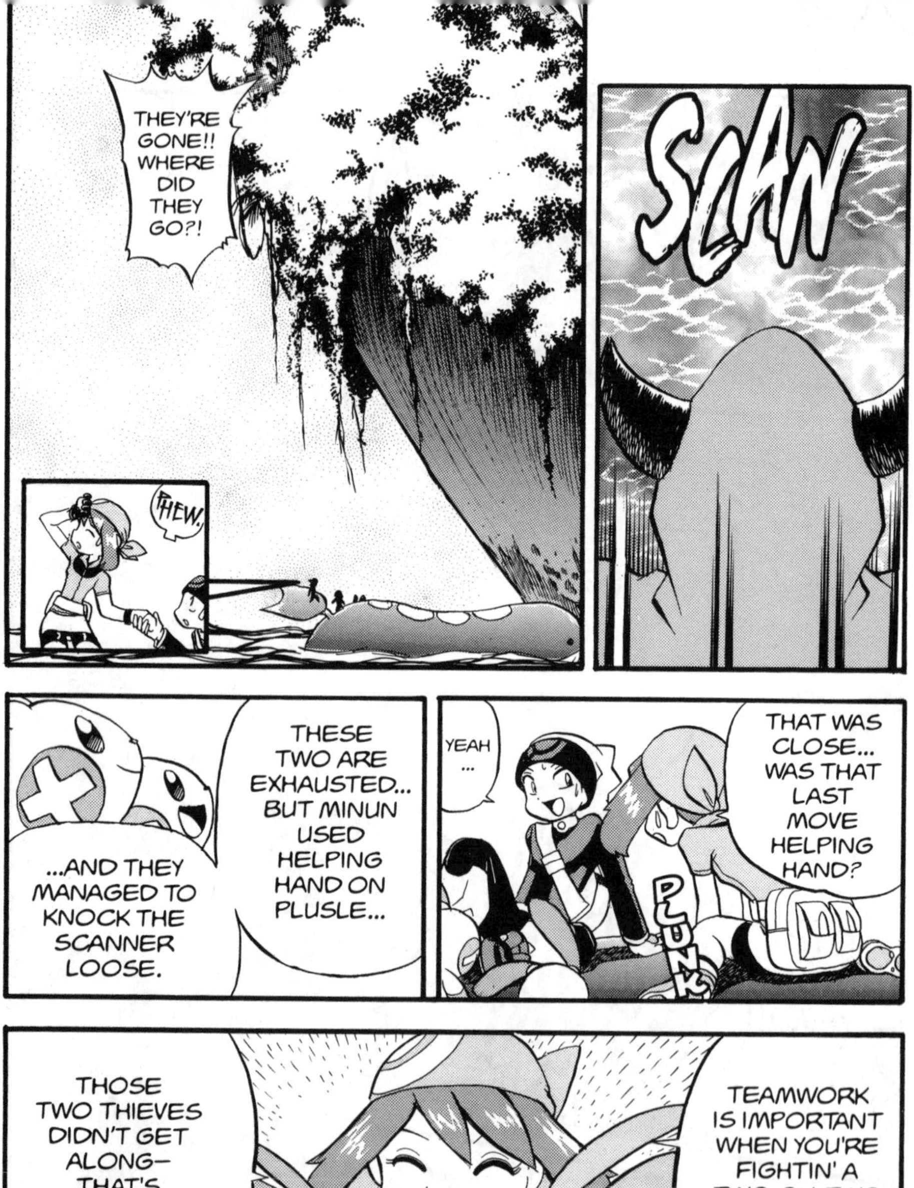
SCAN
THEY'RE GONE!! WHERE DID THEY GO?!
PHEW.
THAT WAS CLOSE... WAS THAT LAST MOVE HELPING HAND?
YEAH ...
PLUNK
THESE TWO ARE EXHAUSTED... BUT MINUN USED HELPING HAND ON PLUSLE...
...AND THEY MANAGED TO KNOCK THE SCANNER LOOSE.
TEAMWORK IS IMPORTANT WHEN YOU'RE FIGHTIN' A TWO-ON-TWO BATTLE!! WE HELPED EACH OTHER OUT!!
THOSE TWO THIEVES DIDN'T GET ALONG— THAT'S WHERE WE HAD THE ADVANTAGE!!

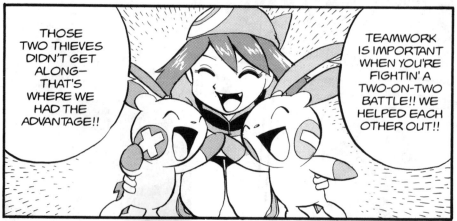

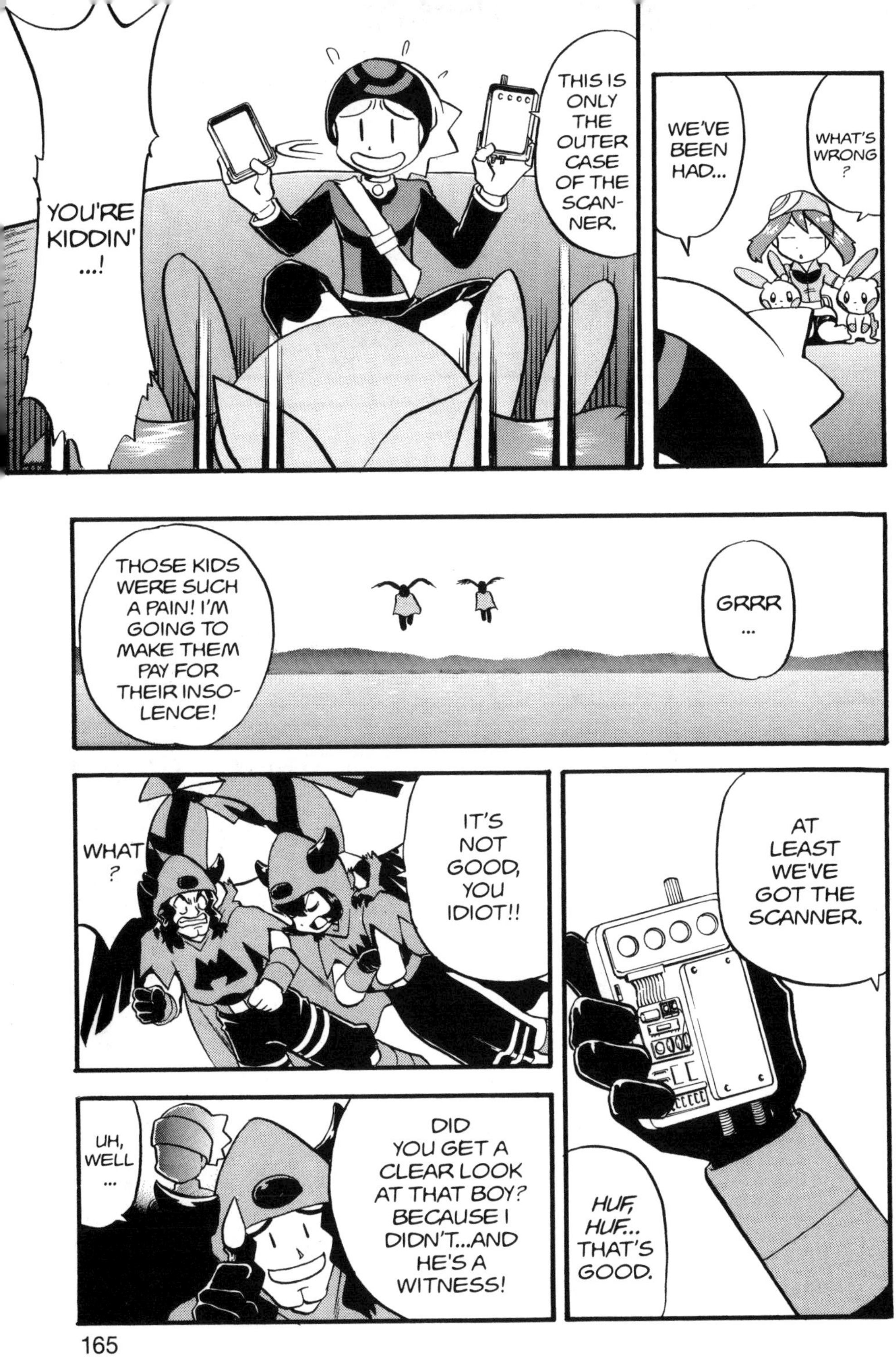
WHAT'S WRONG?
WE'VE BEEN HAD...
THIS IS ONLY THE OUTER CASE OF THE SCAN-NER.
YOU'RE KIDDIN'...!
GRRR...
THOSE KIDS WERE SUCH A PAIN! I'M GOING TO MAKE THEM PAY FOR THEIR INSO-LENCE!
AT LEAST WE'VE GOT THE SCANNER.
HUF, HUF... THAT'S GOOD.
IT'S NOT GOOD, YOU IDIOT!!
WHAT?
DID YOU GET A CLEAR LOOK AT THAT BOY? BECAUSE I DIDN'T...AND HE'S A WITNESS!
UH, WELL...

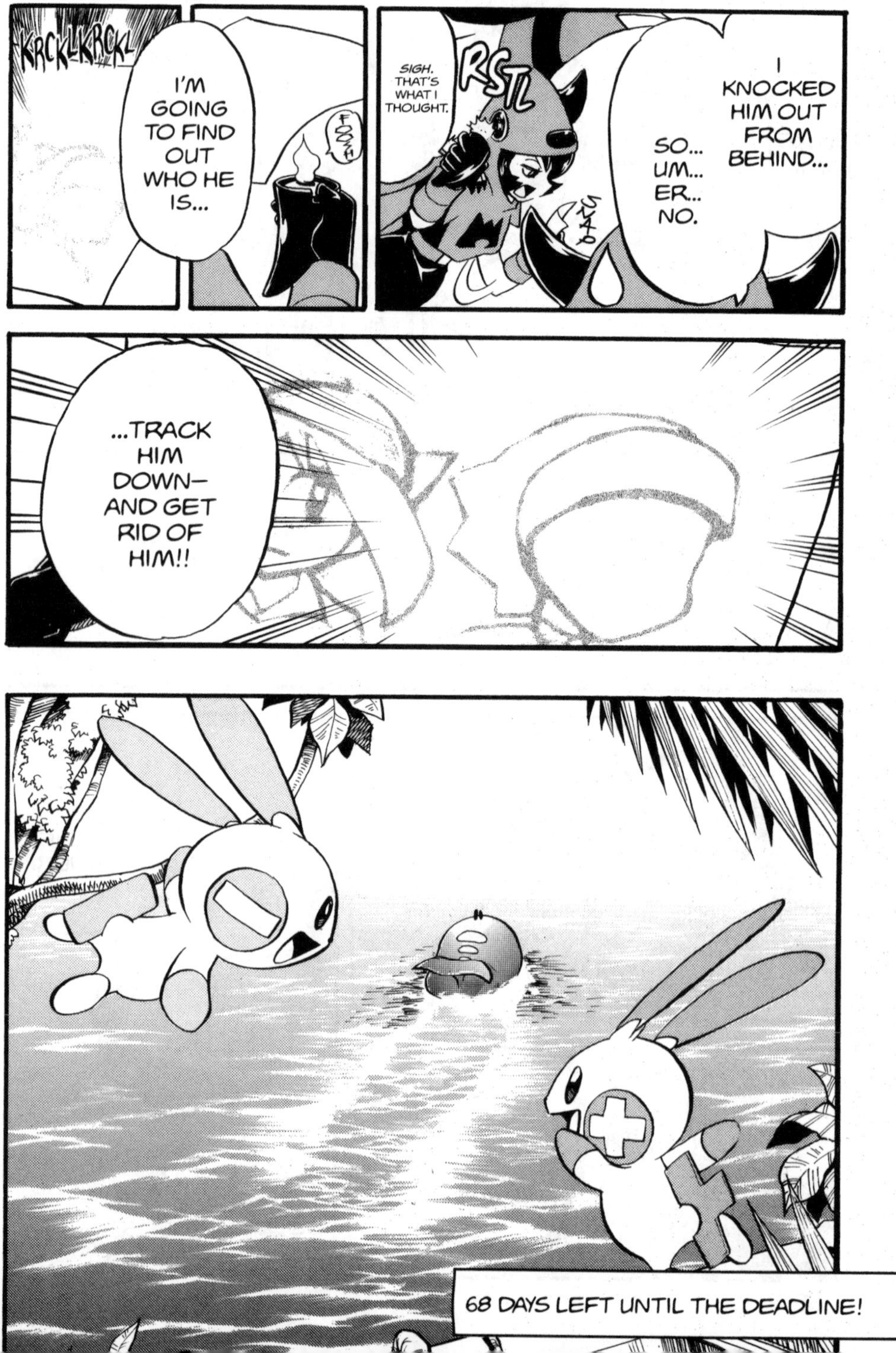
RSTL
I KNOCKED HIM OUT FROM BEHIND...
SO... UM... ER... NO.
SIGH. THAT'S WHAT I THOUGHT.
FOOSH
I'M GOING TO FIND OUT WHO HE IS...
KRCKLKRCKL
...TRACK HIM DOWN—AND GET RID OF HIM!!
68 DAYS LEFT UNTIL THE DEADLINE!

● Adventure 200 ●
Tripped Up by Torkoal

Pokémon Adventures Ruby & Sapphire The Fourth Chapter

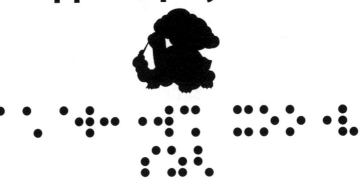

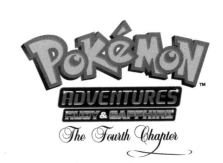

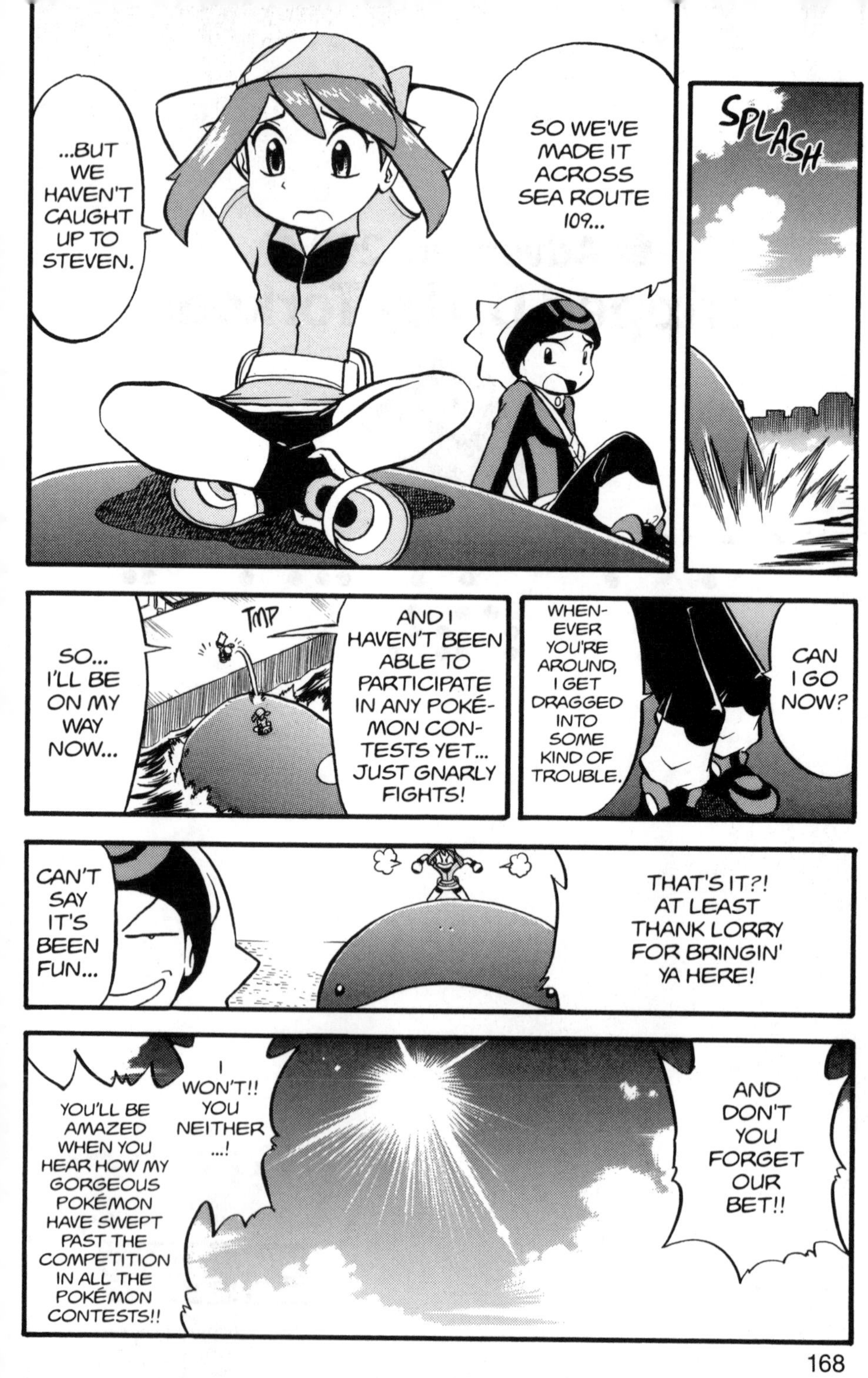
SPLASH
SO WE'VE MADE IT ACROSS SEA ROUTE 109...
...BUT WE HAVEN'T CAUGHT UP TO STEVEN.
CAN I GO NOW?
WHEN-EVER YOU'RE AROUND, I GET DRAGGED INTO SOME KIND OF TROUBLE.
AND I HAVEN'T BEEN ABLE TO PARTICIPATE IN ANY POKÉ-MON CON-TESTS YET... JUST GNARLY FIGHTS!
TMP
SO... I'LL BE ON MY WAY NOW...
THAT'S IT?! AT LEAST THANK LORRY FOR BRINGIN' YA HERE!
CAN'T SAY IT'S BEEN FUN...
AND DON'T YOU FORGET OUR BET!!
I WON'T!! YOU NEITHER ...!
YOU'LL BE AMAZED WHEN YOU HEAR HOW MY GORGEOUS POKÉMON HAVE SWEPT PAST THE COMPETITION IN ALL THE POKÉMON CONTESTS!!

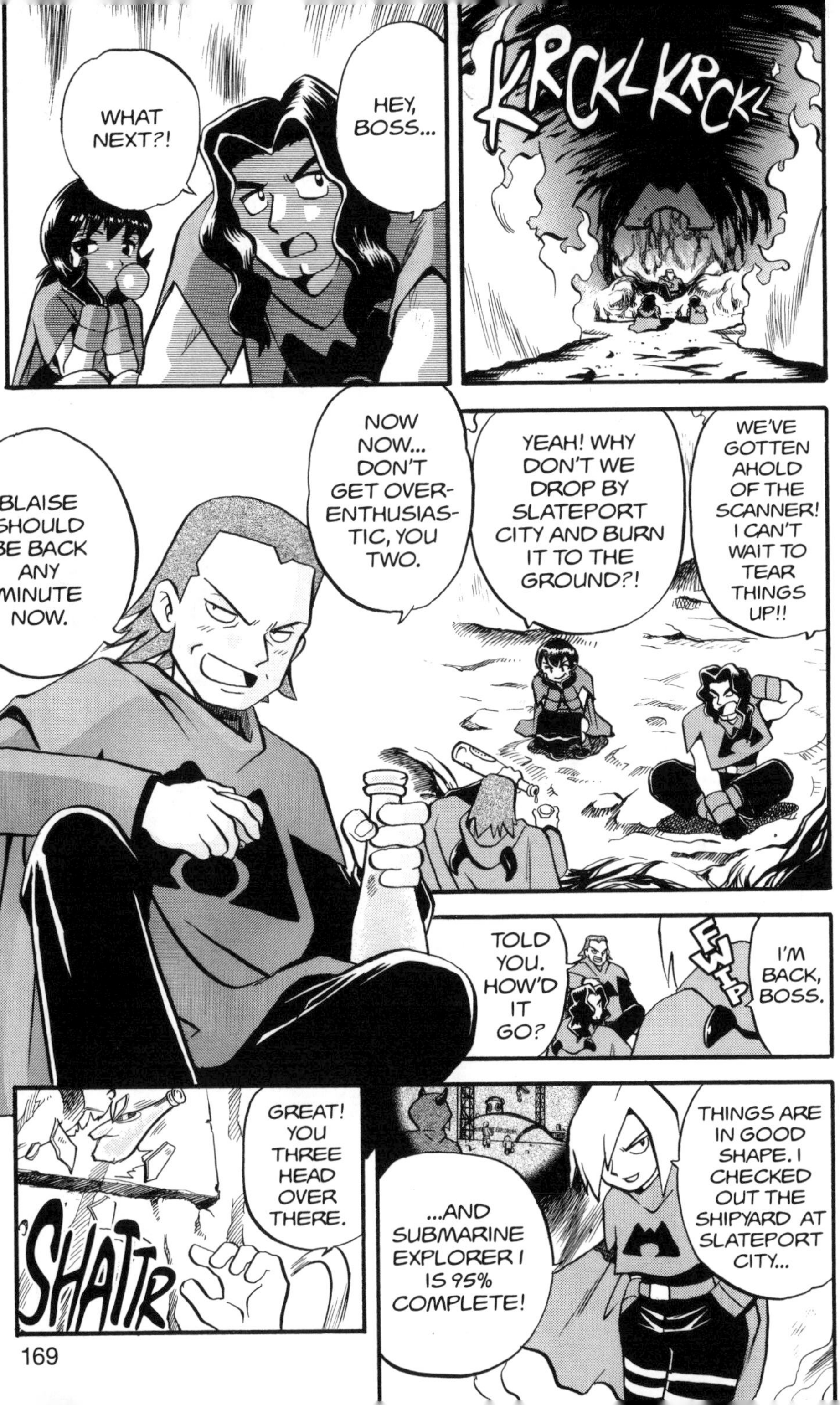
KRCKL KRCKL
HEY, BOSS...
WHAT NEXT?!
WE'VE GOTTEN AHOLD OF THE SCANNER! I CAN'T WAIT TO TEAR THINGS UP!!
YEAH! WHY DON'T WE DROP BY SLATEPORT CITY AND BURN IT TO THE GROUND?!
NOW NOW... DON'T GET OVER-ENTHUSIASTIC, YOU TWO.
BLAISE SHOULD BE BACK ANY MINUTE NOW.
I'M BACK, BOSS.
FWIP
TOLD YOU. HOW'D IT GO?
THINGS ARE IN GOOD SHAPE. I CHECKED OUT THE SHIPYARD AT SLATEPORT CITY...
...AND SUBMARINE EXPLORER I IS 95% COMPLETE!
GREAT! YOU THREE HEAD OVER THERE.
SHATTR

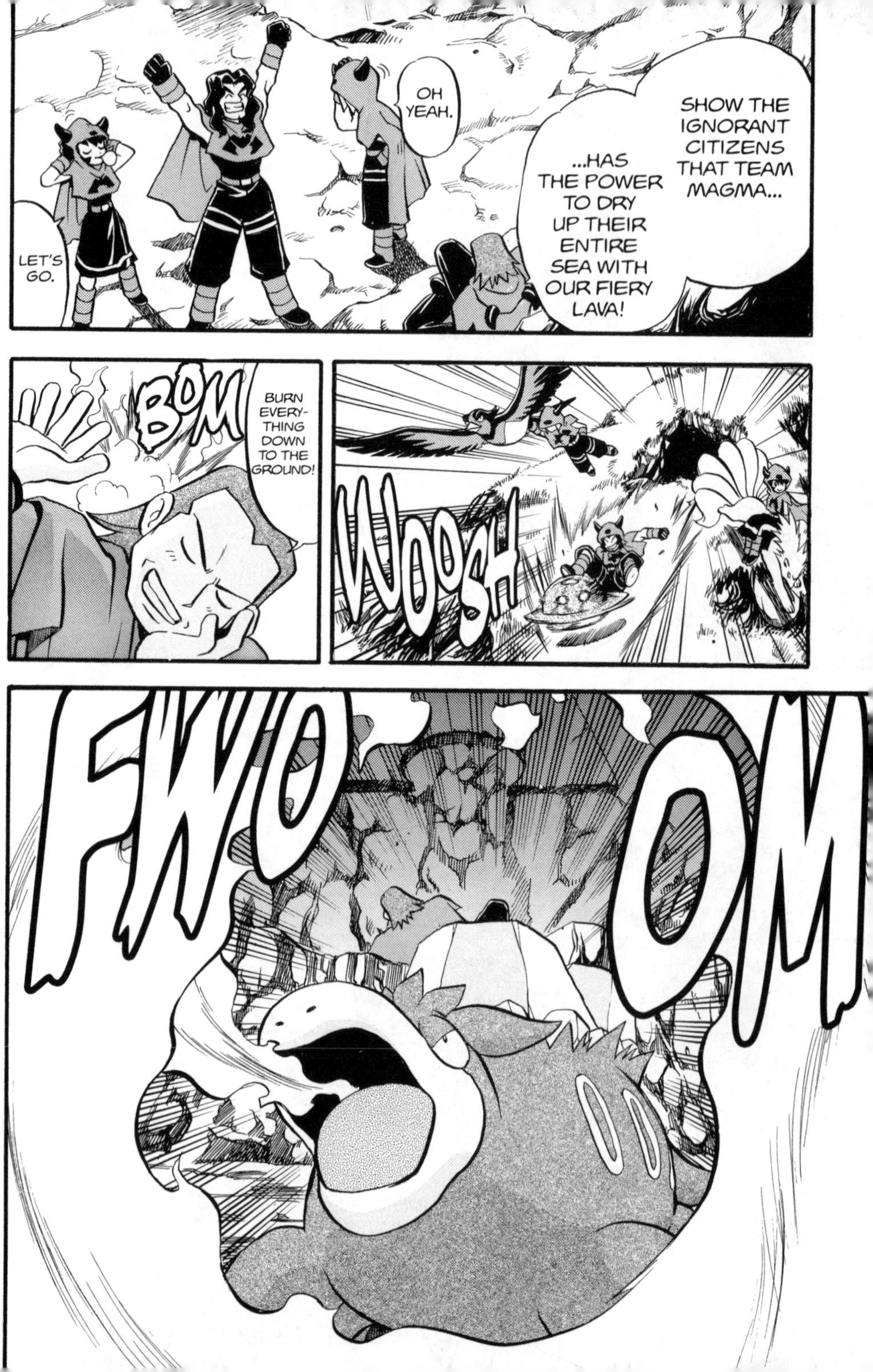
SHOW THE IGNORANT CITIZENS THAT TEAM MAGMA...
...HAS THE POWER TO DRY UP THEIR ENTIRE SEA WITH OUR FIERY LAVA!
OH YEAH.
LET'S GO.
WOOSH
BURN EVERY-THING DOWN TO THE GROUND!
BOM
FWOOM

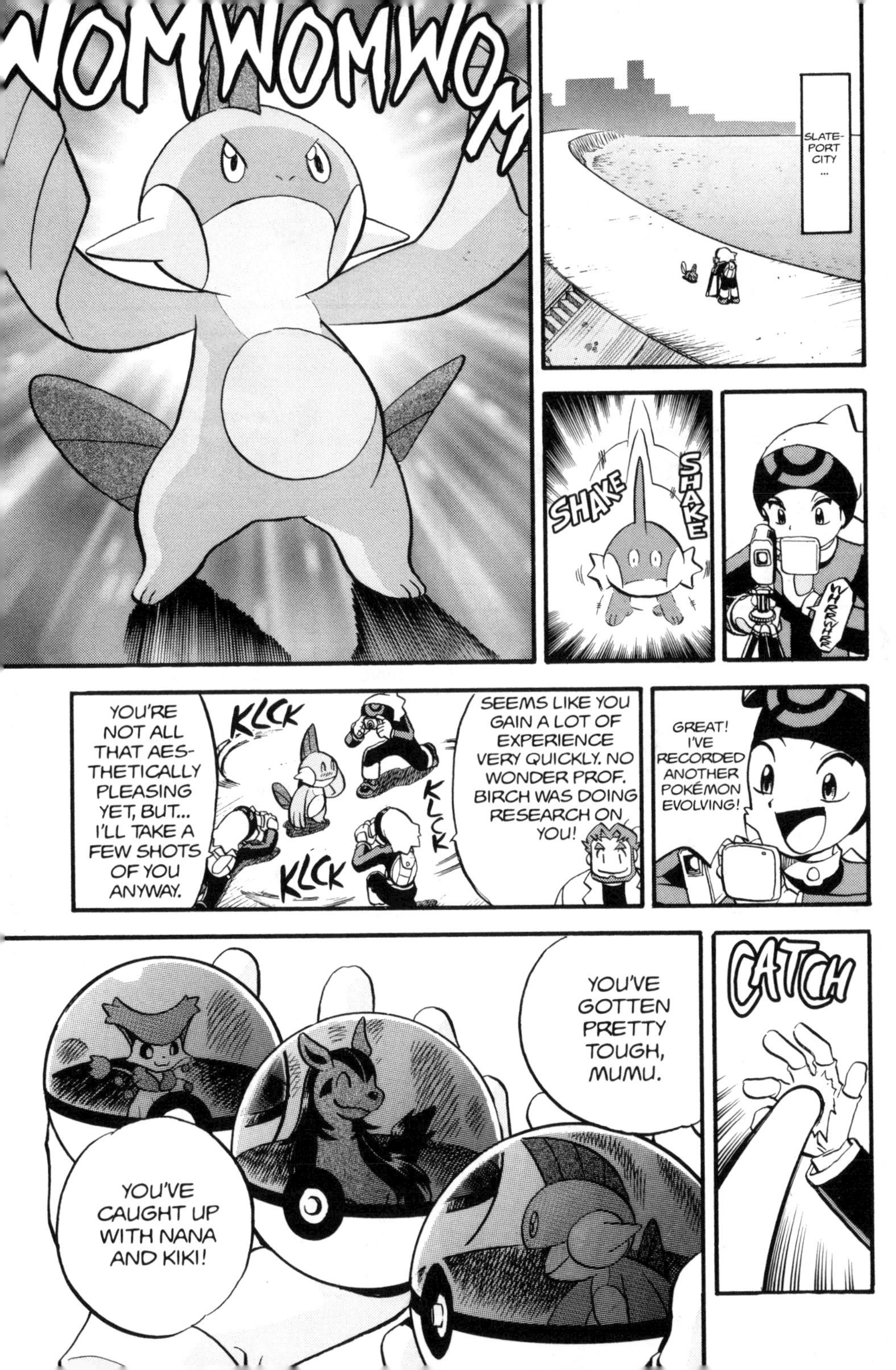
SLATE-PORT CITY ...
WHRWHR
SHAKE
SHAKE
WOMWOMWOM
GREAT! I'VE RECORDED ANOTHER POKÉMON EVOLVING!
SEEMS LIKE YOU GAIN A LOT OF EXPERIENCE VERY QUICKLY. NO WONDER PROF. BIRCH WAS DOING RESEARCH ON YOU!
KLCK
KLCK
KLCK
YOU'RE NOT ALL THAT AES-THETICALLY PLEASING YET, BUT... I'LL TAKE A FEW SHOTS OF YOU ANYWAY.
CATCH
YOU'VE GOTTEN PRETTY TOUGH, MUMU.
YOU'VE CAUGHT UP WITH NANA AND KIKI!

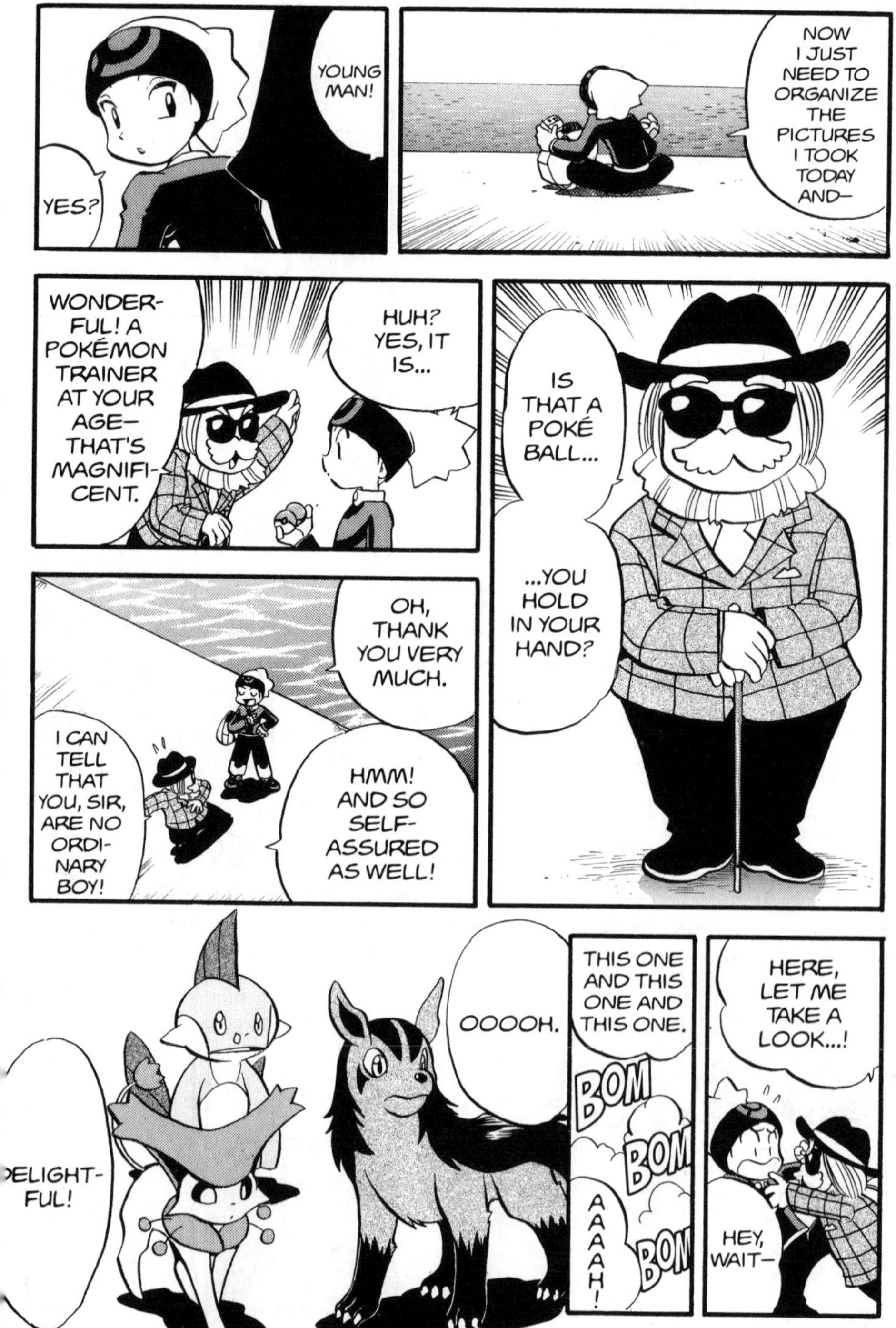
NOW I JUST NEED TO ORGANIZE THE PICTURES I TOOK TODAY AND—
YOUNG MAN!
YES?
IS THAT A POKÉ BALL...
...YOU HOLD IN YOUR HAND?
HUH? YES, IT IS...
WONDER-FUL! A POKÉMON TRAINER AT YOUR AGE—THAT'S MAGNIFI-CENT.
OH, THANK YOU VERY MUCH.
HMM! AND SO SELF-ASSURED AS WELL!
I CAN TELL THAT YOU, SIR, ARE NO ORDI-NARY BOY!
HERE, LET ME TAKE A LOOK...!
HEY, WAIT—
THIS ONE AND THIS ONE AND THIS ONE.
BOM
BOM
BOM
AAAAH!
OOOOH.
DELIGHT-FUL!

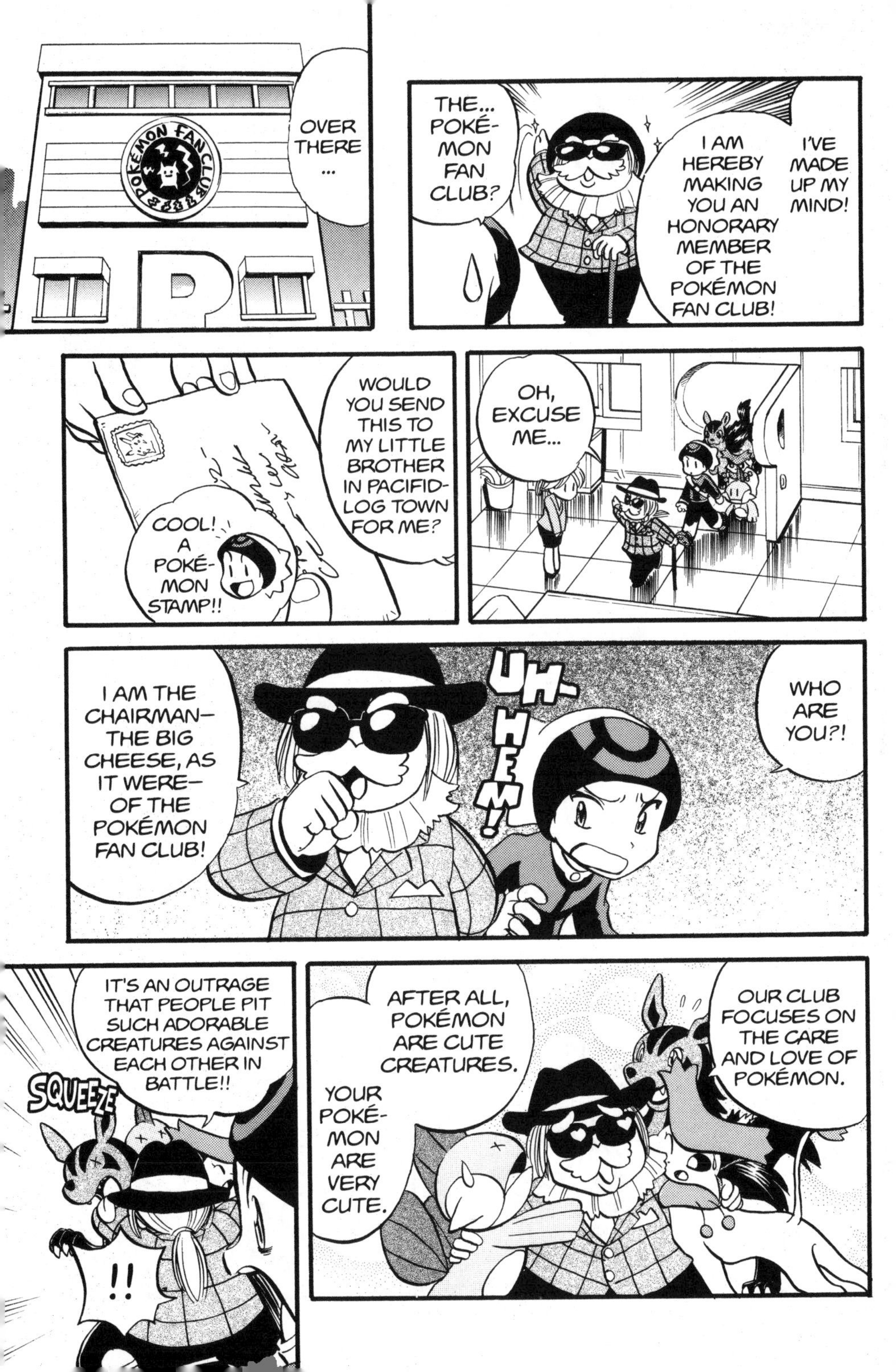
I'VE MADE UP MY MIND!
I AM HEREBY MAKING YOU AN HONORARY MEMBER OF THE POKÉMON FAN CLUB!
THE... POKÉMON FAN CLUB?
POKÉMON FANCLUB
OVER THERE...
OH, EXCUSE ME...
WOULD YOU SEND THIS TO MY LITTLE BROTHER IN PACIFIDLOG TOWN FOR ME?
COOL! A POKÉMON STAMP!!
WHO ARE YOU?!
UH-HEM!
I AM THE CHAIRMAN—THE BIG CHEESE, AS IT WERE—OF THE POKÉMON FAN CLUB!
OUR CLUB FOCUSES ON THE CARE AND LOVE OF POKÉMON.
AFTER ALL, POKÉMON ARE CUTE CREATURES.
YOUR POKÉMON ARE VERY CUTE.
IT'S AN OUTRAGE THAT PEOPLE PIT SUCH ADORABLE CREATURES AGAINST EACH OTHER IN BATTLE!!
SQUEEZE
!!

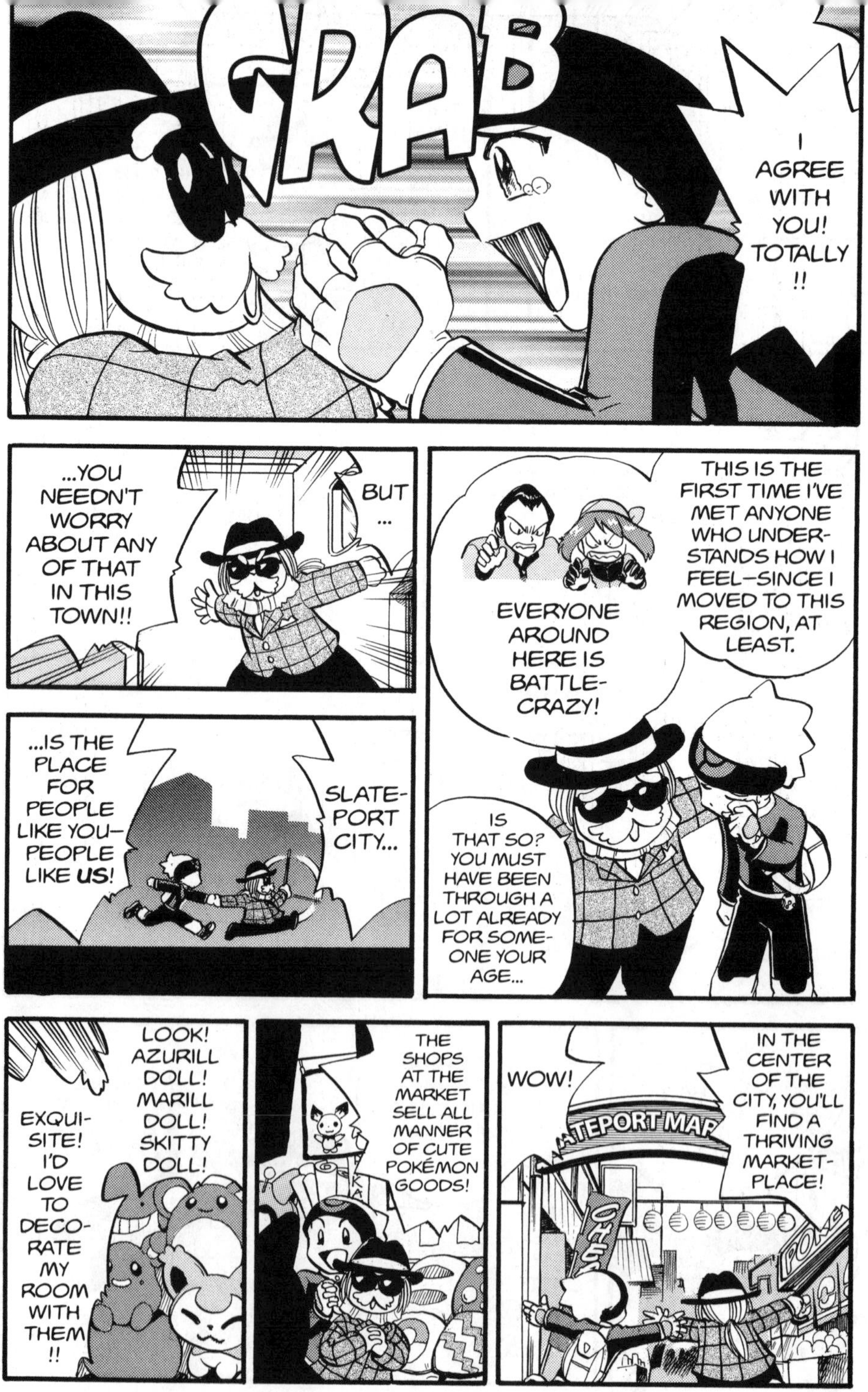
GRAB
I AGREE WITH YOU! TOTALLY!!
THIS IS THE FIRST TIME I'VE MET ANYONE WHO UNDERSTANDS HOW I FEEL—SINCE I MOVED TO THIS REGION, AT LEAST.
EVERYONE AROUND HERE IS BATTLE-CRAZY!
IS THAT SO? YOU MUST HAVE BEEN THROUGH A LOT ALREADY FOR SOMEONE YOUR AGE...
BUT...
...YOU NEEDN'T WORRY ABOUT ANY OF THAT IN THIS TOWN!!
SLATEPORT CITY...
...IS THE PLACE FOR PEOPLE LIKE YOU—PEOPLE LIKE **US**!
IN THE CENTER OF THE CITY, YOU'LL FIND A THRIVING MARKETPLACE!
TEPORT MAR
WOW!
THE SHOPS AT THE MARKET SELL ALL MANNER OF CUTE POKÉMON GOODS!
LOOK! AZURILL DOLL! MARILL DOLL! SKITTY DOLL!
EXQUISITE! I'D LOVE TO DECORATE MY ROOM WITH THEM!!

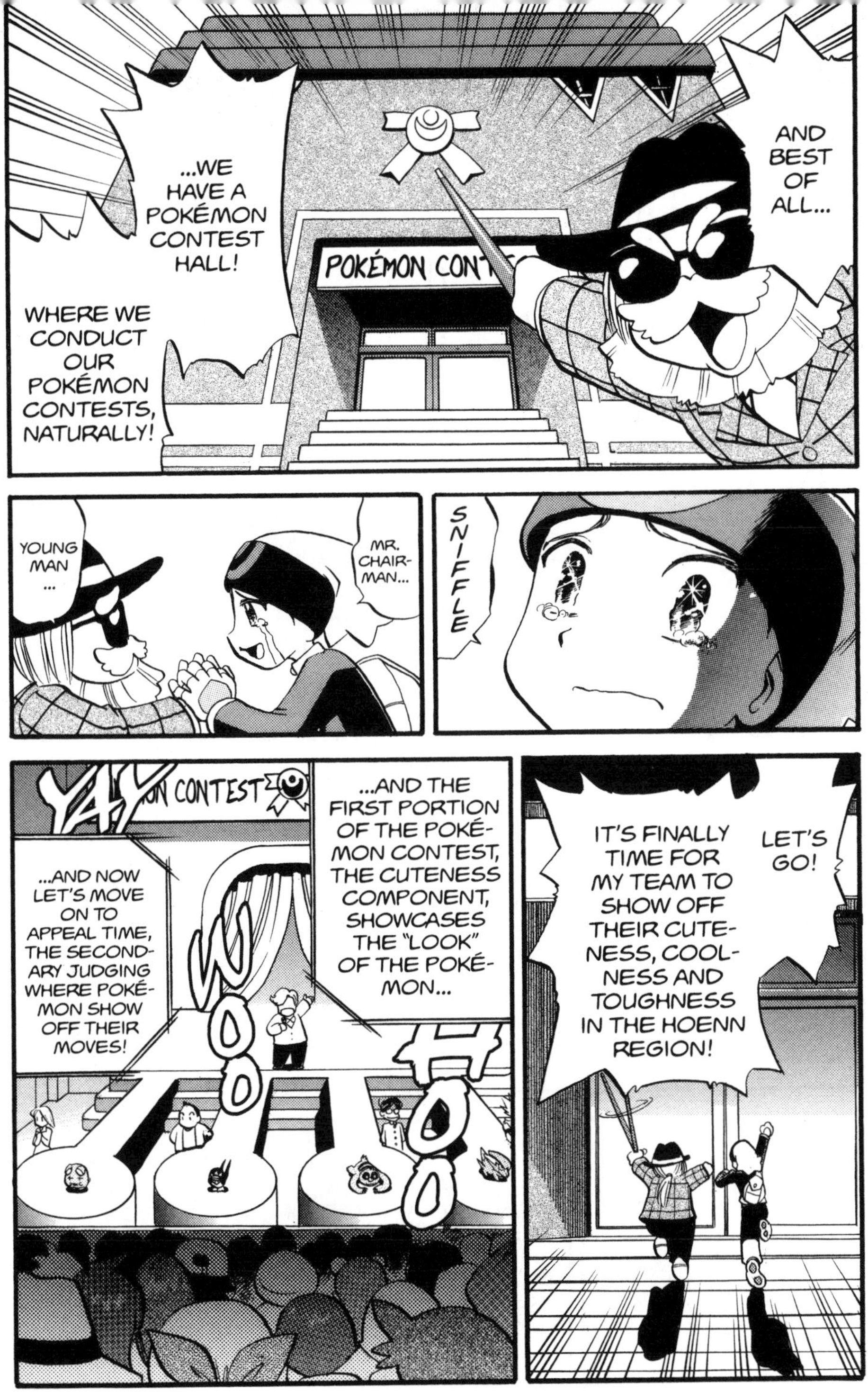

AND BEST OF ALL...
...WE HAVE A POKÉMON CONTEST HALL!
POKÉMON CONTEST
WHERE WE CONDUCT OUR POKÉMON CONTESTS, NATURALLY!
SNIFFLE
MR. CHAIR-MAN...
YOUNG MAN...
LET'S GO!
IT'S FINALLY TIME FOR MY TEAM TO SHOW OFF THEIR CUTE-NESS, COOL-NESS AND TOUGHNESS IN THE HOENN REGION!
...AND THE FIRST PORTION OF THE POKÉ-MON CONTEST, THE CUTENESS COMPONENT, SHOWCASES THE "LOOK" OF THE POKÉ-MON...
YAY
ON CONTEST
...AND NOW LET'S MOVE ON TO APPEAL TIME, THE SECOND-ARY JUDGING WHERE POKÉ-MON SHOW OFF THEIR MOVES!
WOOOO
HOOO

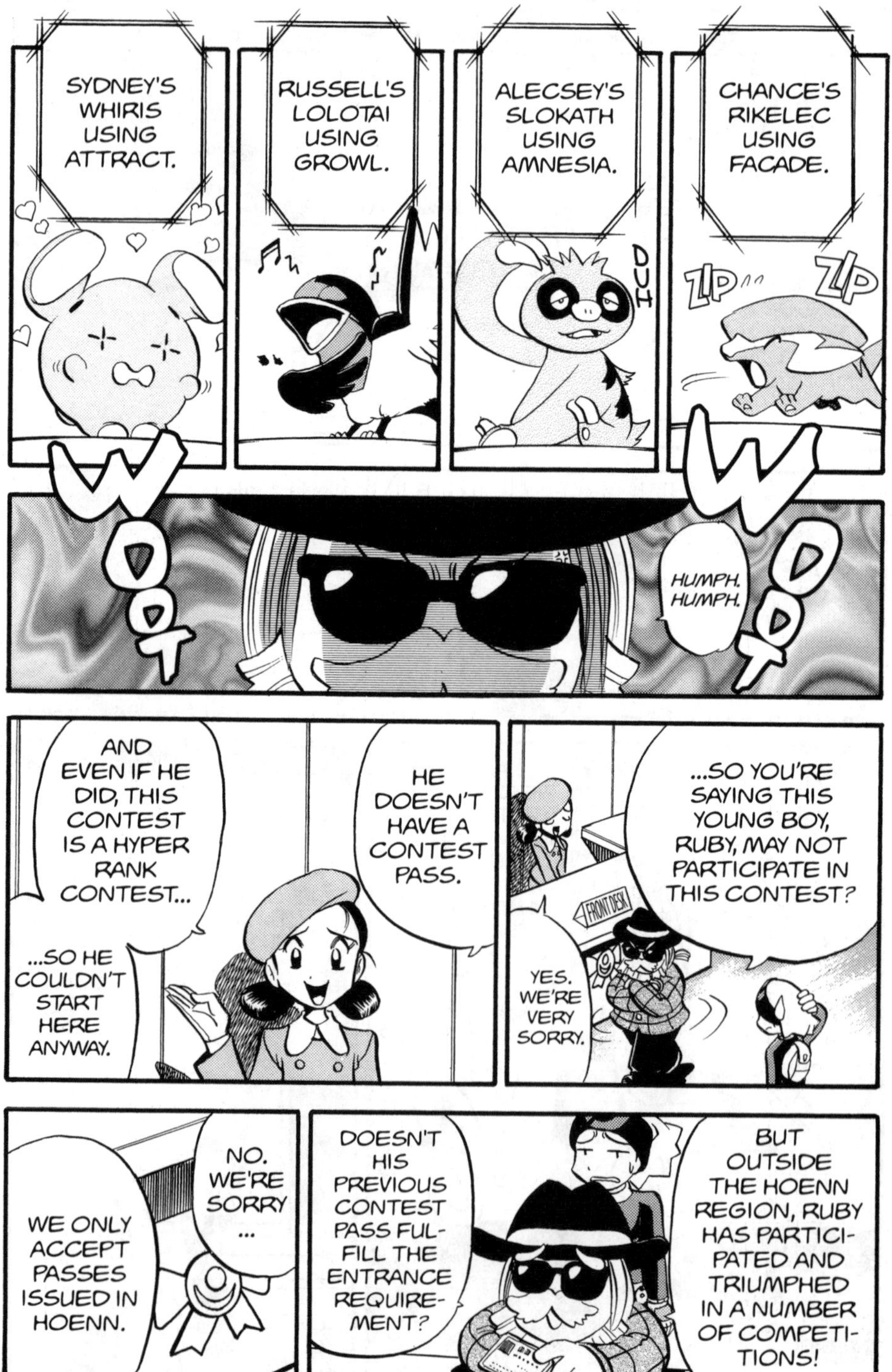
CHANCE'S RIKELEC USING FACADE.
ZIP ZIP
ALECSEY'S SLOKATH USING AMNESIA.
DUH
RUSSELL'S LOLOTAI USING GROWL.
SYDNEY'S WHIRIS USING ATTRACT.
WOOT
HUMPH. HUMPH.
WOOT
...SO YOU'RE SAYING THIS YOUNG BOY, RUBY, MAY NOT PARTICIPATE IN THIS CONTEST?
FRONT DESK
YES. WE'RE VERY SORRY.
HE DOESN'T HAVE A CONTEST PASS.
AND EVEN IF HE DID, THIS CONTEST IS A HYPER RANK CONTEST...
...SO HE COULDN'T START HERE ANYWAY.
BUT OUTSIDE THE HOENN REGION, RUBY HAS PARTICIPATED AND TRIUMPHED IN A NUMBER OF COMPETITIONS!
DOESN'T HIS PREVIOUS CONTEST PASS FULFILL THE ENTRANCE REQUIREMENT?
NO. WE'RE SORRY...
WE ONLY ACCEPT PASSES ISSUED IN HOENN.

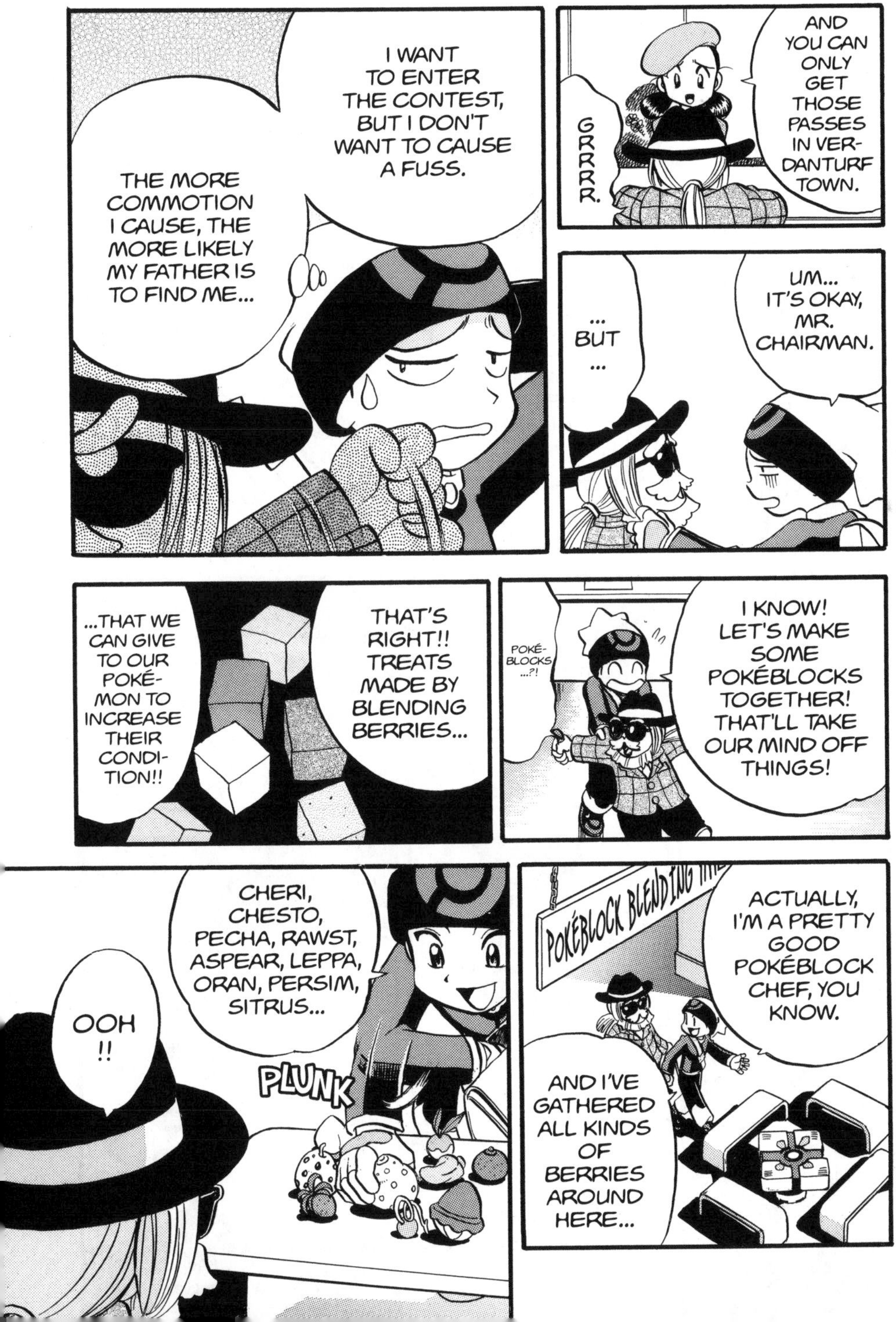
AND YOU CAN ONLY GET THOSE PASSES IN VERDANTURF TOWN.
GRRRR.
UM... IT'S OKAY, MR. CHAIRMAN.
...BUT...
I WANT TO ENTER THE CONTEST, BUT I DON'T WANT TO CAUSE A FUSS.
THE MORE COMMOTION I CAUSE, THE MORE LIKELY MY FATHER IS TO FIND ME...
I KNOW! LET'S MAKE SOME POKÉBLOCKS TOGETHER! THAT'LL TAKE OUR MIND OFF THINGS!
POKÉBLOCKS...?!
THAT'S RIGHT!! TREATS MADE BY BLENDING BERRIES...
...THAT WE CAN GIVE TO OUR POKÉMON TO INCREASE THEIR CONDITION!!
POKÉBLOCK BLENDING
ACTUALLY, I'M A PRETTY GOOD POKÉBLOCK CHEF, YOU KNOW.
AND I'VE GATHERED ALL KINDS OF BERRIES AROUND HERE...
CHERI, CHESTO, PECHA, RAWST, ASPEAR, LEPPA, ORAN, PERSIM, SITRUS...
PLUNK
OOH!!

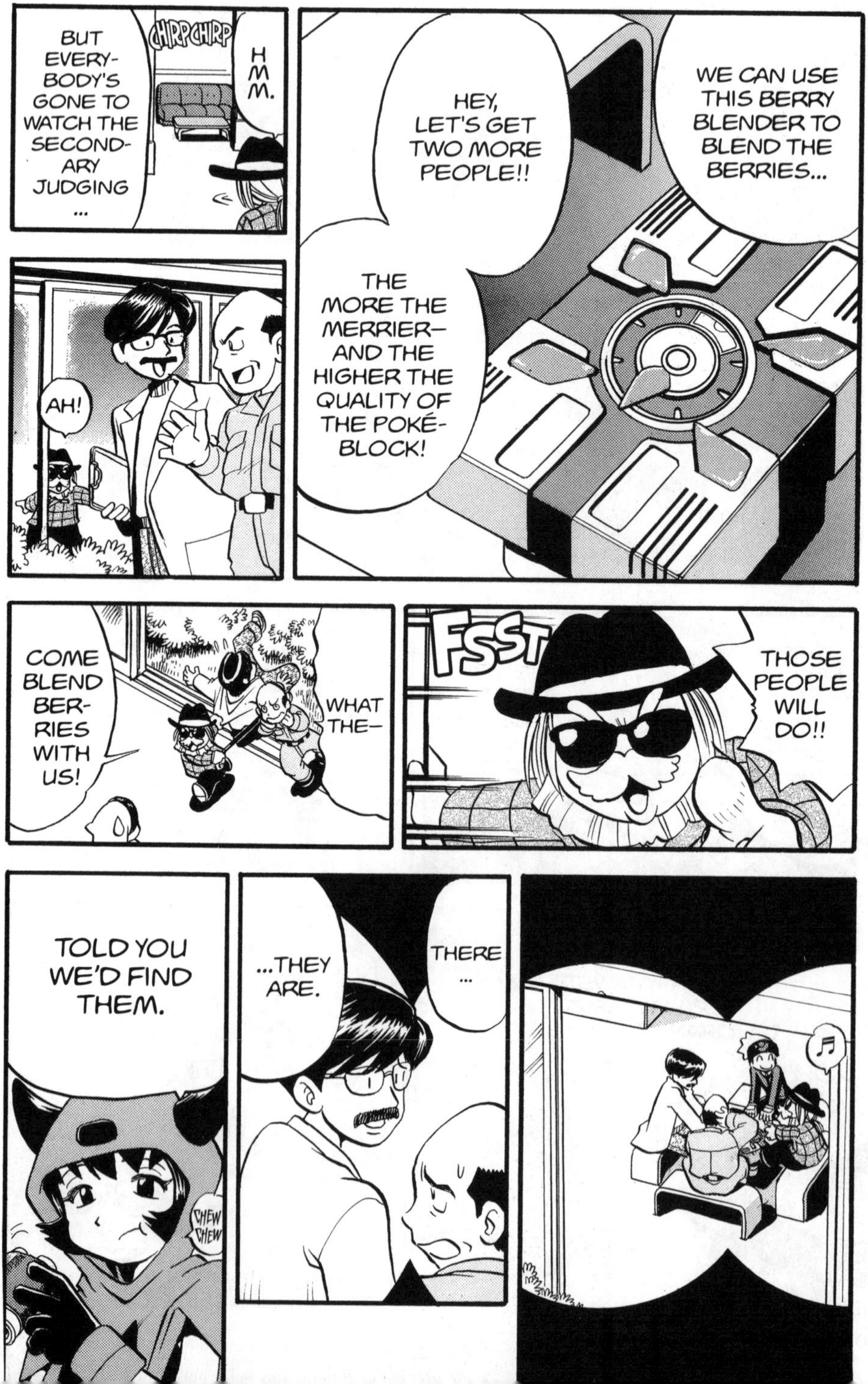
WE CAN USE THIS BERRY BLENDER TO BLEND THE BERRIES...
HEY, LET'S GET TWO MORE PEOPLE!!
THE MORE THE MERRIER— AND THE HIGHER THE QUALITY OF THE POKÉ-BLOCK!
HMM.
CHIRP CHIRP
BUT EVERY-BODY'S GONE TO WATCH THE SECOND-ARY JUDGING ...
AH!
FSST
THOSE PEOPLE WILL DO!!
WHAT THE—
COME BLEND BER-RIES WITH US!
♪
THERE ...
...THEY ARE.
TOLD YOU WE'D FIND THEM.
CHEW CHEW

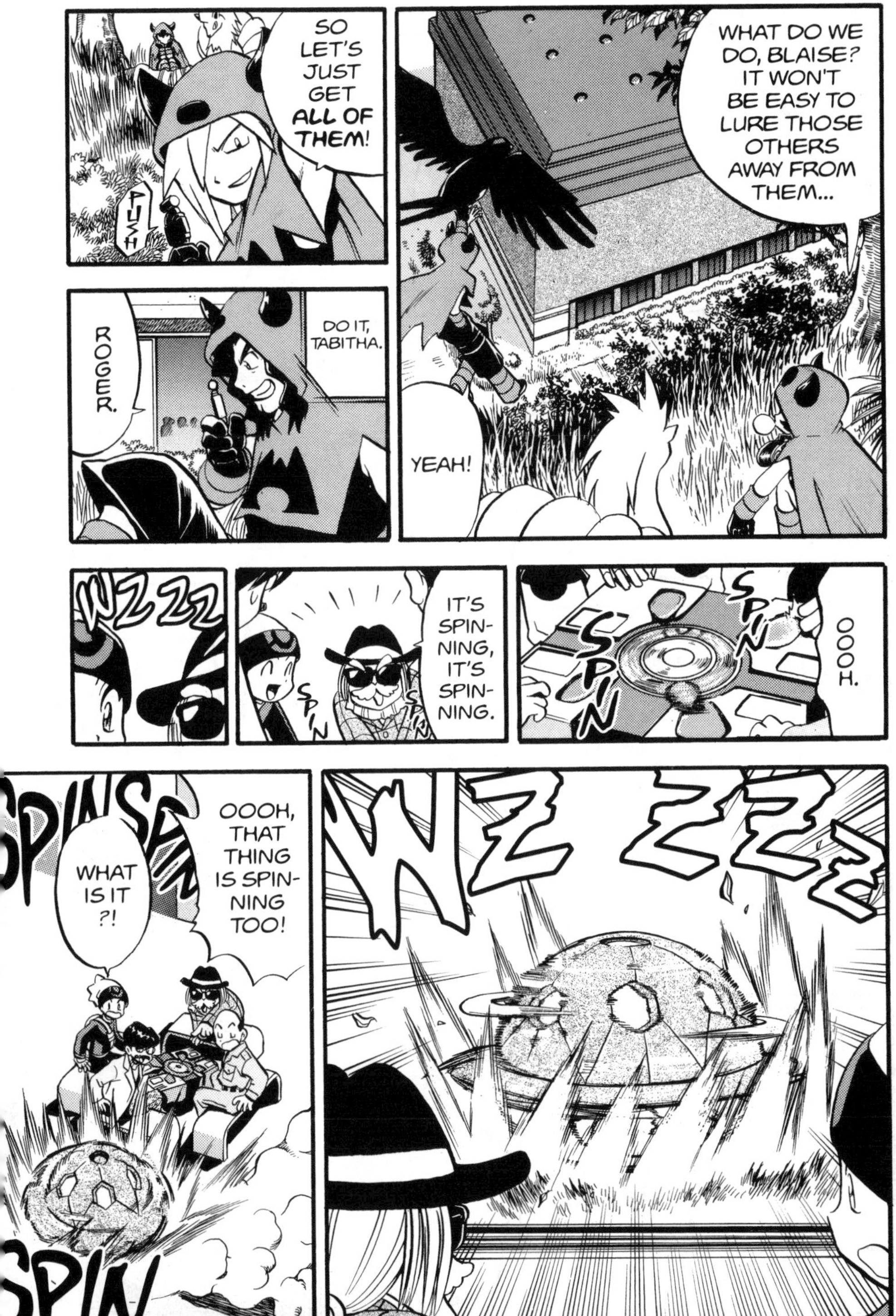
WHAT DO WE DO, BLAISE? IT WON'T BE EASY TO LURE THOSE OTHERS AWAY FROM THEM...
YEAH!
SO LET'S JUST GET **ALL OF THEM**!
PUSH
DO IT, TABITHA.
ROGER.
OOOH.
SPIN
SPIN
IT'S SPIN-NING, IT'S SPIN-NING.
SPIN
SPIN
WZZZ
WZ ZZZ
OOOH, THAT THING IS SPIN-NING TOO!
SPIN SPIN
WHAT IS IT ?!
SPIN

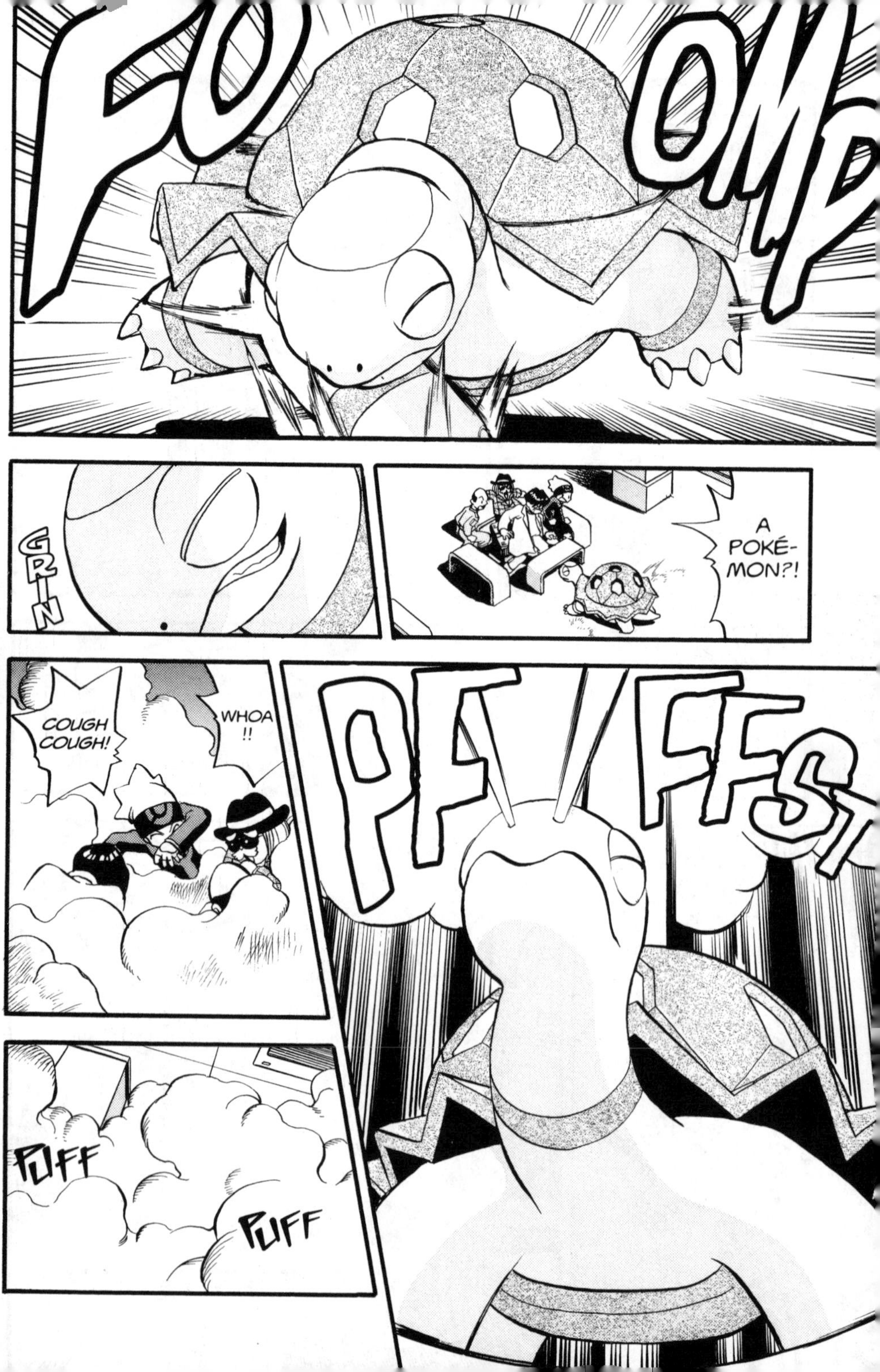
F-O
OMP
A POKÉ-MON?!
GRIN
PF
FFST
WHOA !!
COUGH COUGH!
PUFF
PUFF

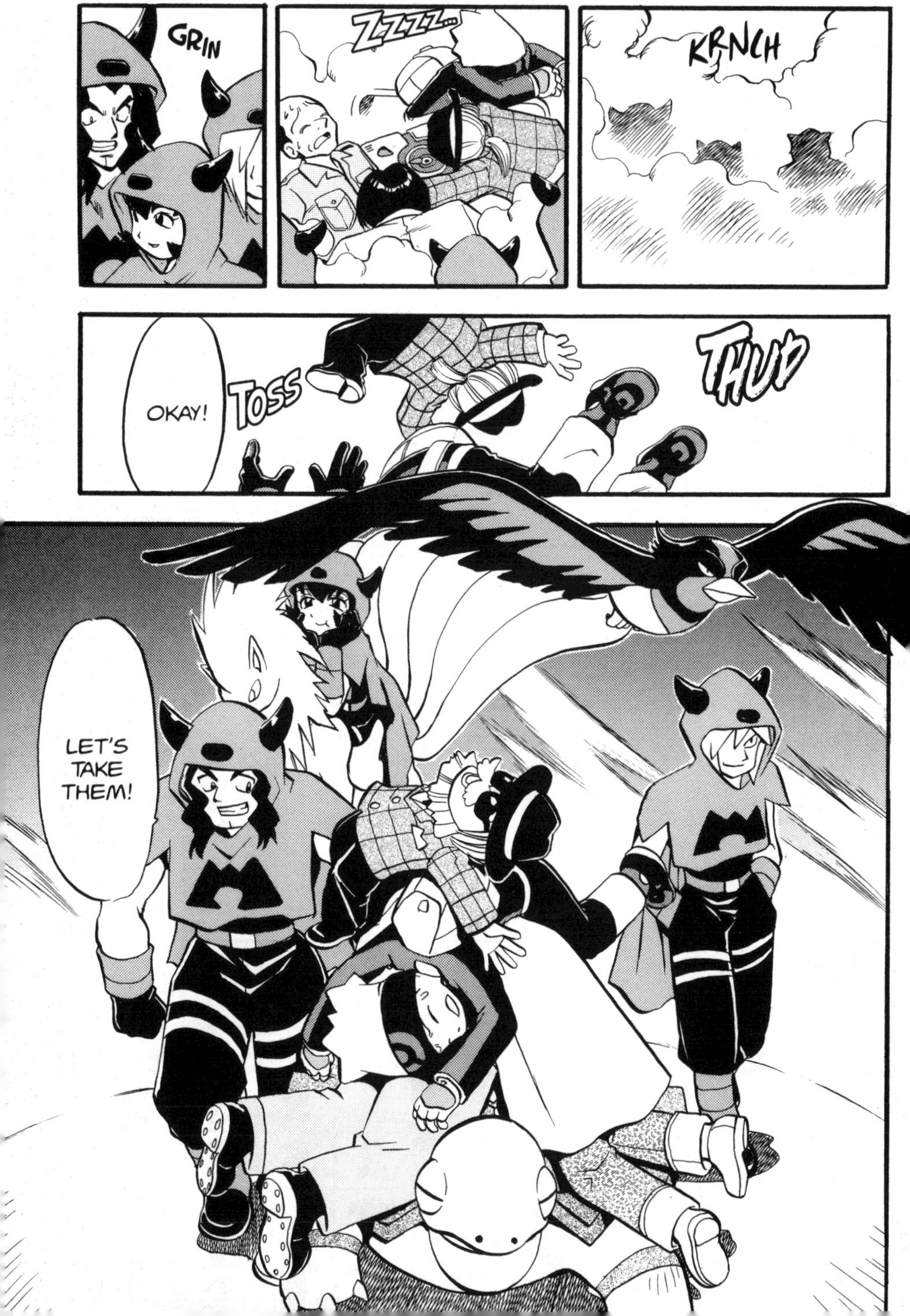
KRNCH
ZZZZ...
GRIN
THUD
TOSS
OKAY!
LET'S TAKE THEM!

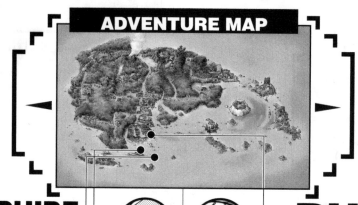

ADVENTURE MAP

SAPPHIRE

CHIC
Combusken ♀
Lv17

RONO
Lairon ♂
Lv33

LORRY
Wailord ♂
Lv41

Sea Route 108

▼

Abandoned Ship

▼

Sea Route 109

▼

Slateport City

RUBY

NANA
Mightyena ♀

KIKI
Delcatty ♀

MUMU
Marshtomp ♂

Stone Badge	Knuckle Badge	Dynamo Badge	Heat Badge
◆	●	●	❀
Balance Badge	**Feather Badge**	**Mind Badge**	**Rain Badge**
●	◗	♥	▲

	Coolness	Beauty	Cuteness	Cleverness	Toughness
Normal	♟	♟	♟	♟	♟
Super	♟	♟	♟	♟	♟
Hyper	✦	✦	✦	✦	✦
Master	✦	✦	✦	✦	✦

● Adventure 201 ●
Slugging It Out with Slugma, Part 1

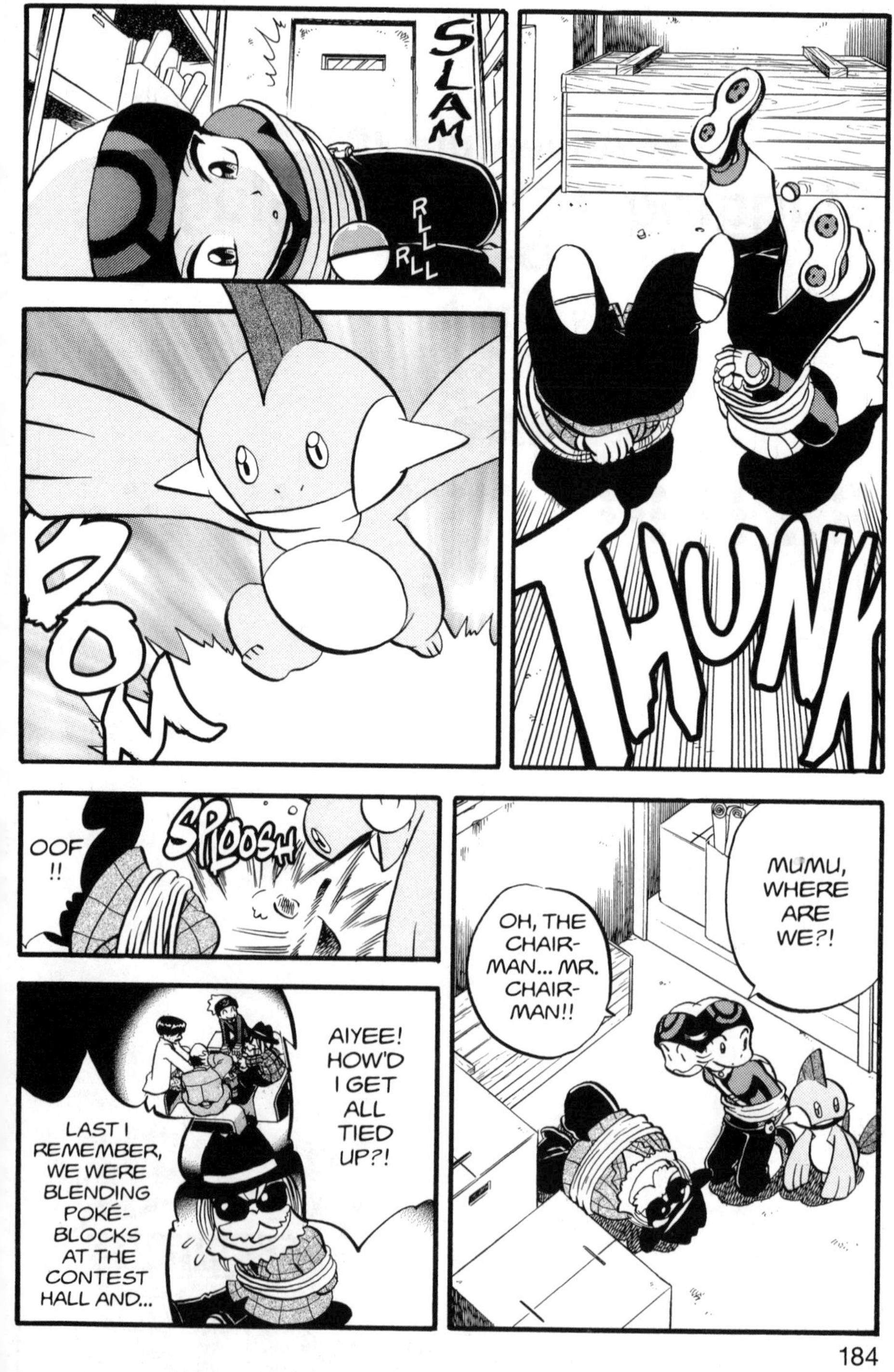
THUNK
SLAM
RLLL RLLL
MUMU, WHERE ARE WE?!
OH, THE CHAIR-MAN... MR. CHAIR-MAN!!
SPLOOSH
OOF !!
AIYEE! HOW'D I GET ALL TIED UP?!
LAST I REMEMBER, WE WERE BLENDING POKÉ-BLOCKS AT THE CONTEST HALL AND...

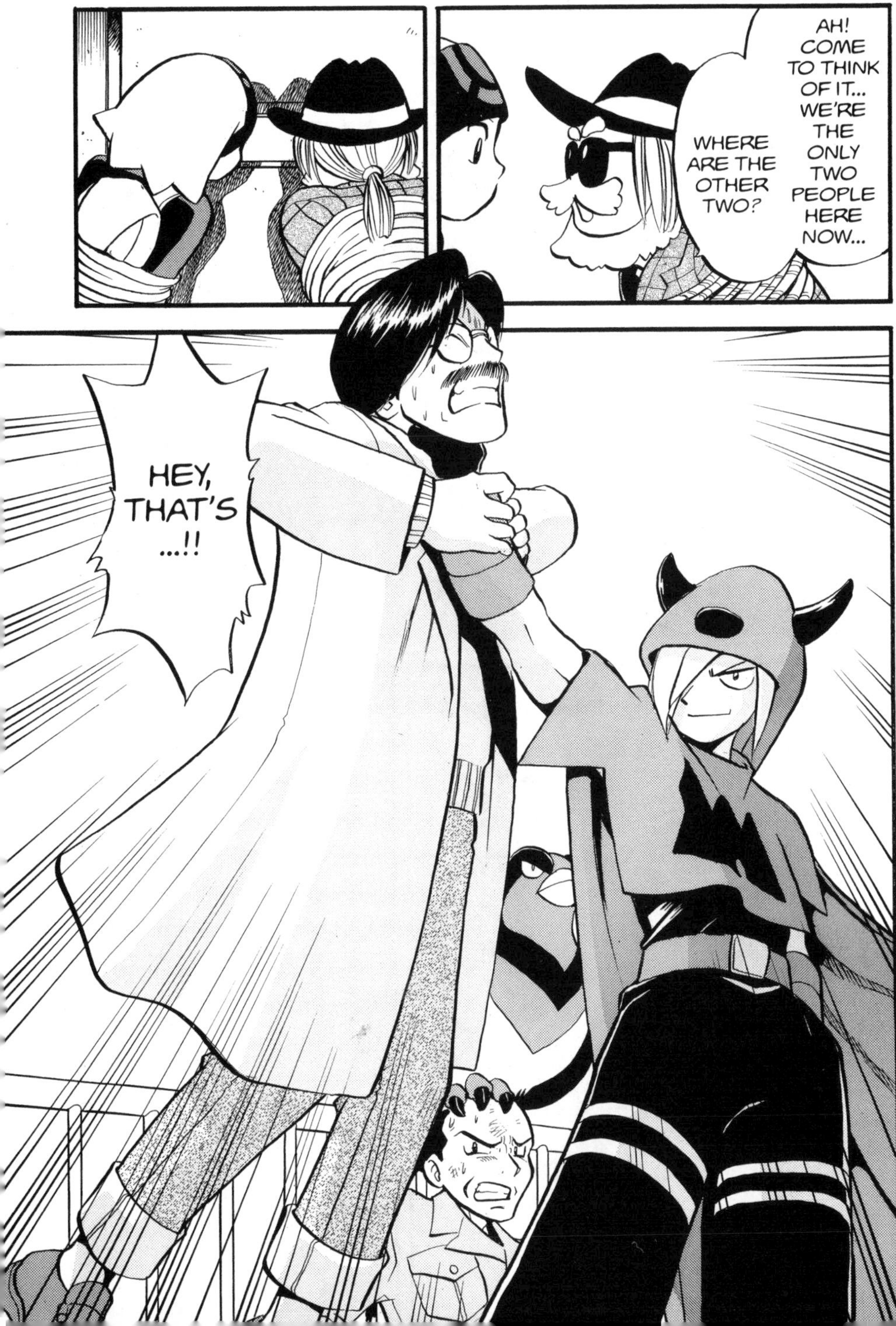
AH! COME TO THINK OF IT... WE'RE THE ONLY TWO PEOPLE HERE NOW...
WHERE ARE THE OTHER TWO?
HEY, THAT'S ...!!

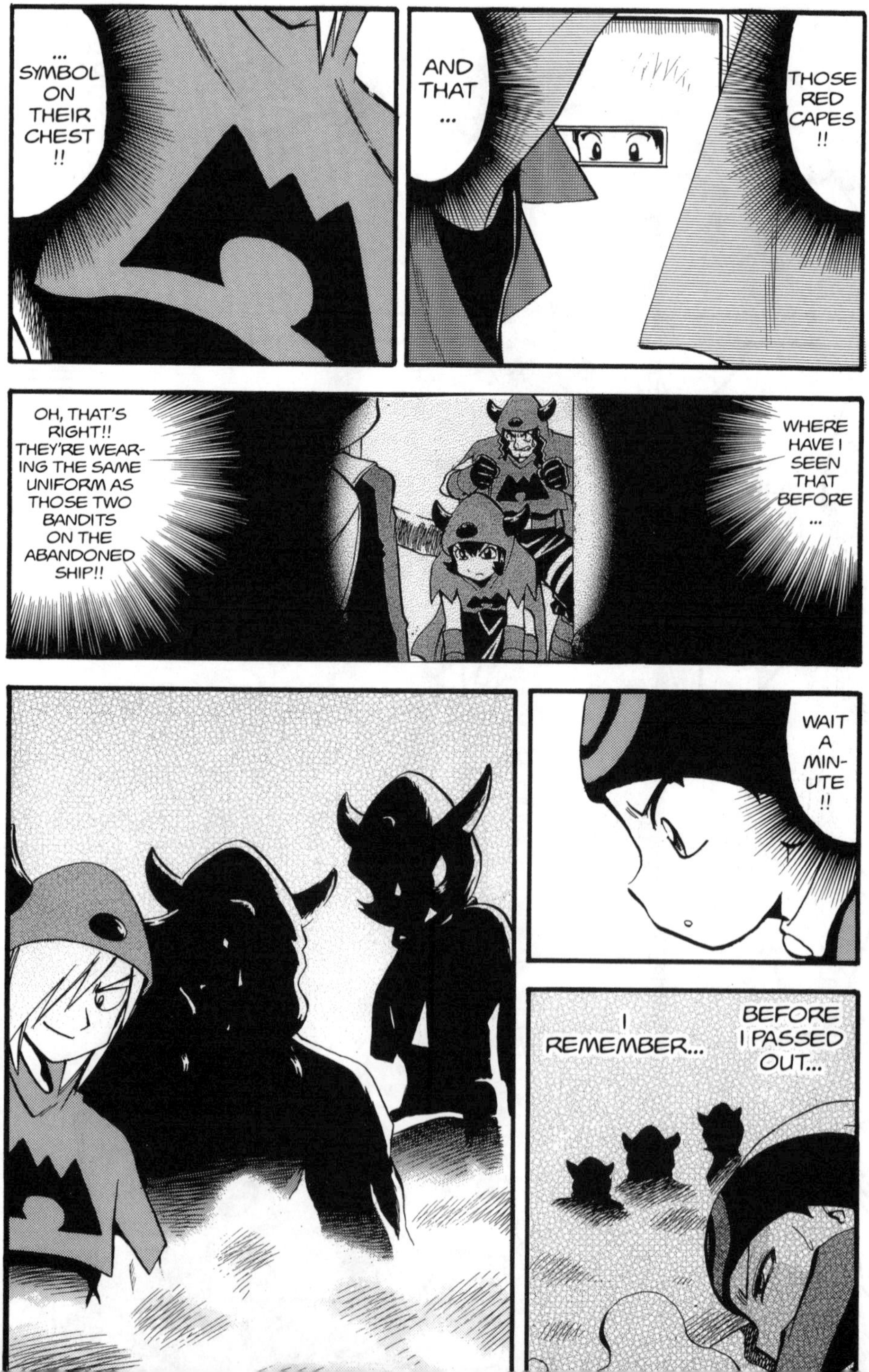
THOSE RED CAPES !!
AND THAT ...
... SYMBOL ON THEIR CHEST !!
WHERE HAVE I SEEN THAT BEFORE ...
OH, THAT'S RIGHT!! THEY'RE WEAR-ING THE SAME UNIFORM AS THOSE TWO BANDITS ON THE ABANDONED SHIP!!
WAIT A MIN-UTE !!
BEFORE I PASSED OUT...
I REMEMBER...

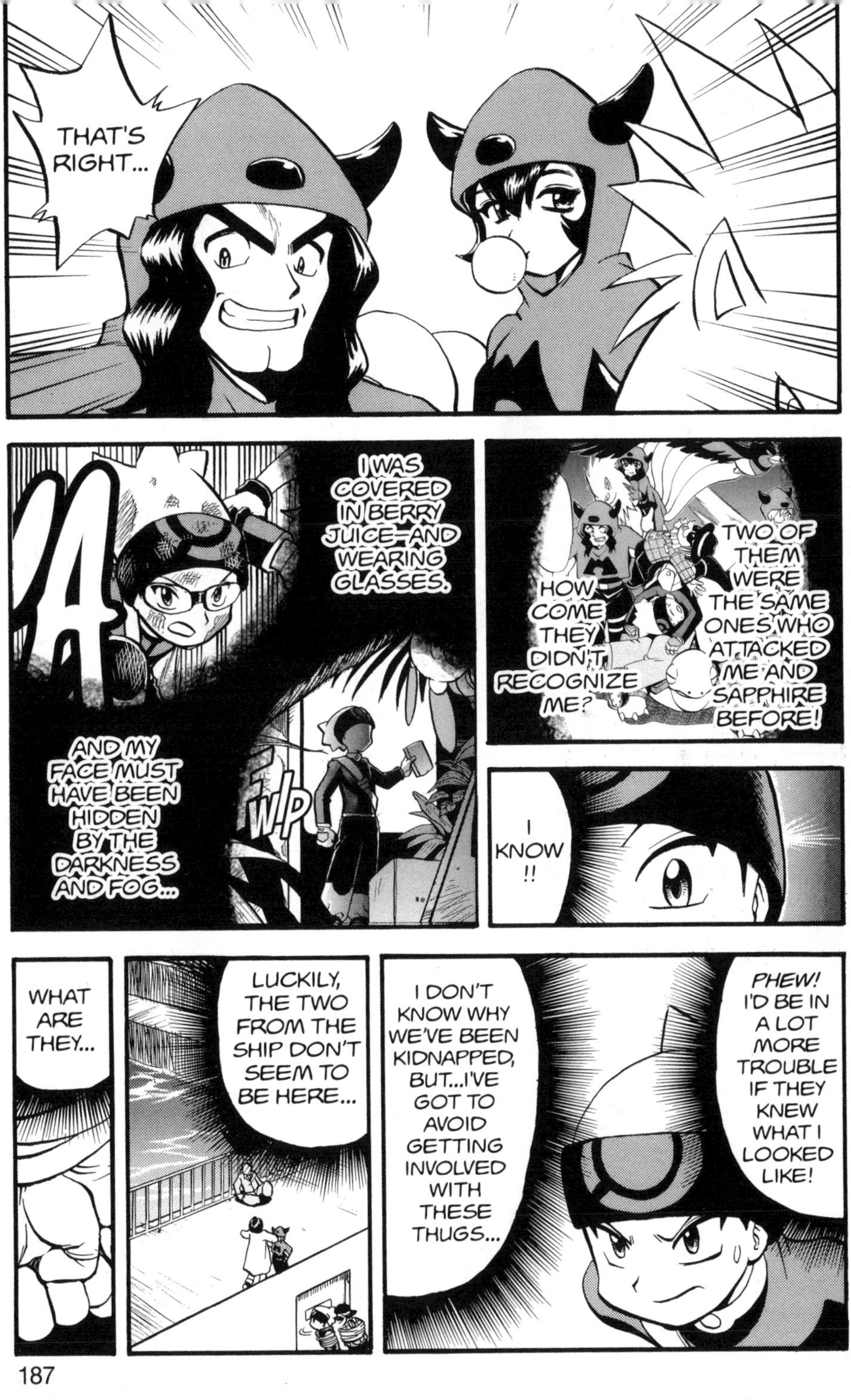
THAT'S RIGHT...
TWO OF THEM WERE THE SAME ONES WHO ATTACKED ME AND SAPPHIRE BEFORE!
HOW COME THEY DIDN'T RECOGNIZE ME?
I KNOW!!
I WAS COVERED IN BERRY JUICE—AND WEARING GLASSES.
FWIP
AND MY FACE MUST HAVE BEEN HIDDEN BY THE DARKNESS AND FOG...
PHEW! I'D BE IN A LOT MORE TROUBLE IF THEY KNEW WHAT I LOOKED LIKE!
I DON'T KNOW WHY WE'VE BEEN KIDNAPPED, BUT...I'VE GOT TO AVOID GETTING INVOLVED WITH THESE THUGS...
LUCKILY, THE TWO FROM THE SHIP DON'T SEEM TO BE HERE...
WHAT ARE THEY...

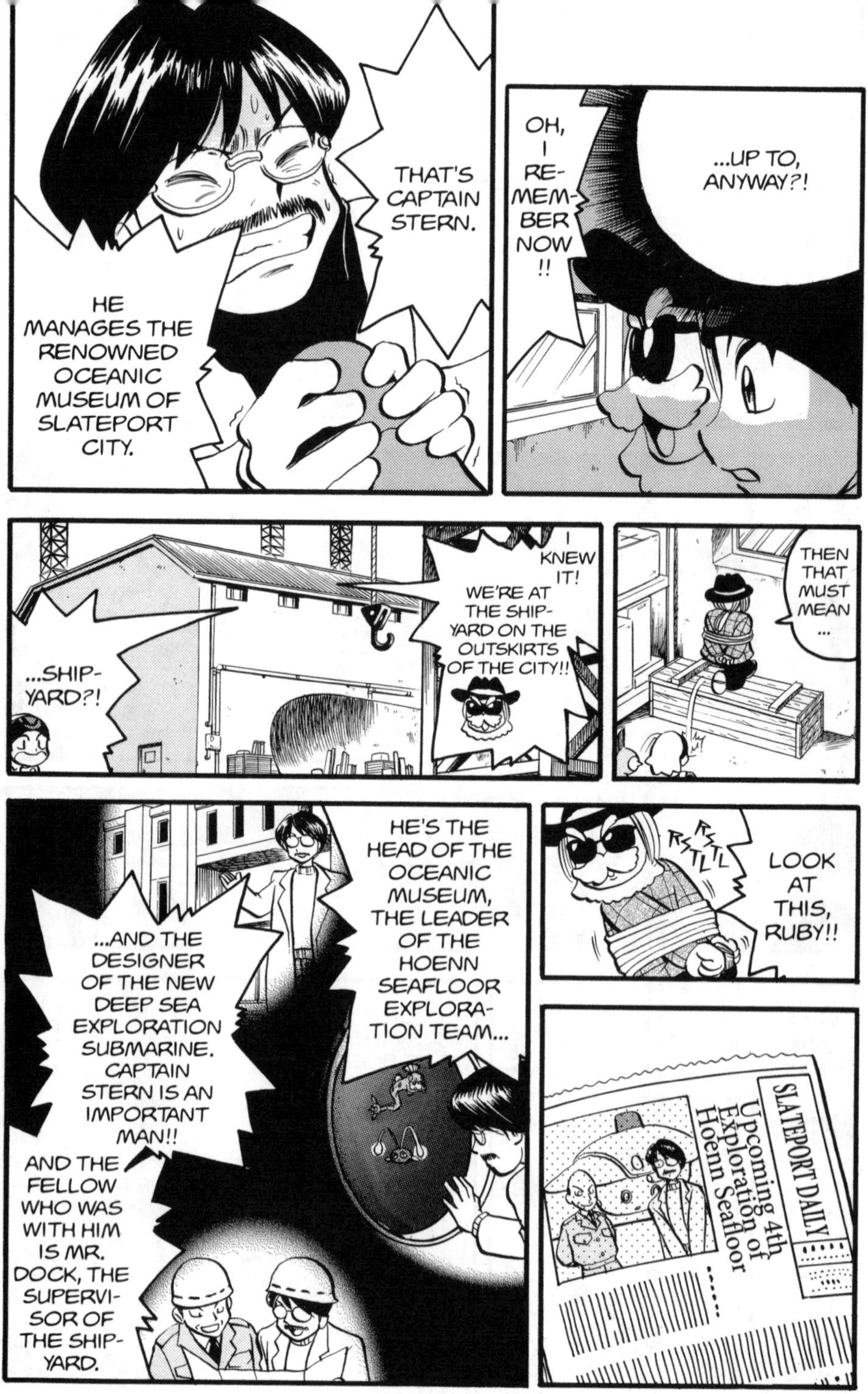

...UP TO, ANYWAY?!
OH, I RE-MEM-BER NOW!!
THAT'S CAPTAIN STERN.
HE MANAGES THE RENOWNED OCEANIC MUSEUM OF SLATEPORT CITY.
THEN THAT MUST MEAN...
I KNEW IT! WE'RE AT THE SHIP-YARD ON THE OUTSKIRTS OF THE CITY!!
...SHIP-YARD?!
RSTL RSTL
LOOK AT THIS, RUBY!!
SLATEPORT DAILY
Upcoming 4th Exploration of Hoenn Seafloor
HE'S THE HEAD OF THE OCEANIC MUSEUM, THE LEADER OF THE HOENN SEAFLOOR EXPLORA-TION TEAM...
...AND THE DESIGNER OF THE NEW DEEP SEA EXPLORATION SUBMARINE. CAPTAIN STERN IS AN IMPORTANT MAN!!
AND THE FELLOW WHO WAS WITH HIM IS MR. DOCK, THE SUPERVI-SOR OF THE SHIP-YARD.

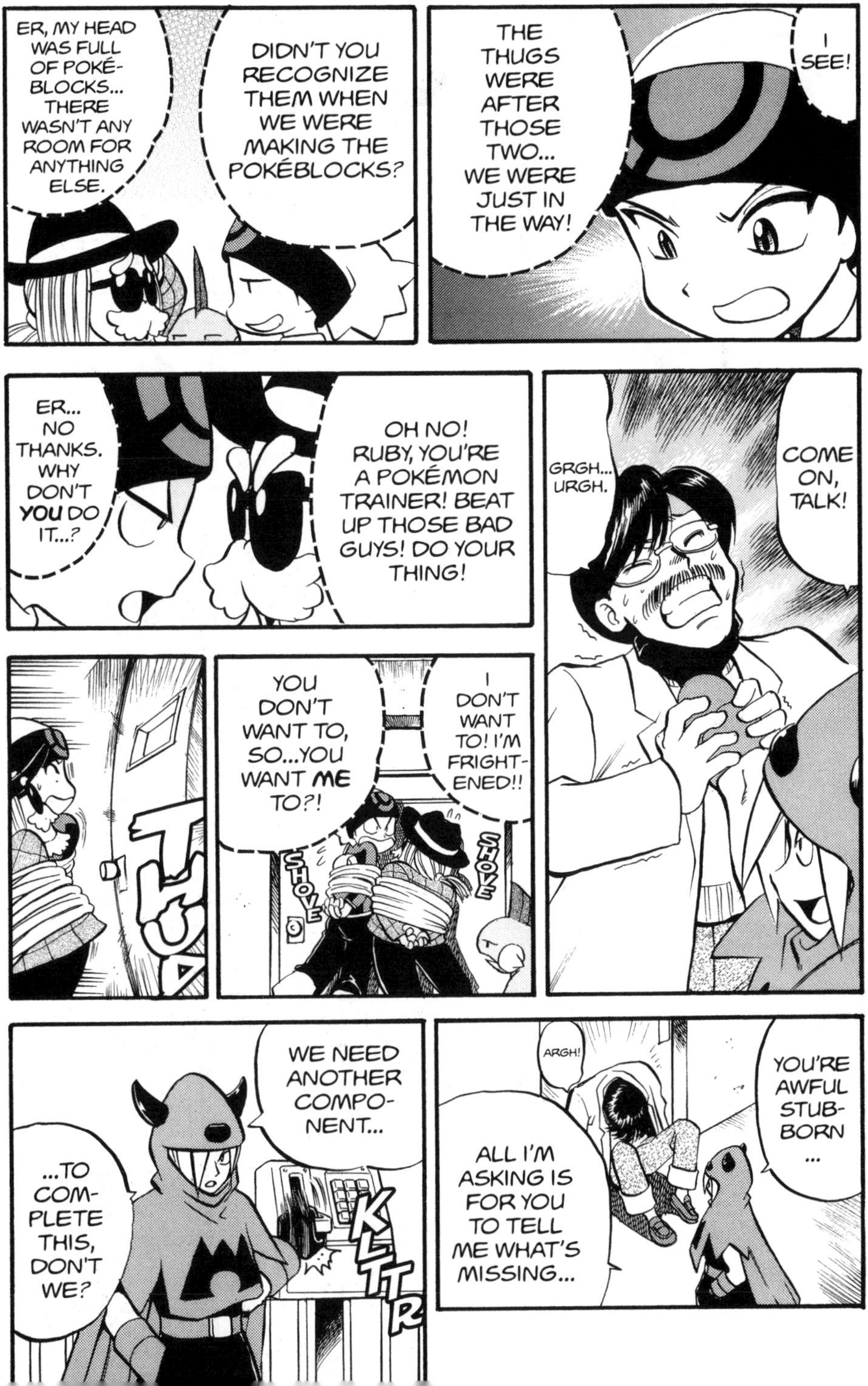
I SEE!
THE THUGS WERE AFTER THOSE TWO... WE WERE JUST IN THE WAY!
DIDN'T YOU RECOGNIZE THEM WHEN WE WERE MAKING THE POKÉBLOCKS?
ER, MY HEAD WAS FULL OF POKÉ-BLOCKS... THERE WASN'T ANY ROOM FOR ANYTHING ELSE.
COME ON, TALK!
GRGH... URGH.
OH NO! RUBY, YOU'RE A POKÉMON TRAINER! BEAT UP THOSE BAD GUYS! DO YOUR THING!
ER... NO THANKS. WHY DON'T **YOU** DO IT...?
I DON'T WANT TO! I'M FRIGHT-ENED!!
YOU DON'T WANT TO, SO...YOU WANT **ME** TO?!
SHOVE
SHOVE
THUD
YOU'RE AWFUL STUB-BORN ...
ARGH!
ALL I'M ASKING IS FOR YOU TO TELL ME WHAT'S MISSING...
WE NEED ANOTHER COMPO-NENT...
...TO COM-PLETE THIS, DON'T WE?
KLTTR

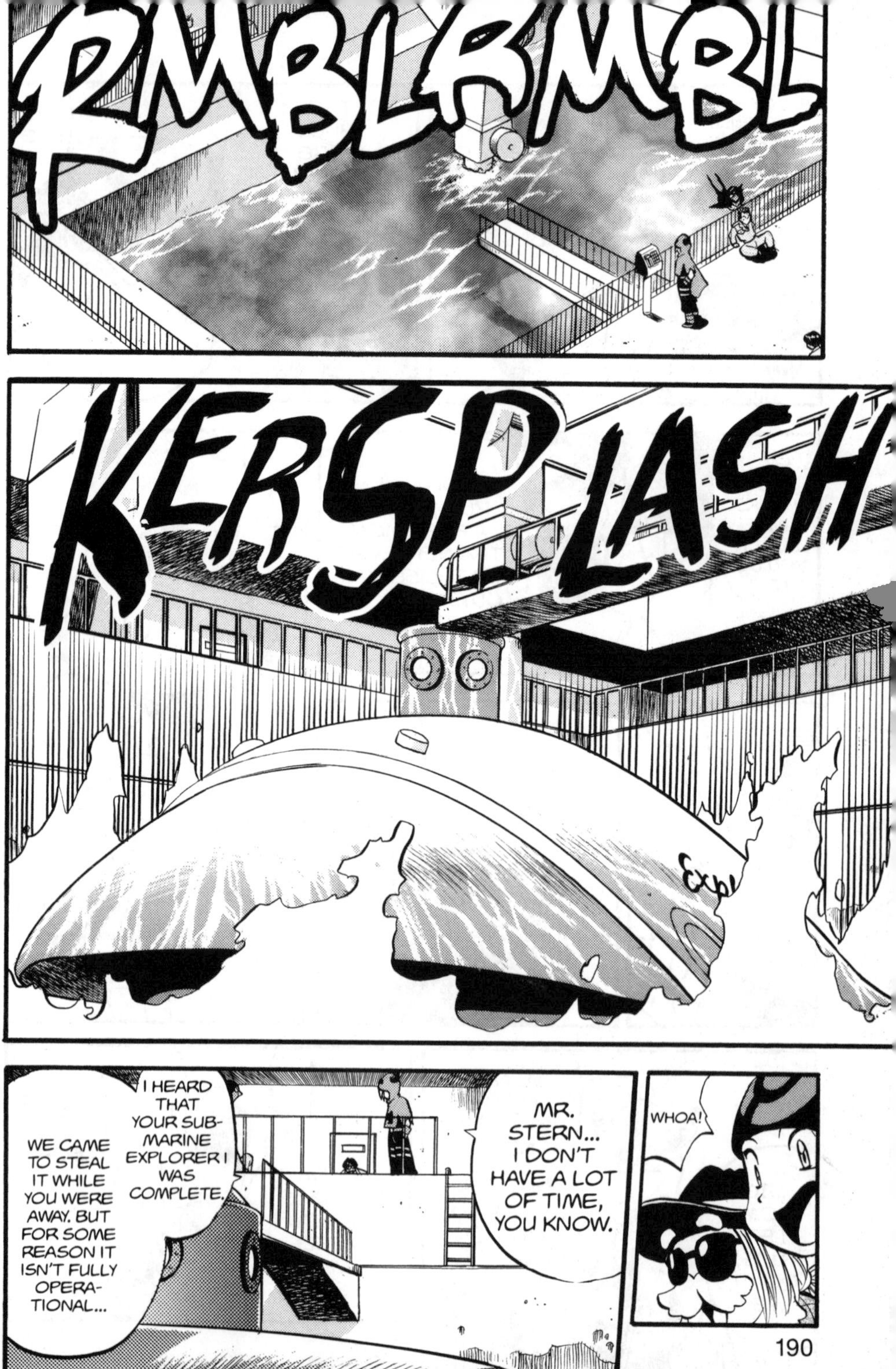
RMBLRMBL
KERSPLASH
WHOA!
MR. STERN... I DON'T HAVE A LOT OF TIME, YOU KNOW.
I HEARD THAT YOUR SUB-MARINE EXPLORER I WAS COMPLETE.
WE CAME TO STEAL IT WHILE YOU WERE AWAY. BUT FOR SOME REASON IT ISN'T FULLY OPERA-TIONAL...

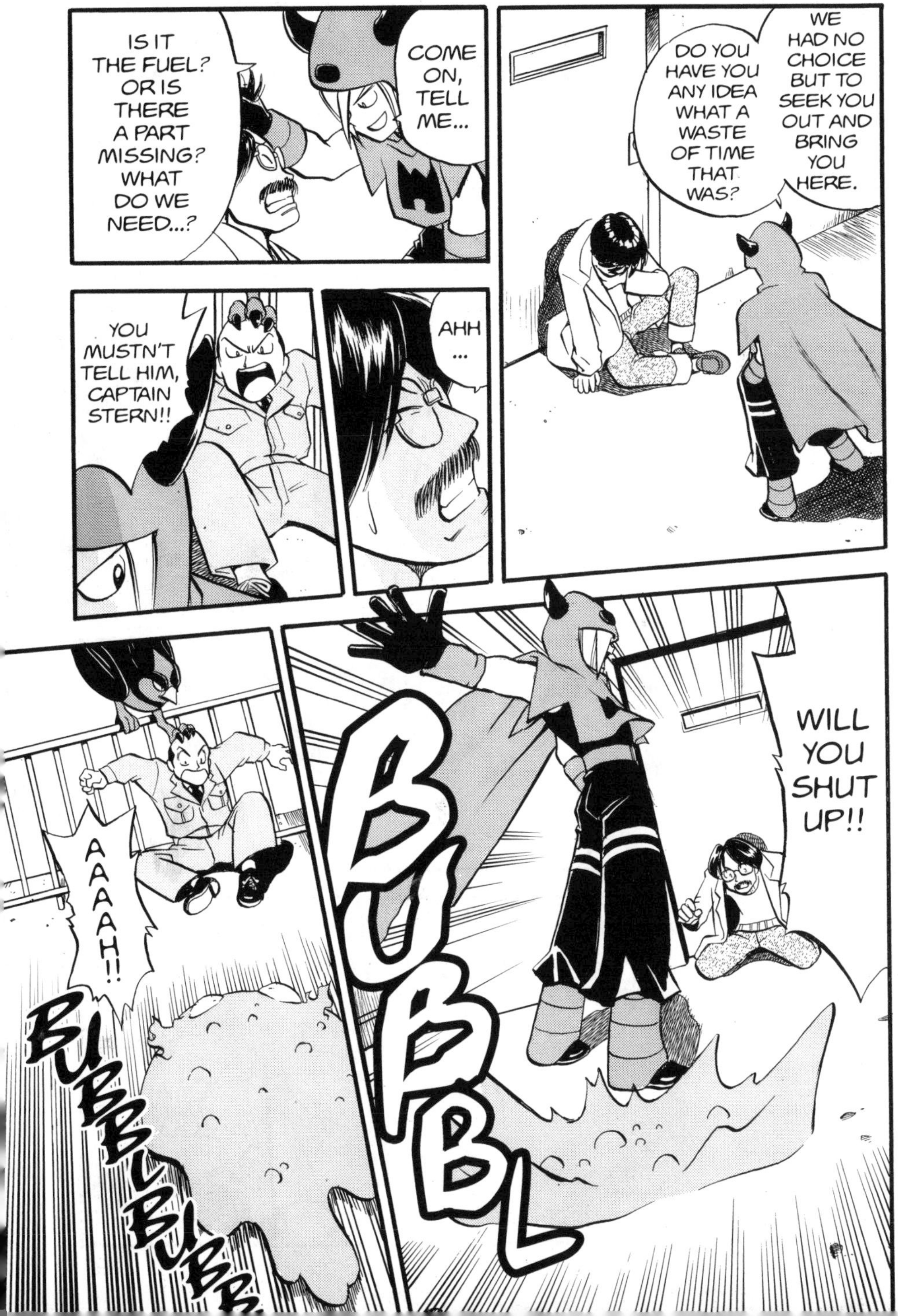
WE HAD NO CHOICE BUT TO SEEK YOU OUT AND BRING YOU HERE.
DO YOU HAVE YOU ANY IDEA WHAT A WASTE OF TIME THAT WAS?
COME ON, TELL ME...
IS IT THE FUEL? OR IS THERE A PART MISSING? WHAT DO WE NEED...?
AHH...
YOU MUSTN'T TELL HIM, CAPTAIN STERN!!
WILL YOU SHUT UP!!
BUBBL
AAAAAH!!
BUBBLUBUBB

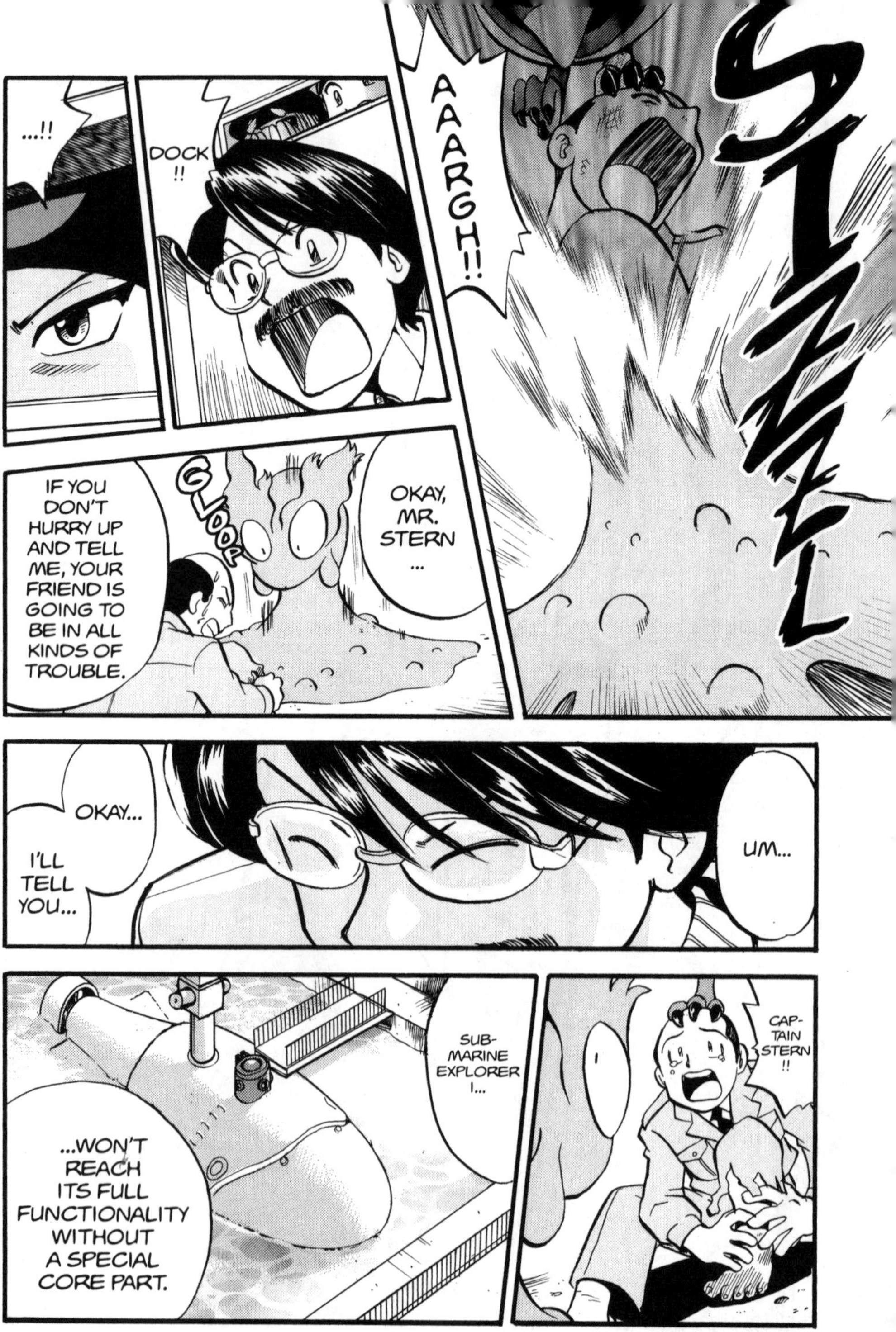
AAARGH!!
DOCK!!
...!!
OKAY, MR. STERN...
GLOOP
IF YOU DON'T HURRY UP AND TELL ME, YOUR FRIEND IS GOING TO BE IN ALL KINDS OF TROUBLE.
UM...
OKAY...
I'LL TELL YOU...
CAP-TAIN STERN!!
SUB-MARINE EXPLORER I...
...WON'T REACH ITS FULL FUNCTIONALITY WITHOUT A SPECIAL CORE PART.

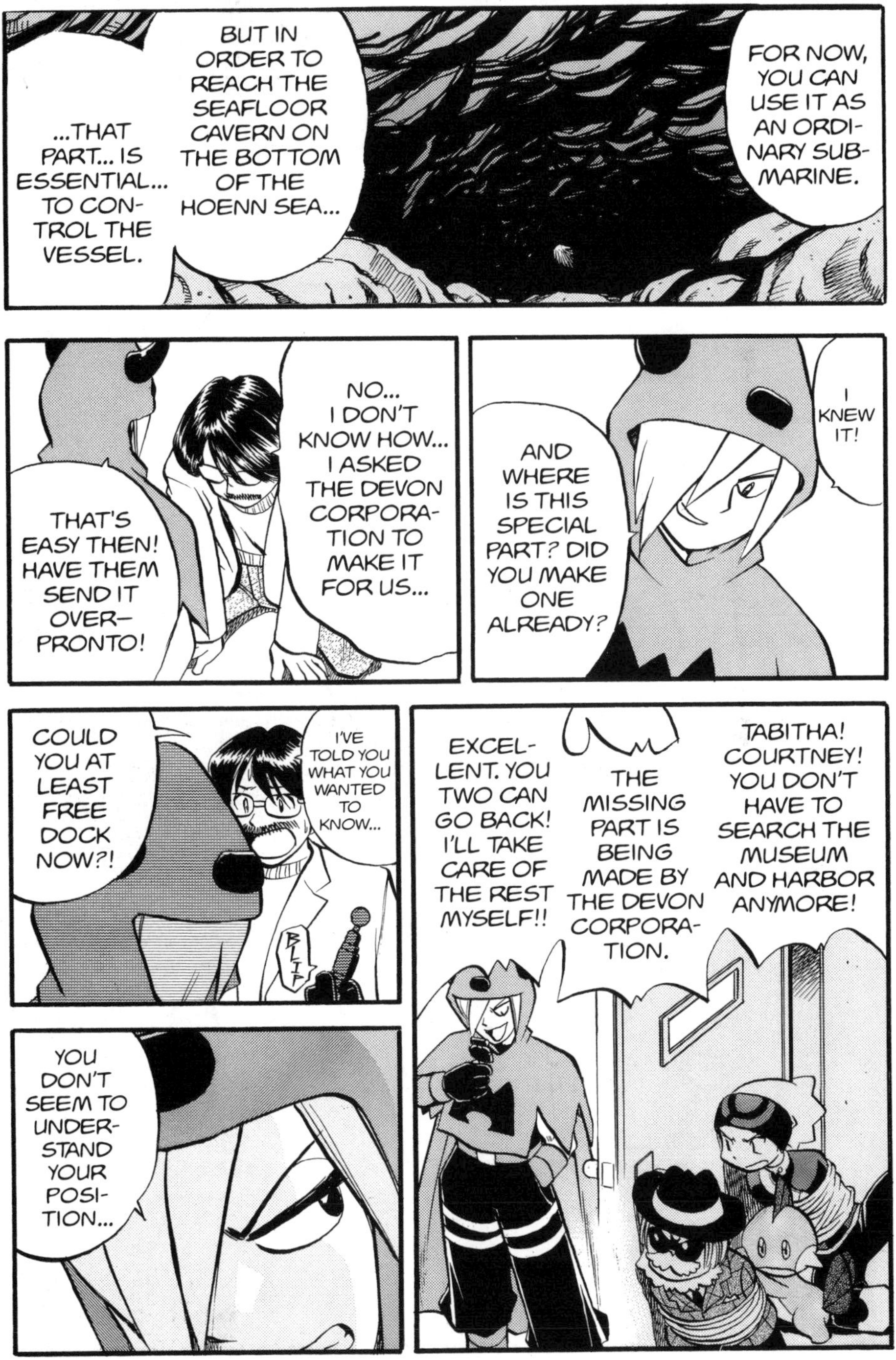
FOR NOW, YOU CAN USE IT AS AN ORDINARY SUBMARINE.
BUT IN ORDER TO REACH THE SEAFLOOR CAVERN ON THE BOTTOM OF THE HOENN SEA...
...THAT PART... IS ESSENTIAL... TO CONTROL THE VESSEL.
I KNEW IT!
AND WHERE IS THIS SPECIAL PART? DID YOU MAKE ONE ALREADY?
NO... I DON'T KNOW HOW... I ASKED THE DEVON CORPORATION TO MAKE IT FOR US...
THAT'S EASY THEN! HAVE THEM SEND IT OVER—PRONTO!
TABITHA! COURTNEY! YOU DON'T HAVE TO SEARCH THE MUSEUM AND HARBOR ANYMORE!
THE MISSING PART IS BEING MADE BY THE DEVON CORPORATION.
EXCELLENT. YOU TWO CAN GO BACK! I'LL TAKE CARE OF THE REST MYSELF!!
I'VE TOLD YOU WHAT YOU WANTED TO KNOW...
COULD YOU AT LEAST FREE DOCK NOW?!
BLIP
YOU DON'T SEEM TO UNDERSTAND YOUR POSITION...

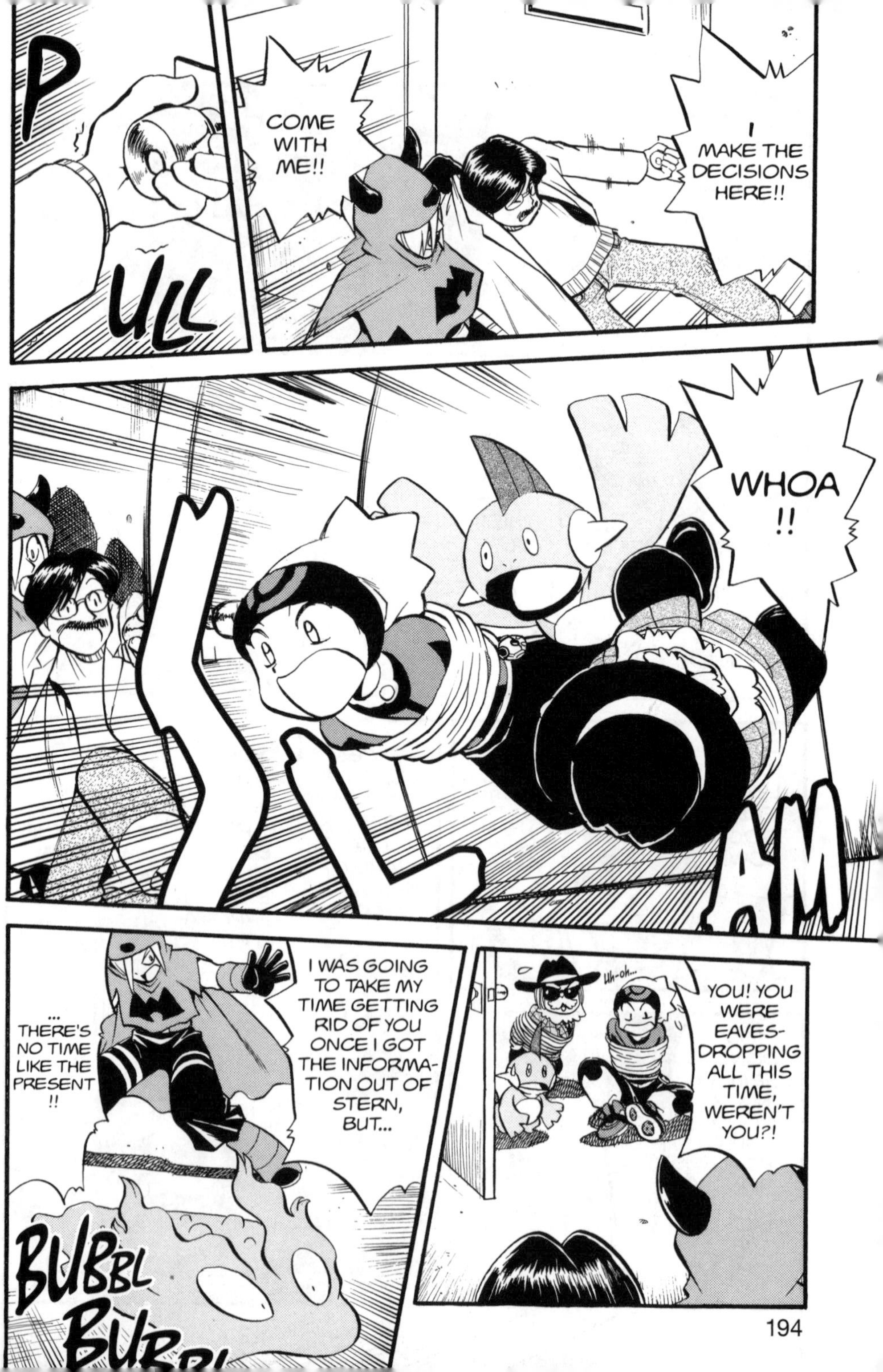
I MAKE THE DECISIONS HERE!!
COME WITH ME!!
PULL
WHOA!!
AM
Uh-oh...
YOU! YOU WERE EAVES-DROPPING ALL THIS TIME, WEREN'T YOU?!
I WAS GOING TO TAKE MY TIME GETTING RID OF YOU ONCE I GOT THE INFORMATION OUT OF STERN, BUT...
...THERE'S NO TIME LIKE THE PRESENT!!
BUBBL
BUBBL

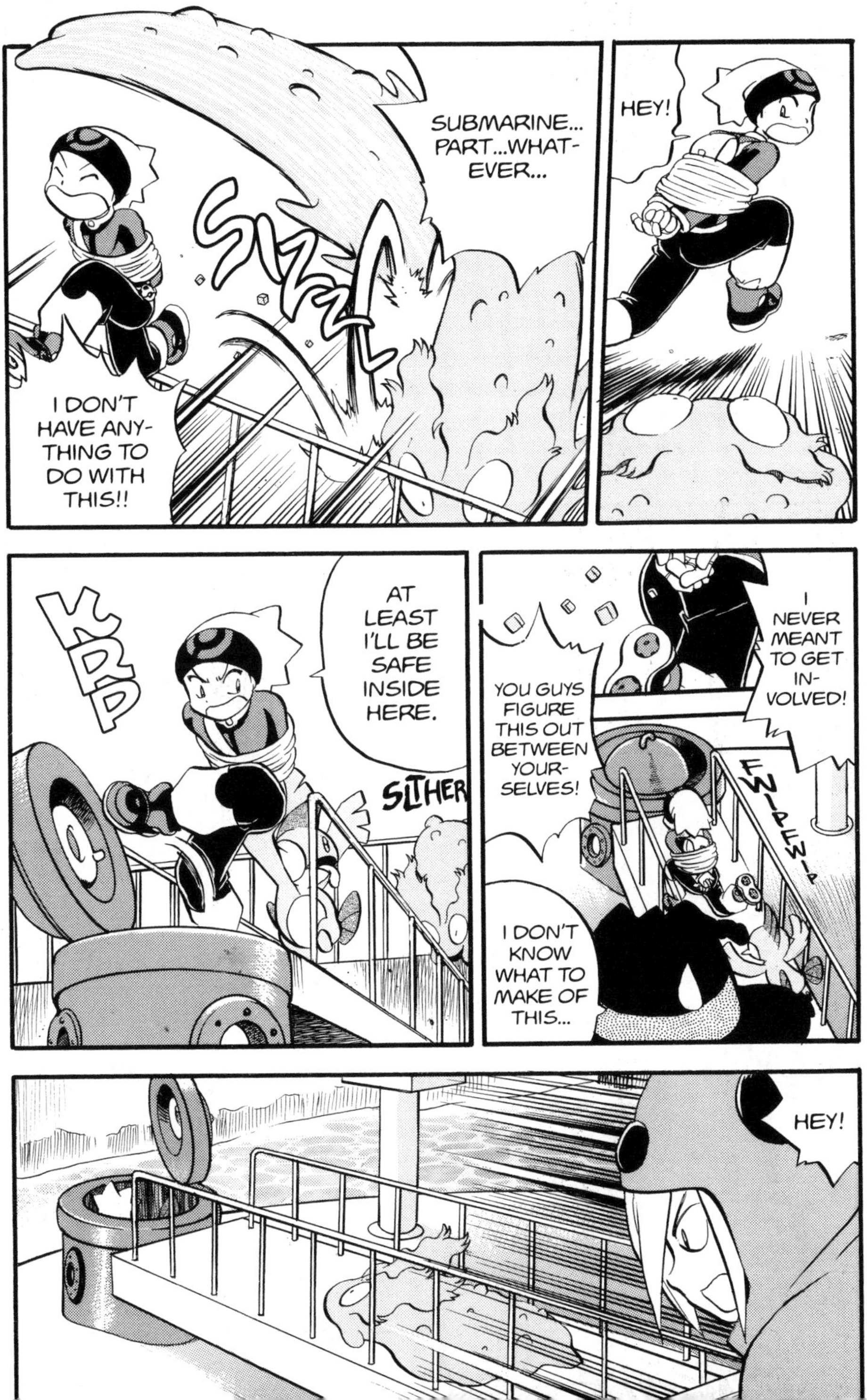
HEY!
SUBMARINE... PART...WHAT-EVER...
SIZZZL
I DON'T HAVE ANY-THING TO DO WITH THIS!!
I NEVER MEANT TO GET IN-VOLVED!
YOU GUYS FIGURE THIS OUT BETWEEN YOUR-SELVES!
FWIPFWIP
I DON'T KNOW WHAT TO MAKE OF THIS...
AT LEAST I'LL BE SAFE INSIDE HERE.
KRP
SLITHER
HEY!

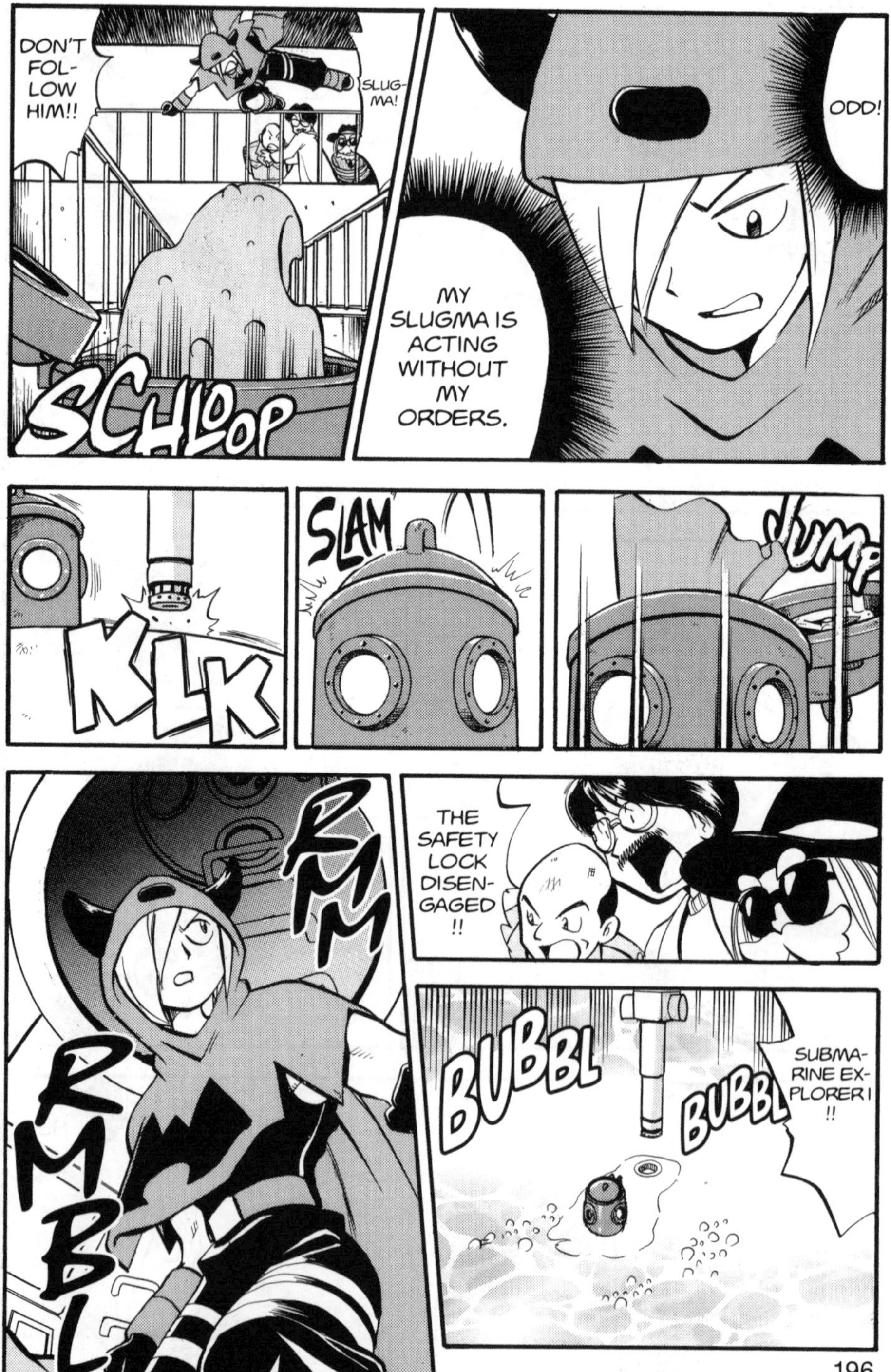
ODD!
MY SLUGMA IS ACTING WITHOUT MY ORDERS.
SLUG-MA!
DON'T FOL-LOW HIM!!
SCHLOOP
DUMP
SLAM
KLK
THE SAFETY LOCK DISEN-GAGED !!
SUBMA-RINE EX-PLORER I !!
BUBBL
BUBBL
RMM
RMMBL

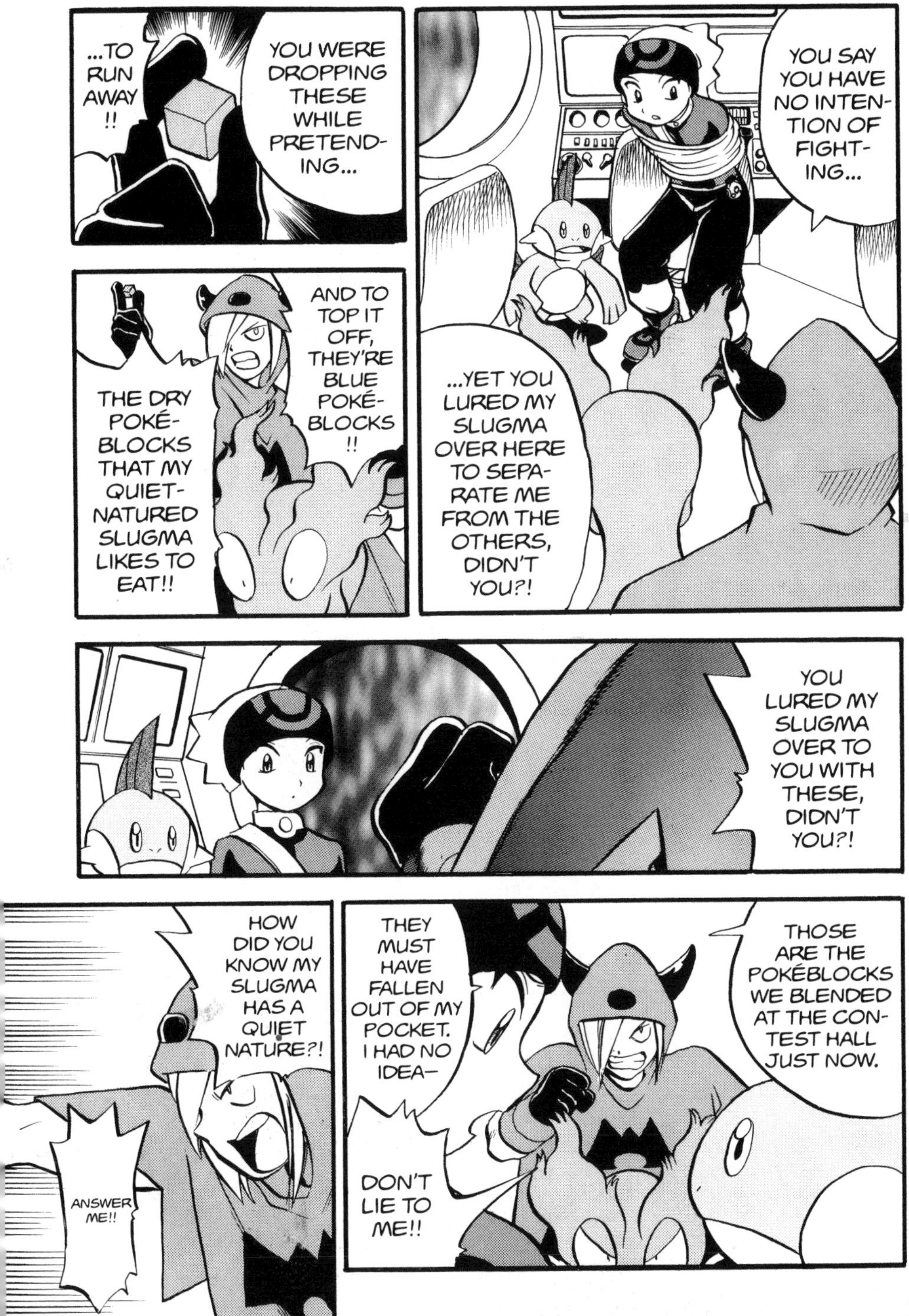

YOU SAY YOU HAVE NO INTENTION OF FIGHTING...
...YET YOU LURED MY SLUGMA OVER HERE TO SEPARATE ME FROM THE OTHERS, DIDN'T YOU?!
YOU WERE DROPPING THESE WHILE PRETENDING...
...TO RUN AWAY!!
AND TO TOP IT OFF, THEY'RE BLUE POKÉBLOCKS!!
THE DRY POKÉBLOCKS THAT MY QUIET-NATURED SLUGMA LIKES TO EAT!!
YOU LURED MY SLUGMA OVER TO YOU WITH THESE, DIDN'T YOU?!
THOSE ARE THE POKÉBLOCKS WE BLENDED AT THE CONTEST HALL JUST NOW.
THEY MUST HAVE FALLEN OUT OF MY POCKET. I HAD NO IDEA—
DON'T LIE TO ME!!
HOW DID YOU KNOW MY SLUGMA HAS A QUIET NATURE?!
ANSWER ME!!

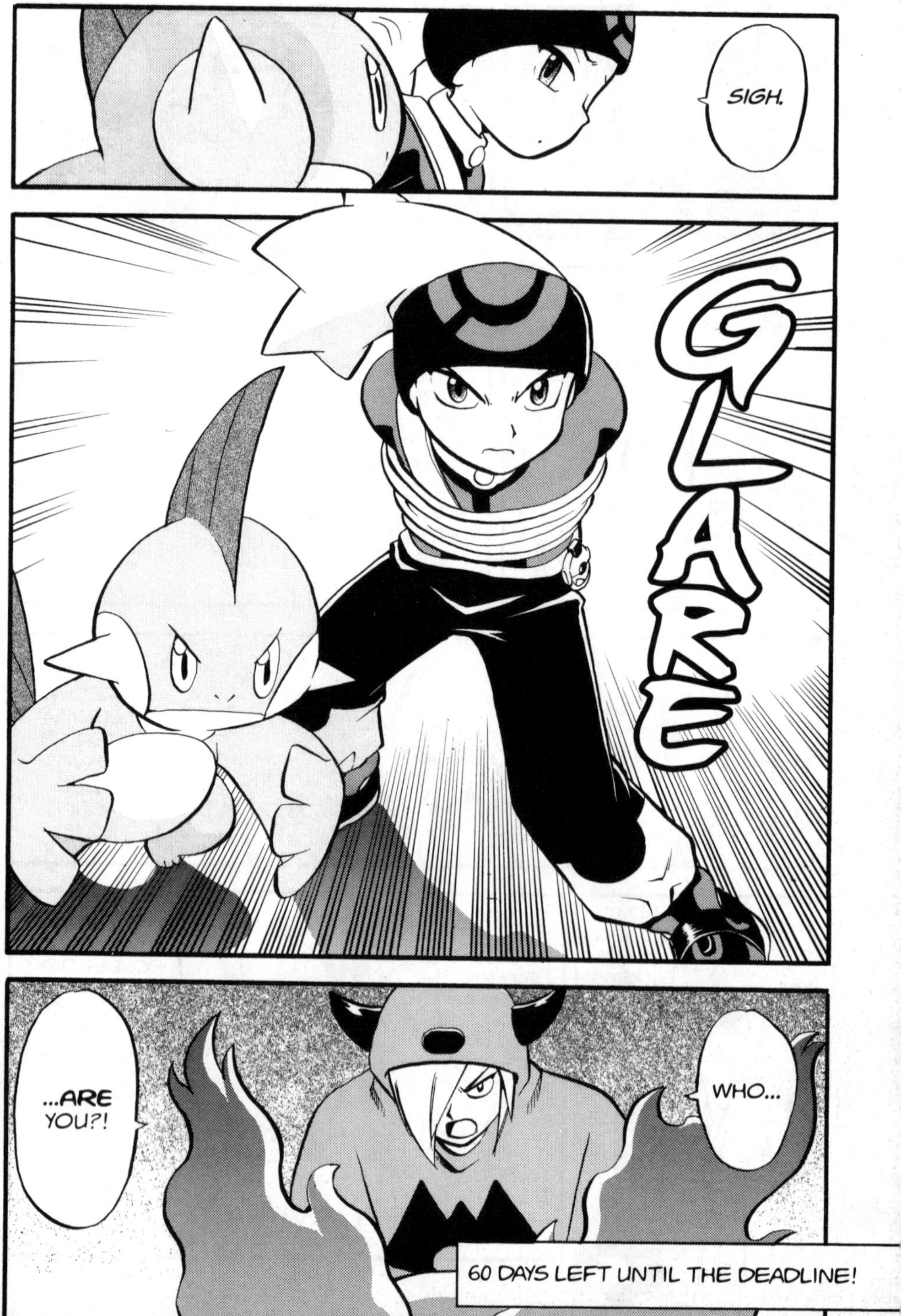
SIGH.
GLARE
WHO...
...ARE YOU?!
60 DAYS LEFT UNTIL THE DEADLINE!

Message from
Hidenori Kusaka

Things have become very convenient with the development of the personal computer. When I started this work, I wrote the story on manuscript paper by hand, but now I type away on my keyboard every day. And when I need to turn in my work, I send it by email. But when we become too dependent on such conveniences, I worry our work might lose its liveliness. Manga is something that is created by hand, so it's like an organic life-form... I especially feel this way when I'm editing the graphic novels.

—2004

Message from
Satoshi Yamamoto

The Ruby and Sapphire story arc is already in its third volume! The main event of this volume is obviously the family conflict between Ruby and Norman!! But personally, I'm more fond of the story line with the Swimmer and the Trick Master. As a matter of fact, I think the Swimmer is the other main character in the family conflict. (What? You don't agree...?)

—2004

● Adventure 202 ●
Slugging It Out with Slugma, Part 2

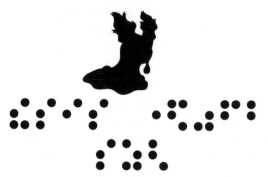

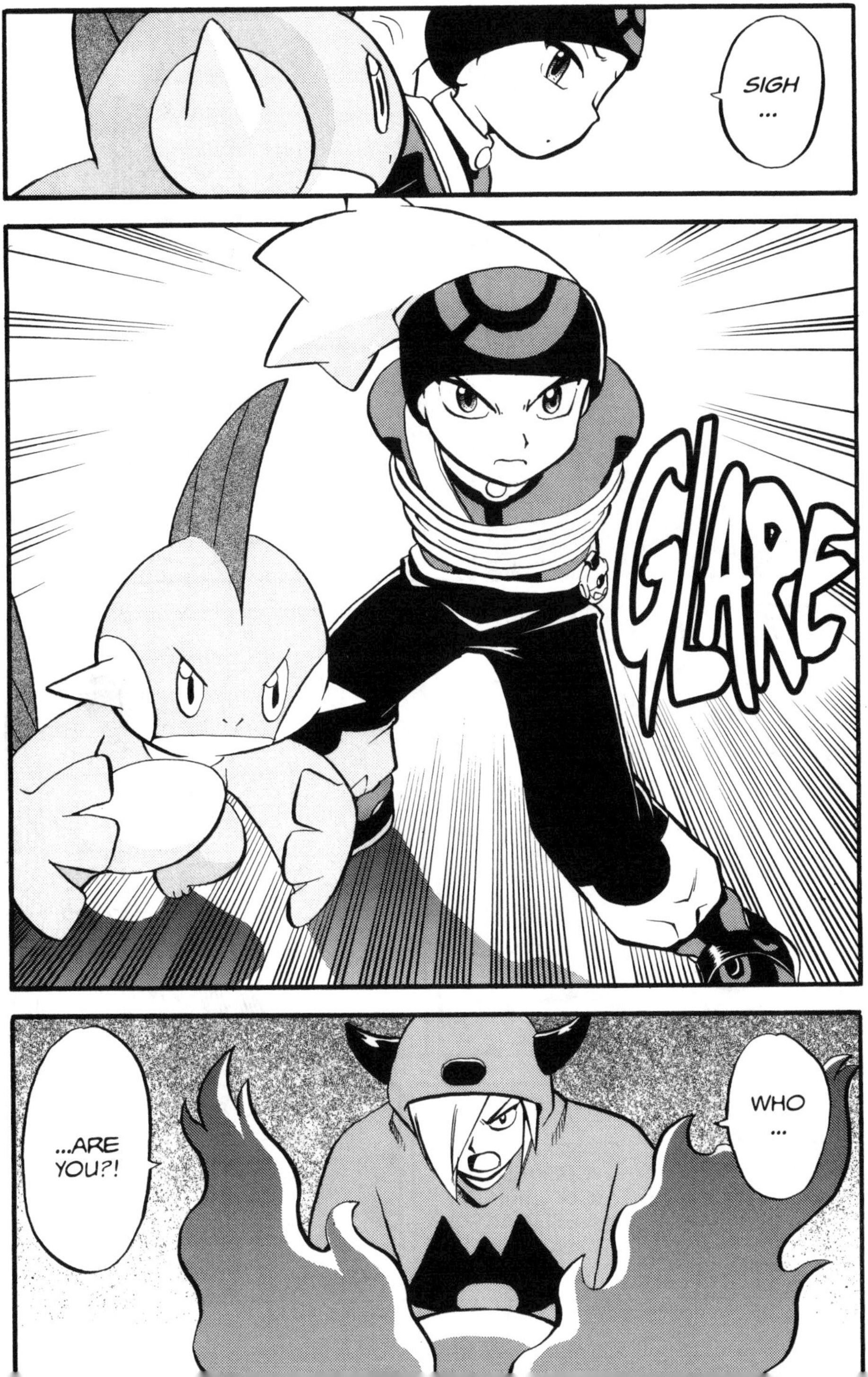
SIGH
...
GLARE
WHO
...
...ARE
YOU?!

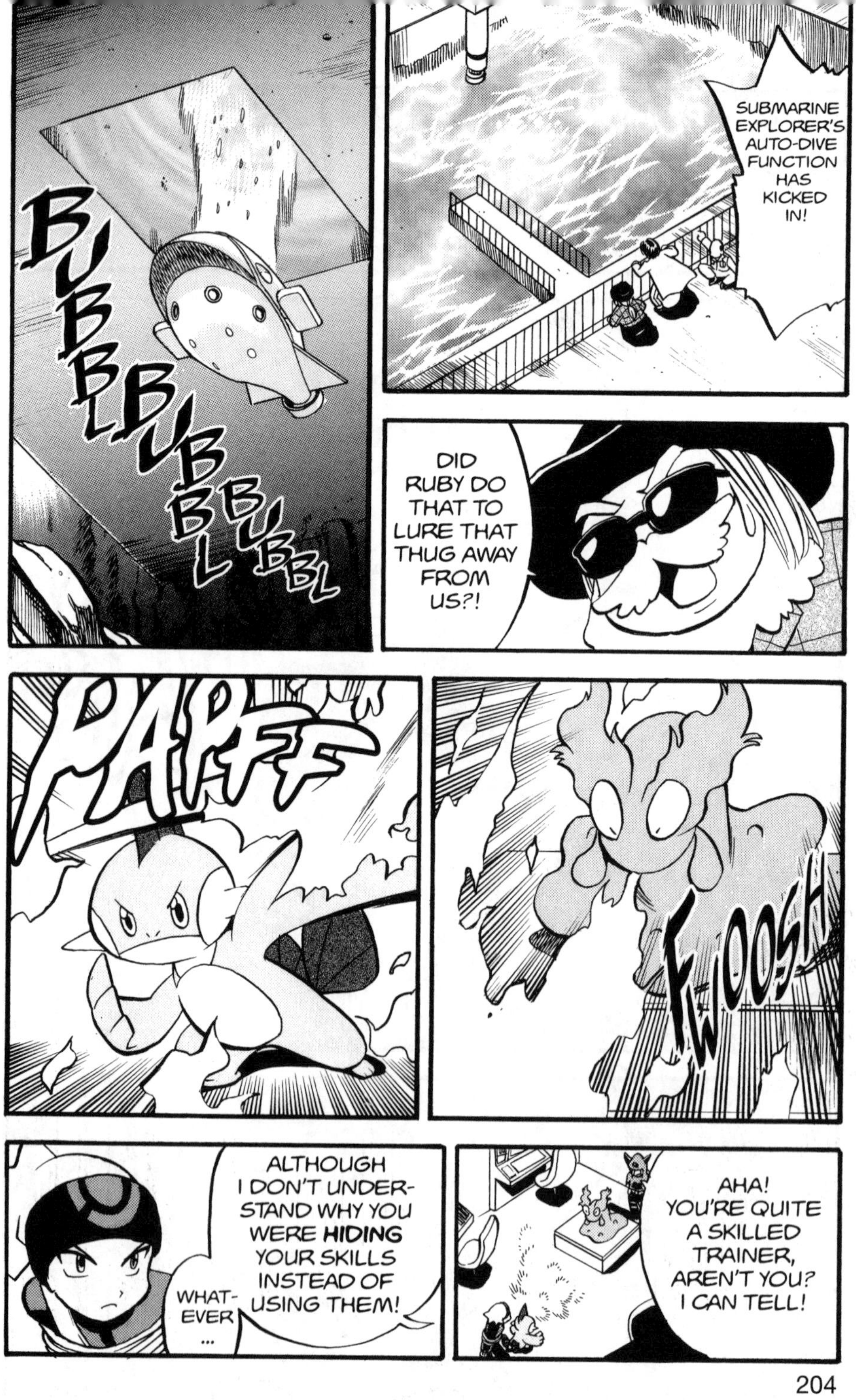
SUBMARINE EXPLORER'S AUTO-DIVE FUNCTION HAS KICKED IN!
DID RUBY DO THAT TO LURE THAT THUG AWAY FROM US?!
BUBBL BUBBL BUBBL
FWOOSH
PAFFF
AHA! YOU'RE QUITE A SKILLED TRAINER, AREN'T YOU? I CAN TELL!
ALTHOUGH I DON'T UNDERSTAND WHY YOU WERE **HIDING** YOUR SKILLS INSTEAD OF USING THEM!
WHATEVER ...

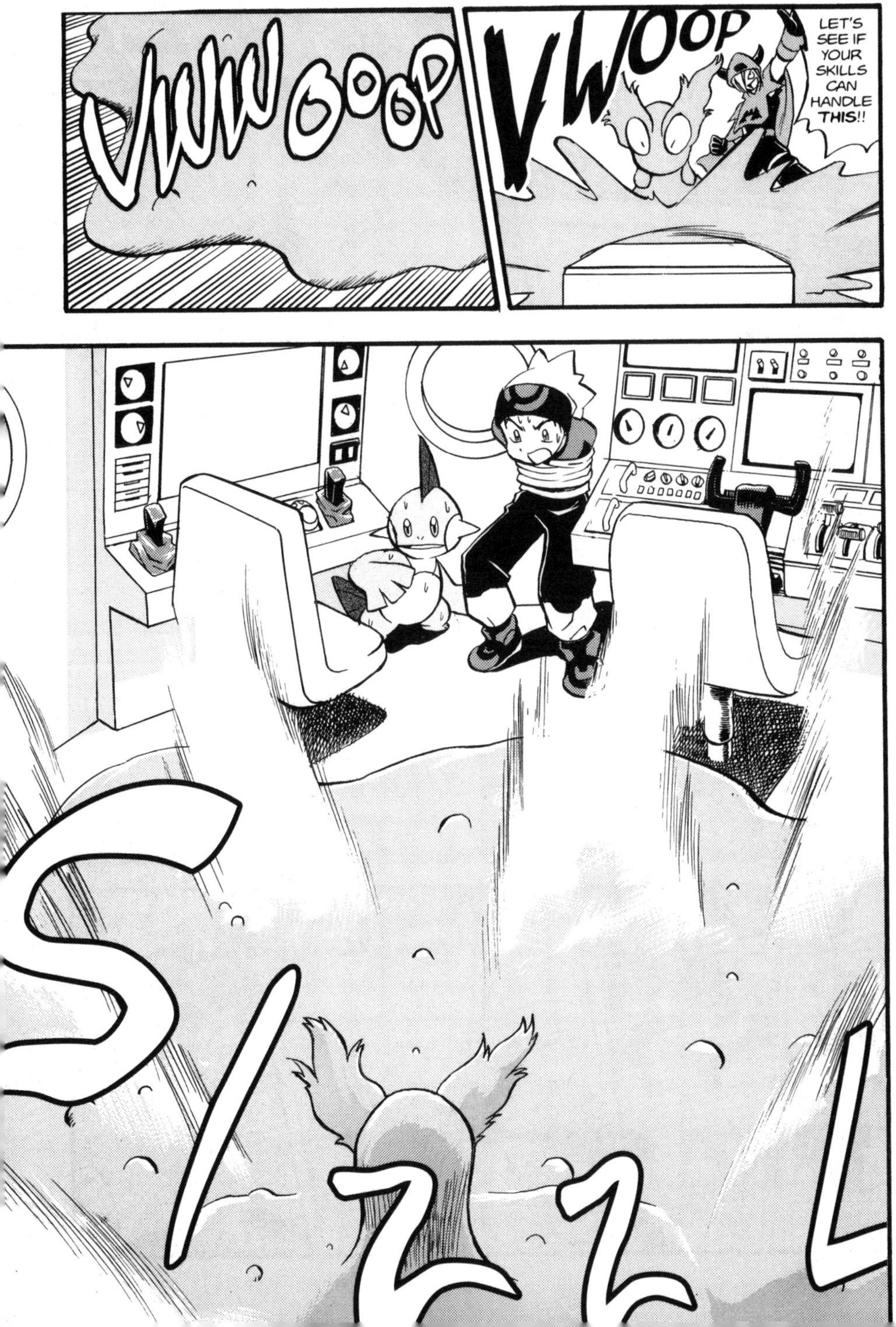
VWOOP
LET'S SEE IF YOUR SKILLS CAN HANDLE **THIS**!!
VWWOOOP
SIZZL

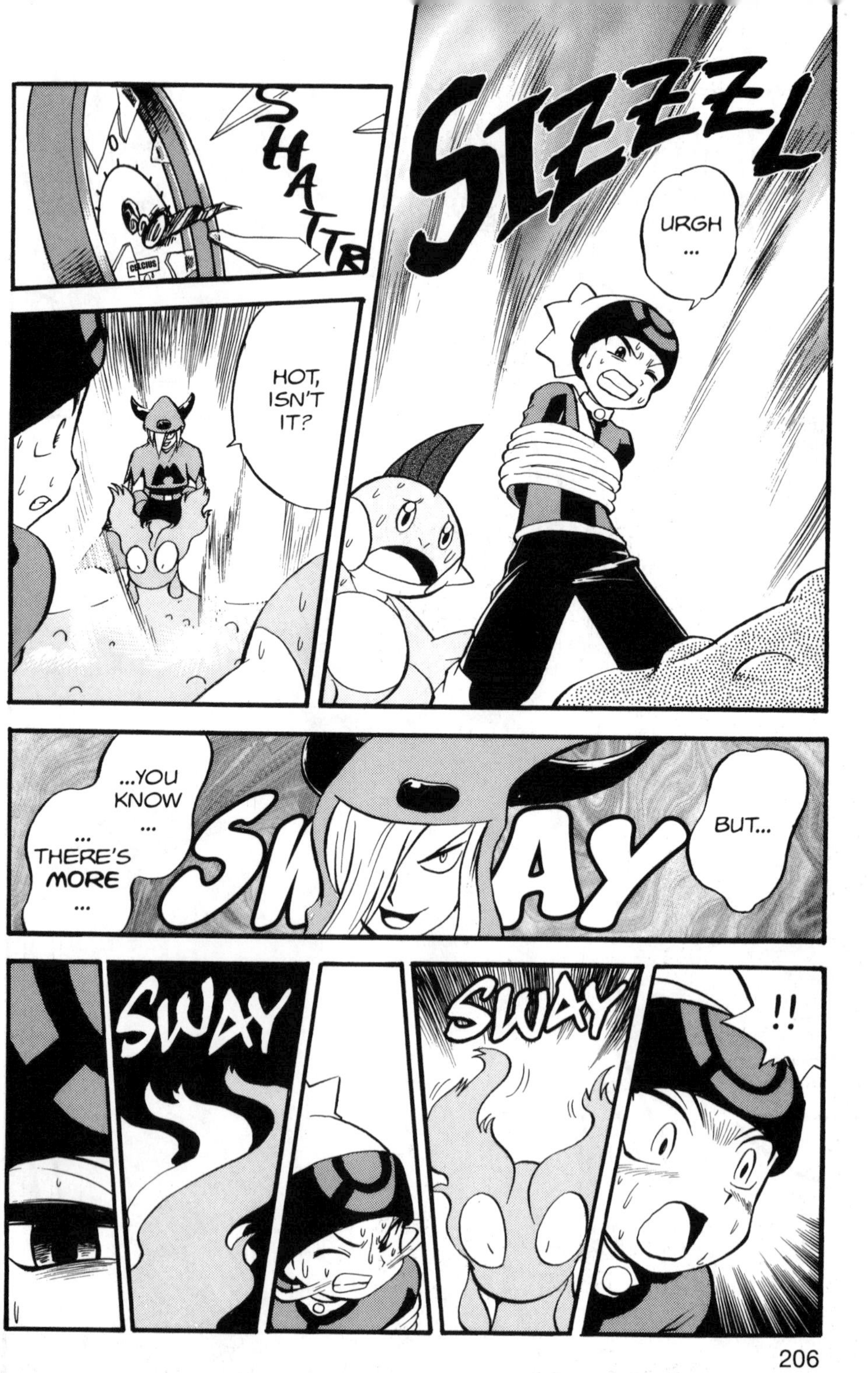

SIZZZL
URGH ...
SHATTR
HOT, ISN'T IT?
BUT...
SWAY
...YOU KNOW ... ... THERE'S MORE ...
!!
SWAY
SWAY

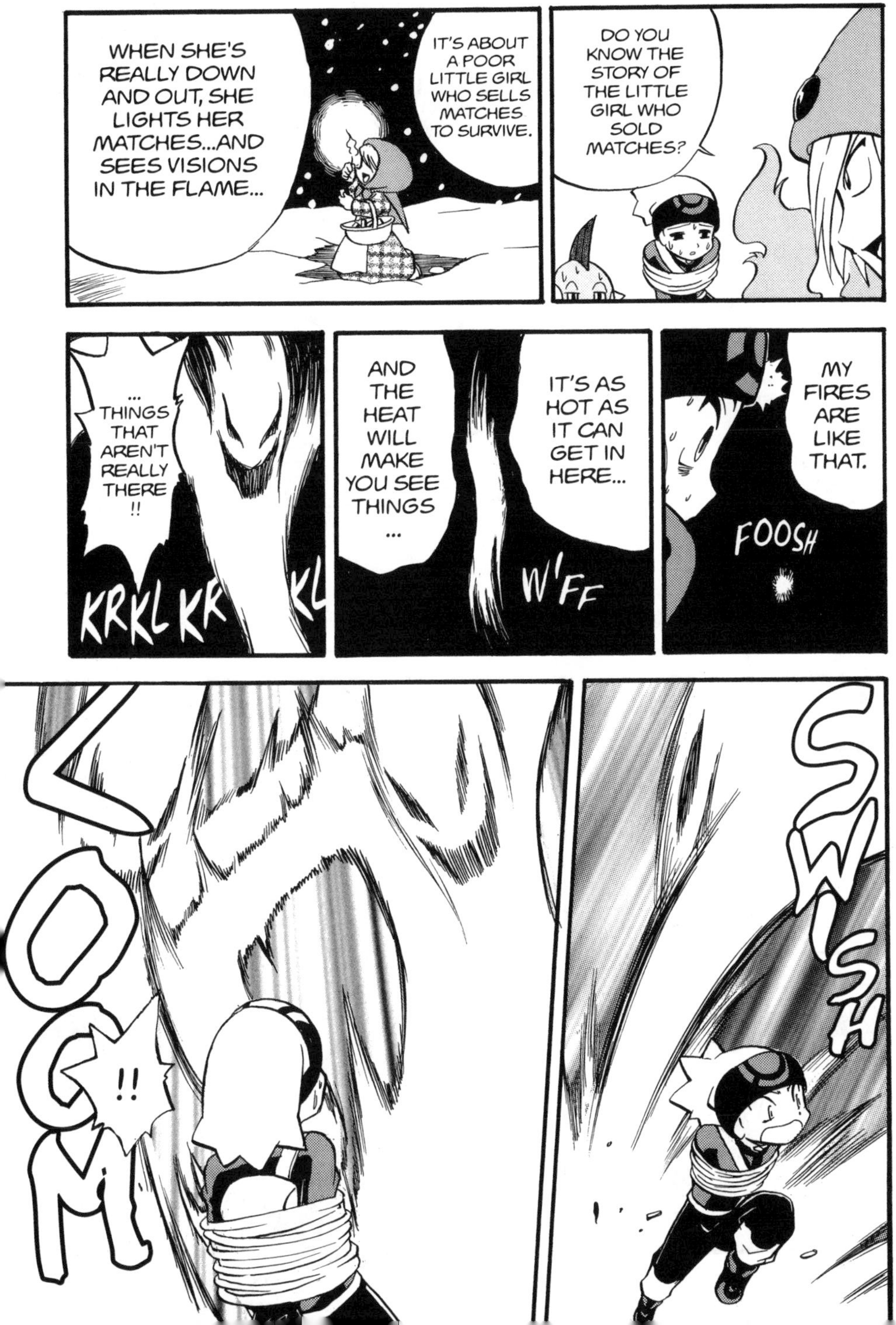
DO YOU KNOW THE STORY OF THE LITTLE GIRL WHO SOLD MATCHES?
IT'S ABOUT A POOR LITTLE GIRL WHO SELLS MATCHES TO SURVIVE.
WHEN SHE'S REALLY DOWN AND OUT, SHE LIGHTS HER MATCHES...AND SEES VISIONS IN THE FLAME...
MY FIRES ARE LIKE THAT.
FOOSH
IT'S AS HOT AS IT CAN GET IN HERE...
AND THE HEAT WILL MAKE YOU SEE THINGS ...
W'FF
... THINGS THAT AREN'T REALLY THERE !!
KRKL KR KL
SWISH
!!
VOOM

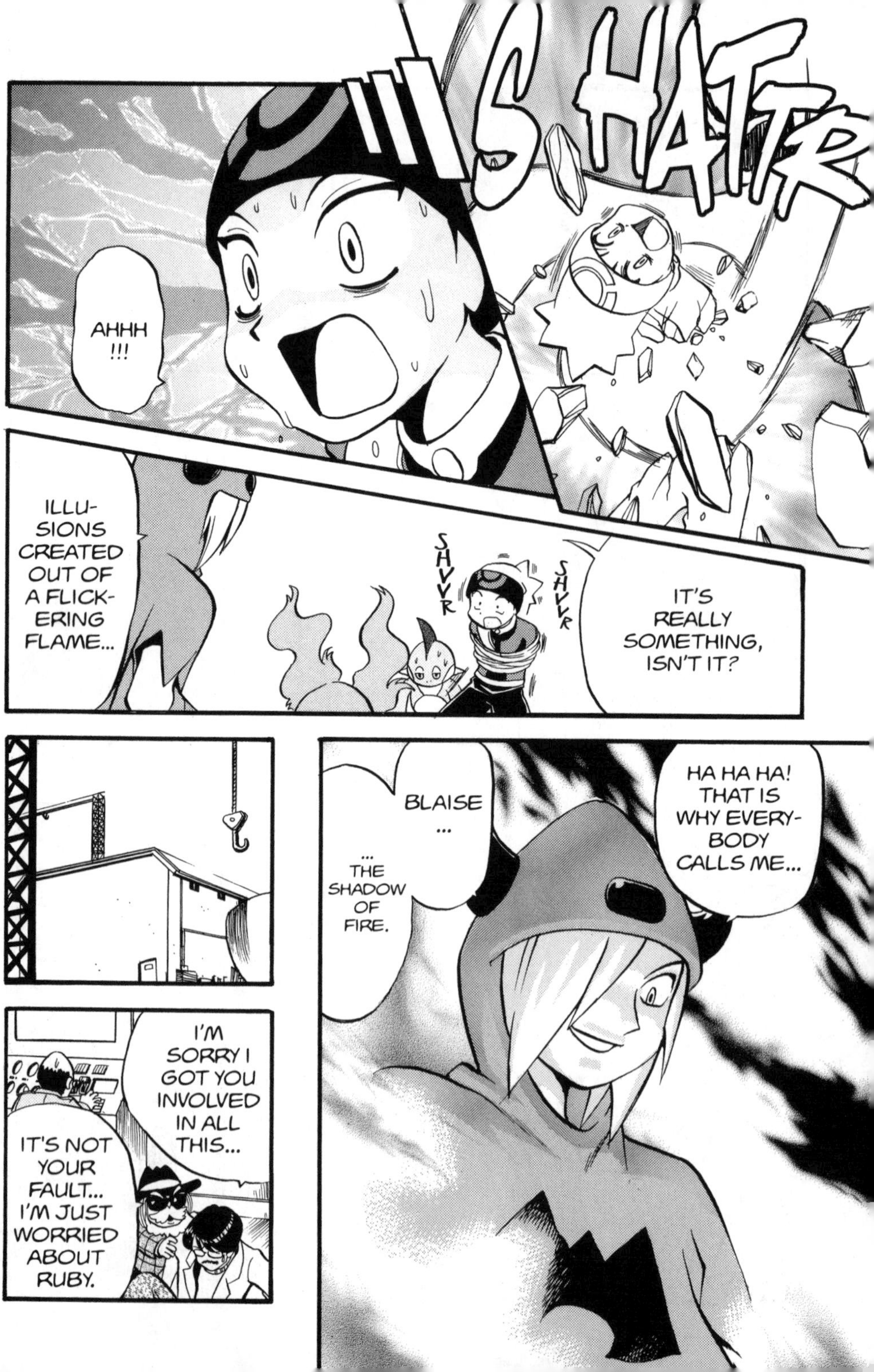
SHATTR
AHHH!!!
IT'S REALLY SOMETHING, ISN'T IT?
SHVVR
SHVVR
ILLUSIONS CREATED OUT OF A FLICKERING FLAME...
HA HA HA! THAT IS WHY EVERYBODY CALLS ME...
BLAISE...
...THE SHADOW OF FIRE.
I'M SORRY I GOT YOU INVOLVED IN ALL THIS...
IT'S NOT YOUR FAULT... I'M JUST WORRIED ABOUT RUBY.

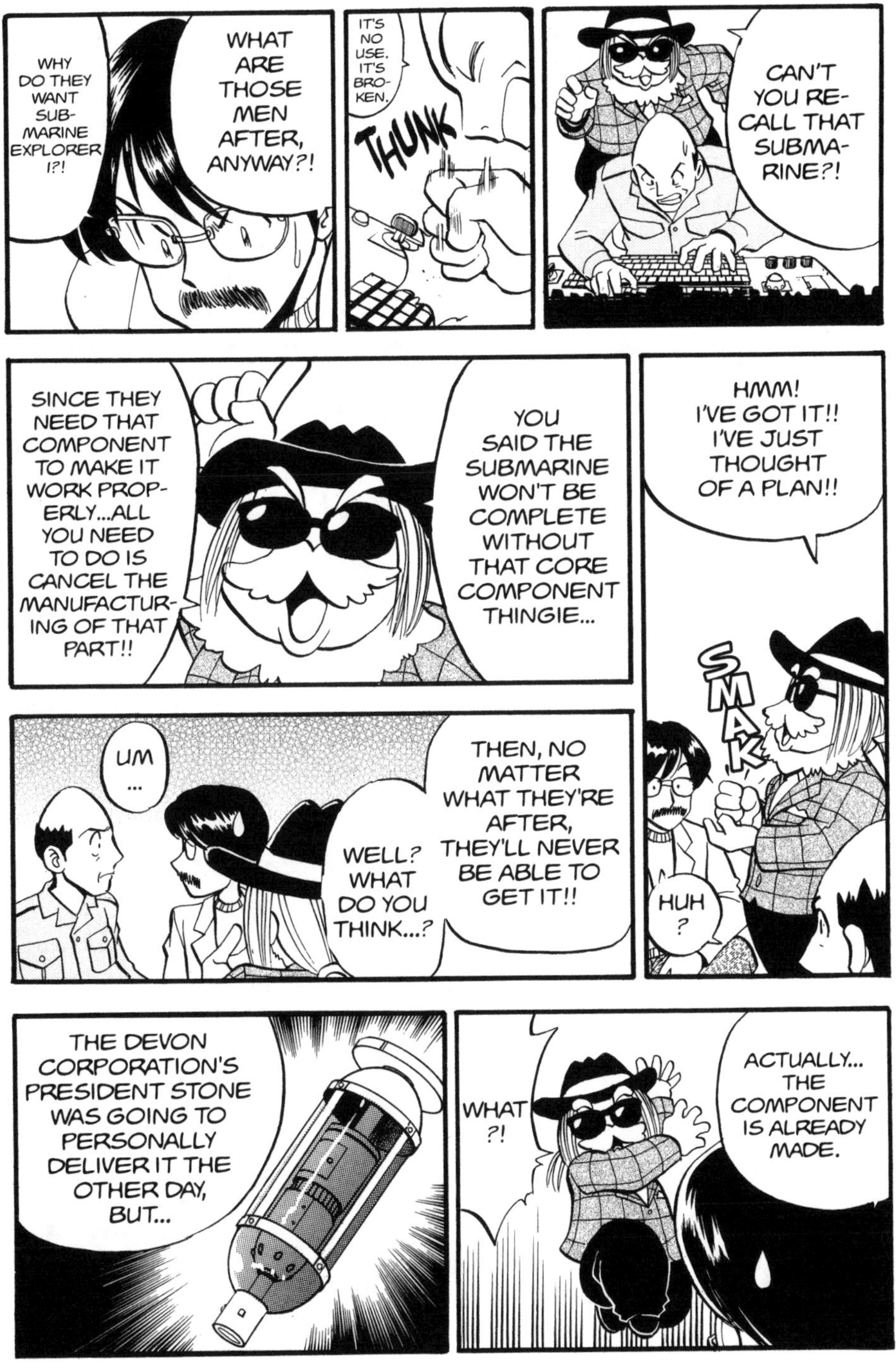
CAN'T YOU RE-CALL THAT SUBMARINE?!
IT'S NO USE. IT'S BROKEN.
THUNK
WHAT ARE THOSE MEN AFTER, ANYWAY?!
WHY DO THEY WANT SUB-MARINE EXPLORER I?!
HMM! I'VE GOT IT!! I'VE JUST THOUGHT OF A PLAN!!
SMAK
HUH ?
YOU SAID THE SUBMARINE WON'T BE COMPLETE WITHOUT THAT CORE COMPONENT THINGIE...
SINCE THEY NEED THAT COMPONENT TO MAKE IT WORK PROP-ERLY...ALL YOU NEED TO DO IS CANCEL THE MANUFACTUR-ING OF THAT PART!!
THEN, NO MATTER WHAT THEY'RE AFTER, THEY'LL NEVER BE ABLE TO GET IT!!
WELL? WHAT DO YOU THINK...?
UM ...
ACTUALLY... THE COMPONENT IS ALREADY MADE.
WHAT ?!
THE DEVON CORPORATION'S PRESIDENT STONE WAS GOING TO PERSONALLY DELIVER IT THE OTHER DAY, BUT...

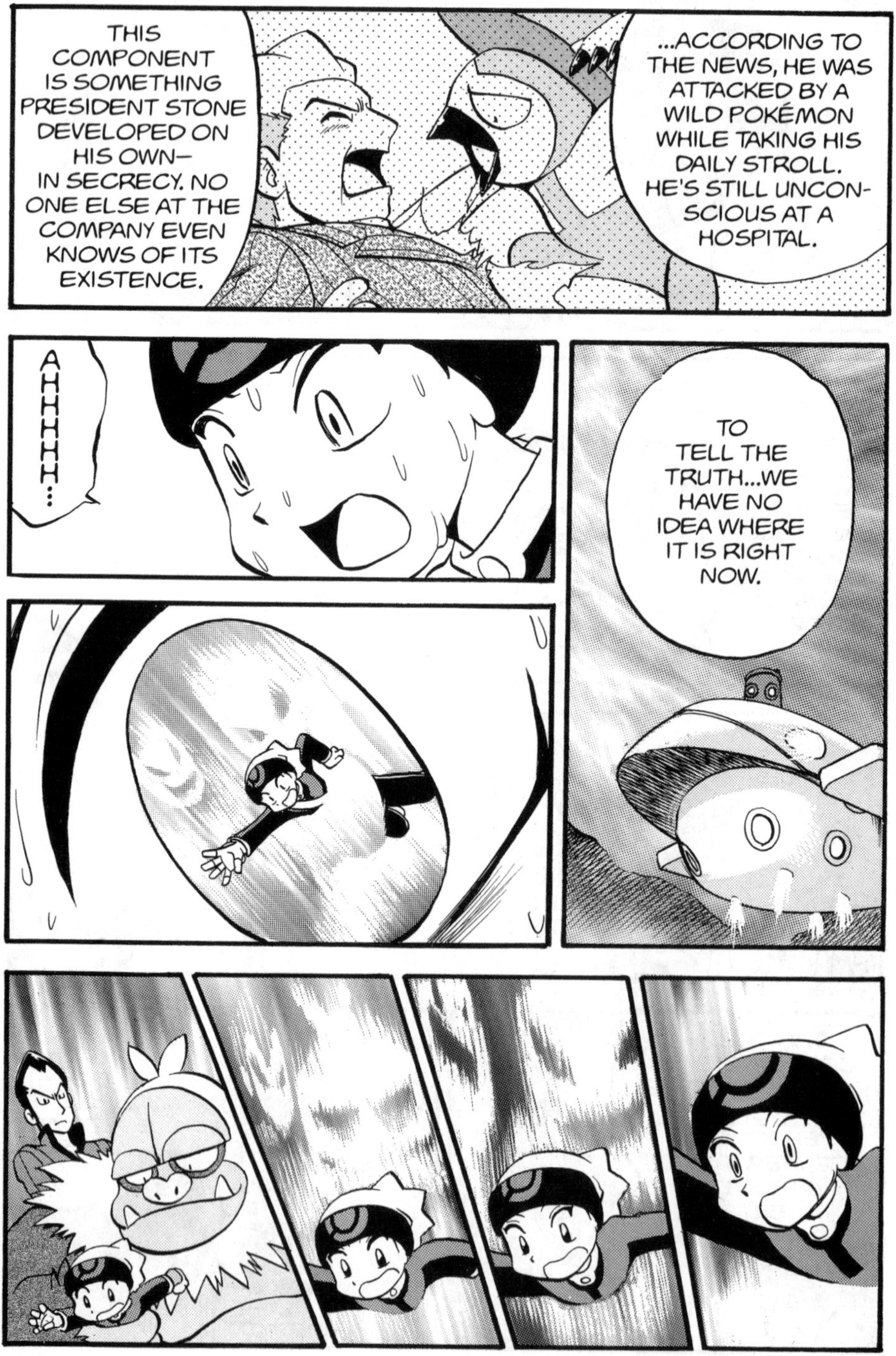
...ACCORDING TO THE NEWS, HE WAS ATTACKED BY A WILD POKÉMON WHILE TAKING HIS DAILY STROLL. HE'S STILL UNCONSCIOUS AT A HOSPITAL.
THIS COMPONENT IS SOMETHING PRESIDENT STONE DEVELOPED ON HIS OWN— IN SECRECY. NO ONE ELSE AT THE COMPANY EVEN KNOWS OF ITS EXISTENCE.
TO TELL THE TRUTH...WE HAVE NO IDEA WHERE IT IS RIGHT NOW.
AHHHHH...

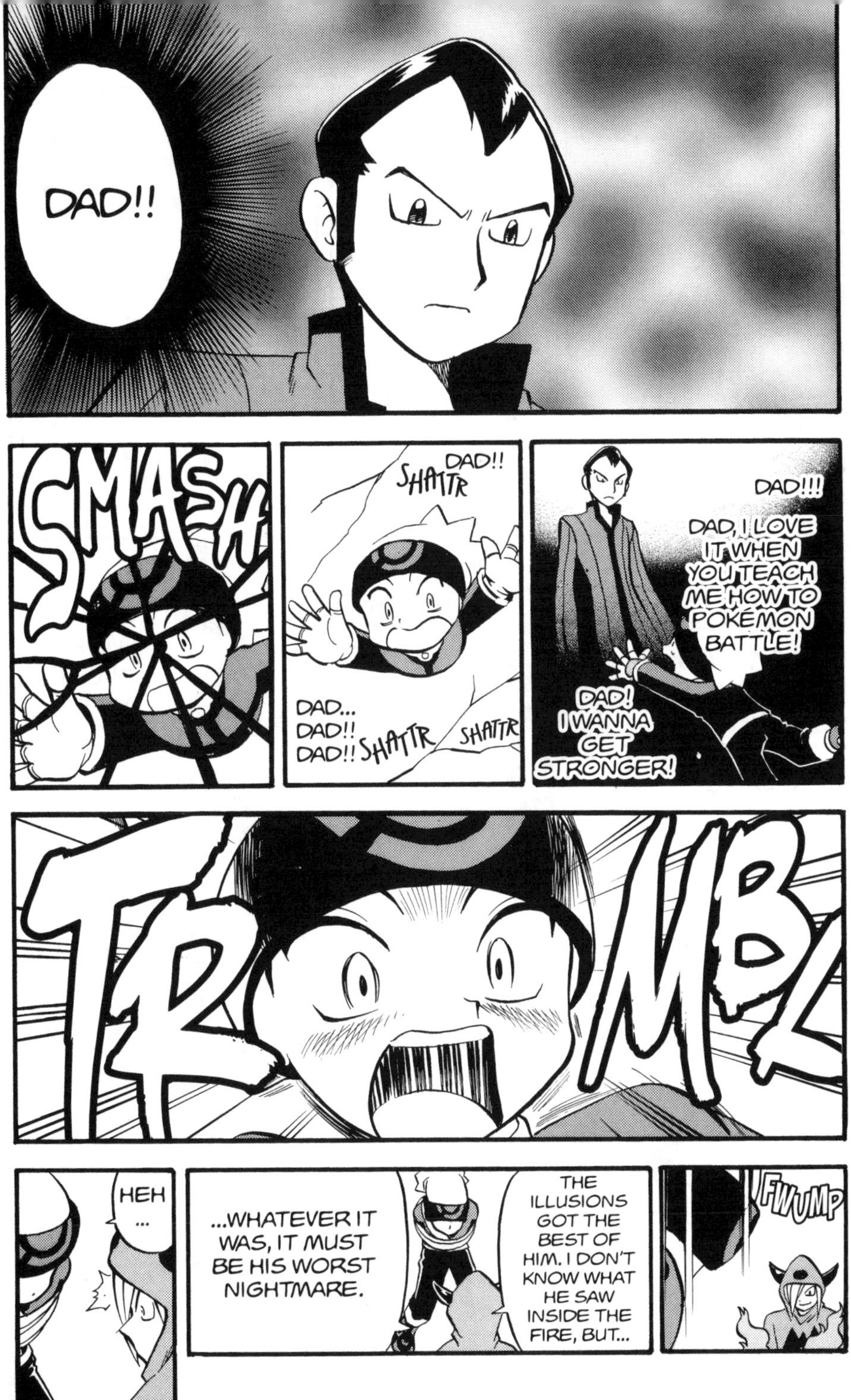
DAD!!
DAD!!!
DAD, I LOVE IT WHEN YOU TEACH ME HOW TO POKÉMON BATTLE!
DAD! I WANNA GET STRONGER!
DAD!!
SHATTR
DAD... DAD!! DAD!!
SHATTR
SHATTR
SMASH
TR
MBL
FWUMP
THE ILLUSIONS GOT THE BEST OF HIM. I DON'T KNOW WHAT HE SAW INSIDE THE FIRE, BUT...
...WHATEVER IT WAS, IT MUST BE HIS WORST NIGHTMARE.
HEH ...

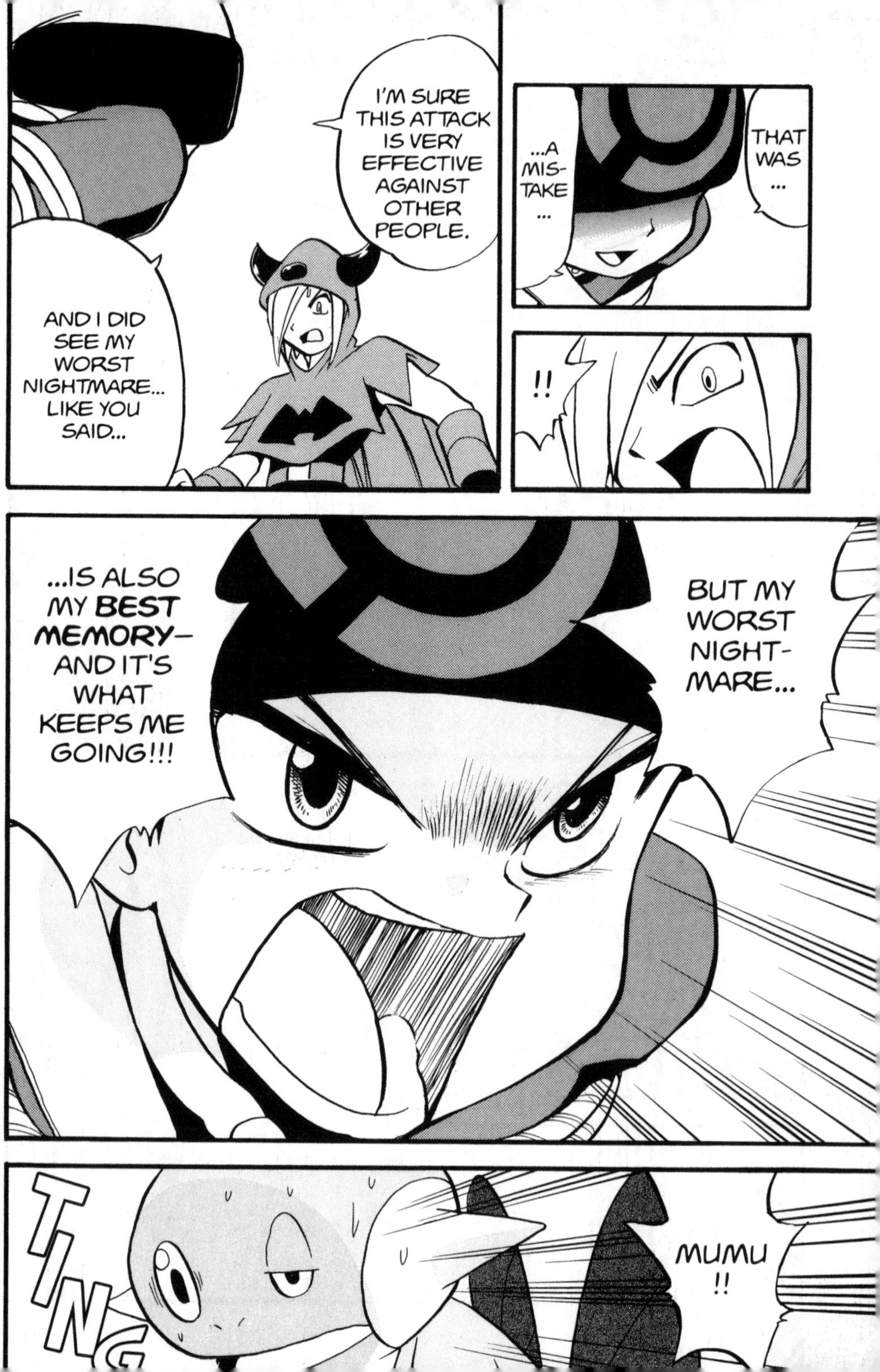
THAT WAS...
...A MIS-TAKE...
!!
I'M SURE THIS ATTACK IS VERY EFFECTIVE AGAINST OTHER PEOPLE.
AND I DID SEE MY WORST NIGHTMARE... LIKE YOU SAID...
BUT MY WORST NIGHT-MARE...
...IS ALSO MY **BEST MEMORY**—AND IT'S WHAT KEEPS ME GOING!!!
MUMU !!
TING

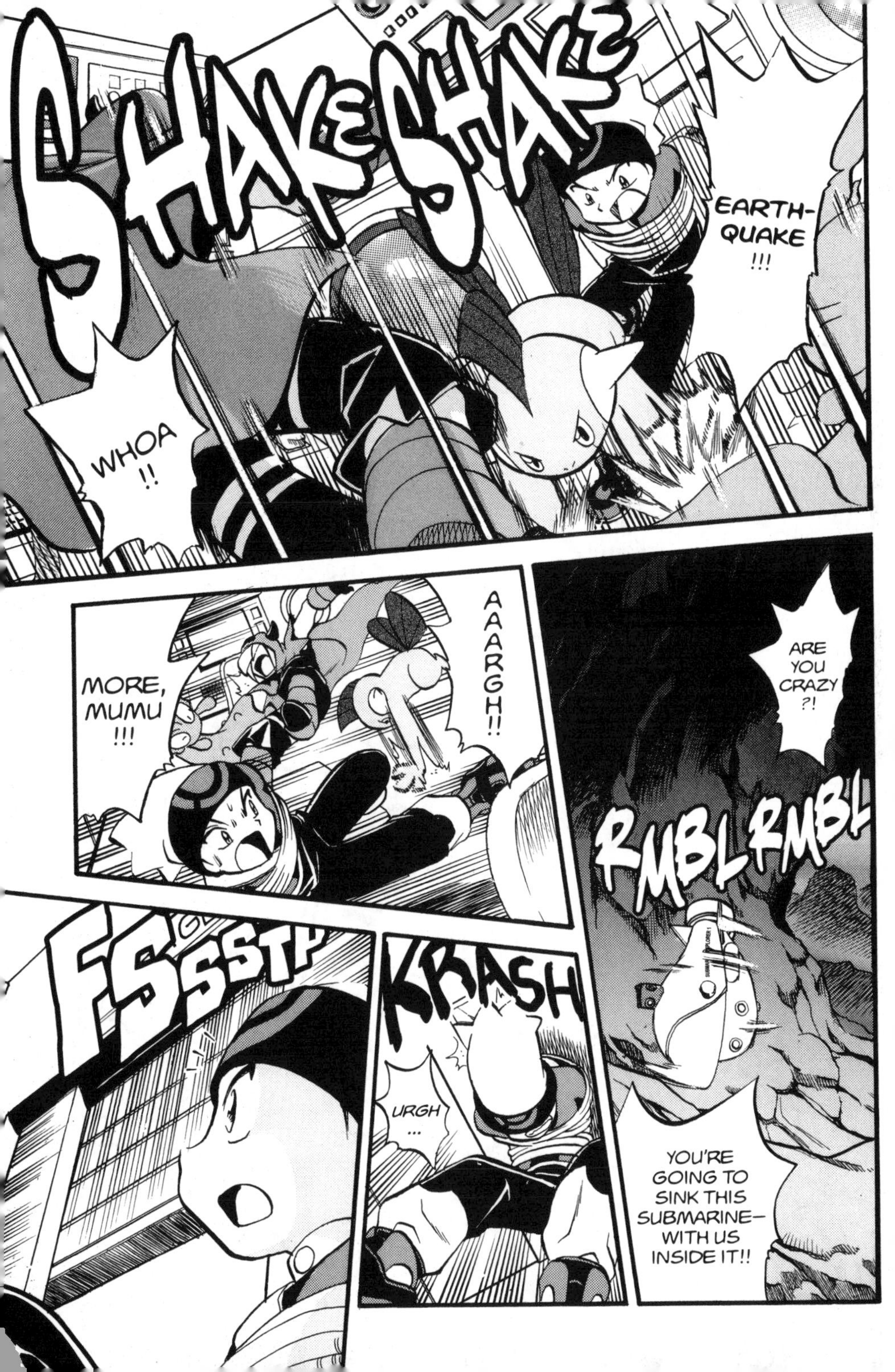
SHAKE SHAKE
EARTHQUAKE!!!
WHOA!!
ARE YOU CRAZY?!
RMBL RMBL
YOU'RE GOING TO SINK THIS SUBMARINE—WITH US INSIDE IT!!
AAAARGH!!
MORE, MUMU!!!
KRASH
URGH...
FSSSTP

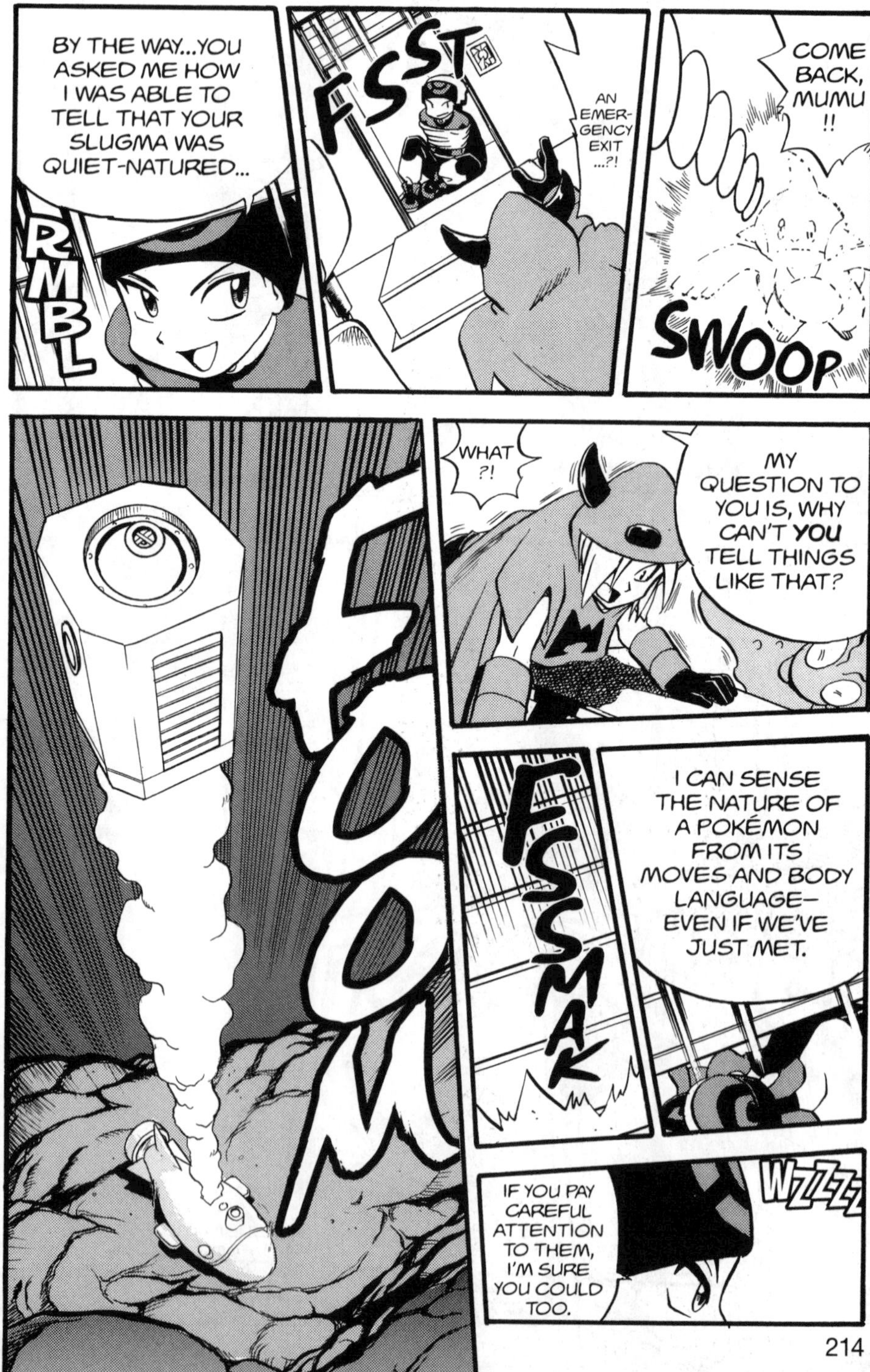
COME BACK, MUMU !!
SWOOP
FSST
AN EMERGENCY EXIT ...?!
BY THE WAY...YOU ASKED ME HOW I WAS ABLE TO TELL THAT YOUR SLUGMA WAS QUIET-NATURED...
RMBL
MY QUESTION TO YOU IS, WHY CAN'T **YOU** TELL THINGS LIKE THAT?
WHAT ?!
I CAN SENSE THE NATURE OF A POKÉMON FROM ITS MOVES AND BODY LANGUAGE— EVEN IF WE'VE JUST MET.
FSSMAK
WZZZZ
IF YOU PAY CAREFUL ATTENTION TO THEM, I'M SURE YOU COULD TOO.
FOOM

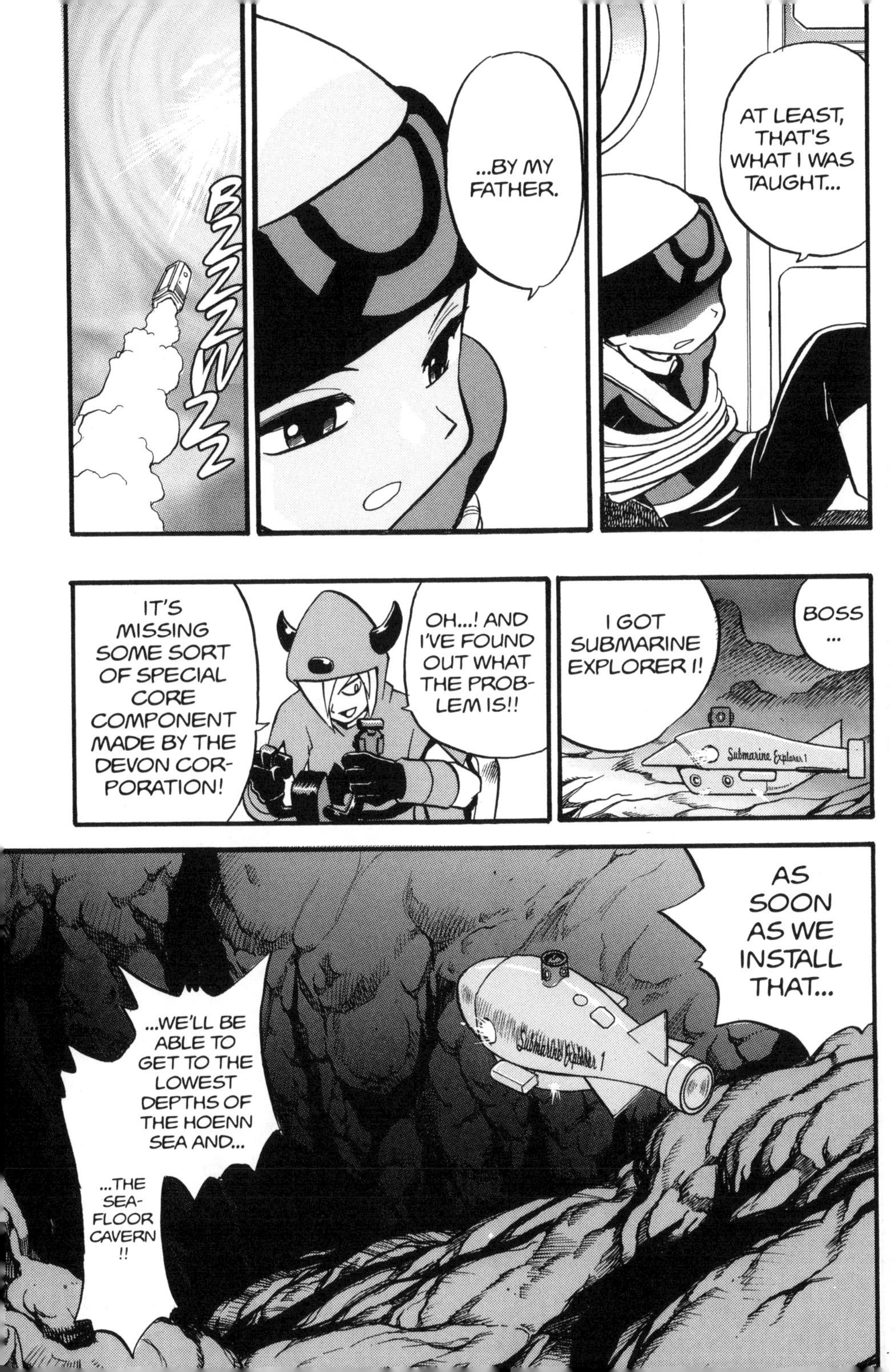
AT LEAST, THAT'S WHAT I WAS TAUGHT...
...BY MY FATHER.
BZZZWZZZ
BOSS...
I GOT SUBMARINE EXPLORER 1!
Submarine Explorer 1
OH...! AND I'VE FOUND OUT WHAT THE PROB-LEM IS!!
IT'S MISSING SOME SORT OF SPECIAL CORE COMPONENT MADE BY THE DEVON COR-PORATION!
AS SOON AS WE INSTALL THAT...
Submarine Explorer 1
...WE'LL BE ABLE TO GET TO THE LOWEST DEPTHS OF THE HOENN SEA AND...
...THE SEA-FLOOR CAVERN !!

ADVENTURE MAP

SAPPHIRE

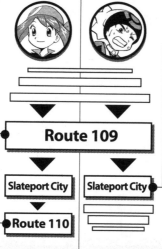

CHIC
Combusken ♀
Lv19

RONO
Lairon ♂
Lv34

LORRY
Wailord ♂
Lv42

Route 109

Slateport City

Route 110

RUBY

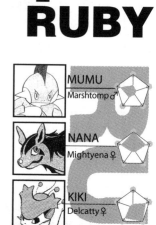

MUMU
Marshtomp ♂

NANA
Mightyena ♀

KIKI
Delcatty ♀

Slateport City

Stone Badge	Knuckle Badge	Dynamo Badge	Heat Badge
Balance Badge	Feather Badge	Mind Badge	Rain Badge

	Coolness	Beauty	Cuteness	Cleverness	Toughness
Normal					
Super					
Hyper					
Master					

● Adventure 203 ●
I'm Your Biggest Fan, Donphan

Pokémon™ Adventures Ruby & Sapphire
The Fourth Chapter

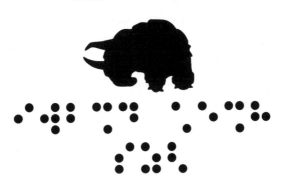

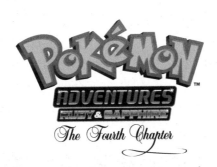

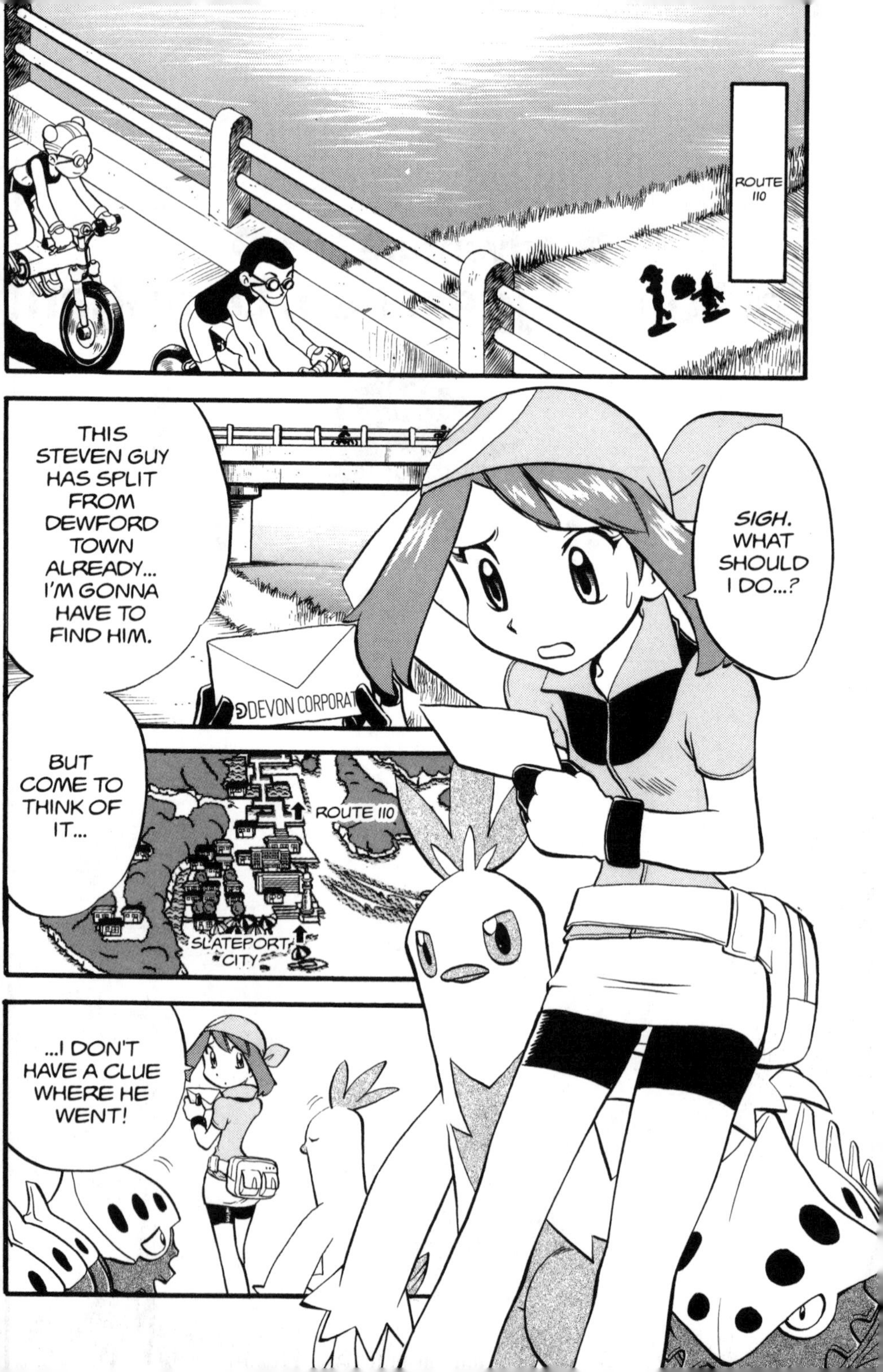
ROUTE 110
SIGH. WHAT SHOULD I DO...?
THIS STEVEN GUY HAS SPLIT FROM DEWFORD TOWN ALREADY... I'M GONNA HAVE TO FIND HIM.
DEVON CORPORAT
BUT COME TO THINK OF IT...
ROUTE 110
SLATEPORT CITY
...I DON'T HAVE A CLUE WHERE HE WENT!

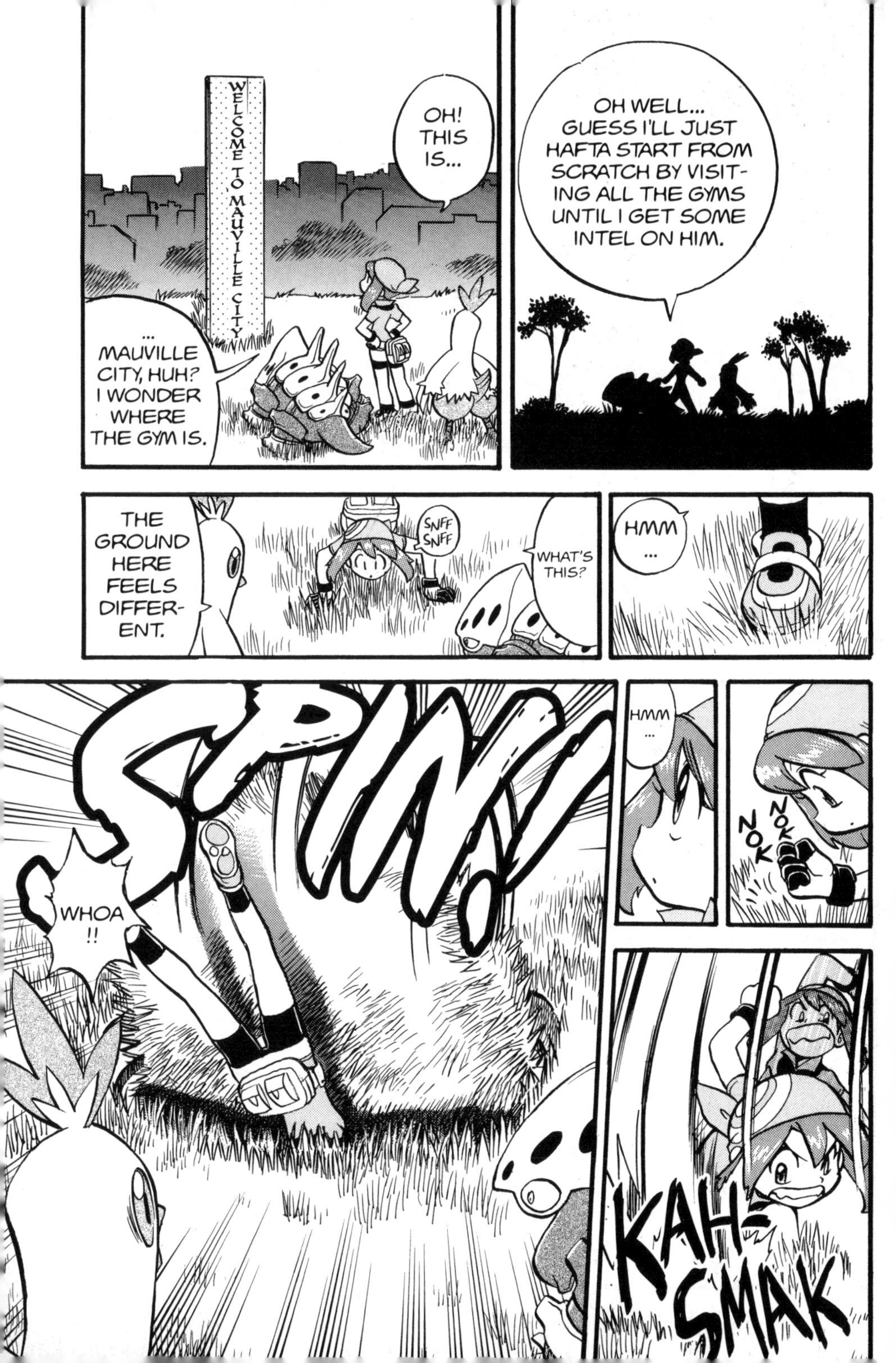
OH WELL... GUESS I'LL JUST HAFTA START FROM SCRATCH BY VISITING ALL THE GYMS UNTIL I GET SOME INTEL ON HIM.
WELCOME TO MAUVILLE CITY
OH! THIS IS...
...MAUVILLE CITY, HUH? I WONDER WHERE THE GYM IS.
HMM ...
WHAT'S THIS?
SNFF SNFF
THE GROUND HERE FEELS DIFFERENT.
NOK NOK
HMM ...
KAH-SMAK
SPIN!
WHOA !!

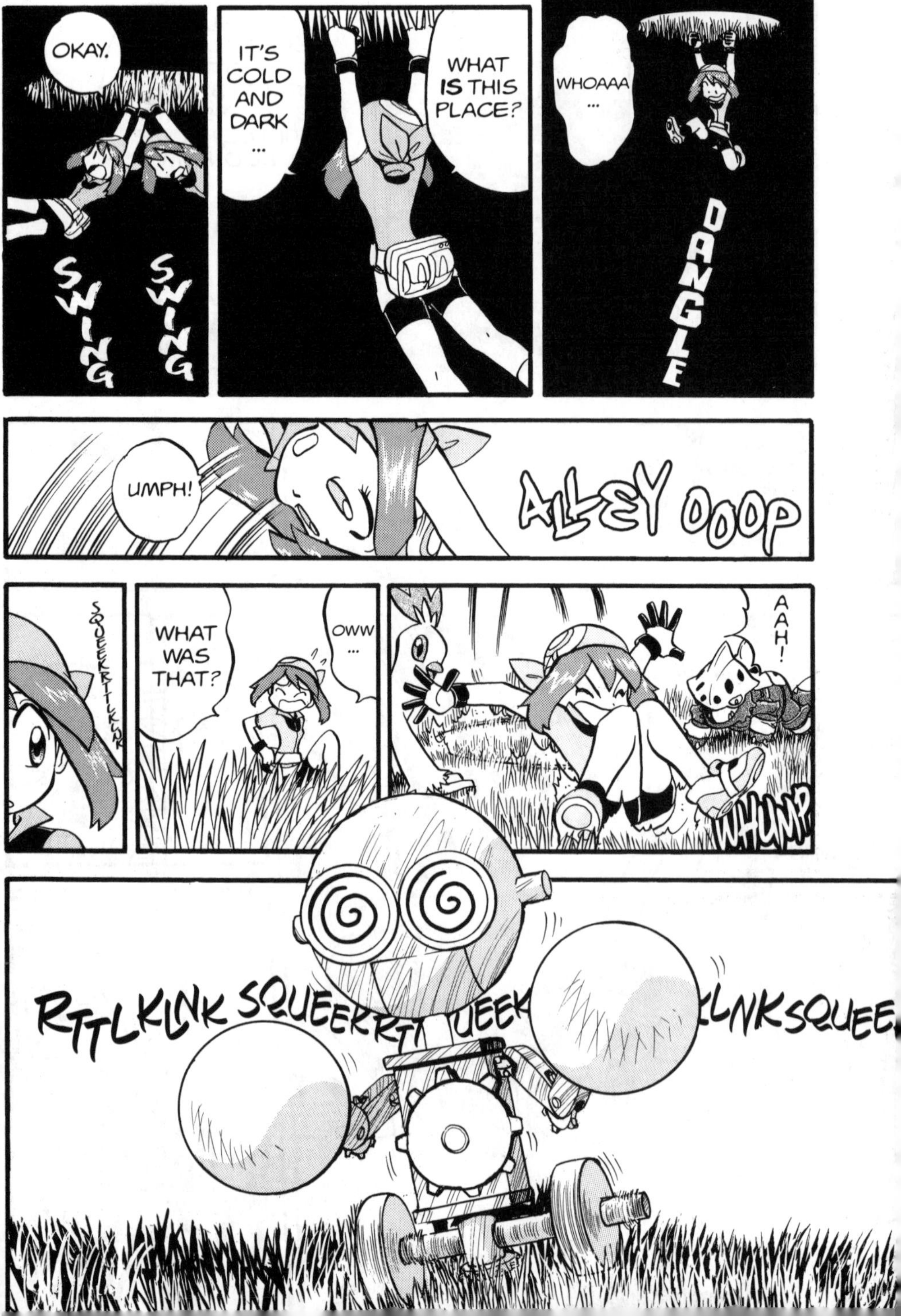
WHOAAA ...
DANGLE
WHAT IS THIS PLACE?
IT'S COLD AND DARK ...
OKAY.
SWING
SWING
ALLEY OOOP
UMPH!
AAH!
WHUMP
OWW ...
WHAT WAS THAT?
SQUEEKRTTLKLNK
RTTLKLNK SQUEEKRTT UEEK
KLNKSQUEE

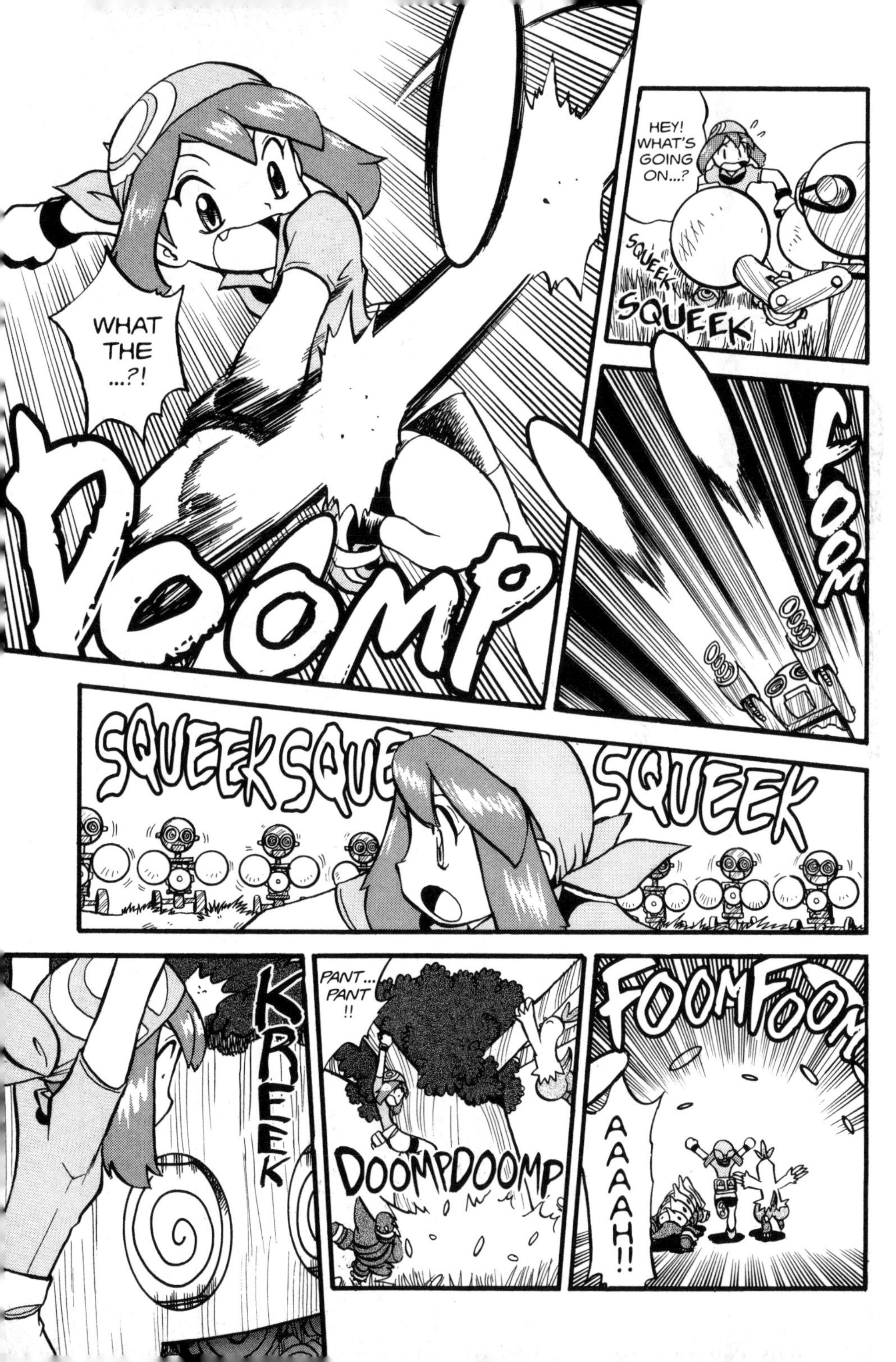

HEY! WHAT'S GOING ON...?
SQUEEK
SQUEEK
FOOOM
WHAT THE ...?!
DOOMP
SQUEEK
SQUEEKSQUE
FOOMFOOM
AAAAH!!
PANT... PANT !!
DOOMPDOOMP
KREEK

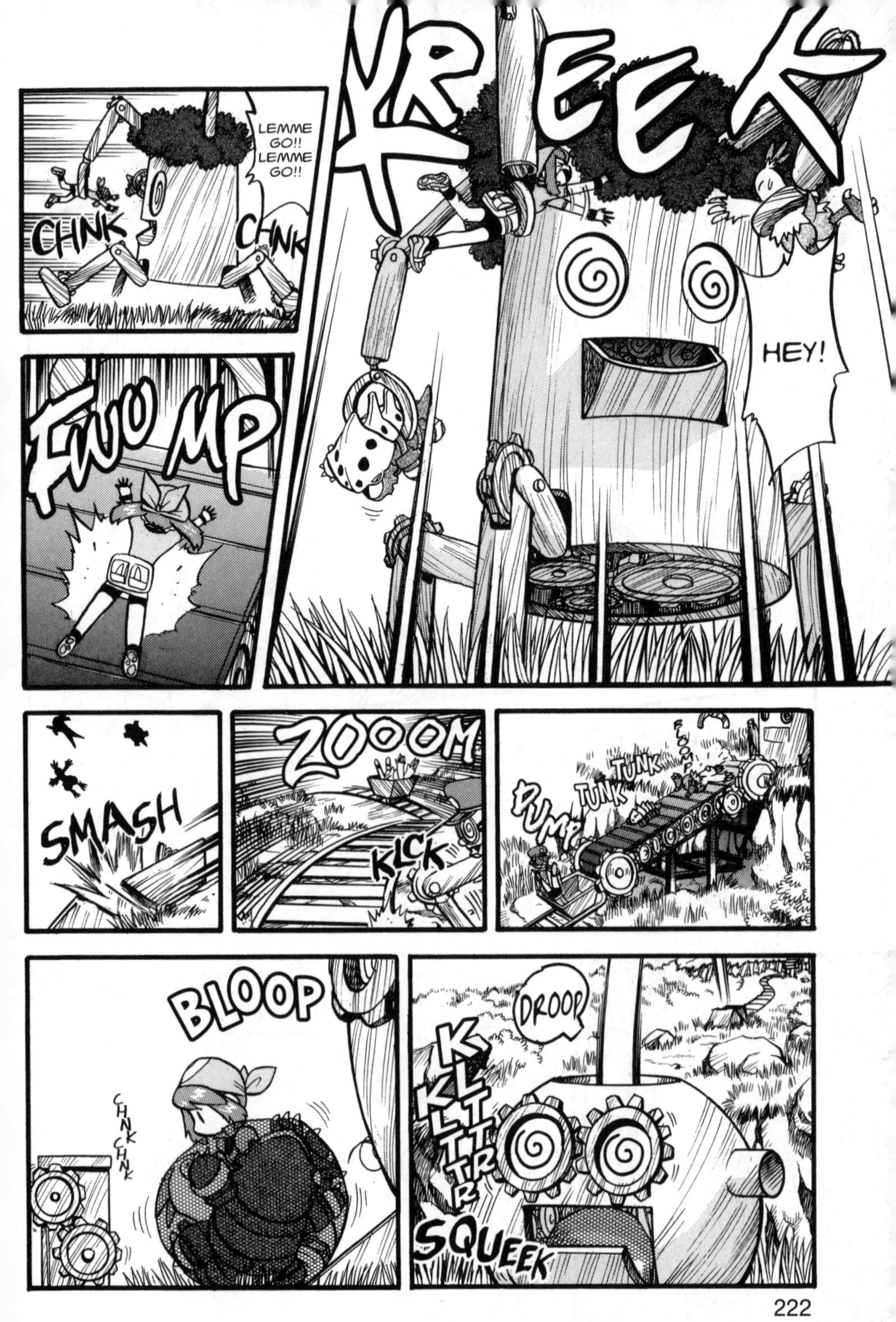
KREEK
HEY!
LEMME GO!! LEMME GO!!
CHNK
CHNK
FWOOMP
BLOOMP
TUNK
TUNK
PUMP
ZOOOM
KLICK
SMASH
DROOP
KKLKLTTRTR
SQUEEK
BLOOP
CHNK CHNK

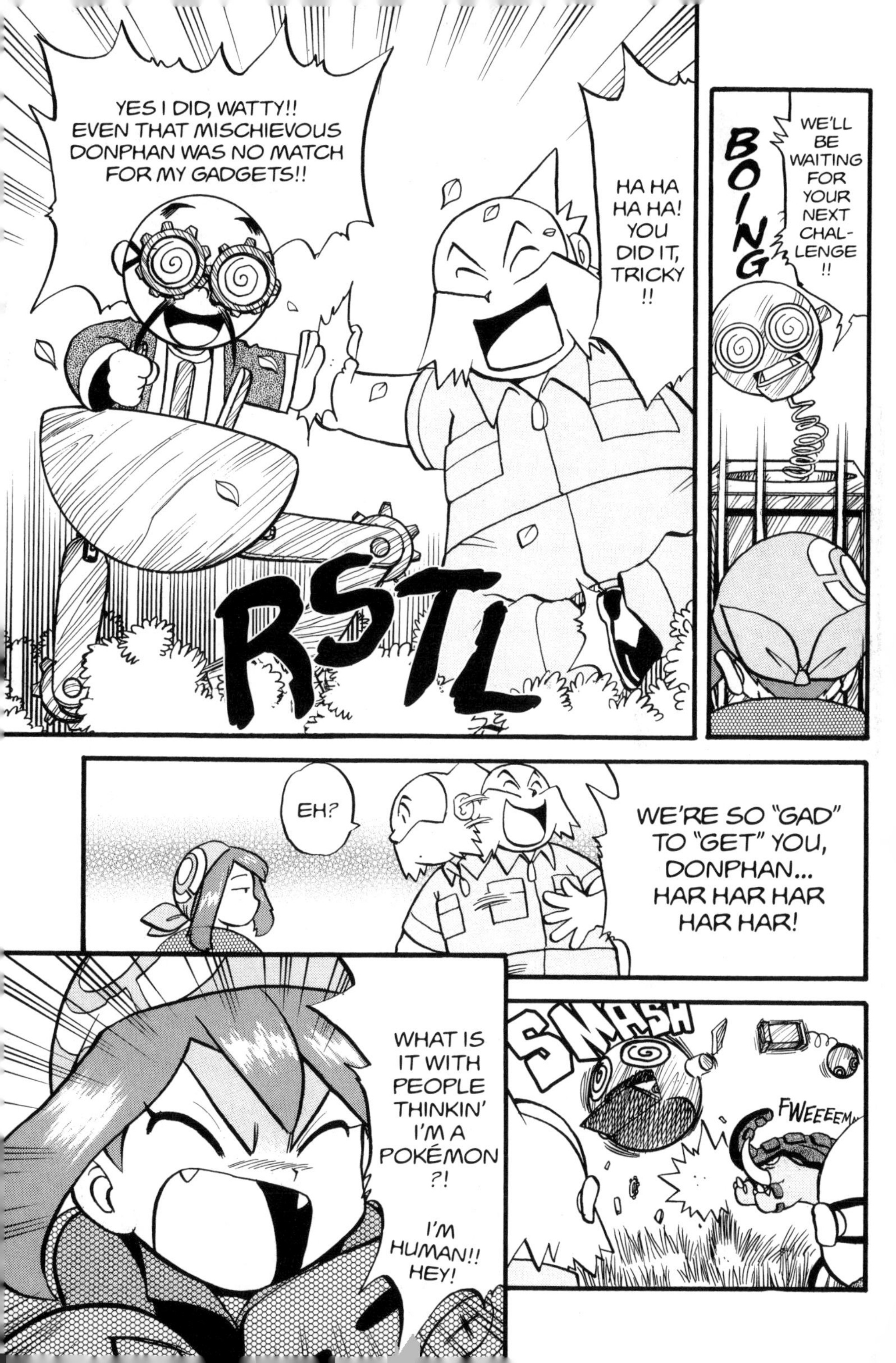
BOING
WE'LL BE WAITING FOR YOUR NEXT CHAL-LENGE!!
HA HA HA HA! YOU DID IT, TRICKY!!
YES I DID, WATTY!! EVEN THAT MISCHIEVOUS DONPHAN WAS NO MATCH FOR MY GADGETS!!
RSTL
WE'RE SO "GAD" TO "GET" YOU, DONPHAN... HAR HAR HAR HAR HAR!
EH?
SMASH
FWEEEEEM
WHAT IS IT WITH PEOPLE THINKIN' I'M A POKÉMON?!
I'M HUMAN!! HEY!

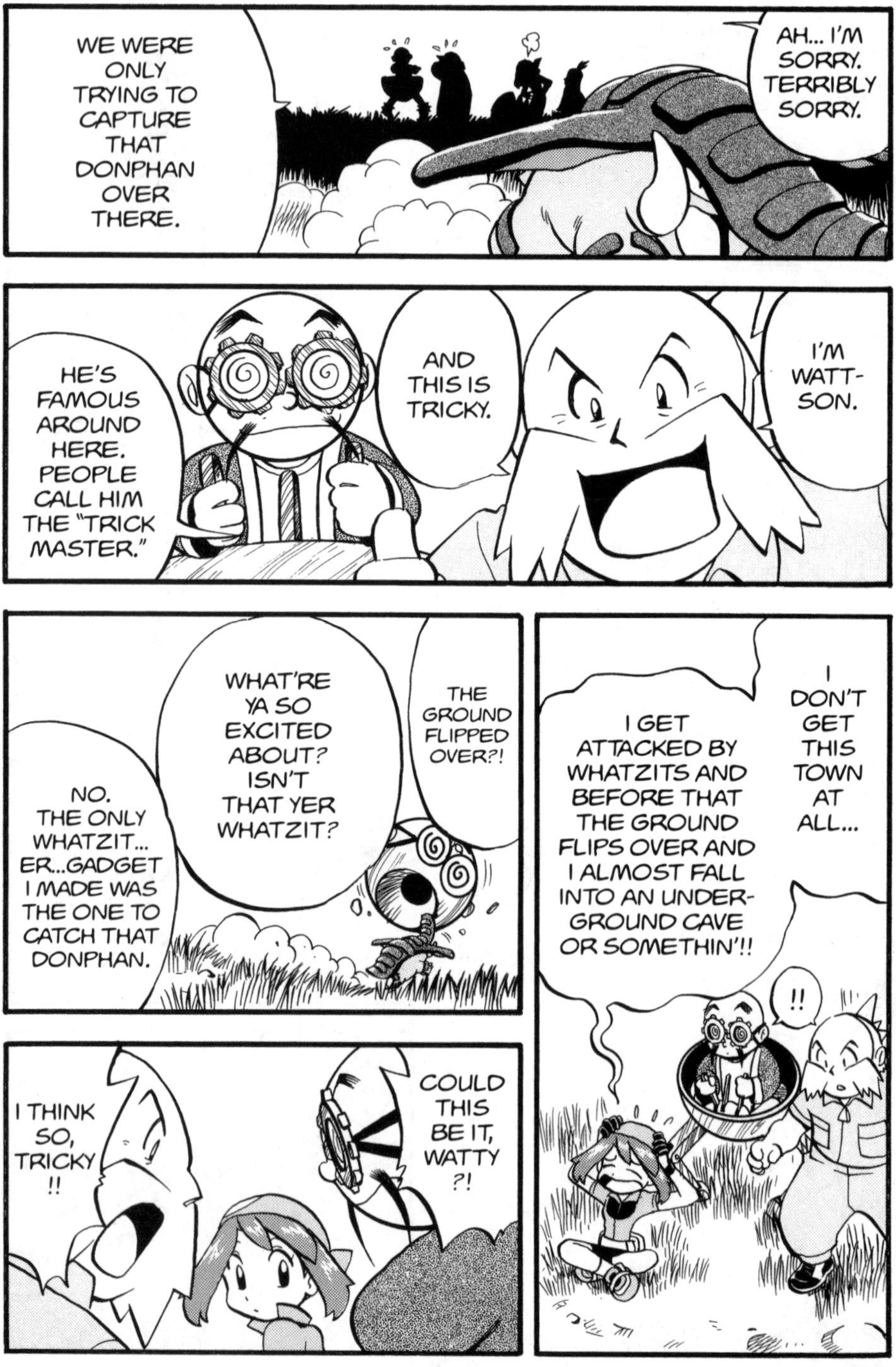
AH... I'M SORRY. TERRIBLY SORRY.
WE WERE ONLY TRYING TO CAPTURE THAT DONPHAN OVER THERE.
I'M WATT-SON.
AND THIS IS TRICKY.
HE'S FAMOUS AROUND HERE. PEOPLE CALL HIM THE "TRICK MASTER."
I DON'T GET THIS TOWN AT ALL...
I GET ATTACKED BY WHATZITS AND BEFORE THAT THE GROUND FLIPS OVER AND I ALMOST FALL INTO AN UNDER-GROUND CAVE OR SOMETHIN'!!
!!
THE GROUND FLIPPED OVER?!
WHAT'RE YA SO EXCITED ABOUT? ISN'T THAT YER WHATZIT?
NO. THE ONLY WHATZIT... ER...GADGET I MADE WAS THE ONE TO CATCH THAT DONPHAN.
COULD THIS BE IT, WATTY?!
I THINK SO, TRICKY!!

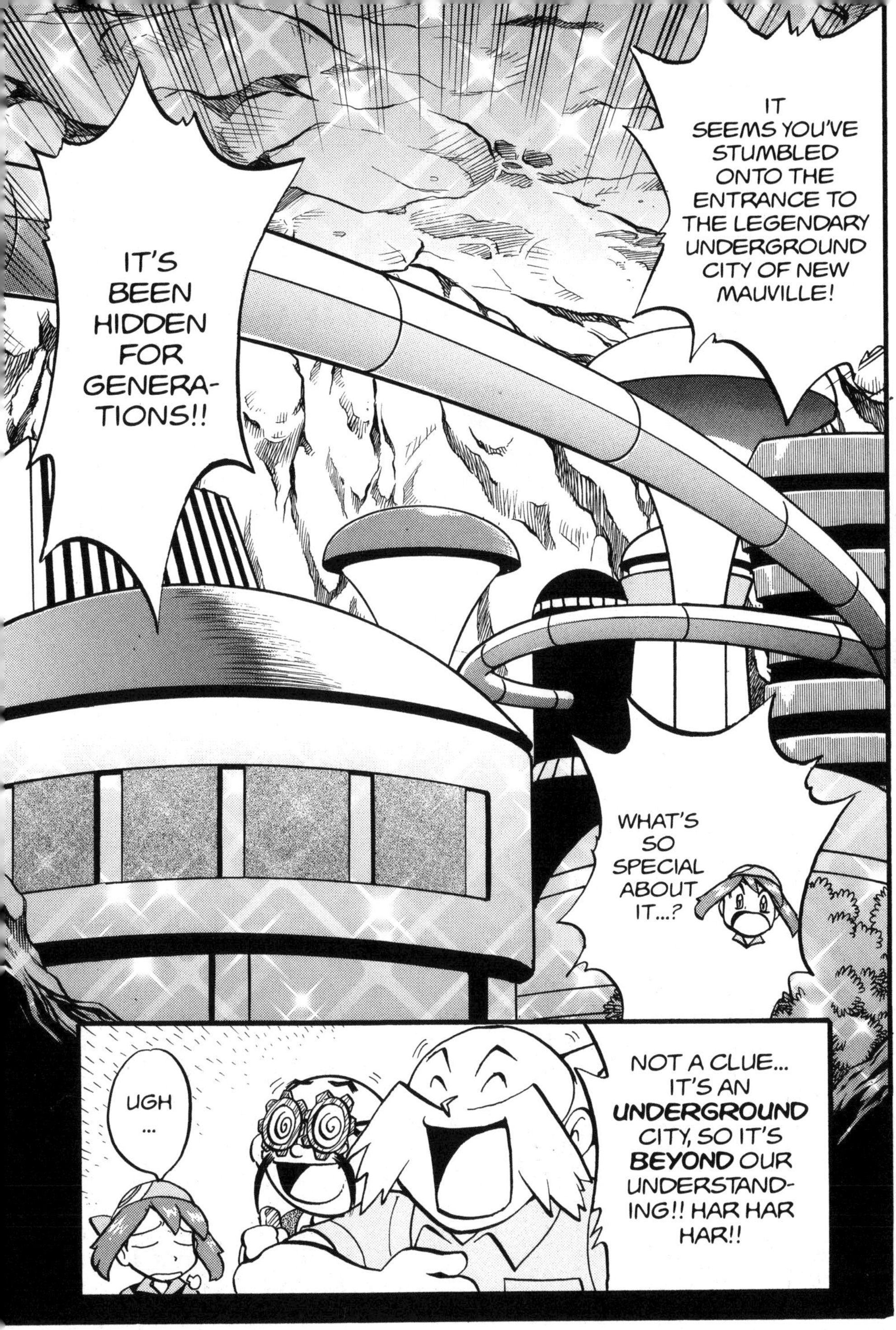
IT SEEMS YOU'VE STUMBLED ONTO THE ENTRANCE TO THE LEGENDARY UNDERGROUND CITY OF NEW MAUVILLE!
IT'S BEEN HIDDEN FOR GENERA-TIONS!!
WHAT'S SO SPECIAL ABOUT IT...?
NOT A CLUE... IT'S AN **UNDERGROUND** CITY, SO IT'S **BEYOND** OUR UNDERSTAND-ING!! HAR HAR HAR!!
UGH ...

● Adventure 204 ●
Plugging Past Electrike, Part 1

POKÉMON™ ADVENTURES RUBY & SAPPHIRE The Fourth Chapter

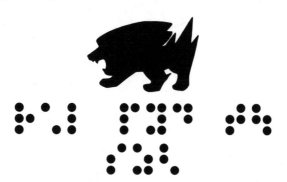

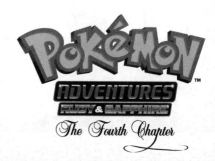

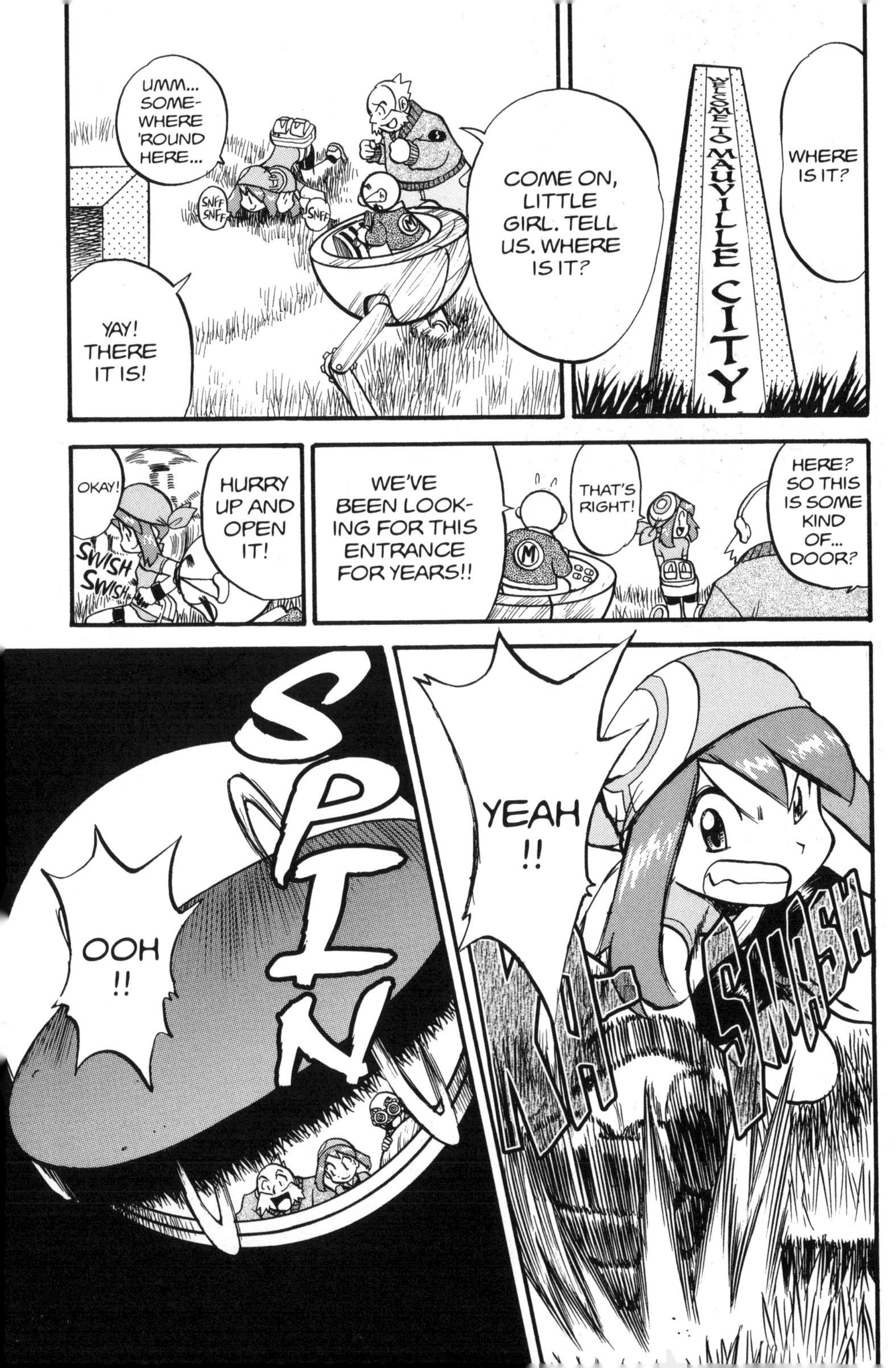
WHERE IS IT?
WELCOME TO MAUVILLE CITY
COME ON, LITTLE GIRL. TELL US. WHERE IS IT?
UMM... SOME-WHERE 'ROUND HERE...
SNFF SNFF
SNFF
YAY! THERE IT IS!
HERE? SO THIS IS SOME KIND OF... DOOR?
THAT'S RIGHT!
WE'VE BEEN LOOK-ING FOR THIS ENTRANCE FOR YEARS!!
HURRY UP AND OPEN IT!
OKAY!
SWISH SWISH
YEAH !!
SWISH
SPIN
OOH !!

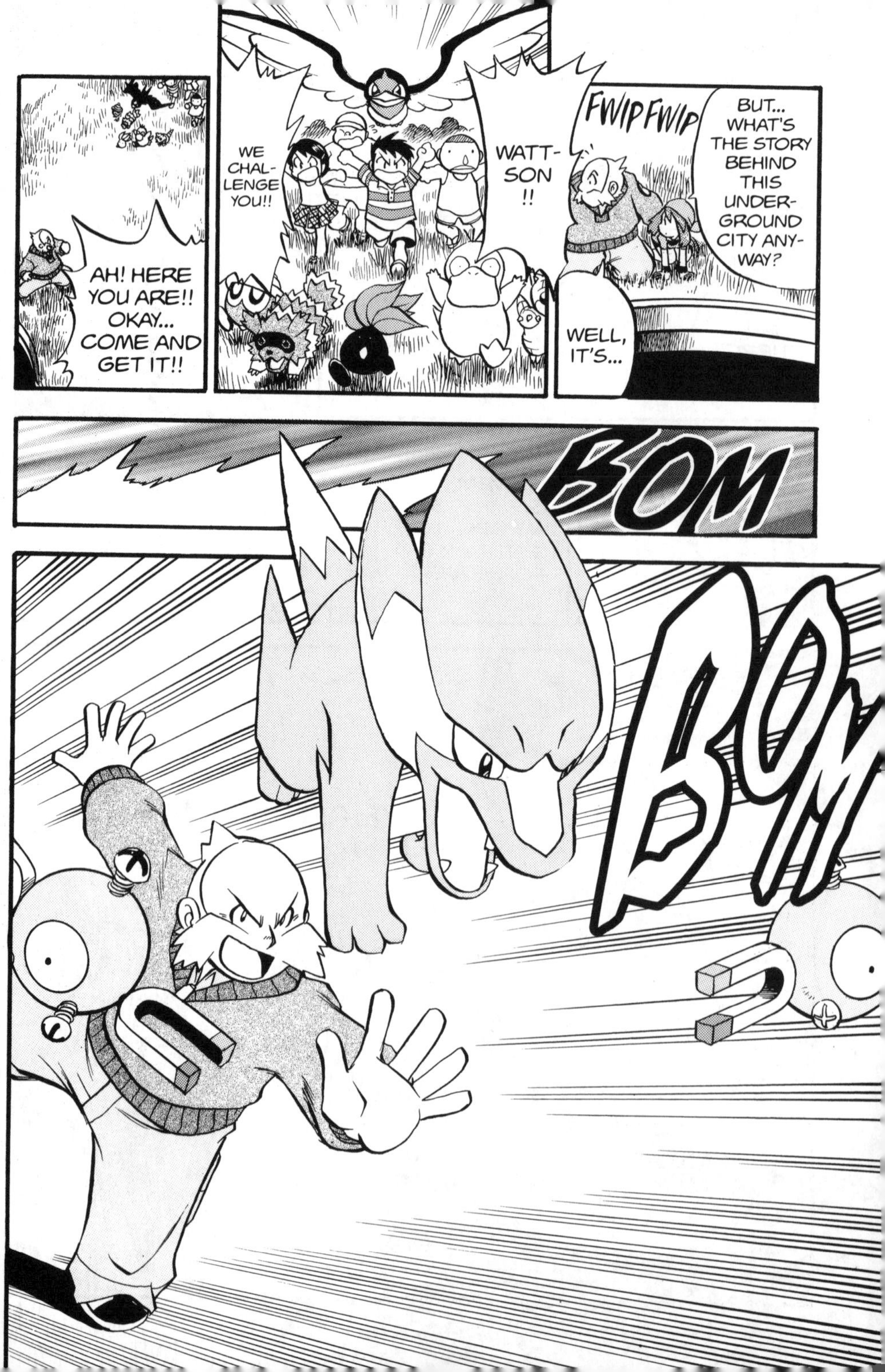
BUT... WHAT'S THE STORY BEHIND THIS UNDER-GROUND CITY ANY-WAY?
FWIP FWIP
WELL, IT'S...
WATT-SON !!
WE CHAL-LENGE YOU!!
AH! HERE YOU ARE!! OKAY... COME AND GET IT!!
BOM
BOM

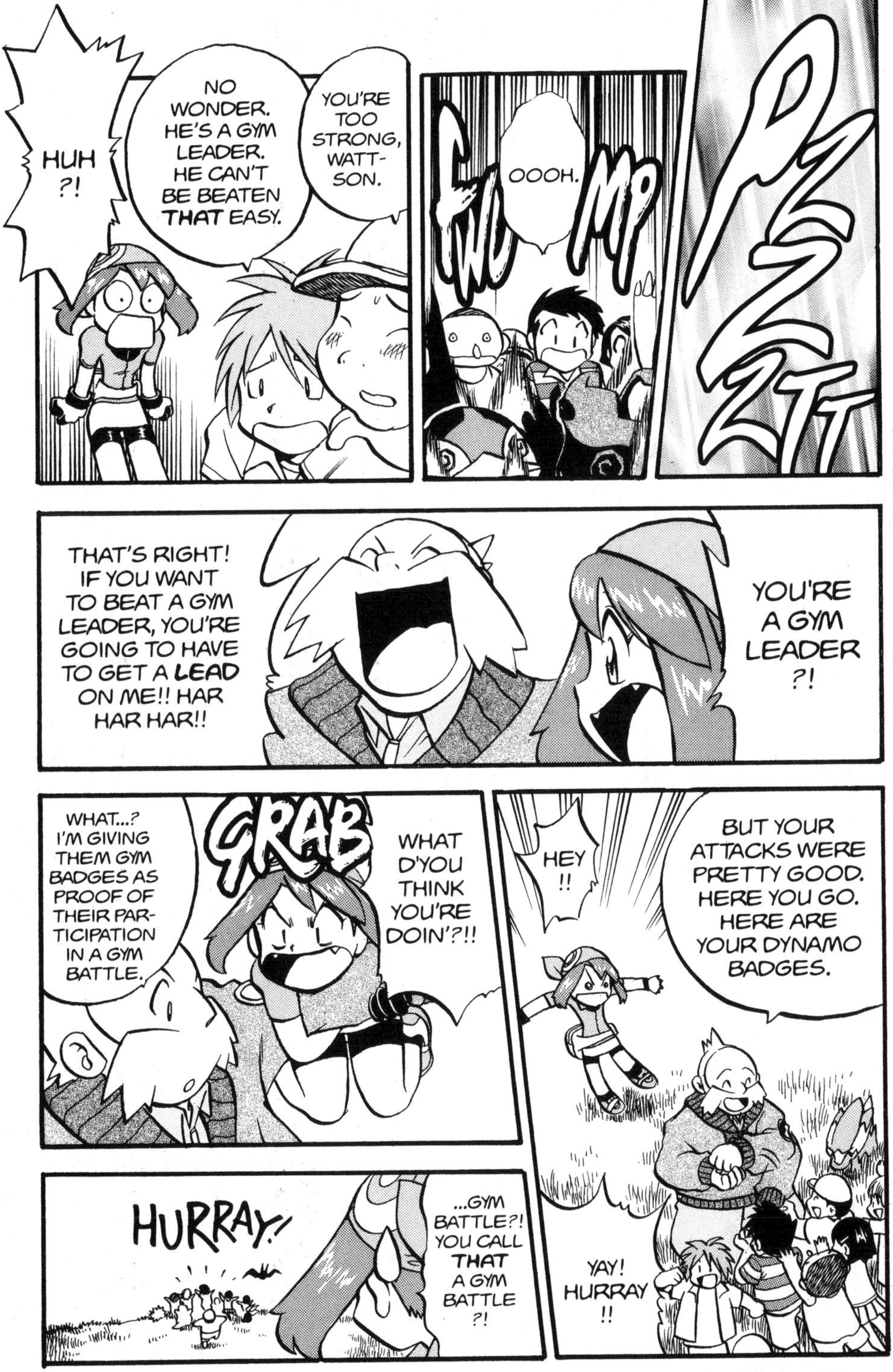
PZZZTT
FWUMP
OOOH.
YOU'RE TOO STRONG, WATTSON.
NO WONDER. HE'S A GYM LEADER. HE CAN'T BE BEATEN THAT EASY.
HUH ?!
YOU'RE A GYM LEADER ?!
THAT'S RIGHT! IF YOU WANT TO BEAT A GYM LEADER, YOU'RE GOING TO HAVE TO GET A LEAD ON ME!! HAR HAR HAR!!
BUT YOUR ATTACKS WERE PRETTY GOOD. HERE YOU GO. HERE ARE YOUR DYNAMO BADGES.
HEY !!
YAY! HURRAY !!
WHAT D'YOU THINK YOU'RE DOIN'?!!
GRAB
WHAT...? I'M GIVING THEM GYM BADGES AS PROOF OF THEIR PARTICIPATION IN A GYM BATTLE.
...GYM BATTLE?! YOU CALL THAT A GYM BATTLE ?!
HURRAY!

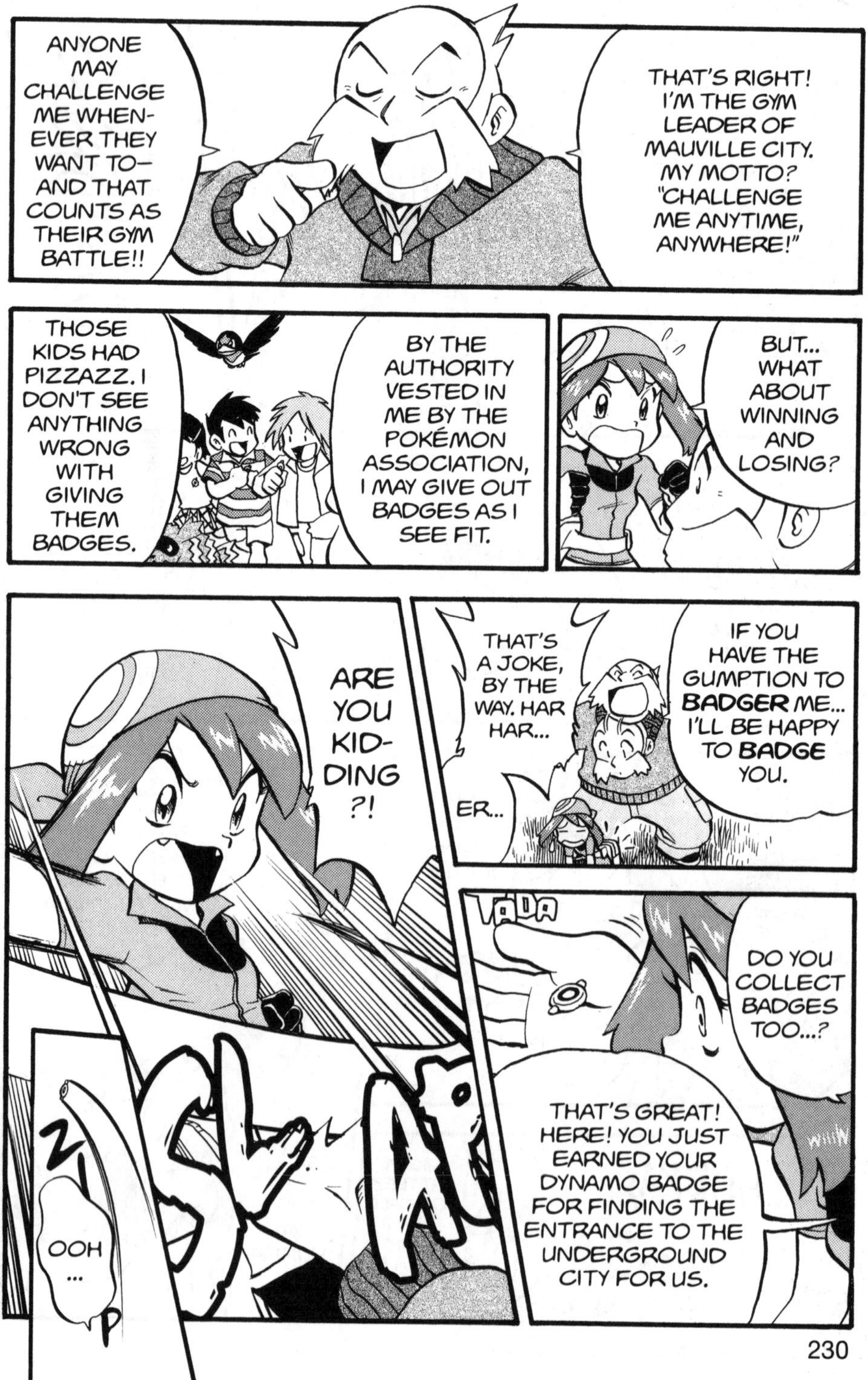
THAT'S RIGHT! I'M THE GYM LEADER OF MAUVILLE CITY. MY MOTTO? "CHALLENGE ME ANYTIME, ANYWHERE!"
ANYONE MAY CHALLENGE ME WHENEVER THEY WANT TO—AND THAT COUNTS AS THEIR GYM BATTLE!!
BUT... WHAT ABOUT WINNING AND LOSING?
BY THE AUTHORITY VESTED IN ME BY THE POKÉMON ASSOCIATION, I MAY GIVE OUT BADGES AS I SEE FIT.
THOSE KIDS HAD PIZZAZZ. I DON'T SEE ANYTHING WRONG WITH GIVING THEM BADGES.
IF YOU HAVE THE GUMPTION TO **BADGER** ME... I'LL BE HAPPY TO **BADGE** YOU.
THAT'S A JOKE, BY THE WAY. HAR HAR...
ER...
TADA
DO YOU COLLECT BADGES TOO...?
THAT'S GREAT! HERE! YOU JUST EARNED YOUR DYNAMO BADGE FOR FINDING THE ENTRANCE TO THE UNDERGROUND CITY FOR US.
ARE YOU KIDDING?!
OOH...

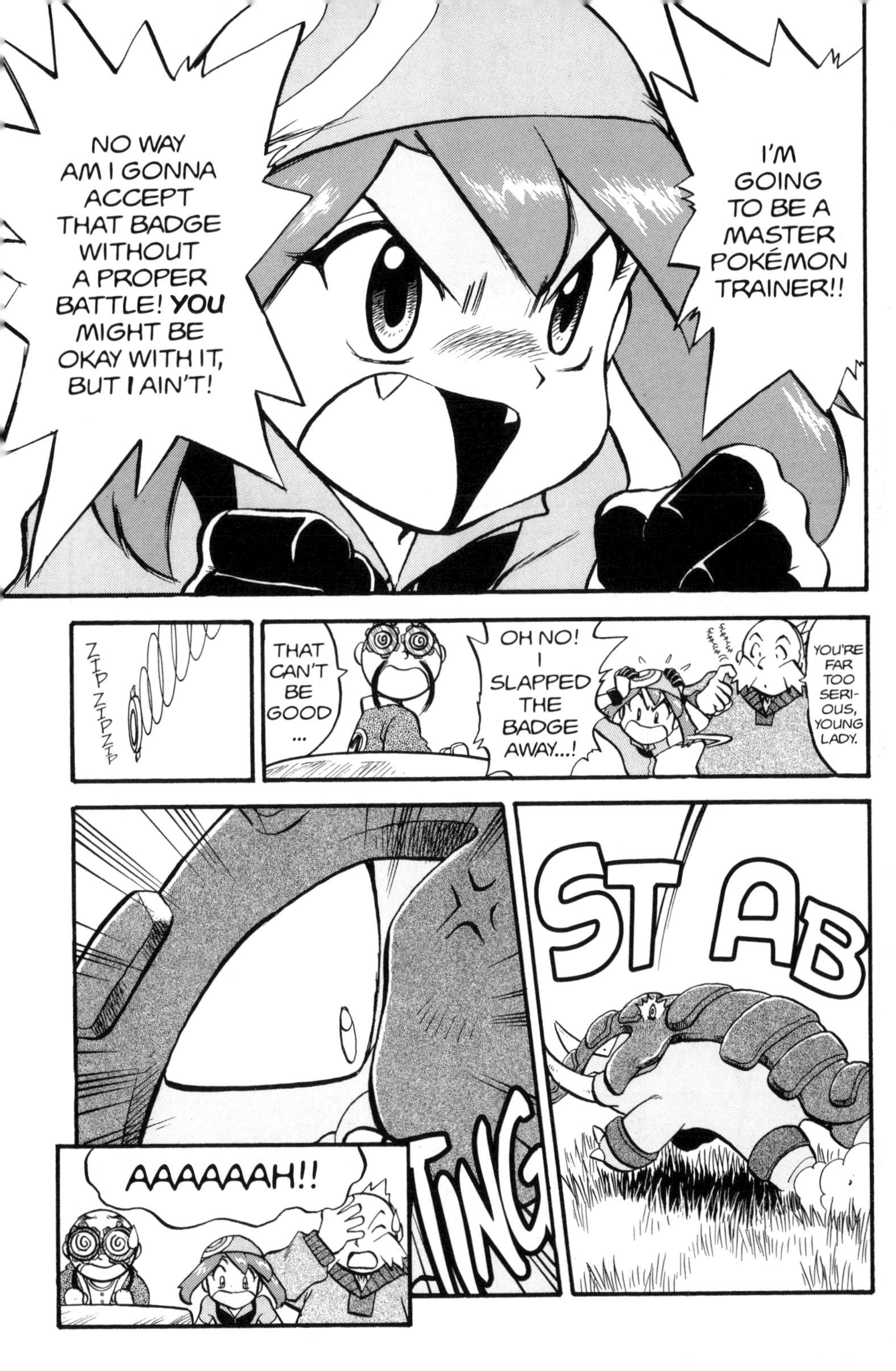

I'M GOING TO BE A MASTER POKÉMON TRAINER!!
NO WAY AM I GONNA ACCEPT THAT BADGE WITHOUT A PROPER BATTLE! **YOU** MIGHT BE OKAY WITH IT, BUT **I** AIN'T!
YOU'RE FAR TOO SERI-OUS, YOUNG LADY.
OH NO! I SLAPPED THE BADGE AWAY...!
THAT CAN'T BE GOOD ...
ZIP ZIPZIPZIP
STAB
TING
AAAAAAH!!

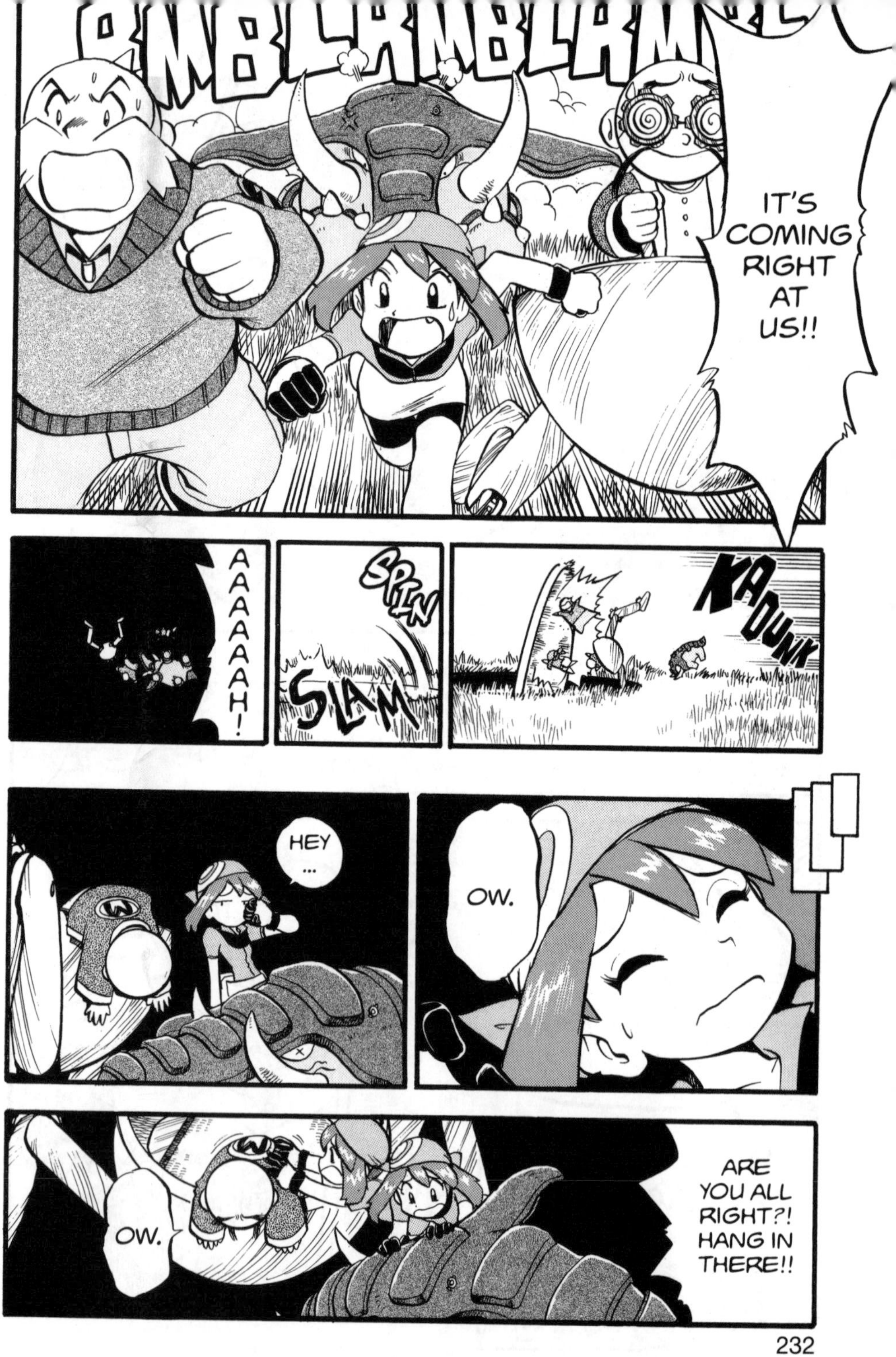
RMBLRMBLRM
IT'S COMING RIGHT AT US!!
KADUNK
SPIN
SLAM
AAAAAAAH!
OW.
HEY ...
ARE YOU ALL RIGHT?! HANG IN THERE!!
OW.

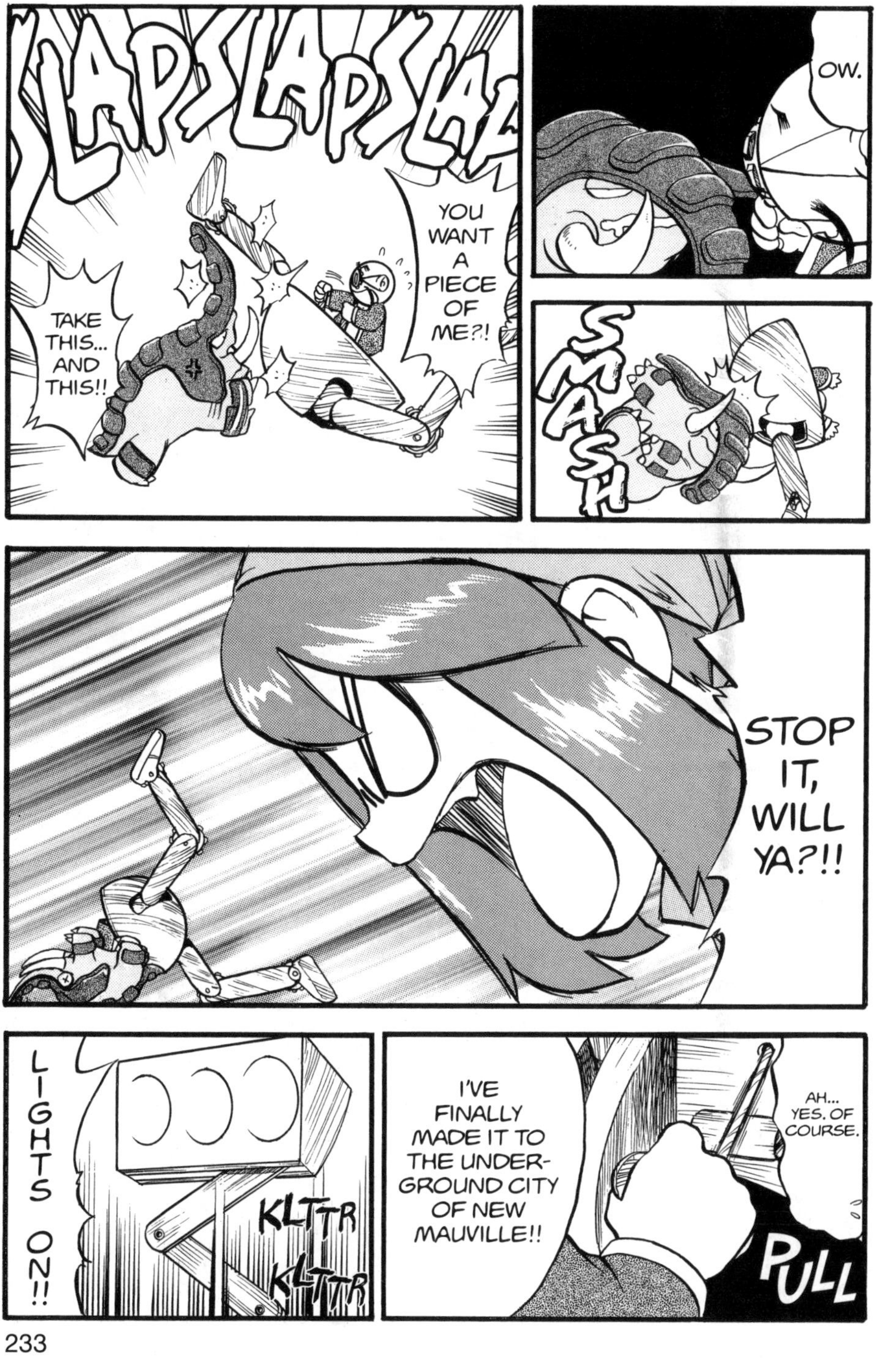
OW.
SMASH
SLAPSLAPSLAP
YOU WANT A PIECE OF ME?!
TAKE THIS... AND THIS!!
STOP IT, WILL YA?!!
AH... YES. OF COURSE.
I'VE FINALLY MADE IT TO THE UNDER-GROUND CITY OF NEW MAUVILLE!!
PULL
LIGHTS ON!!
KLTTR KLTTTR

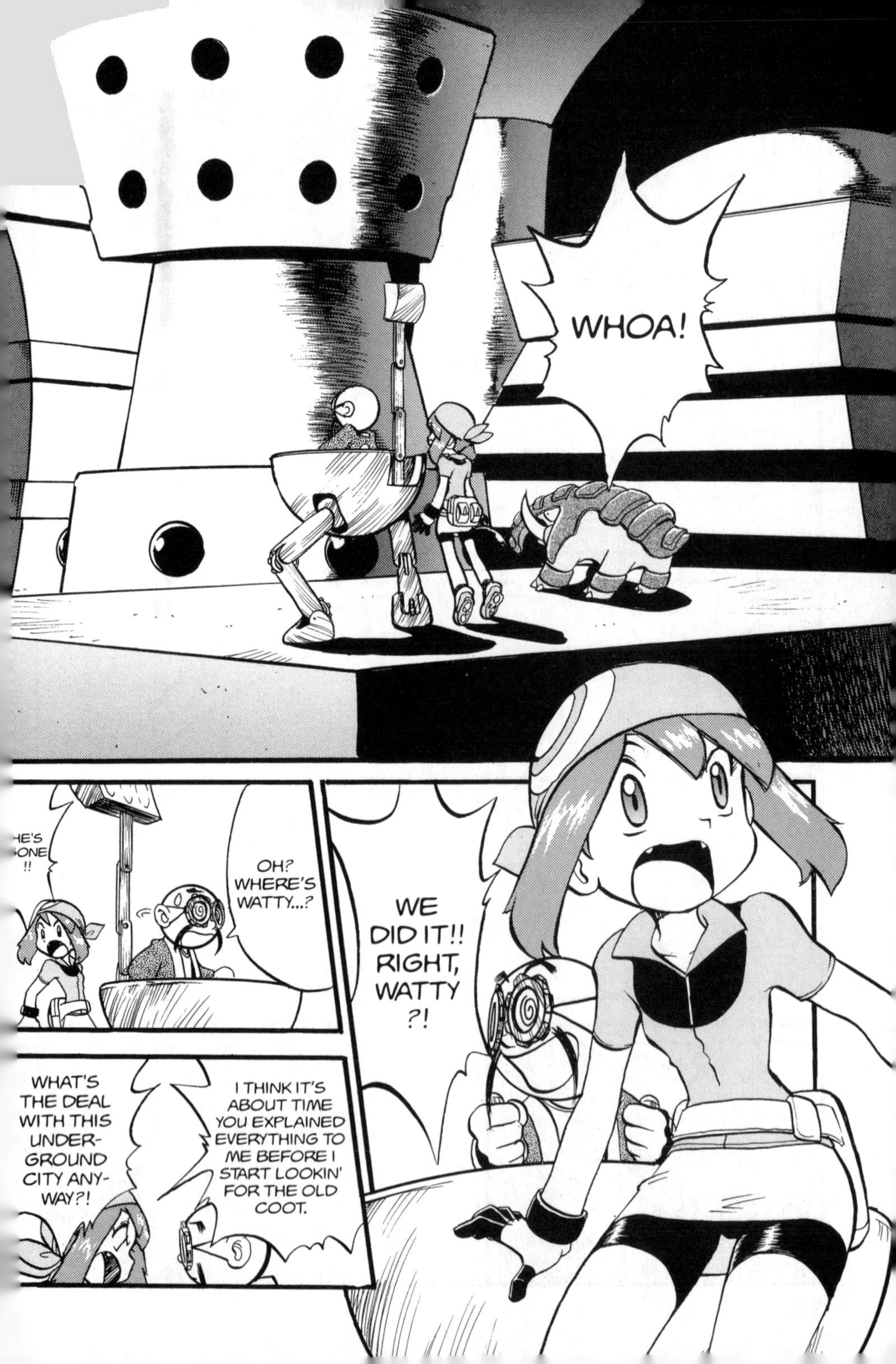
WHOA!
WE DID IT!! RIGHT, WATTY?!
OH? WHERE'S WATTY...?
HE'S GONE!!
I THINK IT'S ABOUT TIME YOU EXPLAINED EVERYTHING TO ME BEFORE I START LOOKIN' FOR THE OLD COOT.
WHAT'S THE DEAL WITH THIS UNDERGROUND CITY ANYWAY?!

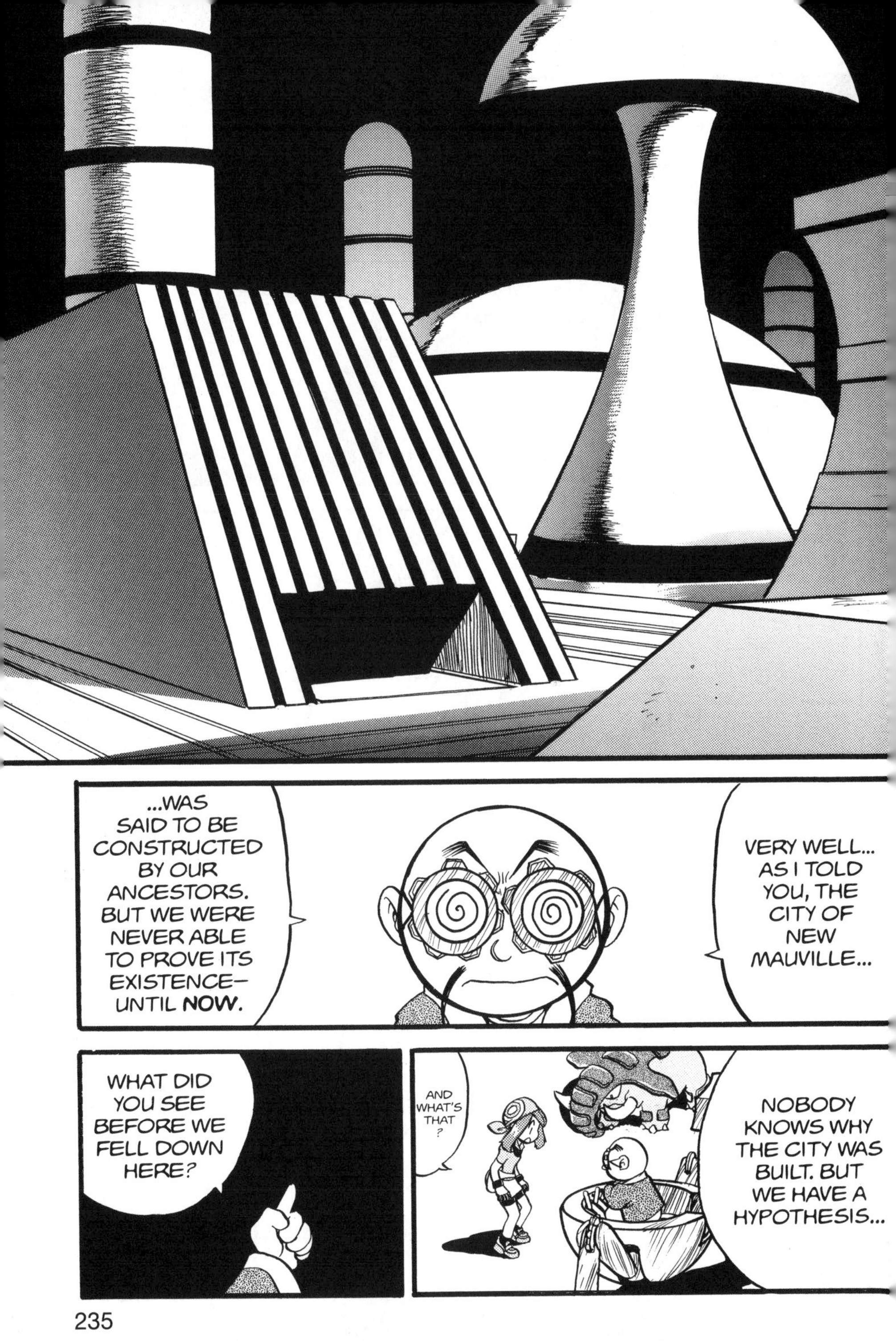
VERY WELL... AS I TOLD YOU, THE CITY OF NEW MAUVILLE...
...WAS SAID TO BE CONSTRUCTED BY OUR ANCESTORS. BUT WE WERE NEVER ABLE TO PROVE ITS EXISTENCE—UNTIL **NOW**.
NOBODY KNOWS WHY THE CITY WAS BUILT. BUT WE HAVE A HYPOTHESIS...
AND WHAT'S THAT?
WHAT DID YOU SEE BEFORE WE FELL DOWN HERE?

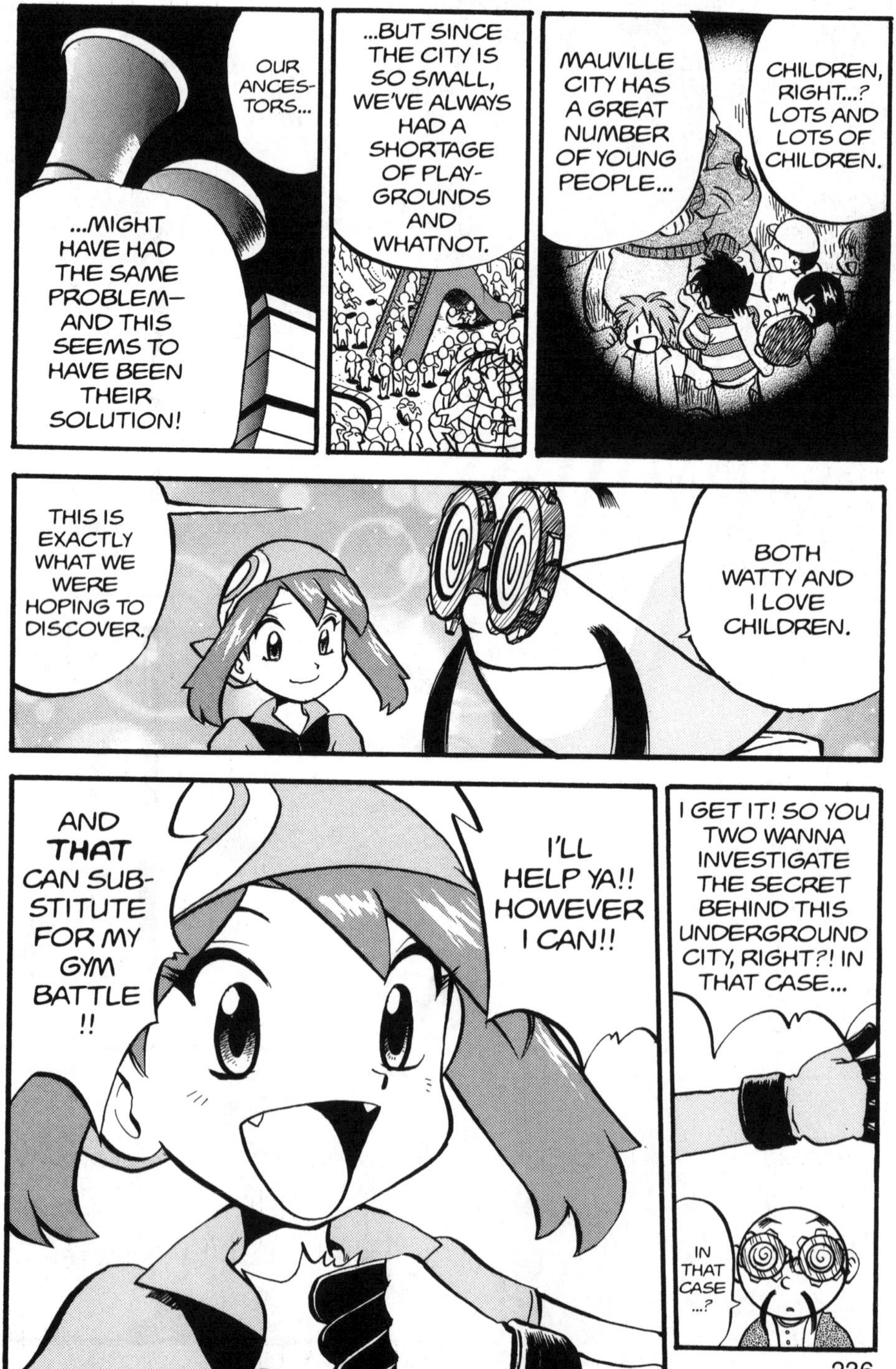
CHILDREN, RIGHT...? LOTS AND LOTS OF CHILDREN.
MAUVILLE CITY HAS A GREAT NUMBER OF YOUNG PEOPLE...
...BUT SINCE THE CITY IS SO SMALL, WE'VE ALWAYS HAD A SHORTAGE OF PLAY-GROUNDS AND WHATNOT.
OUR ANCES-TORS...
...MIGHT HAVE HAD THE SAME PROBLEM— AND THIS SEEMS TO HAVE BEEN THEIR SOLUTION!
BOTH WATTY AND I LOVE CHILDREN.
THIS IS EXACTLY WHAT WE WERE HOPING TO DISCOVER.
I GET IT! SO YOU TWO WANNA INVESTIGATE THE SECRET BEHIND THIS UNDERGROUND CITY, RIGHT?! IN THAT CASE...
IN THAT CASE ...?
I'LL HELP YA!! HOWEVER I CAN!!
AND **THAT** CAN SUB-STITUTE FOR MY GYM BATTLE !!

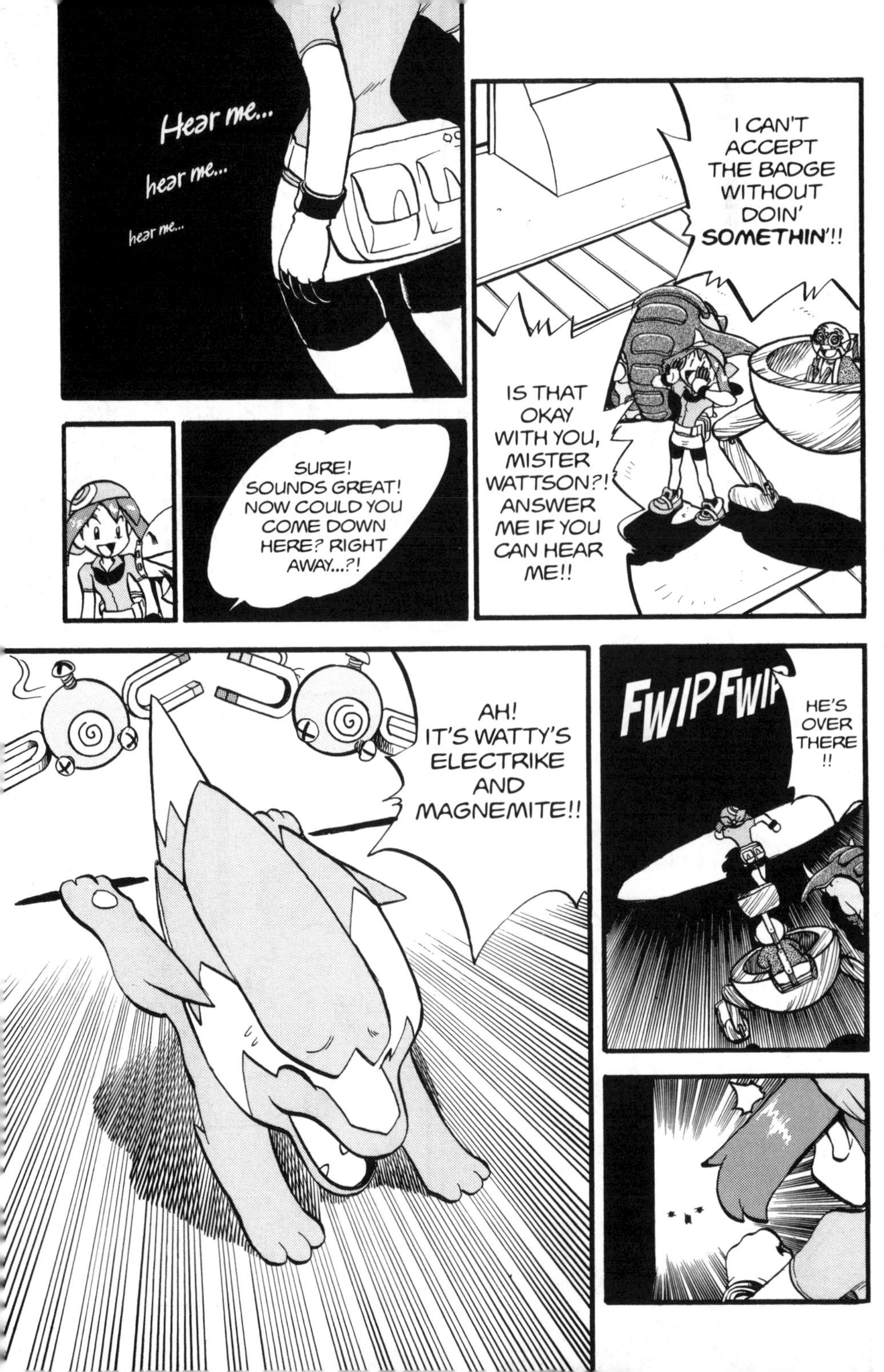
I CAN'T ACCEPT THE BADGE WITHOUT DOIN' **SOMETHIN'**!!
IS THAT OKAY WITH YOU, MISTER WATTSON?! ANSWER ME IF YOU CAN HEAR ME!!
Hear me...
hear me...
hear me...
SURE! SOUNDS GREAT! NOW COULD YOU COME DOWN HERE? RIGHT AWAY...?!
FWIP FWIP
HE'S OVER THERE!!
AH! IT'S WATTY'S ELECTRIKE AND MAGNEMITE!!

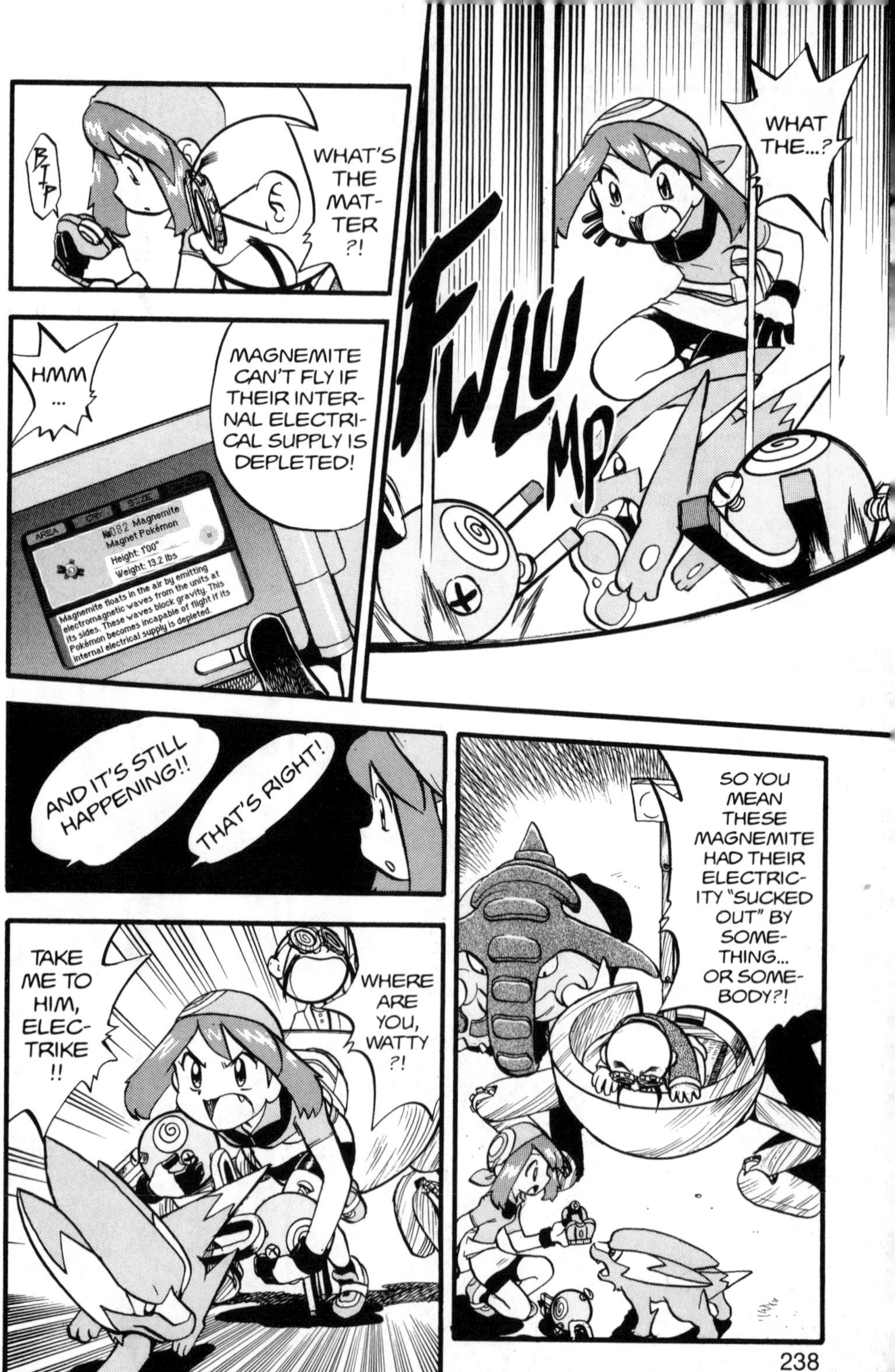
WHAT THE...?
FWLUMP
WHAT'S THE MATTER?!
BIIP
MAGNEMITE CAN'T FLY IF THEIR INTERNAL ELECTRICAL SUPPLY IS DEPLETED!
HMM...
AREA
No082 Magnemite
Magnet Pokémon
Height: 1'00"
Weight: 13.2 lbs
Magnemite floats in the air by emitting electromagnetic waves from the units at its sides. These waves block gravity. This Pokémon becomes incapable of flight if its internal electrical supply is depleted.
SO YOU MEAN THESE MAGNEMITE HAD THEIR ELECTRICITY "SUCKED OUT" BY SOMETHING... OR SOMEBODY?!
THAT'S RIGHT!
AND IT'S STILL HAPPENING!!
WHERE ARE YOU, WATTY?!
TAKE ME TO HIM, ELECTRIKE!!

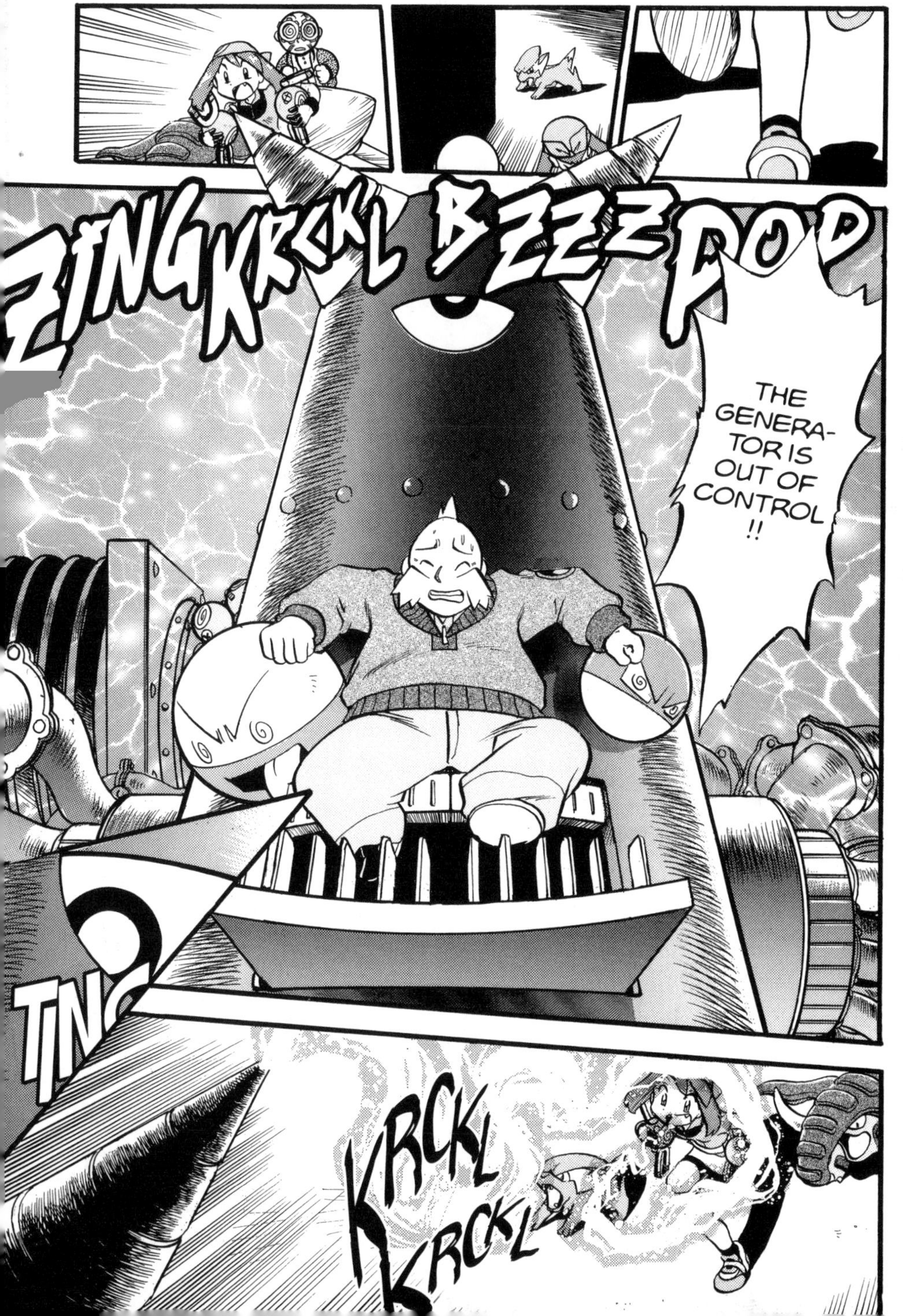
ZING KRCKL BZZZ POP
THE GENERA-TOR IS OUT OF CONTROL !!
TING
KRCKL
KRCKL

● Adventure 205 ●
Plugging Past Electrike, Part 2

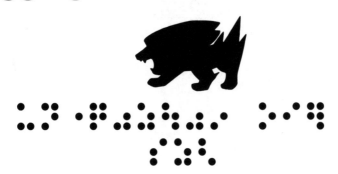

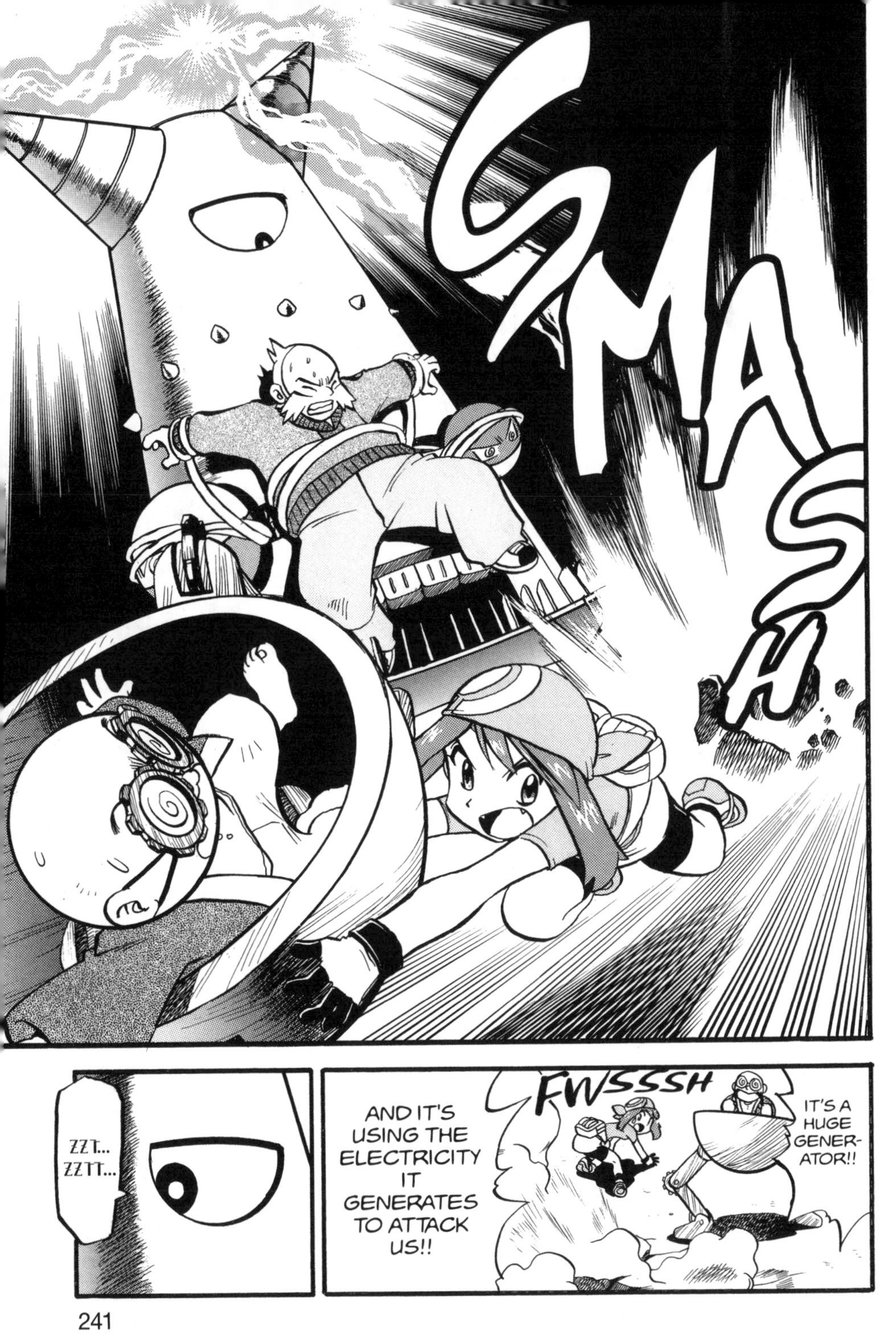
SMASH
IT'S A HUGE GENERATOR!!
FWSSSH
AND IT'S USING THE ELECTRICITY IT GENERATES TO ATTACK US!!
ZZT... ZZTT...

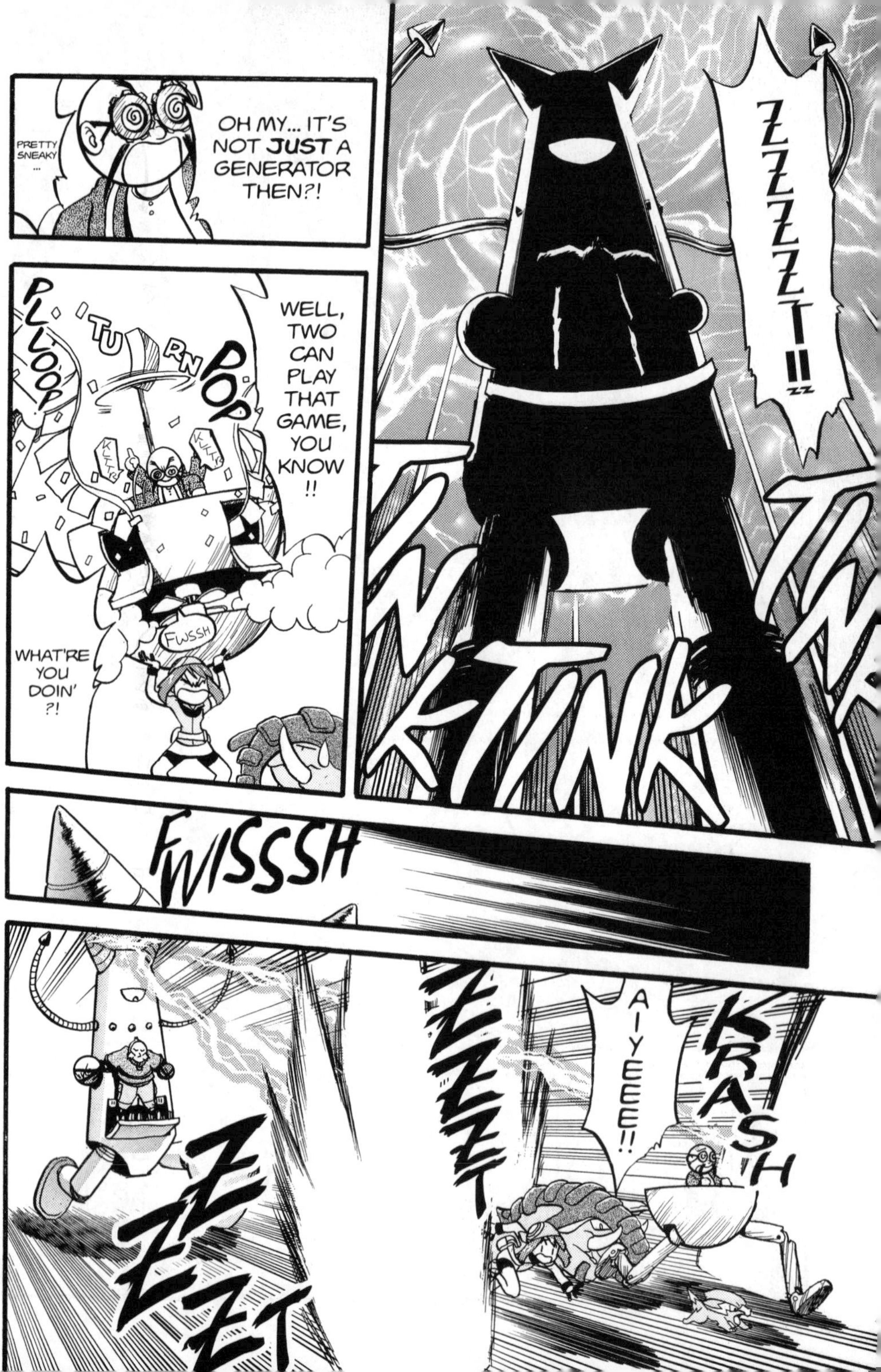
ZZZZZT!!
zz
TINK
OH MY... IT'S NOT **JUST** A GENERATOR THEN?!
PRETTY SNEAKY ...
WELL, TWO CAN PLAY THAT GAME, YOU KNOW!!
PLLOOP!
TURN
POP
FWSSH
WHAT'RE YOU DOIN'?!
FWISSSH
KRASH
AIYEEE!!
ZZZZT
ZZZZT

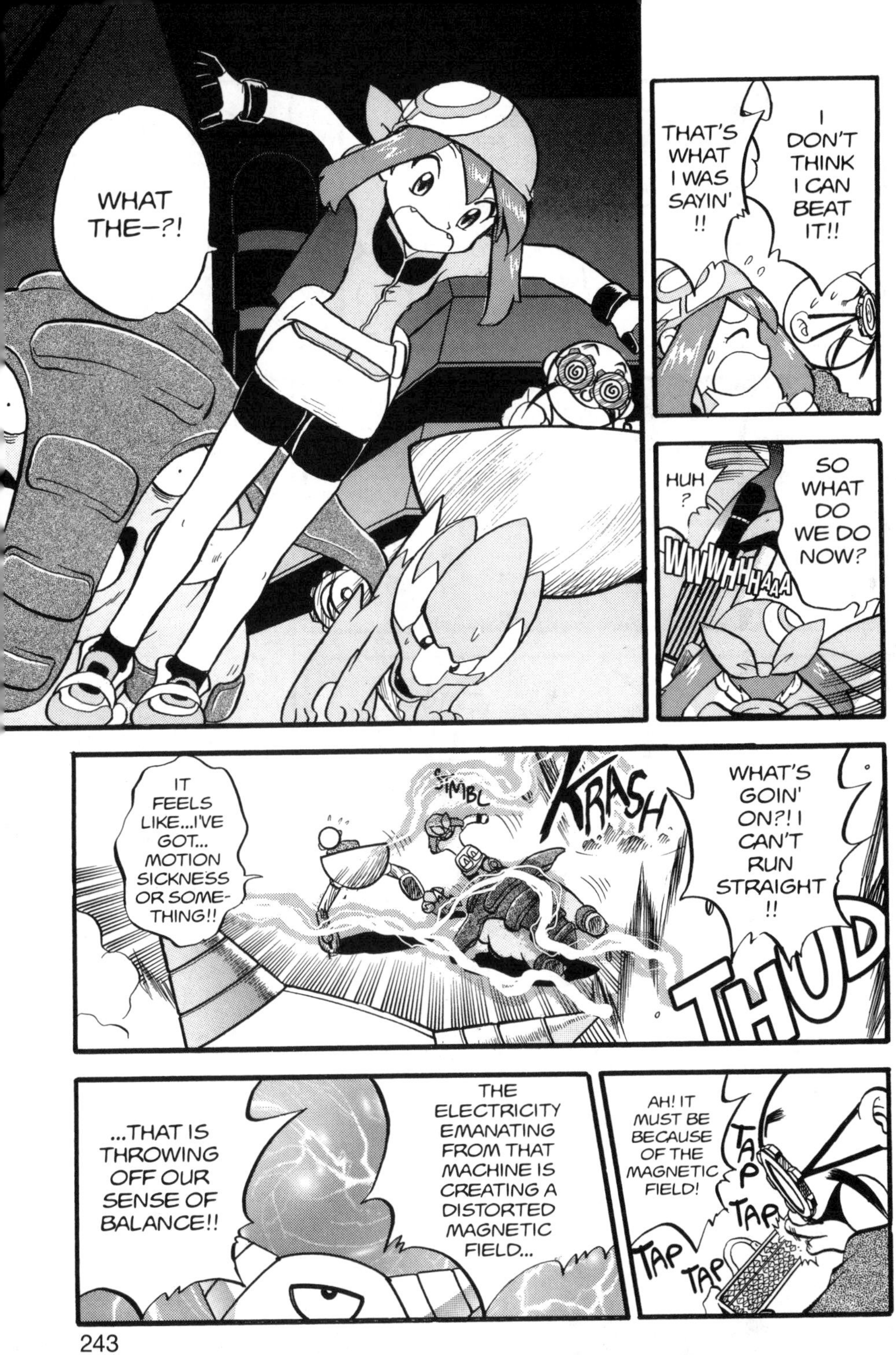
I DON'T THINK I CAN BEAT IT!!
THAT'S WHAT I WAS SAYIN' !!
SO WHAT DO WE DO NOW?
HUH?
WWWHHHAAA
WHAT THE—?!
WHAT'S GOIN' ON?! I CAN'T RUN STRAIGHT !!
THUD
KRASH
IT FEELS LIKE...I'VE GOT... MOTION SICKNESS OR SOME-THING!!
AH! IT MUST BE BECAUSE OF THE MAGNETIC FIELD!
TAP TAP TAP TAP TAP
THE ELECTRICITY EMANATING FROM THAT MACHINE IS CREATING A DISTORTED MAGNETIC FIELD...
...THAT IS THROWING OFF OUR SENSE OF BALANCE!!

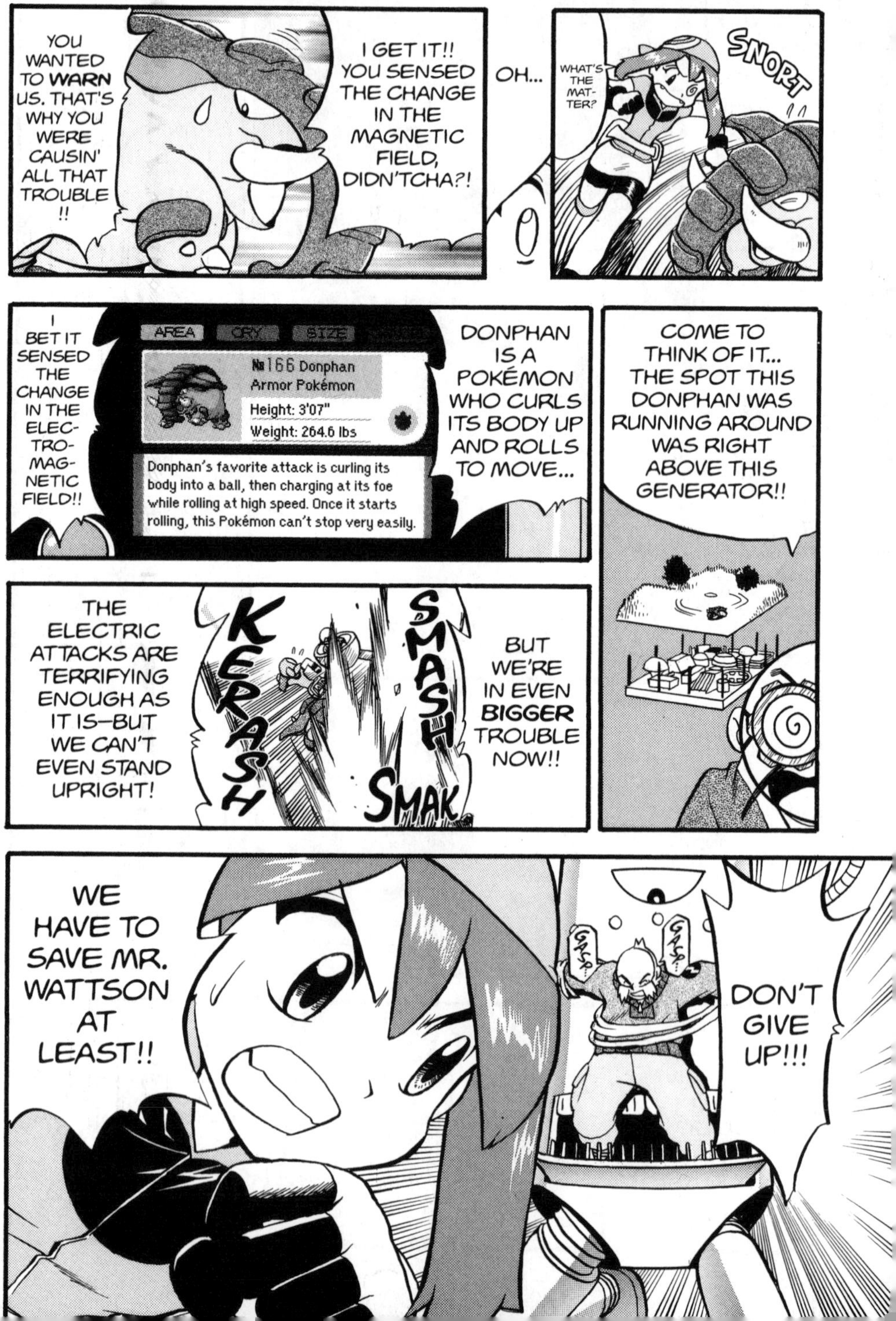
SNORT
WHAT'S THE MAT-TER?
OH...
I GET IT!! YOU SENSED THE CHANGE IN THE MAGNETIC FIELD, DIDN'TCHA?!
YOU WANTED TO **WARN** US. THAT'S WHY YOU WERE CAUSIN' ALL THAT TROUBLE!!
COME TO THINK OF IT... THE SPOT THIS DONPHAN WAS RUNNING AROUND WAS RIGHT ABOVE THIS GENERATOR!!
DONPHAN IS A POKÉMON WHO CURLS ITS BODY UP AND ROLLS TO MOVE...
AREA
CRY
SIZE
№166 Donphan
Armor Pokémon
Height: 3'07"
Weight: 264.6 lbs
Donphan's favorite attack is curling its body into a ball, then charging at its foe while rolling at high speed. Once it starts rolling, this Pokémon can't stop very easily.
I BET IT SENSED THE CHANGE IN THE ELEC-TRO-MAG-NETIC FIELD!!
BUT WE'RE IN EVEN **BIGGER** TROUBLE NOW!!
SMASH
SMAK
KERASH
THE ELECTRIC ATTACKS ARE TERRIFYING ENOUGH AS IT IS—BUT WE CAN'T EVEN STAND UPRIGHT!
DON'T GIVE UP!!!
GASP...
GASP...
WE HAVE TO SAVE MR. WATTSON AT LEAST!!

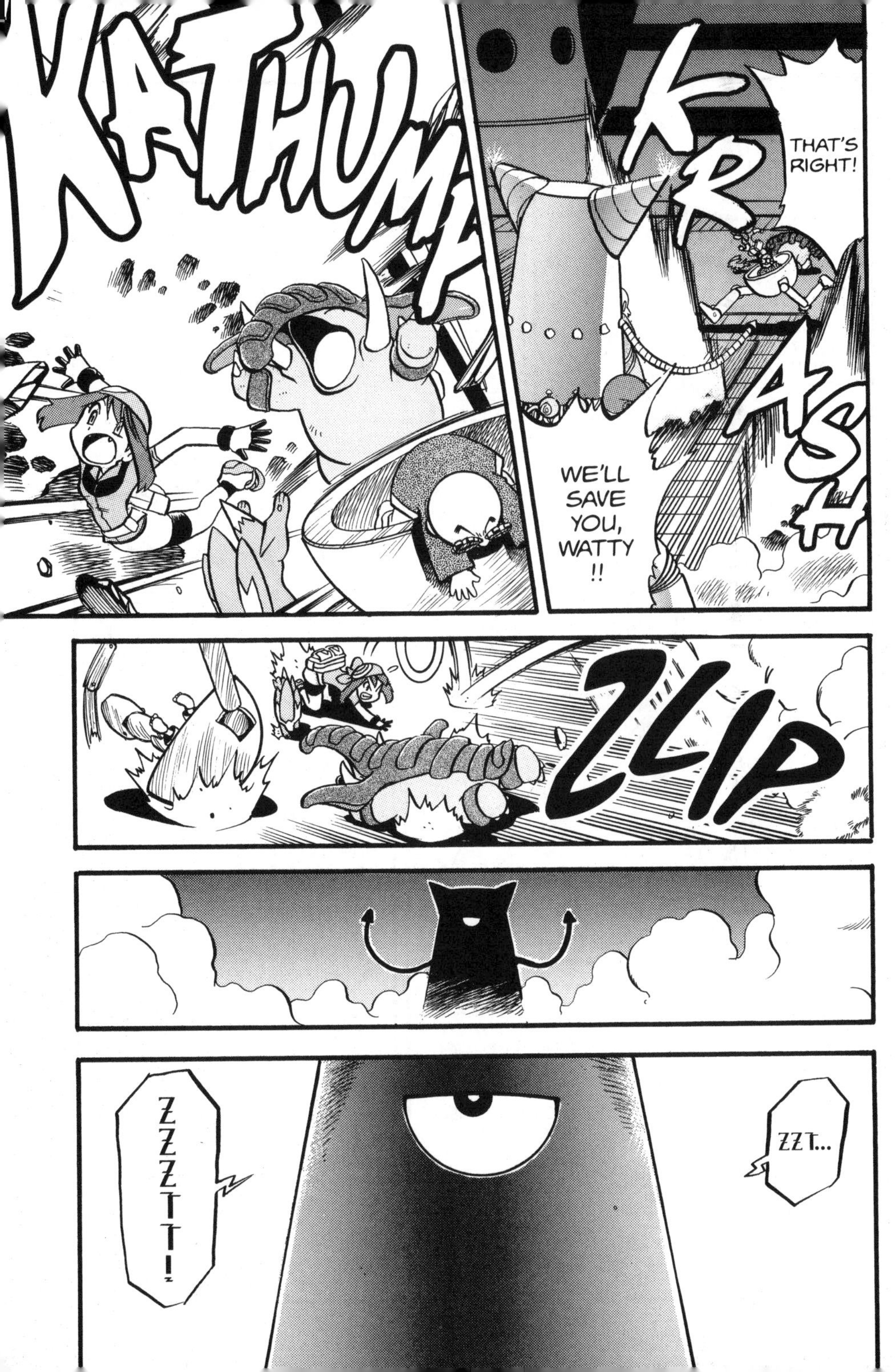
KRASH
THAT'S RIGHT!
WE'LL SAVE YOU, WATTY!!
KATHUMP
ZZIP
ZZT...
ZZZTT!

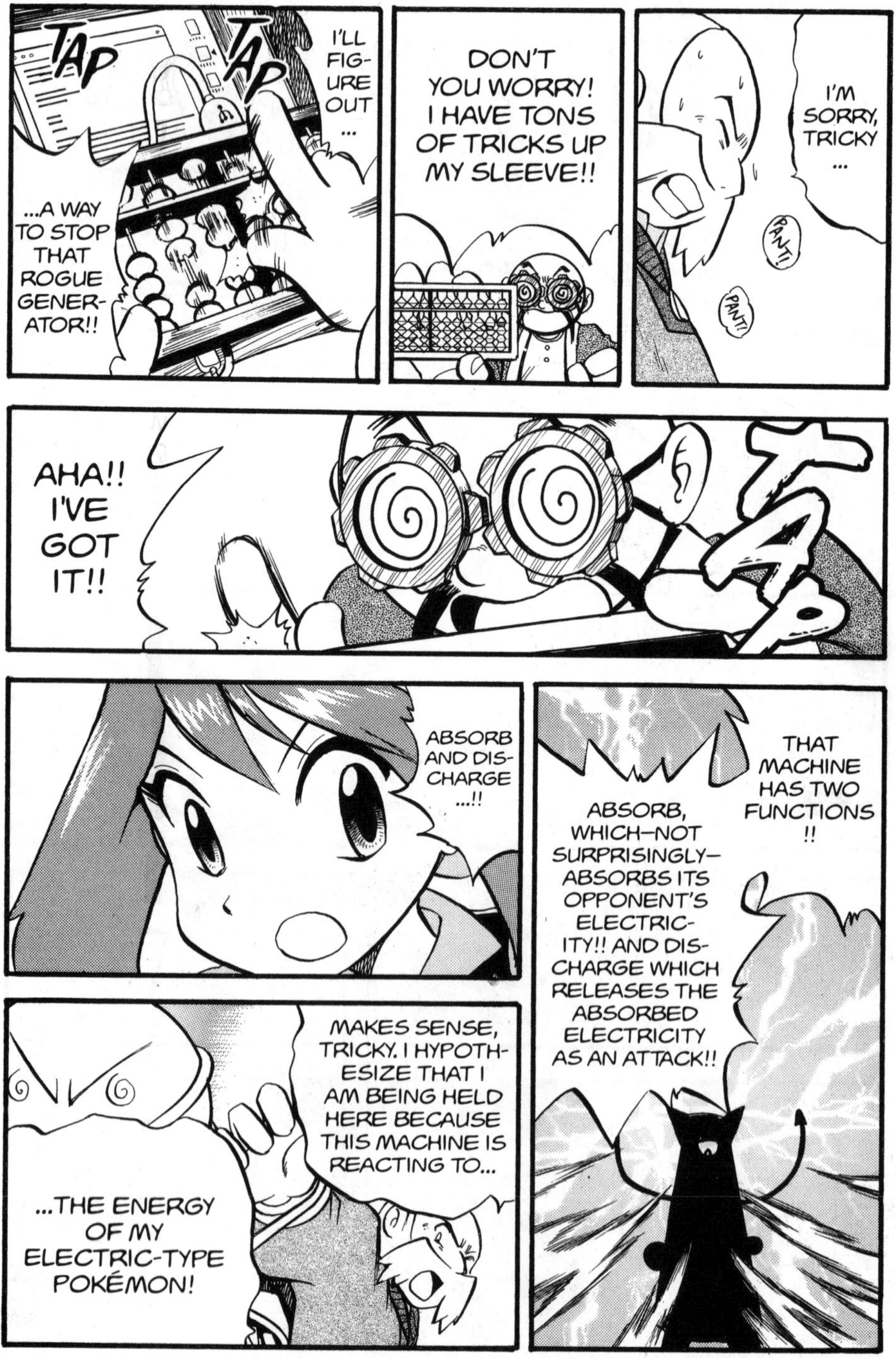
I'M SORRY, TRICKY...
PANT!!
PANT!!
DON'T YOU WORRY! I HAVE TONS OF TRICKS UP MY SLEEVE!!
TAP
TAP
I'LL FIGURE OUT...
...A WAY TO STOP THAT ROGUE GENERATOR!!
TAP
AHA!! I'VE GOT IT!!
THAT MACHINE HAS TWO FUNCTIONS!!
ABSORB, WHICH—NOT SURPRISINGLY—ABSORBS ITS OPPONENT'S ELECTRICITY!! AND DISCHARGE WHICH RELEASES THE ABSORBED ELECTRICITY AS AN ATTACK!!
ABSORB AND DISCHARGE...!!
MAKES SENSE, TRICKY. I HYPOTHESIZE THAT I AM BEING HELD HERE BECAUSE THIS MACHINE IS REACTING TO...
...THE ENERGY OF MY ELECTRIC-TYPE POKÉMON!

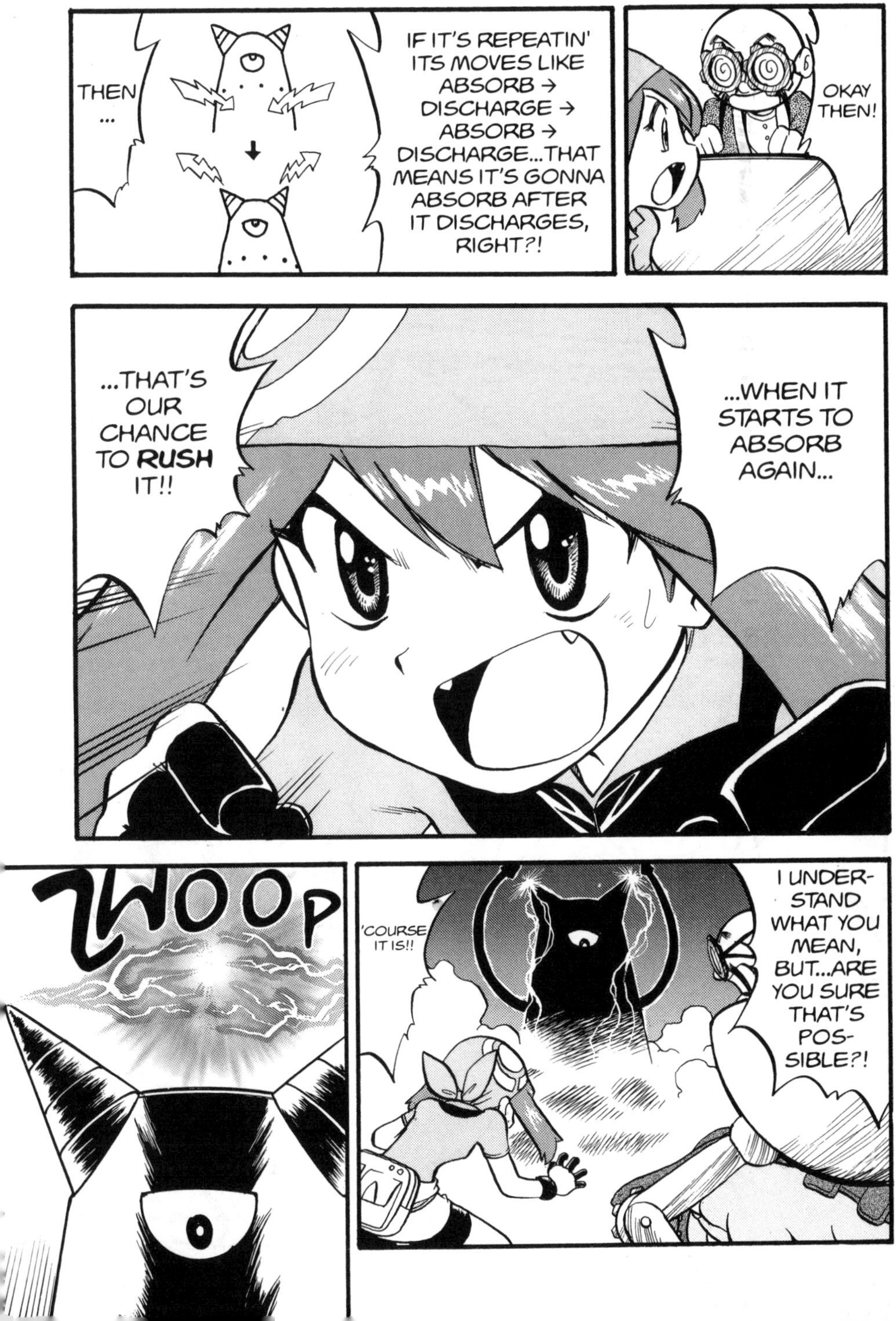
OKAY THEN!
IF IT'S REPEATIN' ITS MOVES LIKE ABSORB → DISCHARGE → ABSORB → DISCHARGE...THAT MEANS IT'S GONNA ABSORB AFTER IT DISCHARGES, RIGHT?!
THEN ...
...WHEN IT STARTS TO ABSORB AGAIN...
...THAT'S OUR CHANCE TO **RUSH** IT!!
I UNDER-STAND WHAT YOU MEAN, BUT...ARE YOU SURE THAT'S POS-SIBLE?!
'COURSE IT IS!!
ZWOOP

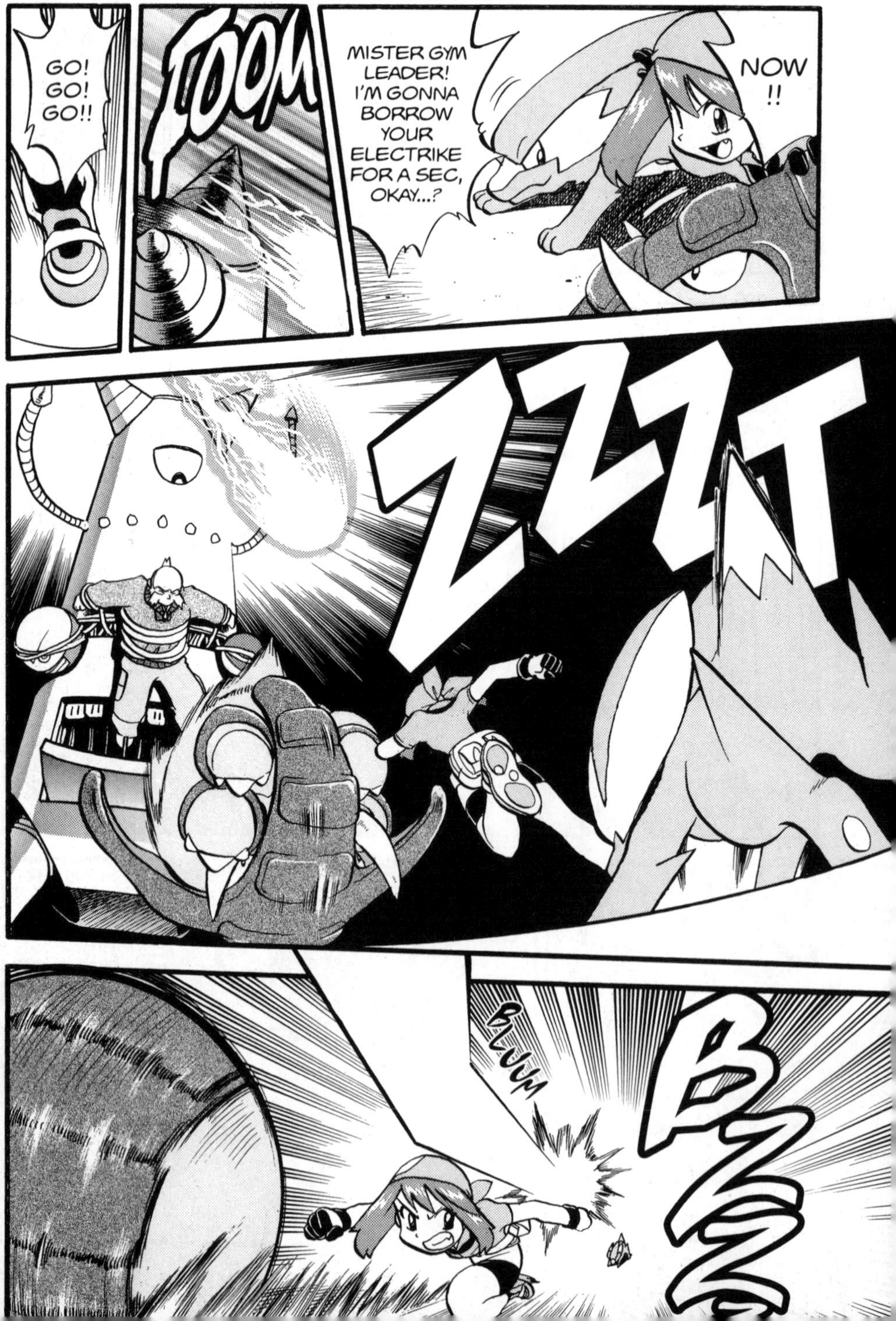
NOW!!
MISTER GYM LEADER! I'M GONNA BORROW YOUR ELECTRIKE FOR A SEC, OKAY...?
FOOM
GO! GO! GO!!
ZZZT
BZZZ
BLUUM

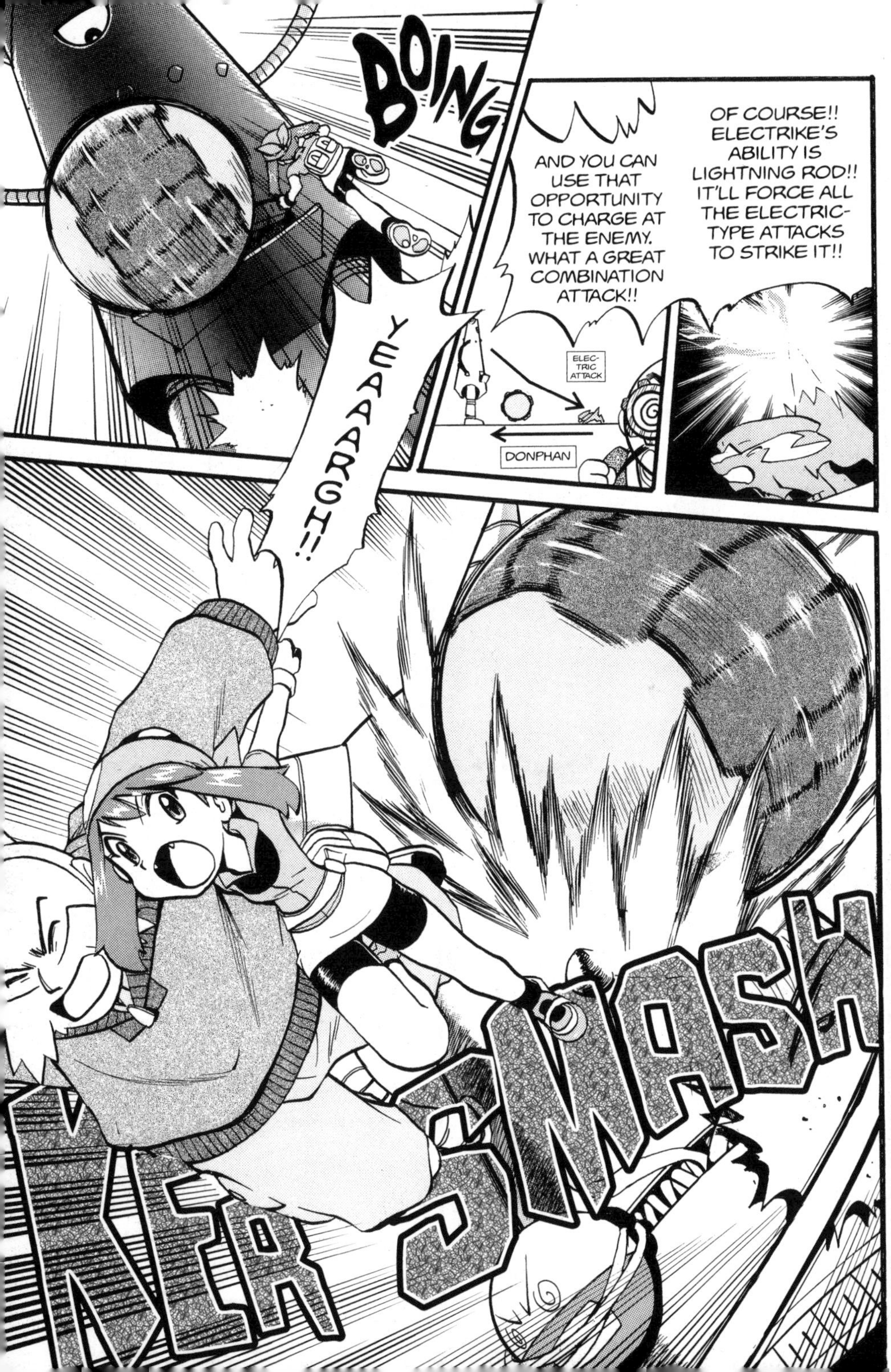
OF COURSE!! ELECTRIKE'S ABILITY IS LIGHTNING ROD!! IT'LL FORCE ALL THE ELECTRIC-TYPE ATTACKS TO STRIKE IT!!
AND YOU CAN USE THAT OPPORTUNITY TO CHARGE AT THE ENEMY. WHAT A GREAT COMBINATION ATTACK!!
ELEC-TRIC ATTACK
DONPHAN
BOING
YEAAAARGH!!
KER SMASH

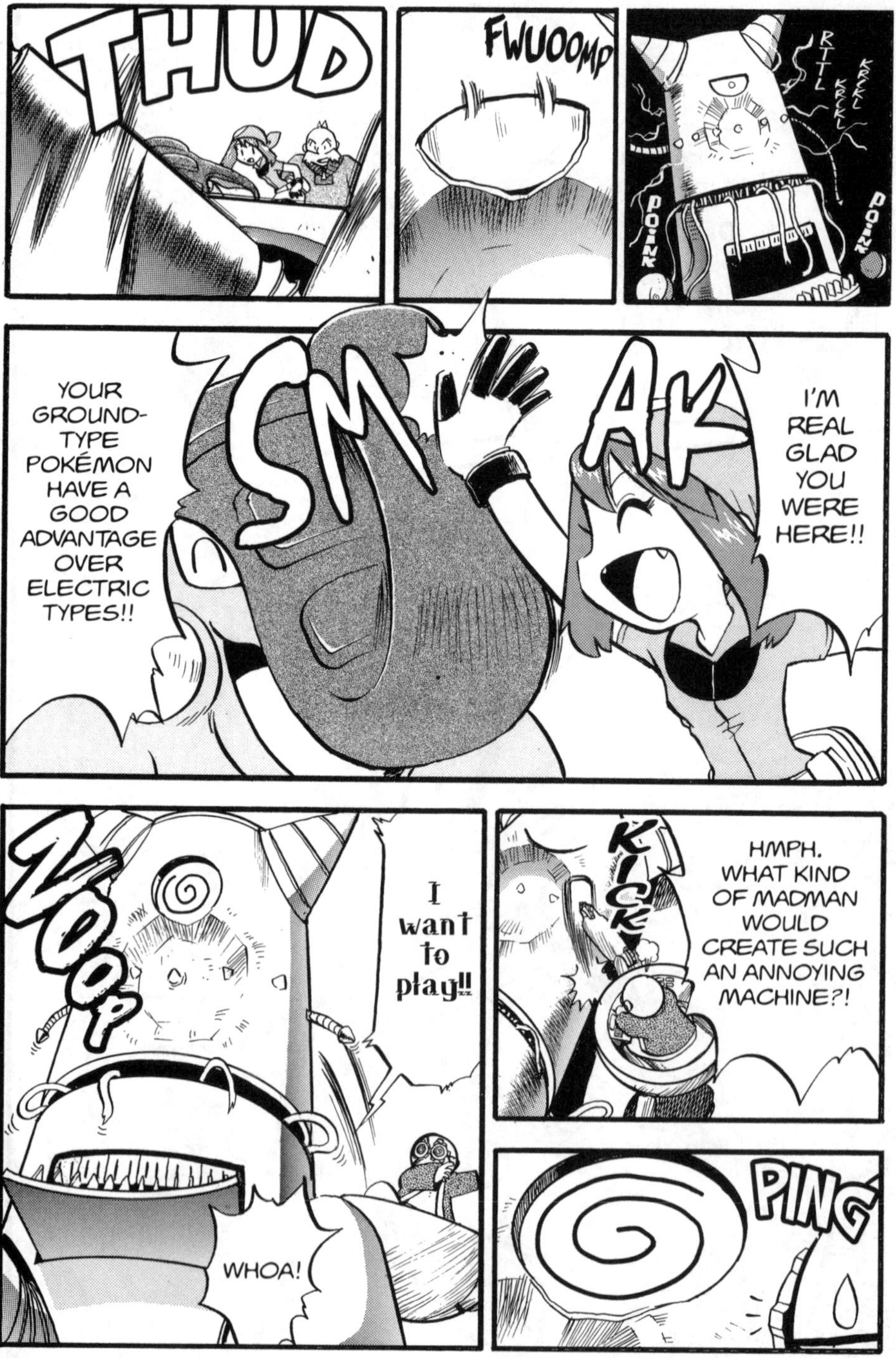
RTTL
KRKKL
KRKKL
POINK
POINK
FWUOOMP
THUD
I'M REAL GLAD YOU WERE HERE!!
SMAK
YOUR GROUND-TYPE POKÉMON HAVE A GOOD ADVANTAGE OVER ELECTRIC TYPES!!
HMPH. WHAT KIND OF MADMAN WOULD CREATE SUCH AN ANNOYING MACHINE?!
KICK
PING
I want to play!!
NOOP
WHOA!

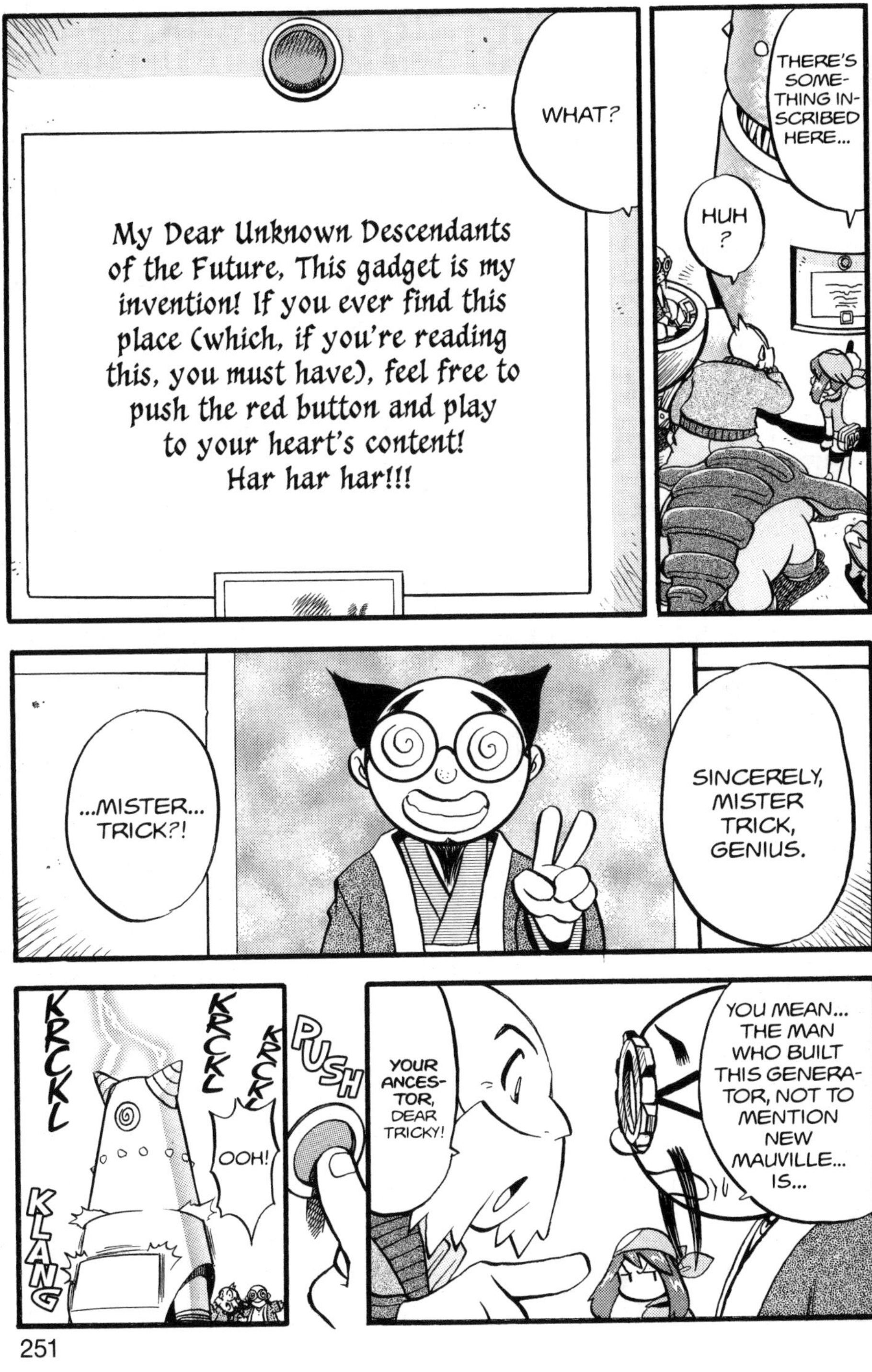
THERE'S SOME-THING IN-SCRIBED HERE...
HUH?
WHAT?
My Dear Unknown Descendants of the Future, This gadget is my invention! If you ever find this place (which, if you're reading this, you must have), feel free to push the red button and play to your heart's content! Har har har!!!
SINCERELY, MISTER TRICK, GENIUS.
...MISTER... TRICK?!
YOU MEAN... THE MAN WHO BUILT THIS GENERA-TOR, NOT TO MENTION NEW MAUVILLE... IS...
YOUR ANCES-TOR, DEAR TRICKY!
PUSH
KRCKL
KRCKL
KRCKL
OOH!
KLANG

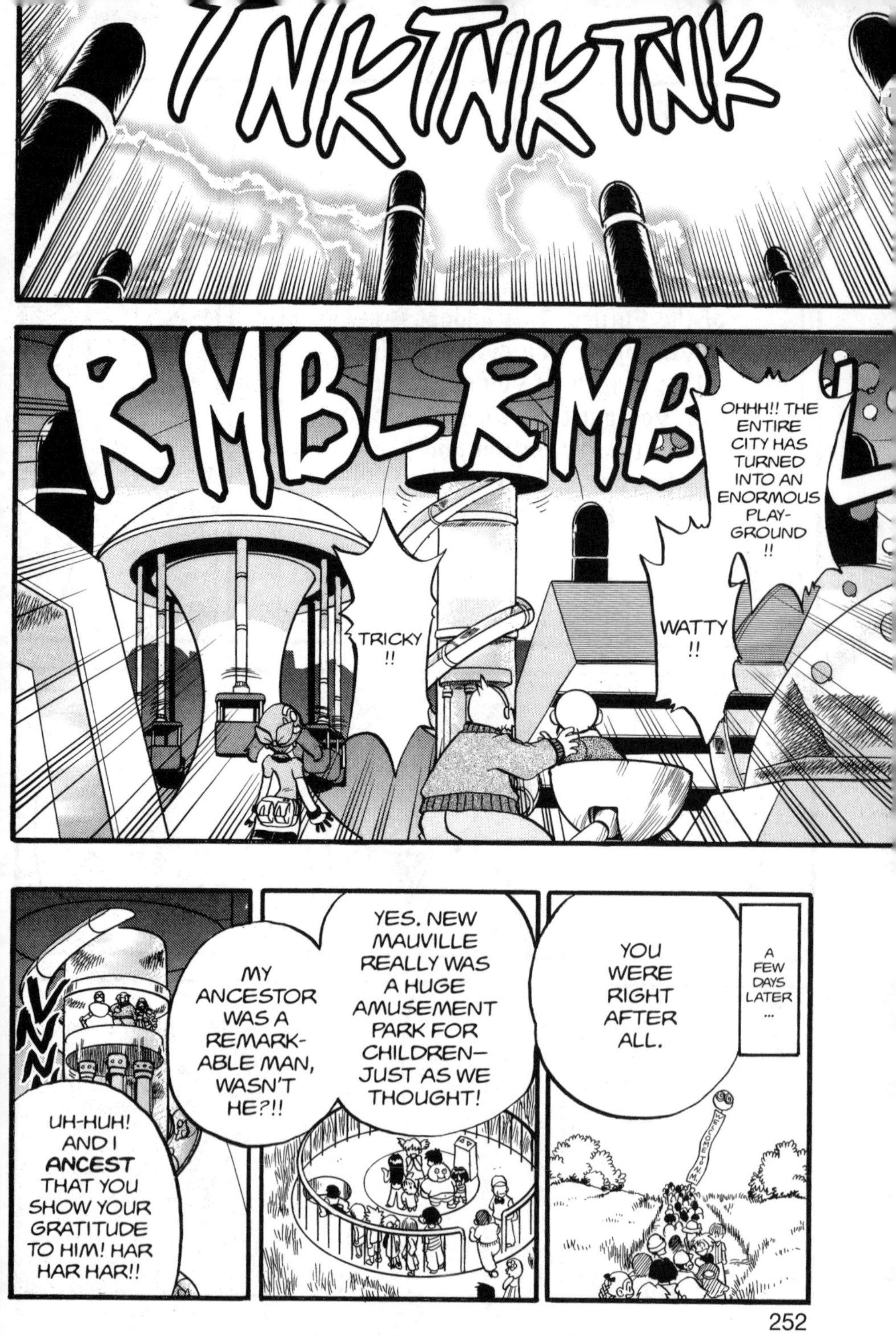
TNKTNKTNK
RMBLRMBL
OHHH!! THE ENTIRE CITY HAS TURNED INTO AN ENORMOUS PLAY-GROUND !!
WATTY !!
TRICKY !!
A FEW DAYS LATER ...
YOU WERE RIGHT AFTER ALL.
YES. NEW MAUVILLE REALLY WAS A HUGE AMUSEMENT PARK FOR CHILDREN— JUST AS WE THOUGHT!
MY ANCESTOR WAS A REMARK-ABLE MAN, WASN'T HE?!!
UH-HUH! AND I **ANCEST** THAT YOU SHOW YOUR GRATITUDE TO HIM! HAR HAR HAR!!

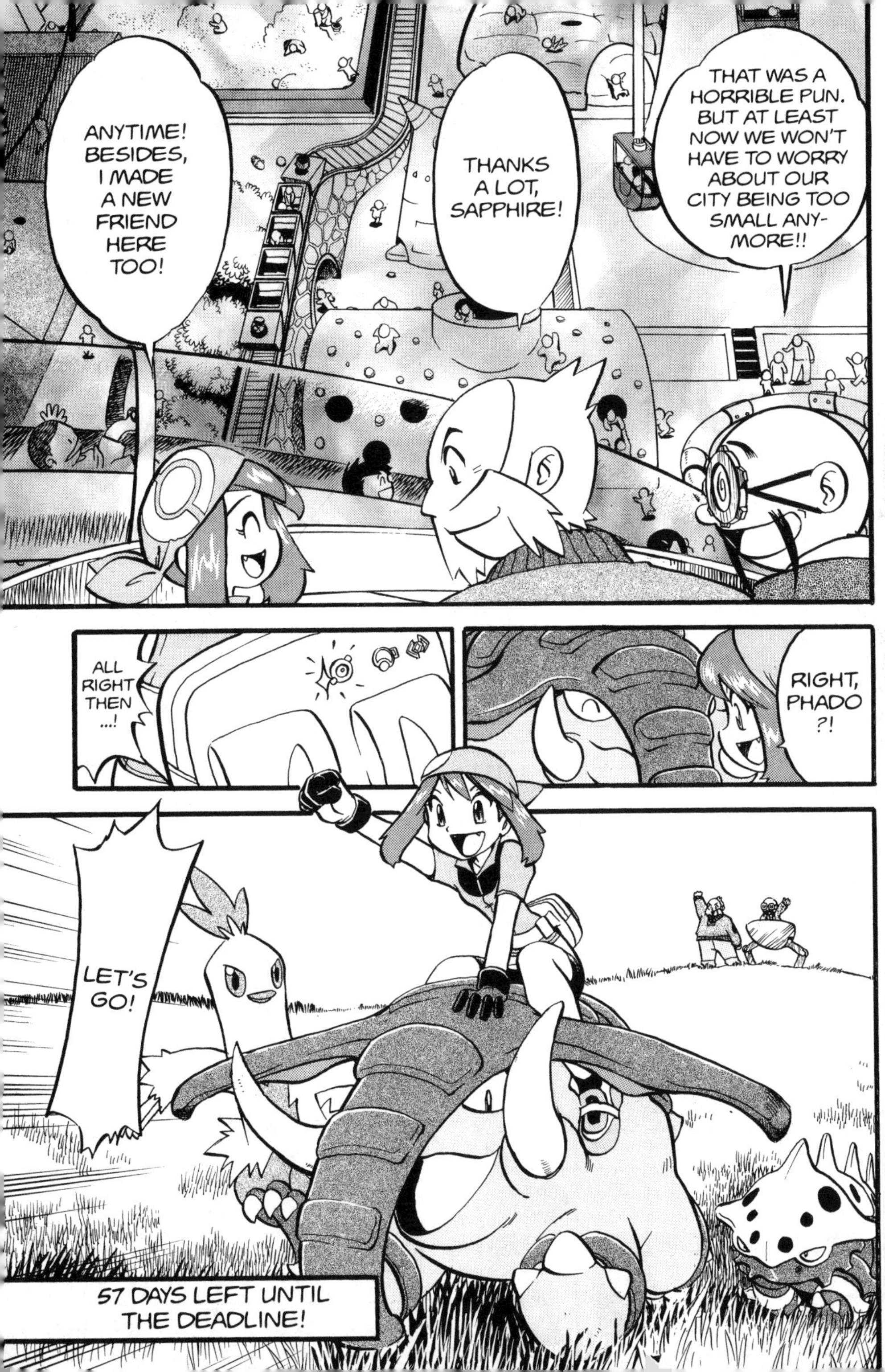
THAT WAS A HORRIBLE PUN. BUT AT LEAST NOW WE WON'T HAVE TO WORRY ABOUT OUR CITY BEING TOO SMALL ANY-MORE!!
THANKS A LOT, SAPPHIRE!
ANYTIME! BESIDES, I MADE A NEW FRIEND HERE TOO!
RIGHT, PHADO?!
ALL RIGHT THEN...!
LET'S GO!
57 DAYS LEFT UNTIL THE DEADLINE!

ADVENTURE MAP

SAPPHIRE

RUBY

Route 109

Slateport City | Slateport City

Route 110

Mauville City

New Mauville

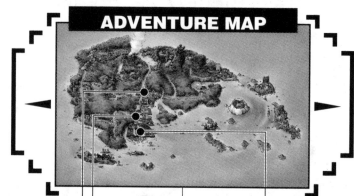

SAPPHIRE

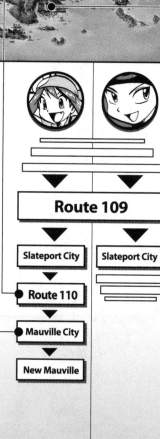

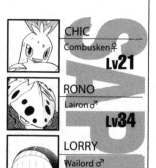

- CHIC — Combusken ♀ — Lv21
- RONO — Lairon ♂ — Lv34
- LORRY — Wailord ♂ — Lv42
- PHADO — Donphan ♂ — Lv39

RUBY

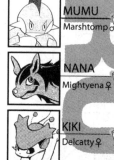

- MUMU — Marshtomp ♂
- NANA — Mightyena ♀
- KIKI — Delcatty ♀

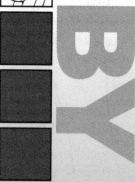

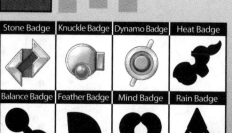

Stone Badge	Knuckle Badge	Dynamo Badge	Heat Badge
Balance Badge	Feather Badge	Mind Badge	Rain Badge

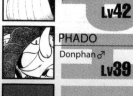

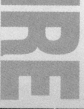

	Coolness	Beauty	Cuteness	Cleverness	Toughness
Normal					
Super					
Hyper					
Master					

● Adventure 206 ●
Not-So-Fetching Feebas

Pokémon™ Adventures Ruby & Sapphire
The Fourth Chapter

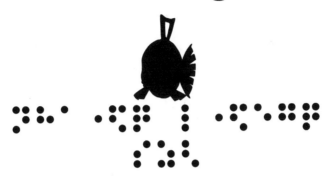

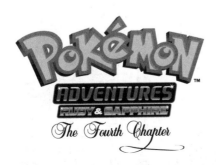

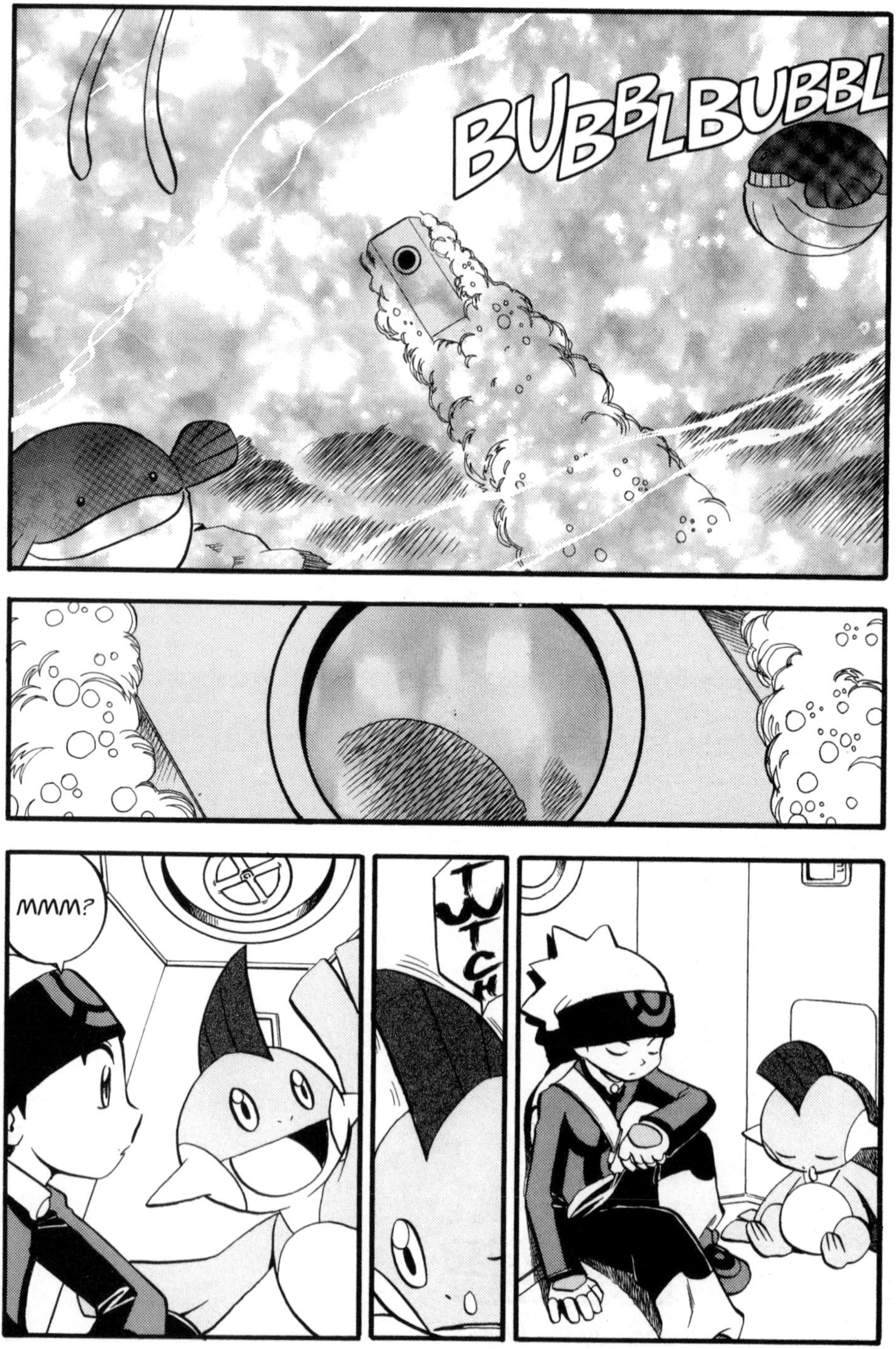
BUBBLBUBBL
TWTCH
MMM?

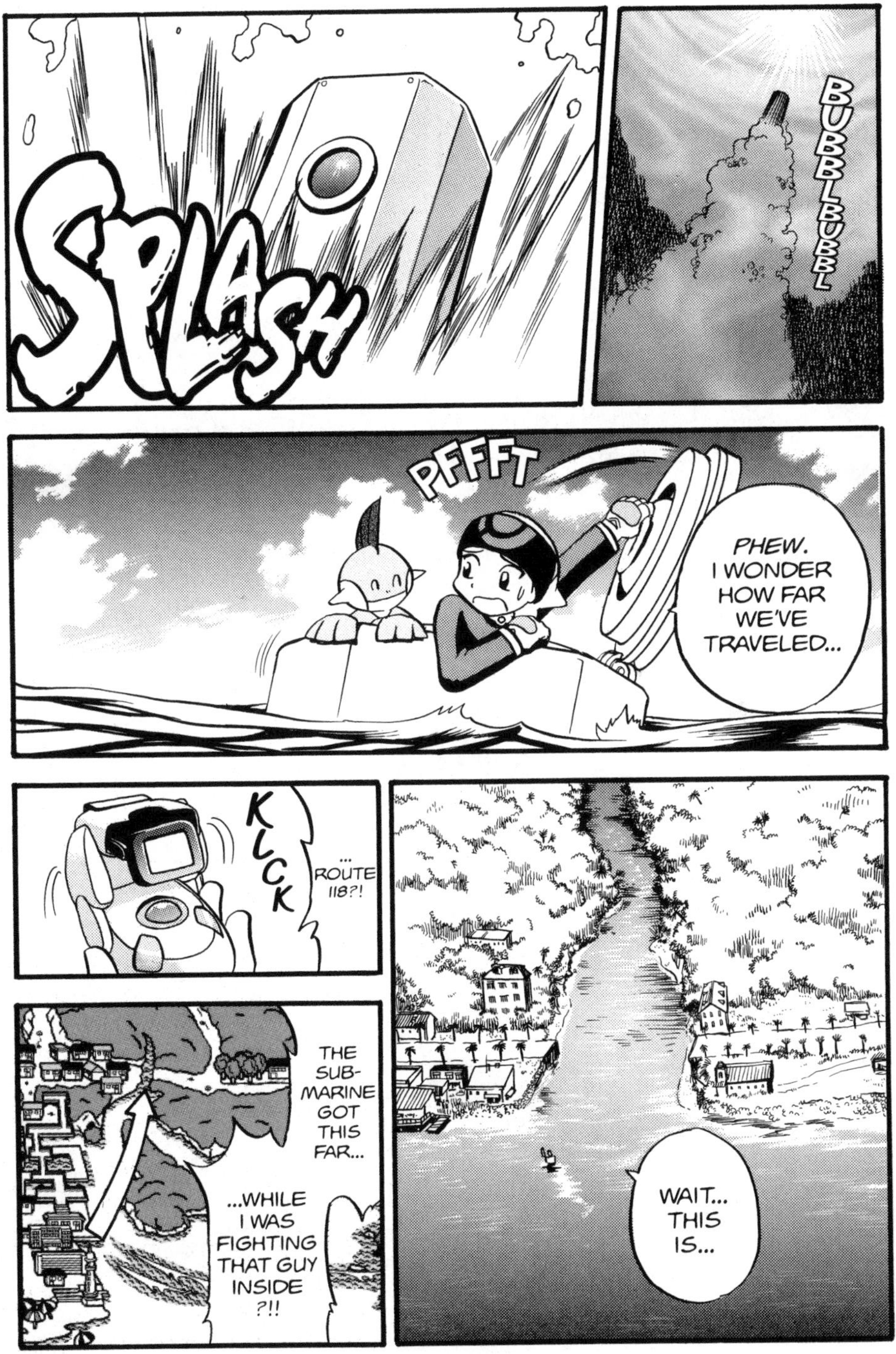
BUBBLBUBBL
SPLASH
PFFFT
PHEW. I WONDER HOW FAR WE'VE TRAVELED...
WAIT... THIS IS...
KLCK
... ROUTE 118?!
THE SUB-MARINE GOT THIS FAR...
...WHILE I WAS FIGHTING THAT GUY INSIDE ?!!

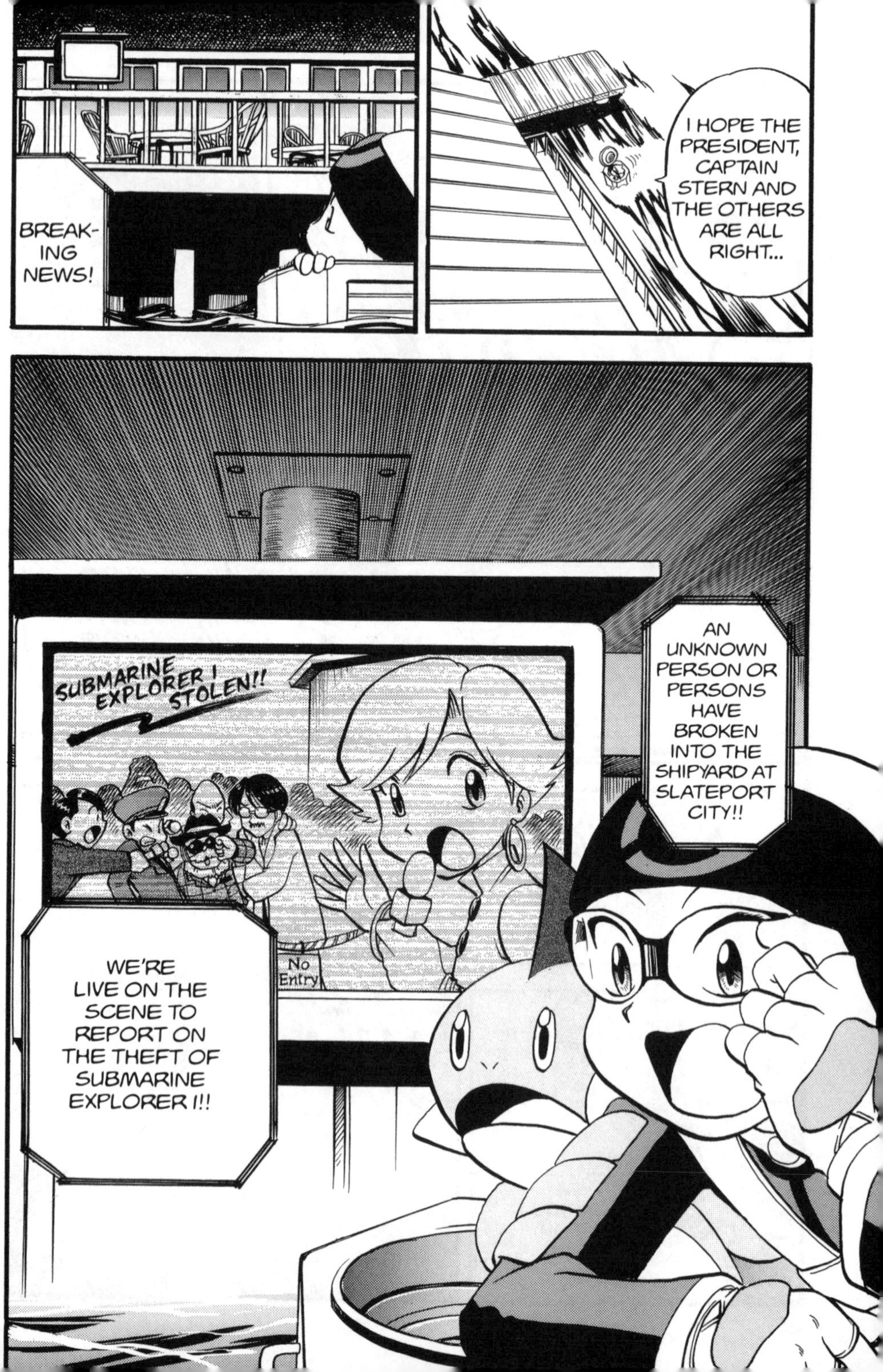
I HOPE THE PRESIDENT, CAPTAIN STERN AND THE OTHERS ARE ALL RIGHT...
BREAK-ING NEWS!
AN UNKNOWN PERSON OR PERSONS HAVE BROKEN INTO THE SHIPYARD AT SLATEPORT CITY!!
SUBMARINE EXPLORER I STOLEN!!
No Entry
WE'RE LIVE ON THE SCENE TO REPORT ON THE THEFT OF SUBMARINE EXPLORER I!!

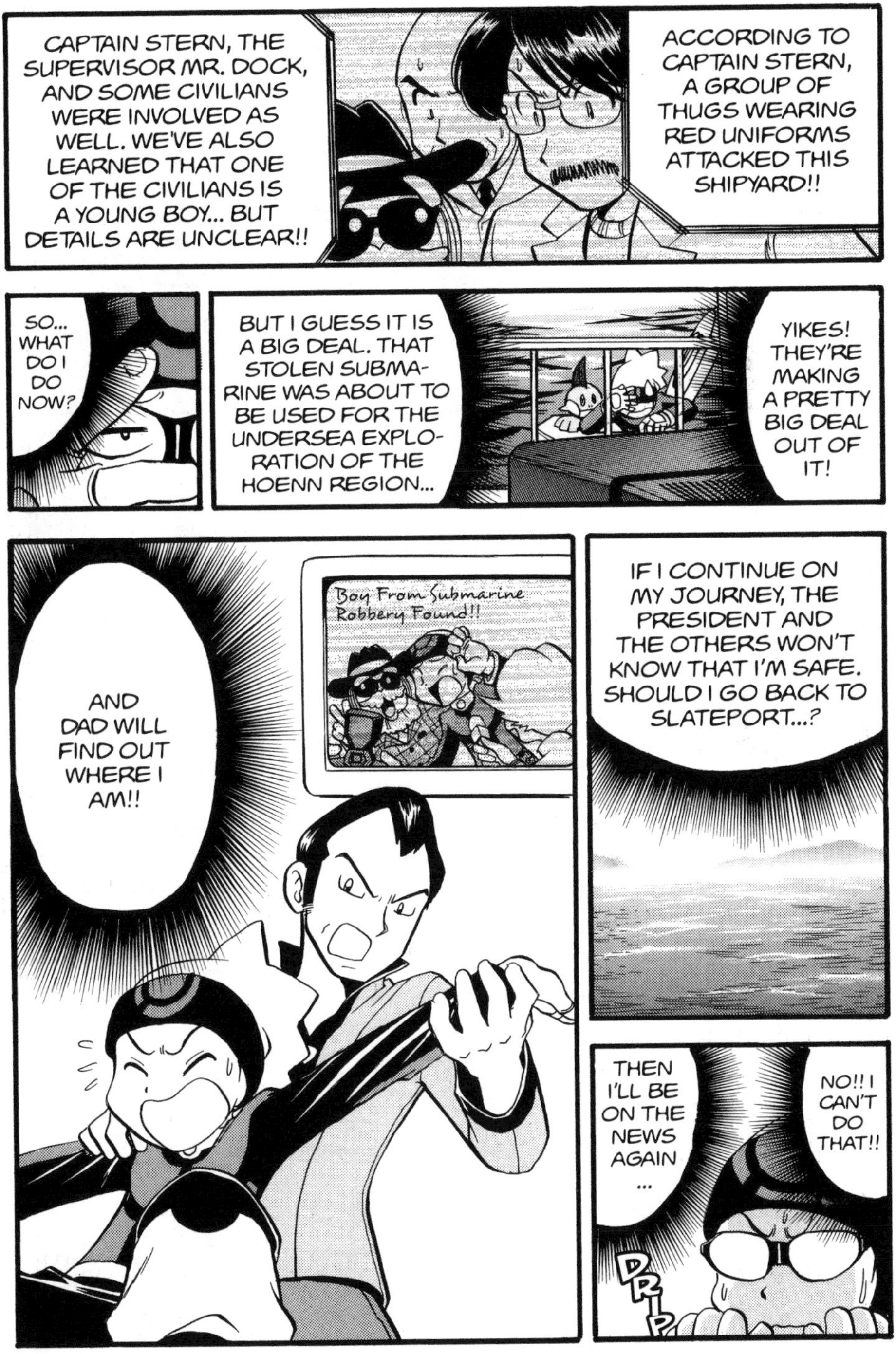
ACCORDING TO CAPTAIN STERN, A GROUP OF THUGS WEARING RED UNIFORMS ATTACKED THIS SHIPYARD!!
CAPTAIN STERN, THE SUPERVISOR MR. DOCK, AND SOME CIVILIANS WERE INVOLVED AS WELL. WE'VE ALSO LEARNED THAT ONE OF THE CIVILIANS IS A YOUNG BOY... BUT DETAILS ARE UNCLEAR!!
YIKES! THEY'RE MAKING A PRETTY BIG DEAL OUT OF IT!
BUT I GUESS IT IS A BIG DEAL. THAT STOLEN SUBMARINE WAS ABOUT TO BE USED FOR THE UNDERSEA EXPLORATION OF THE HOENN REGION...
SO... WHAT DO I DO NOW?
IF I CONTINUE ON MY JOURNEY, THE PRESIDENT AND THE OTHERS WON'T KNOW THAT I'M SAFE. SHOULD I GO BACK TO SLATEPORT...?
THEN I'LL BE ON THE NEWS AGAIN...
NO!! I CAN'T DO THAT!!
DRIP
Boy From Submarine Robbery Found!!
AND DAD WILL FIND OUT WHERE I AM!!

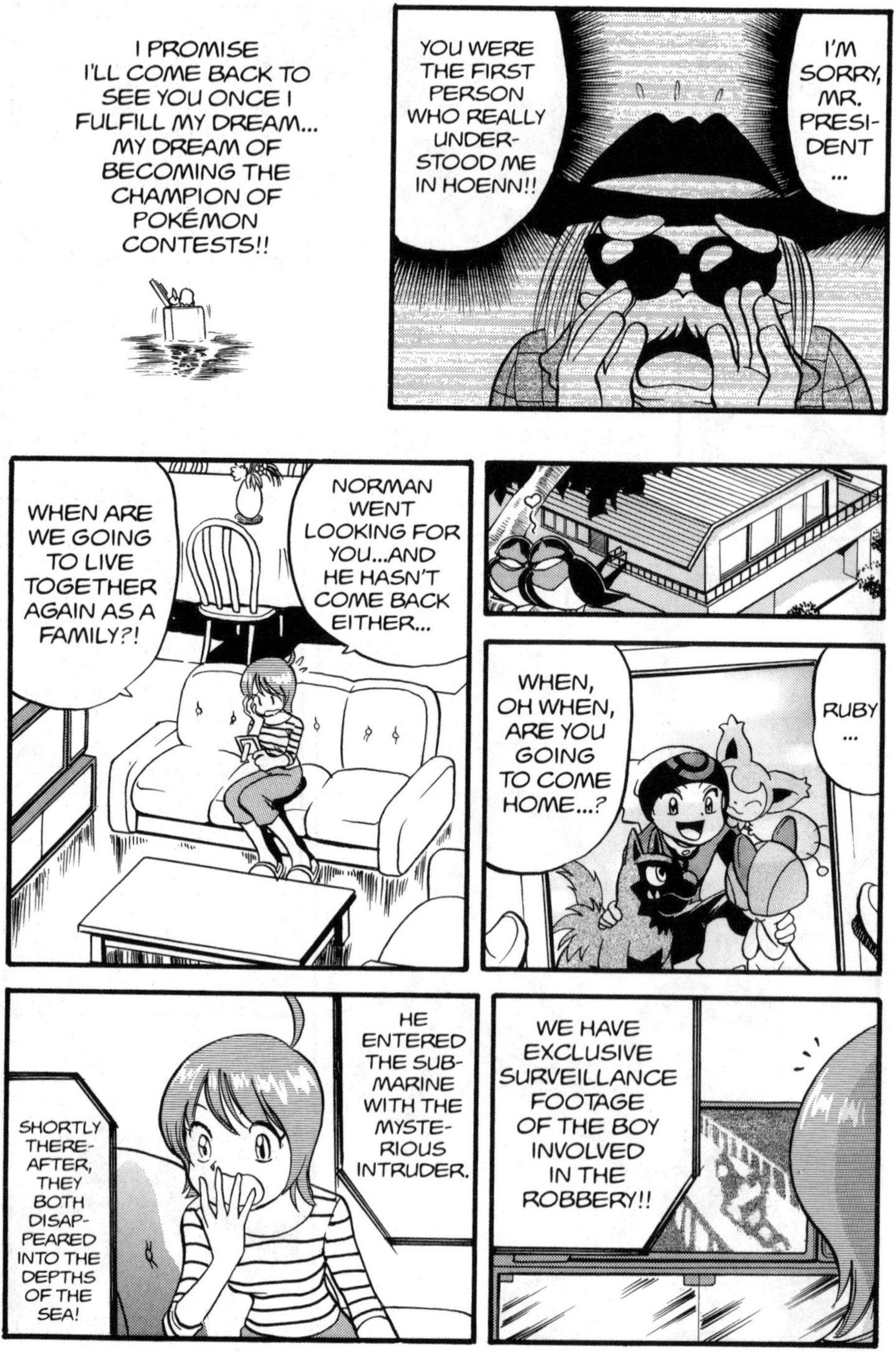
I'M SORRY, MR. PRESIDENT...
YOU WERE THE FIRST PERSON WHO REALLY UNDERSTOOD ME IN HOENN!!
I PROMISE I'LL COME BACK TO SEE YOU ONCE I FULFILL MY DREAM... MY DREAM OF BECOMING THE CHAMPION OF POKÉMON CONTESTS!!
RUBY...
WHEN, OH WHEN, ARE YOU GOING TO COME HOME...?
NORMAN WENT LOOKING FOR YOU...AND HE HASN'T COME BACK EITHER...
WHEN ARE WE GOING TO LIVE TOGETHER AGAIN AS A FAMILY?!
WE HAVE EXCLUSIVE SURVEILLANCE FOOTAGE OF THE BOY INVOLVED IN THE ROBBERY!!
HE ENTERED THE SUBMARINE WITH THE MYSTERIOUS INTRUDER.
SHORTLY THEREAFTER, THEY BOTH DISAPPEARED INTO THE DEPTHS OF THE SEA!

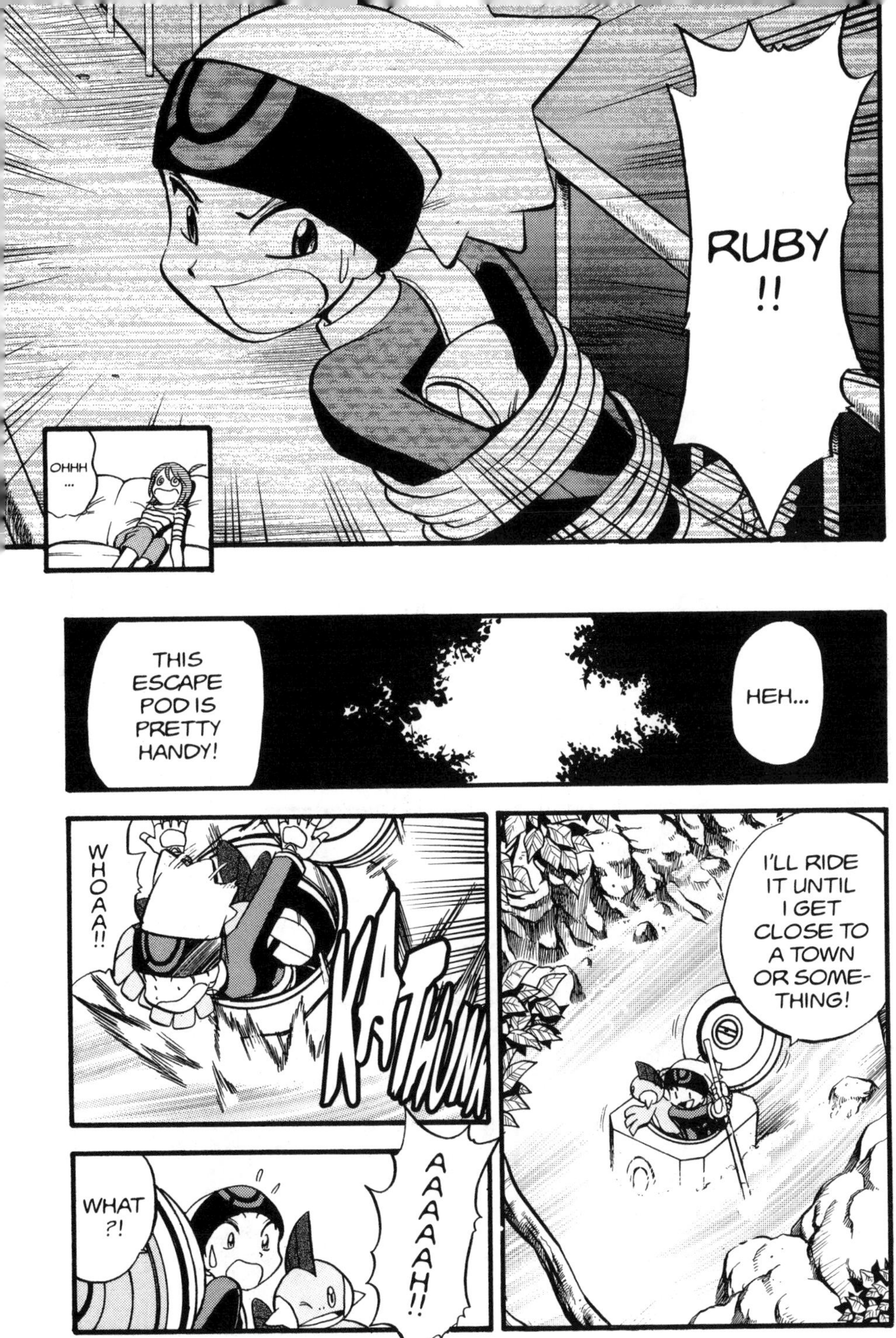
RUBY!!
OHHH...
HEH...
THIS ESCAPE POD IS PRETTY HANDY!
I'LL RIDE IT UNTIL I GET CLOSE TO A TOWN OR SOME-THING!
WHOAAA!!
AAAAAH!!
WHAT?!

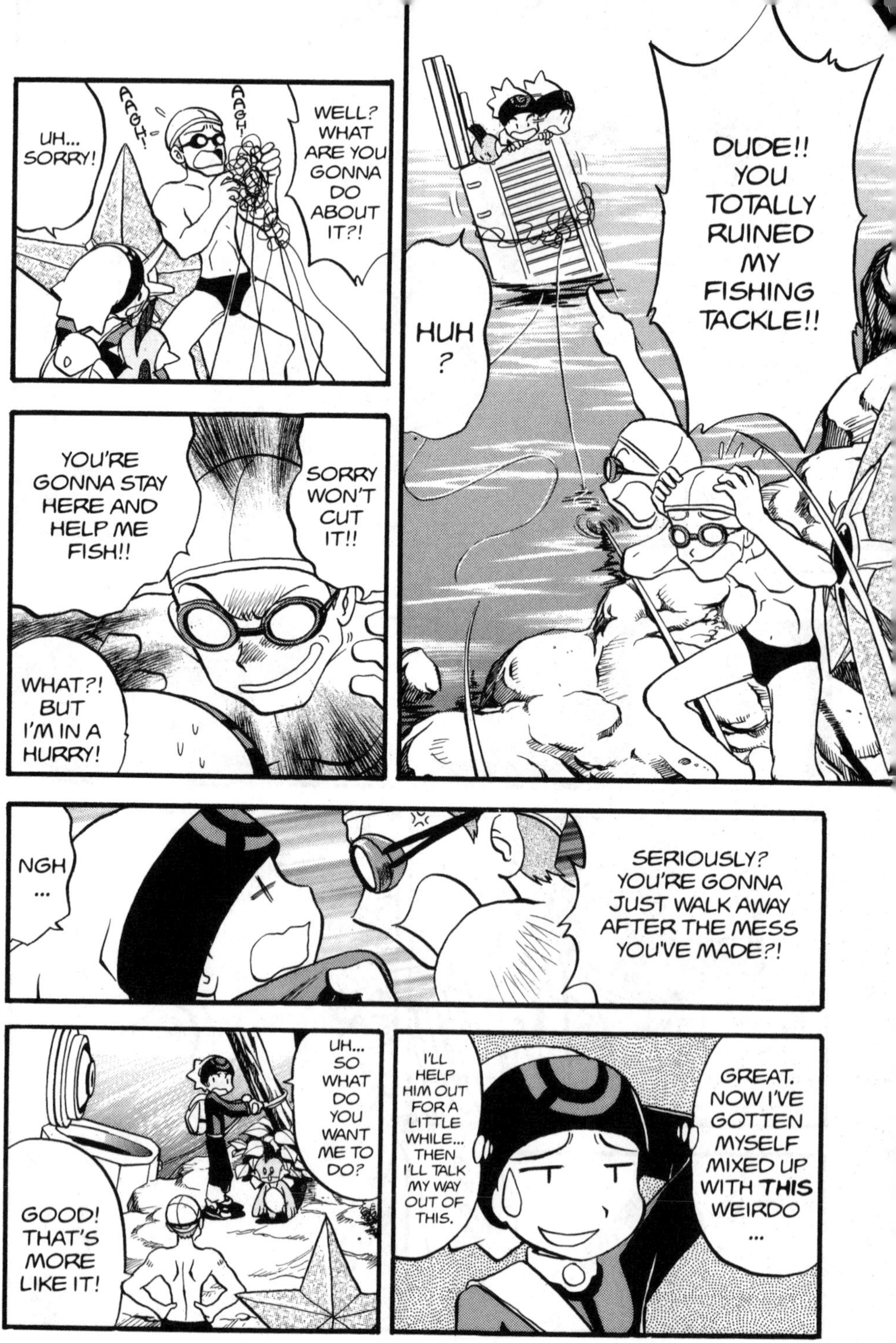
DUDE!! YOU TOTALLY RUINED MY FISHING TACKLE!!
HUH?
WELL? WHAT ARE YOU GONNA DO ABOUT IT?!
AAGH!
AAGH!
UH... SORRY!
SORRY WON'T CUT IT!!
YOU'RE GONNA STAY HERE AND HELP ME FISH!!
WHAT?! BUT I'M IN A HURRY!
SERIOUSLY? YOU'RE GONNA JUST WALK AWAY AFTER THE MESS YOU'VE MADE?!
NGH...
GREAT. NOW I'VE GOTTEN MYSELF MIXED UP WITH **THIS** WEIRDO...
I'LL HELP HIM OUT FOR A LITTLE WHILE... THEN I'LL TALK MY WAY OUT OF THIS.
UH... SO WHAT DO YOU WANT ME TO DO?
GOOD! THAT'S MORE LIKE IT!

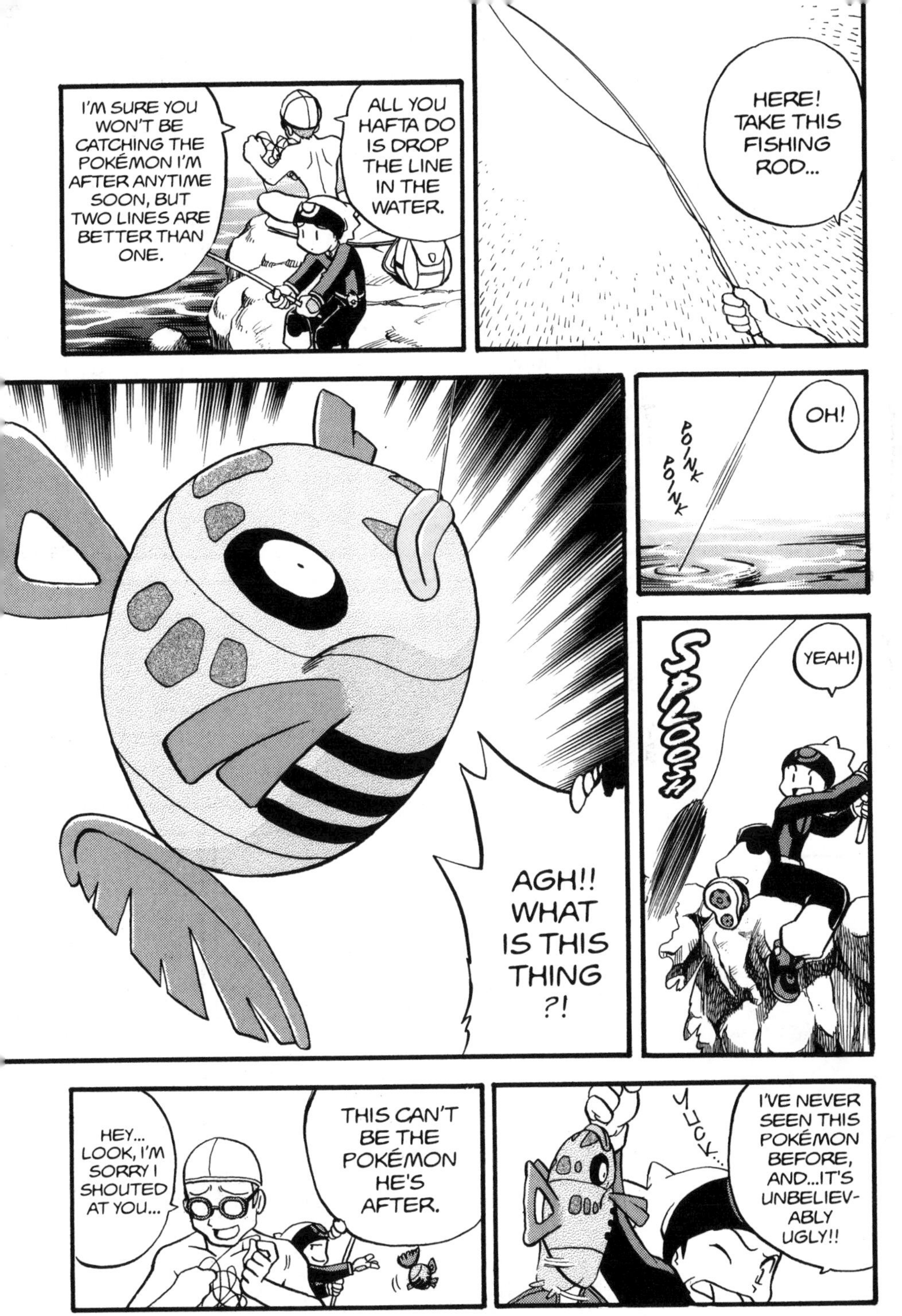
HERE! TAKE THIS FISHING ROD...
ALL YOU HAFTA DO IS DROP THE LINE IN THE WATER.
I'M SURE YOU WON'T BE CATCHING THE POKÉMON I'M AFTER ANYTIME SOON, BUT TWO LINES ARE BETTER THAN ONE.
OH!
POINK POINK
YEAH!
SPLOOSH
AGH!! WHAT IS THIS THING ?!
I'VE NEVER SEEN THIS POKÉMON BEFORE, AND...IT'S UNBELIEV-ABLY UGLY!!
YUCK...
THIS CAN'T BE THE POKÉMON HE'S AFTER.
HEY... LOOK, I'M SORRY I SHOUTED AT YOU...

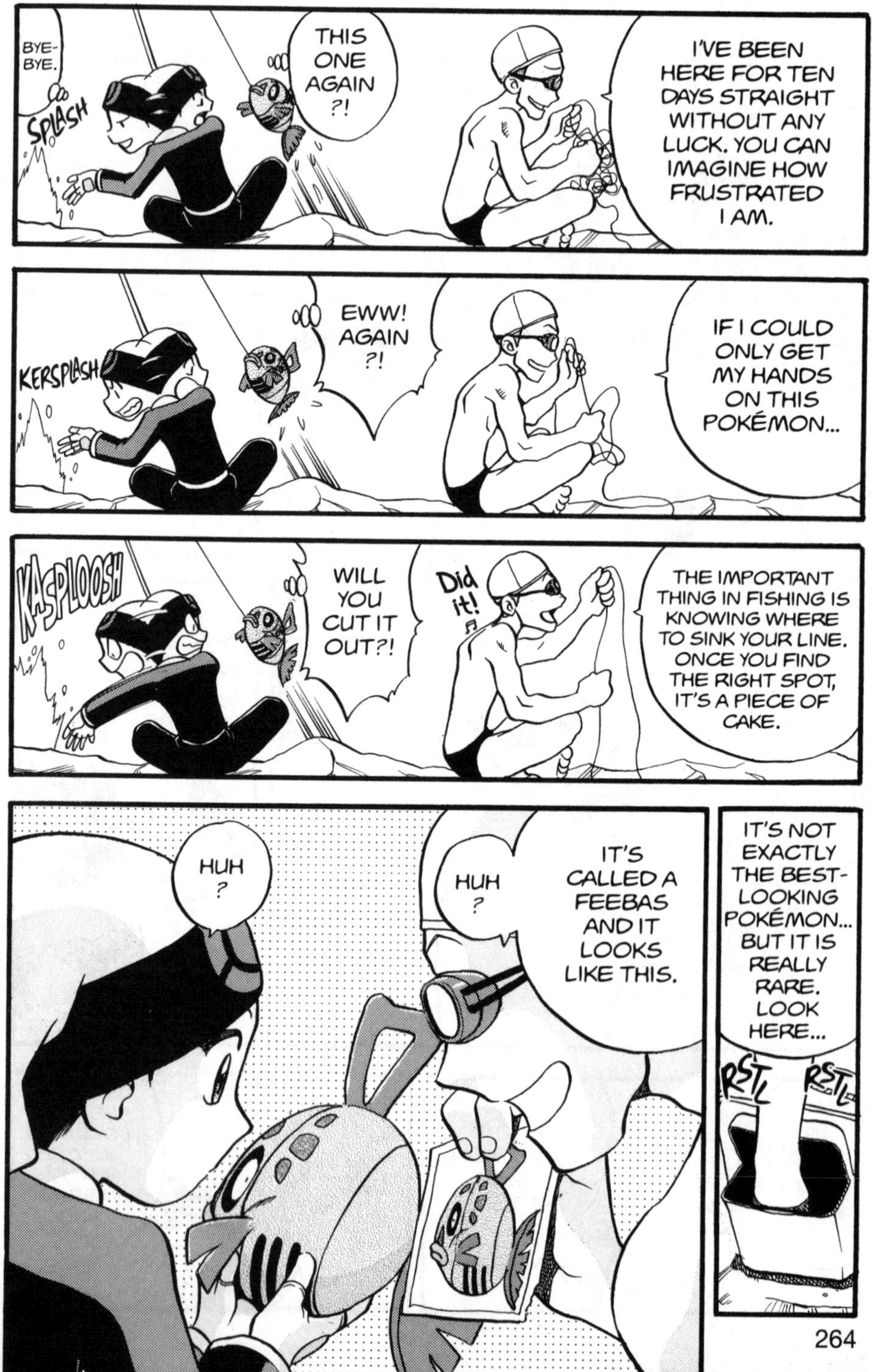
I'VE BEEN HERE FOR TEN DAYS STRAIGHT WITHOUT ANY LUCK. YOU CAN IMAGINE HOW FRUSTRATED I AM.
THIS ONE AGAIN?!
BYE-BYE.
SPLASH
IF I COULD ONLY GET MY HANDS ON THIS POKÉMON...
EWW! AGAIN?!
KERSPLASH
THE IMPORTANT THING IN FISHING IS KNOWING WHERE TO SINK YOUR LINE. ONCE YOU FIND THE RIGHT SPOT, IT'S A PIECE OF CAKE.
Did it!
WILL YOU CUT IT OUT?!
KASPLOOSH
IT'S NOT EXACTLY THE BEST-LOOKING POKÉMON... BUT IT IS REALLY RARE. LOOK HERE...
RSTL RSTL
IT'S CALLED A FEEBAS AND IT LOOKS LIKE THIS.
HUH?
HUH?

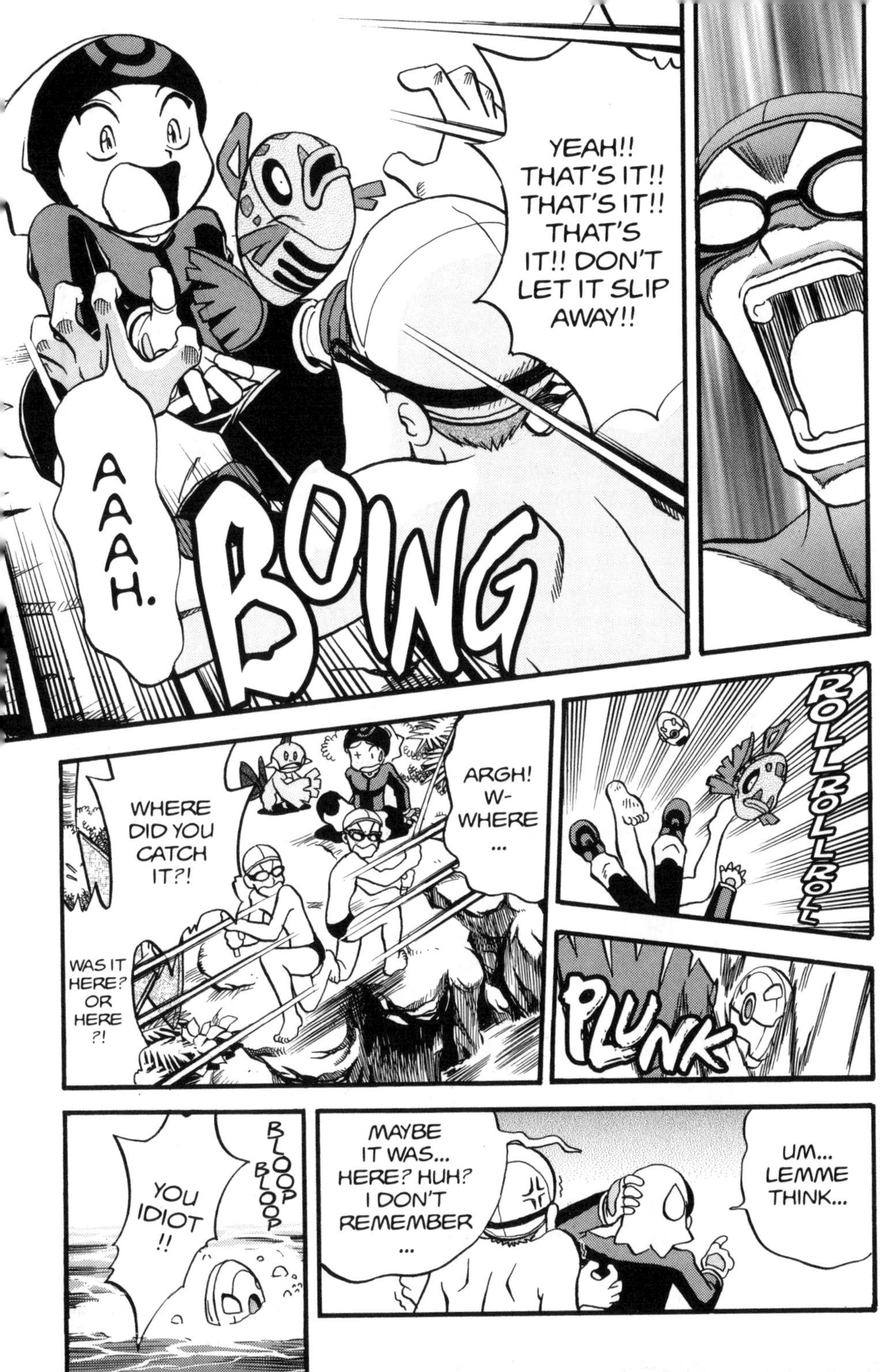
YEAH!! THAT'S IT!! THAT'S IT!! THAT'S IT!! DON'T LET IT SLIP AWAY!!
AAAH.
BOING
ROLLROLLROLL
PLUNK
ARGH! W-WHERE...
WHERE DID YOU CATCH IT?!
WAS IT HERE? OR HERE?!
UM... LEMME THINK...
MAYBE IT WAS... HERE? HUH? I DON'T REMEMBER...
BLOOP BLOOP
YOU IDIOT!!

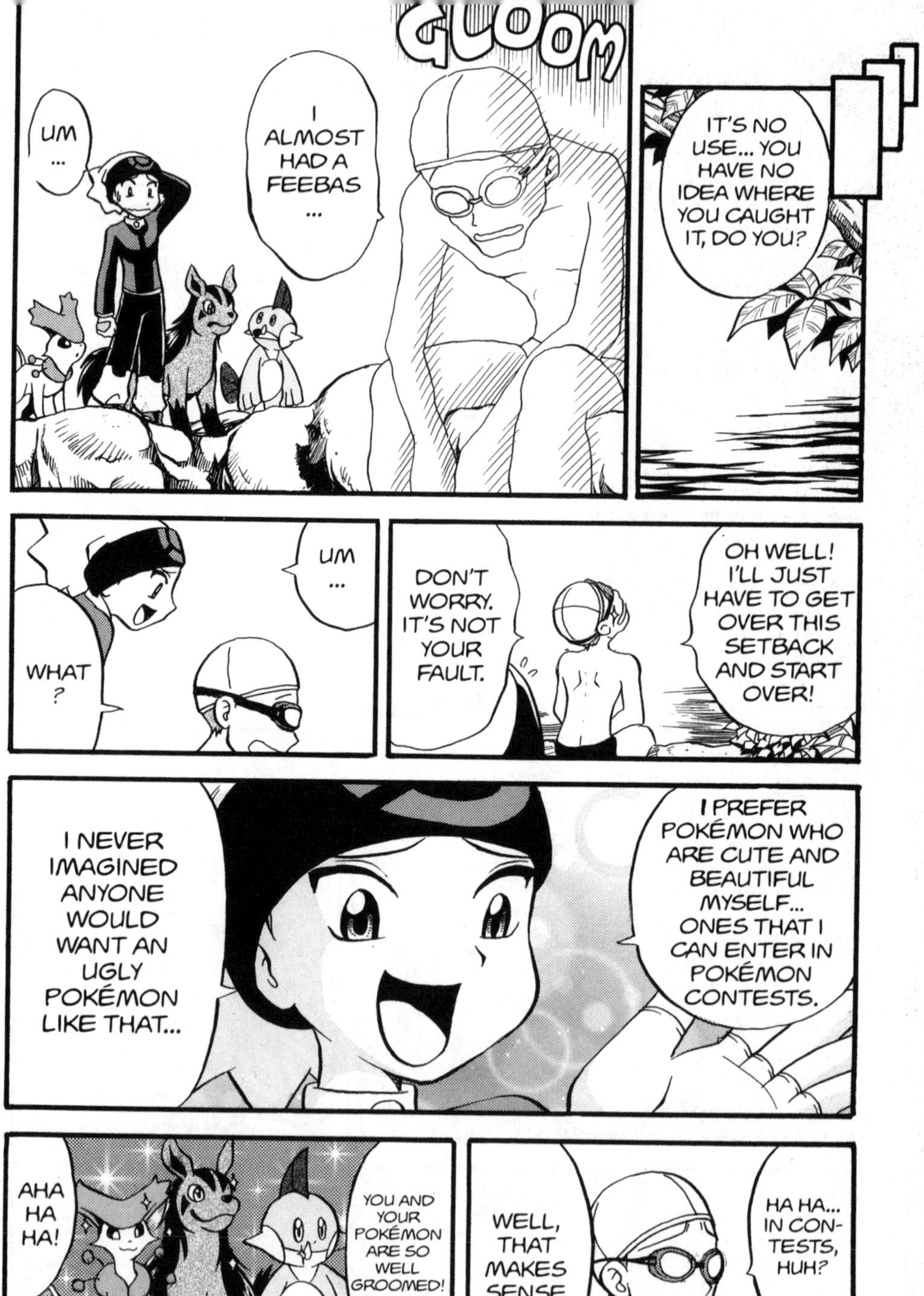
IT'S NO USE... YOU HAVE NO IDEA WHERE YOU CAUGHT IT, DO YOU?
GLOOM
I ALMOST HAD A FEEBAS ...
UM ...
OH WELL! I'LL JUST HAVE TO GET OVER THIS SETBACK AND START OVER!
DON'T WORRY. IT'S NOT YOUR FAULT.
UM ...
WHAT ?
I PREFER POKÉMON WHO ARE CUTE AND BEAUTIFUL MYSELF... ONES THAT I CAN ENTER IN POKÉMON CONTESTS.
I NEVER IMAGINED ANYONE WOULD WANT AN UGLY POKÉMON LIKE THAT...
HA HA... IN CON-TESTS, HUH?
WELL, THAT MAKES SENSE ...
YOU AND YOUR POKÉMON ARE SO WELL GROOMED!
AHA HA HA!

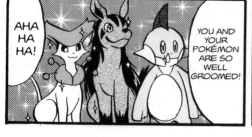

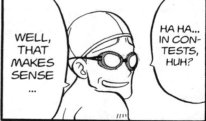

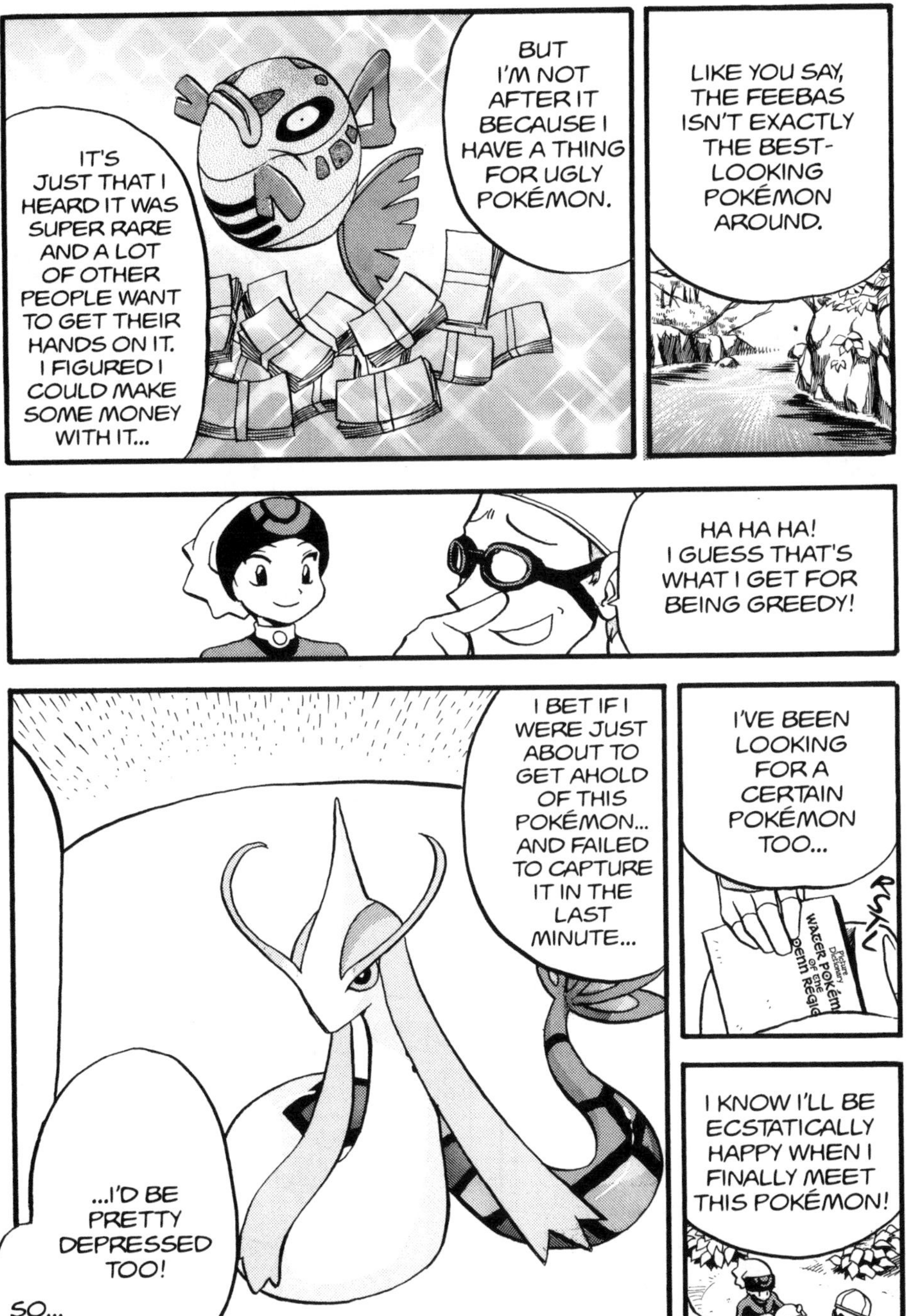
LIKE YOU SAY, THE FEEBAS ISN'T EXACTLY THE BEST-LOOKING POKÉMON AROUND.
BUT I'M NOT AFTER IT BECAUSE I HAVE A THING FOR UGLY POKÉMON.
IT'S JUST THAT I HEARD IT WAS SUPER RARE AND A LOT OF OTHER PEOPLE WANT TO GET THEIR HANDS ON IT. I FIGURED I COULD MAKE SOME MONEY WITH IT...
HA HA HA! I GUESS THAT'S WHAT I GET FOR BEING GREEDY!
I'VE BEEN LOOKING FOR A CERTAIN POKÉMON TOO...
I KNOW I'LL BE ECSTATICALLY HAPPY WHEN I FINALLY MEET THIS POKÉMON!
I BET IF I WERE JUST ABOUT TO GET AHOLD OF THIS POKÉMON... AND FAILED TO CAPTURE IT IN THE LAST MINUTE...
...I'D BE PRETTY DEPRESSED TOO!
SO...

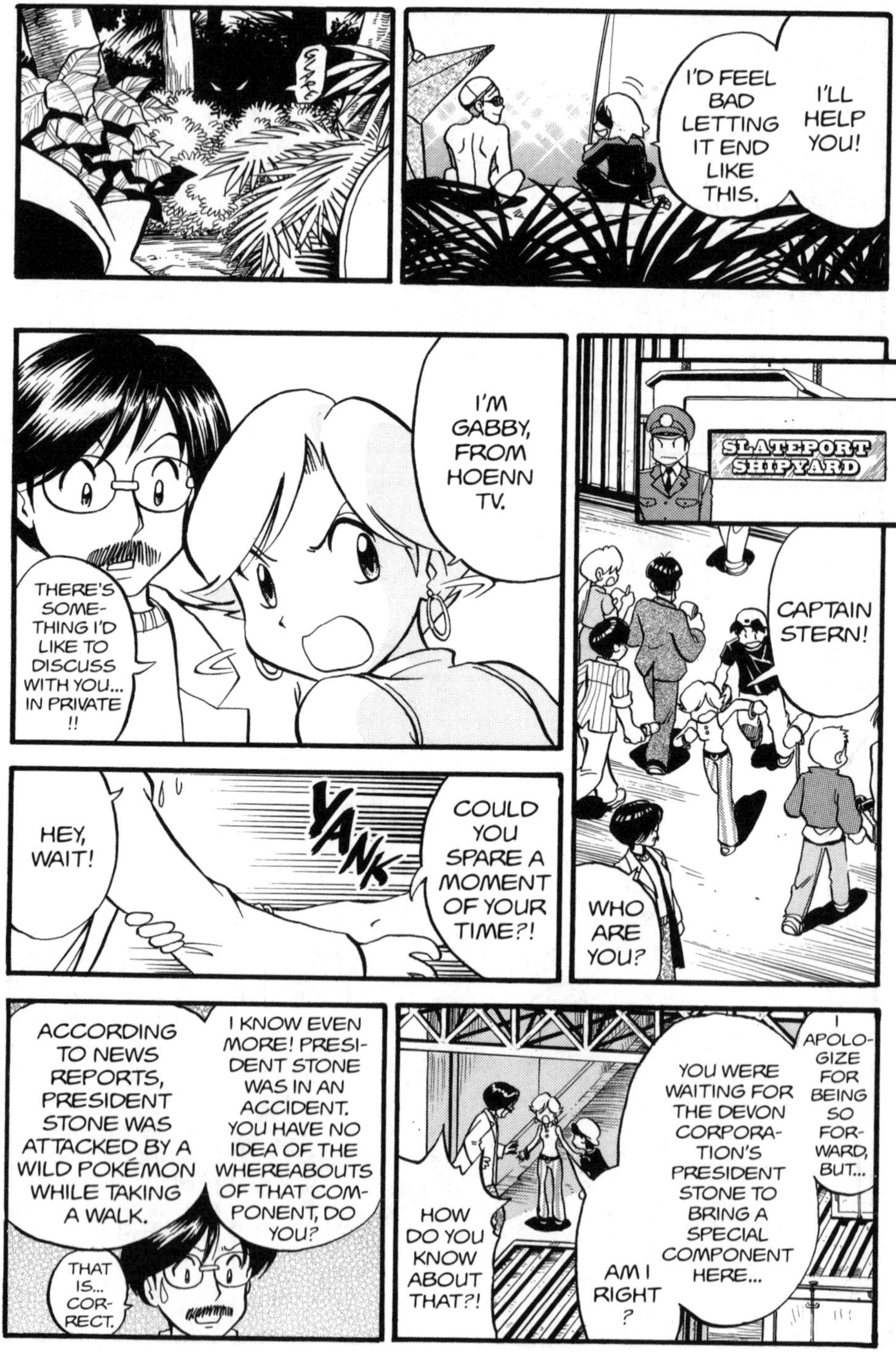

I'LL HELP YOU!
I'D FEEL BAD LETTING IT END LIKE THIS.
SLATEPORT SHIPYARD
CAPTAIN STERN!
WHO ARE YOU?
I'M GABBY, FROM HOENN TV.
THERE'S SOMETHING I'D LIKE TO DISCUSS WITH YOU... IN PRIVATE !!
COULD YOU SPARE A MOMENT OF YOUR TIME?!
YANK
HEY, WAIT!
I APOLOGIZE FOR BEING SO FORWARD, BUT...
YOU WERE WAITING FOR THE DEVON CORPORATION'S PRESIDENT STONE TO BRING A SPECIAL COMPONENT HERE...
AM I RIGHT?
HOW DO YOU KNOW ABOUT THAT?!
I KNOW EVEN MORE! PRESIDENT STONE WAS IN AN ACCIDENT. YOU HAVE NO IDEA OF THE WHEREABOUTS OF THAT COMPONENT, DO YOU?
ACCORDING TO NEWS REPORTS, PRESIDENT STONE WAS ATTACKED BY A WILD POKÉMON WHILE TAKING A WALK.
THAT IS... CORRECT.

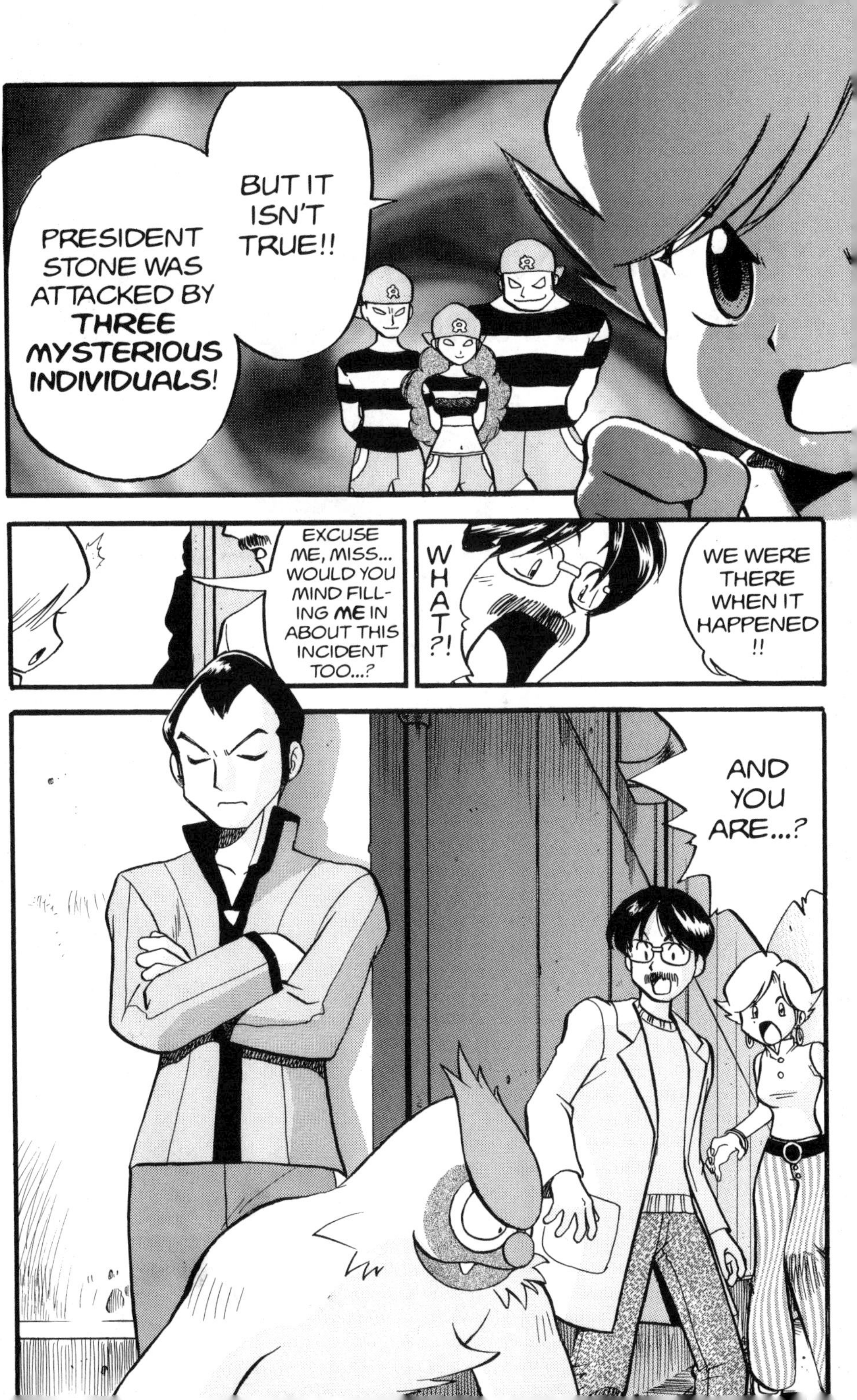
BUT IT ISN'T TRUE!!
PRESIDENT STONE WAS ATTACKED BY **THREE MYSTERIOUS INDIVIDUALS**!
WE WERE THERE WHEN IT HAPPENED!!
WHAT?!
EXCUSE ME, MISS... WOULD YOU MIND FILLING **ME** IN ABOUT THIS INCIDENT TOO...?
AND YOU ARE...?

● Adventure 207 ●

On the Loose and Hyper with Zangoose and Seviper, Part 1

Pokémon™ Adventures Ruby & Sapphire

The Fourth Chapter

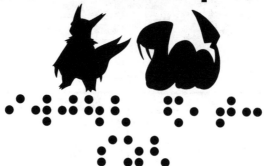

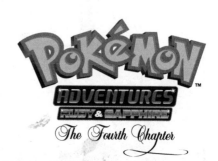

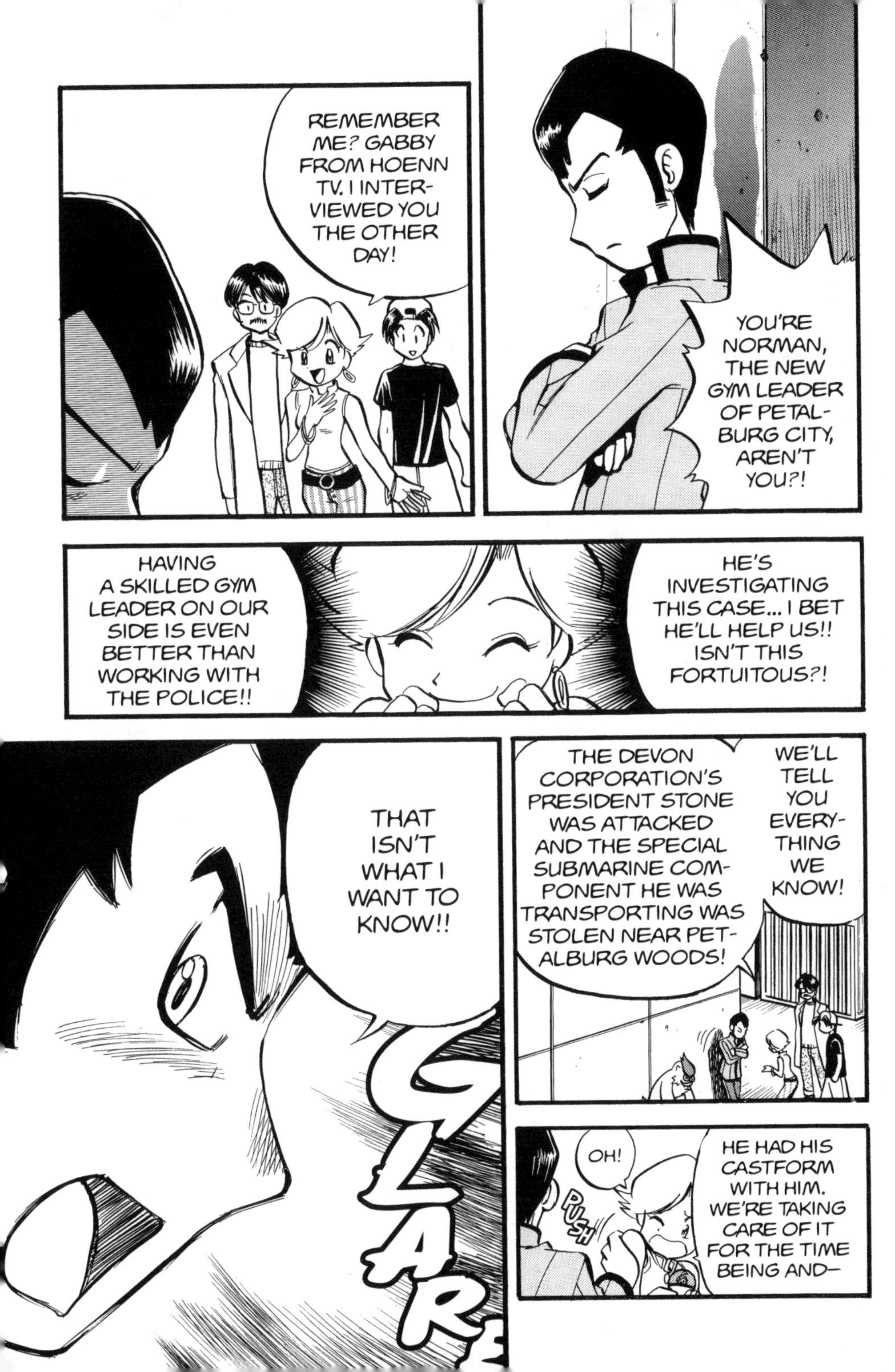
YOU'RE NORMAN, THE NEW GYM LEADER OF PETALBURG CITY, AREN'T YOU?!
REMEMBER ME? GABBY FROM HOENN TV. I INTERVIEWED YOU THE OTHER DAY!
HE'S INVESTIGATING THIS CASE... I BET HE'LL HELP US!! ISN'T THIS FORTUITOUS?!
HAVING A SKILLED GYM LEADER ON OUR SIDE IS EVEN BETTER THAN WORKING WITH THE POLICE!!
WE'LL TELL YOU EVERYTHING WE KNOW!
THE DEVON CORPORATION'S PRESIDENT STONE WAS ATTACKED AND THE SPECIAL SUBMARINE COMPONENT HE WAS TRANSPORTING WAS STOLEN NEAR PETALBURG WOODS!
HE HAD HIS CASTFORM WITH HIM. WE'RE TAKING CARE OF IT FOR THE TIME BEING AND—
OH!
PUSH
THAT ISN'T WHAT I WANT TO KNOW!!
GLAR

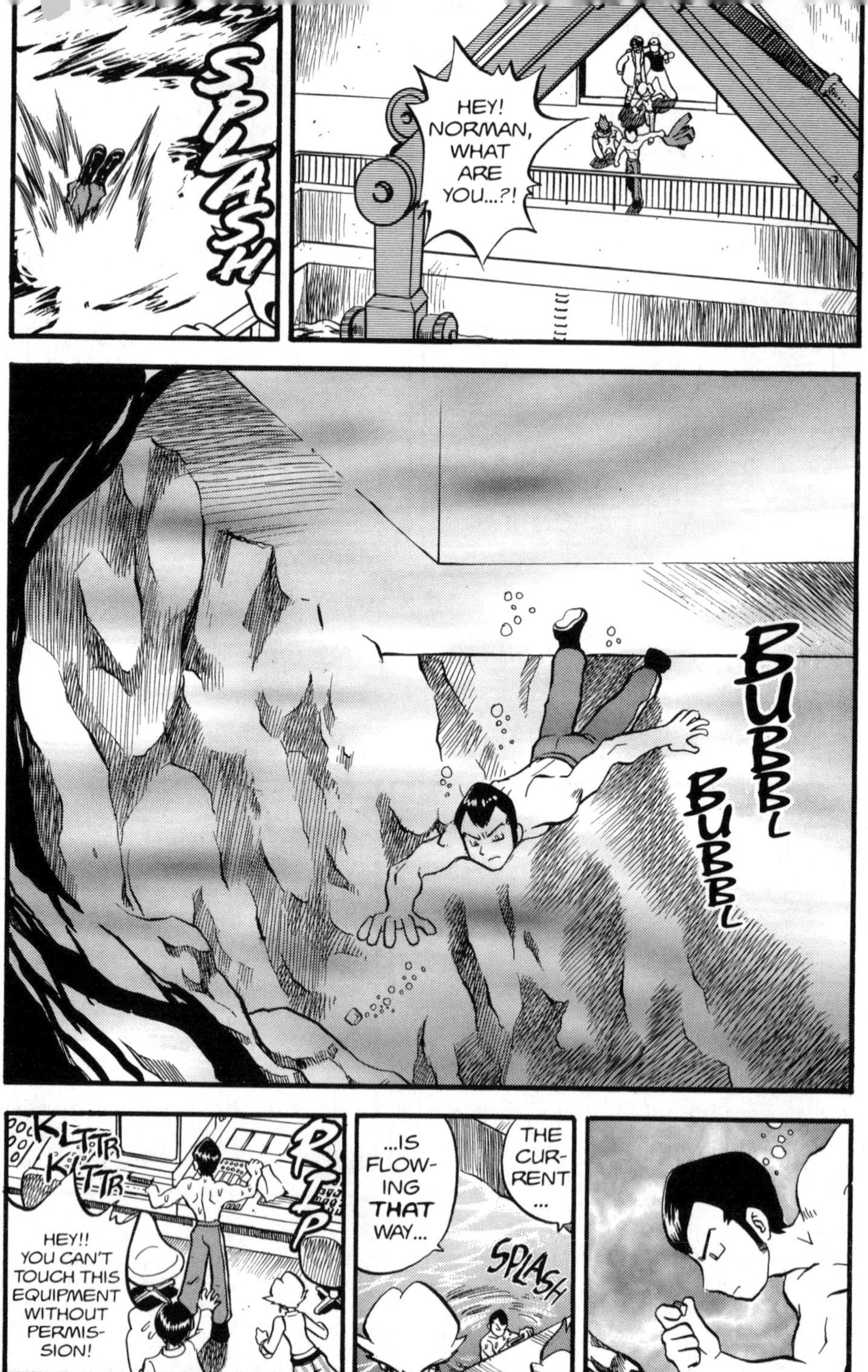
HEY! NORMAN, WHAT ARE YOU...?!
SPLASH
BUBBL
BUBBL
THE CUR-RENT...
...IS FLOWING THAT WAY...
SPLASH
RIP
KLTTTR KLTTTR
HEY!! YOU CAN'T TOUCH THIS EQUIPMENT WITHOUT PERMIS-SION!

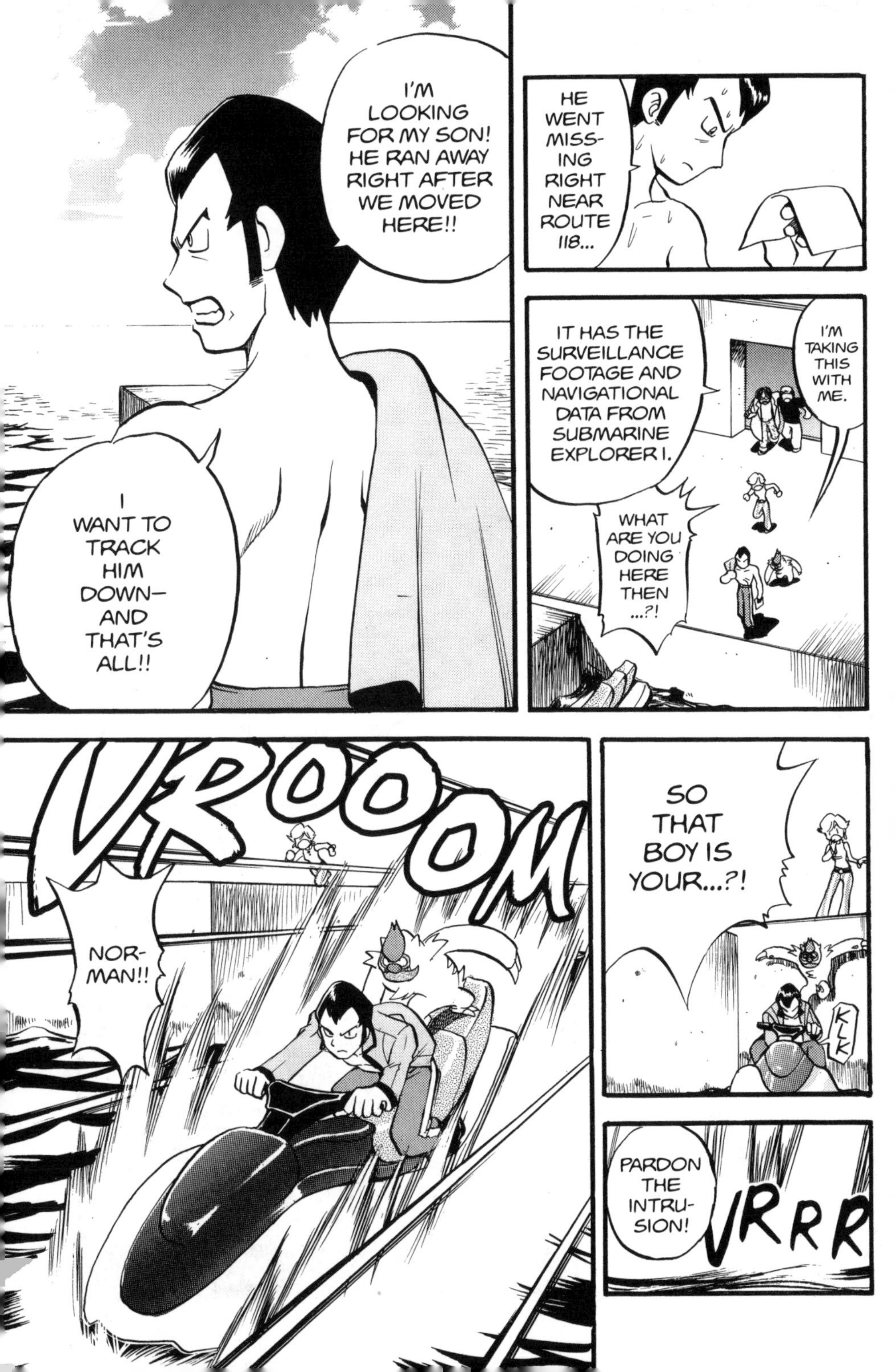
HE WENT MISSING RIGHT NEAR ROUTE 118...
I'M TAKING THIS WITH ME.
IT HAS THE SURVEILLANCE FOOTAGE AND NAVIGATIONAL DATA FROM SUBMARINE EXPLORER 1.
WHAT ARE YOU DOING HERE THEN ...?!
I'M LOOKING FOR MY SON! HE RAN AWAY RIGHT AFTER WE MOVED HERE!!
I WANT TO TRACK HIM DOWN—AND THAT'S ALL!!
SO THAT BOY IS YOUR...?!
KLK
PARDON THE INTRUSION!
VRRR
VROOOM
NORMAN!!

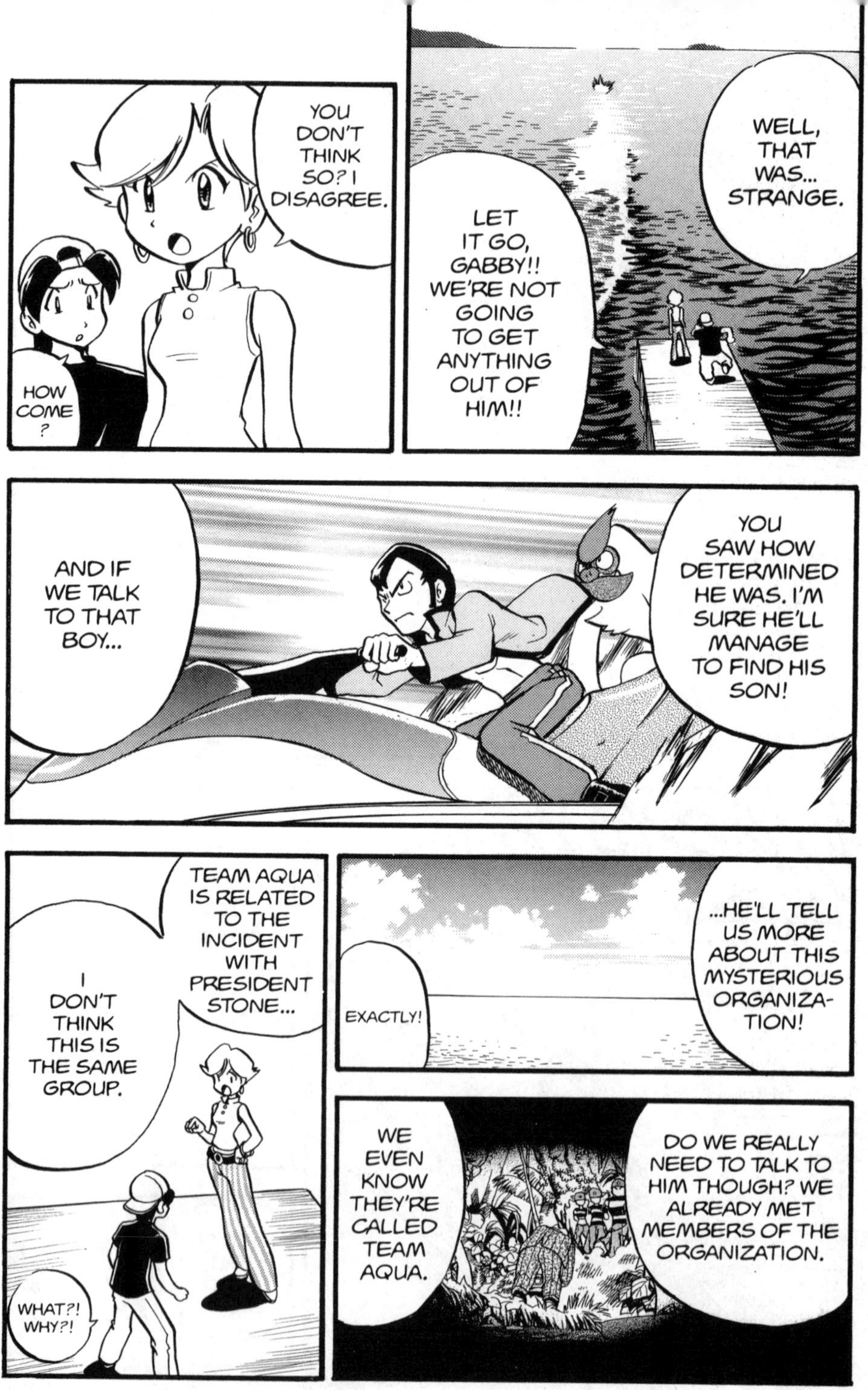
WELL, THAT WAS... STRANGE.
LET IT GO, GABBY!! WE'RE NOT GOING TO GET ANYTHING OUT OF HIM!!
YOU DON'T THINK SO? I DISAGREE.
HOW COME?
YOU SAW HOW DETERMINED HE WAS. I'M SURE HE'LL MANAGE TO FIND HIS SON!
AND IF WE TALK TO THAT BOY...
...HE'LL TELL US MORE ABOUT THIS MYSTERIOUS ORGANIZA-TION!
EXACTLY!
DO WE REALLY NEED TO TALK TO HIM THOUGH? WE ALREADY MET MEMBERS OF THE ORGANIZATION.
WE EVEN KNOW THEY'RE CALLED TEAM AQUA.
TEAM AQUA IS RELATED TO THE INCIDENT WITH PRESIDENT STONE...
I DON'T THINK THIS IS THE SAME GROUP.
WHAT?! WHY?!

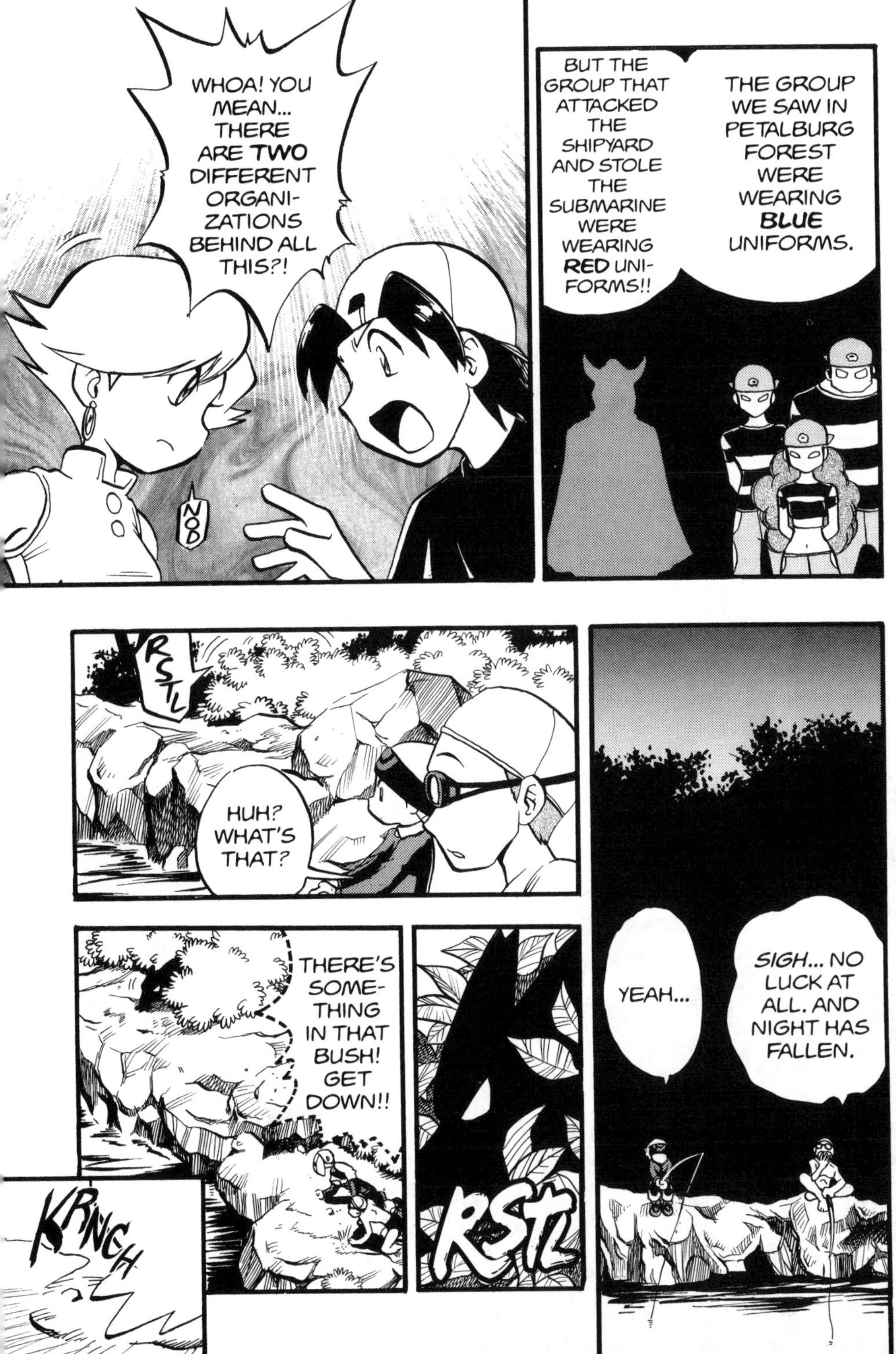
THE GROUP WE SAW IN PETALBURG FOREST WERE WEARING **BLUE** UNIFORMS.
BUT THE GROUP THAT ATTACKED THE SHIPYARD AND STOLE THE SUBMARINE WERE WEARING **RED** UNIFORMS!!
WHOA! YOU MEAN... THERE ARE **TWO** DIFFERENT ORGANIZATIONS BEHIND ALL THIS?!
NOD
SIGH... NO LUCK AT ALL. AND NIGHT HAS FALLEN.
YEAH...
RSTL
HUH? WHAT'S THAT?
RSTL
THERE'S SOMETHING IN THAT BUSH! GET DOWN!!
KRNCH

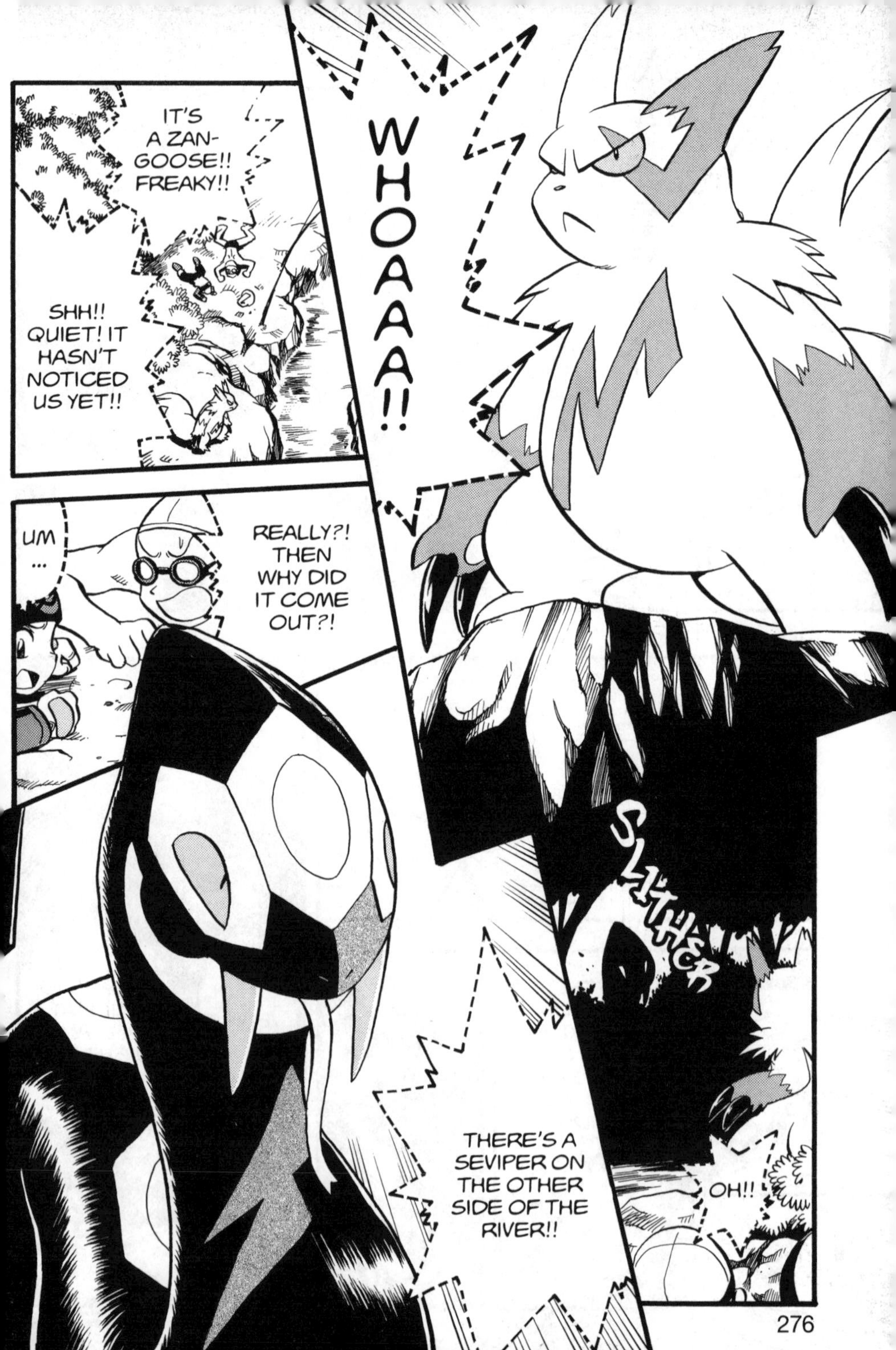
WHOAAA!!
IT'S A ZAN-GOOSE!! FREAKY!!
SHH!! QUIET! IT HASN'T NOTICED US YET!!
REALLY?! THEN WHY DID IT COME OUT?!
UM ...
SLITHER
THERE'S A SEVIPER ON THE OTHER SIDE OF THE RIVER!!
OH!!

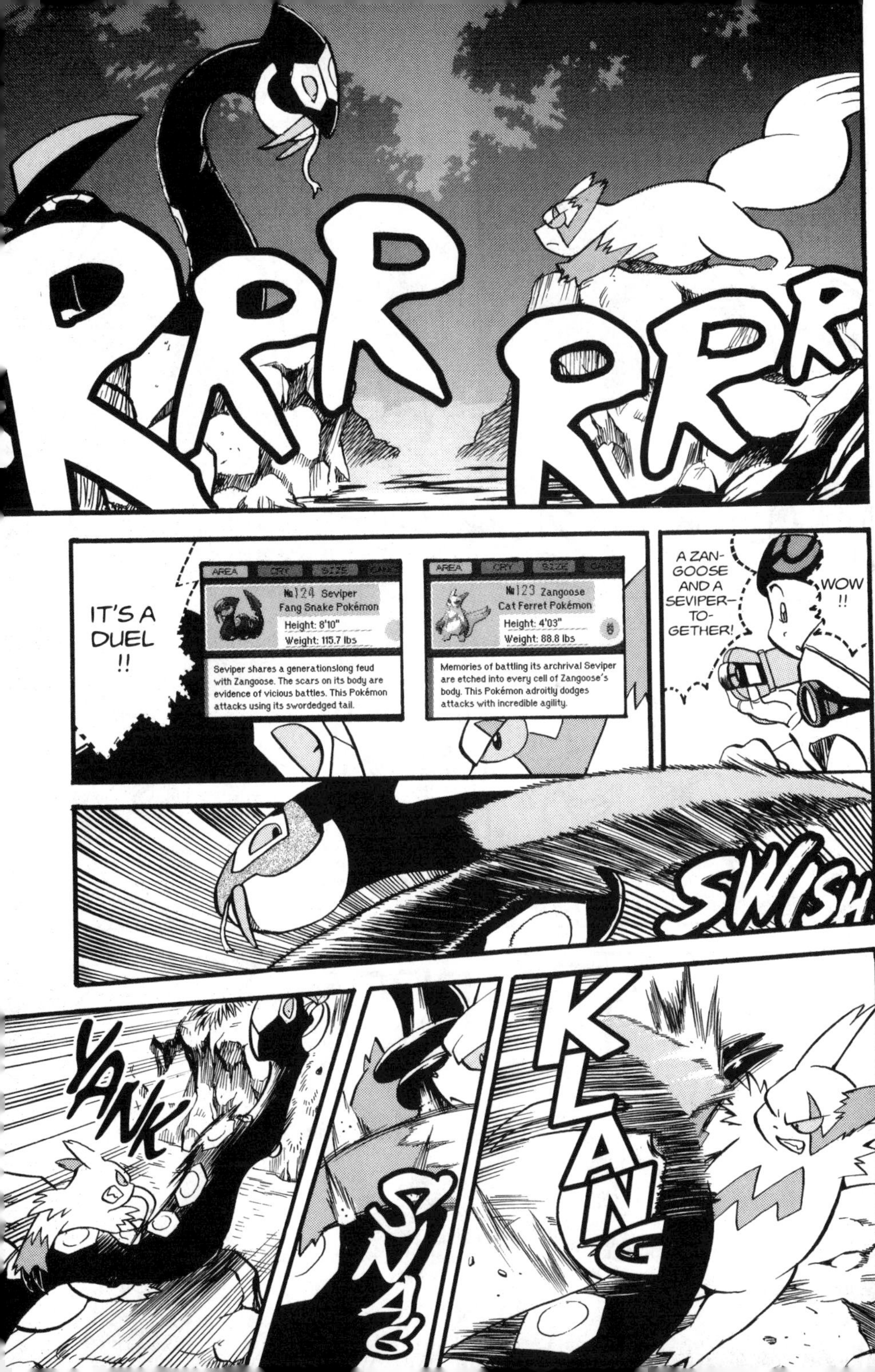
RRRR
RRRR
A ZAN-GOOSE AND A SEVIPER—TO-GETHER!
WOW!!
No123 Zangoose
Cat Ferret Pokémon
Height: 4'03"
Weight: 88.8 lbs
Memories of battling its archrival Seviper are etched into every cell of Zangoose's body. This Pokémon adroitly dodges attacks with incredible agility.
No124 Seviper
Fang Snake Pokémon
Height: 8'10"
Weight: 115.7 lbs
Seviper shares a generationslong feud with Zangoose. The scars on its body are evidence of vicious battles. This Pokémon attacks using its swordedged tail.
IT'S A DUEL!!
SWISH
KLANG
SNAG
YANK

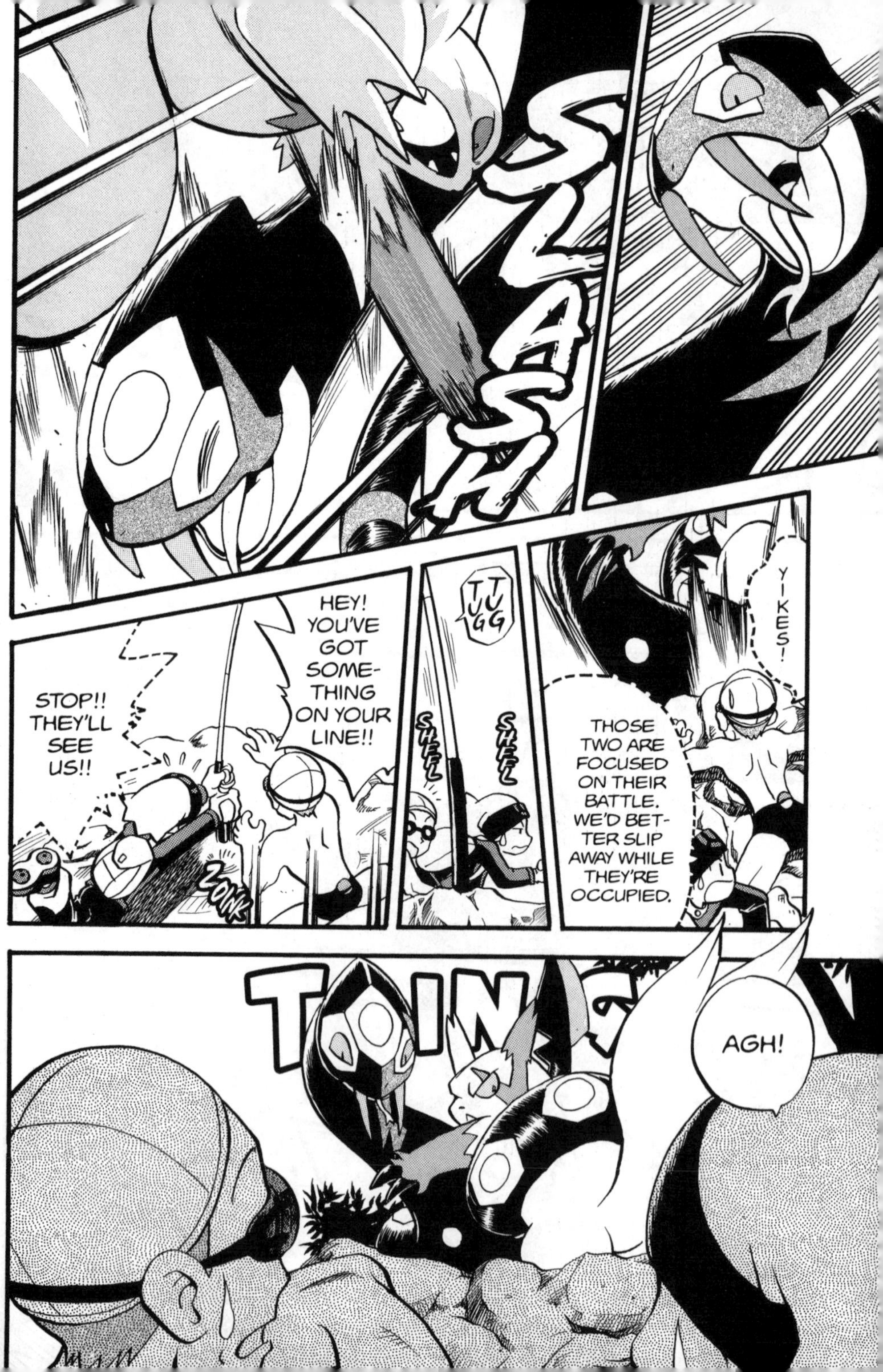
SLASH
YIKES!
THOSE TWO ARE FOCUSED ON THEIR BATTLE. WE'D BETTER SLIP AWAY WHILE THEY'RE OCCUPIED.
TUGG TUGG
SHFFL SHFFL
HEY! YOU'VE GOT SOMETHING ON YOUR LINE!!
STOP!! THEY'LL SEE US!!
ZOINK
TOING
AGH!

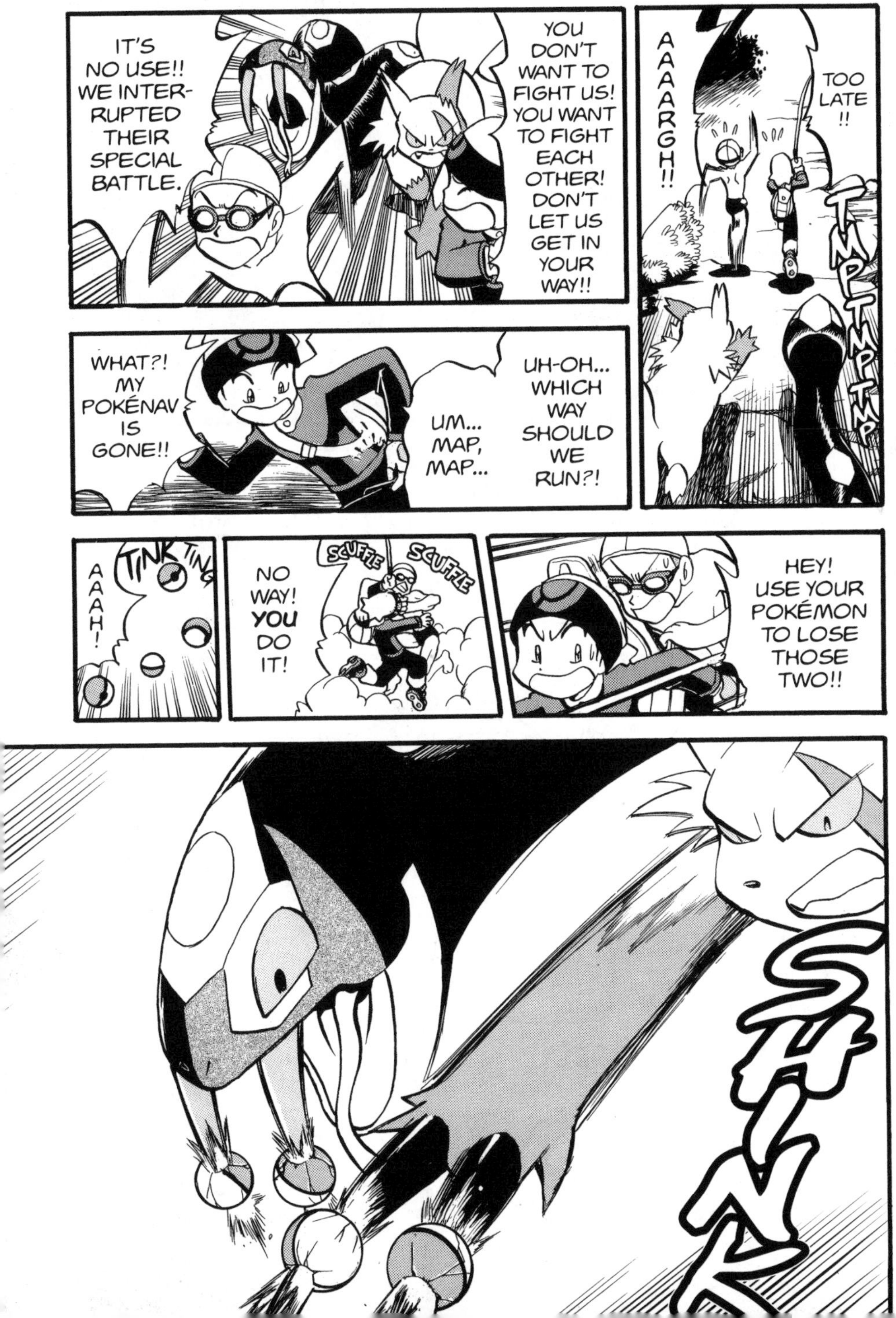
TOO LATE!!
AAAAARGH!!
TMPTMPTMPTMP
YOU DON'T WANT TO FIGHT US! YOU WANT TO FIGHT EACH OTHER! DON'T LET US GET IN YOUR WAY!!
IT'S NO USE!! WE INTER-RUPTED THEIR SPECIAL BATTLE.
UH-OH... WHICH WAY SHOULD WE RUN?!
UM... MAP, MAP...
WHAT?! MY POKÉNAV IS GONE!!
HEY! USE YOUR POKÉMON TO LOSE THOSE TWO!!
SCUFFLE SCUFFLE
NO WAY! **YOU** DO IT!
TINK TING
AAAAH!
SHINK

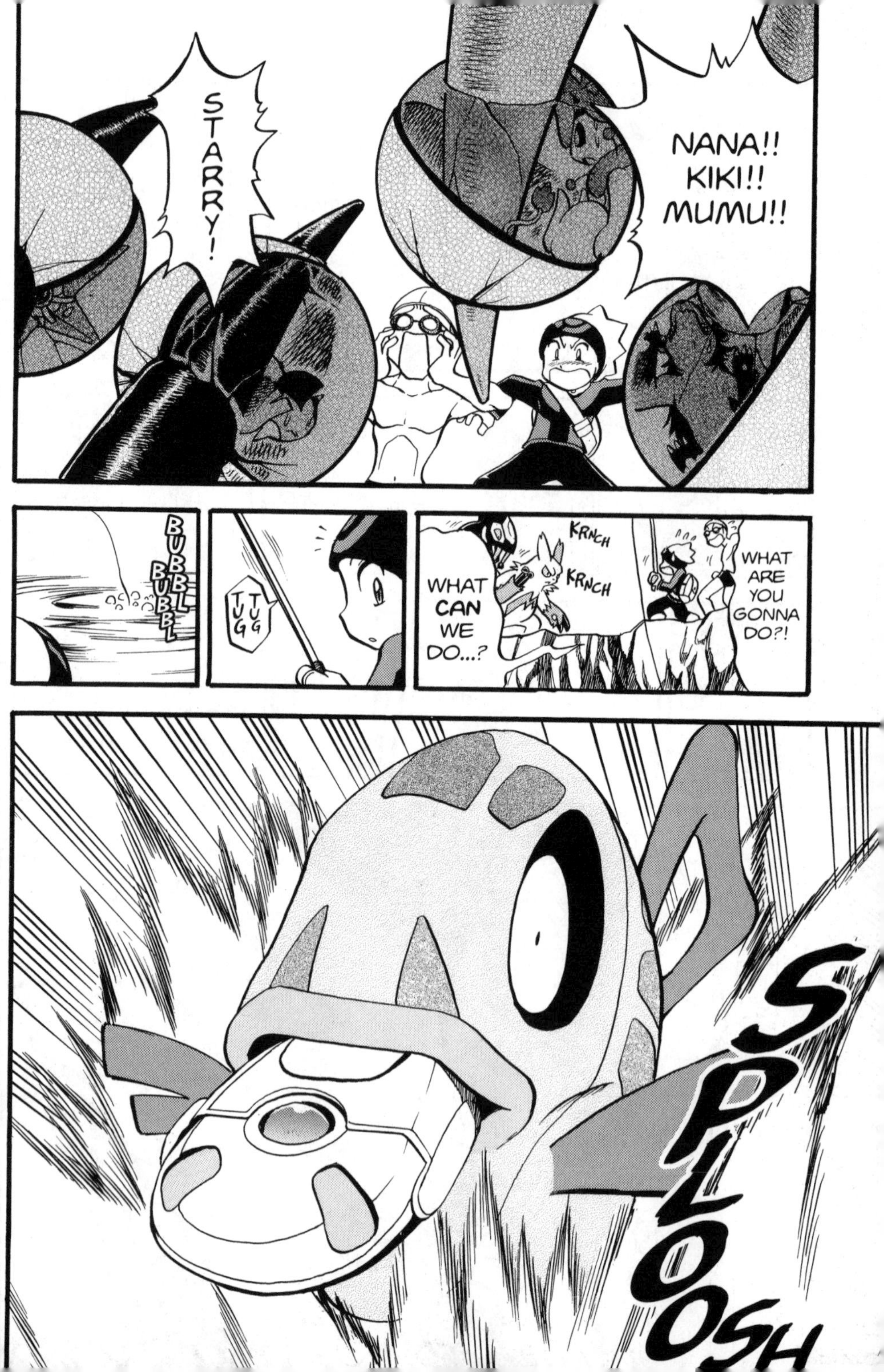
NANA!! KIKI!! MUMU!!
STARRY!
WHAT ARE YOU GONNA DO?!
KRNCH
KRNCH
WHAT CAN WE DO...?
TUG TUG
BUBBL BUBBL
SPLOOSH

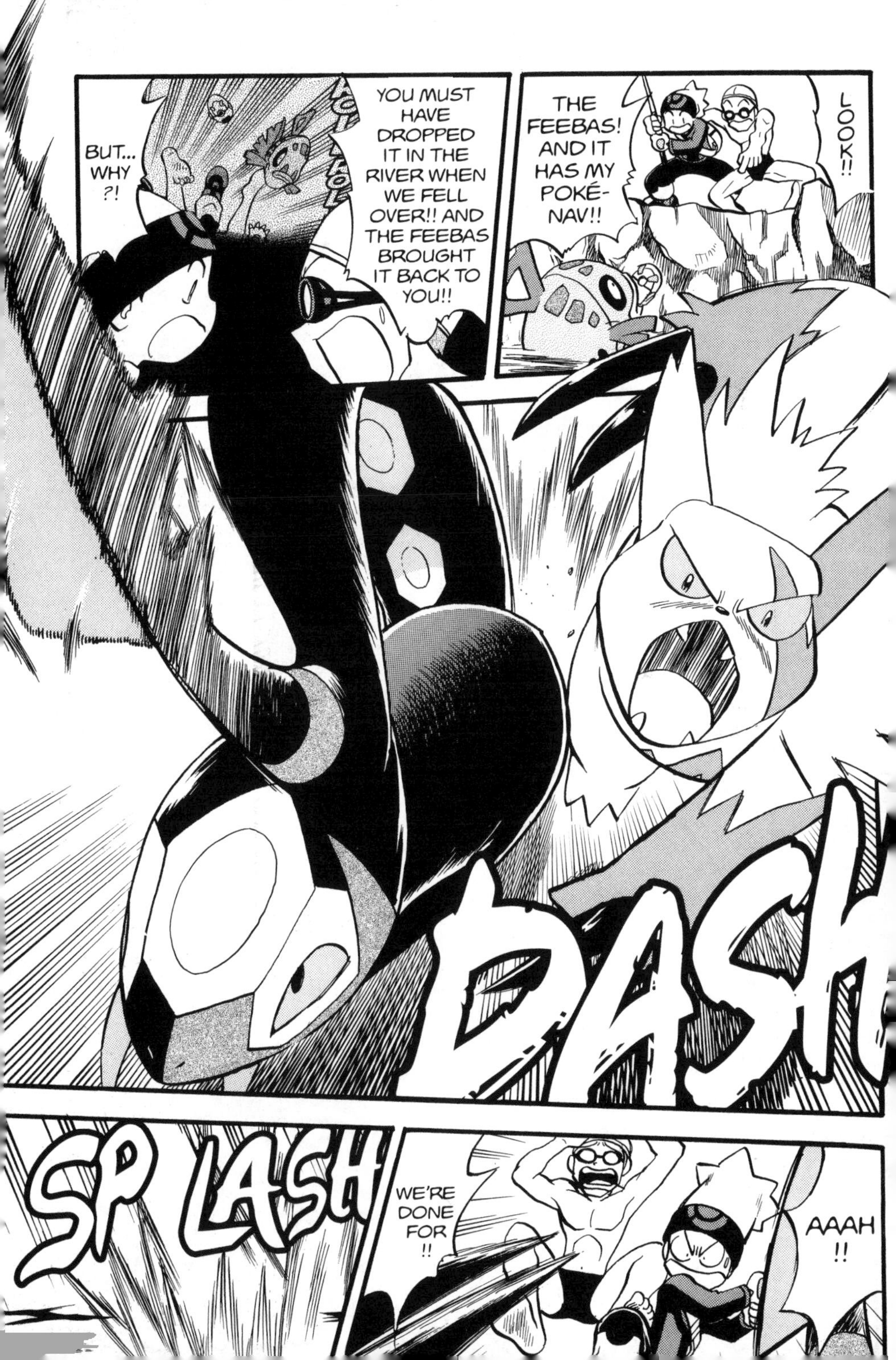
LOOK!!
THE FEEBAS! AND IT HAS MY POKÉ-NAV!!
YOU MUST HAVE DROPPED IT IN THE RIVER WHEN WE FELL OVER!! AND THE FEEBAS BROUGHT IT BACK TO YOU!!
BUT... WHY ?!
DASH
AAAH !!
WE'RE DONE FOR !!
SP LASH

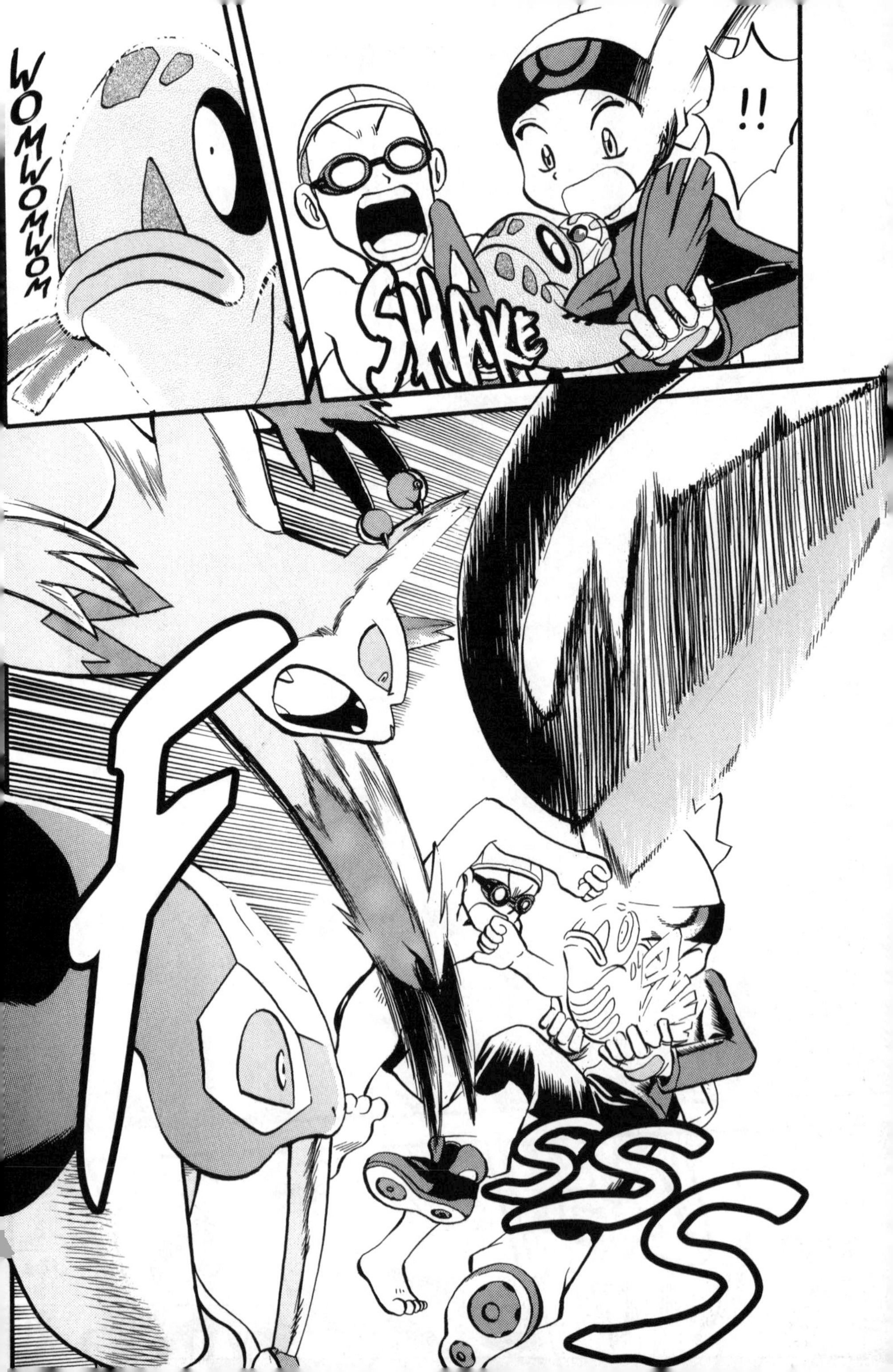

!!
SHAKE
WOMWOMWOM
SSS

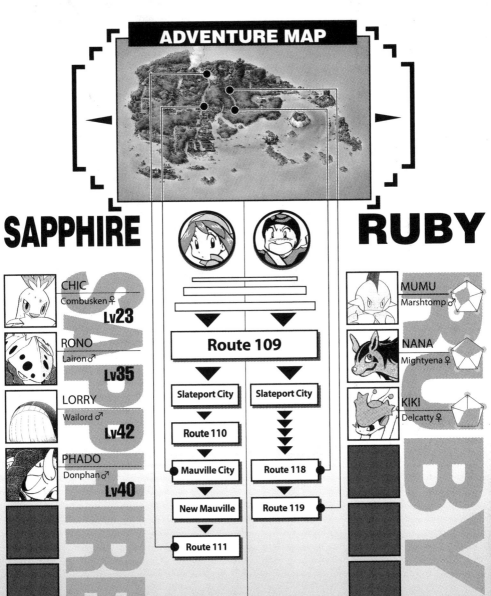

ADVENTURE MAP

SAPPHIRE

CHIC
Combusken ♀
Lv23

RONO
Lairon ♂
Lv35

LORRY
Wailord ♂
Lv42

PHADO
Donphan ♂
Lv40

RUBY

MUMU
Marshtomp ♂

NANA
Mightyena ♀

KIKI
Delcatty ♀

Route 109

Slateport City	Slateport City
Route 110	
Mauville City	Route 118
New Mauville	Route 119
Route 111	

| Stone Badge | Knuckle Badge | Dynamo Badge | Heat Badge |
| Balance Badge | Feather Badge | Mind Badge | Rain Badge |

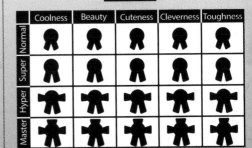

		Coolness	Beauty	Cuteness	Cleverness	Toughness
Normal	Super					
Hyper	Master					

● Adventure 208 ●
On the Loose and Hyper with Zangoose and Seviper, Part 2

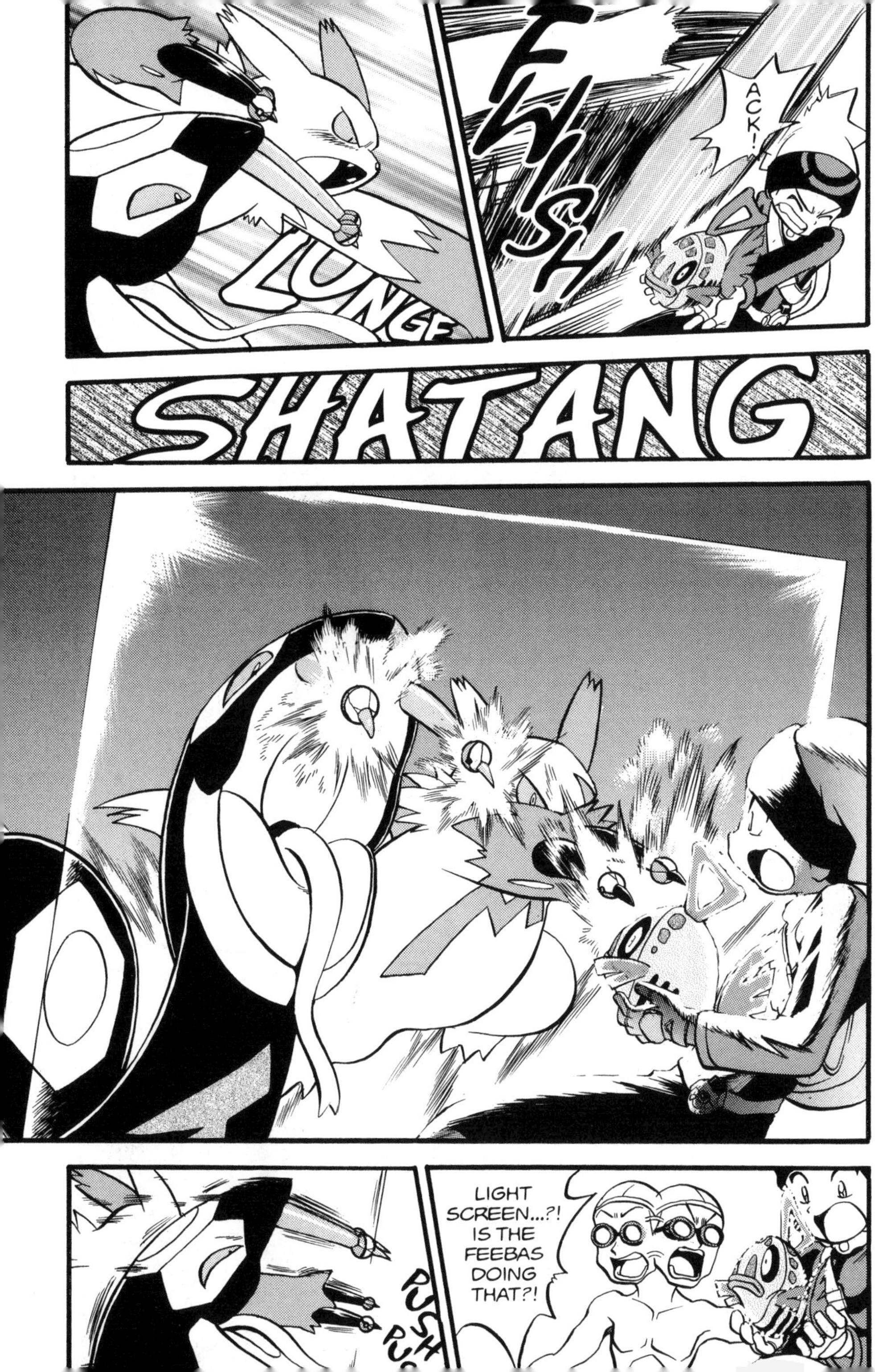
FWISH
ACK!
LUNGE
SHATANG
LIGHT SCREEN...?! IS THE FEEBAS DOING THAT?!
PUSH

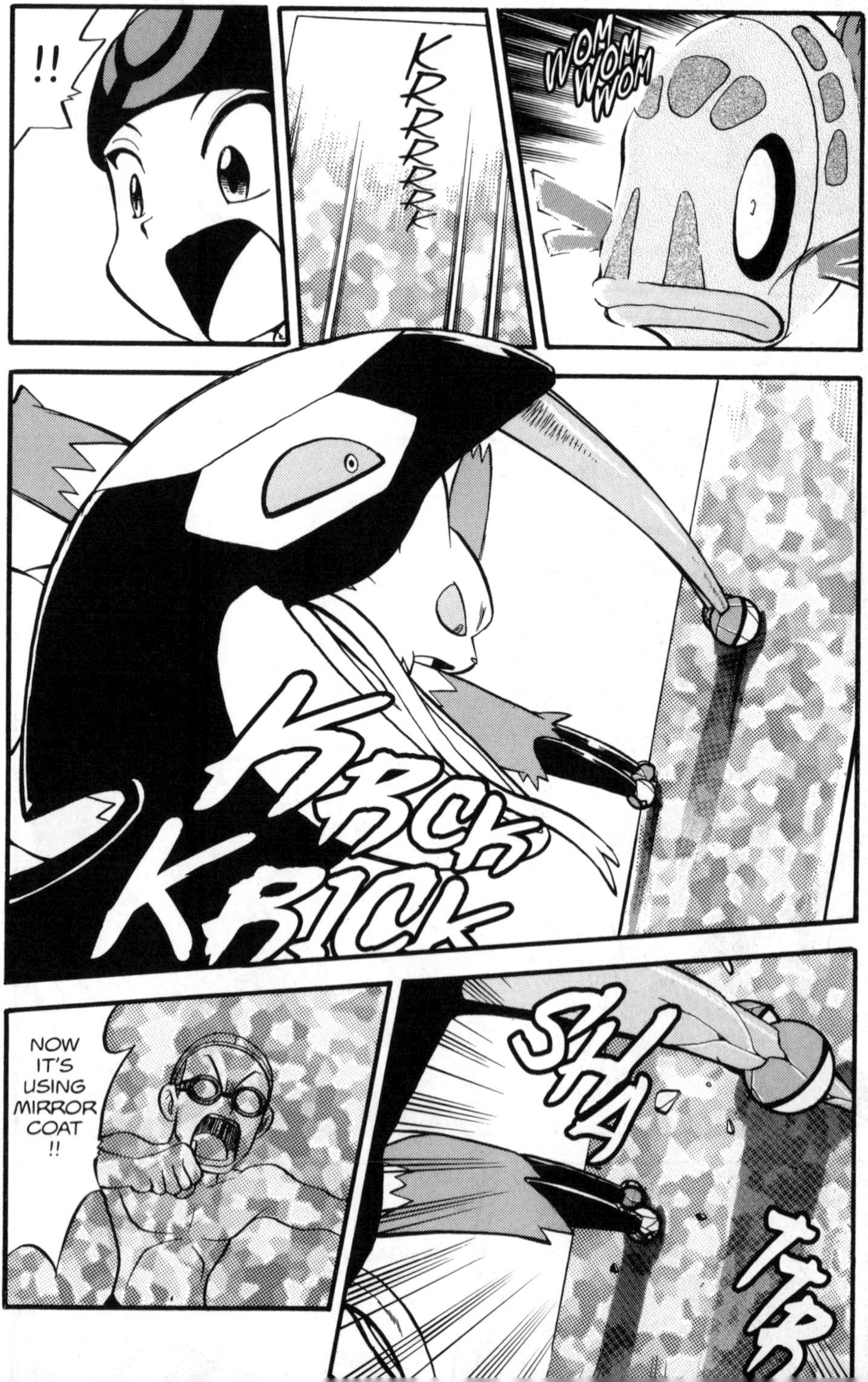
WOM WOM WOM
KRRRRRRK
!!
KRCK
KRICK
SHA
TR
NOW IT'S USING MIRROR COAT !!

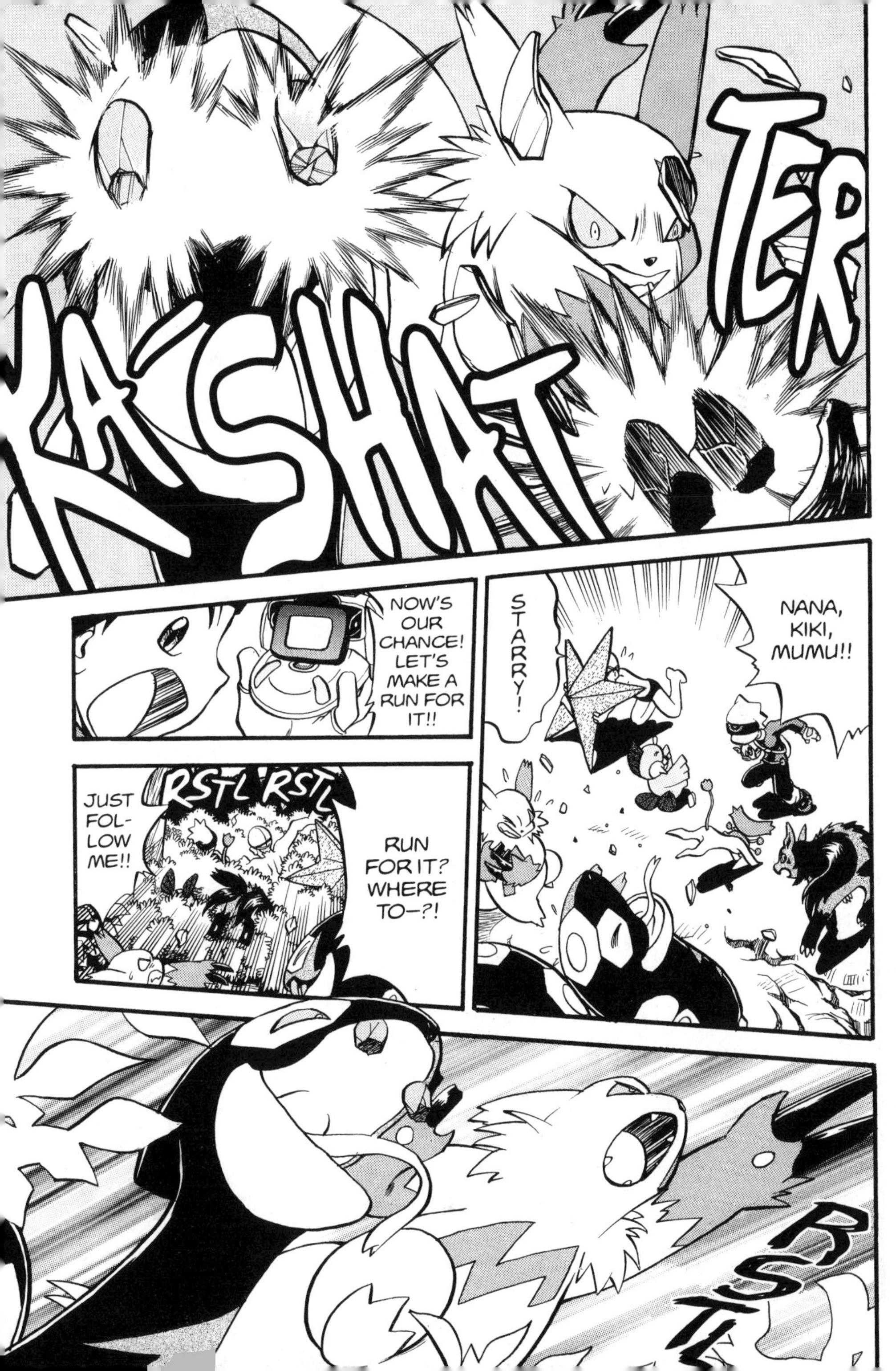

KA-SHAT
TER
NANA, KIKI, MUMU!!
STARRY!
NOW'S OUR CHANCE! LET'S MAKE A RUN FOR IT!!
RSTL RSTL
RUN FOR IT? WHERE TO–?!
JUST FOL-LOW ME!!
RSTL

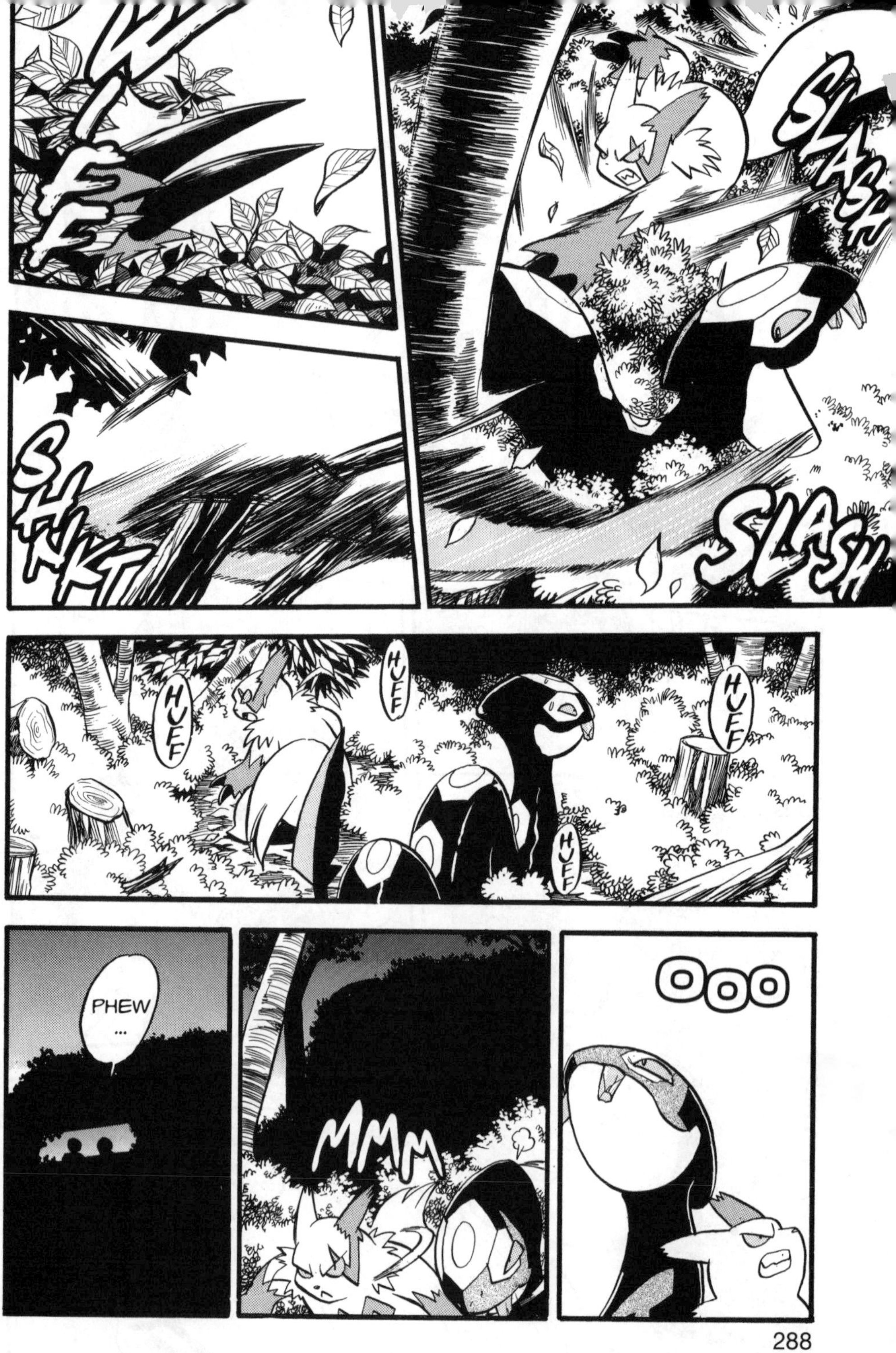

SLASH
SLASH
SHNKT
HUFF
HUFF
HUFF
OOO
MMM
PHEW
...

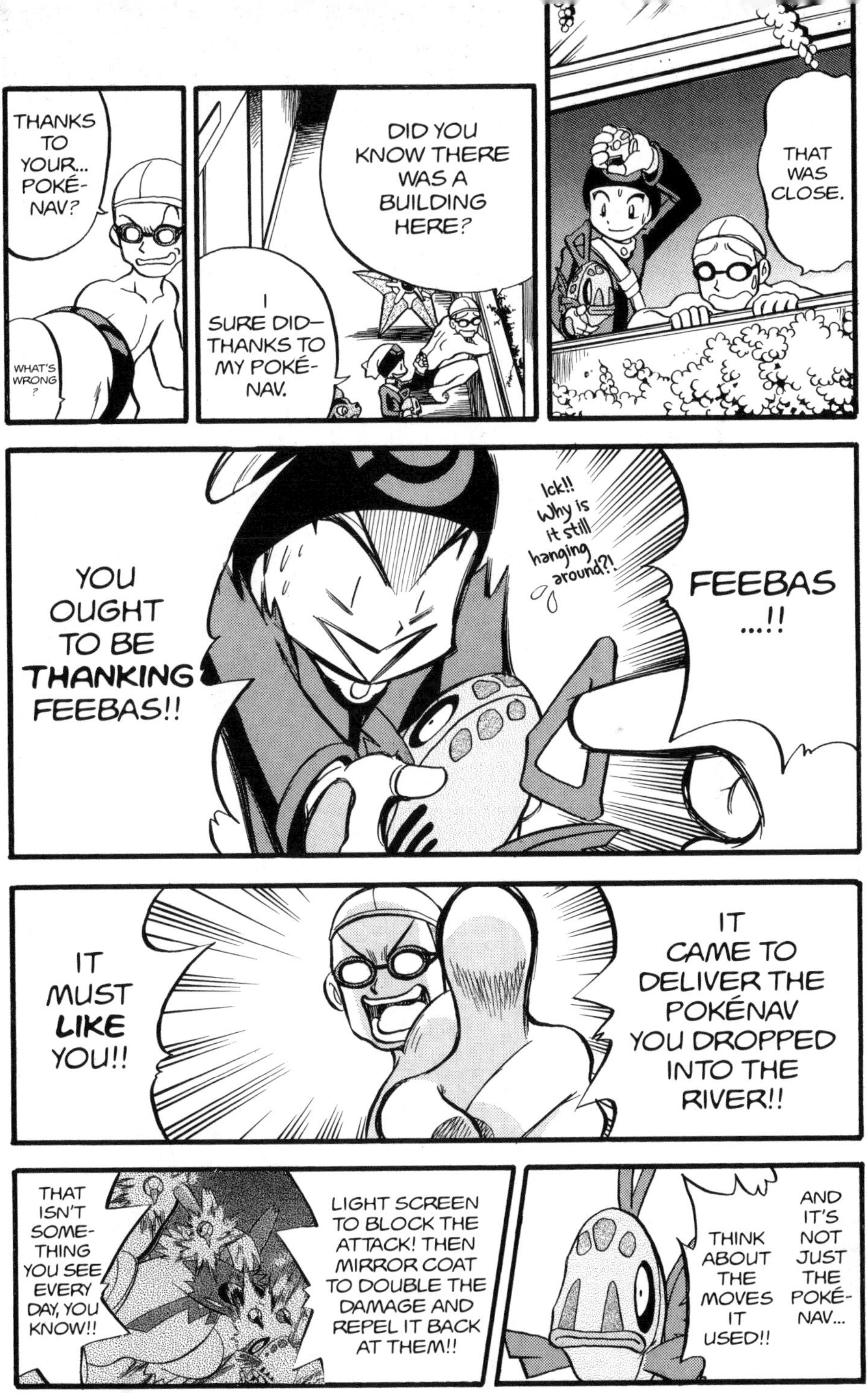
THAT WAS CLOSE.
DID YOU KNOW THERE WAS A BUILDING HERE?
I SURE DID— THANKS TO MY POKÉ-NAV.
THANKS TO YOUR... POKÉ-NAV?
WHAT'S WRONG?
FEEBAS ...!!
Ick!! Why is it still hanging around?!
YOU OUGHT TO BE **THANKING** FEEBAS!!
IT CAME TO DELIVER THE POKÉNAV YOU DROPPED INTO THE RIVER!!
IT MUST **LIKE** YOU!!
AND IT'S NOT JUST THE POKÉ-NAV...
THINK ABOUT THE MOVES IT USED!!
LIGHT SCREEN TO BLOCK THE ATTACK! THEN MIRROR COAT TO DOUBLE THE DAMAGE AND REPEL IT BACK AT THEM!!
THAT ISN'T SOME-THING YOU SEE EVERY DAY, YOU KNOW!!

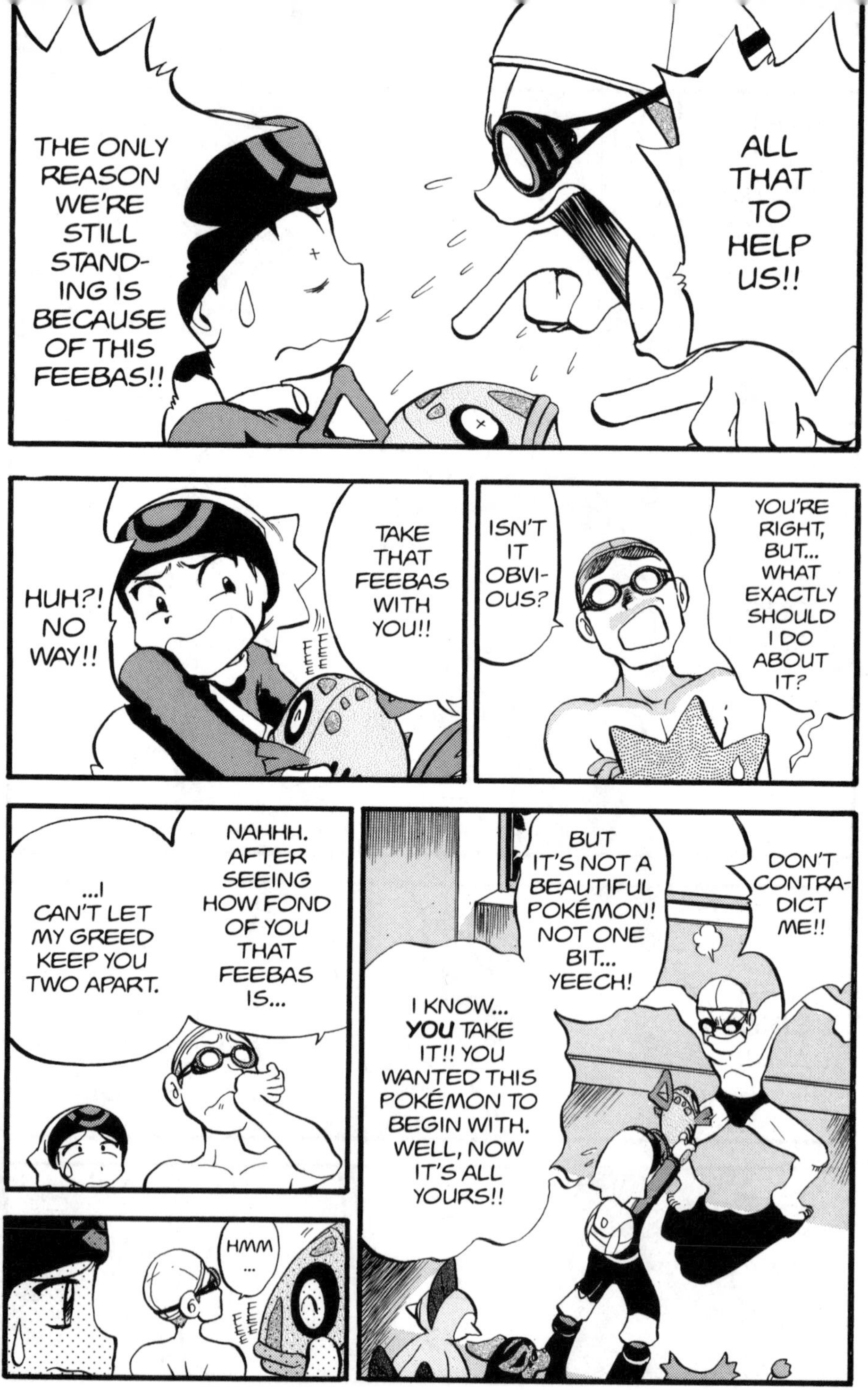
ALL THAT TO HELP US!!
THE ONLY REASON WE'RE STILL STAND-ING IS BECAUSE OF THIS FEEBAS!!
YOU'RE RIGHT, BUT... WHAT EXACTLY SHOULD I DO ABOUT IT?
ISN'T IT OBVI-OUS?
TAKE THAT FEEBAS WITH YOU!!
HUH?! NO WAY!!
DON'T CONTRA-DICT ME!!
BUT IT'S NOT A BEAUTIFUL POKÉMON! NOT ONE BIT... YEECH!
I KNOW... **YOU** TAKE IT!! YOU WANTED THIS POKÉMON TO BEGIN WITH. WELL, NOW IT'S ALL YOURS!!
NAHHH. AFTER SEEING HOW FOND OF YOU THAT FEEBAS IS...
...I CAN'T LET MY GREED KEEP YOU TWO APART.
HMM ...

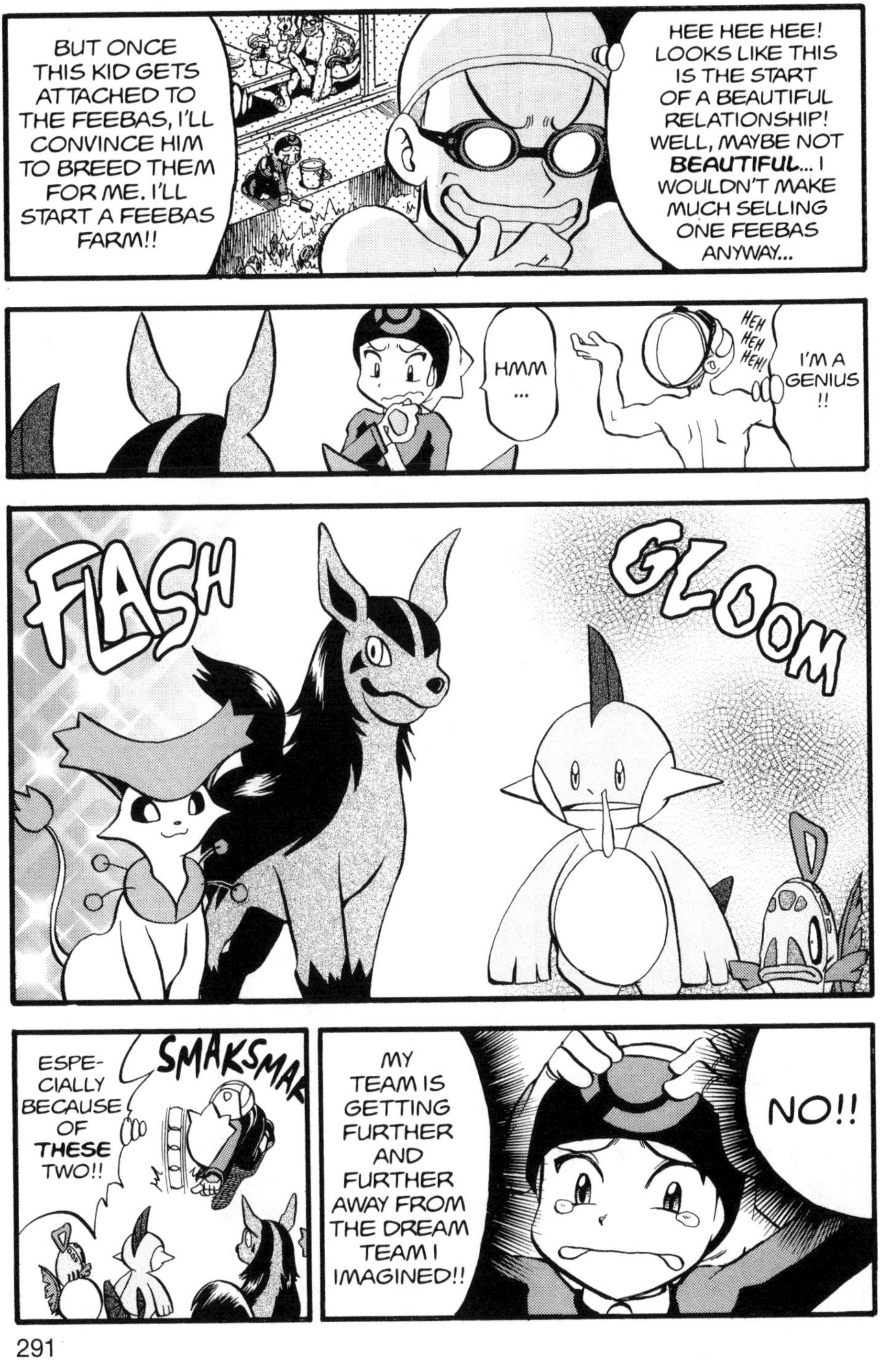
HEE HEE HEE! LOOKS LIKE THIS IS THE START OF A BEAUTIFUL RELATIONSHIP! WELL, MAYBE NOT BEAUTIFUL... I WOULDN'T MAKE MUCH SELLING ONE FEEBAS ANYWAY...
BUT ONCE THIS KID GETS ATTACHED TO THE FEEBAS, I'LL CONVINCE HIM TO BREED THEM FOR ME. I'LL START A FEEBAS FARM!!
I'M A GENIUS!!
HEH HEH HEH!
HMM...
GLOOM
FLASH
NO!!
MY TEAM IS GETTING FURTHER AND FURTHER AWAY FROM THE DREAM TEAM I IMAGINED!!
SMAKSMAK
ESPECIALLY BECAUSE OF THESE TWO!!

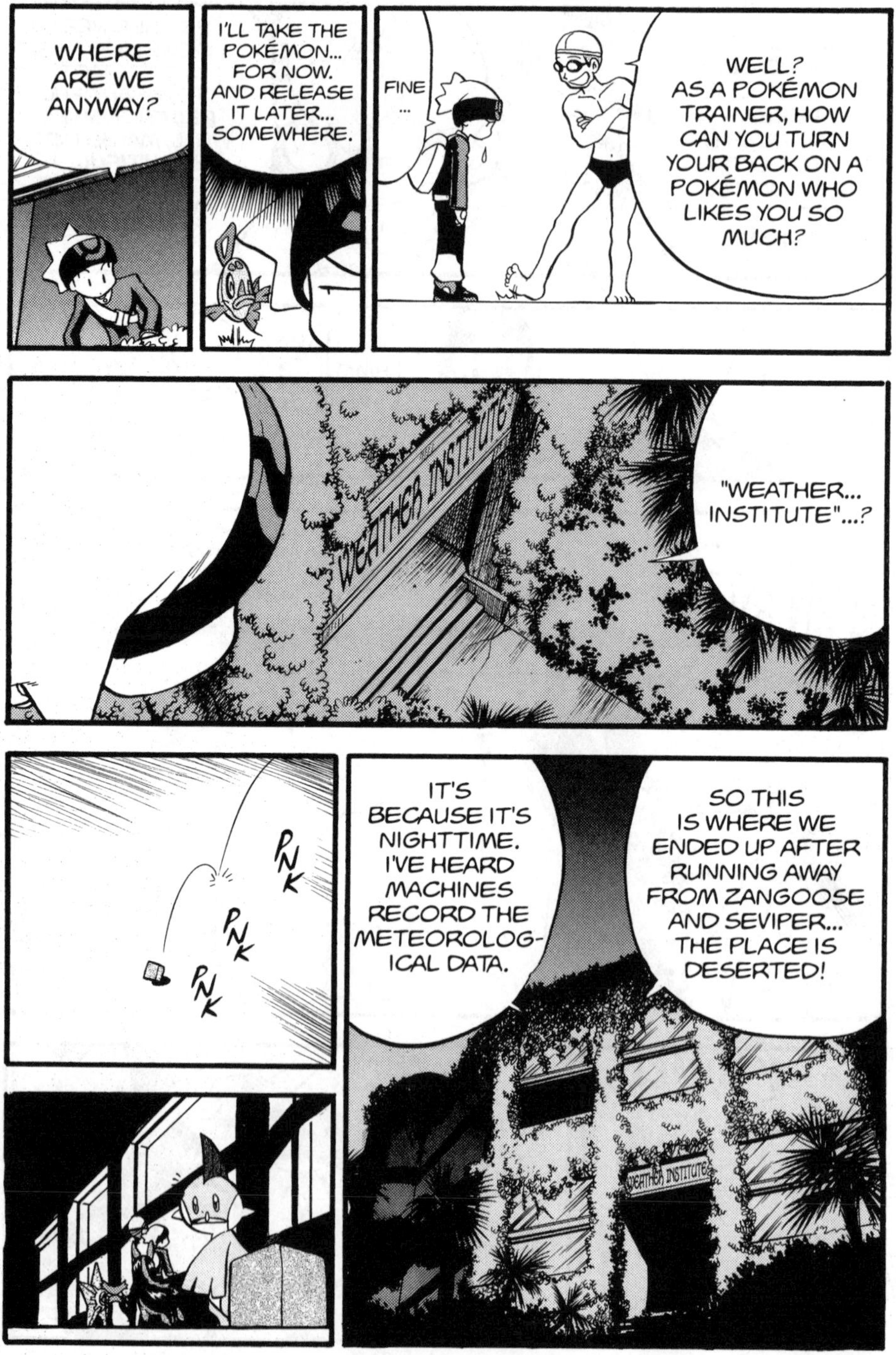
WELL? AS A POKÉMON TRAINER, HOW CAN YOU TURN YOUR BACK ON A POKÉMON WHO LIKES YOU SO MUCH?
FINE ...
I'LL TAKE THE POKÉMON... FOR NOW. AND RELEASE IT LATER... SOMEWHERE.
WHERE ARE WE ANYWAY?
WEATHER INSTITUTE
"WEATHER... INSTITUTE"...?
SO THIS IS WHERE WE ENDED UP AFTER RUNNING AWAY FROM ZANGOOSE AND SEVIPER... THE PLACE IS DESERTED!
IT'S BECAUSE IT'S NIGHTTIME. I'VE HEARD MACHINES RECORD THE METEOROLOGICAL DATA.
WEATHER INSTITUTE
PNK
PNK
PNK

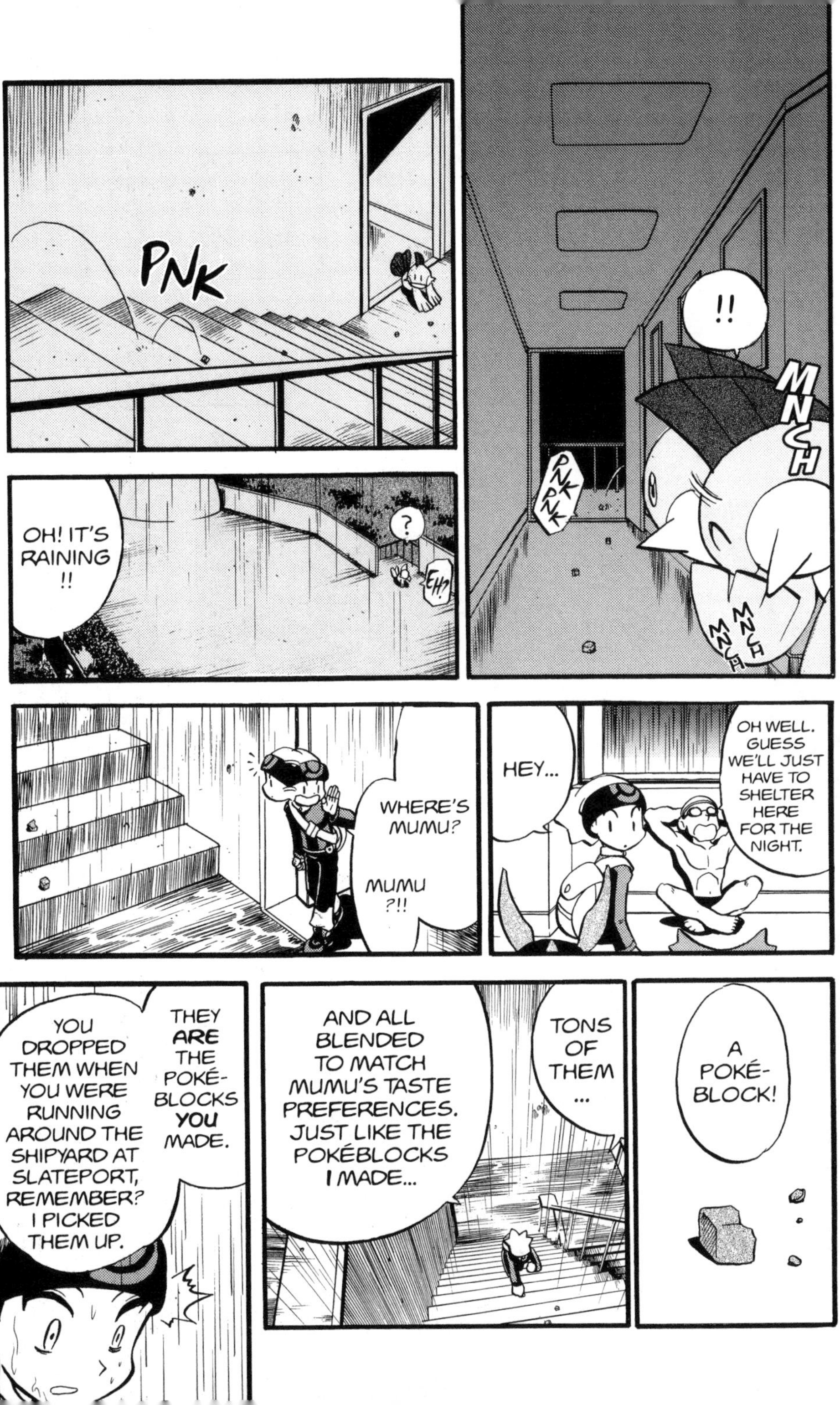
!!
MNCH
PNK PNK
MNCH MNCH
PNK
OH! IT'S RAINING !!
?
EH?
OH WELL. GUESS WE'LL JUST HAVE TO SHELTER HERE FOR THE NIGHT.
HEY...
WHERE'S MUMU?
MUMU ?!!
A POKÉ-BLOCK!
TONS OF THEM ...
AND ALL BLENDED TO MATCH MUMU'S TASTE PREFERENCES. JUST LIKE THE POKÉBLOCKS I MADE...
THEY **ARE** THE POKÉ-BLOCKS **YOU** MADE.
YOU DROPPED THEM WHEN YOU WERE RUNNING AROUND THE SHIPYARD AT SLATEPORT, REMEMBER? I PICKED THEM UP.

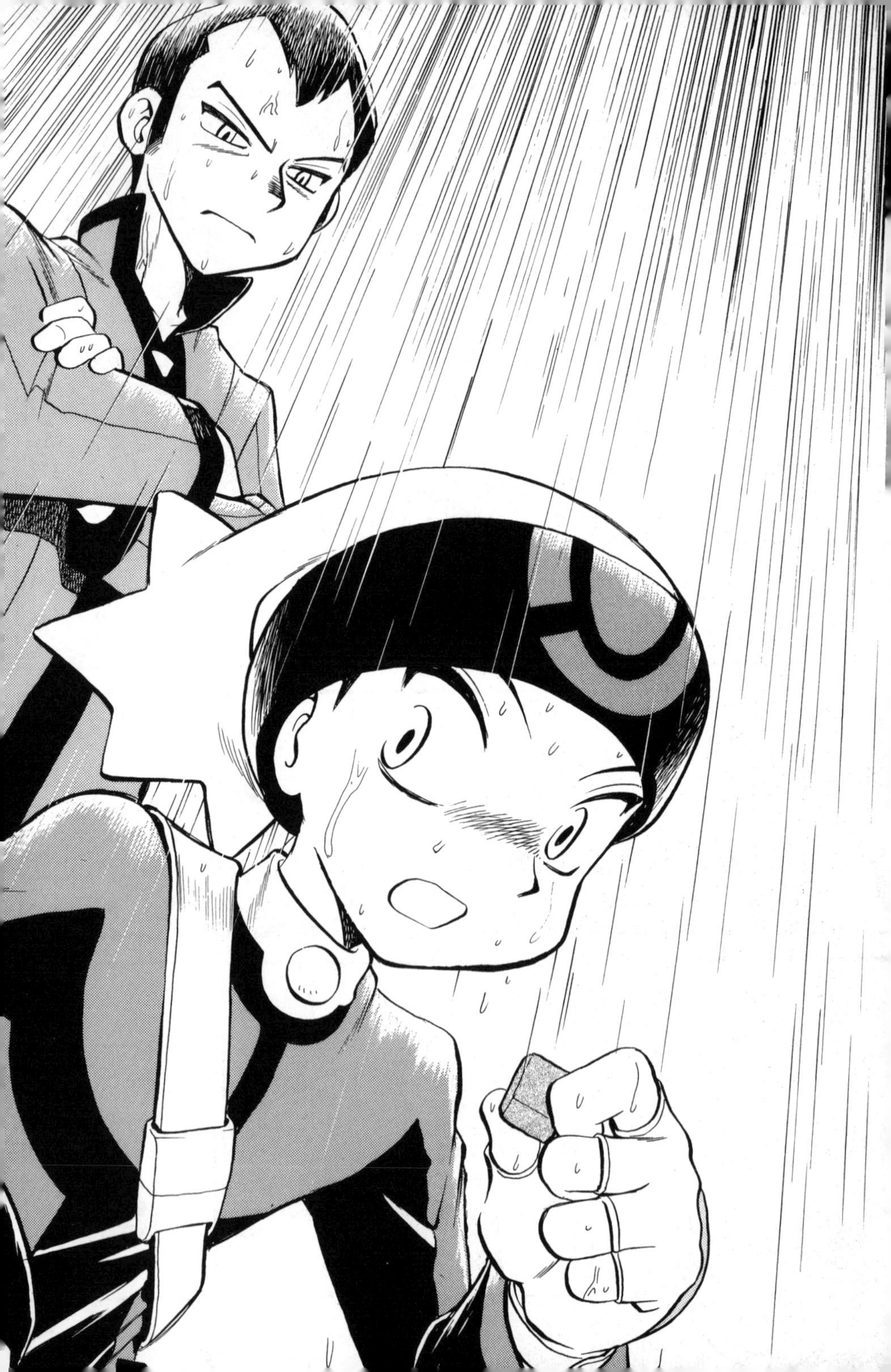

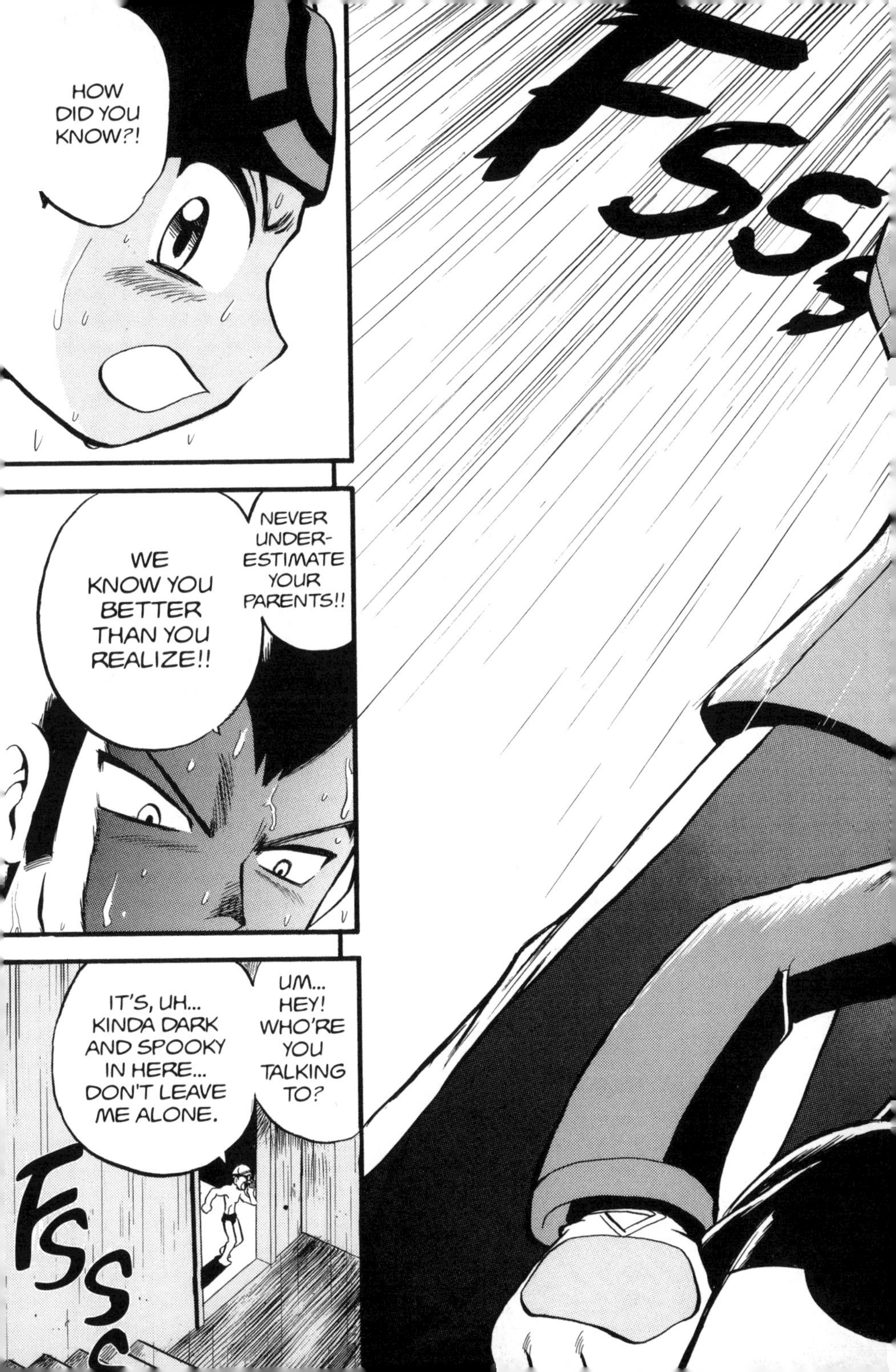
FSS
HOW DID YOU KNOW?!
NEVER UNDER-ESTIMATE YOUR PARENTS!!
WE KNOW YOU BETTER THAN YOU REALIZE!!
UM... HEY! WHO'RE YOU TALKING TO?
IT'S, UH... KINDA DARK AND SPOOKY IN HERE... DON'T LEAVE ME ALONE.
FSS

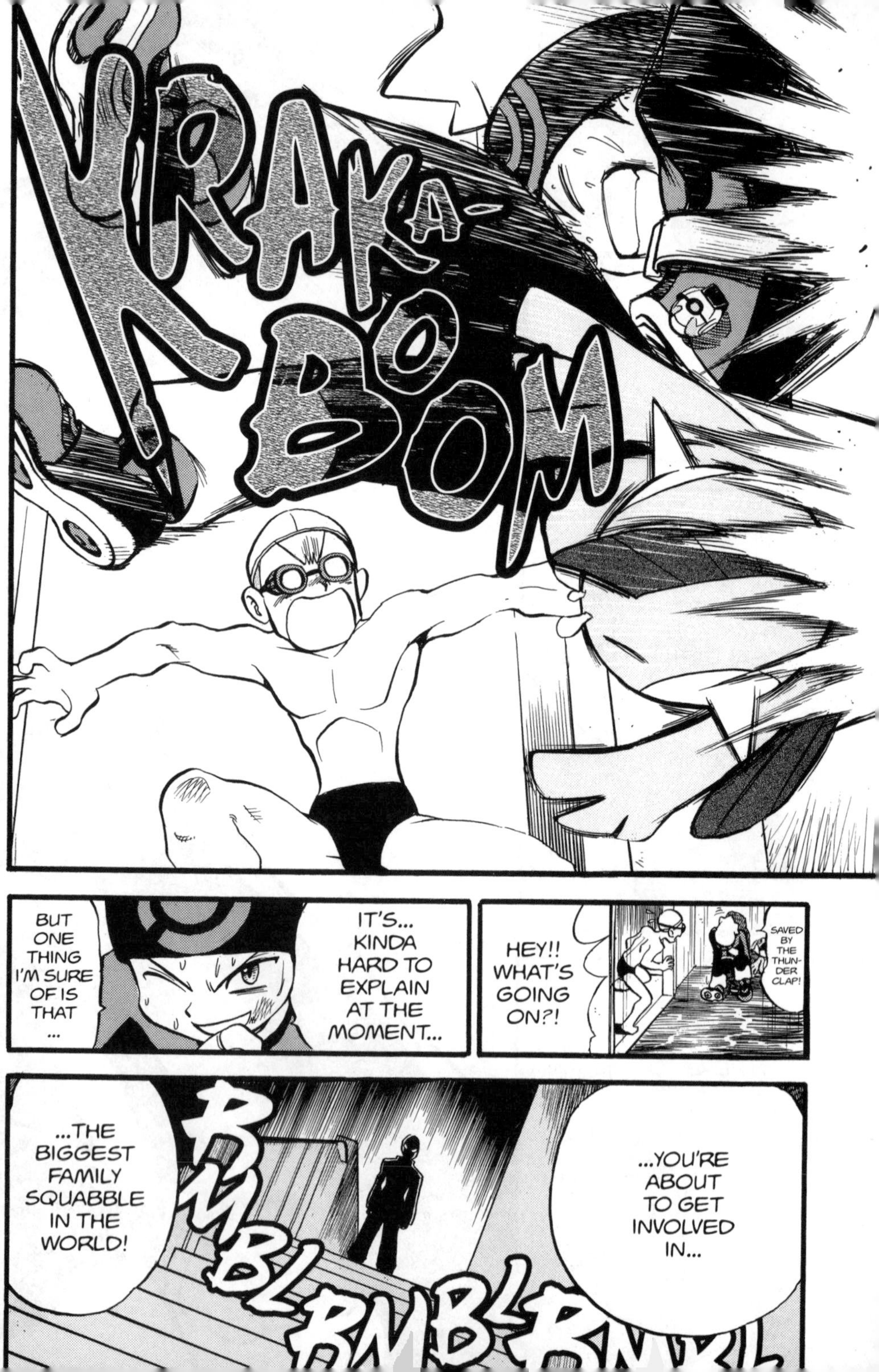
KRAKA-BOOM
SAVED BY THE THUNDER-CLAP!
HEY!! WHAT'S GOING ON?!
IT'S... KINDA HARD TO EXPLAIN AT THE MOMENT...
BUT ONE THING I'M SURE OF IS THAT ...
...YOU'RE ABOUT TO GET INVOLVED IN...
...THE BIGGEST FAMILY SQUABBLE IN THE WORLD!

● Adventure 209 ●
Hanging Around with Slaking, Part 1

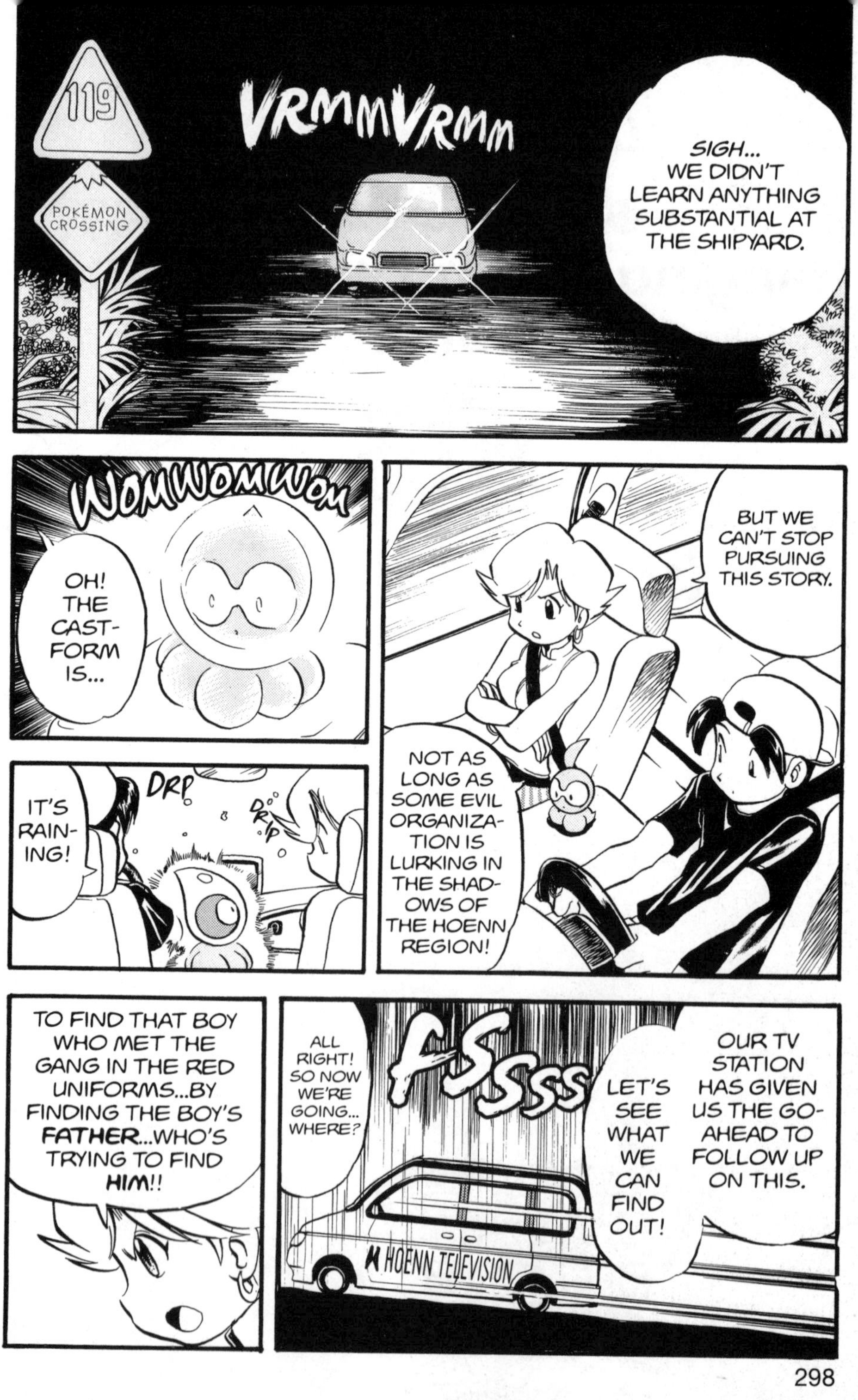

119
POKÉMON CROSSING
VRMMVRMM
SIGH... WE DIDN'T LEARN ANYTHING SUBSTANTIAL AT THE SHIPYARD.
BUT WE CAN'T STOP PURSUING THIS STORY.
NOT AS LONG AS SOME EVIL ORGANIZATION IS LURKING IN THE SHADOWS OF THE HOENN REGION!
WOMWOMWOM
OH! THE CASTFORM IS...
DRP
DRIP
IT'S RAINING!
OUR TV STATION HAS GIVEN US THE GO-AHEAD TO FOLLOW UP ON THIS.
FSSSS
LET'S SEE WHAT WE CAN FIND OUT!
ALL RIGHT! SO NOW WE'RE GOING... WHERE?
HOENN TELEVISION
TO FIND THAT BOY WHO MET THE GANG IN THE RED UNIFORMS...BY FINDING THE BOY'S **FATHER**...WHO'S TRYING TO FIND **HIM**!!

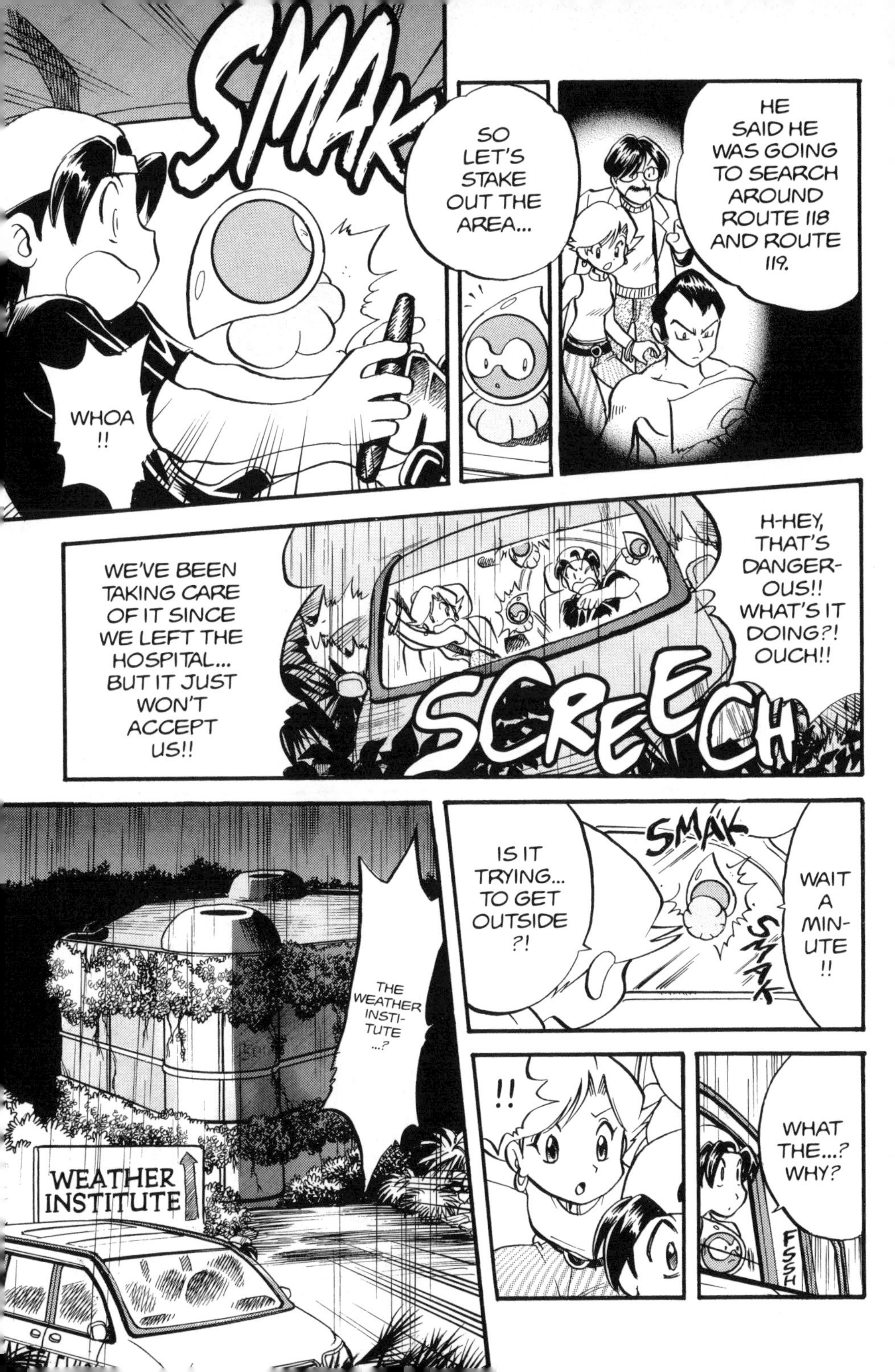
HE SAID HE WAS GOING TO SEARCH AROUND ROUTE 118 AND ROUTE 119.
SO LET'S STAKE OUT THE AREA...
SMAK
WHOA!!
H-HEY, THAT'S DANGER-OUS!! WHAT'S IT DOING?! OUCH!!
WE'VE BEEN TAKING CARE OF IT SINCE WE LEFT THE HOSPITAL... BUT IT JUST WON'T ACCEPT US!!
SCREECH
WAIT A MIN-UTE!!
SMAK
SMAK
IS IT TRYING... TO GET OUTSIDE?!
WHAT THE...? WHY?
FSSH
!!
THE WEATHER INSTI-TUTE...?
WEATHER INSTITUTE

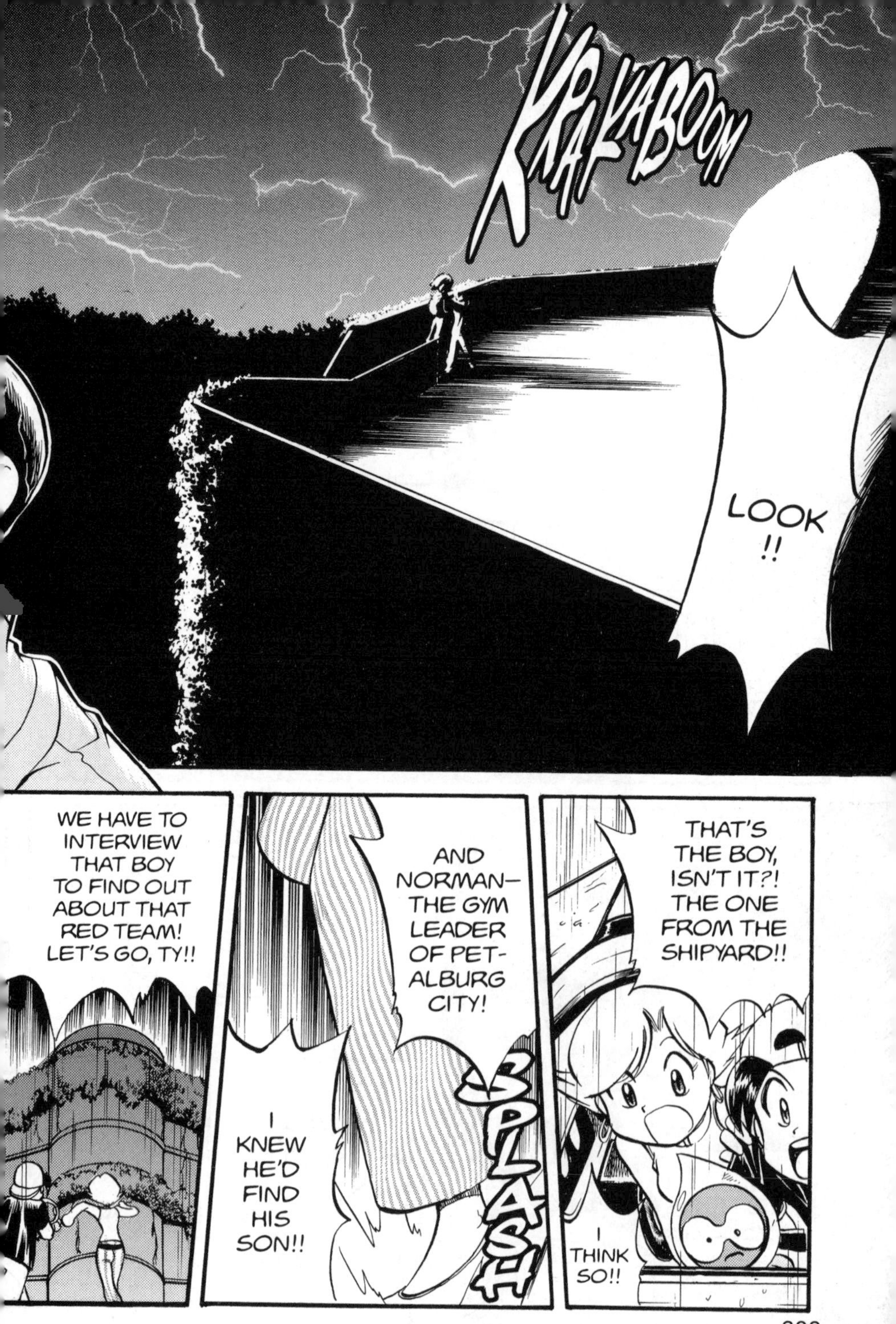
KRAKABOOM
LOOK !!
THAT'S THE BOY, ISN'T IT?! THE ONE FROM THE SHIPYARD!!
I THINK SO!!
AND NORMAN— THE GYM LEADER OF PET-ALBURG CITY!
I KNEW HE'D FIND HIS SON!!
SPLASH
WE HAVE TO INTERVIEW THAT BOY TO FIND OUT ABOUT THAT RED TEAM! LET'S GO, TY!!

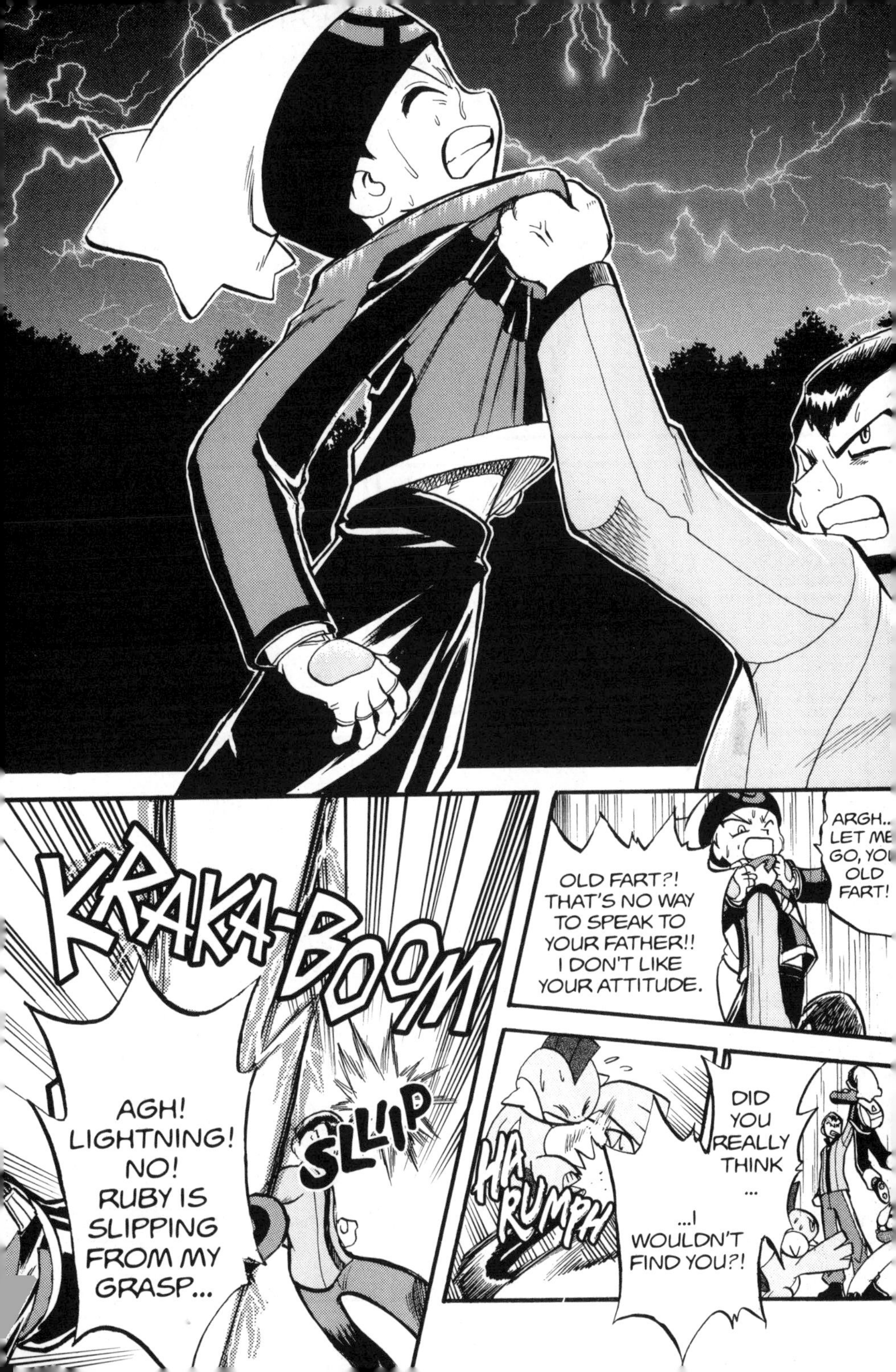

ARGH... LET ME GO, YOU OLD FART!
OLD FART?! THAT'S NO WAY TO SPEAK TO YOUR FATHER!! I DON'T LIKE YOUR ATTITUDE.
DID YOU REALLY THINK ...
...I WOULDN'T FIND YOU?!
HA RUMPH
KRAKA-BOOM
SLLIP
AGH! LIGHTNING! NO! RUBY IS SLIPPING FROM MY GRASP...

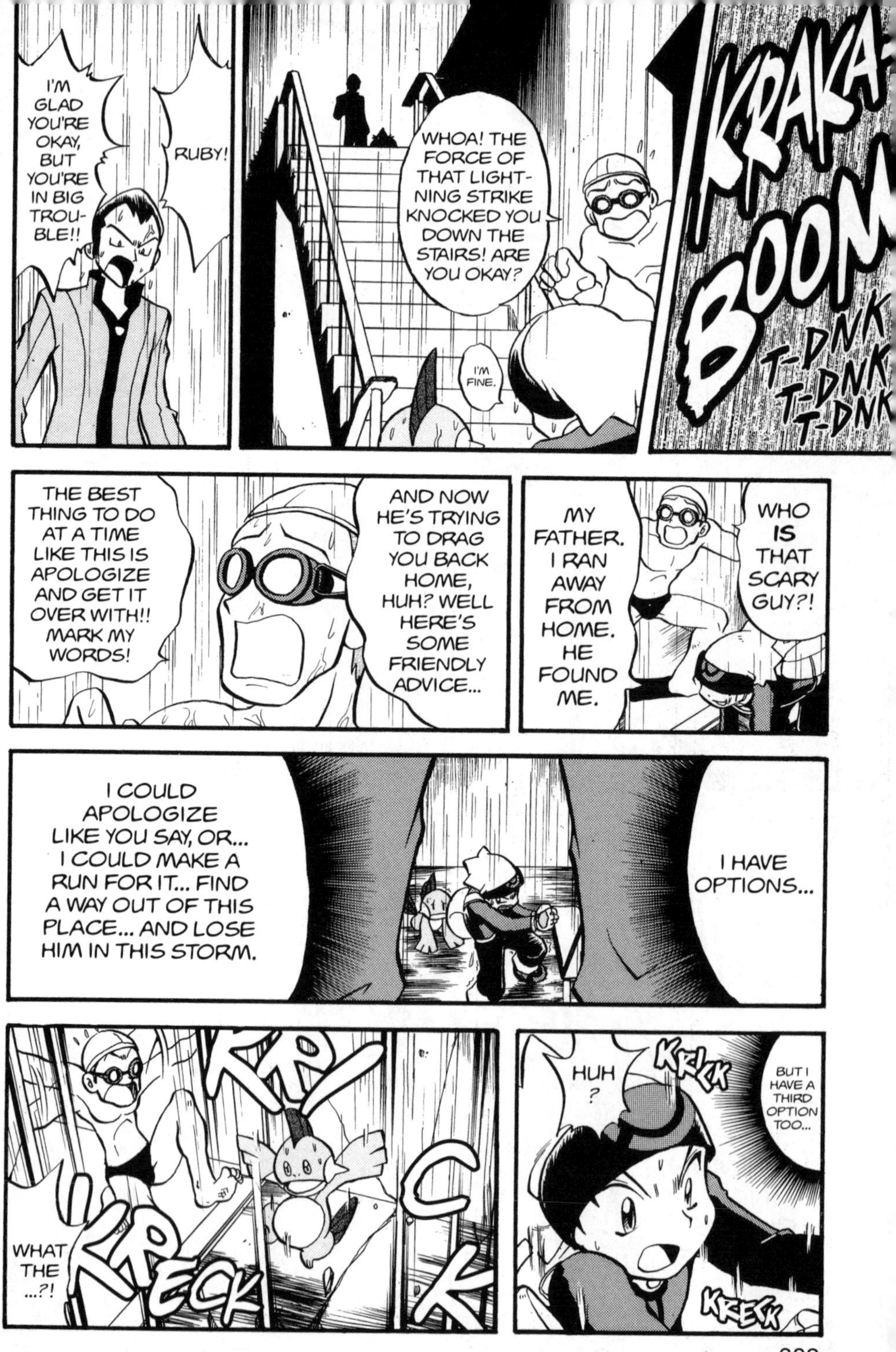
KRAKA-BOOM
T-DNK T-DNK T-DNK
WHOA! THE FORCE OF THAT LIGHTNING STRIKE KNOCKED YOU DOWN THE STAIRS! ARE YOU OKAY?
I'M FINE.
RUBY!
I'M GLAD YOU'RE OKAY, BUT YOU'RE IN BIG TROUBLE!!
WHO **IS** THAT SCARY GUY?!
MY FATHER. I RAN AWAY FROM HOME. HE FOUND ME.
AND NOW HE'S TRYING TO DRAG YOU BACK HOME, HUH? WELL HERE'S SOME FRIENDLY ADVICE...
THE BEST THING TO DO AT A TIME LIKE THIS IS APOLOGIZE AND GET IT OVER WITH!! MARK MY WORDS!
I HAVE OPTIONS...
I COULD APOLOGIZE LIKE YOU SAY, OR... I COULD MAKE A RUN FOR IT... FIND A WAY OUT OF THIS PLACE... AND LOSE HIM IN THIS STORM.
BUT I HAVE A THIRD OPTION TOO...
KRICK
HUH?
KRECK
WHAT THE ...?!

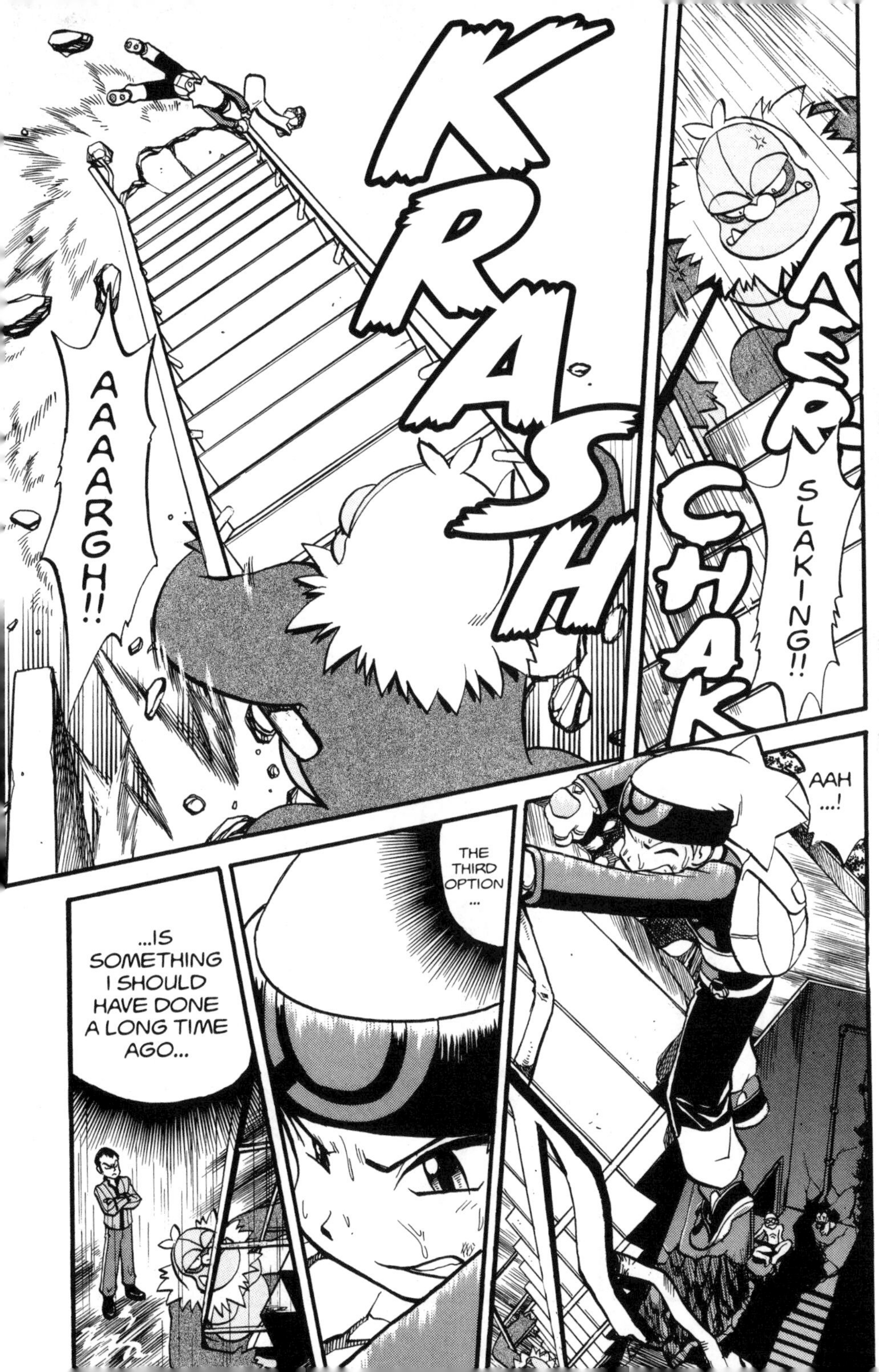
KER-CHAK
SLAKING!!
KRASH
AAAAARGH!!
AAH ...!
THE THIRD OPTION ...
...IS SOMETHING I SHOULD HAVE DONE A LONG TIME AGO...

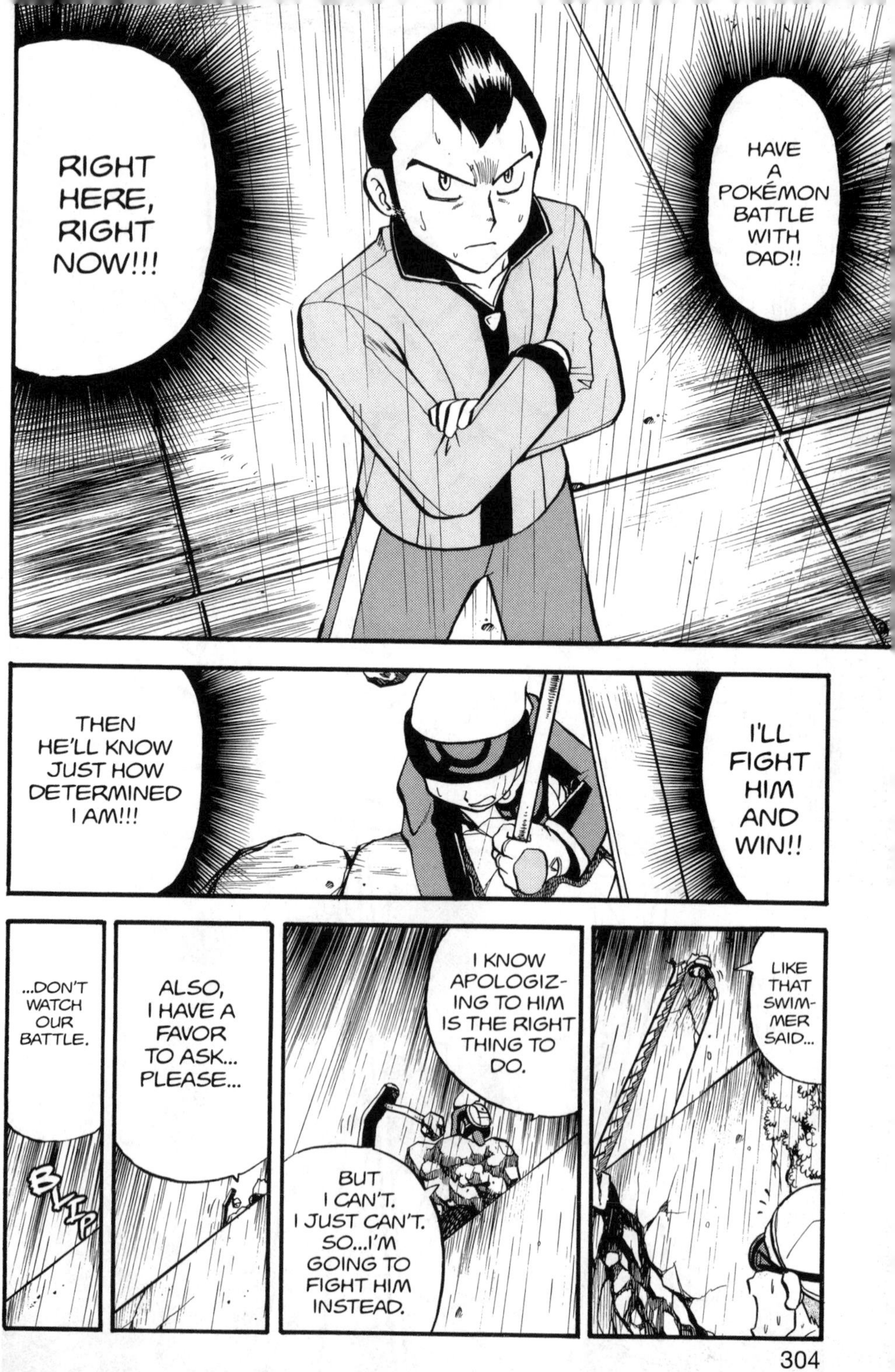
HAVE A POKÉMON BATTLE WITH DAD!!
RIGHT HERE, RIGHT NOW!!!
I'LL FIGHT HIM AND WIN!!
THEN HE'LL KNOW JUST HOW DETERMINED I AM!!!
LIKE THAT SWIMMER SAID...
I KNOW APOLOGIZING TO HIM IS THE RIGHT THING TO DO.
BUT I CAN'T. I JUST CAN'T. SO...I'M GOING TO FIGHT HIM INSTEAD.
ALSO, I HAVE A FAVOR TO ASK... PLEASE...
...DON'T WATCH OUR BATTLE.
BLIP

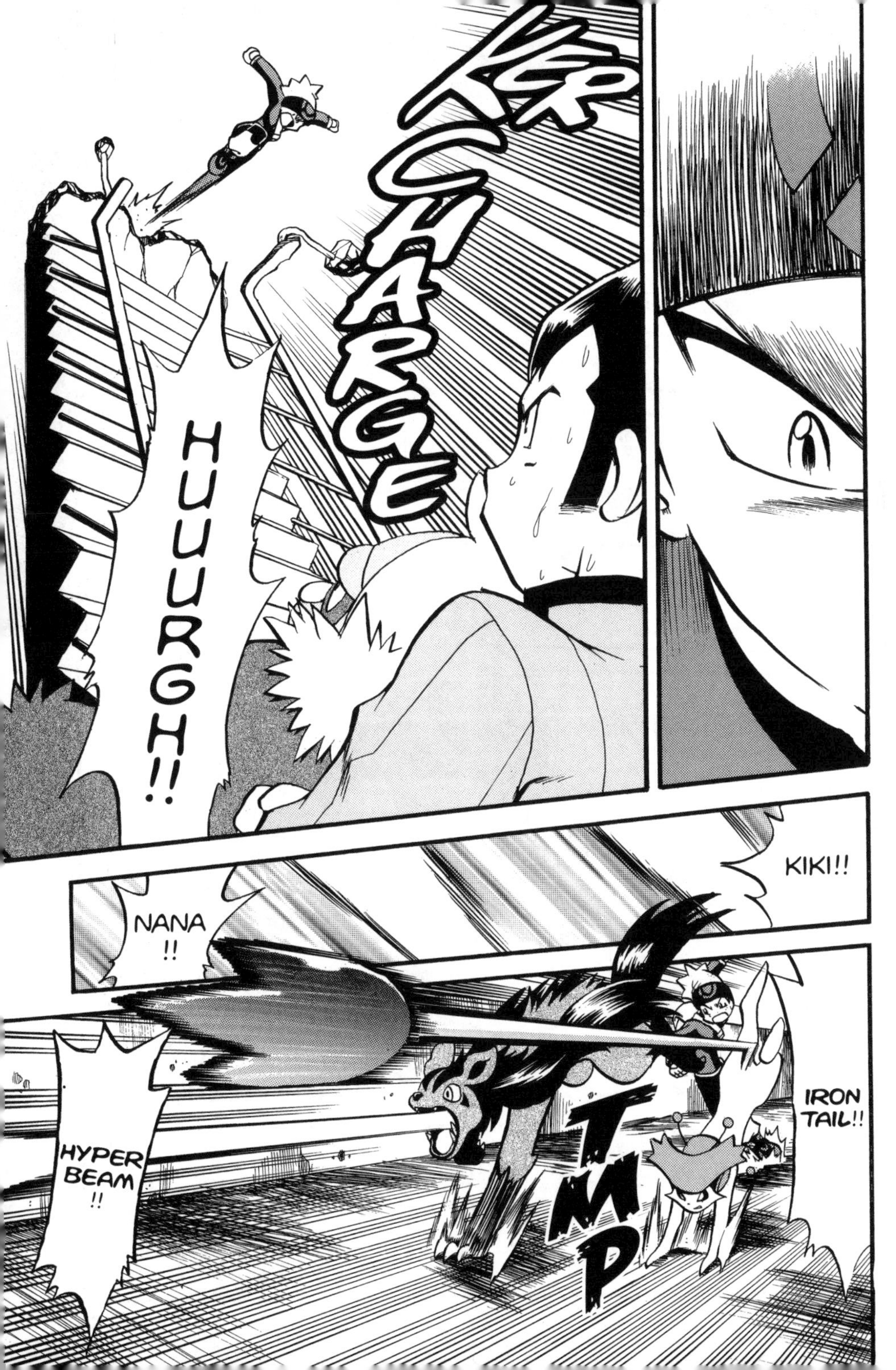
KRCHARGE
HUUURGH!!
KIKI!!
NANA!!
IRON TAIL!!
TMP
HYPER BEAM!!

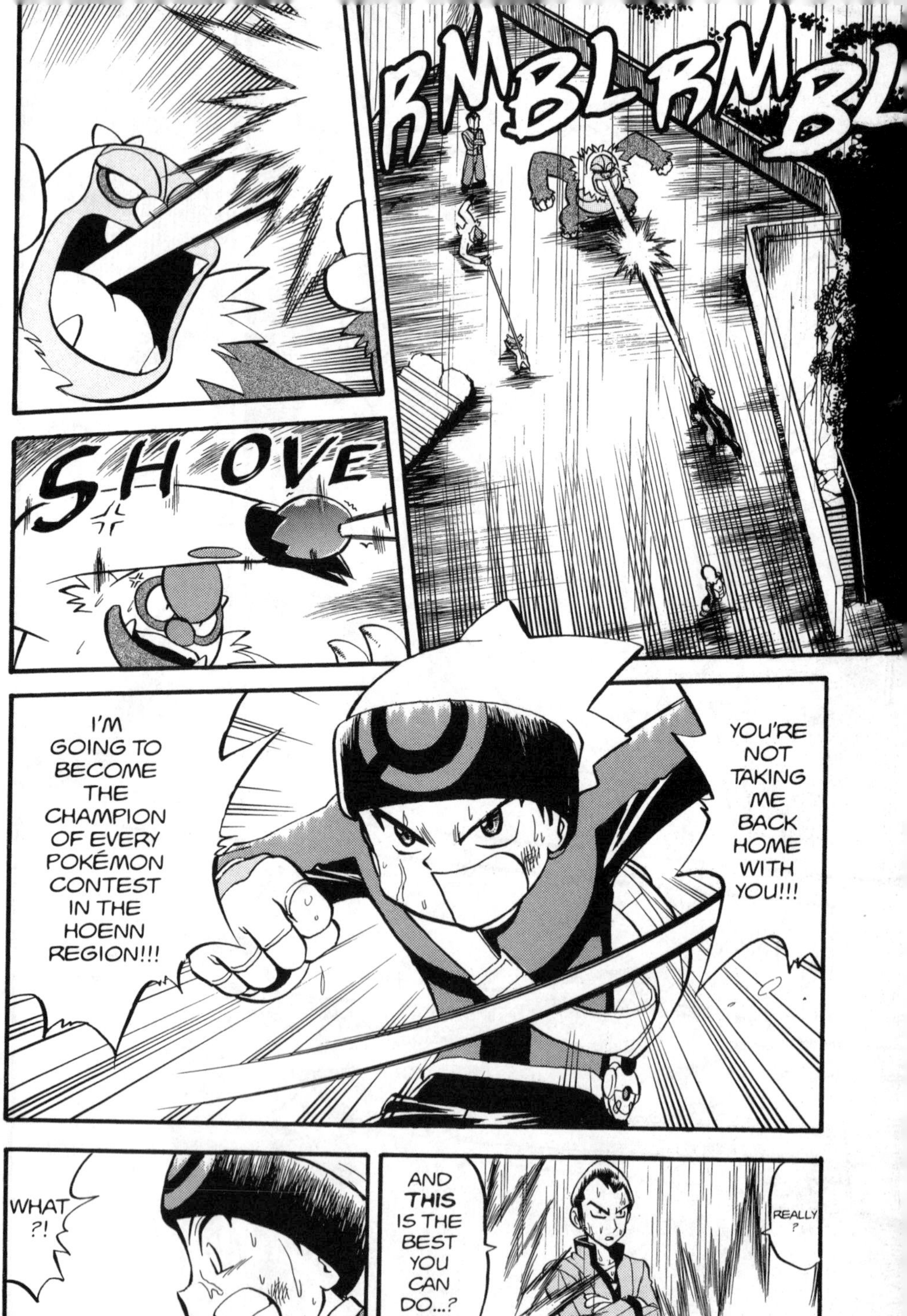
RMBLRMBL
SHOVE
YOU'RE NOT TAKING ME BACK HOME WITH YOU!!!
I'M GOING TO BECOME THE CHAMPION OF EVERY POKÉMON CONTEST IN THE HOENN REGION!!!
REALLY?
AND THIS IS THE BEST YOU CAN DO...?
WHAT?!

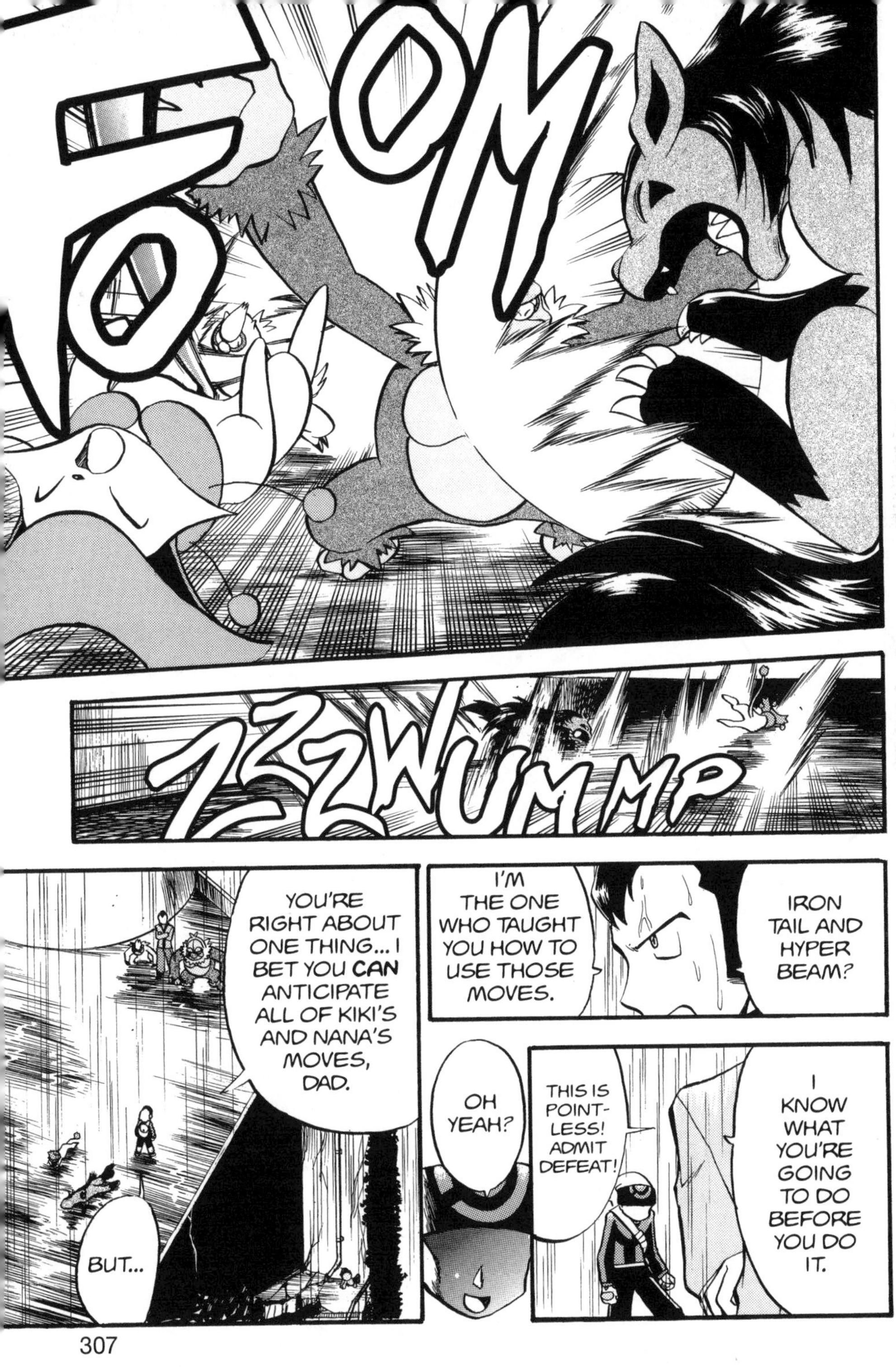
OOM
ZZWUMMP
IRON TAIL AND HYPER BEAM?
I'M THE ONE WHO TAUGHT YOU HOW TO USE THOSE MOVES.
I KNOW WHAT YOU'RE GOING TO DO BEFORE YOU DO IT.
THIS IS POINT-LESS! ADMIT DEFEAT!
YOU'RE RIGHT ABOUT ONE THING... I BET YOU **CAN** ANTICIPATE ALL OF KIKI'S AND NANA'S MOVES, DAD.
OH YEAH?
BUT...

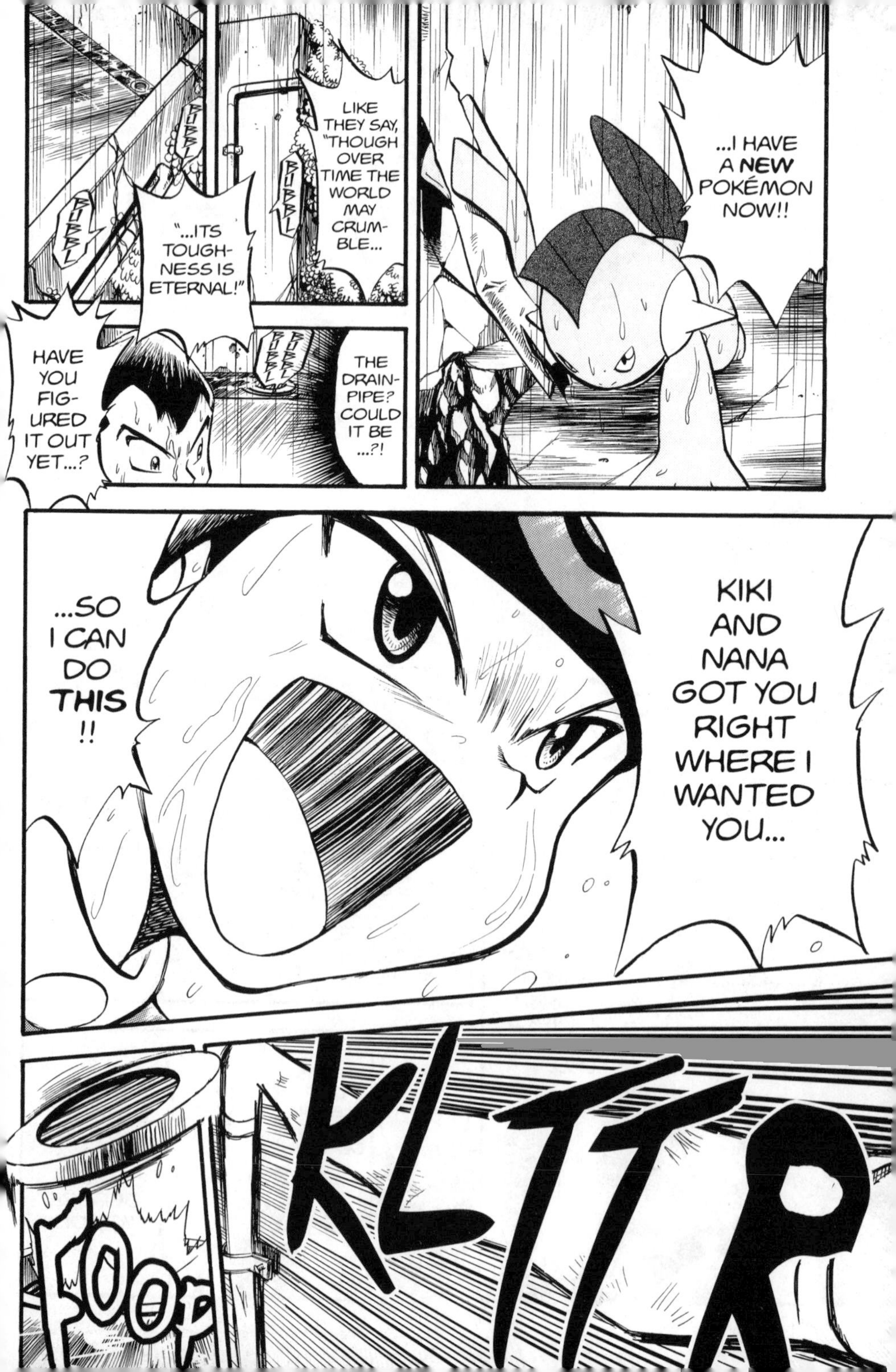

...I HAVE A **NEW** POKÉMON NOW!!
BUBBL
BUBBL
BUBBL
LIKE THEY SAY, "THOUGH OVER TIME THE WORLD MAY CRUMBLE...
"...ITS TOUGHNESS IS ETERNAL!"
BUBBL
BUBBL
THE DRAINPIPE? COULD IT BE ...?!
HAVE YOU FIGURED IT OUT YET...?
KIKI AND NANA GOT YOU RIGHT WHERE I WANTED YOU...
...SO I CAN DO **THIS**!!
KLTTR
FOOP

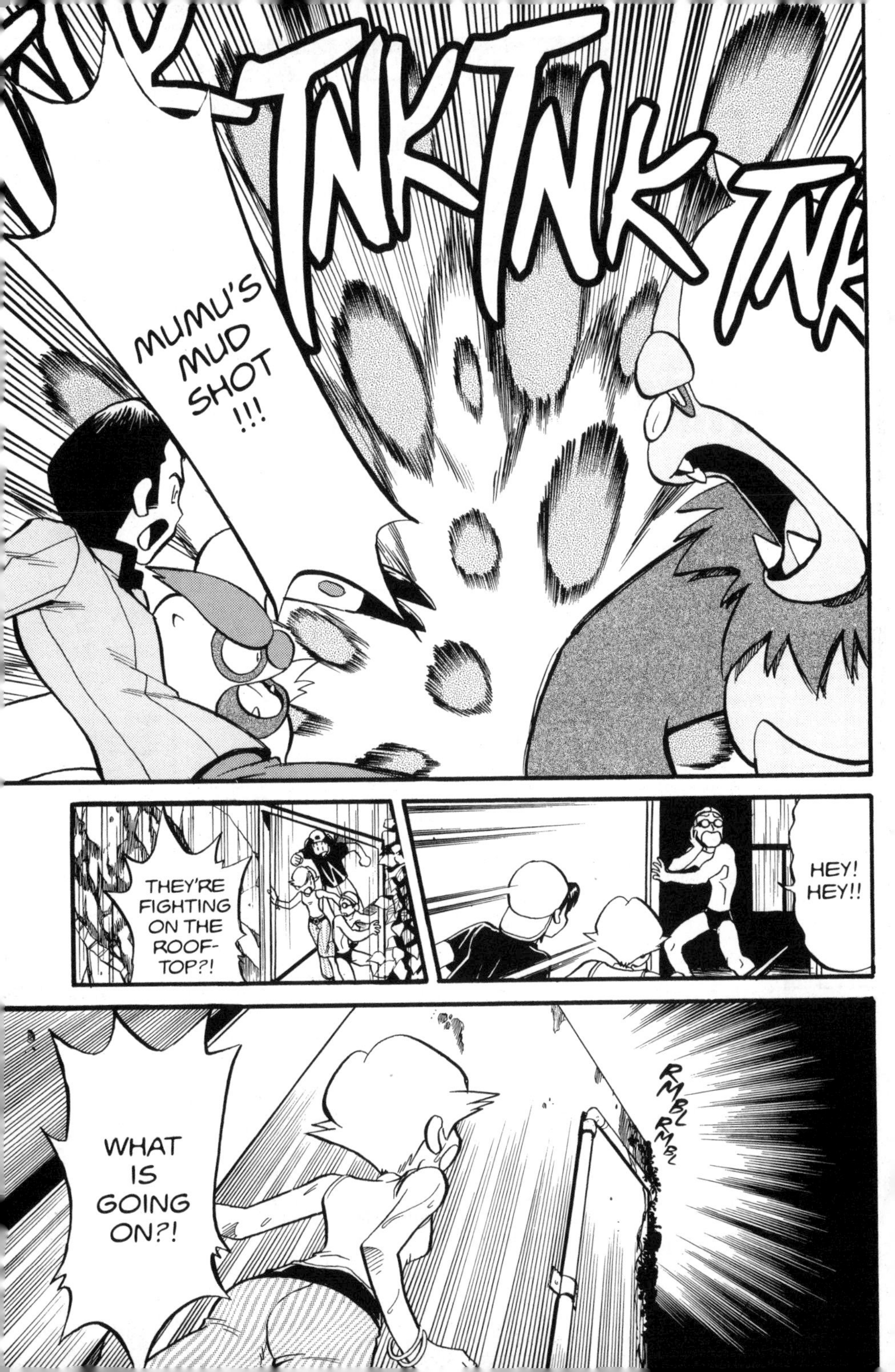
TNK TNK TNK TNK
MUMU'S MUD SHOT !!!
HEY! HEY!!
THEY'RE FIGHTING ON THE ROOF-TOP?!
RMBL RMBL
WHAT IS GOING ON?!

ADVENTURE MAP

SAPPHIRE

CHIC
Combusken ♀
Lv25

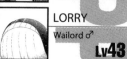

RONO
Lairon ♂
Lv36

LORRY
Wailord ♂
Lv43

PHADO
Donphan ♂
Lv40

RUBY

MUMU
Marshtomp ♂

NANA
Mightyena ♀

KIKI
Delcatty ♀

FEEBAS
Feebas ♀

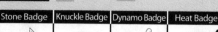

Route 109

Slateport City	Slateport City
Route 110	Route 118
Mauville City	Route 119
New Mauville	Weather Institute
Route 111	

Stone Badge	Knuckle Badge	Dynamo Badge	Heat Badge
Balance Badge	Feather Badge	Mind Badge	Rain Badge

	Coolness	Beauty	Cuteness	Cleverness	Toughness
Normal	🎗	🎗	🎗	🎗	🎗
Super	🎗	🎗	🎗	🎗	🎗
Hyper	✖	✖	✖	✖	✖
Master	✖	✖	✖	✖	✖

● Adventure 210 ●
Hanging Around with Slaking, Part 2

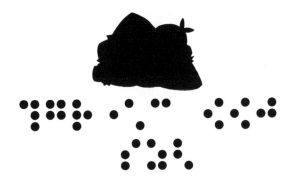

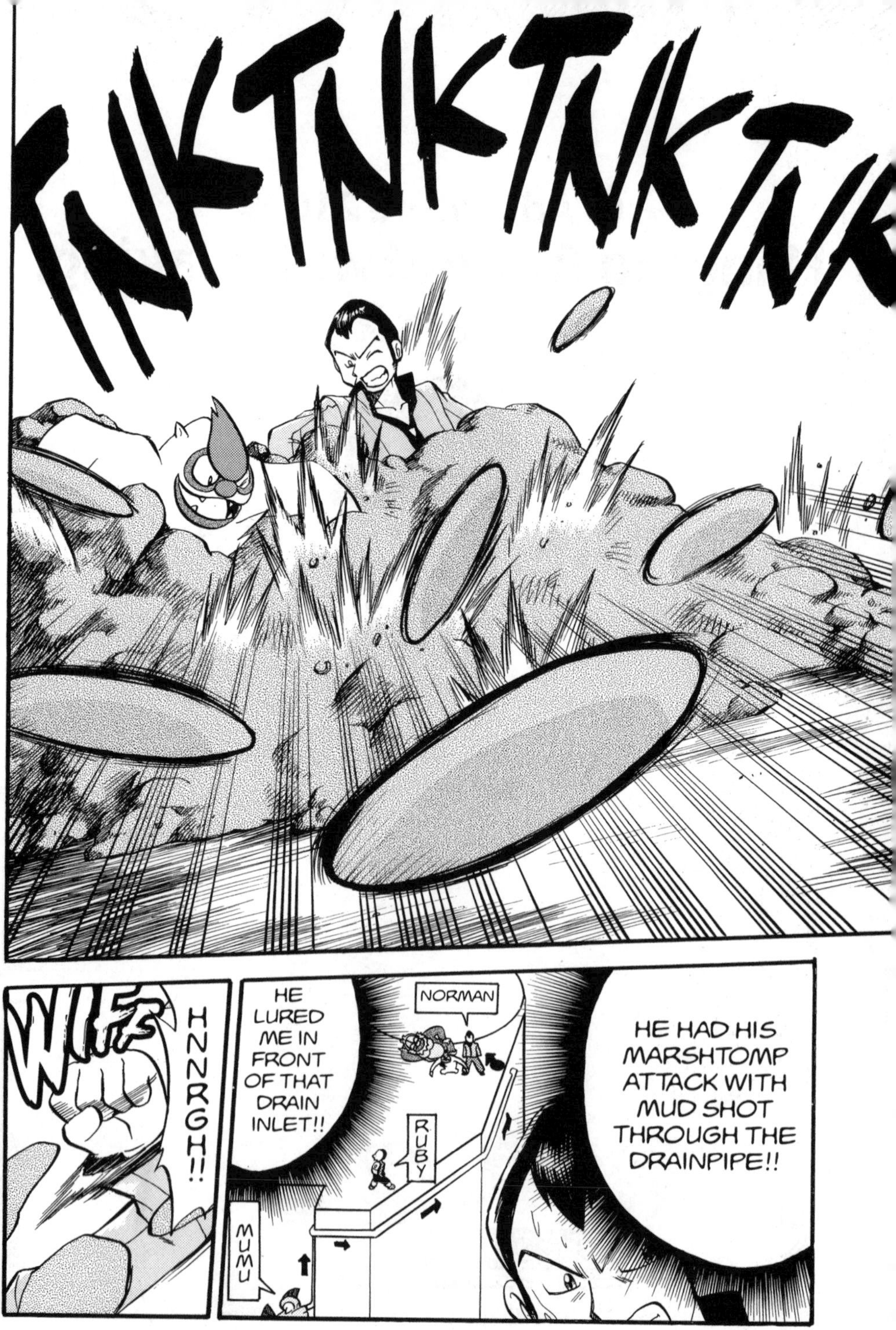
TNK TNK TNK TNK
HE HAD HIS MARSHTOMP ATTACK WITH MUD SHOT THROUGH THE DRAINPIPE!!
HE LURED ME IN FRONT OF THAT DRAIN INLET!!
NORMAN
RUBY
MUMU
HNNRGH!!

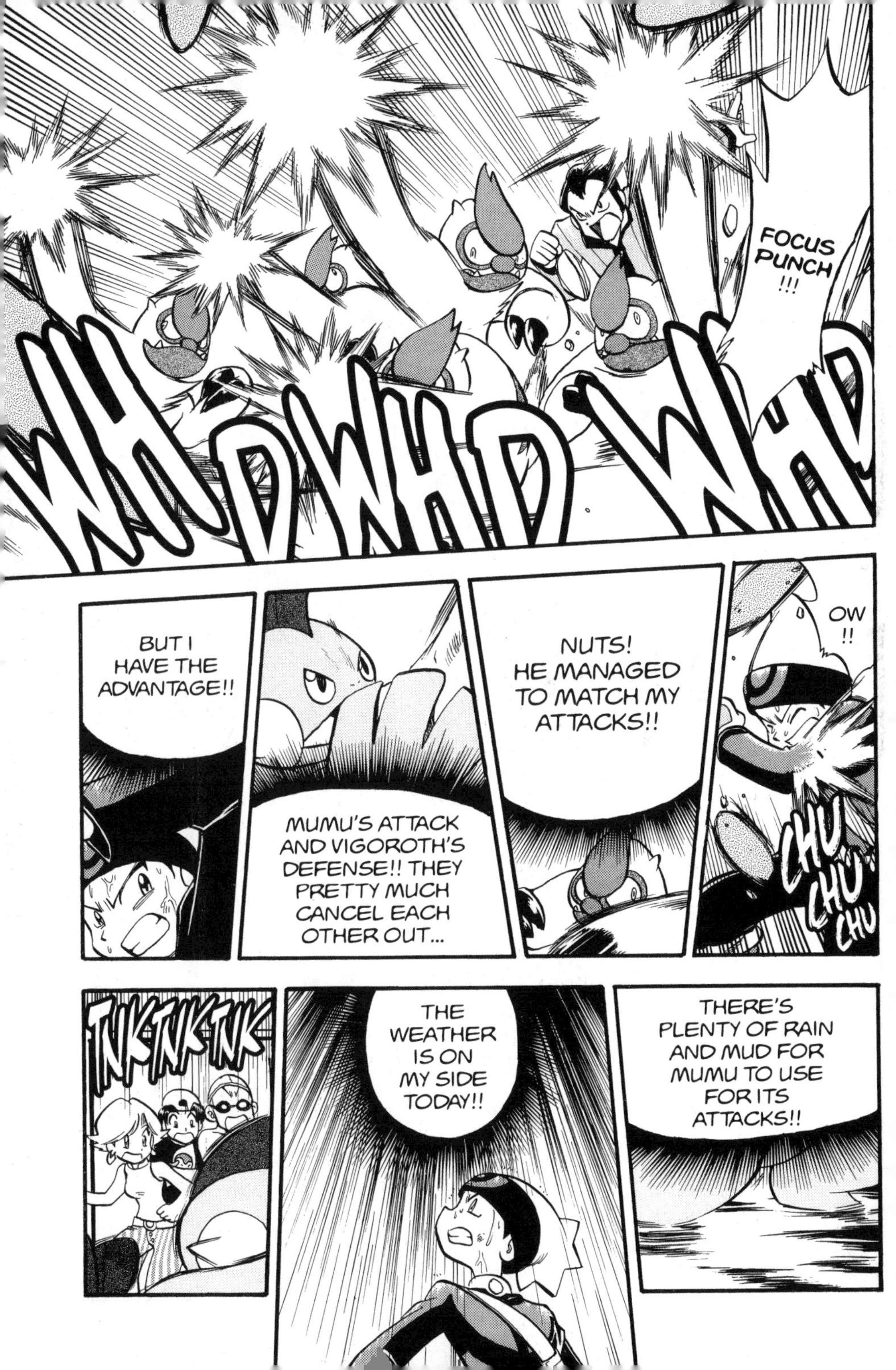
FOCUS PUNCH !!!
WHAP WHAP
OW !!
CHU CHU CHU
NUTS! HE MANAGED TO MATCH MY ATTACKS!!
MUMU'S ATTACK AND VIGOROTH'S DEFENSE!! THEY PRETTY MUCH CANCEL EACH OTHER OUT...
BUT I HAVE THE ADVANTAGE!!
THERE'S PLENTY OF RAIN AND MUD FOR MUMU TO USE FOR ITS ATTACKS!!
THE WEATHER IS ON MY SIDE TODAY!!
TNK TNK TNK

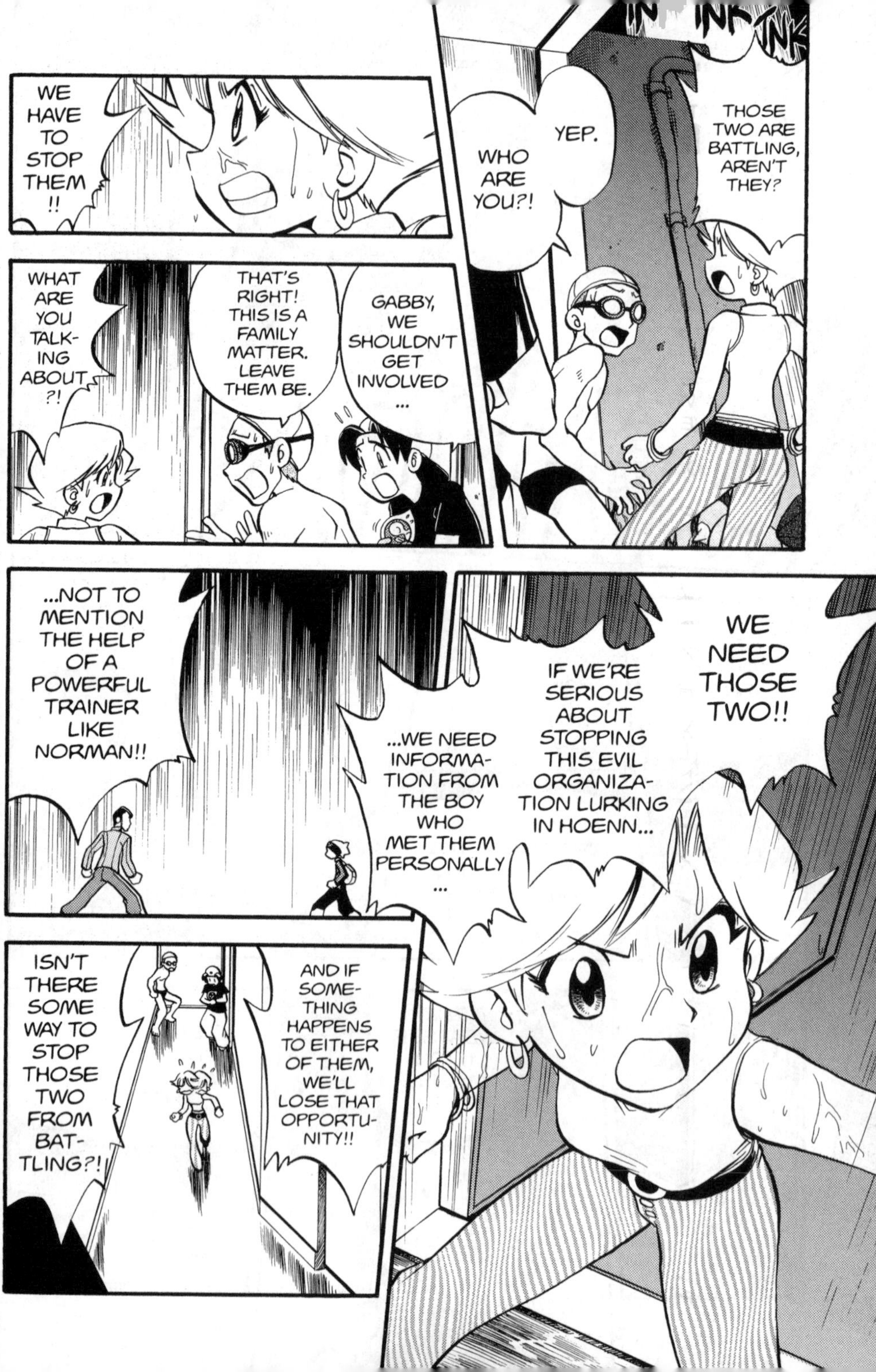
INK INK
THOSE TWO ARE BATTLING, AREN'T THEY?
YEP.
WHO ARE YOU?!
WE HAVE TO STOP THEM!!
GABBY, WE SHOULDN'T GET INVOLVED...
THAT'S RIGHT! THIS IS A FAMILY MATTER. LEAVE THEM BE.
WHAT ARE YOU TALKING ABOUT?!
WE NEED THOSE TWO!!
IF WE'RE SERIOUS ABOUT STOPPING THIS EVIL ORGANIZATION LURKING IN HOENN...
...WE NEED INFORMATION FROM THE BOY WHO MET THEM PERSONALLY...
...NOT TO MENTION THE HELP OF A POWERFUL TRAINER LIKE NORMAN!!
AND IF SOMETHING HAPPENS TO EITHER OF THEM, WE'LL LOSE THAT OPPORTUNITY!!
ISN'T THERE SOME WAY TO STOP THOSE TWO FROM BATTLING?!

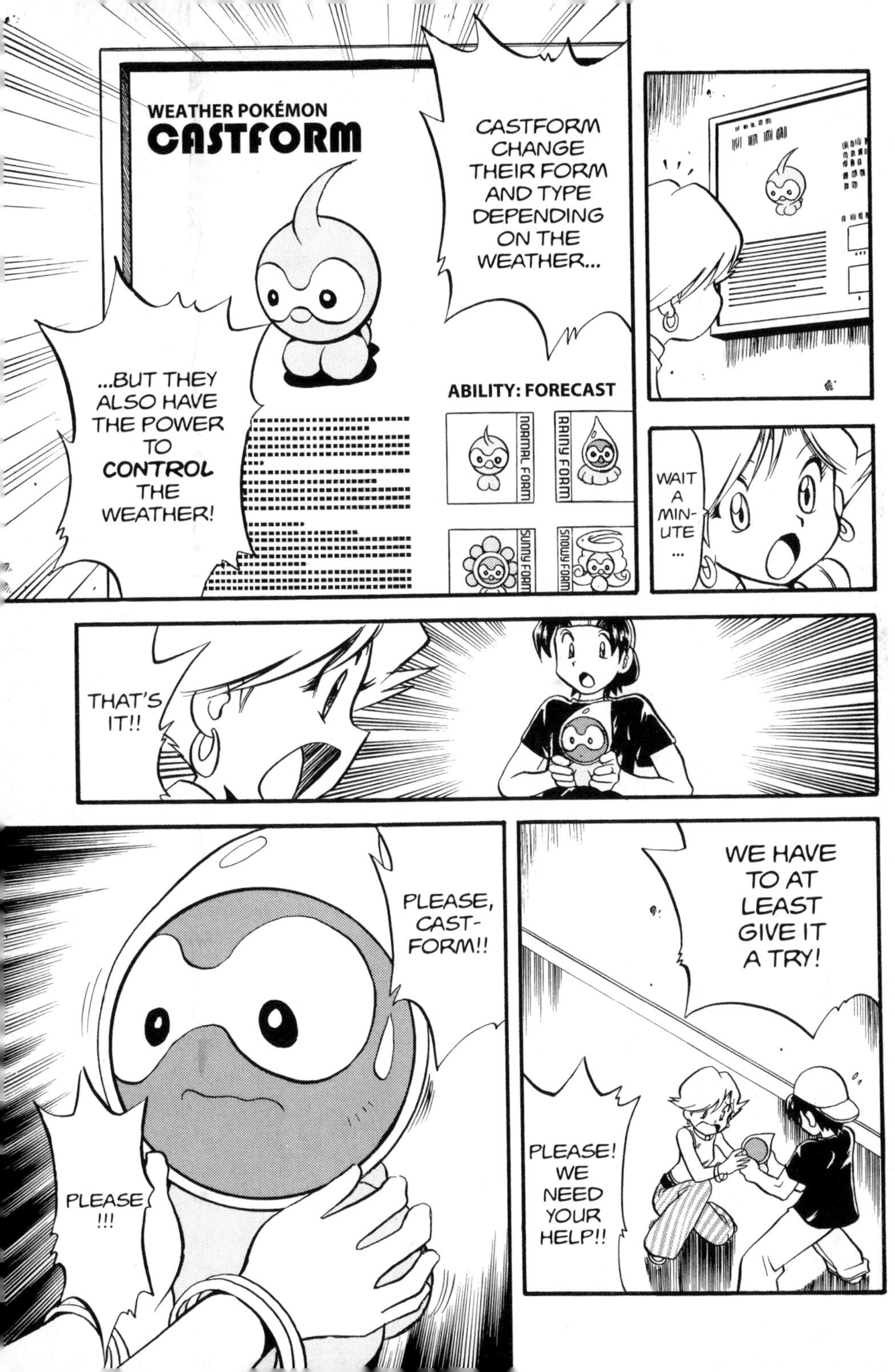
WAIT A MINUTE...
CASTFORM CHANGE THEIR FORM AND TYPE DEPENDING ON THE WEATHER...
WEATHER POKÉMON
CASTFORM
...BUT THEY ALSO HAVE THE POWER TO **CONTROL** THE WEATHER!
ABILITY: FORECAST
RAINY FORM
NORMAL FORM
SNOWY FORM
SUNNY FORM
THAT'S IT!!
WE HAVE TO AT LEAST GIVE IT A TRY!
PLEASE! WE NEED YOUR HELP!!
PLEASE, CAST-FORM!!
PLEASE!!!

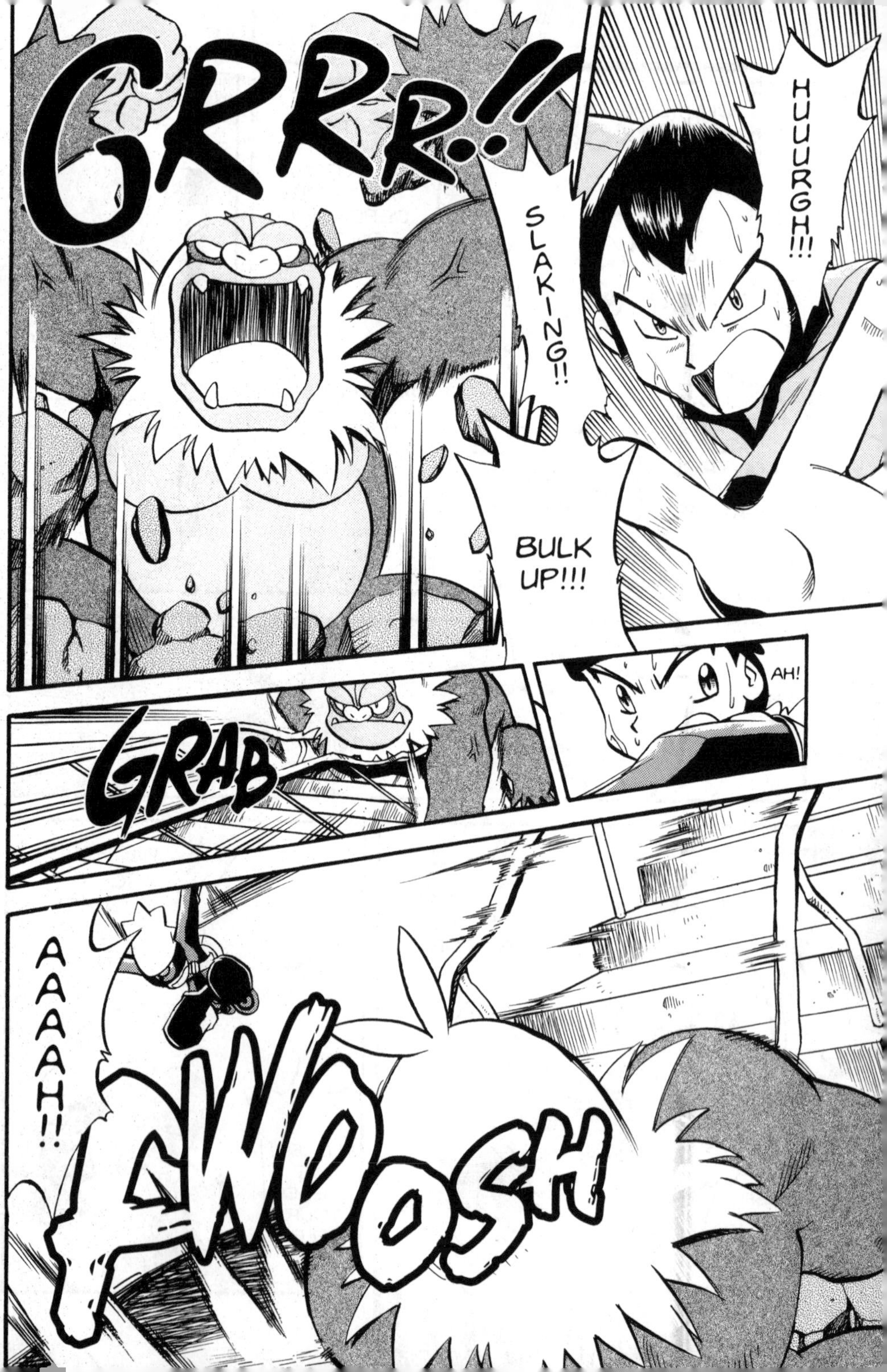
HUUURGH!!!
SLAKING!!
BULK UP!!!
GRRR..!!
AH!
GRAB
AAAAAH!!
WHOOSH

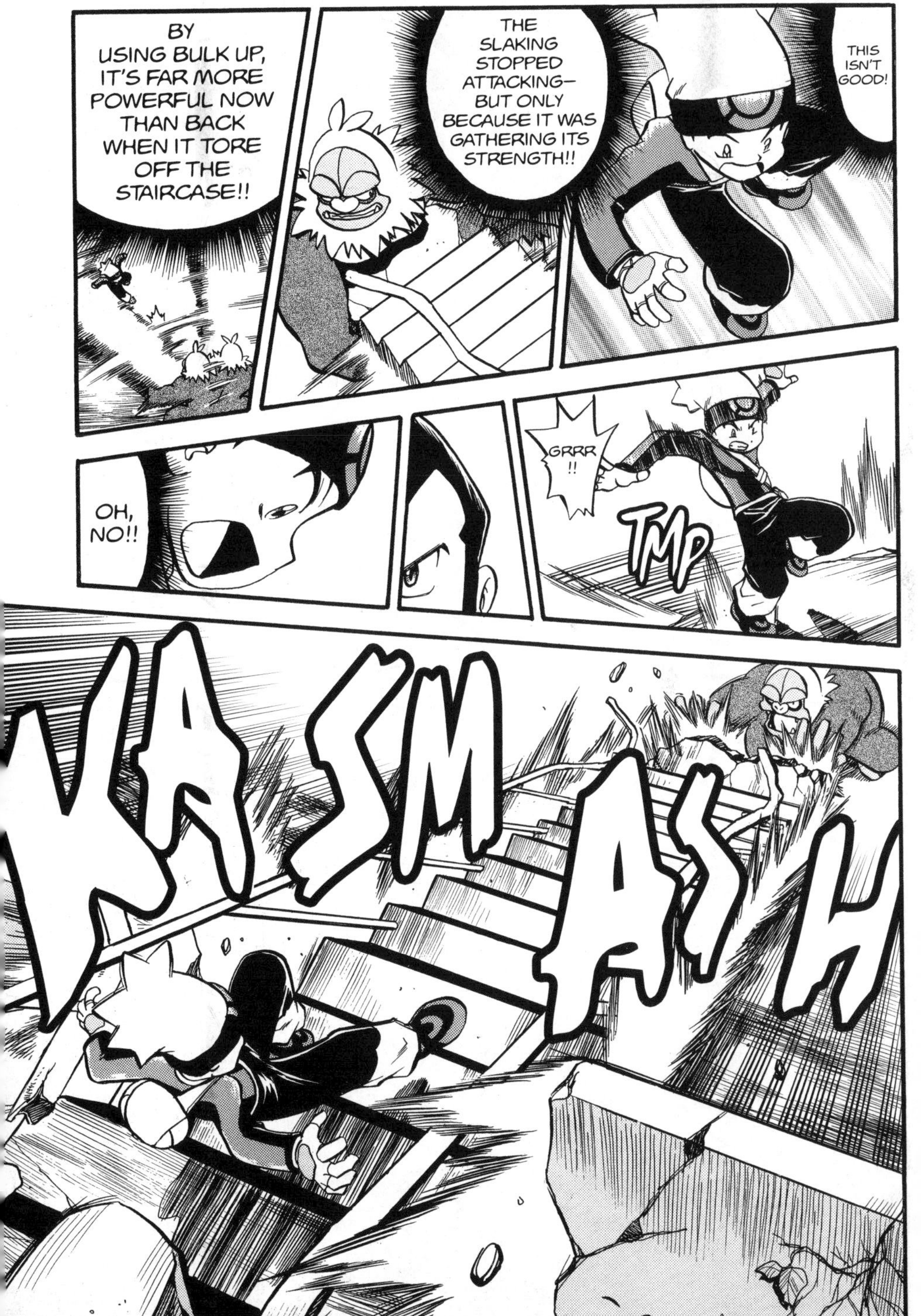
THIS ISN'T GOOD!
THE SLAKING STOPPED ATTACKING— BUT ONLY BECAUSE IT WAS GATHERING ITS STRENGTH!!
BY USING BULK UP, IT'S FAR MORE POWERFUL NOW THAN BACK WHEN IT TORE OFF THE STAIRCASE!!
GRRR!!
TMP
OH, NO!!
KASMASH

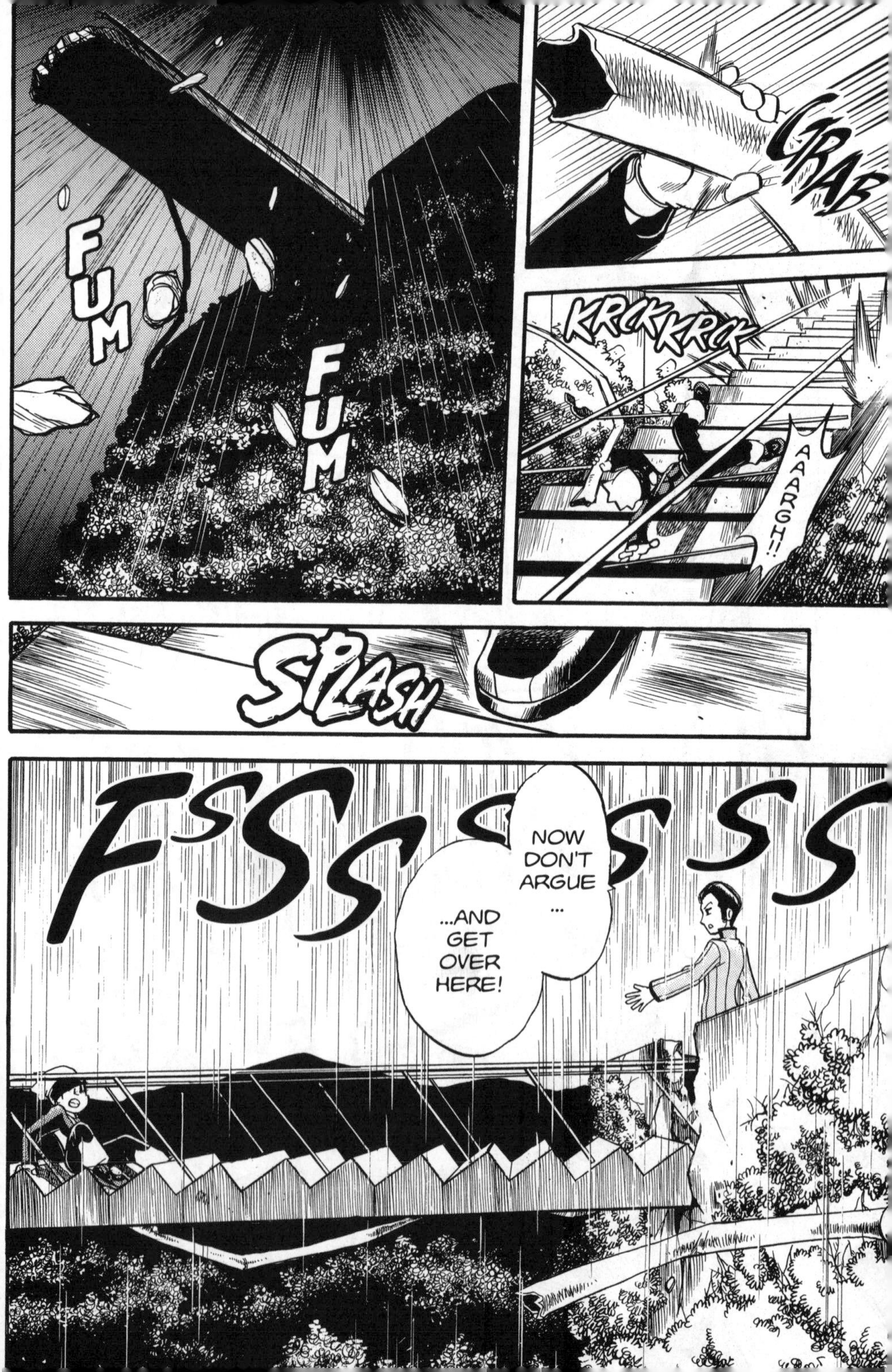
GRAB
KRCK KRCK
AAARGH!!
FUM
FUM
SPLASH
FSSSSSS
NOW DON'T ARGUE ...
...AND GET OVER HERE!

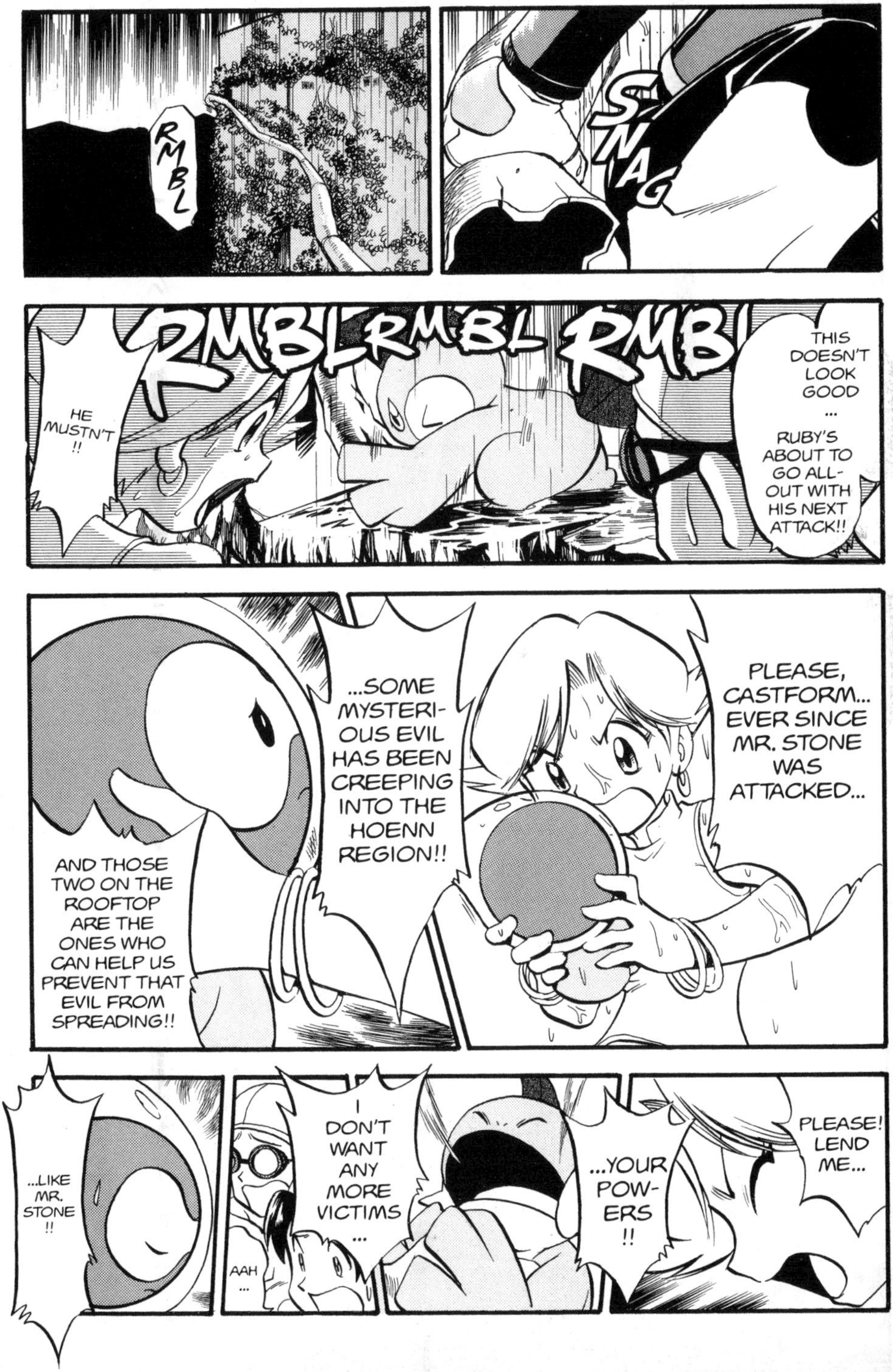
SNAG
RMBL
RMBL RMBL RMBL
THIS DOESN'T LOOK GOOD ... RUBY'S ABOUT TO GO ALL-OUT WITH HIS NEXT ATTACK!!
HE MUSTN'T !!
PLEASE, CASTFORM... EVER SINCE MR. STONE WAS ATTACKED...
...SOME MYSTERIOUS EVIL HAS BEEN CREEPING INTO THE HOENN REGION!!
AND THOSE TWO ON THE ROOFTOP ARE THE ONES WHO CAN HELP US PREVENT THAT EVIL FROM SPREADING!!
PLEASE! LEND ME...
...YOUR POWERS !!
I DON'T WANT ANY MORE VICTIMS ...
AAH ...
...LIKE MR. STONE !!

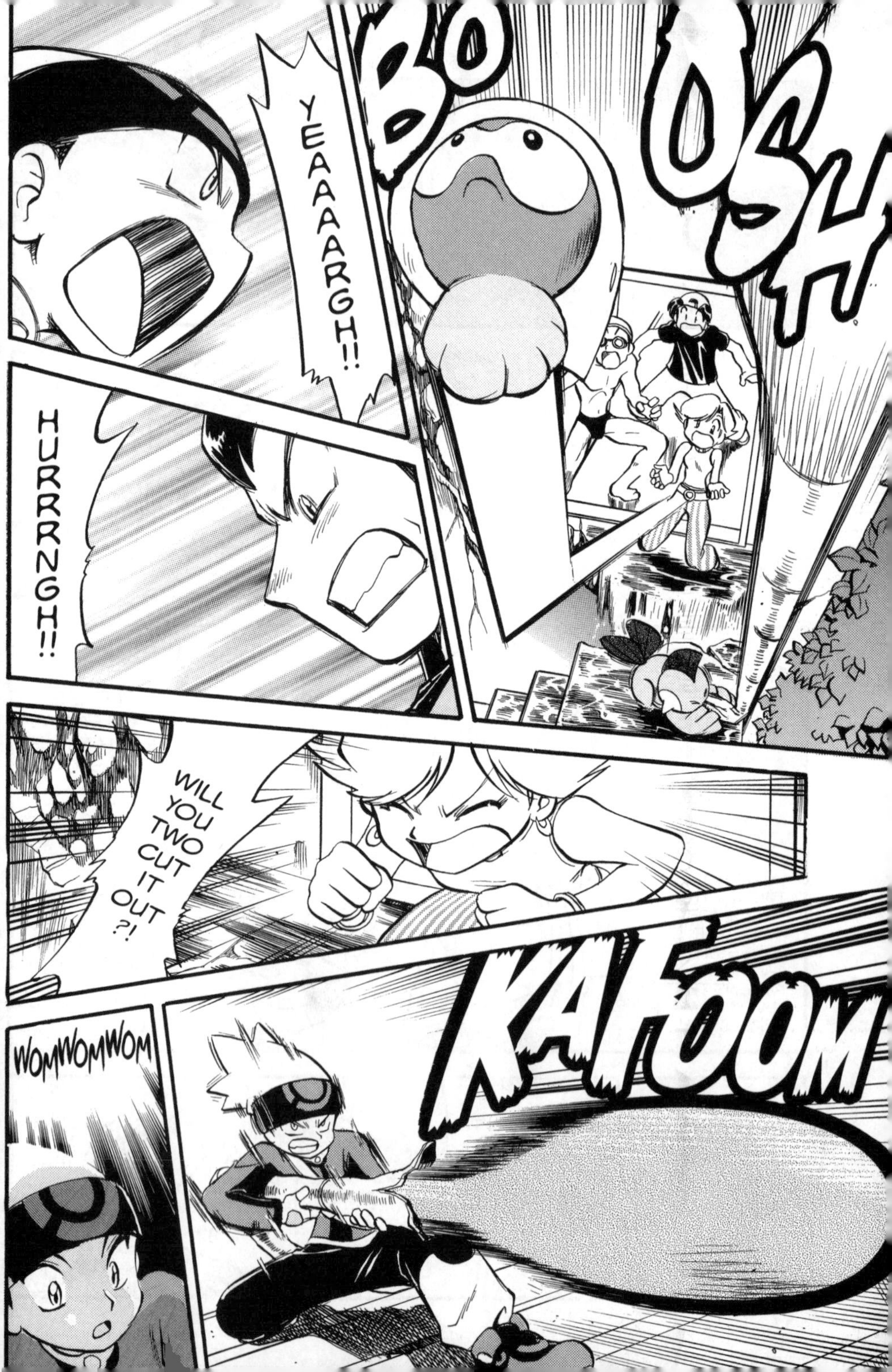
BOOSH
YEAAAAARGH!!
HURRRNGH!!
WILL YOU TWO CUT IT OUT?!
KAFOOM
WOMWOMWOM

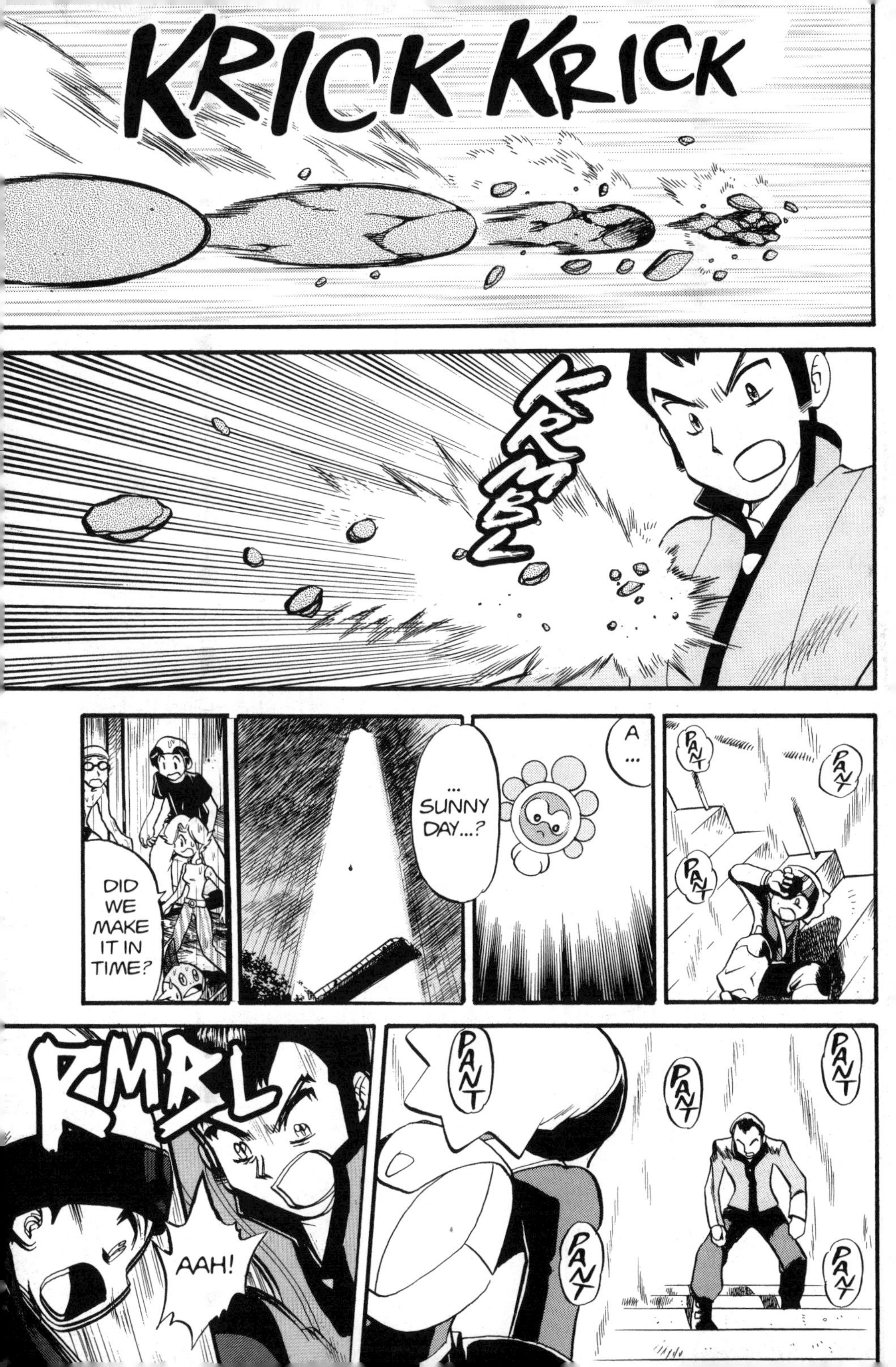
KRICK KRICK
KRMBL
PANT
PANT
PANT
A ...
... SUNNY DAY...?
DID WE MAKE IT IN TIME?
PANT
PANT
PANT
PANT
PANT
RMBL
AAH!

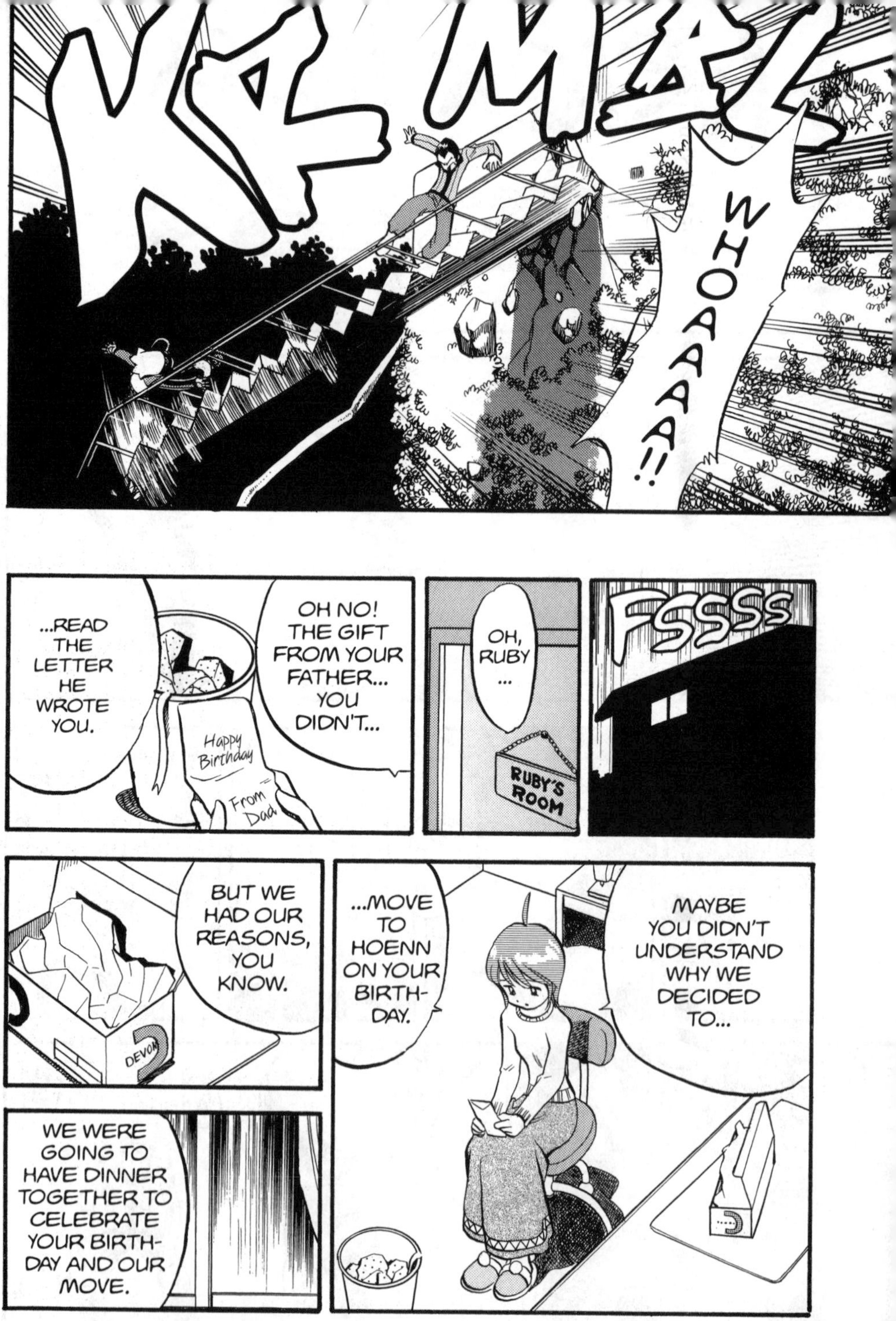
WHOAAAAA!!
FSSSS
OH, RUBY...
RUBY'S ROOM
OH NO! THE GIFT FROM YOUR FATHER... YOU DIDN'T...
...READ THE LETTER HE WROTE YOU.
Happy Birthday
From Dad
MAYBE YOU DIDN'T UNDERSTAND WHY WE DECIDED TO...
...MOVE TO HOENN ON YOUR BIRTH-DAY.
BUT WE HAD OUR REASONS, YOU KNOW.
DEVON
WE WERE GOING TO HAVE DINNER TOGETHER TO CELEBRATE YOUR BIRTH-DAY AND OUR MOVE.

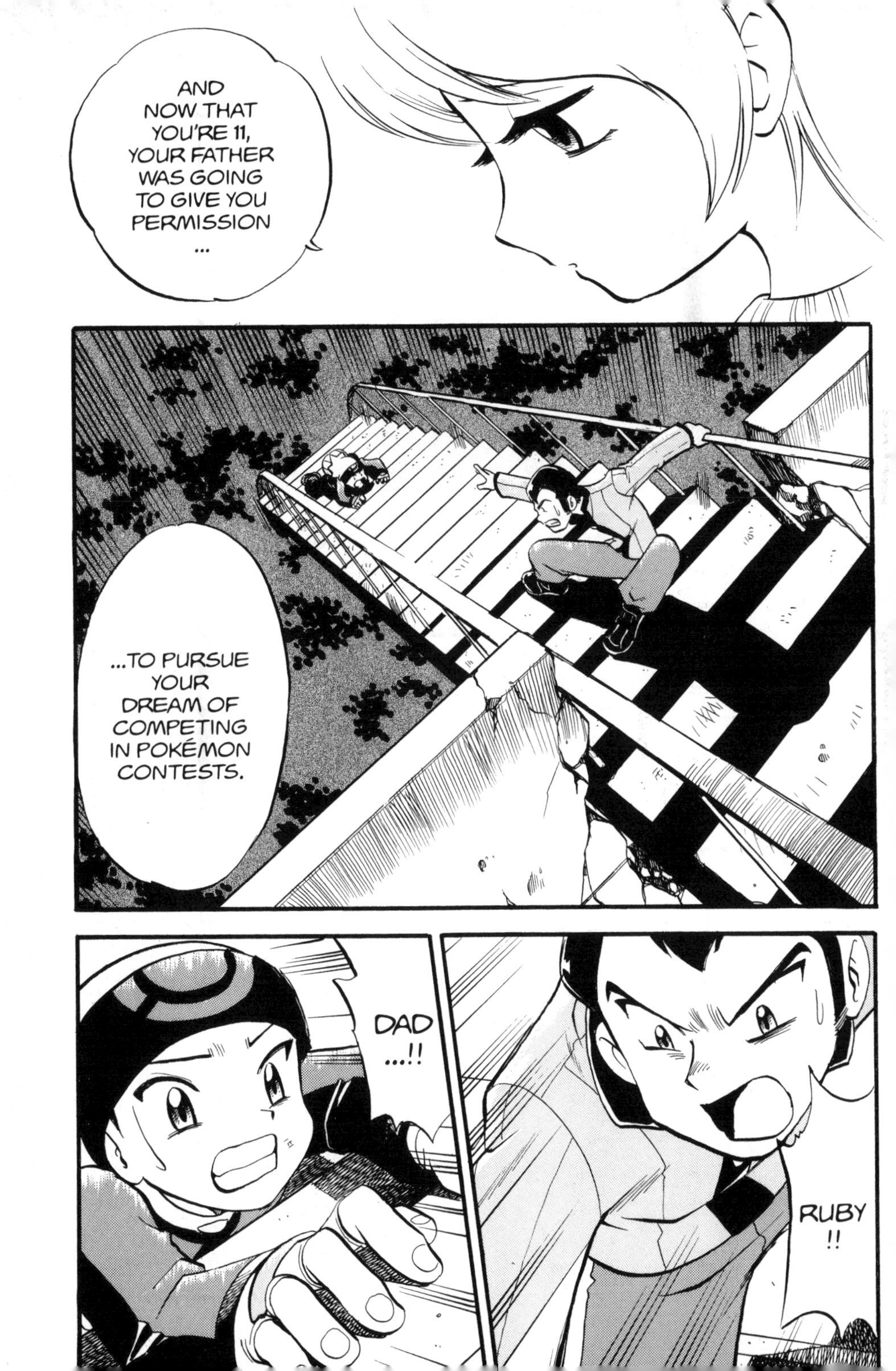
AND NOW THAT YOU'RE 11, YOUR FATHER WAS GOING TO GIVE YOU PERMISSION ...
...TO PURSUE YOUR DREAM OF COMPETING IN POKÉMON CONTESTS.
RUBY !!
DAD ...!!

● Adventure 211 ●

Hanging Around with Slaking, Part 3

POKÉMON™ ADVENTURES RUBY & SAPPHIRE The Fourth Chapter

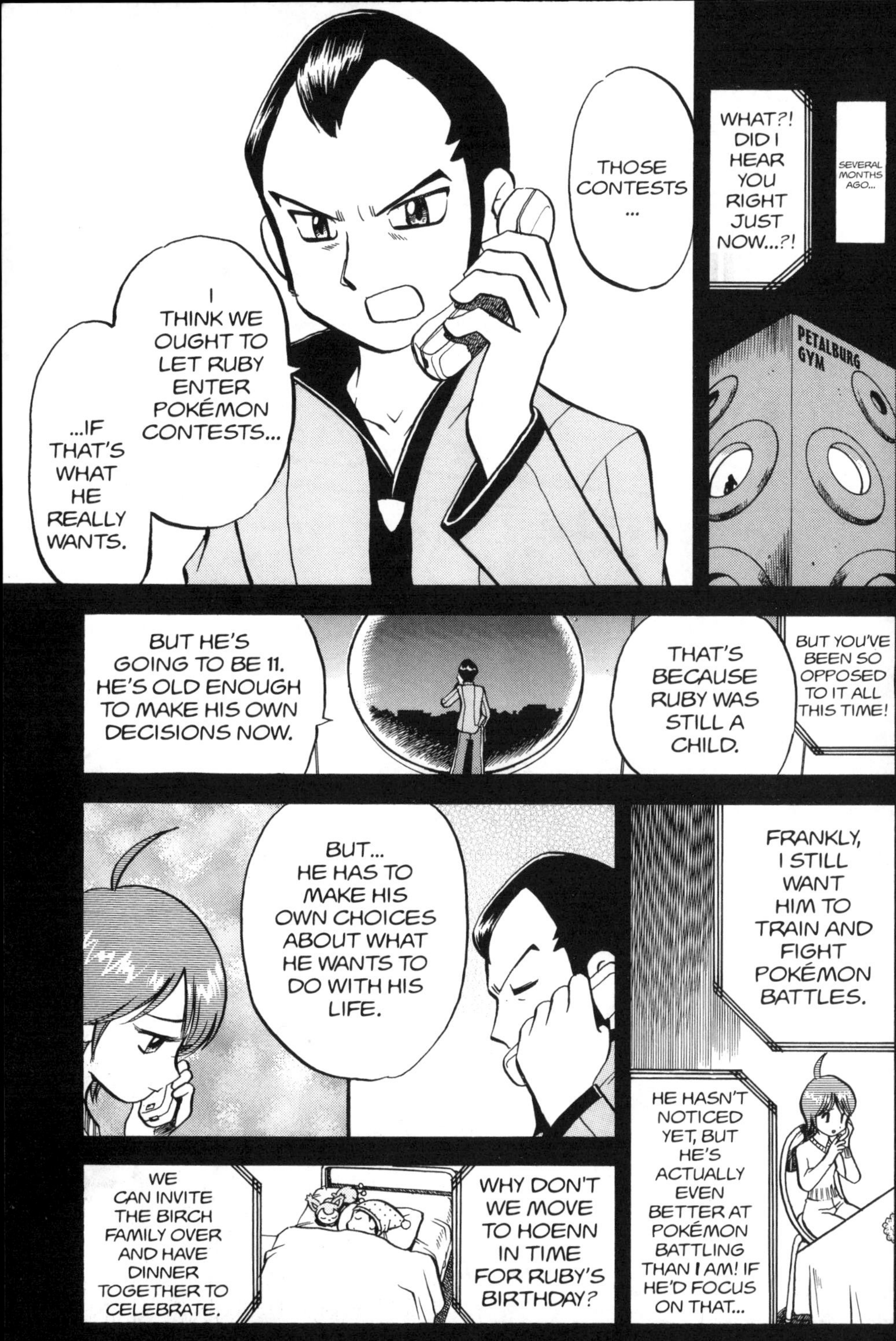
SEVERAL MONTHS AGO...
PETALBURG GYM
WHAT?! DID I HEAR YOU RIGHT JUST NOW...?!
THOSE CONTESTS ...
I THINK WE OUGHT TO LET RUBY ENTER POKÉMON CONTESTS...
...IF THAT'S WHAT HE REALLY WANTS.
BUT YOU'VE BEEN SO OPPOSED TO IT ALL THIS TIME!
THAT'S BECAUSE RUBY WAS STILL A CHILD.
BUT HE'S GOING TO BE 11. HE'S OLD ENOUGH TO MAKE HIS OWN DECISIONS NOW.
FRANKLY, I STILL WANT HIM TO TRAIN AND FIGHT POKÉMON BATTLES.
HE HASN'T NOTICED YET, BUT HE'S ACTUALLY EVEN BETTER AT POKÉMON BATTLING THAN I AM! IF HE'D FOCUS ON THAT...
BUT... HE HAS TO MAKE HIS OWN CHOICES ABOUT WHAT HE WANTS TO DO WITH HIS LIFE.
WHY DON'T WE MOVE TO HOENN IN TIME FOR RUBY'S BIRTHDAY?
WE CAN INVITE THE BIRCH FAMILY OVER AND HAVE DINNER TOGETHER TO CELEBRATE.

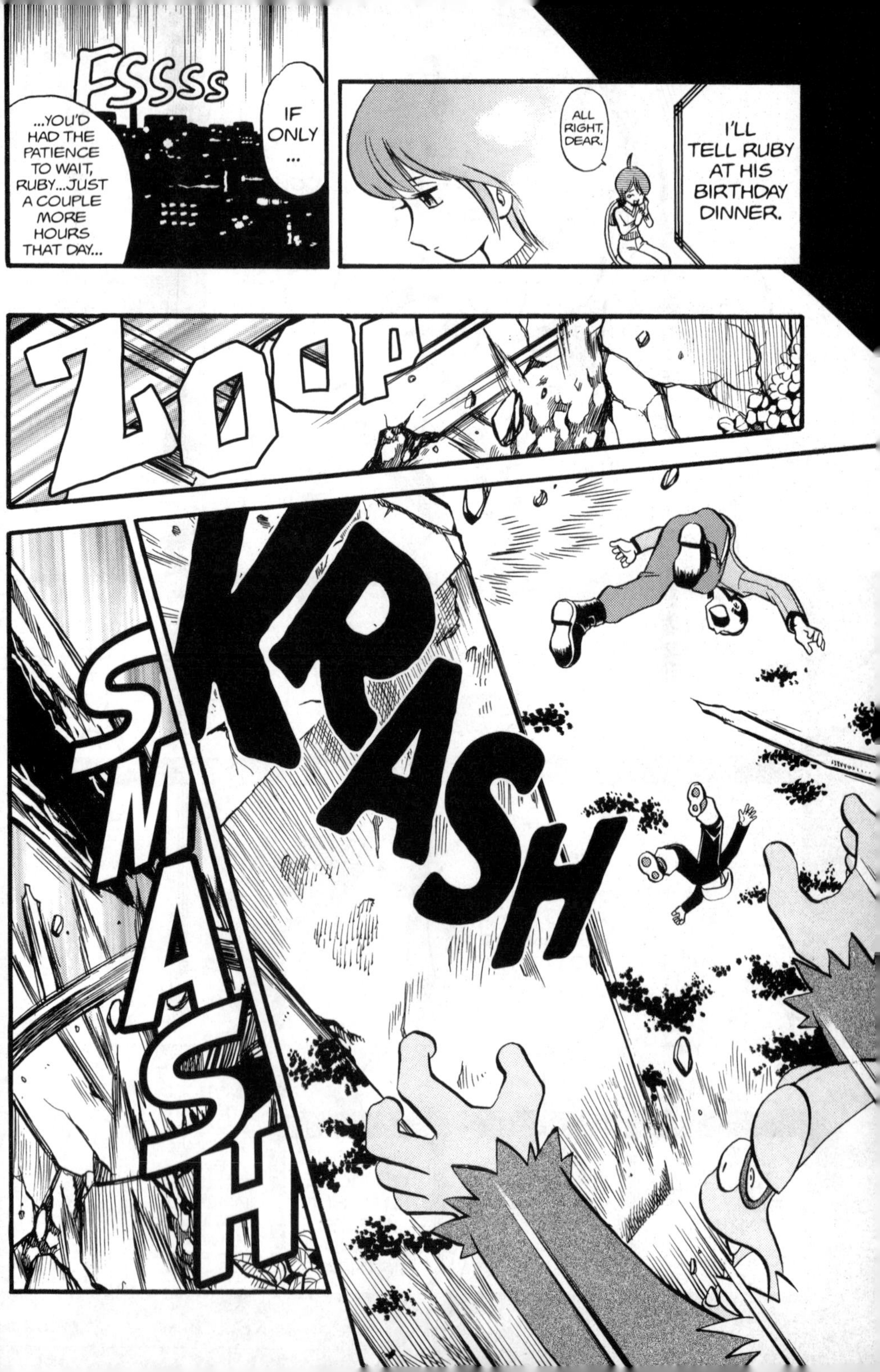
I'LL TELL RUBY AT HIS BIRTHDAY DINNER.
ALL RIGHT, DEAR.
FSSSS
IF ONLY...
...YOU'D HAD THE PATIENCE TO WAIT, RUBY...JUST A COUPLE MORE HOURS THAT DAY...
ZOOOP
KRASH
SMASH

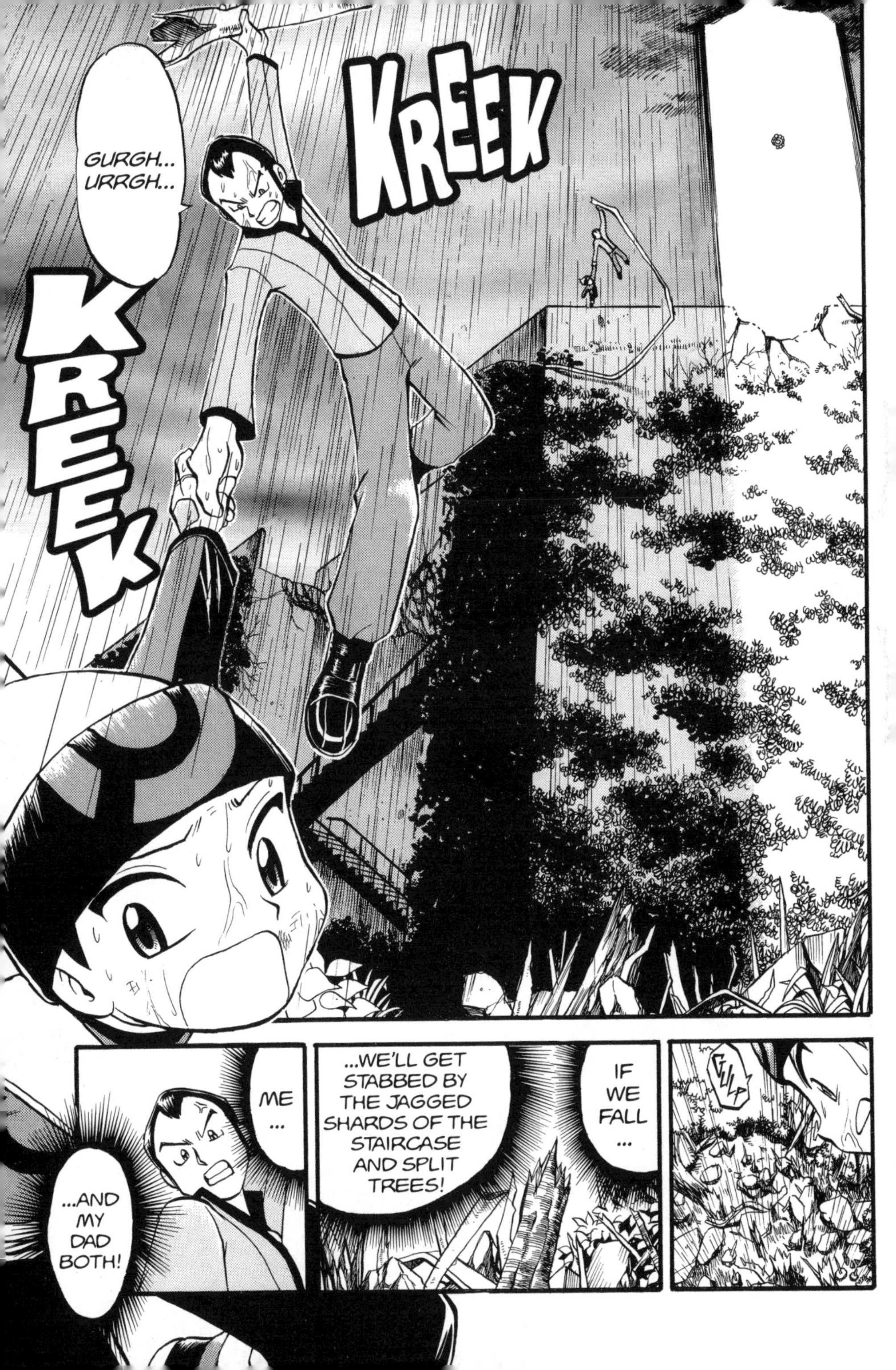
KREEK
GURGH... URRGH...
KREEK
GULP
IF WE FALL ...
...WE'LL GET STABBED BY THE JAGGED SHARDS OF THE STAIRCASE AND SPLIT TREES!
ME ...
...AND MY DAD BOTH!

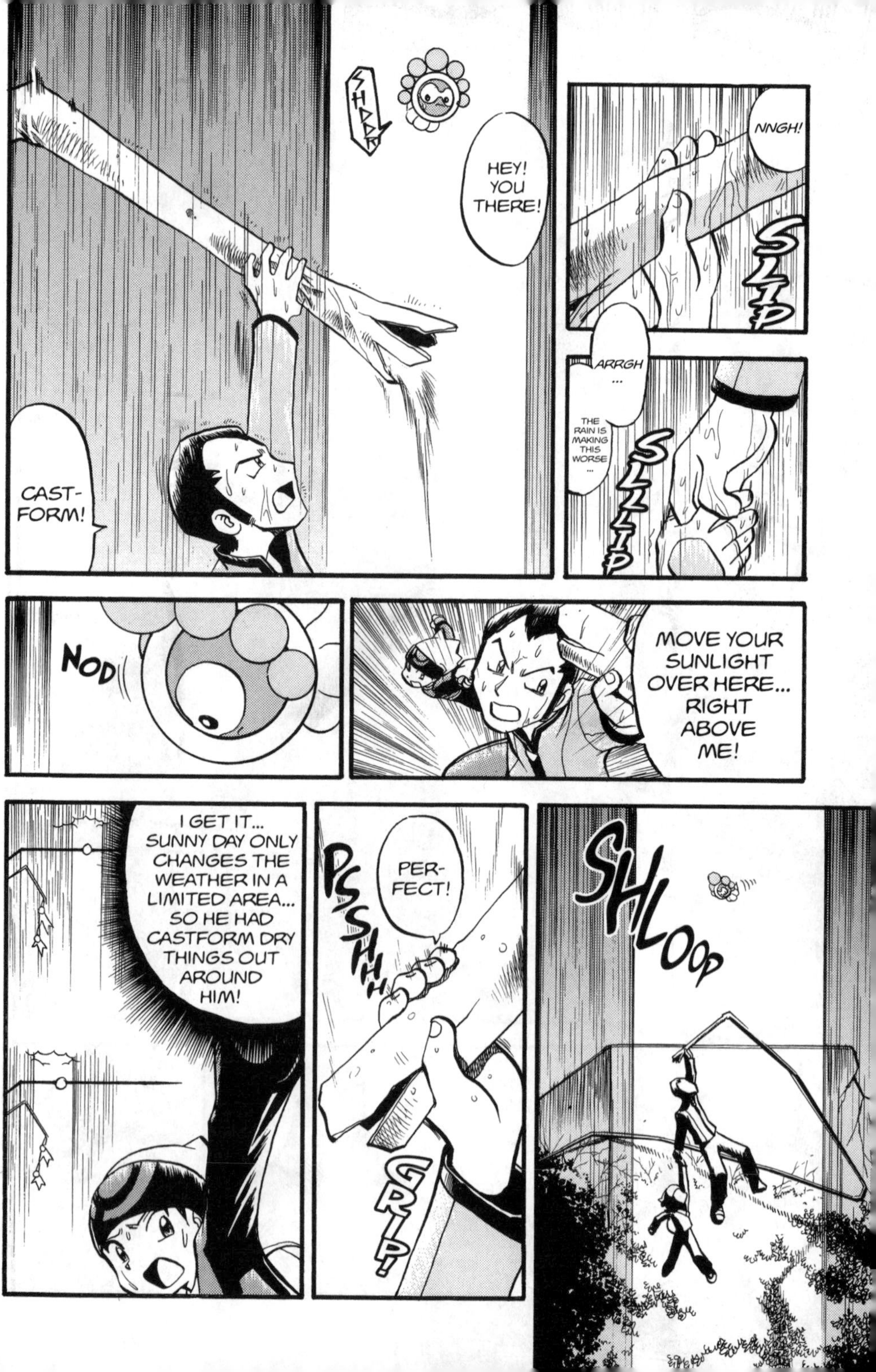

NNGH!
SLIP
ARRGH...
THE RAIN IS MAKING THIS WORSE...
SLLLIP
HEY! YOU THERE!
SHDDR
CAST-FORM!
MOVE YOUR SUNLIGHT OVER HERE... RIGHT ABOVE ME!
NOD
SHLOOP
PER-FECT!
PSSHHH
GRIP!
I GET IT... SUNNY DAY ONLY CHANGES THE WEATHER IN A LIMITED AREA... SO HE HAD CASTFORM DRY THINGS OUT AROUND HIM!

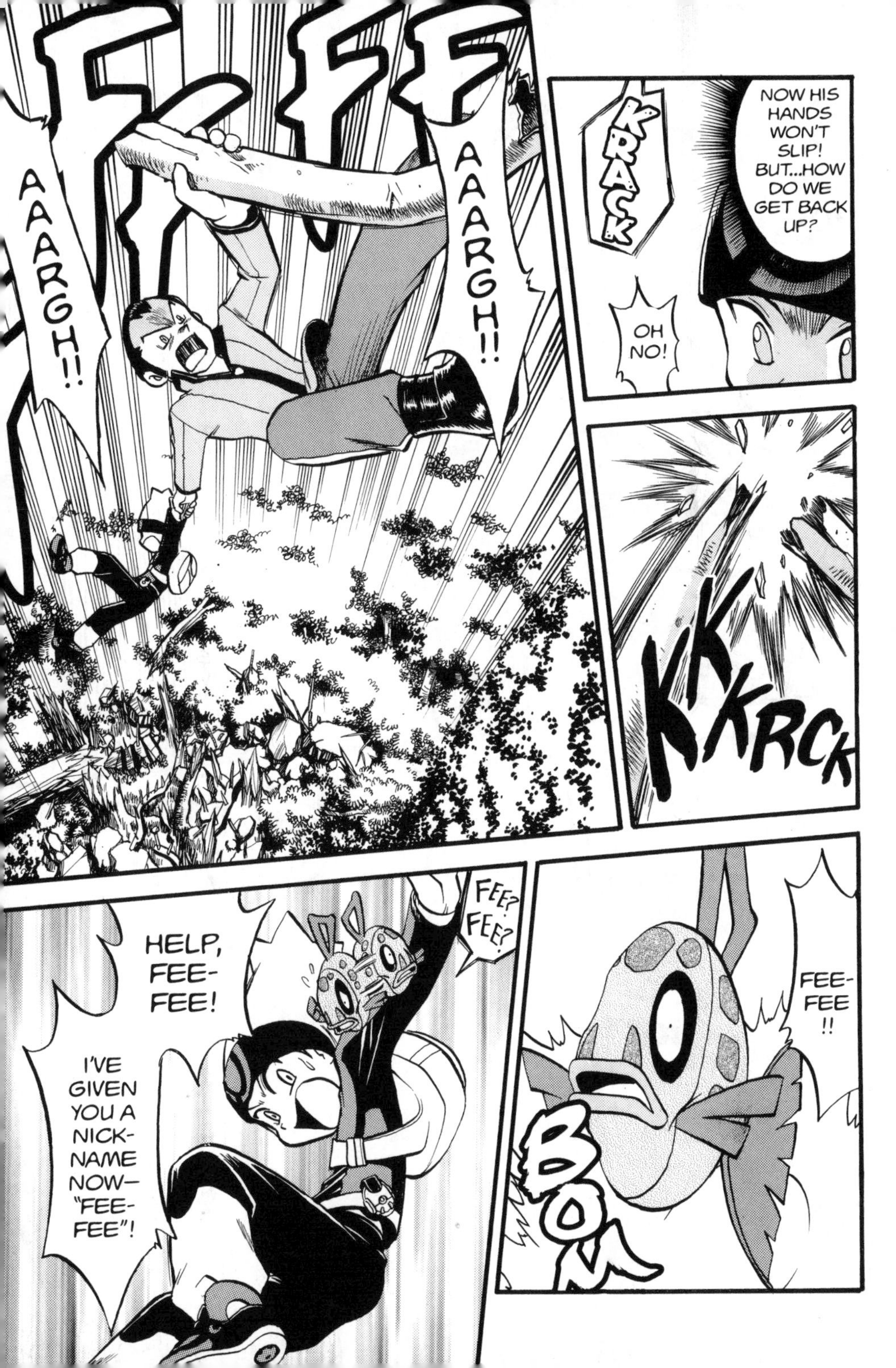

NOW HIS HANDS WON'T SLIP! BUT...HOW DO WE GET BACK UP?
KRACK
OH NO!
KKKRCK
FFFF
AAARGH!!
AAARGH!!
FEE-FEE !!
BO
FEE? FEE?
HELP, FEE-FEE!
I'VE GIVEN YOU A NICK-NAME NOW—"FEE-FEE"!

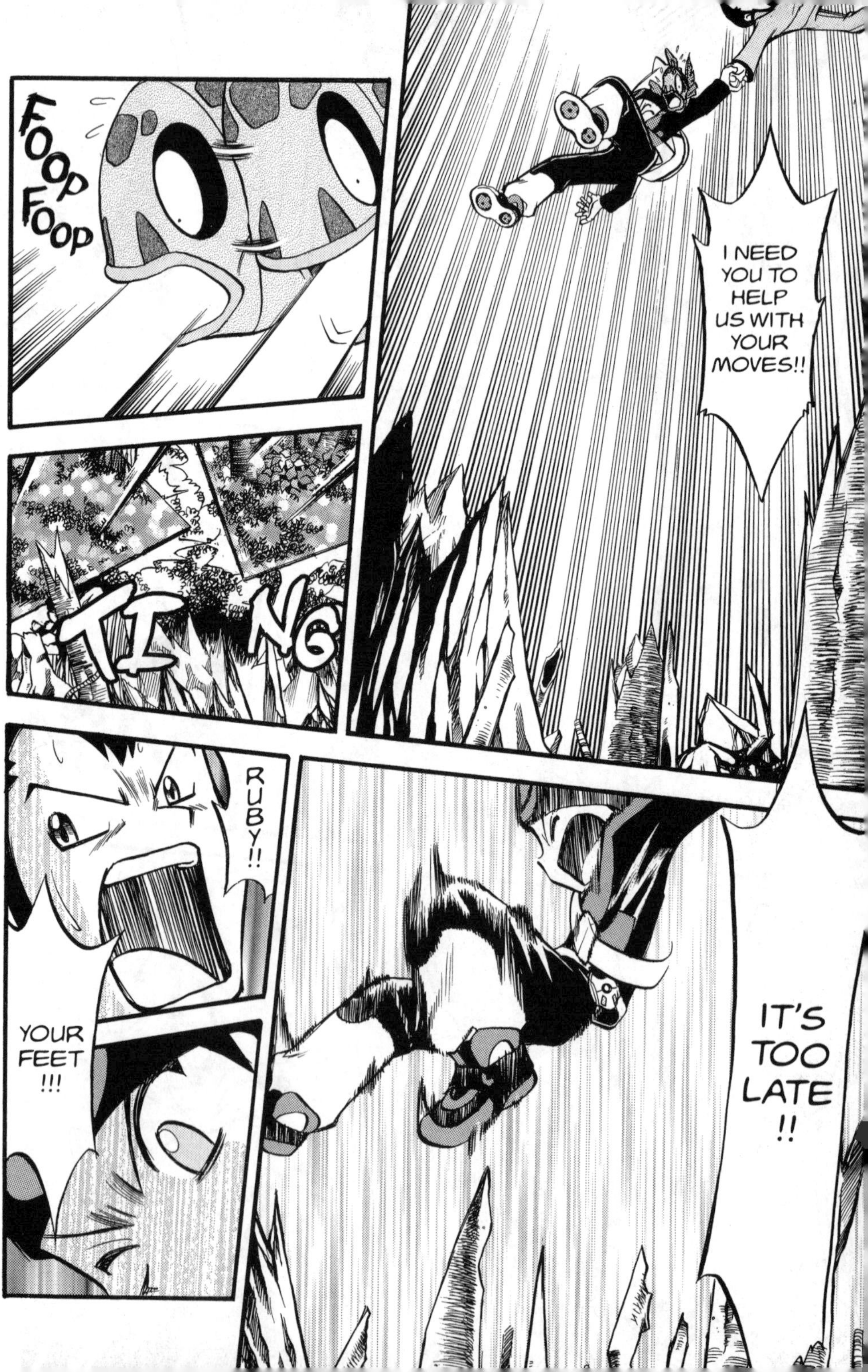
I NEED YOU TO HELP US WITH YOUR MOVES!!
FOOP FOOP
TING
IT'S TOO LATE!!
RUBY!!
YOUR FEET!!!

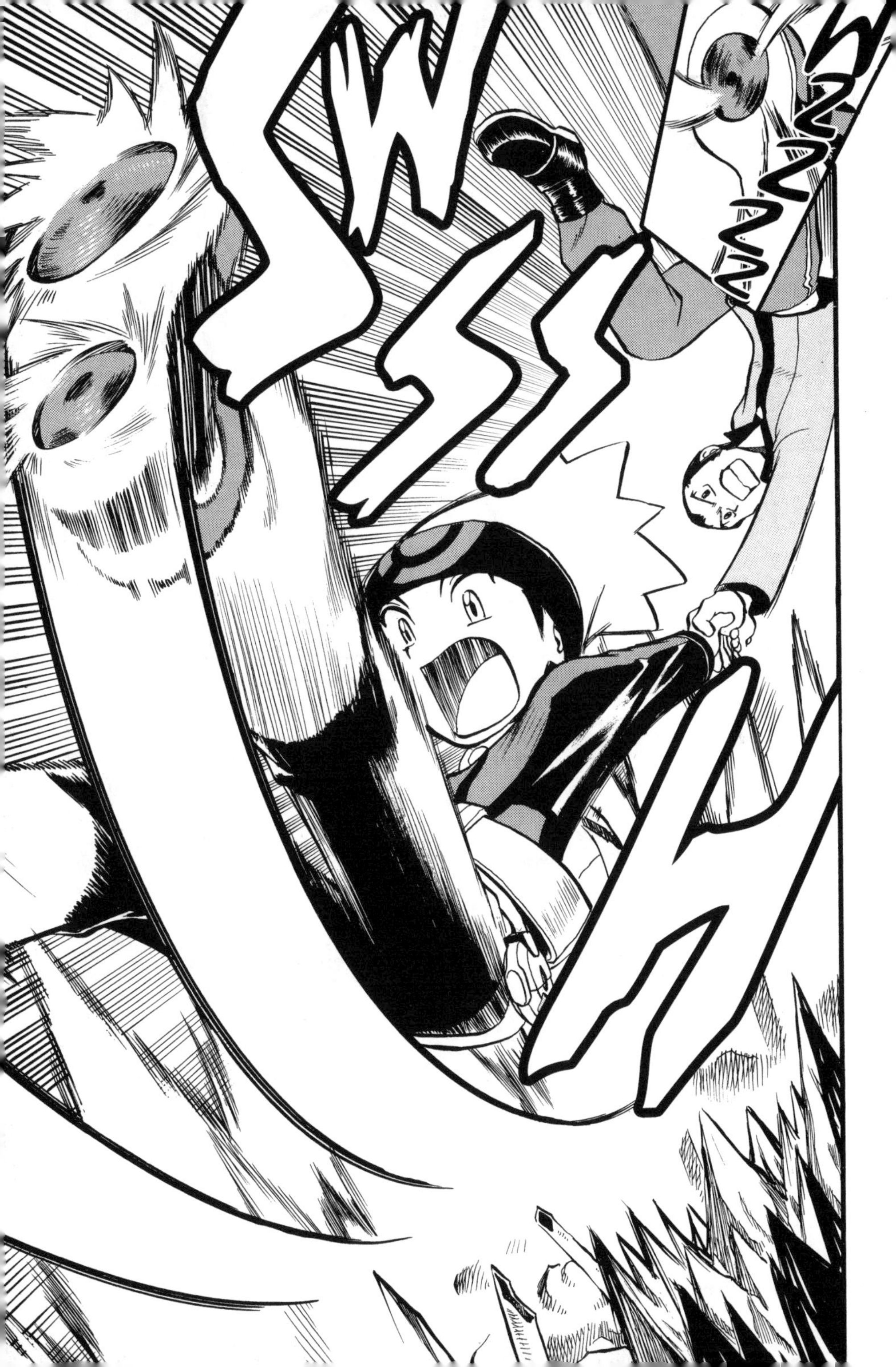

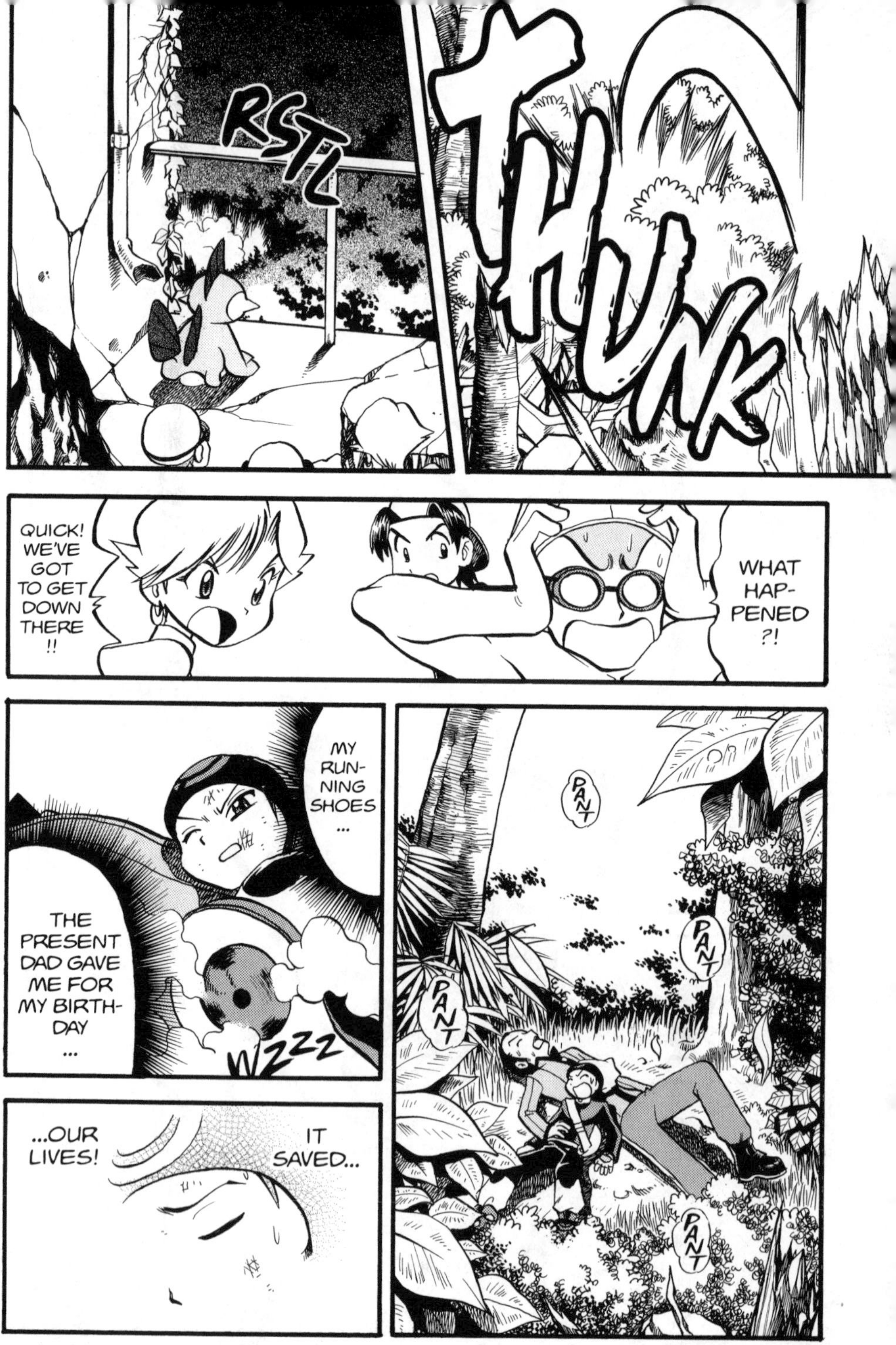
THUNK
RSTL
WHAT HAP-PENED ?!
QUICK! WE'VE GOT TO GET DOWN THERE !!
PANT
PANT
PANT
PANT
MY RUN-NING SHOES ...
THE PRESENT DAD GAVE ME FOR MY BIRTH-DAY ...
WZZZ
IT SAVED...
...OUR LIVES!

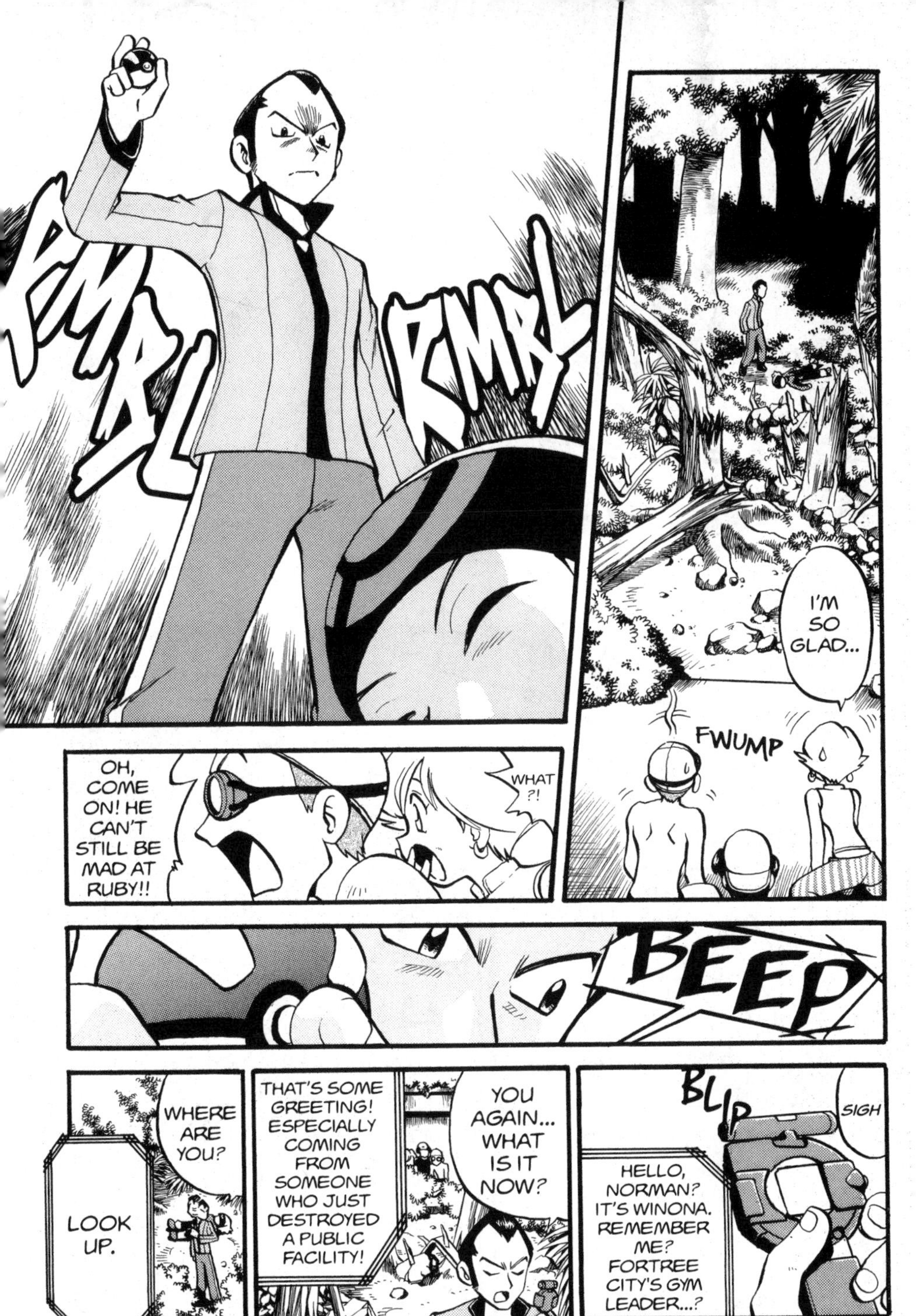
I'M SO GLAD...
FWUMP
RMRL
RMBL
WHAT?!
OH, COME ON! HE CAN'T STILL BE MAD AT RUBY!!
BEEP
SIGH
BLIP
HELLO, NORMAN? IT'S WINONA. REMEMBER ME? FORTREE CITY'S GYM LEADER...?
YOU AGAIN... WHAT IS IT NOW?
THAT'S SOME GREETING! ESPECIALLY COMING FROM SOMEONE WHO JUST DESTROYED A PUBLIC FACILITY!
WHERE ARE YOU?
LOOK UP.

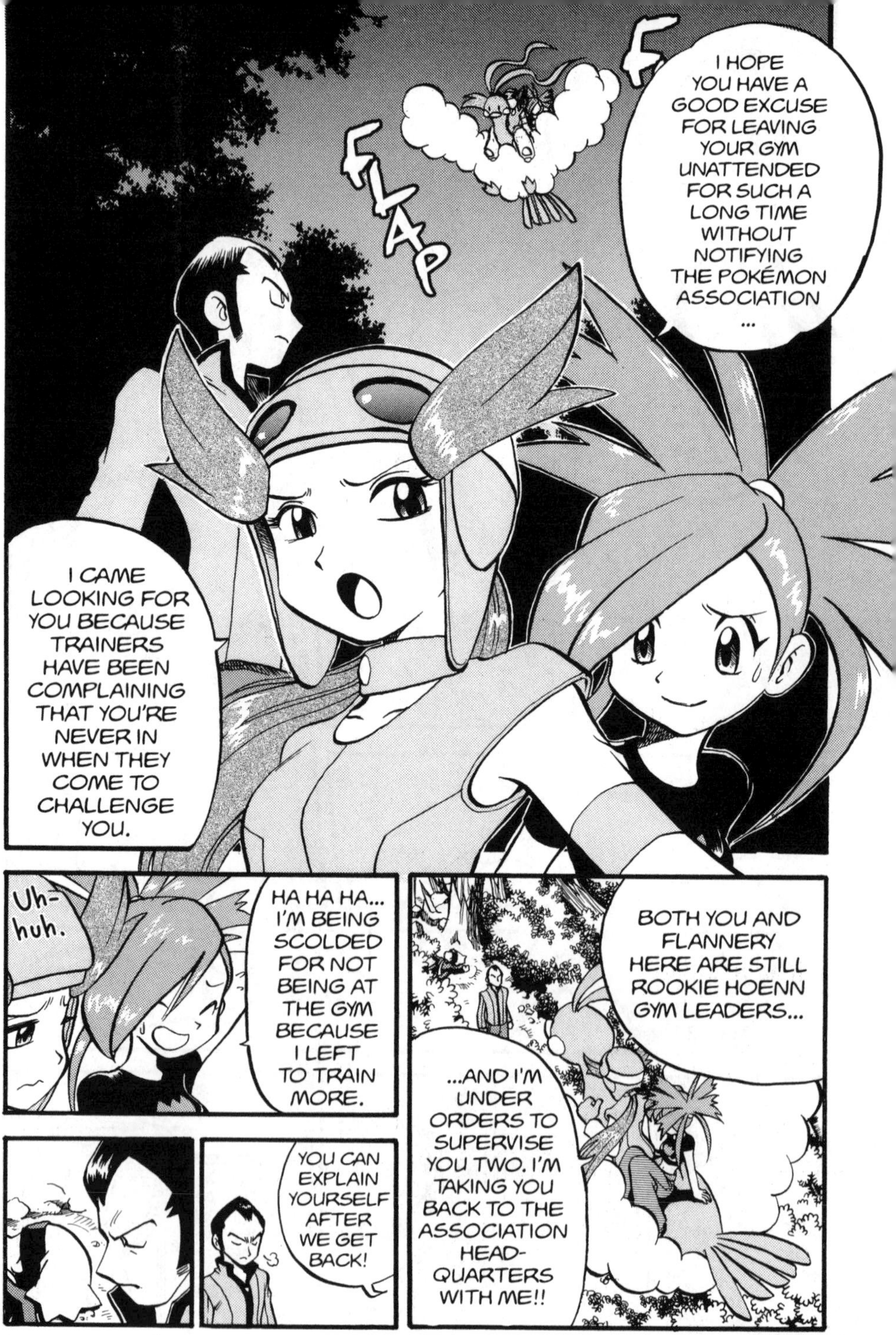
I HOPE YOU HAVE A GOOD EXCUSE FOR LEAVING YOUR GYM UNATTENDED FOR SUCH A LONG TIME WITHOUT NOTIFYING THE POKÉMON ASSOCIATION ...
FLAP
I CAME LOOKING FOR YOU BECAUSE TRAINERS HAVE BEEN COMPLAINING THAT YOU'RE NEVER IN WHEN THEY COME TO CHALLENGE YOU.
BOTH YOU AND FLANNERY HERE ARE STILL ROOKIE HOENN GYM LEADERS...
...AND I'M UNDER ORDERS TO SUPERVISE YOU TWO. I'M TAKING YOU BACK TO THE ASSOCIATION HEAD-QUARTERS WITH ME!!
HA HA HA... I'M BEING SCOLDED FOR NOT BEING AT THE GYM BECAUSE I LEFT TO TRAIN MORE.
Uh-huh.
YOU CAN EXPLAIN YOURSELF AFTER WE GET BACK!

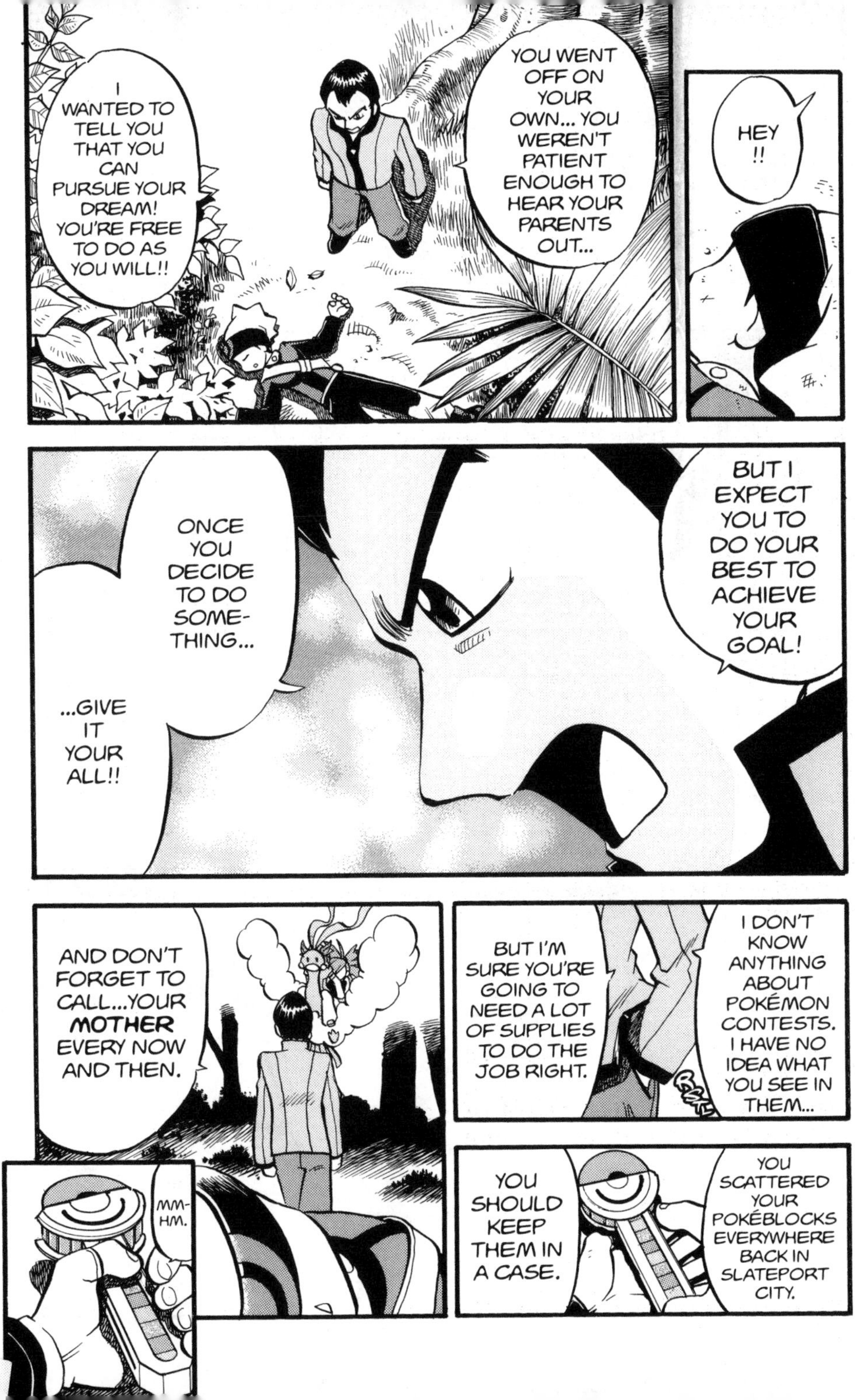
HEY !!
YOU WENT OFF ON YOUR OWN... YOU WEREN'T PATIENT ENOUGH TO HEAR YOUR PARENTS OUT...
I WANTED TO TELL YOU THAT YOU CAN PURSUE YOUR DREAM! YOU'RE FREE TO DO AS YOU WILL!!
BUT I EXPECT YOU TO DO YOUR BEST TO ACHIEVE YOUR GOAL!
ONCE YOU DECIDE TO DO SOME-THING...
...GIVE IT YOUR ALL!!
I DON'T KNOW ANYTHING ABOUT POKÉMON CONTESTS. I HAVE NO IDEA WHAT YOU SEE IN THEM...
BUT I'M SURE YOU'RE GOING TO NEED A LOT OF SUPPLIES TO DO THE JOB RIGHT.
YOU SCATTERED YOUR POKÉBLOCKS EVERYWHERE BACK IN SLATEPORT CITY.
YOU SHOULD KEEP THEM IN A CASE.
AND DON'T FORGET TO CALL...YOUR **MOTHER** EVERY NOW AND THEN.
MM-HM.

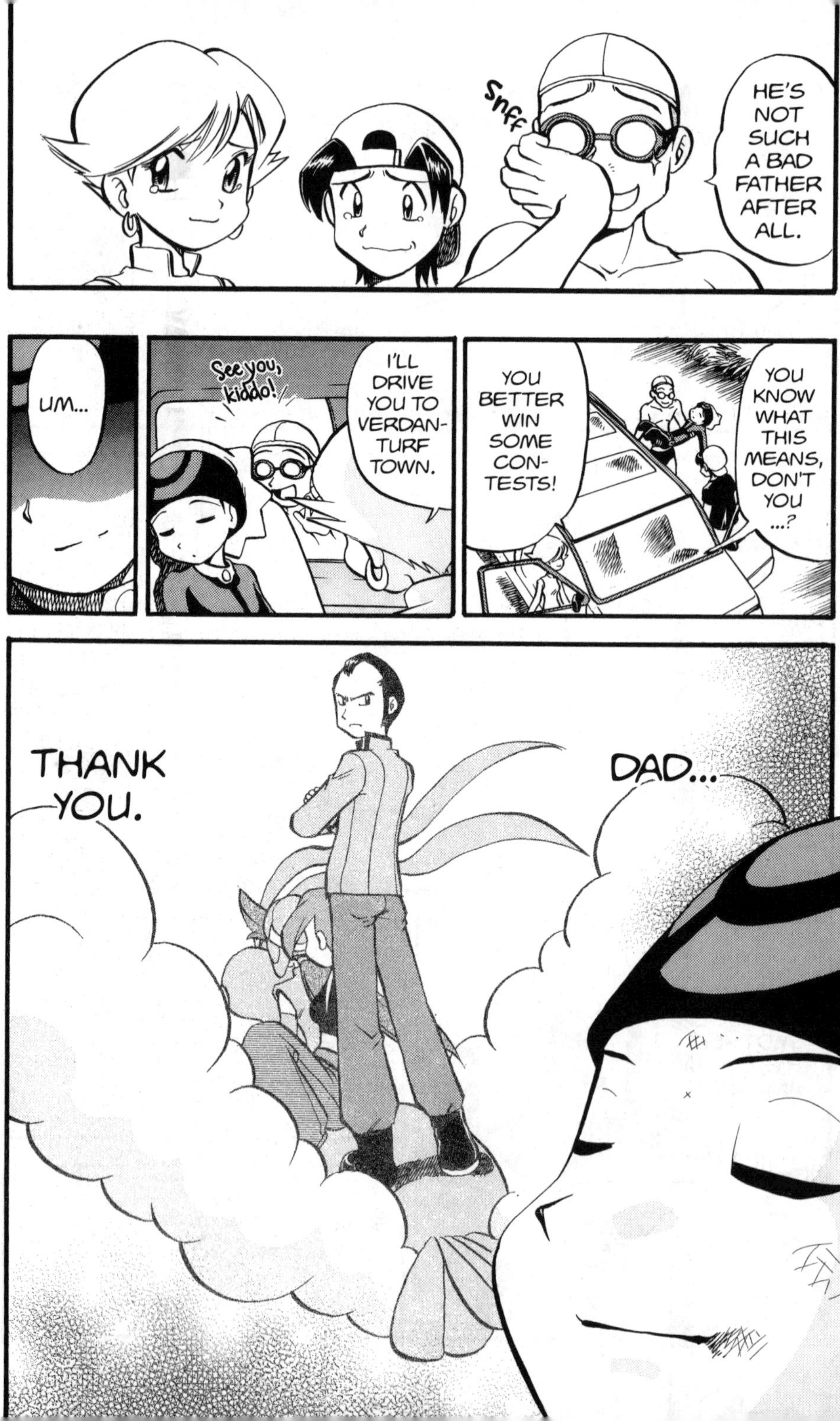
HE'S NOT SUCH A BAD FATHER AFTER ALL.
Snff
YOU KNOW WHAT THIS MEANS, DON'T YOU ...?
YOU BETTER WIN SOME CON-TESTS!
I'LL DRIVE YOU TO VERDAN-TURF TOWN.
See you, kiddo!
UM...
DAD...
THANK YOU.

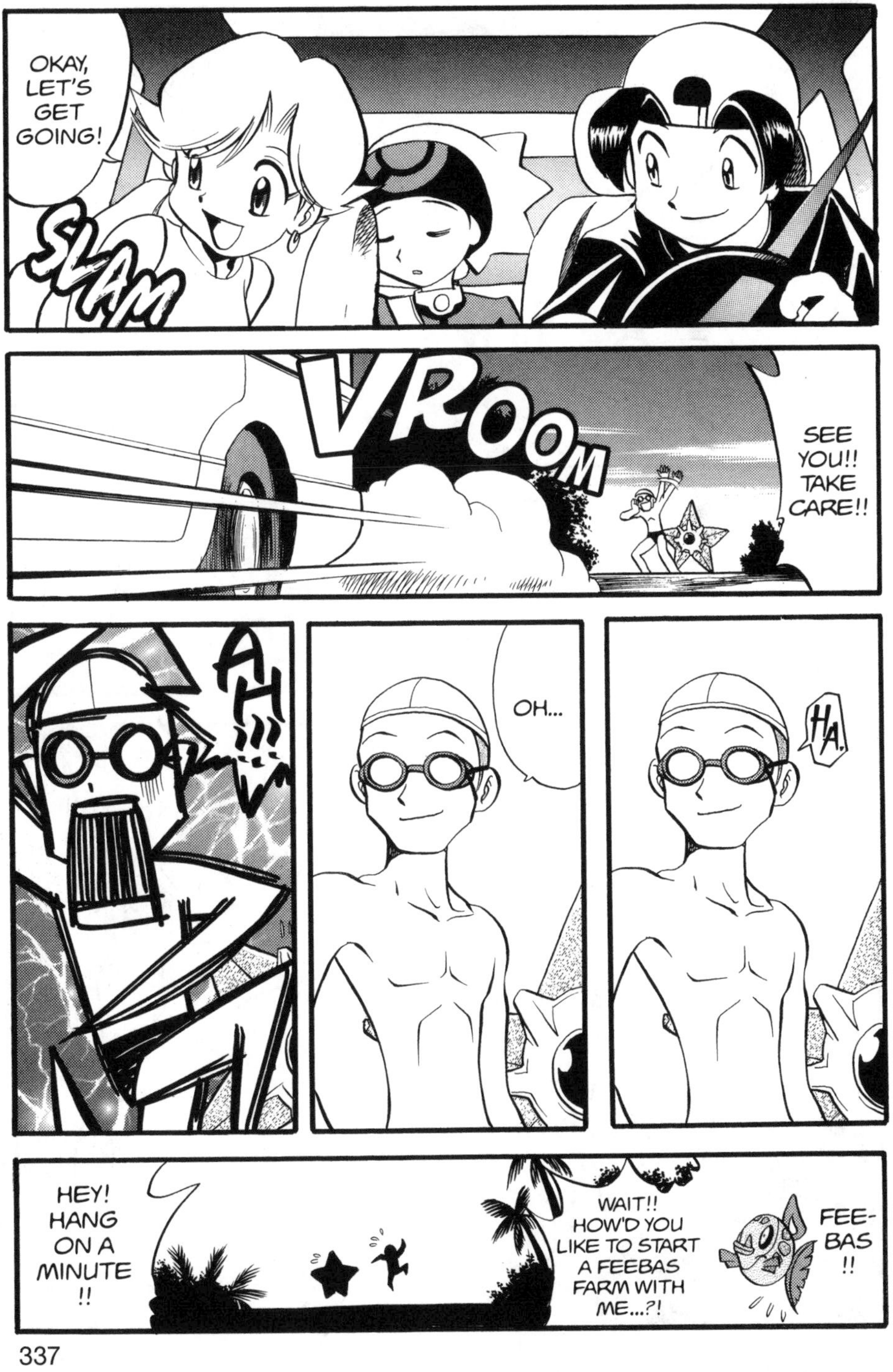

OKAY, LET'S GET GOING!
SLAM
SEE YOU!! TAKE CARE!!
VROOM
HA.
OH...
AH!!!
FEE-BAS!!
WAIT!! HOW'D YOU LIKE TO START A FEEBAS FARM WITH ME...?!
HEY! HANG ON A MINUTE!!

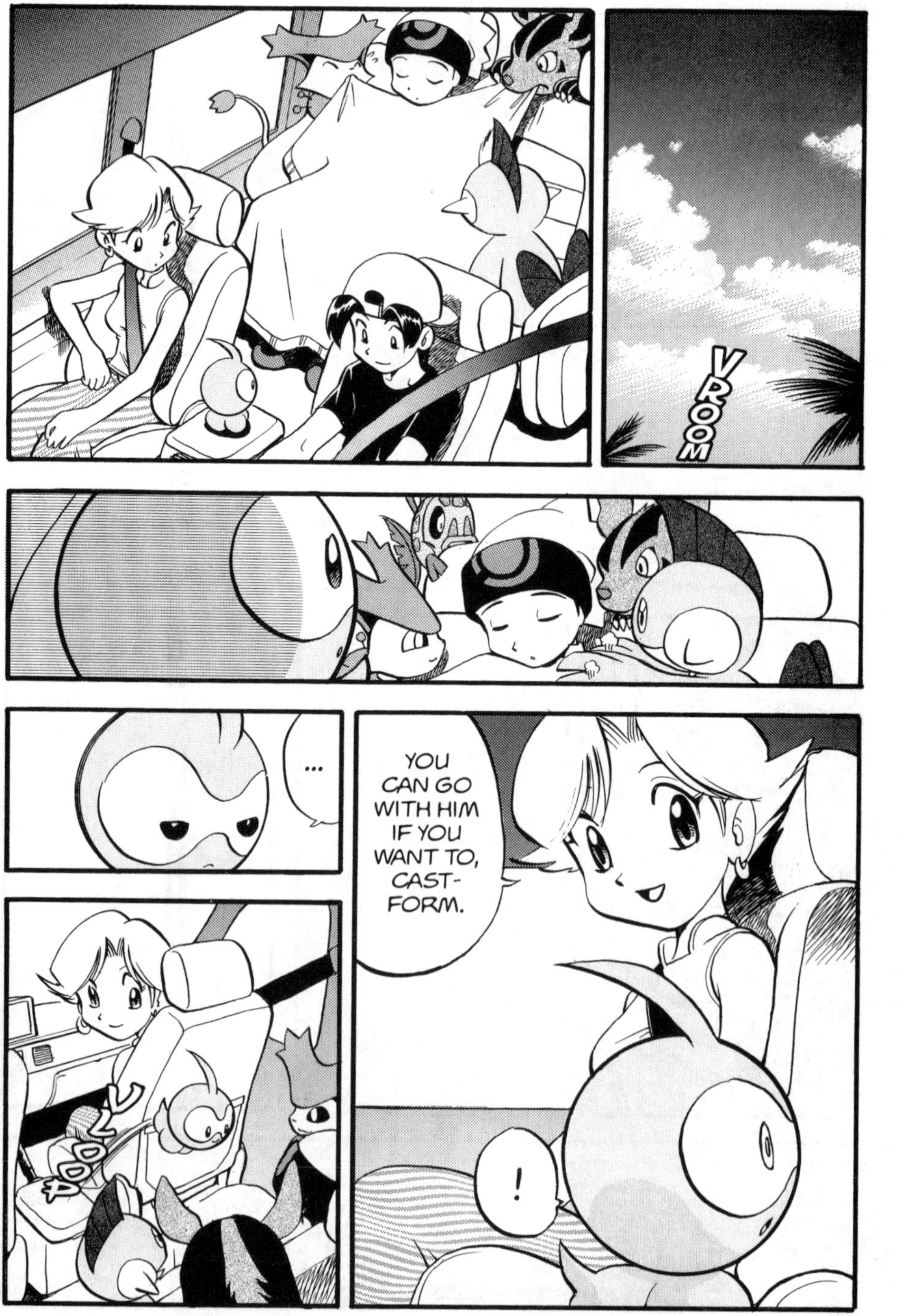

VROOM
YOU CAN GO WITH HIM IF YOU WANT TO, CAST-FORM.
!
...

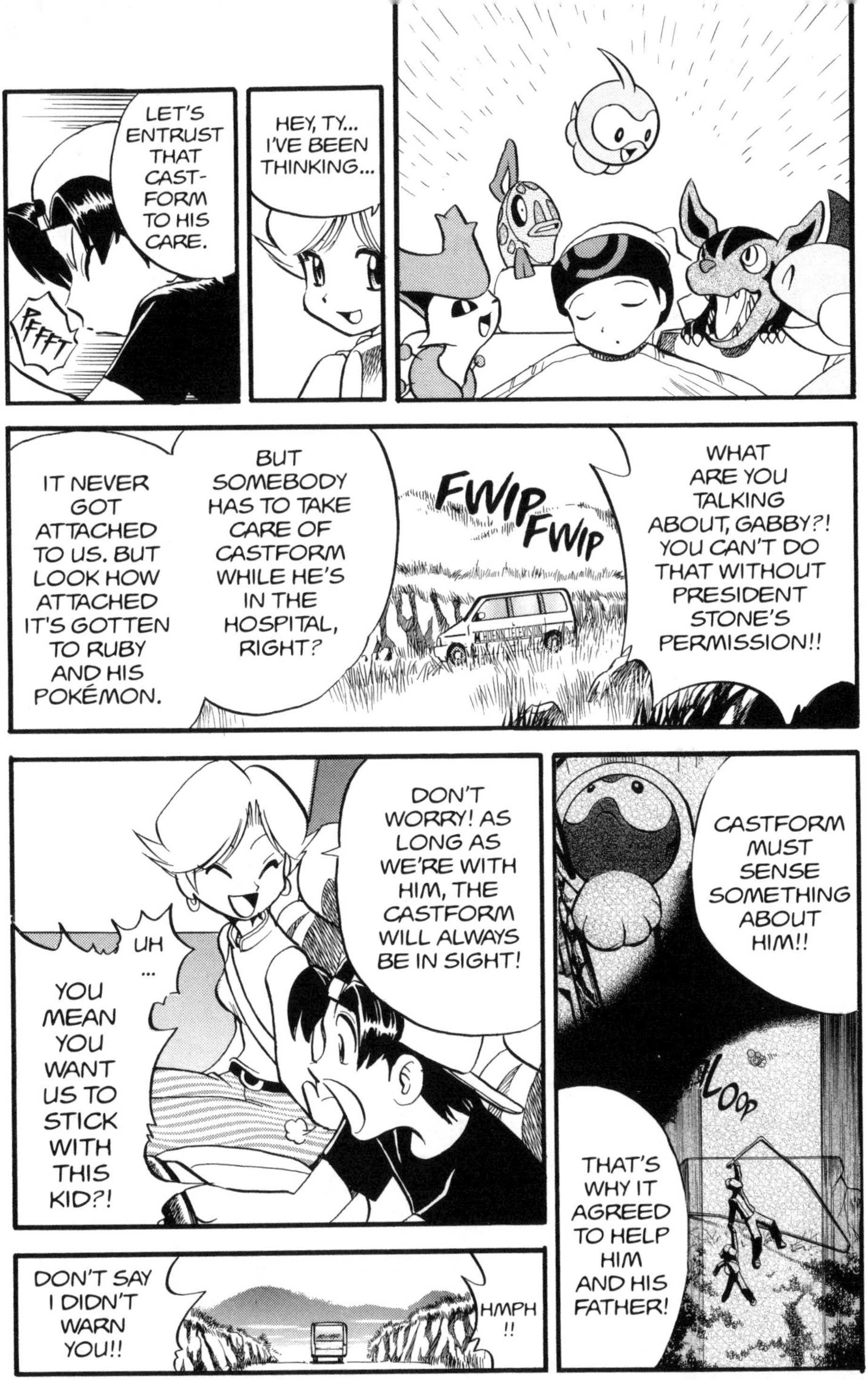
HEY, TY... I'VE BEEN THINKING...
LET'S ENTRUST THAT CASTFORM TO HIS CARE.
PFFFT
WHAT ARE YOU TALKING ABOUT, GABBY?! YOU CAN'T DO THAT WITHOUT PRESIDENT STONE'S PERMISSION!!
FWIP FWIP
BUT SOMEBODY HAS TO TAKE CARE OF CASTFORM WHILE HE'S IN THE HOSPITAL, RIGHT?
IT NEVER GOT ATTACHED TO US. BUT LOOK HOW ATTACHED IT'S GOTTEN TO RUBY AND HIS POKéMON.
CASTFORM MUST SENSE SOMETHING ABOUT HIM!!
LOOP
THAT'S WHY IT AGREED TO HELP HIM AND HIS FATHER!
DON'T WORRY! AS LONG AS WE'RE WITH HIM, THE CASTFORM WILL ALWAYS BE IN SIGHT!
UH ...
YOU MEAN YOU WANT US TO STICK WITH THIS KID?!
HMPH !!
DON'T SAY I DIDN'T WARN YOU!!

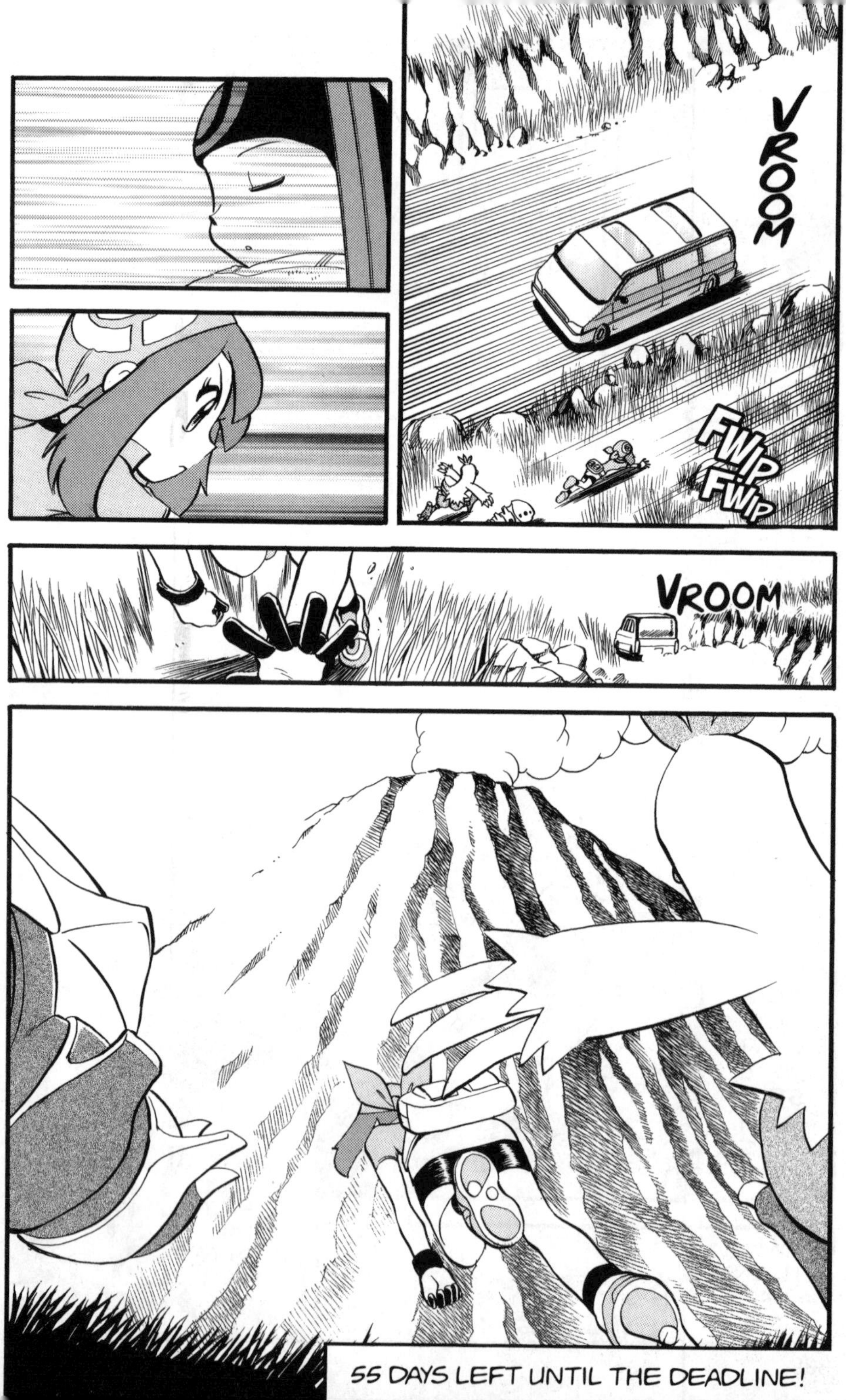
VROOM
FWIP FWIP
VROOM
55 DAYS LEFT UNTIL THE DEADLINE!

ADVENTURE MAP

SAPPHIRE

RUBY

Route 109

SAPPHIRE	RUBY
Slateport City	Slateport City
Route 110	
Mauville City	Route 118
New Mauville	Route 119
Route 111	Weather Institute

SAPPHIRE

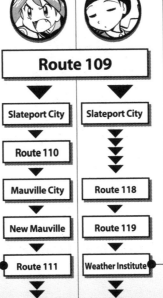

CHIC
Combusken ♀
Lv27

RONO
Lairon ♂
Lv37

LORRY
Wailord ♂
Lv43

PHADO
Donphan ♂
Lv41

RUBY

MUMU
Marshtomp ♂

NANA
Mightyena ♀

KIKI
Delcatty ♀

FEEFEE
Feebas ♀

CASTFORM
Castform ♀

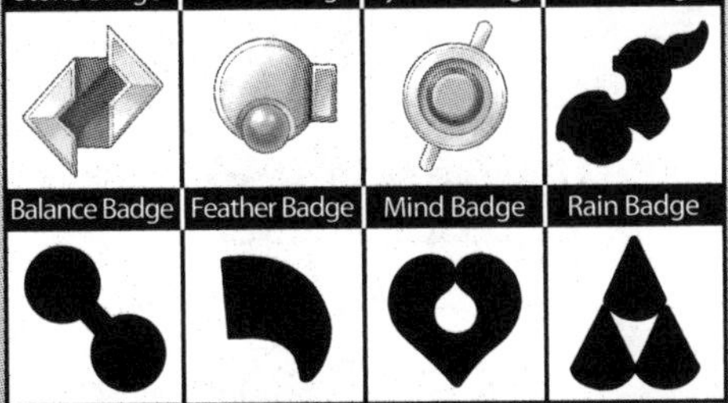

Stone Badge	Knuckle Badge	Dynamo Badge	Heat Badge
Balance Badge	Feather Badge	Mind Badge	Rain Badge

	Coolness	Beauty	Cuteness	Cleverness	Toughness
Normal					
Super					
Hyper					
Master					

● Adventure 212 ●
Bubble, Bubble Toil and Azumarill, Part 1

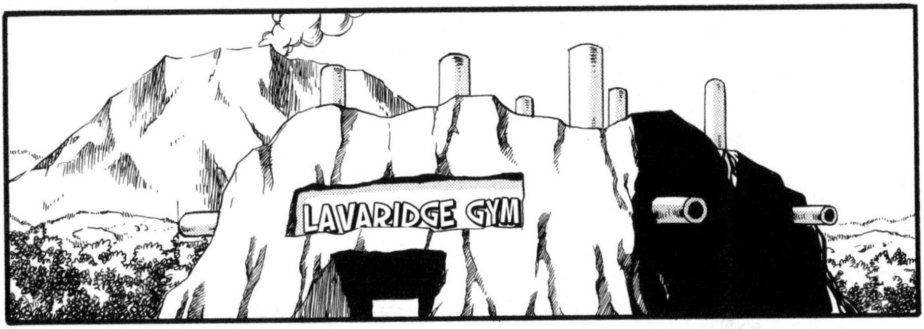
LAVARIDGE GYM

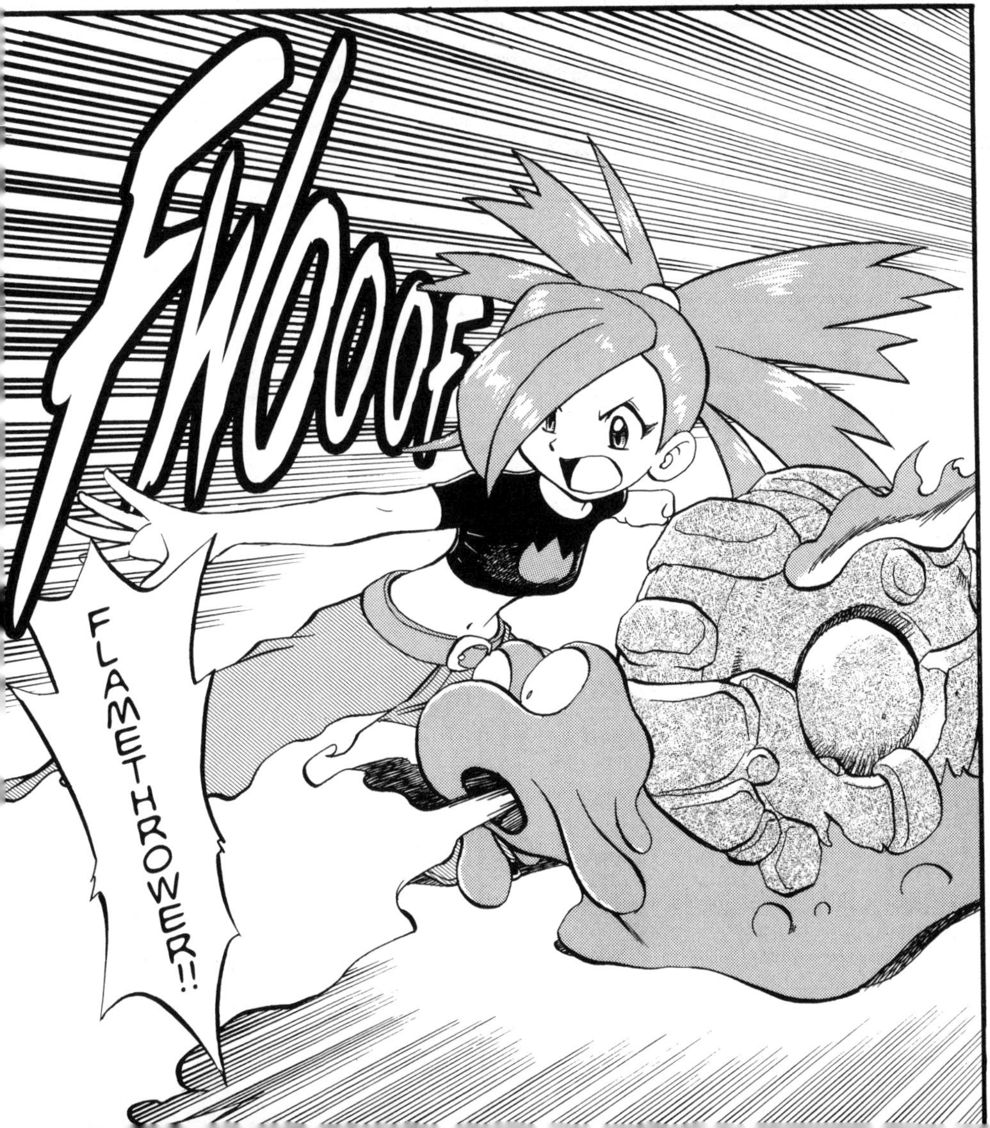
FWOOOF
FLAMETHROWER!!

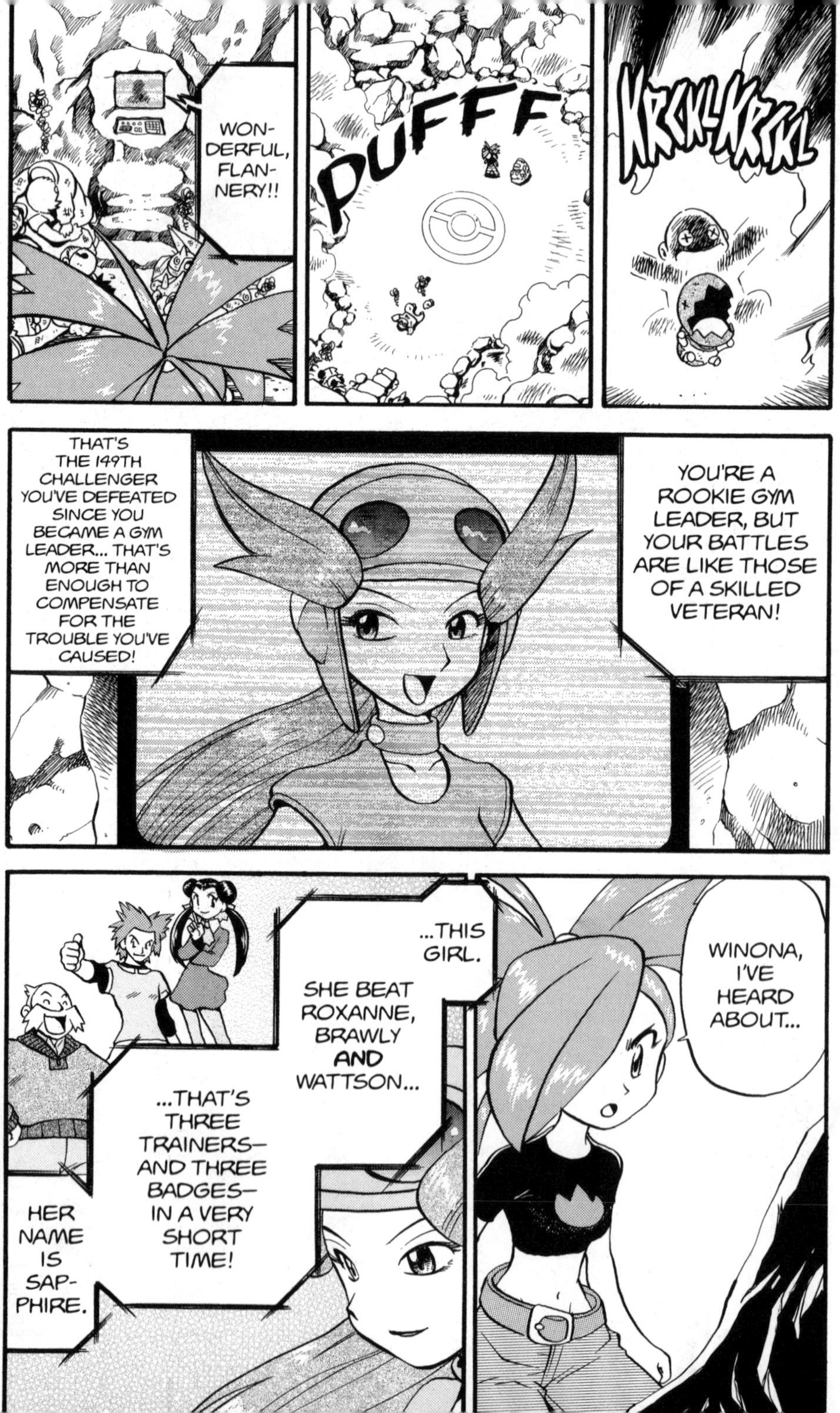
KRCKL-KRIKL
PUFFFF
WON-DERFUL, FLAN-NERY!!
YOU'RE A ROOKIE GYM LEADER, BUT YOUR BATTLES ARE LIKE THOSE OF A SKILLED VETERAN!
THAT'S THE 149TH CHALLENGER YOU'VE DEFEATED SINCE YOU BECAME A GYM LEADER... THAT'S MORE THAN ENOUGH TO COMPENSATE FOR THE TROUBLE YOU'VE CAUSED!
WINONA, I'VE HEARD ABOUT...
...THIS GIRL.
SHE BEAT ROXANNE, BRAWLY **AND** WATTSON...
...THAT'S THREE TRAINERS—AND THREE BADGES—IN A VERY SHORT TIME!
HER NAME IS SAP-PHIRE.

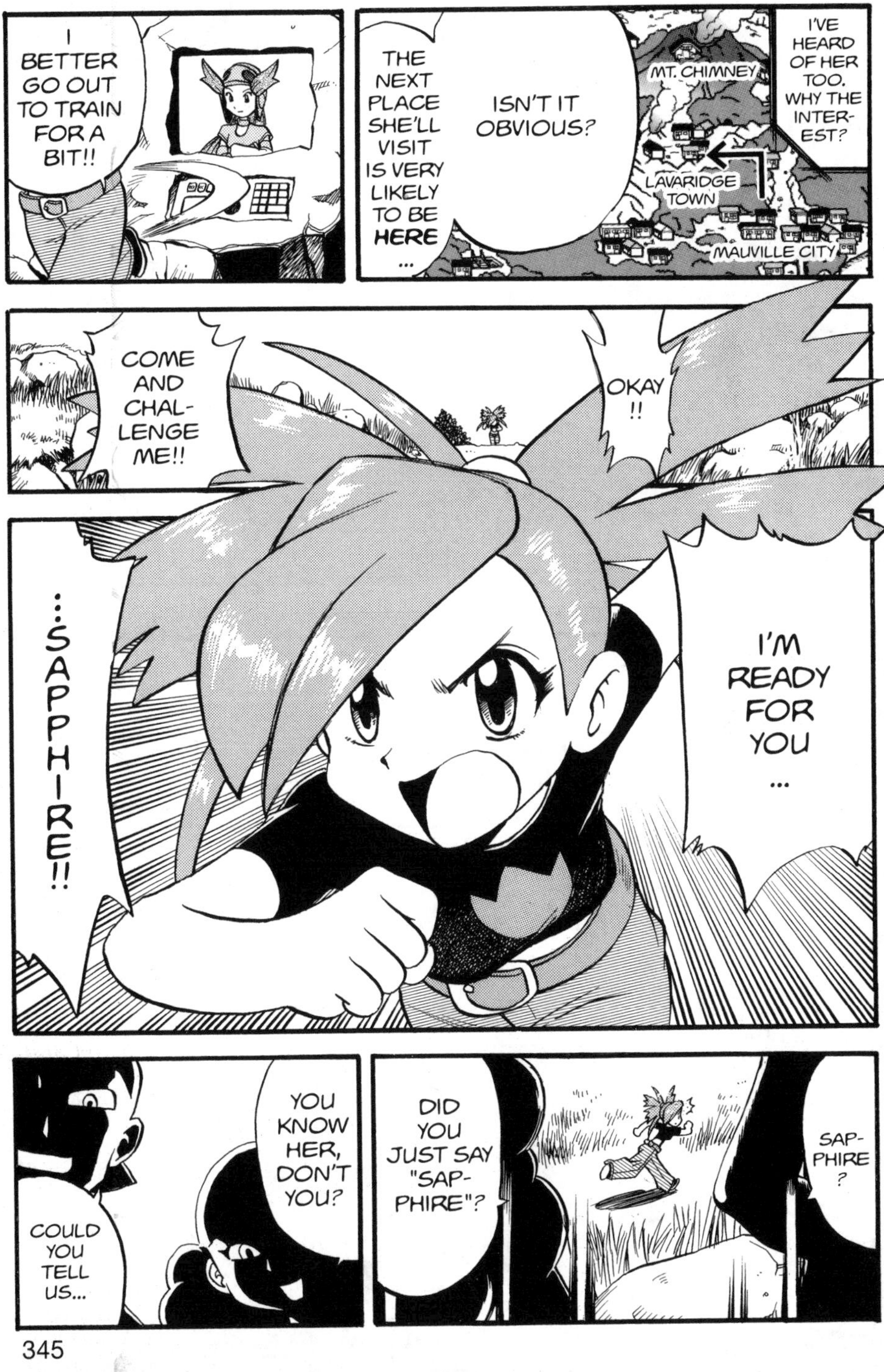
I'VE HEARD OF HER TOO. WHY THE INTEREST?
MT. CHIMNEY
LAVARIDGE TOWN
MAUVILLE CITY
ISN'T IT OBVIOUS?
THE NEXT PLACE SHE'LL VISIT IS VERY LIKELY TO BE **HERE** ...
I BETTER GO OUT TO TRAIN FOR A BIT!!
OKAY!!
COME AND CHALLENGE ME!!
I'M READY FOR YOU ...
...SAPPHIRE!!
SAPPHIRE?
DID YOU JUST SAY "SAPPHIRE"?
YOU KNOW HER, DON'T YOU?
COULD YOU TELL US...

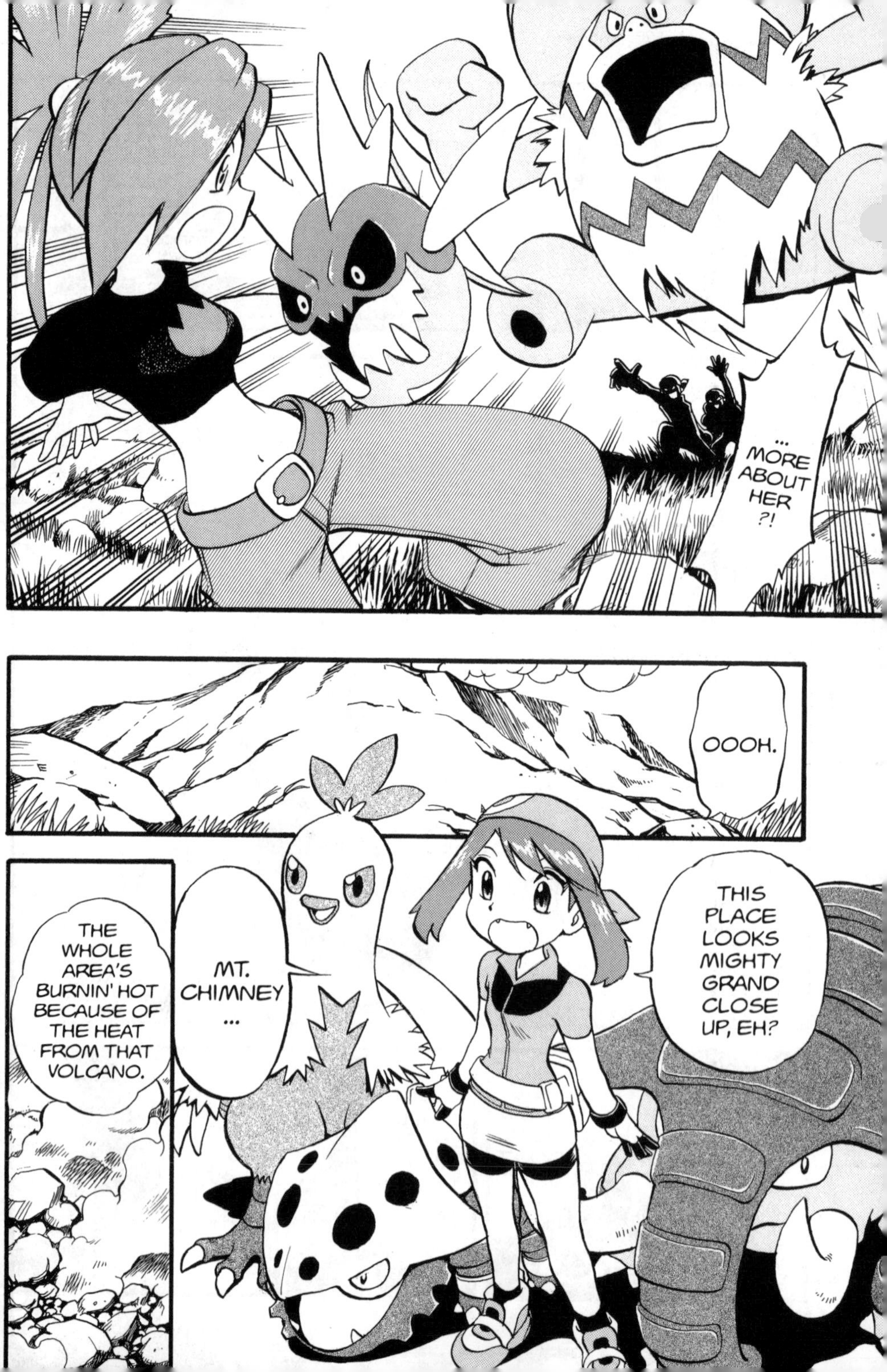
... MORE ABOUT HER?!
OOOH.
THIS PLACE LOOKS MIGHTY GRAND CLOSE UP, EH?
MT. CHIMNEY ...
THE WHOLE AREA'S BURNIN' HOT BECAUSE OF THE HEAT FROM THAT VOLCANO.

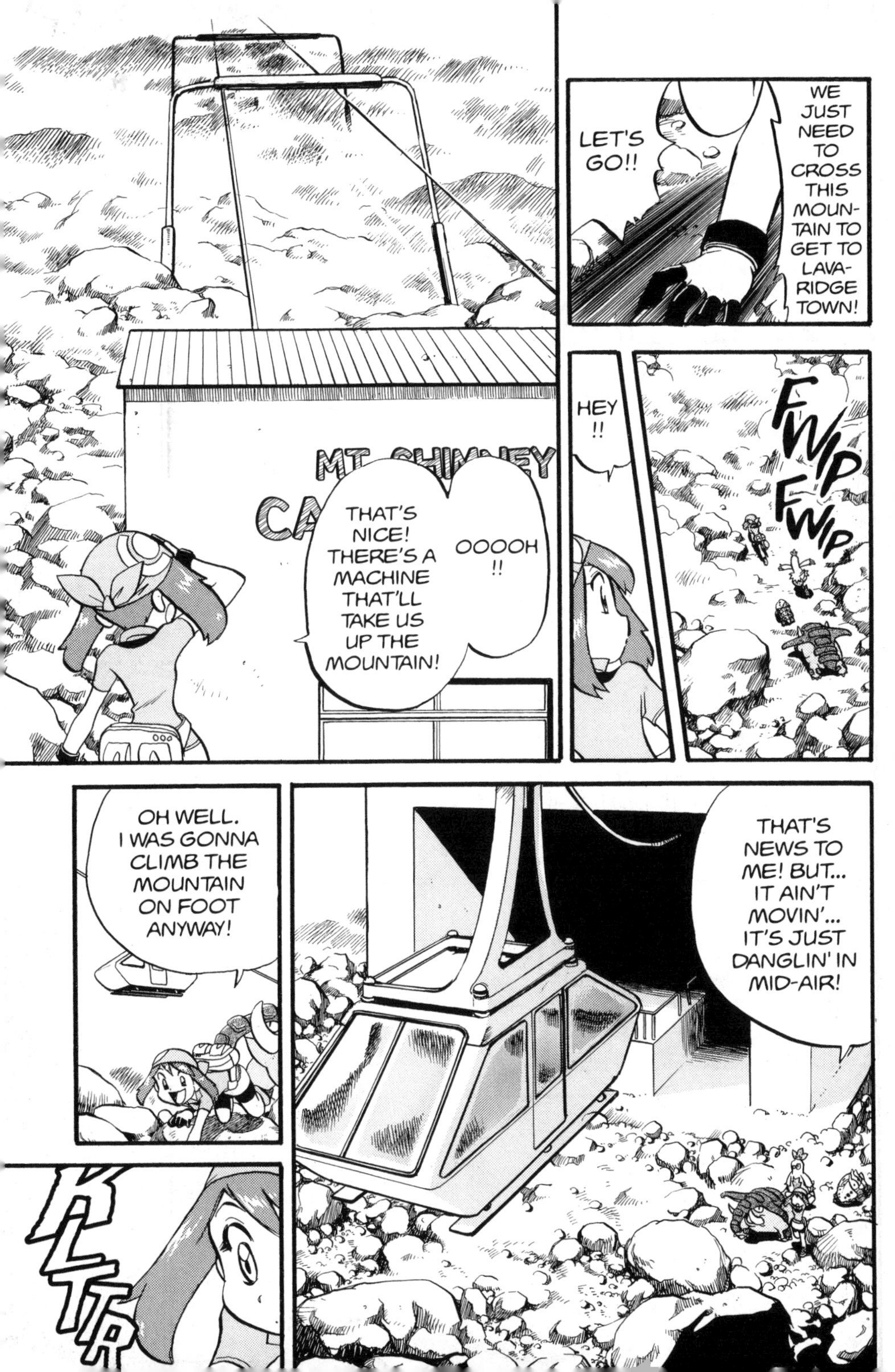
WE JUST NEED TO CROSS THIS MOUNTAIN TO GET TO LAVA-RIDGE TOWN!
LET'S GO!!
FWIP FWIP
HEY!!
OOOOH!!
THAT'S NICE! THERE'S A MACHINE THAT'LL TAKE US UP THE MOUNTAIN!
THAT'S NEWS TO ME! BUT... IT AIN'T MOVIN'... IT'S JUST DANGLIN' IN MID-AIR!
OH WELL. I WAS GONNA CLIMB THE MOUNTAIN ON FOOT ANYWAY!
KLTTR

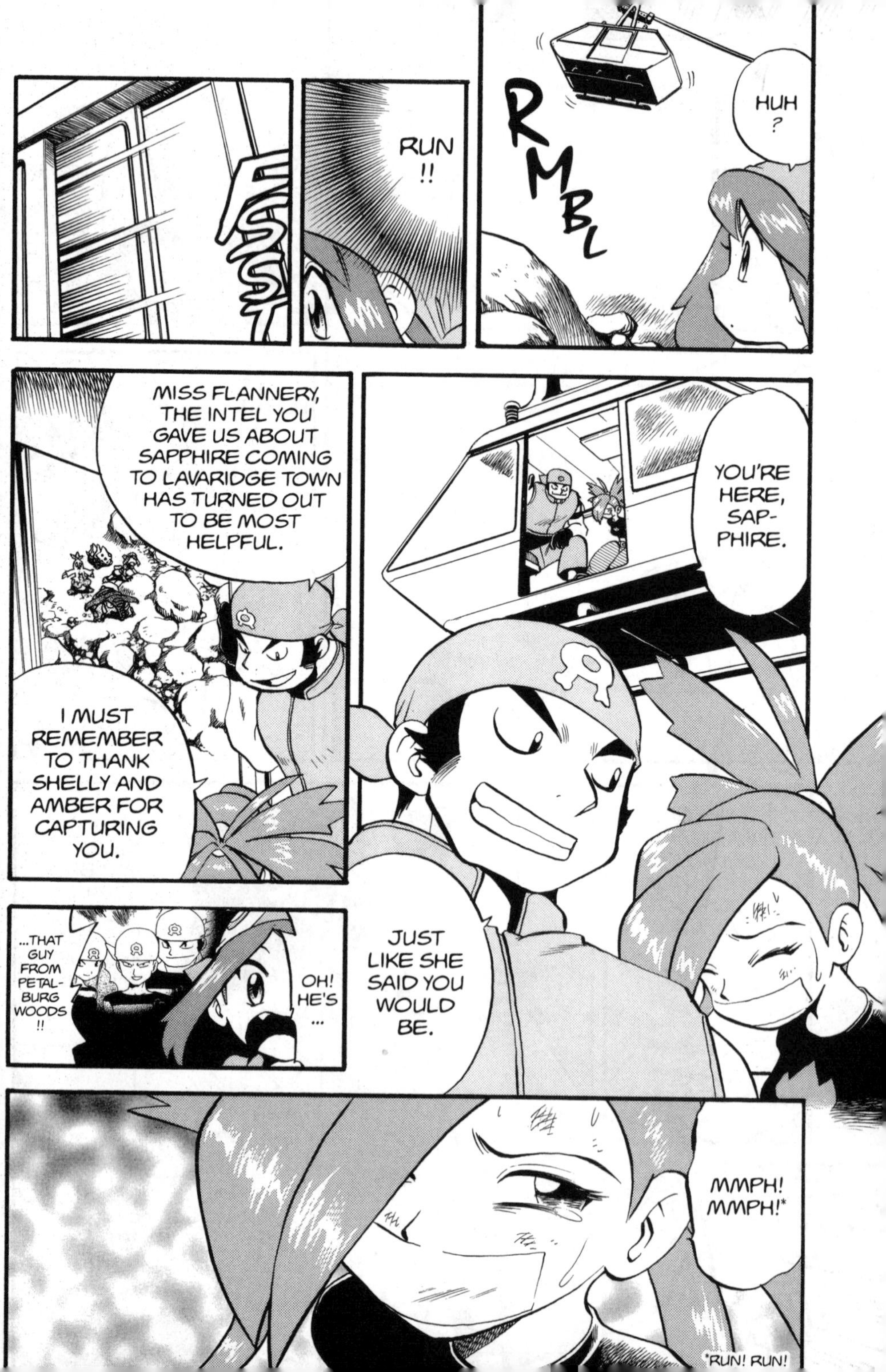
RMBL
HUH?
RUN!!
YOU'RE HERE, SAPPHIRE.
JUST LIKE SHE SAID YOU WOULD BE.
MISS FLANNERY, THE INTEL YOU GAVE US ABOUT SAPPHIRE COMING TO LAVARIDGE TOWN HAS TURNED OUT TO BE MOST HELPFUL.
I MUST REMEMBER TO THANK SHELLY AND AMBER FOR CAPTURING YOU.
OH! HE'S...
...THAT GUY FROM PETALBURG WOODS!!
MMPH! MMPH!*
*RUN! RUN!

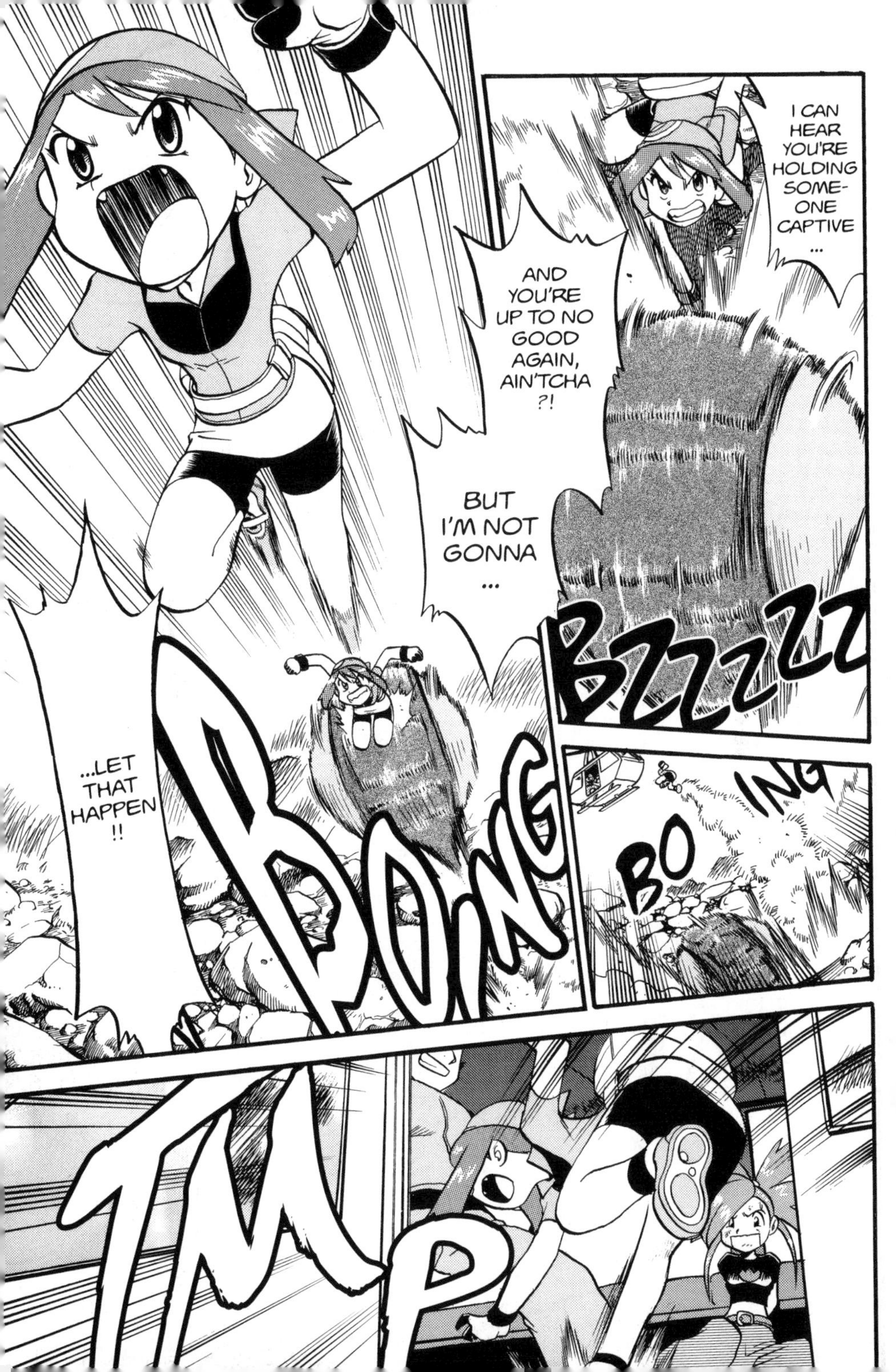
I CAN HEAR YOU'RE HOLDING SOME-ONE CAPTIVE ...
BZZZZZ
BO ING
AND YOU'RE UP TO NO GOOD AGAIN, AIN'TCHA ?!
BUT I'M NOT GONNA ...
...LET THAT HAPPEN !!
BOING
TMP

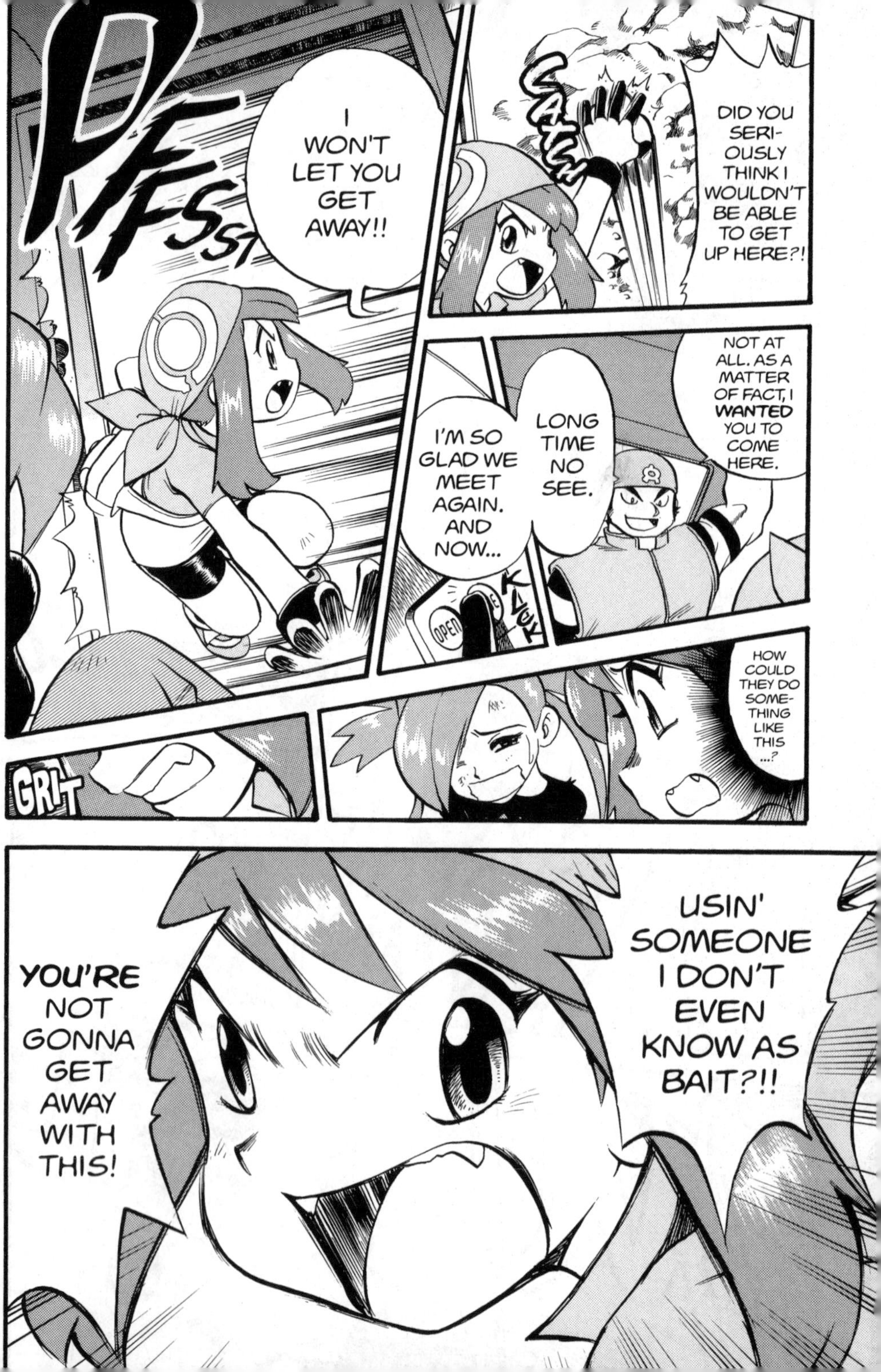
DID YOU SERIOUSLY THINK I WOULDN'T BE ABLE TO GET UP HERE?!
NOT AT ALL. AS A MATTER OF FACT, I **WANTED** YOU TO COME HERE.
LONG TIME NO SEE.
I'M SO GLAD WE MEET AGAIN. AND NOW...
I WON'T LET YOU GET AWAY!!
HOW COULD THEY DO SOMETHING LIKE THIS...?
GRIT
USIN' SOMEONE I DON'T EVEN KNOW AS BAIT?!!
YOU'RE NOT GONNA GET AWAY WITH THIS!

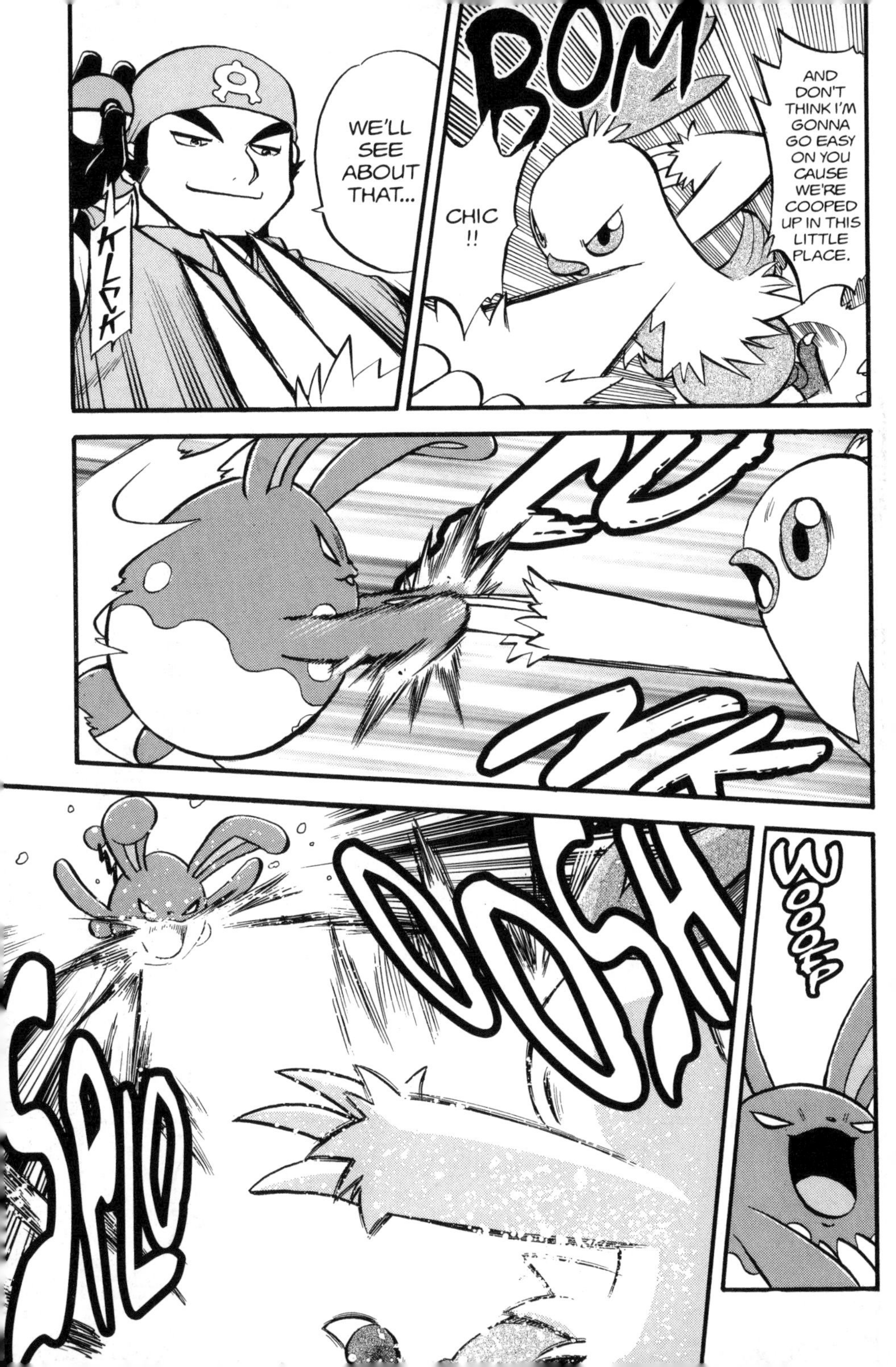
BOM
AND DON'T THINK I'M GONNA GO EASY ON YOU CAUSE WE'RE COOPED UP IN THIS LITTLE PLACE.
CHIC !!
WE'LL SEE ABOUT THAT...

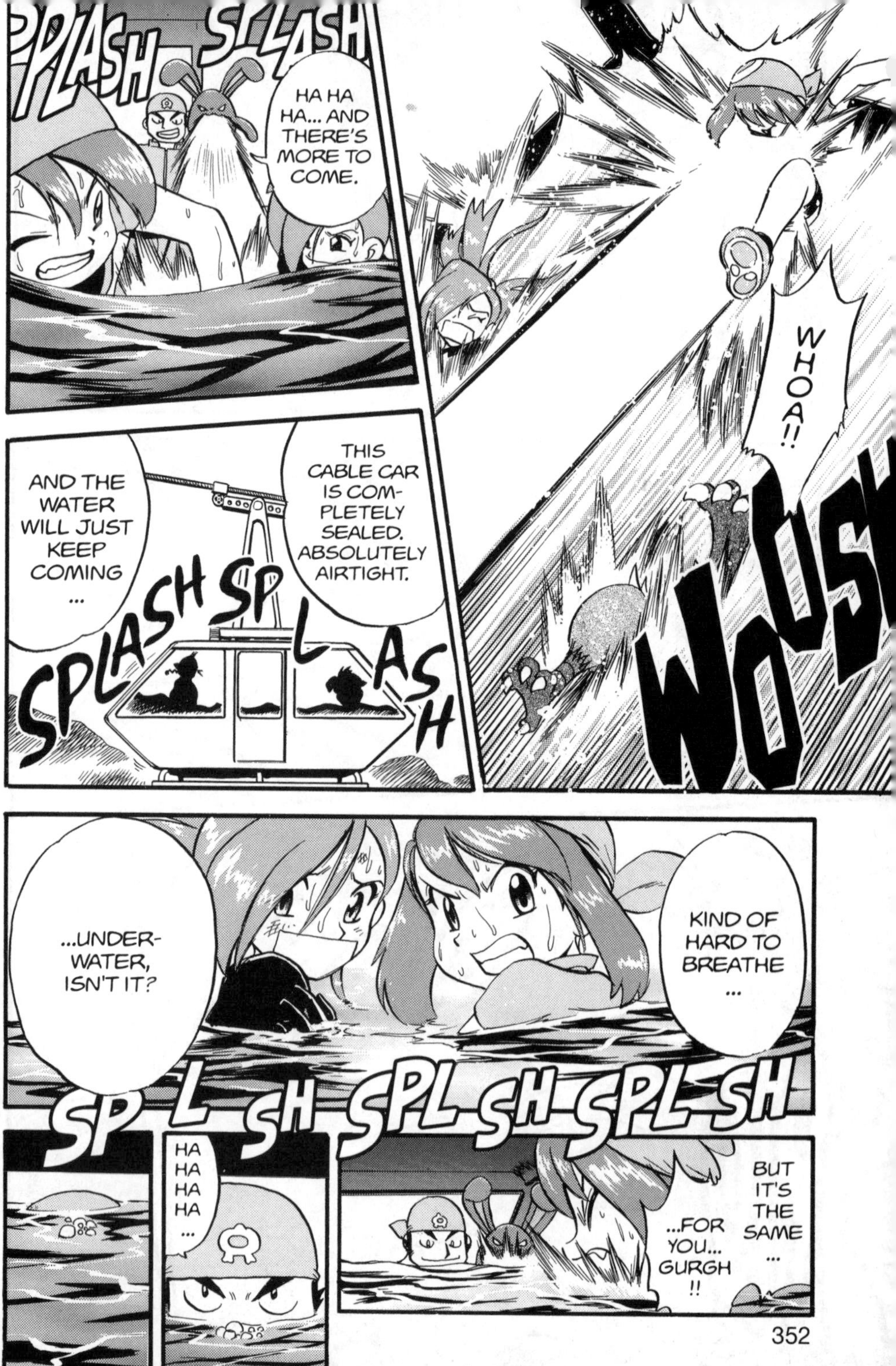
WHOA!!
WOOS
SPLASH SPLASH
HA HA HA... AND THERE'S MORE TO COME.
THIS CABLE CAR IS COM-PLETELY SEALED. ABSOLUTELY AIRTIGHT.
AND THE WATER WILL JUST KEEP COMING ...
SPLASH SPLASH
KIND OF HARD TO BREATHE ...
...UNDER-WATER, ISN'T IT?
SP L SH SPL SH SPL SH
BUT IT'S THE SAME ...
...FOR YOU... GURGH !!
HA HA HA HA ...

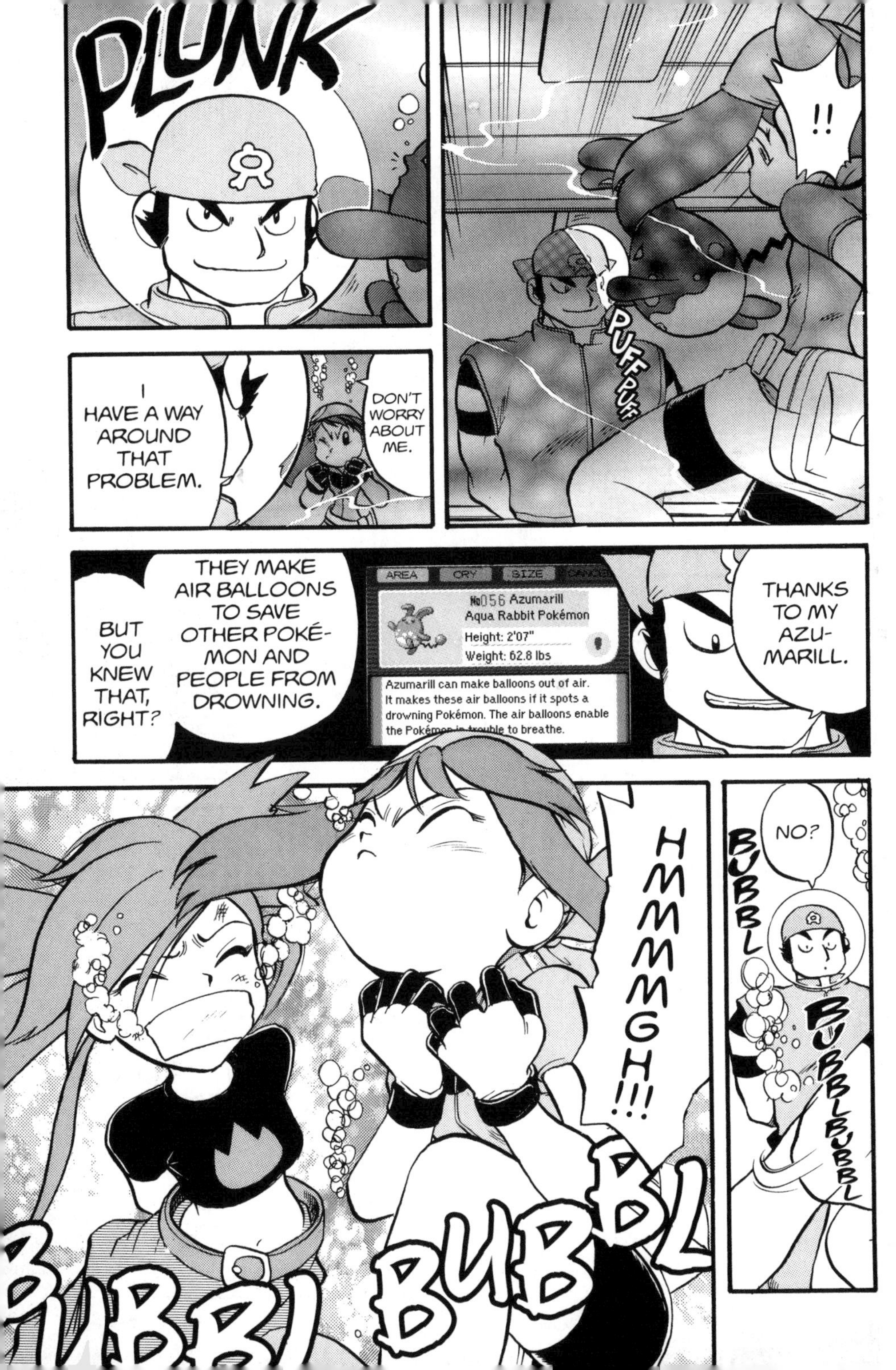

!!
PUFF PUFF
PLUNK
DON'T WORRY ABOUT ME.
I HAVE A WAY AROUND THAT PROBLEM.
THANKS TO MY AZUMARILL.
AREA CRY SIZE CANCEL
№056 Azumarill
Aqua Rabbit Pokémon
Height: 2'07"
Weight: 62.8 lbs
Azumarill can make balloons out of air. It makes these air balloons if it spots a drowning Pokémon. The air balloons enable the Pokémon in trouble to breathe.
THEY MAKE AIR BALLOONS TO SAVE OTHER POKÉMON AND PEOPLE FROM DROWNING.
BUT YOU KNEW THAT, RIGHT?
BUBBL
NO?
BUBBLBUBBL
HMMMMMGH!!!
BUBBL

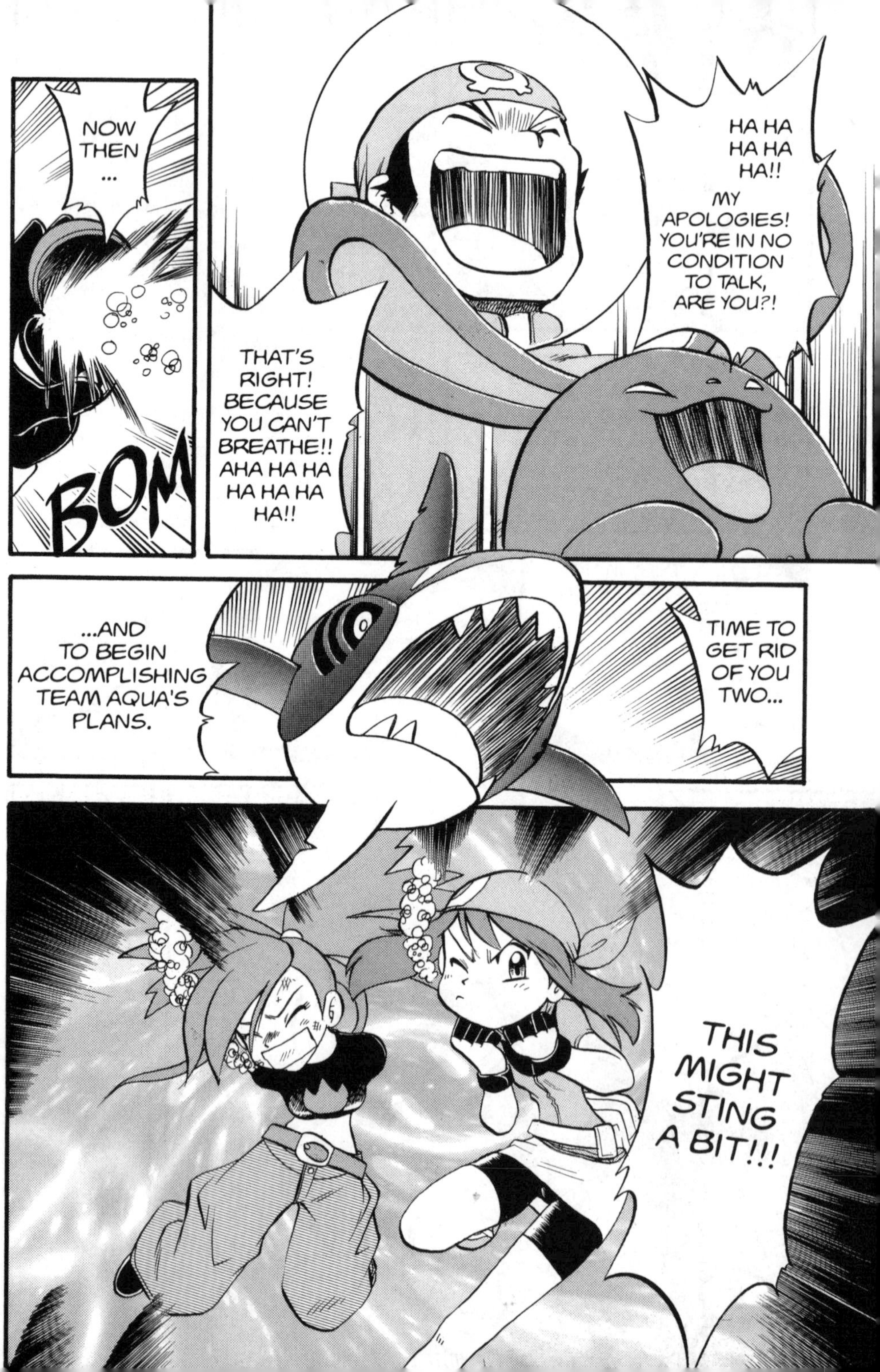
HA HA HA HA HA!!
MY APOLOGIES! YOU'RE IN NO CONDITION TO TALK, ARE YOU?!
THAT'S RIGHT! BECAUSE YOU CAN'T BREATHE!! AHA HA HA HA HA HA HA!!
NOW THEN ...
BOM
TIME TO GET RID OF YOU TWO...
...AND TO BEGIN ACCOMPLISHING TEAM AQUA'S PLANS.
THIS MIGHT STING A BIT!!!

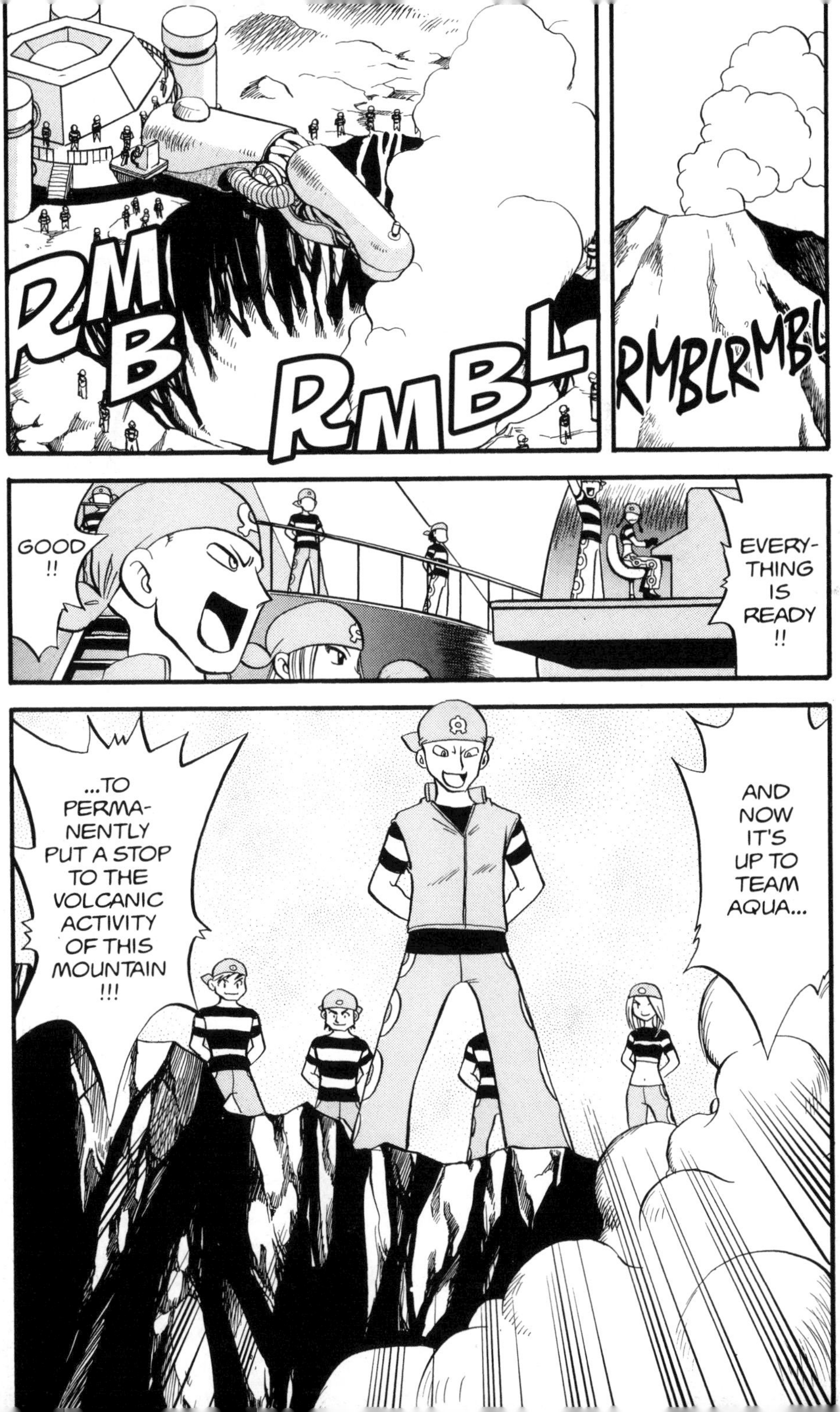
RMBLRMBL
RMB
RMBL
EVERYTHING IS READY!!
GOOD!!
AND NOW IT'S UP TO TEAM AQUA...
...TO PERMANENTLY PUT A STOP TO THE VOLCANIC ACTIVITY OF THIS MOUNTAIN!!!

● Adventure 213 ●

Bubble, Bubble Toil and Azumarill, Part 2

Pokémon™ Adventures Ruby & Sapphire The Fourth Chapter

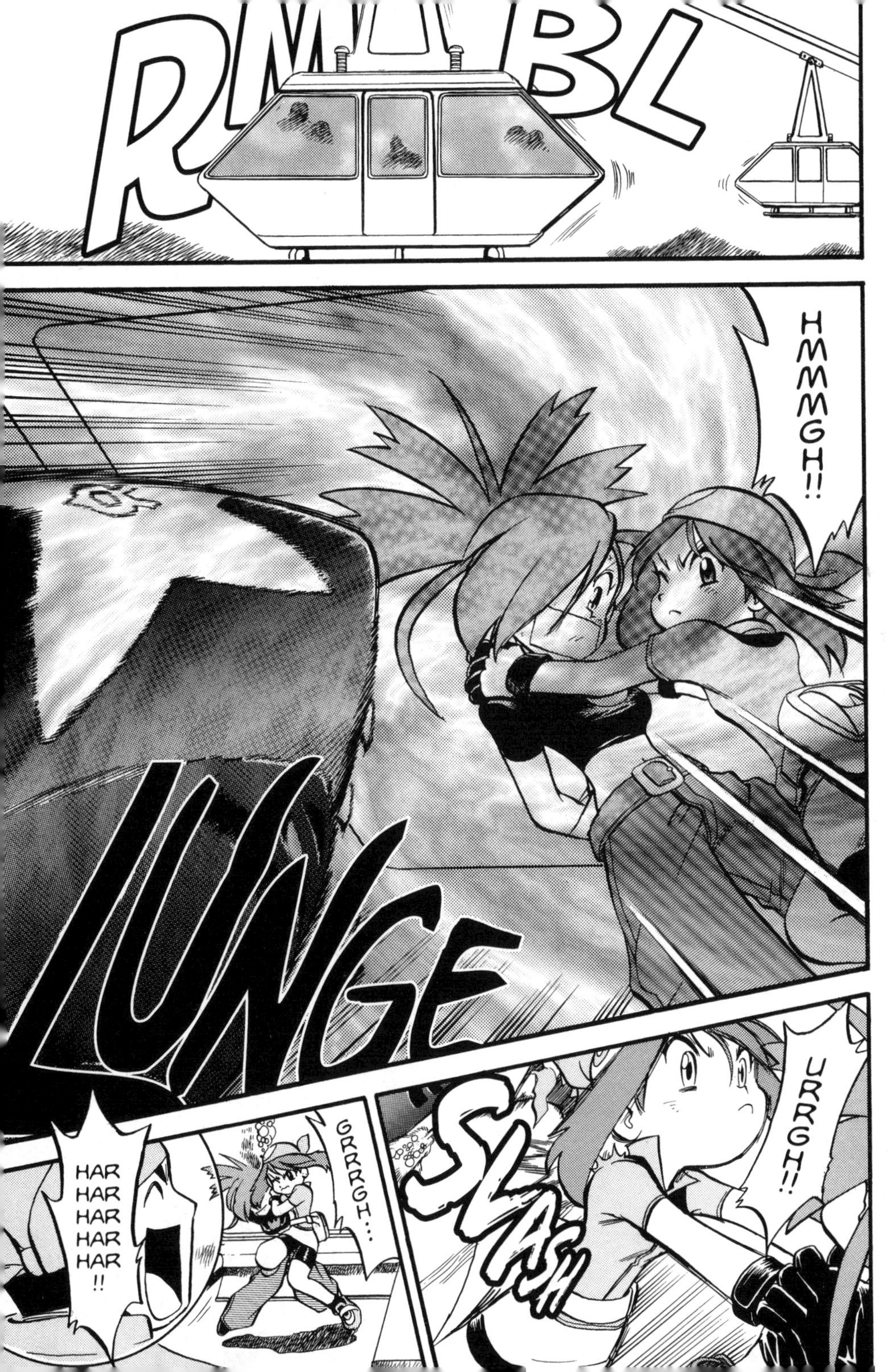
RMBL
HMMMGH!!
LUNGE
URRGH!!
SLASH
GRRRGH...
HAR HAR HAR HAR HAR!!

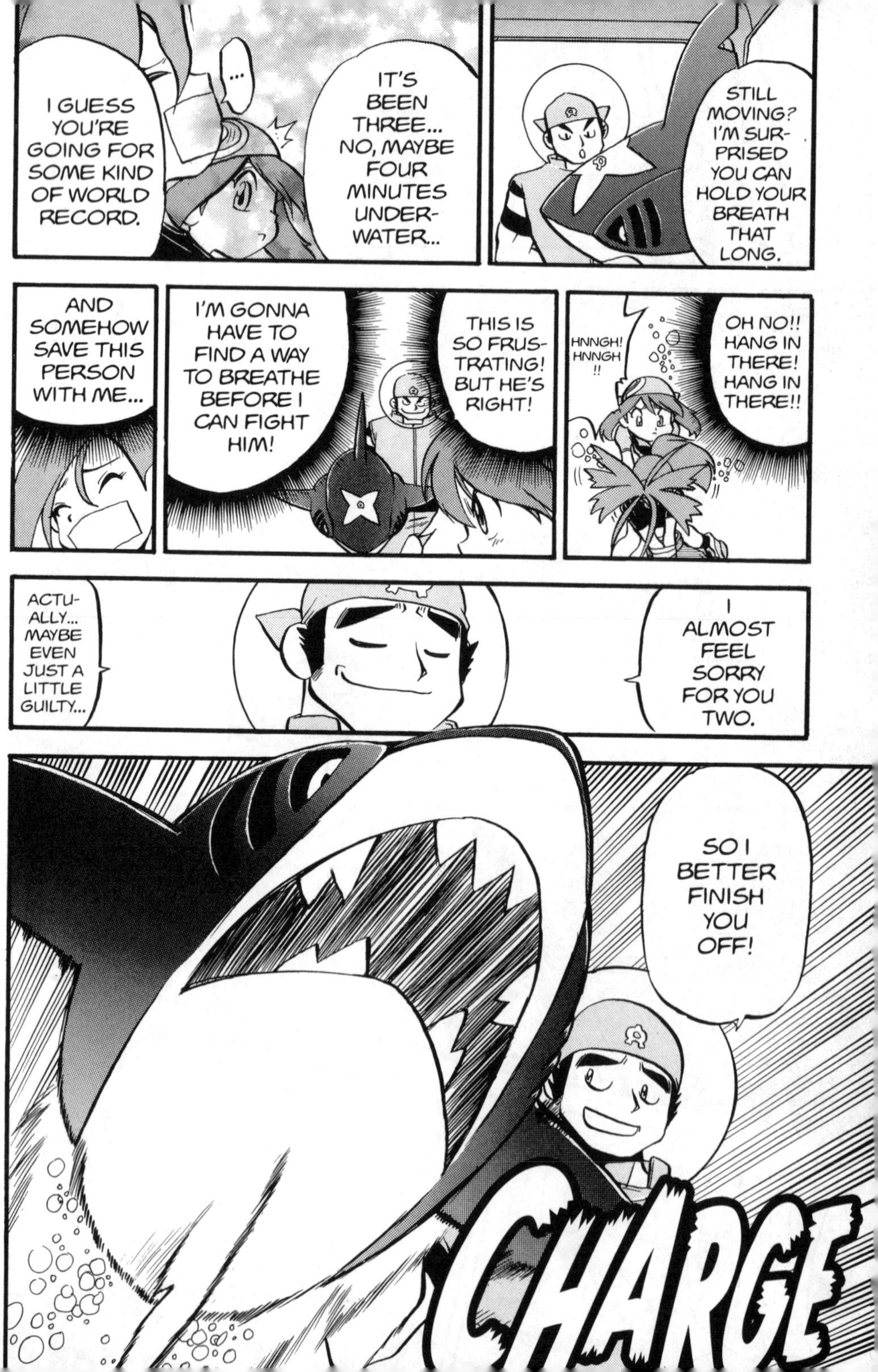
STILL MOVING? I'M SURPRISED YOU CAN HOLD YOUR BREATH THAT LONG.
IT'S BEEN THREE... NO, MAYBE FOUR MINUTES UNDERWATER...
...
I GUESS YOU'RE GOING FOR SOME KIND OF WORLD RECORD.
OH NO!! HANG IN THERE! HANG IN THERE!!
HNNGH! HNNGH!!
THIS IS SO FRUSTRATING! BUT HE'S RIGHT!
I'M GONNA HAVE TO FIND A WAY TO BREATHE BEFORE I CAN FIGHT HIM!
AND SOMEHOW SAVE THIS PERSON WITH ME...
I ALMOST FEEL SORRY FOR YOU TWO.
ACTUALLY... MAYBE EVEN JUST A LITTLE GUILTY...
SO I BETTER FINISH YOU OFF!
CHARGE

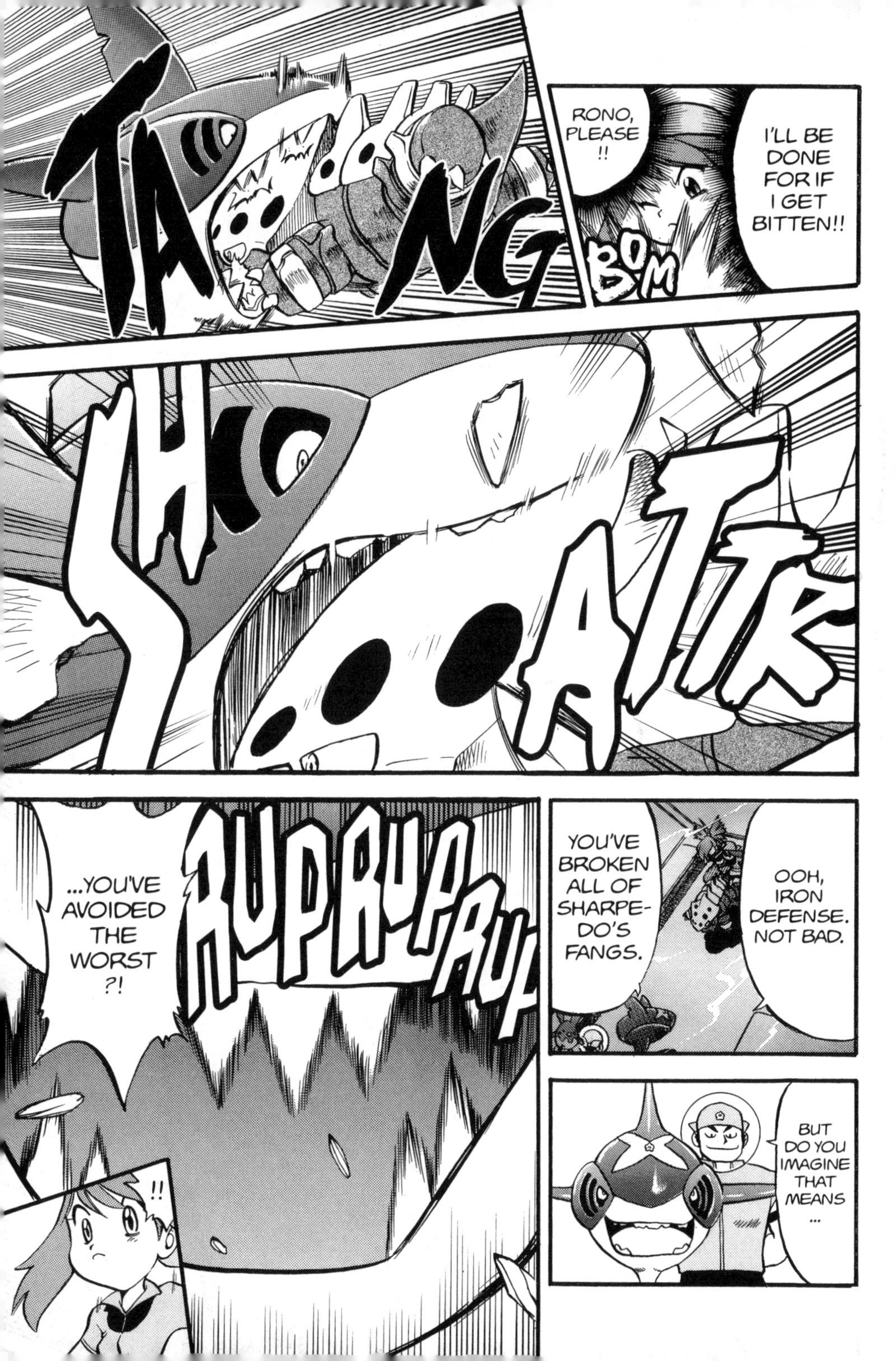
I'LL BE DONE FOR IF I GET BITTEN!!
RONO, PLEASE!!
BOM
TANG
SHATTR
OOH, IRON DEFENSE. NOT BAD.
YOU'VE BROKEN ALL OF SHARPE-DO'S FANGS.
BUT DO YOU IMAGINE THAT MEANS ...
RUPRUPRUP
...YOU'VE AVOIDED THE WORST?!
!!

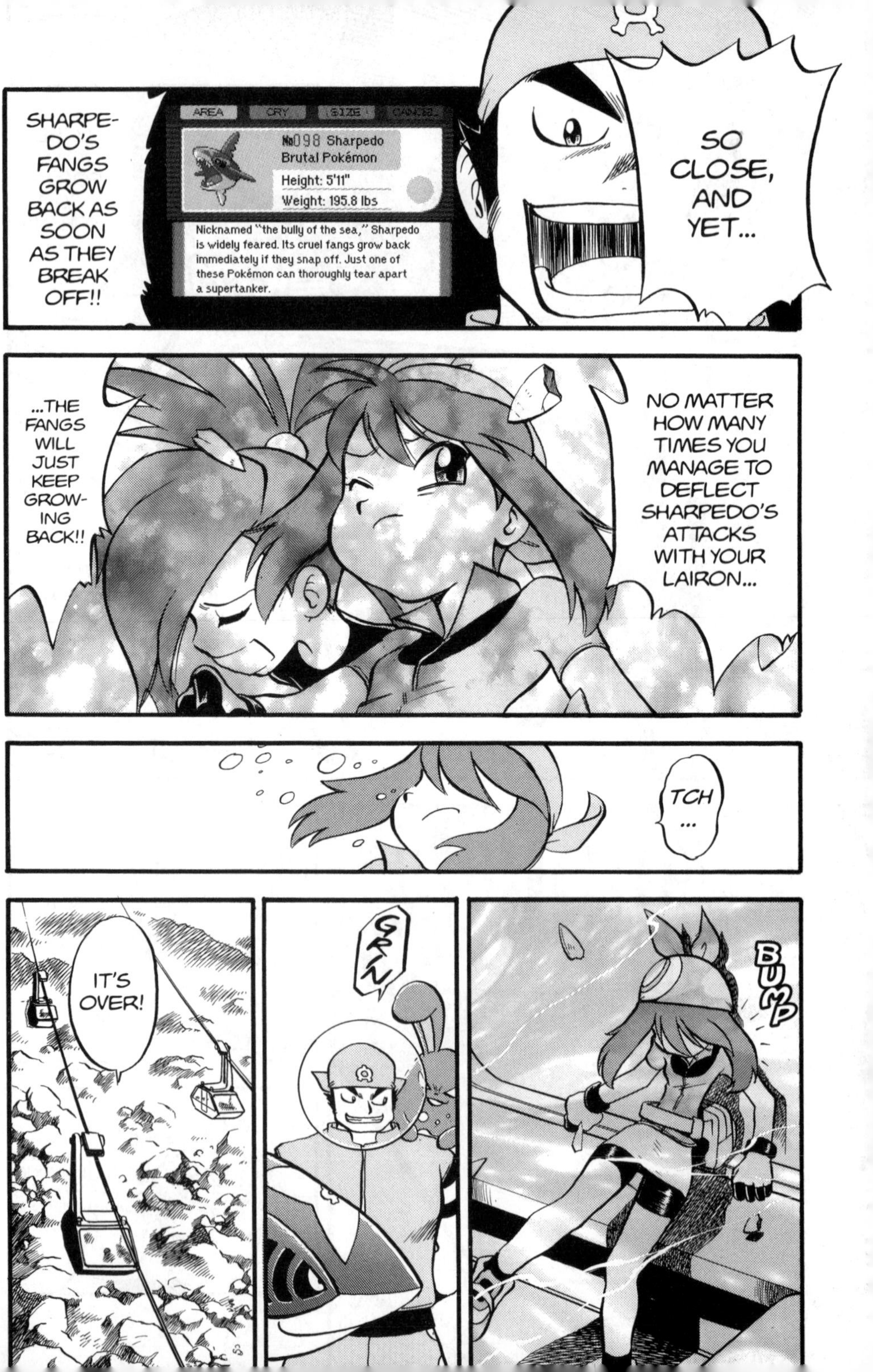
SO CLOSE, AND YET...
SHARPE-DO'S FANGS GROW BACK AS SOON AS THEY BREAK OFF!!
AREA
CRY
SIZE
CANCEL
№098 Sharpedo
Brutal Pokémon
Height: 5'11"
Weight: 195.8 lbs
Nicknamed "the bully of the sea," Sharpedo is widely feared. Its cruel fangs grow back immediately if they snap off. Just one of these Pokémon can thoroughly tear apart a supertanker.
NO MATTER HOW MANY TIMES YOU MANAGE TO DEFLECT SHARPEDO'S ATTACKS WITH YOUR LAIRON...
...THE FANGS WILL JUST KEEP GROW-ING BACK!!
TCH ...
BUMP
GRIN
IT'S OVER!

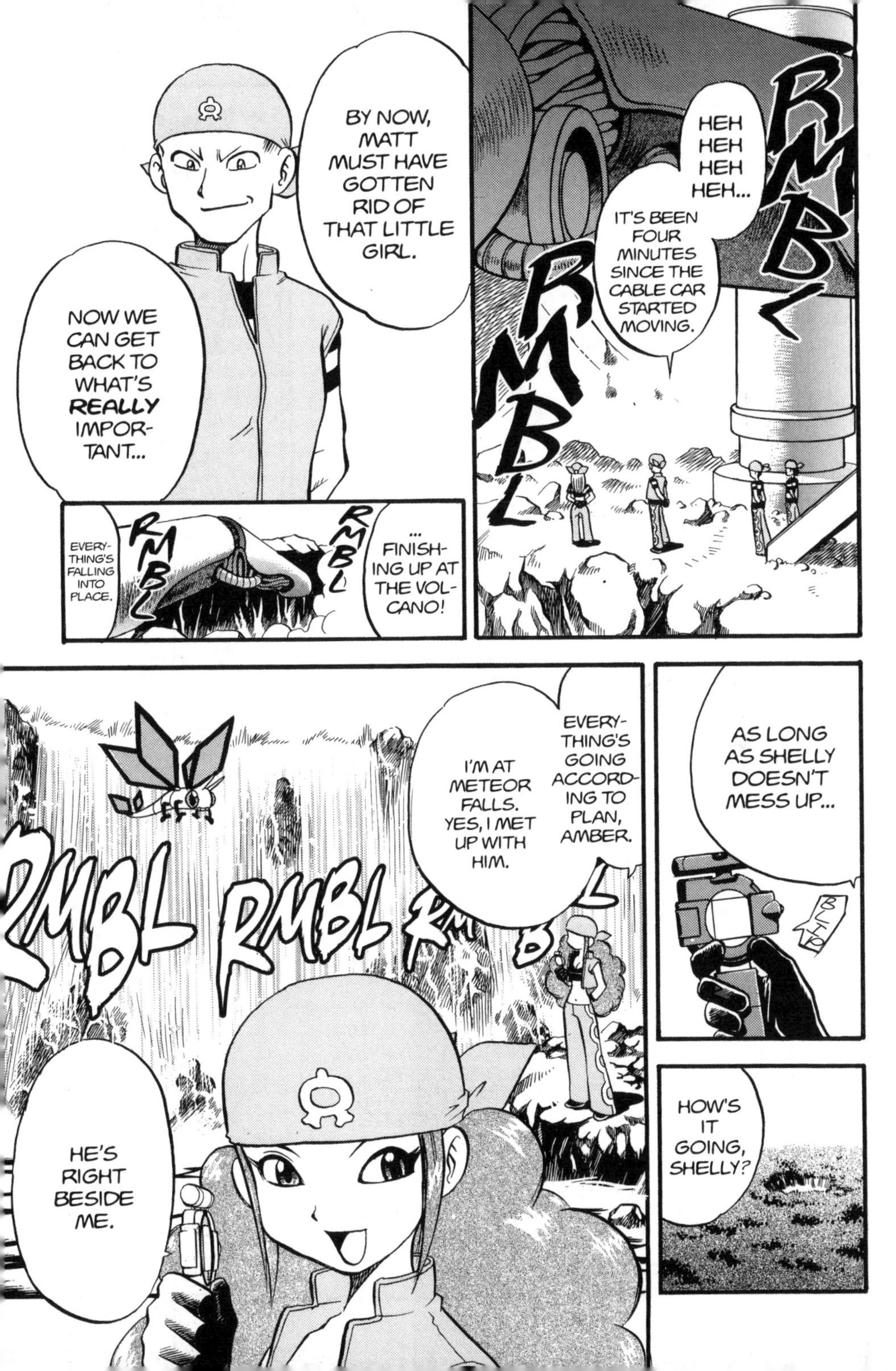
RMBL
HEH HEH HEH HEH...
IT'S BEEN FOUR MINUTES SINCE THE CABLE CAR STARTED MOVING.
RMBL
BY NOW, MATT MUST HAVE GOTTEN RID OF THAT LITTLE GIRL.
NOW WE CAN GET BACK TO WHAT'S **REALLY** IMPORTANT...
RMBL
... FINISHING UP AT THE VOLCANO!
RMBL
EVERYTHING'S FALLING INTO PLACE.
AS LONG AS SHELLY DOESN'T MESS UP...
BLIK
HOW'S IT GOING, SHELLY?
RMBL RMBL RMBL
EVERYTHING'S GOING ACCORDING TO PLAN, AMBER.
I'M AT METEOR FALLS. YES, I MET UP WITH HIM.
HE'S RIGHT BESIDE ME.

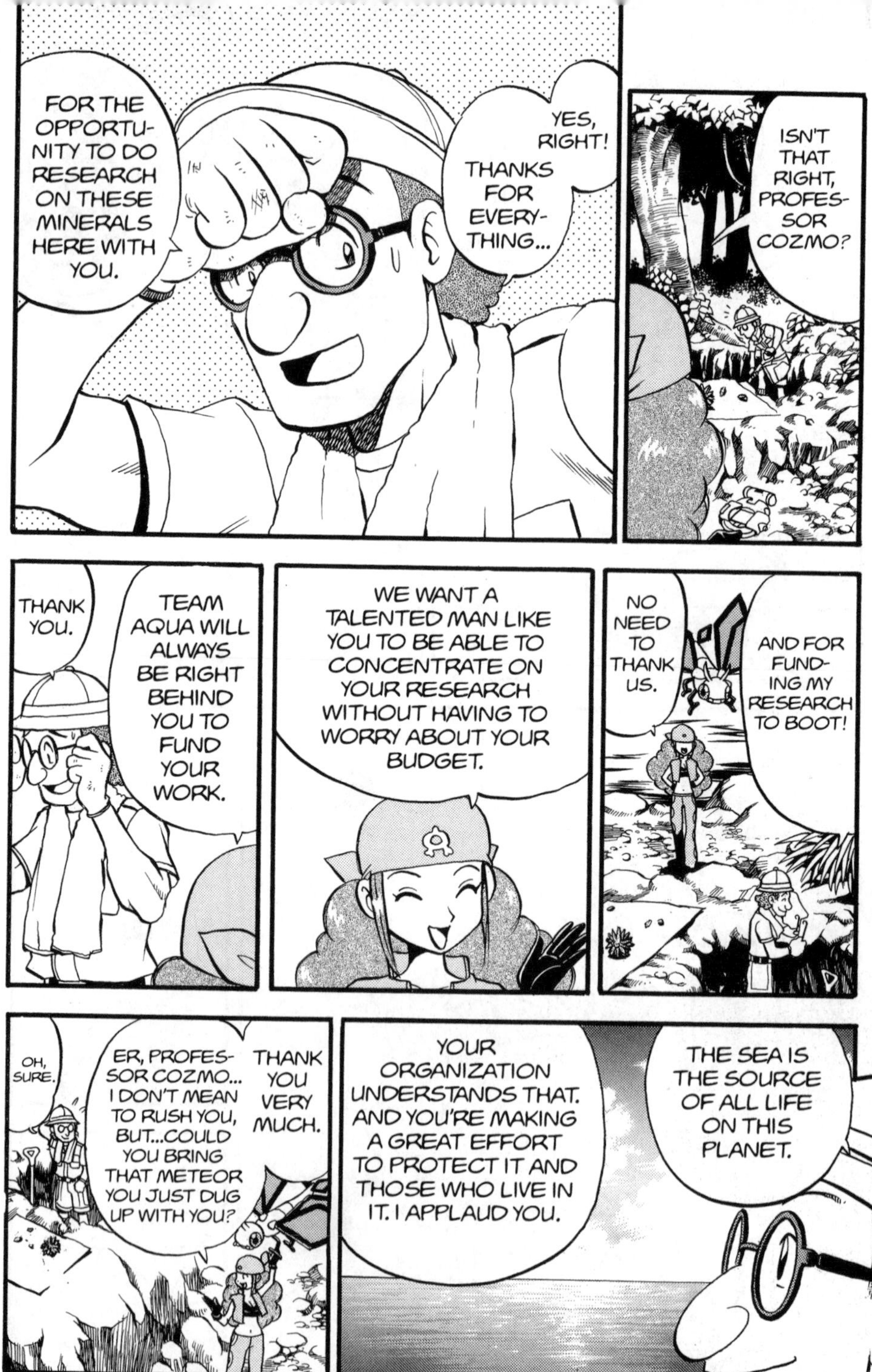
ISN'T THAT RIGHT, PROFES-SOR COZMO?
YES, RIGHT!
THANKS FOR EVERY-THING...
FOR THE OPPORTU-NITY TO DO RESEARCH ON THESE MINERALS HERE WITH YOU.
AND FOR FUND-ING MY RESEARCH TO BOOT!
NO NEED TO THANK US.
WE WANT A TALENTED MAN LIKE YOU TO BE ABLE TO CONCENTRATE ON YOUR RESEARCH WITHOUT HAVING TO WORRY ABOUT YOUR BUDGET.
TEAM AQUA WILL ALWAYS BE RIGHT BEHIND YOU TO FUND YOUR WORK.
THANK YOU.
THE SEA IS THE SOURCE OF ALL LIFE ON THIS PLANET.
YOUR ORGANIZATION UNDERSTANDS THAT. AND YOU'RE MAKING A GREAT EFFORT TO PROTECT IT AND THOSE WHO LIVE IN IT. I APPLAUD YOU.
THANK YOU VERY MUCH.
ER, PROFES-SOR COZMO... I DON'T MEAN TO RUSH YOU, BUT...COULD YOU BRING THAT METEOR YOU JUST DUG UP WITH YOU?
OH, SURE.

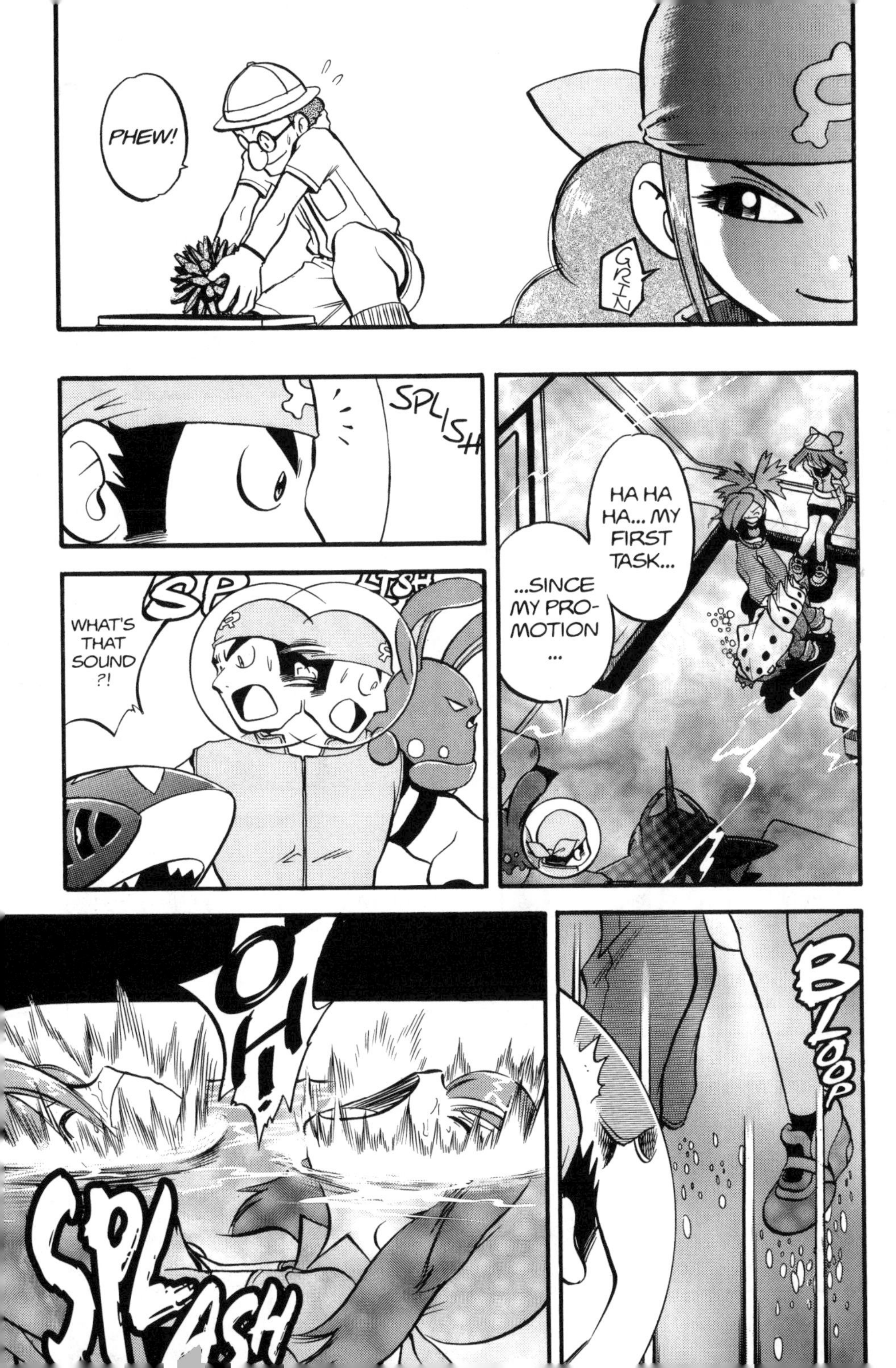
GRIN
PHEW!
HA HA HA... MY FIRST TASK...
...SINCE MY PRO-MOTION ...
SPLISH
SP
LISH
WHAT'S THAT SOUND ?!
BLOOOP
OH!
SPLASH

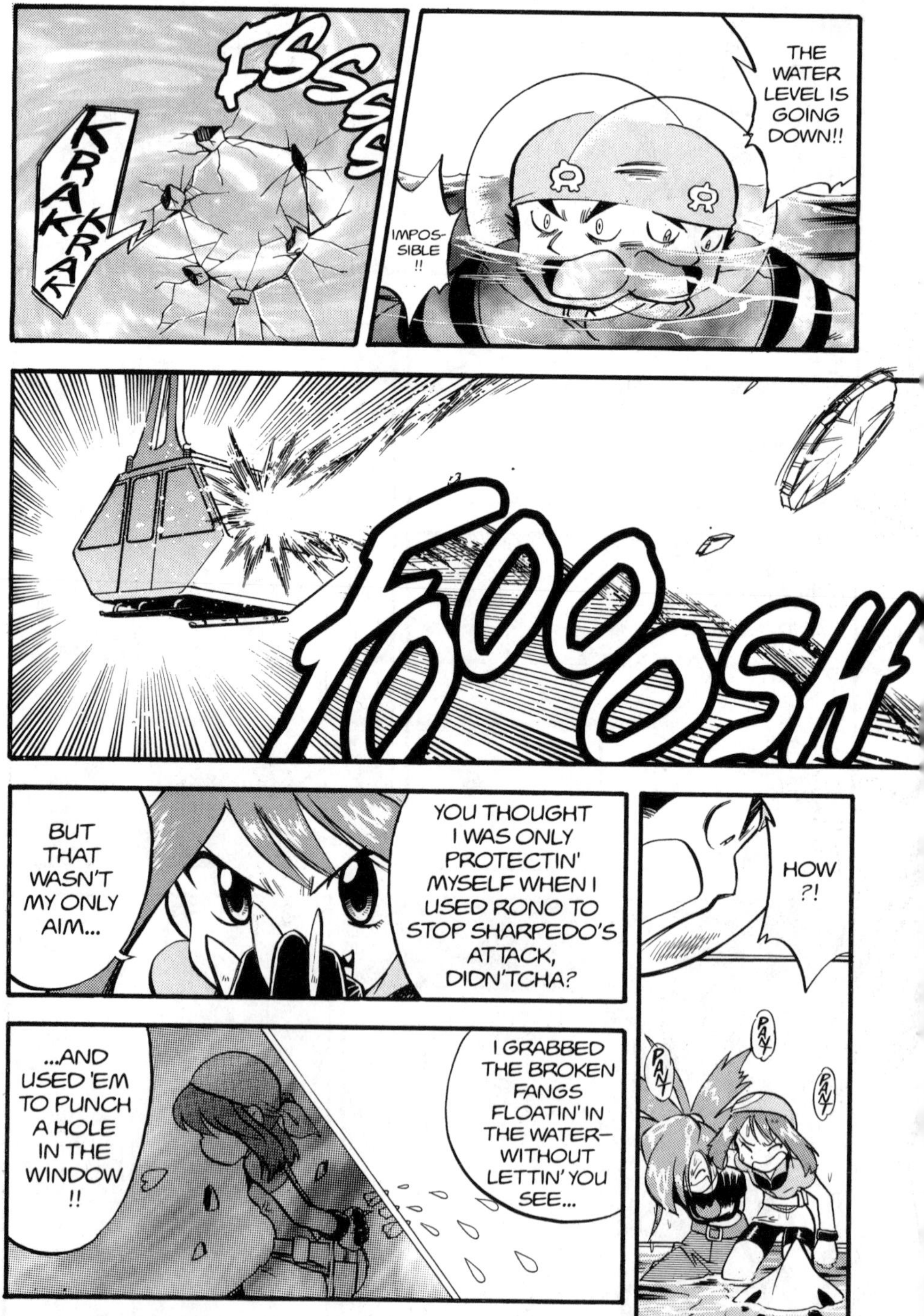
THE WATER LEVEL IS GOING DOWN!!
IMPOSSIBLE!!
FSSSS
KRAK KRAK
FOOOSH
HOW?!
PANT
PANT
PANT
YOU THOUGHT I WAS ONLY PROTECTIN' MYSELF WHEN I USED RONO TO STOP SHARPEDO'S ATTACK, DIDN'TCHA?
BUT THAT WASN'T MY ONLY AIM...
I GRABBED THE BROKEN FANGS FLOATIN' IN THE WATER—WITHOUT LETTIN' YOU SEE...
...AND USED 'EM TO PUNCH A HOLE IN THE WINDOW!!

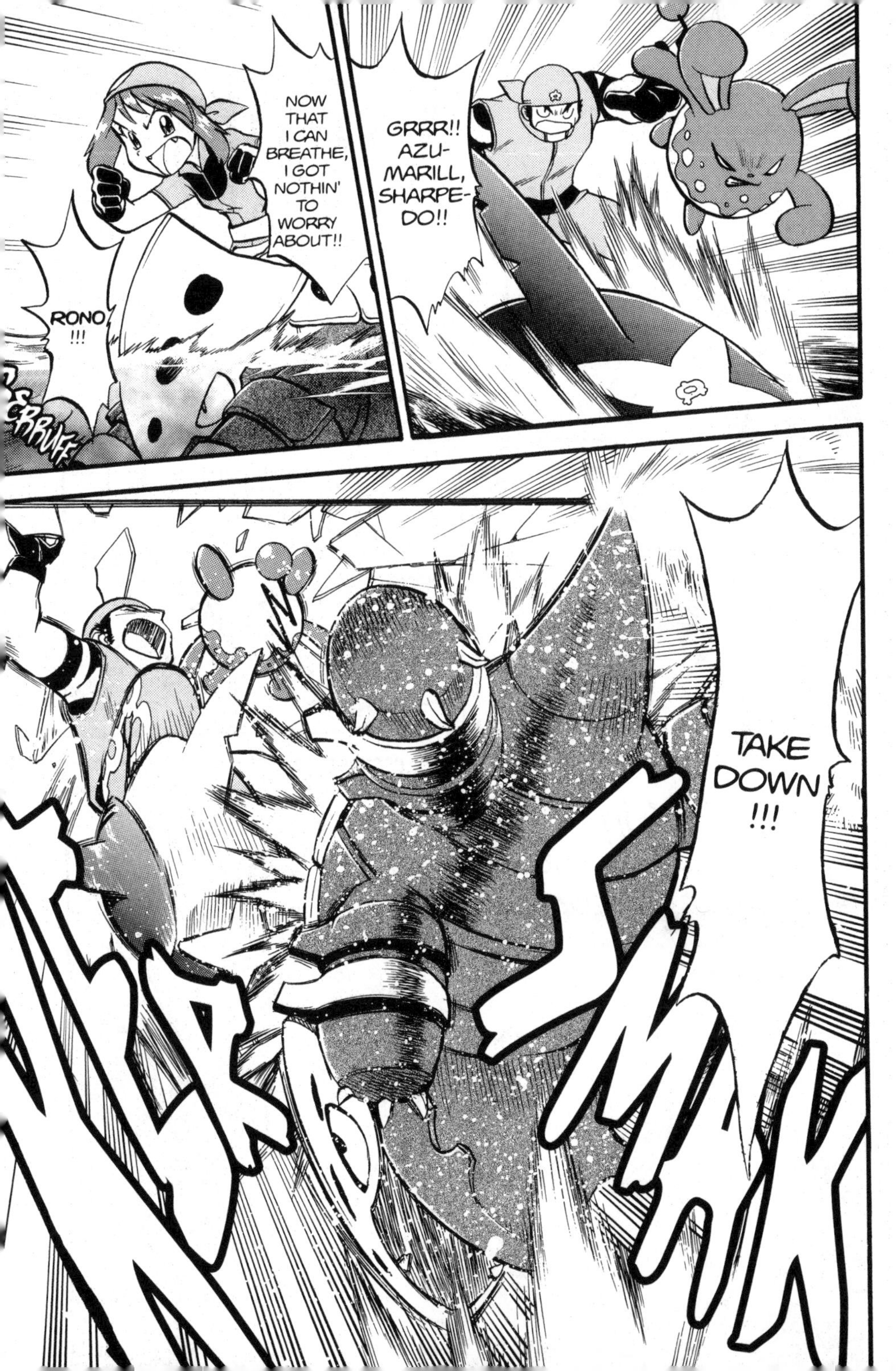
GRRR!! AZU-MARILL, SHARPE-DO!!
NOW THAT I CAN BREATHE, I GOT NOTHIN' TO WORRY ABOUT!!
RONO !!!
TAKE DOWN !!!

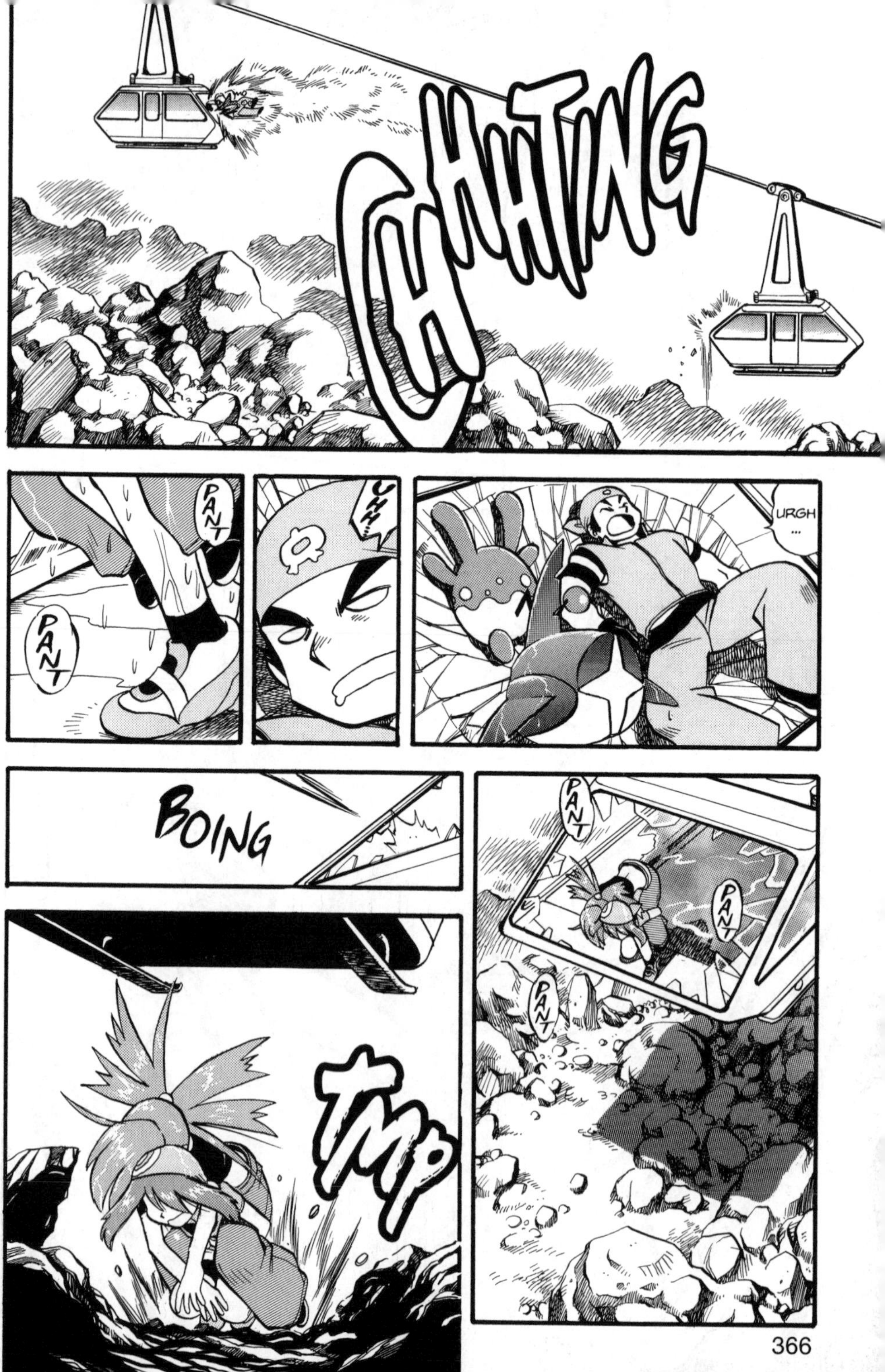
CHHTING
URGH...
UHH...
PANT
PANT
PANT
PANT
PANT
BOING
TMP

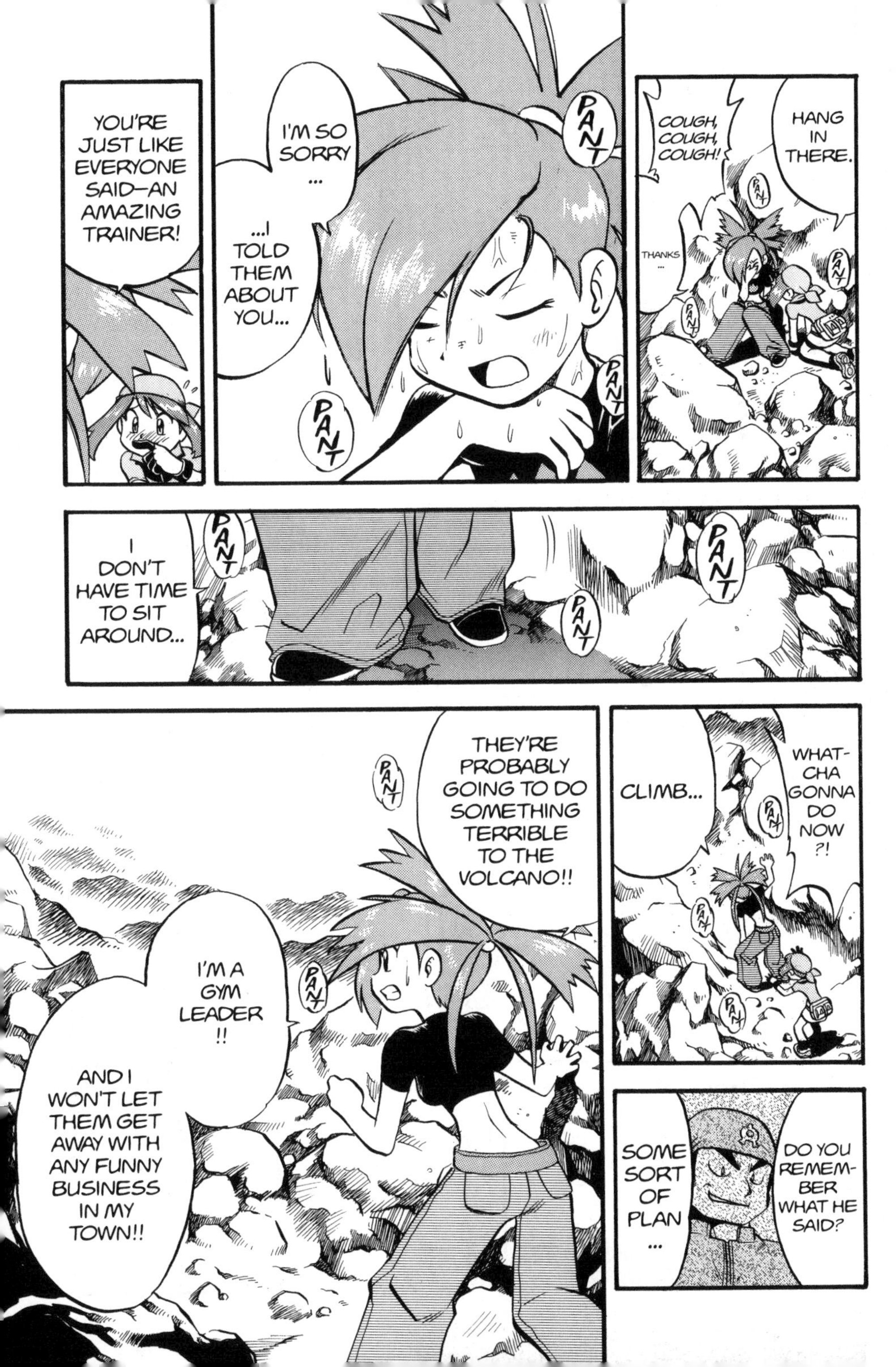
HANG IN THERE.
COUGH, COUGH, COUGH!
PANT
THANKS ...
PANT
PANT
PANT
I'M SO SORRY ...
...I TOLD THEM ABOUT YOU...
PANT
PANT
YOU'RE JUST LIKE EVERYONE SAID—AN AMAZING TRAINER!
PANT
PANT
PANT
I DON'T HAVE TIME TO SIT AROUND...
WHAT-CHA GONNA DO NOW ?!
CLIMB...
PANT
PANT
PANT
DO YOU REMEMBER WHAT HE SAID?
SOME SORT OF PLAN ...
THEY'RE PROBABLY GOING TO DO SOMETHING TERRIBLE TO THE VOLCANO!!
PANT
PANT
I'M A GYM LEADER !!
AND I WON'T LET THEM GET AWAY WITH ANY FUNNY BUSINESS IN MY TOWN!!

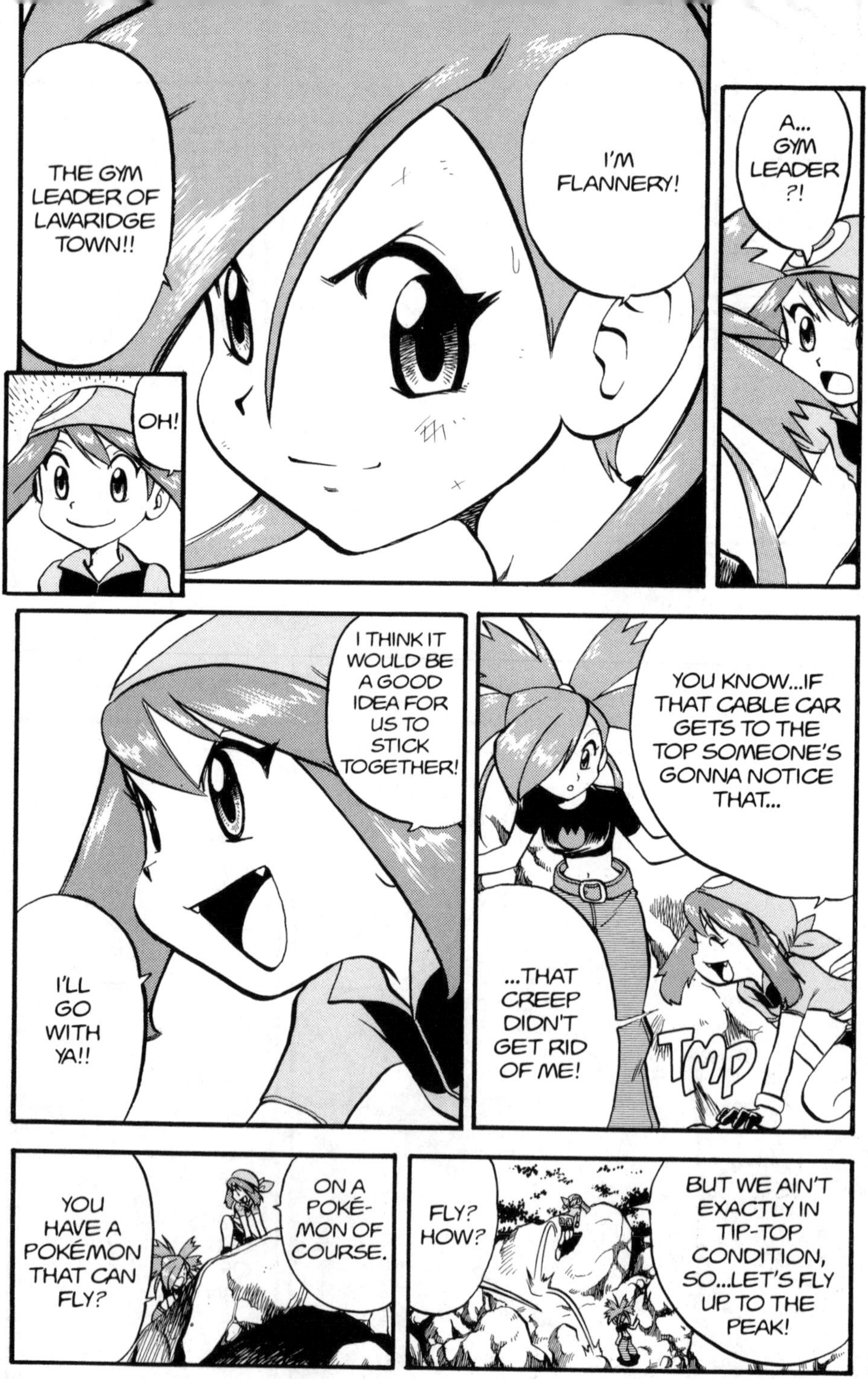
A... GYM LEADER ?!
I'M FLANNERY!
THE GYM LEADER OF LAVARIDGE TOWN!!
OH!
YOU KNOW...IF THAT CABLE CAR GETS TO THE TOP SOMEONE'S GONNA NOTICE THAT...
...THAT CREEP DIDN'T GET RID OF ME!
TMP
I THINK IT WOULD BE A GOOD IDEA FOR US TO STICK TOGETHER!
I'LL GO WITH YA!!
BUT WE AIN'T EXACTLY IN TIP-TOP CONDITION, SO...LET'S FLY UP TO THE PEAK!
FLY? HOW?
ON A POKÉ-MON OF COURSE.
YOU HAVE A POKÉMON THAT CAN FLY?

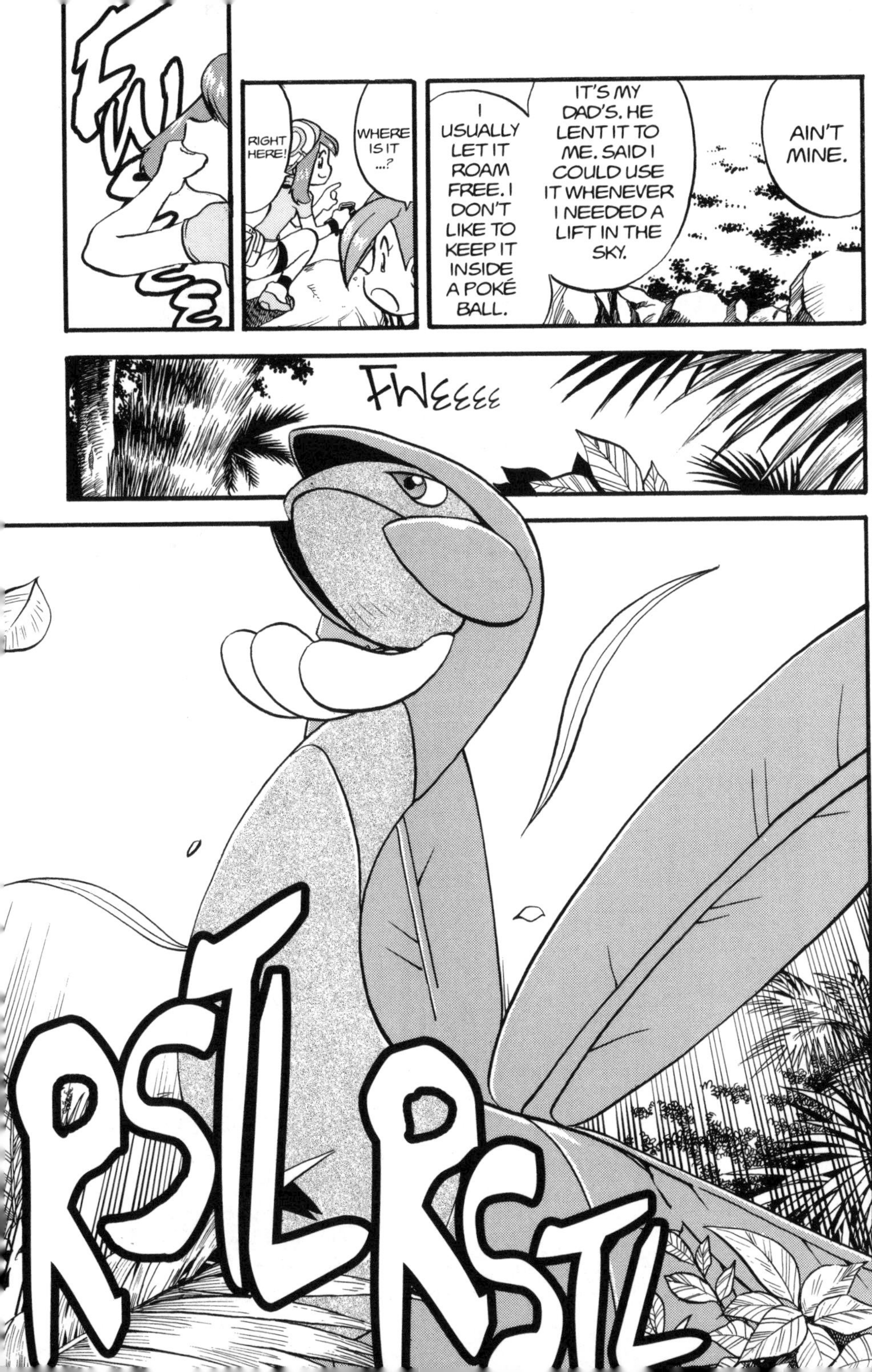
AIN'T MINE.
IT'S MY DAD'S. HE LENT IT TO ME. SAID I COULD USE IT WHENEVER I NEEDED A LIFT IN THE SKY.
I USUALLY LET IT ROAM FREE. I DON'T LIKE TO KEEP IT INSIDE A POKÉ BALL.
WHERE IS IT ...?
RIGHT HERE!
FWEEEE
RSTL RSTL

● Adventure 214 ●
Assaulted by Pelipper, Part 1

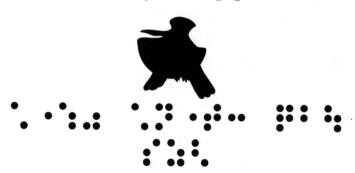

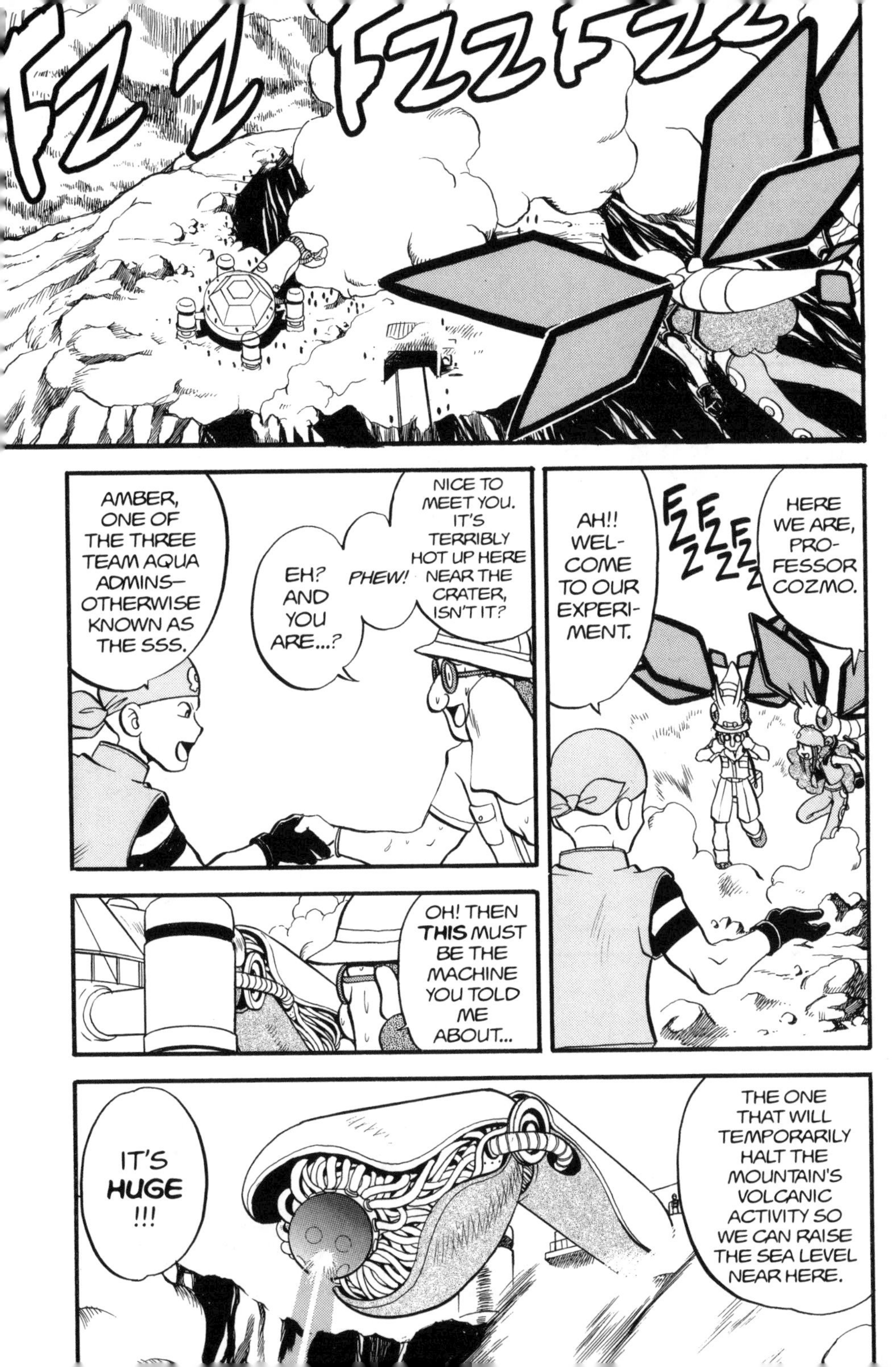
FZZ FZZFZZ
HERE WE ARE, PROFESSOR COZMO.
FZZFZZFZZ
AH!! WELCOME TO OUR EXPERIMENT.
NICE TO MEET YOU. IT'S TERRIBLY HOT UP HERE NEAR THE CRATER, ISN'T IT?
PHEW!
EH? AND YOU ARE...?
AMBER, ONE OF THE THREE TEAM AQUA ADMINS—OTHERWISE KNOWN AS THE SSS.
OH! THEN **THIS** MUST BE THE MACHINE YOU TOLD ME ABOUT...
THE ONE THAT WILL TEMPORARILY HALT THE MOUNTAIN'S VOLCANIC ACTIVITY SO WE CAN RAISE THE SEA LEVEL NEAR HERE.
IT'S **HUGE** !!!

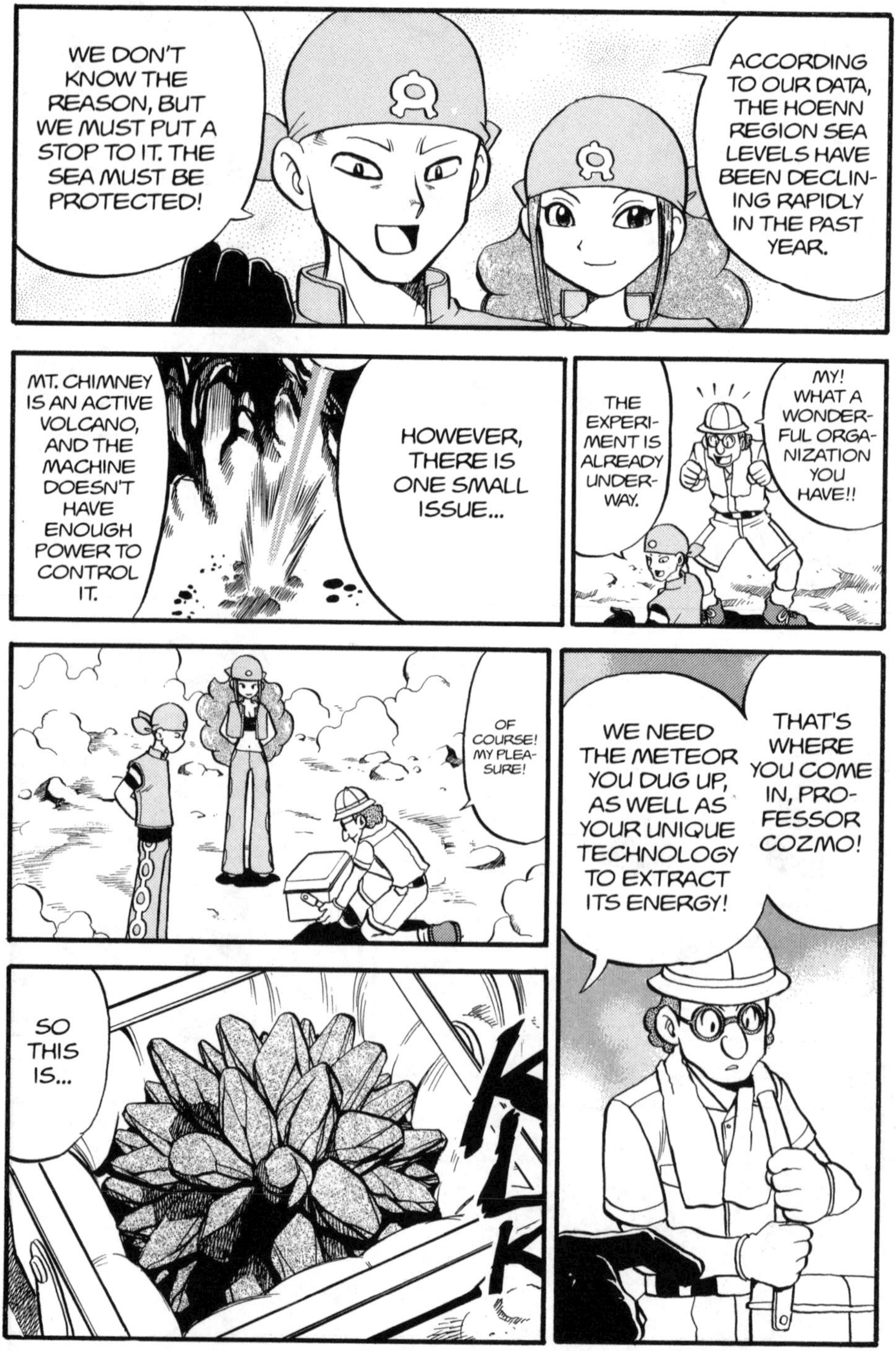
ACCORDING TO OUR DATA, THE HOENN REGION SEA LEVELS HAVE BEEN DECLINING RAPIDLY IN THE PAST YEAR.
WE DON'T KNOW THE REASON, BUT WE MUST PUT A STOP TO IT. THE SEA MUST BE PROTECTED!
MY! WHAT A WONDERFUL ORGANIZATION YOU HAVE!!
THE EXPERIMENT IS ALREADY UNDERWAY.
HOWEVER, THERE IS ONE SMALL ISSUE...
MT. CHIMNEY IS AN ACTIVE VOLCANO, AND THE MACHINE DOESN'T HAVE ENOUGH POWER TO CONTROL IT.
THAT'S WHERE YOU COME IN, PROFESSOR COZMO!
WE NEED THE METEOR YOU DUG UP, AS WELL AS YOUR UNIQUE TECHNOLOGY TO EXTRACT ITS ENERGY!
OF COURSE! MY PLEASURE!
SO THIS IS...

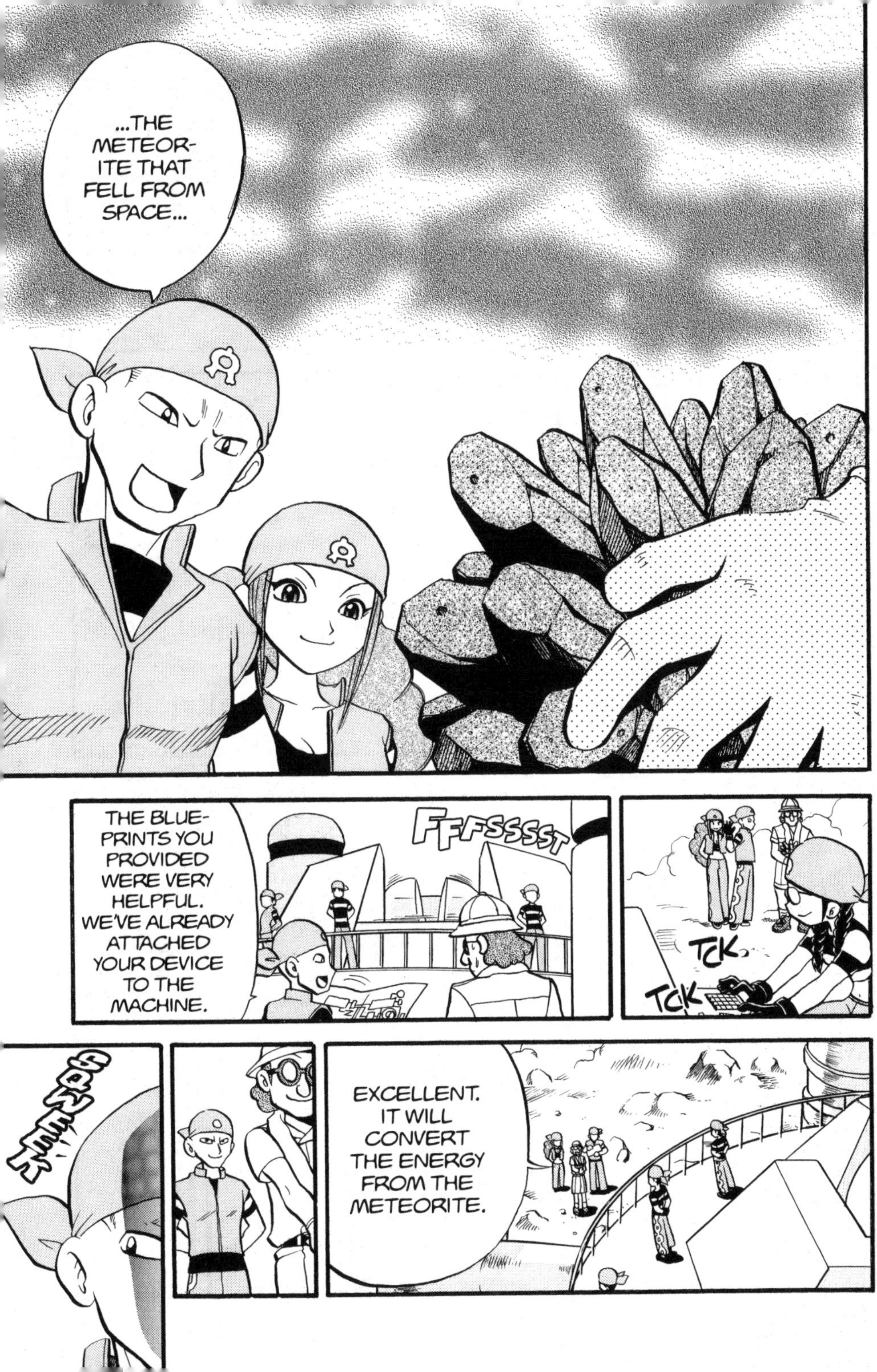
...THE METEORITE THAT FELL FROM SPACE...
TCK
TCK
FFFSSSST
THE BLUEPRINTS YOU PROVIDED WERE VERY HELPFUL. WE'VE ALREADY ATTACHED YOUR DEVICE TO THE MACHINE.
EXCELLENT. IT WILL CONVERT THE ENERGY FROM THE METEORITE.

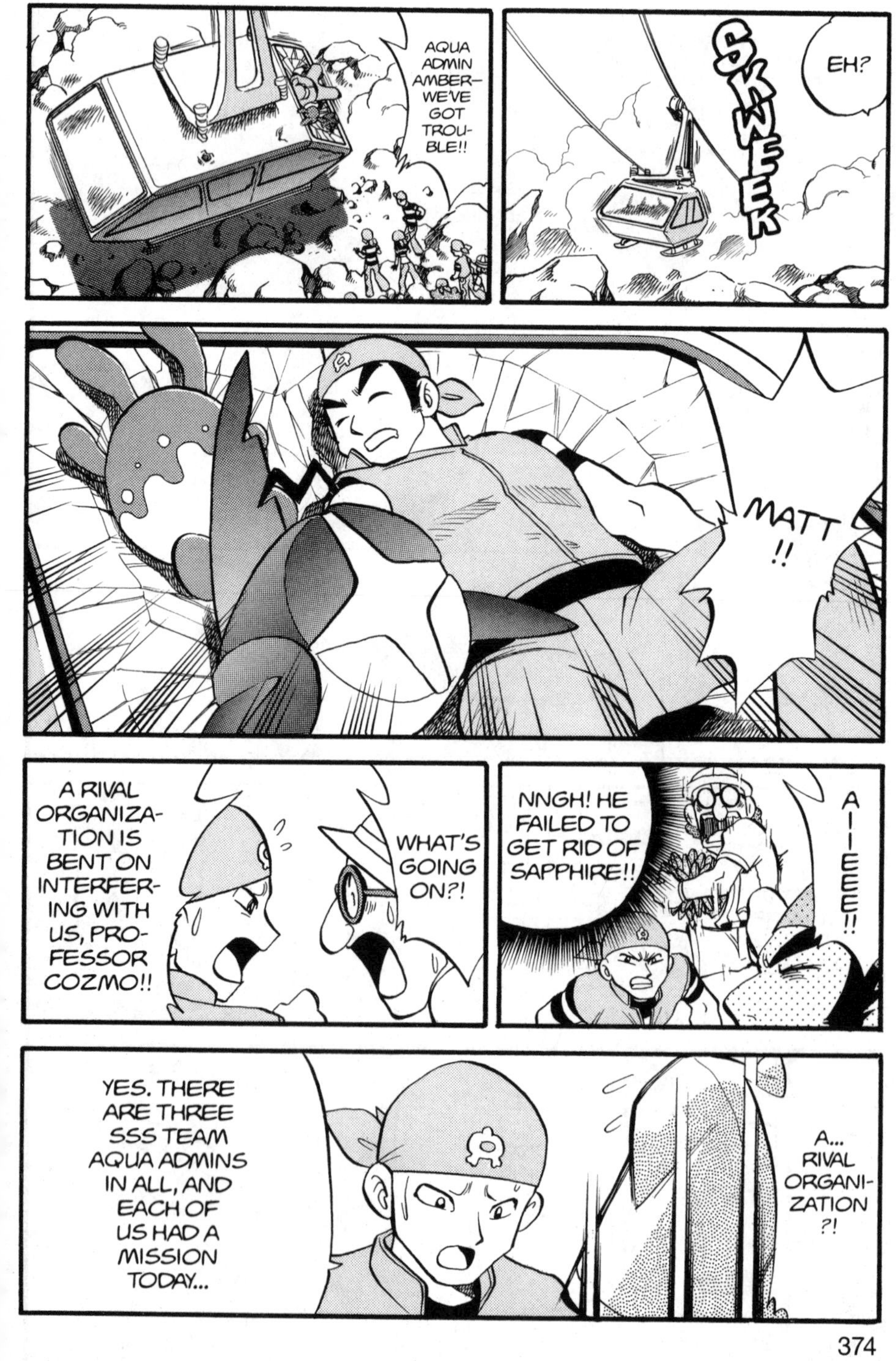
EH?
SKWEEK
AQUA ADMIN AMBER— WE'VE GOT TROUBLE!!
MATT!!
AIIEEEE!!
NNGH! HE FAILED TO GET RID OF SAPPHIRE!!
WHAT'S GOING ON?!
A RIVAL ORGANIZATION IS BENT ON INTERFERING WITH US, PROFESSOR COZMO!!
A... RIVAL ORGANIZATION?!
YES. THERE ARE THREE SSS TEAM AQUA ADMINS IN ALL, AND EACH OF US HAD A MISSION TODAY...

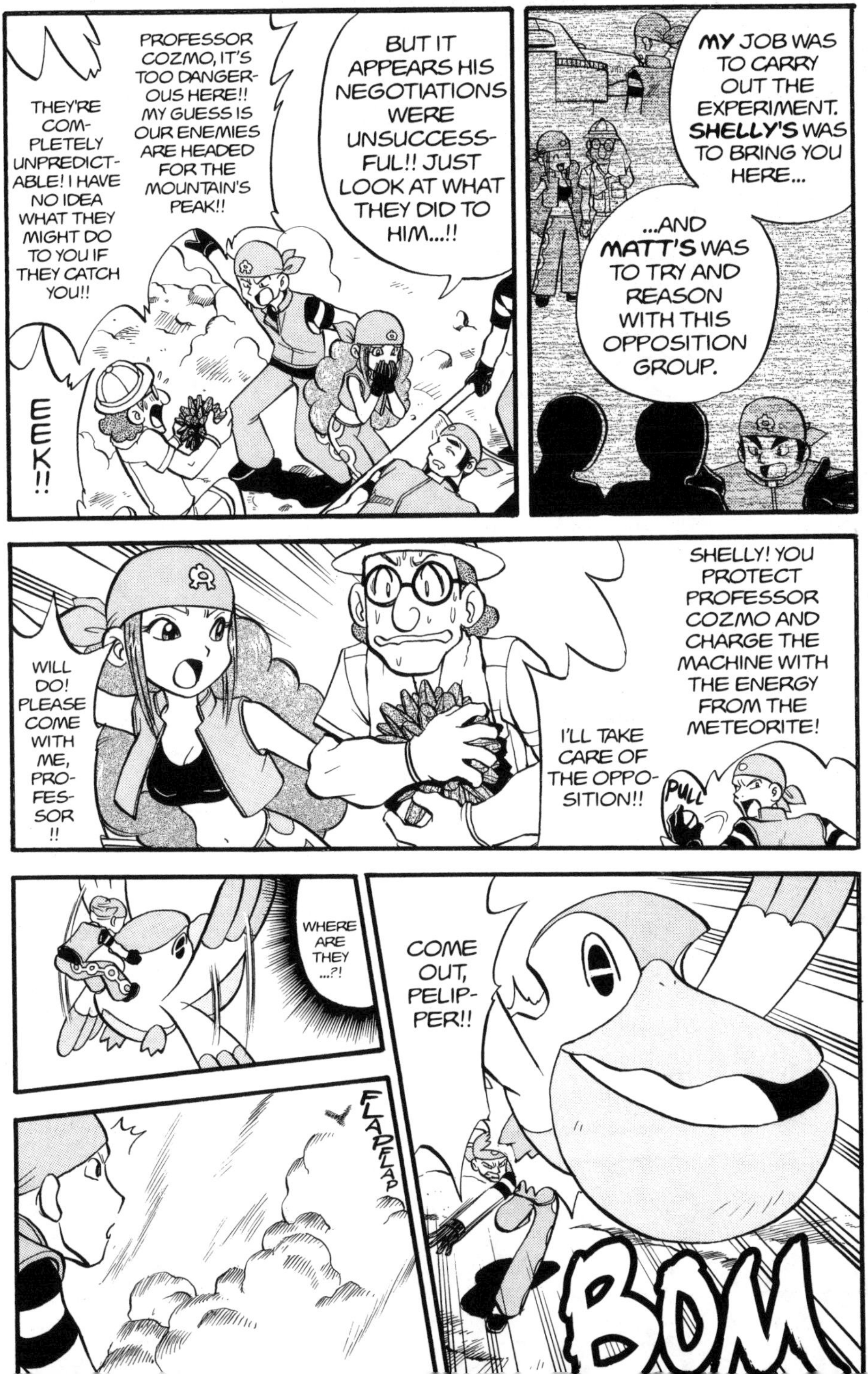
MY JOB WAS TO CARRY OUT THE EXPERIMENT. SHELLY'S WAS TO BRING YOU HERE...
...AND MATT'S WAS TO TRY AND REASON WITH THIS OPPOSITION GROUP.
BUT IT APPEARS HIS NEGOTIATIONS WERE UNSUCCESS-FUL!! JUST LOOK AT WHAT THEY DID TO HIM...!!
PROFESSOR COZMO, IT'S TOO DANGER-OUS HERE!! MY GUESS IS OUR ENEMIES ARE HEADED FOR THE MOUNTAIN'S PEAK!!
THEY'RE COM-PLETELY UNPREDICT-ABLE! I HAVE NO IDEA WHAT THEY MIGHT DO TO YOU IF THEY CATCH YOU!!
EEEK!!
SHELLY! YOU PROTECT PROFESSOR COZMO AND CHARGE THE MACHINE WITH THE ENERGY FROM THE METEORITE!
I'LL TAKE CARE OF THE OPPO-SITION!!
PULL
WILL DO! PLEASE COME WITH ME, PRO-FES-SOR!!
COME OUT, PELIP-PER!!
BOM
WHERE ARE THEY ...?!
FLAPFLAP

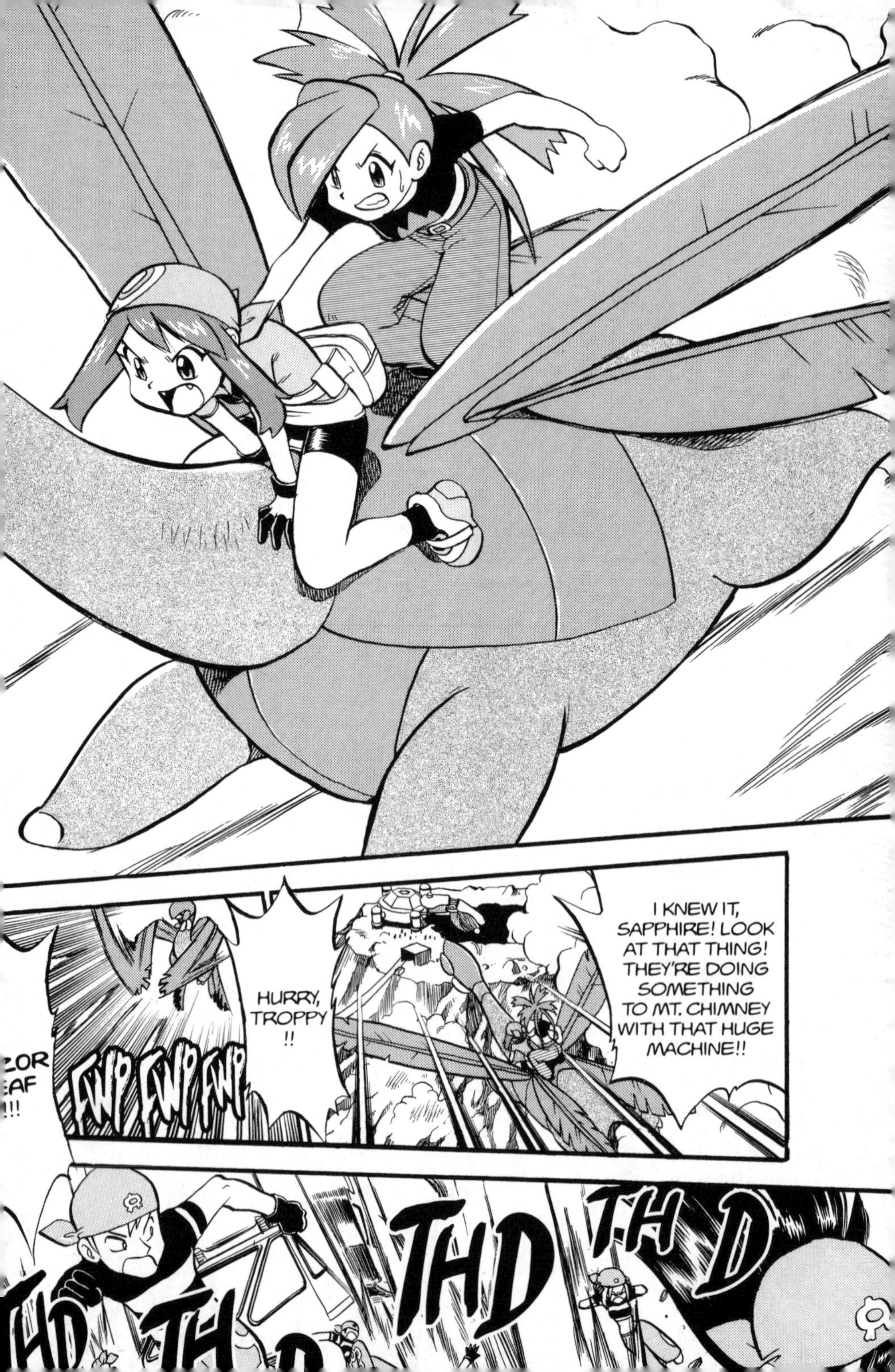
I KNEW IT, SAPPHIRE! LOOK AT THAT THING! THEY'RE DOING SOMETHING TO MT. CHIMNEY WITH THAT HUGE MACHINE!!
HURRY, TROPPY!!
FWP FWP FWP
THD
THD
THD

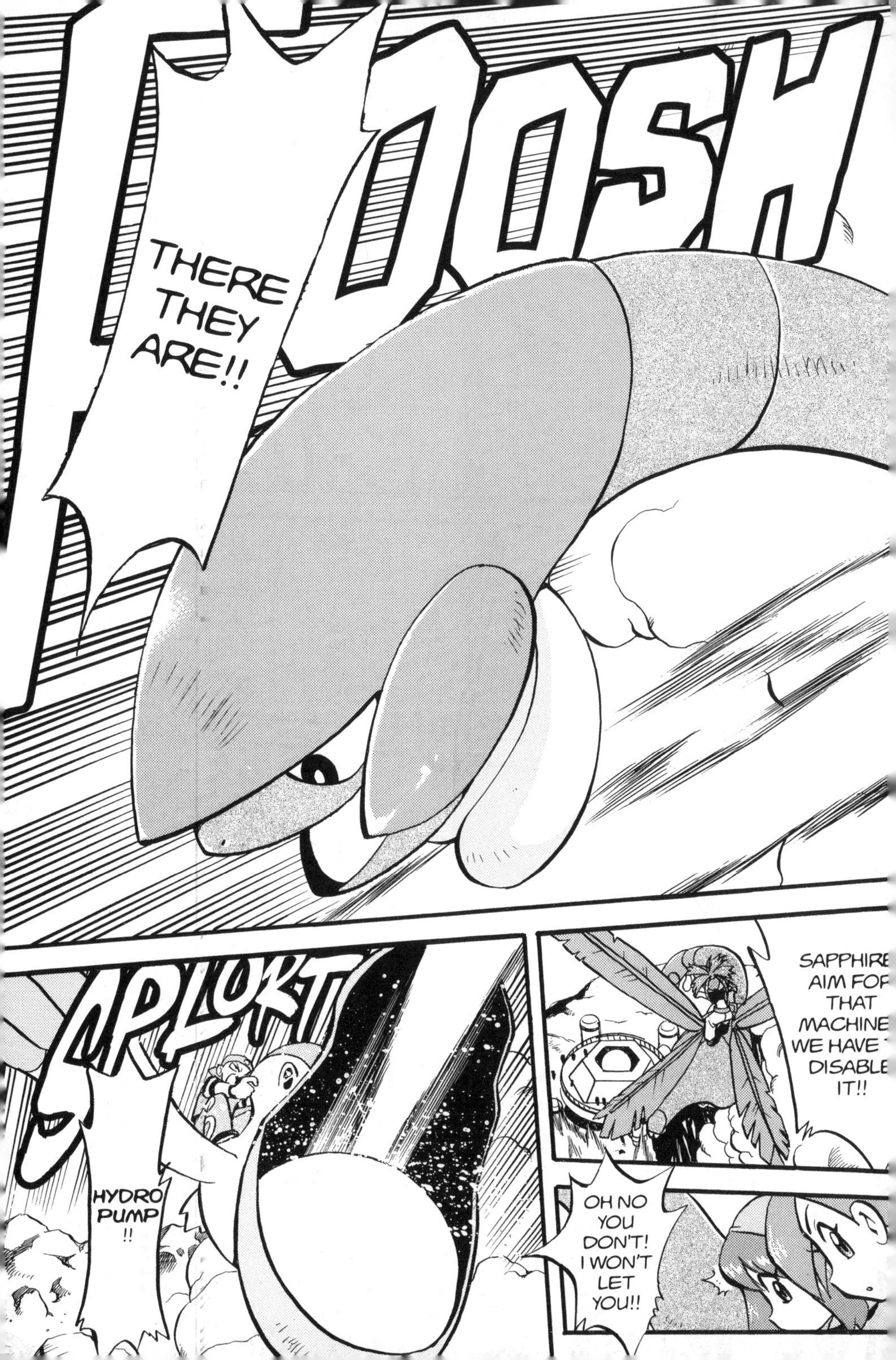
OOSH
THERE THEY ARE!!
SAPPHIRE AIM FOR THAT MACHINE WE HAVE T DISABLE IT!!
OH NO YOU DON'T! I WON'T LET YOU!!
APLORT
HYDRO PUMP !!

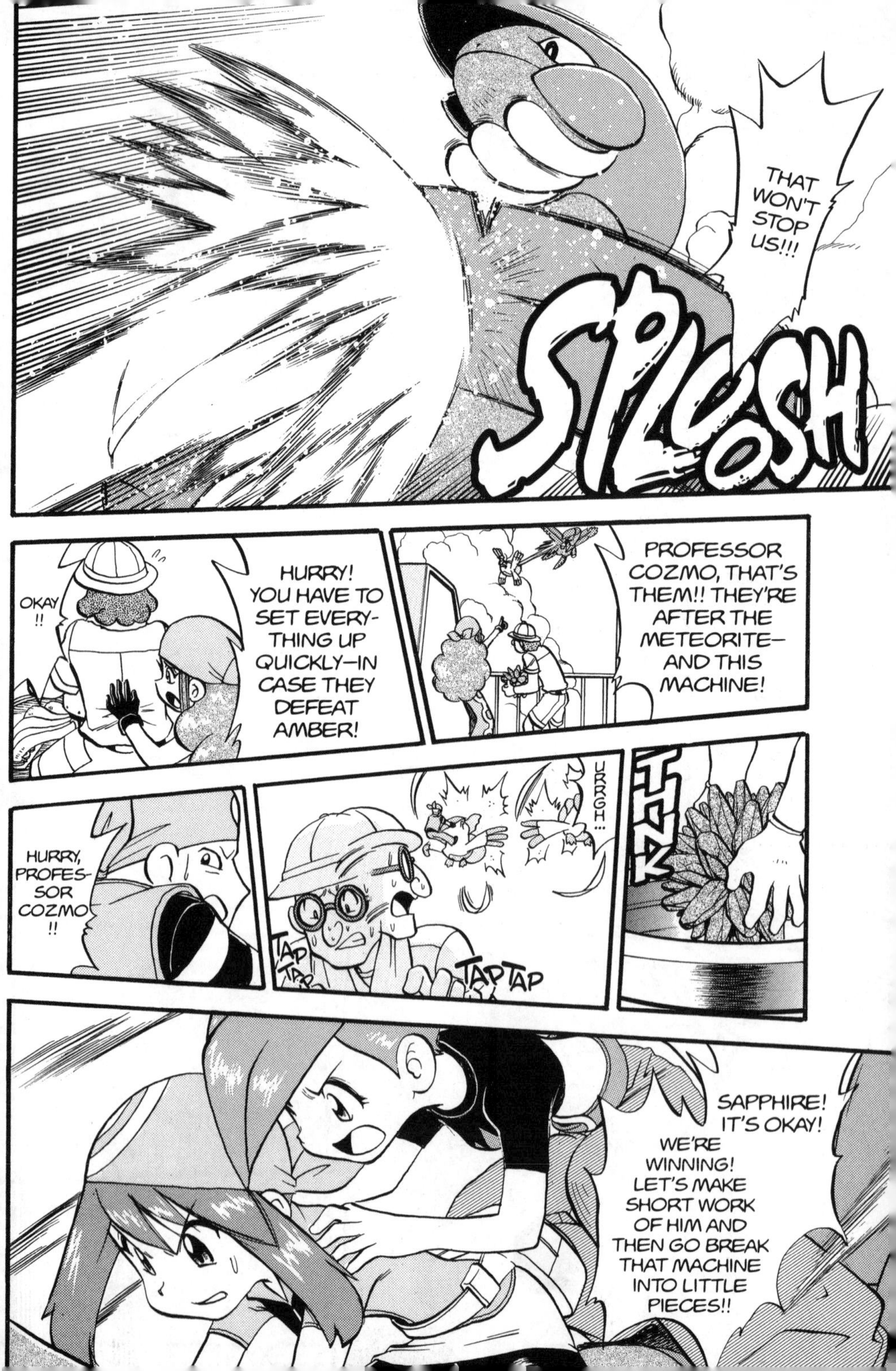
THAT WON'T STOP US!!!
SPLOOSH
PROFESSOR COZMO, THAT'S THEM!! THEY'RE AFTER THE METEORITE—AND THIS MACHINE!
HURRY! YOU HAVE TO SET EVERYTHING UP QUICKLY—IN CASE THEY DEFEAT AMBER!
OKAY!!
THUNK
URRGH...
TAP TAP
TAPTAP
HURRY, PROFESSOR COZMO!!
SAPPHIRE! IT'S OKAY! WE'RE WINNING! LET'S MAKE SHORT WORK OF HIM AND THEN GO BREAK THAT MACHINE INTO LITTLE PIECES!!

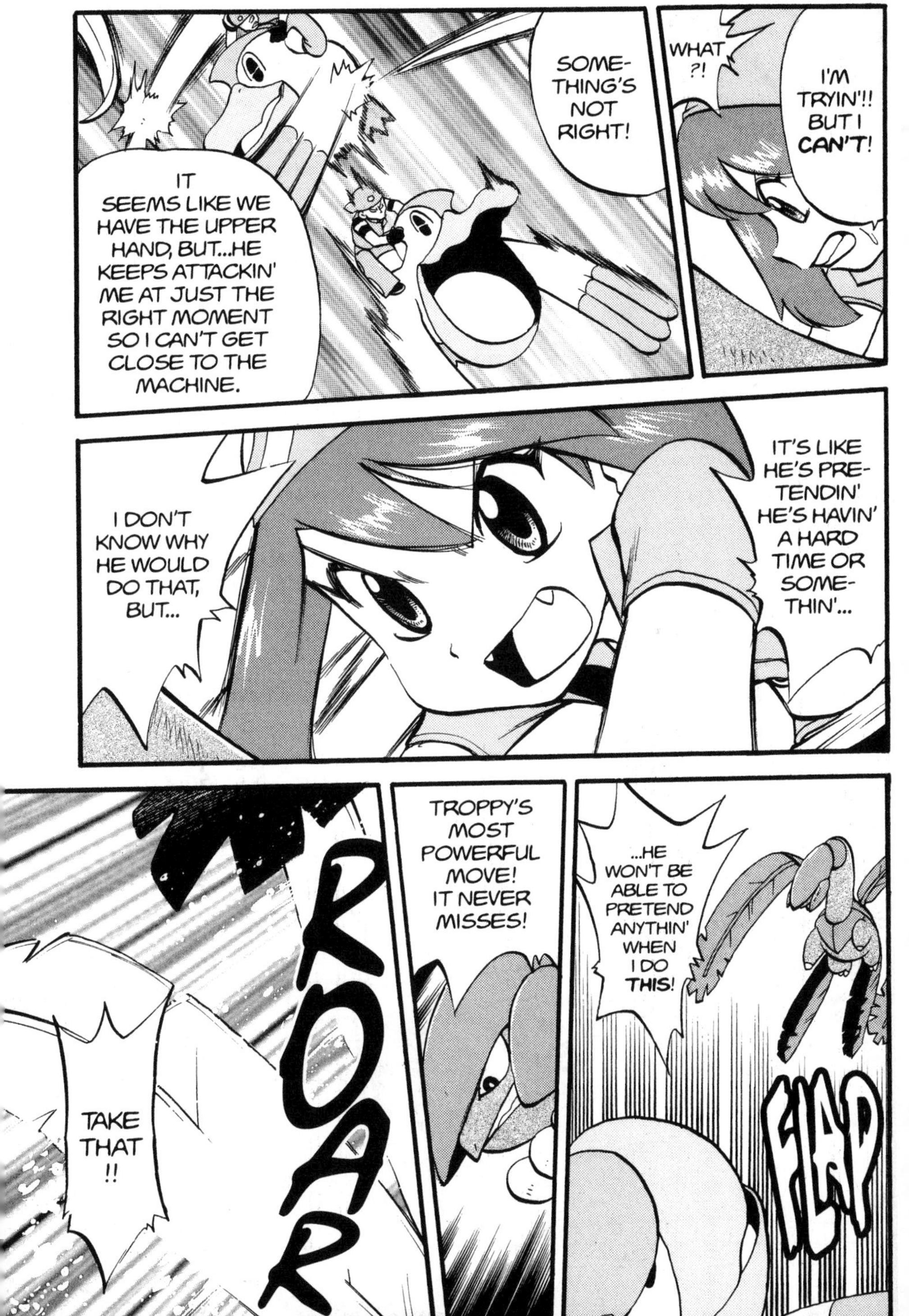
WHAT ?!
I'M TRYIN'!! BUT I CAN'T!
SOME-THING'S NOT RIGHT!
IT SEEMS LIKE WE HAVE THE UPPER HAND, BUT...HE KEEPS ATTACKIN' ME AT JUST THE RIGHT MOMENT SO I CAN'T GET CLOSE TO THE MACHINE.
IT'S LIKE HE'S PRE-TENDIN' HE'S HAVIN' A HARD TIME OR SOME-THIN'...
I DON'T KNOW WHY HE WOULD DO THAT, BUT...
...HE WON'T BE ABLE TO PRETEND ANYTHIN' WHEN I DO THIS!
FLAP
TROPPY'S MOST POWERFUL MOVE! IT NEVER MISSES!
ROAR
TAKE THAT !!

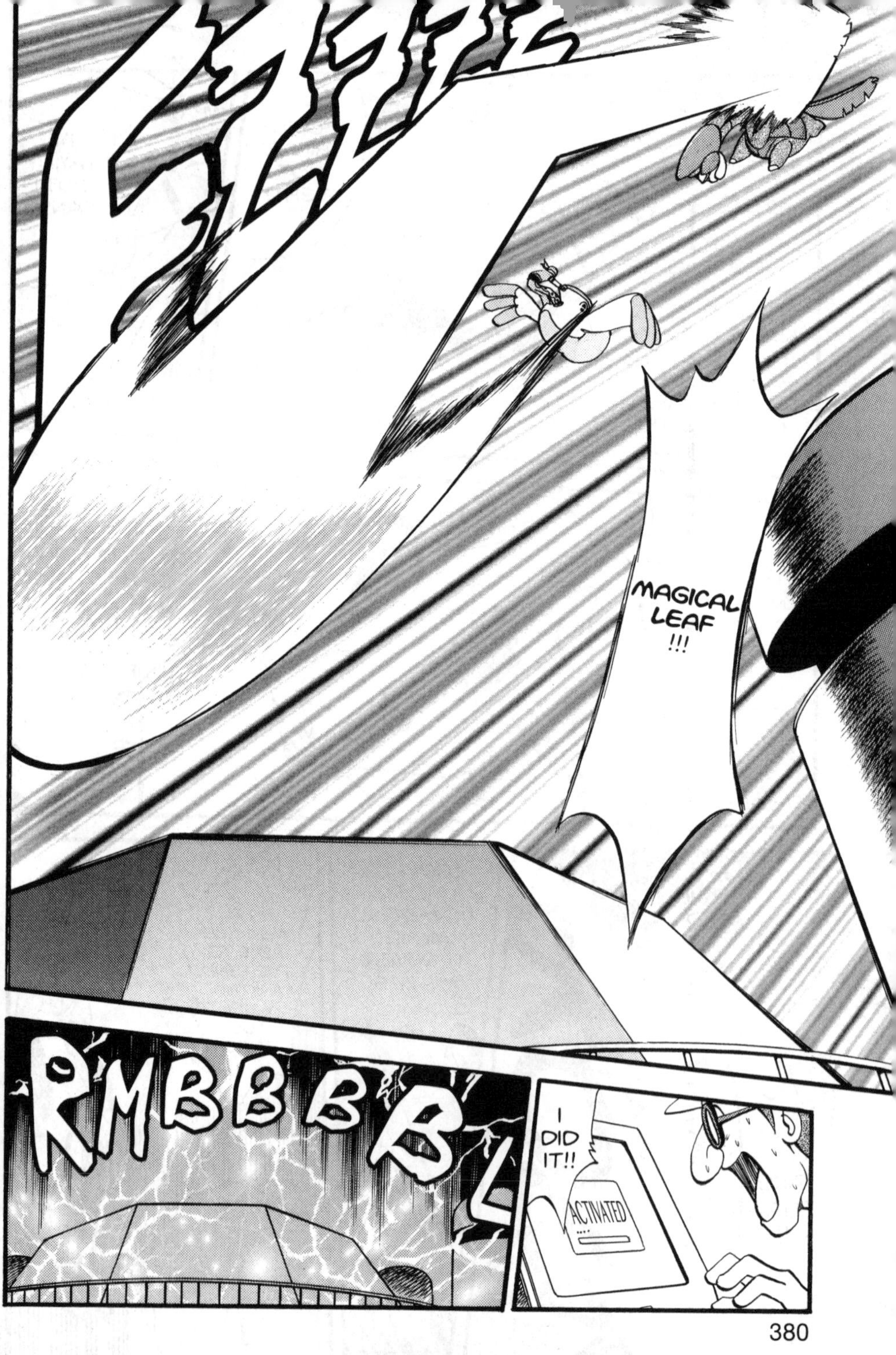
MAGICAL LEAF !!!
I DID IT!!
ACTIVATED
RMBBBBL

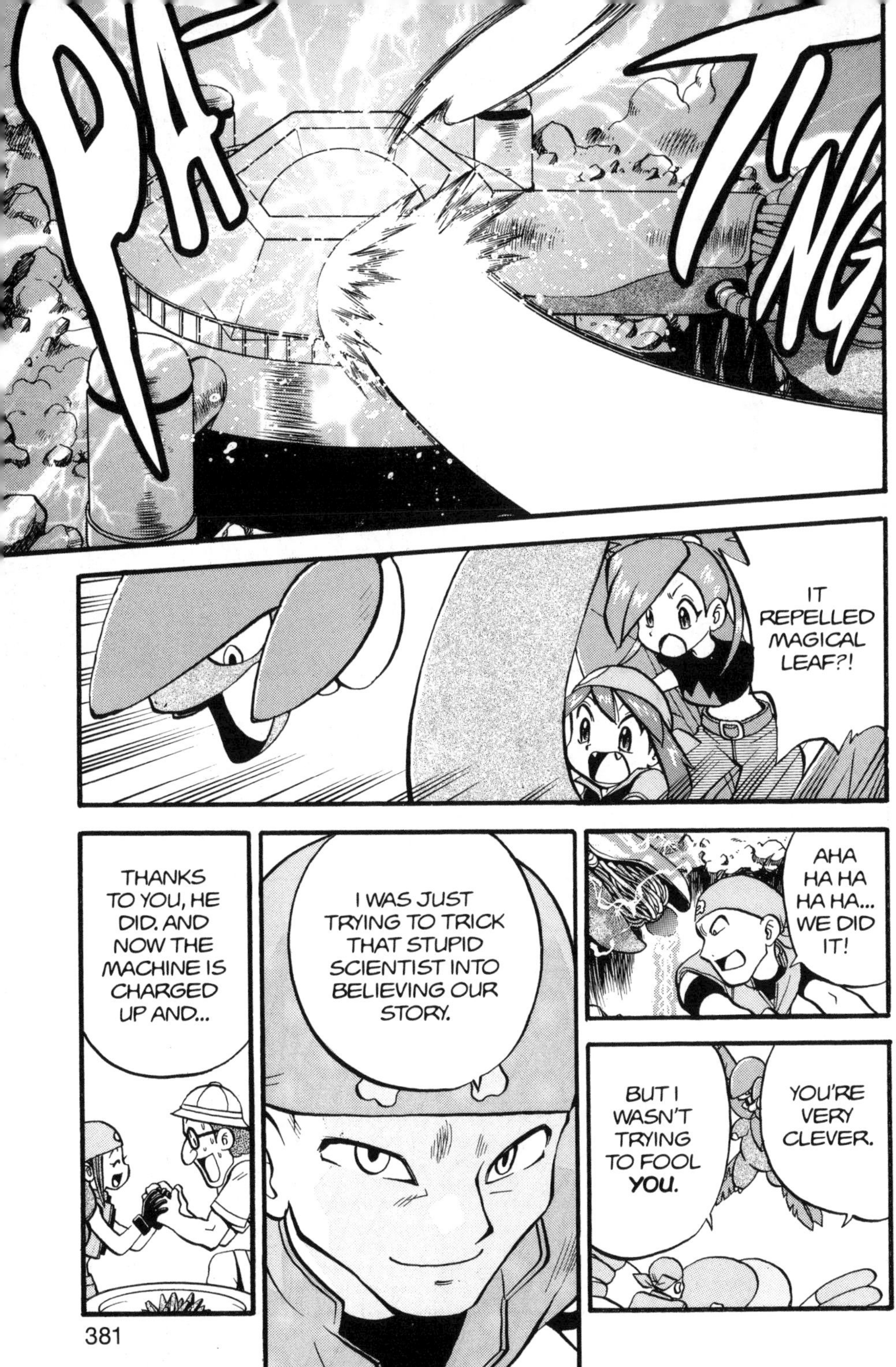
PA
TWNG
IT REPELLED MAGICAL LEAF?!
AHA HA HA HA HA... WE DID IT!
YOU'RE VERY CLEVER.
BUT I WASN'T TRYING TO FOOL **YOU**.
I WAS JUST TRYING TO TRICK THAT STUPID SCIENTIST INTO BELIEVING OUR STORY.
THANKS TO YOU, HE DID. AND NOW THE MACHINE IS CHARGED UP AND...

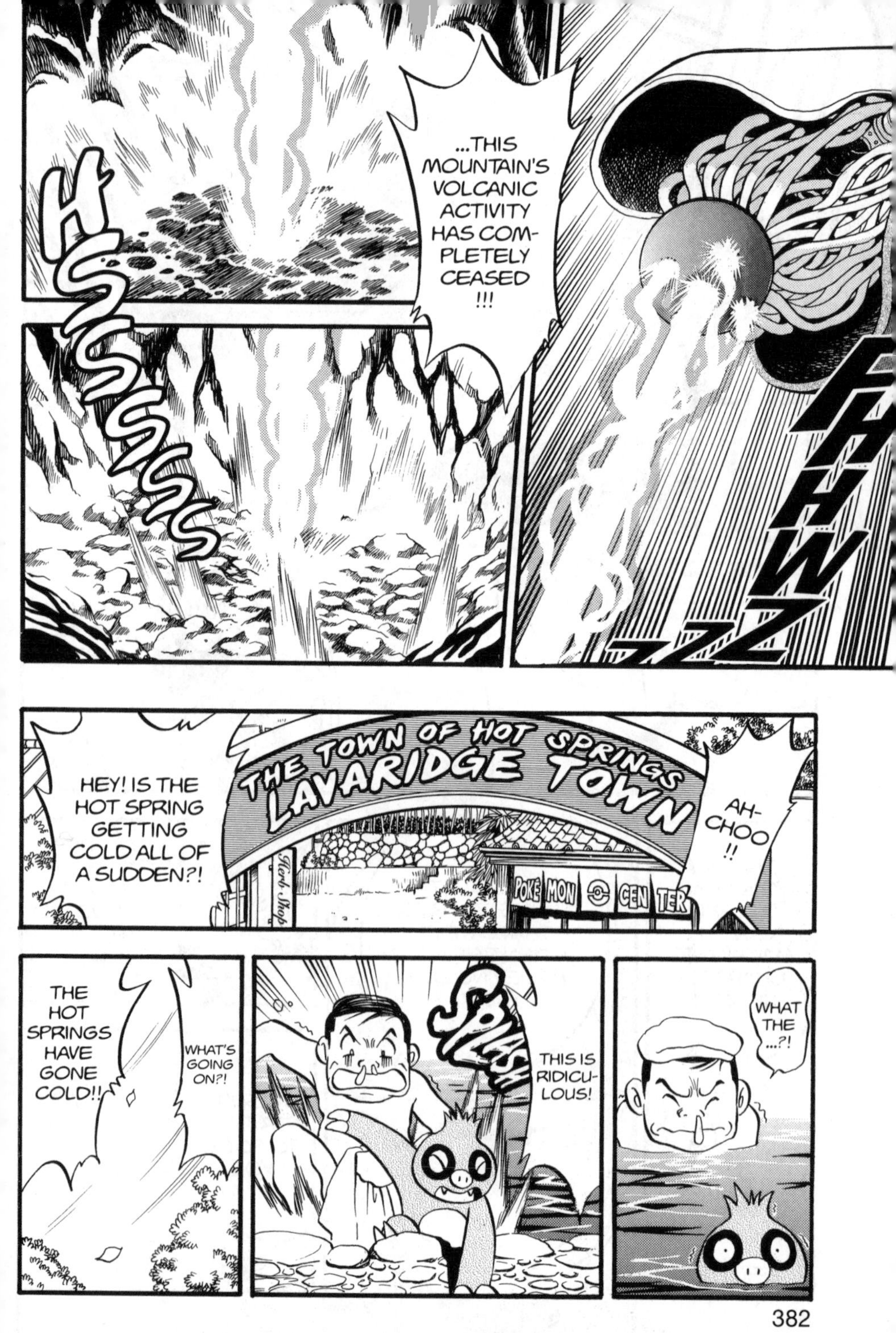
...THIS MOUNTAIN'S VOLCANIC ACTIVITY HAS COMPLETELY CEASED!!!
HSSSSSS
THE TOWN OF HOT SPRINGS
LAVARIDGE TOWN
AH-CHOO!!
HEY! IS THE HOT SPRING GETTING COLD ALL OF A SUDDEN?!
POKÉMON CENTER
Herb Shop
WHAT THE ...?!
SPLASH
THIS IS RIDICULOUS!
WHAT'S GOING ON?!
THE HOT SPRINGS HAVE GONE COLD!!

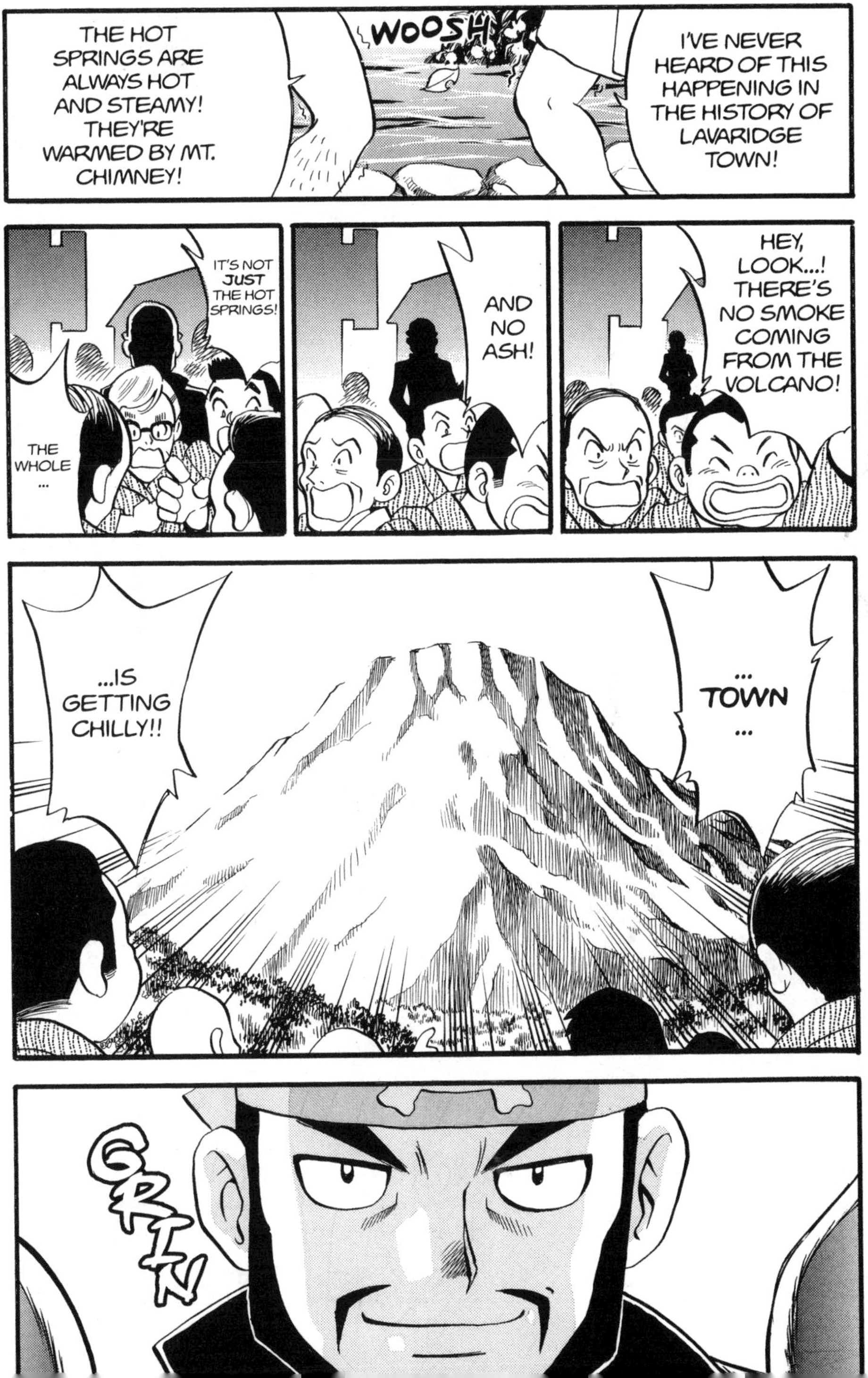
I'VE NEVER HEARD OF THIS HAPPENING IN THE HISTORY OF LAVARIDGE TOWN!
WOOSH
THE HOT SPRINGS ARE ALWAYS HOT AND STEAMY! THEY'RE WARMED BY MT. CHIMNEY!
HEY, LOOK...! THERE'S NO SMOKE COMING FROM THE VOLCANO!
AND NO ASH!
IT'S NOT JUST THE HOT SPRINGS!
THE WHOLE ...
... TOWN ...
...IS GETTING CHILLY!!
GRIN

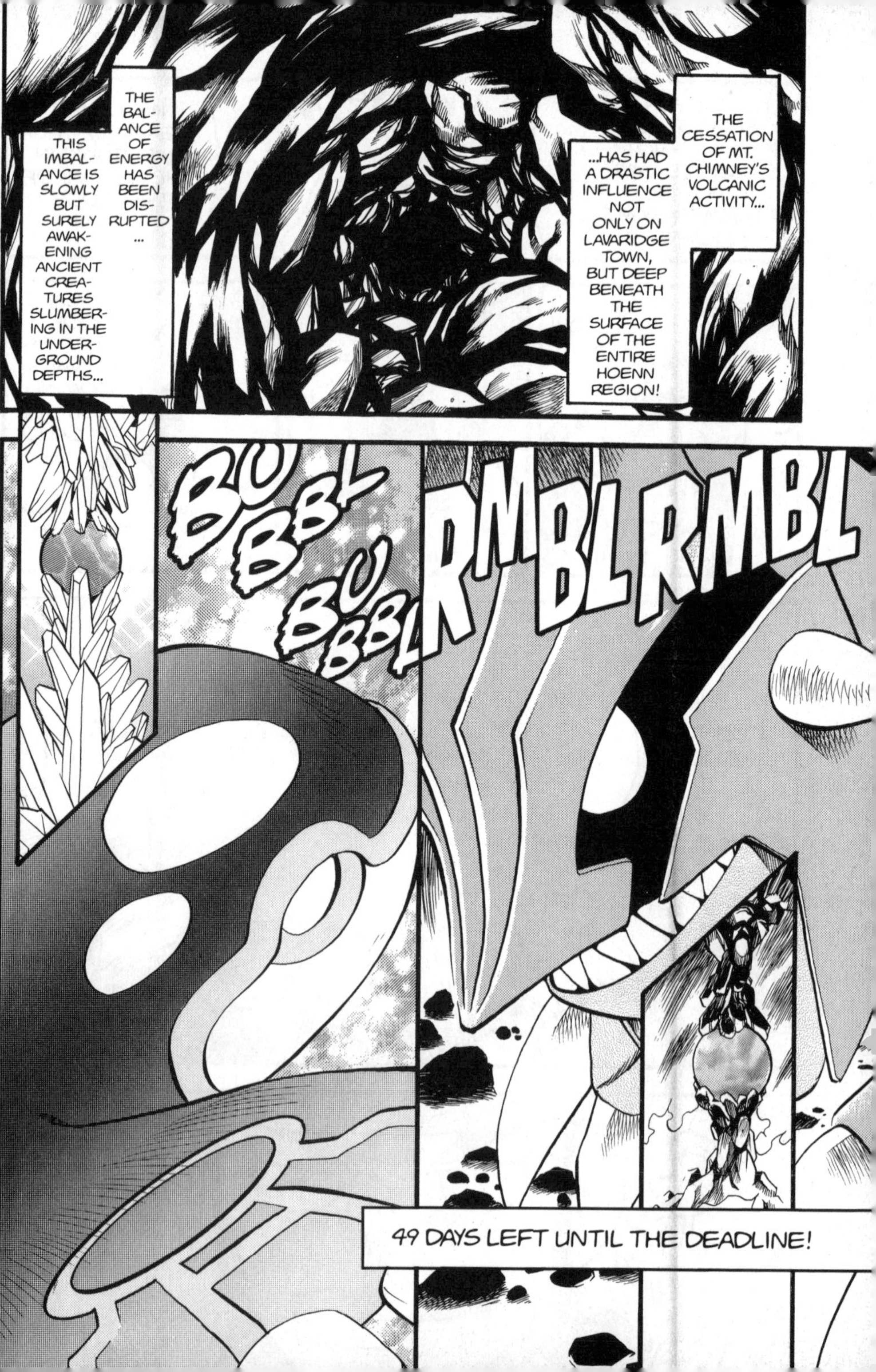
THE CESSATION OF MT. CHIMNEY'S VOLCANIC ACTIVITY...
...HAS HAD A DRASTIC INFLUENCE NOT ONLY ON LAVARIDGE TOWN, BUT DEEP BENEATH THE SURFACE OF THE ENTIRE HOENN REGION!
THE BALANCE OF ENERGY HAS BEEN DISRUPTED...
THIS IMBALANCE IS SLOWLY BUT SURELY AWAKENING ANCIENT CREATURES SLUMBERING IN THE UNDERGROUND DEPTHS...
RMBL RMBL
49 DAYS LEFT UNTIL THE DEADLINE!
BUBBL BUBBL

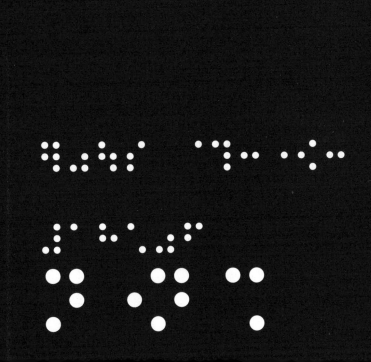

Message from
Hidenori Kusaka

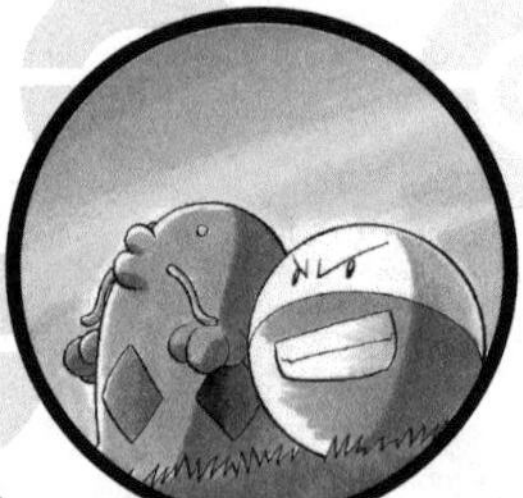

You can play with *Pokémon FireRed* and *Pokémon LeafGreen* in all sorts of ways, so I've been playing these games for a really long time. Communication is an important aspect of these Pokémon games. Unfortunately, at the moment I don't have anybody to play with. But I'll get my chance at large events, which are attended by lots of players. In fact, I'm off to one of them now with my game console!

—2004

Message from
Satoshi Yamamoto

It's been four years since I started working on *Pokémon Adventures*. This is the first long series that I've done, and volume 18 marks my ninth volume! I like a lot of the episodes and characters, but I get encouragement by always telling myself, "This latest volume is the best!" (*laugh*)

—2004

● Adventure 215 ●
Assaulted by Pelipper, Part 2

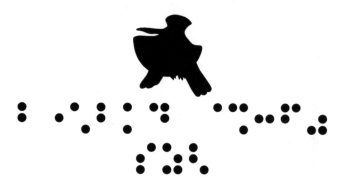

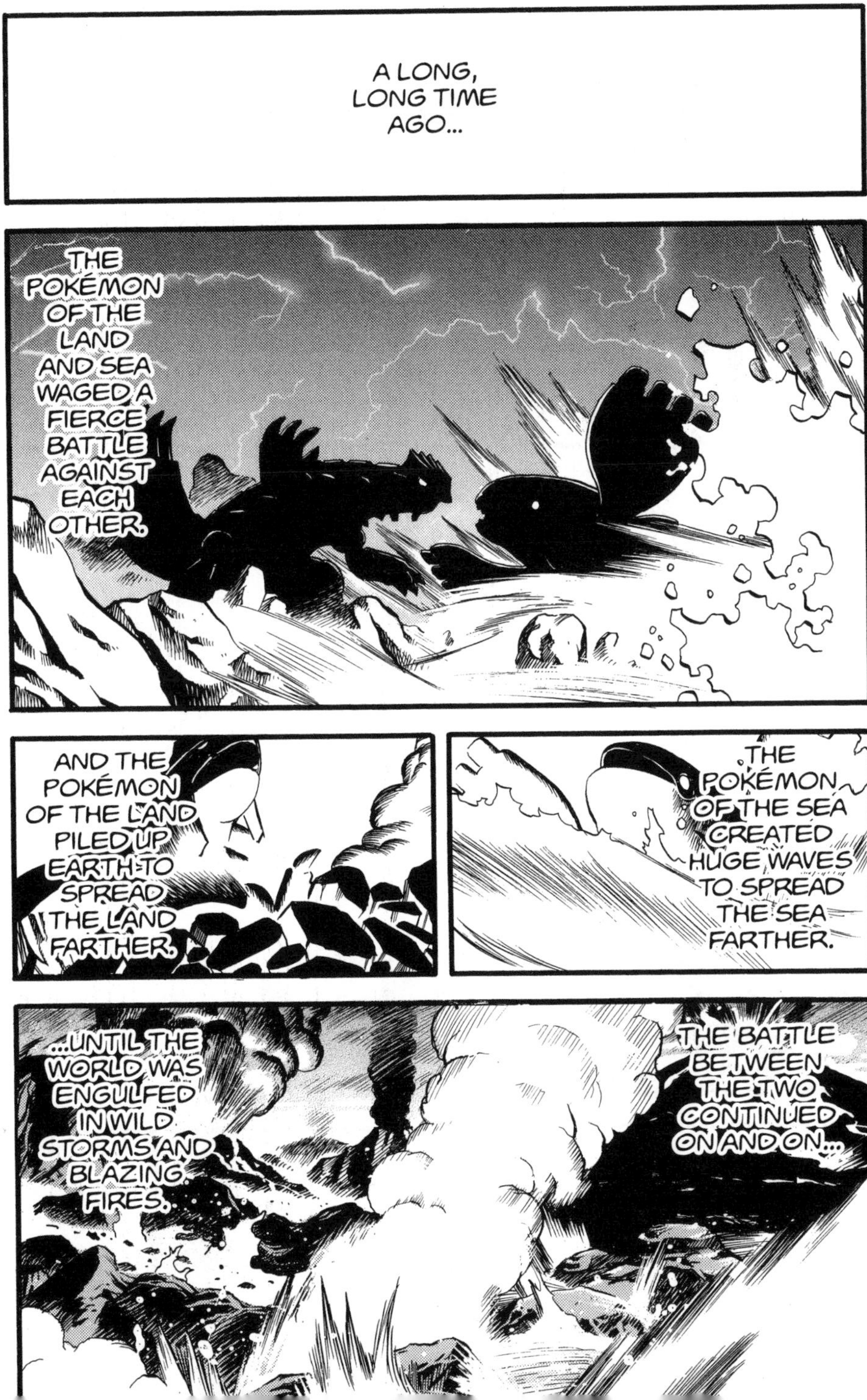
A LONG, LONG TIME AGO...
THE POKÉMON OF THE LAND AND SEA WAGED A FIERCE BATTLE AGAINST EACH OTHER.
THE POKÉMON OF THE SEA CREATED HUGE WAVES TO SPREAD THE SEA FARTHER.
AND THE POKÉMON OF THE LAND PILED UP EARTH TO SPREAD THE LAND FARTHER.
THE BATTLE BETWEEN THE TWO CONTINUED ON AND ON...
...UNTIL THE WORLD WAS ENGULFED IN WILD STORMS AND BLAZING FIRES.

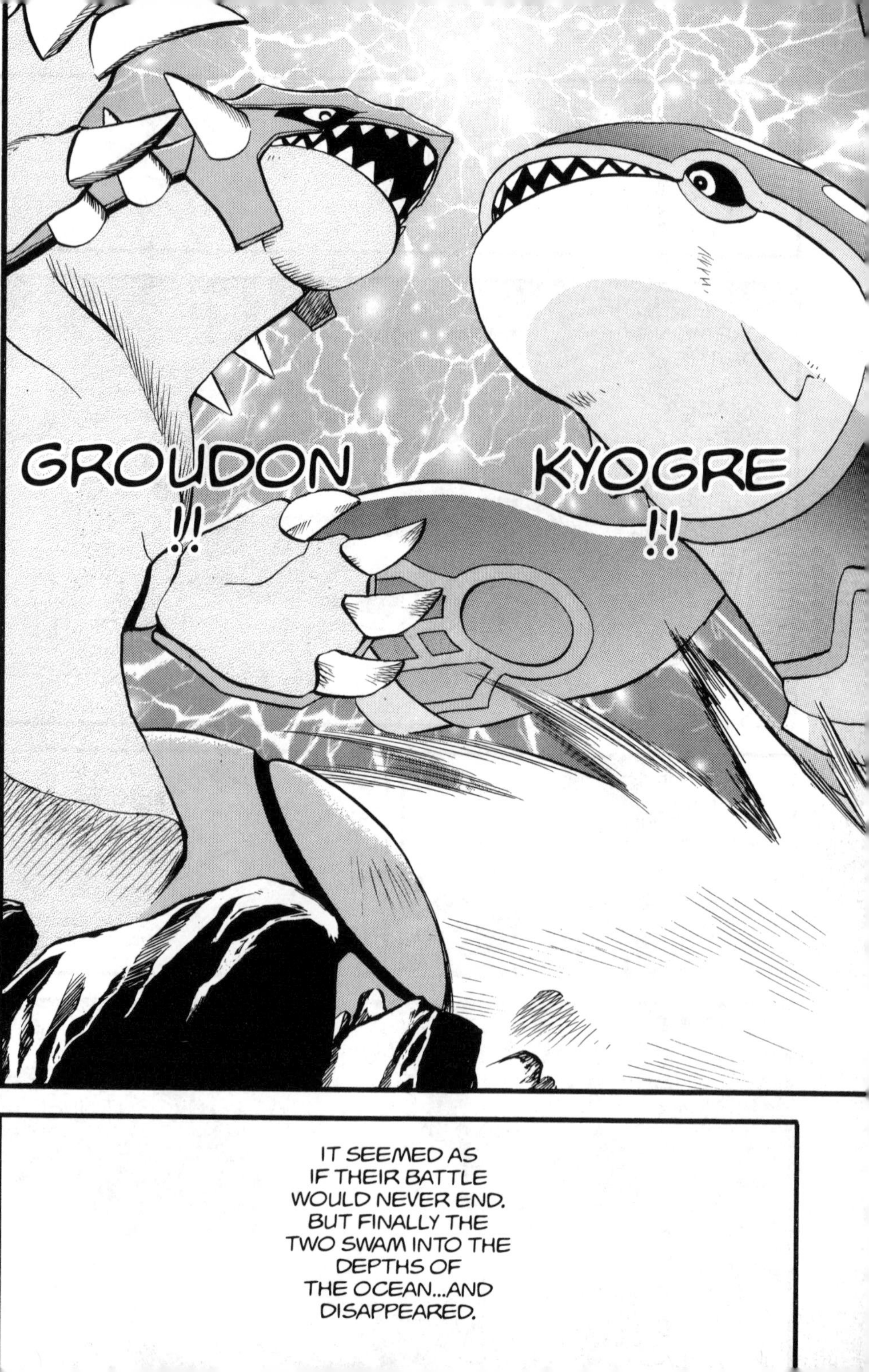
KYOGRE !!
GROUDON !!
IT SEEMED AS IF THEIR BATTLE WOULD NEVER END. BUT FINALLY THE TWO SWAM INTO THE DEPTHS OF THE OCEAN...AND DISAPPEARED.

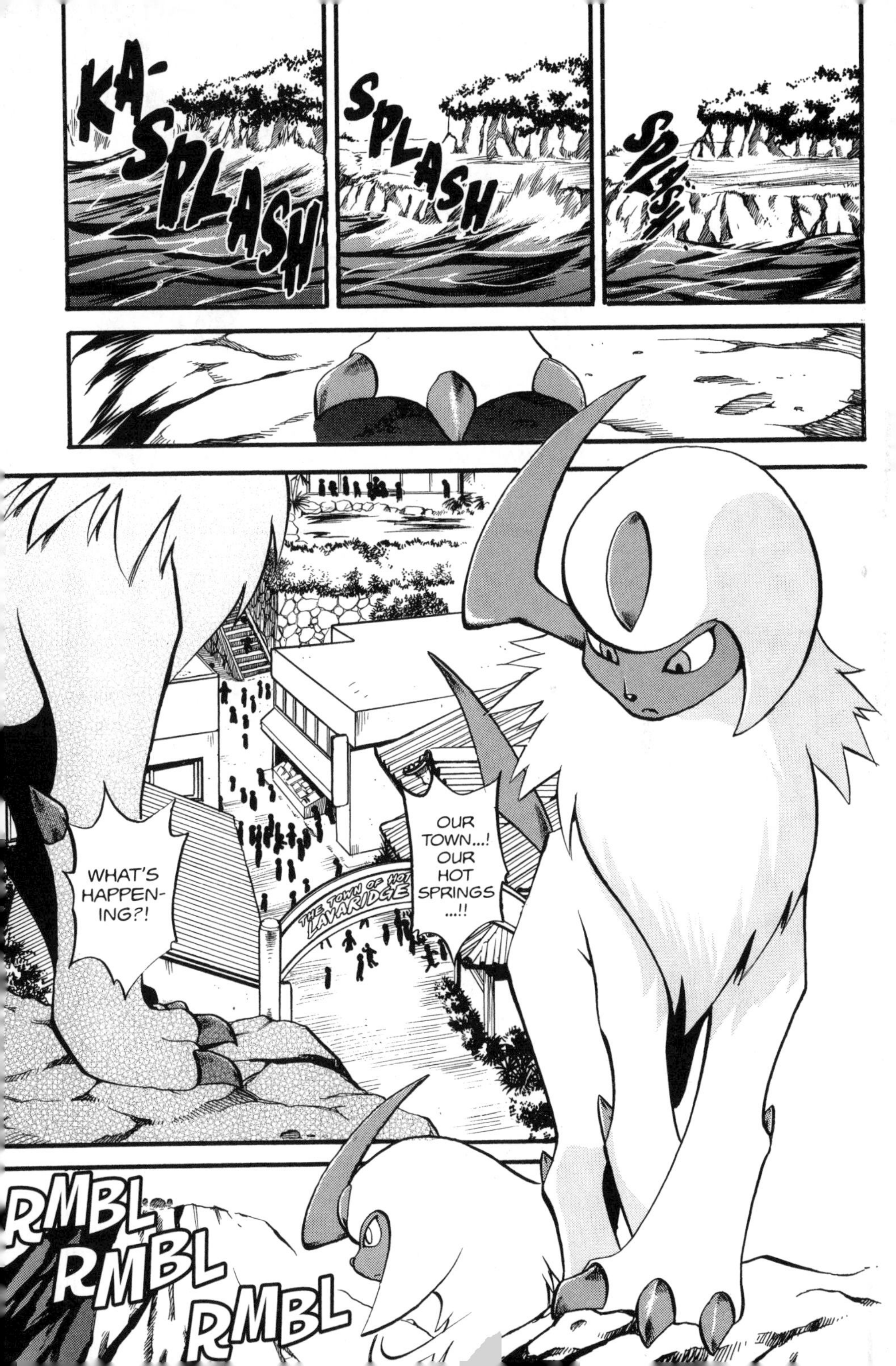
SPLASH
SPLASH
KA-SPLASH
OUR TOWN...! OUR HOT SPRINGS ...!!
THE TOWN OF HOT LAVARIDGE
WHAT'S HAPPEN-ING?!
RMBL RMBL RMBL

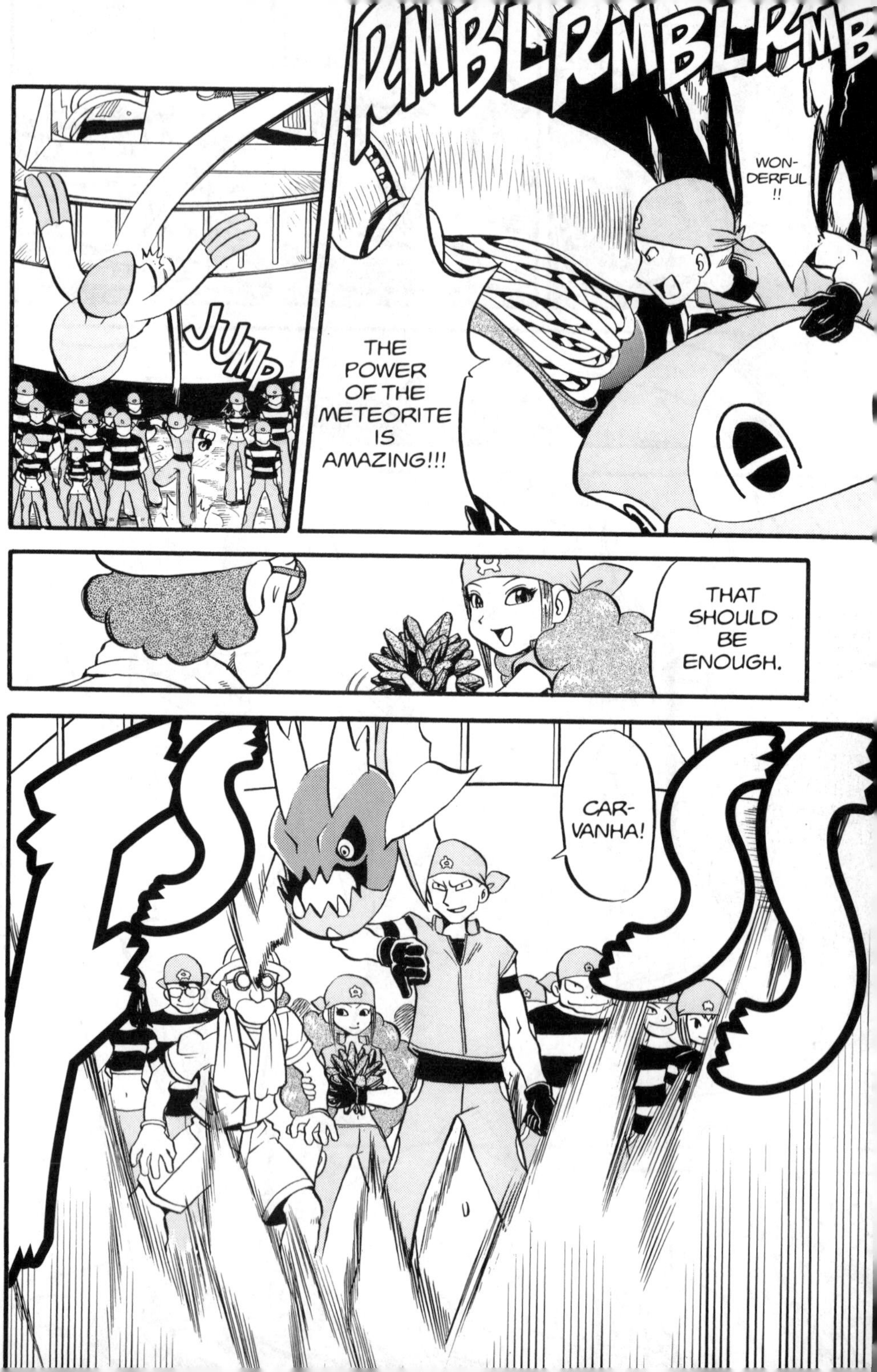
RMBLRMBLRMB
WON-DERFUL!!
THE POWER OF THE METEORITE IS AMAZING!!!
JUMP
THAT SHOULD BE ENOUGH.
CAR-VANHA!
FSSS

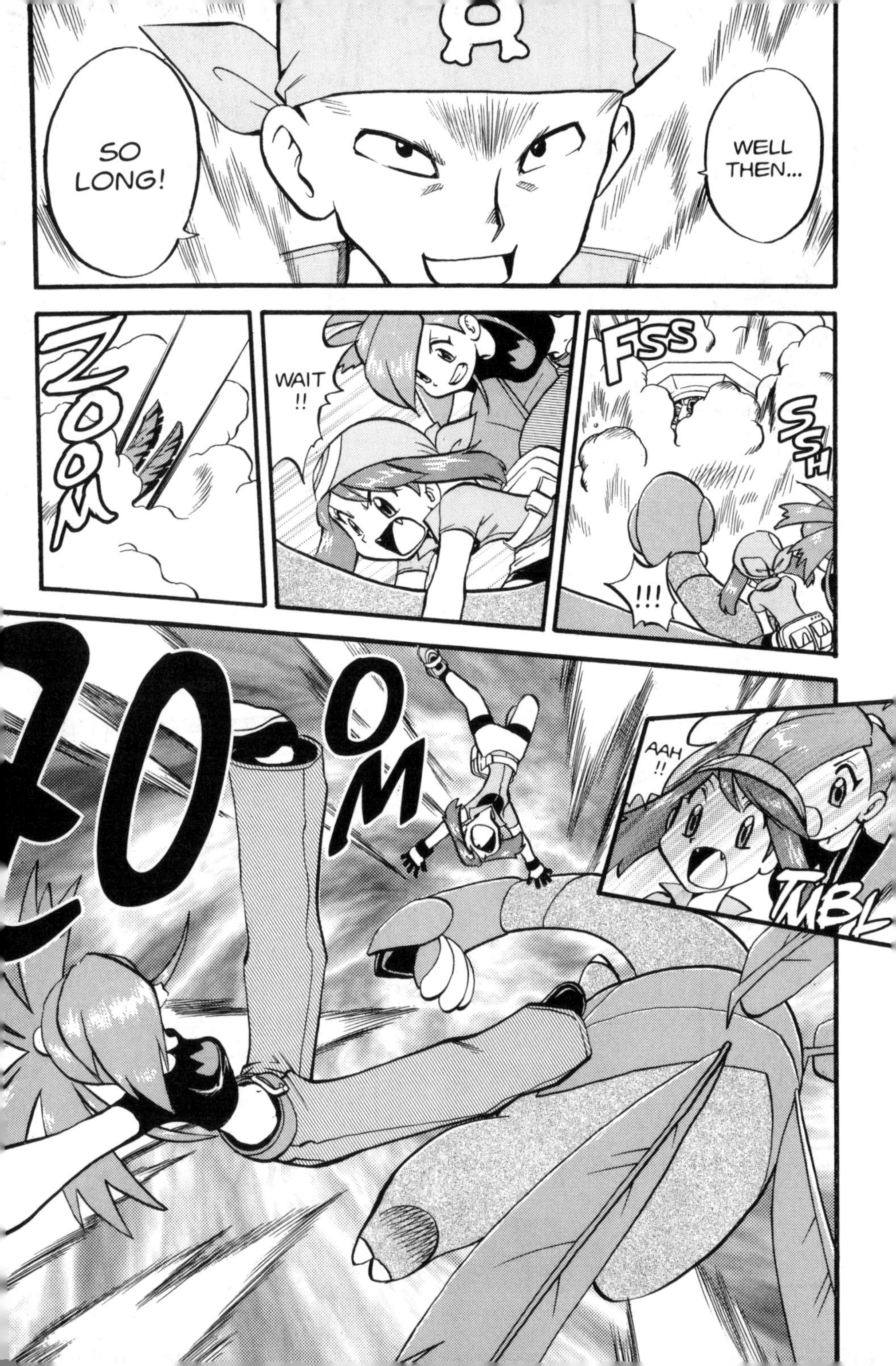

WELL THEN...
SO LONG!
FSS
SSH
!!!
WAIT !!
ZOOM
AAH !!
TUMBL
OOM

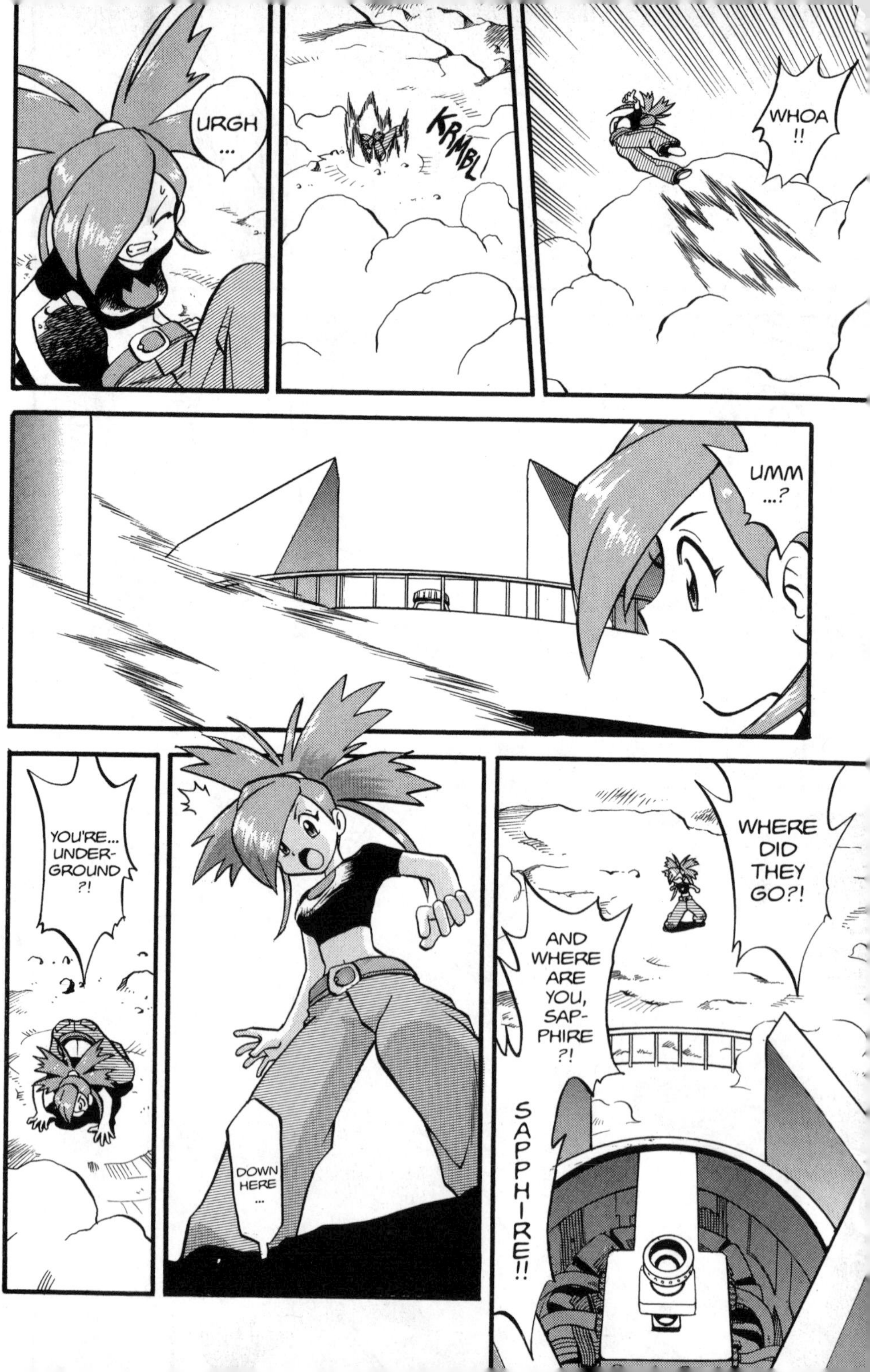
WHOA !!
KRMBL
URGH ...
UMM ...?
WHERE DID THEY GO?!
AND WHERE ARE YOU, SAPPHIRE?!
SAPPHIRE!!
DOWN HERE ...
YOU'RE... UNDERGROUND?!

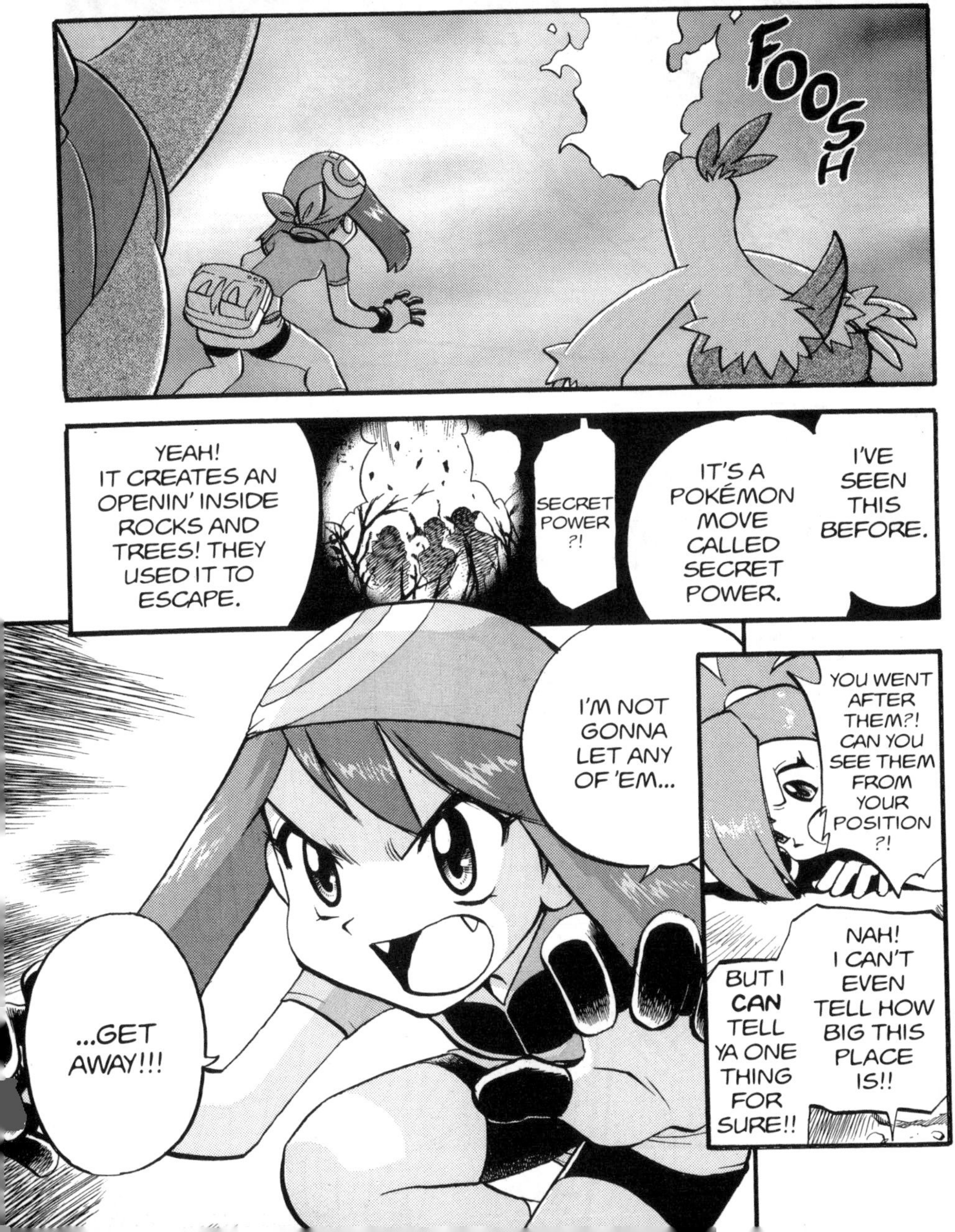
FOOSH
I'VE SEEN THIS BEFORE.
IT'S A POKÉMON MOVE CALLED SECRET POWER.
SECRET POWER ?!
YEAH! IT CREATES AN OPENIN' INSIDE ROCKS AND TREES! THEY USED IT TO ESCAPE.
YOU WENT AFTER THEM?! CAN YOU SEE THEM FROM YOUR POSITION ?!
NAH! I CAN'T EVEN TELL HOW BIG THIS PLACE IS!!
BUT I **CAN** TELL YA ONE THING FOR SURE!!
I'M NOT GONNA LET ANY OF 'EM...
...GET AWAY!!!

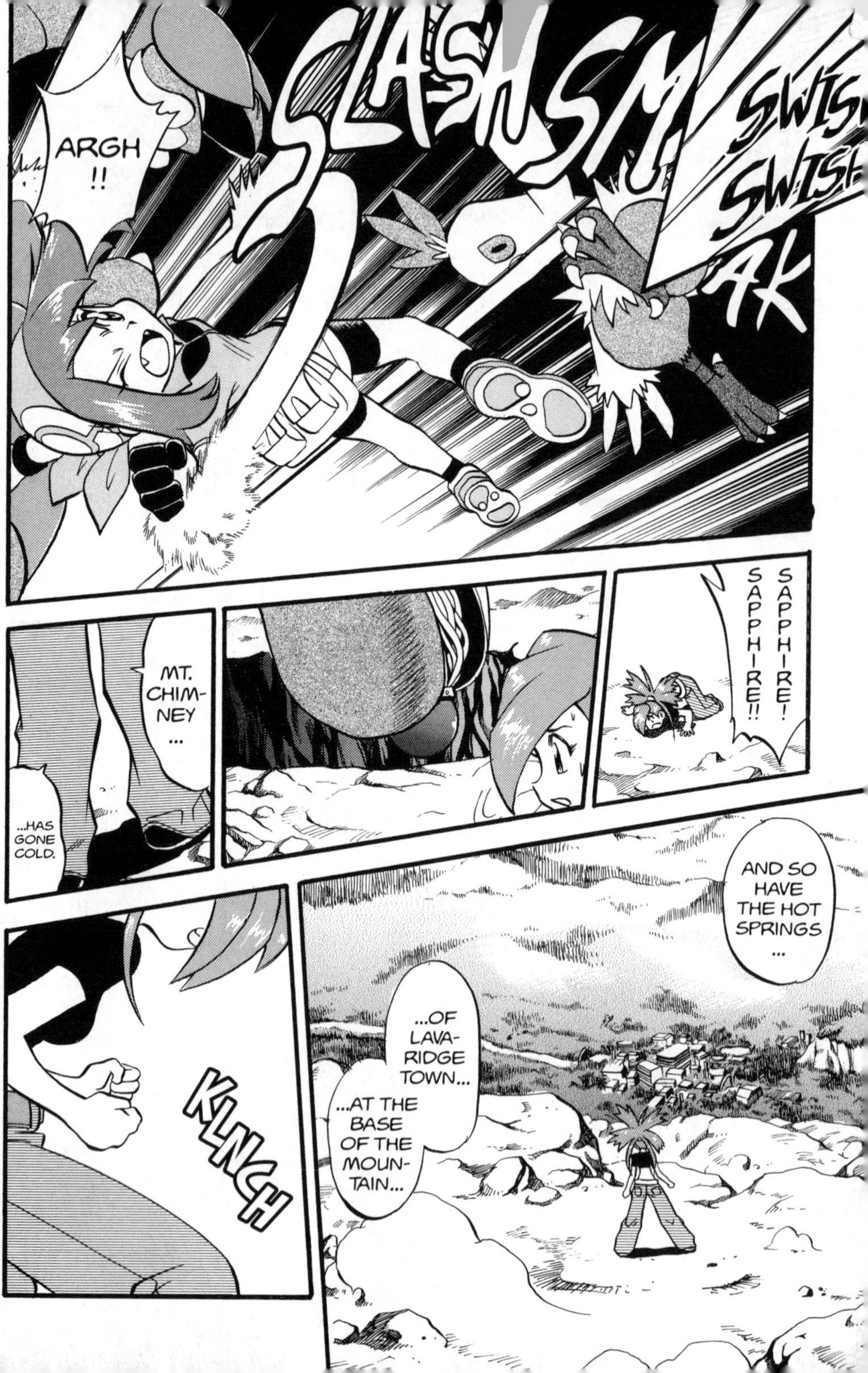
SWISH SWISH
CLASH
ARGH !!
SAPPHIRE!
SAPPHIRE!!
MT. CHIMNEY ...
...HAS GONE COLD.
AND SO HAVE THE HOT SPRINGS ...
...OF LAVARIDGE TOWN...
...AT THE BASE OF THE MOUNTAIN...
KLNCH

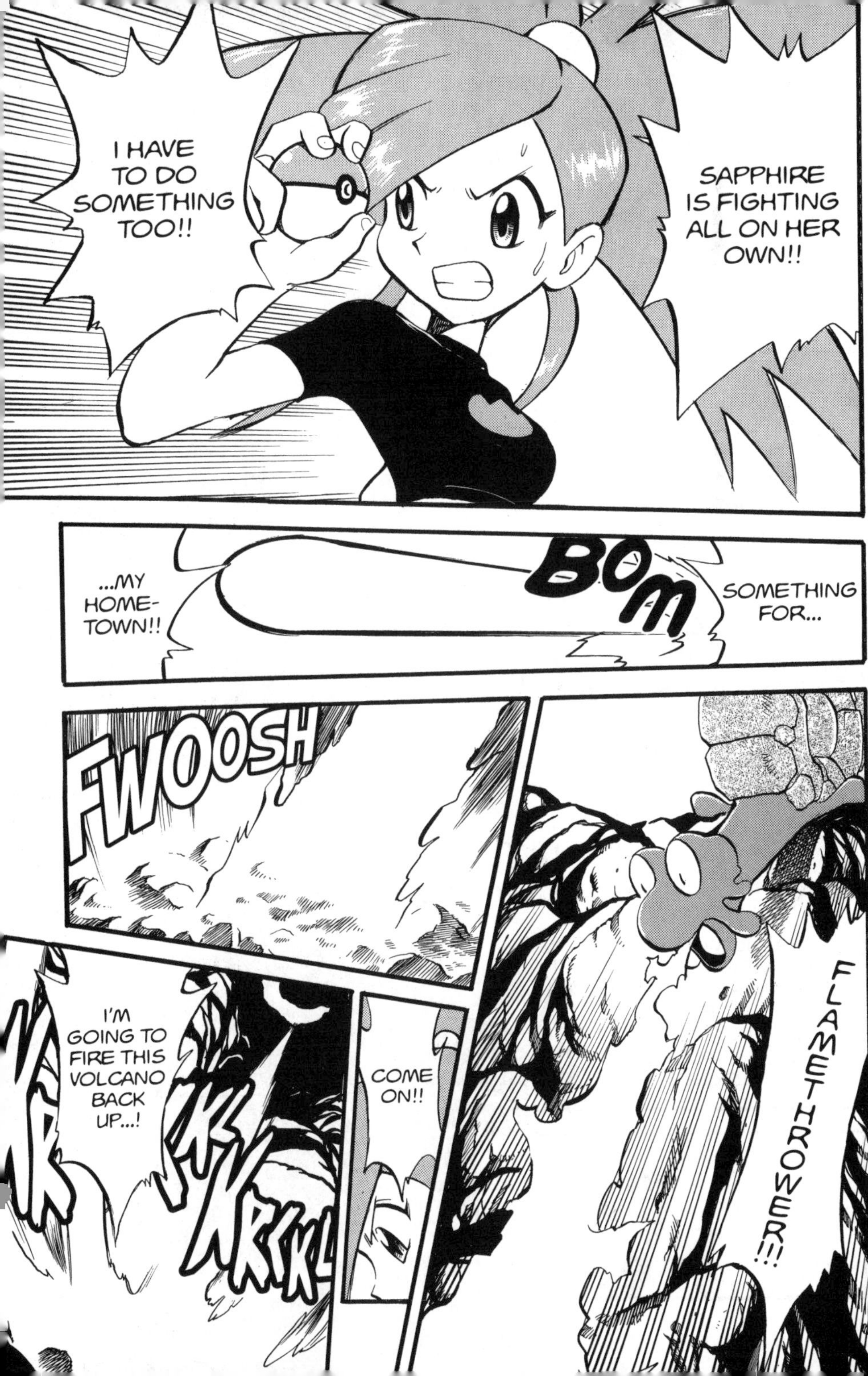

SAPPHIRE IS FIGHTING ALL ON HER OWN!!
I HAVE TO DO SOMETHING TOO!!
SOMETHING FOR...
BOM
...MY HOMETOWN!!
FLAMETHROWER!!!
FWOOSH
COME ON!!
I'M GOING TO FIRE THIS VOLCANO BACK UP...!
KRKL

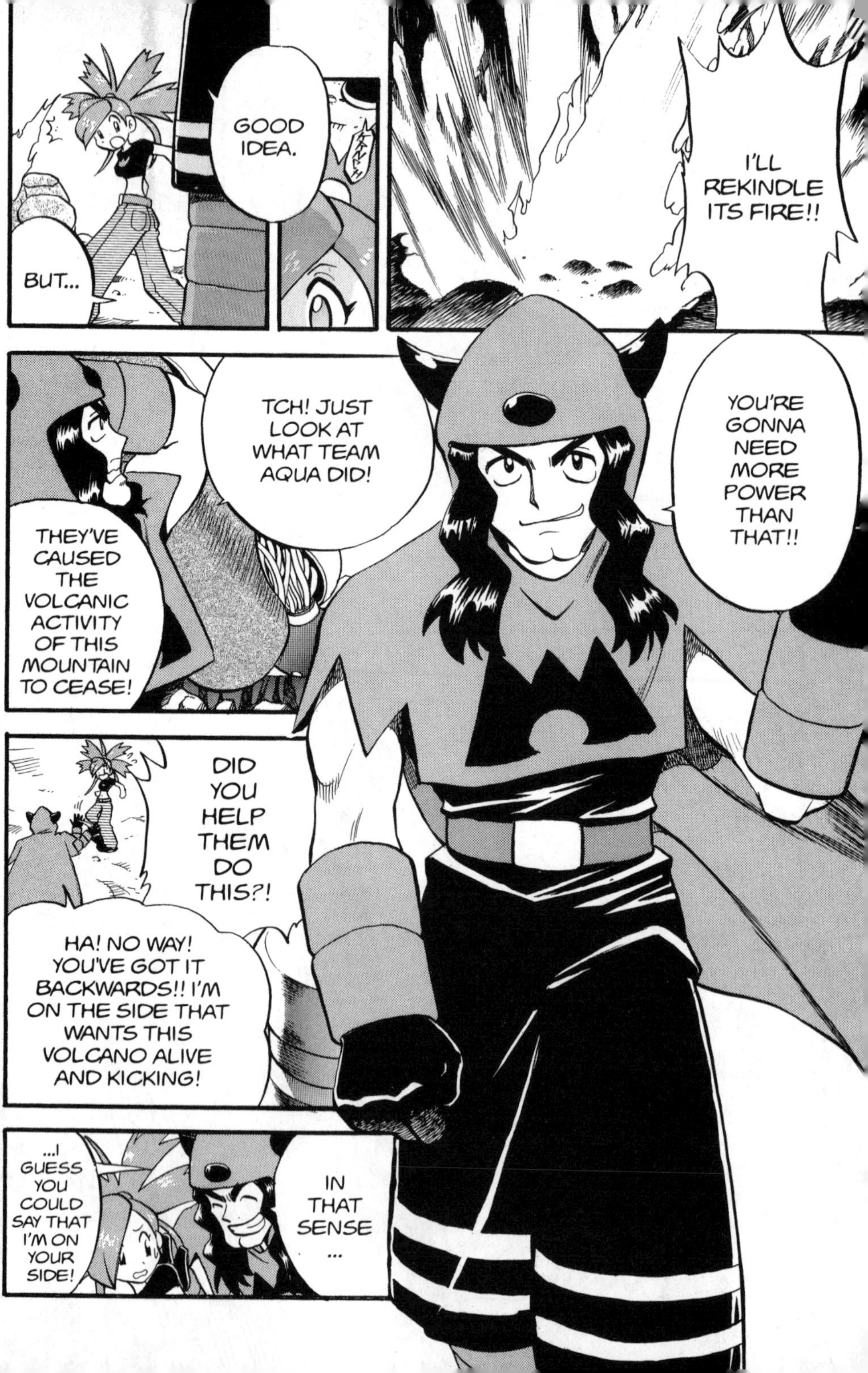
I'LL REKINDLE ITS FIRE!!
GOOD IDEA.
BUT...
YOU'RE GONNA NEED MORE POWER THAN THAT!!
TCH! JUST LOOK AT WHAT TEAM AQUA DID!
THEY'VE CAUSED THE VOLCANIC ACTIVITY OF THIS MOUNTAIN TO CEASE!
DID YOU HELP THEM DO THIS?!
HA! NO WAY! YOU'VE GOT IT BACKWARDS!! I'M ON THE SIDE THAT WANTS THIS VOLCANO ALIVE AND KICKING!
IN THAT SENSE...
...I GUESS YOU COULD SAY THAT I'M ON YOUR SIDE!

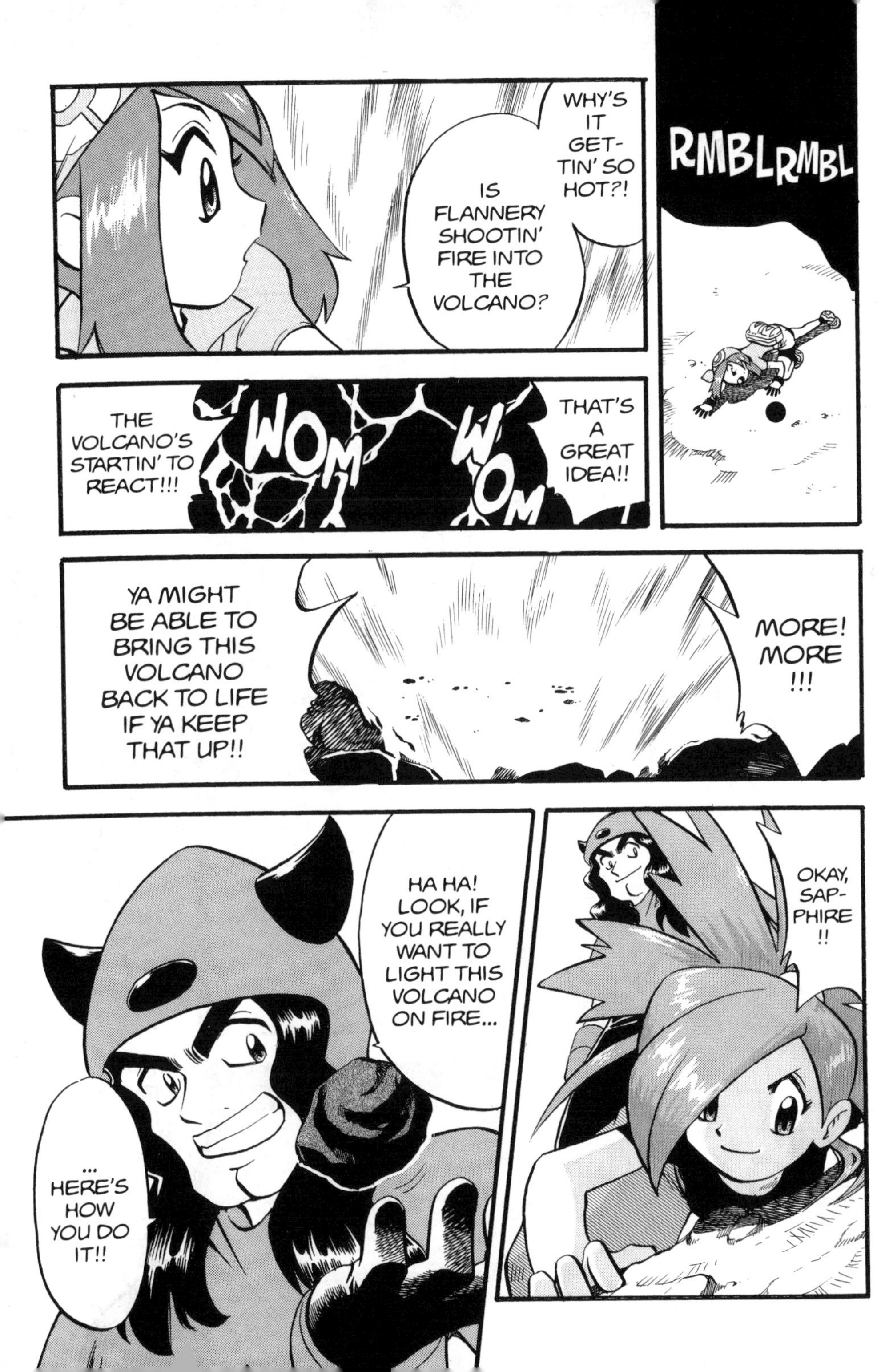
RMBL RMBL
WHY'S IT GET-TIN' SO HOT?!
IS FLANNERY SHOOTIN' FIRE INTO THE VOLCANO?
THAT'S A GREAT IDEA!!
WOM WOM
THE VOLCANO'S STARTIN' TO REACT!!!
MORE! MORE!!!
YA MIGHT BE ABLE TO BRING THIS VOLCANO BACK TO LIFE IF YA KEEP THAT UP!!
OKAY, SAP-PHIRE!!
HA HA! LOOK, IF YOU REALLY WANT TO LIGHT THIS VOLCANO ON FIRE...
...HERE'S HOW YOU DO IT!!

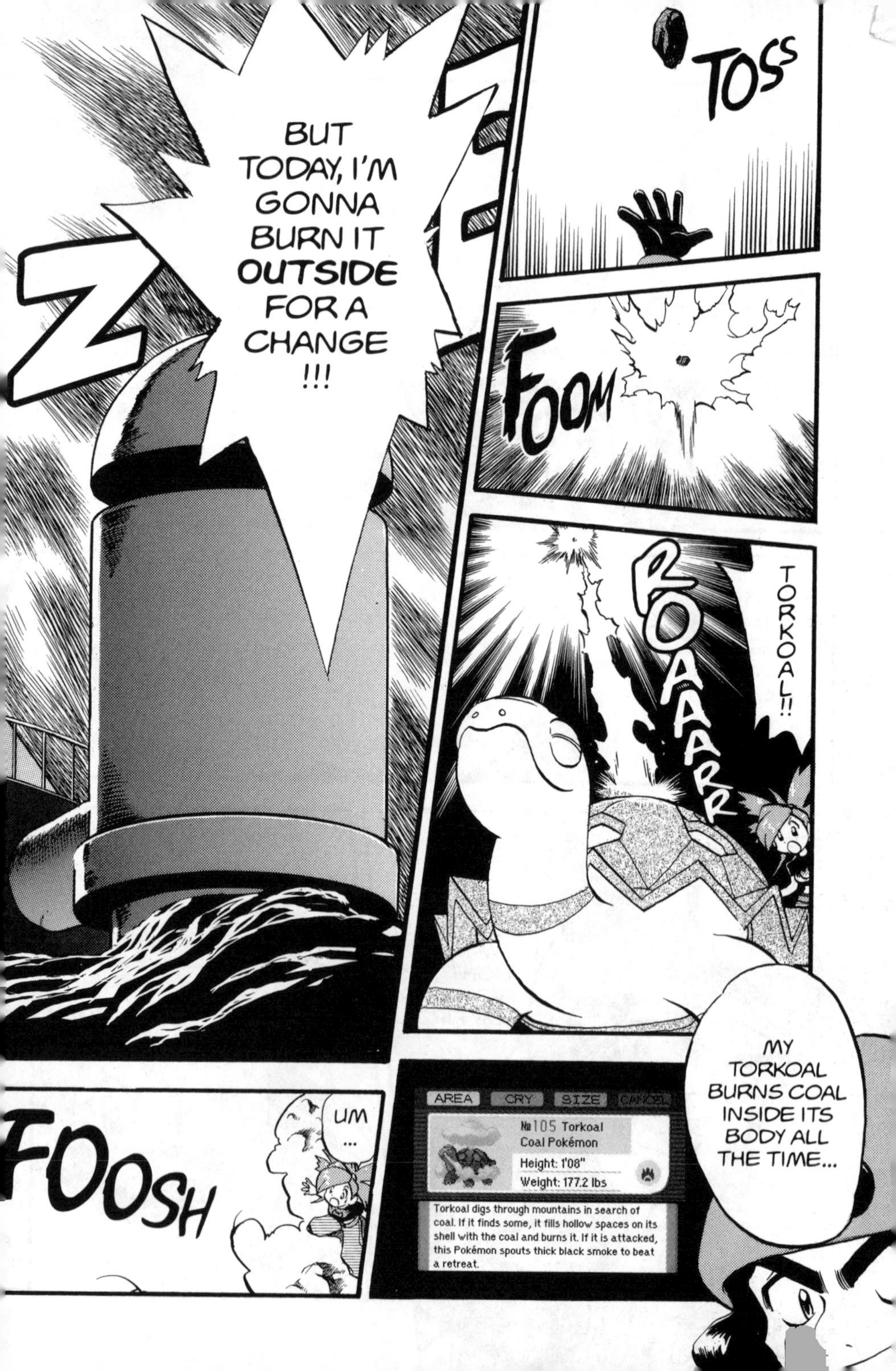
TOSS
FOOM
ROAAARR
TORKOAL!!
BUT TODAY, I'M GONNA BURN IT **OUTSIDE** FOR A CHANGE!!!
MY TORKOAL BURNS COAL INSIDE ITS BODY ALL THE TIME...
AREA CRY SIZE CANCEL
№105 Torkoal
Coal Pokémon
Height: 1'08"
Weight: 177.2 lbs
Torkoal digs through mountains in search of coal. If it finds some, it fills hollow spaces on its shell with the coal and burns it. If it is attacked, this Pokémon spouts thick black smoke to beat a retreat.
UM ...
FOOSH

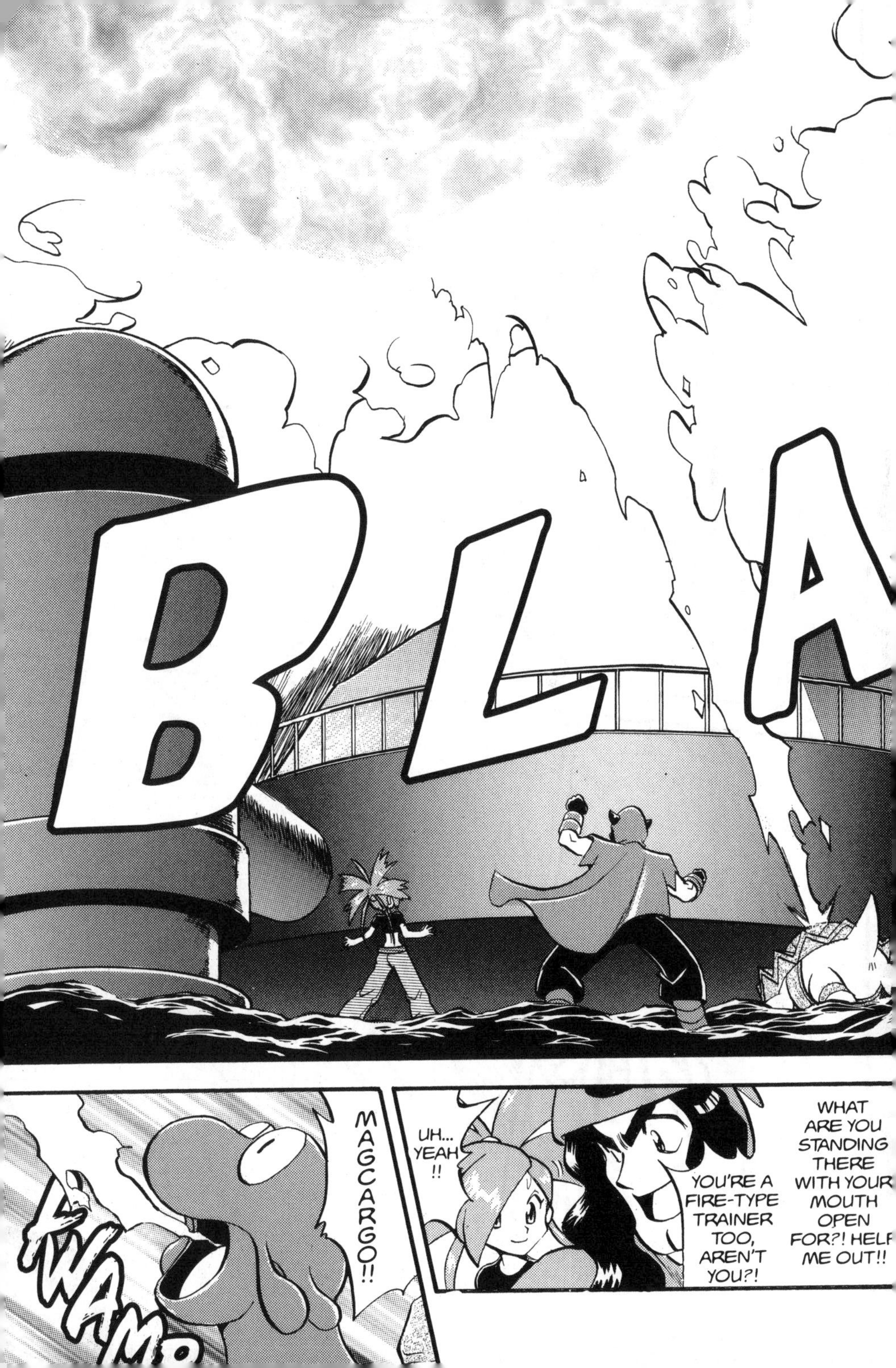
BLA
WHAT ARE YOU STANDING THERE WITH YOUR MOUTH OPEN FOR?! HELP ME OUT!!
YOU'RE A FIRE-TYPE TRAINER TOO, AREN'T YOU?!
UH... YEAH!!
MAGCARGO!!
KWAMP

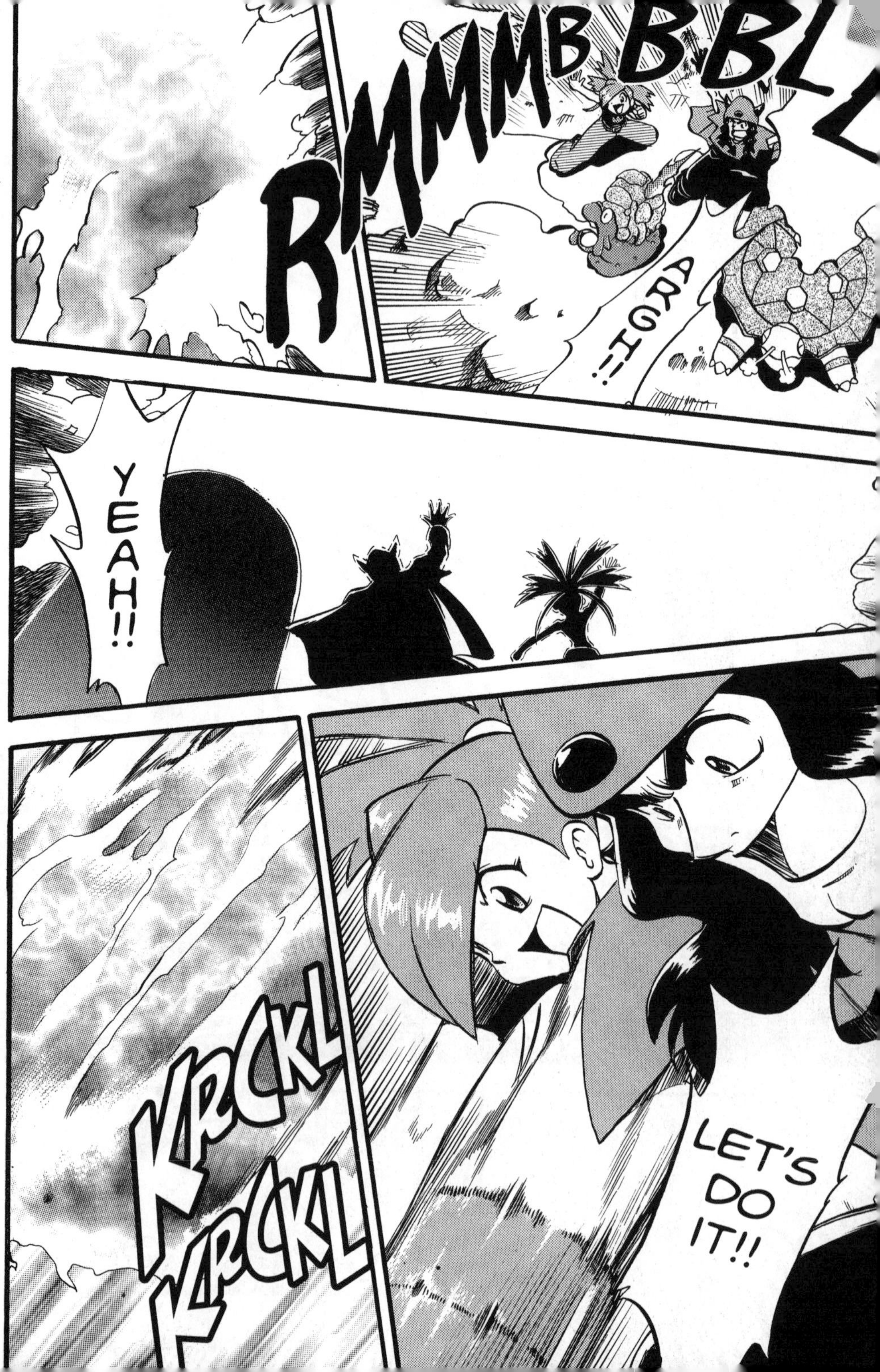
RMMMB BBL
ARGH!!
YEAH!!
LET'S DO IT!!
KRCKL KRCKL

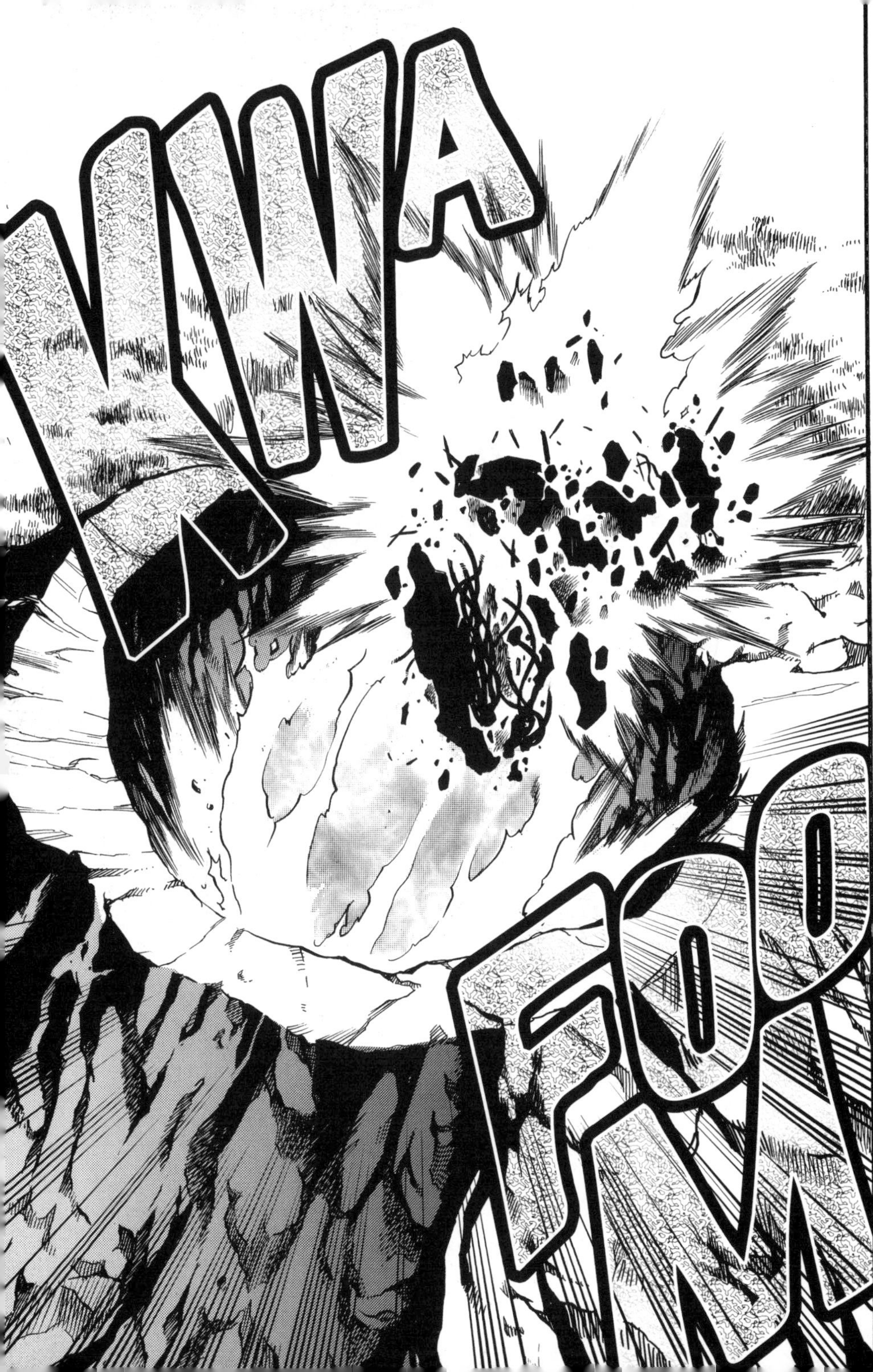
KWA
FOOM

● Adventure 216 ●

Mixing It Up with Magcargo

Pokémon Adventures Ruby & Sapphire

The Fourth Chapter

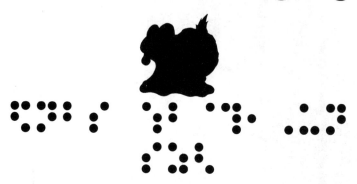

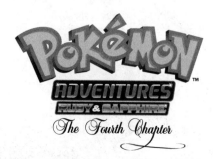

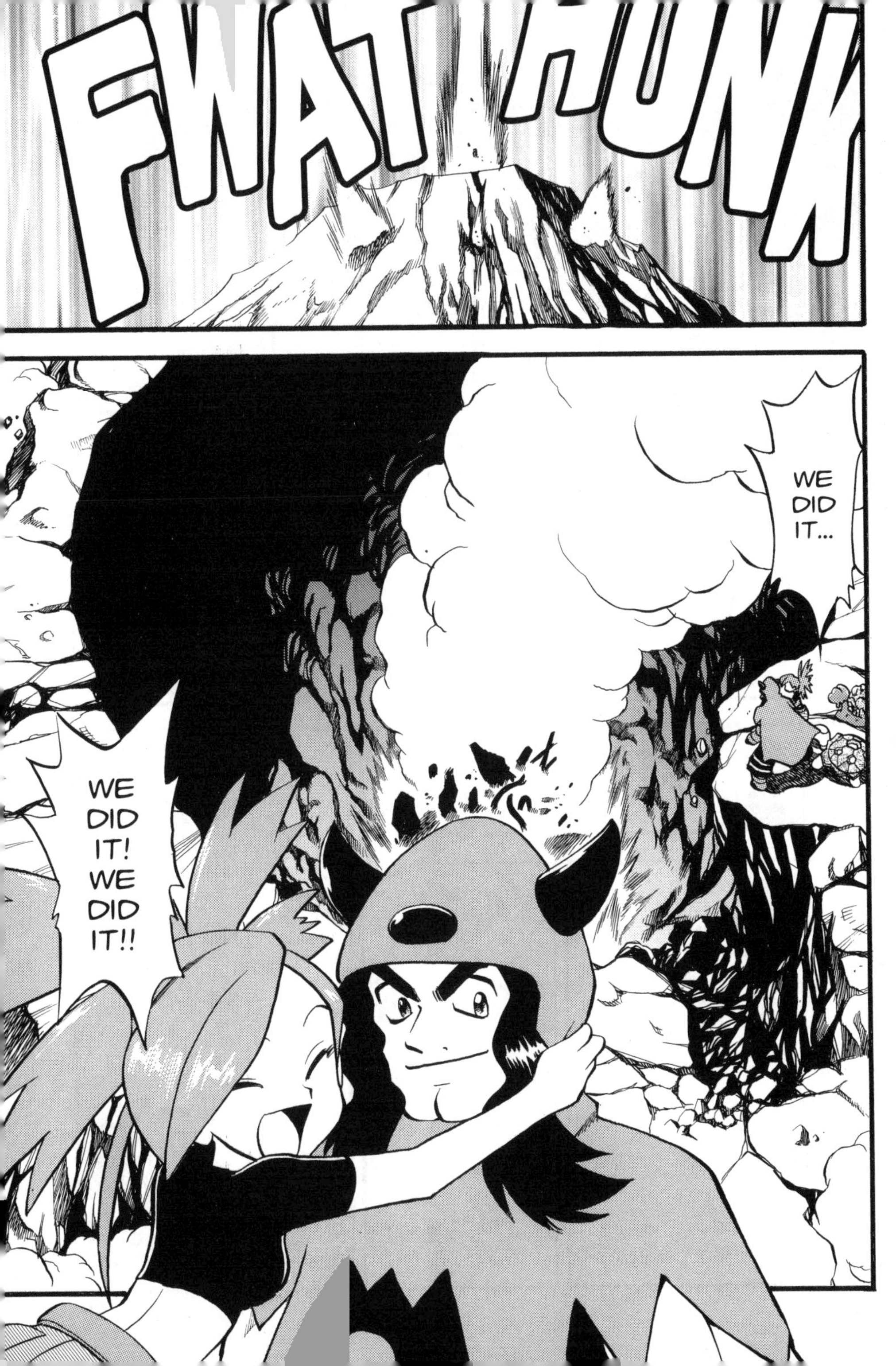
FWATHUNK
WE DID IT...
WE DID IT! WE DID IT!!

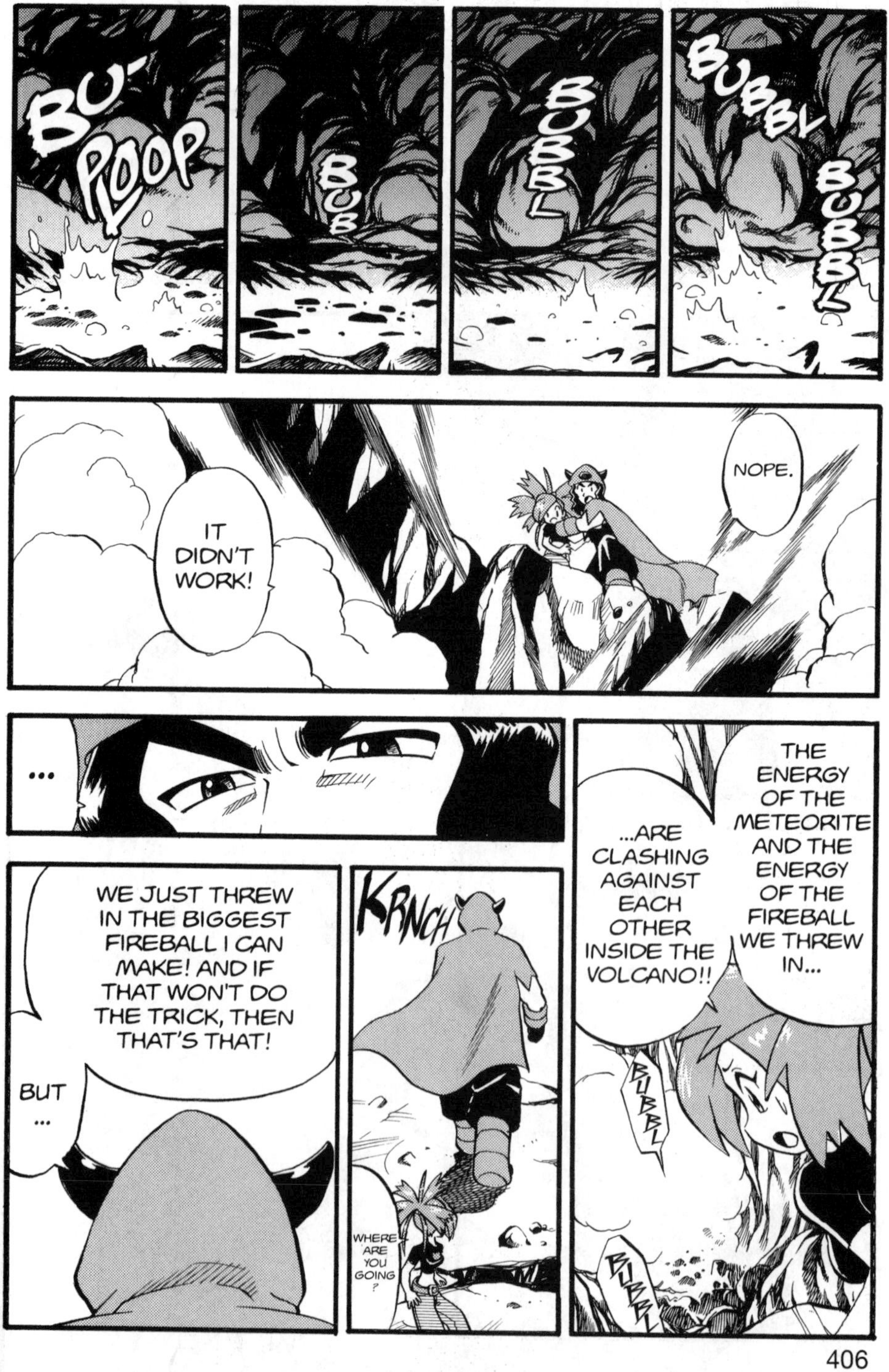
BUBBY
BUBBL
BUBBL
BUB
BU-
PLOOP
IT DIDN'T WORK!
NOPE.
THE ENERGY OF THE METEORITE AND THE ENERGY OF THE FIREBALL WE THREW IN...
...ARE CLASHING AGAINST EACH OTHER INSIDE THE VOLCANO!!
BUBBL
BUBBL
...
KRNCH
WHERE ARE YOU GOING?
WE JUST THREW IN THE BIGGEST FIREBALL I CAN MAKE! AND IF THAT WON'T DO THE TRICK, THEN THAT'S THAT!
BUT ...

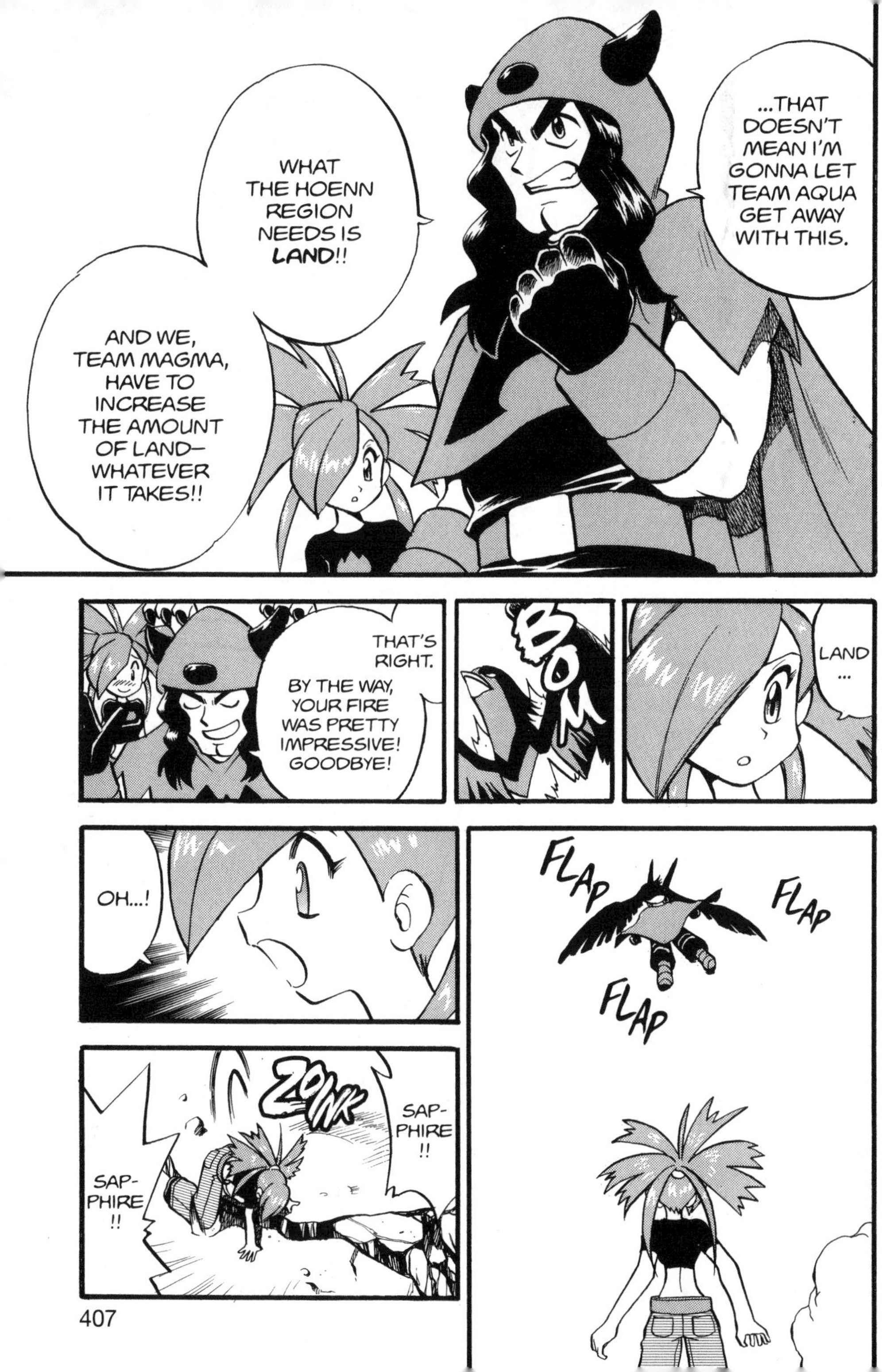
...THAT DOESN'T MEAN I'M GONNA LET TEAM AQUA GET AWAY WITH THIS.
WHAT THE HOENN REGION NEEDS IS **LAND**!!
AND WE, TEAM MAGMA, HAVE TO INCREASE THE AMOUNT OF LAND—WHATEVER IT TAKES!!
LAND ...
BOM
THAT'S RIGHT.
BY THE WAY, YOUR FIRE WAS PRETTY IMPRESSIVE! GOODBYE!
FLAP
FLAP
FLAP
OH...!
ZONK
SAP-PHIRE !!
SAP-PHIRE !!

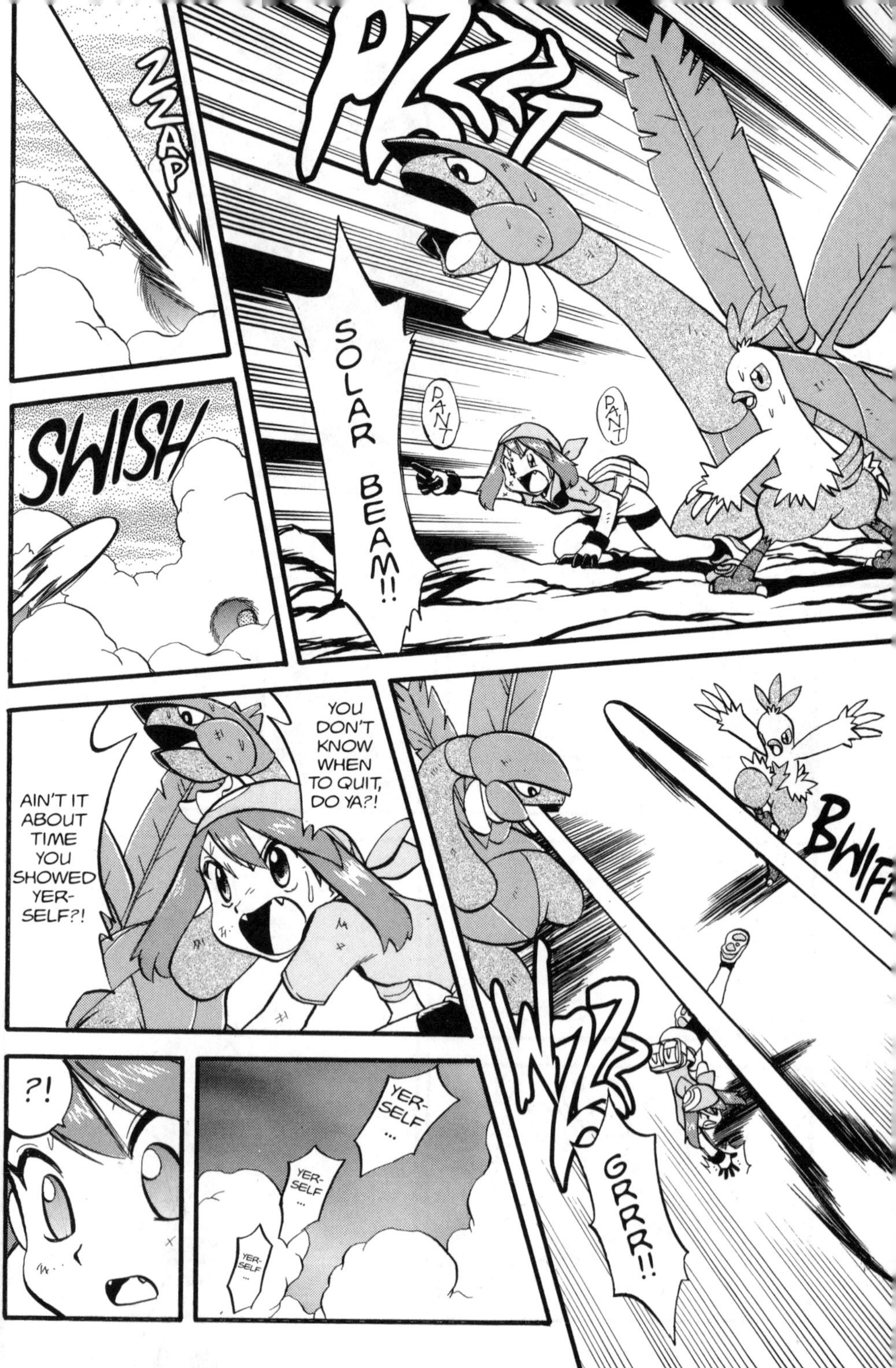
PZZT
SOLAR BEAM!!
PANT
PANT
ZZZAP
SWISH
BWIFF
WZZZ
GRRR!!
YOU DON'T KNOW WHEN TO QUIT, DO YA?!
AIN'T IT ABOUT TIME YOU SHOWED YER-SELF?!
YER-SELF...
YER-SELF...
YER-SELF...
?!

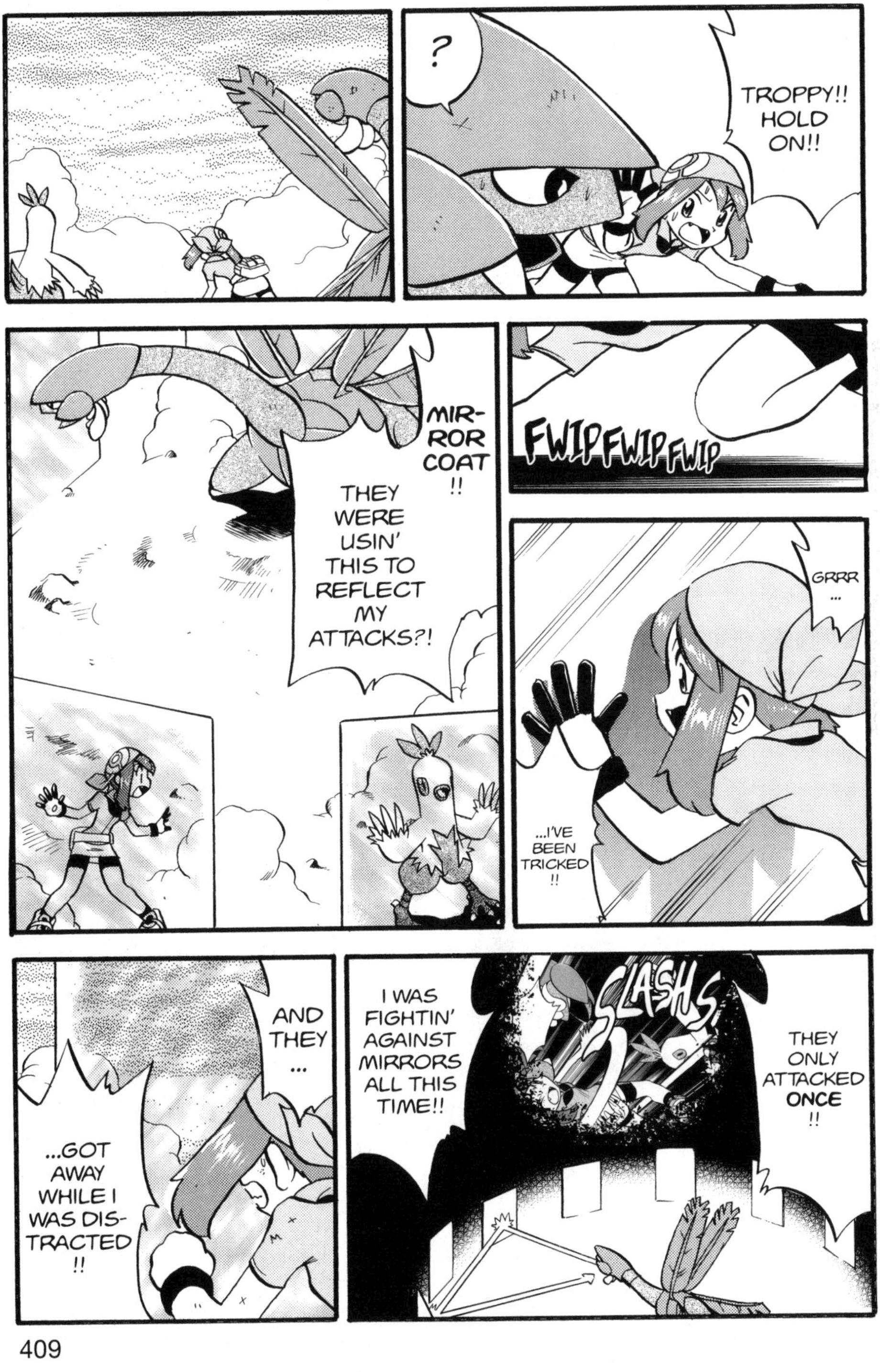

TROPPY!! HOLD ON!!
?
FWIP FWIP FWIP
GRRR...
...I'VE BEEN TRICKED!!
MIRROR COAT!!
THEY WERE USIN' THIS TO REFLECT MY ATTACKS?!
THEY ONLY ATTACKED ONCE!!
SLASH
I WAS FIGHTIN' AGAINST MIRRORS ALL THIS TIME!!
AND THEY...
...GOT AWAY WHILE I WAS DISTRACTED!!

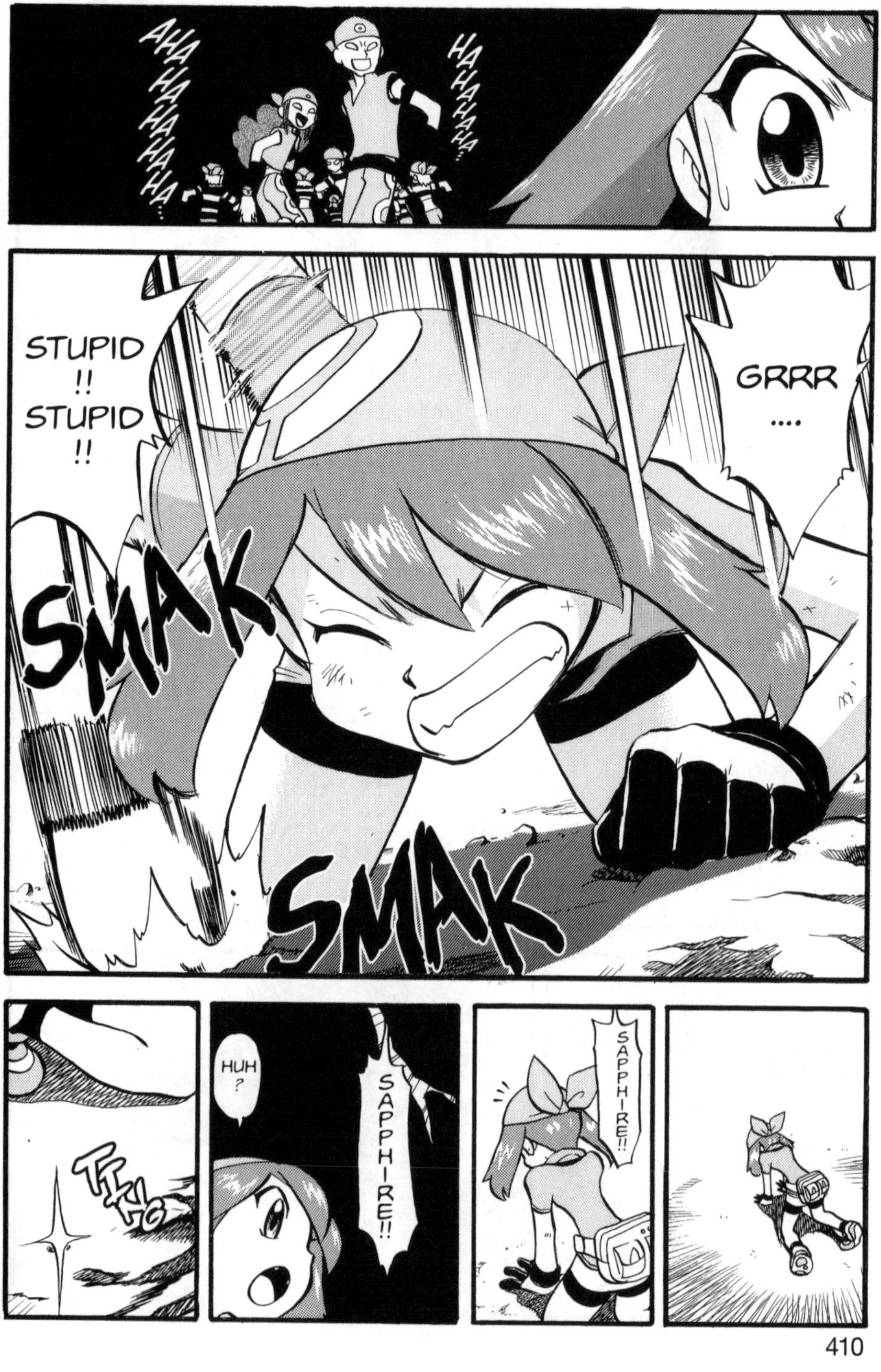
HAHAHAHAHA...
AHAHAHAHAHAHAHA...
GRRR....
STUPID!! STUPID!!
SMAK
SMAK
SAPPHIRE!!
SAPPHIRE!!
HUH?
TING

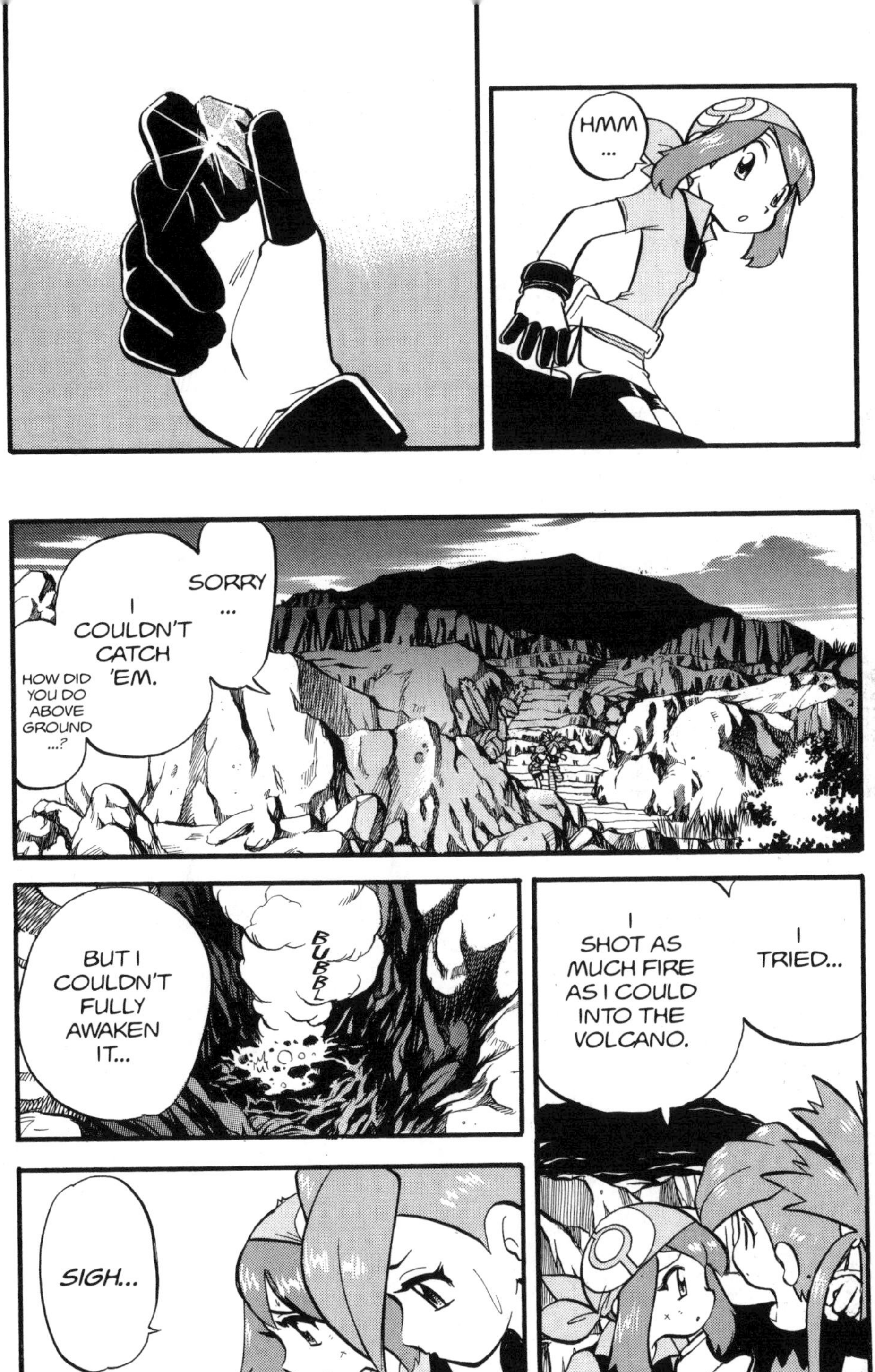
HMM ...
SORRY ... I COULDN'T CATCH 'EM.
HOW DID YOU DO ABOVE GROUND ...?
I TRIED...
I SHOT AS MUCH FIRE AS I COULD INTO THE VOLCANO.
BUBBL
BUT I COULDN'T FULLY AWAKEN IT...
SIGH...

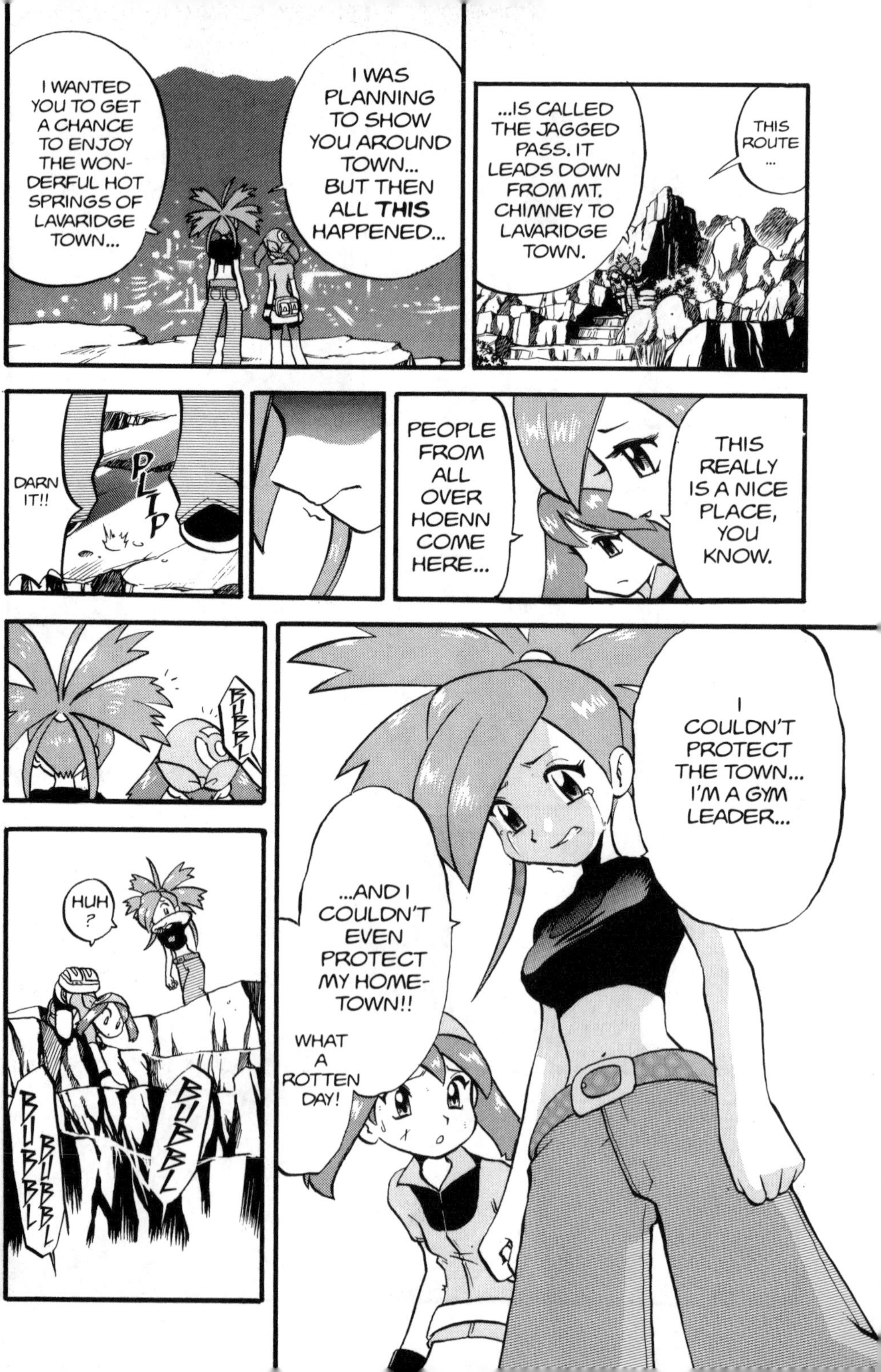
THIS ROUTE ...
...IS CALLED THE JAGGED PASS. IT LEADS DOWN FROM MT. CHIMNEY TO LAVARIDGE TOWN.
I WAS PLANNING TO SHOW YOU AROUND TOWN... BUT THEN ALL **THIS** HAPPENED...
I WANTED YOU TO GET A CHANCE TO ENJOY THE WON-DERFUL HOT SPRINGS OF LAVARIDGE TOWN...
THIS REALLY IS A NICE PLACE, YOU KNOW.
PEOPLE FROM ALL OVER HOENN COME HERE...
PLIP
DARN IT!!
I COULDN'T PROTECT THE TOWN... I'M A GYM LEADER...
...AND I COULDN'T EVEN PROTECT MY HOME-TOWN!!
WHAT A ROTTEN DAY!
BUBBL
HUH?
BUBBL
BUBBL
BUBBL

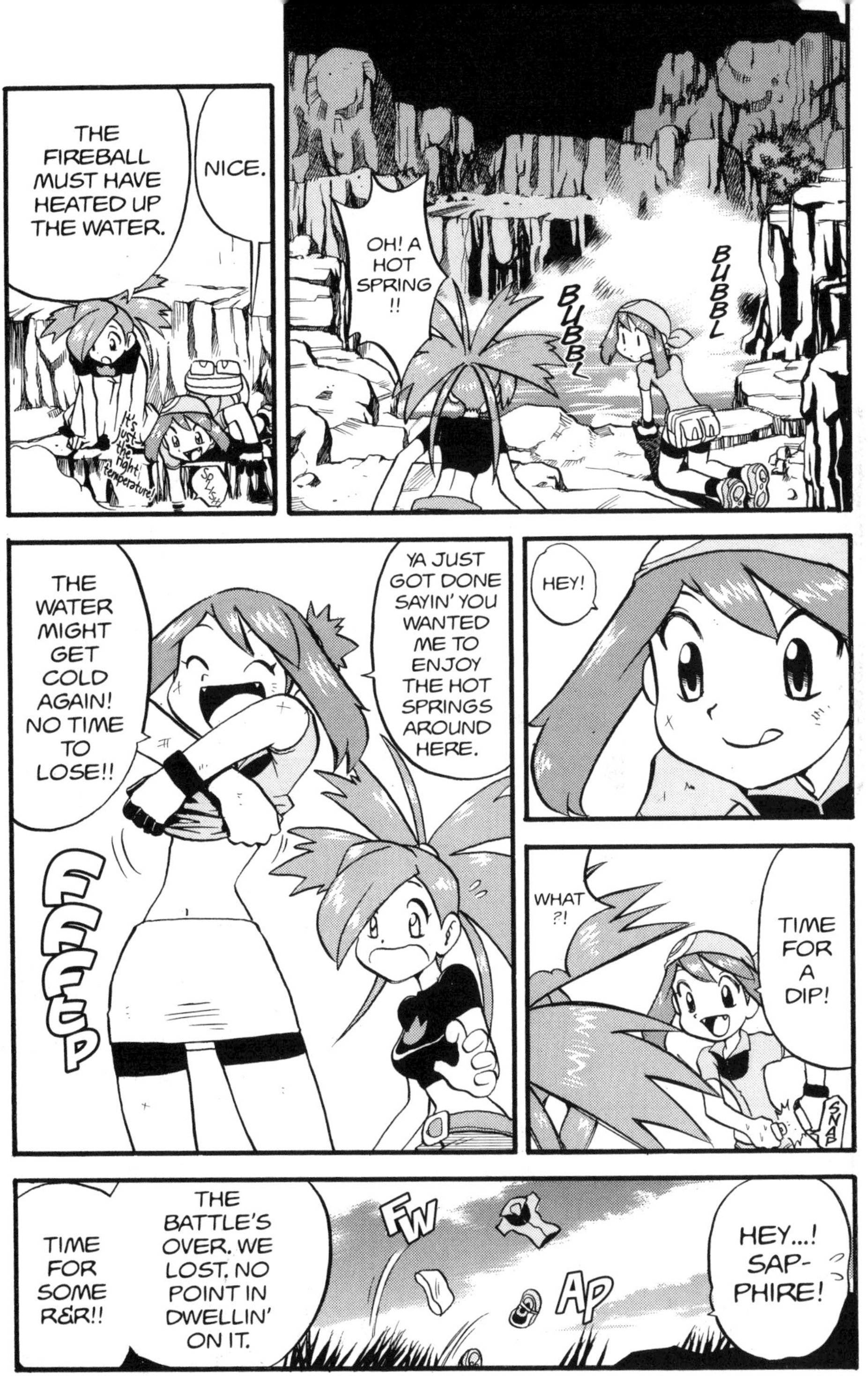

OH! A HOT SPRING !!
BUBBL
BUBBL
NICE.
THE FIREBALL MUST HAVE HEATED UP THE WATER.
It's just the right temperature!
SPLISH
HEY!
TIME FOR A DIP!
WHAT?!
SNAP
YA JUST GOT DONE SAYIN' YOU WANTED ME TO ENJOY THE HOT SPRINGS AROUND HERE.
THE WATER MIGHT GET COLD AGAIN! NO TIME TO LOSE!!
HEY...! SAPPHIRE!
AP
FW
THE BATTLE'S OVER. WE LOST. NO POINT IN DWELLIN' ON IT.
TIME FOR SOME R&R!!

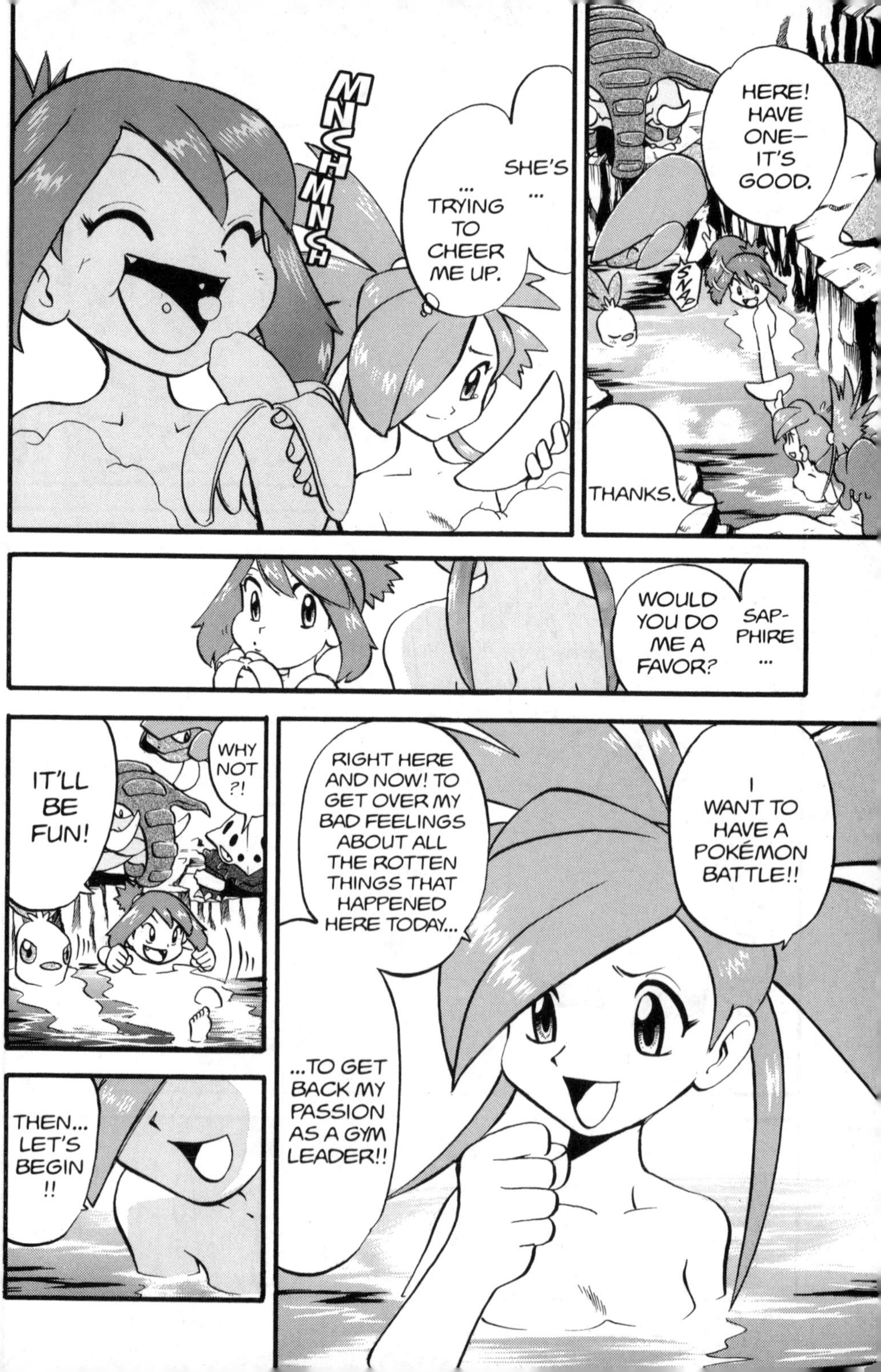
HERE! HAVE ONE— IT'S GOOD.
THANKS.
MNCH MNCH
SHE'S ...
... TRYING TO CHEER ME UP.
SAP-PHIRE ...
WOULD YOU DO ME A FAVOR?
I WANT TO HAVE A POKÉMON BATTLE!!
RIGHT HERE AND NOW! TO GET OVER MY BAD FEELINGS ABOUT ALL THE ROTTEN THINGS THAT HAPPENED HERE TODAY...
...TO GET BACK MY PASSION AS A GYM LEADER!!
WHY NOT ?!
IT'LL BE FUN!
THEN... LET'S BEGIN !!

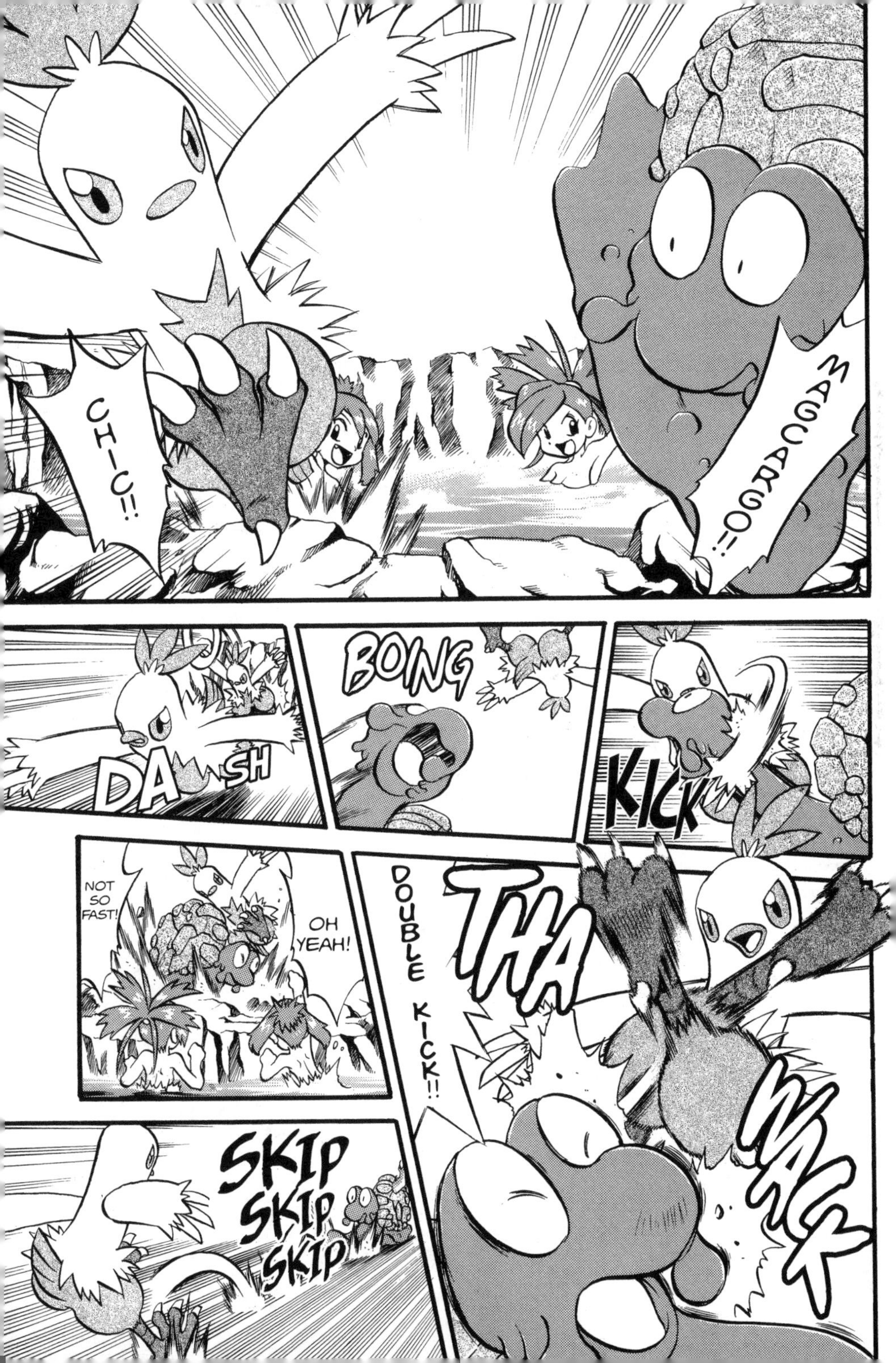
MAGCARGO!!
CHIC!!
KICK
BOING
DASH
THA
DOUBLE KICK!!
WACK
NOT SO FAST!
OH YEAH!
SKIP SKIP SKIP

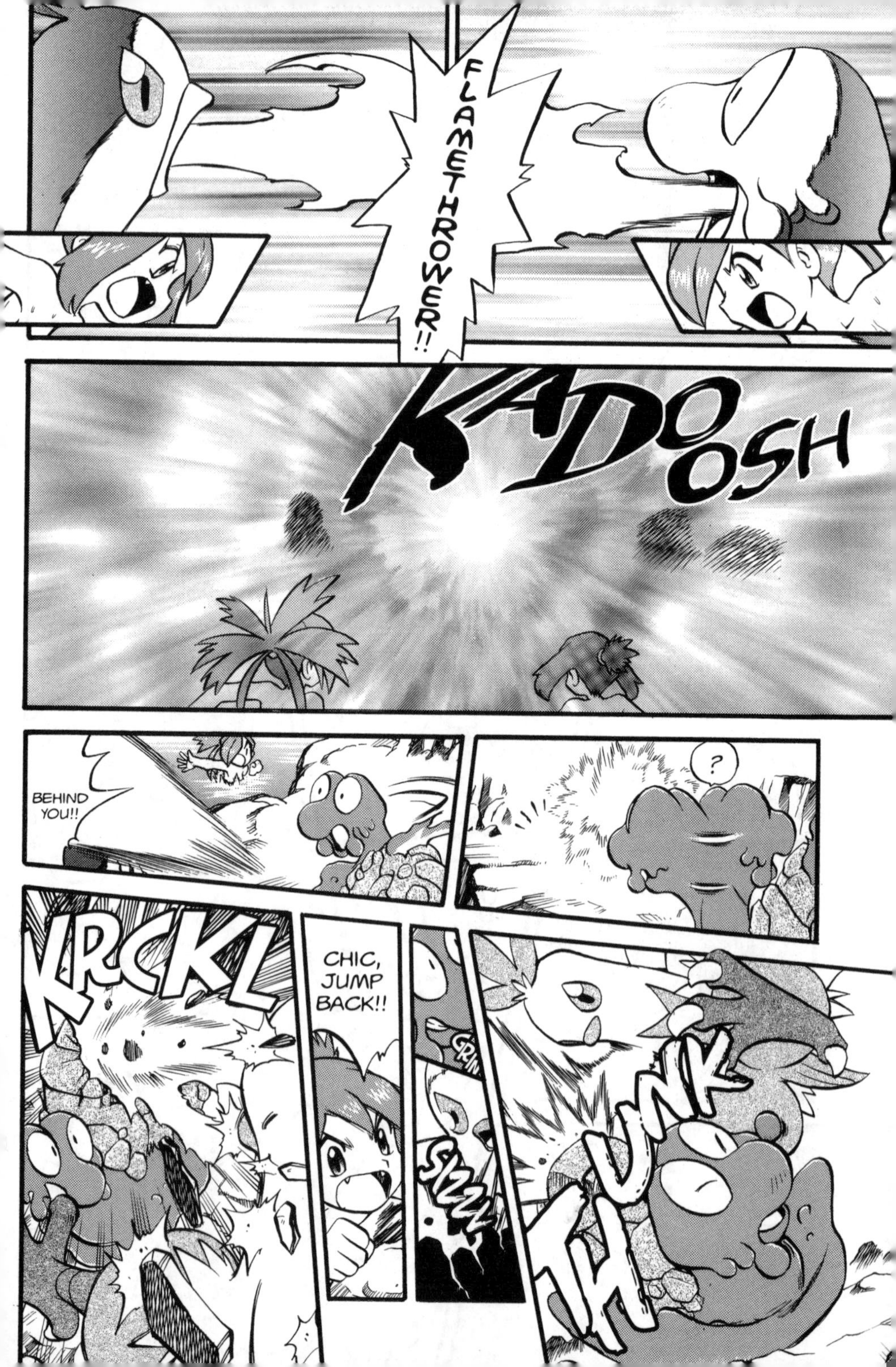
FLAMETHROWER!!
KADOOSH
?
BEHIND YOU!!
THUNK
GRIN
SWSH
CHIC, JUMP BACK!!
KRCKL

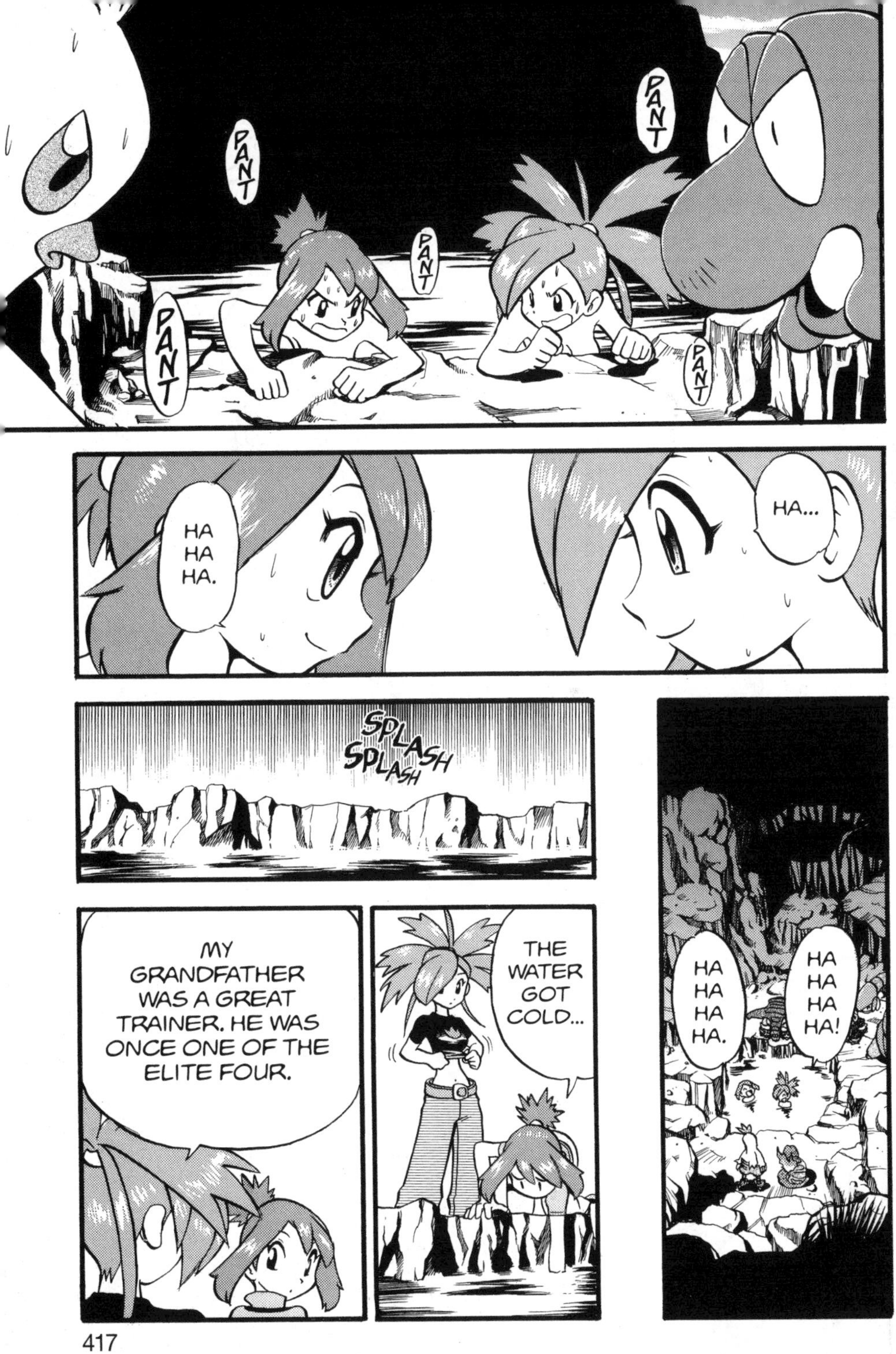
PANT
PANT
PANT
PANT
PANT
HA...
HA HA HA.
HA HA HA HA!
HA HA HA HA.
SPLASH SPLASH
THE WATER GOT COLD...
MY GRANDFATHER WAS A GREAT TRAINER. HE WAS ONCE ONE OF THE ELITE FOUR.

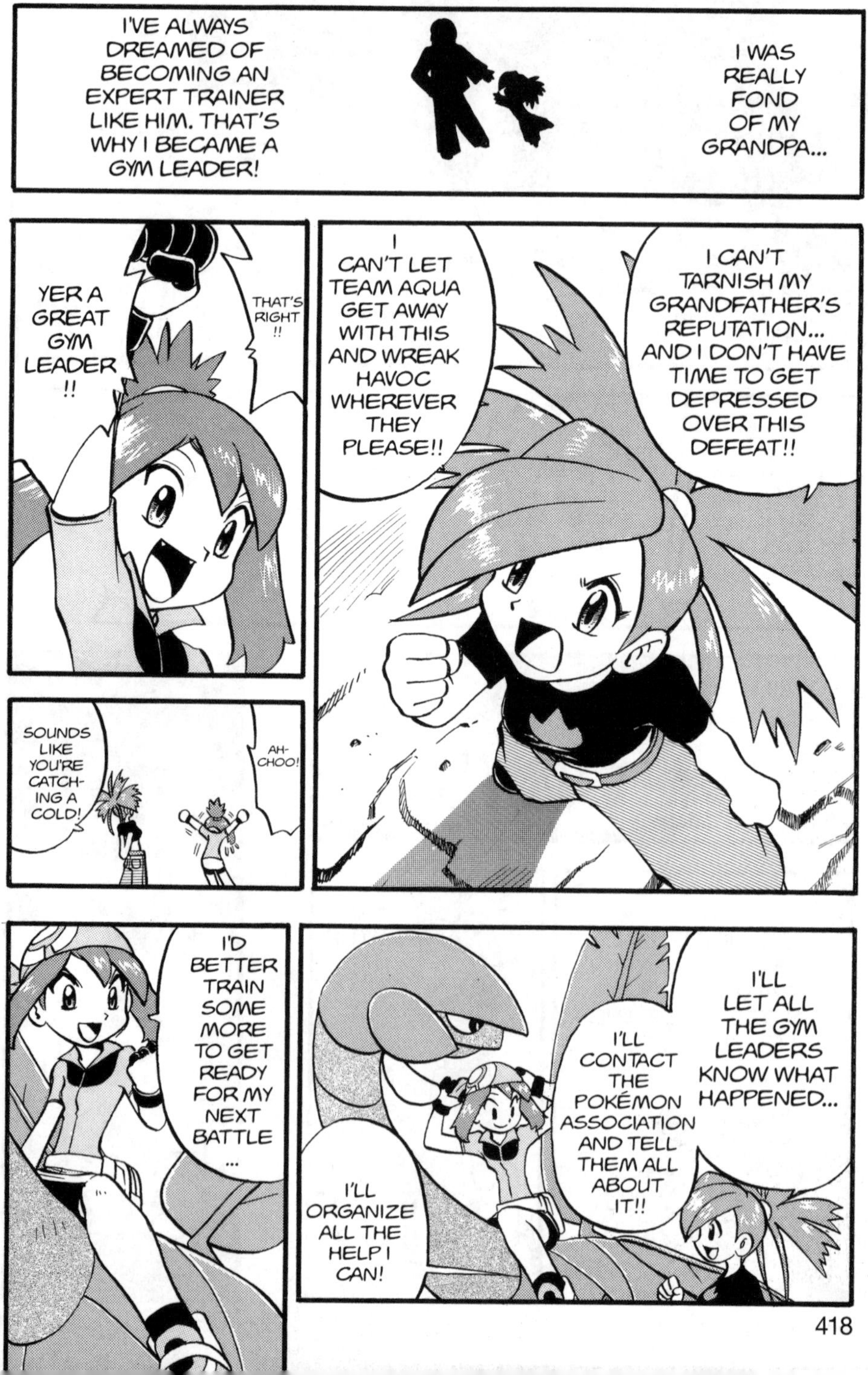
I WAS REALLY FOND OF MY GRANDPA...
I'VE ALWAYS DREAMED OF BECOMING AN EXPERT TRAINER LIKE HIM. THAT'S WHY I BECAME A GYM LEADER!
I CAN'T TARNISH MY GRANDFATHER'S REPUTATION... AND I DON'T HAVE TIME TO GET DEPRESSED OVER THIS DEFEAT!!
I CAN'T LET TEAM AQUA GET AWAY WITH THIS AND WREAK HAVOC WHEREVER THEY PLEASE!!
THAT'S RIGHT!!
YER A GREAT GYM LEADER!!
AH-CHOO!
SOUNDS LIKE YOU'RE CATCHING A COLD!
I'LL LET ALL THE GYM LEADERS KNOW WHAT HAPPENED...
I'LL CONTACT THE POKÉMON ASSOCIATION AND TELL THEM ALL ABOUT IT!!
I'LL ORGANIZE ALL THE HELP I CAN!
I'D BETTER TRAIN SOME MORE TO GET READY FOR MY NEXT BATTLE...

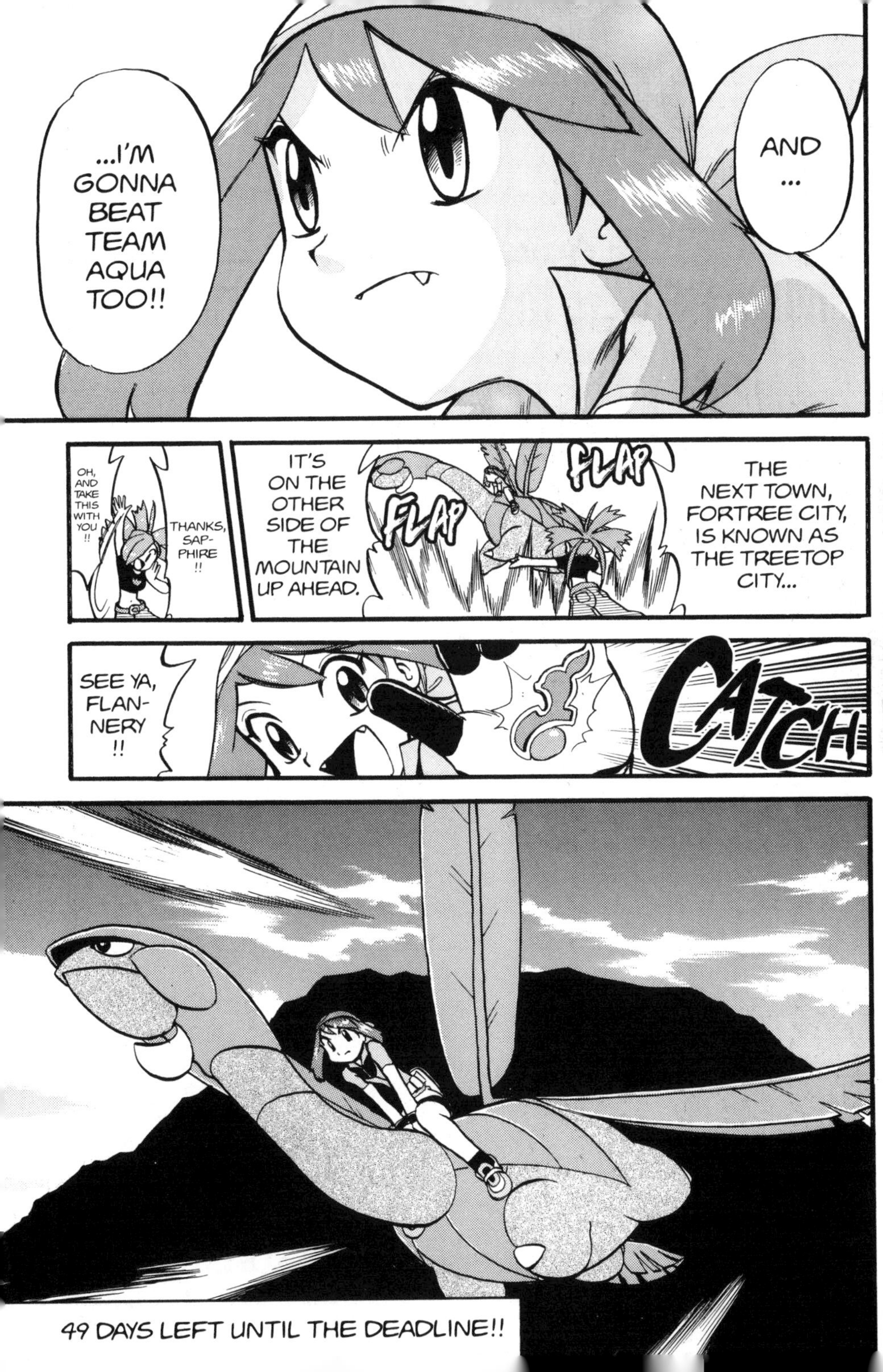
AND ...
...I'M GONNA BEAT TEAM AQUA TOO!!
THE NEXT TOWN, FORTREE CITY, IS KNOWN AS THE TREETOP CITY...
FLAP
FLAP
IT'S ON THE OTHER SIDE OF THE MOUNTAIN UP AHEAD.
THANKS, SAPPHIRE !!
OH, AND TAKE THIS WITH YOU !!
CATCH
SEE YA, FLANNERY !!
49 DAYS LEFT UNTIL THE DEADLINE!!

● Adventure 217 ●
Mind-Boggling with Medicham

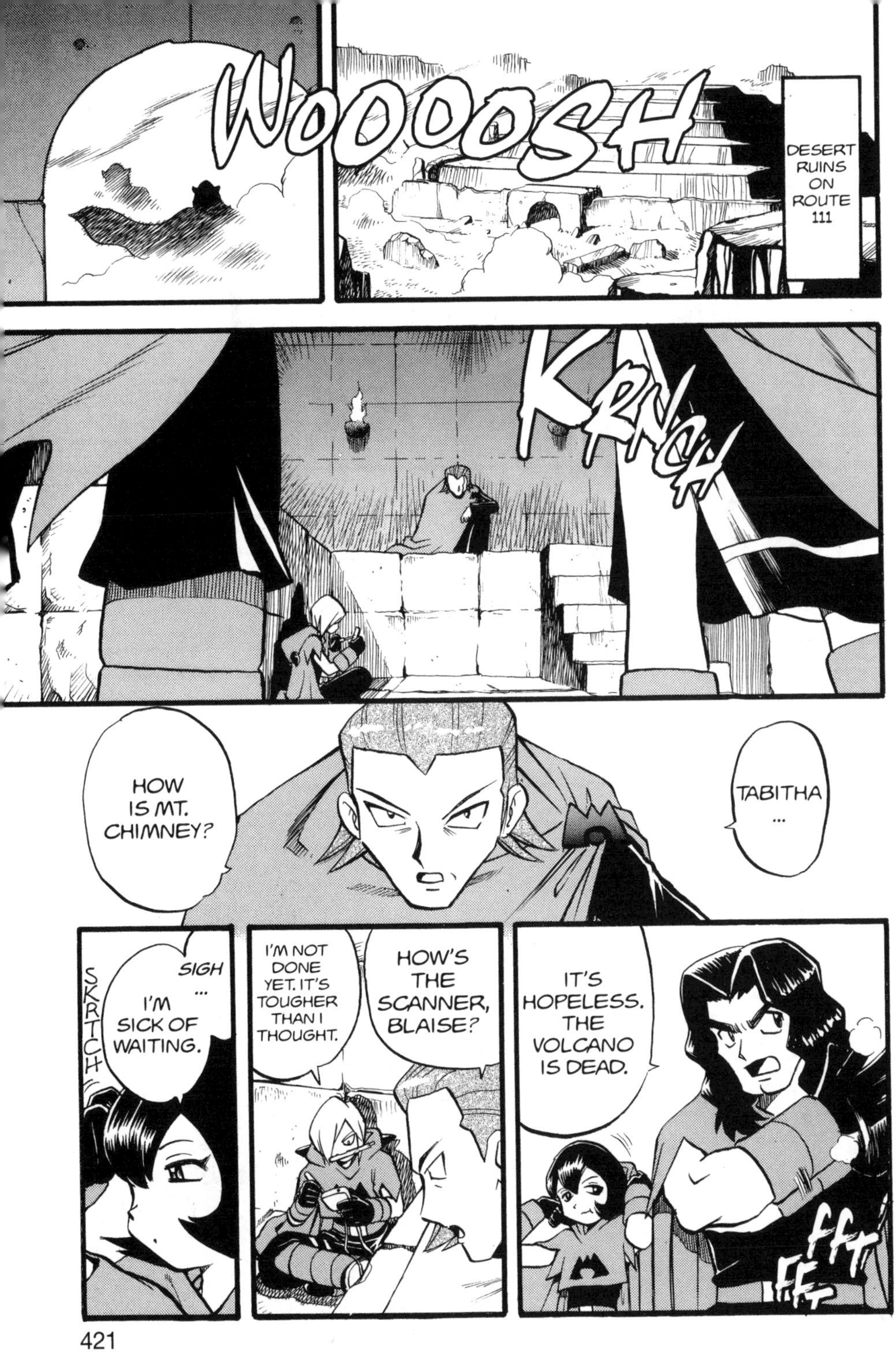
DESERT RUINS ON ROUTE 111
WOOOOSH
KRNCH
TABITHA ...
HOW IS MT. CHIMNEY?
IT'S HOPELESS. THE VOLCANO IS DEAD.
FFT FFT
HOW'S THE SCANNER, BLAISE?
I'M NOT DONE YET. IT'S TOUGHER THAN I THOUGHT.
SIGH ...
I'M SICK OF WAITING.
SKRTCH

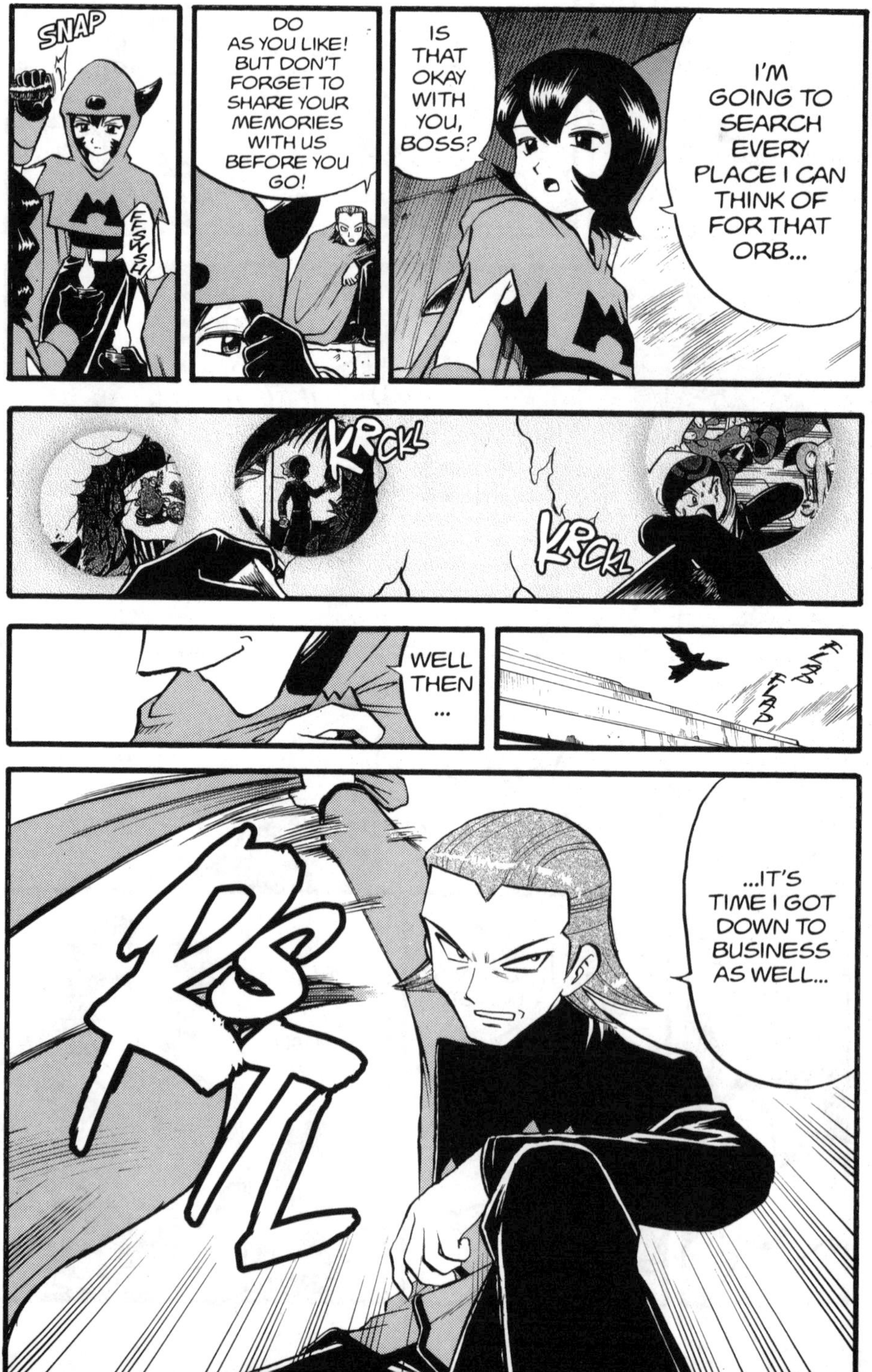
I'M GOING TO SEARCH EVERY PLACE I CAN THINK OF FOR THAT ORB...
IS THAT OKAY WITH YOU, BOSS?
DO AS YOU LIKE! BUT DON'T FORGET TO SHARE YOUR MEMORIES WITH US BEFORE YOU GO!
SNAP
FFSWSH
KRCKL
KRCKL
FLAP
FLAP
WELL THEN...
...IT'S TIME I GOT DOWN TO BUSINESS AS WELL...
RSTL

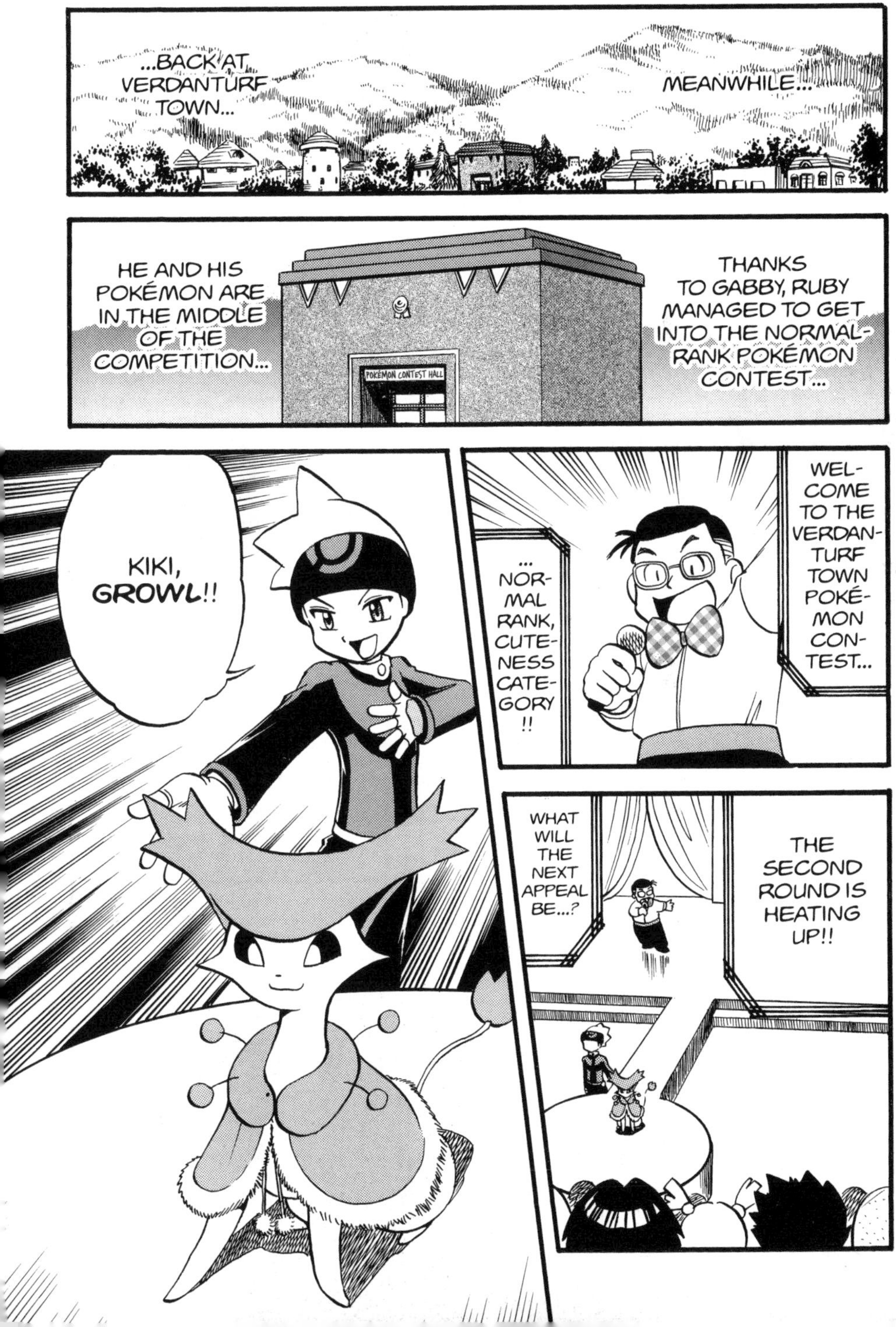
MEANWHILE...
...BACK AT VERDANTURF TOWN...
THANKS TO GABBY, RUBY MANAGED TO GET INTO THE NORMAL-RANK POKÉMON CONTEST...
POKÉMON CONTEST HALL
HE AND HIS POKÉMON ARE IN THE MIDDLE OF THE COMPETITION...
WEL-COME TO THE VERDAN-TURF TOWN POKÉ-MON CON-TEST...
...NOR-MAL RANK, CUTE-NESS CATE-GORY!!
THE SECOND ROUND IS HEATING UP!!
WHAT WILL THE NEXT APPEAL BE...?
KIKI, GROWL!!

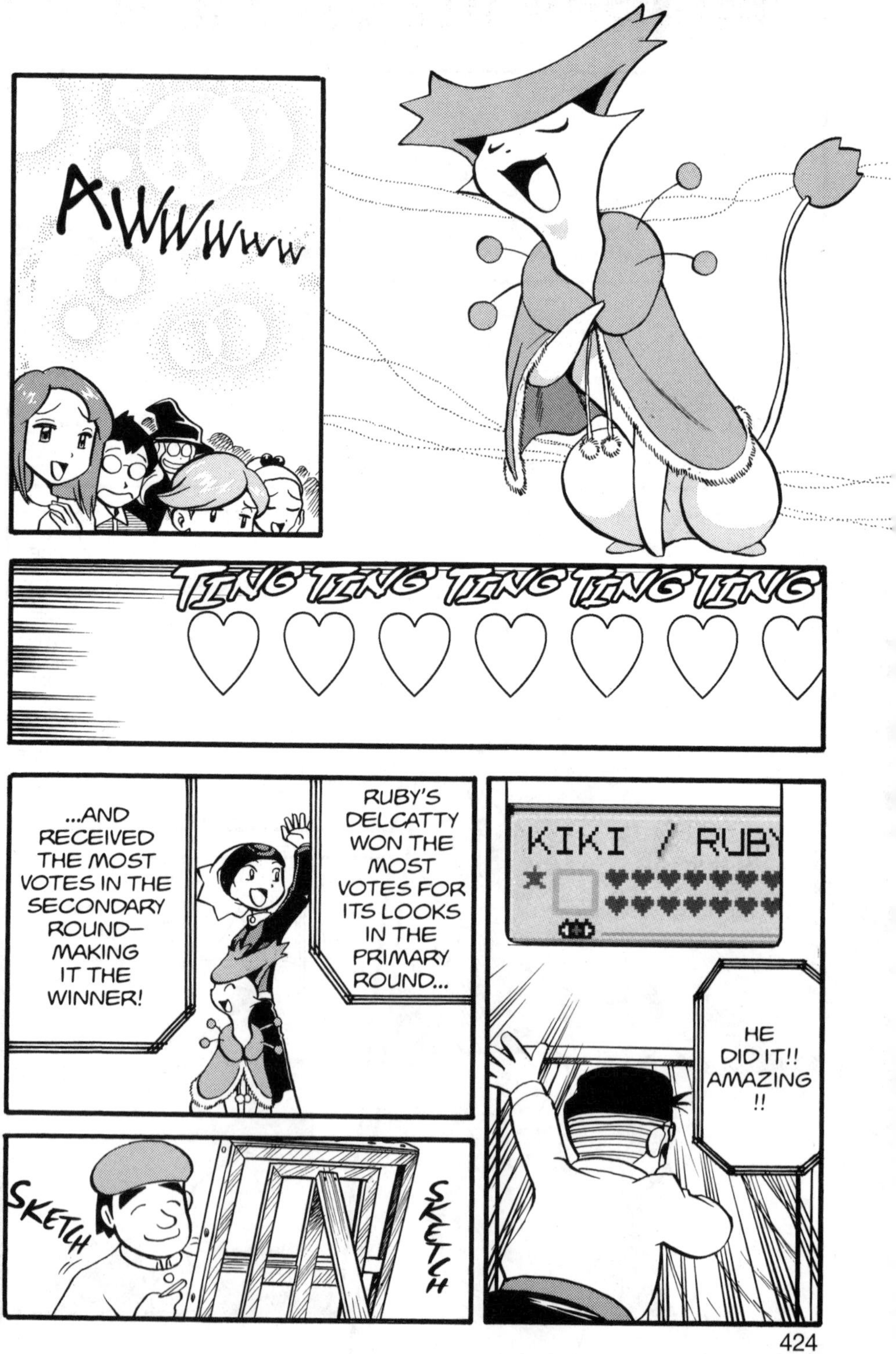
AWWWWWW
TING TING TING TING TING
KIKI / RUBY
HE DID IT!! AMAZING !!
RUBY'S DELCATTY WON THE MOST VOTES FOR ITS LOOKS IN THE PRIMARY ROUND...
...AND RECEIVED THE MOST VOTES IN THE SECONDARY ROUND—MAKING IT THE WINNER!
SKETCH
SKETCH

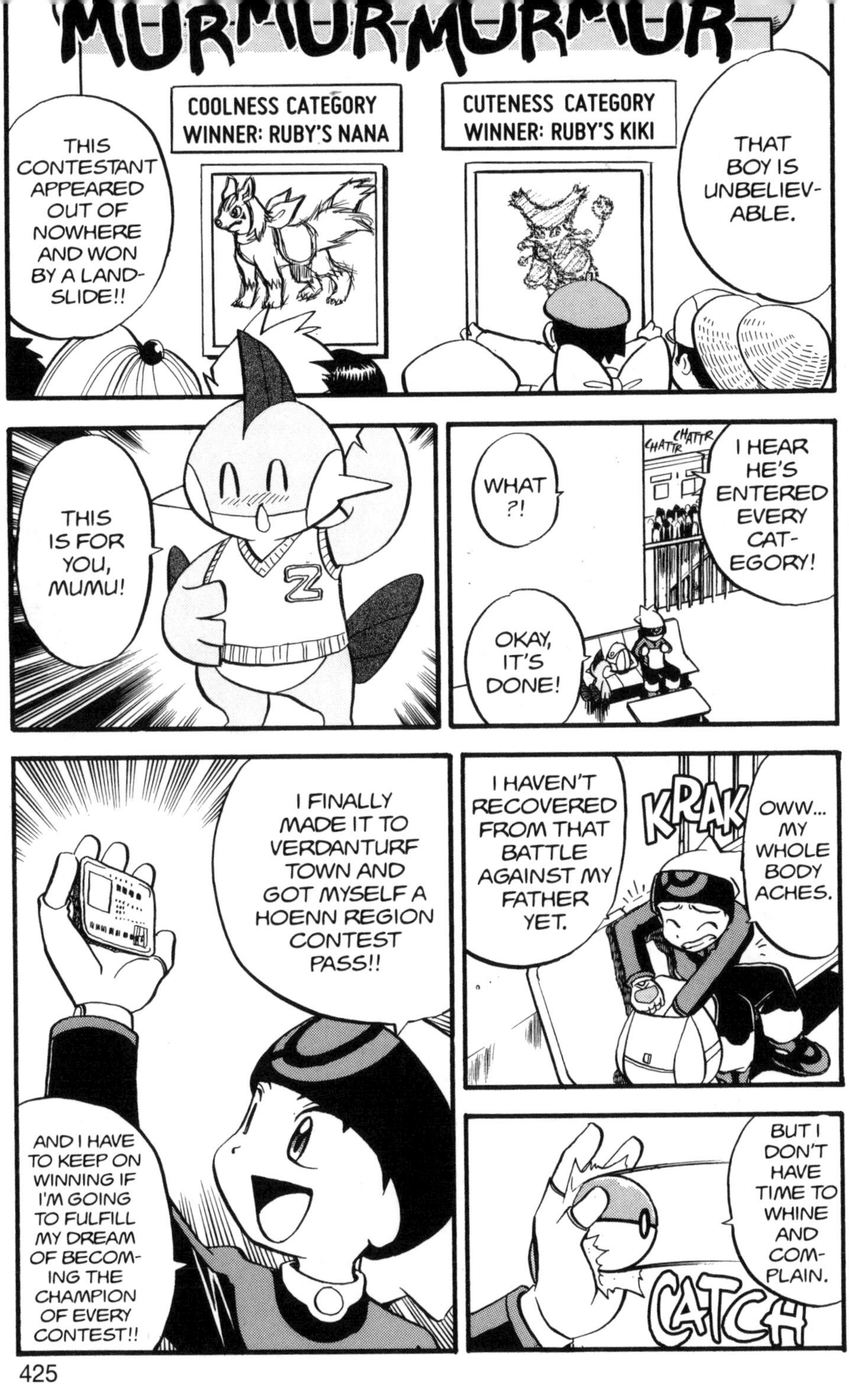
MURMURMURMUR
CUTENESS CATEGORY WINNER: RUBY'S KIKI
COOLNESS CATEGORY WINNER: RUBY'S NANA
THAT BOY IS UNBELIEV-ABLE.
THIS CONTESTANT APPEARED OUT OF NOWHERE AND WON BY A LAND-SLIDE!!
CHATTR CHATTR
I HEAR HE'S ENTERED EVERY CAT-EGORY!
WHAT?!
OKAY, IT'S DONE!
THIS IS FOR YOU, MUMU!
OWW... MY WHOLE BODY ACHES.
KRAK
I HAVEN'T RECOVERED FROM THAT BATTLE AGAINST MY FATHER YET.
BUT I DON'T HAVE TIME TO WHINE AND COM-PLAIN.
CATCH
I FINALLY MADE IT TO VERDANTURF TOWN AND GOT MYSELF A HOENN REGION CONTEST PASS!!
AND I HAVE TO KEEP ON WINNING IF I'M GOING TO FULFILL MY DREAM OF BECOM-ING THE CHAMPION OF EVERY CONTEST!!

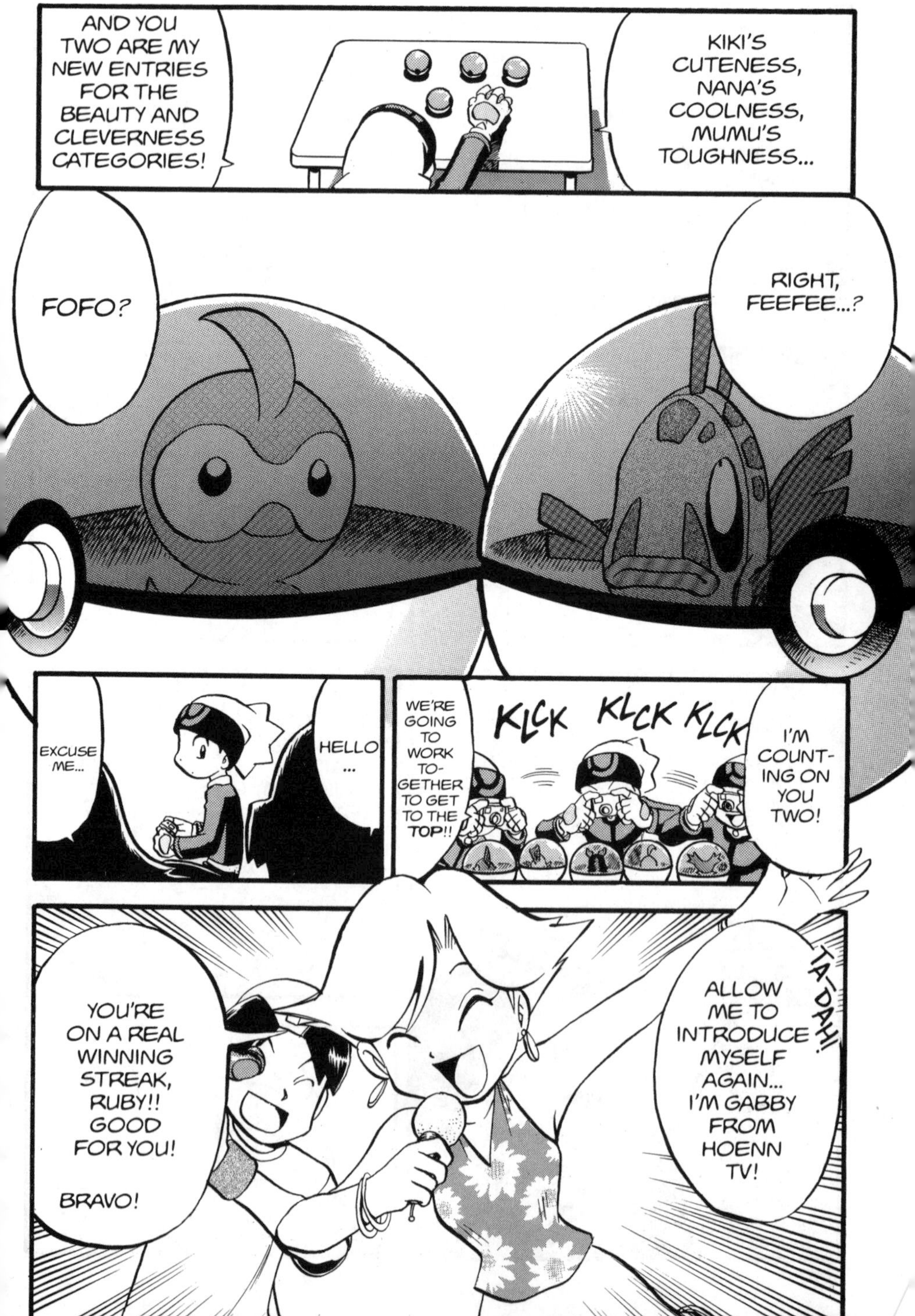

KIKI'S CUTENESS, NANA'S COOLNESS, MUMU'S TOUGHNESS...
AND YOU TWO ARE MY NEW ENTRIES FOR THE BEAUTY AND CLEVERNESS CATEGORIES!
RIGHT, FEEFEE...?
FOFO?
I'M COUNT-ING ON YOU TWO!
KLCK KLCK KLCK
WE'RE GOING TO WORK TO-GETHER TO GET TO THE **TOP**!!
HELLO ...
EXCUSE ME...
TA-DAH!
ALLOW ME TO INTRODUCE MYSELF AGAIN... I'M GABBY FROM HOENN TV!
YOU'RE ON A REAL WINNING STREAK, RUBY!! GOOD FOR YOU!
BRAVO!

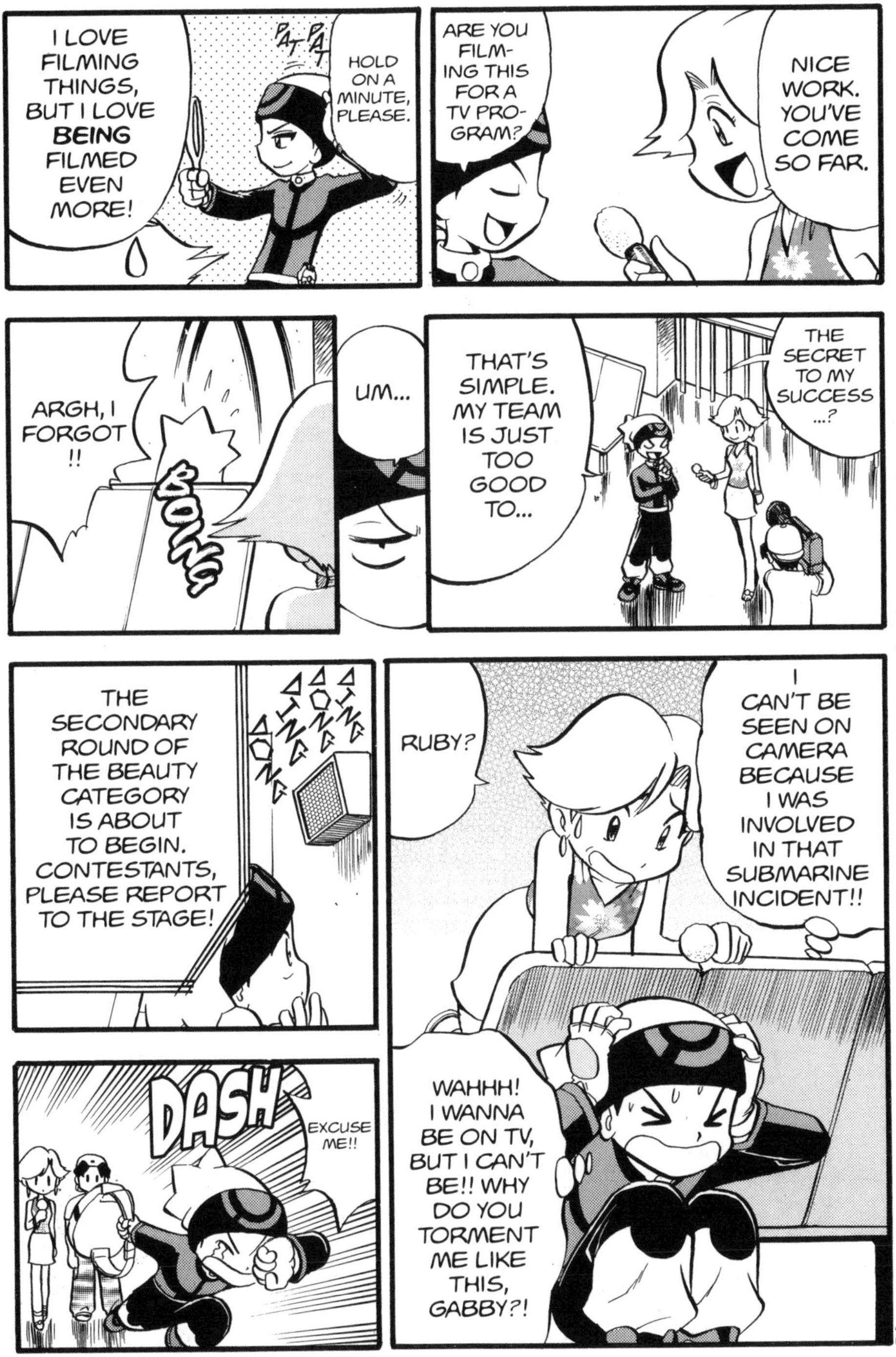
NICE WORK. YOU'VE COME SO FAR.
ARE YOU FILMING THIS FOR A TV PROGRAM?
HOLD ON A MINUTE, PLEASE.
PAT PAT
I LOVE FILMING THINGS, BUT I LOVE **BEING** FILMED EVEN MORE!
THE SECRET TO MY SUCCESS ...?
THAT'S SIMPLE. MY TEAM IS JUST TOO GOOD TO...
UM...
BONG
ARGH, I FORGOT !!
I CAN'T BE SEEN ON CAMERA BECAUSE I WAS INVOLVED IN THAT SUBMARINE INCIDENT!!
RUBY?
WAHHH! I WANNA BE ON TV, BUT I CAN'T BE!! WHY DO YOU TORMENT ME LIKE THIS, GABBY?!
DING DONG DING DONG
THE SECONDARY ROUND OF THE BEAUTY CATEGORY IS ABOUT TO BEGIN. CONTESTANTS, PLEASE REPORT TO THE STAGE!
DASH
EXCUSE ME!!

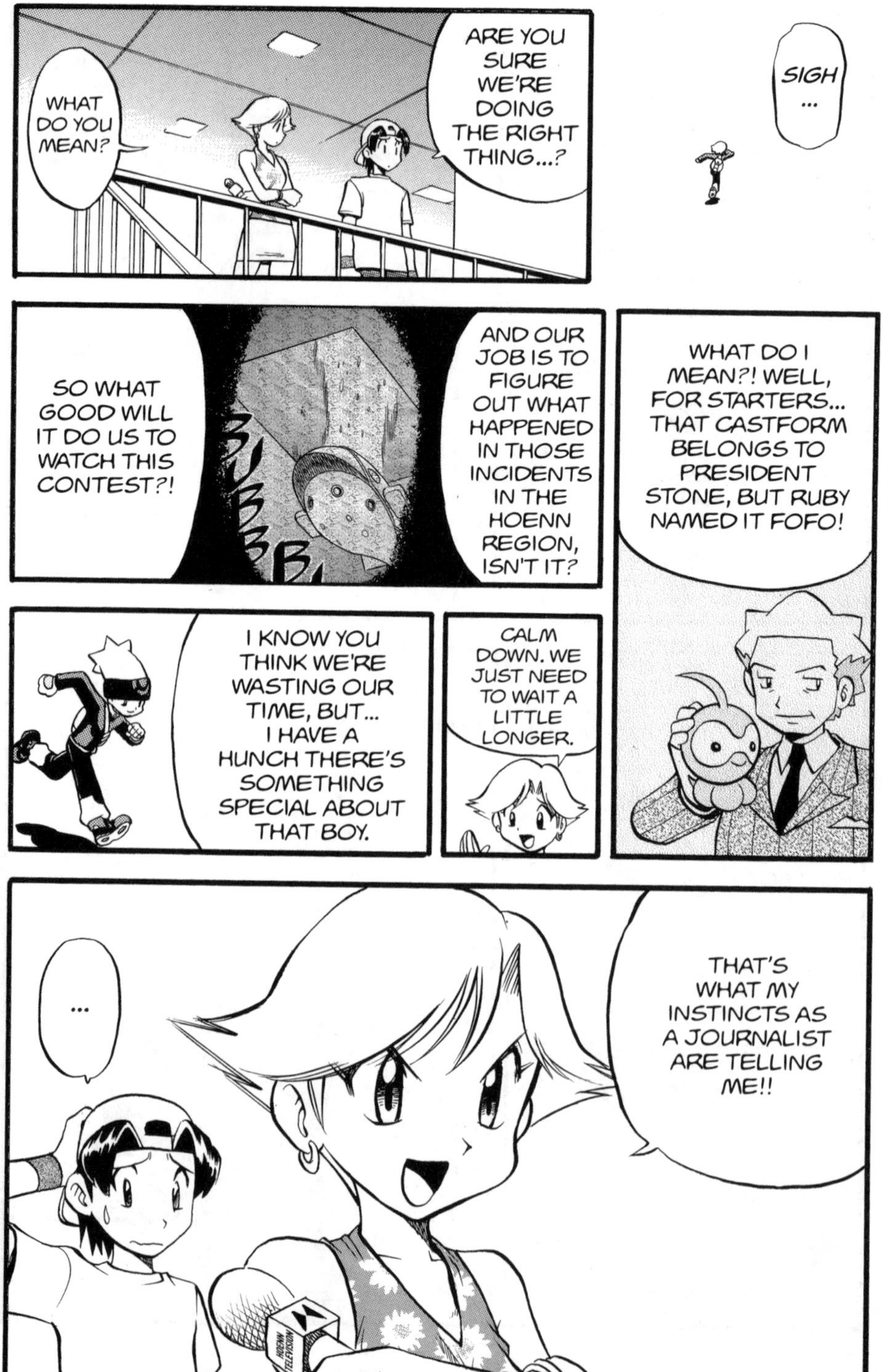
SIGH ...
ARE YOU SURE WE'RE DOING THE RIGHT THING...?
WHAT DO YOU MEAN?
WHAT DO I MEAN?! WELL, FOR STARTERS... THAT CASTFORM BELONGS TO PRESIDENT STONE, BUT RUBY NAMED IT FOFO!
AND OUR JOB IS TO FIGURE OUT WHAT HAPPENED IN THOSE INCIDENTS IN THE HOENN REGION, ISN'T IT?
SO WHAT GOOD WILL IT DO US TO WATCH THIS CONTEST?!
CALM DOWN. WE JUST NEED TO WAIT A LITTLE LONGER.
I KNOW YOU THINK WE'RE WASTING OUR TIME, BUT... I HAVE A HUNCH THERE'S SOMETHING SPECIAL ABOUT THAT BOY.
THAT'S WHAT MY INSTINCTS AS A JOURNALIST ARE TELLING ME!!
...

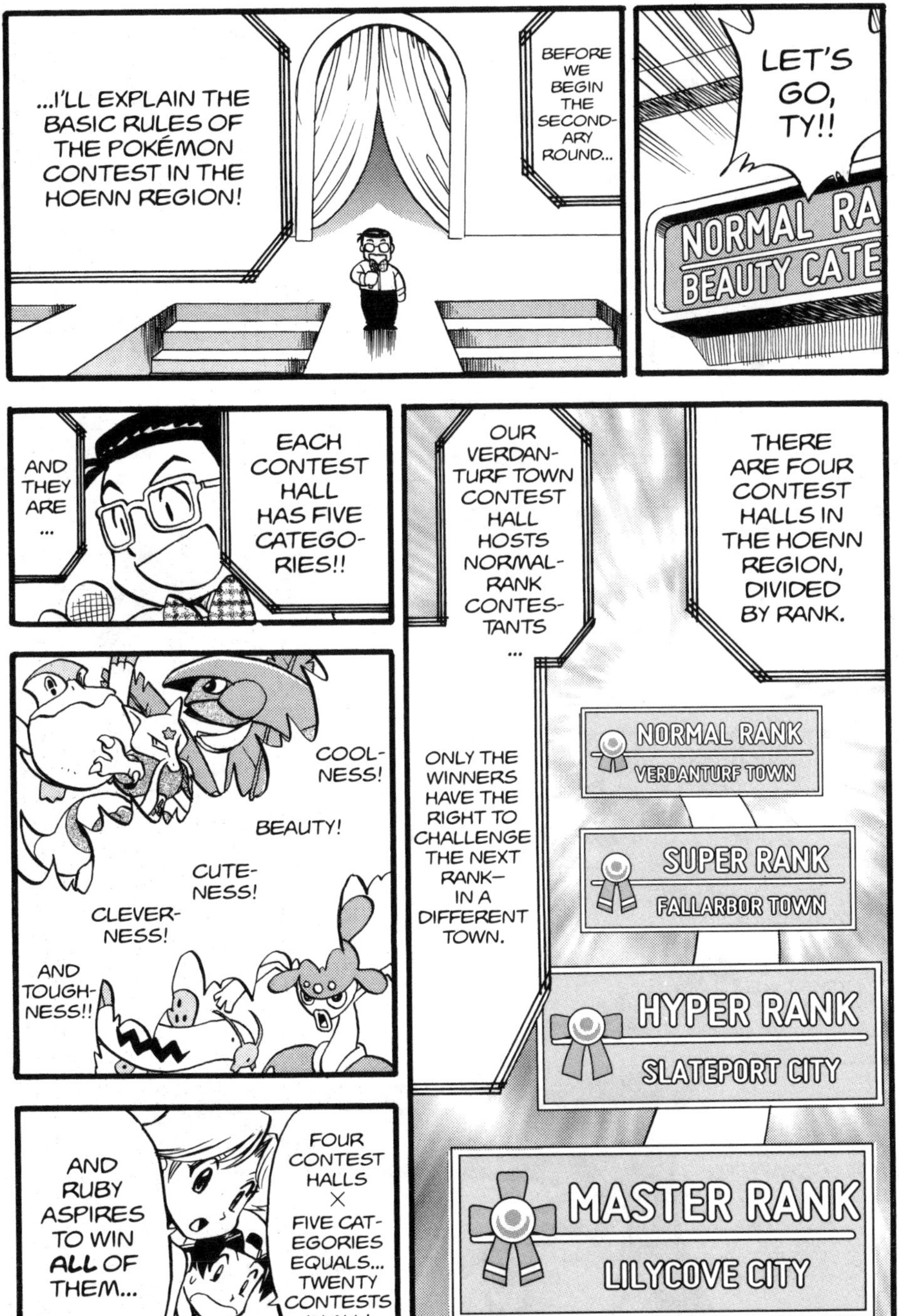
LET'S GO, TY!!
NORMAL RA
BEAUTY CATE
BEFORE WE BEGIN THE SECOND-ARY ROUND...
...I'LL EXPLAIN THE BASIC RULES OF THE POKÉMON CONTEST IN THE HOENN REGION!
THERE ARE FOUR CONTEST HALLS IN THE HOENN REGION, DIVIDED BY RANK.
OUR VERDAN-TURF TOWN CONTEST HALL HOSTS NORMAL-RANK CONTES-TANTS...
ONLY THE WINNERS HAVE THE RIGHT TO CHALLENGE THE NEXT RANK—IN A DIFFERENT TOWN.
NORMAL RANK
VERDANTURF TOWN
SUPER RANK
FALLARBOR TOWN
HYPER RANK
SLATEPORT CITY
MASTER RANK
LILYCOVE CITY
EACH CONTEST HALL HAS FIVE CATEGO-RIES!!
AND THEY ARE...
COOL-NESS!
BEAUTY!
CUTE-NESS!
CLEVER-NESS!
AND TOUGH-NESS!!
FOUR CONTEST HALLS × FIVE CAT-EGORIES EQUALS... TWENTY CONTESTS IN ALL!
AND RUBY ASPIRES TO WIN **ALL** OF THEM...

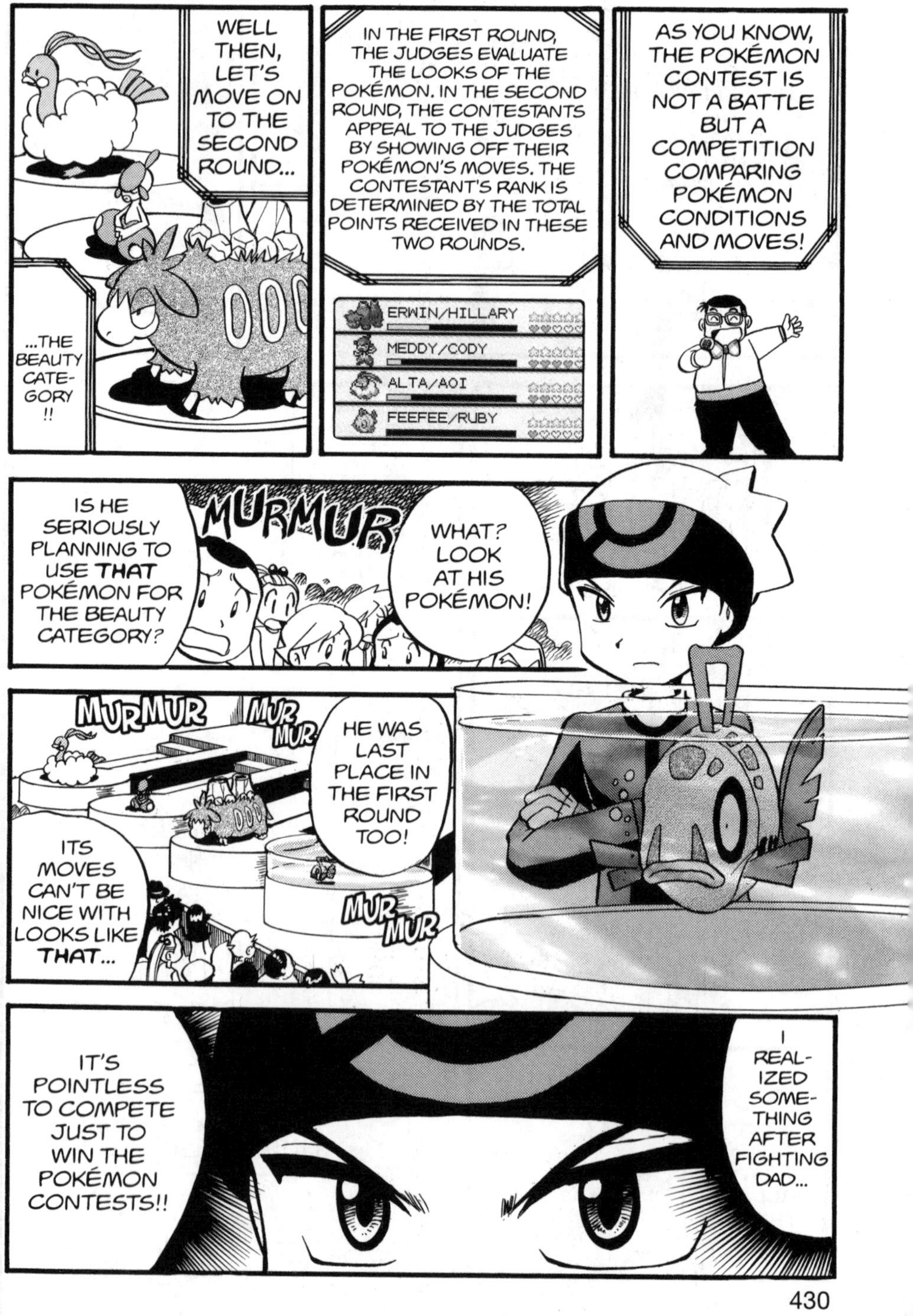
AS YOU KNOW, THE POKéMON CONTEST IS NOT A BATTLE BUT A COMPETITION COMPARING POKéMON CONDITIONS AND MOVES!
IN THE FIRST ROUND, THE JUDGES EVALUATE THE LOOKS OF THE POKéMON. IN THE SECOND ROUND, THE CONTESTANTS APPEAL TO THE JUDGES BY SHOWING OFF THEIR POKéMON'S MOVES. THE CONTESTANT'S RANK IS DETERMINED BY THE TOTAL POINTS RECEIVED IN THESE TWO ROUNDS.
ERWIN/HILLARY
MEDDY/CODY
ALTA/AOI
FEEFEE/RUBY
WELL THEN, LET'S MOVE ON TO THE SECOND ROUND...
...THE BEAUTY CATE-GORY !!
WHAT? LOOK AT HIS POKéMON!
MURMUR
IS HE SERIOUSLY PLANNING TO USE **THAT** POKéMON FOR THE BEAUTY CATEGORY?
HE WAS LAST PLACE IN THE FIRST ROUND TOO!
MUR MUR
MURMUR
ITS MOVES CAN'T BE NICE WITH LOOKS LIKE **THAT**...
MUR MUR
I REAL-IZED SOME-THING AFTER FIGHTING DAD...
IT'S POINTLESS TO COMPETE JUST TO WIN THE POKéMON CONTESTS!!

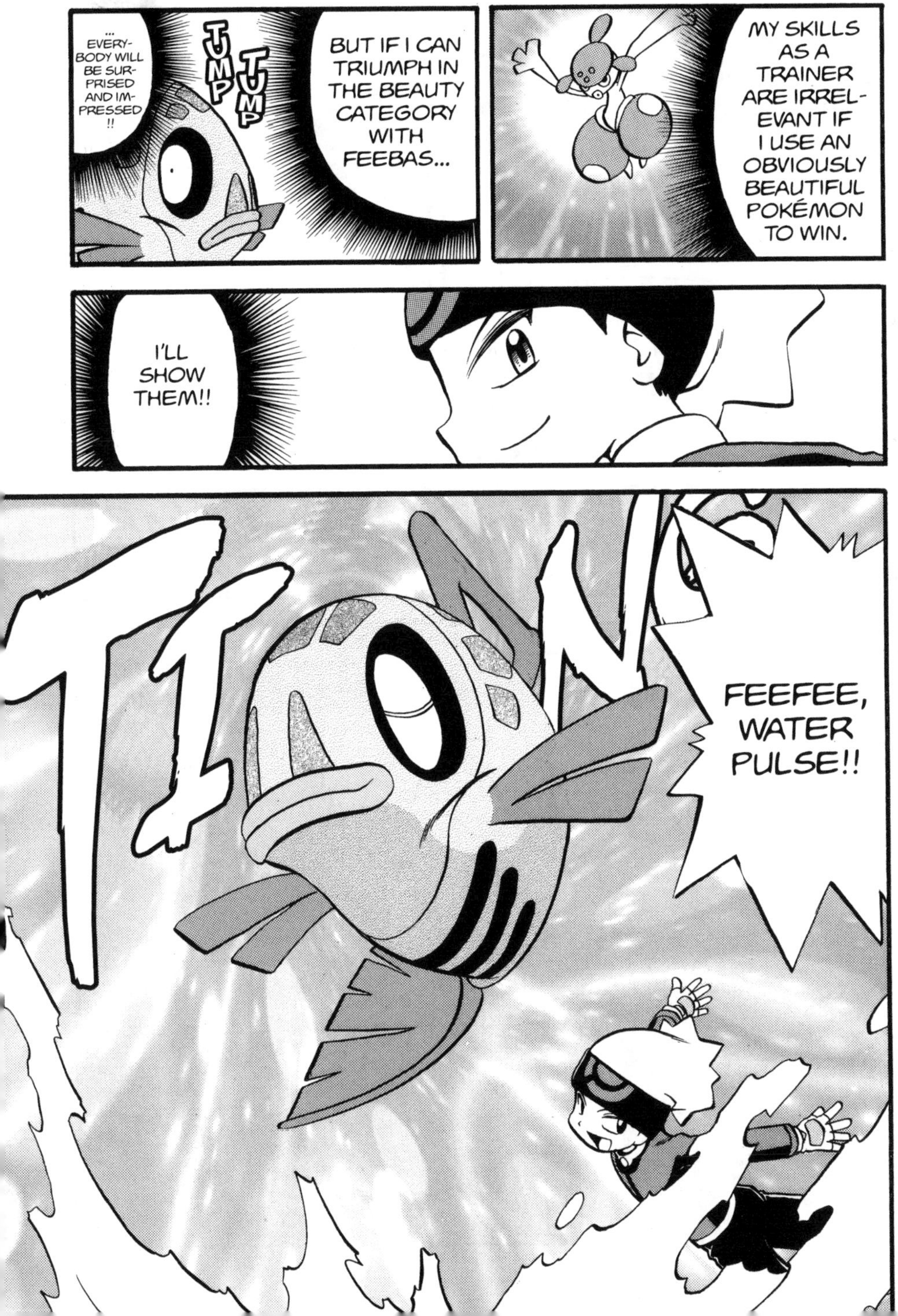
MY SKILLS AS A TRAINER ARE IRREL-EVANT IF I USE AN OBVIOUSLY BEAUTIFUL POKÉMON TO WIN.
BUT IF I CAN TRIUMPH IN THE BEAUTY CATEGORY WITH FEEBAS...
...EVERY-BODY WILL BE SUR-PRISED AND IM-PRESSED!!
TUMP TUMP
I'LL SHOW THEM!!
FEEFEE, WATER PULSE!!

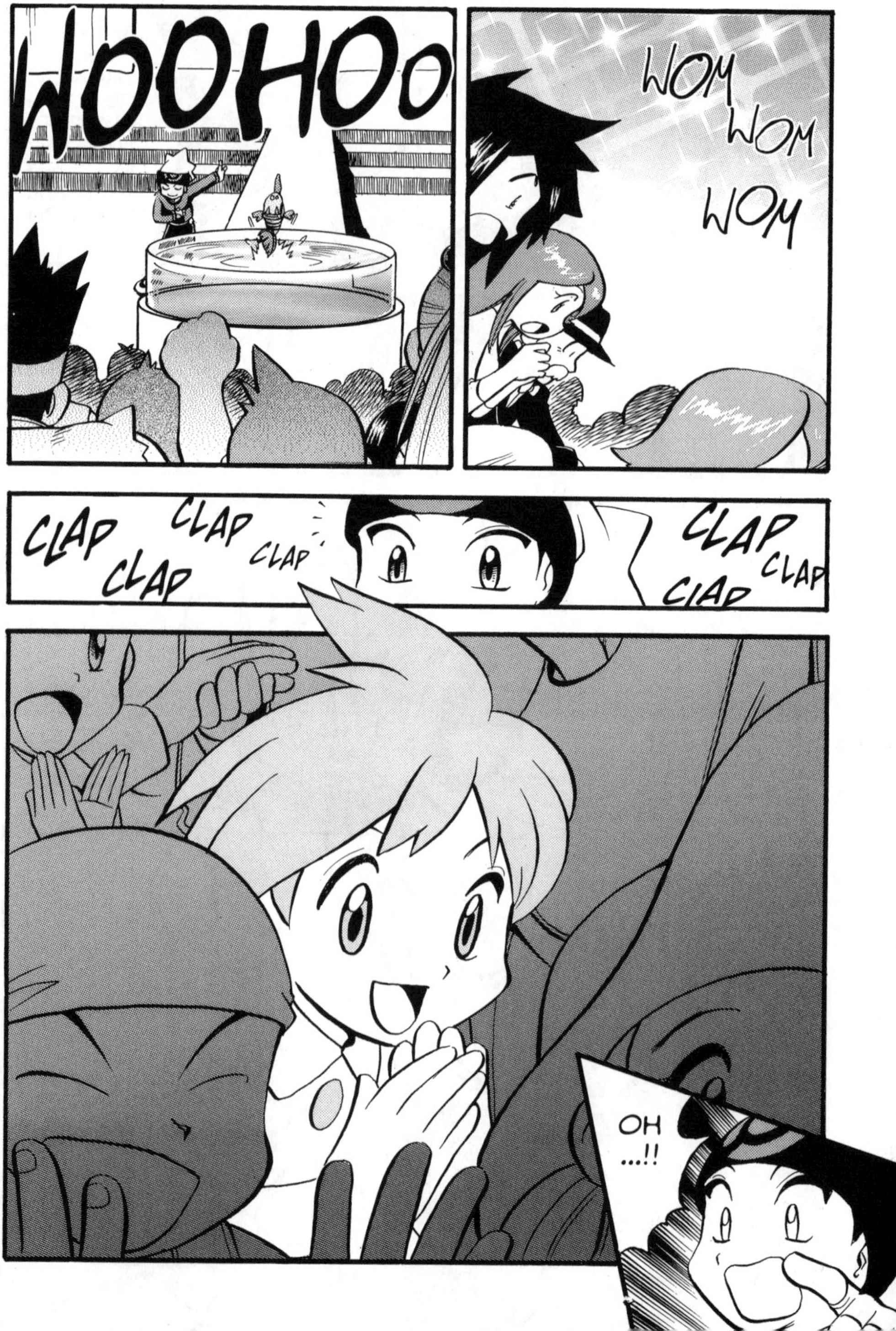
WOM
WOM
WOM
WOOHOO
CLAP
CLAP
CLAP
CLAP
CLAP
CLAP
CLAP
OH
...!!

● Adventure 218 ●

It's Absol-lutely a Bad Omen

Pokémon™ Adventures Ruby & Sapphire

The Fourth Chapter

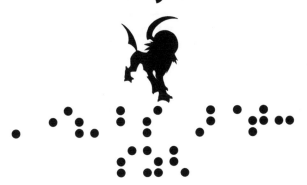

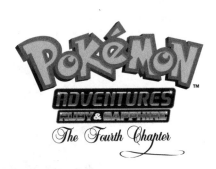

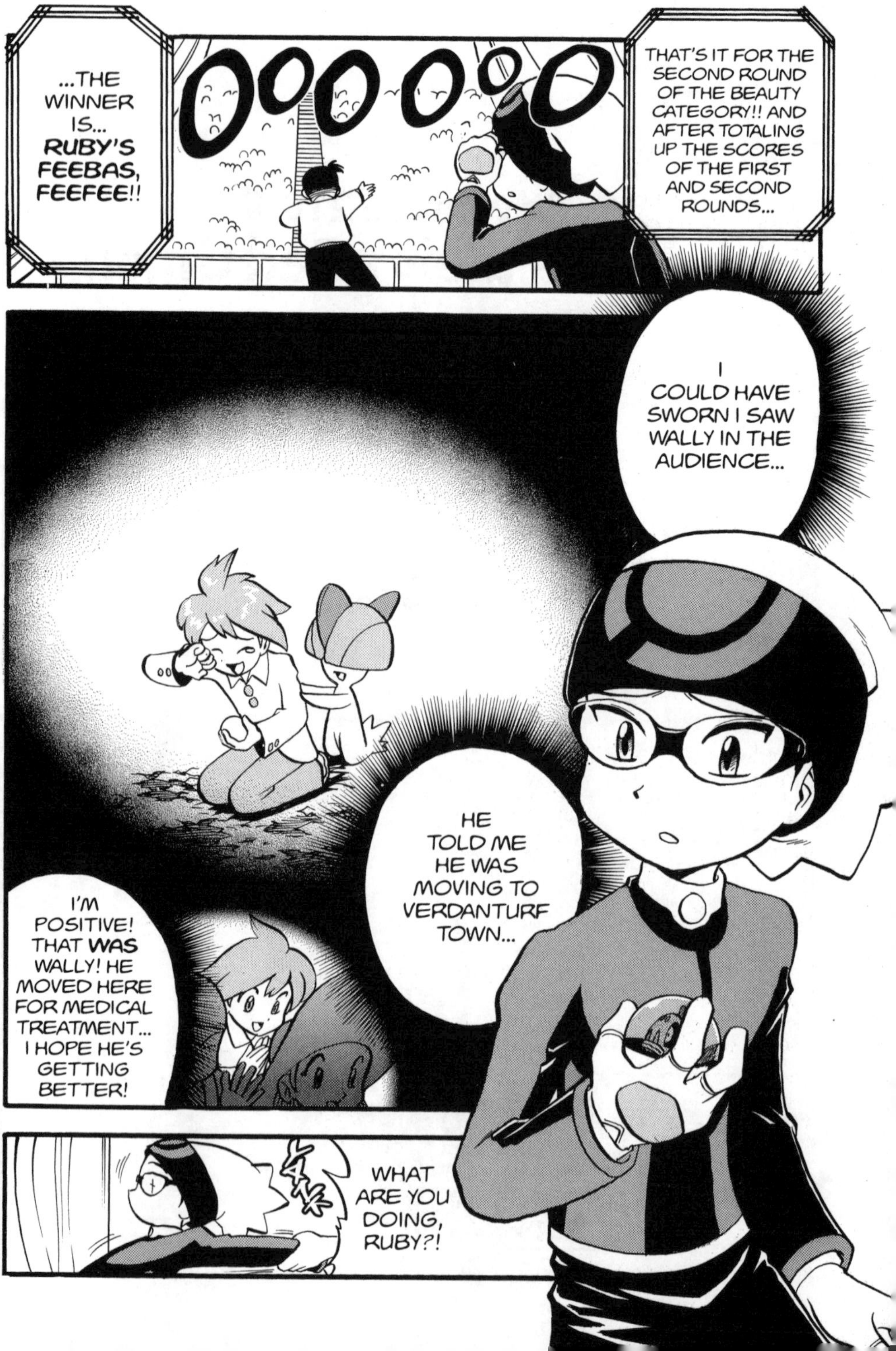
THAT'S IT FOR THE SECOND ROUND OF THE BEAUTY CATEGORY!! AND AFTER TOTALING UP THE SCORES OF THE FIRST AND SECOND ROUNDS...
OOOOOO
...THE WINNER IS... **RUBY'S FEEBAS, FEEFEE!!**
I COULD HAVE SWORN I SAW WALLY IN THE AUDIENCE...
HE TOLD ME HE WAS MOVING TO VERDANTURF TOWN...
I'M POSITIVE! THAT **WAS** WALLY! HE MOVED HERE FOR MEDICAL TREATMENT... I HOPE HE'S GETTING BETTER!
WHAT ARE YOU DOING, RUBY?!
YANK

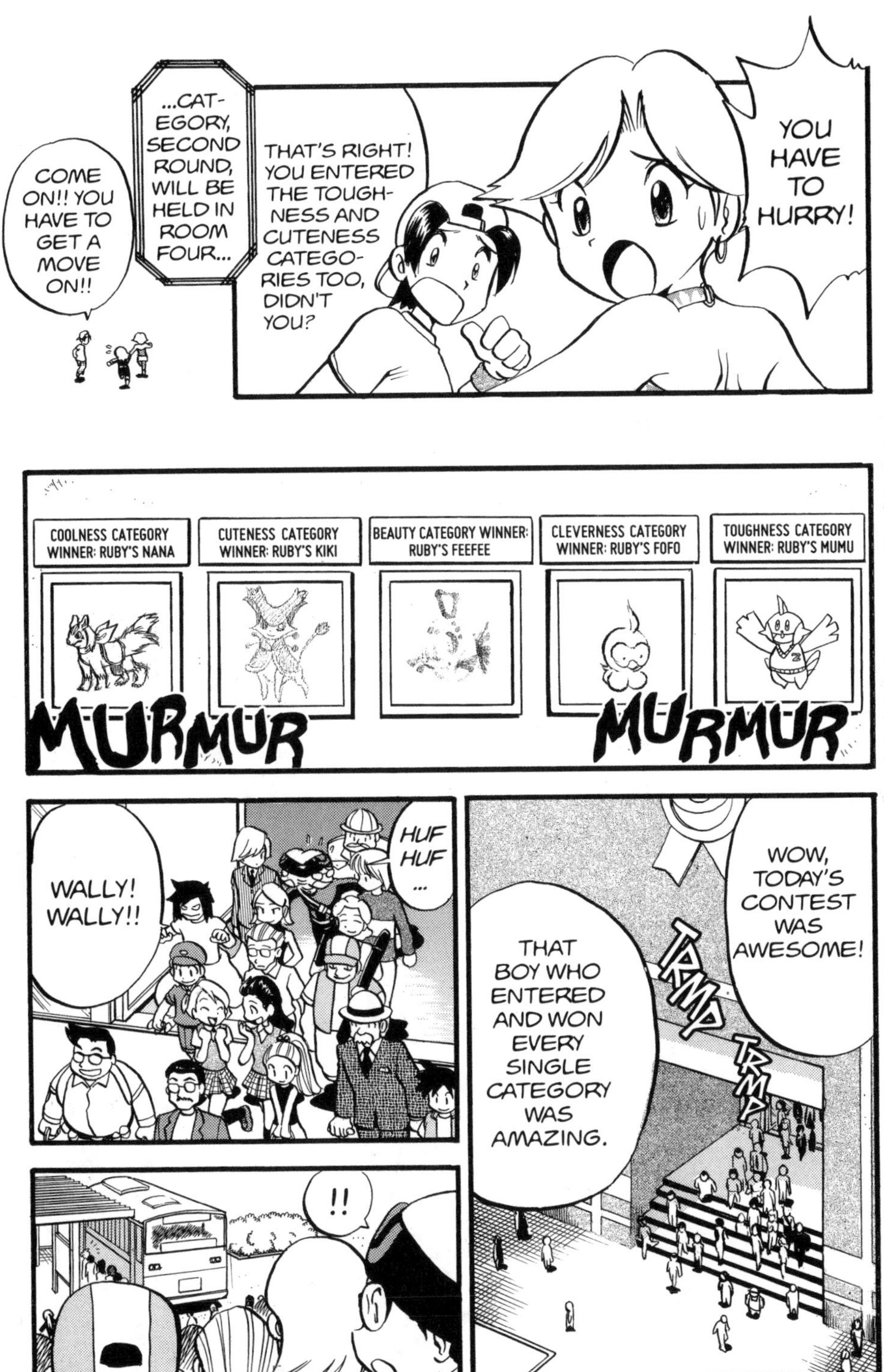
YOU HAVE TO HURRY!
THAT'S RIGHT! YOU ENTERED THE TOUGHNESS AND CUTENESS CATEGORIES TOO, DIDN'T YOU?
...CATEGORY, SECOND ROUND, WILL BE HELD IN ROOM FOUR...
COME ON!! YOU HAVE TO GET A MOVE ON!!
TOUGHNESS CATEGORY WINNER: RUBY'S MUMU
CLEVERNESS CATEGORY WINNER: RUBY'S FOFO
BEAUTY CATEGORY WINNER: RUBY'S FEEFEE
CUTENESS CATEGORY WINNER: RUBY'S KIKI
COOLNESS CATEGORY WINNER: RUBY'S NANA
MURMUR
MURMUR
WOW, TODAY'S CONTEST WAS AWESOME!
THAT BOY WHO ENTERED AND WON EVERY SINGLE CATEGORY WAS AMAZING.
TRMP
TRMP
HUF HUF ...
WALLY! WALLY!!
!!

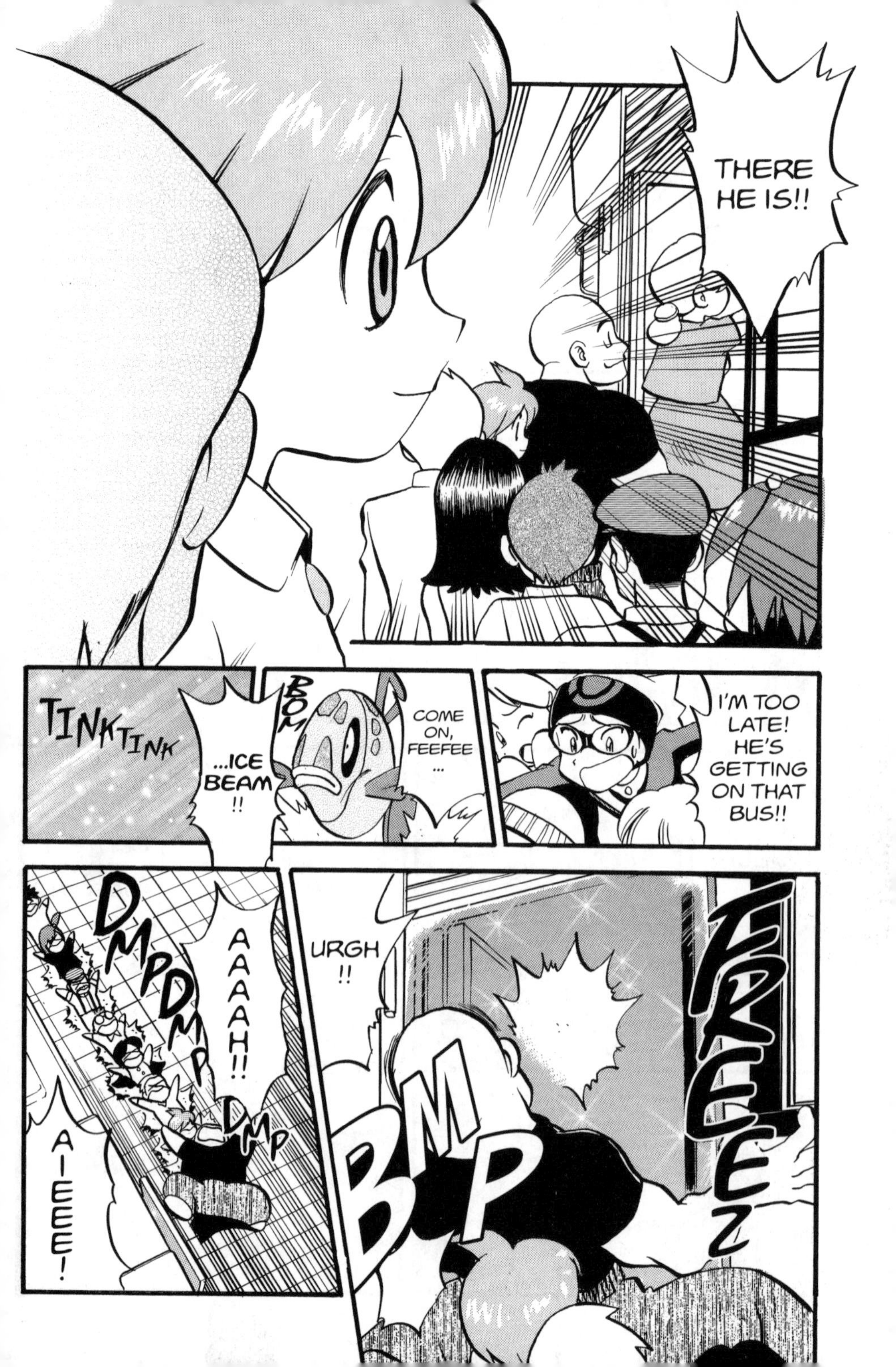
THERE HE IS!!
I'M TOO LATE! HE'S GETTING ON THAT BUS!!
COME ON, FEEFEE ...
BOM
...ICE BEAM!!
TINKTINK
URGH!!
BMP
FREEEZ
AAAAAH!!
DMPDMPDMP
DMP
A-IEEE!

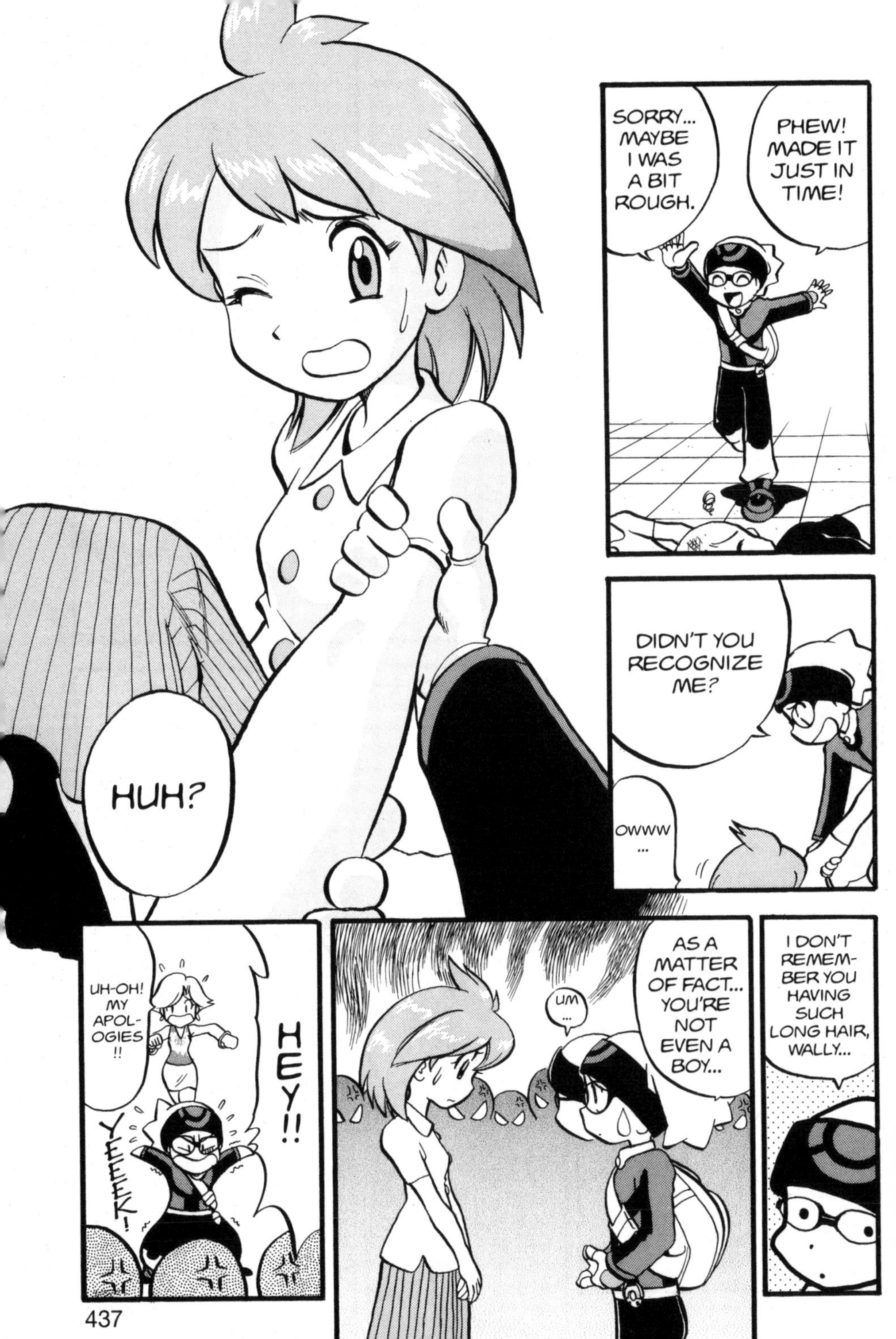
PHEW! MADE IT JUST IN TIME!
SORRY... MAYBE I WAS A BIT ROUGH.
DIDN'T YOU RECOGNIZE ME?
OWWW ...
HUH?
I DON'T REMEM-BER YOU HAVING SUCH LONG HAIR, WALLY...
AS A MATTER OF FACT... YOU'RE NOT EVEN A BOY...
UM ...
HEY!!
UH-OH! MY APOL-OGIES !!
YEEEK!

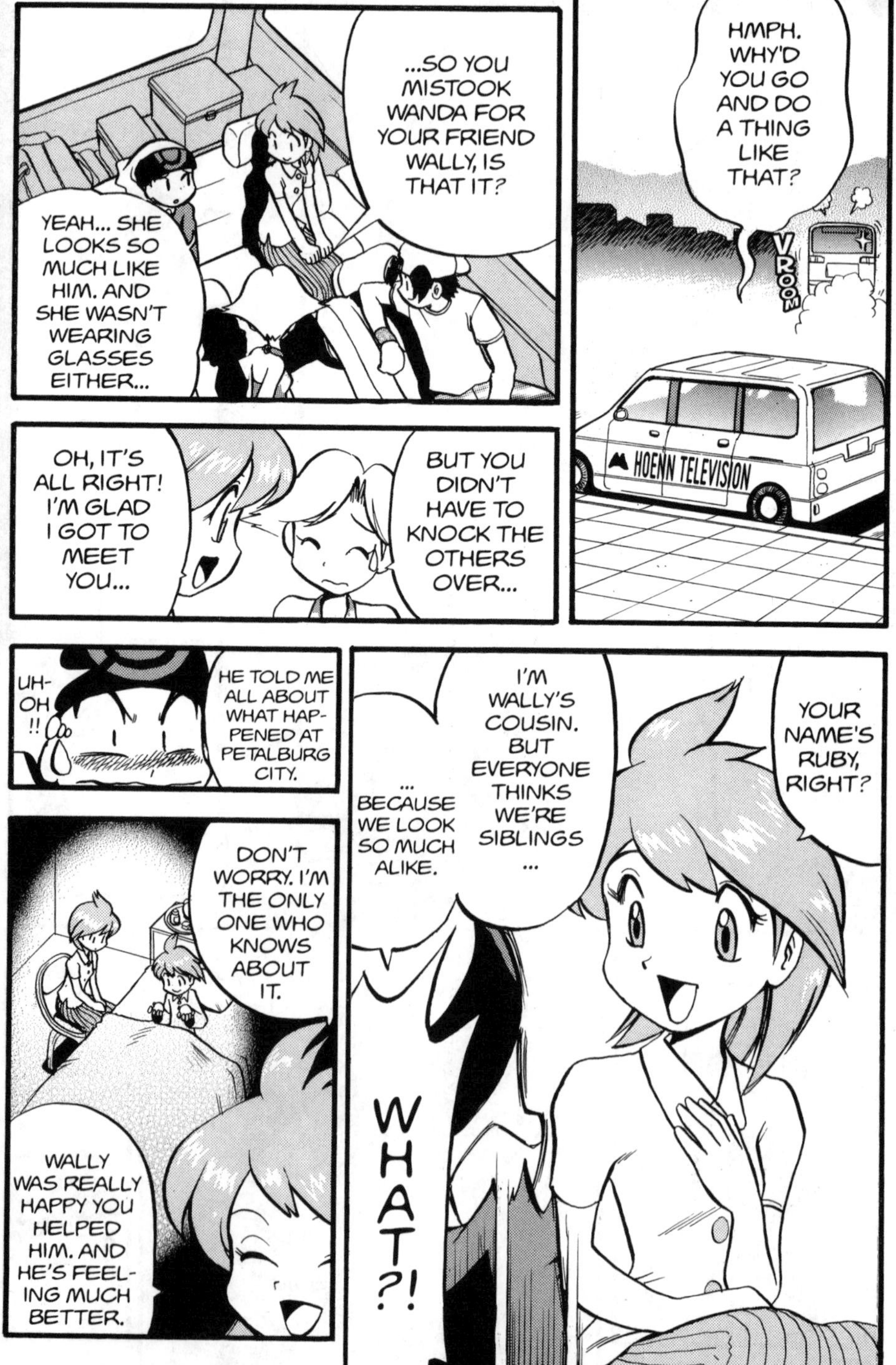
HMPH. WHY'D YOU GO AND DO A THING LIKE THAT?
VROOM
HOENN TELEVISION
...SO YOU MISTOOK WANDA FOR YOUR FRIEND WALLY, IS THAT IT?
YEAH... SHE LOOKS SO MUCH LIKE HIM. AND SHE WASN'T WEARING GLASSES EITHER...
BUT YOU DIDN'T HAVE TO KNOCK THE OTHERS OVER...
OH, IT'S ALL RIGHT! I'M GLAD I GOT TO MEET YOU...
YOUR NAME'S RUBY, RIGHT?
I'M WALLY'S COUSIN. BUT EVERYONE THINKS WE'RE SIBLINGS...
...BECAUSE WE LOOK SO MUCH ALIKE.
WHAT?!
HE TOLD ME ALL ABOUT WHAT HAPPENED AT PETALBURG CITY.
UH-OH!!
DON'T WORRY. I'M THE ONLY ONE WHO KNOWS ABOUT IT.
WALLY WAS REALLY HAPPY YOU HELPED HIM. AND HE'S FEELING MUCH BETTER.

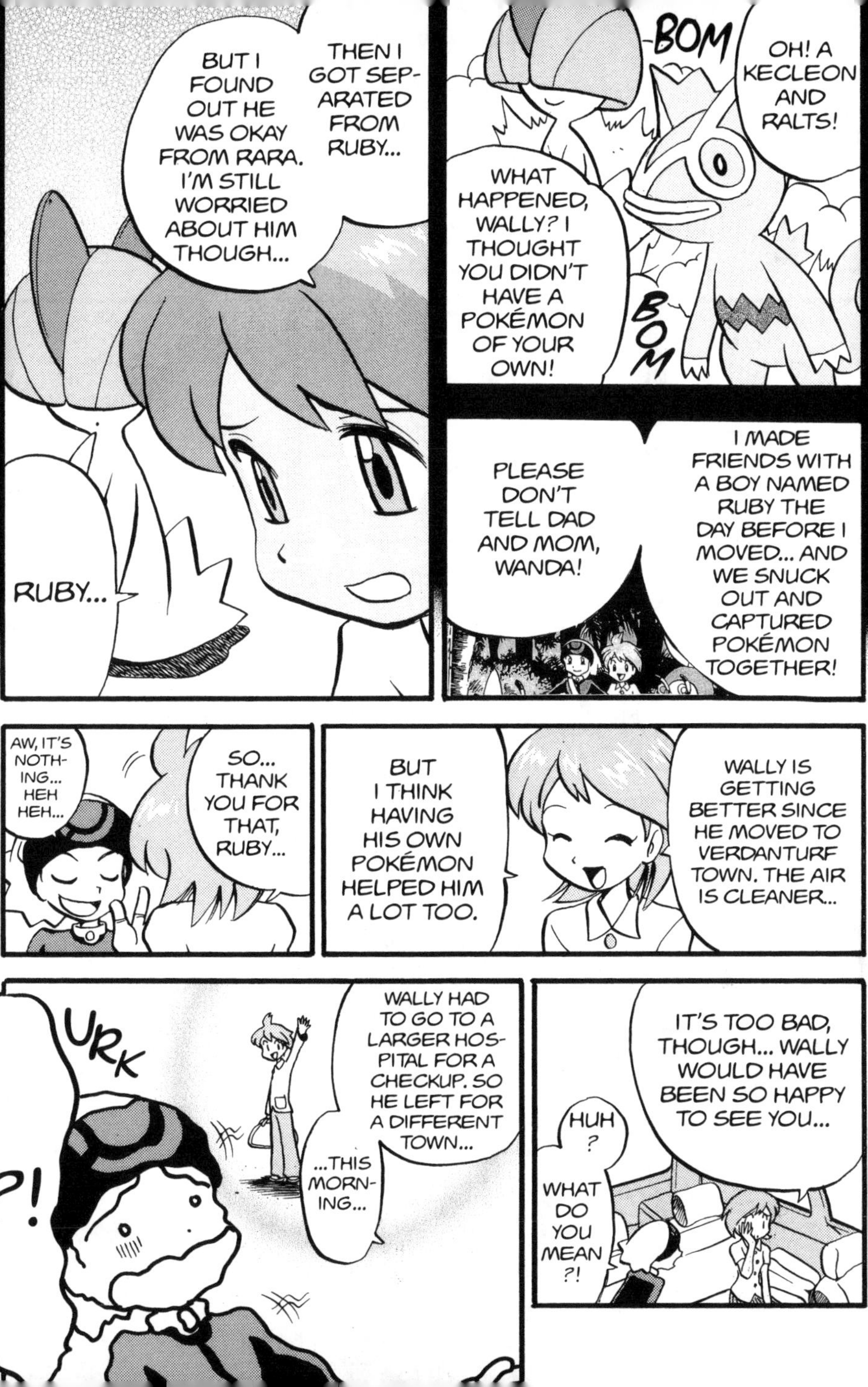
-BOM
OH! A KECLEON AND RALTS!
WHAT HAPPENED, WALLY? I THOUGHT YOU DIDN'T HAVE A POKÉMON OF YOUR OWN!
BOM BOM
I MADE FRIENDS WITH A BOY NAMED RUBY THE DAY BEFORE I MOVED... AND WE SNUCK OUT AND CAPTURED POKÉMON TOGETHER!
PLEASE DON'T TELL DAD AND MOM, WANDA!
THEN I GOT SEP-ARATED FROM RUBY...
BUT I FOUND OUT HE WAS OKAY FROM RARA. I'M STILL WORRIED ABOUT HIM THOUGH...
RUBY...
WALLY IS GETTING BETTER SINCE HE MOVED TO VERDANTURF TOWN. THE AIR IS CLEANER...
BUT I THINK HAVING HIS OWN POKÉMON HELPED HIM A LOT TOO.
SO... THANK YOU FOR THAT, RUBY...
AW, IT'S NOTH-ING... HEH HEH...
IT'S TOO BAD, THOUGH... WALLY WOULD HAVE BEEN SO HAPPY TO SEE YOU...
HUH?
WHAT DO YOU MEAN?!
WALLY HAD TO GO TO A LARGER HOS-PITAL FOR A CHECKUP. SO HE LEFT FOR A DIFFERENT TOWN...
...THIS MORN-ING...
URK
?!

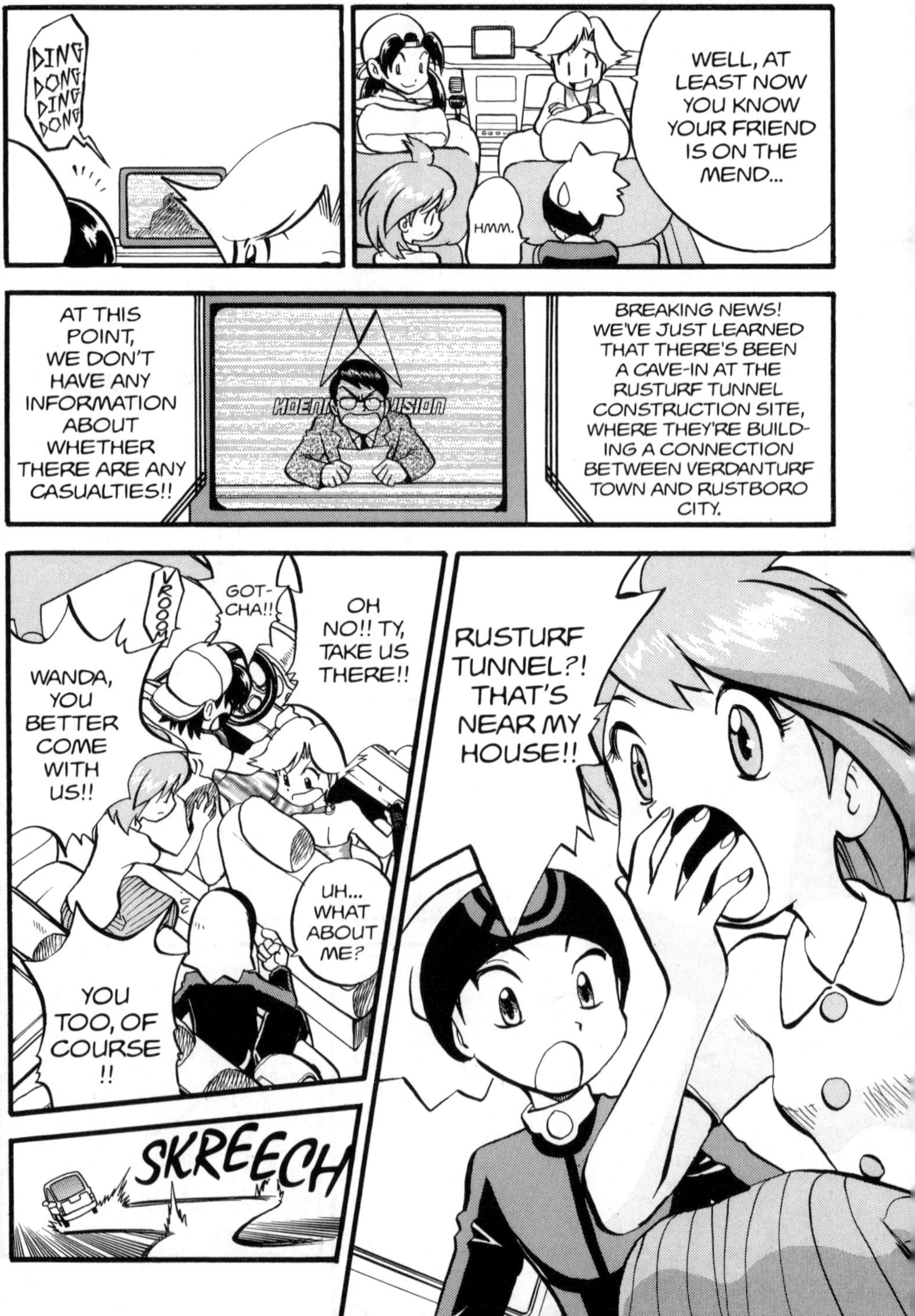

WELL, AT LEAST NOW YOU KNOW YOUR FRIEND IS ON THE MEND...
HMM.
DING DONG DING DONG
BREAKING NEWS! WE'VE JUST LEARNED THAT THERE'S BEEN A CAVE-IN AT THE RUSTURF TUNNEL CONSTRUCTION SITE, WHERE THEY'RE BUILDING A CONNECTION BETWEEN VERDANTURF TOWN AND RUSTBORO CITY.
AT THIS POINT, WE DON'T HAVE ANY INFORMATION ABOUT WHETHER THERE ARE ANY CASUALTIES!!
RUSTURF TUNNEL?! THAT'S NEAR MY HOUSE!!
OH NO!! TY, TAKE US THERE!!
GOT-CHA!!
VROOOM
WANDA, YOU BETTER COME WITH US!!
UH... WHAT ABOUT ME?
YOU TOO, OF COURSE!!
SKREECH

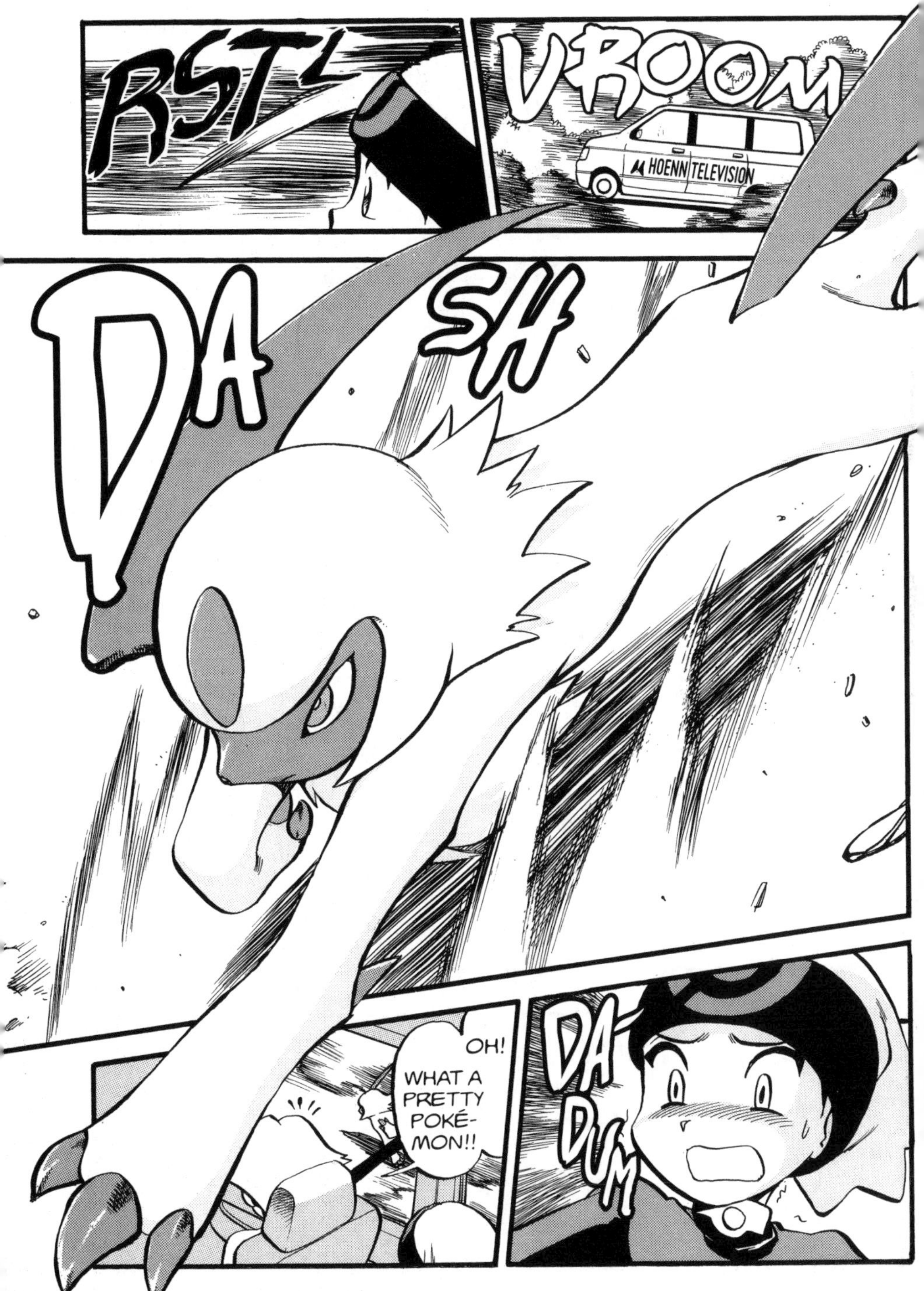
VROOM
HOENN TELEVISION
RST
DASH
DA DUM
OH! WHAT A PRETTY POKÉMON!!

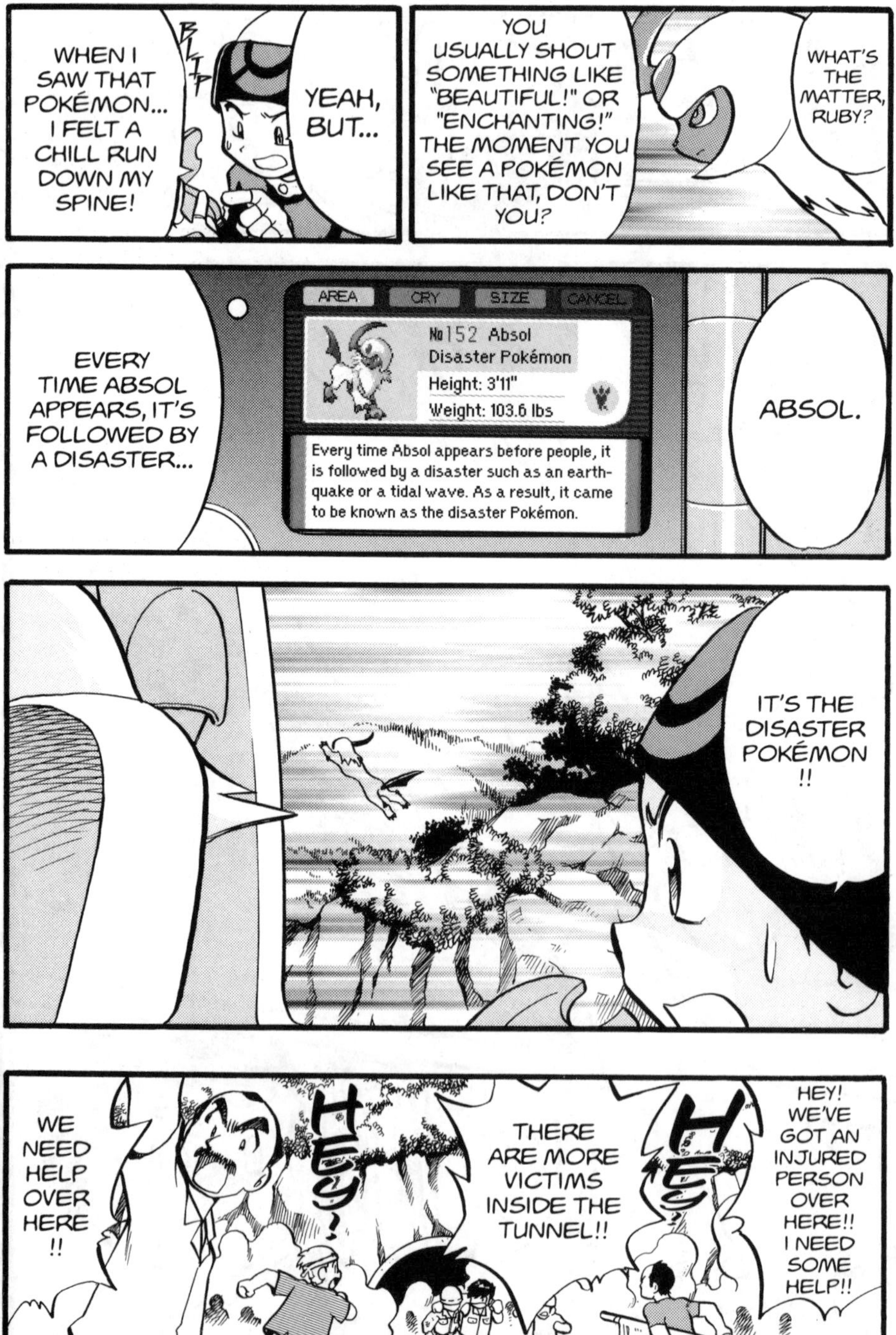
WHAT'S THE MATTER, RUBY?
YOU USUALLY SHOUT SOMETHING LIKE "BEAUTIFUL!" OR "ENCHANTING!" THE MOMENT YOU SEE A POKÉMON LIKE THAT, DON'T YOU?
YEAH, BUT...
WHEN I SAW THAT POKÉMON... I FELT A CHILL RUN DOWN MY SPINE!
ABSOL.
AREA
CRY
SIZE
CANCEL
№152 Absol
Disaster Pokémon
Height: 3'11"
Weight: 103.6 lbs
Every time Absol appears before people, it is followed by a disaster such as an earthquake or a tidal wave. As a result, it came to be known as the disaster Pokémon.
EVERY TIME ABSOL APPEARS, IT'S FOLLOWED BY A DISASTER...
IT'S THE DISASTER POKÉMON !!
HEY! WE'VE GOT AN INJURED PERSON OVER HERE!! I NEED SOME HELP!!
HEY!?
THERE ARE MORE VICTIMS INSIDE THE TUNNEL!!
HEY!?
WE NEED HELP OVER HERE !!

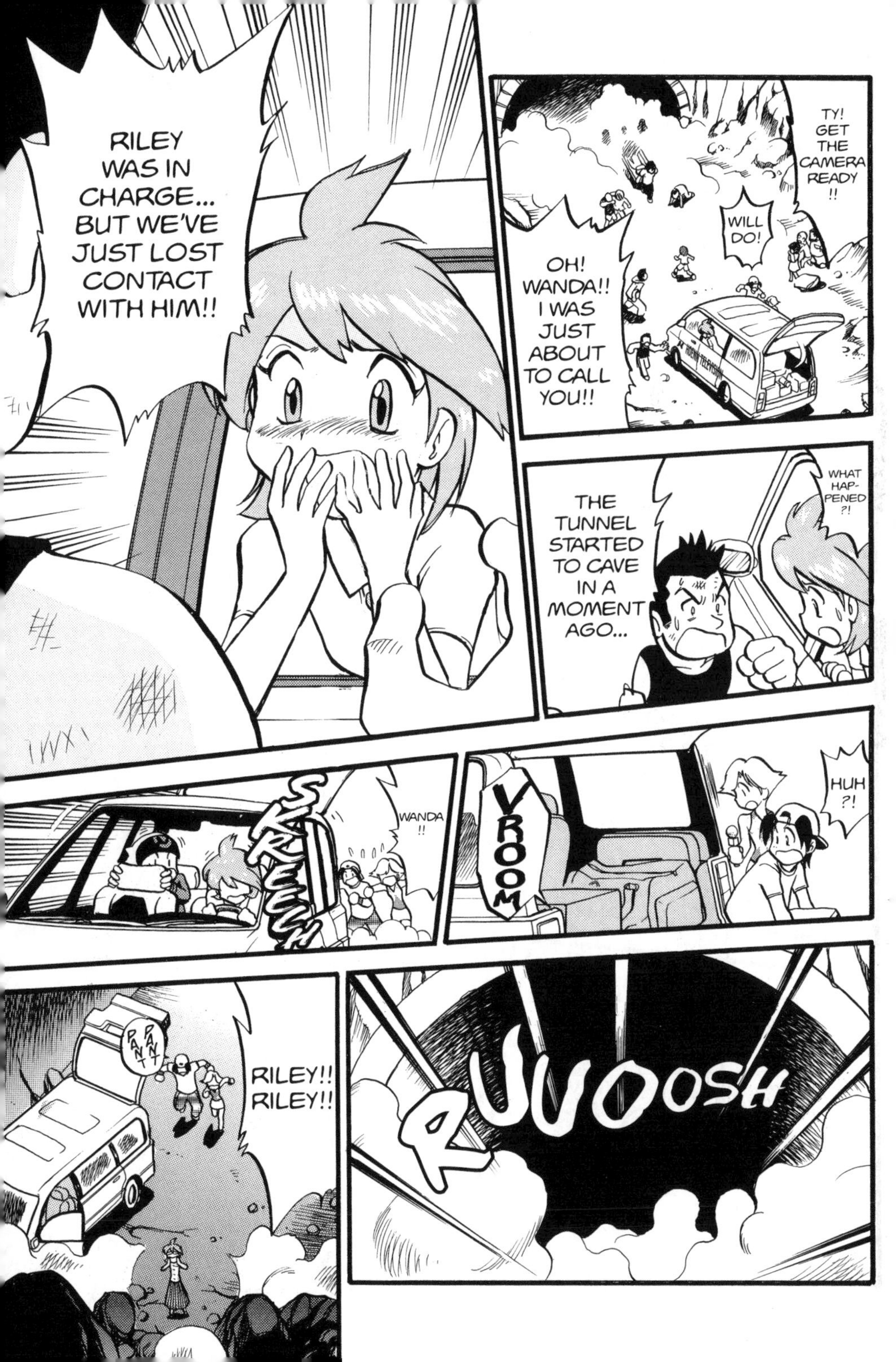
TY! GET THE CAMERA READY!!
WILL DO!
OH! WANDA!! I WAS JUST ABOUT TO CALL YOU!!
WHAT HAP-PENED?!
THE TUNNEL STARTED TO CAVE IN A MOMENT AGO...
RILEY WAS IN CHARGE... BUT WE'VE JUST LOST CONTACT WITH HIM!!
HUH?!
VROOM
WANDA!!
SKREECH
RUUOOSH
PANT PANT
RILEY!! RILEY!!

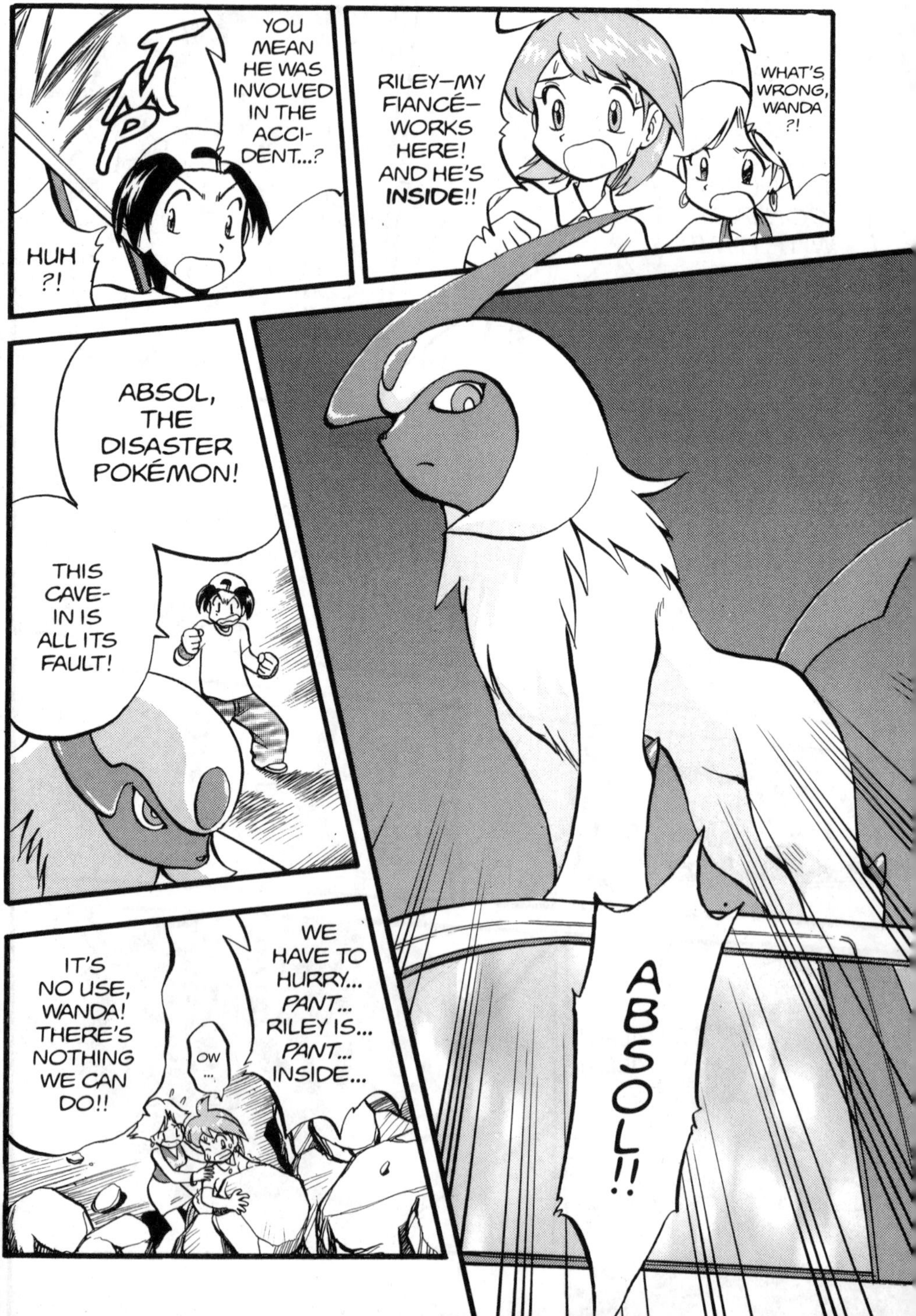
WHAT'S WRONG, WANDA?!
RILEY—MY FIANCÉ—WORKS HERE! AND HE'S **INSIDE**!!
YOU MEAN HE WAS INVOLVED IN THE ACCI-DENT...?
TMP
HUH?!
ABSOL!!
ABSOL, THE DISASTER POKÉMON!
THIS CAVE-IN IS ALL ITS FAULT!
WE HAVE TO HURRY... *PANT*... RILEY IS... *PANT*... INSIDE...
OW...
IT'S NO USE, WANDA! THERE'S NOTHING WE CAN DO!!

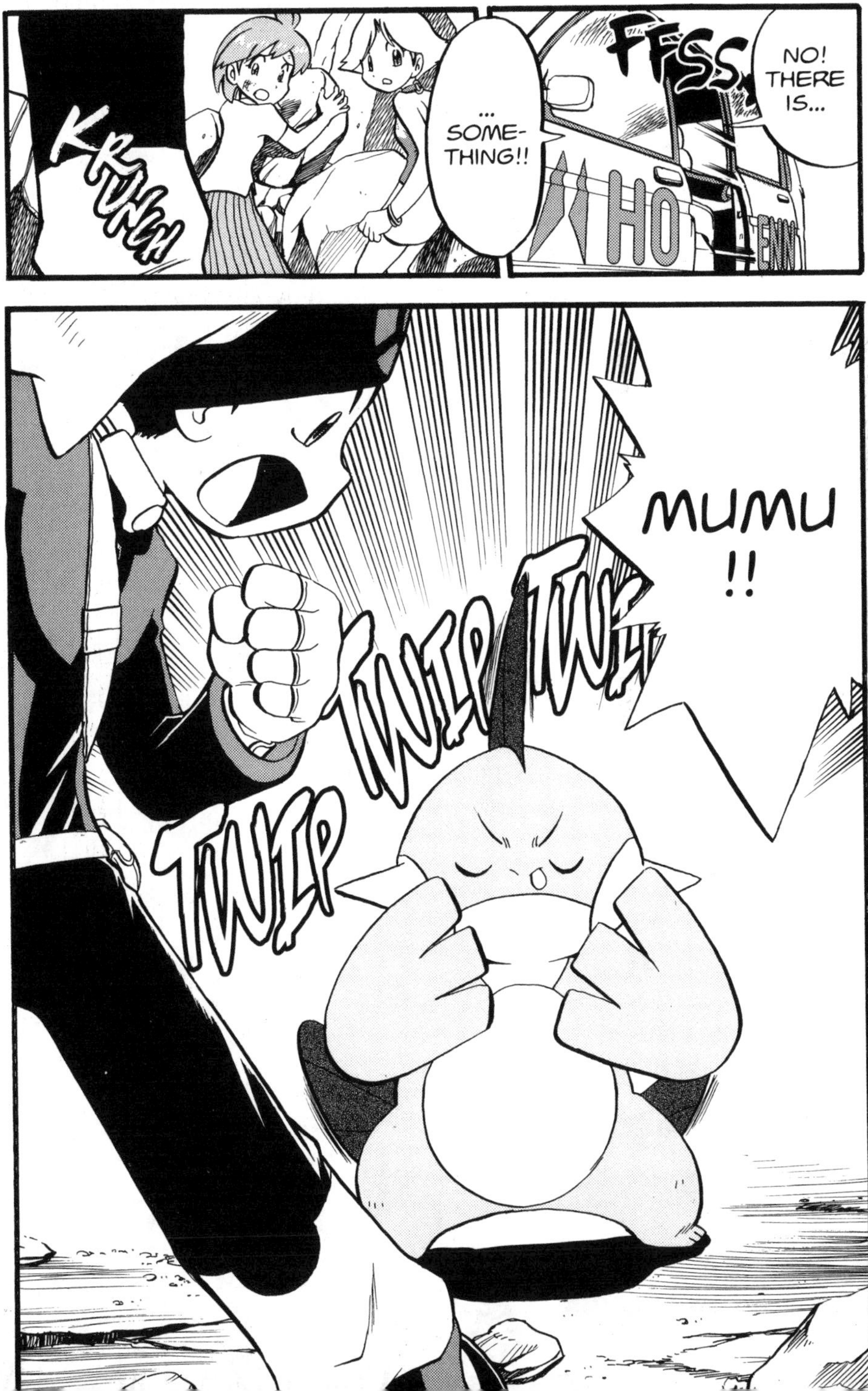
NO! THERE IS...
FFSS
... SOME-THING!!
KRUNCH
MUMU !!
TWIP TWIP TWIP

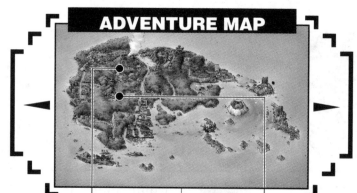

ADVENTURE MAP

SAPPHIRE

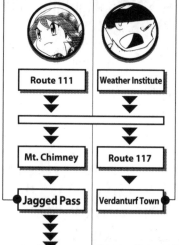

Route 111 ▼ ▼ Mt. Chimney ▼ Jagged Pass ▼

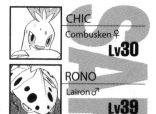

CHIC
Combusken ♀
Lv30

RONO
Lairon ♂
Lv39

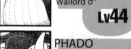

LORRY
Wailord ♂
Lv44

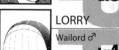

PHADO
Donphan ♂
Lv42

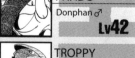

TROPPY
Tropius ♂
Lv41

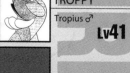

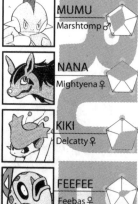

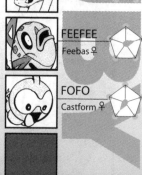

Stone Badge	Knuckle Badge	Dynamo Badge	Heat Badge
Balance Badge	Feather Badge	Mind Badge	Rain Badge

RUBY

Weather Institute ▼ ▼ Route 117 ▼ Verdanturf Town

MUMU
Marshtomp ♂

NANA
Mightyena ♀

KIKI
Delcatty ♀

FEEFEE
Feebas ♀

FOFO
Castform ♀

	Coolness	Beauty	Cuteness	Cleverness	Toughness
Normal					
Super					
Hyper					
Master					

● Adventure 219 ●

What Would You Do for a Whismur?

Pokémon™ Adventures Ruby & Sapphire

The Fourth Chapter

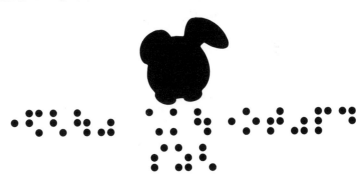

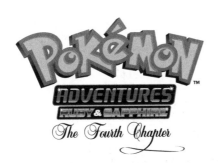

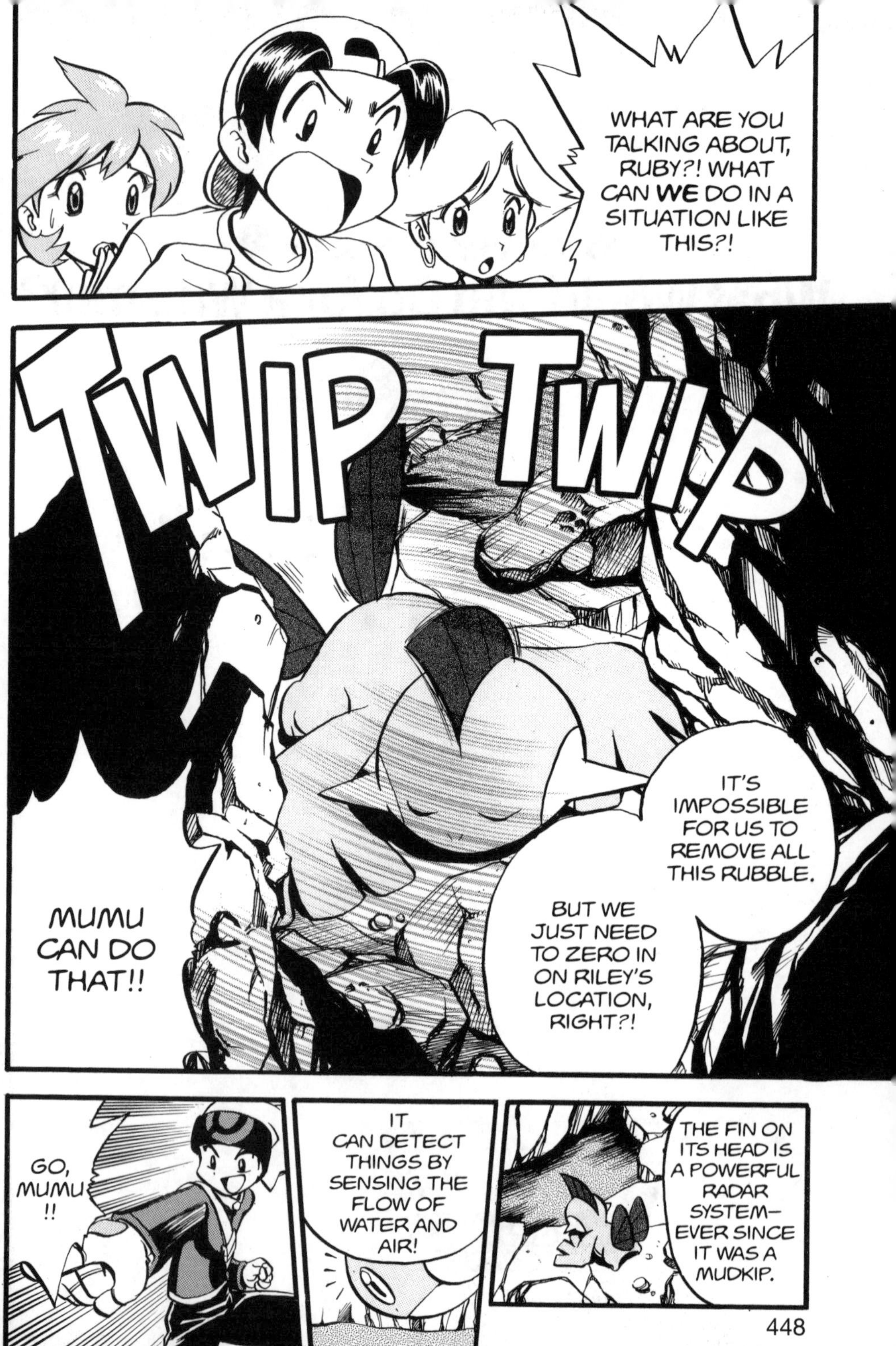
WHAT ARE YOU TALKING ABOUT, RUBY?! WHAT CAN WE DO IN A SITUATION LIKE THIS?!
TWIP
TWIP
IT'S IMPOSSIBLE FOR US TO REMOVE ALL THIS RUBBLE.
BUT WE JUST NEED TO ZERO IN ON RILEY'S LOCATION, RIGHT?!
MUMU CAN DO THAT!!
THE FIN ON ITS HEAD IS A POWERFUL RADAR SYSTEM—EVER SINCE IT WAS A MUDKIP.
IT CAN DETECT THINGS BY SENSING THE FLOW OF WATER AND AIR!
GO, MUMU!!

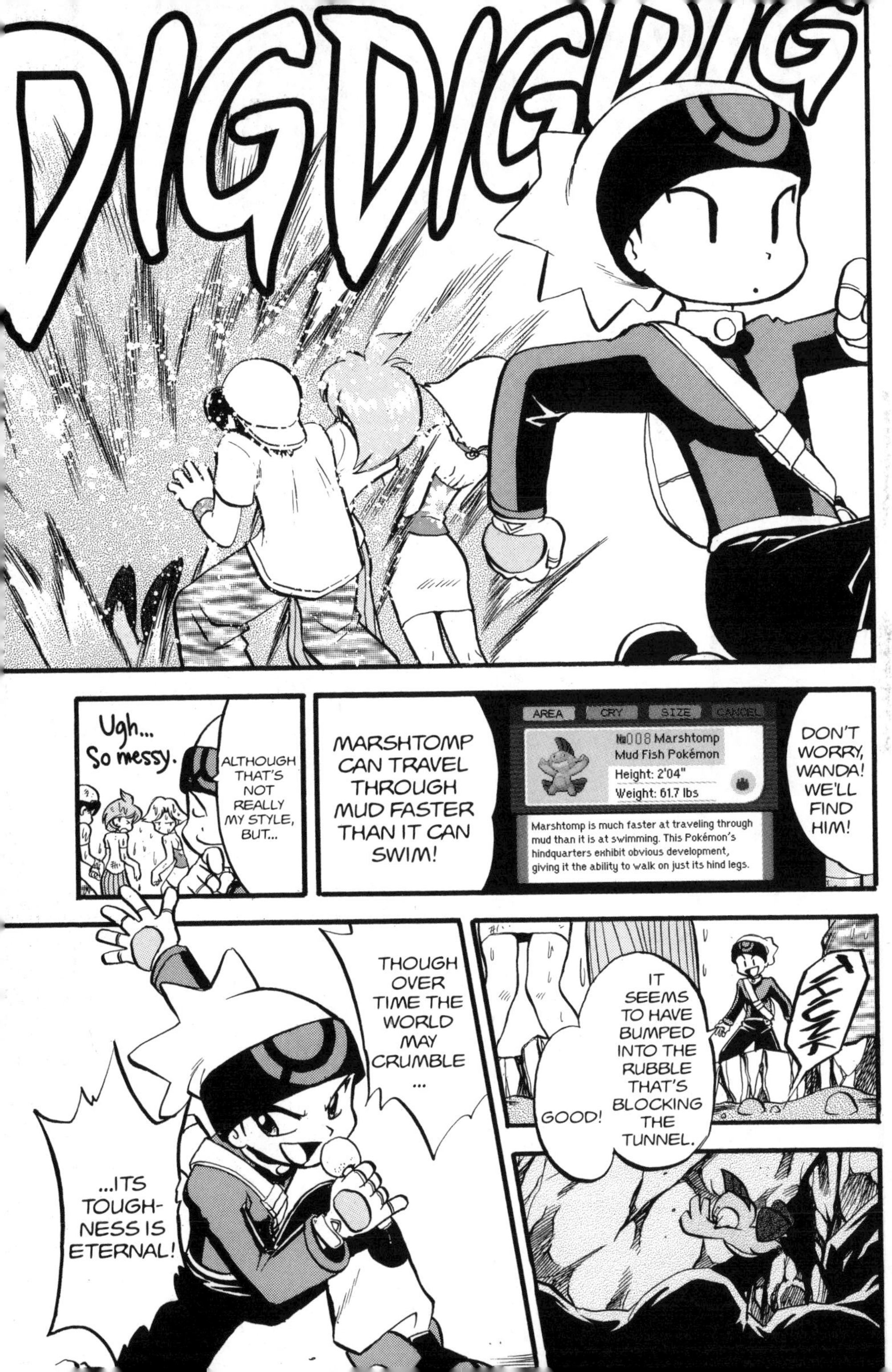
DIGDIGDUG
DON'T WORRY, WANDA! WE'LL FIND HIM!
MARSHTOMP CAN TRAVEL THROUGH MUD FASTER THAN IT CAN SWIM!
AREA CRY SIZE CANCEL
№008 Marshtomp
Mud Fish Pokémon
Height: 2'04"
Weight: 61.7 lbs
Marshtomp is much faster at traveling through mud than it is at swimming. This Pokémon's hindquarters exhibit obvious development, giving it the ability to walk on just its hind legs.
ALTHOUGH THAT'S NOT REALLY MY STYLE, BUT...
Ugh... So messy.
THUNK
IT SEEMS TO HAVE BUMPED INTO THE RUBBLE THAT'S BLOCKING THE TUNNEL.
GOOD!
THOUGH OVER TIME THE WORLD MAY CRUMBLE...
...ITS TOUGHNESS IS ETERNAL!

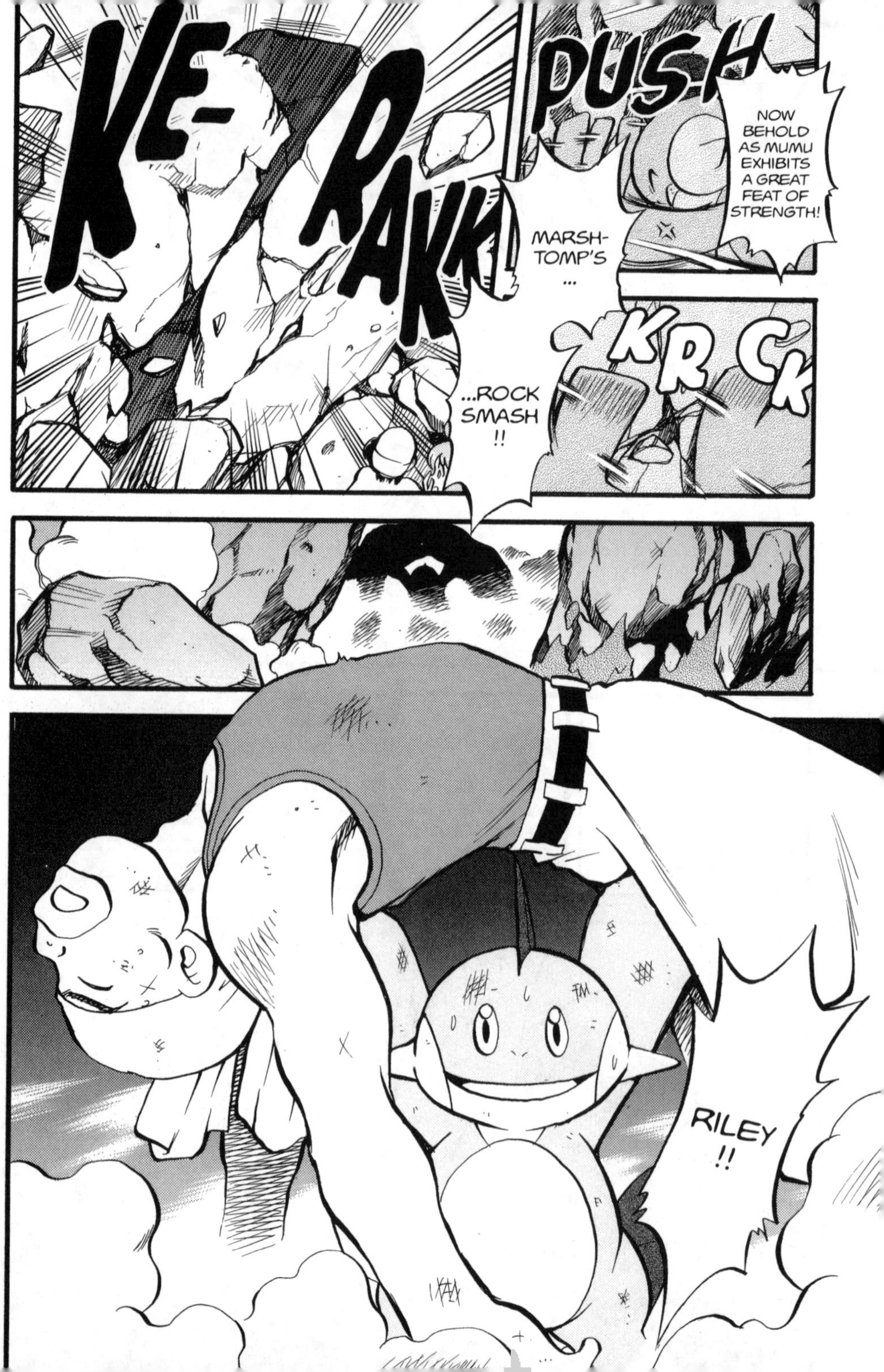

PUSH
NOW BEHOLD AS MUMU EXHIBITS A GREAT FEAT OF STRENGTH!
MARSH-TOMP'S ...
KRCK
...ROCK SMASH !!
KE-RAKK!
RILEY !!

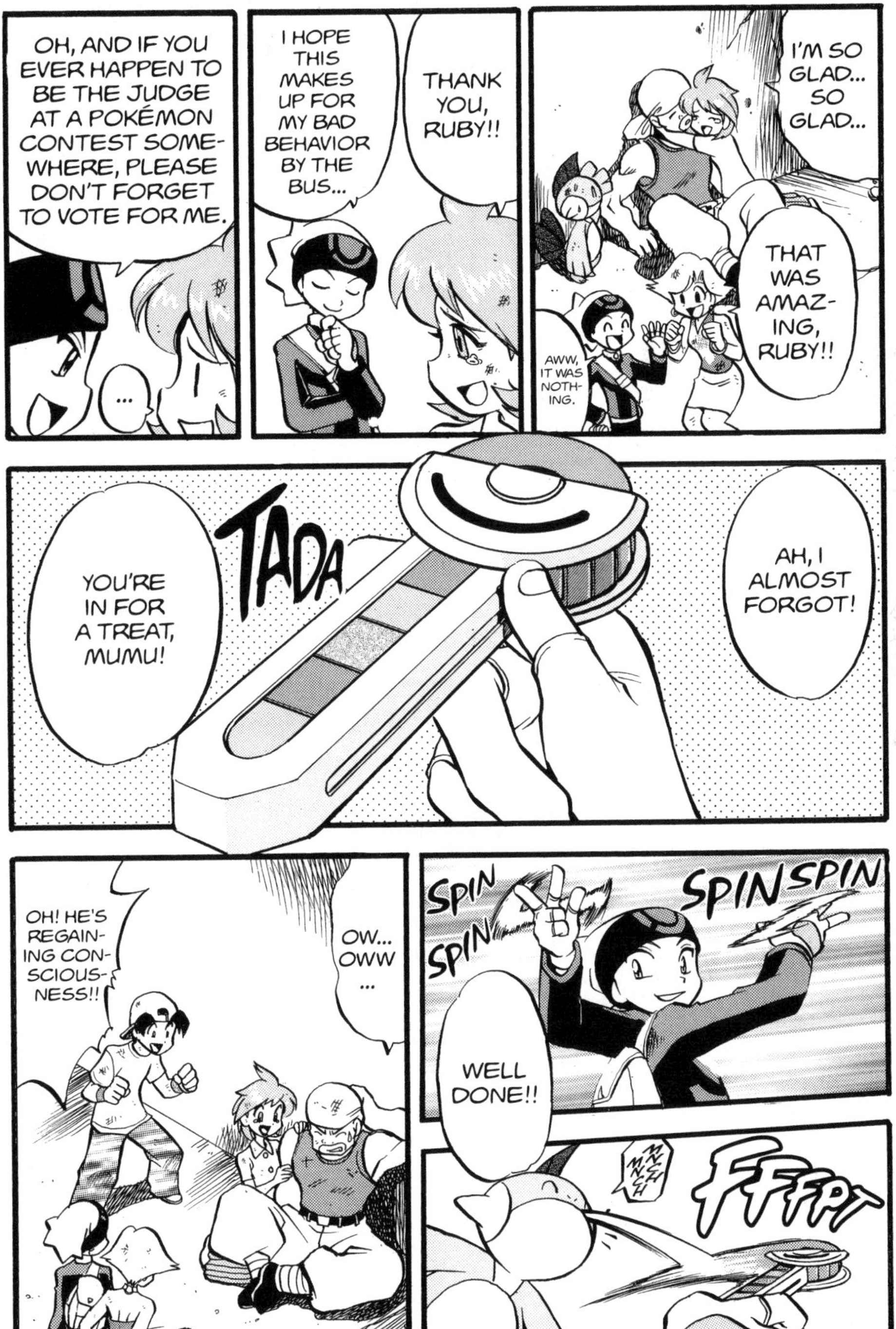
I'M SO GLAD... SO GLAD...
THAT WAS AMAZ-ING, RUBY!!
AWW, IT WAS NOTH-ING.
THANK YOU, RUBY!!
I HOPE THIS MAKES UP FOR MY BAD BEHAVIOR BY THE BUS...
OH, AND IF YOU EVER HAPPEN TO BE THE JUDGE AT A POKÉMON CONTEST SOME-WHERE, PLEASE DON'T FORGET TO VOTE FOR ME.
...
AH, I ALMOST FORGOT!
TADA
YOU'RE IN FOR A TREAT, MUMU!
SPIN SPIN
SPIN SPIN
WELL DONE!!
FFFPT
MNCH MNCH
OW... OWW ...
OH! HE'S REGAIN-ING CON-SCIOUS-NESS!!

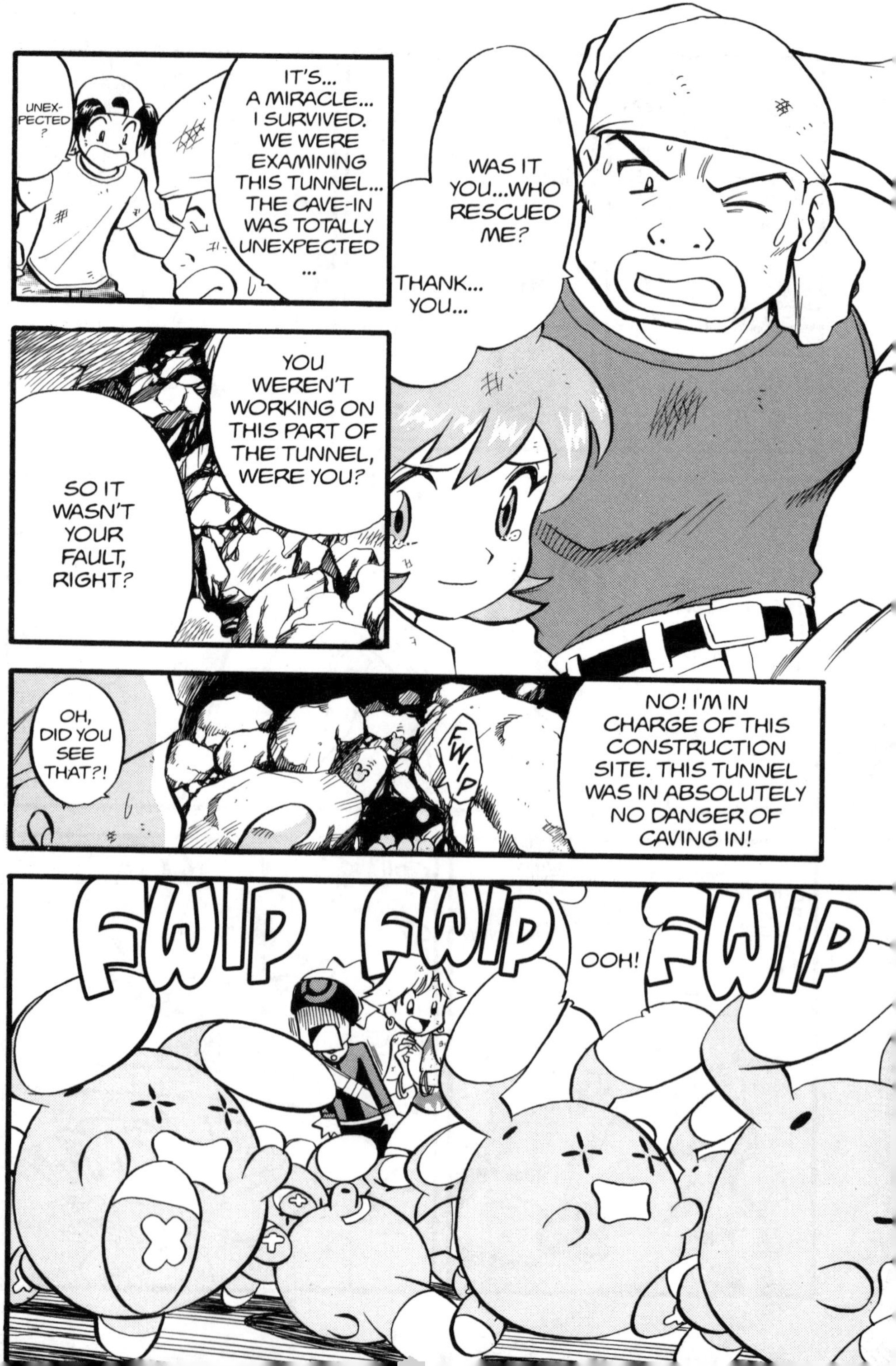
WAS IT YOU...WHO RESCUED ME?
THANK... YOU...
IT'S... A MIRACLE... I SURVIVED. WE WERE EXAMINING THIS TUNNEL... THE CAVE-IN WAS TOTALLY UNEXPECTED...
UNEX-PECTED?
YOU WEREN'T WORKING ON THIS PART OF THE TUNNEL, WERE YOU?
SO IT WASN'T YOUR FAULT, RIGHT?
NO! I'M IN CHARGE OF THIS CONSTRUCTION SITE. THIS TUNNEL WAS IN ABSOLUTELY NO DANGER OF CAVING IN!
FWIP
OH, DID YOU SEE THAT?!
FWIP
OOH!
FWIP
FWIP

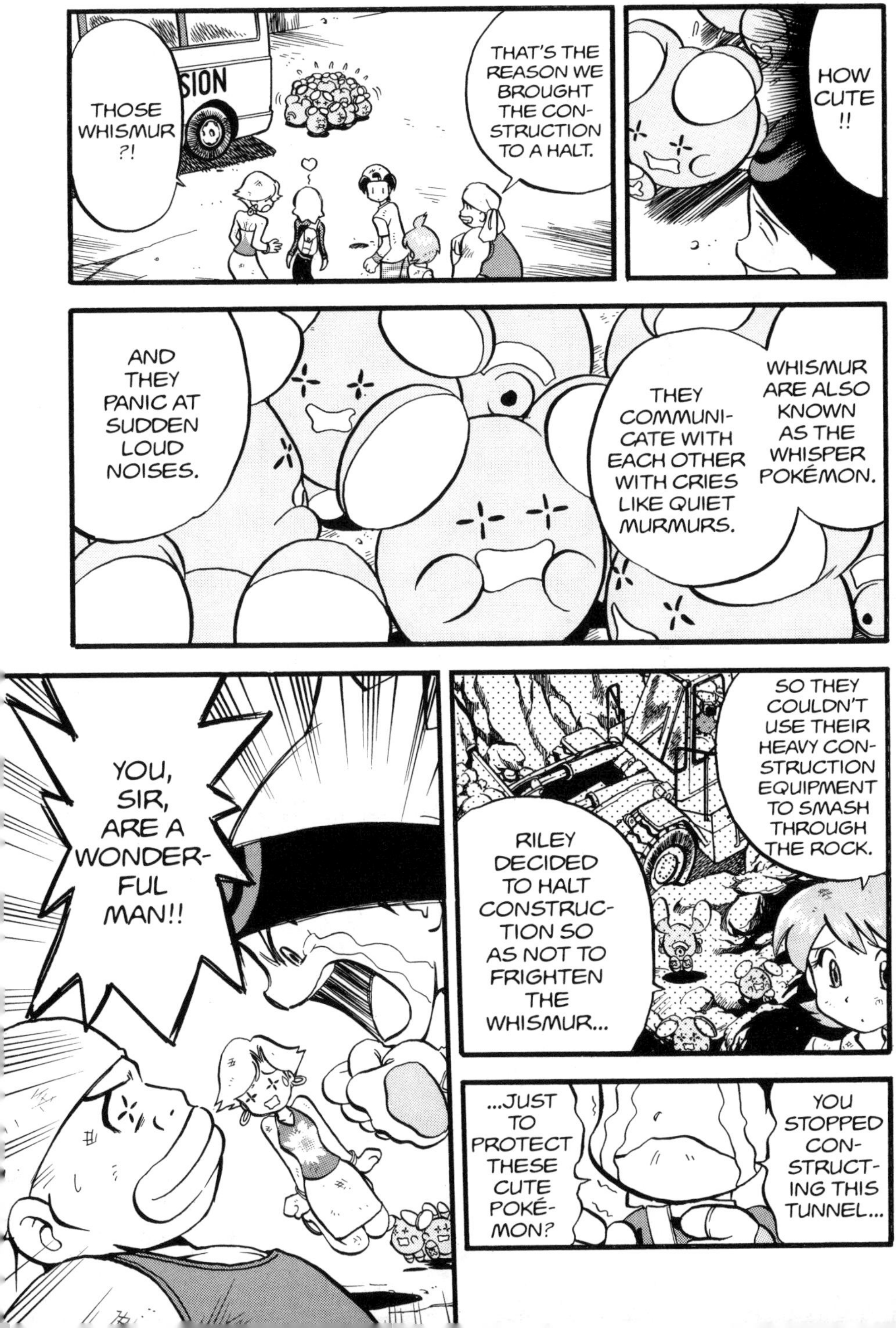
HOW CUTE !!
THAT'S THE REASON WE BROUGHT THE CONSTRUCTION TO A HALT.
SION
THOSE WHISMUR ?!
WHISMUR ARE ALSO KNOWN AS THE WHISPER POKÉMON.
THEY COMMUNICATE WITH EACH OTHER WITH CRIES LIKE QUIET MURMURS.
AND THEY PANIC AT SUDDEN LOUD NOISES.
SO THEY COULDN'T USE THEIR HEAVY CONSTRUCTION EQUIPMENT TO SMASH THROUGH THE ROCK.
RILEY DECIDED TO HALT CONSTRUCTION SO AS NOT TO FRIGHTEN THE WHISMUR...
YOU STOPPED CONSTRUCTING THIS TUNNEL...
...JUST TO PROTECT THESE CUTE POKÉMON?
YOU, SIR, ARE A WONDERFUL MAN!!

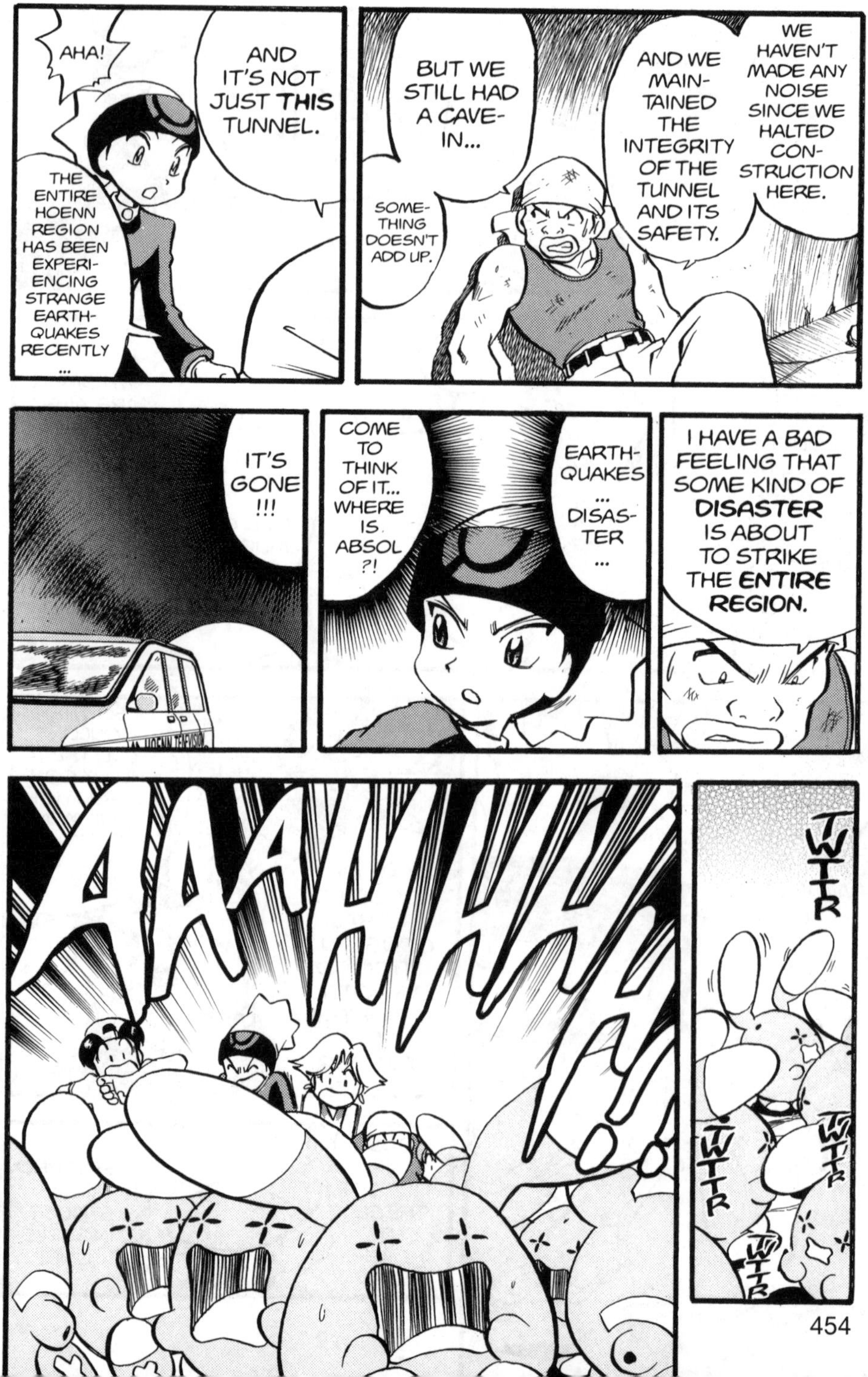

WE HAVEN'T MADE ANY NOISE SINCE WE HALTED CON-STRUCTION HERE.
AND WE MAIN-TAINED THE INTEGRITY OF THE TUNNEL AND ITS SAFETY.
BUT WE STILL HAD A CAVE-IN...
SOME-THING DOESN'T ADD UP.
AND IT'S NOT JUST **THIS** TUNNEL.
AHA!
THE ENTIRE HOENN REGION HAS BEEN EXPERI-ENCING STRANGE EARTH-QUAKES RECENTLY ...
I HAVE A BAD FEELING THAT SOME KIND OF **DISASTER** IS ABOUT TO STRIKE THE **ENTIRE REGION.**
EARTH-QUAKES ... DISAS-TER ...
COME TO THINK OF IT... WHERE IS ABSOL ?!
IT'S GONE !!!
HOENN TELEVISION
TWTTR
TWTTR
TWTTR
TWTTR
AAHHHHH

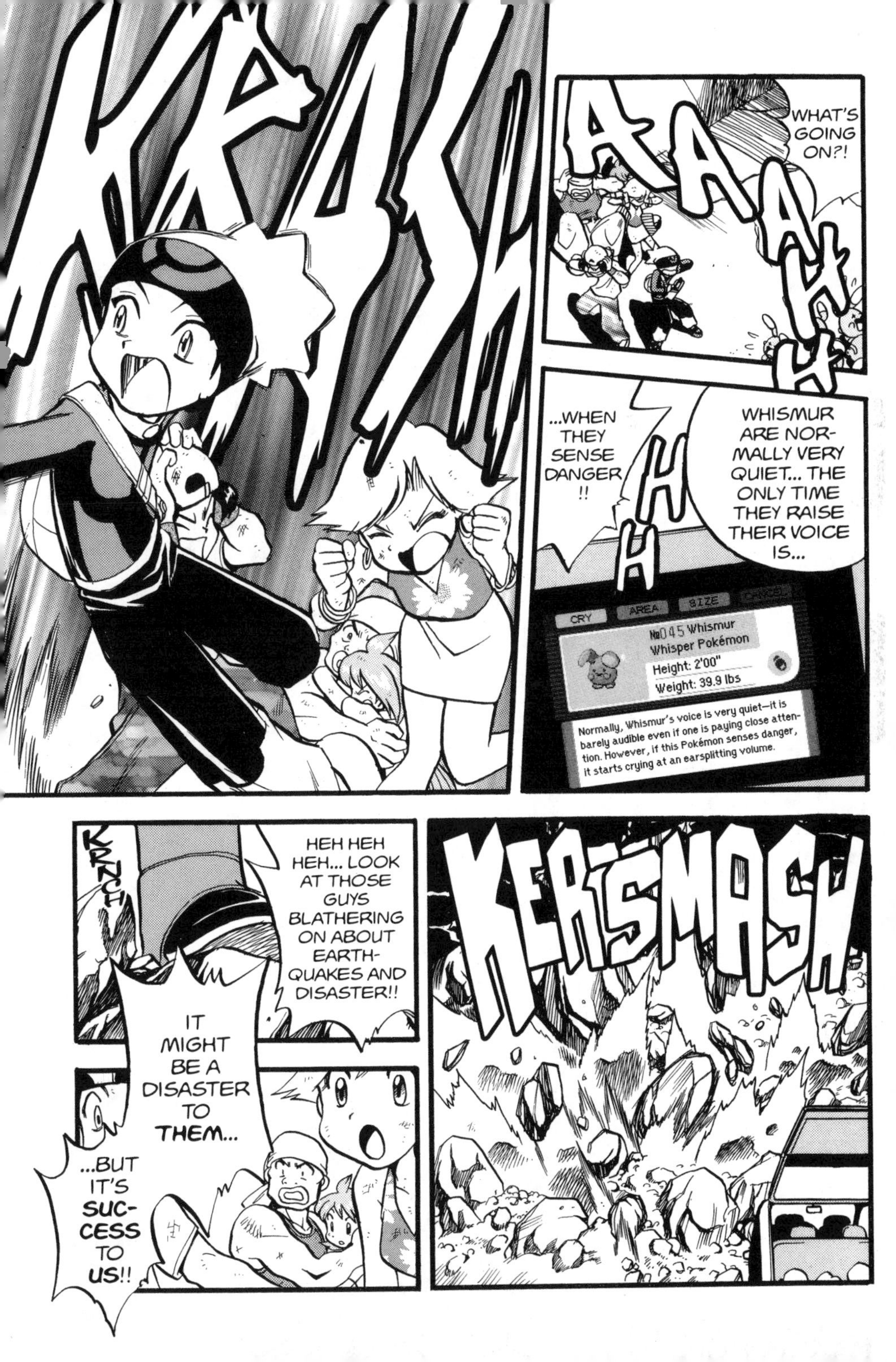
WHAT'S GOING ON?!
WHISMUR ARE NORMALLY VERY QUIET... THE ONLY TIME THEY RAISE THEIR VOICE IS...
...WHEN THEY SENSE DANGER!!
CRY
AREA
SIZE
CANCEL
No045 Whismur
Whisper Pokémon
Height: 2'00"
Weight: 39.9 lbs
Normally, Whismur's voice is very quiet—it is barely audible even if one is paying close attention. However, if this Pokémon senses danger, it starts crying at an earsplitting volume.
KERSMASH
KRNCH
HEH HEH HEH... LOOK AT THOSE GUYS BLATHERING ON ABOUT EARTHQUAKES AND DISASTER!!
IT MIGHT BE A DISASTER TO THEM...
...BUT IT'S SUCCESS TO US!!

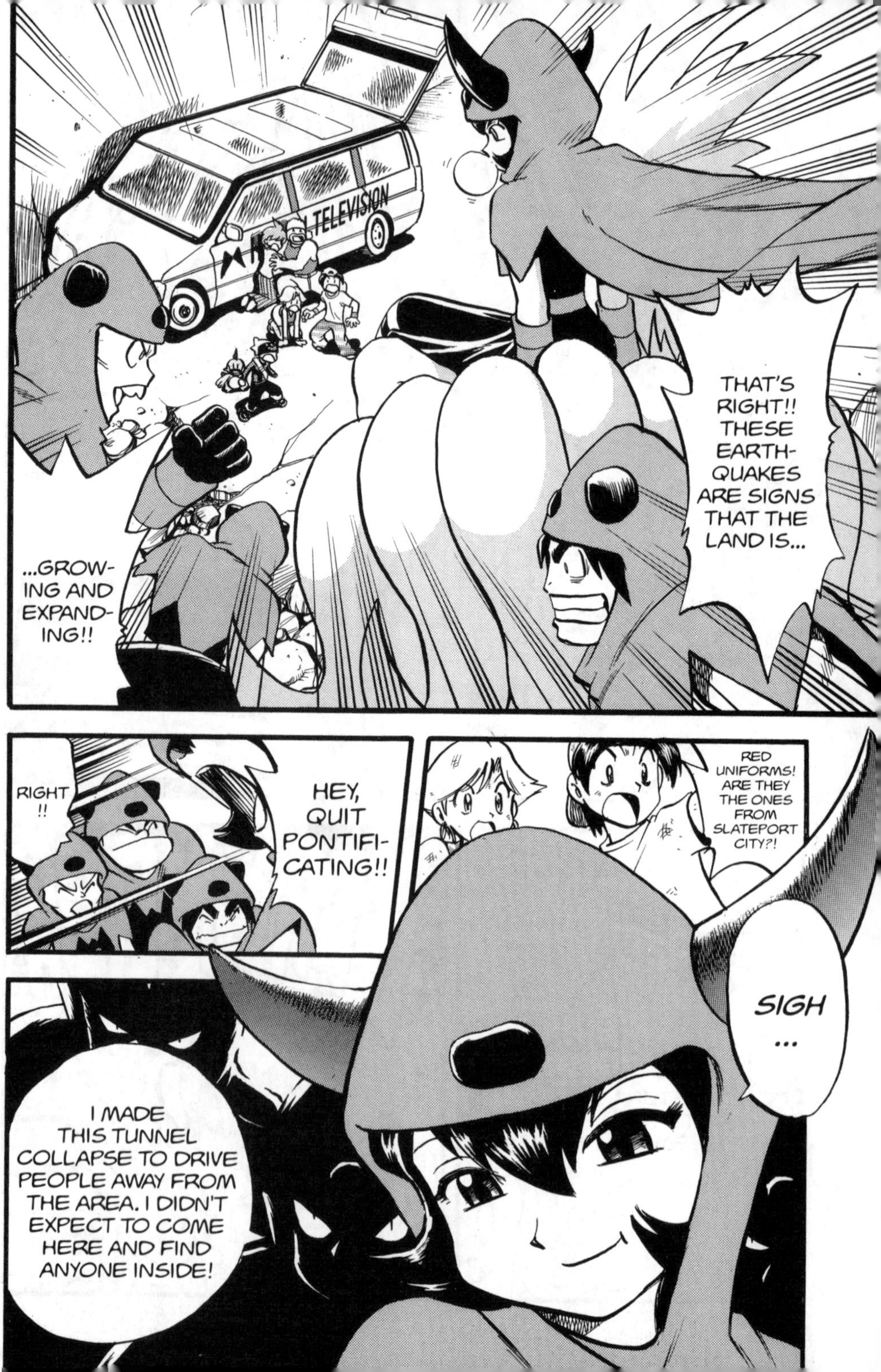
TELEVISION
THAT'S RIGHT!! THESE EARTH-QUAKES ARE SIGNS THAT THE LAND IS...
...GROW-ING AND EXPAND-ING!!
RED UNIFORMS! ARE THEY THE ONES FROM SLATEPORT CITY?!
HEY, QUIT PONTIFI-CATING!!
RIGHT!!
SIGH...
I MADE THIS TUNNEL COLLAPSE TO DRIVE PEOPLE AWAY FROM THE AREA. I DIDN'T EXPECT TO COME HERE AND FIND ANYONE INSIDE!

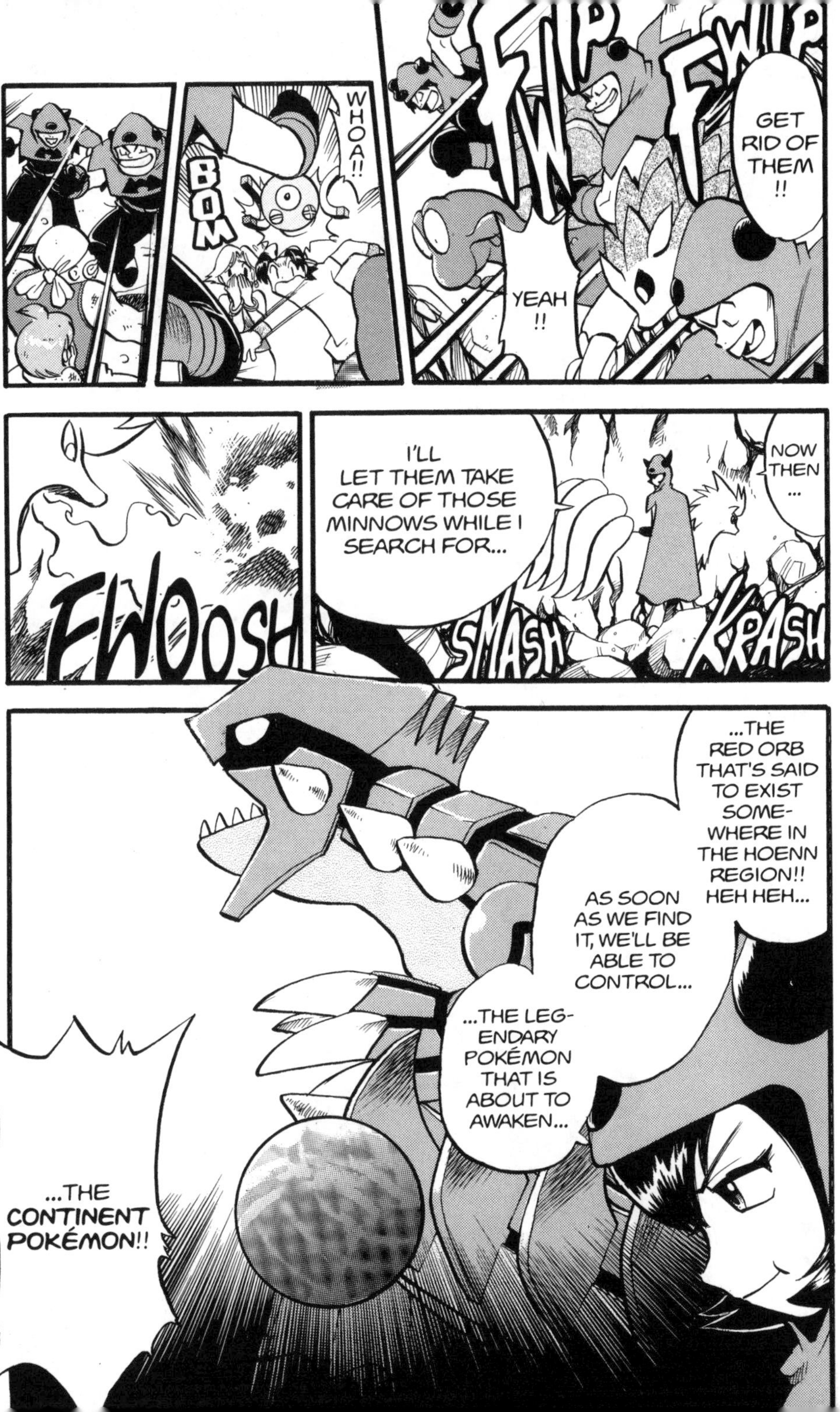
FWIP
FWIP
GET RID OF THEM!!
YEAH!!
WHOA!!
BOM
NOW THEN...
I'LL LET THEM TAKE CARE OF THOSE MINNOWS WHILE I SEARCH FOR...
SMASH
KRASH
FWOOSH
...THE RED ORB THAT'S SAID TO EXIST SOME-WHERE IN THE HOENN REGION!! HEH HEH...
AS SOON AS WE FIND IT, WE'LL BE ABLE TO CONTROL...
...THE LEG-ENDARY POKÉMON THAT IS ABOUT TO AWAKEN...
...THE CONTINENT POKÉMON!!

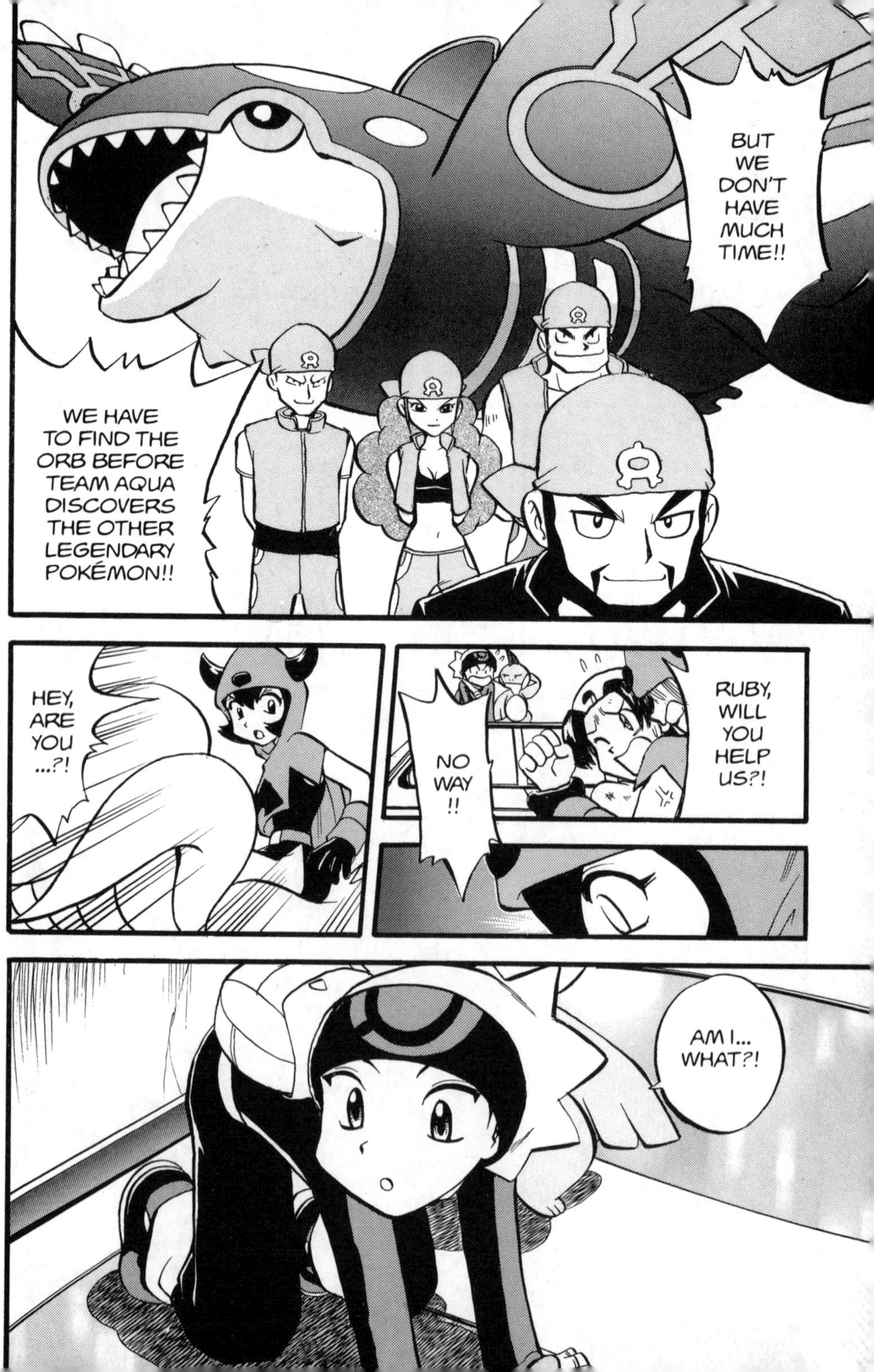
BUT WE DON'T HAVE MUCH TIME!!
WE HAVE TO FIND THE ORB BEFORE TEAM AQUA DISCOVERS THE OTHER LEGENDARY POKÉMON!!
RUBY, WILL YOU HELP US?!
NO WAY!!
HEY, ARE YOU ...?!
AM I... WHAT?!

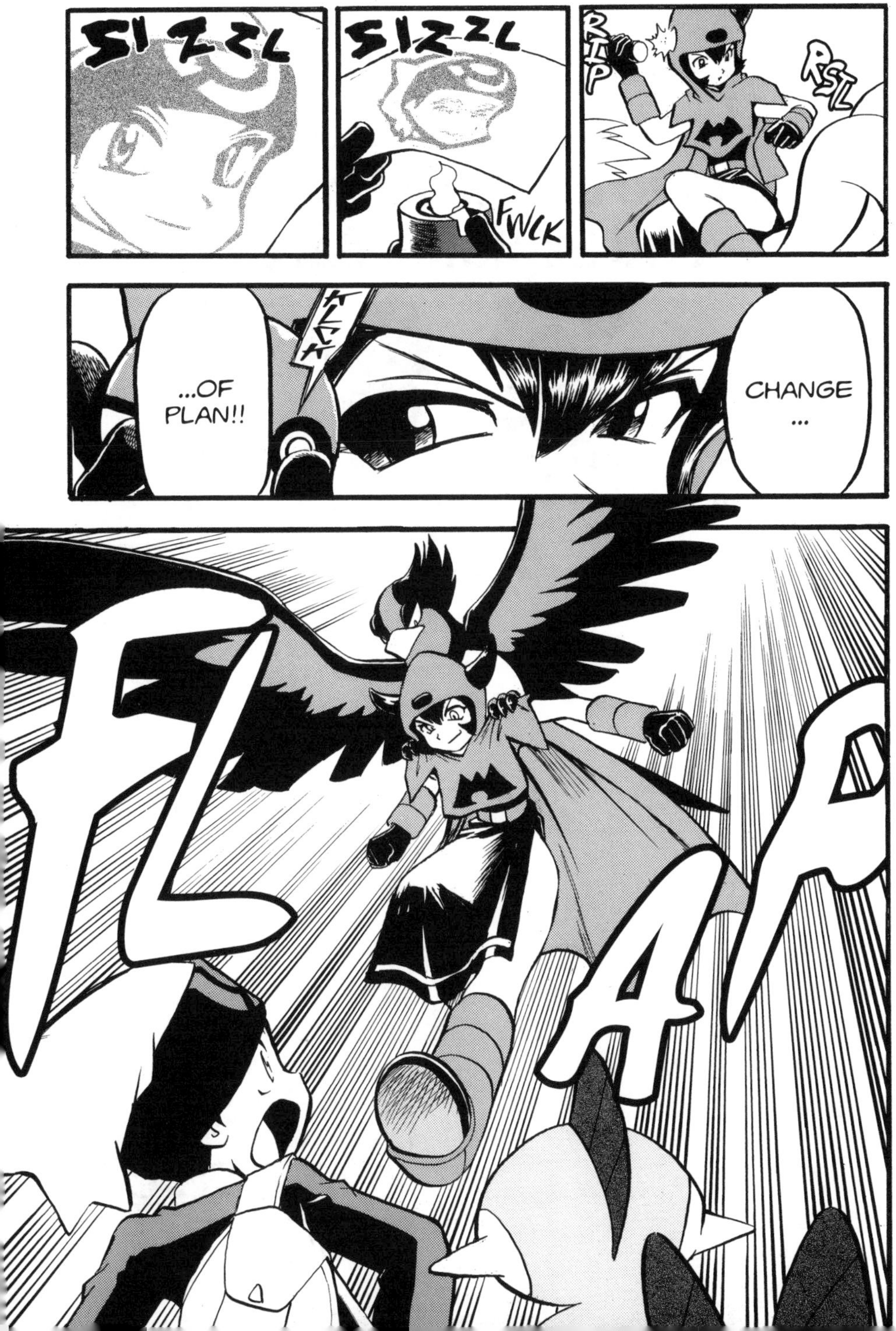
RIP
RSL
SIZZL
FWICK
SIZZL
CHANGE ...
KLICK
...OF PLAN!!
FLAP

● Adventure 220 ●
Going to Eleven with Loudred and Exploud, Part 1

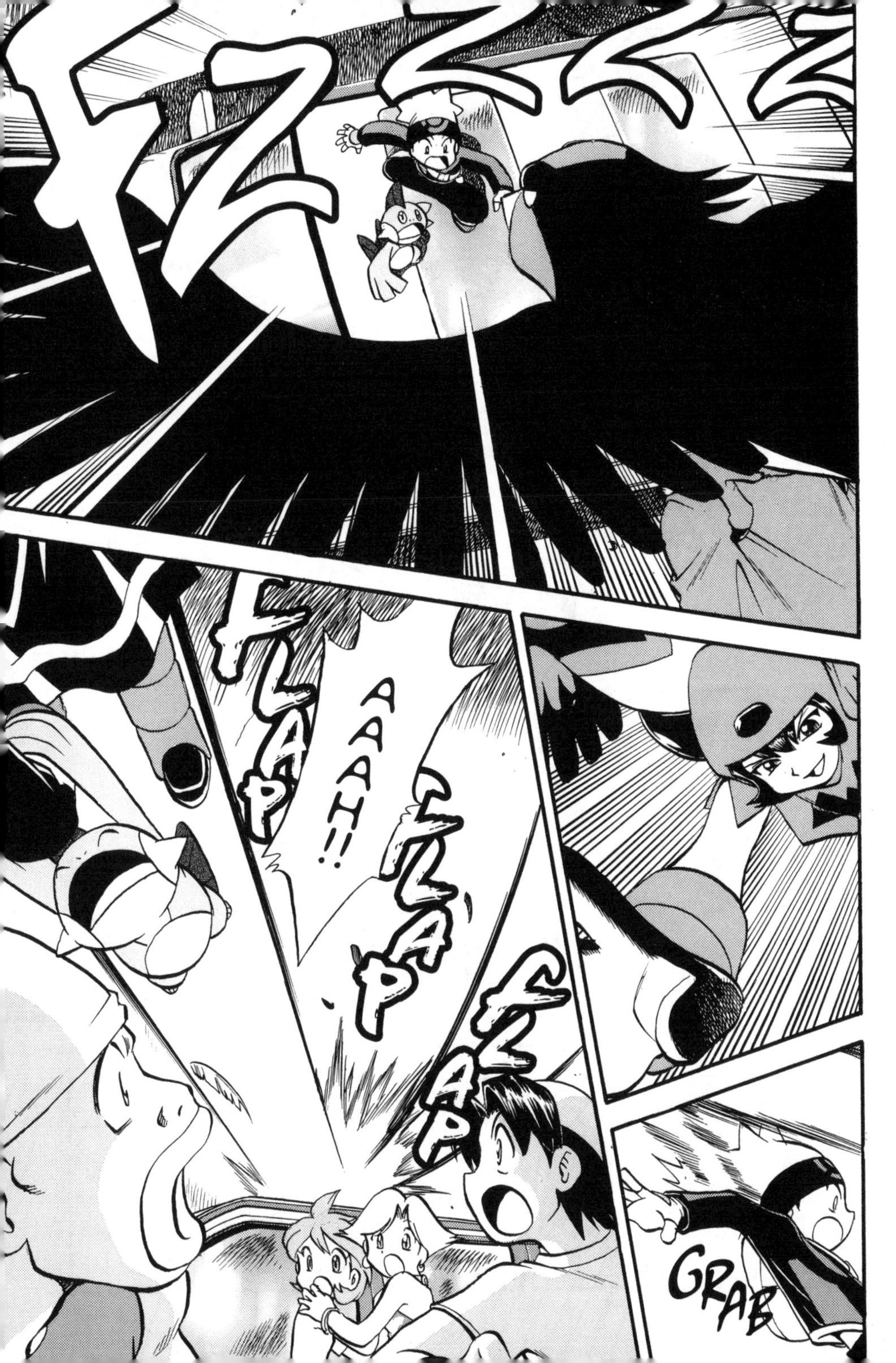
FZZZZZ
FLAP
AAAAH!!
FLAP
FLAP
GRAB

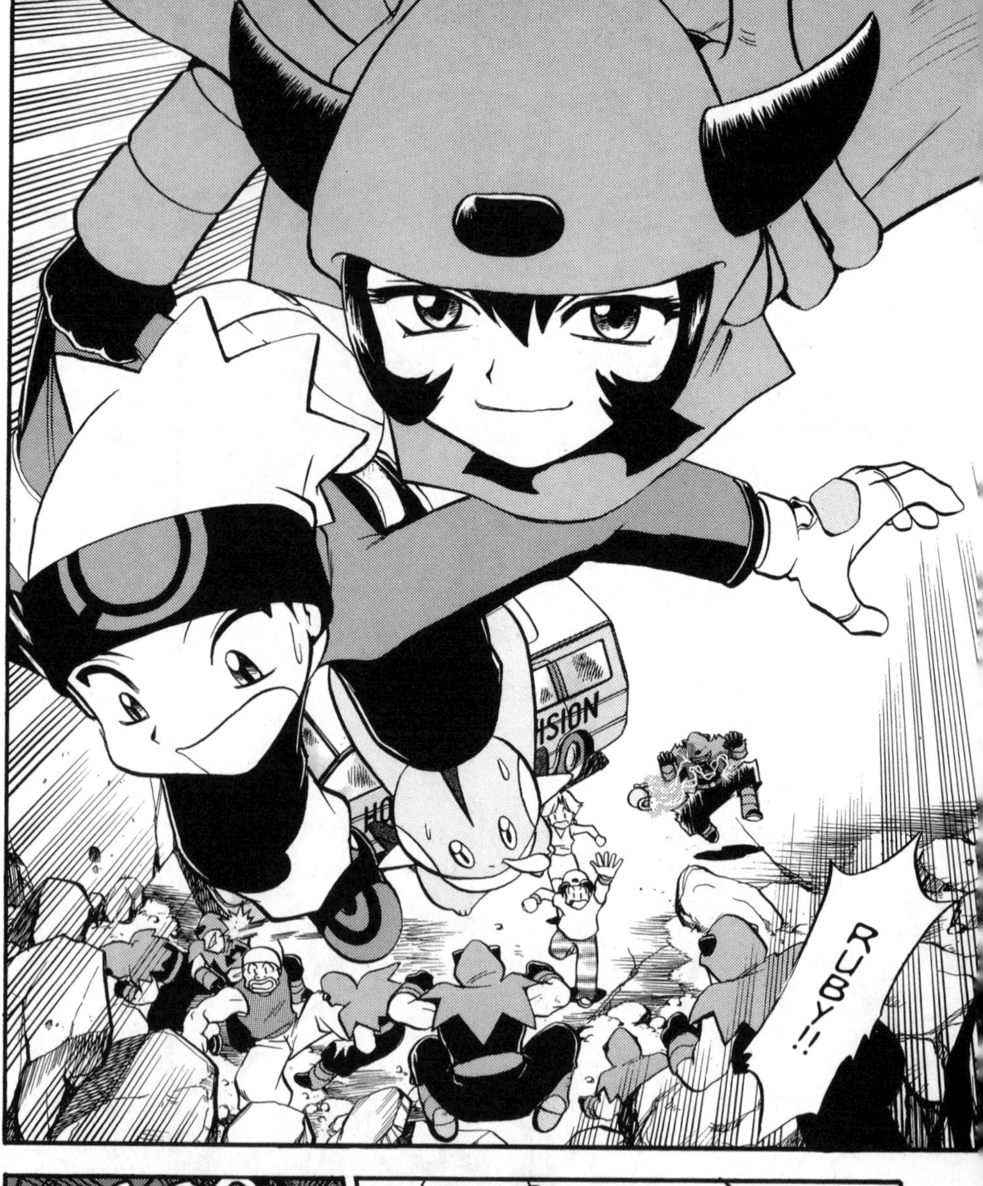
HION
HO
RUBY!!

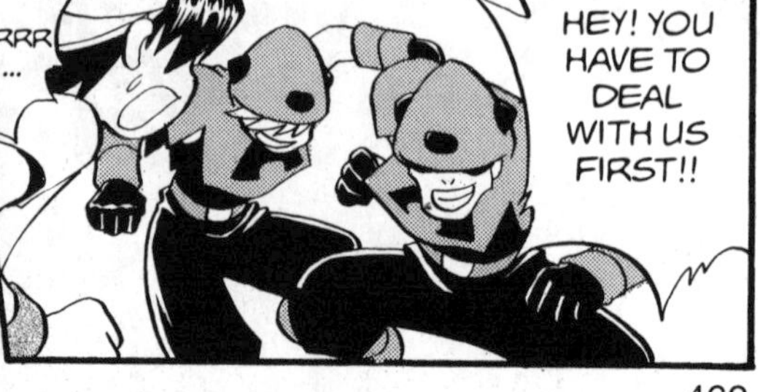
GRRR
...
HEY! YOU HAVE TO DEAL WITH US FIRST!!

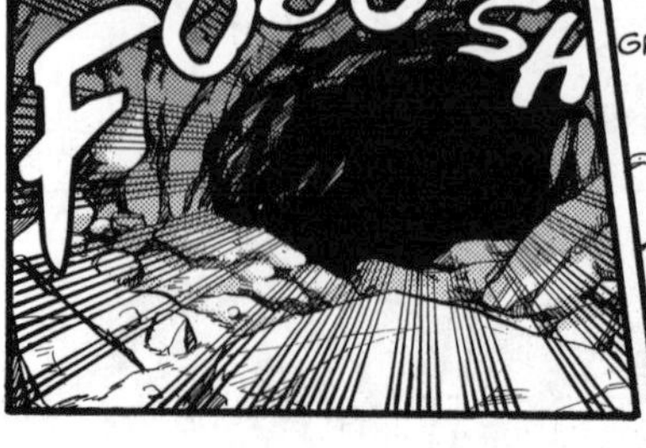
FOOOSH

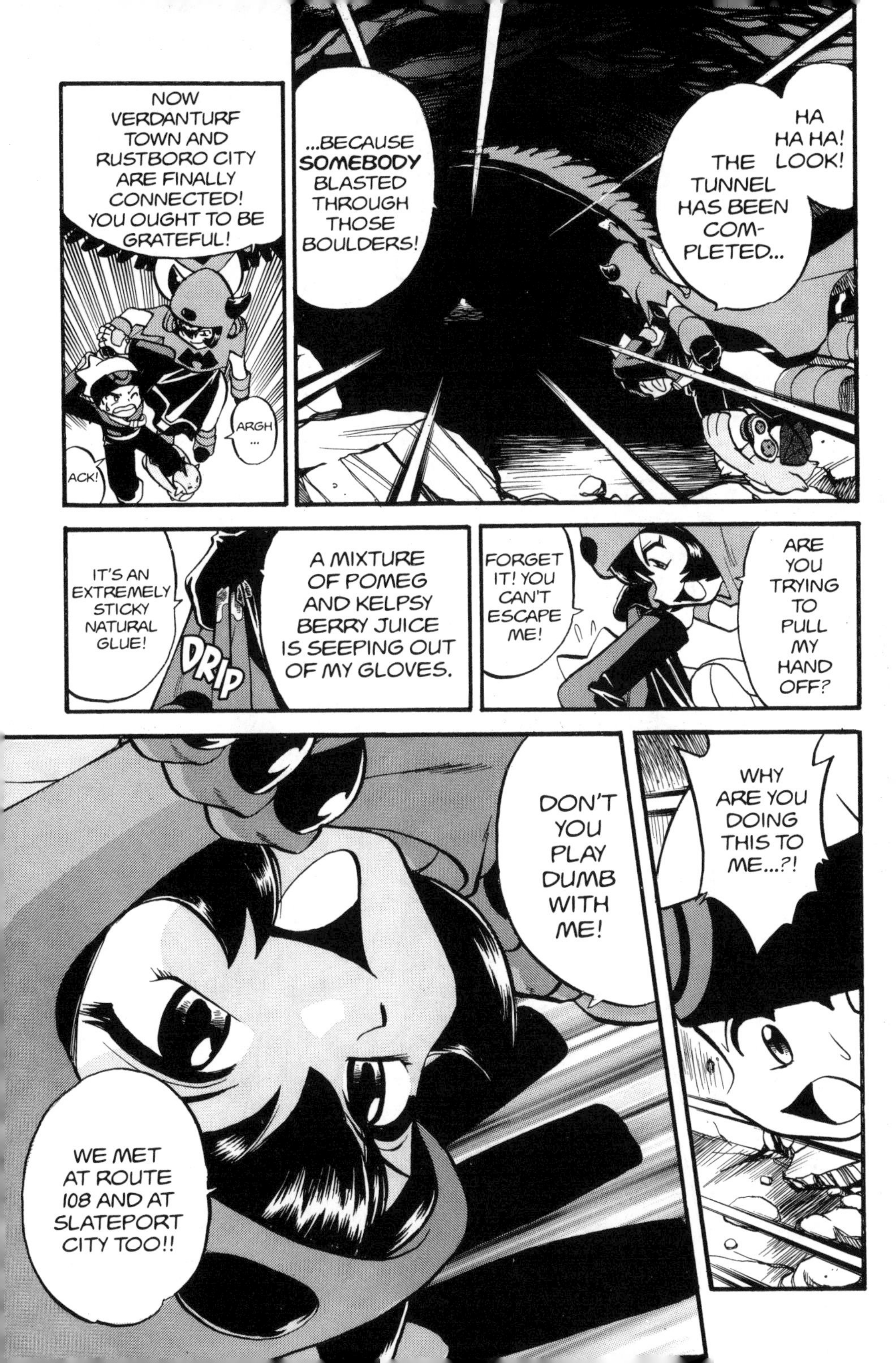
HA HA HA! LOOK!
THE TUNNEL HAS BEEN COMPLETED...
...BECAUSE **SOMEBODY** BLASTED THROUGH THOSE BOULDERS!
NOW VERDANTURF TOWN AND RUSTBORO CITY ARE FINALLY CONNECTED! YOU OUGHT TO BE GRATEFUL!
ARGH...
ACK!
ARE YOU TRYING TO PULL MY HAND OFF?
FORGET IT! YOU CAN'T ESCAPE ME!
A MIXTURE OF POMEG AND KELPSY BERRY JUICE IS SEEPING OUT OF MY GLOVES.
DRIP
IT'S AN EXTREMELY STICKY NATURAL GLUE!
WHY ARE YOU DOING THIS TO ME...?!
DON'T YOU PLAY DUMB WITH ME!
WE MET AT ROUTE 108 AND AT SLATEPORT CITY TOO!!

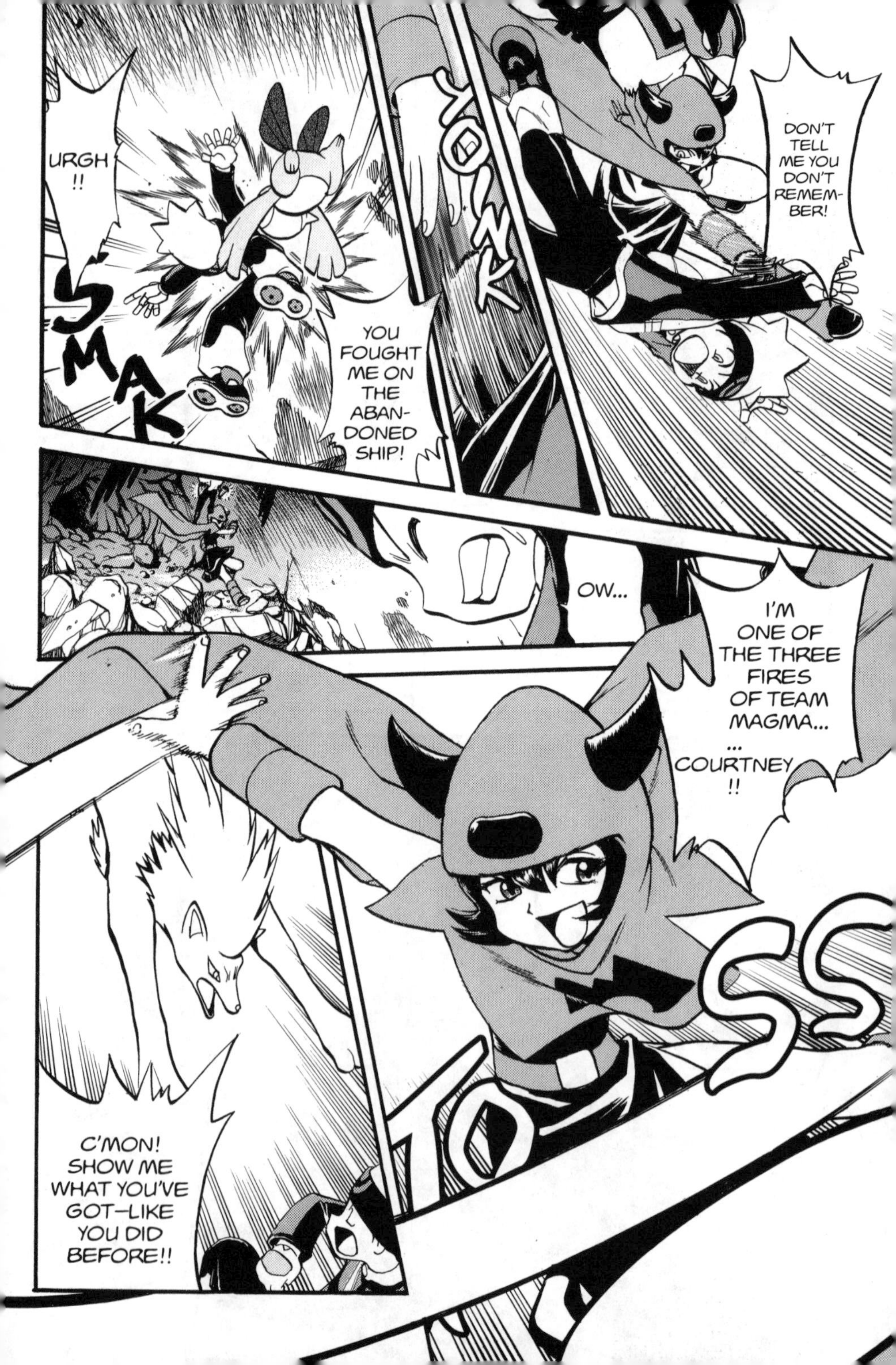
DON'T TELL ME YOU DON'T REMEM-BER!
YOINK
YOU FOUGHT ME ON THE ABAN-DONED SHIP!
URGH !!
SMAK
OW...
I'M ONE OF THE THREE FIRES OF TEAM MAGMA... ... COURTNEY !!
SS
C'MON! SHOW ME WHAT YOU'VE GOT—LIKE YOU DID BEFORE!!

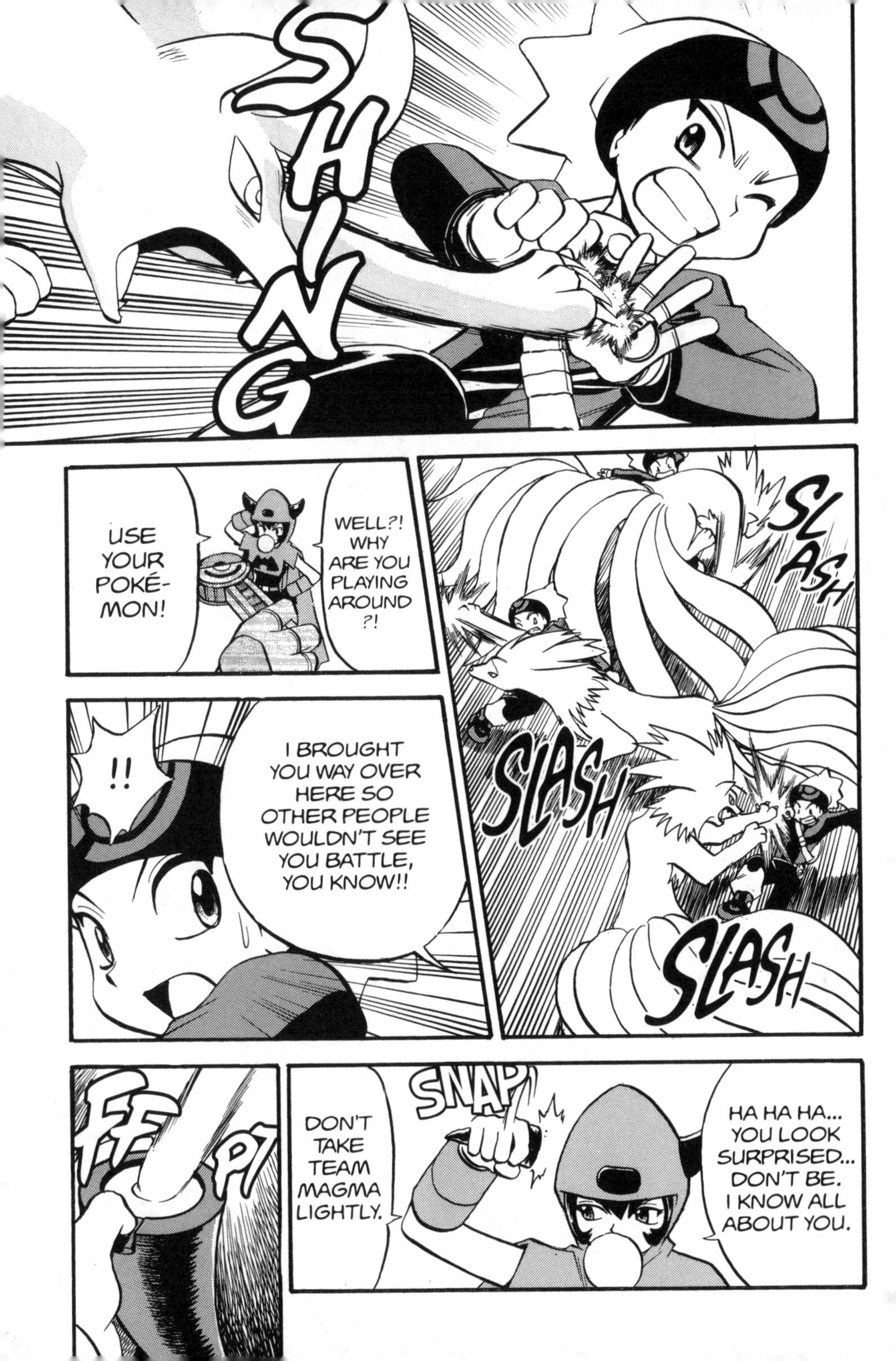
SHING
SLASH
SLASH
SLASH
WELL?! WHY ARE YOU PLAYING AROUND ?!
USE YOUR POKÉMON!
I BROUGHT YOU WAY OVER HERE SO OTHER PEOPLE WOULDN'T SEE YOU BATTLE, YOU KNOW!!
!!
HA HA HA... YOU LOOK SURPRISED... DON'T BE. I KNOW ALL ABOUT YOU.
SNAP
DON'T TAKE TEAM MAGMA LIGHTLY.
FF PT

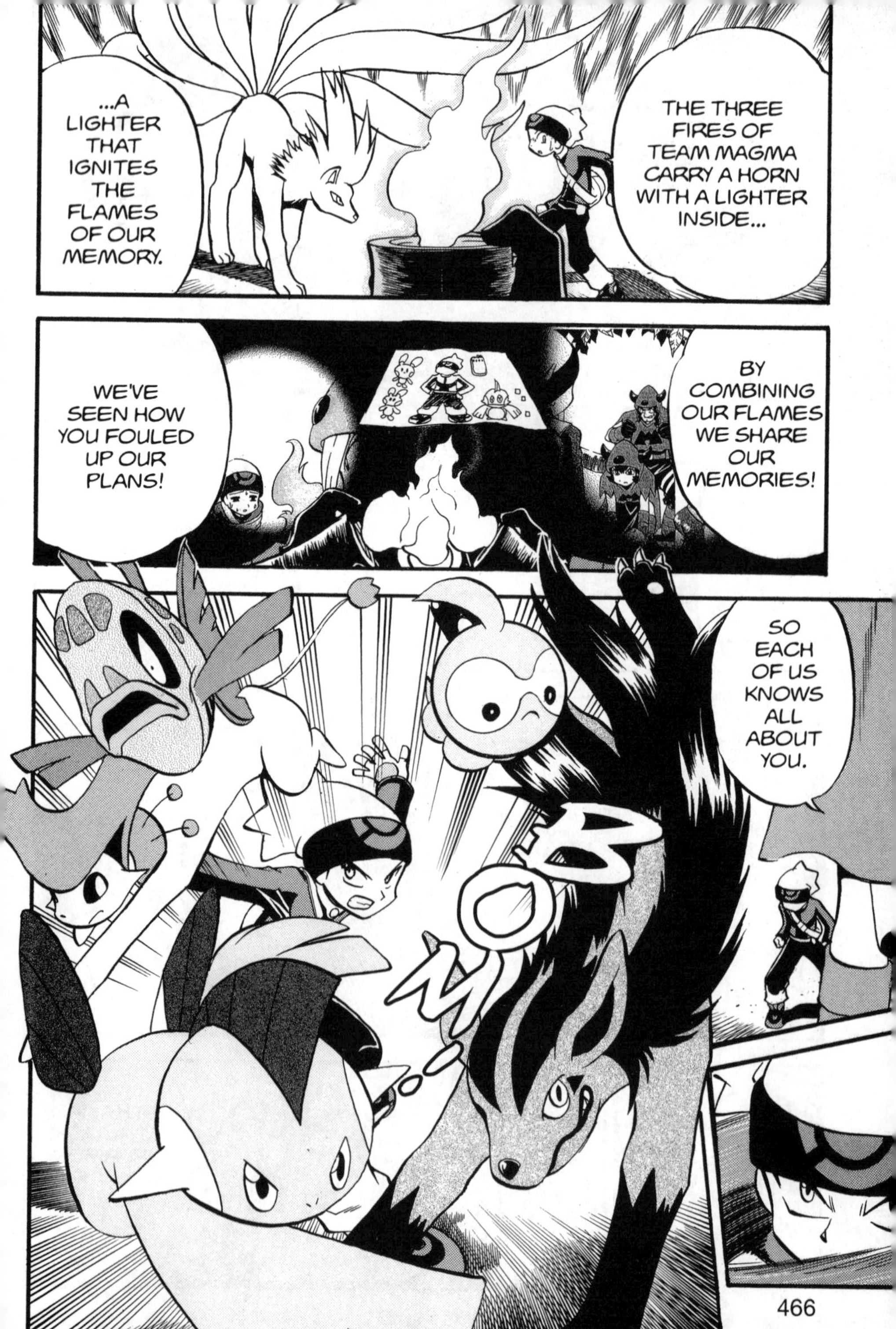
THE THREE FIRES OF TEAM MAGMA CARRY A HORN WITH A LIGHTER INSIDE...
...A LIGHTER THAT IGNITES THE FLAMES OF OUR MEMORY.
BY COMBINING OUR FLAMES WE SHARE OUR MEMORIES!
WE'VE SEEN HOW YOU FOULED UP OUR PLANS!
SO EACH OF US KNOWS ALL ABOUT YOU.

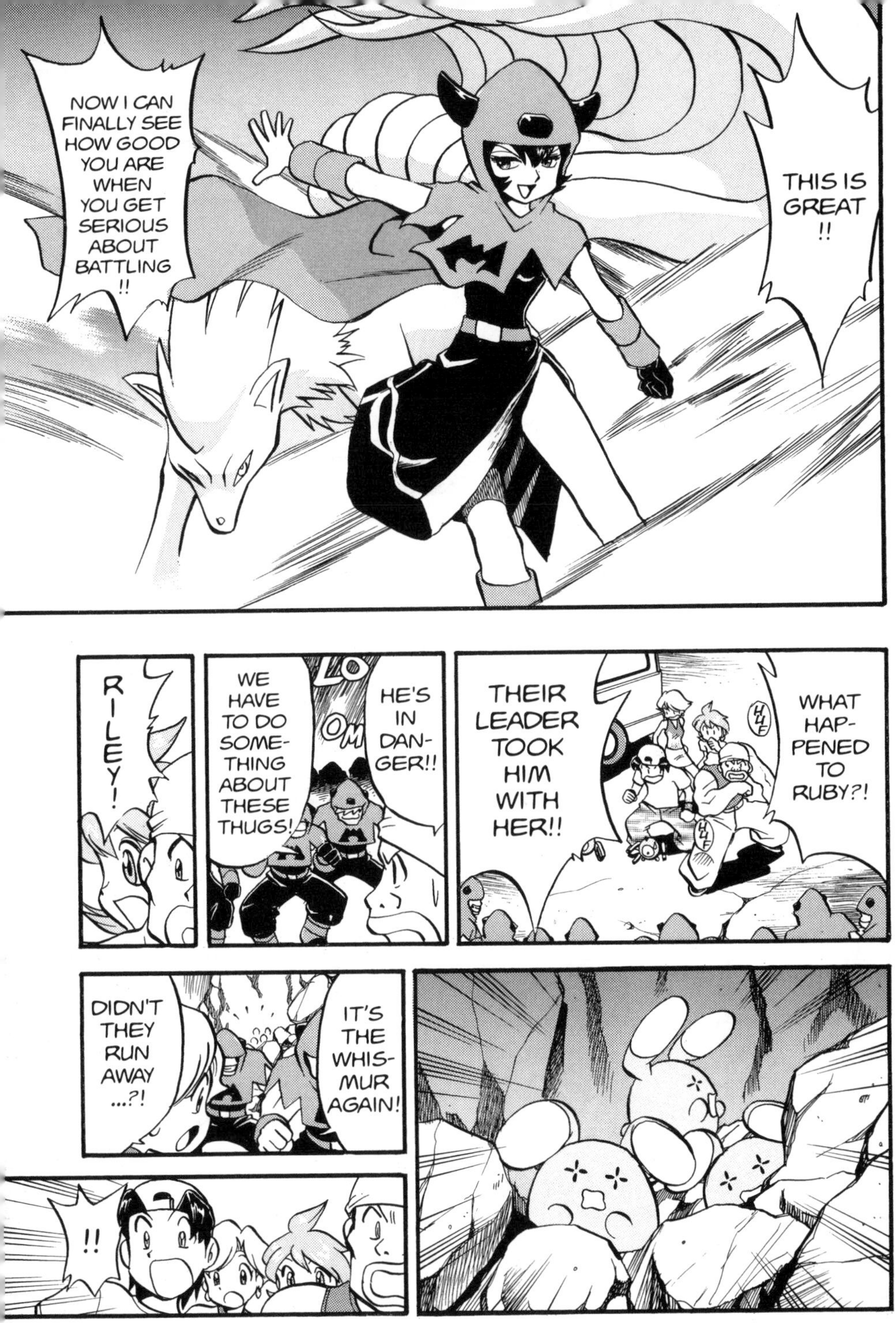
THIS IS GREAT!!
NOW I CAN FINALLY SEE HOW GOOD YOU ARE WHEN YOU GET SERIOUS ABOUT BATTLING!!
WHAT HAPPENED TO RUBY?!
HUF
HUF
THEIR LEADER TOOK HIM WITH HER!!
HE'S IN DANGER!!
WE HAVE TO DO SOMETHING ABOUT THESE THUGS!
RILEY!
IT'S THE WHISMUR AGAIN!
DIDN'T THEY RUN AWAY...?!
!!

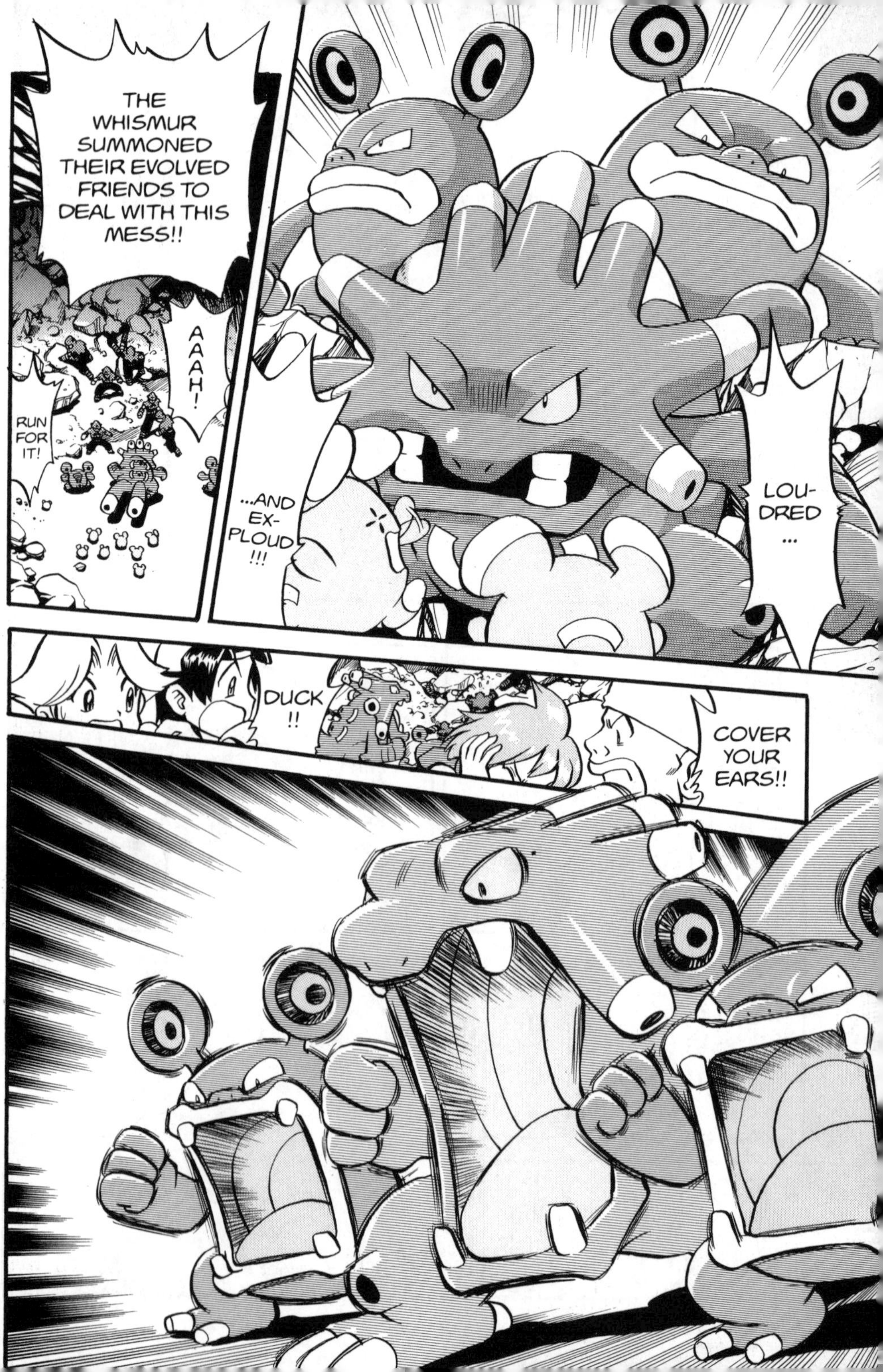

LOU-DRED...
...AND EX-PLOUD!!!
THE WHISMUR SUMMONED THEIR EVOLVED FRIENDS TO DEAL WITH THIS MESS!!
AAAAH!
RUN FOR IT!
COVER YOUR EARS!!
DUCK!!

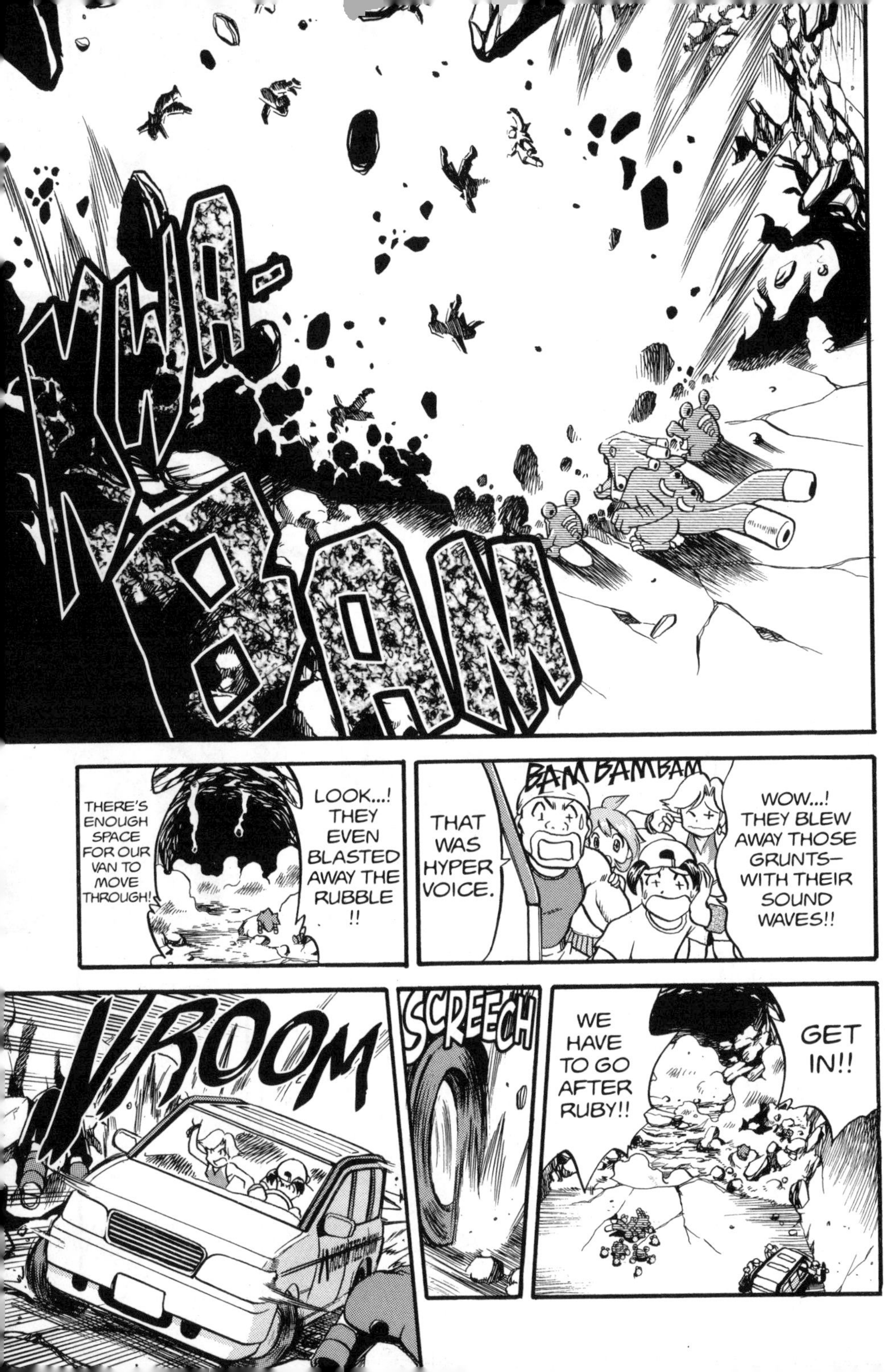
KWA-BAM
BAM BAMBAM
WOW...! THEY BLEW AWAY THOSE GRUNTS— WITH THEIR SOUND WAVES!!
THAT WAS HYPER VOICE.
LOOK...! THEY EVEN BLASTED AWAY THE RUBBLE!!
THERE'S ENOUGH SPACE FOR OUR VAN TO MOVE THROUGH!
GET IN!!
WE HAVE TO GO AFTER RUBY!!
SCREECH
VROOM

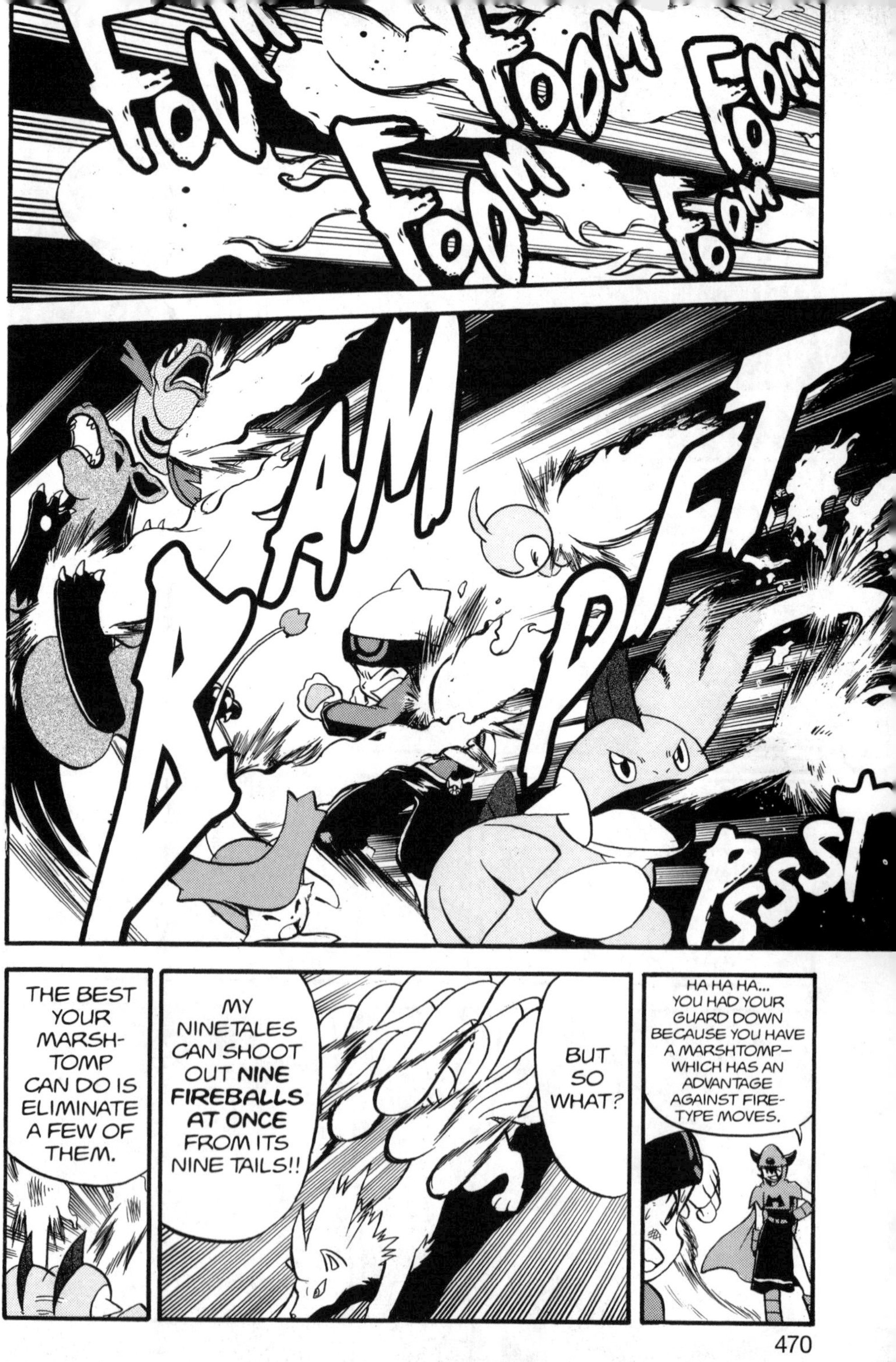
FOOM
FOOM
FOOM
FOOM
FOOM
BAM
PFT
PSSST
HA HA HA... YOU HAD YOUR GUARD DOWN BECAUSE YOU HAVE A MARSHTOMP—WHICH HAS AN ADVANTAGE AGAINST FIRE-TYPE MOVES.
BUT SO WHAT?
MY NINETALES CAN SHOOT OUT **NINE FIREBALLS AT ONCE** FROM ITS NINE TAILS!!
THE BEST YOUR MARSH-TOMP CAN DO IS ELIMINATE A FEW OF THEM.

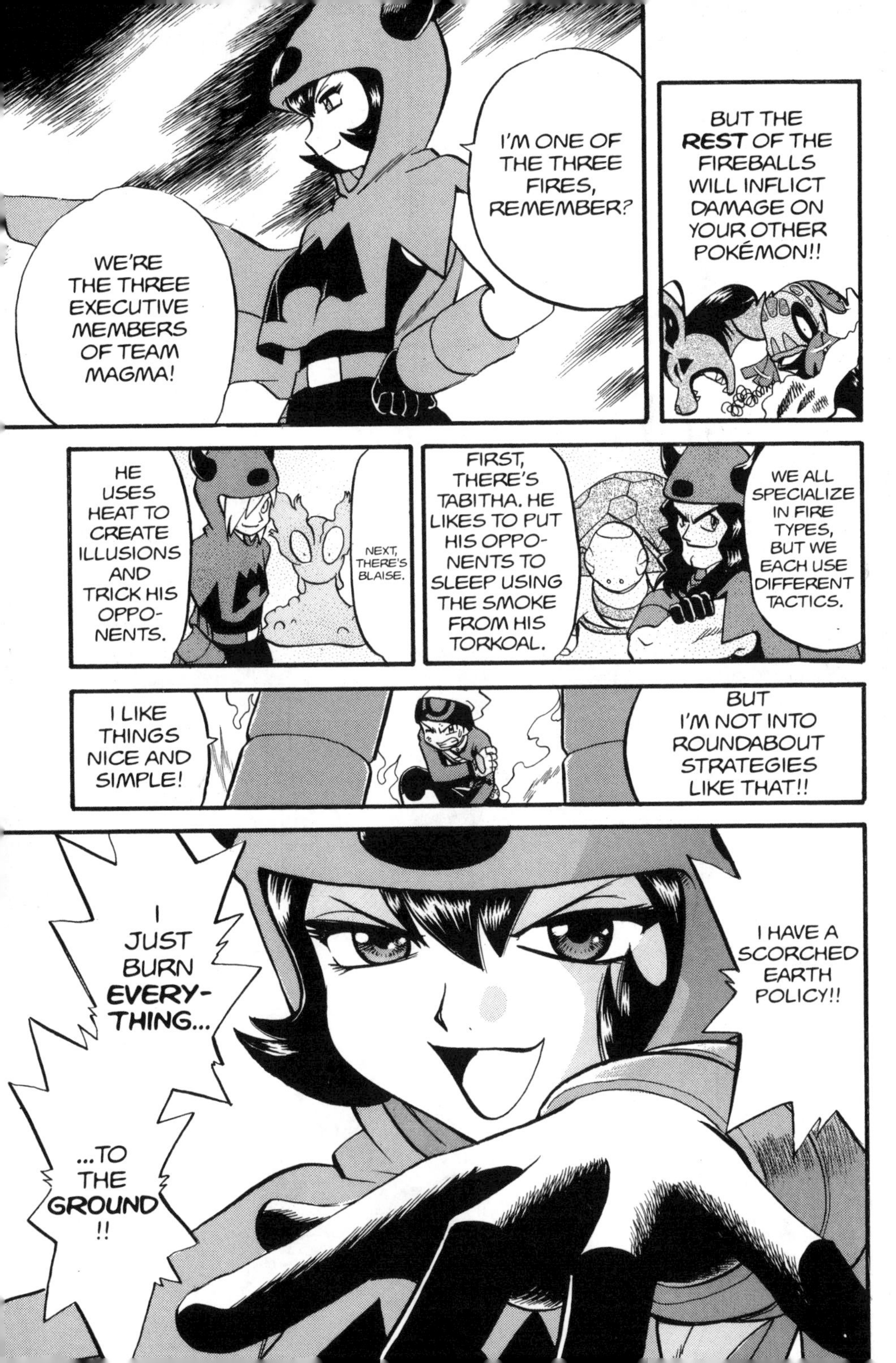
BUT THE REST OF THE FIREBALLS WILL INFLICT DAMAGE ON YOUR OTHER POKÉMON!!
I'M ONE OF THE THREE FIRES, REMEMBER?
WE'RE THE THREE EXECUTIVE MEMBERS OF TEAM MAGMA!
WE ALL SPECIALIZE IN FIRE TYPES, BUT WE EACH USE DIFFERENT TACTICS.
FIRST, THERE'S TABITHA. HE LIKES TO PUT HIS OPPO-NENTS TO SLEEP USING THE SMOKE FROM HIS TORKOAL.
NEXT, THERE'S BLAISE.
HE USES HEAT TO CREATE ILLUSIONS AND TRICK HIS OPPO-NENTS.
BUT I'M NOT INTO ROUNDABOUT STRATEGIES LIKE THAT!!
I LIKE THINGS NICE AND SIMPLE!
I HAVE A SCORCHED EARTH POLICY!!
I JUST BURN EVERY-THING...
...TO THE GROUND!!

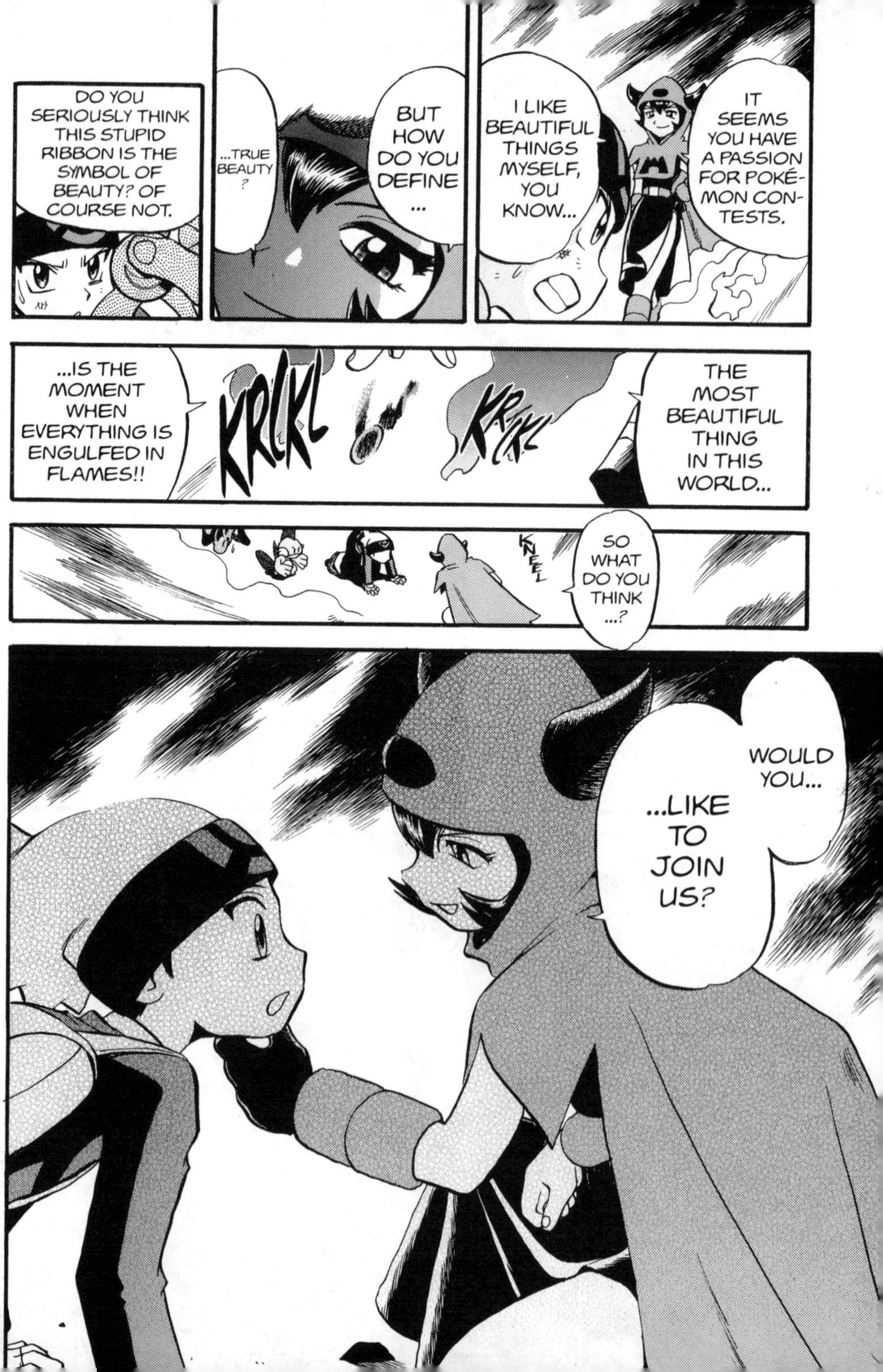
IT SEEMS YOU HAVE A PASSION FOR POKÉMON CONTESTS.
I LIKE BEAUTIFUL THINGS MYSELF, YOU KNOW...
BUT HOW DO YOU DEFINE ...
...TRUE BEAUTY ?
DO YOU SERIOUSLY THINK THIS STUPID RIBBON IS THE SYMBOL OF BEAUTY? OF COURSE NOT.
THE MOST BEAUTIFUL THING IN THIS WORLD...
KRKL
KRKL
...IS THE MOMENT WHEN EVERYTHING IS ENGULFED IN FLAMES!!
SO WHAT DO YOU THINK ...?
KNEEL
WOULD YOU...
...LIKE TO JOIN US?

ADVENTURE MAP

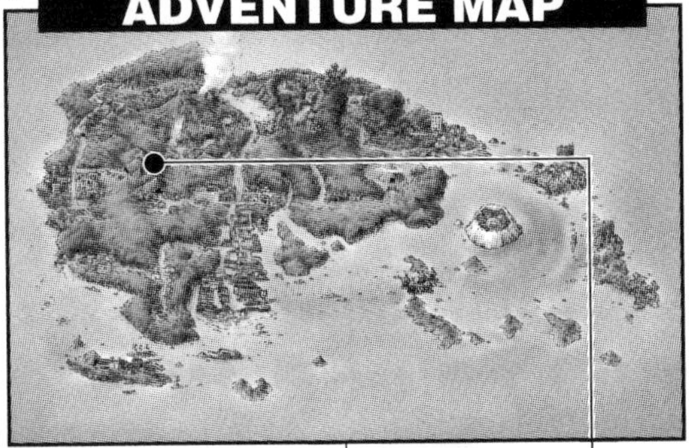

SAPPHIRE

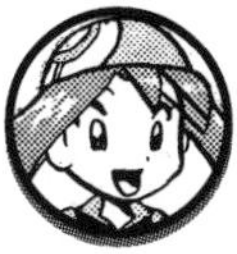

Route 111
▼
▼
Mt. Chimney
▼
Jagged Pass
▼

RUBY

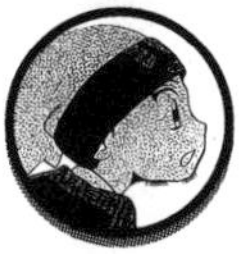

Weather Institute
▼
▼
Route 117
▼
Verdanturf Town
▼
Rusturf Tunnel

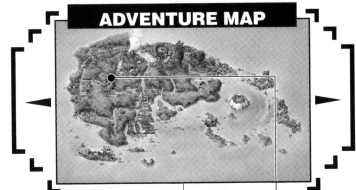

SAPPHIRE

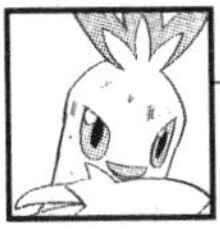

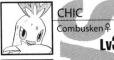

CHIC
Combusken ♀
Lv31

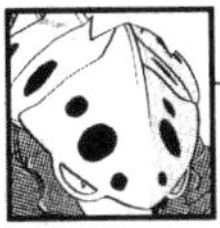

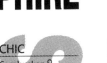

RONO
Lairon ♂
Lv40

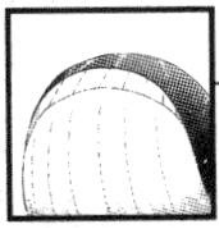

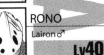

LORRY
Wailord ♂
Lv45

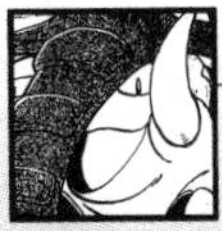

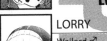

PHADO
Donphan ♂
Lv43

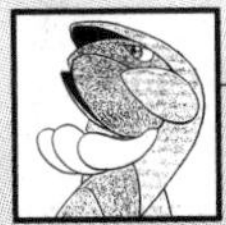

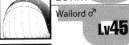

TROPPY
Tropius ♂
Lv42

RUBY

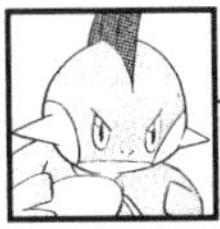

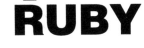

MUMU
Marshtomp ♂

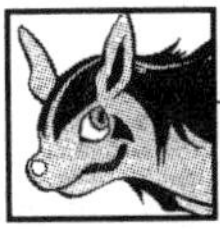

NANA
Mightyena ♀

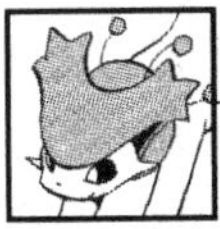

KIKI
Delcatty ♀

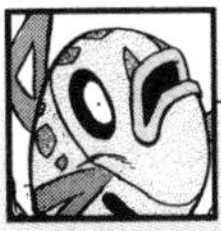

FEEFEE
Feebas ♀

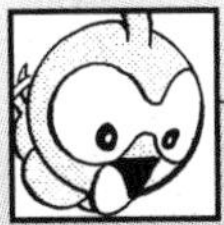

FOFO
Castform ♀

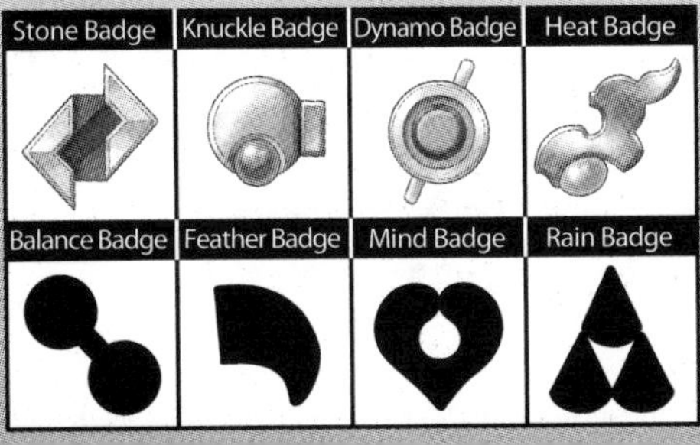

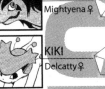

Stone Badge
Knuckle Badge
Dynamo Badge
Heat Badge
Balance Badge
Feather Badge
Mind Badge
Rain Badge

	Coolness	Beauty	Cuteness	Cleverness	Toughness
Normal					
Super					
Hyper					
Master					

● Adventure 221 ●
Going to Eleven with Loudred and Exploud, Part 2

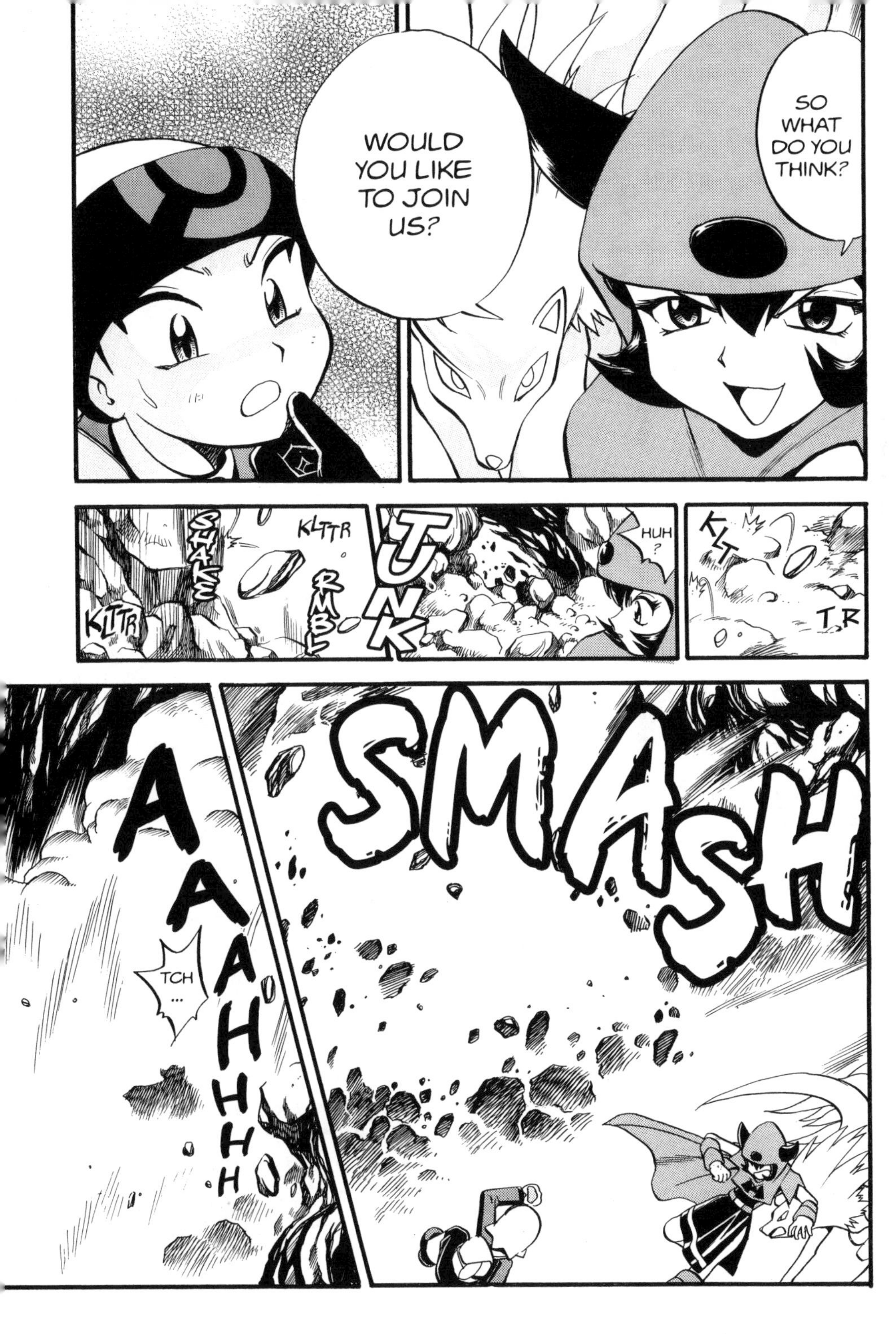
SO WHAT DO YOU THINK?
WOULD YOU LIKE TO JOIN US?
KLT
TR
HUH?
JUNK
KLTTR
RMBL
SHAKE
KLTTR
SMASH
AAAHHHHH
TCH...

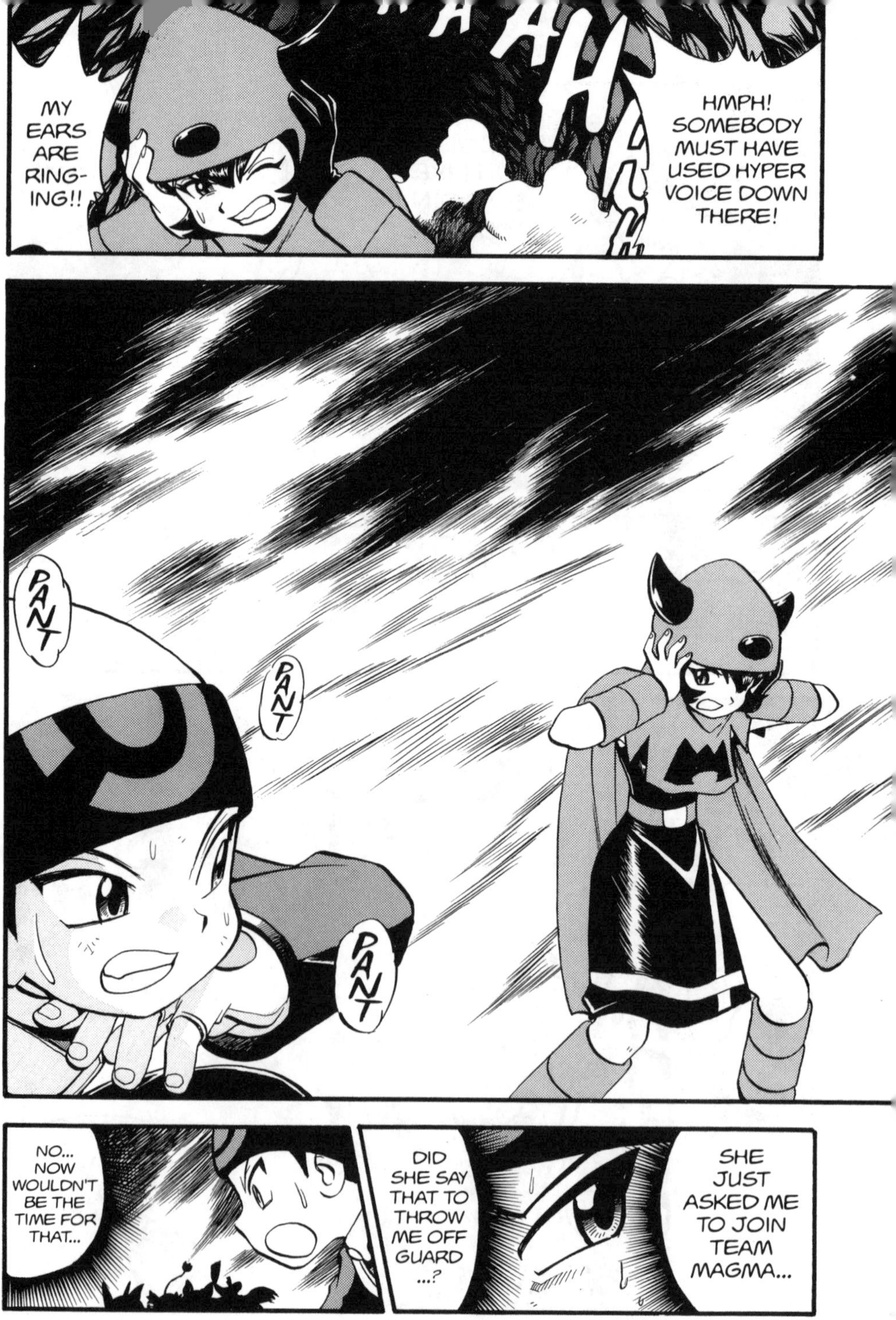
HMPH! SOMEBODY MUST HAVE USED HYPER VOICE DOWN THERE!
MY EARS ARE RING-ING!!
PANT
PANT
PANT
SHE JUST ASKED ME TO JOIN TEAM MAGMA...
DID SHE SAY THAT TO THROW ME OFF GUARD ...?
NO... NOW WOULDN'T BE THE TIME FOR THAT...

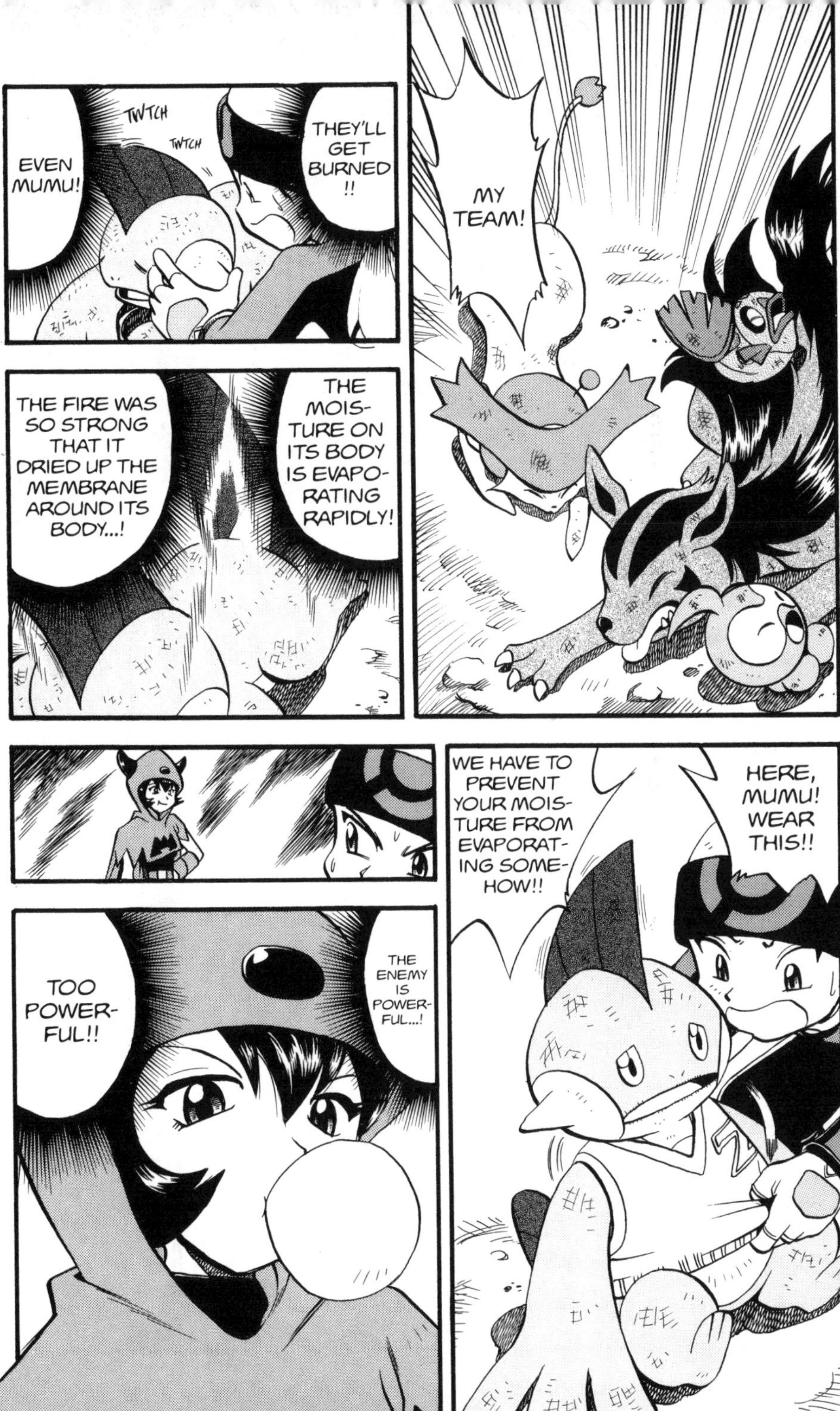
MY TEAM!
THEY'LL GET BURNED!!
TWTCH
TWTCH
EVEN MUMU!
THE MOISTURE ON ITS BODY IS EVAPORATING RAPIDLY!
THE FIRE WAS SO STRONG THAT IT DRIED UP THE MEMBRANE AROUND ITS BODY...!
HERE, MUMU! WEAR THIS!!
WE HAVE TO PREVENT YOUR MOISTURE FROM EVAPORATING SOMEHOW!!
THE ENEMY IS POWERFUL...!
TOO POWERFUL!!

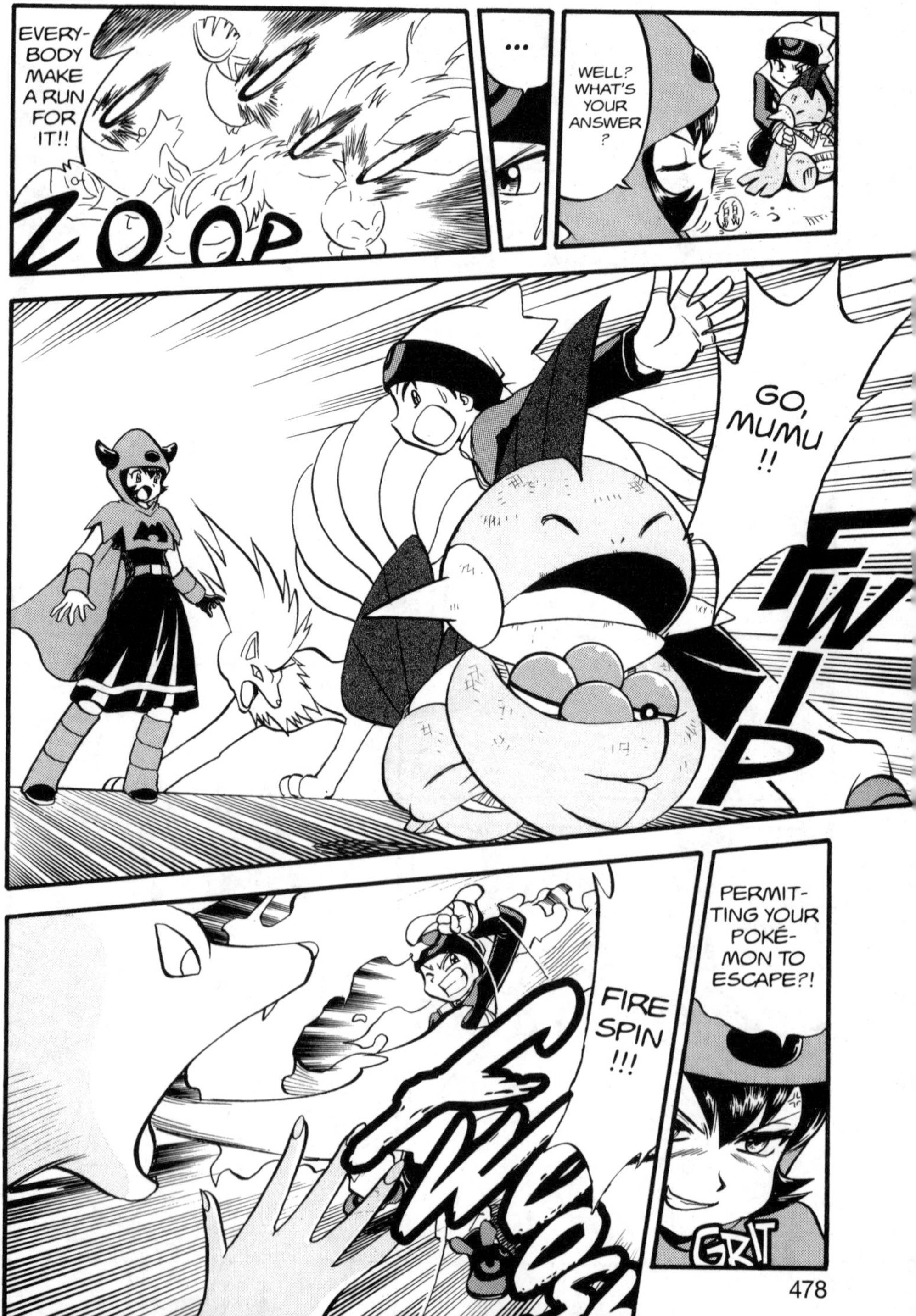
WELL? WHAT'S YOUR ANSWER?
...
EVERYBODY MAKE A RUN FOR IT!!
ZOOP
GO, MUMU!!
FWIP
PERMITTING YOUR POKÉMON TO ESCAPE?!
GRIT
FIRE SPIN!!!

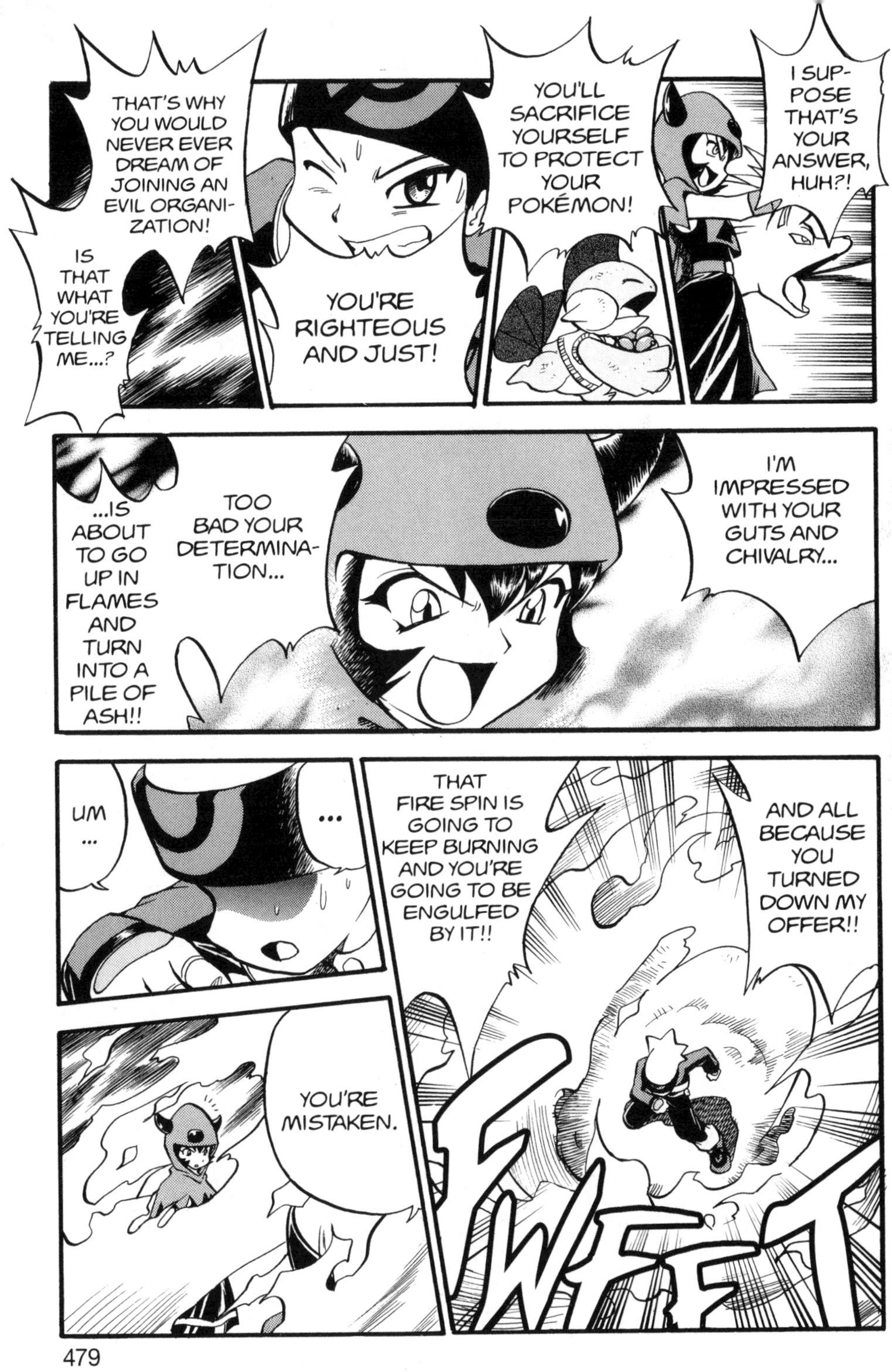
I SUP-POSE THAT'S YOUR ANSWER, HUH?!
YOU'LL SACRIFICE YOURSELF TO PROTECT YOUR POKÉMON!
YOU'RE RIGHTEOUS AND JUST!
THAT'S WHY YOU WOULD NEVER EVER DREAM OF JOINING AN EVIL ORGANI-ZATION!
IS THAT WHAT YOU'RE TELLING ME...?
I'M IMPRESSED WITH YOUR GUTS AND CHIVALRY...
TOO BAD YOUR DETERMINA-TION...
...IS ABOUT TO GO UP IN FLAMES AND TURN INTO A PILE OF ASH!!
THAT FIRE SPIN IS GOING TO KEEP BURNING AND YOU'RE GOING TO BE ENGULFED BY IT!!
AND ALL BECAUSE YOU TURNED DOWN MY OFFER!!
SWFFT
...
UM ...
YOU'RE MISTAKEN.

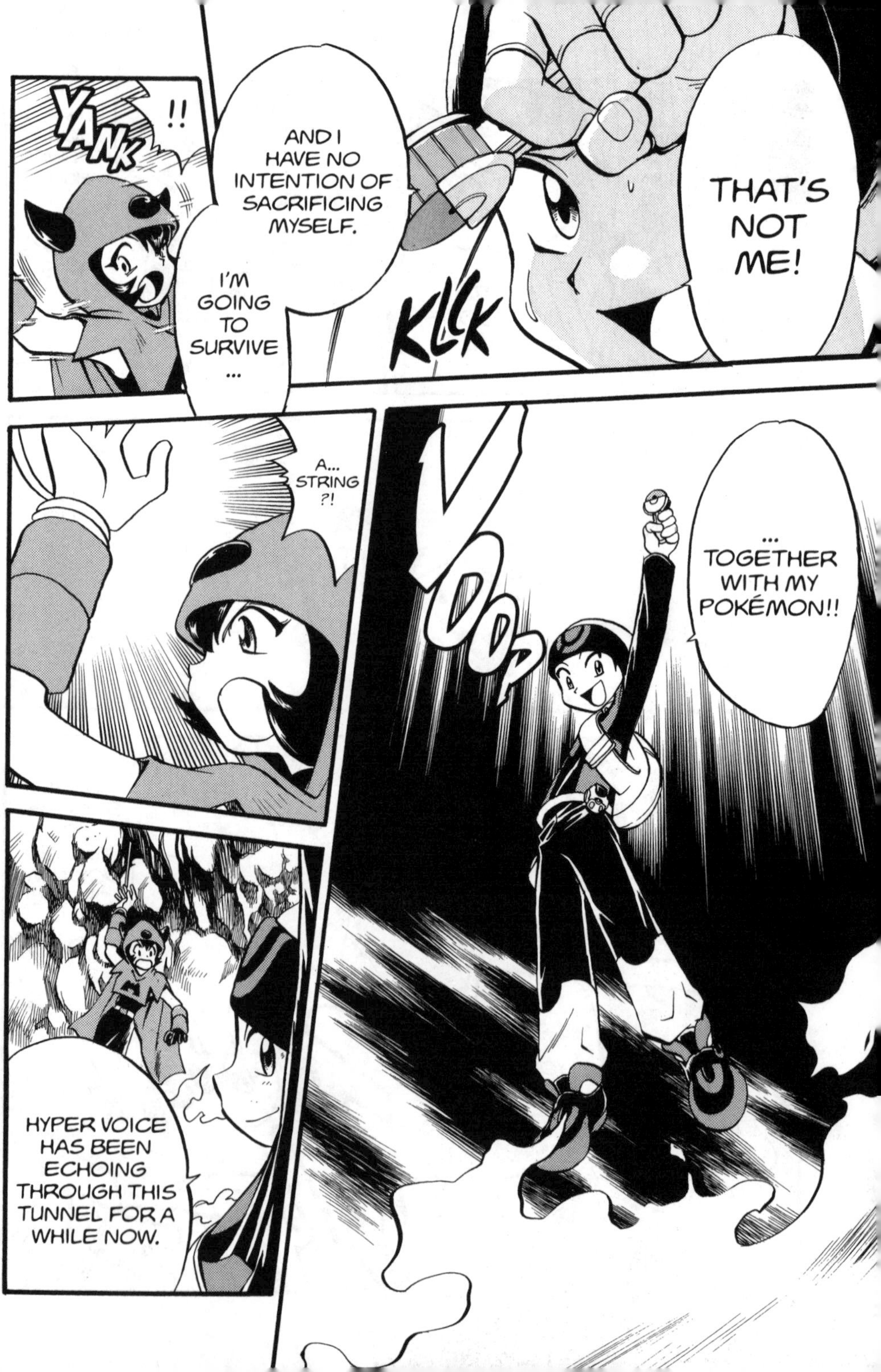
THAT'S NOT ME!
KLICK
AND I HAVE NO INTENTION OF SACRIFICING MYSELF.
I'M GOING TO SURVIVE ...
YANK
!!
... TOGETHER WITH MY POKÉMON!!
VOOOP
A... STRING ?!
HYPER VOICE HAS BEEN ECHOING THROUGH THIS TUNNEL FOR A WHILE NOW.

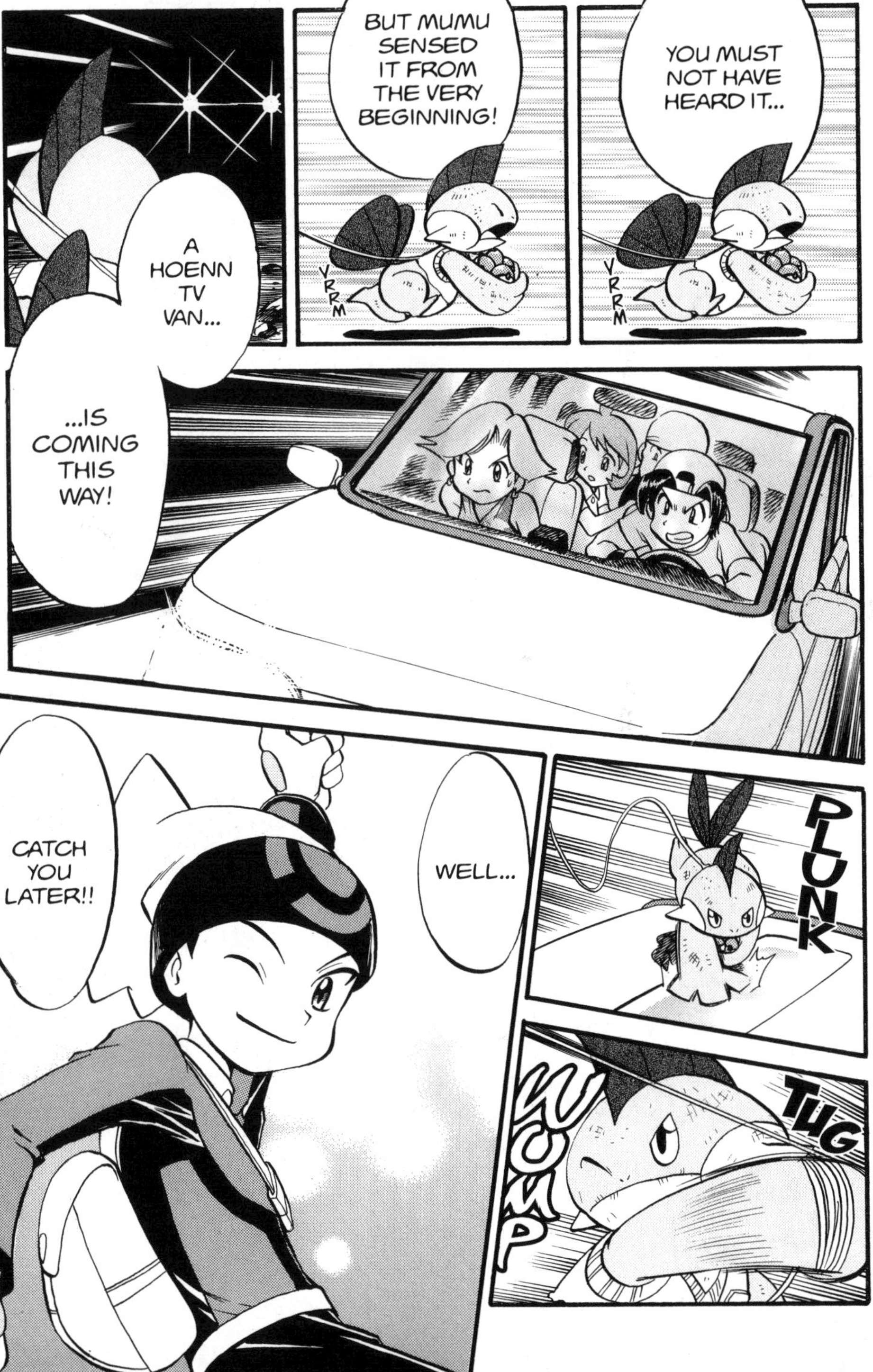
YOU MUST NOT HAVE HEARD IT...
VRRM
BUT MUMU SENSED IT FROM THE VERY BEGINNING!
VRRM
A HOENN TV VAN...
...IS COMING THIS WAY!
PLUNK
TUG
WUMP
WELL...
CATCH YOU LATER!!

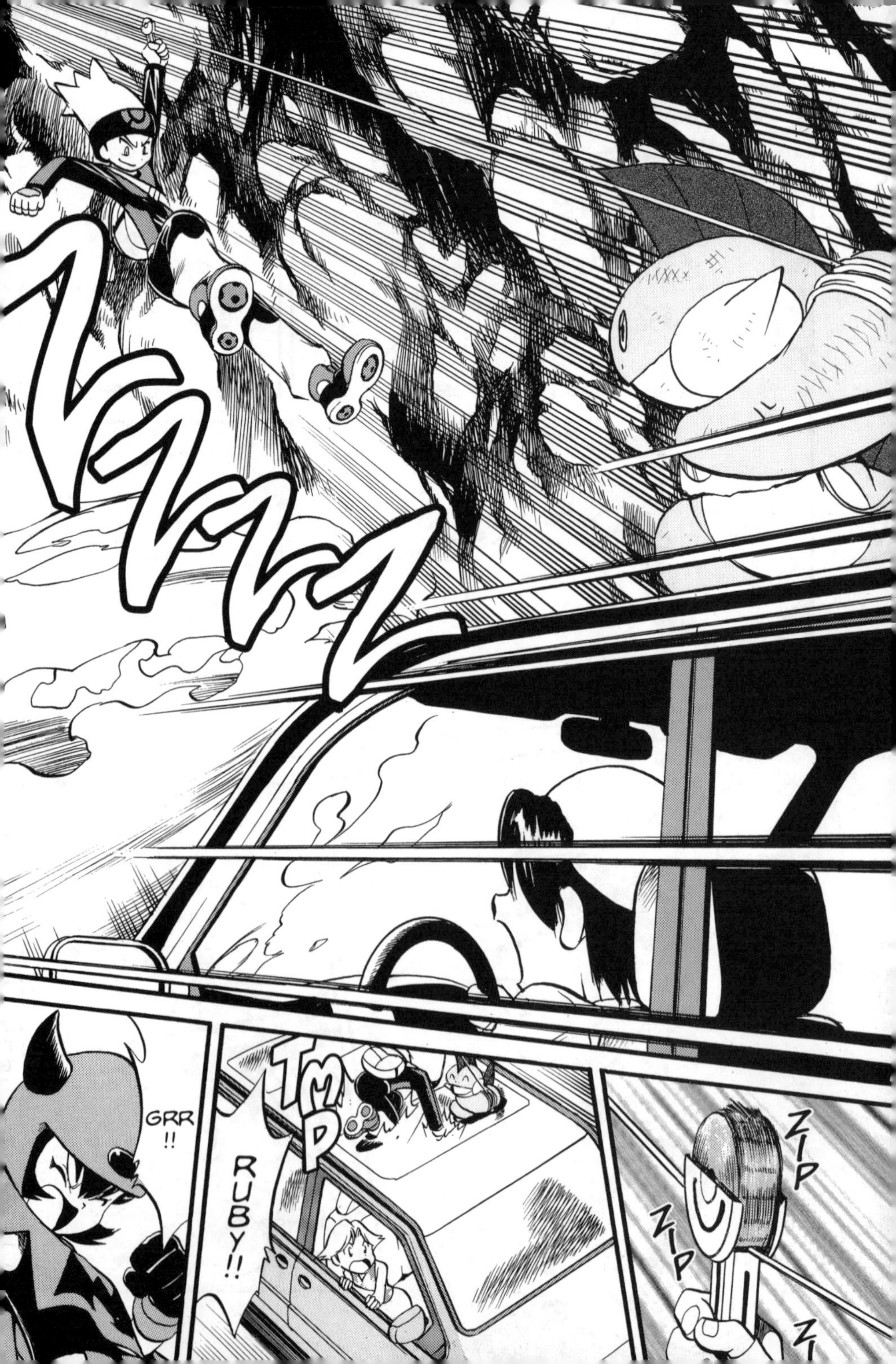
ZIP
ZIP
ZI
TMP
RUBY!!
GRR !!

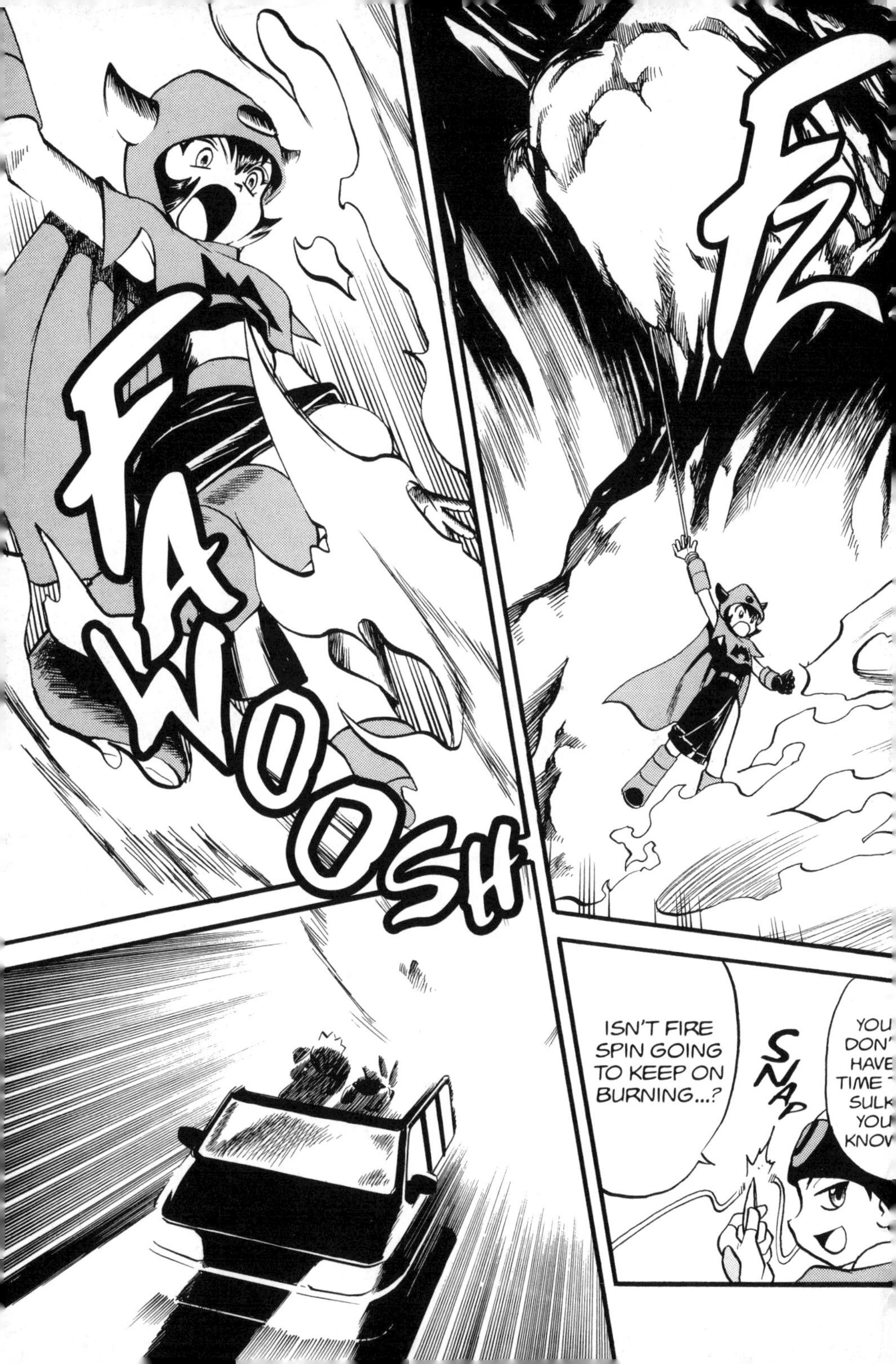
FWOOSH
YOU DON' HAVE TIME SULK YOU KNOW
SNAP
ISN'T FIRE SPIN GOING TO KEEP ON BURNING...?

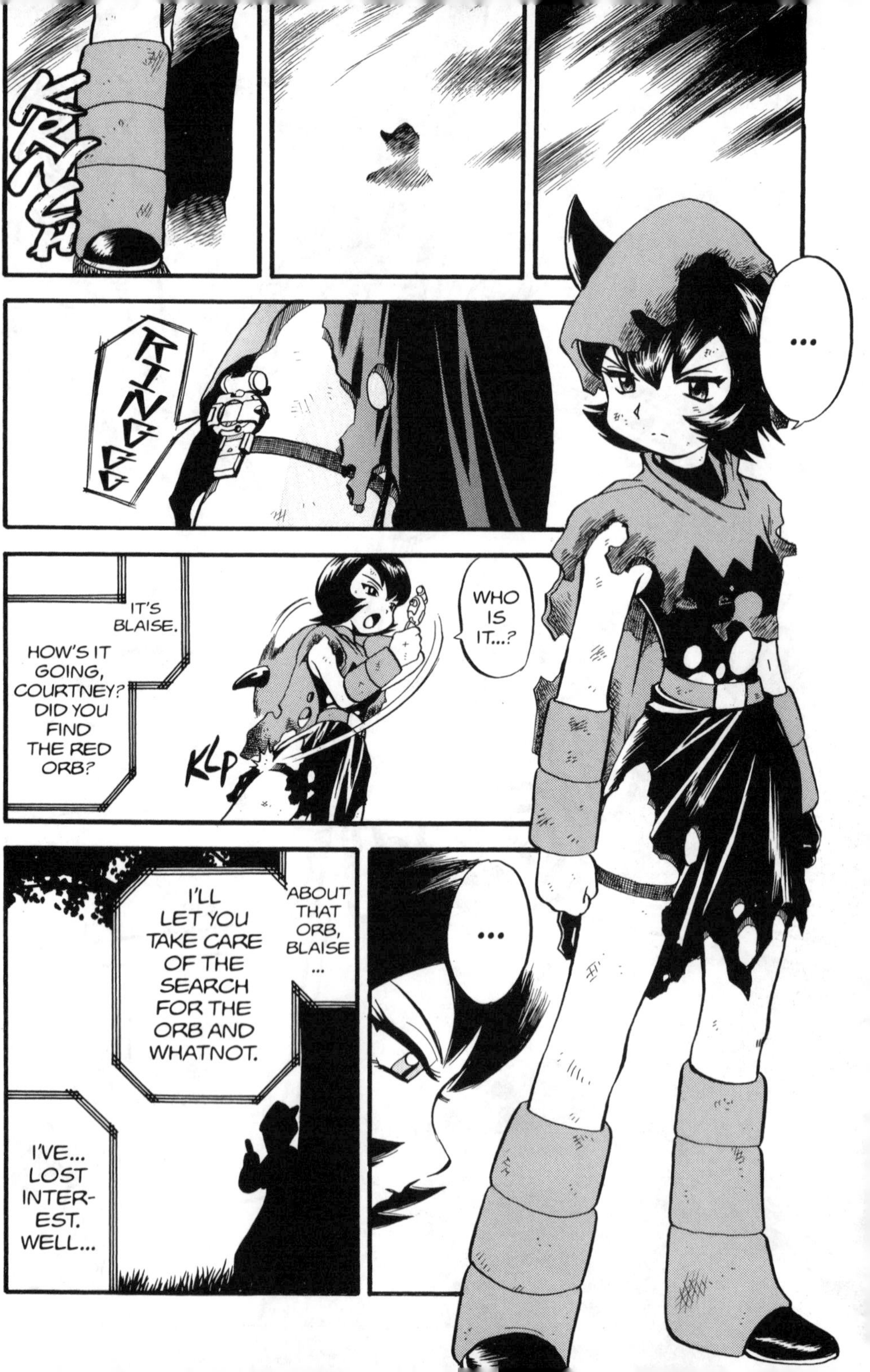
KRNCH
...
RINGGG
WHO IS IT...?
IT'S BLAISE.
HOW'S IT GOING, COURTNEY? DID YOU FIND THE RED ORB?
KLP
...
ABOUT THAT ORB, BLAISE ...
I'LL LET YOU TAKE CARE OF THE SEARCH FOR THE ORB AND WHATNOT.
I'VE... LOST INTER-EST. WELL...

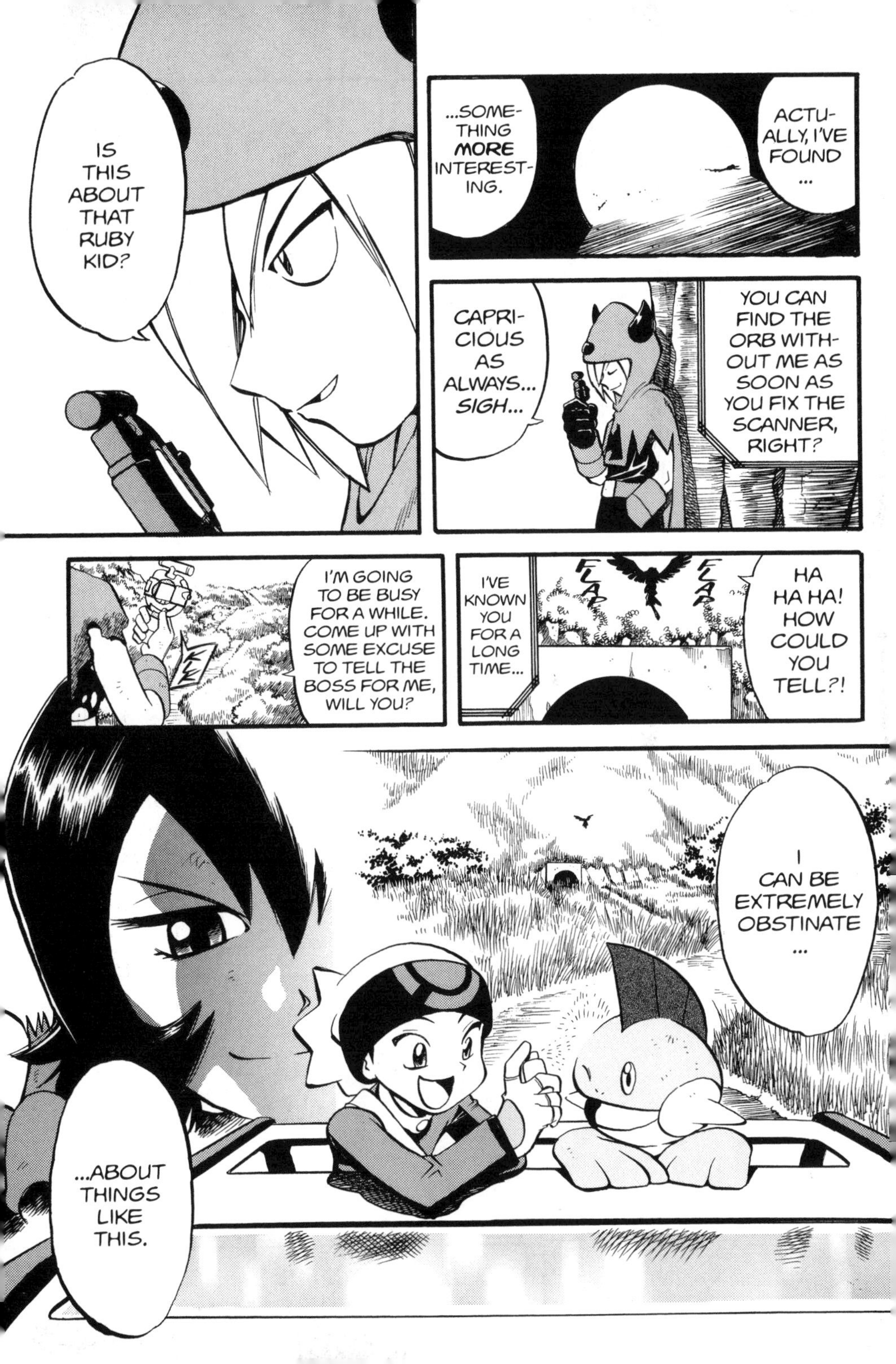
ACTUALLY, I'VE FOUND ...
...SOMETHING **MORE** INTERESTING.
YOU CAN FIND THE ORB WITHOUT ME AS SOON AS YOU FIX THE SCANNER, RIGHT?
CAPRICIOUS AS ALWAYS... *SIGH*...
IS THIS ABOUT THAT RUBY KID?
HA HA HA! HOW COULD YOU TELL?!
FLAP
FLAP
I'VE KNOWN YOU FOR A LONG TIME...
I'M GOING TO BE BUSY FOR A WHILE. COME UP WITH SOME EXCUSE TO TELL THE BOSS FOR ME, WILL YOU?
I CAN BE EXTREMELY OBSTINATE ...
...ABOUT THINGS LIKE THIS.

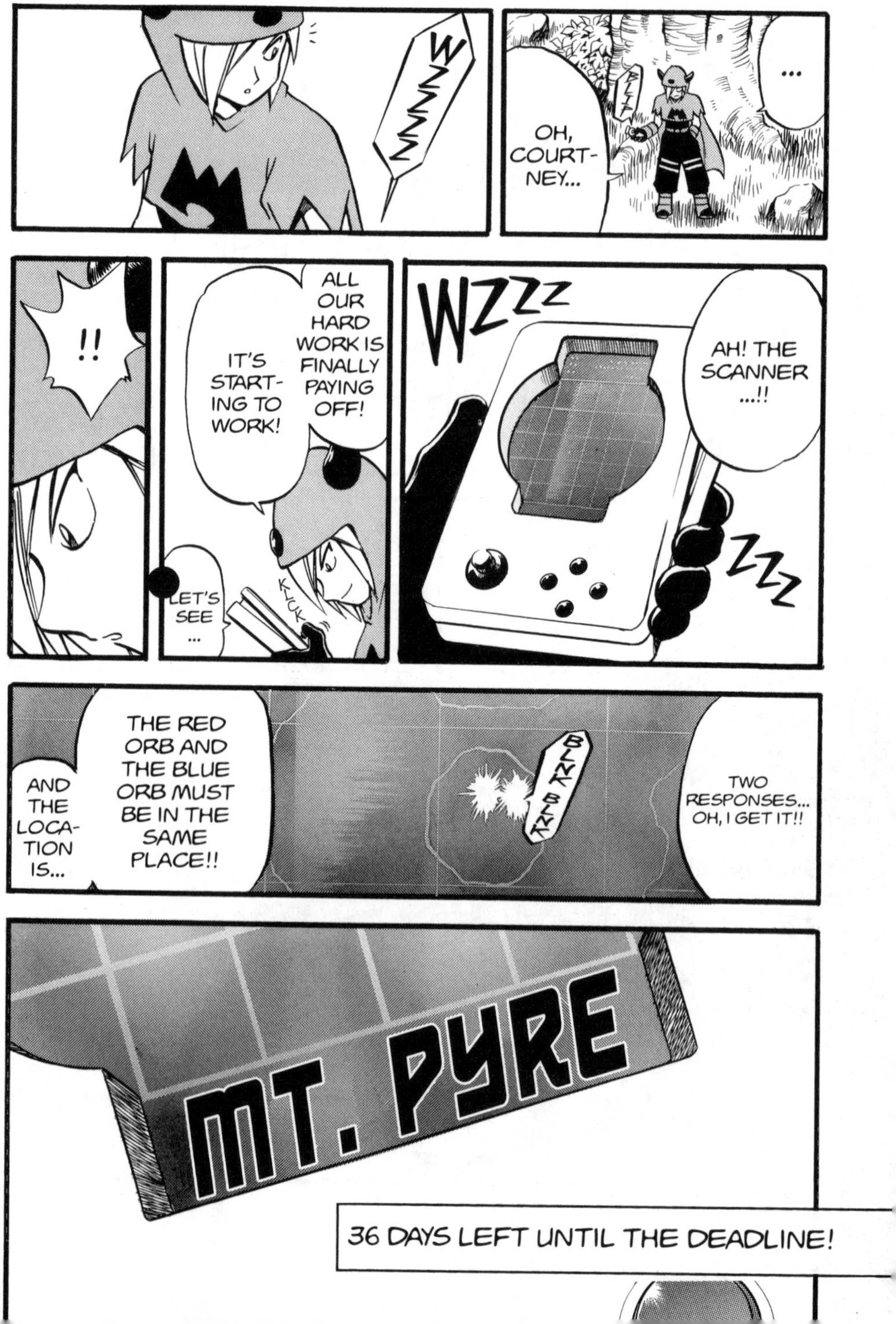
...
BLIT
OH, COURTNEY...
WZZZZZ
AH! THE SCANNER ...!!
WZZZ
ZZZ
ALL OUR HARD WORK IS FINALLY PAYING OFF!
IT'S STARTING TO WORK!
KLICK
LET'S SEE ...
!!
TWO RESPONSES... OH, I GET IT!!
BLNK BLNK
THE RED ORB AND THE BLUE ORB MUST BE IN THE SAME PLACE!!
AND THE LOCATION IS...
MT. PYRE
36 DAYS LEFT UNTIL THE DEADLINE!

● Adventure 222 ●

Short Shrift for Shiftry

Pokémon™ Adventures Ruby & Sapphire

The Fourth Chapter

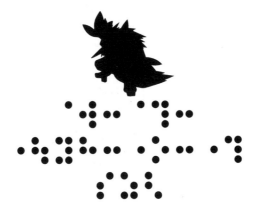

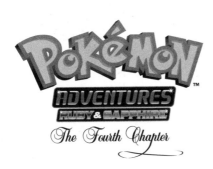

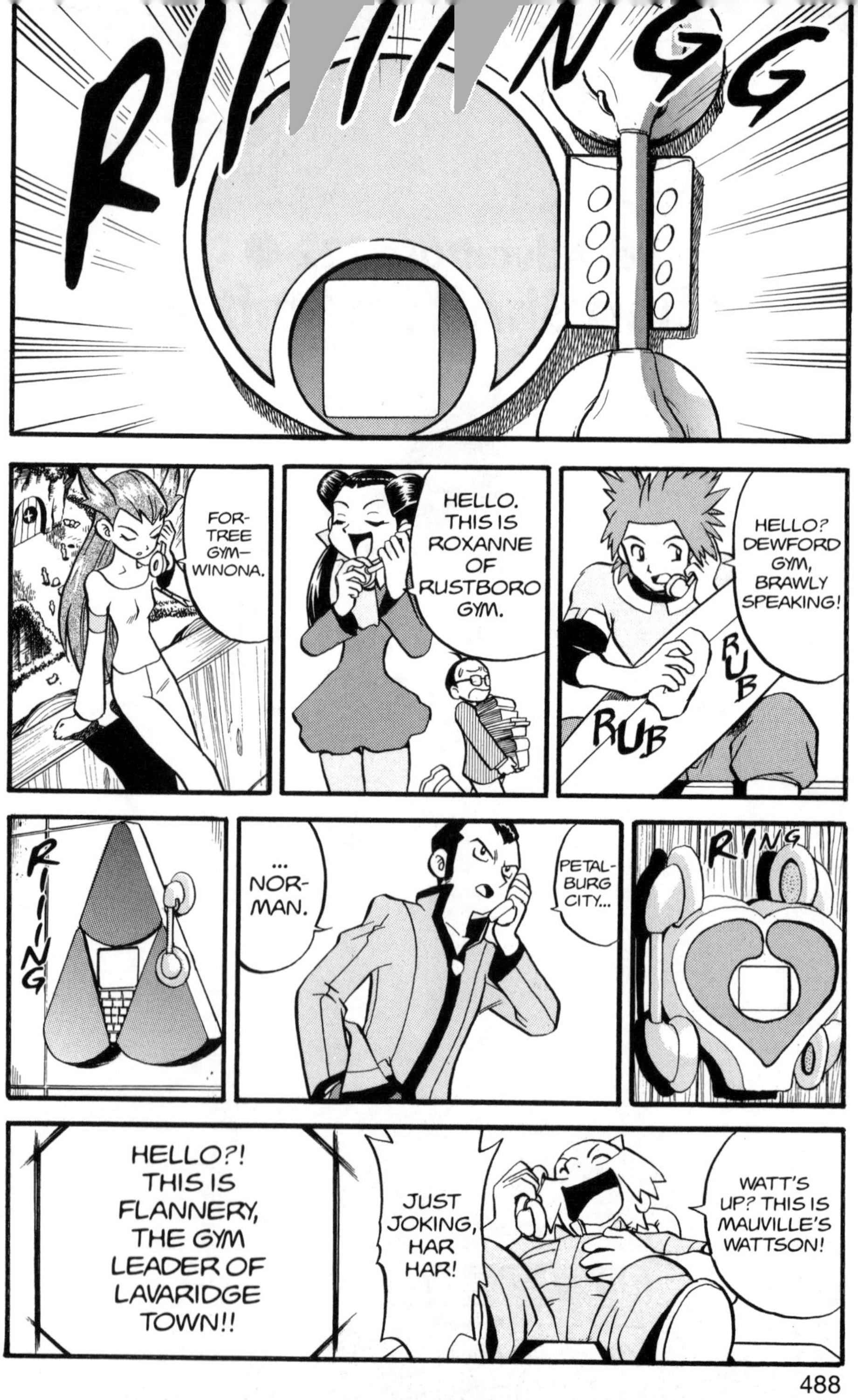

RIIIINGG
HELLO? DEWFORD GYM, BRAWLY SPEAKING!
RUB
RUB
HELLO. THIS IS ROXANNE OF RUSTBORO GYM.
FOR-TREE GYM— WINONA.
RING
PETAL-BURG CITY...
... NOR-MAN.
RIIIING
WATT'S UP? THIS IS MAUVILLE'S WATTSON!
JUST JOKING, HAR HAR!
HELLO?! THIS IS FLANNERY, THE GYM LEADER OF LAVARIDGE TOWN!!

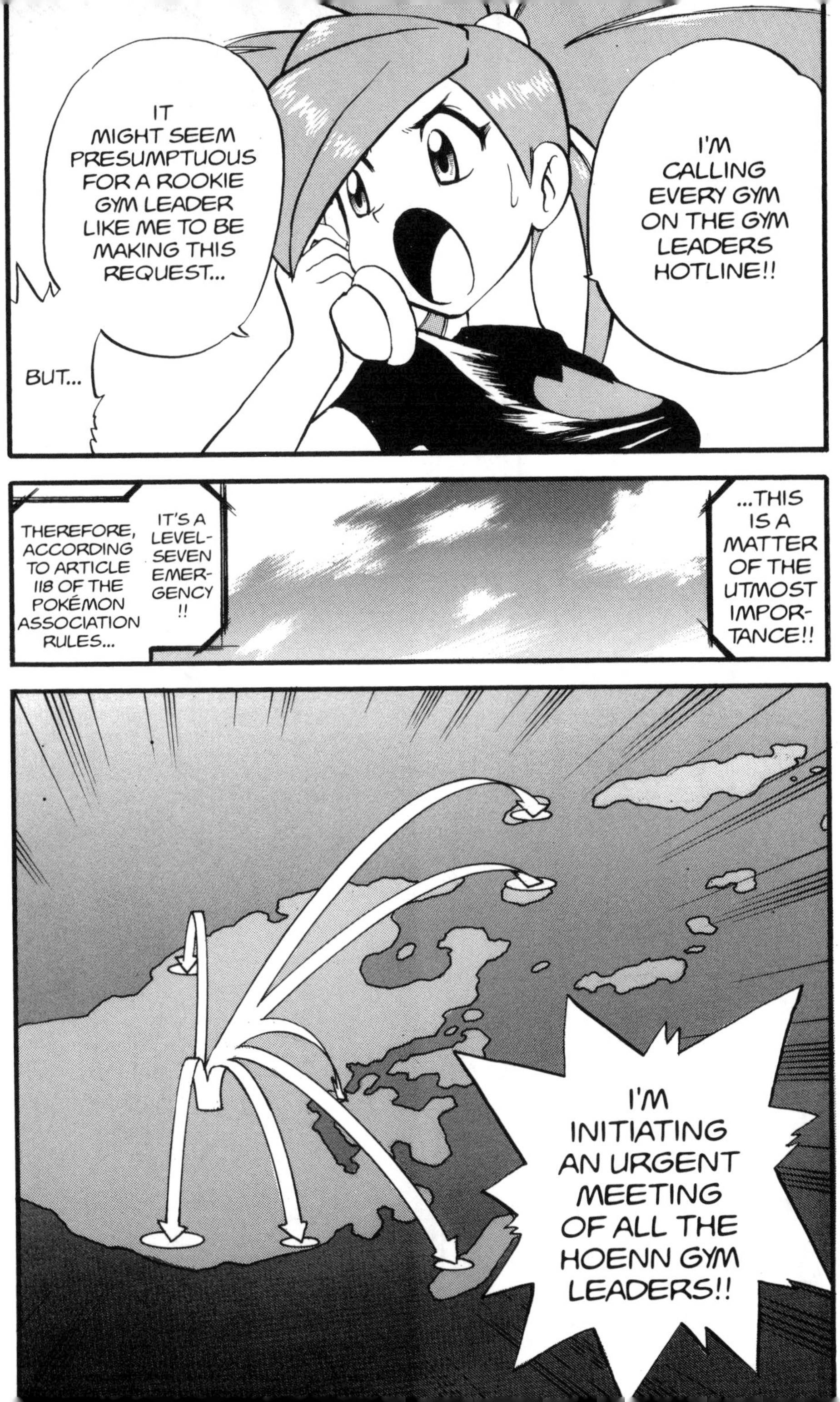
I'M CALLING EVERY GYM ON THE GYM LEADERS HOTLINE!!
IT MIGHT SEEM PRESUMPTUOUS FOR A ROOKIE GYM LEADER LIKE ME TO BE MAKING THIS REQUEST...
BUT...
...THIS IS A MATTER OF THE UTMOST IMPORTANCE!!
IT'S A LEVEL-SEVEN EMERGENCY!!
THEREFORE, ACCORDING TO ARTICLE 118 OF THE POKÉMON ASSOCIATION RULES...
I'M INITIATING AN URGENT MEETING OF ALL THE HOENN GYM LEADERS!!

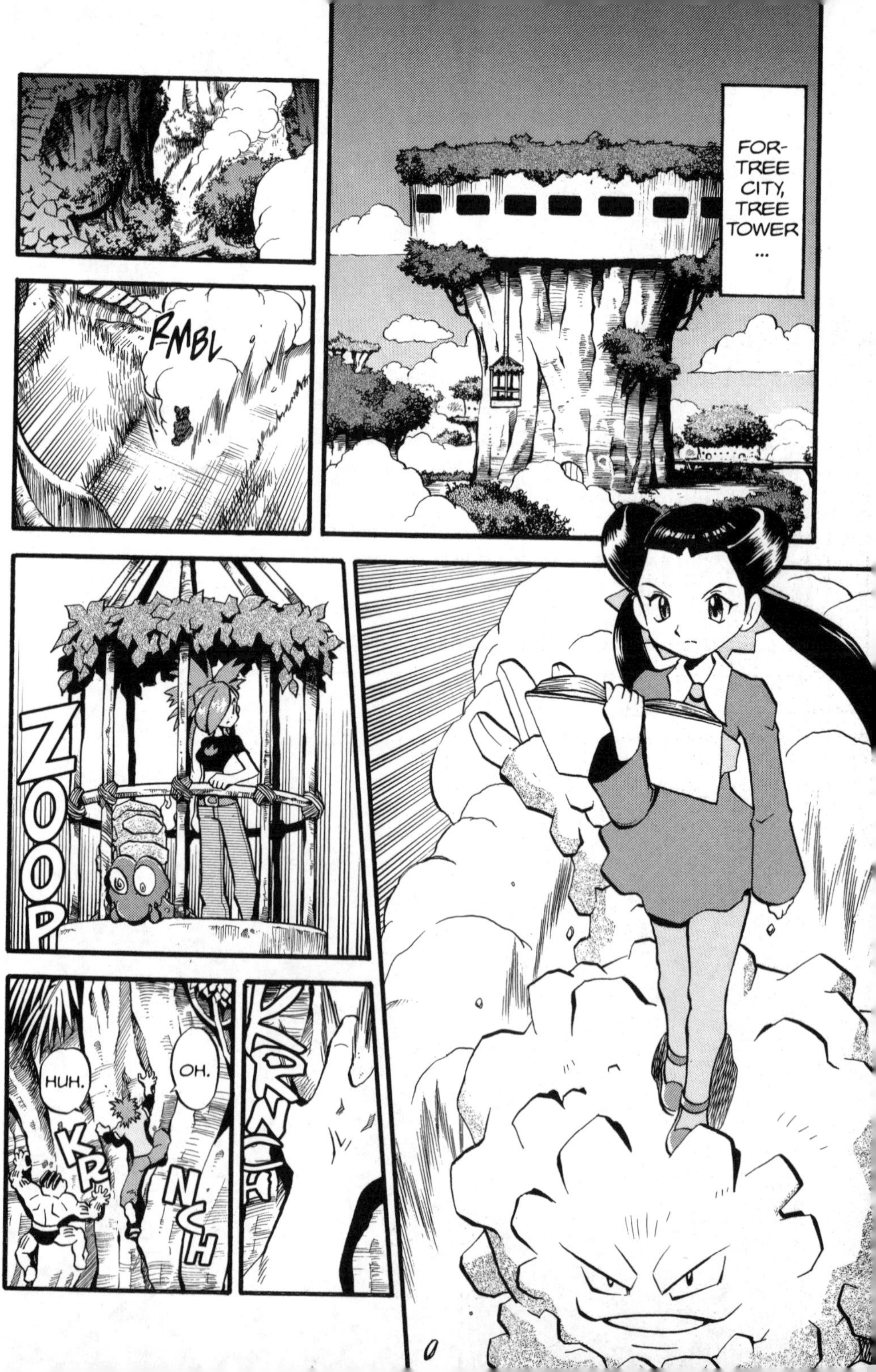
FOR-TREE CITY, TREE TOWER ...
RMBL
ZOOP
KRNCH
OH.
HUH.
KRNCH

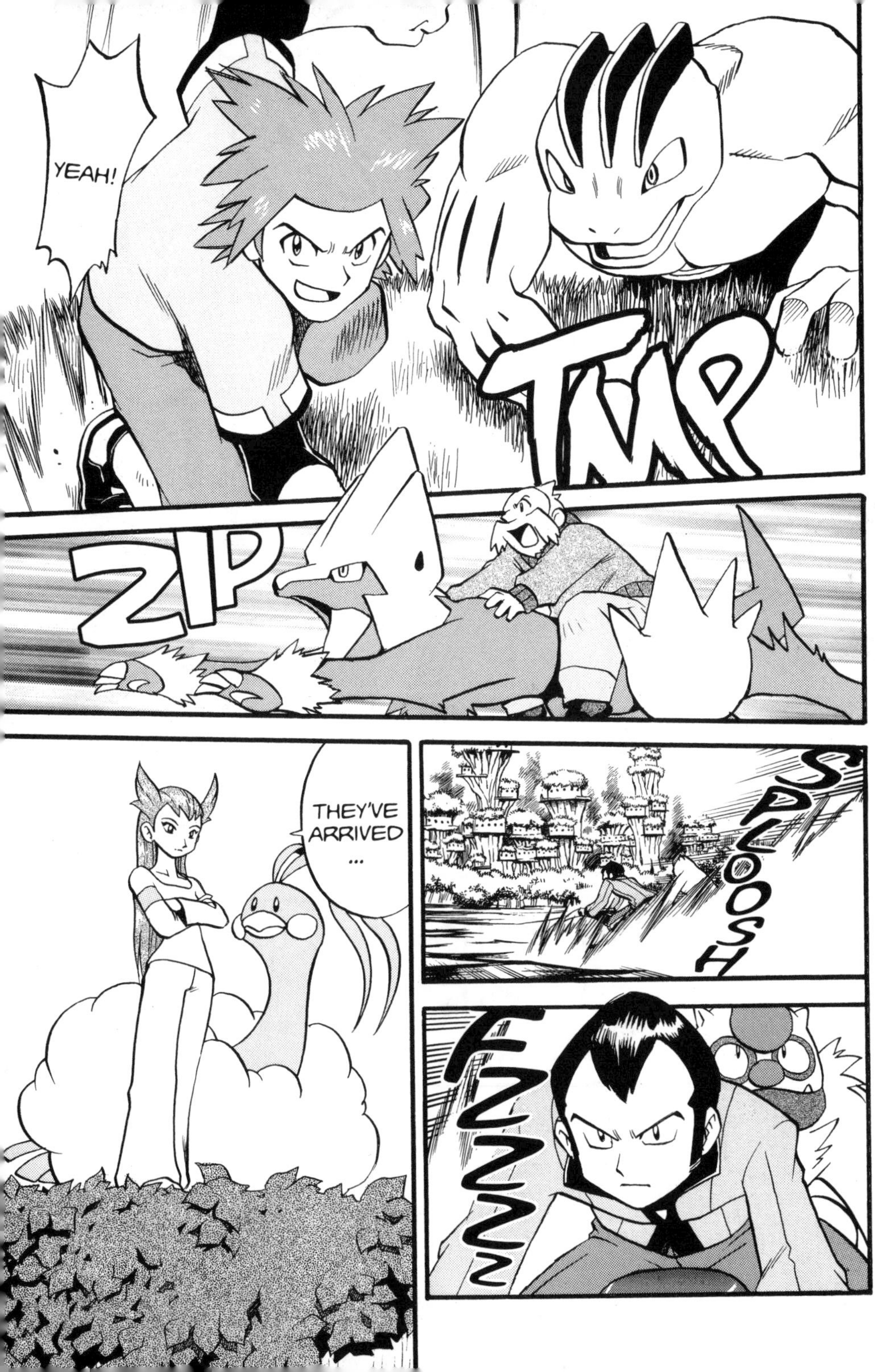
YEAH!
TMP
ZIP
SPLOOSH
FZZZZ
THEY'VE ARRIVED ...

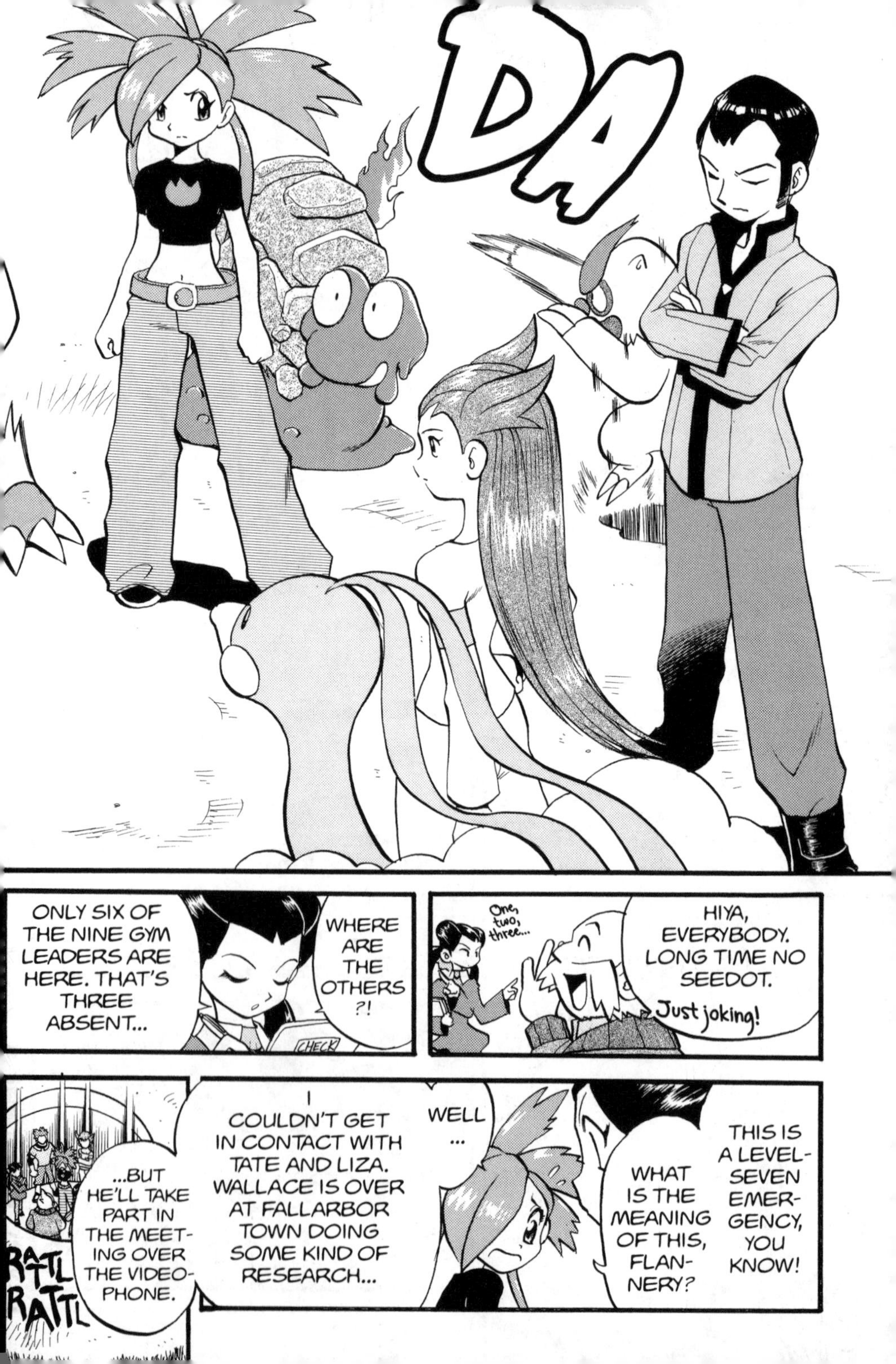
DA
HIYA, EVERYBODY. LONG TIME NO SEEDOT.
Just joking!
One, two, three...
WHERE ARE THE OTHERS ?!
ONLY SIX OF THE NINE GYM LEADERS ARE HERE. THAT'S THREE ABSENT...
CHECK
THIS IS A LEVEL-SEVEN EMERGENCY, YOU KNOW!
WHAT IS THE MEANING OF THIS, FLANNERY?
WELL ...
I COULDN'T GET IN CONTACT WITH TATE AND LIZA. WALLACE IS OVER AT FALLARBOR TOWN DOING SOME KIND OF RESEARCH...
...BUT HE'LL TAKE PART IN THE MEETING OVER THE VIDEOPHONE.
RATTL RATTL

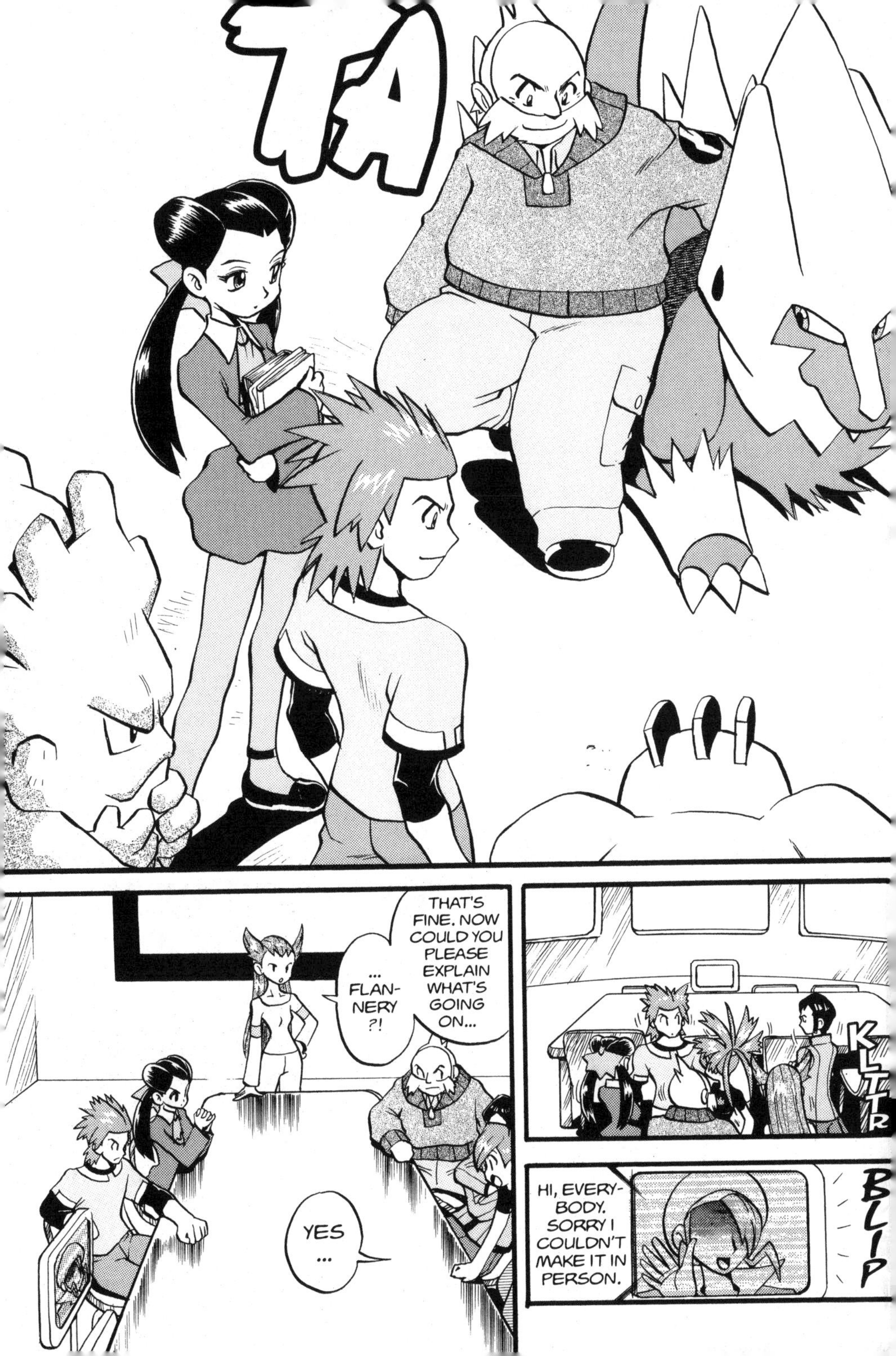
TA
KLTTR
BLIP
HI, EVERYBODY. SORRY I COULDN'T MAKE IT IN PERSON.
THAT'S FINE. NOW COULD YOU PLEASE EXPLAIN WHAT'S GOING ON...
...FLANNERY?!
YES...

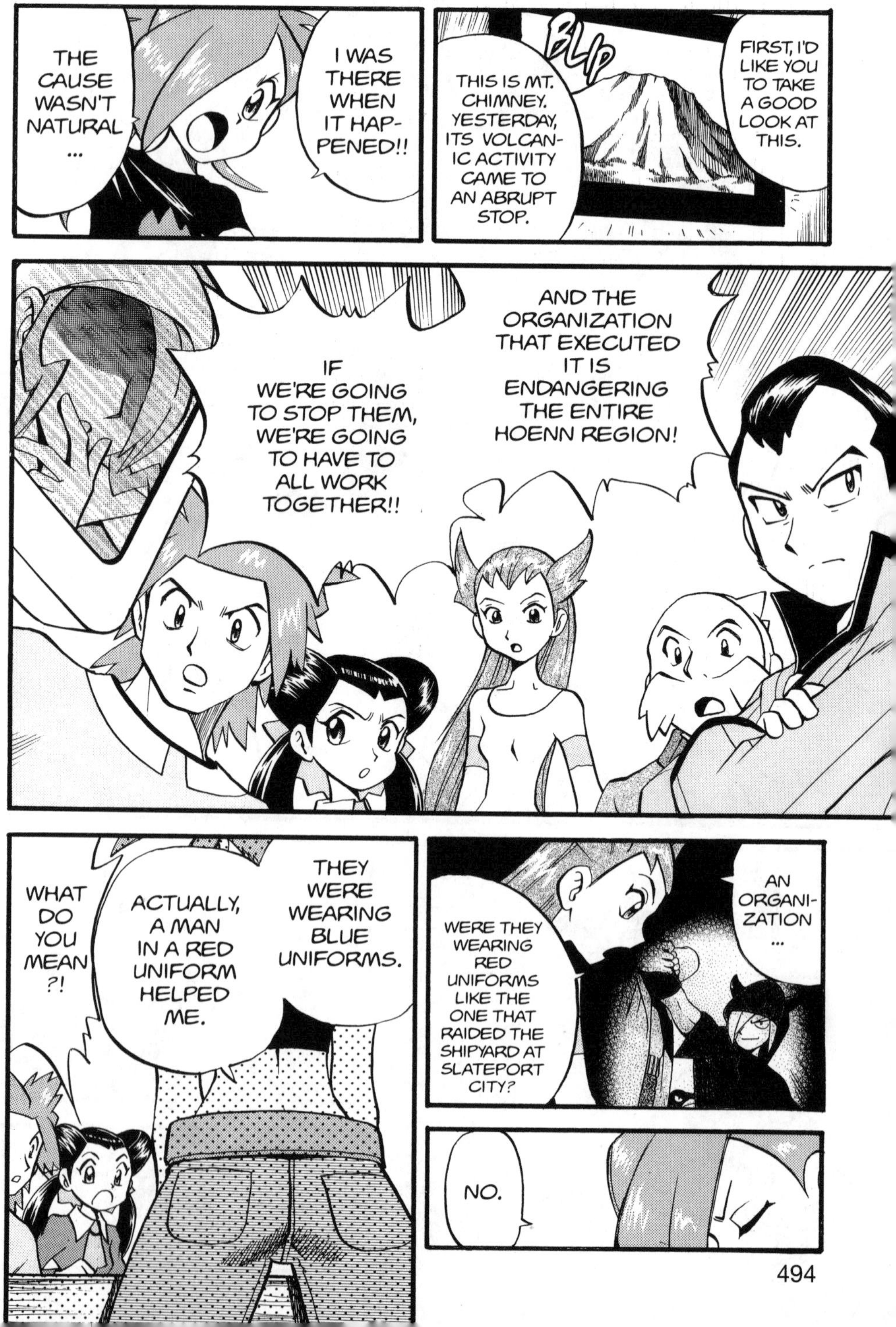
FIRST, I'D LIKE YOU TO TAKE A GOOD LOOK AT THIS.
BLIP
THIS IS MT. CHIMNEY. YESTERDAY, ITS VOLCANIC ACTIVITY CAME TO AN ABRUPT STOP.
I WAS THERE WHEN IT HAPPENED!!
THE CAUSE WASN'T NATURAL...
AND THE ORGANIZATION THAT EXECUTED IT IS ENDANGERING THE ENTIRE HOENN REGION!
IF WE'RE GOING TO STOP THEM, WE'RE GOING TO HAVE TO ALL WORK TOGETHER!!
AN ORGANIZATION...
WERE THEY WEARING RED UNIFORMS LIKE THE ONE THAT RAIDED THE SHIPYARD AT SLATEPORT CITY?
NO.
THEY WERE WEARING BLUE UNIFORMS.
ACTUALLY, A MAN IN A RED UNIFORM HELPED ME.
WHAT DO YOU MEAN?!

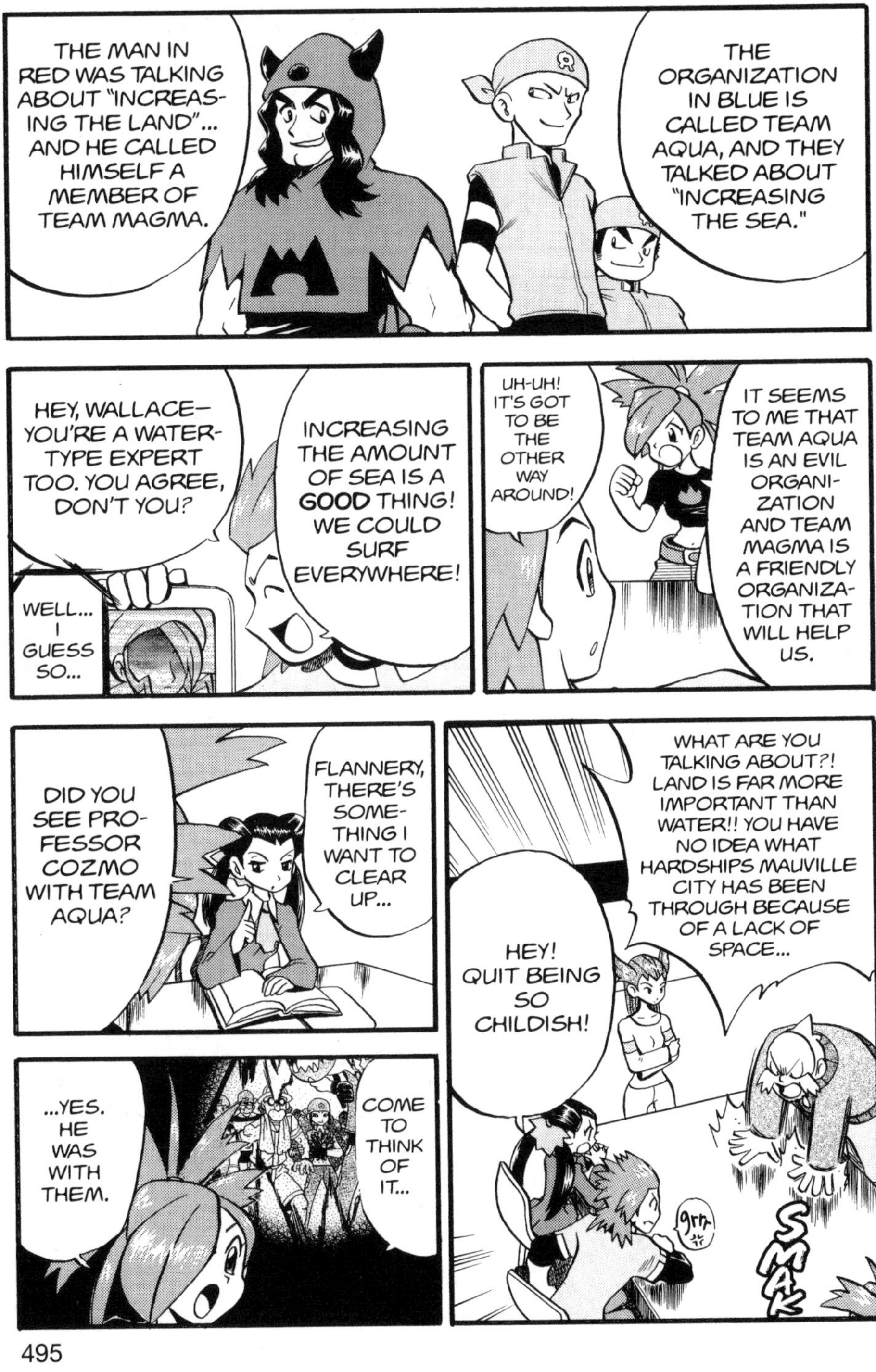
THE ORGANIZATION IN BLUE IS CALLED TEAM AQUA, AND THEY TALKED ABOUT "INCREASING THE SEA."
THE MAN IN RED WAS TALKING ABOUT "INCREASING THE LAND"... AND HE CALLED HIMSELF A MEMBER OF TEAM MAGMA.
IT SEEMS TO ME THAT TEAM AQUA IS AN EVIL ORGANIZATION AND TEAM MAGMA IS A FRIENDLY ORGANIZATION THAT WILL HELP US.
UH-UH! IT'S GOT TO BE THE OTHER WAY AROUND!
INCREASING THE AMOUNT OF SEA IS A **GOOD** THING! WE COULD SURF EVERYWHERE!
HEY, WALLACE— YOU'RE A WATER-TYPE EXPERT TOO. YOU AGREE, DON'T YOU?
WELL... I GUESS SO...
WHAT ARE YOU TALKING ABOUT?! LAND IS FAR MORE IMPORTANT THAN WATER!! YOU HAVE NO IDEA WHAT HARDSHIPS MAUVILLE CITY HAS BEEN THROUGH BECAUSE OF A LACK OF SPACE...
HEY! QUIT BEING SO CHILDISH!
grr
SMAK
FLANNERY, THERE'S SOMETHING I WANT TO CLEAR UP...
DID YOU SEE PROFESSOR COZMO WITH TEAM AQUA?
COME TO THINK OF IT...
...YES. HE WAS WITH THEM.

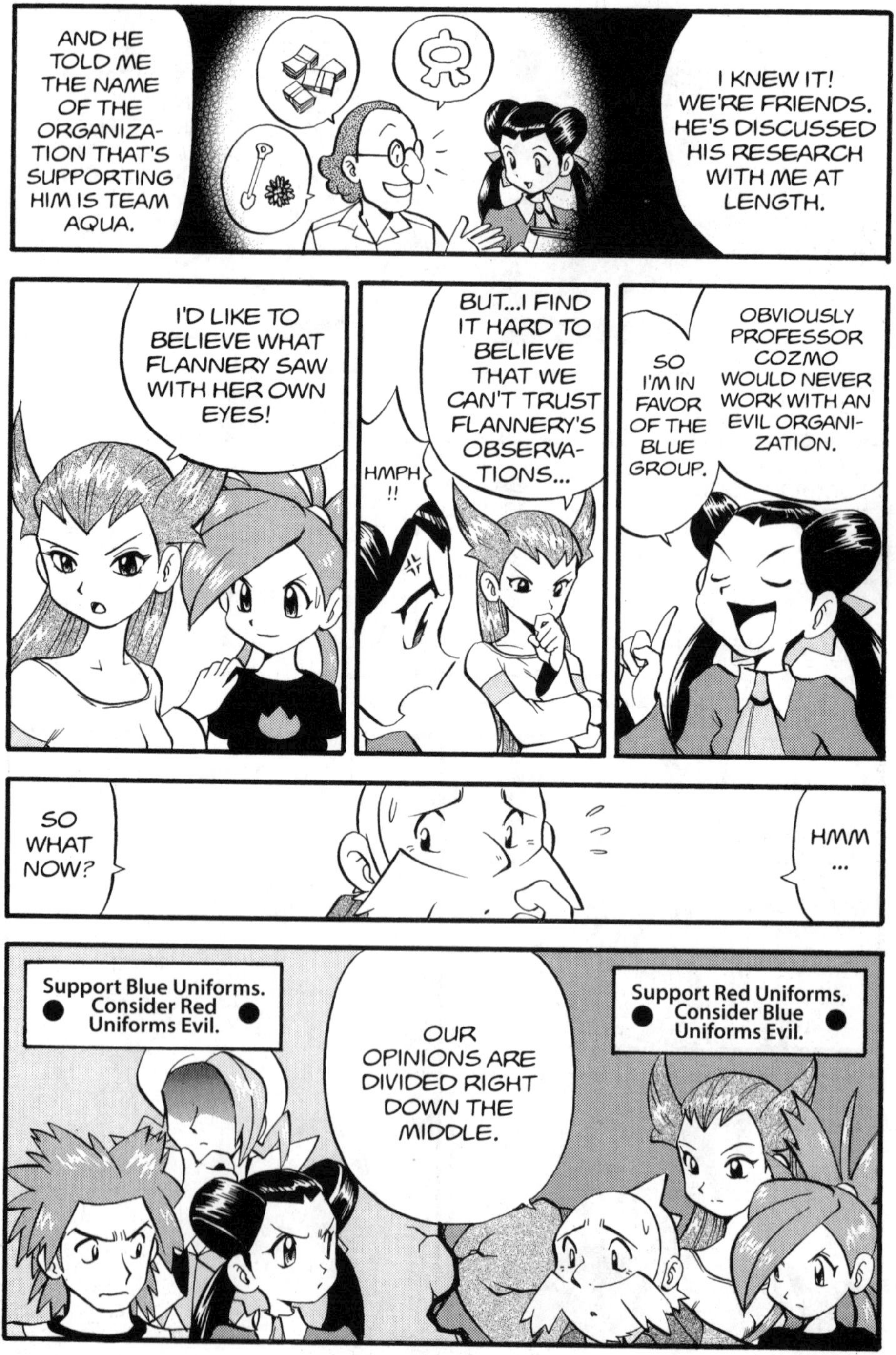
I KNEW IT! WE'RE FRIENDS. HE'S DISCUSSED HIS RESEARCH WITH ME AT LENGTH.
AND HE TOLD ME THE NAME OF THE ORGANIZATION THAT'S SUPPORTING HIM IS TEAM AQUA.
OBVIOUSLY PROFESSOR COZMO WOULD NEVER WORK WITH AN EVIL ORGANIZATION.
SO I'M IN FAVOR OF THE BLUE GROUP.
BUT...I FIND IT HARD TO BELIEVE THAT WE CAN'T TRUST FLANNERY'S OBSERVATIONS...
HMPH !!
I'D LIKE TO BELIEVE WHAT FLANNERY SAW WITH HER OWN EYES!
HMM ...
SO WHAT NOW?
Support Red Uniforms. Consider Blue Uniforms Evil.
OUR OPINIONS ARE DIVIDED RIGHT DOWN THE MIDDLE.
Support Blue Uniforms. Consider Red Uniforms Evil.

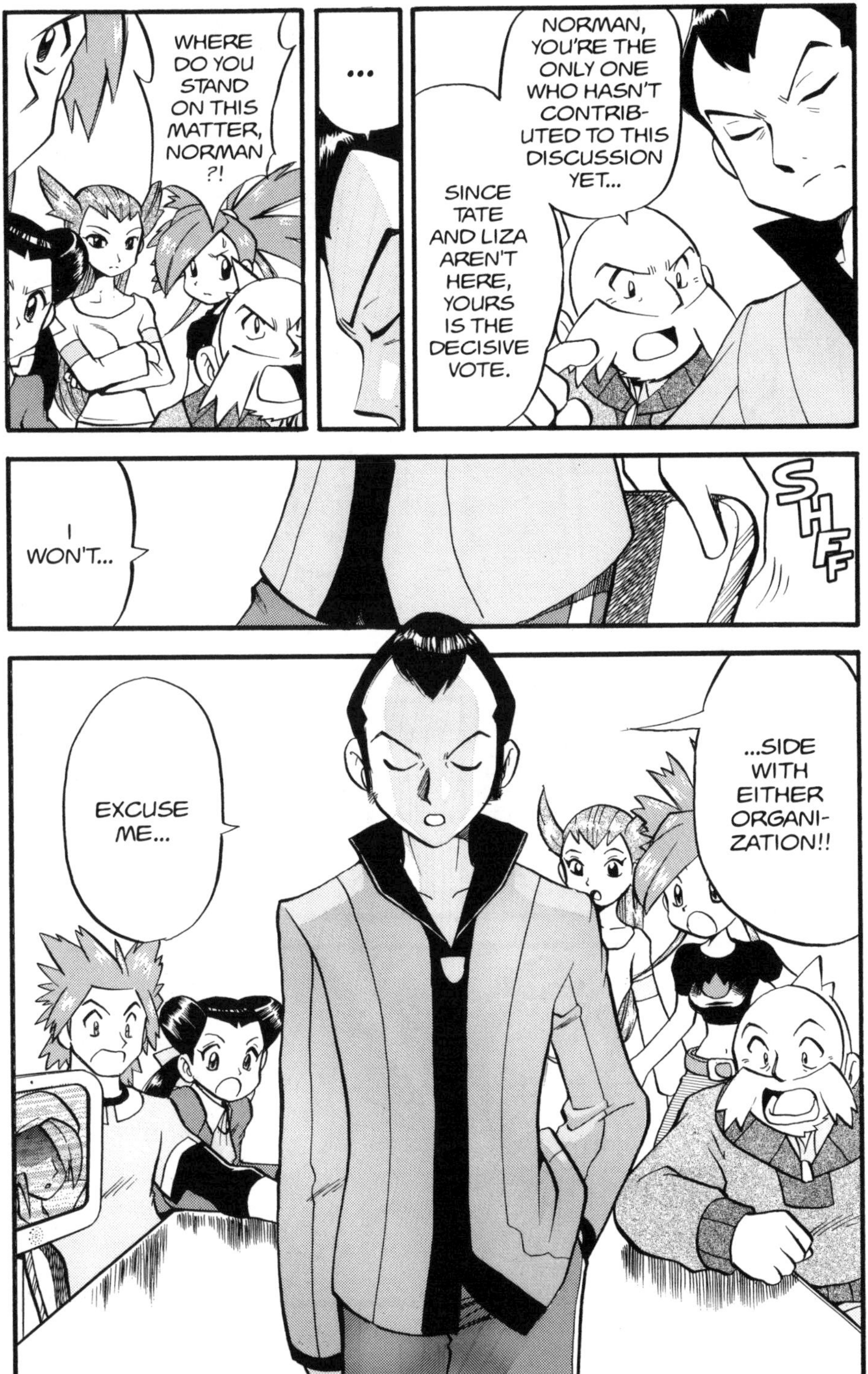

NORMAN, YOU'RE THE ONLY ONE WHO HASN'T CONTRIB-UTED TO THIS DISCUSSION YET...
SINCE TATE AND LIZA AREN'T HERE, YOURS IS THE DECISIVE VOTE.
...
WHERE DO YOU STAND ON THIS MATTER, NORMAN?!
SHFF
I WON'T...
...SIDE WITH EITHER ORGANI-ZATION!!
EXCUSE ME...

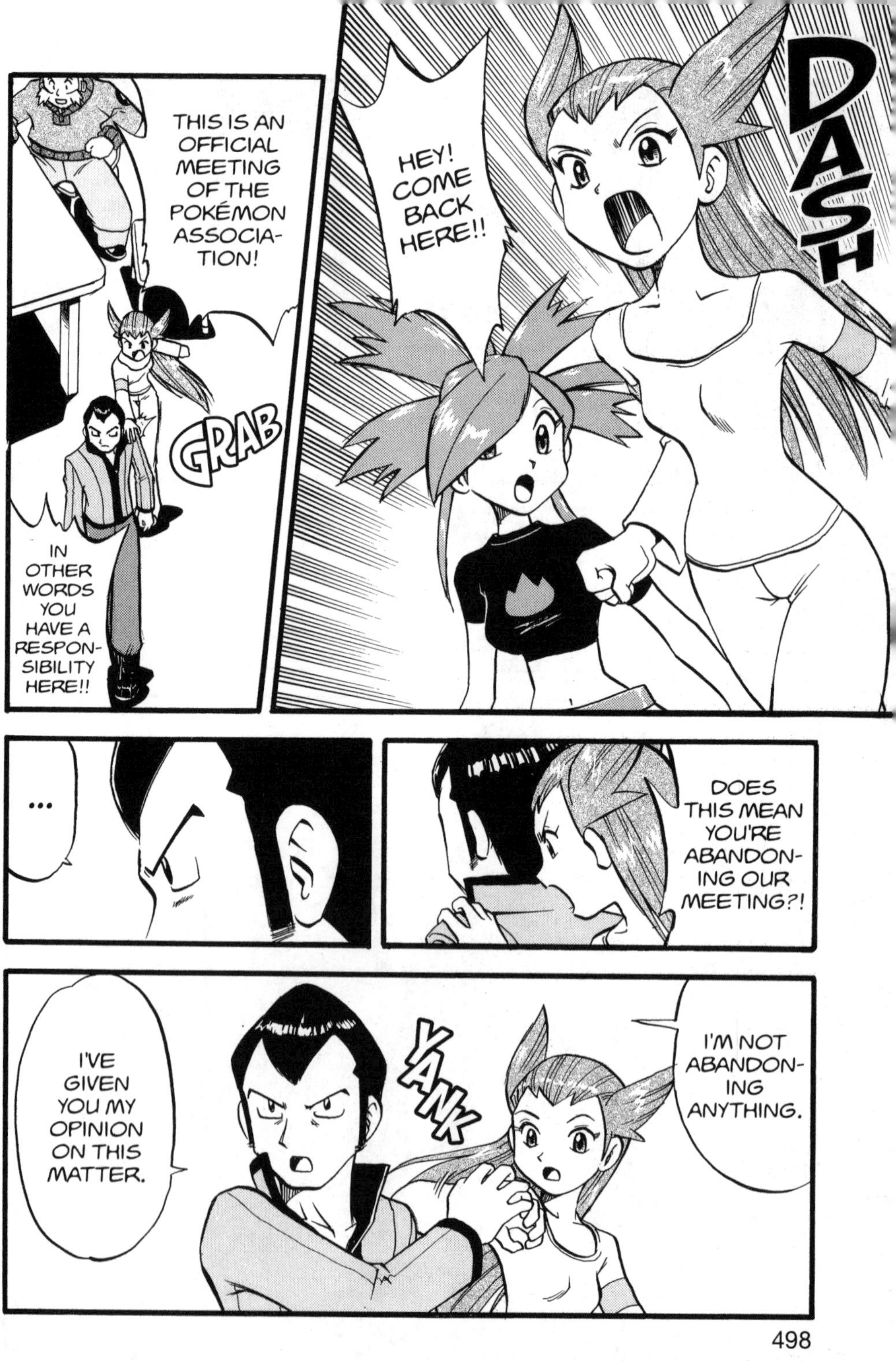
DASH
HEY! COME BACK HERE!!
THIS IS AN OFFICIAL MEETING OF THE POKÉMON ASSOCIATION!
GRAB
IN OTHER WORDS YOU HAVE A RESPONSIBILITY HERE!!
DOES THIS MEAN YOU'RE ABANDONING OUR MEETING?!
...
I'M NOT ABANDONING ANYTHING.
YANK
I'VE GIVEN YOU MY OPINION ON THIS MATTER.

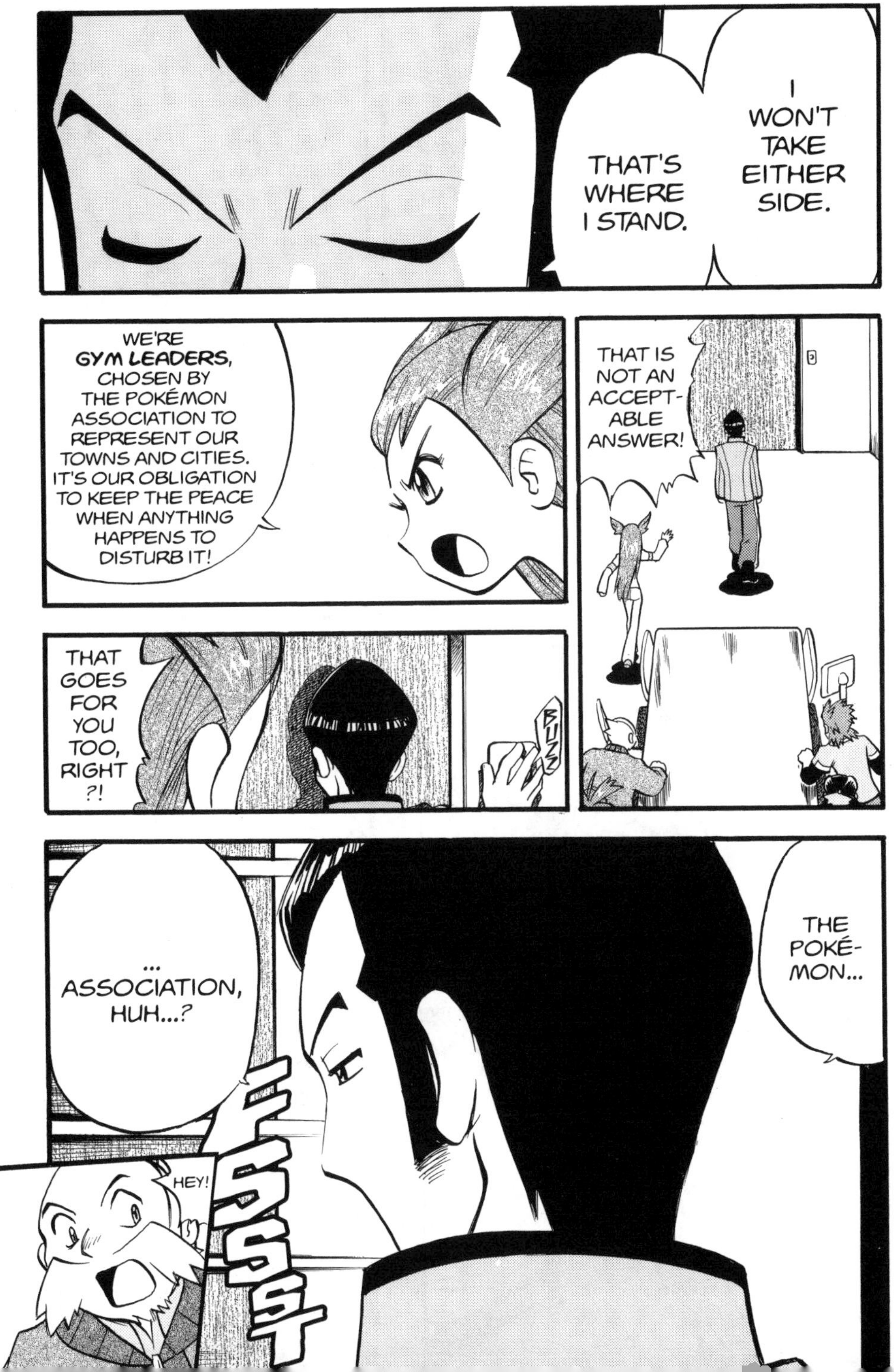
I WON'T TAKE EITHER SIDE.
THAT'S WHERE I STAND.
THAT IS NOT AN ACCEPT-ABLE ANSWER!
WE'RE **GYM LEADERS**, CHOSEN BY THE POKÉMON ASSOCIATION TO REPRESENT OUR TOWNS AND CITIES. IT'S OUR OBLIGATION TO KEEP THE PEACE WHEN ANYTHING HAPPENS TO DISTURB IT!
THAT GOES FOR YOU TOO, RIGHT?!
BUZZ
THE POKÉ-MON...
...ASSOCIATION, HUH...?
HEY!
FSSST

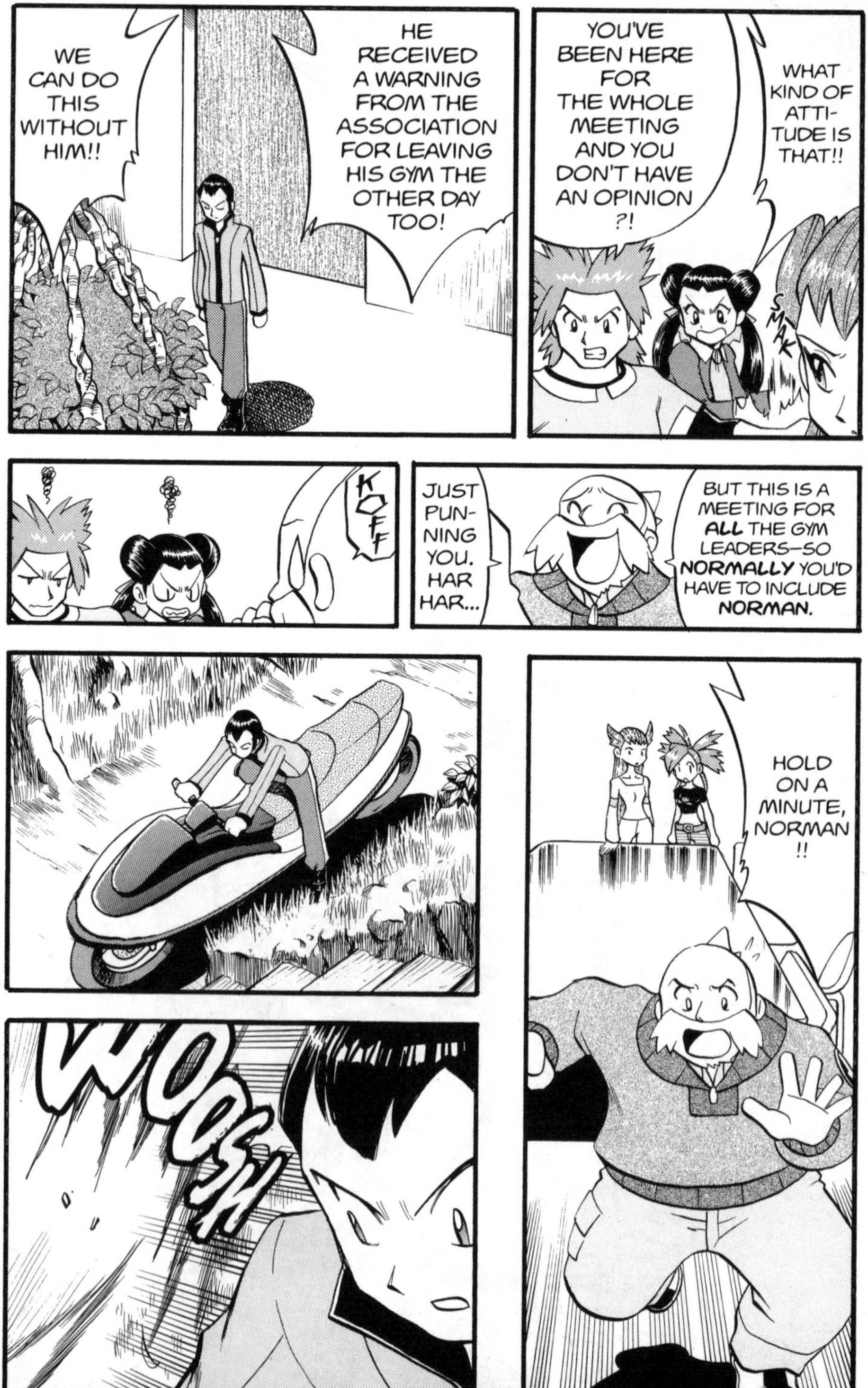
YOU'VE BEEN HERE FOR THE WHOLE MEETING AND YOU DON'T HAVE AN OPINION ?!
WHAT KIND OF ATTI-TUDE IS THAT!!
SMAK
HE RECEIVED A WARNING FROM THE ASSOCIATION FOR LEAVING HIS GYM THE OTHER DAY TOO!
WE CAN DO THIS WITHOUT HIM!!
BUT THIS IS A MEETING FOR **ALL** THE GYM LEADERS—SO **NORMALLY** YOU'D HAVE TO INCLUDE **NORMAN**.
JUST PUN-NING YOU. HAR HAR...
KOFF
HOLD ON A MINUTE, NORMAN !!
WHOOSH

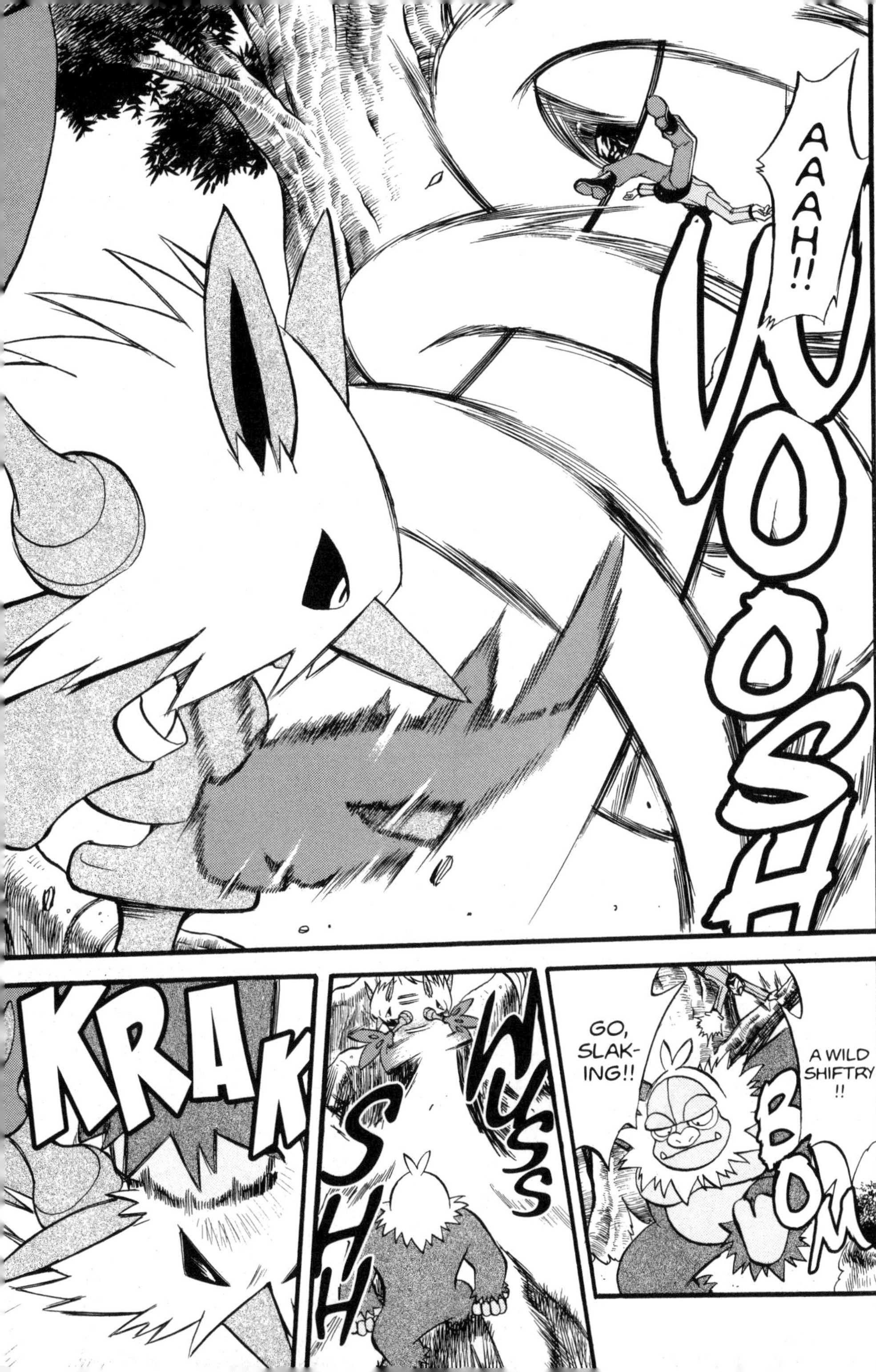
AAAH!!
WOOOSH
A WILD SHIFTRY !!
BOOM
GO, SLAK-ING!!
WUSSS
SHH
KRAK

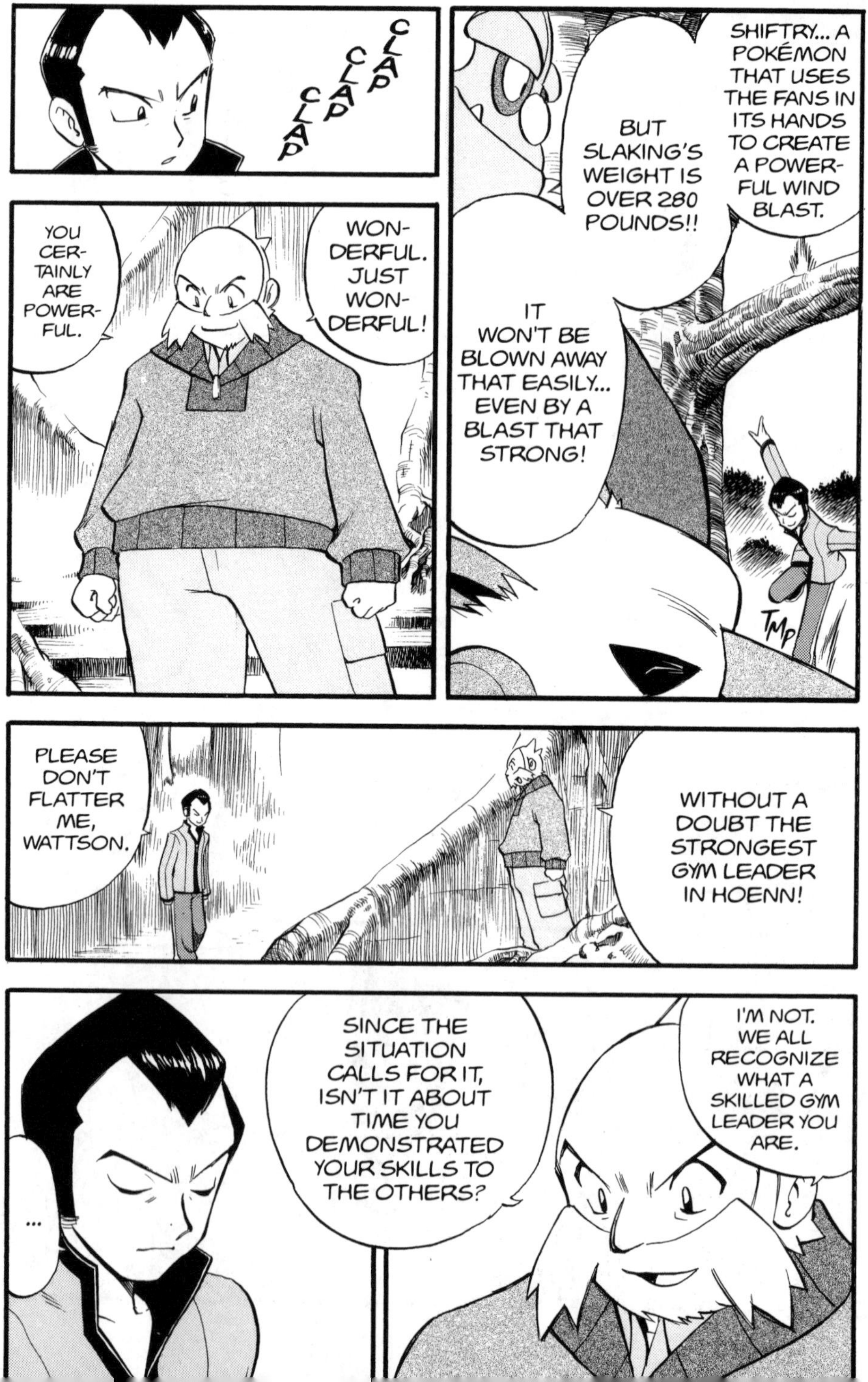
SHIFTRY... A POKÉMON THAT USES THE FANS IN ITS HANDS TO CREATE A POWERFUL WIND BLAST.
BUT SLAKING'S WEIGHT IS OVER 280 POUNDS!!
IT WON'T BE BLOWN AWAY THAT EASILY... EVEN BY A BLAST THAT STRONG!
TMP
CLAP CLAP CLAP
WONDERFUL. JUST WONDERFUL!
YOU CERTAINLY ARE POWERFUL.
WITHOUT A DOUBT THE STRONGEST GYM LEADER IN HOENN!
PLEASE DON'T FLATTER ME, WATTSON.
I'M NOT. WE ALL RECOGNIZE WHAT A SKILLED GYM LEADER YOU ARE.
SINCE THE SITUATION CALLS FOR IT, ISN'T IT ABOUT TIME YOU DEMONSTRATED YOUR SKILLS TO THE OTHERS?
...

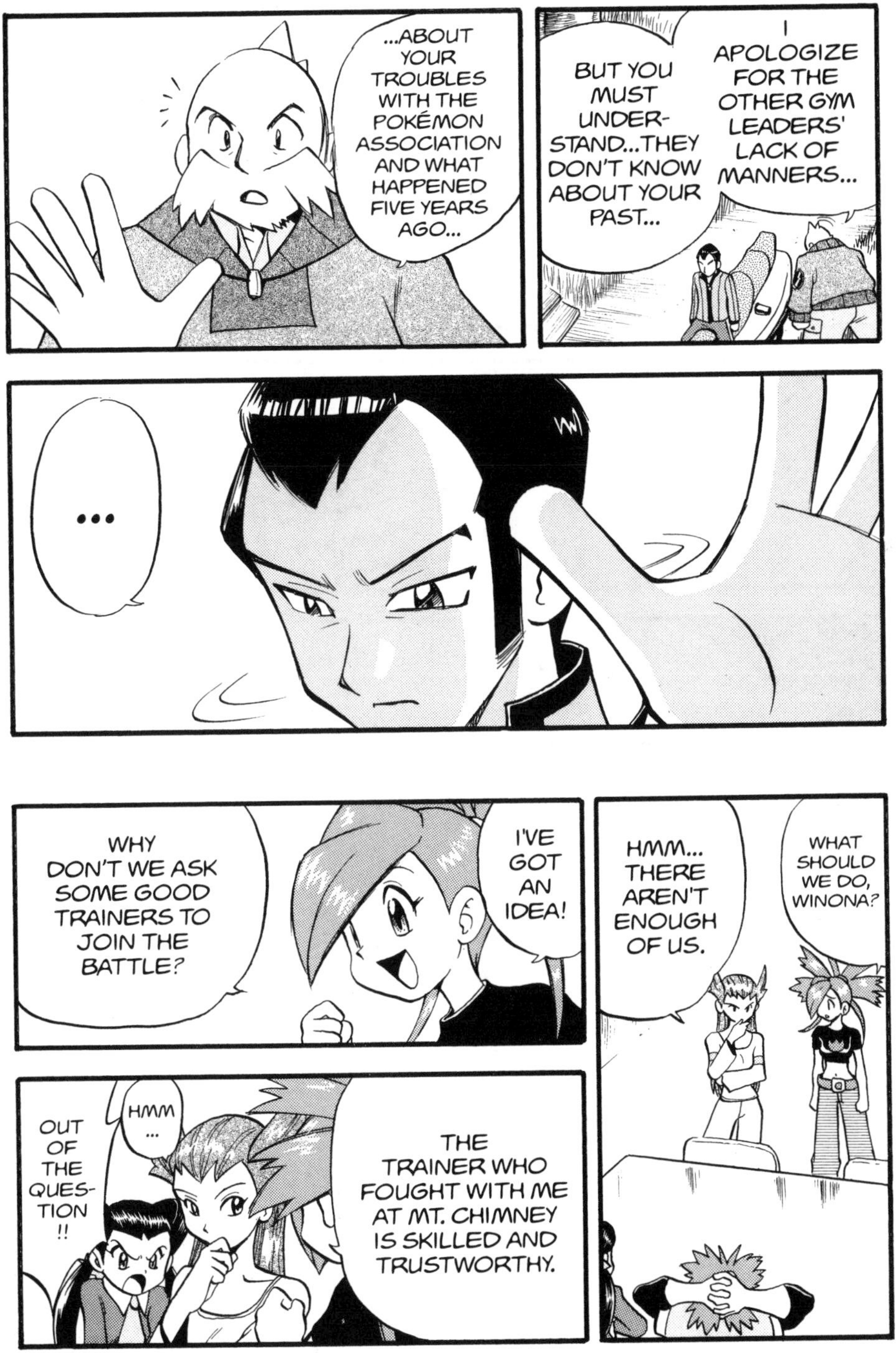
I APOLOGIZE FOR THE OTHER GYM LEADERS' LACK OF MANNERS...
BUT YOU MUST UNDER-STAND...THEY DON'T KNOW ABOUT YOUR PAST...
...ABOUT YOUR TROUBLES WITH THE POKÉMON ASSOCIATION AND WHAT HAPPENED FIVE YEARS AGO...
...
WHAT SHOULD WE DO, WINONA?
HMM... THERE AREN'T ENOUGH OF US.
I'VE GOT AN IDEA!
WHY DON'T WE ASK SOME GOOD TRAINERS TO JOIN THE BATTLE?
THE TRAINER WHO FOUGHT WITH ME AT MT. CHIMNEY IS SKILLED AND TRUSTWORTHY.
HMM ...
OUT OF THE QUES-TION !!

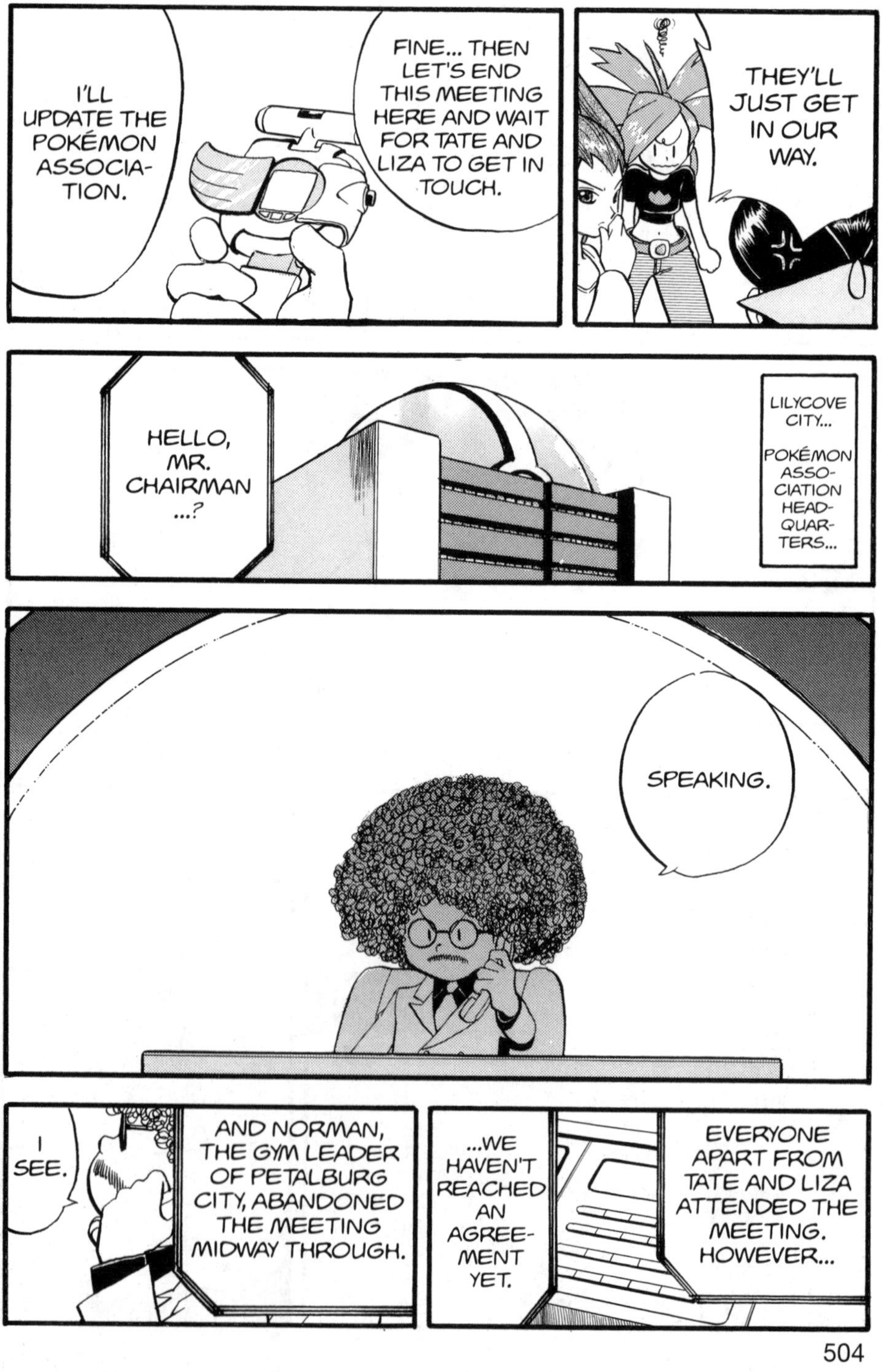
THEY'LL JUST GET IN OUR WAY.
FINE... THEN LET'S END THIS MEETING HERE AND WAIT FOR TATE AND LIZA TO GET IN TOUCH.
I'LL UPDATE THE POKÉMON ASSOCIA-TION.
LILYCOVE CITY... POKÉMON ASSO-CIATION HEAD-QUAR-TERS...
HELLO, MR. CHAIRMAN ...?
SPEAKING.
EVERYONE APART FROM TATE AND LIZA ATTENDED THE MEETING. HOWEVER...
...WE HAVEN'T REACHED AN AGREE-MENT YET.
AND NORMAN, THE GYM LEADER OF PETALBURG CITY, ABANDONED THE MEETING MIDWAY THROUGH.
I SEE.

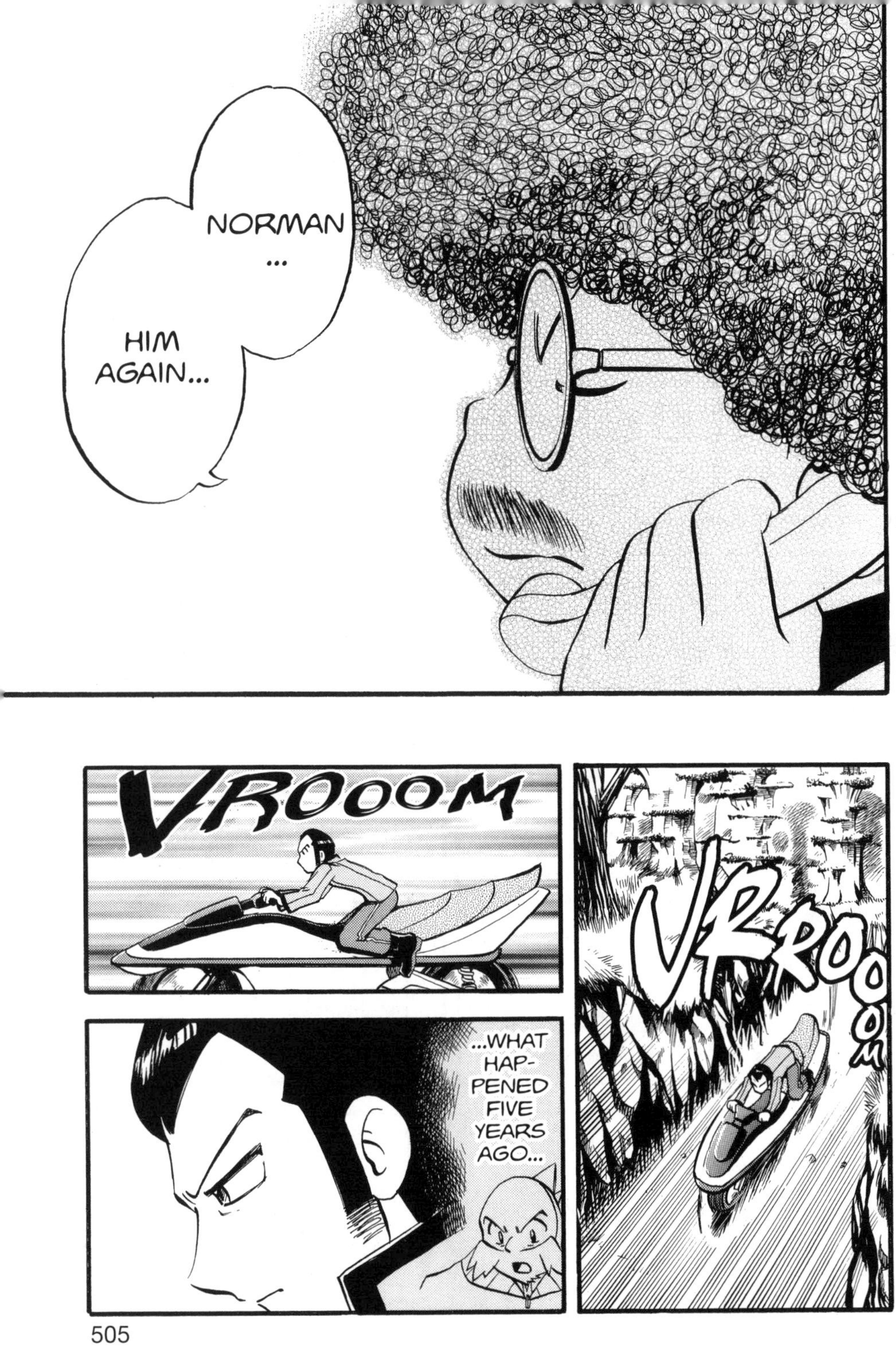
NORMAN ...
HIM AGAIN...
VRROOOOM
VROOOM
...WHAT HAP-PENED FIVE YEARS AGO...

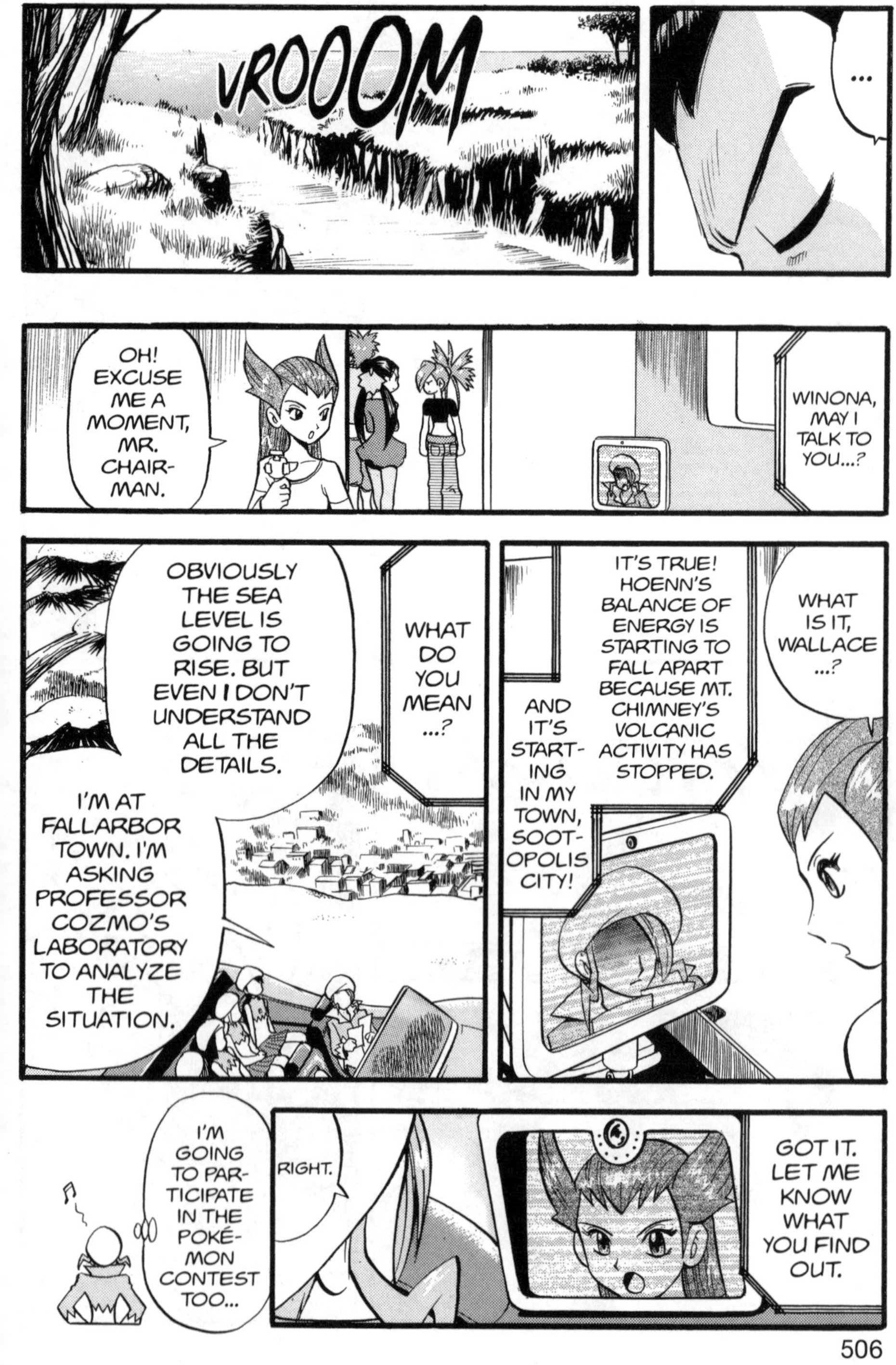
...
VROOOM
WINONA, MAY I TALK TO YOU...?
OH! EXCUSE ME A MOMENT, MR. CHAIRMAN.
WHAT IS IT, WALLACE...?
IT'S TRUE! HOENN'S BALANCE OF ENERGY IS STARTING TO FALL APART BECAUSE MT. CHIMNEY'S VOLCANIC ACTIVITY HAS STOPPED.
AND IT'S STARTING IN MY TOWN, SOOTOPOLIS CITY!
WHAT DO YOU MEAN...?
OBVIOUSLY THE SEA LEVEL IS GOING TO RISE. BUT EVEN I DON'T UNDERSTAND ALL THE DETAILS.
I'M AT FALLARBOR TOWN. I'M ASKING PROFESSOR COZMO'S LABORATORY TO ANALYZE THE SITUATION.
GOT IT. LET ME KNOW WHAT YOU FIND OUT.
RIGHT.
I'M GOING TO PARTICIPATE IN THE POKÉMON CONTEST TOO...

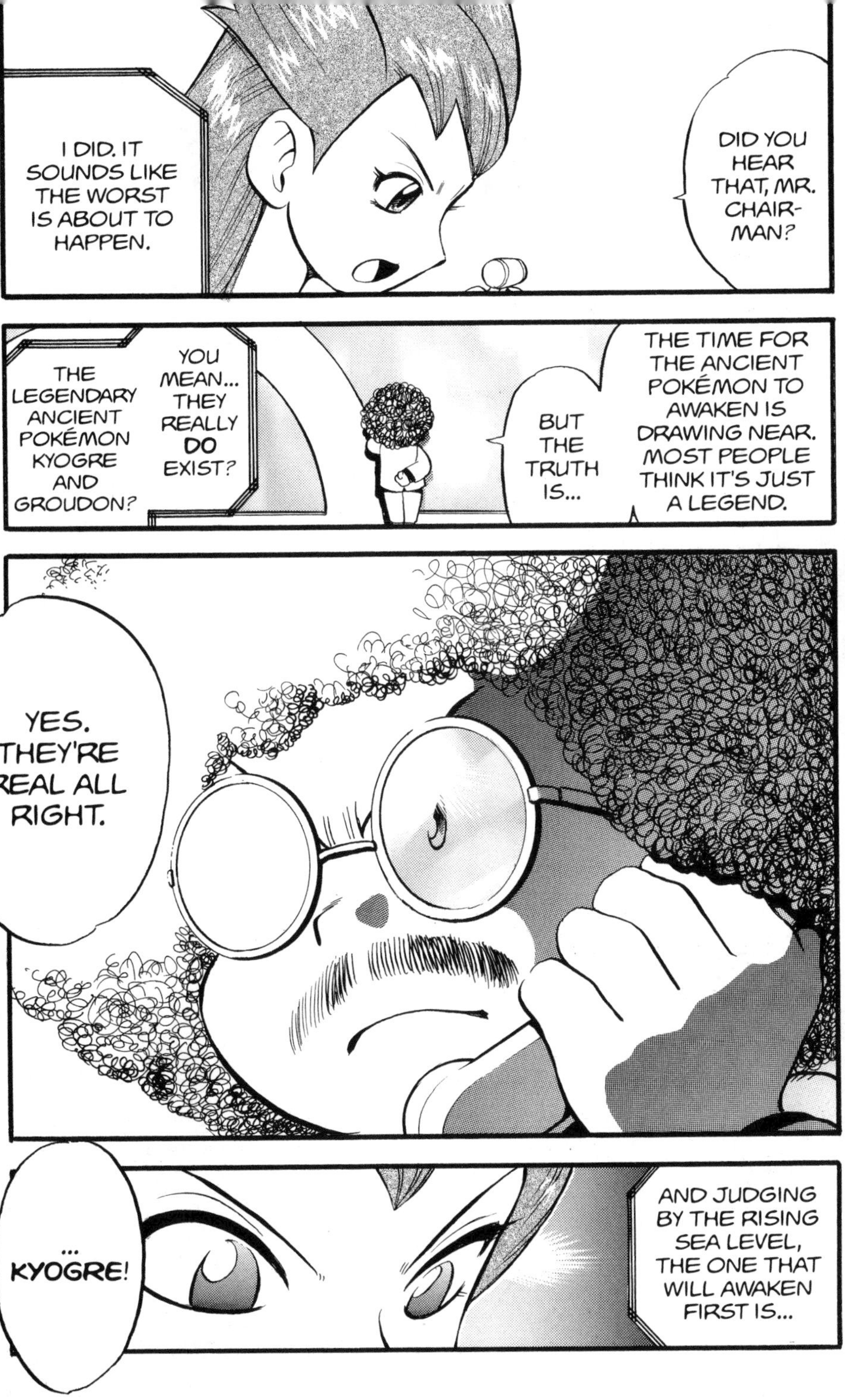
DID YOU HEAR THAT, MR. CHAIRMAN?
I DID. IT SOUNDS LIKE THE WORST IS ABOUT TO HAPPEN.
THE TIME FOR THE ANCIENT POKÉMON TO AWAKEN IS DRAWING NEAR. MOST PEOPLE THINK IT'S JUST A LEGEND.
BUT THE TRUTH IS...
YOU MEAN... THEY REALLY **DO** EXIST?
THE LEGENDARY ANCIENT POKÉMON KYOGRE AND GROUDON?
YES. THEY'RE REAL ALL RIGHT.
AND JUDGING BY THE RISING SEA LEVEL, THE ONE THAT WILL AWAKEN FIRST IS...
...**KYOGRE!**

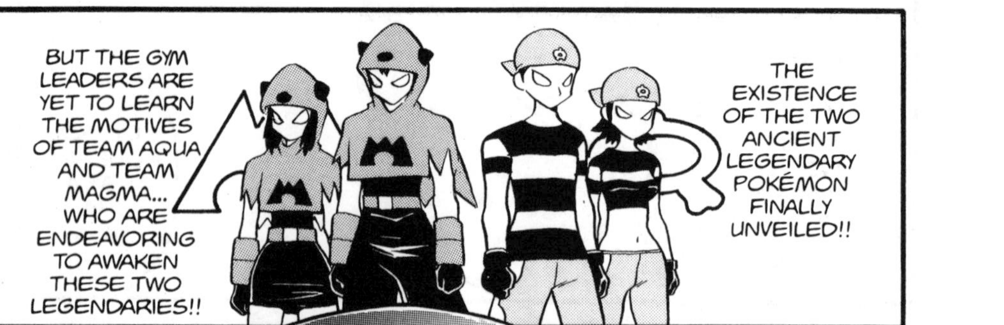
THE EXISTENCE OF THE TWO ANCIENT LEGENDARY POKÉMON FINALLY UNVEILED!!
BUT THE GYM LEADERS ARE YET TO LEARN THE MOTIVES OF TEAM AQUA AND TEAM MAGMA... WHO ARE ENDEAVORING TO AWAKEN THESE TWO LEGENDARIES!!
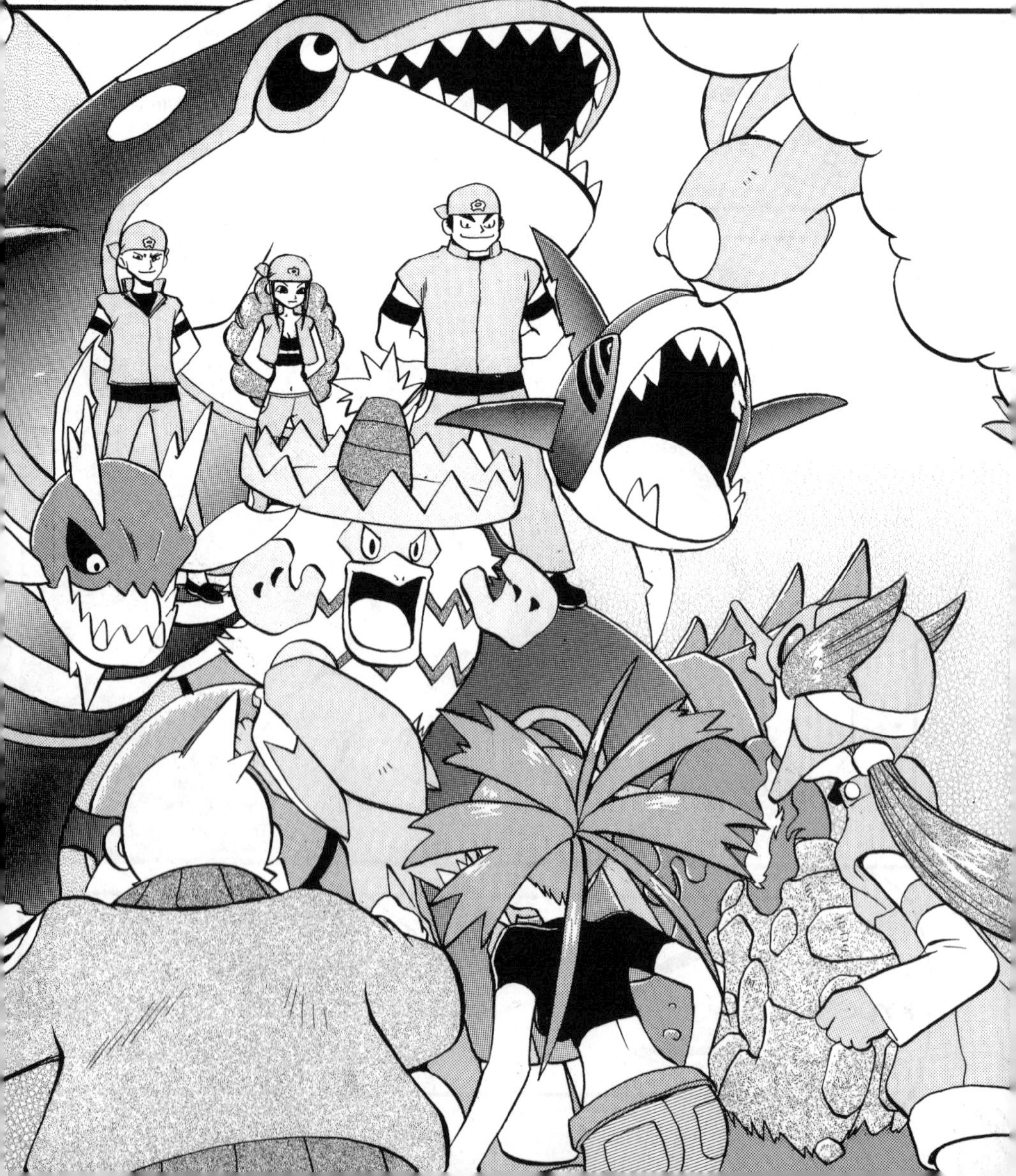

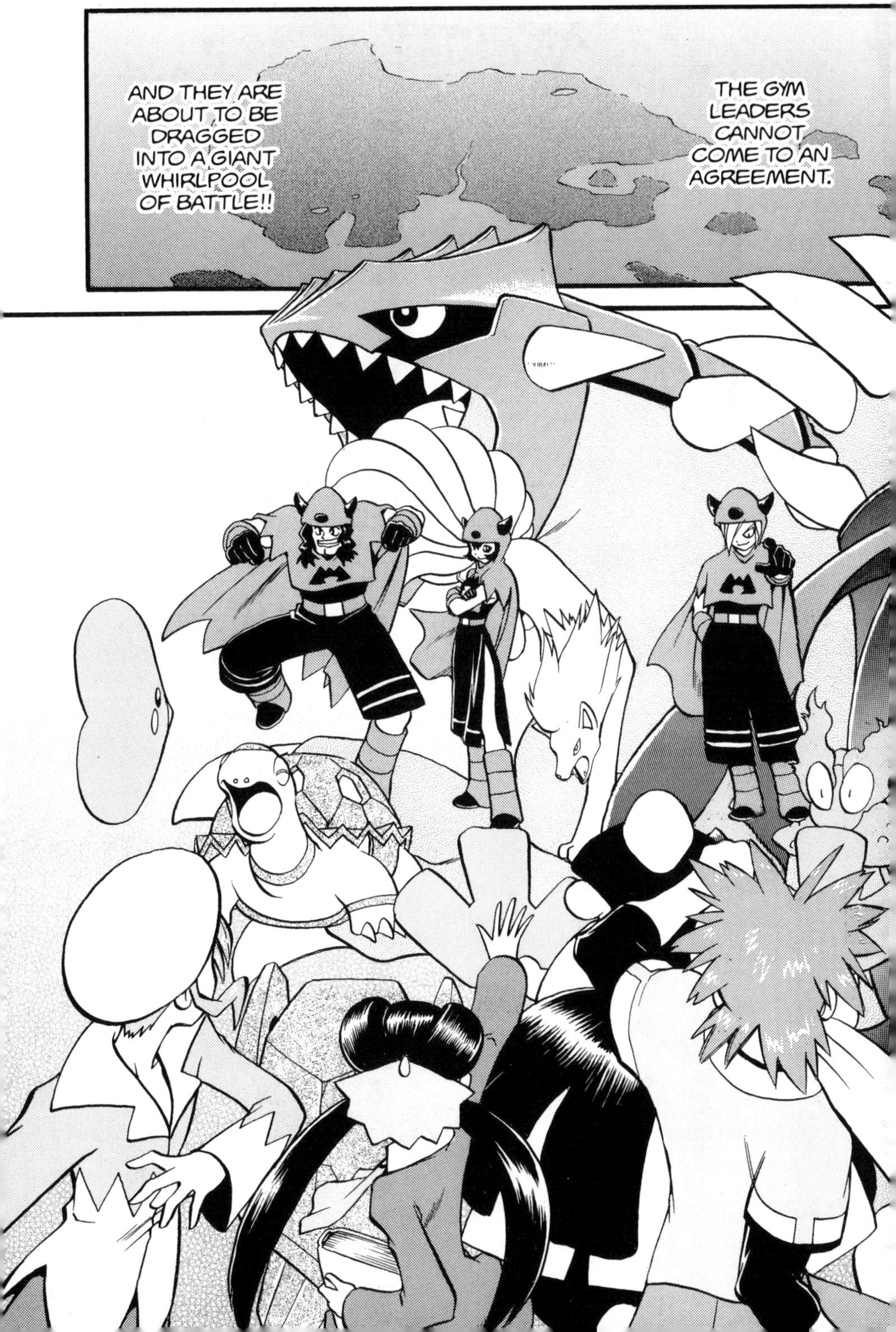
THE GYM LEADERS CANNOT COME TO AN AGREEMENT.
AND THEY ARE ABOUT TO BE DRAGGED INTO A GIANT WHIRLPOOL OF BATTLE!!

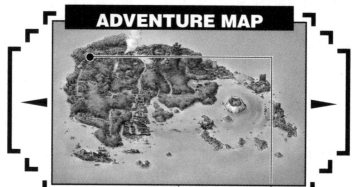

ADVENTURE MAP

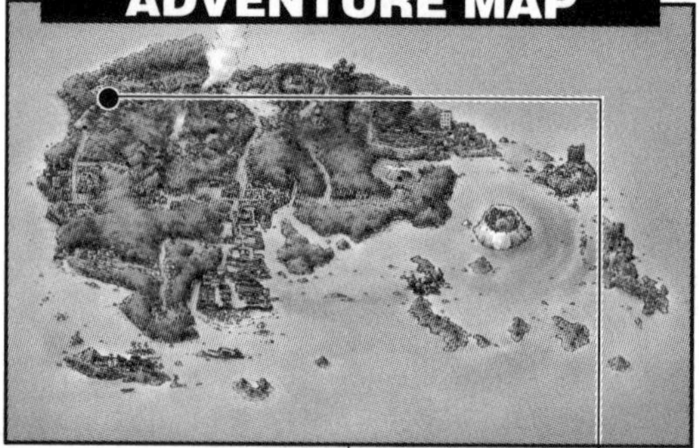

SAPPHIRE

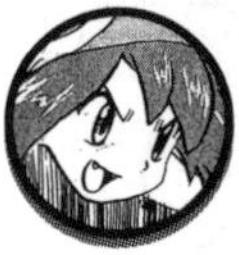

RUBY

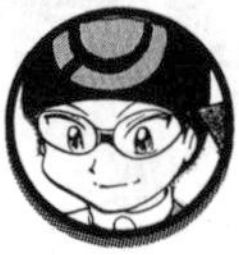

SAPPHIRE	RUBY
Mt. Chimney	Route 117
Jagged Pass	Verdanturf Town
	Rusturf Tunnel
	Rustboro City
	Route 115
	Route 114

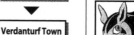

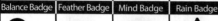

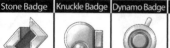

SAPPHIRE

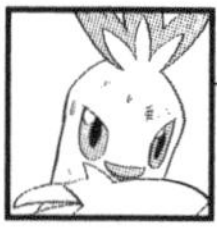

CHIC
Combusken ♀
Lv33

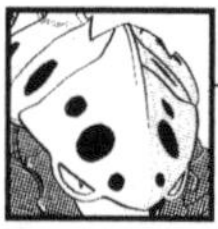

RONO
Lairon ♂
Lv41

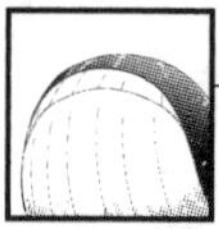

LORRY
Wailord ♂
Lv46

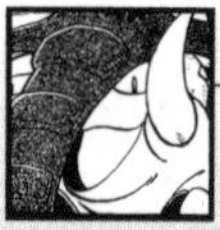

PHADO
Donphan ♂
Lv44

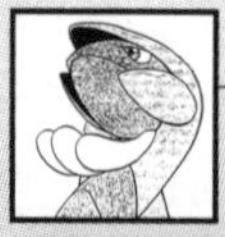

TROPPY
Tropius ♂
Lv43

RUBY

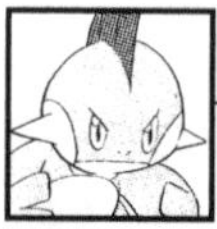

MUMU
Marshtomp ♂

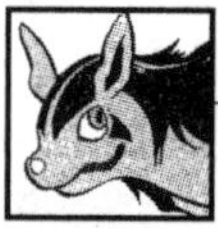

NANA
Mightyena ♀

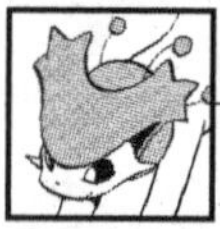

KIKI
Delcatty ♀

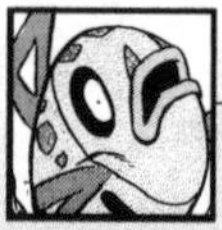

FEEFEE
Feebas ♀

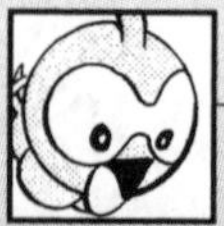

FOFO
Castform ♀

Stone Badge	Knuckle Badge	Dynamo Badge	Heat Badge
Balance Badge	Feather Badge	Mind Badge	Rain Badge

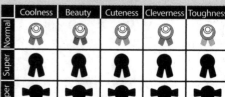

	Coolness	Beauty	Cuteness	Cleverness	Toughness
Normal					
Super					
Hyper					
Master					

● Adventure 223 ●
I More than Like You, Luvdisc, Part 1

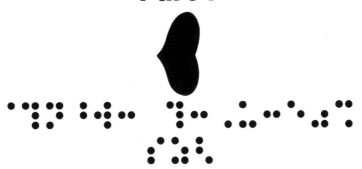

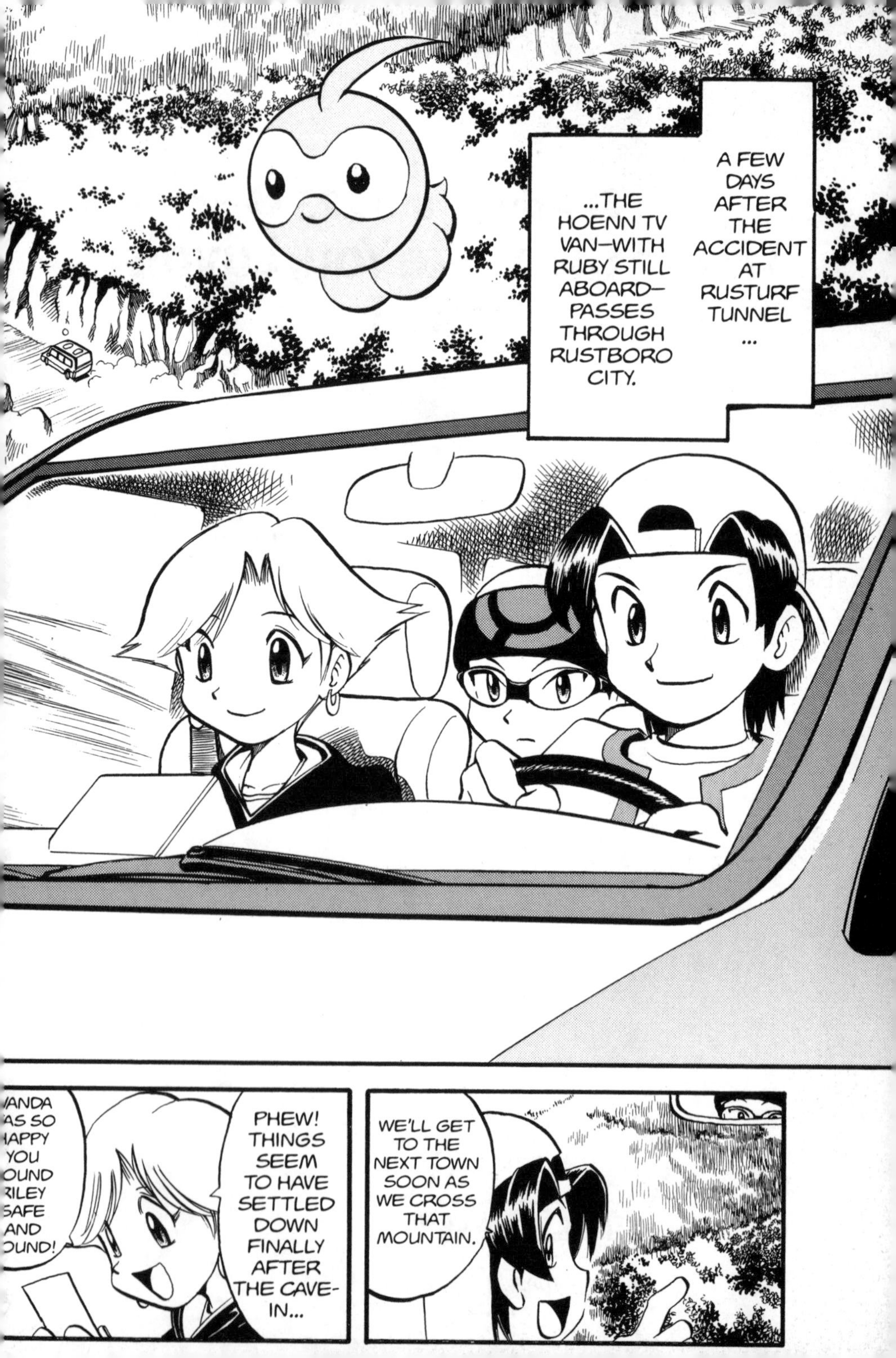
A FEW DAYS AFTER THE ACCIDENT AT RUSTURF TUNNEL ...
...THE HOENN TV VAN—WITH RUBY STILL ABOARD—PASSES THROUGH RUSTBORO CITY.
WE'LL GET TO THE NEXT TOWN SOON AS WE CROSS THAT MOUNTAIN.
PHEW! THINGS SEEM TO HAVE SETTLED DOWN FINALLY AFTER THE CAVE-IN...
ANDA AS SO HAPPY YOU OUND RILEY SAFE AND OUND!

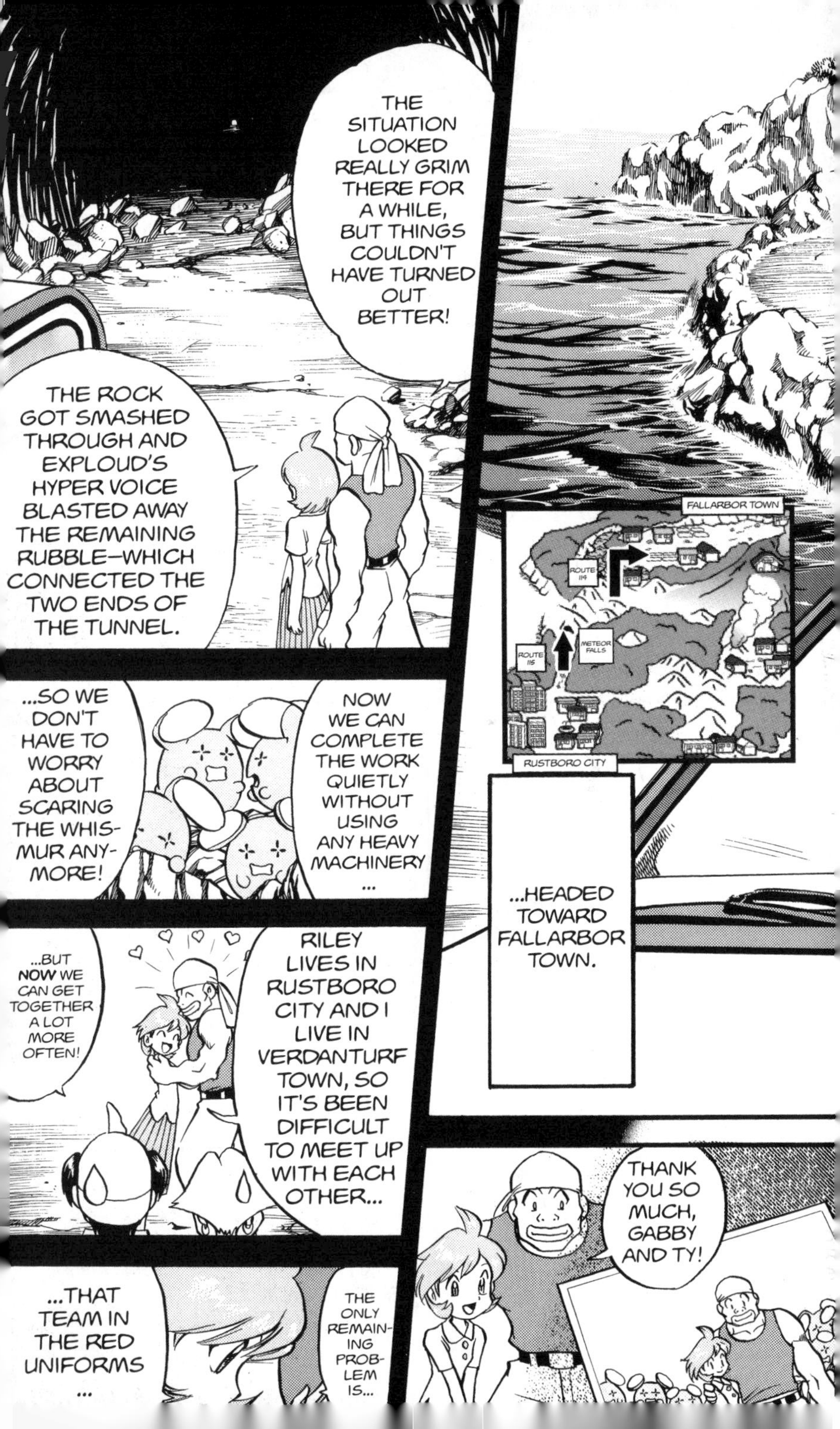
FALLARBOR TOWN
ROUTE 114
ROUTE 115
METEOR FALLS
RUSTBORO CITY
...HEADED TOWARD FALLARBOR TOWN.
THANK YOU SO MUCH, GABBY AND TY!
THE SITUATION LOOKED REALLY GRIM THERE FOR A WHILE, BUT THINGS COULDN'T HAVE TURNED OUT BETTER!
THE ROCK GOT SMASHED THROUGH AND EXPLOUD'S HYPER VOICE BLASTED AWAY THE REMAINING RUBBLE—WHICH CONNECTED THE TWO ENDS OF THE TUNNEL.
NOW WE CAN COMPLETE THE WORK QUIETLY WITHOUT USING ANY HEAVY MACHINERY...
...SO WE DON'T HAVE TO WORRY ABOUT SCARING THE WHIS-MUR ANY-MORE!
RILEY LIVES IN RUSTBORO CITY AND I LIVE IN VERDANTURF TOWN, SO IT'S BEEN DIFFICULT TO MEET UP WITH EACH OTHER...
...BUT **NOW** WE CAN GET TOGETHER A LOT MORE OFTEN!
THE ONLY REMAIN-ING PROB-LEM IS...
...THAT TEAM IN THE RED UNIFORMS...

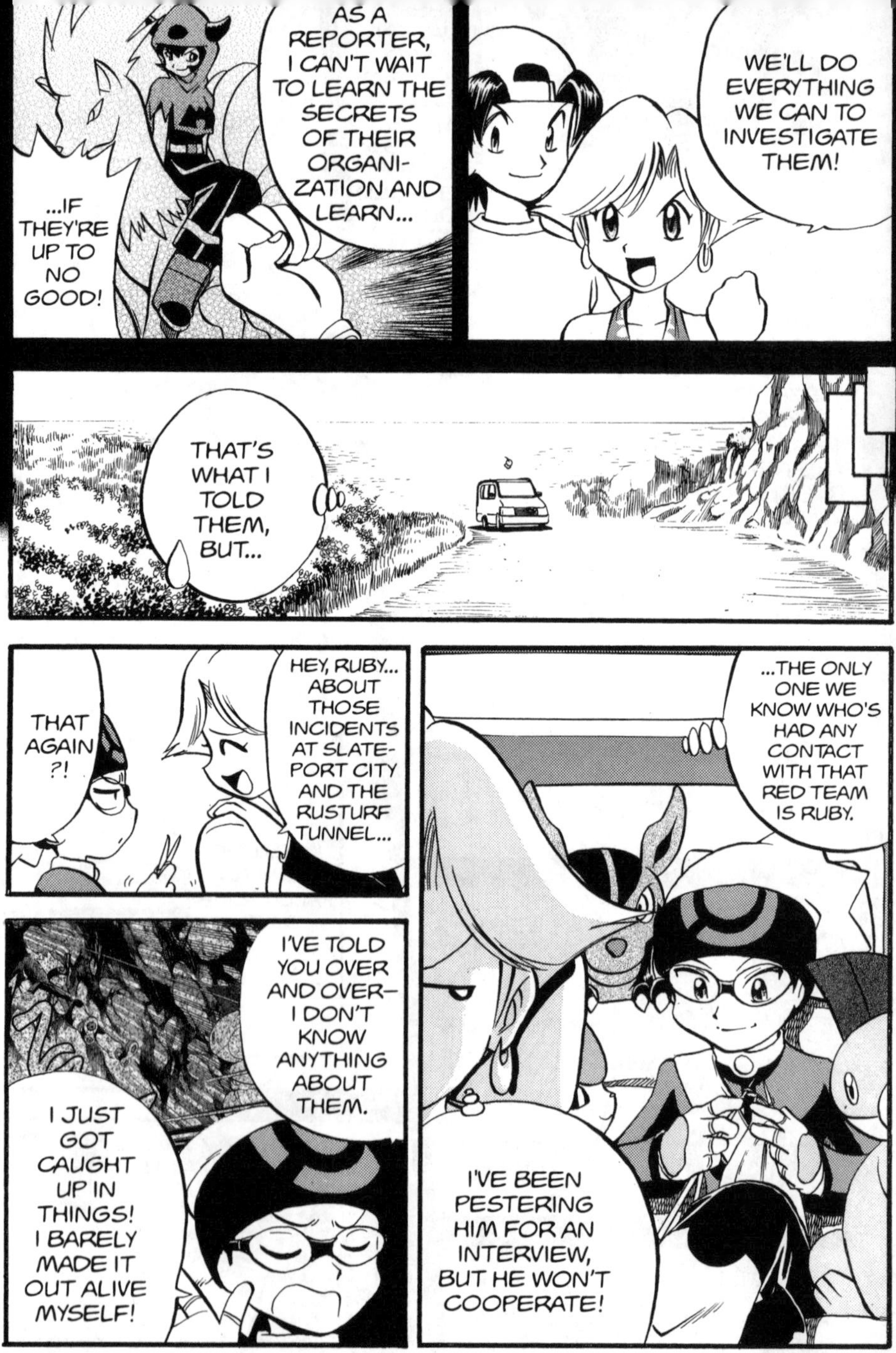
WE'LL DO EVERYTHING WE CAN TO INVESTIGATE THEM!
AS A REPORTER, I CAN'T WAIT TO LEARN THE SECRETS OF THEIR ORGANI-ZATION AND LEARN...
...IF THEY'RE UP TO NO GOOD!
THAT'S WHAT I TOLD THEM, BUT...
...THE ONLY ONE WE KNOW WHO'S HAD ANY CONTACT WITH THAT RED TEAM IS RUBY.
I'VE BEEN PESTERING HIM FOR AN INTERVIEW, BUT HE WON'T COOPERATE!
HEY, RUBY... ABOUT THOSE INCIDENTS AT SLATE-PORT CITY AND THE RUSTURF TUNNEL...
THAT AGAIN?!
I'VE TOLD YOU OVER AND OVER—I DON'T KNOW ANYTHING ABOUT THEM.
I JUST GOT CAUGHT UP IN THINGS! I BARELY MADE IT OUT ALIVE MYSELF!

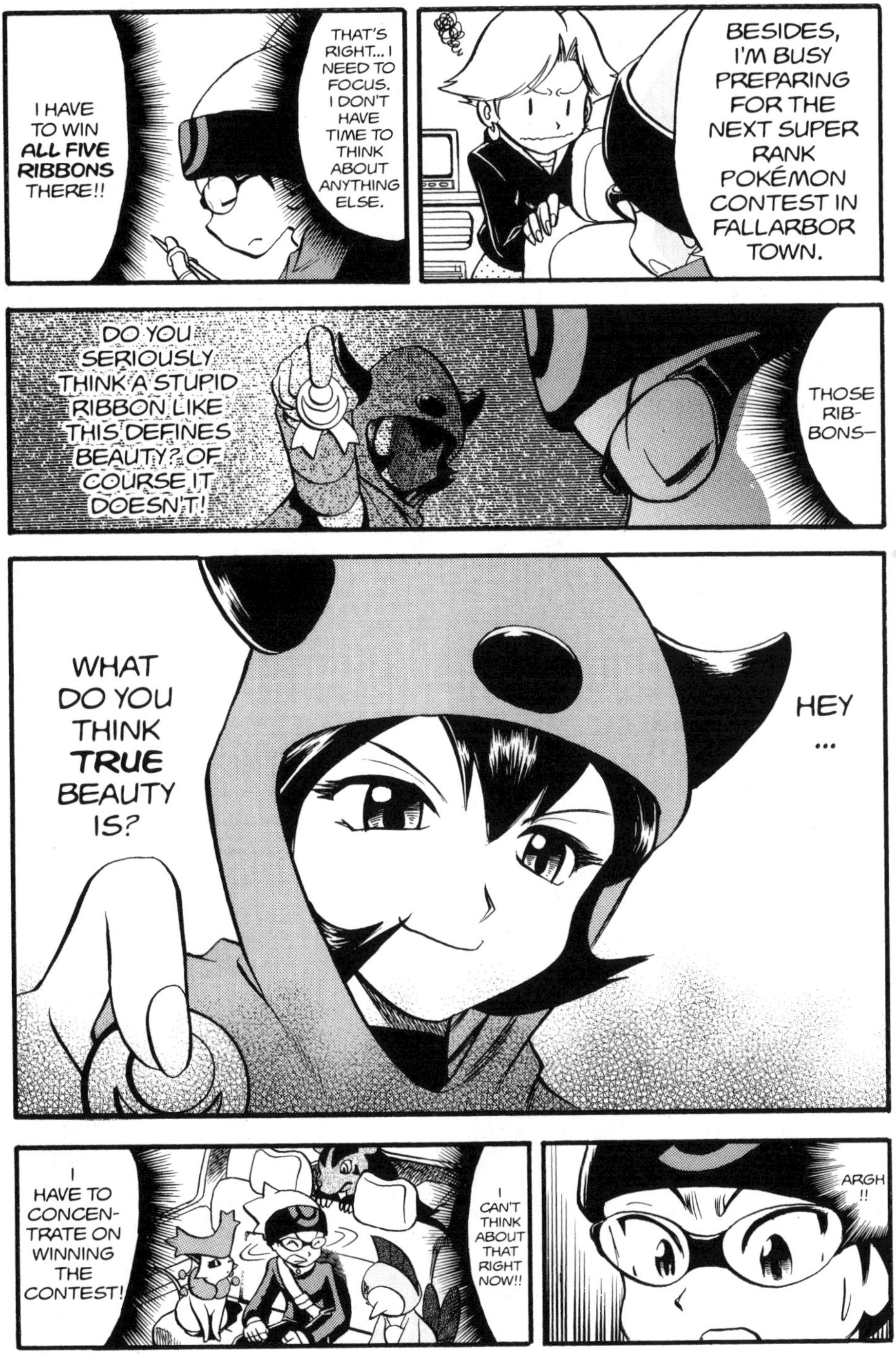
BESIDES, I'M BUSY PREPARING FOR THE NEXT SUPER RANK POKÉMON CONTEST IN FALLARBOR TOWN.
THAT'S RIGHT... I NEED TO FOCUS. I DON'T HAVE TIME TO THINK ABOUT ANYTHING ELSE.
I HAVE TO WIN **ALL FIVE RIBBONS** THERE!!
THOSE RIB-BONS—
DO YOU SERIOUSLY THINK A STUPID RIBBON LIKE THIS DEFINES BEAUTY? OF COURSE IT DOESN'T!
HEY ...
WHAT DO YOU THINK **TRUE** BEAUTY IS?
ARGH !!
I CAN'T THINK ABOUT THAT RIGHT NOW!!
I HAVE TO CONCEN-TRATE ON WINNING THE CONTEST!

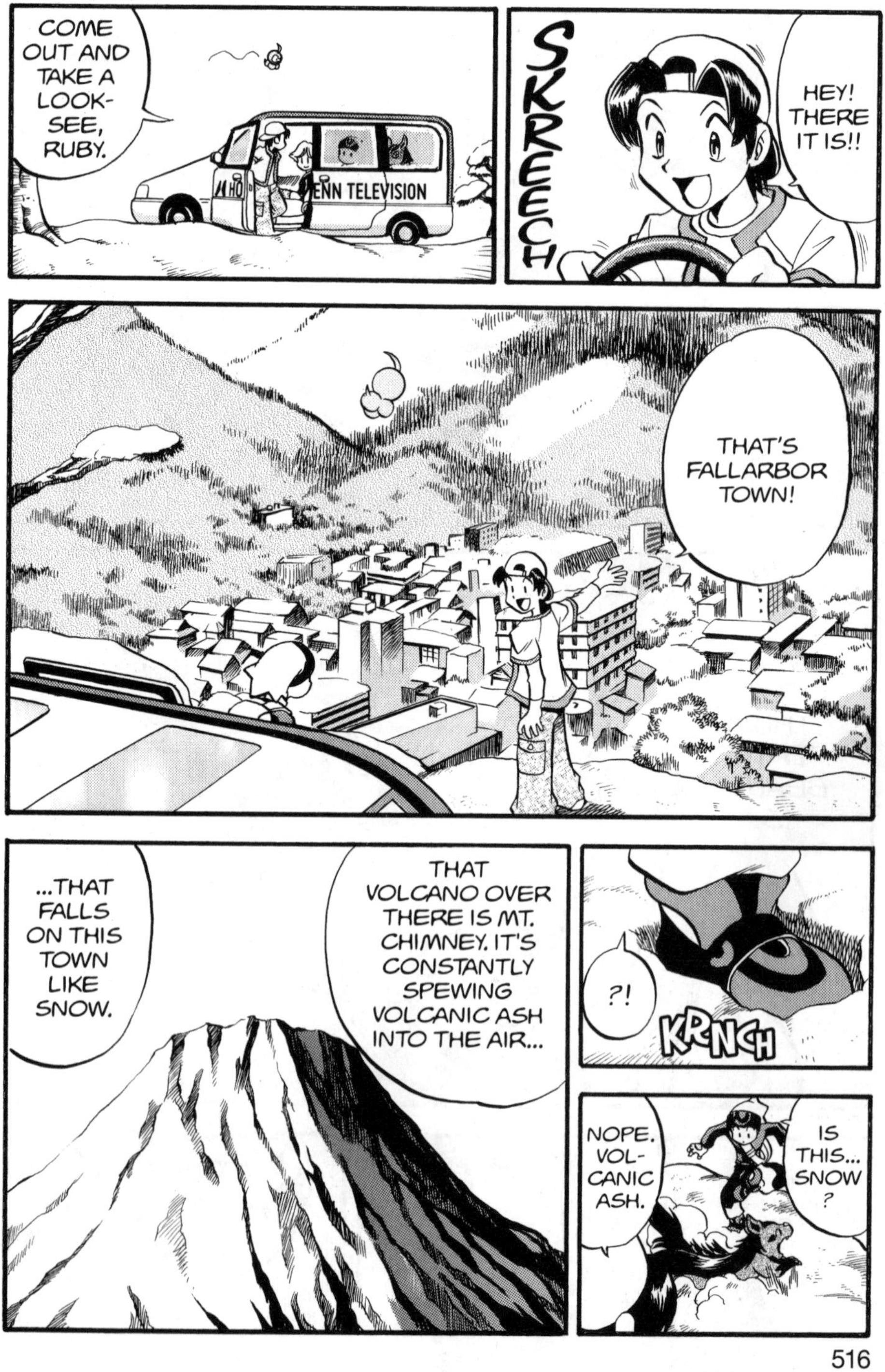
SKREECH
HEY! THERE IT IS!!
COME OUT AND TAKE A LOOK-SEE, RUBY.
THAT'S FALLARBOR TOWN!
?!
KRNCH
IS THIS... SNOW?
NOPE. VOLCANIC ASH.
THAT VOLCANO OVER THERE IS MT. CHIMNEY. IT'S CONSTANTLY SPEWING VOLCANIC ASH INTO THE AIR...
...THAT FALLS ON THIS TOWN LIKE SNOW.

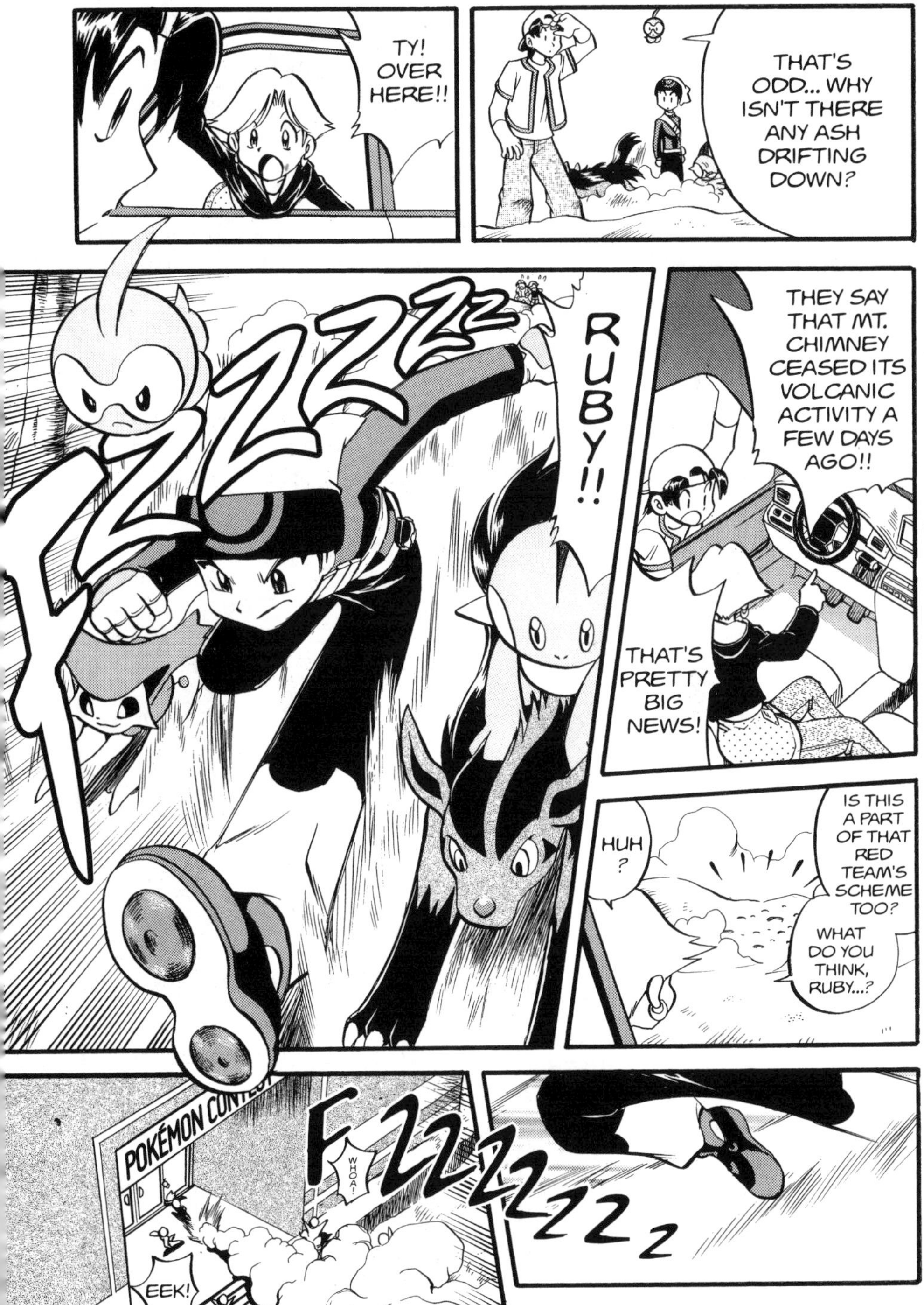
THAT'S ODD... WHY ISN'T THERE ANY ASH DRIFTING DOWN?
TY! OVER HERE!!
THEY SAY THAT MT. CHIMNEY CEASED ITS VOLCANIC ACTIVITY A FEW DAYS AGO!!
THAT'S PRETTY BIG NEWS!
IS THIS A PART OF THAT RED TEAM'S SCHEME TOO?
HUH?
WHAT DO YOU THINK, RUBY...?
FZZZZZZ
RUBY!!
FZZZZZZZZ
WHOA!
POKÉMON CONTEST
EEK!

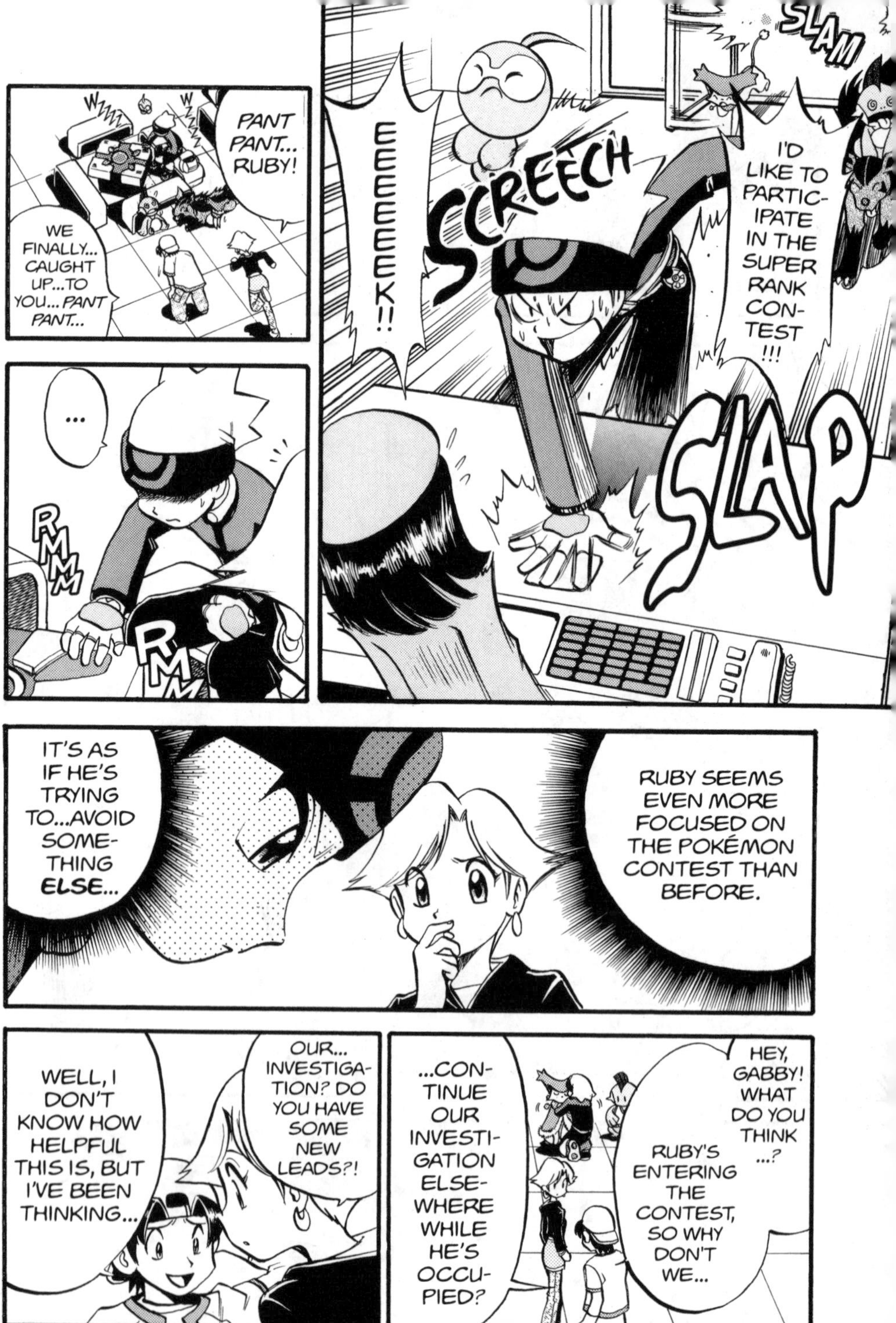
SLAM
I'D LIKE TO PARTICIPATE IN THE SUPER RANK CONTEST!!!
EEEEEEEK!!
SCREECH
SLAP
PANT PANT... RUBY!
WE FINALLY... CAUGHT UP...TO YOU...PANT PANT...
...
RMMM
RMM
RUBY SEEMS EVEN MORE FOCUSED ON THE POKÉMON CONTEST THAN BEFORE.
IT'S AS IF HE'S TRYING TO...AVOID SOMETHING **ELSE**...
HEY, GABBY! WHAT DO YOU THINK...?
RUBY'S ENTERING THE CONTEST, SO WHY DON'T WE...
...CONTINUE OUR INVESTIGATION ELSEWHERE WHILE HE'S OCCUPIED?
OUR... INVESTIGATION? DO YOU HAVE SOME NEW LEADS?!
WELL, I DON'T KNOW HOW HELPFUL THIS IS, BUT I'VE BEEN THINKING...

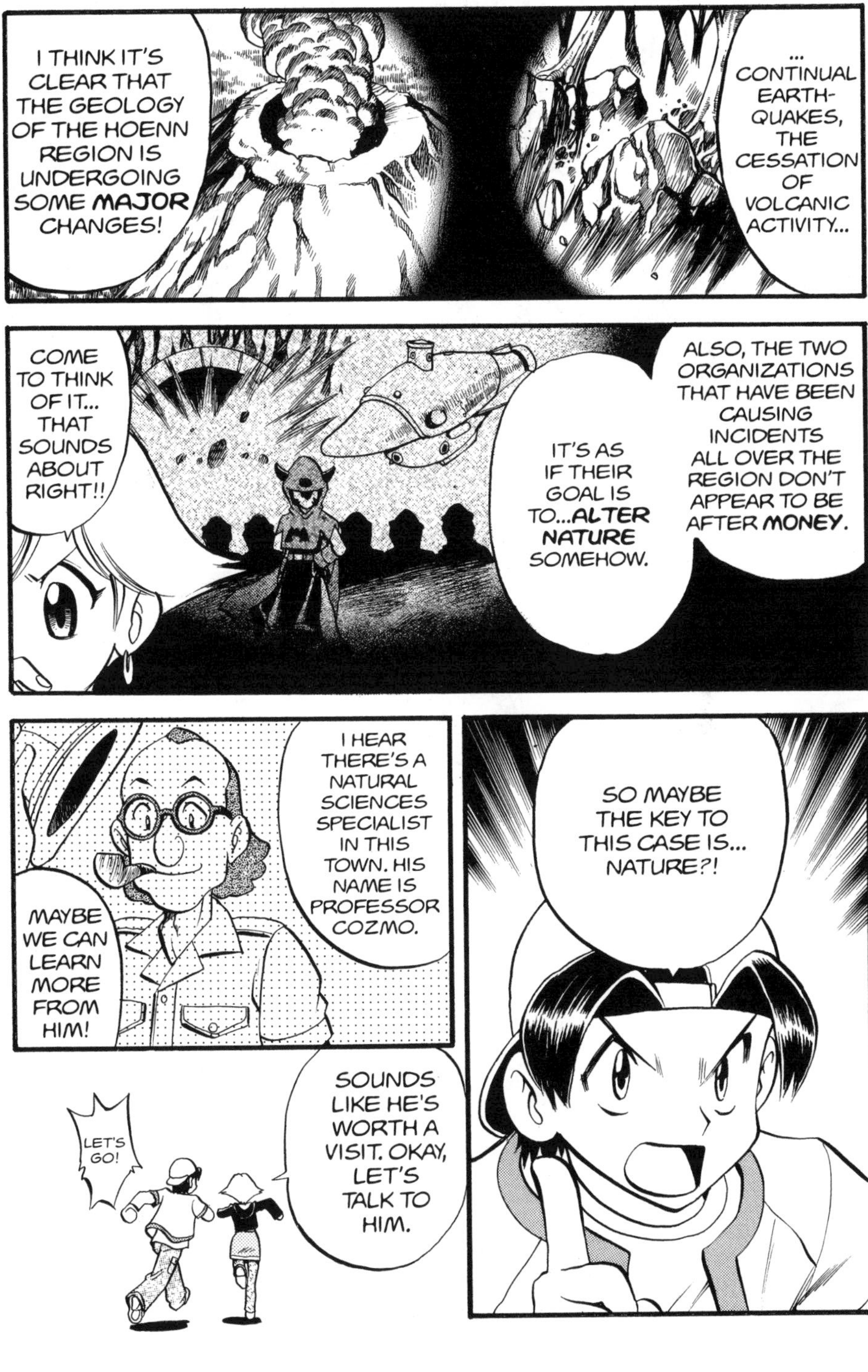
... CONTINUAL EARTH-QUAKES, THE CESSATION OF VOLCANIC ACTIVITY...
I THINK IT'S CLEAR THAT THE GEOLOGY OF THE HOENN REGION IS UNDERGOING SOME **MAJOR** CHANGES!
ALSO, THE TWO ORGANIZATIONS THAT HAVE BEEN CAUSING INCIDENTS ALL OVER THE REGION DON'T APPEAR TO BE AFTER **MONEY**.
IT'S AS IF THEIR GOAL IS TO...**ALTER NATURE** SOMEHOW.
COME TO THINK OF IT... THAT SOUNDS ABOUT RIGHT!!
SO MAYBE THE KEY TO THIS CASE IS... NATURE?!
I HEAR THERE'S A NATURAL SCIENCES SPECIALIST IN THIS TOWN. HIS NAME IS PROFESSOR COZMO.
MAYBE WE CAN LEARN MORE FROM HIM!
SOUNDS LIKE HE'S WORTH A VISIT. OKAY, LET'S TALK TO HIM.
LET'S GO!

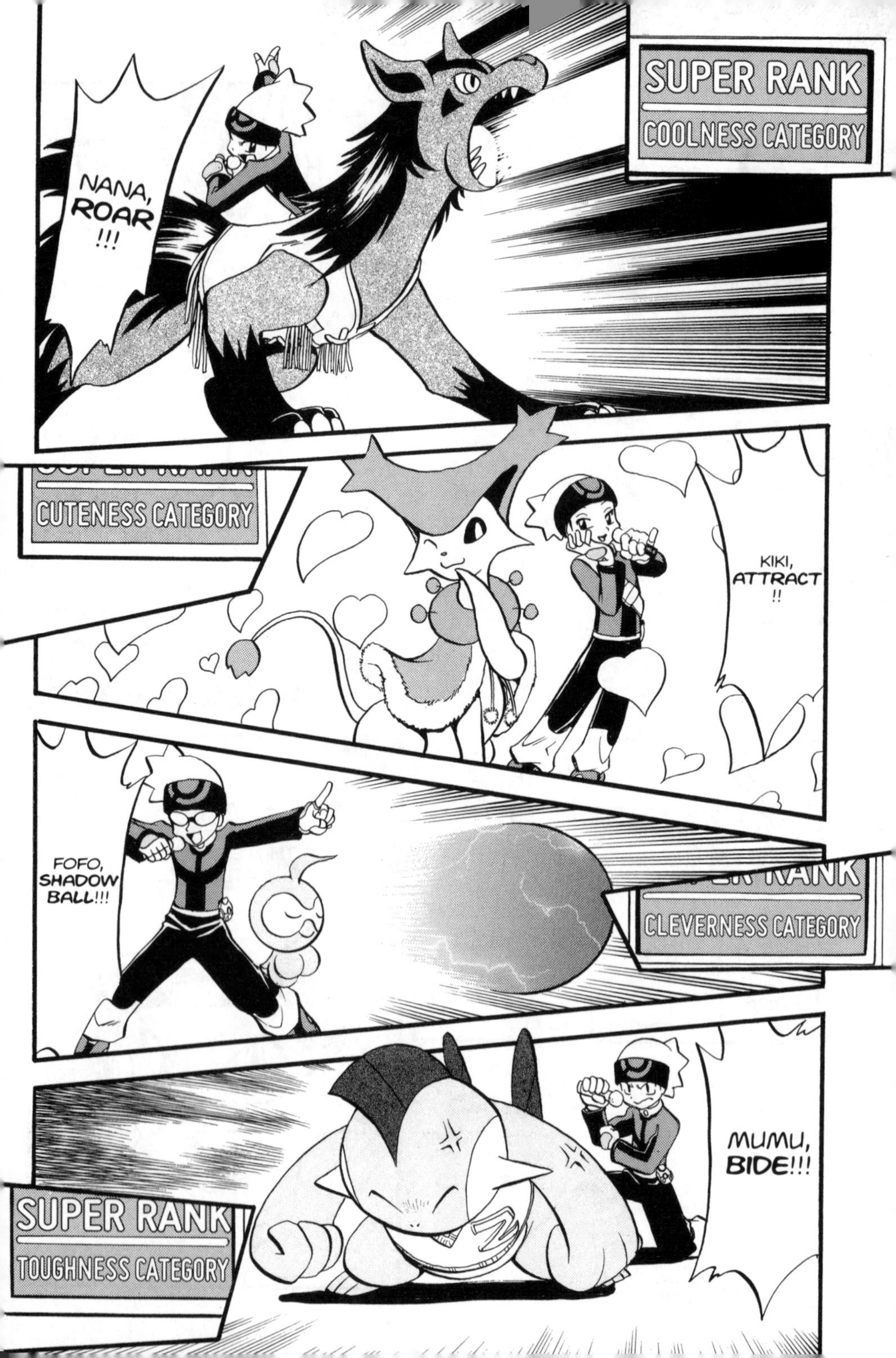
SUPER RANK
COOLNESS CATEGORY
NANA, ROAR!!!
KIKI, ATTRACT!!
CUTENESS CATEGORY
CLEVERNESS CATEGORY
FOFO, SHADOW BALL!!!
MUMU, BIDE!!!
SUPER RANK
TOUGHNESS CATEGORY

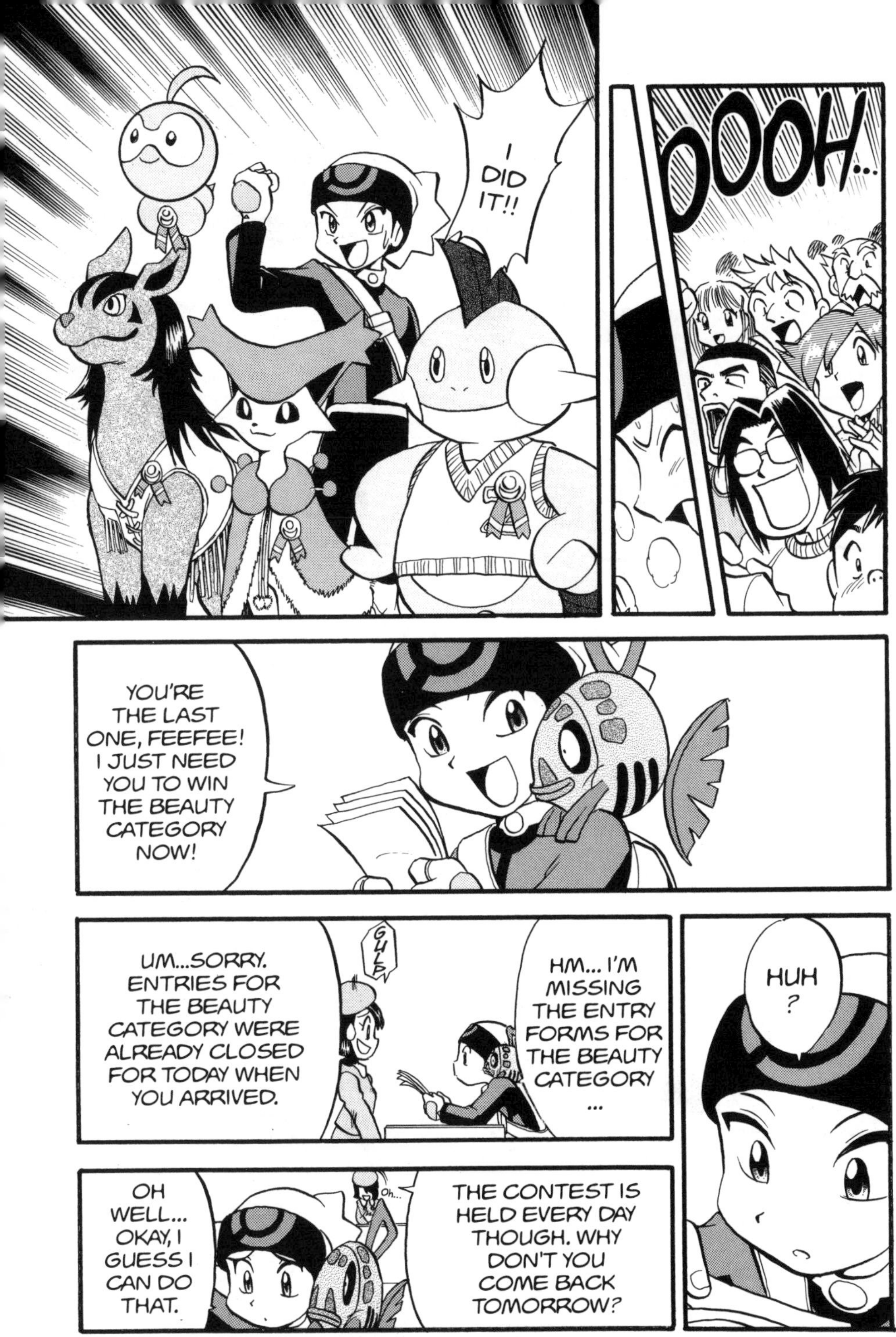
OOOH...
I DID IT!!
YOU'RE THE LAST ONE, FEEFEE! I JUST NEED YOU TO WIN THE BEAUTY CATEGORY NOW!
HUH ?
HM... I'M MISSING THE ENTRY FORMS FOR THE BEAUTY CATEGORY ...
GULP
UM...SORRY. ENTRIES FOR THE BEAUTY CATEGORY WERE ALREADY CLOSED FOR TODAY WHEN YOU ARRIVED.
THE CONTEST IS HELD EVERY DAY THOUGH. WHY DON'T YOU COME BACK TOMORROW?
Oh...
OH WELL... OKAY, I GUESS I CAN DO THAT.

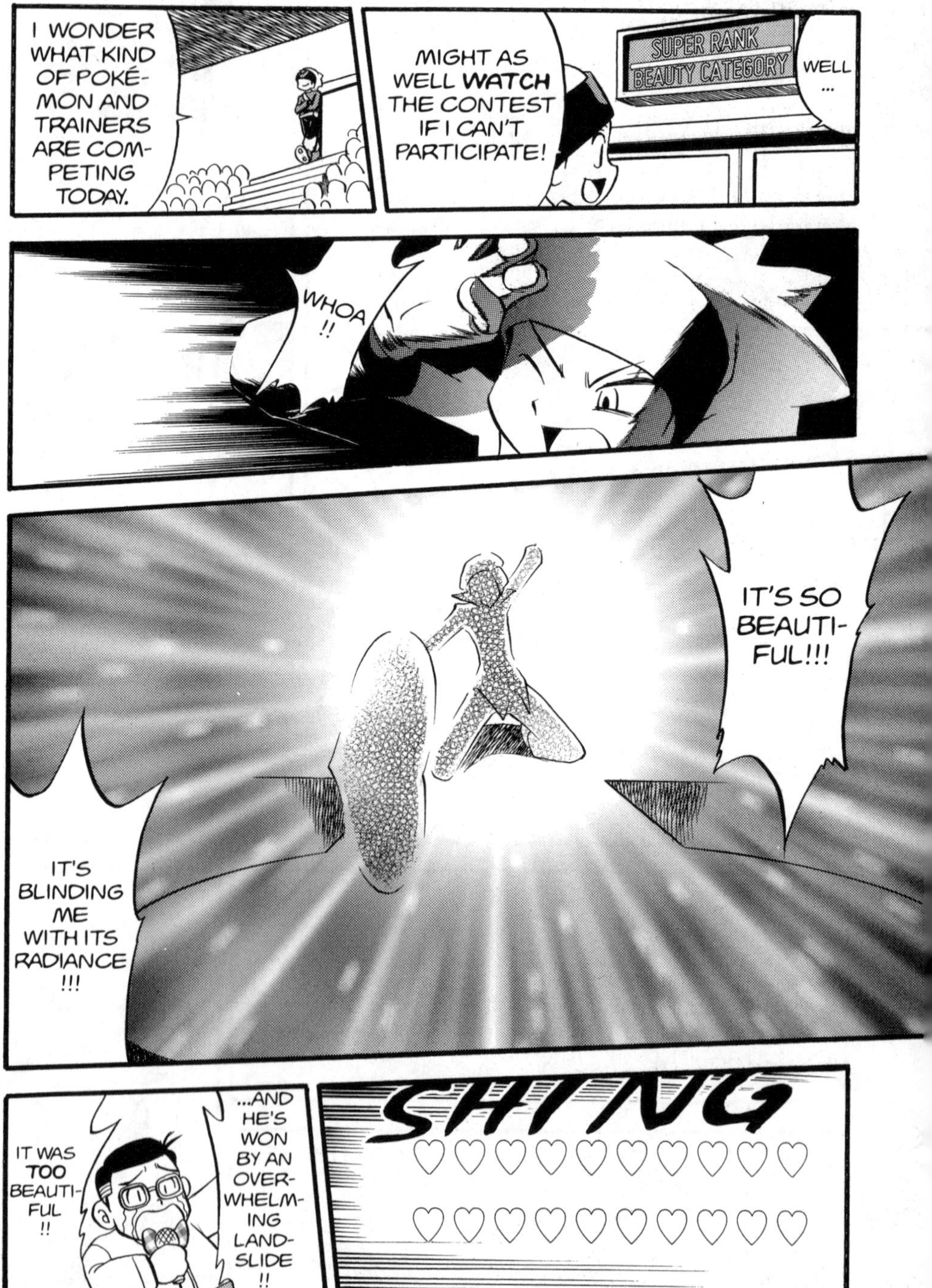
WELL ...
SUPER RANK BEAUTY CATEGORY
MIGHT AS WELL **WATCH** THE CONTEST IF I CAN'T PARTICIPATE!
I WONDER WHAT KIND OF POKÉMON AND TRAINERS ARE COMPETING TODAY.
WHOA!!
IT'S SO BEAUTIFUL!!!
IT'S BLINDING ME WITH ITS RADIANCE!!!
SHING
...AND HE'S WON BY AN OVERWHELMING LANDSLIDE!!
IT WAS **TOO** BEAUTIFUL!!

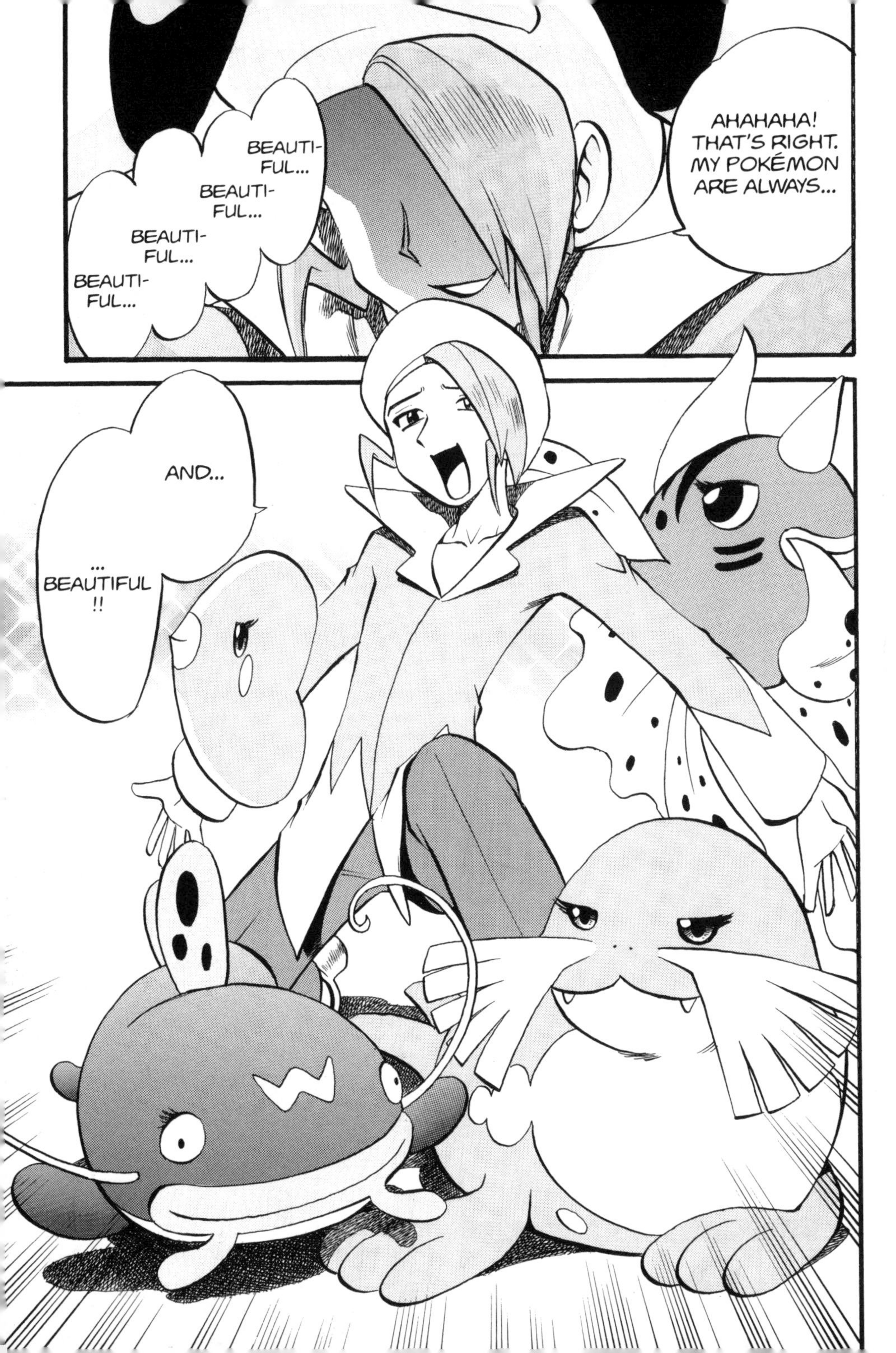
AHAHAHA! THAT'S RIGHT. MY POKÉMON ARE ALWAYS...
BEAUTI-FUL... BEAUTI-FUL... BEAUTI-FUL... BEAUTI-FUL...
AND...
...BEAUTIFUL!!

ADVENTURE MAP

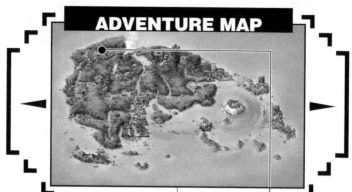

SAPPHIRE

- Mt. Chimney
- Jagged Pass

Name	Pokémon	Level
CHIC	Combusken ♀	Lv35
RONO	Lairon ♂	Lv41
LORRY	Wailord ♂	Lv46
PHADO	Donphan ♂	Lv45
TROPPY	Tropius ♂	Lv44

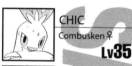

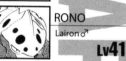

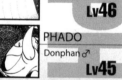

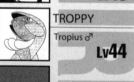

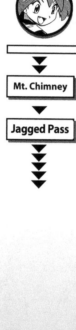

RUBY

- Route 117
- Verdanturf Town
- Rusturf Tunnel
- Rustboro City
- Route 115
- Route 114
- Fallarbor Town

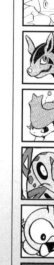

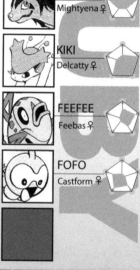

Name	Pokémon
MUMU	Marshtomp ♂
NANA	Mightyena ♀
KIKI	Delcatty ♀
FEEFEE	Feebas ♀
FOFO	Castform ♀

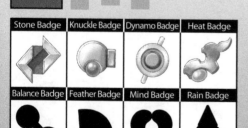

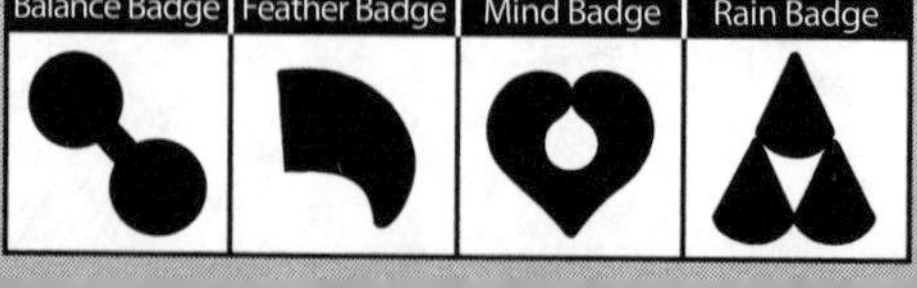

Stone Badge
Knuckle Badge
Dynamo Badge
Heat Badge
Balance Badge
Feather Badge
Mind Badge
Rain Badge

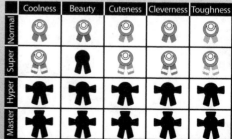

Coolness
Beauty
Cuteness
Cleverness
Toughness
Normal
Super
Hyper
Master

● Adventure 224 ●

I More than Like You, Luvdisc, Part 2

Pokémon Adventures™ Ruby & Sapphire

The Fourth Chapter

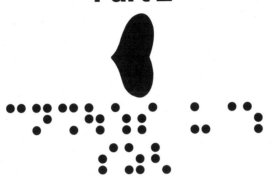

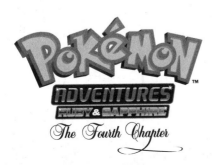

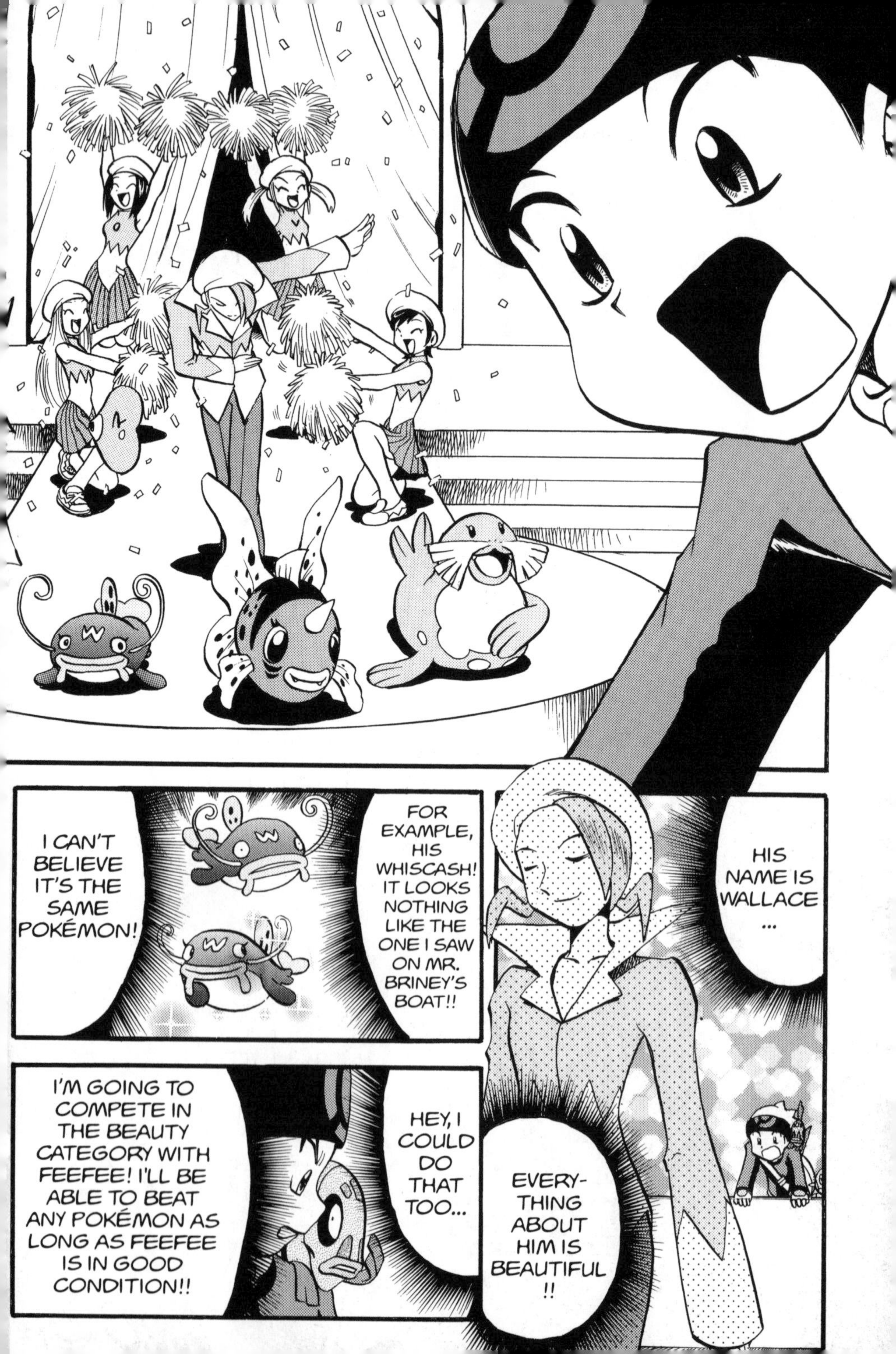
HIS NAME IS WALLACE ...
EVERY-THING ABOUT HIM IS BEAUTIFUL !!
FOR EXAMPLE, HIS WHISCASH! IT LOOKS NOTHING LIKE THE ONE I SAW ON MR. BRINEY'S BOAT!!
I CAN'T BELIEVE IT'S THE SAME POKÉMON!
HEY, I COULD DO THAT TOO...
I'M GOING TO COMPETE IN THE BEAUTY CATEGORY WITH FEEFEE! I'LL BE ABLE TO BEAT ANY POKÉMON AS LONG AS FEEFEE IS IN GOOD CONDITION!!

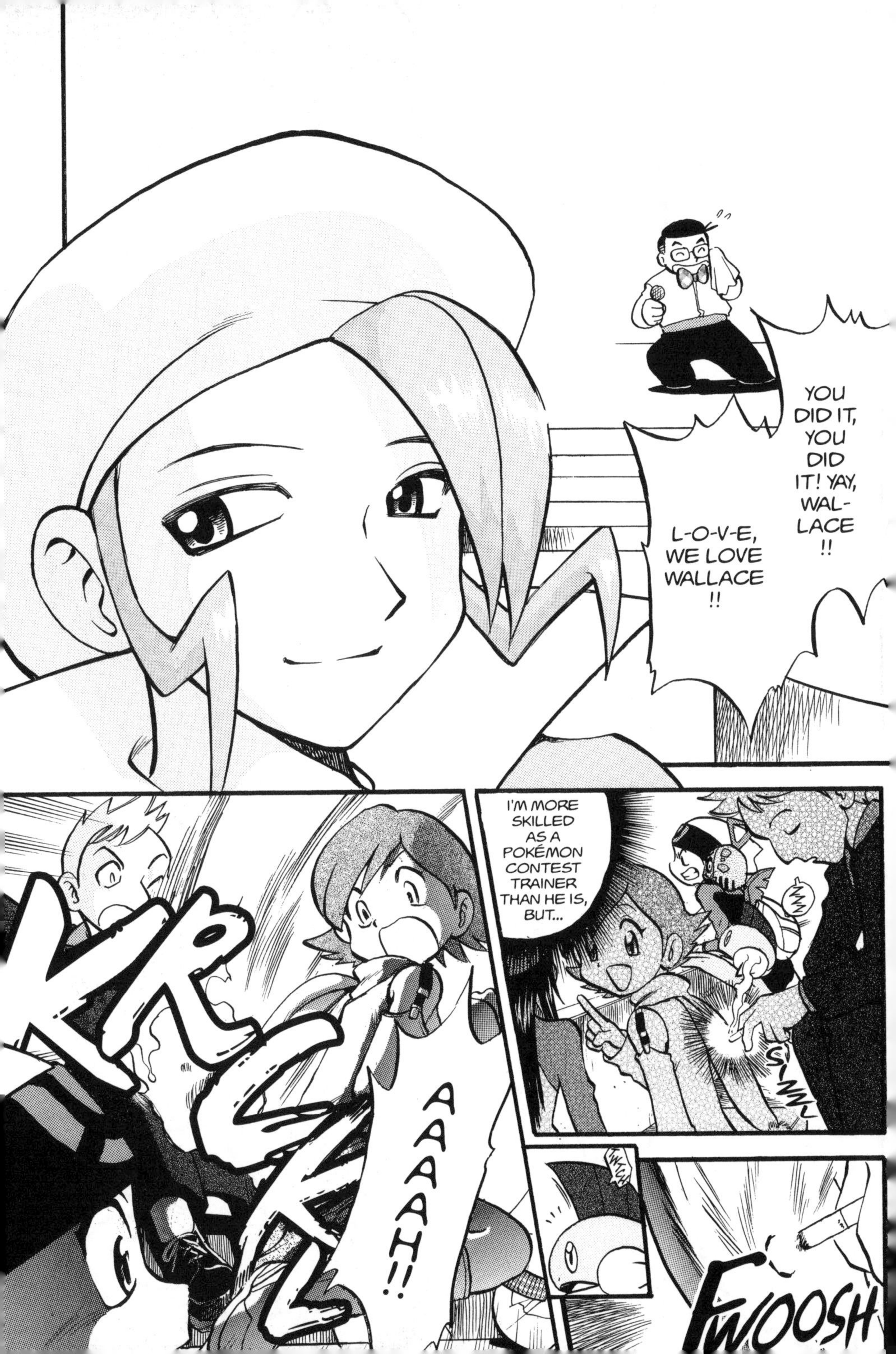
YOU DID IT, YOU DID IT! YAY, WAL-LACE!!
L-O-V-E, WE LOVE WALLACE!!
I'M MORE SKILLED AS A POKÉMON CONTEST TRAINER THAN HE IS, BUT...
ZZZ
SIZZZL
FWOOSH
TWITCH
AAAAAH!!

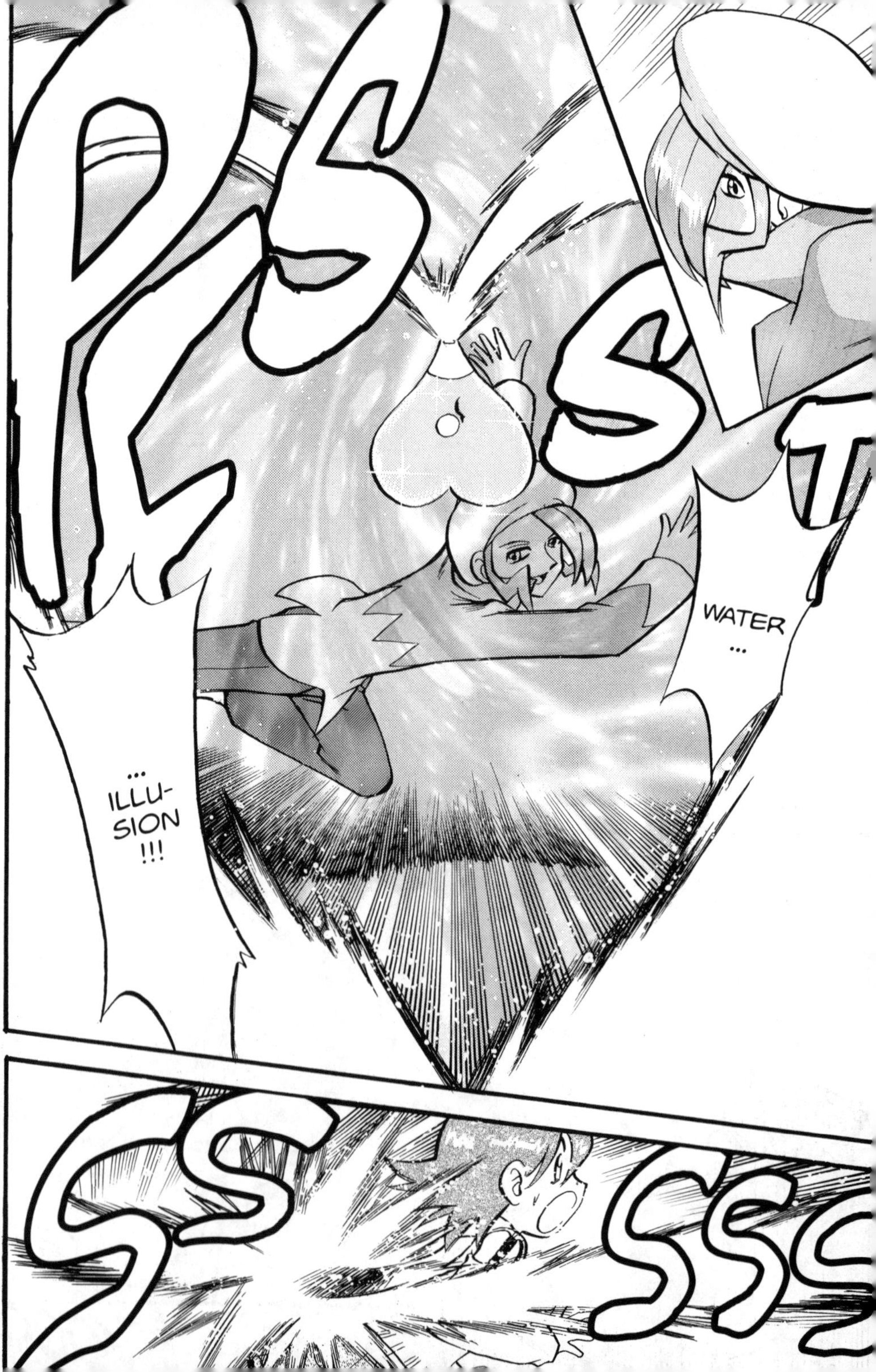
WATER ...
... ILLU-SION !!!

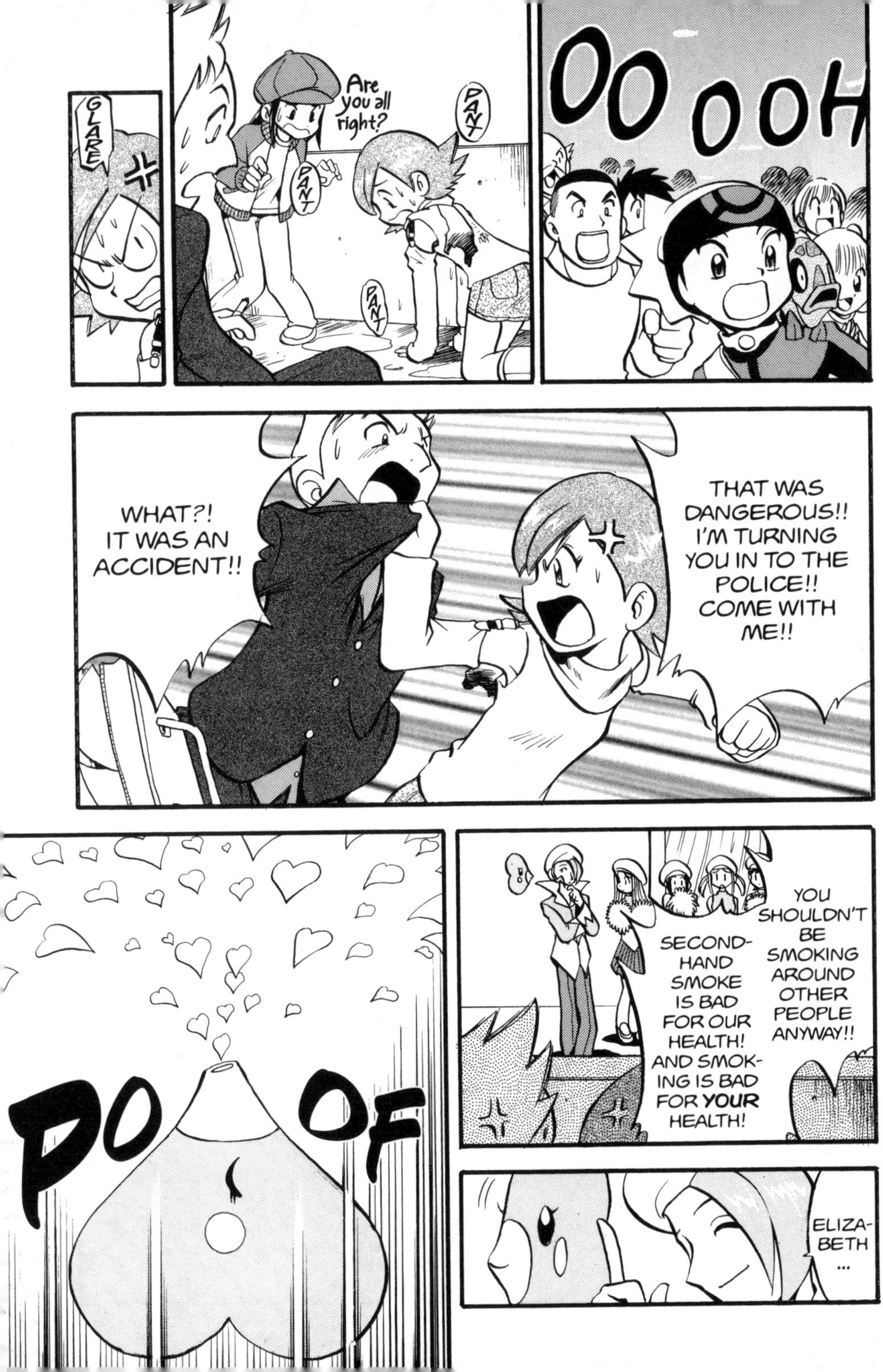
OOOOOH
PANT
Are you all right?
PANT
PANT
GLARE
THAT WAS DANGEROUS!! I'M TURNING YOU IN TO THE POLICE!! COME WITH ME!!
WHAT?! IT WAS AN ACCIDENT!!
YOU SHOULDN'T BE SMOKING AROUND OTHER PEOPLE ANYWAY!!
SECOND-HAND SMOKE IS BAD FOR OUR HEALTH! AND SMOKING IS BAD FOR **YOUR** HEALTH!
ELIZA-BETH ...
POOF

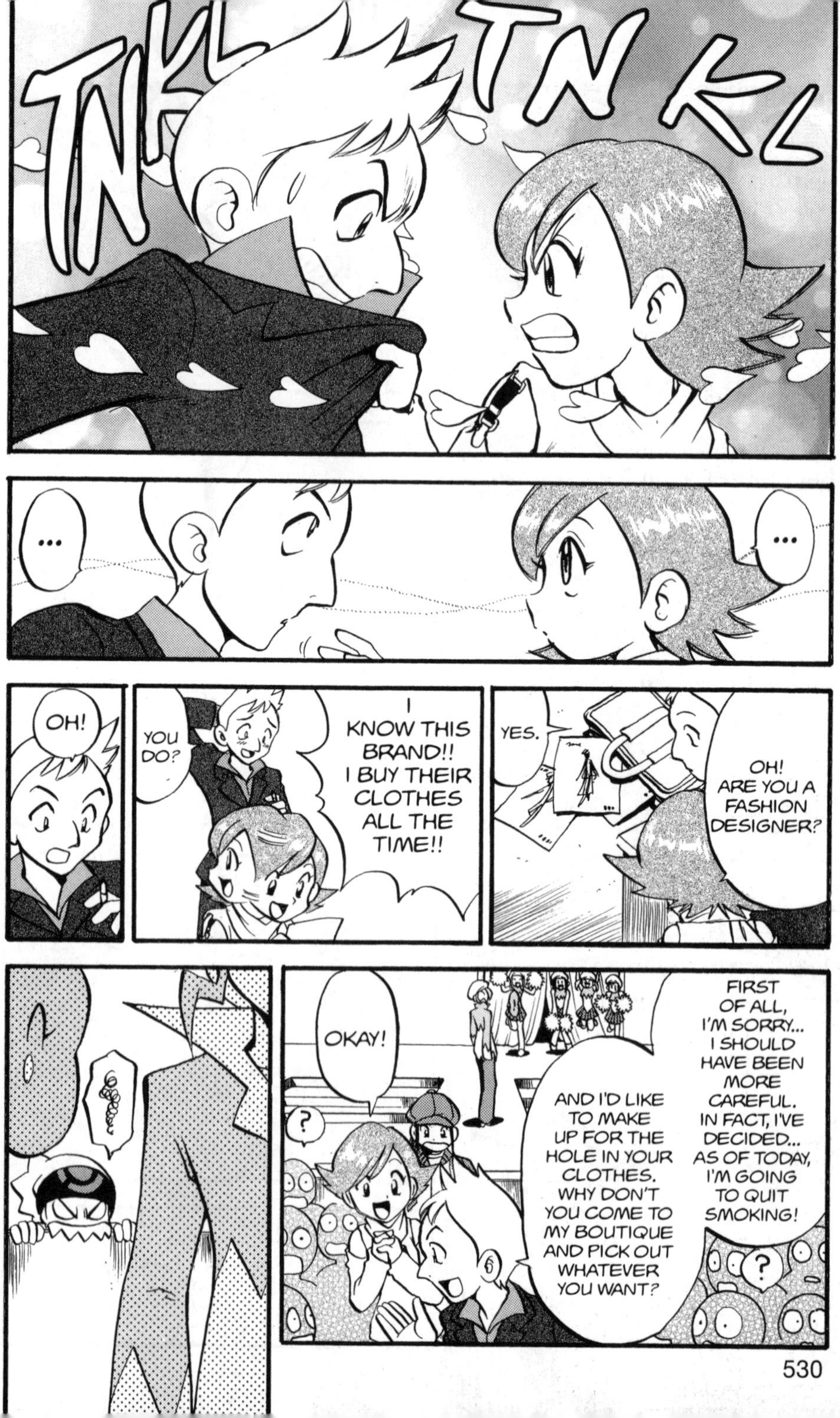
TNKL TN KL
...
...
OH! ARE YOU A FASHION DESIGNER?
YES.
I KNOW THIS BRAND!! I BUY THEIR CLOTHES ALL THE TIME!!
YOU DO?
OH!
FIRST OF ALL, I'M SORRY... I SHOULD HAVE BEEN MORE CAREFUL. IN FACT, I'VE DECIDED... AS OF TODAY, I'M GOING TO QUIT SMOKING!
AND I'D LIKE TO MAKE UP FOR THE HOLE IN YOUR CLOTHES. WHY DON'T YOU COME TO MY BOUTIQUE AND PICK OUT WHATEVER YOU WANT?
?
OKAY!
?

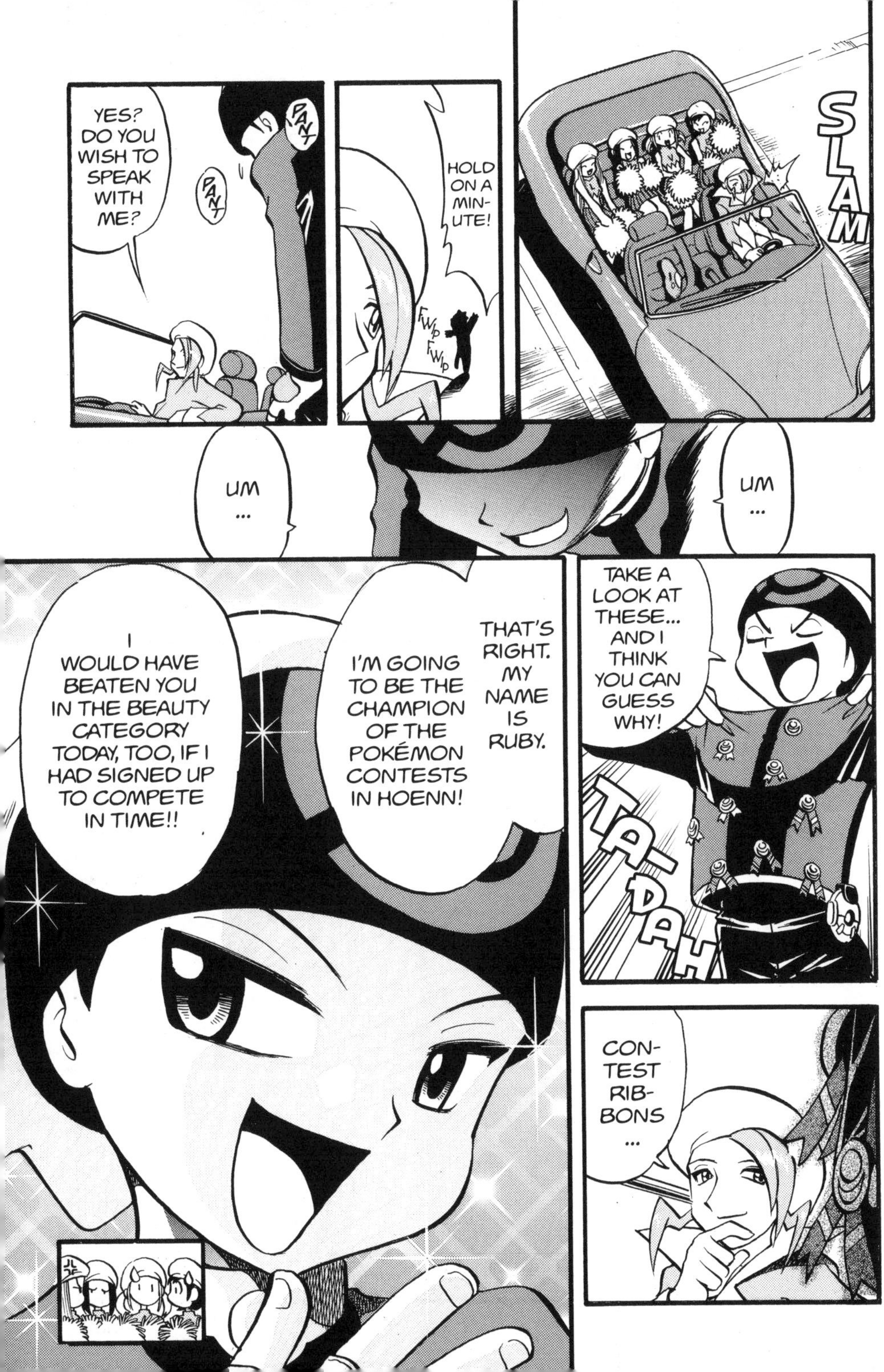
SLAM
HOLD ON A MIN-UTE!
FWIP FWIP
PANT
PANT
YES? DO YOU WISH TO SPEAK WITH ME?
UM ...
UM ...
TAKE A LOOK AT THESE... AND I THINK YOU CAN GUESS WHY!
TA-DAH
CON-TEST RIB-BONS ...
THAT'S RIGHT. MY NAME IS RUBY.
I'M GOING TO BE THE CHAMPION OF THE POKÉMON CONTESTS IN HOENN!
I WOULD HAVE BEATEN YOU IN THE BEAUTY CATEGORY TODAY, TOO, IF I HAD SIGNED UP TO COMPETE IN TIME!!

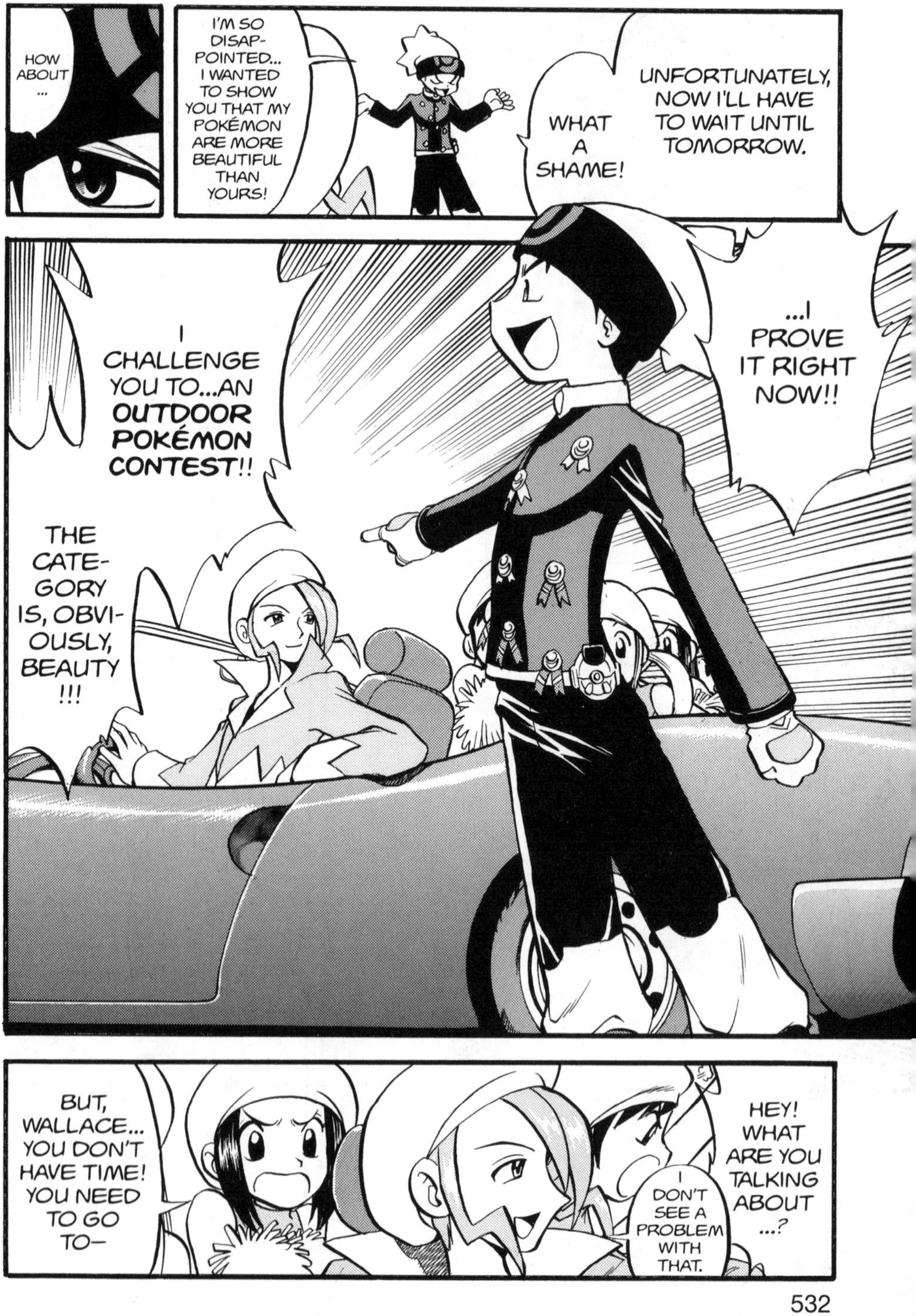
UNFORTUNATELY, NOW I'LL HAVE TO WAIT UNTIL TOMORROW.
WHAT A SHAME!
I'M SO DISAPPOINTED... I WANTED TO SHOW YOU THAT MY POKÉMON ARE MORE BEAUTIFUL THAN YOURS!
HOW ABOUT ...
...I PROVE IT RIGHT NOW!!
I CHALLENGE YOU TO...AN **OUTDOOR POKÉMON CONTEST**!!
THE CATEGORY IS, OBVIOUSLY, BEAUTY !!!
HEY! WHAT ARE YOU TALKING ABOUT ...?
I DON'T SEE A PROBLEM WITH THAT.
BUT, WALLACE... YOU DON'T HAVE TIME! YOU NEED TO GO TO—

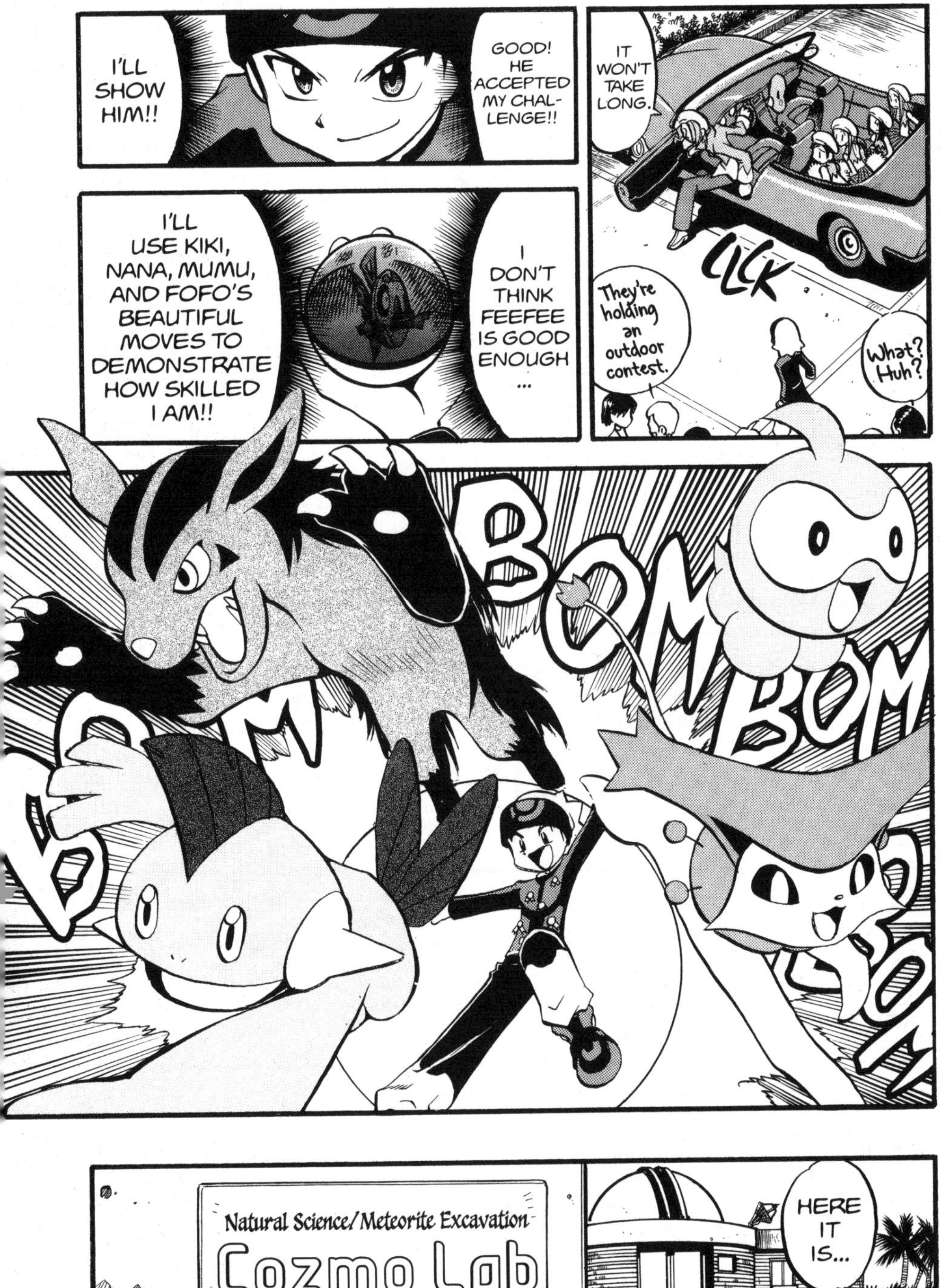
IT WON'T TAKE LONG.
CLICK
They're holding an outdoor contest.
What? Huh?
GOOD! HE ACCEPTED MY CHAL-LENGE!!
I'LL SHOW HIM!!
I DON'T THINK FEEFEE IS GOOD ENOUGH ...
I'LL USE KIKI, NANA, MUMU, AND FOFO'S BEAUTIFUL MOVES TO DEMONSTRATE HOW SKILLED I AM!!
BOM
BOM
BOM
BOM
BOM
HERE IT IS...
Natural Science/Meteorite Excavation
Cozmo Lab

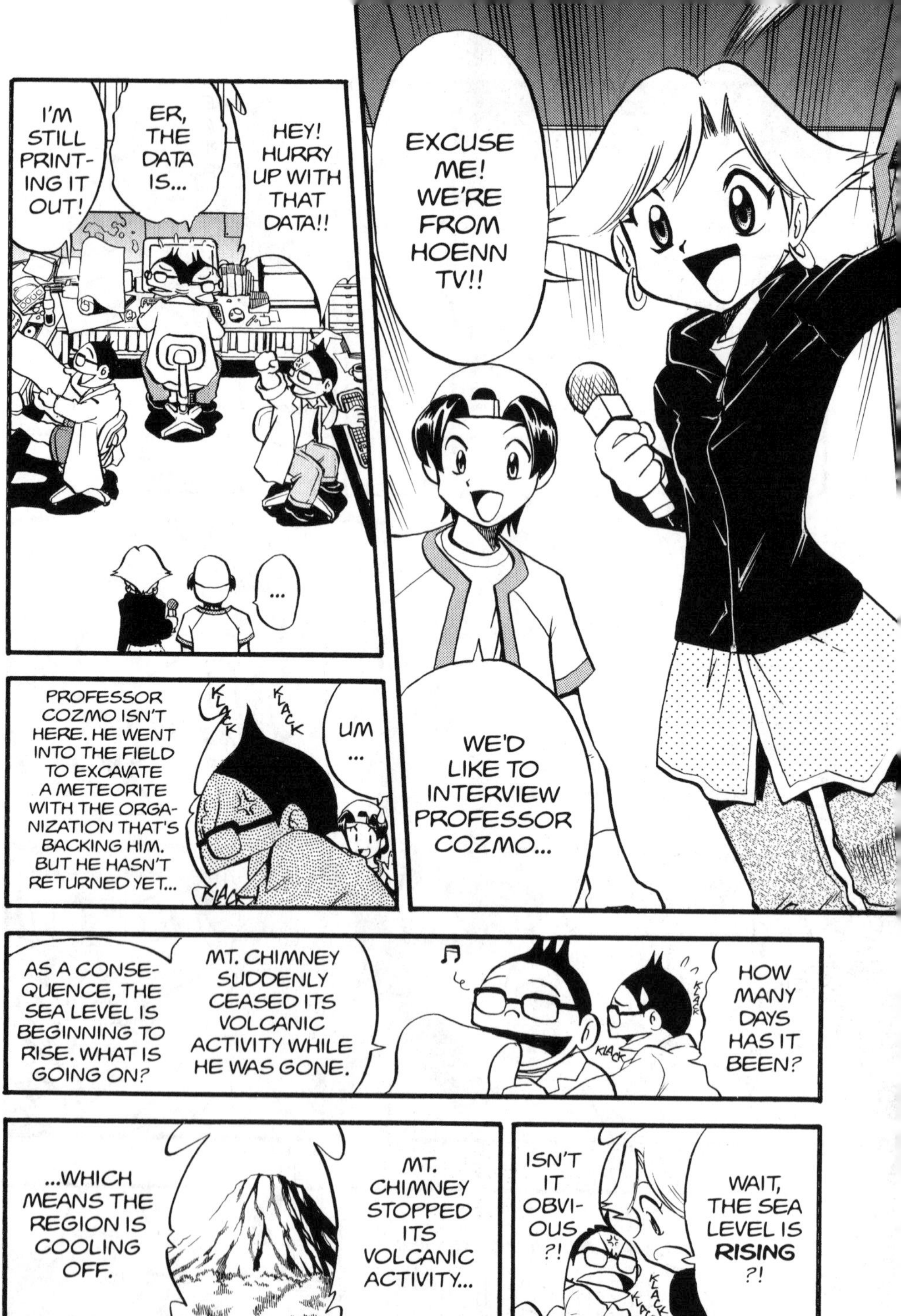
EXCUSE ME! WE'RE FROM HOENN TV!!
WE'D LIKE TO INTERVIEW PROFESSOR COZMO...
HEY! HURRY UP WITH THAT DATA!!
ER, THE DATA IS...
I'M STILL PRINTING IT OUT!
...
UM ...
KLACK
KLACK
PROFESSOR COZMO ISN'T HERE. HE WENT INTO THE FIELD TO EXCAVATE A METEORITE WITH THE ORGANIZATION THAT'S BACKING HIM. BUT HE HASN'T RETURNED YET...
KLACK
HOW MANY DAYS HAS IT BEEN?
KLACK
KLACK
MT. CHIMNEY SUDDENLY CEASED ITS VOLCANIC ACTIVITY WHILE HE WAS GONE.
AS A CONSEQUENCE, THE SEA LEVEL IS BEGINNING TO RISE. WHAT IS GOING ON?
WAIT, THE SEA LEVEL IS **RISING**?!
ISN'T IT OBVIOUS?!
KLACK
KLACK
MT. CHIMNEY STOPPED ITS VOLCANIC ACTIVITY...
...WHICH MEANS THE REGION IS COOLING OFF.

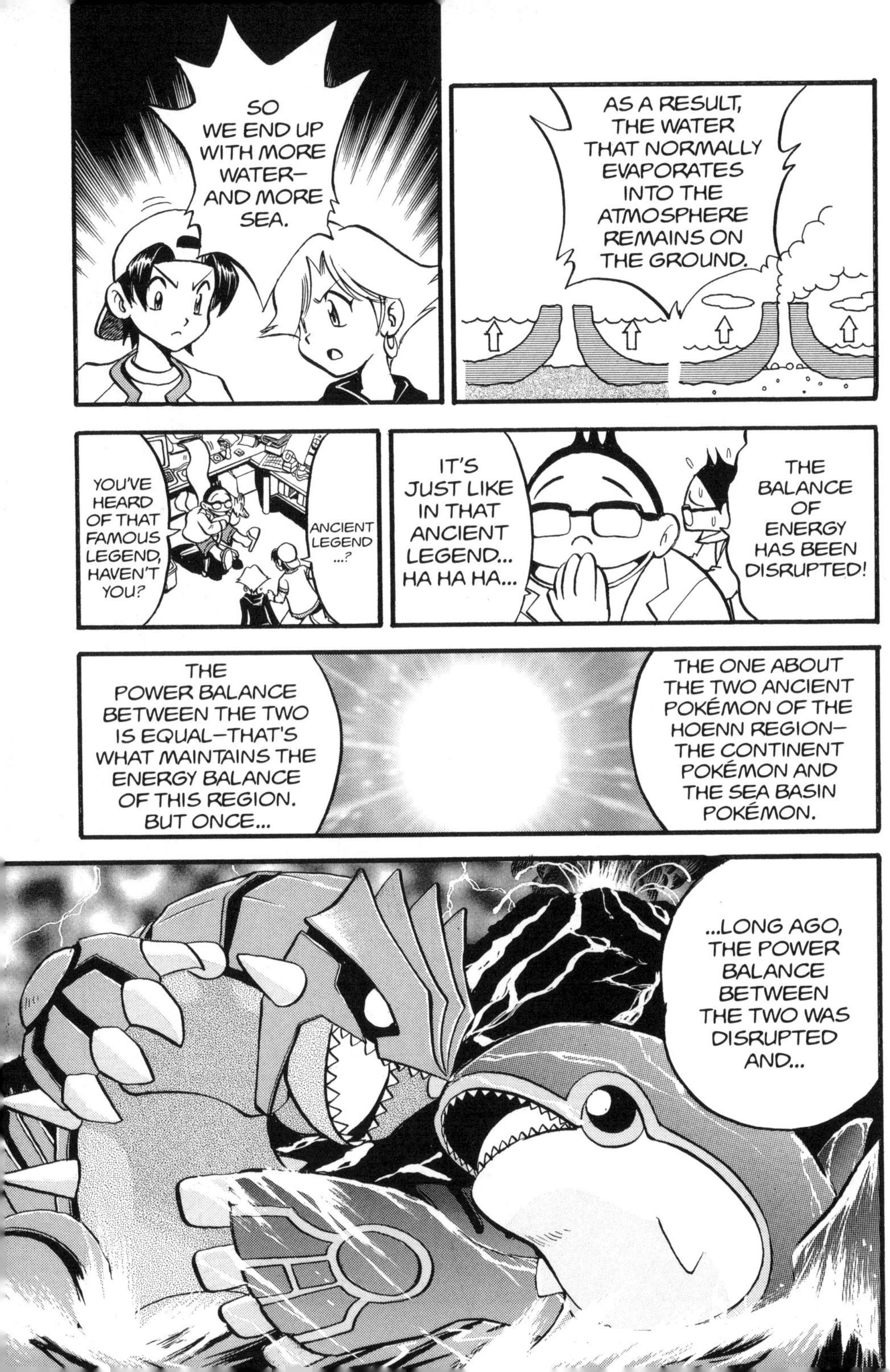
AS A RESULT, THE WATER THAT NORMALLY EVAPORATES INTO THE ATMOSPHERE REMAINS ON THE GROUND.
SO WE END UP WITH MORE WATER— AND MORE SEA.
THE BALANCE OF ENERGY HAS BEEN DISRUPTED!
IT'S JUST LIKE IN THAT ANCIENT LEGEND... HA HA HA...
ANCIENT LEGEND ...?
YOU'VE HEARD OF THAT FAMOUS LEGEND, HAVEN'T YOU?
THE ONE ABOUT THE TWO ANCIENT POKÉMON OF THE HOENN REGION— THE CONTINENT POKÉMON AND THE SEA BASIN POKÉMON.
THE POWER BALANCE BETWEEN THE TWO IS EQUAL—THAT'S WHAT MAINTAINS THE ENERGY BALANCE OF THIS REGION. BUT ONCE...
...LONG AGO, THE POWER BALANCE BETWEEN THE TWO WAS DISRUPTED AND...

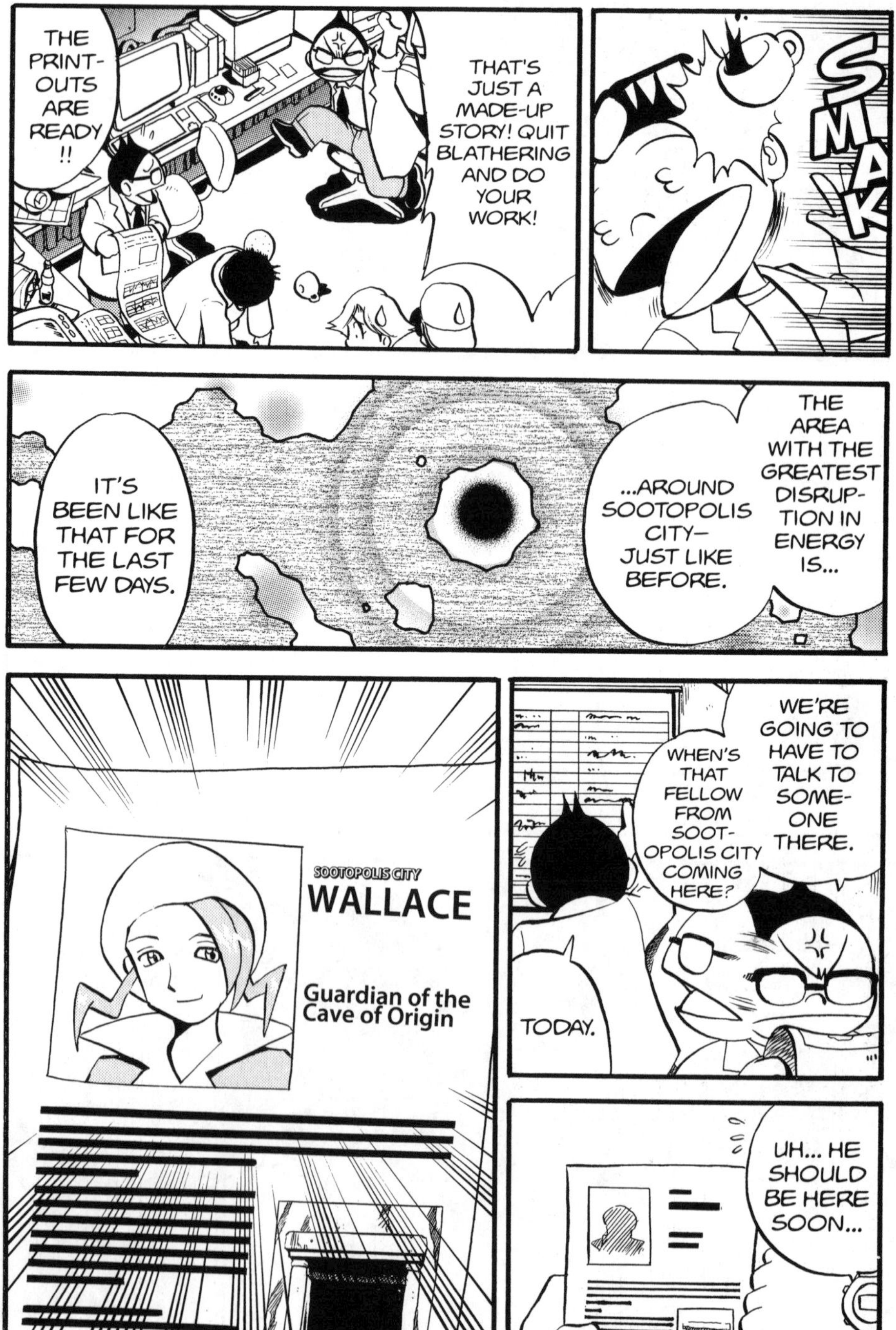

SMAK
THAT'S JUST A MADE-UP STORY! QUIT BLATHERING AND DO YOUR WORK!
THE PRINT-OUTS ARE READY!!
THE AREA WITH THE GREATEST DISRUPTION IN ENERGY IS...
...AROUND SOOTOPOLIS CITY—JUST LIKE BEFORE.
IT'S BEEN LIKE THAT FOR THE LAST FEW DAYS.
WE'RE GOING TO HAVE TO TALK TO SOMEONE THERE.
WHEN'S THAT FELLOW FROM SOOTOPOLIS CITY COMING HERE?
TODAY.
UH... HE SHOULD BE HERE SOON...
SOOTOPOLIS CITY
WALLACE
Guardian of the Cave of Origin

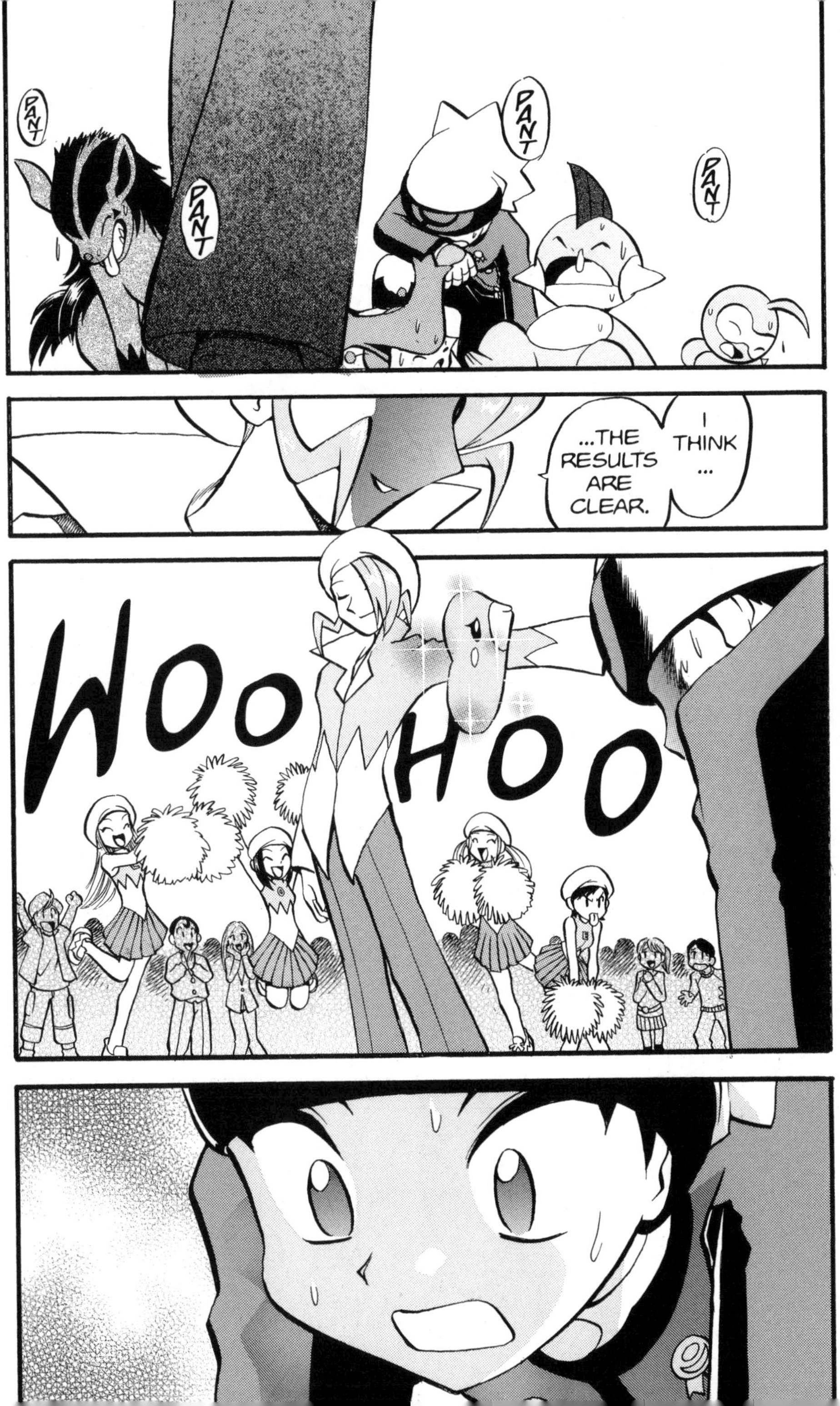
PANT
PANT
PANT
PANT
I THINK ...
...THE RESULTS ARE CLEAR.
WOO HOO

● Adventure 225 ●

Tanks, but No Tanks, Anorith and Lileep

Pokémon™ Adventures Ruby & Sapphire

The Fourth Chapter

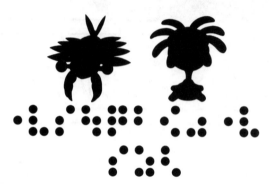

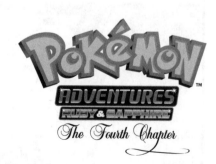

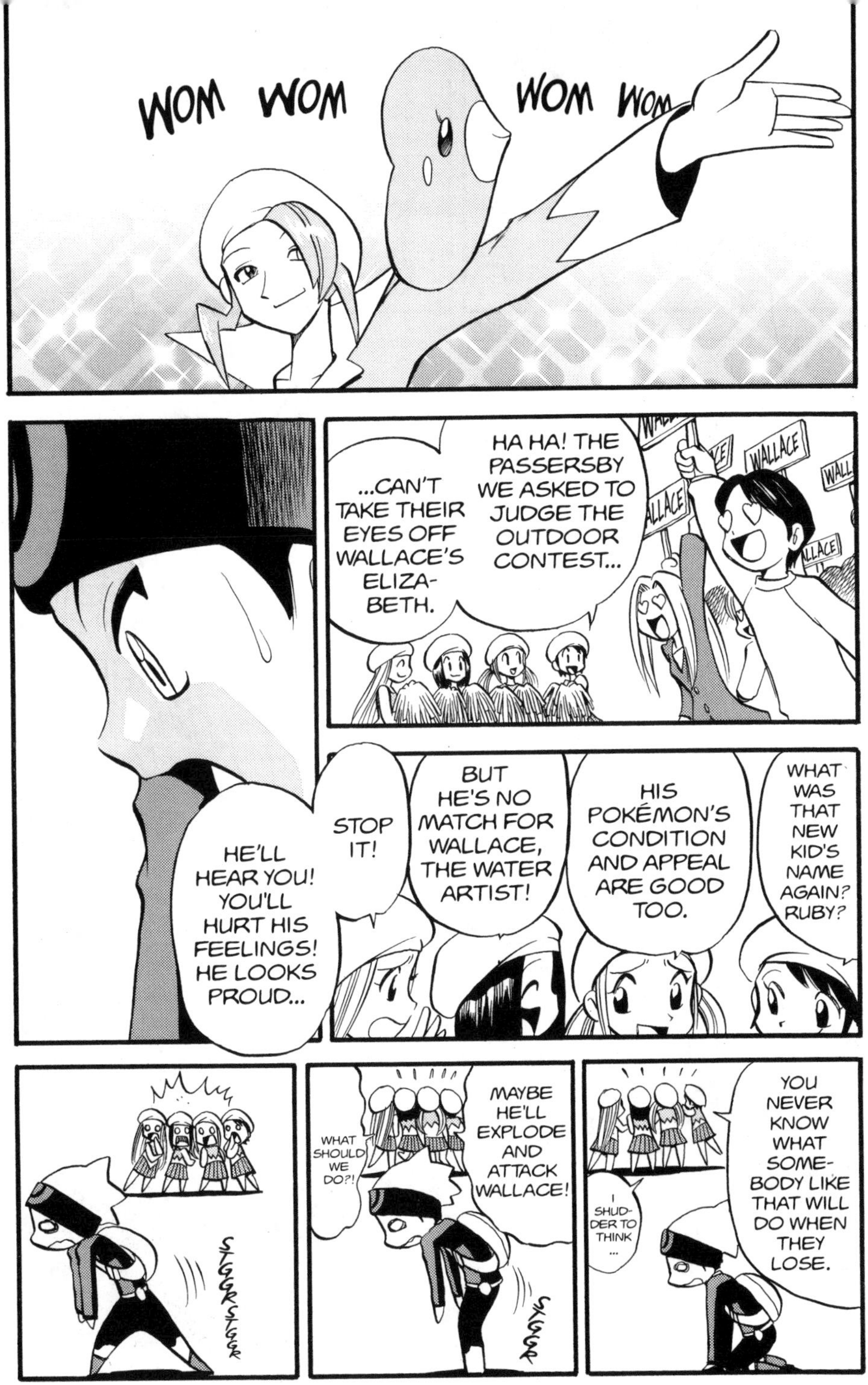
WOM WOM WOM WOM
HA HA! THE PASSERSBY WE ASKED TO JUDGE THE OUTDOOR CONTEST...
...CAN'T TAKE THEIR EYES OFF WALLACE'S ELIZA-BETH.
WALLACE
WHAT WAS THAT NEW KID'S NAME AGAIN? RUBY?
HIS POKÉMON'S CONDITION AND APPEAL ARE GOOD TOO.
BUT HE'S NO MATCH FOR WALLACE, THE WATER ARTIST!
STOP IT!
HE'LL HEAR YOU! YOU'LL HURT HIS FEELINGS! HE LOOKS PROUD...
YOU NEVER KNOW WHAT SOME-BODY LIKE THAT WILL DO WHEN THEY LOSE.
I SHUD-DER TO THINK...
MAYBE HE'LL EXPLODE AND ATTACK WALLACE!
WHAT SHOULD WE DO?!
STGGR
STGGR STGGR

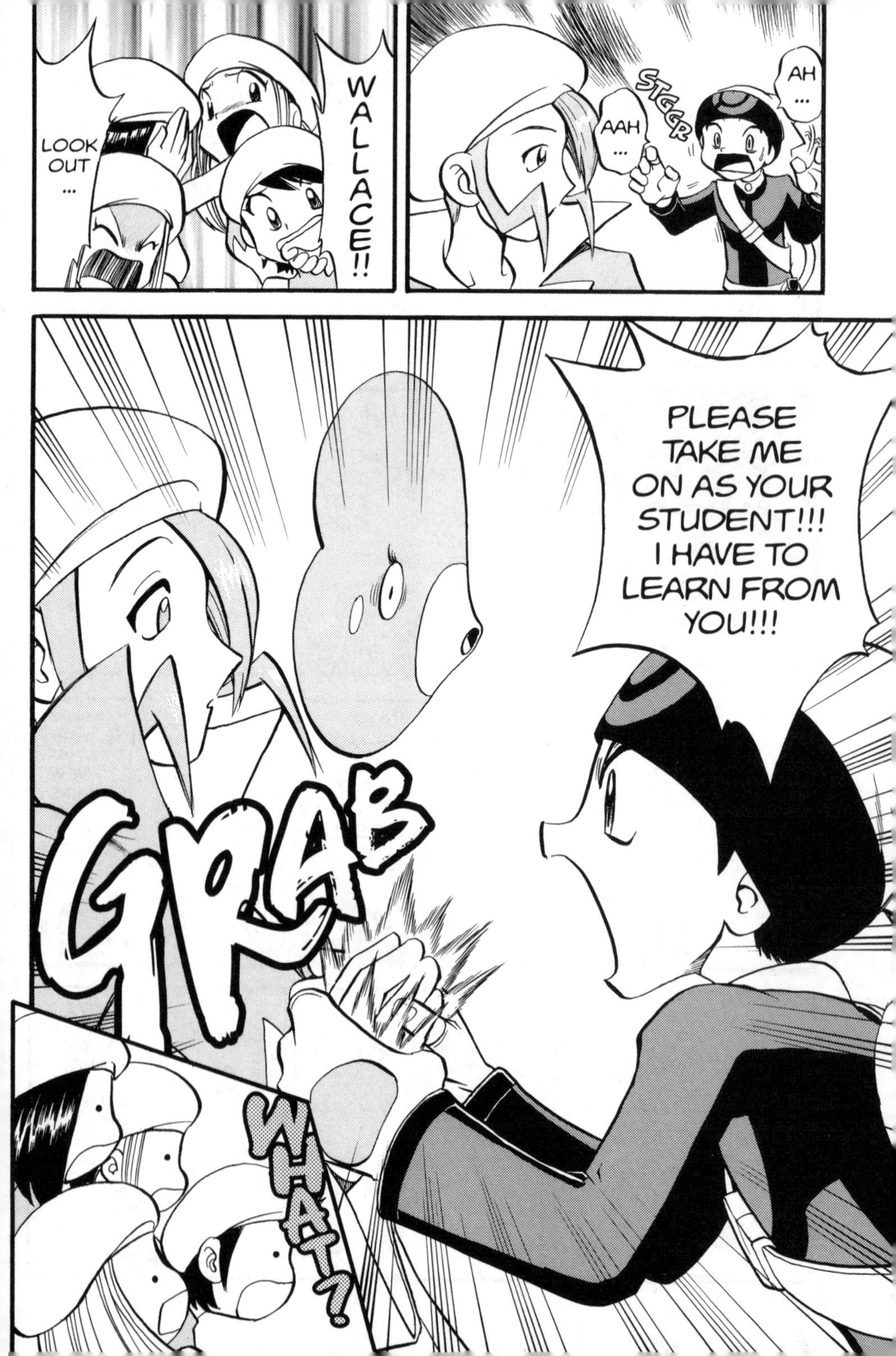
AH ...
STGGR
AAH ...
WALLACE!!
LOOK OUT ...
PLEASE TAKE ME ON AS YOUR STUDENT!!! I HAVE TO LEARN FROM YOU!!!
GRAB
WHAT?!

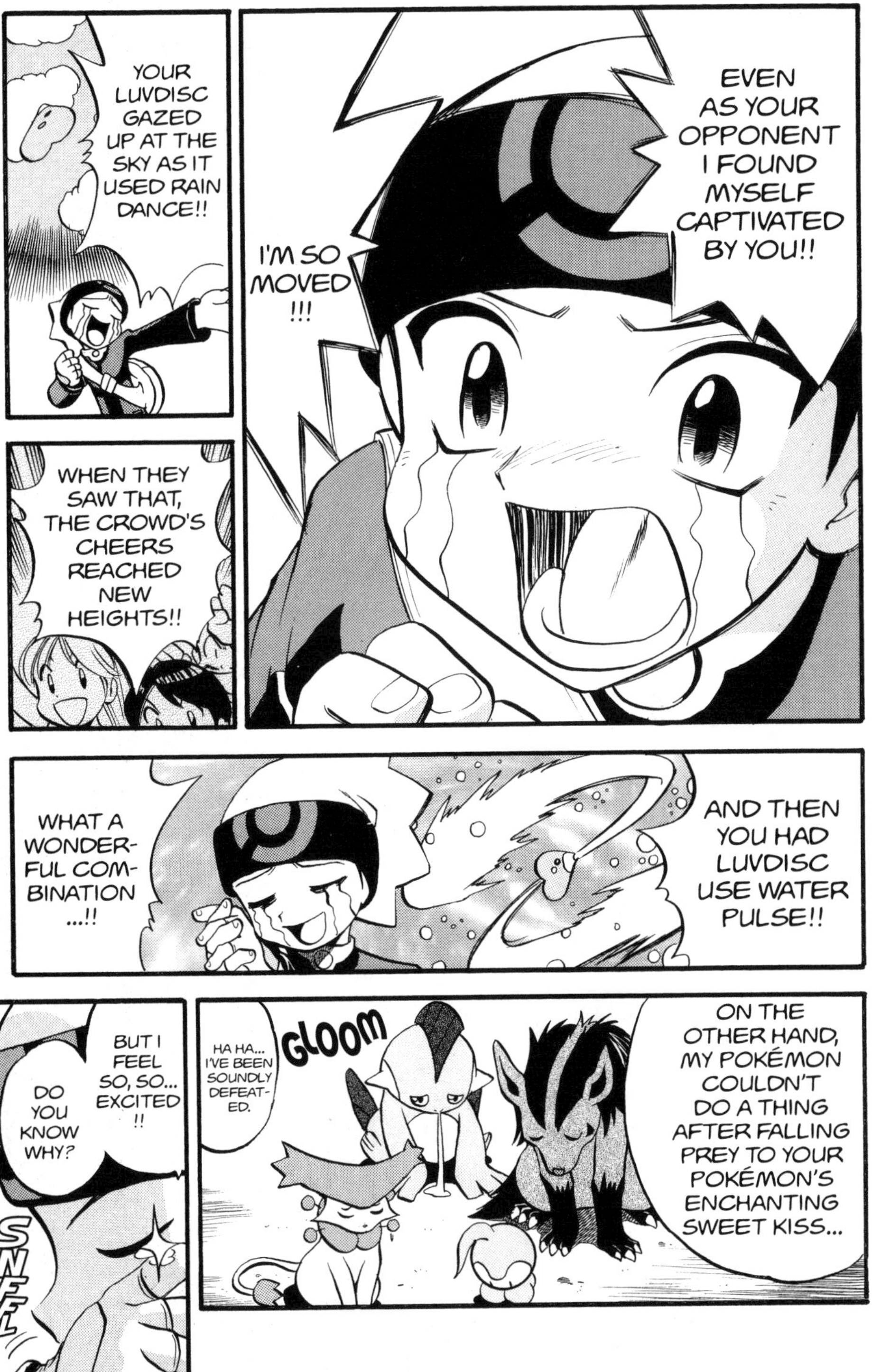
EVEN AS YOUR OPPONENT I FOUND MYSELF CAPTIVATED BY YOU!!
I'M SO MOVED!!!
YOUR LUVDISC GAZED UP AT THE SKY AS IT USED RAIN DANCE!!
WHEN THEY SAW THAT, THE CROWD'S CHEERS REACHED NEW HEIGHTS!!
AND THEN YOU HAD LUVDISC USE WATER PULSE!!
WHAT A WONDER-FUL COM-BINATION ...!!
ON THE OTHER HAND, MY POKÉMON COULDN'T DO A THING AFTER FALLING PREY TO YOUR POKÉMON'S ENCHANTING SWEET KISS...
GLOOM
HA HA... I'VE BEEN SOUNDLY DEFEAT-ED.
BUT I FEEL SO, SO... EXCITED!!
DO YOU KNOW WHY?
SNFFL

EH?

BECAUSE I'VE MET A MASTER POKÉMON CONTEST TRAINER LIKE YOU!

MASTER... MASTER!!

MASTER!!

YOU'LL HAVE TO HONE YOUR SKILLS BY YOURSELF.

I'M SORRY, BUT I DON'T TAKE ON STUDENTS.

WIZZZZZ

I WON'T GIVE UP!!

URROOMM

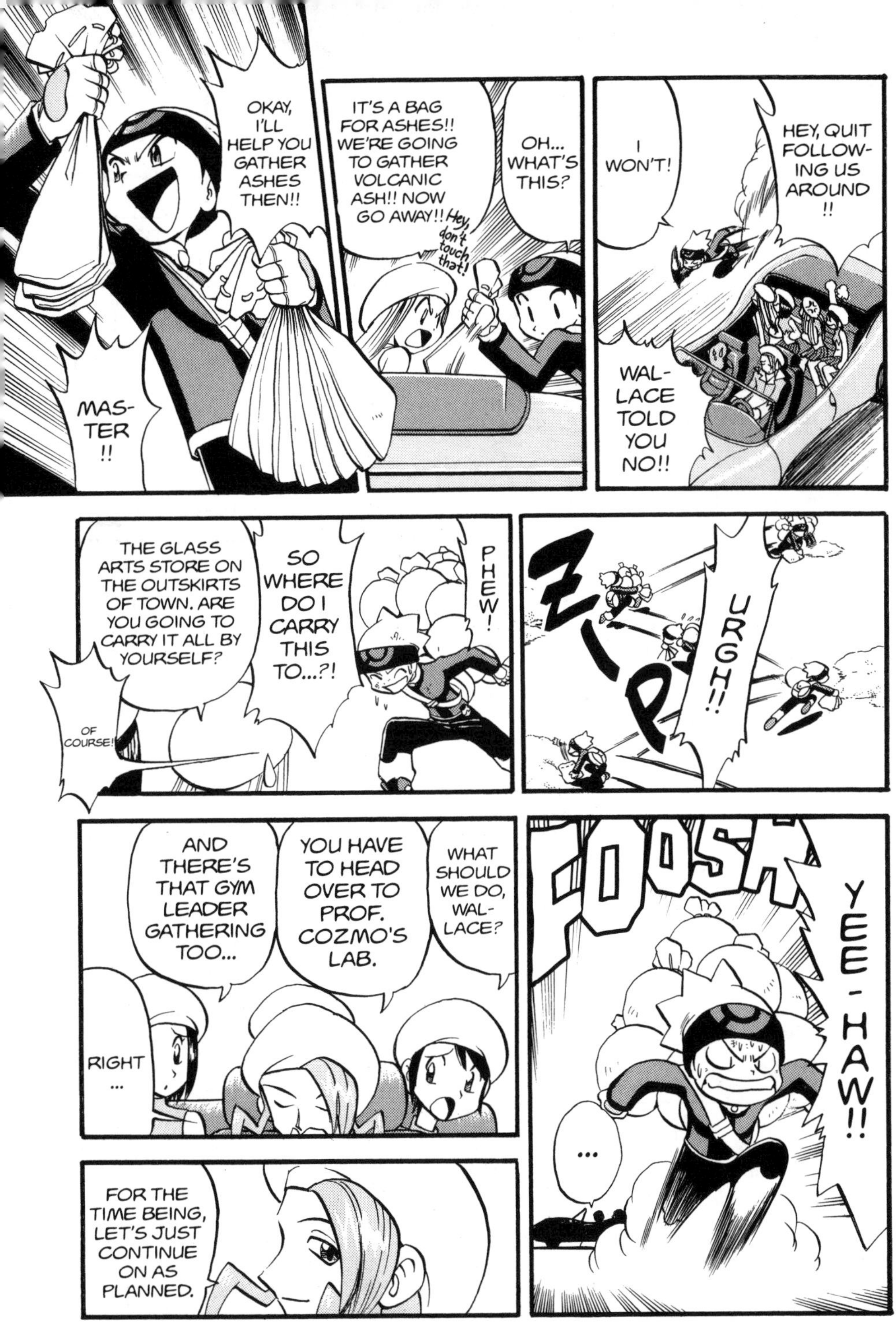
HEY, QUIT FOLLOWING US AROUND!!
I WON'T!
WALLACE TOLD YOU NO!!
OH... WHAT'S THIS?
IT'S A BAG FOR ASHES!! WE'RE GOING TO GATHER VOLCANIC ASH!! NOW GO AWAY!!
Hey, don't touch that!
OKAY, I'LL HELP YOU GATHER ASHES THEN!!
MASTER!!
URGH!!
ZIP
PHEW!
SO WHERE DO I CARRY THIS TO...?!
THE GLASS ARTS STORE ON THE OUTSKIRTS OF TOWN. ARE YOU GOING TO CARRY IT ALL BY YOURSELF?
OF COURSE!
FOOSH
YEE-HAW!!
...
WHAT SHOULD WE DO, WALLACE?
YOU HAVE TO HEAD OVER TO PROF. COZMO'S LAB.
AND THERE'S THAT GYM LEADER GATHERING TOO...
RIGHT...
FOR THE TIME BEING, LET'S JUST CONTINUE ON AS PLANNED.

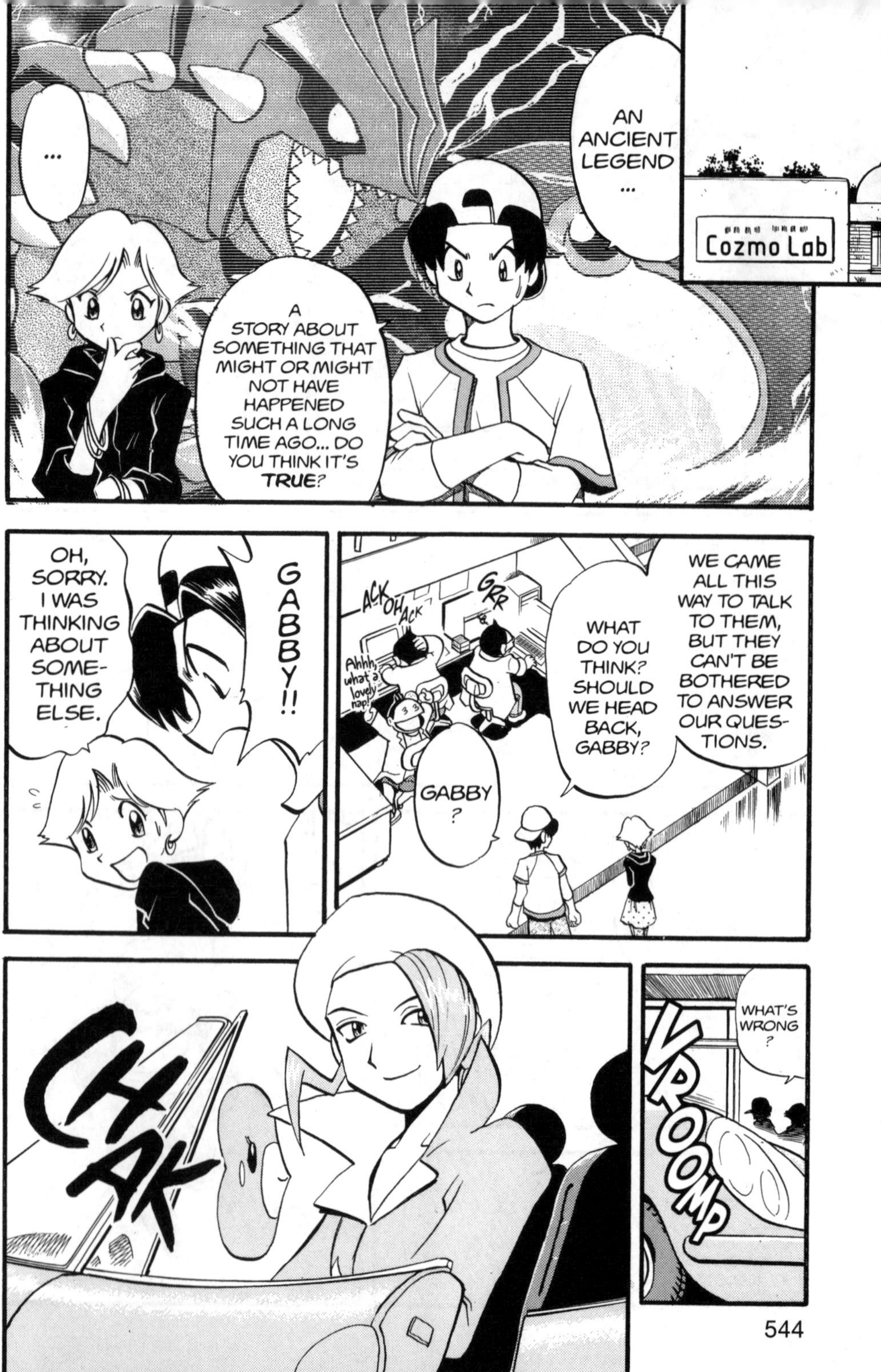

Cozmo Lab
AN ANCIENT LEGEND ...
A STORY ABOUT SOMETHING THAT MIGHT OR MIGHT NOT HAVE HAPPENED SUCH A LONG TIME AGO... DO YOU THINK IT'S TRUE?
...
WE CAME ALL THIS WAY TO TALK TO THEM, BUT THEY CAN'T BE BOTHERED TO ANSWER OUR QUESTIONS.
WHAT DO YOU THINK? SHOULD WE HEAD BACK, GABBY?
GRR
ACK OH ACK
Ahhh, what a lovely nap!
GABBY?
GABBY!!
OH, SORRY. I WAS THINKING ABOUT SOMETHING ELSE.
WHAT'S WRONG?
VROOOMP
CHAK

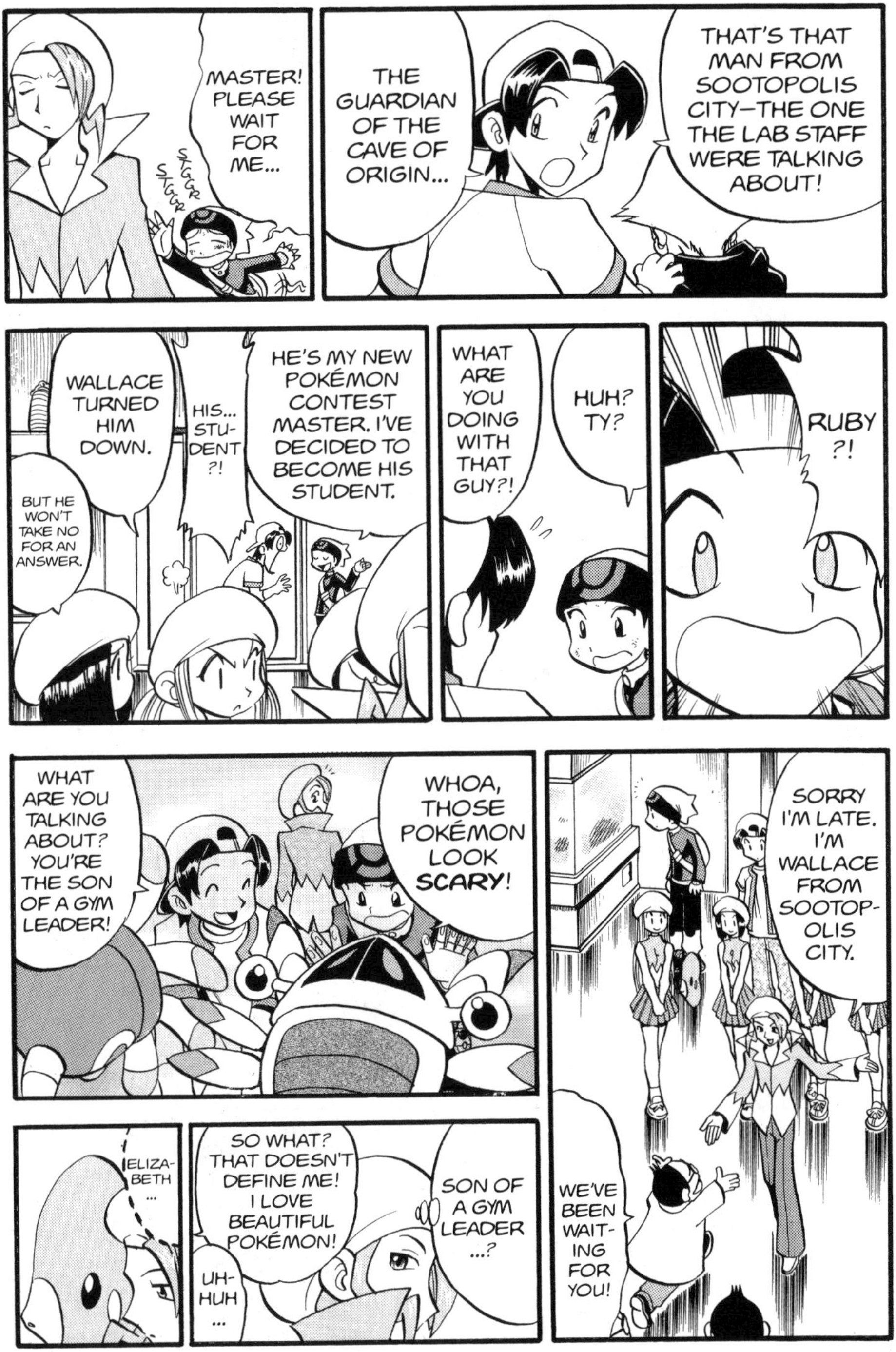

THAT'S THAT MAN FROM SOOTOPOLIS CITY—THE ONE THE LAB STAFF WERE TALKING ABOUT!
THE GUARDIAN OF THE CAVE OF ORIGIN...
MASTER! PLEASE WAIT FOR ME...
STGGR STGGR
RUBY?!
HUH? TY?
WHAT ARE YOU DOING WITH THAT GUY?!
HE'S MY NEW POKÉMON CONTEST MASTER. I'VE DECIDED TO BECOME HIS STUDENT.
HIS... STU-DENT?!
WALLACE TURNED HIM DOWN.
BUT HE WON'T TAKE NO FOR AN ANSWER.
SORRY I'M LATE. I'M WALLACE FROM SOOTOP-OLIS CITY.
WE'VE BEEN WAIT-ING FOR YOU!
WHOA, THOSE POKÉMON LOOK **SCARY**!
WHAT ARE YOU TALKING ABOUT? YOU'RE THE SON OF A GYM LEADER!
SON OF A GYM LEADER...?
SO WHAT? THAT DOESN'T DEFINE ME! I LOVE BEAUTIFUL POKÉMON!
UH-HUH...
ELIZA-BETH...

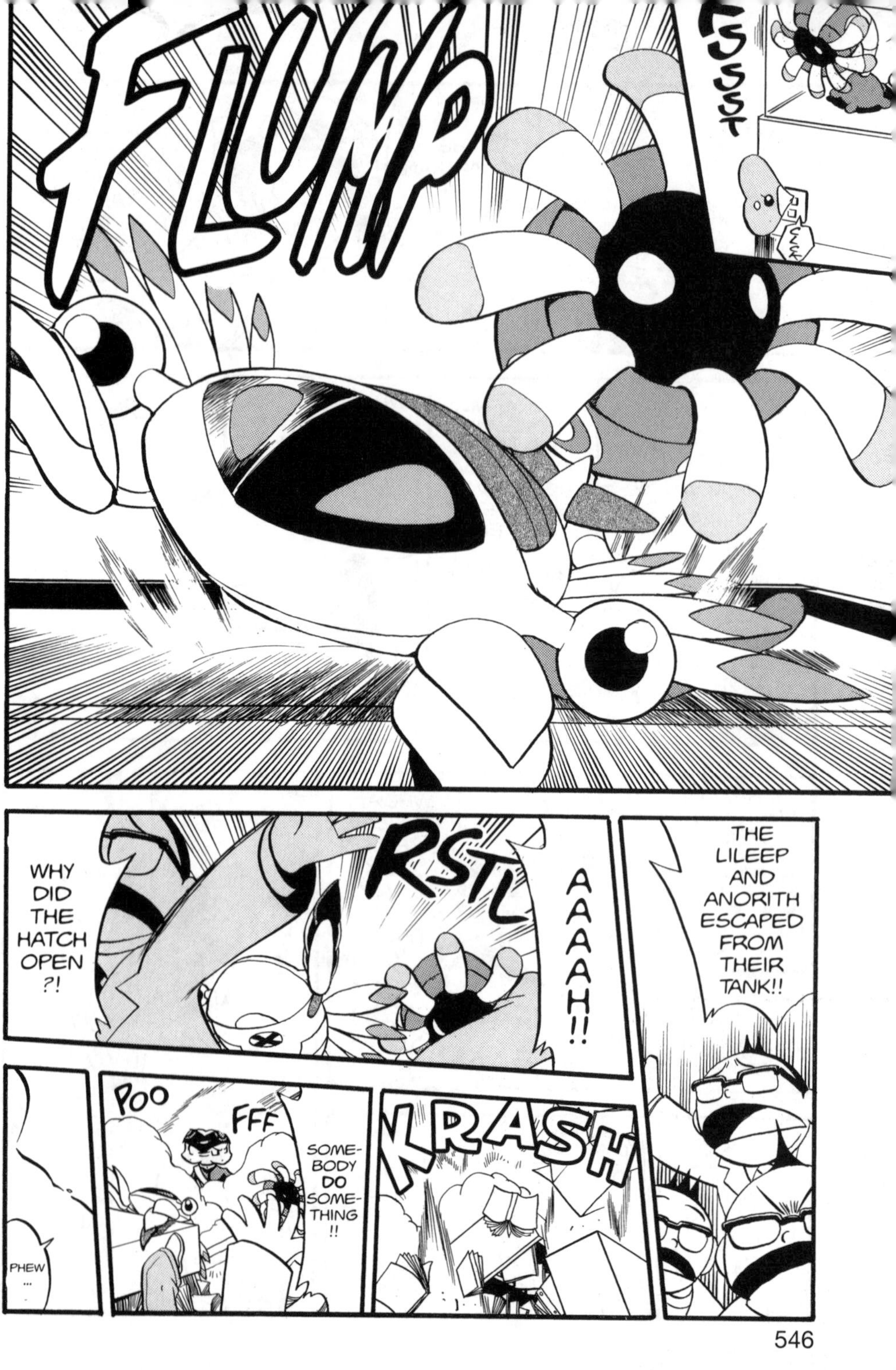
FLUMP
FSSST
THE LILEEP AND ANORITH ESCAPED FROM THEIR TANK!!
AAAAAH!!
RSTL
WHY DID THE HATCH OPEN?!
KRASH
SOMEBODY DO SOMETHING!!
POO
FFF
PHEW...

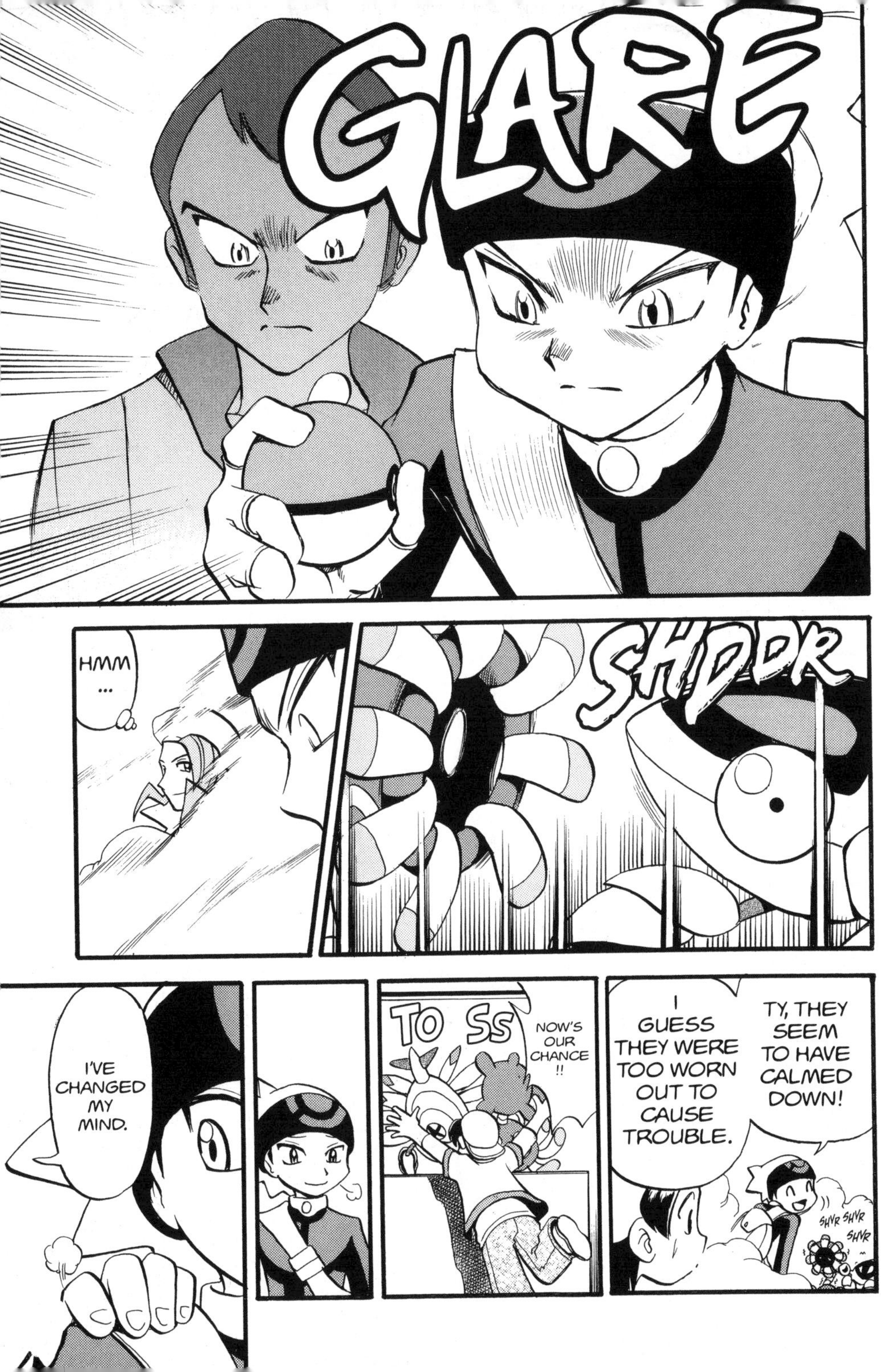
GLARE
SHDDR
HMM ...
TY, THEY SEEM TO HAVE CALMED DOWN!
I GUESS THEY WERE TOO WORN OUT TO CAUSE TROUBLE.
SHVR SHVR SHVR
TO Ss
NOW'S OUR CHANCE !!
I'VE CHANGED MY MIND.

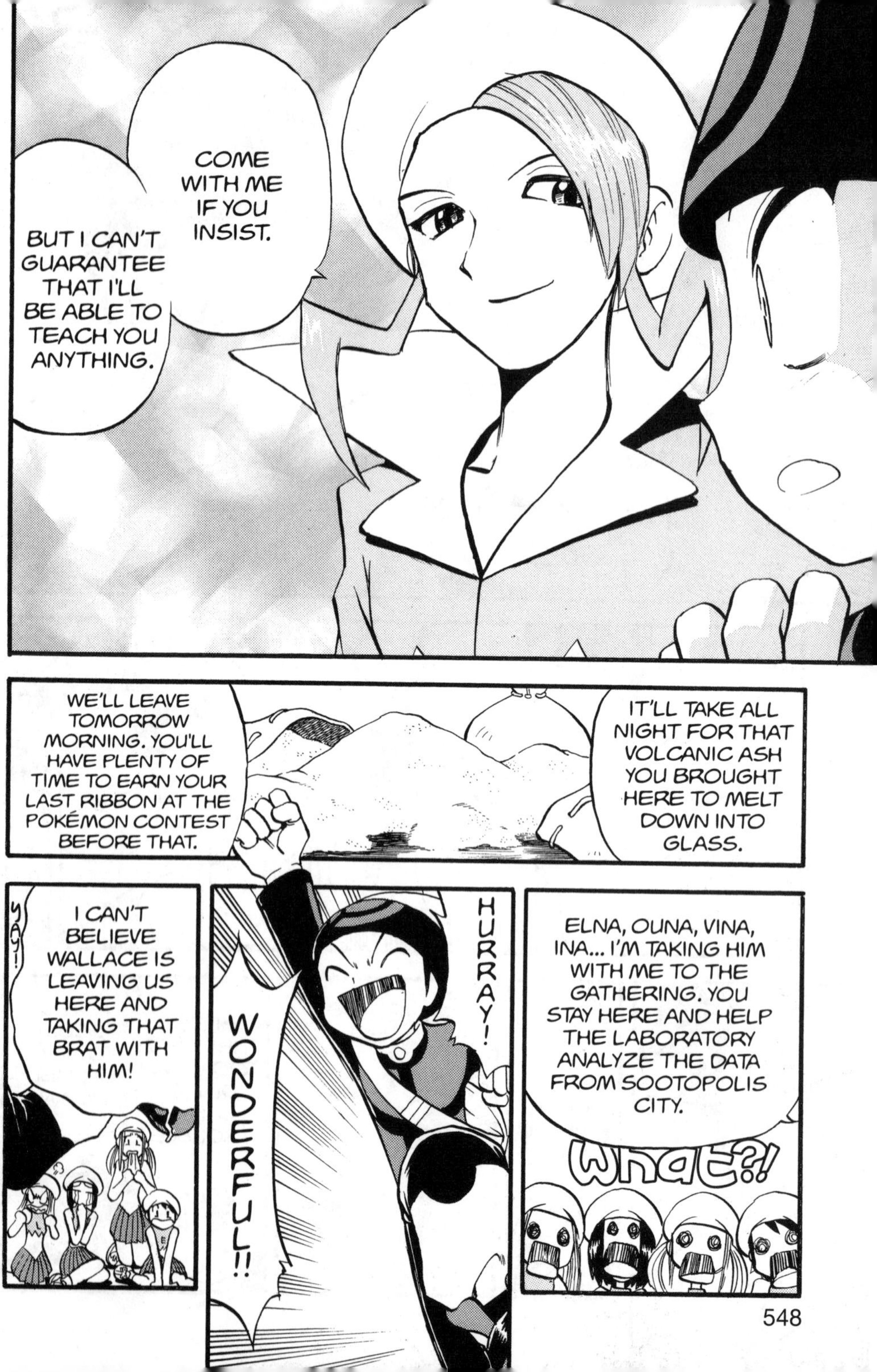
COME WITH ME IF YOU INSIST.
BUT I CAN'T GUARANTEE THAT I'LL BE ABLE TO TEACH YOU ANYTHING.
IT'LL TAKE ALL NIGHT FOR THAT VOLCANIC ASH YOU BROUGHT HERE TO MELT DOWN INTO GLASS.
WE'LL LEAVE TOMORROW MORNING. YOU'LL HAVE PLENTY OF TIME TO EARN YOUR LAST RIBBON AT THE POKÉMON CONTEST BEFORE THAT.
ELNA, OUNA, VINA, INA... I'M TAKING HIM WITH ME TO THE GATHERING. YOU STAY HERE AND HELP THE LABORATORY ANALYZE THE DATA FROM SOOTOPOLIS CITY.
What?!
HURRAY!
WONDERFUL!!
YAY!
I CAN'T BELIEVE WALLACE IS LEAVING US HERE AND TAKING THAT BRAT WITH HIM!

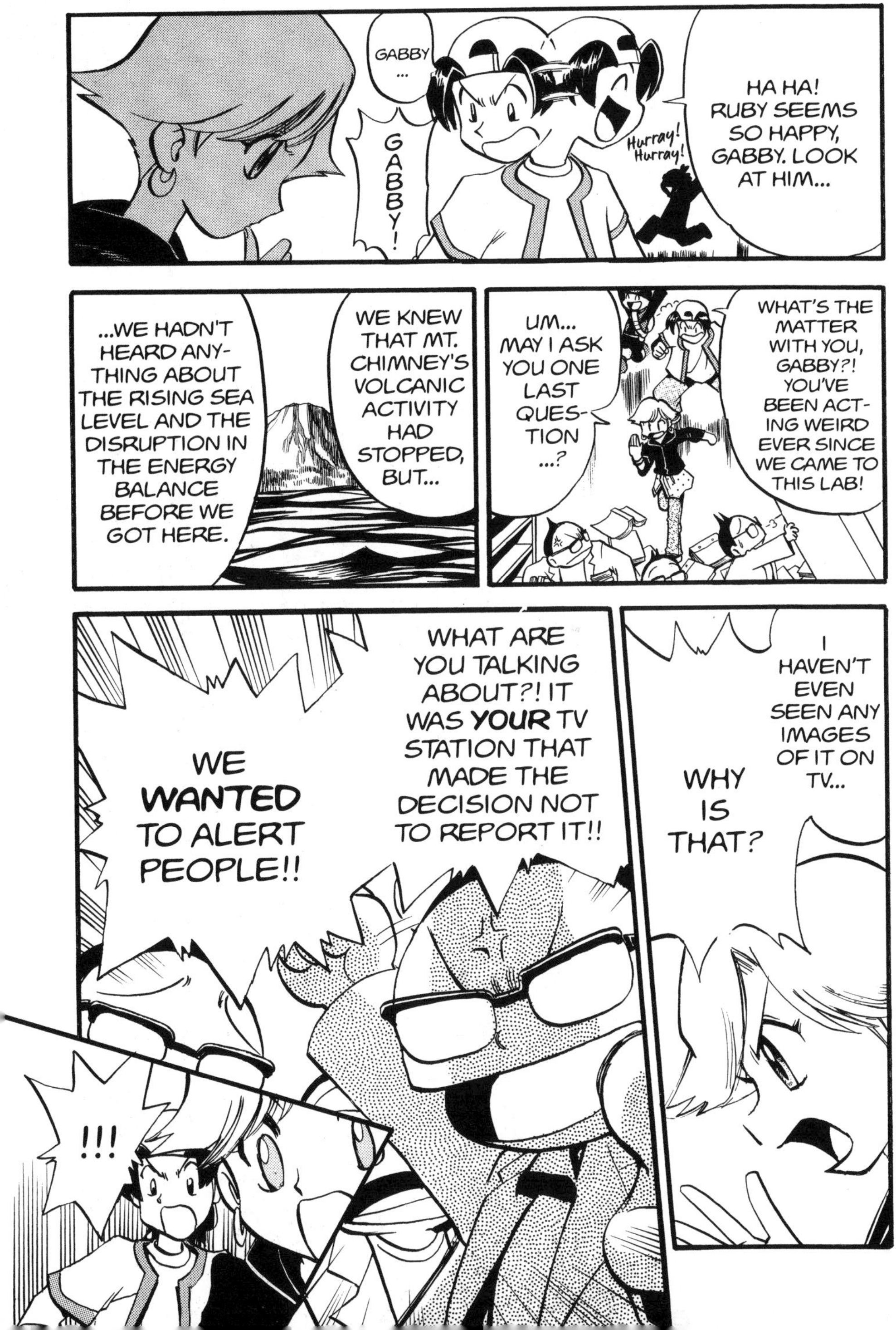
HA HA! RUBY SEEMS SO HAPPY, GABBY. LOOK AT HIM...
Hurray! Hurray!
GABBY!
GABBY ...
WHAT'S THE MATTER WITH YOU, GABBY?! YOU'VE BEEN ACTING WEIRD EVER SINCE WE CAME TO THIS LAB!
UM... MAY I ASK YOU ONE LAST QUESTION ...?
WE KNEW THAT MT. CHIMNEY'S VOLCANIC ACTIVITY HAD STOPPED, BUT...
...WE HADN'T HEARD ANYTHING ABOUT THE RISING SEA LEVEL AND THE DISRUPTION IN THE ENERGY BALANCE BEFORE WE GOT HERE.
I HAVEN'T EVEN SEEN ANY IMAGES OF IT ON TV...
WHY IS THAT?
WHAT ARE YOU TALKING ABOUT?! IT WAS **YOUR** TV STATION THAT MADE THE DECISION NOT TO REPORT IT!!
WE **WANTED** TO ALERT PEOPLE!!
!!!

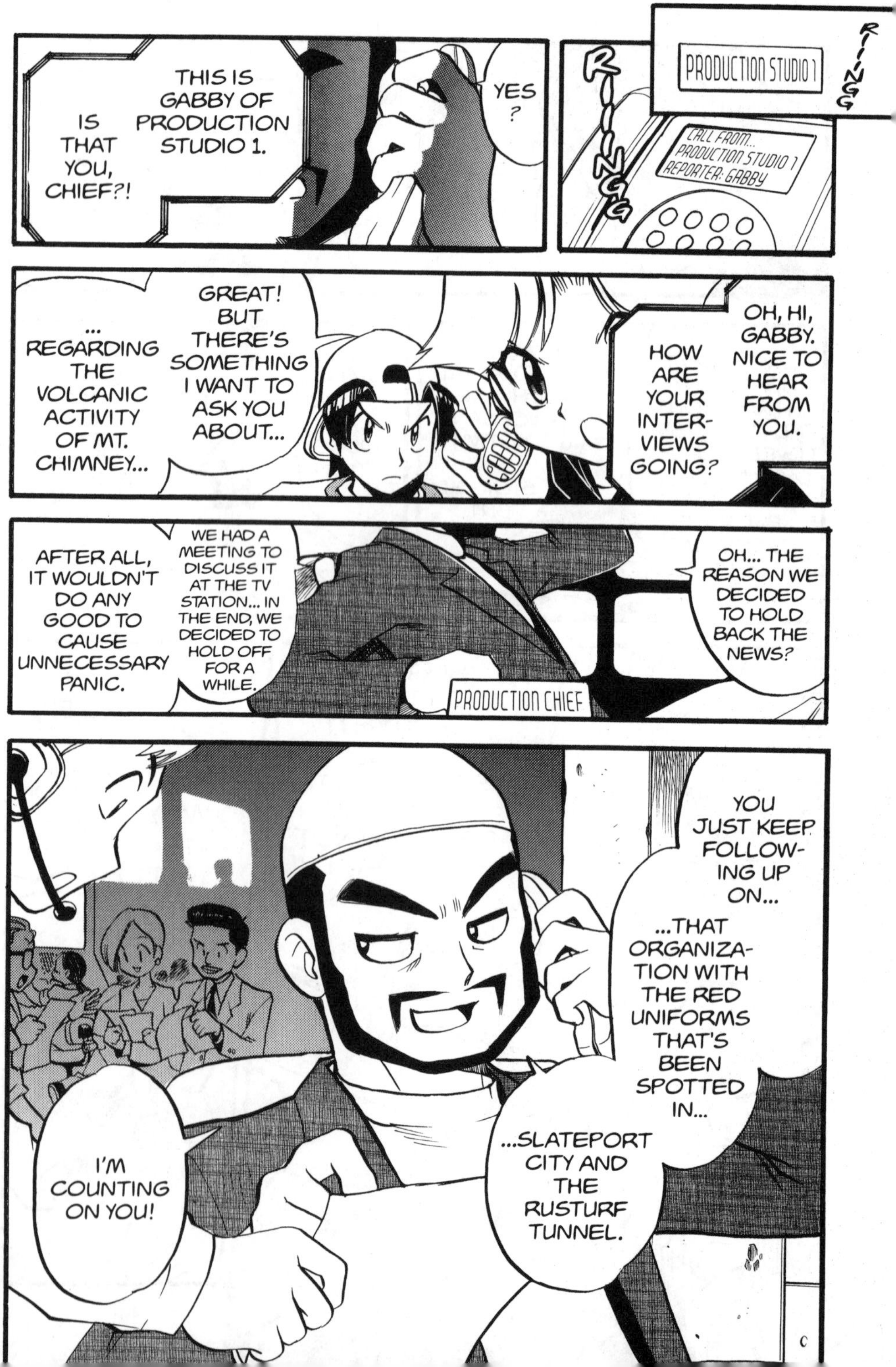
PRODUCTION STUDIO 1
RIIINGG
RIIINGG
CALL FROM... PRODUCTION STUDIO 1 REPORTER: GABBY
YES?
THIS IS GABBY OF PRODUCTION STUDIO 1.
IS THAT YOU, CHIEF?!
OH, HI, GABBY. NICE TO HEAR FROM YOU.
HOW ARE YOUR INTER-VIEWS GOING?
GREAT! BUT THERE'S SOMETHING I WANT TO ASK YOU ABOUT...
...REGARDING THE VOLCANIC ACTIVITY OF MT. CHIMNEY...
OH... THE REASON WE DECIDED TO HOLD BACK THE NEWS?
PRODUCTION CHIEF
WE HAD A MEETING TO DISCUSS IT AT THE TV STATION... IN THE END, WE DECIDED TO HOLD OFF FOR A WHILE.
AFTER ALL, IT WOULDN'T DO ANY GOOD TO CAUSE UNNECESSARY PANIC.
YOU JUST KEEP FOLLOW-ING UP ON...
...THAT ORGANIZA-TION WITH THE RED UNIFORMS THAT'S BEEN SPOTTED IN...
...SLATEPORT CITY AND THE RUSTURF TUNNEL.
I'M COUNTING ON YOU!

COLLECTOR'S EDITION

Volume 6

Story by **HIDENORI KUSAKA**
Art by **SATOSHI YAMAMOTO**

©2021 Pokémon.
©1995–2004 Nintendo / Creatures Inc. / GAME FREAK inc.
TM, ®, and character names are trademarks of Nintendo.
POCKET MONSTERS SPECIAL Vols. 16–18
by Hidenori KUSAKA, Satoshi YAMAMOTO
©1997 Hidenori KUSAKA, Satoshi YAMAMOTO
All rights reserved.
Original Japanese edition published by SHOGAKUKAN.
English translation rights in the United States of America, Canada, the United Kingdom,
Ireland, Australia, New Zealand and India arranged with SHOGAKUKAN.

Translation/HC Language Solutions, Tetsuichiro Miyaki
English Adaptation/Bryant Turnage
Lettering/Annaliese "Ace" Christman
Original Series Design/Shawn Carrico
Original Series Editor/Annette Roman
Collector's Edition Production Artist/Christy Medellin
Collector's Edition Design/Julian [JR] Robinson
Collector's Edition Editor/Joel Enos

The stories, characters and incidents mentioned in this publication are entirely fictional.

Printed in the U.S.A.

Published by VIZ Media, LLC
P.O. Box 77010
San Francisco, CA 94107

10 9 8 7 6 5 4 3 2 1
First printing, February 2021

viz.com

THIS IS THE LAST PAGE.

THIS BOOK READS RIGHT TO LEFT.